THE CHRONICLES OF DRAGON

COLLECTION

CRAIG HALLORAN

The Chronicles of Dragon Collection
By Craig Halloran

Copyright © 2015 by Craig Halloran
Print Edition

TWO-TEN BOOK PRESS
P.O. Box 4215, Charleston, WV 25364

Hardback ISBN: 978-1-941208-37-7
eBook ISBN: 978-1-941208-40-3
Paperback ISBN: 978-1-941208-41-0

http://www.thedarkslayer.net

Illustrations by David Schmelling and Joe Shawcross
Map by Gillis Bjork
Edited by Cherise Kelley

The Chronicles of Dragon: *The Hero, The Sword, and The Dragons* Copyright © 2012 by Craig Halloran
The Chronicles of Dragon: *Dragon Bones and Tombstones* Copyright © March 2013 by Craig Halloran
The Chronicles of Dragon: *Terrot at the Temple* Copyright © March 2013 by Craig Halloran
The Chronicles of Dragon: *Clutch of the Cleric* Copyright © December 2013 by Craig Halloran
The Chronicles of Dragon: *Hunt for the Hero* Copyright © December 2013 by Craig Halloran
The Chronicles of Dragon: *Siege at the Settlements* Copyright © March 2014 by Craig Halloran
The Chronicles of Dragon: *Strife in the Sky* Copyright © March 2014 by Craig Halloran
The Chronicles of Dragon: *Fight and the Fury* Copyright © December 2013 by Craig Halloran
The Chronicles of Dragon: *War in the Winds* Copyright © August 2014 by Craig Halloran
The Chronicles of Dragon: *Finale* Copyright © September 2014 by Craig Halloran

All rights reserved. No part of this publication may be reproduced, stored in a retrieval system or transmitted, in any form, or by any means, electronic, mechanical, recorded, photocopied, or otherwise, without the prior permission of the copyright owner, except by a reviewer who may quote brief passages in a review.

Publisher's Note
This book is a work of fiction. Names, characters, places, and incidents either are the product of the author's imagination or are used fictitiously, and any resemblance to actual persons, living or dead, events, or locales is entirely coincidental.

NALZAMBOR
Key Location Guide

TABLE OF CONTENTS

The Chronicles of Dragon

The Hero, The Sword, and The Dragons

-BOOK 1-

CRAIG HALLORAN

To my son, Nathaniel Conan. Words can never express how much you mean to me, but I wrote you a book anyway.

CHAPTER

1

I WAS RUNNING HARD, PUSHING MYSELF past human limits, to the only place I knew could help. Home. I already could tell that my wound was fatal, and with every step the loss of blood made me more woozy. Orcs were hot on my trail, at least a dozen, howling for my head. I was certain they would not stop; they were stubborn and stupid, slow as well, but I was smart and fast. I was a dragon, after all... in a very man-like sort of way. By appearance, I was a man: big, long-haired, and rangy—more than capable of whipping a few lousy dragon-poaching orcs, until they got the drop on me. So now I was running for my life, my dragon heart pounding in my chest like a galloping horse mile after mile until I had no choice but to come to a stop. I looked down at the crossbow bolts protruding from my side, through my back.

"Egad!" I exclaimed, checking the wounds. The blood had already stained a patch in my armor, and I knew it was still worse than it looked. Every breath I took was pain filled and biting. I knew I was bleeding inside, and I had to stop it or die. I pulled the lid from my canteen and drank, which did little to quench my thirst, but it brought some relief. I reached inside my satchel, my little bag of tricks, and fumbled for a vial.

Over the years, I've picked up a few useful things, like potions. Magic potions. They can do many things. Turn you invisible. Make you bigger. Smarter. Faster. Stronger. And even heal. In this particular case, it was a healing potion, in a vial as big as my index finger, which was pretty big, but it only looked to have about one drop left as I shook it before my eyes.

"Ugh," I moaned, the pain not getting any better, "I don't think this will do it." I looked down at my wounds and tried to decide: should I take out the wooden shafts first, or afterward? I'd been hurt before, plenty of times, but this festering wound was a tricky one.

"Just do what you always do, Dragon."

That's what I call myself, and I talk to myself a lot. My real name is much longer, difficult to pronounce and spell, but part of it is Nath. So, if a commoner ever asks, Nath Dragon is my name; saving dragons (and other things) is my game.

I tore a piece of bark from a tree, pinched it between my teeth, and bit down. Beads of sweat erupted from my forehead as I began pulling the first bolt through my skin. The good thing about them being crossbow bolts was they weren't as big as arrows, but they sure did pack a punch. I groaned, certain I was going to die as I ripped the rest of the shaft free.

I felt sick. My skin turned clammy, and the sound of the woodland crickets became loud and irritating. In the woods there are many dangers, and I wasn't anywhere close to being out of harm's way. Anything could pick up the trail of the wounded: overbearing bugbears, wily wood elves, pesky witches, dog-faced gnolls, transforming wolves, tricky sprites, were-shadows, or even worse ... dragons. Yes, there are bad dragons, too, but it wasn't likely I'd run into two dragons in one day, or that a dragon would want to fool with me, for that matter. But they did, on occasion; I'd seen it for myself. The most beautiful and dangerous creatures in the world. The noblest and greediest, too.

"Do it, Dragon!" I was gritting my teeth on the tasteless bark once more. The pain was excruciating, each bloody inch I tugged free twice as painful as the last. *Don't black out.* A wave of wooziness assailed me as I got the last bolt free and slipped to my hands and knees, trembling like a leaf. I put the healing vial to my lips and watched that last pink drop slide down the tube and land on my tongue. Elation. Exasperation. It coursed through me, head to toe, mending every fiber, sealing every unnatural pore. The relief was astounding, but the healing incomplete. As quick as it started, it had stopped, but at least I wouldn't be dripping blood anymore. Spitting it, perhaps.

Clatch-Zip!

Clatch-Zip!

Two bolts ripped past my face and quavered in a nearby tree.

"Stupid bloody orcs!"

I pushed myself to my feet with a groan and began sprinting through the woods, each step feeling like a punch in my stomach. I had to get home, find my father, and explain to him how I had gotten whipped by orcs, which never would have happened if I'd been allowed to kill them in the first place.

Zip! Zip! Zip!

My legs churned harder and harder as I began to outdistance my pursuers, cutting across the grassy plain, and the barrage of bolts began to subside. So on I ran, the sounds of the angry orcs fading away, leaving only the wind in my ears and the sharp throbbing pangs in my stomach. I just hoped I had enough strength left to return home.

Of course, my father probably wouldn't be too pleased by my return, either. I had his sword that I named Fang, a beautiful glimmering object of steel and magic woven together like its own living thing. Well, it wasn't given to me; I sort of borrowed it, and by then I was pretty sure my father would know it was missing. He wasn't the most understanding when it came to such things, either.

So I ran, through the shallow waters, over grassy gnolls, by shining cities whose towers almost reached the clouds, each long stride a hair shorter than the last, until I made it to just within my keen eye's shot of the Mountain of Doom and collapsed.

CHAPTER
2

As the sun rose, warming the chin hairs on my haggard face, the last thing I remembered was the blackness of the coming night. For all I knew, I'd been asleep for a day. I don't think a screaming ogre could have woken me. At the moment, everything felt fine. Then I moved.

"Ug," I said. I wiped the morning drool from my mouth and spat out the tangy taste of my blood. I still had miles to go, and I wasn't so certain I could make it. Upright as I could be, I staggered forward. My stiff legs were no longer capable of churning after days of running off and on, but I knew I had to keep going, seek help, and not die.

Ahead was the Mountain of Doom, which isn't its real name, but a shorter name I'd given it because I never cared to take the time to say things properly. I swear, long names are given to things just so others will have something to talk about or just to give some little wretch yearning for knowledge something significant to do. I can spell it, backward as well as forward, but I'm not going to. Learning it once was more than enough already, and I see no need to repeat myself. It's just a word. But, the Mountain of Doom, my home, is beyond words. It's something you just have to see for yourself, and if you ever do, and you're wise, you'll gape in wide-eyed wonder, turn, and run away.

The base of the mountain is miles wide, maybe a league or two. I used to have to run around its base as a boy, every crevice treacherous, loosely footed of shale, and streams of lava hot enough to burn your leg to the bone in an instant. That area is called the marsh of sulfur. The peak's nose reaches into the sky, snow caps blending into those cloudy skies, such as it was that day, before disappearing. Steam. Smoke. Those gases billowing from cave mouths, some small, others large and even enormous, seemed to illustrate that the mountain was more than a clump of rock and clay, but a living and breathing part of the world itself.

I wiped the sweat from my brow and fought for secure footing over the shale as I made it two miles deeper into the rising heat. The heat didn't bother me; I was used to that, but it wrought damage on my glorious mane of recently mangled hair.

I stood straddling the crest of a ravine, where a small stream of lava was flowing below. The face on the mountain, a frightful grimace it seemed, some said was a coincidence or a design of arcane wizards that once took harbor there. Or it was a massive scarecrow created by dwarves that wanted to be left alone. It was, without question in my mind, the face of a dragon. A massive cave filled with rows of teeth could be seen, smoke rolling from its mouth. The eyes shimmered with fire, and the nose holes dripped lava. It would be hard to argue that it didn't look like a dragon, that it was just happenstance, an illusion, something the feeble minded shared to encourage fear to be spread by other feeble minds.

I sighed. It was pretty much the reason no one ever came here, very often, and lived. Mile after mile I trudged along in agony, deeper into the valley of living lava until I had nowhere else to go but up. I looked back, the green grasses and tall trees no longer within sight, the rising mist now hid my view of the gentler, softer world.

The base of the mountain was sheer, black rock, no smoke, nor stairs, nor solid footholds. Not smooth, but rough, and spanning hundreds of feet high. This was the part that kept the adventurers at bay: the curious, the daring, the foolish, and the greedy that wanted the dragon's hoard, rumored to be large enough to fill every household in an entire kingdom or more. It was impossible to get in, but to get out, with loads of treasure, it would take at least a thousand of the stoutest men to do that. Unless of course you knew a secret way, which it so happens I did know.

A natural archway greeted me like an old friend as I fell onto my knees before it. No runes, no nothing, just a familiarity that I had from long ago. I began to speak to it, my raspy voice struggling to be clear, as my tongue was thick and swollen with fever. Word after word, minute after minute I chanted in a language more ancient than man, more difficult than women, more lengthy than a river. It took thirty minutes before I finished, and nothing happened.

"Open," I tried to shout, slamming my fists into the rock. My voice was gone now, withered away like the ashes of a burning log, my efforts spent in failure. *Nooooooooo!* I collapsed, holding my belly, the taste of blood filling my mouth, my last flavor before dying.

The archway shook and quaked, angry. From the corner of my watery eye, I saw a sheet of rock lifting. *Thank goodness.* I lay there, in pain, misery, and suffering, eyeing the portal open to safety, but unable to move. How long, I did not know. The archway shuddered and buckled, and the doorway began to sink down, a mouth closing, lips soon to seal shut. *Move!* But I could not. It seemed my death was likely to come first.

CHAPTER

3

SOMETHING POWERFUL GRABBED MY ARM and started dragging me though the portal as the doorway closed shut like a clap of thunder. Gruff hands rolled me over and pushed on the bloody patch on my armor.

I screamed so loud my voice began to crack.

"See, yer alive," a strong voice said, less hearty, more grim "...for the moment. Now let's get you patched up, restored to full health, so your father can be guilt free before he kills ya."

"Thanks, Brenwar," I groaned, "you always know what to say to make me feel better."

"Har!" He reached down and grabbed both my hands. "Up you go!" He almost jerked my arms from the sockets as he ripped me up from the floor. I looked down at Brenwar, with a frown as big as his, glowering in pain. My dwarven friend was as big and stout as a sand-filled barrel, raven-bearded, and armored in heavy metals from his chin to his toes. You'd think he'd sound like a wagon load of scrap metal when he walked, but all I heard as I followed was the sound of well-oiled leather rubbing together. I followed him up a cavernous stairwell designed for monsters, not men, spiraling upward without end. I knew where I was, but wasn't certain where Brenwar was going.

"In here," he said, stopping at an opening I swore hadn't been there a moment ago and shoving me inside. "Wait." His booted feet stomped up the stairs, echoing, then fading away.

I was in an alcove where a lone torch hung, its orange light offering a warm illumination to the scenes of many dragon murals painted across all the walls. I gasped as one of the images of the painting came to life. A female dragon, tall as me, slender and batting her eyes, walked over, her tail tickling my chin. I knew she was a female because her belly scales were lighter than the others. Male dragons tend to be darker. But if you truly know dragons, as I do, the eyes were a dead giveaway. The females have lashes on their lids, nothing too pronounced, but noticeable all the same.

Her scales, copperish and pink, reflected the most beautiful colors, and her comely face offered a smile. In her hands was a vial, the same as the one I drank from days before, that she tilted to my lips. I gulped it down, fell onto a pillow big enough for a cow, and let the magical mending begin.

I burned, inside and out, with satisfaction. My weary bones were revitalized. My innards—dormant, agonized and bleeding—now regenerated. My vitality was back. My aching feet were no longer sore. I felt as strong as a horse as I tore off my armor, stretched out my mighty frame on the pillow, and shouted at the top of my lungs with glee.

I swear the lady dragon giggled before she pecked me on my head.

"Thank you," I said, combing my hair from my eyes. The dragoness was beautiful, her features soft behind her armor and razor sharp claws. After all, beautiful things have to defend themselves. I waved as I watched her disappear back into the mural among her kind, a queen defending in a glorious battle of dragons charging across the sun glazed sky.

"Ah!" I elated.

I fell back on the pillow, wanting to sleep, as my mind told me I needed rest, but my body was ready to go.

"A bath perhaps," I said to myself, getting up, grabbing my gear and sword.

A gruff voice disagreed. "You can have your bath later, Nat—"

I glared at Brenwar.

"Er, I mean, Dragon. Your father waits." The husky dwarf walked over and took Fang from my hands. "I'll take that."

I held my head in my hand. I could leave now, if I wanted. I was healed and all the better for it. My father, he wouldn't come after me. He never did. He threatened to chase me down, but usually just sent Brenwar instead, who was slow. A team of galloping horses wouldn't make him fast.

"So be it," I said in resignation. Up through the Mountain of Doom I followed, one heavy step at a time, the revitalized feeling in my organs replaced with a queasy feeling. My energy, one moment endless, was now gone. Oh, I was fine, my health fully operational, but that didn't do much good in the presence of an angry father who I had been reluctant to listen to for quite some time. When we stopped in front of a massive set of doors that stood almost five stories tall, Brenwar looked up at me with a hard look in his eyes and said, "I told him you needed bathed, but he insisted that you come now." He reached up and patted me on my lower back. "I'll see to it your bathed before the funeral. It's been an honor knowing you, Dragon." With that, Brenwar, my only true friend in the entire mountain, pushed the door open far enough for me to squeeze through, and like a fat rat out of a metal can, he scurried away.

And there I stood, at the threshold of all thresholds, looking back over my shoulder for escape, but finding none. If I had some dragon scales by now, things would probably be all right, but I didn't. With great hesitation and a trembling heart, I stepped inside.

CHAPTER

4

IMAGINE THE THRONE ROOMS OF the greatest kings in the world combined and all their wealth lying at their feet. That's nothing compared to my father's throne room, and those kings are nothing compared to my father. There he sat on his golden throne, treasure covering the floor as far as eye could see, glimmering and twinkling in the light of the lanterns. Like a man he sat, more than three stories tall, monstrous wings folded behind his back, dragon head resting in the palm of his clawed hand, eyes closed. There had never been a king that big.

I pushed the door closed with a loud *wump*, stirring the golden coins that slipped from their pile towards the floor. To my relief, my father, a heavy sleeper, did not stir, yet my heart pounded in my chest. I supposed that it should be pounding in my chest, but I had figured that feeling, that nervous feeling you get as you tread into the unknown, would fade away with age. It hadn't. I pushed the hair back from my eyes and proceeded forward.

My father, the largest living thing in the world so far as I knew, was scaled in red mostly, a brick red, with trims of gold along his armored belly, wings, and claws. His taloned toe alone was almost as big as me, and I was big, for a man anyway.

"Come closer," he said from the side of his mouth. The power of his voice sent tremors through the room, upsetting more piles of precious metals and jewels.

I kept going, taking my time, having no desire to begin the conversation but very eager to end it. I stopped a good fifty feet away, craning my neck upward, trying to find the first word to say. My tongue was thick in my mouth, and I thought of all the brave deeds I had done, but it all seemed so minute before my father.

He snorted the air, opened his dragon's maw, and said, "You smell dirty. Like an orc."

That bothered me. He always had to say something that bothered me.

"It's good to see you too, Father," I shouted back, my words barely a gerbil's compared to his. And I was loud, loud as an ogre when I wanted to be.

One eye popped open, brown like a man's, but flecked in gold and glaring. The other eye opened as well, the same as the other, its intent no less hostile than the first. My father leaned back on his throne, long powerful neck stretching between the massive marble pillars behind him, which held the ceiling. He was glorious and powerful; his mere presence began to charge my blood. I was proud to have a father like that, but I hadn't told him so in a long time.

"Ah ... the fear in your sweat is gone already I see and replaced by your spiteful tongue," he said, moving very little, poised rather, pleasant, as if he was being served dinner. "Still, it is good to see you, Son, as always."

That part got to me a little, but only because I knew he meant it. The way he said it was the truth.

Everything he said was true, I knew, whether I wanted to agree to it or not. My father, which is what I called him, because his real name would take the better part of the day to say, had a voice of a most peculiar quality. Powerful and beautiful like a crashing waterfall. Wise and deep with all the wisdom in the world combined. Soothing and uplifting. But my proud ears had gotten accustomed to it over the years.

"Yes, well, Father, it's good to see you, too. There's nothing quite like taking a long journey home. Scraping and clawing for your life, bleeding out your last drop," I laid it on thick, "gasping for your last breath, only to be saved at the last moment of life, healed, only to be jostled and dragged here without a moment's rest." I began pacing back and forth, hands on hips, throwing my neck back. "And you complain, of all things, that I have not had a bath."

Ever seen a dragon smile, one with a mouthful of teeth as long as you? That's what I was seeing now, and it bothered me.

"Well, you know how I feel about those foul creatures, and I was excited to see you, smelling like orc's blood or not, and it's been so long, several weeks at least," my father said.

Now my father was being ridiculous. Dragons are never in a hurry to do anything. It takes them a minute just to blink. They aren't slow, by any means or measure, no matter how big they are, but they take their good time doing anything. Hours are minutes to them, if even that long.

I plopped down on a huge stack of gemstones, inspecting a few before tossing them away.

"Father, it's been almost a decade," I said, agitated. "Have you even moved since the last time I was here?"

"Certainly, Son, I've moved quite a bit since you've been here."

"I see." He never moved, except when it was time to feed, which wasn't very often. He hadn't moved since I was a boy, either. "Father, what would you know of me?" I had to push things, be impolite; it was the only way to make this conversation go quicker.

"I see things as well, Nath …"

"No don't!" I yelled, but it was too late. He began pronouncing my full name, which is as long as a river, syllable after syllable, ancient, poetic and powerful. I listened; minute after minute, mesmerized, my aggravation beginning to subside. My name was a beautiful thing: prosperous and invigorating.

"… nan," he finished, over an hour later. "Have you gained any scales?"

There it was. The dreaded question about my scales. Here I was, a son of the greatest dragon, but without a single scale. Despite all the right I had done, it seemed I'd done my own fair share of wrong as well.

"No!"

My father snorted. I saw a look of disappointment in his eyes, and I felt disappointed as well. I'd failed. Despite all my great deeds in the lands of Nalzambor, I was not living up to expectations.

He sighed, and it seemed such a terrible thing.

"How long, Son?"

I kicked at the piles of treasure.

"Two hundred years."

Like a man, my father reached up and grabbed his skull with his four fingered hands. I knew what was coming next.

"Son, the first hundred years of your life were the most wonderful of mine. You did everything I said. You listened. You learned. You grew. And when you became old enough, I let you choose. Stay in the mountain and continue to grow, or risk losing everything you are just to see the rest of the world." He shook his head. "I never should have given you that choice."

"I wanted to see things for myself. It was my right. You told me I needed to understand the world of men," I argued.

"Yes, I did. But I told you not to get too close. Don't get caught up in their ways. You are not one of them. You are one of us."

"How can I be sure? I still look like a man. I talk like a man."

He stopped me, head leering over at me, his eyes showing a glimmer of the infernos within.

"True, Son, but I warned you not to *act* like a man. I showed you what dragons do, how they act, how they respond."

I rose to my feet and resumed my pacing through the hoard, coins jingling beneath my feet.

"Maybe I don't want to devour herds of sheep and goats like a beast. I like my food cooked and making use of knives and forks. It's civilized. Unlike the dragons that rampage the flocks."

Father said, "The herds are for feeding, man and dragon alike. Forgive me for forgetting to use my knife." He waggled a talon at me. "If you had your scales, you'd understand, Son. You are meant to be a good dragon, the same as me."

I wanted to please my father. I really did. But, as the years passed and the hairs on my skin became more coarse, I had an aching doubt that I was ever going to become a dragon. There were many things that I could do that men could not. Living long was one of them, but I never felt sure.

"Father, how can I know that I am a dragon? If I was a dragon, certainly I'd have scales by now. The others do."

"Son, you are not like the others. You are like me. As I've explained, there are dragons like the rest, and there are dragons like us. I am the keeper of this world, a protector of men as well as the dragons. But I won't live forever, and who will protect them when I'm gone? It has to be you."

Me. Yes, I knew it was supposed to be me. Deep down in my heart, I knew it was true. But one would think I'd have a sister or brother to share the responsibility. I continued to pout.

"What about my mother? Will you ever reveal her to me?"

"Oh, stop. You were hatched from an egg."

"I was not hatched from an egg like a goose!" I yelled. It infuriated me, him saying that. I knew I had a mother, and I suspected she was mortal, but my father, truthful and wise, had been holding something back all along. And it infuriated me that I did not know.

"More like a little crocodile," he said, joking. "You had scales when you were born, we… er, I was so proud. But after a few years, they fell away." His voice saddened. "And that's when I knew."

He had slipped! There was indeed a mother; I was certain of it. But, I could not remember her face or anything of her at all. Was she a dragon or a mortal?

"Knew what?" I asked, even though I had already heard the answer before.

His voice was heavy as he said, "That you would be the child that replaced me. That the responsibility was yours, whether you liked it or not. As I did not have a choice, Son, neither have you. There is only one great dragon in the world, and if it isn't me, it must be you. Without us, the world is doomed."

That was it: the ship's anchor strapped onto my back. The burden of an impossible responsibility that weighed me down to my knees. *I didn't ask for this.*

CHAPTER

5

THE MORE HE KEPT TALKING, the smaller I felt. It was a big part of the reason that I didn't come home to visit too much. He told me about the Dragon Wars, where one brood of dragons battled another for the sake of mankind. Every race: man, elf, dwarf, gnolls, orcs, and ogres had been in danger those days, but the dragons, the good ones like my father, won out. It all happened long before I came, and it was impossible to believe that there had been such devastation. Mankind, all of the races that is, had been on the border of extinction. My father had sacrificed everything to prevent that, and he had the scars and missing scales to prove it. Still, it was all hard to believe, that life on Nalzambor had been so cold and hopeless.

I stretched on a sofa, as soft and exquisite as one could be, and listened again. There must have been something I was missing. Why didn't I have my scales? And yet again, he told me why he thought I didn't.

"For every life you take, you must save another, or more. It does not matter if they are good or evil, who can really tell? There is good in everything, evil as well ...."

I knew better: orcs were evil. Gnolls, orcs, and bugbears, too. And renegade dragons, remnants of the Dragon Wars, were, too. It never made any sense to me to let them live.

He knew what I was thinking. "It's not just the orcs, Son. Men and elves can be just as bad. Have you not seen how they treat people? Would you treat your people like that? Outrageous."

It made sense. I'd spent so much time among them that I rarely noticed anymore. Some of their kind, men liked, and some they didn't like. They would feud and war with one another. Brag and boast about their riches, their kingdoms and princesses. I just laughed at them. They hadn't seen anything like I had, so their commentary was quite meaningless to me, but the company was very entertaining.

"My father was the same as me and you. He made this throne, but this treasure was here long before he came, even his father before him. And like us, they were born dragons that turned to men. You are not like your brothers and sisters, nor was I. They care little for the world of mankind, but it's important that we do. Men and dragons need one another. It's how life is."

I never really understood why dragons needed men, except to make treasure, which was still one of those things I enjoyed searching for in my journeys. I met many great men, elves, and dwarves, but I never saw any reason why we needed them. They tended sheep and cattle. Made objects that I assumed dragons were too big to craft. That was another thing. I never saw a dragon build anything.

"When I was your age, I was a bigger man, stronger, faster than the others. Our dragon hearts account for that. Like a horse's times two. I was cocky, too, for a while. I befriended the dwarves and learned about blacksmithing and forged the sword you've become so fond of over the years."

I jumped to my feet.

"You made Fang?"

"Indeed."

"But, if you weren't supposed to kill anybody, then why did you make the sword?"

"Because it's a symbol of truth, hope and strength. The men respected a man that swung a blade. And I never said you couldn't kill, just that it's only a last resort. But again, take a life, safe a life or more."

"How many did you kill?"

"Enough to remember, each and every one. Seeing life diminishing in a dying creature's eyes is a sad thing, indeed. We are here to save lives, not take them."

I thought about that.

"But don't we save lives when we take the lives of those endangering others?"

"How can you know for sure? At what cost, Son? Men will always fight and feud, whether we help them or not. They'll listen for a while, then wage war with one another. In all of your heroics, how much have you really changed?"

It was true. Battles were won and lost. Good men died, and bad ones lived. Evil withered in the dirt only to rise again into a strong and mighty tower. There was nothing that held it back for long. Not war. Not power. Not peace. This was the part that gave me a headache. Holding back against evil, the despicable beast.

"Save the ones you can, Son. Expect no rewards nor 'thank-you's, and move on, which I don't think you are very eager to do."

I liked being with people, but they aged quickly, and sooner or later I would always have to move on. It was hard to watch them fight so hard for a life that wasn't long lasting. And maybe that was what I liked most about men. Every day mattered to them. Each one was new, never the same, filled with new adventures over every horizon. Men, good and bad, knew how to live.

I let out a long sigh. I still had no idea how to get my scales.

"I can see in your eyes that you are frustrated, Nath—"

"NO! Don't say it again!" I held my hands up.

"Sorry, Son. You should stay among your brothers and sisters awhile. I'd enjoy your company. Maybe my guidance will sink in."

He was talking another hundred years at least.

"No," I stammered, a good bit angry at myself, "I want to earn my scales. I want to be a dragon!"

My father leaned back, dragon claws clasping his knees, and said, "Take the sword. The one you borrowed. It was going to be a gift anyway, but you slipped out of here like a halfling rogue before I could gift it to you. Take Brenwar," my father's tone darkened, and so did his smoldering eyes, "and do not return this time without your scales."

"What? I can't come back?"

An impatient tone took over his voice like a dam about to break.

"NO! Take with you that which you need. You've earned that much at least, but do not return without your scales."

I shouted back. "Earned it for what?"

"Saving our kin. The dragons. Like I've told you to. Focus on the dragons. The little green one, Ezabel, was quite grateful for your intrusion. She sends her best. And she's not the only one."

"Really?" I said, surprised.

"Son, have I ever lied?"

"No," I said.

"Or been wrong?"

I remained silent. I wasn't ready yet to admit that, so I shrugged.

My father shook his neck, a column of red armor over pure muscle. Then he said, "I don't just sit here as you think and leave every once in a while to gorge myself on cattle. I do many things you aren't aware of. I see things that you cannot."

That was new, but I wasn't so sure I believed it. If he ever did pop out of the mountain, I was certain the entire world would know, each and every one would be screaming like the world was on fire. I know that I would be if I wasn't his son. Then I realized he'd gotten me off track.

"Am I really banished as you say?" I asked, unable to disguise my worry.

"Yes," he said, his voice stern. "It's time you decided. Do you want to be a dragon or a man? Which is more important to you, Son?"

It was a hard question to answer, and it shouldn't have been. Among the dragons, I wasn't so special, but among the people I stood out. The women, smelling like blossoming rosebuds, running their delicate fingers in my hair, whispering words in my ear that would make a bugbear blush. I liked it.

And the elves, when you came across them, were so pure and delicate in beauty. Their mannerisms were quaint, direct, their cores as strong as deep tree roots. A bit arrogant though, and I'd be lying if I said I didn't enjoy humbling them from time to time.

The dwarves, brash and bold, like my dearest friend Brenwar, were the fiercest fighters and stubbornest competitors of all. Hardy, grim, and a little mirthful, I found nothing but comfort among their kind.

"Ahem." My father interrupted my thoughts. "Do you really have to think about it so much? By now the choice should be clear!"

I waved my hands up in front of me, saying, "Oh, no-no-no father. It's dragons. I want to be with the dragons. It's just that I find myself feeling so sorry for the others." I lied to some small degree. I also wasn't so sure I wanted to sit where he sat forever, even with all the treasures of the world at my feet. There had to be more to what he did.

Father lowered his head all the way down to the floor, his face a dozen feet from mine, hitting me with a snort of hot air. I felt like an insect when he said, "I've been in your shoes and walked the same path, and I know what you are thinking. You think like a man. It's time to grow up and think like a dragon. Now, with all my heart and wisdom, it is time for me to go. Take care, Son."

He reared up, went around the throne, and melded into an enormous mural of himself that was painted brilliantly on the wall. All of a sudden I felt alone. His presence, for the first time in my life, seemed gone. It was clear that he was serious about my scales, and I'd better be getting serious as well.

I spent the next few hours shuffling through the piles, loading a sack with anything I thought might help me, knowing full well it was up to me, no matter how many tricks I had in my pack. I departed, taking one last long look back at the mural of my father and wishing that I was on the other side of the grand painting as well. Brenwar awaited me, leaning against a wall, arms folded over his barrel chest, bushy black brows raised with alarm.

"You live!" he said, more in a grumble, but a surprised one.

"Ha! You didn't really think he'd kill me, did you?"

"I would've."

"For what?" I demanded.

Brenwar slammed my scabbarded sword into my chest.

"For stealing."

"Borrowing," I said, correcting him. "Besides, it was mine to take anyway."

"I know."

"You did?" I said, surprised. "But how di—"

"Just keep walking, Chatter Box. I'm ready to go. I feel so blasted small in this place. And there's no ale or dwarves…"

Brenwar kept going on, but I couldn't listen. My mind was too busy wondering if this would be my last time at home or not. My scales! I had my doubts I could do it, but determined I was, and a good bit deflated, too. How could I ever be a great dragon like my father? I didn't even have one scale.

CHAPTER

6

BRENWAR'S STOUT LEGS WERE TOO slow to keep up with my long legged pace, so we rode on horseback. Otherwise, he'd complain the entire way. I wasn't usually in such a hurry, so I normally preferred to walk, but I felt a degree of haste these days. Northward we went, towards the five great cities.

The Human city of Quintuklen was filled with magnificent castles and shining towers that overlooked vast rich and reaching farmlands.

The dwarven city of Morgdon was a mass of stone blocks and metal works, like a dwarven made mountain, grim and impenetrable.

The elven city, Elomelorrahahn, which I just called Elome, the most majestic of all, was hidden in the fog and forests.

The Free City, Narnum, hosted all the races, at least all those not so monstrous, damaging or tormented. It was a trade city, where all the merchants from all the races came to do business, and I found it the most exciting of them all.

The most dreaded, not so vast, nor appealing, was Thraagramoor, or just Thraag, grim as a mudslide, crumb poor, and run by the orcs, ogres, and goblin sorts.

"Well," Brenwar said, "which way will it be?"

The Mountain of Doom lay in the south, leagues and days from the others. The cities were each two weeks' ride from the other. They formed a rough circle, with Narnum, the Free City, hosting the middle. Everything in between was unprotected and dangerous land.

"Free City, as if you didn't know," I said, hoisting my canteen to my lips.

"I thought we were to be rescuing dragons and such? There'll be no dragons in that city."

"Ah, but is there not talk of dragons wherever we go?" I was grinning.

"I say we go to Morgdon first, then. My kin will be happy to see you again." He stroked his beard. "Not so much as me, but they'll be glad."

Visiting with dwarves was almost as bad as visiting with dragons, except the dwarves were always working, drinking, smoking or frowning. Their voices were gruff, their conversations short, but they also took time to host their guests. They liked to talk about the things they built and the battles they fought in—with vivid detail. But if you'd heard one dwarf story, you'd heard them all. I was polite when I said, "How about on the way back then, Brenwar?"

He grunted, kicked his short little legs into the ribs of his horse, and charged forward. "To Narnum it is then, Nath! But by my beard, they'd better not have run out of dwarven ale, else I'll drag you back to Morgdon by your ears!"

I couldn't help but smile as he spurred his mount, the hot air of the sun billowing in my recently chopped hair thanks to those dreaded orcs. It would grow back before we made it to Narnum City, where I could find an elven barber to refine it with a dash of magic here and there.

We traveled dusk to dawn, over the plains, through the woodlands, over some mountains, through some small lake towns, and well past the ruins. All the way we chatted with caravans and merchant trains. It was spring, and farmers, miners, and merchants were moving along the dusty and cobblestoned roads, taking their wares to every city in the north.

As usual, I heard the same rumors of war, for there were battles and skirmishes everywhere. There were soldiers from many races, all eager to lay down their lives to make money for their families. Brave men we met, and I admired them all. Of course, there were others, too, up to no good. Some spoiled and bold and others as crooked as a busted dog's tail. But, I didn't chat too long. I had heard it all before. I'd fought in wars, myself.

Nearing the end of the tenth day, my hips were sore from all the hard riding, and words couldn't describe my elation when I saw the tiniest tip of a spire in the middle of Narnum City.

"Brenwar! We're almost there. Two hours' ride at most, wouldn't you say?"

"Aye, I can't see it, but I know the road as well as you. I knew when we were five hours away three hours ago." He snorted. "I knew we were a day away a day ago. I see no reason for celebration. It's not like we haven't been here before."

"Ah, it's just better to actually see it. Having the goal in sight. Can't you ever get excited about anything?"

"I'll be excited when I have a barrel of ale under my bones and a full tankard as big as my head. It looks the same as it always has: not dwarven."

Well, I was happy. The past few months I'd been outside the cities, tracking down dragon poachers and hunters. Life wasn't all fun and games for me, despite all my advantages, but when I went to the city, I made the most of it. And anyway, a place like Narnum, a mix of everything in the world, was where I went to find the ones who tried to hunt dragons.

This city in particular was different from the rest. A mix of everyone tried to thrive here, and for the most part it worked out. All of the races, good and bad, had a say in Narnum, which for lack of a better word was nothing more than a giant market place ruled by many dukes and earls that feuded with one another most of the time, paying little attention to the troubles of the people if they were not their own. There was never enough for most of them, and what they gained, they quickly lost. At least that's how I'd seen it over the past two hundred years.

A tower rose over three hundred feet tall, like an ivory tusk had burst from the ground. It was a beautiful thing. Massive windows adorned its circular walls where an outward staircase spiraled upward like a green vine. I could see tiny bodies moving and peering through the bay windows. I dreamed about the day I'd be able to fly around that tower, wings spread wide, soaring through the air. But for now I was a ground pounder, same as the dwarves and men.

The closer we got, the more people we saw: dozens becoming hundreds, hundreds becoming thousands as we approached the only great city that had no walls. A river flowed through the city, east to west. I could see the tall buildings, some reaching over a dozen stories tall, but most were not so tall at all. There were guardsmen and garrisons all along the way. The protection of the city was well paid for. The citizens, hard workers, liked it that way, and I didn't fault them. I'd want my efforts protected as well.

The roads were paved with cobblestones and brick. The markets thrived with activity as we trotted deeper into the city. A half-elven auctioneer worked the stage in the marketplace, selling pieces of jewelry to a crowd of excited onlookers. He was dashing, not as dashing as me, but his lips were as fast as a hummingbird's wings. Banners marking the neighborhoods fluttered in the air. Children played in the fountains, and some begged for coins. Women aplenty hung from the windows, whistling at me, to Brenwar's chagrin.

"Quit ta' flirting' will you! Let's find a tavern, eat, drink and make grumpy!" He was hollering at me.

One buxom gal was yelling my way, "Handsome warrior, will you come and stay with me tonight? I've the softest lips in all of Narnum."

"I can see that," I said, momentarily mesmerized.

The women kept calling to me, one compliment following the other.

One shoved the other, saying, "No, my lips are softer."

"You are so gorgeous, and look at those broad shoulders! I will massage them all night."

"Your handsome eyes, are they your mother's or father's? I've never seen gold in a man's eyes, not even an elf's. So splendid and superb," a comely gal with long lashes noted, posturing from her window.

I stood and gaped at all of the wonderful things coming from their painted lips. I couldn't help myself.

Smack!

Brenwar jostled me hard in my side.

"Come on, Nath Dragon!"

I didn't budge … spellbound. Flattery was a weakness of mine, something my father had warned me about, but it didn't seem to ever sink in. I didn't want to fight what they were saying and saw no reason to, either.

"In a minute," I shrugged. "As you were saying, Ladies."

They all laughed and giggled as Brenwar took my horse by the reins and dragged me away.

"Fool!" he grumbled. "You'll never learn, will you?"

"I hope not," I said, waving at the ladies, whose attentions faded from me and coated the next traveler with their wares and pleasantries. I frowned.

"Whatcha frowning fer? You'd think you'd learn by now." He thumped his bearded chest with his fist. "Next time, I'll lead us in. You always go the same way. You're as drawn to those sirens as an orc is to stink."

"Am not!"

Through the city I went, my passions subdued, the sun dipping over the horizon. I led us into a less traveled part of the down, through some alleys and well off the commoner's path.

"Let's try this one," I said, pointing at a tavern, dark and dangerous, three stories tall, constructed of timber, and roofed in red clay tile. It gave me a shivering feeling. "There's plenty of trouble to find in there." So in I went, oblivious to the stranger's eyes that followed me from the road.

CHAPTER
7

THERE WAS MUSIC, HOLLERING, AND tale telling inside, and I liked that. Mostly men, of a questionable pedigree, long gazes and hard faces. The smell of roasted pheasant filled the air, and I was ready to eat. Brenwar pushed his way past me and saddled up to the bar.

"Ye got dwarven ale?" He asked a tall man, bald and wearing a black apron.

I took a seat alongside him, paying no attention to the stares glaring on my back. This city was used to travelers of all sorts coming and going all times of the night, but this place was one of those that kept close to their own.

"The same for me and two full pheasants, not charred, either." The two coins that I plunked on the table widened the barkeep's restless eyes. "And your undivided attention when I ask."

The barkeep slipped away, a small woman appearing moments later with two tankards of frothing ale as big as her head. Brenwar gulped his down in several large swallows, let out a tremendous belch, and looked at me.

"You can have mine," I said, turning my attention away from the bar and towards all the people inside.

Two men, one a bald giant, another part orc, each laden in muscle, arm wrestled over the wiles of a dainty girl with a look of trouble in her eye. A coarse group of men and women sat at a long table near the stone fireplace in the back, the adventuring sort, somewhat like me, some of them casting nervous glances over their shoulders.

An elven man wearing light purple garb and long pale green hair sulked in the corner and played a black lute of many strings for a small group of swooning women. His music was wonderful and strong. All in all, the tavern, a roomy little hole, was nothing compared to so many other taverns that tended to be much larger and more occupied. Still, it offered what I'd been looking for: trouble.

Three orcs sat in the back, beady eyes glancing my way and back. Another man, long and gaunt, sat huddled in the corner, fingering a blade, his tongue licking his lips as he gazed at me like some kind of meal.

At one end of the bar was a fair haired woman, a long sword strapped on her full hips, her tongue as coarse as the hulking man she accompanied, the one who had sneered at me earlier. I wasn't so sure they presented the kind of trouble I was looking for, but they were trouble. The kind that conspire and thieve. Rob grave yards, fight fiends and ghouls for gold. Kidnap women, sell children, and don't look back on their deeds with regret. Of course, my father would tell me not to be so judgmental, but I could detect evil, and it hung as heavy as a wet blanket in here. But did they trifle with dragons? That was what I was here to find out.

Brenwar's elbow rocked me in the ribs.

"Time to eat," he said.

Two steaming hot pheasants greeted my senses with a delightful aroma. One thing you could say about these run down taverns of disreputable ilk: they tended to have tasty food. My stomach rumbled, and my mouth watered. I hadn't realized how hungry I was until I started eating, tearing off big hunks at a time. Brenwar grunted and almost smiled, trying to keep the juicy bird meat out of his beard.

"Say," I said to the barkeep, shoving a gold coin his way, "I'm in need of some *dragon* accessories."

The man glared at me and said, "I don't know a thing about that, and it's best you take such business elsewhere." He shoved the coin back

I shoved it back saying, "Beg your pardon, Sir. Then a bottle of wine will do."

He hesitated, took the coin, and pulled a bottle down from the top shelf, setting it down and pointing to the door. "Once it's gone—you're gone." His eyes grazed the pommel of my sword on my back. "No dragon talk in my place." He turned and left.

"Cripes!" Brenwar said, wiping his mouth on his sleeve. "Why don't you just scare off every dragon poacher in town? Why don't you go ask for some orc accessories as well?" He glared at the orcs, still huddled in the corner, grunting with dissatisfaction over something.

I slapped him on the shoulder and said, "You eat and drink; I'll do the rest."

As we sat and gorged ourselves on bird meat and wine, I felt the tone in the room shifting. The patrons that sat near us began to fade away elsewhere. Many of the patrons seemed to stiffen, some leaving, and more notorious sorts arriving. The men began to bristle and brag, their comments of their exploits designed to catch my ear. Like most bad people, it seemed they didn't like me. Despite my rugged armor and attempt to blend in, I looked more than formidable. So far as I could tell, I was the tallest man in the room, my shoulders, arms and chest as knotted and broad as the rest. What they hadn't noticed about me before, they had noticed now. But I didn't come here looking for a fight. Or did I?

I tapped the big brute at the end of the bar on the shoulder.

"Do that again, and I'll cut off your hand," he warned.

"No doubt you would try," I said, smiling over at the fair-haired woman with the curious and inviting eyes. "I'm in need of dragon accessories."

"Get out of here!" He shoved me away.

Dragon accessories were a profitable business. A single scale was almost worth a piece of gold. Dragon teeth, scales, skin, claws and horns, whether they contained magic or not, were highly prized possessions that adorned many wealthy citizens. It was a practice that made me sick, seeing my kind displayed for fashion. Dragons were the same as the other races, but treated like something different. Of course, not all dragons were good, but most people viewed them all as bad.

I shoved him back.

"You touch me again; you'll be the one to lose your hands." No one shoves me around.

The fair-haired woman forced her way between us, pushing her angry man friend back with both hands, saying, "No blood here tonight." Then she whirled on me, poking her finger in my chest. "Go and sit down. I don't know what game you're playing, but I'll not stand for any talk of dragons. We fight for gold, not poach."

"I can see that now. But I pay well. Pardon me," I said with a slight bow, retaking my seat. *That ought to get them going,* I thought.

The man and woman warriors grumbled with each another, then departed, but she gave me one long look over her shoulder as they went. Now, me and Brenwar sat and waited. The barkeep continued to glower at me, but he didn't throw me out as long as we kept paying, and Brenwar was still eating and drinking. So I sat, noted all the scowls, and waited and waited and waited. I was a dragon, so waiting wasn't such a bad thing for me. But words travel faster than the wind sometimes. That's when two lizard men wandered in, both taller than me, crocodile green, dressed like men, and armored like soldiers. Their yellow eyes attached themselves to me first as they ripped their daggers out and charged.

CHAPTER

8

LIZARDMEN. BIG, STRONG AND FAST, like me, except not nearly as smart, but that didn't really matter when all they wanted to do was kill you.

I slung my barstool into one, cracking it into timbers over its head.

"Blasted reptile! Ye spilled my drink," Brenwar bellowed, clubbing another on its head with his tankard.

Slowed, but not stunned, the lizard sprang on top of me, driving me hard to the floor. I locked my fingers on its wrists as it tried to drive its dagger into my throat. Its red lizard tongue licked out as it hissed, angry and fateful. The lizard men weren't many in the world, usually pawns to greater evil, but effective pawns no less. I drove my knee up into its stomach with little effect as its blade strained inches above my neck.

"Dieeeesss, dragonsssss!" it said with a heave.

It felt like the veins were going to burst in my arms when I shoved back with all my strength. Over the sound of the blood rushing behind my ears, I could hear a rising clamor and more hissing voices. Not good. Yet Brenwar's bellows were clear.

"NO!" I yelled back. In a blink, I freed one hand and punched its long nose, rocking back its head.

Whap! Whap! Whap!

The lizard man jerked away from my stinging blows, but my hands felt like they were punching a wall. Still, lizard men hate getting hit in the nose, so do most lizards, for that matter. My blood was running hot now, the warrior in me suddenly alive as I jumped on its back and smashed its face into the floor. The dagger clattered from its grasp, and I snatched it up and rolled back to my feet.

Brenwar had the other one on the ground in a chokehold.

Crack!

And now it was dead, but the first two weren't the last. Three more were charging my way, not with daggers, but heavy broadswords this time. I can't imagine what I would have said that would have drawn so much attention.

Shing!

There was an audible gasp in the room as I whipped Fang's glowing blade through the air. Every eye was wide and wary, and I had to remember I had no friends here except Brenwar. The lizard men stopped for a moment, but they were well trained soldiers ordered to move forward.

The first lizard man charged past Brenwar, sword arcing downward and clashing hard into mine, juttering my arms.

Bap!

I punched its nose, rammed my knee in its gut, and jammed my sword into the thigh of the one behind it, drawing a pain filled hiss from its lizard lips. Two more were down, and the third had an angry dwarven man latched on its back. I raised my sword to deliver a lethal blow. I know, I know. My father warned me that killing is only a last resort, but I don't care what anyone says: lizard men and orcs don't count.

"Stop!" The Barkeep screamed. "STOP!"

No one moved, not even the lizard men.

Crack!

Well, that was one lizard man that wasn't going to move again for sure as Brenwar rode its dead body down to the floor.

"YOU, with the magic sword, get out of my TAVERN!"

"Me? But they attacked me!"

My longsword Fang hummed in my hand, its blade glimmering with a radiant light like the first crack of dawn. I brought the tip of its edge towards the barkeep's nose. I wasn't in any mood to be accused of something I didn't do.

He held his hands up, but tipped his chin up towards the folks behind me. I had a bad feeling as I turned to look. The two arm wrestlers stood now, each with a short sword in hand, eyes narrowed and ready to jump. The orcs, once three and now six, had drifted closer. The adventurers at the long table now stood. A staff glowed in one's hand, a sword glimmered in another. One warrior, grim faced and wearing chainmail, had a crossbow pointed at my chest. One woman, small and slender, stood poised on a chair, a handful of throwing knives bared. There were more, too, each focused on me, ready to fight or kill if need be.

"You can all try to take me if you want, but you won't all survive. Is your life worth the risk or not?" I glared back at the barkeep. "Your patrons can't pay if they're dead."

It was a bluff. I wouldn't have killed any of them, except the orcs. I swear they don't count. Neither do the lizard men, three of which had begun crawling back out the way they came. Lizard men didn't get along with me. We went way back. Well, I didn't mention it before, but I've been around awhile, and when you live a long time and do what I do, you tend to make enemies. I had plenty to go around. Chances were that one of my enemies knew I was here and had sent in a squadron of goons to kill me.

"Just go," the bartender pleaded, his eyes nervous now.

I looked at the two dead lizard men on the floor and asked, "What about them?"

"I'll take care of them. The lizards don't hold any worth with the authorities."

Brenwar had resumed his eating, his blocky mailed shoulder hunched back over his pheasant. I was still itching for a fight. The tension in the air had not slackened. My legs were still ready to spring. That's when the man in the corner stood up and walked towards the center of the room. Long and gaunt, hooded in a dark cloak, he seemed more of a ghost than a man. All eyes now fell on the man that held a hefty sack in one hand and dropped it on the table to the sound of clinking coins.

Slowly, he pulled his hood back, revealing a shaven head that was tattooed with symbols and signs I knew all too well. He was a Cleric of Barnabus, a cult of men obsessed with the dragons. Meddlers in a dark and ancient magic. I hadn't expected to come across one so soon. His voice was loud and raspy as he pointed at me and said:

"This bag of gold to the one that brings me his head!"

Clatch-Zip!

A crossbow bolt darted towards my ducking head and caught the barkeep full in the shoulder.

"What!" Brenwar roared, readying his dwarven war hammer, sharp at one end, like an anvil on the other.

"Don't let that cleric escape, Brenwar!" I said, smacking the muscled goons' blades with Fang. I clipped one in the leg and took a rock hard shot in the jaw from the other. He gloated. I retaliated, cracking him upside his skull with the flat of my blade.

"Agh!" I cried out in pain. A row of small knives were imbedded in my arm, courtesy of the little rogue woman. I'd have to deal with her later. I had to get the cleric, who was scurrying away towards the door. Brenwar was a barricade at the door, a host of orcs swarming at him.

"Let's dance, you smelly beasts!" he yelled, hitting one so hard it toppled the others.

He could handle himself, and I had bigger problems: the party of adventurers had surrounded me. Well, mercenaries seemed to be more likely the term for them. I leapt back as the lanky fighter with the brilliant sword tried to cut me in half. He was a young man, confident in his skills.

Clang! Clang! Clatter!

He lacked my power or speed as I tore his sword free from his grasp.

Slice!

I clipped muscle from his sword arm and sent him spinning to the floor.

Then everything went wrong.

The little woman jammed a dagger in my back. The wizard fired a handful of missiles into my chest, and the crossbowman, now wielding a hammer, slung it into my chest. That's why I wear armor, forged by the dwarves at that. My breastplate had saved me from dying more than a dozen times, but I'd gotten careless. I should have negotiated with this hardy brood, but I wanted to fight instead. I was mad. I was Nath Dragon, the greatest hero in the land, as far as I was concerned. It was time they saw that.

I banged the tip of my sword on the hard oaken floor. The metal hummed and vibrated with power.

THAAAAROOOOONG!!!

Glass shattered. Men and women fell to the floor, covering their ears, all except me and Brenwar, who stood on top of a pile of what looked to be dead orcs. I could see him yelling at me, but I could not hear. His lips mouthed the words, "Shut that sword off!"

I sheathed my singing blade, and the sound stopped immediately. The entire tavern looked like it had been turned upside down. Everyone living was moaning or wailing. The loudest among them? The Cleric of Barnabus. Huddled up in a fetal position, shivering like a leaf.

Fang's power was pretty helpful when it came to ending a fight with no one dying, but it didn't work on every race, or most of the time, for that matter. Fang only did what it wanted to do. My father said the sword had a mind of its own, and I was pretty sure that was true. I grabbed the cleric by the collar of his robe and dragged him over the bar. Brenwar had the cleric's bag of gold in his hand when he came off and plopped it on the bar. The barkeep, grimacing in pain from the crossbow bolt in his shoulder that was meant for me, smiled as the dwarf filled his hands with the gold and spilled them on the bar. "Fer the damages. The rest I'll be keeping."

"So long," I said, tying and gagging the cleric and hoisting him over my shoulder. "And thanks. This man will have just what I'm looking for."

The remaining patrons, still dazed and confused, holding their heads and stomachs, paid no mind at all as I left. They should have learned a lesson today: never pick a fight with an opponent you don't know anything about; it just might be a dragon.

CHAPTER
9

NO ONE OUTSIDE SEEMED TO mind as we pushed our way through the bewildered crowd of the neighborhood, loaded our prisoner on my horse, and galloped towards a part of town I knew better. The authorities weren't likely to give much chase, if they even bothered at all. Some parts of the city were void of the common rules of order.

"Here," I said to Brenwar, turning my steed inside a large barn of stables.

A stable hand, a young man, straw colored hair, and sandaled, greeted us with an eerie glance at my wriggling captive.

"No questions," I said, handing him a few coins.

"No problem," he said with a smile as broad as an ogre's back.

Stables and barns are good places to do business, or interrogations, for that matter. No echoes, and the smell of manure tends to offend most people, keeps them away. I shoved the cleric from my saddle, and Brenwar dragged him inside the stables over the straw and stood watch outside.

As I said, the Clerics of Barnabus are an evil lot, and we go way back. The fact that one had already come after me was a stroke of luck, both good and bad. Bad, because they almost got me killed. Good, because this man would lead me to their next nefarious plot. Normally, some desperate person would tell me something or find someone that would, when I asked after dragon articles. I'd follow their information, and sometimes that led to a dead end, but oft times it led me to where I was going. The Clerics of Barnabus, it seemed, had become privy to my ways. And when it came to dragons, they had eyes and ears everywhere. From then on, I had to be more careful how I went about gathering information.

Now the hard part. Interrogation. Taking information from an unwilling mind by force. It wasn't a very dragon-like way of doing things, but it didn't always have to be brutal.

I pinned the man up against the wall by the neck and jerked the rag from his mouth. His impulse to scream was cut short as my fingers squeezed around his throat.

"Urk!"

"That's a good little evil cleric. Keep quiet, and I'll let you breathe." I squeezed a little harder, forcing his eyes open wider. "I talk. You answer, quietly. Understand?"

He blinked.

That was pretty much all he could do, and I took it as a definitive yes. I could tell by the tattoos on his head that this acolyte was only a few notches above a lackey of the cult. He had some magic, but nothing I couldn't handle.

"See my dwarven friend over there?" I said.

Brenwar peered inside, holding a manure shovel in his hand.

"Look at what he does to people that don't cooperate."

He took the shovel, blacksmith hands holding both ends of the wooden handle, and grunted.

Snap!

The skin on the cleric's already gaunt face paled. His eyes blinked rapidly.

"Now, I'd say that shovel's thicker than your skinny bones. So, I suggest you answer my questions, in detail, or you'll be going home in a wheelbarrow."

The man's chin quivered. I couldn't ask for a better result.

"Y-You're, you're N-Nath Dragon. Aren't you?"

"You didn't know that already?"

"I was told it was you, but I did not believe until I saw for myself. Someone mentioned you'd come into town. I followed you in. Fully ready to see you dead. There is such a high bounty on your head. But, you move so fast. Impossible. Unnatural. I knew I'd lost as soon as it started, but I had no choice but to try," he said grinning sheepishly.

I slapped him in the face.

"Please, no flattery if you want to walk again."

Evil ones always try to beguile and convince a person their distorted intentions are only for the best, or out of necessity. It's tough to sell me if you're a man, but an attractive woman is a different story, and I knew right there and then I had best be more careful.

"We hate you, Nath Dragon! We'll have your head by dawn!"

"My, it seems you've forgotten what happened to my dear friend and the shovel. Brenwar!"

"No!" The evil cleric pleaded. "No. I can't have my arms and legs splintered. I'd rather die. Make a deal with me."

"No."

"Hear me out. I know where many dragons are kept, near this city. Small ones."

He had my attention. The little ones, some as small as hawks, others bigger than dogs, weren't easy to catch, but easy to keep. The thought of them being caged infuriated me. I pushed harder on his throat.

"You tell me now, and not a single bone of yours will be broken."

He nodded. I eased the pressure.

"Take the trail to Orcen Hold."

Finnius the Cleric of Barnabus lived, and Nath Dragon and his dwarven companion, Brenwar, were long gone. But still he struggled in his bindings, and his knee throbbed like an angry heart where the dwarf had whacked him with the busted shovel.

"Let me help you with that," a woman said. Her dark grey robes matched his, but she had short raven-colored hair, and thin lips of a pale purple.

She pulled the gag from his mouth and helped him to his feet.

"Have you done well, acolyte Finnius?" she asked, cutting the bonds from his wrists.

"I did exactly as you ordered, High Priestess." He rubbed his reddened wrists. "They are halfway to Orcen Hold by now. Your plan, Priestess, I'm certain will be successful. In a few more hours, Nath Dragon will be ours."

She rubbed her hand over his bald head and smiled.

"You'll be needing more tattoos after this, Finnius. I had my doubts you would pull this off, but it seems you did quite well. Assuming, of course, they arrive as expected."

"Oh they will, Priestess. Nath's eyes were as fierce as a dragon's when I said it. He'll not be stopped."

She walked away and said, "That's what I'm counting on. This day, the Clerics of Barnabus will forever change the life of Nath Dragon."

Finnius limped along behind her toward the front of the stables, where the stable hand greeted her from a distance. A long serpent's tail slipped out from underneath her robes. Striking like a snake, it knocked the boy clear from his feet, smacking him hard into the wall. Finnius swallowed hard and hurried along.

CHAPTER

10

ORCEN HOLD. NOT NEARLY AS bad as it sounds, but still bad, miles north east from Narnum towards the orcen city of Thraagamor. It's a stronghold, filled with brigands and mercenaries, all swords and daggers for hire that sometimes form an army whose side you never know they were on.

It isn't just orcs, either, or even mostly orcs for that matter, but men and some of the other races as well. The name most likely kept unwanted do-gooders like me away. I'd never been there before, but the world was vast, and even in my centuries of life, I still couldn't have been everywhere. That would still take some time.

Brenwar and I rode our mounts up a steep road that winded up a hillside, rather than around it, which would have been wholly more adequate. On the crest of the hill, no more than a mile high, I could see there was a massive fort of wood posts and block, jutting into the darkening sky. Pigeons scattered in the air, wings flapping before settling back along the edges of the walls. Pigeons are crumb snatching carrion, never a good sign, rather a bad one, as the black and white speckled birds are drawn to filth. Of course, what would one expect from a place named Orcen Hold?

I pulled my hood over my head as the drizzling rain became a heavy down pour, soaking me to the bone in less than a minute. I hated being wet, or drenched, or saturated in any kind of water that I hadn't planned on. You'd think a tough man like me would be used to it by now, but I saw no reason to like it. I like the sun, the heat on my face, the sweat glistening on my skin.

As the horses clopped through the mud, we made our way around the last bend, stopped, and looked up. Orcen Hold was a good bit bigger than it had looked from below. A veritable city that could host thousands, where I assumed at most were just a few hundred. Well-fortified. There were watch towers along the walls with soldiers spread out, crossbows ready to cut any unwanted intruders down. Ahead, the main gate, two twenty foot high doors, stood open behind a small moat. I couldn't shed the foreboding feeling that overcame me any more easily than the water soaking my back. It didn't seem like the kind of place where two men entered and got to leave… alive, anyway.

Still, we trotted over the drawbridge, through the doors, and underneath the portcullis that hung over us like a massive set of iron jaws.

"Yer sure ye want to do this?" Brenwar's beard was dripping with rain.

"I'd do just about anything to get us out of this rain."

Behind the walls over Orcen Hold lay a small city, not refined, but functional. The roads, normally covered with brick and stone customary of most cities, were dirt, now turned to mud. The buildings, ramshackle and ruddy, were tucked neatly behind plank wood walkways. People were milling about, dashing through puddles and across the streets from one porch to the other. Some shouted back and forth, in arguments of some sort. The children, possibly the most mottled ones I'd ever seen, played in the mud, their faces, grimy, poor, and hungry. And the smell. I could only assume it would have been worse without the rain, so for a moment I was thankful for the rain.

The Troll's Toe. That was the place we were looking for. The Cleric of Barnabus, Finnius was his name, had proven to be a very unwilling participant after he let loose the location called Orcen Hold. His tongue had frozen in his clenched jaws. A well placed spade to the knee, courtesy of Brenwar, and he'd told me what I was certain I needed to know.

The light was dim as the sinking sun continued to dip behind the clouds and disappear, turning an otherwise hot day cold. The wind began to bang the wooden signs that hung from chains in front of the buildings, making the dreary trek from an unknown city worse.

The firelight that gleamed from behind the dingy windows was a welcoming sight despite the coarse faces that glared at us with more remorse than curiosity. Blasted orcs. If it weren't for them, I swear that life on Nalzambor would be an excellent party.

"There," Brenwar said, pointing his stubby finger in the rain. "Seems we've found what yer looking for. But Nath, it's not too late to turn back. I'd say we're outnumbered here, uh, about a thousand to one."

"I thought you liked those kinds of odds?" I said, trying to wipe the rain from my face.

"Er … well, I do. But, this place reeks. If I'm to die, I'd like it to be somewhere a little closer to my home."

"Die?"

Brenwar looked a little bit ashamed when he said, "I just want to make sure I get a proper funeral. I'll not have a bunch of orcs burying me in the sewer. Or you, either, for that matter."

Brenwar was a bit obsessive about his funeral. It's a special thing for a dwarf. If they had their way, they'd die in battle, but they just wanted to be remembered for it. Brenwar, an older man by dwarven standards, had lived longer than even me and more than likely had a couple hundred years to go. He'd been with me so long, it didn't seem that he could ever die. But I'd seen other dwarves as great as him perish before.

The wind picked up, banging the sign to the Troll's Toe hard against the rickety building frame as we hitched our horses and went inside. Warm air and the smell of bread dough and stale ale greeted us as we sat down at a small table away from the firelight. The crowded room was momentarily quiet, more on account of Brenwar's presence than mine. It wasn't often you saw a dwarf in Orcen Hold, but Brenwar's bushy bearded face wasn't the only one. Still, I couldn't shake the feeling we were all on our own.

CHAPTER

11

IT WAS A ROUGH BUNCH, as bad as I'd ever seen. Tattooed, scarred, ornery, peg-legged, eye-patched, and hook-handed, it looked like the perfect place to get in trouble. The men were as coarse and rude as the orcs and half-orcs that snorted and blustered around the bar. The women were as crass as the men, singing and dancing on a small stage, their voices as soothing as a glass of boiling water.

"Now what?" Brenwar asked, looking back over his shoulder.

"We wait," I said, waving over a waitress with hips as big as an ogre's.

"What will it be, weary travelers?" She had a gap-toothed smile.

"Two of whatever tastes best with your ale," Brenwar spouted. "Human food, not the orcen mishmash that tastes like mud and worms."

She tried to make a pretty smile, but it was quite frightening when she said, "As you wish, Dwarven Sire."

"I think she likes you," I said.

"I certainly don't see why she wouldn't," he said, watching her prance away.

I sat there, sulking and soaking, damp hood still covering my face. It wasn't as if anyone would recognize me, but I'd still stick out like a sore thumb. There was something about my eyes and looks that drew stares, and for the most part, I like that kind of attention, but here, it was the kind of attention I didn't want. I just needed to lay low and wait until the opportunity presented itself. In a pain-filled voice, Finnius had assured us that I would know.

My appetite was barren, but the food wasn't half bad as I sat there and picked at it. Something about the greasy meat and cheeses they served in the worst of places always made me want to come back for more. It was getting late though, less than an hour from the middle of the night, and my wet clothes finally began to dry. The rain no longer splattered on the window panes, and I could again see the moon's hazy glow. I craned my neck at the chatter about dragons that lingered in the air, but it was hard to make anything out over all the singing voices and carousing.

Brenwar nudged me, pointing over towards a mousy man with hunched shoulders whispering among the tables. I watched him, his lips flapping in a feverish and convincing fashion. Some shoved him away, while others minded his words with keen interest. He had my interest as well. *Dragons.* I could see the word on his lips as plain as the nose on his face. I wasn't a lip reader or mind reader, but when it came to anything about dragons I could just tell.

Like a busy rodent, he darted from one table to the next, collecting coins and scowls, while directing the people towards the back of the room where I watched them disappear behind the fireplace mantle. *Don't ask for it. Wait for it.* That's what the cleric Finnius had said. It made sense, too. Asking would only rouse suspicion.

"You think he'll make it our way or not?" Brenwar combed some food from his beard.

The little man's head popped up our way, as if he'd heard Brenwar's question. He scurried towards us, his ferret face nervous, eyes prying into the shadows beneath my hood. Brenwar shoved him back a step.

"Some privacy, Man."

The small man hissed a little, then spoke fast.

"Dragon fights. Five gold. Dragon fights. Five gold. Last chance. One. Two. Three ..." his fingers were collapsing on his hand. "Four. Fi—"

"Sure," I said, sliding the coins over the table.

He frowned.

"Five for you!" he said, offended, scowling at Brenwar. "Seven for the dwarf!"

"Why you little—", Brenwar made a fist.

"Six," I insisted. You have to barter with dealers like these or else they won't respect you, and that can lead to trouble.

"Fine," he said, snatching the additional coins I pushed his way. He left two tokens, each wooden with a dragon face carved into it. "Under thirty minutes. Be late and no see."

I looked over at Brenwar as the little wispy-haired man left and said, "I suppose we should go, then."

Brenwar finished off the last of his ale and wiped his mouth.

"I suppose," he said, casting an odd look over at the large stone fireplace. "It's underground, it is. I feel the draft and the shifting of the stones. We're over a cave, or something carved from the mountain. Bad work. Not dwarven." He got up and patted his belly. "Probably collapse on us, it will. They probably let the orcs build the tunnel."

"You'll dig us out if it does, won't you?" I followed him behind the mantle. He didn't say a word.

One thing about Nalzambor, there were always new places to go. It was impossible to ever see what was behind every door in every city, and for the most part it was exciting. The chill from the damp clothes and biting air had worn off now, and the hearth of the stone fireplace was like a warm summer day. I put my hand on the rock, nice and toasty, which made me think of when I used to lie alongside my father's belly when I was a boy. He'd tell the most excellent stories, and even though they usually lasted more than a week, I never got bored of them.

We followed a man and woman of questionable character down a narrow winding stairwell.

"Bah. Orcen engineers. There should be no such thing," Brenwar complained, his heavy feet thundering down the steps.

At the bottom, two half-orcen men waited, armored in chainmail from head to toe, and two more stood behind them, spears at the ready. The tips of my fingers tingled. I realized I still had my sword, and Brenwar his war axe, but the pair before us, with steel swinging on their hips, paid their tokens and moved on, down a tunnel where many loud voices were shouting. The half-orcen man snatched my token from my hand and sneered.

"Take down your hood."

Brenwar stiffened at my side, hands clutching his weapon with white knuckles.

I looked down into the half-orcen eyes and growled, "I paid my share. No one said hoods weren't allowed. You have something against hoods?"

His lip curled back, but he couldn't tear his eyes away. I wouldn't let him. I looked deeper into him. I could see his hate and fear. There was little good in him, but enough man left for him to step aside.

"Go ahead," he said, blinking hard and moving on to the next people.

Making our way down the tunnel cut through the rock, I could feel the cool draft air nipping at my sweating neck. The sound of voices was getting louder now. A mix of races I could hear. Men mostly, but orcs, too, and a few dwarves as well. We emerged into a cavernous room, part cave, part auditorium, with seats carved from stone that formed a crude arena. The excited voices were shouting at a shimmering black curtain that covered an object in the center about twenty feet high and thirty feet wide. The hair on my neck stiffened as I pushed my way through the crowd that circled and pressed around the wall that surrounded it.

"Kill the dragon!" someone cried, jostling my senses.

An outcry of agreement followed, along with a series of cheers. I could feel more bodies pressing against mine, a frenzied and gambling horde. From above, a powerful voice, amplified beyond the powers of nature, shouted out.

"SILENCE!"

I'd never seen so many loud and obnoxious people fall silent at once, yet they did, looking upward at the sound of the voice. A man, as tall as he was wide, stood in robes laced in arcane symbols, glittering different colors in the light. A dragon's claw, a big one, jostled around his fat neck as he ran his pudgy fingers through a mop of brown hair. He seemed tired, expressionless, and bored. He yawned, his mouth opening three times bigger than it looked.

Brenwar nudged me, saying, "That ain't no man."

Whatever he was, he kept on speaking.

"SILENCE!"

He said it once again, long and drawn out. At this rate, I'd never see what was underneath the curtain.

"LET ... THE ... DRAGON ... GAMES ... BEEEEEEE ... GIIIIIN!"

There was a clap of thunder and a flash of light, followed by a series of gasps.

I gawped at what I saw next. A cage. A series of iron works constructed into a see-through dome of metal. But that wasn't what got me. I'd seen plenty of cages before. Instead, it was who was perched inside on a swing. A dragon, no taller than a dwarf, glimmering with orange and yellow scales, clawed wings covering his face and body. He shone like a diamond inside a room full of coal. My nerves turned to sheets of ice when the big fat man said.

"SEND ... IN ... THE ... TROLLS!"

CHAPTER

12

I T SEEMED SO OUT OF place to imagine such things as trolls fighting a dragon, albeit a small one, to the death. My inner self was recoiling, uncertain what to do, when the cage doors opened on a tunnel, to a rousing course of cheers. A troll—ten kinds of ugly all wrapped up into a ruddy piece of brawny flesh towering at ten feet tall—stood there, pounding its fist into its hand. The smacking was so loud it popped my ears. I tore my eyes away from the troll that lumbered, arms swinging into the walls, shaking the cage on its way into the chamber. The dragon was as still as a crane on his perch, unmoving. *Good boy*, I thought. I could tell he was a boy by the scales on his belly, a little darker than the orange and yellow scales on his body, unlike the girls, who were usually lighter than the rest.

The troll, naked except for a burlap loin cloth, narrowed its small eyes on the dragon and let out a terrible yell, loud and getting louder. A battle cry of sorts. A chorus of bestial fury. The dragon remained at peace on his perch, not showing the slightest degree of motion.

The crowed quieted. All eyes as full as the moon and fixated on the dragon. My own heart was pounding in my chest like a team of galloping horses. The troll, every bit as dangerous as it was dumb, lumbered around the dragon, like a predator sizing up its prey. Despite their lack of intelligence, trolls aren't impulsive, but once they make a decision, which usually involves something other than them dying, they stick to it.

"What's going on?" Brenwar muttered.

"I'm not sure."

"KILL THE DRAGON!" someone cried.

That's when the chants began, a rising crescendo of fury, and like a frenzied ape the troll beat its chest, charging the unmoving dragon, massive fists raised up and ready to deal a lethal blow.

The dragon's wings popped open, his serpentine neck striking out as he began breathing a stream of white lava.

The troll screamed in agony, thrashing under the weight of the dragon's breath that coated it from head to toe with brilliant white burning oil. The troll's flesh charred and smoked, its efforts to escape diminishing. The heat was like sticking your face too close to a campfire, from where I stood. The crowd roared so loud I couldn't hear myself think. I slapped Brenwar on the back, unable to hide my elation as the little dragon finished, leaving nothing left of the troll but the smoldering bones and an uncanny stink.

Brenwar looked up at me, eyes as big as stones, and said, "Did you see that? I've never seen a dragon with breath like that!"

Dragons. There were all kinds. Different makes and families, and each kind had a special weapon or two of its own. The orange dragons, called blazed ruffies, were one of the noblest and deadliest of them all. I had to get this one out, and out soon. He was still young, and it would be at least a day before his breath returned.

"That should do it," I said. "Let's stick around and see what we can do to sneak this dragon out of here."

There was a lot of murmuring, most good, some bad. It seemed most of the people that liked to take chances had been smart enough to bet on the dragon. I was expecting everyone to leave, but most of them were sticking around and talking. Of course, how often do you get to see a live dragon fight? Their fascination sickened me.

I looked above as the fat man whose mouth was too large for his face spoke again.

SEND ... IN ... MORE ... TROLLS!

My heart sunk down into my toes. "What?" I couldn't hide my exclamation. Wooden double doors opened on the other side of the cage into the tunnel again. Two trolls, this time carrying shields, clubs and wearing helmets, charged the orange dragon on the perch. The crowd screamed. I screamed. The dragon didn't stand a chance. He'd last another minute or two at most.

"We've got to get him out of there, Brenwar!" I yelled.

The dragon zoomed from his perch, dashing between the legs of one troll who swung, missed and bashed the other. Dragons are fast, no matter how big they are. But no dragon with spent breath and little room to fly could last for long in that cage.

"Find a way in, Brenwar!"

As soon as I pushed one person away, two more appeared. The crowd was in a frenzy, trying to get a closer look. The cage, so far as I could see, didn't have a door or opening except into the tunnel on the other side. I heard a sound like a rattlesnake's rattle. The Ruffie clawed his way up one troll's back, tearing its flesh up like dirt, drawing an inhuman howl. He perched on one troll's head and taunted the other with the rattle snake sound made by tiny fins that buzzed by his ears.

WANG!

One troll struck the other on its metal helmet just as the dragon darted away. It looked like two clumsy dogs trying to catch a mouse. One troll would swing, miss, and hit the other. That wouldn't last forever. Dragons, for all their speed and skill, tire quickly after their dragon breath is spent. They are magic, and magic needs time to recharge. Trolls, however, tire about as easily as a wall of stone. Those two wouldn't stop or slow until they were dead.

"Brenwar!"

I couldn't see him, but I could see people falling like stones, a path of people parting within the throng before closing up again.

The voice from above came again.

"STOP ... THEM!"

I saw him, the fat mage, like a toad on a stool, pointing straight at me. The crowd, dazzled by the spectacular fight, gave the man little notice, but the guards, the ones armed to the teeth, they were ready and coming after me. If they got me, I'd never get to the dragon in time, and I still hadn't figured out a way inside the cage.

"MOVE!" I shouted, but the people paid me no mind.

That's when I heard it, an awful sound, the sound of a dragon crying out, his shrieking so loud it hurt my ears. A troll had ahold of his wing. The dragon fought and fluttered, talons tearing into the troll's flesh, but its grip held firm. That's when something snapped inside me. A geyser of power erupted within my bones. Fang, my sword, was glowing white hot in my hands. I was surrounded, but my mind was no longer my own. The guards and men were falling under the wrath of my blade. I ignored the fear-filled screams and howls of fury. I could not tell one man from another. All I wanted to do was save the dragon, and nothing was going to stop me.

There was blood and fury in my eyes as I swung Fang into the iron cage. Fang cut into the iron as I chopped like a lumberjack gone mad. *Hack! Hack! Hack!* I was through, a troll's massive back awaiting me. I sent Fang through its spine and caught a glimmer of the dragon slithering away. Brenwar was yelling. I turned in time to see the other troll's club coming for me. I dove. *Whump!* The club missed my head. I rolled. *Whump!* It almost broke my back as I scrambled away. *Crack!* The troll fell over dead, thanks to the help of Brenwar's war hammer catching it in the skull.

"Come on!" He pulled me to my feet. Ahead, the large wooden double doors, at least ten inches thick, barred our escape from the coming wrath of who knows what.

Brenwar charged, war-hammer raised over his head, bellowing, "BARTFAAAAST!"

There was a clap of thunder, the splintering of wood, and a giant hole in the doors that had momentarily barred our path. The dragon was gone like a bolt of orange lightning.

"Follow that dragon," I yelled, following Brenwar down the tunnel.

The dwarven fighter's short legs churned like a billy goat's as he charged down one tunnel and through another. My instincts fired at the sound of armored soldiers coming after us down the tunnel.

"Do you know where you're going, Brenwar?" I cried from behind him.

Brenwar snorted, "I'm a dwarf, aren't I? Not a tunnel made that can lose me."

We found ourselves running down a long corridor, where a wooden door had been busted open that led outside into the pouring rain. The pounding of armored boot steps was coming our way, barking orders and calling for our heads. It was time to make a stand.

A group of heavily armed soldiers rounded the corner, armored in chainmail from head to toe, the silver tips of their spears glinting in the torch light.

"Get him," one ordered from behind, thrusting his sword in the air.

I whipped Fang's keen edge around my body and yelled back.

"The first one that comes within ten feet of me is dead!"

The soldiers stopped, looking with uncertainty towards one another. That's when I noticed the blood dripping from my sword. Their eyes were on it as well, and a hollow feeling crept over me. How many had I killed? Everything was a blur. Perhaps it was troll's blood, but it didn't' seem dark enough.

"Skewer that man!" The commander's face was red. "If you don't follow orders, then you're dead men anyway. We've got strength in numbers. Attack!"

The first two spearmen lowered their weapons at my belly and advanced. All I wanted to do was buy time. Just a few seconds more. I leaped in, batting one spear away with my sword and yanking the spear away from the next man. The soldiers shuffled back. Now I faced them with a sword in one hand and a spear hoisted over my shoulder.

"The next soldier to advance will catch this in his belly," I said, motioning with the spear.

"Cowards! Charge him! Charge him now!"

The unarmed spearman stepped back as another took his place.

I launched my spear into his leg. The man let out a cry of pain as he tumbled to the ground.

I ducked as a spear whizzed past my face.

"Charge!"

I hoisted Fang over my head and said, "Stop! I surrender!"

No one moved, every eye intent on me.

The commander shouted from the back, "Drop your sword, then!"

Slowly, I lowered my arms. But I had another plan. I'd use Fang's magic to blast back my enemies as I'd done in the tavern.

"What are you smiling for?" The commander moved forward.

"I'm just glad to put an end to the violence, is all. Oh, and you might want to hold your ears."

"What for?"

I banged the tip of Fang's blade on the stone corridor's floor.

Ting.

Nothing happened. I tried it again.

Ting.

Drat!

"Fang, what are you doing?" I shook my sword.

The commander was not amused. "You going to drop that sword, or not?"

I was flat-footed now with nowhere to go but out. I grasped my sword in both my hands and pulled it in front of my face.

"I've changed my mind. I'm going to fight you all. To the death!" I let out a battle cry and charged forward. All of the soldiers hunkered down. In stride, I pivoted on my right foot, twisted the other way, and dashed outside the busted doorway into the rain.

I was drenched the moment I made it out into the river of mud that was supposed to be a street. I heard a horse nicker nearby and dashed that way. Brenwar, my horse in tow, was galloping down the road, hooves splashing in the water.

"Run, Dragon!"

The heavy boots were trampling behind me as I sprinted alongside Brenwar, grabbed ahold of the saddle on my horse, and pulled myself up.

"Great timing," I yelled up towards Brenwar as we began our gallop away. "I couldn't have done better myself—*ulp*!"

Something that burned like fire slammed into my back. Another spear sailed past my head, followed by another. The pain was excruciating as I galloped onward with a spear in my back, holding on for dear life.

It was dawn before we stopped riding. I could barely keep my head up, and I swore I'd black out any second. We didn't slow, not once, taking trails little known to most. I'd been that certain our pursuers were many. I was restless when we stopped along a silvery stream and gave the horses a moment to drink.

"Finally stopping are we? Think we lost them?" Brenwar said.

I slid from my saddle, grimacing.

"What's the matter with you, Nath? You look like … Egad! Is that a spear in your back?"

He hurried over and inspected my wound.

"Ouch! I don't need speared again, Brenwar!"

"Why didn't you say something, you fool! You could've bled to death."

"It's not that bad," I gasped. "Only a javelin, right?"

"Sure, and I'm a fairy's uncle. Still, it's a small one. Not barbed for hunting. It's wedged between your armor and your back. Hold this." Brenwar put my horse reins in my mouth.

"What for," I tried to say.

"Just bite down. I've got to pull the spear out."

I shook my head.

Brenwar yanked out the spear. I screamed. It felt like my entire back was pulled out, and I fell to my knees.

"I'm going to need to stitch that up. And quick. Are you sure you are feeling sound? That's a dangerous wound. Another inch it'd be inside a lung."

It hurt, but I'd been stitched up by Brenwar before. Besides, I had some salve that would accelerate the healing.

"All done," he grumbled as he poked his finger in my face, "and next time, tell me something."

"Thanks, Brenwar." I rolled my shoulder, and my back still burned like fire. At least the rain had passed.

"You sure you're feeling well? You don't look well."

"I've been recently skewered. I'd assume that's it."

"Pah ... Yer fine, I guess," he said, walking away.

The sun, warm on my face, a feeling that normally gave me comfort, gave me none. Brenwar, usually full of boasts after a battle, was quiet. I picked up a stone and skipped it from my side of the stream to the other.

"Another dragon saved," I said. "A fairly powerful ruffie, at that."

"Aye," Brenwar said, refilling his canteen. "Some fight, too. Works up the ole' appetite, it does." He thumped his armored belly with his fist. "How about I snare a rabbit or two?"

"I've got my bow."

"Are ye daft? Ye didn't bring yer bow," he argued, his busy face widening with worry.

"What?" I said, "You look like you just swallowed a halfling. Brenwar ..."

The world wobbled beneath me. Bright spots burst in my eyes: pink, green and yellow. Brenwar's arms stretched and stretched and stretched toward me, beyond me. His face spun like a pinwheel and was gone. Silence. Blackness. I fell, I think.

Finnius stood alongside the High Priestess of the Clerics of Barnabus with a nervous look in his rodent eyes. He'd seen men dead before, but not so many, not like this. He couldn't imagine how Nath Dragon had done all this, but the witnesses, the ones that survived the horror, assured him he had. The arena beneath the Troll's Toe in Orcen Hold looked like a battlefield. A battle that they had clearly lost, not to mention losing a dragon as well. The High Priestess, however, didn't seem worried. Arms folded over her chest, a dark twinkle in her eyes, a smile cropping up from the corner of her mouth, she said, "It won't be long, Finnius. Nath Dragon will be mine."

CHAPTER
13

It was dark. I smelled burning wood. Meat roasting over a fire. My eyes opened to a brilliant starlit sky, and I felt whole again. I rolled over to where a campfire blazed and Brenwar kneeled, turning rabbit meat on a spit.

"Dinner time already?" I got up and walked over.

Brenwar looked at me like I'd come back from the dead.

"What? Has it been a day or more? You look like I've been sleeping for a week." I stretched my arms out and yawned. "I must admit though, it feels like I've slept for a week, maybe longer. I guess saving dragons is bound to catch up with you."

"Or turning into one," he said. At least, I thought that was what he said.

"Brenwar, is that some kind of joke?"

I looked at him, the sky, and the moon before turning back towards the stream that was no longer there. A very bad feeling overcame me, like a part of my life was missing.

"Say, how'd I get here? Where's the water? Brenwar, how long have I been out?"

He mumbled something.

"Louder," I insisted.

"Three months! Three months, Nath Dragon! And I've been out here counting daisies and trapping furry little animals." He rose to his feet and poked me in the chest. "Now, three months isn't long for a dwarf, but it's not short by any measure, either."

"Why didn't you wake me, then?"

He jumped up on his feet and yelled, "Don't you think I tried? I could've set you on fire, and you wouldn't have moved! I should have let the harpies carry you off."

"Harpies?"

"Pah," he said, waving me off.

I raked my fingers through my hair and checked the beard that had grown on my face. I scratched it with my nails that were unusually long, on my right hand anyway. I held my hand out and stared. Brenwar's downcast face stayed down, kicking at the dirt as I looked at the black scales on the fingers of my dragon-like hand.

"Gagh!" I said, jumping away from myself.

I looked at my other hand, the left, and it was fine, but my right—black glimmering scales and thick yellow claws like my father's—was a thing of beauty. A rush of energy and excitement went through me as I jumped high in the air and screamed with delight. I felt like a child again.

"I can go home again, Brenwar! I've gotten my scales! Or some scales."

I ran my new and old fingers over my face.

"Brenwar, is my face unchanged?"

He nodded.

I was relieved, but I wasn't certain whether I should have been or not. I shed the blanket from my shoulder, and everything but my right arm was fine, or human at least, and I still wasn't sure if that was a good thing or not. I checked behind me.

"Do I have a tail?"

"No!"

"Why so glum then, Brenwar? I've gotten scales!" I said, marveling at my arm.

He shrugged and said, "Don't know."

He was being stubborn, naturally, but something bothered me.

"What?"

"I ain't seen no man become a dragon before," he said, taking the rabbit from the spit. "Hungry?"

I gazed at my arm, its diamond-like scales shimmering in the twilight, like broken pieces of coal. I could feel power, true power, like I'd never felt before. I swore my right arm was twice as strong as my left, and my left was already stronger than most men's.

"Come, then, Brenwar! I can't wait a moment longer. It's time to go see my father!"

"So be it then, Nath."

The trek through the Sulfur Marsh at the bottom of the Mountain of Doom had never gone quicker as Brenwar and I made our way through the secret passageway. Most of the time, when I came home I was either half-dead, which had been the case the last time, or filled with dread because I had not gained any scales. Despite my father's and my disagreements over the past two centuries, I never wanted to disappoint him. This time, however, I had the upper hand. I had my scales, and my days as a man were numbered.

I took a moment to pause in reflection as I stood outside my father's chamber doors. The detail in the doors and the rest of the caves and tunnels appeared to have a greater meaning to me now. The brass framework interwoven in ornate patterns on the wooden doors said something to me. The symbols carried power.

"So," Brenwar's gruff voice interrupted my thoughts, "are you going inside, or are you going to stand there and gawk? It's a dwarven door, you know. You'd think you'd never seen it before." His thick fingers were playing with his beard. He seemed nervous, if that was at all possible.

"It's fine work. I just never noticed before. Do you think I should knock?"

"There's a first time for everything."

True, in all my years, I hadn't bothered to knock before. I wasn't certain why it was different this time, but it was. This time, of all times, the little things seemed to matter.

I looked down at Brenwar's face, then at the door, and lifted my fist to knock. Both doors swung open on their own.

"ENTER, SON, AND MY FRIEND THE DWARF."

I led, my chin held high, like the time I'd saved my first dragon. I felt like a boy again, new and refreshed, a spring in my step because the hard feelings at failed efforts were gone.

My father, the grandest dragon of them all, sat on his throne, his eyes burning like fire. I'd never seen such an expression on him before. Fearsome. Deadly. Secrets as ancient as the world itself protected beneath the impenetrable scales and horns on his skull. His voice was like a volcano about to erupt, turning my swaggering gate into a shuffle.

"COME CLOSER."

The gold pieces piled up were slipping like shale, and the entire cavern seemed to shake. I was thirty yards from the foot of his throne when I opened my mouth to speak; my day of glory had come.

"STOP!"

I froze. Something was wrong. Brenwar dropped to a knee beside me, head down.

My father sat there, monstrous claws clasped in his lap, a side of his razor sharp teeth bare.

"REMOVE YOUR ARMOR."

"With great joy, Father," I said, unstrapping the buckles on my chest plate. Certainly, he had to have noticed my dragon's hand at least, yet he said nothing. Perhaps, there was to be more of a ceremony with the full showing. I tossed my armor and garments aside, standing with my naked chest out, my incredible black-scaled arm up high.

My father sucked his breath through his teeth, his face smoldering with fury, and roared so loud I thought the mountain had exploded.

I fell to the ground, holding my ears, crying out and pleading for mercy. I couldn't think or focus; I just screamed as I felt like the entire world was going to end. A sharp cracking sound exploded nearby as one of the marble columns fell. The room filled with heat so hot I could barely breathe. My whole world had gone wrong. I'd never been so terrified.

Somehow, I rose to my feet despite all the feeling in my legs being gone. My hands were still clamped over my ears as I watched my father continue his angry bellow. Brenwar was almost covered in treasure, his face devoid of expression, eyes watering like he'd seen a horrible ghost.

I yelled out, "What is wrong, Father?"

His roar stopped, but my ears kept on ringing.

His voice was lower now.

"What have you done?"

I stood, shaking, stupefied, and gawping.

"What have you done?" My father asked again, the rage in his voice gone, but the molten steel tone remaining. "Have you ever seen a black-scaled dragon?"

I looked at my arm, shook my head, and said, "No."

Then, I realized something must be horribly wrong.

"The Ruffie you saved has been here and told me what you have done. I hoped that it was not true, though I knew that it was. Did you even realize that you killed so many?"

The truth was, I didn't have any idea how many I killed at all. I hadn't even thought about it.

My father looked down, and I felt like it was the last time I'd ever see him again. My heart began to sputter in my chest as I fell to my knees, tears streaming down my cheeks, and begged, "No, father, I'm so sorry. Let me fix this."

"It's too late for that. You have cursed yourself. You are no longer welcome in Dragon Home. You'll take no swords, no gold, no magic … not anything. You are on your own. If there is any hope left, you'll have to find it on your own. I've told you all I can. Now go, to never return unless those scales are a different color."

My father gave me one long lasting look with nothing but sadness and disappointment in his eyes. I'd failed him, I knew it, for the last time. I felt smaller than the tiniest coin in the room as he turned, walked away and disappeared back into the mural.

Alone, I wept my way through my father's throne room, never looking back, through Dragon Home, through the Sulfur Marsh, until I wept no more.

Bearded and lonely, I sat inside a cave at least a hundred leagues from my father, as another season passed while I contemplated my failure in self-pity. No men killed. No dragons saved. My cursed black scales remained.

If there is any hope left, you'll have to find it on your own, my father had said.

He'd said many things, and it was time I put them together. I rose from the crag where I had stooped and bellowed the fiercest bellow I could muster. It was time to figure out what I must do to become a dragon, a very good one, at that. Like my father.

From out of nowhere, Brenwar showed up and tossed a beautiful sword at my feet. It was Fang.

"Brenwar! How did you get this?" I asked in alarm and jubilation.

"Yer father only said *you* couldn't take anything from his cavern. He didn't say anything about me." He winked and added. "And that isn't all I got, either."

Thus begins the Chronicles of Dragon.

Dragon Bones and Tombstones

-Book 2-

CRAIG HALLORAN

PROLOGUE

STARLIGHT. THE LAND OF NALZAMBOR was filled with stars, more than could be counted, more than could be seen. The biggest one, the most brilliant, lingered behind the moon like the twinkling eye of a dragon. But now was not the time to pay attention to such beautiful things. Not the shimmering waters, the soft grasses, the gentle breeze or trees filled with fruit a plenty. No, such things didn't matter now in the mystic land of Nalzambor, at least not when death, despite all the beauty, still whispered in the air.

CHAPTER

1

I SAT HIGH IN THE BRANCHES, spying the orcen camp below. Brenwar and I had spent weeks trying locate it. Brenwar wasn't with me. He didn't climb trees, not unless he really had to.

Below, the gruff voices bellowed and drank, celebrating their prized catch: an evergreen dragon. I could see her well from my perch. She was a rare flower, a thing of beauty among the decay of mankind. Small and young, the creature's body was less than that of a man. Her tail, slender and serpentine, curled around her body as she lay still. Green, a brilliant green like emeralds, was the color of her scales. Her underbelly was not fully developed, yet it was armored in citrine yellow. Long-necked, with a small nose and snout, she had two leathery wings folded over her back. Her chest was rising and falling like she was out of breath. I could sense her fear, alone and helpless. I had to free her; after all, that's what I did. Or at least, what I was supposed to be doing.

I watched and waited. Certainly, Brenwar's signal would come at any moment. I hated waiting. And the watching part was another matter. Watching orcs—all of which were brawny, fatty and boar-like in the face with little tusks jutting from the bottom of the mouths—was offensive. They were crude.

One sat on a log by the fire, picked his nose, poured a nasty stew in his mouth and belched. Another was plucking the lice from his beard while a different one picked lice from his hair and tossed it in the iron pot of stew. Their purpose in my world was a mystery because I'd yet to see anything good from a single one of them, ever.

Where are you, Brenwar?

The moon rose to a full zenith, a full bright yellow, and it wasn't long before the party of orcs began to drift into sleep.

Two orcen guards stood watch alongside a wagon that housed the metal cage that contained the dragon. Both were alert, chests out and spears ready. I knew from experience that the slightest abnormality in the camp would make them sound the alarm. Sneaking up on them wasn't a very good idea. I could get one shot off with my bow, killing one, but getting the second shot off before the alarm sounded would be difficult. And I had to remember that I was not supposed to kill.

My back was beginning to ache, and my legs were becoming numb. I needed to move. Brenwar, on the other hand, well, he could stand like a statue for days. I've seen him do it. He could beat a stone in a standing still contest. But me, no. I was a man of action, and I had things to do. A dragon was suffering, endangered, helpless. It made me feel miserable, too. With or without Brenwar, I was going to free the dragon. I didn't rustle a single leaf as I climbed down. A stiff breeze blew my hair in my eyes. It was good, being downwind from the camp. The orcs had snouts almost as good as hounds, and I had to be careful they didn't catch wind of me. Of course, on the flip side, I got plenty a nose full of their foul dander.

Wretched things.

I never ate bacon because of them, and I love meat, in all its forms and flavors.

I hunched down behind the tree I'd been sitting in and watched as one of the orcs poked at the dragon with the butt of his spear. It lit a fire in me as I watched the little dragon's tail tighten around her body. The orcs' mocking laughter and mockery stirred the warrior within me. My impulses took over. My anger rose.

Control, Nath. Keep it under control.

I reached for my bow, Akron. Compact in size, forged by magic, it hung from the armor on my back. I snapped it into place.

Snap. Clatch. Snap.

The bow string coiled into place like a living thing. Akron, a wonderful weapon made in the forges of the elves, a gift from long ago. I spit on the tip of my arrow and rubbed it in. The black arrowhead began to glow with a yellow fire as I nocked it. My dragon arm was steady, solid as a red oak. My aim was true as I listened to the stretching sound of the bowstring. The orcs' throats were as clear as the nose on my face.

Save the dragon. Kill them all if you have to.

Oh, how much I wanted to. But killing, no matter how evil the opponents, wasn't the best way to earn my scales. I hated that part. It was so hard to understand.

Small breath. Release.

Twang!

A streak of yellow light whizzed through the night, soaring past the orcs' heads and into the lock on the dragon's cage. The orcs jumped like their feet were on fire, gawping at the arrow juttering inside the metal lock.

The dragon remained still.

One orc grabbed his head, bewildered, studying the arrow in the lock.

Wait for it.

I nocked the next arrow.

Boom!

The arrow exploded. The orcs fell to the ground. The sound wasn't so loud, except it came in the dead of night, and in all likelihood I had woken up everything sleeping for a quarter mile. As I watched the pieces of the large metal lock scatter everywhere, the green dragon came to life, her small winged arms clawing at the cage. The dazed orcs scrambled back on their feet, fighting to secure the cage door, one putting his body into it, the other trying to lock it with something else.

Twang!

The orc screamed as the arrow imbedded in its ankle.

Twang!

I sent the other howling to the ground as I caught it in its hip.

Two down, none dead, but the dragon was still trapped inside.

Drat!

The camp was a flurry of activity now. Orcs rose from under their blankets, ripped their swords from their belts, and began barking orders. The dragon thrashed inside her cage. The latch, lock or no lock, was still holding. I moved. Bounding across the camp, ducking under a chopping axe, I lowered my shoulder, bowling the next orc over. In a single bound, I made it to the wagon and pulled the cage door free.

A thunderous cry of alarm went up as the dragon's long neck jutted out, stepping from the cage, spreading her magnificent wings in the moonlight. With a single whoosh, she darted into the sky and disappeared from sight. They're fast. So am I, but the problem is—I can't fly!

"You're welcome!" I yelled, for all the good it did. Of all the dragons I saved, none ever thanked me. Not that they could talk. Some could. Most couldn't, and I only knew a few that did. But one would think, for all the times I helped them, they'd at least come back and help me, but they never came.

"Kill him!" The orcs yelled, surrounding me.

I leapt into the wagon and pulled out Fang, its blade glimmering like wide fire. Still, none fled. The orcs were stubborn like that, always letting their greedy intentions get the better of them. The orcs were not cowardly, just stupid. They closed in, weapons brandished, their faces eager for my blood. An orc with a face like cottage cheese let out an angry cry, and they charged.

I leapt on top of the cage as a battle axe whacked a chunk out of the wagon where I was standing. One by one, they jumped into the wagon, heavy swings nipping at my toes as I danced and batted their steel away, careful my feet would not slip between the bars. It was chaos, as one fought over top of the other, trying to tear my legs from underneath me and cut me down in a tide of my own blood.

The dragon I freed, as with all dragons, was worth a lot. Worth enough for these thugs and rogues to gorge themselves on ale and food for months, maybe even a year. If you ever want to make somebody really mad, just take their money.

The nearest orc bellowed as I sank my blade, Fang, into its shoulder. Fang is short for its real name that is as hard to pronounce as it is to spell, at least for me. Impossibly long. What else should I expect of a sword made by my father? *Chop! Chop! Clang!*

Their blows rattled the cage, tearing more wood from the wagon. I wobbled on my legs as two more of the beastly orcs heaved the wagon in an attempt to shake me to the ground. It was getting hot now, my breath heavy as my sword arm became heavy from deflecting all their blows. My muscles were being put to the test as I struck quick, clipping an ear, before dancing away from another's broad stroke. I slipped. My foot went down between the cage bars, catching my knee on the metal, filling my head with an explosion of pain. I cried out.

"We've got him! Kill him!"

Three orcs surrounded me, trying to pin my arms down. I cracked one in the nose with the sword's pommel and punched another in the jaw. Its head rocked back, but my fist stung from the blow. The orc wrapped its meaty arms around my throat, arcing like a bow, bending me backward over the cage.

It was suffocating. The sweaty thing had me, and I could smell its breath that was as foul as garbage. I heaved. It heaved back as I cried out in agony. My leg, still pinned between the cage bars, was ready to snap. My sword, Fang, was useless. I let it slip through my fingers, hanging onto the pommel, revealing a small dagger within that I called Dragon Claw.

Slice!

I stabbed its belly. It recoiled and teetered from the wagon. Bloody dagger in hand, I jabbed it into the second orc's arm. It had power, determination. It was me or him. I had the feeling that before I poked another dozen holes in its arm, my leg would break. The pressure was building, and I felt the tendons in my knee stretching. I swung at him with my dagger, but I could not reach him.

"Let go! Beast! Let go!" My lungs were bursting inside my chest as I cleared my leg from the cage and dodged another blow. I hopped to the ground, rolled over Fang and re-inserted Dragon Claw in the pommel.

Now, ten orcs still lived, each snorting in open hostility, not a one willing to yield, though the one

I stabbed in the belly might have been dying, based off the pain-filled groans I could hear. Unfortunate, but it happens. I fought for my breath. It was time to speak.

"This has gone far enough, orcs. I've scratched you, maimed you, but I can do much, much worse," I said, pulling back my shoulders and standing taller than their tallest, and orcs are big, bigger than men on average. My voice was as big as me, but that didn't really matter if the orcs were too stupid to recognize Common. I could always speak in orcen if I wished, but why lower my standards? They might take that as a compliment.

"So, what will it be, little piggies?" I said, twirling Fang's glowing blade through the air. "Limp home and live," I shrugged. "Or die." Which was a bluff, because I'm not supposed to kill them, remember? If anything, they'd figure I was as bad a shot with a bow as I was at swinging my sword.

Dripping blood from their injuries, lathered in sweat—orcs sweated more than anything I knew—they gathered closer. I'd played the game too long. It was time to get serious.

Dragon saved. Disappear? Disarm? Oh, what to do? Where in Nalzambor is Brenwar! Fang glimmered in the grip of my fingers, a bright piece of steel that shimmered with radiant living light. It felt alive in my hand. It was hefty, its flat blade wide, its hilt big enough for two hands, but in my grasp it was as light as a stick, perfect in weight and balance.

Shing!

I struck the belt buckle of the nearest orc, dropping his pants over his ankles. The rest jumped back. But as far as they were concerned, it was another miss.

Oh great, they're going to attack.

They came at me like a sweaty swarm of hornets, steel stingers in their grasp, ready to skewer me alive.

I was big, an easy target, but I was fast, too.

"Kill him!" the orc said, kneeling down and trying to pick his pants up from the ground. I think Kill is a very common word for orcs, meaning the same in their language as mine. I ducked just in time as a sword whistled over my head. I rolled under the wagon to the other side. My blood, still pumping from the moment this all started, was just warming up. The warrior in me had lost patience when I popped up on the other side and began swinging.

Crack!

I clipped one under the chin with the butt of my sword.

Glitch!

I stabbed another in the thigh, bringing a forthcoming howl and limp.

Slice!

Another orc clutched its bleeding arm where I cut clean through the triceps. I meant to do that.

Parry!

Clang!

A battle axe clattered into the back of the wagon, drawing astonished grunts. I shifted behind the next attacker that was poised to poke a hole in my back with a spear.

Chop!

I sliced though the shaft of the spear, drove my sword into its shoulder, and spun away from another two-handed blow.

Parry.

Clang!

Fang tore its blade from its grasp.

Glitch!

I stabbed it in the chest and watched it, beady eyes now wide, fall over and die.

Oops!

Yes, I'm not supposed to kill other people, in order to earn my scales, but I don't consider orcs people. And no one can really say whether or not killing something evil prevents me from getting my scales. And my father said I could kill if my life was in danger. I was pretty sure it was.

I punched an orc in the face with my dragon fist, my right arm. Stabbed Fang into the shoulder with my left arm. It was like having a weapon in each hand, but my dragon arm and Fang had issues, and I'll talk about that later.

I kept the pressure up, my lungs burning, sweat dripping from my hair into my face as I watched all the remaining orcs try to scramble away from my wrath. Like most people, they were hard headed until faced with the possibility of an inevitable death. Then, only then they became reasonable.

The orcs cried out. Bleeding from one wound, some ran; others began to grovel and pray. I ignored them. They could live … for now. Though I was certain it was a mistake. I fought for my breath and thirsted.

"Thanks for the help, Fang," I said to my sword. I swear it could hear me.

Fang responded with the hyper-low hum of a tuning fork. That was the magic within. Ancient. Mysterious and wonderful.

I ran my battle numbed fingers over the two dragon faces on the brass fit pommel, their gemstone eyes red and green. I took a deep breath and slipped it back into the scabbard that hung at my side.

I looked back at the orcs, their expressions defeated, yet evil. I could have told them, "Let the dragons alone or I'll be back," but what good would that do? Now it was time to depart and find Brenwar. I felt good as I dashed into the woods and disappeared into the night. One more dragon in the land saved from the clutches of evil, and sometimes from the clutches of the self-proclaimed good as well.

You see, dragons are hard to find, but not so hard to catch. They, like most people, like shiny things: gems, pearls, gold, diamonds, silver, and did I mention gold? Dragons love gold as much as I hate orcs. If you can find one and leave a pile of gold near their nest, cave, nook or hole, chances are, like a trout and a silvery lure, they'll try to snatch it. Drop a net over them, and they're yours, but beware. With claws as sharp as swords, teeth as cutting as knives and breath as dangerous as anything you ever saw, they aren't so easy to take alive. That evergreen dragon was a little one, but there are others twenty times her size.

My good deed was done, and I turned to walk away.

Clatch-Zip!

Something exploded in my leg.

"Argh!"

Fool! I stumbled to the ground. My chest and stomach were burning like fire. It felt like my entire core was being torn apart as I rose to my feet and ran. I looked down to see a crossbow bolt sticking through my thigh. It hurt. It was a good shot. I dashed into the woods, one foot stumbling past the other, branches slapping my face. *Orcs!* That's the problem with leaving them alive: if you do, they don't usually stop until you're dead.

CHAPTER

2

ANOTHER BOLT WHIZZED PAST MY head. I half-crawled, half-limped, and somehow dove behind the cover of a Red Oak tree.

Thunk! Thunk!

I made it!

"Drat!" I said, reaching down and yanking the bolt from the back of my leg. "Stupid orcs! How'd they catch up on me so fast!"

I stood up, groaning, my back against the tree, one bolt sailing past, followed by another. I listened. It sounded like there were only two of them, but there might have been three, rustling in the bushes and half-grunting, half-whispering their plans to one another. It seemed they had me right where they wanted me: trapped, with nowhere to run, not that I could. Well, certainly I could outsmart a few orcs.

Whop!

Bam!

Boom!

I stiffened. What was that? What was that, indeed. The sounds of battle didn't come from me, but beyond the tree. I stood with Fang in my grip and peeked around the bend in the tree.

"Come out from behind there, Nath Dragon!"

I let out a sigh. It was Brenwar, standing tall, for a dwarf at least, three orcs crumpled at his feet.

"Hah!" I said, limping forward, using Fang as a crutch. "It's about time you showed up, Brenwar!"

He eyed me, and I knew what was next: a lecture. Brenwar liked to lecture me on the things I did wrong, but this time it would be different. This time he was wrong and I was right.

Brenwar hefted his war-axe over the plate armor on his shoulder.

His voice was gruff when he said, "I told you to wait for my signal, Dragon."

One of the orcs started to move.

Brenwar whacked it in the head with his hammer. "But you couldn't wait, could you? Just a few more minutes was all I needed. But once again, you rushed headlong into danger without thinking about the consequences." He eyed the blood dripping from my leg.

I slid Fang back in its sheath and folded my arms across my chest. "My leg will be fine. It's not that bad." I tried not to grimace, but I did. "And none of this would have happened if you would have been there in the first place."

Brenwar was scowling now.

I threw my arms up. This wasn't my fault. It was his. "I couldn't wait forever. You know how I feel about that. Seeing a dragon caged infuriates me."

An angry growl rose in his throat.

I could feel the heat coming off of him, hot like a furnace.

"I'm not talking about your leg, NATH!"

He stepped over a fallen long and punched me so hard in my chest I could feel it through my armor.

"You killed two orcs, Fool!" He hit me again, same spot, but harder.

I fell to the ground.

"You killed—AGAIN!"

So I did. But it was in self-defense, and Father said that was all right, if you had to. Now my own anger was beginning to rise. No one pushes me around. No dwarf. No man. No orc and no dragon. I started to rise, but a jabbing pain throbbed in my leg. So I pointed at him instead.

"Don't do that again, Brenwar! What I did was in self-defense. It's as much the orcs' fault as it is mine."

Brenwar slammed the blade of his war-axe into the log.

I winced. He was angry, much more so than I.

He sat on the log and looked me square in the eye.

"Patience, Nath. I was on my way. If you would have just waited, you wouldn't have had to kill any of them. I'd have distracted them while you freed the dragon. Just like we've been doing for months now." He shook his head as he tugged at his beard with his iron-fingers. "Now look at you."

"What?" I said, checking over myself. I didn't see anything wrong other than the hole in my leg. "Is it my face?" I patted it over. "Do you have my mirror? Brenwar, where's the mirror?"

Brenwar just stared at me, pupils blank, eyes expressionless.

"There's something wrong, alright," he said.

I was mortified. Was it possible I'd gained black dragon-eyes or a black dragon's snout? Everything felt the same, but I could not help but wonder. "Brenwar, tell me! What is it?"

He muttered something.

"What!"

Brenwar did something he rarely does unless he's finished a few tankards of ale. He smiled. Or at least I thought he did. It was hard to tell underneath his black beard that looked like wool from a lamb.

"Are you jesting with me?" I asked, standing back up, ignoring the pain. As my anger rose, I looked down on him. "Brenwar, why would you do such a thing! It's not something to be joking about. Not at all."

He let out a short chuckle, pointed at me, and said, "You'll think better of it next time, before you start carving into orcs or any other kind. Ha! You should have seen your eyes! You should be worried. And you should be thanking me, too. Your father told me to keep you in line. And you're out of line right now."

I stormed away. The pain in my leg wasn't so bothersome when I was angry, but it still hurt. But something else ached worse. My heart. I ripped a hunk of a tree out with my dragon-clawed hand, took a seat behind it, and wiped the dampness from my eyes. I missed my father and my home in the Mountain of Doom. And even though I'd been gone away years longer, it already seemed like I'd been gone forever. There was no worse feeling than knowing you could never go home again.

I sat there and sulked for the next few hours. My heart was heavy, and my angry thoughts turned sad as the moons dipped from view with the sun. Brenwar was right of course; he always was. You would think that after two-hundred years of life I'd know much better by now, but I had such a hard time controlling myself. I hated dragon poachers and all their kind, and I'd be lying if I didn't admit to loving the lust for battle. I had to be better, be wiser if I was going to solve the riddle that had become of my arm and hand. I had to turn my scales any color other than black.

"You ready?" Brenwar said, stepping into view.

I nodded.

"Brenwar, how many dragons must I free to get things back to normal? We've freed so many dragons recently, at least seven that I count. Father said that for every life you take, a life you must save, or something like that. I've saved more lives than I've killed. In all of these months, only those two orcs have I killed, and only because I was trying to save myself from death."

He shook his head and grunted.

"Well thanks, Brenwar," I said, shaking my head. I knew it wasn't up to him to solve my problems. I gazed at my right arm, the dragon arm. It seemed a great way to compensate a man that was left-handed. If anything, it did things that my left could not do. It was stronger, faster, and though I shouldn't admit it, it was a magnificent thing.

Whop!

I ducked down. Brenwar slammed his axe into the tree, inches above my head.

"Have you gone mad, Brenwar! You almost took my head off!"

He ripped his war hammer out of the tree and yelled at me.

"I should be taking our arm off, Nath! It's your problem!"

"I know that!" I shouted back. I wasn't an idiot. Why would he say such a thing?

"No, you fool! That's not what I mean. If you could just see yourself looking at it. You like it! You crave it! Your eyes are like a dwarf's in a gold rush: hungry as a bear for honey. Thirsty as a fish out of water." He waggled his dwarven hammer in my face. "You have a dangerous look in those eyes of yours. The kind men get when they have enough power and want more."

I laughed him off as he walked away. "You're being ridiculous, Brenwar." I carved my initials in a rock with my dragon claw. It was another one of those awesome things I liked to do. I got up to smiling as I followed him, saying, "I don't like it." *I love it!*

CHAPTER

3

TRAVEL WAS SLOW GOING FOR the next couple of days, and Brenwar had barely said a word, which wasn't odd for a dwarf, but I could still tell he held a grudge.

I stopped, pulled off my boots, and dumped some gravel from them. We were in the Shale Hills, a network of ravines and green forests with hill tops and valleys covered in a blue-grey shale.

"Hold up, Brenwar," I said, stuffing my boot back on.

The journey would have been more pleasant on horseback, but we'd given them up two rescues ago. Brenwar said they made too much noise. I agreed, much to my regret now. My wounded leg was still in agony. I'd used up the last healing vial on the last adventure. But I wasn't letting it slow us down. I poured out the shale from my second boot, stuffed it back on, and began my tracking of Brenwar.

His tracks, faint but discernible to my eye, led me to a stream that gently flowed over a bed of smooth shale. It was a nice place, lots of ferns, red and green, both sides lined by pines. On the other side of the stream sat Brenwar: refilling his canteen, taking a drink, then refilling it again. He eyed me, shook his head, and turned away. I was starting to get sick of this now.

"Brenwar, are you done pouting at me? Not communicating isn't going to solve my problem. A little advice, such as where we are going, wouldn't be so bad right now." I skipped a stone across the stream. "Of course, I could always rescue dragons all by myself."

"Is that so!"

Well, it was so, but I wasn't going to say that. Brenwar taught me everything I know about tracking, but I fared pretty well on my own now. The fact that I was part dragon gave me an edge even he didn't have, but his centuries of experience provided him with an edge that I had not yet developed. Besides, I needed Brenwar to keep me under control. I needed that, but I wouldn't admit it to him.

I sloshed across the water and stuck my nose down in his face. He still hadn't answered a question of mine. And I was beginning to suspect maybe it wasn't me, but rather the questions he didn't want to answer. "Brenwar, why did you take so long to arrive back at the orcen camp?"

He started to turn away, but I stopped him.

"Let go, Dragon. It wasn't so long," he huffed. "It hardly makes a difference how long it was now, anyway." He started to pull away.

I exclaimed, "I waited up in the tree for hours!"

He huffed. "So."

"No, no, no, no, Brenwar. Not a couple of hours—several hours. You've never left me hanging around that long before."

I got in his face.

He tried to look away.

I could see it in his eyes: he was hiding something. There was certainly something he didn't want to tell me. I wanted to know what that was. It was driving me crazy now.

"Tell me, Brenwar, or I'll ask you every minute of the journey. I'll talk like a chatter boxing gnome if I must. You know how good I am at it."

"Alright then!" He shoved himself back and shook his head. "I had to go."

I gave him a funny look. It didn't make any sense to me what he meant.

"Go where?" I said.

He grunted, gestured with his hands, looked around and whispered, "I—Had—To—Go." He nodded towards the ground.

"Huh?"

He made another gesture I didn't comprehend. Then another.

"Oh!" I didn't know what to think at first, but like a sock in the belly it hit me. I started laughing so hard that I fell over. My voice was echoing from one end of the ravine to the other.

"Will you quit laughing, you idiot! You'll bring the entire hills upon us!" He tried to stop me. "Quit that!"

It didn't do any good. I couldn't get rid of the thought of Brenwar being late because he had to go to the bathroom!

"Did you pile or pee?" I asked, only to erupt in laughter once more. "BRAWAH-AH-AH-HA!"

"Pah! Both, if you must know!"

I was still laughing when I said, "Well, it's nothing to be embarrassed about." I was being sincere.

"Ho! It's not like that happens often at all… er," he was twisting his beard and rubbing the back of his head, "…it happens, now just leave me alone."

He walked away, leaving me alone with my laughter. Great Dragons! I hadn't laughed like that in ages. There was nothing quite like a belly full of joy to take away the aches and pains of the soul. I caught my breath, giggled a little more, and sat up on the stream bank.

It took a while before Brenwar sauntered back.

"Let's go, Laughing Dragon."

I held my finger up.

"Certainly, but my question remains unanswered. You only told me part of the answer. You told me the circumstance, but I still don't understand why having to relieve yourself took so long. Hours, at least?"

He grumbled and kicked at the ground.

"Did you have to go really far away? Were your bowels bound up? Was there—"

"No! No! And No!" he said, looking as if he wanted to hit me again. "I'm a dwarf! We don't go all the time. We can hold our water weeks at a time if we want to! And when we go, it takes some time, concentration, and privacy. Happy are we now, Nosey Dragon!"

"Ah!" I held my finger up once more, not my dragon finger, mind you. "One more question, though."

He folded his arms across his chest and sighed.

"What is it?"

I reached out and he helped me to my feet.

"Is that why you're always so grumpy?"

Up the stream we went, hour after hour, from dusk until dawn. Brenwar was speaking more, well maybe a few words per hour. When he's onto something, he's all business about it, and according to him, he had heard long ago that many dragons were held captive deep in the Shale Hills.

"How many?" I asked him.

He shrugged and said, "How should I know?"

Well, I hoped it wasn't too many. In most cases, we only rescued one dragon at a time, but I'd rescued as many as three on one occasion. Little ones: one bronze, one green, one red, their scales like shiny mineral stones.

But dragons weren't all just one color. They had different abilities, as well. Some could fly. Others could swim, and some could even cast spells. That's right, and you shouldn't be surprised because they are magical creatures, after all. Even I had magic like that, but I didn't have the hang of it, yet.

I stopped in the stream, the waters rushing over my boots. Some loose shale was sliding down a hill. Brenwar was looking at me and I at him. Something was coming down the hill. Something big. I made my way into the reeds along the bank. Brenwar did the same. I readied my bow, Akron, and waited.

Whatever caused the disturbance on the hillside wasn't moving now, but in my bones I could feel that something was coming. It was dusk, and many creatures in the forest came out at that time to hunt. I filled my nostrils and exhaled in relief. It wasn't one of the giant races, but I wasn't comfortable that I couldn't smell anything, either. That left me uncertain. Curious, too.

I shifted around in the reeds and water, trying to get a better look up the hill. It was dim, the time of day that the dipping sunlight casts the darkest shadows. There was no moon or sun to adjust your sight. That's when your other senses come in. You can't always trust your eyes, but your nose and ears can serve you just as well, if you let them. I stepped farther out of the reeds. The wind rustled the leaves in the trees. The waters gurgled at my feet, but I heard the faintest sound. A heavy step. Two heavy steps. I thought what was coming was big, certainly bigger than me, which doesn't mean much.

"Dragon," a voice said in a hushed whisper, "get back here."

It was Brenwar, but I wasn't going to listen. I had my bow, and I was fast, so if something was going to try and eat me it would have to catch me first. Up and down stream I noticed the last glimmers of sunlight. I was more than halfway across when something emerged from the woods. A dark mass on two legs with arms as long as its feet crept through and huddled by the waters. Its head was large, more shoulders than neck, almost the size of a horse's, but more like a man. It looked right through me then scooped a handful of water into its mouth. The icy look in its eyes froze me, and how it did not see me, I didn't know. It just wasn't one of those things I recall ever seeing before.

I held my arm out behind me and made a sign of caution. I was sure Brenwar's keen eyes would pick it out. The creature's head turned my way again, tilted, and paused. Now my heart was racing. I saw the white of its teeth. A set of fangs in particular. Its body stiffened, and something fluttered at its side. It looked as if the ape-like creature had—*wings!* It came closer, wading into the stream, big fists splashing in the water.

I didn't move. I didn't dare move. The last thing you should do when you are facing the unknown is panic. Or move, until you figure out what that move is going to be. My bow was ready. It was just another extension to my body after years of practice and training. If the winged ape made any sudden moves, I would shoot a pointed feather into it. But this thing was big, much bigger than me, and I wasn't going to start a fight with it if I didn't have to. It's not like it was an orc or a lizard man. If that were the case, I'd have shot ten times already.

It growled, spread its wings, pounded its chest, and charged.

Chapter

4

MY FIRST SHOT ZINGED OVER the ape's head. Not because my aim was off, but because it wasn't. That thing was fast. Really fast, almost as fast as me, I hated to admit. My second shot hit it in the pack of muscles in its shoulder and bounced off like a toothpick hitting a wall of stone. You see, there's a difference between the three types of arrows I use: non-magic arrows for hunting, *moorite* ones that can shoot through almost anything, and enchanted ones with special abilities. I didn't need a magic one ninety-nine times out of a hundred, but I needed one right now.

Drat!

And the third shot, a magic arrow from my quiver, well that wasn't going to happen. The ape was too close, too quick, and just a few yards from rushing into me. I hooked my bow Akron over my shoulders. The dwarven armor Brenwar made me had a design for that. I braced myself for impact, reaching down to wrap my hand around the hilt of my sword, Fang.

Too late, Dragon!

Brenwar jumped from the reeds and slammed his war-hammer into the ape's chest, drawing forth a howl of anger. Brenwar was a couple hundred pounds of solid brawn facing eight hundred pounds of raw muscle.

The ape snatched Brenwar from the waters of the stream, hoisted him over its head, and hurled him like a log that disappeared into the woods.

Brenwar would never live that down if we lived to tell about it, and I wasn't ready to die without recounting it one last time.

I ripped Fang from his scabbard and thrust at the ape's belly.

It jumped over top of me, landed in the stream, and kicked me in the back with its feet.

I slammed into a boulder, and Fang almost slipped from my grip. I held on as I fought to regain the wind that was knocked out of me. Whatever that thing was, it was strong, fast—a real monster. Not as big as many I've faced but still bigger than me.

It came at me again, face full of fury, its black eyes intelligent and cunning. A real killer.

I chopped.

It twisted.

I stabbed.

It jumped.

I cut.

It ducked.

I pressed the attack.

It howled as I clipped its arm. It shuffled backward, spread its wings, and flew away, disappearing into the night.

Eyes skyward, I stood, alone, basking in the light of my sword's glow, looking skyward. Where did that thing go? I whirled around as Brenwar burst forth from the brush, brandishing his hammer.

"Where is that thing! Nobody! Not nothing, not anything throws a dwarf without permission! Especially when yer not a dwarf!"

"I think I scared it away," I said, sheathing my sword. My leg was aching more now than ever and started to bleed again. "What was that, Brenwar? Any idea at all?"

The once quiet forest was alive and well now. The night owls hooted, and the pixies were singing. Of course, the pixies often disguised themselves as crickets and such. It was really hard to tell the difference.

"I don't know what that was," Brenwar said. "It's not any part of the lore that I know, and the dwarves are well-schooled on all the creatures and monsters of this world." He stormed up the stream. "But whatever it is, I'm going to see that it doesn't throw a dwarf anymore. Not ever! I'll have its head, I will!"

I unhooked Akron and loaded a magic arrow. I wasn't going to take any chances. Whatever that thing was, well, I'm certain it would have torn me apart without Fang's help. And don't get me wrong: I've been in plenty of fights without my sword. This thing was different. And its eyes left an uncomfortable impression on me. And that was dangerous. That worried me.

Ahead, Brenwar had started a new path out of the water and along the tree line. It seemed he didn't want to take any more chances being out in the open. As for me, I remained in the middle of the water, bow with arrow, scanning the skyline, behind and below. If that thing was up there, I still wanted it to see me. The fight in me wasn't finished just yet, as my senses and instincts were challenged. It was one of those things that my father had instructed me to work on. He said I needed self-control, and I'm sure he was right, but I needed to test myself, too. I wanted to be ready for anything, and I always felt like I was.

The moon had risen over the tree tops now and shined over the water. The heavy spots of clouds spotted the sky like dull grey orbs that absorbed the moonlight. My magic arrow tip twinkled like a sliver of mercy, so bright and shiny it was. The arrows could penetrate just about anything as the tips were of a dwarven made metal called *moorite*. Brenwar had made the arrows for me himself, and his people had blessed them with accuracy and strength. No winged ape was going to dodge one of these. No, it better not come back, but I hoped it would. I wanted to know what that thing was.

"Brenwar," I said, "do you want to camp? It's getting late."

"I suppose," he replied, "But I'm not making a fire. I'll not have that black fiend sneak up on me at night."

I couldn't agree more. There was no need for a fire on such a warm night, and for the most part we made fire to roast the critters that we hunted. We had other things packed up to eat, of the dwarven assortment. Stripes of dried beef and a round disk of blessed bread that would fill your belly for hours. It didn't make for the tastiest of meals, and you had to wash it down with a lot of water, but it would get you through the day. I wasn't hungry at the moment anyway. Besides, there was nothing like fishing in the morning and the smell of fish meet roasting over an open fire. And this stream was full of trout bigger than my feet. I could feel them swimming by as I waded in the waters.

"You should rest that wounded leg," Brenwar suggested.

I nodded and gave in.

The next morning, I woke up after a restless sleep that left me feeling empty and edgy. As a dragon, I have to admit that we like our sleep, even though dragons don't require it. I did, however, because I was still more man than dragon. But that night my dreams were filled with darkness. The winged-ape was there, a shadow in the background. There was a graveyard as well and dragons, many dragons, some living and many dead.

"Ye were restless," Brenwar said, as he roasted a large trout I'd caught earlier.

Brenwar didn't sleep much. He slept and guarded somehow, a dwarven art I never had much interest in. It was one of the advantages to having him around like this. And it probably was another good explanation as to why dwarves could be so cranky. They didn't sleep much. But they did sleep, just not for very long, or unless it was after one of their harvest festivals when they'd eat, drink and be merry for weeks on end and sleep for days, even weeks after that.

"No, I didn't sleep well at all," I said, tightening the bandage on my leg, "but the rest isn't bothering me, that black creature is. I want to know what that thing was, Brenwar. It was dangerous."

He tossed me a hunk of cooked fish meat and said, "We're rescuing dragons, not hunting monsters. I don't think that creature is a threat to us. I just think we surprised it, is all. It's someone else's problem now. Eat. I'm ready to go."

"Ah, you just don't want it to toss you around again."

"That's enough, Dragon! I'm in no mood for your humor, and you better not be telling anyone about that," Brenwar warned. "I've got plenty of tales I could tell about you, but I don't."

I smiled. "Fair enough, Friend. Consider the incident stricken from my lips forever, but not forgotten."

We filled our bellies with fish and broke camp. My irritation subsided, and my stiff leg began to loosen as the bright sun of the new day warmed my face. It seemed to lift that cloud of darkness within.

"So, where do you think these dragons are that we're going after? What have you heard?"

"There's always poachers in the hills, hiding something or another. I just figured we'd go and poke our noses around. It's well known that these hills hide many things, both good and evil."

Brenwar's answer was pretty vague, but the dwarves didn't often get into the details, unless you were talking about building, mining or blacksmithing. Then they became a waterfall of information, and I must admit, I didn't really want a lengthy explanation, either, but I needed some kind of guidance.

After an hour more of hiking, we'd abandoned the stream and resumed our climb up the loose foot hills. Tiny bits of shale had found their way into my boots and were digging into my toes, but I trudged along behind Brenwar. He was surefooted and steady, not likely to be slowed by anything. Still, it bothered me that he hadn't said much about where we were going.

In the dragon business, I came across information in the cities and villages. People talked. People talked a lot, and even the best kept secrets were never a secret, just something spoken of less than more. But at the mere mention of dragons, if someone knew something, in most cases their eyes lit up. Sometimes it took patience, other times charm, bribes, or a stern convincing, but it often gave me another direction to go on. Once I found the right path, I could figure out the rest of the clues from there.

We crested another hilltop, miles now above the stream, the hundred-foot high evergreen trees swaying in the wind. I tied my mane of red-brown hair behind my head and took a drink from my canteen. So far as I could tell, we were in the middle of nowhere. Just some forest leagues away from civilization, and I had a feeling Brenwar wanted it that way. I was certain he was keeping me out of trouble by keeping me from the cities. It hurt to think about it, actually.

I missed the cities, but my dragon arm caused me to stick out like a sore thumb. I had a way to cover it up if I had to, but what would all of those fawning women think? A man with a dragon arm. As much as I loved it, I was insecure about it. I didn't want people to think it was a cursed thing.

Brenwar headed down the hilltop and started towards another. The forest, unlike most, didn't have all the signs of life of the others. Other than the trees, the rocky ground didn't leave roots for the small plants that fed the critters and buck. That made the hunting more scarce and made the hills seem more dangerous. It was a natural place, but grim and foreboding with the black ground against the green.

I woke up from the dullness of the journey when I heard the sound of an axe chopping into wood. I couldn't imagine why anyone would be cutting down trees this deep in the forest. But stranger things happened in Nalzambor I figured, as Brenwar and I treaded down the hill to investigate.

I couldn't see a person, but the chopping sounds remained steady. On silent feet, I closed in, only to discover the echoes had drifted farther down the hill. I motioned for Brenwar. I was going to lead this time.

The chopping stopped. I didn't hear, smell or see anything out of the ordinary. But as the wind drifted into my nose, I smelled something out of the ordinary in the forest. Brenwar had a look of concern on his face as I began to back out of the clearing.

Snap! Snap!

Too late! A net rose beneath our feet, jerking us from the ground and binding us like fish more than a dozen feet over the ground. We were trapped.

CHAPTER

5

"YOU SHOULD HAVE LET ME lead!" Brenwar fussed and struggled in the net as we hung there like a giant's lunch.

I fully expected a small army of orcs or lizard men to surround as I fought to get my knife. I couldn't reach it.

"Grab my knife, Dragon," ordered Brenwar.

"I can't reach it. You try and grab mine," I ordered back.

"I can't even see it. Cripes, I think you're on top of me. Get off me! I'm not a stool."

We thrashed at our bonds, but all the wiggling did was ensnare us deeper in the heavy cords. The net was made for bigger prey than us, perhaps an animal, but it could be cut.

"Of all the Halls in Morgdon, I'll not be trapped like some kind of morsel!" Brenwar exclaimed. "Get me out of here, Dragon! I'm not going to die in such a helpless predicament as this."

"You get us out of here."

"You sprung the trap, not me!"

Our packs were full of plenty of gear that would help—if I could get to them. I could feel Brenwar's pack beneath my seat. That wasn't going to work. My left arm was pinned at my side, but my dragon arm was free enough to reach behind my back. The long claws on my dragon fingers caught my attention. I had an idea. I began sawing at the net's cords with my claws.

"What are you doing up there?" Brenwar asked.

"I'm trying to free us. That's what you want, isn't it?"

"With what are you freeing us?"

I didn't reply. Brenwar admonished me about using my black dragon arm for anything, no matter what it was. But I didn't see the harm in it. It was a part of me. It wasn't like it was evil or had a mind of its own. Not like Fang, anyway.

"Ah, Brenwar, what choice do I have? It's the only way to get us free right now."

"No, it isn't."

"Then what is?"

I continued to saw in silence. That's when they showed up. Two figures in dark cloaks approached, bows aimed at our bellies. At least, I thought it was two. As the net continued a slow rotation over the ground, I'd see one, then the other. Hoods were pulled over the tops of their heads, and their cloaks dangled over their toes. I wasn't certain what to say, trying to figure out if silence was the best answer, uncertain if they'd speak first or not. But my nose told me this: it wasn't orcs, or lizard men, either, so that was a plus.

"Um ... could I trouble you, Stranger, to let us down? It seems we've accidentally triggered a wildebeest trap."

I heard the tension on the bow strings stretching and bit my tongue. The pair weren't playing around, and perhaps we were trespassing, and I wasn't so certain my clever tongue could get us out of here. I cleared my throat when I noticed the pudgy fingers wrapped around the bow.

"That's a very nice elven-made bow you have, Sir. Some of the finest craftsmanship I've ever seen." I was trying to be complimentary. The bow was elven but hardly worth commentary. "And those shoes, are they elven made as well?" That's when I noticed one nod at the other. Both of them were beefy and similar in dress: elven clothes, ornate, blending and fanciful. It seemed these two brigands had either robbed or bartered for them and were hiding from something up here.

"Cut him down," one said to the other in Elvish.

"Dragon," Brenwar said in a whisper. "They speak Elvish. But they can't be elves. You ever seen a fat elf before?"

"No—Eeeee-Yah!" I cried out, falling to the ground. I landed on Brenwar. I think it would have been softer if I landed on a bench of stone. "A little warning first would be nice!"

The two characters stood over us, bows ready, as I picked my way out of the net and assisted Brenwar. The two of them were speaking in Elvish, and quite naturally I could understand every word they said. I knew all of the languages, mostly. So in Elvish I spoke back.

"Thank you for letting us down," I said with a small bow. It always helps to be polite and sincere when arrows are pointing at you. "And I apologize for springing your trap. What were you trying to catch? If indeed this is your trap."

They backed away and spread out a little farther from us and one another. The pair were almost as tall as men, each heavy set. They moved their girth with grace and ease, and I could see the clothes underneath their cloaks were woodsman-like but splendid in design. I just couldn't figure what men were doing in elven clothes and speaking Elvish, at that. My, if an elf saw this, they would frown upon it. The elves—wonderful, sophisticated, proper, beautiful and in most cases arrogant—would possibly kill a man for this.

They didn't say a word, so I continued in Elvish.

"If it's all the same to you, we'll be getting out of your way."

"Hold your position," a voice said, a mixture of polish and salt in his tone. He sounded elven. "I'd be curious to know what you're doing in these hills."

"These hills don't belong to you," Brenwar fired back. Dwarves and elves don't get along so well. "I'd be just as curious to know what you are doing here."

Both of the men flipped back their hoods.

I blinked my eyes.

"Brenwar, are you seeing what I'm seeing?"

He nodded.

Both men had long brown hair, almost as gorgeous as mine, but not quite. Their features were without a blemish or mark, their eye brows perched in neat lines, and not a single crease in their foreheads. High cheek bones and strong chins, all distinctions of the elves—except one thing.

"You're the fattest elves I've ever seen!" I said. The words just came out. I couldn't help it.

Brenwar's belly rumbled with laughter.

"I knew they weren't perfect! I knew it!"

Both of the elves folded their arms across their chests and gave us disappointed looks. I felt like a child for a moment, realizing how rude I was. There were all kinds of big people in the world, but fat elves? No. They were all so lean and graceful. I'd never seen an ounce of girth on one of them, and I'd seen plenty of elves in my day.

Fat Elf One walked over and looked down on Brenwar.

"Be silent, Dwarf. Else I'll seal that big mouth hole shut."

Brenwar's laughter stopped.

"I'd like to see you try," he warned. "No elf can best me, not fat or skinny. Ye better mind your choice of words if you want to see your next meal, you puffy face!"

"You bearded hog!"

"Ye've got a fanny like an orcen woman!" Brenwar stuck his fingers out. "Two of them!"

As much as I hated to, I stepped in the middle. It was pretty clear these elves, as odd as they seemed, weren't our enemies. And they didn't seem like the type we wanted to make enemies of, either. They were formidable underneath their girth. Seasoned and deadly.

"Let's start over again, shall we?" I said. "I'm Nath Dragon, and this is Brenwar Bolderguild."

Fat Elf One stepped away, while Fat Elf Two came by his side and said in Common, "I am Shum." He bowed. "This is my brother Hoven." His brother nodded.

The big hipped and rangy pair just looked at us, and I wasn't certain whether I should speak or wait for them. But I did have a one predominant question on my mind.

"Oh," Shum broke the silence, "I'm guessing you want to know why we're so … eh … large for elves."

I scratched my head. I didn't want to admit to things. After all, it would be rude, but seeing an elf in such shape was unique. "Well, forgive me, but I've seen many elves and—"

He held out his hand.

"Not all elves are as vain as you know them. In our case, we are thicker thewed and bigger boned, a gift to some, a curse to others."

"Are there more of you?" I asked.

"Oh certainly. We have families: young, old, big and small like the rest. But we move much and befriend little. A tiny conclave that comes and goes. We prefer the vast lands and all their riches. We are the Wilder Elves. And we are also part of the Elven Roaming Rangers of Nalzambor."

I couldn't believe my ears.

CHAPTER

6

BRENWAR LOOKED AT ME, AND I looked at him. The Roaming Rangers of Nalzambor were a band of the most elusive people in the world. A heralded group of do-gooders whose deeds were whispered in all corners of the world. It was no wonder we were snared in their net. They were said to be the renowned hunters and trappers in the land. And now we stood in the midst of two of them, neither of which was very intimidating. Perhaps they were lying.

"You can't be serious?"

"Indeed I am," Shum said, his face calm and resolute. "I imagine you'd expect someone different, but I tell you we are who we say we are."

"Well, your brother Hoven hasn't said anything," Brenwar said, adjusting the buckles on his armor.

"He's discreet, Brenwar Bolderguild."

"And I've never heard of Wilder Elves, either," I said.

"Nor should you have. Of course, I'm certain you aren't aware of all the dragon kind either, are you, Nath Dragon?"

I smiled. I couldn't help it when I found out that someone had heard of me. It made my heart swell. I extended my dragon arm. "Is it that obvious?"

Both elves drew close to me, eyeing my arm in fascination. Hoven reached out, touched it, shook his head, and backed away.

"Forgive my brother, but he gets excited at times."

"You call that excited?" Brenwar said.

"For him it is," Shum said. "Come with me. I've some food prepared, if you'd like to eat.

The food was good, the cave setting quaint, tucked back in the hills. The elves certainly knew how to cook their venison.

Shum passed over a small bowl filled with nuts and berries. Brenwar scoffed at it.

"The whispers serve you well, Nath Dragon. Your hair, eyes, build, all as the rumors describe, yet there's been no mention of your arm as of yet."

"Nor should there be," I said, eyeing him. "So, are you going to tell us what you were trying to trap out there? That was a pretty big net. A winged-ape, perhaps?"

Shum and Hoven's eyes widened like moons. They both leaned in.

"You've seen him!"

"Aye, fought him off, we did."

"Where? Where did you see him?"

I had their full attention now. Both of the elves were hungry for every last detail. But I wasn't going to tell them anything if they didn't tell me what I wanted to know first.

"What is it, and why are you after it?" I asked.

Shum shifted in his spot, his double chin dipping, eyes narrowing a little.

"I cannot say. Dragon, tell me, did you wound him? Did he wound you?"

I leaned forward.

"An arrow shattered on its hide. My sword licked at its skin, grazing it a few times, but I did get did get one good lick in. It grabbed Brenwar and—"

"Dragon!" Brenwar warned.

I held my tongue and then finished.

"And it was gone. Shot into the moonlight and disappeared. In all truth, Shum, the beast, monster or whatever it was… well, it was glorious and dangerous."

The tension in the air evaporated. Their faces looked relieved. I couldn't tell if it was a good or a bad thing. Something wasn't right. Awkward, I'd say.

"So, what do you call this beast?" I asked.

"It doesn't have a name. It is a new threat, you might say, and Hoven and I are charged with its capture. I don't think anyone that faces it in combat would live. And I must say, Nath Dragon, the fact that you're still standing after facing off with it is inspiring. All the others who've encountered it are dead."

Shum was sincere. Both the elves feared it. It seemed their charge was a life or death matter.

"How long have you been tracking it? Perhaps we can help." I said.

Shum shook his head and said, "Years. We haven't seen it in years, either. We just follow the signs and the stories. It seems the creature does have an affinity to these hills, however. It dwells here at times. Of that much, we are certain. But its terrors are reported all over the lands."

"There are many terrors, "Brenwar said.

"And that makes him all the more difficult to track." Shum rose to his feet. "I'm grateful for the information, and perhaps I can be of some assistance to you as well."

"You sure you don't want our help?" I said, rising.

"It's our problem. I see no need for you to endanger yourselves. But we do share much in common as trackers. You want dragons, and I want that monster. I honor what you do, Nath Dragon, rescuing the great lizards."

I didn't like the name lizard, but he meant it in a reverent way, so I let him continue.

"We've seen dragons in the Shale, but not many. Still, where the rivers meet and beyond the horizon over the mountain lies a graveyard. They say many bones can be found there, of all the races and all the monsters, even dragons. Treasure hunters and adventurers traverse from time to time, but the risk is high." He stood up and stretched his long arms. "Poachers lie in these hills as well. They have hidden outposts and make many traps for dragons. The dragons like the seclusion here, but not that the poachers have invaded. Their lives are in danger. Of course, we've come across many dead poachers, as well... many scorched to the bone."

"And what of the winged-ape, Shum? What happens if we come across its path again?"

Shum and Hoven's piercing eyes locked on mine, and they both shook their heads.

"Run. Hide. Don't cross with it again if you want to live, Nath Dragon. The creature is dangerous. Much more so than it appears. Consider yourself fortunate."

Brenwar bristled at the remark and said, "And we're supposed to believe two potbellied elves can take it and we can't? Hah! Now that's a laugh."

"Watch your boast, Dwarf," Shum warned. "Roaming Rangers are some of the best fighters in all of Nalzambor. I suggest you save your energy for the trials you face ahead. We are not your enemy, and you should be glad of that."

Shum donned his cloak and extended his hand. Elves were tall in some cases, even taller than me. Shum and his brother, Hoven, were half a head shorter, but just as heavy, if not heavier. We braced arms, and I could feel the power in his grip.

I said, "Thanks for the warning, Brothers. And thanks for the information."

Without another word, they departed, two ghosts disappearing into the dimness of the forest. I wondered if I'd ever see them again. The Wilder Elves. The Roaming Rangers. One thing was certain: they were hiding something. I was pretty good at detecting that. But what it was, I wasn't sure.

"Let's go, Brenwar. And I'll lead this time. We've got some dragons to save."

CHAPTER

7

IT TOOK A DAY AND a half before we made it to where the two rivers merged. They weren't big rivers, but small ones, the kind you could throw a stone across, or skip one if you were really good. Which I was.

Brenwar sat on top of a tree stump as I shook the last bit of shale from my boots. Lucky for me, the terrain changed where the rivers met. The travel would be on softer ground—dirt and moss, ferns and flowers—once we crossed the river and headed up the mountain. I was still bothered by the encounter with the Roaming Rangers, though.

"Brenwar, what did you make of those two?"

"They looked a pair of pretty ogres."

"No, that's not what I meant. Don't you find it odd that they don't want us to fight that winged-ape? Wouldn't you think that if it was so dangerous, they would want us to help them kill it?"

He hopped from his stump.

"An insult, it was. Thinking the two of us couldn't take that thing. We've faced greater dangers than that. I've faced greater dangers on my own, and I still have my arms, legs and head to show for it."

"Agreed."

I squatted over the river's edge and doused my face with water. It was an insult to think they didn't need our help, or that we were over matched. After all, I had chased the creature off. Of course, that was with fang in my hand. If I hadn't had it, I wondered if things would have turned out differently.

"Do you think we'll ever see them or it again?"

"Doesn't matter, Dragon. You focus on the dragons. You don't need to meddle in other ones' matters."

Brenwar was right. There's nothing I'd rather than do than toil in the affairs of the other races. I loved coming to their rescue. I loved to hear the stories they told about me. It was an addicting elixir, the sounds of my accolades like honey on my tongue. I couldn't help but want to assist them. However, my father had told me time and time again that men, elves, dwarves and all kinds have to help themselves at times.

"Well, I still would like to see them again. My, big hips and bellies on elves. I never would have imagined it in my lifetime."

"Me neither, but I couldn't care less if I never saw them again," Brenwar said, refilling his canteen.

"Why?"

He gave me a dirty look and said, "'Cause they're elves."

I laughed then took a forlorn look back over my shoulder. If we came back this way, and I would do everything in my power to see to it that we would, I was going to check on them. After all, the Roaming Rangers were renowned trackers, but Nath Dragon was a tracker of his own renown as well. And if they couldn't find that winged-ape, then my bet was that I could.

With the Wilder Elves miles behind us, it was time to focus on finding dragons now. They were family, and it was my charge to rescue them from their own greedy and self-destructive habits. That's right; I wasn't the only dragon with issues; there were plenty of others as well. For example, some dragons became so greedy and obsessed with precious items they'd kill for them. And thanks to them, most dragons had bad reputations with the peoples of Nalzambor.

As a matter of fact, you might be wondering why most dragons didn't reside in Dragon Home, or rather the Mountain of Doom. That's because, like me, that were curious, and often sought a hoard, a life, or treasure of their own. Face it, dragons didn't like to share. Still, plenty maintained a peaceful existence beyond the halls in Dragon Home. Of course, that's probably because they slept so much.

Up we walked, down we walked, around the mountain we went when a glimmer of steel caught my eye.

"See this?" I said, kneeling down and picking up the handle of a broken sword.

"Aye," Brenwar added, "a battle was near."

Farther up the base of the mountain we went, which was more like a slanted forest on a hill. I found some blood on the leaves and on the ground. I readied my bow and listened. The wind whispered in my ears, and the scent of death was near.

"Do you smell that?" I asked.

"All too well." Brenwar brandished his war hammer. "Let's go."

On cat's feet, I weaved in and out of the trees, my senses on high alert, my bow ready with a magic arrow. I wasn't taking any chances with that winged-ape getting a jump on me again. But my blood was charged for a fight. I could still smell the hair and breath of the beast. It was strong in my memory.

I stopped. There was breathing ahead, somewhere in the trees. An unseen enemy beyond.

Brenwar gave me a signal and moved farther up in the woods out of sight.

I pushed a branch and leaves from my face. A clearing lay ahead in the forest where a battle had indeed been fought. There was a charred body and another one broken and dead. The breath I'd heard moments earlier was gone. So far as I could tell, the danger was long gone.

I stepped into the clearing to continue my investigation. The bodies, charred and still smoking, were goblins. I hated goblins, too, and I bet that doesn't surprise you. They were some of the most notorious dragon poachers of all. I ran my fingers over an impression in the ground. *Dragon tracks!* My heart thumped harder in my chest. Looking at all the signs, broken branches and stirred up dirt, I'd say at least twenty goblins had trapped one dragon and dragged him down. But what kind of dragon was it?

The body smoking on the ground was my best clue. The goblin's leather armor was dry and brittle. Its sword was fused to its hand, and all of its hairs were singed from its body as if it had been hit by a lightning bolt. A blue razor. That was the type of dragon I thought it was. Fast, fast as lightning, and its breath, a jolt from the heavens. I hadn't seen one in decades.

"Brenwar," I said. No response. He must have been onto something, but I wasn't worried. There was never a reason to worry about Brenwar, and if he thought you did, he'd be insulted. There was a glint of light in the dirt at my feet, like a piece of shining metal. A dragon scale. I picked it up, as big as two of my fingers, a metallic blue. It was a blue razor, alright, a dragon more known for its speed than strength. Blue razors didn't grow to be very big, no bigger than a horse, and judging by the tracks, this one wasn't much bigger than a pony. Now, you would think that a dragon would be really hard for something as stupid as a goblin to catch, but goblins aren't stupid, just ugly. Orcs are stupid. That's why they're dangerous. Don't forget that.

The goblins, or in this case, goblin poachers, had been hunting dragons for centuries, and they'd developed tools and weapons to use. They used netting and slings to trap the dragon's wings, and all the rest they did by force. The goblin charred to a crisp on the ground was given the honor, as his goblin leaders would have convinced him, to absorb the dragon's breath. Volunteering his own death to capture a dragon would bring the fallen goblin's family great honor.

I could see the entire scuffle between dragon and goblin playing out in my head. The blue razor sniffing out a small hoard of treasure and gathering it with his small hands into a pouch under his wings. I bet you didn't know that, did you? Dragons have pouches and other secrets as well. The goblins shooting a net over the dragon, pinning his wings so he couldn't fly to escape. Next, the first goblin charges at him only to be scorched alive. Another goblin attacks and is downed under the power of the striking dragon's claws. His breath exhausted on the first goblin, the sheer number of goblins overwhelms him. I was sad thinking about the dragon's capture. If Brenwar and I had come sooner, maybe we could have prevented it.

There was dragon blood in the dirt as well. Not much, but enough to know the dragon was injured, and in jeopardy. On a positive note, dragons are worth much more alive than dead. At least ten times more, and it made perfect sense that the goblins would be searching for buyers.

Brenwar emerged from the woods, scratching his black beard as he said, "I found wagon tracks and a large path up ahead. They've been moving half a day, if that."

I slipped my magic arrow back into my quicker and hooked Akron.

"Let's get moving then," I said.

I stepped, stopped and turned. I could feel eyes on me. The hair on my neck rose. The breathing that had come and gone was back, but heavier and louder than before.

"Don't move," a coarse voice warned from somewhere behind my back.

CHAPTER

8

I FROZE. IT WASN'T MY INCLINATION to freeze; that wasn't natural. Not when someone had a bowstring stretched and pointed at my back. At least, I supposed my aggressor did. No, I wanted to move and move fast, but Brenwar's eyes suggested otherwise. Whoever was behind me needed serious consideration.

"Arms up, I suppose?" I said. I'd been in this situation before. They always wanted your arms and hands where they could see them.

"Just turn around and keep your hands where I can see them," it demanded.

See, I told you they'd want to see my hands. So I spread my arms out to my sides as far as I could reach them and turned.

It was a goblin. And it was one a little higher up on the frightful scale. Goblins come in a variety. Some are taller than dwarves, others as tall as a man. Some heavy, some thin. Not much different than men, except they never bathe, and they have an affection for mud and dirt. They abhor crossing a river and will languish and brag to one another of their grimy coats. If you ever want to make a goblin mad, really mad, give him a bath. It's torture. They hate water.

This goblin stood tall, his muscles thick, hands meaty, greasy brown hair hanging over his shoulders. He wore leather armor and a necklace of small bones tied around his neck. One of his long pointed ears was cut off, and the other displayed a painful looking earring, chained to his nose. Even goblins have their own sense of fashion, I suppose. But the worst thing about this goblin was that he had the drop on me.

"A dragon poacher," I said, "except it seems that you are missing a dragon."

I got the feeling he didn't care for where my conversation was headed. The aim of the goblin's arrow rose from my chest to my face. He wasn't going to miss.

"Drop all your gear—both you and the dwarf—and toss it over, quickly."

Brenwar was rumbling behind me.

"There's only one. Take him."

I objected.

"You aren't the one with an arrow pointed at you."

The goblin's eyes narrowed, and he let out an awful hiss.

"Foolish dwarf, more are coming, don't you know. I'm the scout. Now leave your gear, and I'll let you go. Tut-tut!"

Goblins aren't patient, nor kind nor merciful. If they say they won't hurt you, they're probably lying. If they say they have more support coming, they are lying. Goblins are liars. They'll say anything to get what they want and then cut your throat, but they'd rather cut your throat first.

This goblin, judging by his size, figured he'd shoot me down and then battle Brenwar. I didn't want to get shot, not from this close. Besides, I'd already been shot just a couple days ago.

"Dragon," Brenwar said, "I'm not yielding to any goblin."

You see, this is one of the problems you have traveling with dwarves: they aren't going to bargain with anyone, especially with those evil races. Brenwar would rather that he or I died first.

The goblin spat a big glob on the ground and smiled wide. I swear I could see bugs crawling around his teeth.

"The dwarf is foolish," the goblin pulled back the bow string, "and you get to die."

Twang!

I plucked the arrow from the air, inches from my nose. The look on the goblin's face said it all as I held the arrow in my dragon arm.

"Impossible!" I gaped in my own incredulity. I hadn't even had time to think; I'd just reacted, or at least my arm had, anyway.

Brenwar pounced on the goblin, his stone-hard fists raining down blows, knocking the goblin unconscious. He kicked the goblin in the ribs once more for good measure and dusted off his hands.

"Did you see that?" I said, marveling at the arrow.

"I saw it, alright. Luck is all, Dragon. All you had to do was duck."

I tried to recall the last thing I'd been thinking. *Duck! Dodge! Dive! Evade!* Any of those things I was committed to, but catching an arrow? Well, that never entered my mind. I squeezed the arrow in my grip and snapped the shaft with my dragon thumb. What else could my amazing arm do?

"Quit playing with it, will you?" Brenwar tied up the goblin with some rope and stuffed a gag in its mouth. "We've got to find dragons now. This one stayed behind for some reason, or was tracking back. Methinks they're worried they might be followed."

"Other poachers, you think?"

"It wouldn't be the first time." Brenwar slung the goblin over his shoulder. "You know that. Now carry my sack. Daylight's burning."

"What are you going to do with the goblin, Brenwar?" I held my nose. "It stinks."

"Evil stinks. You should be used to it by now." He started hoofing it up the mountain. "When it comes to, I'll beat what we need out of it, but there ain't no sense in waiting for that when the poachers have a lead on us."

I slung Brenwar's pack over my shoulder along with mine. His pack was twice as heavy. Of course, most of the stuff was mine anyway, so I shouldn't complain. But it didn't do my ailing leg much good. So I tried to block out my discomfort, opting to marvel at my incredible arm all I could. It was fast! Insanely so, and I liked it.

"Quit looking at it," Brenwar growled, forcing us deep up the mountain and into the woods.

CHAPTER

9

AFTER THE FIRST FEW MILES, my wounded leg was in agony, and I'd forgotten all about my dragon arm. I just wanted to stop. I had no idea how Brenwar carried so much, no problem, no complaint, no issue at all. I wiped the sweat from my eyes and groaned. I could see the trail of the goblins. Moving a dragon over the faint and rugged pathways wouldn't be easy, but they had their ways. Judging by things, there were many to carry the load, too, so at least I had a good idea about the sizable force we'd run into. They were careful to cover their tracks, but it wasn't enough.

Ahead, Brenwar stopped. The goblin had awoken and now was wriggling in its bonds, eyeballing us with hatred. Brenwar's shoulders heaved up, and the goblin fell to the ground with a *wump*.

"Interrogation time," Brenwar said, a row of white teeth showing over his beard.

Now, you might be thinking that an interrogation could be cruel and painful. And that it might conflict with the higher standards that I'd set in life. And you're right; they can, and they will sometimes. Of course, that's what Brenwar's for.

I dropped the two packs on the ground and started rubbing my aching shoulders. "Finally."

Brenwar jerked the rag from the goblin's mouth and drew back to wallop it in the nose.

"Easy Brenwar," I said, "let's give it a chance to speak first."

Brenwar stayed close, eyes intent on the goblin's mouth. Goblins have many tricks, and they only need a few seconds to send a warning.

"Nah, I don't trust him." Brenwar wrapped his fingers around its throat. "Just ask yer questions and make it quick."

The first question was the obvious choice.

"How many in your troop?"

"Heh … heh … I'll not tell—*urk!*"

Its eyes widened as Brenwar squeezed. I could see its grimy coat of skin begin to turn red in the cheeks.

I checked the dirt under my dragon claw nails. My, my black claws were so shiny.

"Oh goblin," I wagged my finger in his face, "I don't think you want to toy with us again. Now, when I ask you a question, I suggest that you answer, with all the forthcoming integrity I've come to expect from your race."

Brenwar's fingers slacked.

"I don't have integrity," the goblin said. "Goblins don't know what that is."

"Ah, an honest goblin, that is a good thing. Perhaps we can compromise on the information I require then."

It cocked its ugly head. It seemed as if it wanted to scratch its head and consider what I had suggested. Goblins were always open to bargain, especially when it concerned their lives.

"C-Compromise," it said, eyes sliding over towards Brenwar then back to me. "What kind?"

Now that was good. The goblin was open to negotiate, but I think it had more to do with its own self-preservation than anything else.

"You tell me where they are taking the dragon and what to expect, and I'll add a few coins to your purse."

"What!" Brenwar objected. "You'll not be giving the rotten life such a thing. I'll not pay for answers I can get for myself.

"No! No! NO!" the goblin cried. "Take the coins I will. I like the coins. Fair deal. Fair deal. I like my life. I'll give you all the information you require, just don't let the dwarf hurt me."

Even the biggest of goblins could turn out to be the biggest of whiners and babies. One thing was for certain: every creature valued its own life in Nalzambor. The problem was they didn't all value the lives of others.

I tossed the first gold coin at its feet.

It licked its lips.

"Tell me where they are going and how many?"

Sure, a single coin didn't seem like much of a sacrifice in comparison for a dragon, but this goblin wouldn't see any of the profits anyway. He'd be lucky to get so much as a few coppers or a silver for his efforts. Poor goblins. And whatever they'd sell the dragon for, they could have gotten a hundred times more.

"Around the mountain where the sun sets, there's a city in the cliffs that overlooks the valley. Small city, cut from stone, ancient and abandoned long ago. Our hideout is there."

It seemed simple enough, assuming there was such a place. But I needed to know more about what they intended for the dragon. I tossed another gold coin at his feet.

"Nath …" Brenwar growled at me. "That's quite enough!"

I held my hand out.

"Are other dragons kept there?"

It was a good question. For all I knew, they might have a dozen up there.

It shook its head.

"How many dragons have you sold?"

I didn't want to ask them how many they'd killed. I didn't want to know.

"Three."

I couldn't hide my sneer. My guilt was also beginning to overwhelm me. If only I had gotten here sooner.

I kneeled in front of the ugly creature and held the biggest gold coin it had ever seen in front of its face. Its beady eyes blinked repeatedly in the reflecting gold light, and a drop of drool fell from its lips onto its chest.

"Who have you been selling the dragon to?"

It didn't answer.

I didn't like that. I enclosed the gold coin in my hand.

"Do you want this coin or not?"

It nodded. "Yes. Yes. Yes."

"Who are you selling the dragons to?" I shook my dragon fist in its face.

It closed its eyes and turned its chin away. Whoever they were doing business with, the goblin had greater fear of them than of me, or Brenwar.

I caught the light of the gold coin and reflected it into the goblin's eyes.

Its eyes popped open. Its breathing became loud and heavy as it made a raspy sigh.

"With this coin you can start another life, far, far away. We won't say a thing."

It was in turmoil now. Its eyes shifted between me, Brenwar and the coin. But something was holding it back, something dark and powerful. I could see the fear in its eyes, and goblins didn't scare easily.

"Tie him to the tree then, Brenwar. It seems he would rather suffer than enjoy a fistful of gold," I said, picking up the other coins and dropping them into my pouch.

"I'd be happy to. But I don't think that's a very nice thing to do to a tree." He looked around. "I'll see if I can find a fallen log instead, or maybe a rock."

I shrugged. "Whatever you think is best. I just want to get going."

The goblin's face was contorted with emotion.

"I'll tell! I'll tell! Please, show me my coins again."

"A change of heart, I see." I set all the coins in my hand, the biggest one in the middle. "Well?"

"The Clerics of Barnabus."

My heart stopped in my chest.

Chapter

10

"FINNIUS!" SHE SCREAMED.

Finnius's heart jumped as he emerged from a side room in the great hall, rubbing the ornate tattoos shaved in his head, then wringing his hands. He was medium in build with a slight hitch in his step. His large eyes probing and evil, he approached with caution.

"Yes, High Priestess," he said, bowing.

She sat on her throne, shoulders back, chin up, shifting on the tangerine colored cushion and tapping her perfectly white teeth, an impatient look on her face. On either side of her, two bald headed men sat cross-legged, muttering incantations under their breath. Finnius felt his heart flutter.

She was different. Radiant. Exotic. Evil incarnate. She was the High Priestess of Barnabus, Selene. The acolytes of Barnabus—loyal, dutiful, and deadly—would do anything she asked, anything she asked at all. But at the moment, their task had escaped them. Finnius knew her wrath would not be contained much longer.

She smoothed her dark robes over her chest as she rose from her chair and walked down the steps. Six lizard men with barbed spears stood tall, heads bowed as she passed. Her black dragon tail spilled out from under the hem of her robe and cracked one lizard man across the face, spinning him to the floor.

"Walk with me," she said.

Finnius shuffled a half-step behind, watching her tail disappear under her robes.

She led him into the depths of the temple, down a stone stair case, and into a torch-lit room. The lizard men and acolytes kneeled down. Two eight-foot tall lizard men stood guard at a tall heavy iron door. He had little desire to go in there, but he had no choice in the matter. On the bright side, it wasn't a torture chamber, but what lay within was far deadlier.

"Open it," she ordered.

Her voice was commanding and persuasive, a rushing river with the power of a waterfall. He'd seen her speak and crack stone walls. He loved it and feared it, but he wanted such power for himself, as well. Of course, he wanted her just as much. After all, she was the High Priestess, as pretty and evil as they come.

He unhitched the ring of keys from his belt and unlocked the door. One lizard man slid the bar from the door while the other pushed it open, before stepping out of the way. Selene took the lead, the cool draft billowing the dark hair along her face. Finnius fell in step behind her as the door was closed after them. Selene snapped her fingers, and a row of smokeless torches flared to life. They had an orange hue and only lit one side of the tunnel that seemed too long to be underground.

"Finnius" she said, slowing her pace, "how many dragons have we captured this season?"

His mouth became dry as an empty well. *She knows this already, but I must squirm, anyway.*

She always asked questions. Probing for failure. Searching for a reason to pounce.

He cleared his throat.

"Eleven."

"Ah, I see, and how many did we acquire last season?"

"Ahem ... eh ... Twenty."

He felt himself shrink when she stopped, turned, and looked down in his eyes. He scratched a dry patch of skin on his hand and swallowed hard.

She folded her elegant arms across her chest. "Hmmm ... so we have caught fewer dragons this season than the last, yet we have more resources at our disposal than ever before." Her voice rose up to a higher volume. Her pleasant expression faded. "How could that be, Finnius?"

Finnius could hear his heart thumping in his ears now. He knew why. She knew why, so why did she have to ask? Even worse, why did he have to answer? He remembered the last acolyte who'd failed to answer a similar question before. He'd been brought into this tunnel with the Priestess, and never emerged. Finnius was that cleric's replacement.

I don't know. I don't know. I don't know.

He wanted to say that. The truth was he couldn't actually say for sure, but that is what the last cleric had said. He looked her in the eye.

"Nath Dragon."

Selene's perfect lips curled, and her nostrils flared. She was getting taller now; he was certain of it as he watched her face contort in the orange light. It was dragon-like. Mysterious. Then gone.

"Nath Dragon, indeed," she said, putting her arm over his shoulder and leading him down the corridor where another large door waited. "Come."

This lone door was as tall as the last, a black slab of stone, no key holds, locks or bars, just a smooth surface. Butterflies fluttered in his stomach, and sweat beaded his forehead. *Always something different and dangerous every time.* He drew little reassurance from her arm around his shoulder, despite how thrilling it was to have her touch him. *She can't be killing me. She just can't be. She needs me. Doesn't she?*

She stepped in front of him, raised her arms up, and loudly proclaimed a series of mystic words. It was in a language even he didn't comprehend, and all his attempts to pronounce it himself met with failure.

The black door shimmered and wavered. Selene reached out for his hand, smiling. He was trembling when he took it and she pushed him in.

CHAPTER

11

LET THE GOBLIN GO. WELL, abandoned him to his bonds, actually. But that gave Brenwar and me enough time to distance ourselves from him.

The journey around the mountain was long, the brush heavy, the bugs becoming more irritating the deeper we ventured. I'd already spit three bugs from my mouth. But, my leg wasn't so bad now, not with Brenwar carrying most of the burden again, and it was getting better. After all, I healed pretty fast.

"What are ye thinking, Dragon?" Brenwar asked, pushing past some vines.

The Clerics of Barnabus. That's what I was thinking. Fiends of all kinds. My enemy of enemies. The mere mention of them left a fowl taste on my tongue. It was like swallowing hot vinegar every time I heard them mentioned. I clenched my teeth and balled up my hands. I hated them.

"The Clerics, Brenwar. We need to put a stop to them. We need to crush them all."

"I know."

It seemed every poacher in Nalzambor was paid by the clerics now. Kings of the dragon trade. The Clerics enslaved the dragons. They killed the dragons. They tortured them as well. They wanted the dragons' magic. It was the remnants of dragons that they sold: bones, talons, teeth, scales and even parts from the flesh within. The power within dragons allowed them to cast many spells. The thought of it all lit a fire in my belly.

I continued.

"Everywhere we go, they turn up. We need to track them down one day, Brenwar. We need to save the dragons from their clutches, once and for all."

Brenwar stopped me with a disapproving look and sniffed the air. I could smell it, too. We were closing in. The goblins were close, just a few miles ahead now, I'd say.

I gritted my teeth and took the lead.

"Time to free the dragon."

The travel around the mountain's base was long. From where I stood, I couldn't see the peak for all the trees, but the mountain wasn't so big, not as big as Dragon Home, the Mountain of Doom. I had to admit, I missed that grisly exterior more now than ever. I even wondered what my father was doing. Was he worried? Mad? Or had he given up on me entirely? It all tugged at my heart.

I climbed up onto a crag above the trail we'd followed the goblins on. Below was a wonderful view of the valley the goblin poacher had told us about. It was miles away, but I could still see the birds darting in and out of the tree tops, and I could smell the water that ran down the mountain to form a lake or swamp down there. Most likely a swamp. Goblins have a penchant for stagnant water, but for the most part they drink a homemade concoction called Swill. A cup of dirt would taste better, judging by the smell.

"We need to see its face," I said, as Brenwar crawled up the rocks beside me. Dwarves didn't like to climb. They'd rather just carve a tunnel through a mountain than go above or around it. They swore it would save time in the long run, which it might, but we couldn't take years to dig a tunnel.

"Sun's setting." Dark clouds had formed about. "Storm's coming. Best we get moving. The face will be black as coal in the dark, assuming there is one."

In less than an hour, we made it to the bottom of the mountain and saw the goblin hide-out for the first time. The rain was a heavy drizzle now. I shielded my eyes from the drops.

The mountain was flat on this side. A cliff face. A network of ledges and doorways. So far as I could tell, the mountain hideout could harbor hundreds if not thousands of goblins. Finding a dragon in there would not be easy. But at the moment there was a greater concern.

"How are we going to get in there?" I asked. "There are no stairs or footholds that I can see." I held my hand over my eyes. "But I don't see any guards, either. Do you?"

"No. But, I bet I can find a way in," Brenwar said. "If there's a secret door in the stone, I'll find it. There could be another entrance they use, too. We'll just have to go back and follow the trail."

Just like in the Mountain of Doom, there could be a well-concealed entrance. But walking right up to it wasn't the best idea. I was certain there would be guards or a guardian. Probably not anything we couldn't handle, but alerting them of our presence would be the problem.

"I have an idea. Follow me."

We pushed our way through the forest until we came across the stream that came from the mountain and formed a waterfall that plunged into the valley. The water was clear below, a small lake surrounded by a lush and beautiful forest. It was unlikely goblins ventured in the valley, not near such crystal clear water. It was a break.

I looked at Brenwar, who said, "I know what you're thinking, Dragon. I like it. Let's go."

It took a little bit of time before we made it to where the valley bottomed out and the waterfall formed the lake. It was dark now, the warmth of the sun gone, replaced by a chill in the air. The sound of the waterfall was loud, steady and soothing. Not a bad place to sit and fish for a while. I'd have to remember to come back here one day, when all the goblins were gone.

I climbed over the rocks, Brenwar at my back, and we plunged underneath the water of the falls. I shivered. The water was cold coming from the mountain top, and being cold wasn't one of my favorite things. Behind the waterfall, it was pitch black. I pushed my wet hair from my face and drew Fang from its sheath. A soft illumination reflected off the damp stones behind the falls. I squinted my eyes, peering in the dimness.

"I don't see anything."

Brenwar huffed. "It's because you don't know what to look for." He ran his hands over the stones, feeling, pushing, and probing nooks and crevices. Anything below the ground or leading into it the dwarves are experts of. If there was a way under the mountain, the water would lead the way, but it was dangerous if you didn't know what you were doing. Plenty of adventurers drowned this way. I really hoped we wouldn't have to swim to get into this cave, assuming I was right and there was one.

"Here it is," Brenwar said. One second he was standing in the light, the next he was gone.

"Where'd you go?" I asked.

"Come on, will you!" his voice echoed from behind the dripping rocks.

"Huh," I muttered, squeezing through a dark crevice I'd overlooked. I'm a dragon. I'm not very keen on dull rocks and such things.

It was muddy and damp by the time I traversed the crevice and made my way inside. The cave was small, just a little taller than me, with passageways in several directions. Brenwar took a deep draw in through his nose, moving from one passage to the other. He tipped his chin and led, boots splashing.

Now, of all places, I was stuck in a series of caves beneath the mountain with a glowing sword in my hand, fighting for footholds and hand grips, not being able to tell if we were going up or down. I had to trust Brenwar with that. But I'd be lying if I said the dark caves didn't worry me. I wanted to get back outside already. I'll take the rain over darkness any day.

"I hope it doesn't flood," Brenwar said.

I could see the waters rising at my feet.

"What do you mean?"

Brenwar looked down at the water and said, "The rains must be getting heavy now." He shrugged. "Nothing to worry about now, we're flooded in."

My breath grew thin.

"What?"

CHAPTER

12

TWIST. TURN. CRAWL. CLIMB. SCRAPE and sweat. It was like that every agonized step of the way. I wiped the mud from my face and accidentally rubbed it into a scrape I'd gotten on my cheek. I could only imagine what a mess my hair was now. I should have tied a few knots in it. I felt like I was suffocating down here, too.

"Are we there yet?" I asked. It might have been the hundredth time for all I know. I lost count after thirty.

Brenwar didn't slow, climbing up over a ledge, plodding through a shallow lake, whistling a cheerful tune. He couldn't be more happy underground. He was like a pig in mud. Me, I couldn't get out of there fast enough. I'd rather fight a hundred goblins. Something about being in these caves with no sense of direction got the better of me. I wasn't in control, and without Brenwar I might get lost, probably would, actually.

Now, you're probably thinking that dragons live in caves, and that's true, many do, and it's not so bad when you have a lot of room, and you know your way through. But this, no thanks. I liked having the open air to look at and everything beyond.

"Here," Brenwar said, standing in a spring of water burbling at his feet, pointing upward.

I could see a faint light, a brown hole you might say, among the all-encompassing black. It flickered. My heart leapt in my chest. A torch or lantern was near.

"You think we're at the top?"

"Think? I know it. Just twenty yards below that hide out." He thumped his chest. "I told you so."

I sheathed Fang and allowed my eyes to adjust to the darkness. I could see the ceiling better now. A circle of dim light. It illuminated the both of us now.

"What do you think that is?"

Brenwar pointed.

"A well. See all these stones?"

There was part of a formation that had crumbled at the base. It was possible that the people who had built the hideout abandoned the place once the source of water dried up or was destroyed. Most ruins had thrived at one time or another, but time, war, famine and the elements destroyed the greatest cities in the world. It happens as sure as the sun and moon set in the sky every single day.

"So," in the dark I said, "how do we get up there?"

"I brought us here. It's up to you to do the rest."

"You don't think there's another entrance farther?"

"No. There's no other entrance at all. This is the one. Trust me. I know."

I rubbed my chin and gave some serious thought to this one. I couldn't jump twenty feet in the air, and I couldn't fly, either.

Brenwar growled, fumbled through his pack, and pulled something out. A rope. A grappling hook was attached to it.

"You could have mentioned that you had that among your assets before. It would have spared me troublesome thoughts."

"Do I have to think of everything, Dragon? What would you do without me?"

"I guess I would have just gone through the front door."

"This was your idea," he huffed.

Brenwar whirled the hook on the rope and slung it upward toward the hole. *Clank.*

I slapped him on the back.

"Great shot!"

I tugged the rope and nodded.

"You go first," he said. "I've done more than enough already."

Up I went, hand over hand, foot after foot until I could clearly see the outline of the well that once stood. I hung in midair and listened. I always gave it sixty seconds or so. You had to make sure the coast was clear. No sounds, no rustles, no footsteps or voices. It seemed we'd found as good a place to enter as any. I climbed over the mouth of the well and shook the rope. I could hear Brenwar coming, but it would take him awhile. Dwarves aren't the fastest climbers—or the fastest anything, for that matter. But I couldn't complain. So far, so good.

That's when I heard voices. My hand dropped to my hilt. Goblins. Two of them, chatting back and forth, coming my way.

"Guards!" I whispered into the well. Brenwar only had about ten more feet to go. "Drop if you have to."

"I'm not going to drop—"

"Sssssh!"

The room I was in was big, at one time a common area of sorts, long abandoned with very few places to hide. I glided towards the wall farthest from the well and squatted in the shadows. Yes indeed, the goblins were a patrol, making their rounds. I suspected it, but my wishful thinking had gotten the better of me. I couldn't let them see the grappling hook or Brenwar. I had to stop them, or the alarm would be sounded and the entire hideout would swarm with goblins.

Here they came, side by side, both big, the size of men, wearing helmets and armed with spears. They didn't look my way, but one was carrying a torch, the other's yellow eyes were fixed on the well.

I reached for my bow, then thought the better of it. I could hit one, but I couldn't kill it fast enough. Its screams would send a warning. *Drat!* That left me with Fang. Oh, if I could just sneak up and chop them down it would be so easy. That wouldn't be such a good idea, either. Too risky. That left me with my wits. My brain. Oh … and my dragon arm. What wonders would it allow me to get away with? Could I get away with it in time?

"Huh. You smell something, Brother?" one goblin said to the other.

It sniffed the air.

This was it. They'd be onto us any second. I had to spring.

Then, the speaking goblin farted and said, "I bet you do now. Heh-heh."

The other took a deep snort and said, "I can do better than that," and let one rip.

I didn't know whether to laugh or be sick as the foul odor wafted to my nostrils. *Yech!*

They both let out some rugged chuckles and took seats on the well's stony rim, the grappling hook right between them, and farted again.

I don't think Brenwar's going to like that.

"Ah! Ah! Ah! Ooh!" the goblin laughed and patted his belly. "I'm hungry." He reached inside a pouch, stuffed some bugs in his mouth, and crunched them up. "Mmmmm. Take some."

I needed to kill them now. I wanted to kill them now. And the foul smell started to make my eyes water and my stomach nauseous. What I really wanted to do was run. I had to escape the stink.

"What is this, Brother?"

Oh no! The goblin had discovered the grappling hook.

"Eh … hmmm, that looks like a—*urk!*"

It looked like one of the goblins was sucked down the well. The other opened its mouth to scream. I flew across the room and cracked it across the jaw before the first syllable came out. Its yellow eyes rolled up in its head just before Brenwar jerked it down inside the well and climbed out.

"Great goblin farts!" Brenwar exclaimed, holding his nose, stamping his boots.

"Quiet," I warned, holding my nose as well. "I wouldn't call them great."

"Well, what would you call them?"

My stomach wrenched in my belly, and I spit up into the well.

"The words evade me; now let's get out of this stink hole."

As I stepped away, Brenwar jerked me back.

"Let's lighten the load," he said, slipping off his pack and setting it over in the shadows.

I tossed him mine. Brenwar set them side by side, unfolded a cloth that got bigger and bigger, and covered the packs up. He muttered some words, and our covered packs blended in with the stone. It was another one of those delights he'd brought from my father's throne room: a Cloth of Concealment, and it was helpful all the time.

He lumbered over, swinging his arms, war hammer ready.

"Better get going; it won't be long before they miss those two."

I looked back at the well. I'd say we had an hour at most.

"Let's go."

The hideout was a network of rooms and tunnels, some lit, some not, carved from stone. From room to room, corridor to corridor, there were sparse furnishings, few decorations, and here and there, runes were written on the walls. Nothing extraordinary. It seemed many races had used this place as a hideout over time, though. We moved in the shadows, darting from alcove to alcove avoiding the light and the sounds of anything coming. Other than the two guards we'd encountered, there was nothing. No chatter, no shuffling of feet, not even the crick of a cricket or the scurry of a rodent.

I stopped a moment and gathered my thoughts. The goblins must have felt safe in their hideout, and maybe only a couple of guards were needed to make the rounds. Still, it was weird. It wasn't usually this easy sneaking into any place, and even though we had put some thought into it and come through the utmost back door, something was eating at me.

Brenwar jostled me with his elbow and sniffed the air.

"Smell that," he said.

Ah, indeed I did. It was goblin brew. The making of swill. The mix of sweat. We were getting close to the goblins, but where was the dragon? "Follow me."

Now, when it comes to saving dragons, there is only one thing you need to concern yourself with: getting them free of the net, shackles or cage they're in. If you pull that off, any dragon is smart enough and fast enough to do the rest on his or her own. In a flash, they'll be gone, which probably explains why they never thanked me or stuck around to help. Which always bothered me. After all, I was putting my life on the line, and I had the scars to show for it.

"TUMBA—TUMBA—TUMBA—TUMBA ..."

It seemed the goblins were singing, or celebrating, perhaps. I'm guessing that dragon, a rare blue razor, would be very valuable. But they weren't going to collect a single coin. I would see to that. I swore it!

We squatted down behind a balcony that overlooked a great hall. Peeking over the ledge, I could see boiling vats of goblin gruel and swill bubbling on beds of red hot coals. There was a throne at the end of the hall, where a massive humanoid sat, covered from head to toe in deep purple robes. The goblins ate, drank, sang and wrestled with one another... at least thirty of them that I could see. It was a celebration.

"That's a lot of goblins," I said.

"Aye."

I felt a knife in my heart when I noticed the dragon curled up inside a heavy iron cage. A girl, at that. My keen eyes picked up the lighter belly and long dark eyelashes. That made me sad and mad at the same time.

"Let's move," I said, unfolding my bow, Akron. Its workings snapped to, the bowstring coiling around the wood and into place. I was ready. I was ready to take them all on.

Brenwar grabbed my elbow and pulled me back. I jerked away.

"Easy, Dragon. Give them more time to celebrate. They'll by drunk soon enough. Easier to strike them."

Well, soon enough wouldn't be soon enough for me, but I conceded.

"And what happens when the patrol doesn't return?"

"Well, let's hope they don't remember."

I kept my eyes on the robed figure on the simple stone throne. Mysterious and powerful he or she seemed, yet unmoving. The figure felt evil, though. I felt compelled to launch a magic arrow into that hooded skull. Take down the leader and they all fall down. Darn that need not to kill! I resisted, slipped my arrow back in my quiver, and against all my compulsions, I waited.

CHAPTER
13

DRAGONS. CAGED. QUIET. UNHAPPY. FINNIUS had never seen so many of them before. The door he'd been shoved through, the one he swore he'd taken before, had led him elsewhere. Where had Selene taken him? He dabbed his handkerchief on his head. *Mercy! It's hot in here.* He tugged and rapidly jerked at the neck of his sweat-soaked robes.

"What do you think?" Selene said, reaching out and stroking the whiskers of a cat-faced dragon. Finnius stayed back.

It was as big as a horse, feline in its features, with a dark red belly and red-scaled. Two tails whipped back and forth, banging against the walls and the iron on the cage, its eyes penetrating and evil.

"Care to pet it?"

Finnius kept his arms folded in his sleeves. There was no way he would pet that thing. He was close enough already. But how did he answer without sounding too fearful?

"I'm just fine, High Priestess. But, if you insist." He shuffled forward.

A wry smile came across Selene's lips as she said, "Your caution is warranted. Come any closer... and he'll kill you."

Finnius backed away, his face recoiling.

"You should have seen what happened to the last one who got too close." Selene patted the dragon on the nose, drawing a part purr, part roaring sound. "The poor man sizzled and fried. Skin bubbled right off of him."

Catching the dragon's eye, he gulped. Its eyes glowed with a sinister yellow light.

"Er ... how exactly did that happen, if I may ask?"

"Some other time. Now walk with me."

The room was more or less an underground stable, but instead of being filled with horses, it was filled with dragons. All of which were restrained by one form or another. A chain was cuffed to each neck. A muzzle on all of their snouts, except for the catlike red one. It was different that the rest. A creature of its own free will.

She flipped her hair over her shoulders as she made her way to a smaller stall. A green dragon the size of a large dog was curled up in a ball. Shackled and muzzled the same as the rest.

"How well do you know your dragons, Finnius?" Selene said.

A question. Any answer could be wrong or right. It all depended on the mood Selene was in, which seemed to be pretty good at this time. But he'd seen her put a fellow acolyte to sleep before, permanently, for saying, "Yes," which was the correct response, but she'd wanted to hear, "No." He cleared his throat.

"Just what I have read, which, I am sorry to say, is little."

"And what have you read about what we have here?"

"A green lily?"

"Good, keep going."

"Well, unlike most dragons, it feeds off plants, not animals. Can be snared with honey or gold. Flies less and walks more, with a preference to hide in the heights of the trees."

"Ah … well done, Finnius."

He smiled a little.

"And can you tell me the most important part about this dragon?"

Finnius pulled his shoulders back a little and lifted his chin up.

"The breath weapon. A stream of yellow powder. Like pollen. It paralyzes."

"Not bad, Acolyte. Not bad at all. But that's not all it can do." She pointed at the back of the dragon. A row of yellow scales flared up and down its back. "Those humps. Poisonous. Rare and pure. Assassins will pay a very high price for that."

"How do you extract it?" he asked.

"There is only one way to do that. You have to kill it."

A little something tugged at Finnius's heart just then.

"Is there something wrong?"

What was that, sympathy? It couldn't be.

"Pardon, High Priestess. Eh … I was of the impression you were keeping them alive. Just some confusion on my part."

She shook her head, saying, "Come."

He followed. He'd probably follow her anywhere. Drawn like a frog to a lily pad. He could not help it.

She took a seat along a bench in the back of the stables and patted a spot for him.

"Dragons are much like people. Well, they're better than people in most regards. They can be guided down the paths of good or evil. Some are born of evil dragons, but most are born of good dragons. Do you recall the Great Dragon War?"

Who didn't remember the legends about those wars when people and dragons battled side by side for the preservation of good natured Nalzambor? The entire mission of the Clerics of Barnabus was to begin that war again and triumph this time. But in order to do so, they would need more dragons. Whoever controlled the dragons controlled the entire world. Free dragons, free world. Enslave the dragons … destroy the world.

Finnius dabbed his head again before stuffing his handkerchief under his robes. His sweating slowed from drops to a fine haired trickle. Finally, he felt comfortable. "Yes, High Priestess."

Selene's face darkened, and her eyes were like burning coals.

"We lost then, our numbers decimated because we were careless." She poked him in the shoulder. "One, we didn't have enough dragons." She poked him again. "Two, we didn't kill enough before we started."

He could see the regret in her eyes, the anger, a fire deep in her mind, as if the battle was still going on. In a sense, it still was. Most of the world didn't know that, though. The strange thing was that she spoke as if she had been there. But, the Great Dragon War took place hundreds of years ago. Selene looked much too young to have lived that long.

She continued.

"As for the green lily dragon, well, if he doesn't submit to my will, turn from his better nature, then what is left of him will fetch a fine price on the markets. Those yellow humps, just a couple of them garner enough gold to fund a war."

There was that feeling in his gut again. *Sympathy? It can't be.*

"No chance he'd be sold as a pet?"

"The poison is worth more than all the rest of him."

Dragon hide. Claws. Scales. Teeth. Wings. Every bit of it was a high-priced commodity.

"And the blood?" he asked.

She didn't answer at first. She just sat and sat and sat, making part of him wish he were elsewhere, anywhere but there.

After several minutes passed, Finnius cleared his throat.

"Ah," she said, "I keep all of that." She stretched out her arms as she got up and said, "Keep up the effort, Finnius, and I'll show you things you never could have dreamed of. But for now, I'm going to reveal a little more. I'm going to show you what is next in store for Nath Dragon."

CHAPTER

14

THE REVELING OF THE GOBLINS didn't show any signs of slowing, and I was tired of waiting. And their chants were getting annoying.

"TUMBA—TUMBA—TUMBA—TUMBA …"

I wanted to shoot them all. Stupid sing-songy goblins. Brenwar might disagree with me, but he pretty much disagreed with me most of the time. The longer the goblins sang, drank, ate and fought one another, the worse I felt for the dragon.

As she lay curled up in her cage, the goblins danced around the bars and taunted her. And why not? After all, they had captured her. But the swill they drank gave them a little too much courage. Now, if I'd seen a lock on the cage, I could have shot it with an arrow and shattered it. But this cage was solid steel bars bolted down into the stone. No lock or door in sight. The truth was, I didn't have any idea how we'd get the dragon out until we got down there. I punched Brenwar in the arm.

His popped open his eye and asked, "What are ye' thinking, Dragon?"

"How are we going to get the dragon out? She's sealed in that cage."

"Well, we might just have to kill them all first, and figure it out later. Or we can interrogate another after another until we figure it out."

"You think you can take thirty goblins and whatever or whoever that thing on the throne is?"

He peeked over the wall.

"Certainly."

Now it was my turn to grunt. The throned man, humanoid or whatever it was, bothered me. It had barely moved an inch the entire time I'd been here. It just sat in its robes, hands and feet covered, moving its head in slow nods and shakes when the goblins spoke to it. It was big, too, bigger than me, not that it bothered me. I wondered if it was the winged-ape.

"Do you think it's a mage or a cleric? A sage or druid?"

Brenwar rested his war hammer on his chest, leaned back along the wall, and shrugged.

"It doesn't matter what it is…" he licked his thumb and ran it along his blade. "It will be dead soon enough."

Being around Brenwar didn't make my urges to fight any easier. He was a bad influence. I just didn't understand why I was held to a higher standard. Brenwar was good and noble, but he could kill in battle without regret or consequence, it seemed. But as Father told me, "To each kind their own purposes. Your purpose is different than theirs."

My eyes went back and forth between the dragon and the man on the throne. The thing on the throne bothered me. Mages, wizards, warlocks, and witches were all a cunning bunch. They loved traps and wards and little creatures called familiars. The familiars really kept a close eye on things and could be most anything, in most cases small: cats, birds, lizards, snakes, monkeys or even a mouse. That's just a few samples, and they can be much odder things. So I'm always careful around any animals that look at me too long, but so far, in this hideout I'd hardly seen a thing. Everything had been going well, too well.

"Something's wrong," I said.

Brenwar eyed me. He'd been around me long enough to know my instincts are often right.

The commotion in the grand hall came to a stop.

I felt my spine tighten from my waist to my neck. The hairs on my neck stood on end when I saw two goblins dragging another goblin in. And it wasn't just any goblin, either. It was the one we'd throttled and bribed in the woods. The goblins shoved the broken prisoner onto his knees before the throne. Its body shook as it fought against its bonds and cried out for mercy. I got the feeling that it would have been better off if we'd killed it ourselves. We could have been merciful at least.

"Brenwar, I think our time is up."

The figure on the stone chair leaned forward. The goblin cried out, only to be silenced with a sharp blow to the back of its head from a goblin soldier.

One of the guards set the coins I'd given it down on the steps. I could see the big one sitting in the middle, twinkling in the torchlight like a tiny sun.

The goblin spilled his guts. I could hear the conversation, and the goblin told all that he knew, which wasn't so bad. For all he knew, or they knew, we weren't within miles of the place. How would we get in, anyway? The figure in the robes sat upright at the mention of my dragon arm, however. The figure stood up taller than I even figured. Seven feet high at least. Then another pair of goblins, from another direction, rushed in. One was holding a grappling hook.

"Uh oh," Brenwar said, checking the straps on his armor.

I slid two arrows from my quiver. I nocked one, and bit down on the other.

I knew things had been too easy.

CHAPTER

15

I GOT MY FIRST GOOD LOOK at the figure in the robes. Its hands and fingers were large, clawed and hairy, like a bugbear or gnoll. The figure reached down, grabbed the prisoner goblin by the neck, and hoisted him high in the air. Every goblin slunk back. Some froze, and the hot air seemed too cool, with icy intensity. The goblin's feet twitched in the air as the figure carried him down the steps for all to see. Then, in a loud male voice, the figure spoke words of power... ancient and mystic.

A sliver of ice went down my spine. *A magic user! Always unpredictable.*

His hands burst into flame, and the goblin's face caught fire as it screamed, twitched and died. A pungent smell wafted my way, burnt goblin skin and hair. The figure dropped the goblin to the floor, where it fell apart like pieces of a charred tree. The magic user held his arm up for all to see. It was radiant with red, yellow and blue flames that danced from one hand to the other. He was a formidable one, to control magic like that. Still, what he was, I wasn't so sure.

The magic user clapped his hands together. The fires extinguished as he spoke in a thick voice.

"Find them."

At least it was a man, but what kind of man I wasn't certain.

"I'm shooting him," I said.

"No, wait," Brenwar warned. "There'll be less of them to shoot in a moment. They'll be searching these endless tunnels for hours trying to find us, if we're careful. Shoot now, and they all swarm us."

Point taken, but I didn't like it. I wanted to move. I needed to get down there and see if Fang could hew through that dragon cage. Below, the goblins, most of them half-drunk or worse, fumbled through their gear and stumbled into the surrounding tunnels. One moment footsteps echoed everywhere, the next moment they faded away. Three goblins remained, surrounding the dragon's cage, armed with battle axes, swords and spears. I noticed the throne of the magic user was vacant. The magic user was nowhere in sight. The gold coins on the steps were still there, however. *Excellent!*

"I've got a plan."

Brenwar eyed me and said, "You do?"

Remember those gold coins I gave that goblin? Well, they aren't coins. They're something else. An item from Father's treasure trove I learned to use long ago. I muttered some words of magic of my own. My human finger tips tingled as I twirled them around. One by one, each coin rose on its edge and began to roll.

Brenwar huffed under his beard, "Magic." Then, he moved on. He had some idea what I was thinking. He usually did.

Tink. Tink. Tink.

Down the steps they came rolling over the stone floor, towards the dragon cage. The goblins eyed the coins, one looking at the other, curiosity filling their blurry yellow eyes.

"Just keep watching," I muttered under my breath.

The coins circled the cage once, then stopped upright and each fell before a different goblin. They wanted to grab those coins, each of them; I could feel it. One scratched his head. The other bent forward. The third kept an eye on the throne before stooping closer.

Poof. Poof. Poof.

Each coin burst into a cloud of gold dust that coated a goblin from head to toe. They coughed, hacked, and clutched at their necks before falling over. Not dead, mind you. Just sleeping.

Those coins, well, as I said, they came in handy. I'd figured if that goblin we met ever came back to the hideout and ratted us out, we'd need all the help we could get. So, I planted my own surprise just in case. I hopped off the balcony, landing like a cat on the main floor as the gold dust settled.

One of the goblins started snoring.

The dragon, well, she was sitting up in her cage, tail swaying back and forth. She was so beautiful, her scales like shiny blue shields with jagged streaks of black. Her long lashes batted as she stared at me. . She was fine.

"It won't be long," I said. "I'll have you out of here soon."

I tugged at the metal on the bars. It was thicker than I could bend. There was no cage door, either, just where the iron was bolted to the stone. Perhaps Brenwar's hammer could bust it up, or perhaps my sword could cut through it.

"Stand back," I said, drawing Fang.

The dragon reared back and struck at me with an angry hiss. Her razor sharp teeth snapped at me.

"What?" I said. "You have to trust me." I drew Fang back again.

She hissed. Louder this time. Opened her mouth to release her breath. I lowered Fang and backed away.

Brenwar appeared at my side, pushed me back, and said, "It's magic."

"What do you mean?"

"See the markings on the floor?"

Oh, now I saw them. Arcane symbols and designs were beneath the dragon's feet. The cage was woven with similar designs as well. It left me cold. These dragon poachers were more than what they appeared to be. That was when the unsettling feeling crept back in between my neck and shoulders.

"Heh-Heh-Heh ... go ahead," a disturbing voice said. "Go ahead, cut into the cage and see what happens."

It was the voice of the magic user, who now stood on the balcony where Brenwar and I had stood earlier.

"The only person who can open that cage is me. And if anyone else tries to open it by any other means, it will be very, very painful for the dragon. Deathly so."

The figure flicked a lance of energy from his fingers. It sailed over my ducking head, striking the cage bars. The Blue Racer roared and fluttered her wings, curling back up on the floor in a tight knot.

"Drop your weapons unless you want to see the dragon start to smoke," the magic user warned.

Over the years, I'd faced, fought, dropped, kicked and punched my share of wizards, shamans and illusionists. And like I said, they were a crafty bunch. And sometimes, when they got the drop on you, it was best to do as you were told. I looked around. All the goblins that were gone had returned now, and then some.

"I'm not surrendering to any goblin, Dragon," Brenwar growled under his beard.

I set Fang on the ground and held my hands up.

"I don't think there's much choice."

CHAPTER

16

WITH THE ESSENCE OF THE dragon's life linked to her cage, there wasn't much choice other than to give up. The pair of goblin soldiers took my sword and bow along with Brenwar's hammer while the others surrounded us. Above, the magic user jumped from the balcony and descended slowly, robes softly touching the floor.

The goblins held our arms while two others started to bind them.

"Leave them be," the magic user proclaimed. "And bring them to my throne."

The magic user took his seat as we were shoved onto the steps.

"Don't do that again, Goblin!" Brenwar warned, rising back to his feet, only to be shoved down again. "That's it!"

Brenwar stuffed his heel in one's belly and shattered the knee of the next, making it let out a cry of pain.

"Enough!" The magic user said. "Let the prisoner be."

Finally, the man pulled back his hood.

"I am Corzan the Necromancer. Lord of the Burrow Goblins."

Lord of the Burrow Goblins? Hah! I wanted to laugh, but could not. I could laugh at a goblin, yes, but him, no. He worried me. My eyes met his. What I saw was unsettling.

Corzan had the devilish features of a goblin but was still a man. His face was ill-tempered and scarred. A sorcerer of many battles won and lost. His eyes were dark, intelligent and probing. But, he didn't look like a necromancer. No, too rough around the edges, very atypical of his ilk. His hair was long, thin, and black as coal, and his side burns came down to form a beard that hung inches below his chin. His ears were clipped in metal points at the top and bottom. I'd never seen that style before, but it looked uncomfortable. His strange hands were coarse haired and rough, with dark metal arm bands wrapped around his wrists. He sighed as he folded his fingers and set them down in his lap, showing the humanity that he must have possessed at some time before. His serene gesture gave me no additional comfort at all. He was trouble.

"So, I can only assume you have come to steal my dragon?"

"It's not *your* dragon, Corzan. Dragons are free creatures. Such is the way on Nalzambor. Dragon poaching is a crime, well known in all the world."

"Hah!" He slapped the stone arm of his throne. "Dragon poaching has been around all my life and always will be. The people of this world capture, hunt and eat the other creatures to decorate their tables. Cows, sheep, horses, goats—and no one complains. I don't see how dragons are any different."

That last phrase really got me going. My nerves inflamed as I stepped forward.

"Dragons aren't animals! They are the oldest race on Nalzambor. Vastly superior to the likes of you—Poachers."

Corzan motioned with his arm and said, "And yet one sits in my cage. Hah, I hardly consider them superior. Quite easy to catch, skin and eat, like any other rodent."

Red-faced, I stepped forward again, only to have four goblins lower their spears at my belly. I had Brenwar to think about, too. And getting myself killed wasn't going to do the dragon any good. I had to settle down. Think things out. I let my anger subside.

"So, you are Nath Dragon, I see. Every bit as ill-tempered as the troubadours sing. It's nice to see it for myself, but something is different." His eyes shimmered with light as he waved his hand.

My dragon arm shot up in the air. I fought to pull it down, but could not. I'd lost control.

"What are you doing, Corzan? Let me go!"

"Fascinating!" Corzan said, eyeing my arm like a splendid robe of wizards. "Hah, it seems maybe my comments about the dragon might be wrong. Either that, or you are part-animal. Of course, I'm sure you consider yourself part-dragon." He returned to his seat. "There you go."

I gasped as my arm was freed. I didn't know what happened, but this necromancer wasn't one to fool with. No one had ever taken control of my body before.

"How did you do that?" I said, rubbing my dragon arm.

"Like I said, I'm a necromancer, and I know things about dragons." Corzan pulled out his necklace of bronze dragon scales and claws. "Certainly you of all people understand the mystic powers of these things."

He was right. Dragon parts could be used against the dragons, to control them and make them do one's will. Many dragons had been used to commit evil acts against their will, while some dragons didn't mind doing evil. Just like the Necromancer bound the blue dragon to his cell, he'd done something similar to me. I wasn't sure how, but I did realize with my dragon arm I might be more vulnerable that I previously understood.

"Impressive, Corzan, but I'm still here, and I can only assume you want something from me." I might as well be nice about it. "Care to share?"

"Very well, Nath Dragon… your enemies are close."

I looked around.

"I can see that."

"No, we are not your enemy. Just your captors. The Clerics of Barnabus, now they are your enemies."

My stomach churned at the mention of their name.

"And you would be selling this dragon to my enemies, which would make you my enemy. All the dragon poachers are my enemies. So please, don't try to use clever words to imply that you are not my enemy, Corzan."

"As you wish," He shrugged. "If it makes you feel better to be my sworn enemy, then I guess I can live with that. But, the Clerics of Barnabus are not my allies, either. I have my own ambitions, Dragon. My own wants, needs and desires. Lord of the Burrow goblins? Do you think I was born for that?" He slammed his fist down on his throne. "No! I am cursed by it!" He clutched his hairy fingers. "Look at these hands. Have you ever seen a man with such hands before?"

"Have you ever seen one with a dragon arm before?"

Corzan brightened. A glimmer of humanity returned back in his eyes.

"Huh… touché. But, honestly, a dragon arm or goblin hands, which would you take?"

I smiled and said, "I think you know the answer to that. Now, can you back up and tell me about this issue with the Clerics?"

"They pay well for the dragons, but information on you as well. They want you dead, but I need you alive."

"Pardon?" I should have been elated by the statement, but I wasn't. *Alive for what?* "First things first." I pointed at the blue razor.

"I trapped the dragon to trap you. And my plan worked out all so well, thanks to your friend, the dwarf."

"Me!" Brenwar objected. "I had nothing to do with that. He lies."

"Oh, don't be so hard on yourself, Brenwar Bolderguild. My familiar made the suggestion to you when you were miles away."

"What familiar?" I asked.

Corzan held out his hands.

"Come, come to me, little creature," Corzan beckoned.

I followed Corzan's eyes to Brenwar's black beard.

"What's every one looking at?" Brenwar said, bunching up.

That's when I saw it. A tiny face popped out of his beard. A pixie! As it crawled out, its mosquito-like wings came to life. Brenwar gawped, swung, and missed as it darted over to Corzan and landed on his shoulder. I could hear the faintest whisper on its tiny black lips now. "Dragons beyond the shale."

"Would it kill you to comb that thing every once in a while?" I said.

Brenwar pointed at the pixie, saying, "Nothing lives in a dwarf's beard without permission. You'll be paying for that, you little pixie—you will." He slapped his hands together.

The pixie squeaked and dove into Corzan's hood.

You see, I told you about those familiars. It just proved Corzan knew we were here all along, but what did he need me for?

"So, let me understand this. The Clerics put a bounty on me. And you wanted to catch me to turn in to the Clerics? Or did you have something more zany in mind?"

"The price on your head is high, but I don't value gold. I value magic, and they cannot offer me any more than I can get for myself. No, what I need is something else entirely. And the Clerics, well they gave me an idea on how I could obtain what I do not have."

I folded my arms across my chest and said, "And what might that be?"

"There is an object of power, an artifact that I cannot acquire." He licked his lips. "I want you to get it for me."

"And what makes you think I can get it if you can't?"

"I think my evil nature denies me access to such things."

"So you've tried?"

"And failed, so to speak."

"So," I said, "What and where is it?"

"At the top of this mountain is an ancient graveyard. Inside a tomb is an object of power. A Thunderstone. Bring it back to me."

The recesses of my mind sparked with memory. A Thunderstone. My father had mentioned those before. There were many of them scattered in the world, each with different powers of its own. This was something worth looking into—not so much for Corzan but for myself.

"So, just walk in there, get it, and bring it back. What's up there that I need to know about?"

"A guardian, is all."

"What kind of guardian?"

Corazon formed a smile that could crack stone as he tapped his fingertips together.

"A troublesome one."

"Pretty vague. So, am I to venture to the graveyard and battle this troublesome guardian unarmed?"

Corzan rubbed his chin with his hairy hand.

"No. You can have your weapons and gear. You can take your friend. Just bring me the Thunderstone, and I'll let you and the dragon go."

Let us go. I didn't think so. Magic users were notorious for going back on their word, both good and evil. They always had some stipulation that they failed to mention. So Corzan's words were no good. But I didn't have much choice in the matter, either.

"How much time do I have?"

"Not much. The Clerics of Barnabus will be here in two days, if not sooner. The climb up the steep mountain is long and treacherous. Still, you have plenty of time."

"And what happens if I'm not back before then?"

"I would suggest you return before they come if you want this dragon freed. They won't want any delays, and I've no desire to agitate them."

"And what will you do when they arrive and the dragon is gone?"

Corzan laughed, a wicked sound that suggested I'd been duped.

"If I have the stone, that won't be an issue. Just bring it to me, and all things will fall in order. Do we have an agreement?"

Never make deals with wizards, magic users, sorcerers and especially necromancers. Never... Ever!

Everyone said that, but they still made them.

A wizard's word is never good.

That's another one I heard all the time. The best thing you could do when dealing with a magic user was to not put it in writing and watch your behind.

"We have one," I said.

"Get your gear and go, Nath Dragon. And be wary of the scales."

CHAPTER

17

STILL IN THE RAIN, WE made our way up the mountain like two ants on a giant's belly, the top too far to see. The climb wasn't so difficult, not for me anyway, but Brenwar struggled to keep up.

"Slow down, I don't have those long legs like yours," Brenwar huffed from behind me.

Like I said, dwarves would rather dig than climb. Digging just wasn't prudent at this time. And I'd already spent an hour convincing Brenwar that climbing was better than trying to find another secret tunnel. Of course, he seemed to inspect every rock along the way.

"I'm going as slow as I can," I yelled back.

"Well don't go too slow."

"But you said to slow down. Now you don't want me to go too slow?"

Below me, I could see Brenwar looking below him. It was a long way down to where we started, a simple slip would be the beginning of a long painful tumble.

"Just keep moving," he grumbled.

Like I said, it wasn't the worst climb for me, but I had Brenwar tethered by rope to me just in case. He didn't like that—I could tell—but he didn't protest, either.

"Just tug if you want me—"

"Keep moving!"

Up I went.

Two days. That seemed like plenty of time to make it up the mountain and back. It would only take half a day to make it to the top and less than that to make it back down. I couldn't imagine retrieving a Thunderstone would take much longer. Except for the issue with the guardian. Whatever that might be. And why Corzan couldn't handle it, but could handle me, I didn't understand. Magic items, for the most part, could be used by good or evil. There was something he wasn't telling me. So it must be something I could do that he could not. Good for me.

I clutched the ledge with my dragon-clawed hand and pulled myself up to the next ridge. Brenwar's stubby fingers made it to the lip, and I pulled him up by the back of his armor.

He rolled up to one knee, wiped the rainwater from his eyes, and combed out his beard with his fingers. He shook his head at me before turning away. That pixie had gotten to him.

The valley below us was a wondrous sight of black forest underneath the lantern of the moonlight. Even with all the rain, it was still something to behold. So peaceful, one wouldn't expect any danger up here.

"Look," Brenwar said, untying the rope around his waist.

The ledge we were on was moss covered, with tracks that looked like an old road.

"Better than climbing," I said as I readied my bow.

Something caught my eye. In the distant moonlight, I saw something sail across the sky, flapping its wings like a bird of prey before disappearing into the night. It could have been a dragon, but all I could think of was the winged-ape. Still, it was hard to tell in all the darkness and rain. Even with my keen eyes. For all I knew, it was just a really big bat.

The trail we took was steep, winding around the mountain like a giant snake. I wondered what had carved it from the mountain and why it didn't go all the way to the bottom. Oddly, it had started at the top. Perhaps they, whoever they were, had started at the top but never made it to the bottom. I'd seen stranger things.

The cold rain pelted my face like tiny icicles, and the whipping wind made my bones feel brittle. It was moment like this that I missed the city, so soft and warm and amenable. And the women, oh how I missed their soft lips and compliments. It had been a while since I'd seen one, but fortunately many had burned a lasting impression in my memory. It was funny how my thoughts drifted to women at times like this.

The more I walked, the more my leg ached, until I finally had to stop and take a seat. The moonlight faded as it passed to the other side of the mountain, leaving us alone in the pitch black. It was like a cold, windy tomb, alone on the mountain, biting and unforgiving. I longed for the sun already, but that was hours away, and we still had miles to go at least. I dipped my head down and closed my eyes, trying to think of the sunnier times.

"You should rest, Dragon." Brenwar said. "It's been a long time, and your limp is getting worse."

"Is it that noticeable?"

"It is to me. How about I take a look at it?"

I could hear the sound of concern in Brenwar's voice, and the truth was my leg should have healed up by now. But every so often you got a stubborn wound; one that festered and throbbed like a pulsating cyst. Still, pain was a steady reminder of what the blue razor was going through. I could live with a little pain; I felt guilty for even stopping. I closed my eyes again. I just needed a little rest. I brushed my mane of hair away from my face

"Just give me a few minutes, Brenwar. I'll be fine."

A minute couldn't have passed before everything fell quiet. The wind stopped. The rain as well. I felt the hairs on my neck standing.

"That's odd." Wiping my soaked hair from my face, I opened my eyes. "We've been on top of many mountains, but I've never known the wind to stop before."

"Me neither," Brenwar said, extending his arm.

I groaned all the way back up to my feet. So far as I knew, nothing could stop the wind. Sure, controlling the wind was one thing, but stopping it was another. Of course, the wind could stop itself I suppose. Father always said the Earth, Wind, Water and Fire all had minds of their own.

"Follow me," I said.

I churned up the trail, every step as heavy as the last, determined to make it to the top by dawn. As suddenly as the wind had stopped, it returned, brisk, more so than before. It gave me little relief, as my gut told me something was wrong. After all, we were heading to a graveyard, and there was no telling what kind of spirits and forces resided there. Cold rain splattering my face, I pushed on.

At last, we crested the top, and the rays of the rising sun caught my eyes. The warmth on my face invigorated me.

"Glad that's over," I said, putting my hands on my hips. "It should be easier going down than coming up." I slapped Brenwar on the shoulder. "Let's take a look around, shall we?"

The mountain top was a grassy plain that stretched as far as I could see. In the distance, I saw the greater mountain ranges of Nalzambor and their snowcapped peaks. The grass and weeds were tall, the ground barren in some places, and I had to walk awhile until the first tombstone appeared. It was tall and marked in a language I could not read—and I could read a lot of languages, but I'd never seen anything like this before.

"Can you make anything of this?" I said.

Brenwar squinted at the headstone when he snarled.

"Giants!"

I took a closer look.

"No, it's not giants. Too small. And just because you can't read it doesn't mean it's giants."

As we walked, the tombstones appeared in more clusters. Some cracked, others broken, many almost completely covered in moss and roots. On stone marking in particular was three stories tall and half as wide. I couldn't imagine how such a large stone made its way to the top of the mountain, but giants could account for that.

"Told you, giants," Brenwar said.

I shrugged. If there were any giants, they'd have to have died long ago. But I didn't care about that. I just wanted to find the tomb that held the Thunderstone. I rubbed the back of my head. I didn't see what why it should be so difficult for Corzan to come up here and get it himself.

"Find anything?"

"No!" Brenwar said.

"Well, you should be able to find a tomb anywhere beneath this cemetery."

For an hour, Brenwar had stomped over the grass, the ground, the stone sarcophagi… and I would suspect he'd have found something by now, but he hadn't. So many graves, hundreds of them at least. Some small enough for a halfling, others big enough for ogres. He glared at me, hoisted his hammer over his head, and brought it down.

"NO!" I yelled.

Too late. Brenwar's hammer smashed into the shell of a stone sarcophagus.

CRACK!

It sounded like the earth split open.

"Are you trying to wake the dead! Have you gone mad!"

"There's a giant in there!" He yelled back.

"A dead giant, maybe! Brenwar, why did you do that?"

Chest out, war-hammer hanging in his grip, he laughed at me.

"Take a look for yourself."

There it was: a staircase leading down.

"Well done," I said.

"Never doubt a dwarf."

I pinched my nose. "Ew… that's bad." I looked at him and said, "You first, then."

He looked at me.

I said, "Well it's your discovery."

"Certain—"

A cloud of dark smoke crept out from within. A grey fog above fell over us. Both of us coughed as we stepped back. That eerie feeling returned as the wind died again. Death. Something was shuffling up the stairs, and it wasn't alone.

CHAPTER

18

THERE'S NOTHING WORSE THAN THE smell of rotting flesh in the morning. Nose pinched, stomach knotted, I backed from the dark mist as I slid Fang from his sheath. I retched. And that's when the first ghoul appeared.

Ghouls. Creepy long fingered fiends with yellow skin and bright green eyes. They spilled out from the hole in all shapes and sizes, arms outstretched, mouths frothing, each making its own ghastly sigh. They were men once, now turned to something darker, lingering between life and death by cursed threads of magic. My first impulse was to run, let them spill out, scatter—and then take them one by one—but it was too late for that. Like a hive of bees, they swarmed and struck fast.

"Fiends!" Brenwar roared. "I'll stomp you back into your dark hole. Come on!"

Brenwar smashed one in the face and another in the chest, knocking it to the ground. It was a good start, but where there had been ten, now there were twenty. We were in danger, grave danger. Forgive the pun.

"Let's get out of this, Brenwar! Quit swinging and start running!"

I toppled one over with a cut to its knee. The best thing I could do was slow them down. They weren't so easy to kill. Ghouls are terrors. Ghastly things that crawl in and out of dark places in the night. The truth is, I'd never seen one in daylight before, and never so many all at once. The daylight gave us a little bit of an edge, but the fog didn't help. Where that came from, I'd never know.

Two closed in on either side of me, as fast as well trained soldiers. Ghouls, unlike most undead things, are pretty fast, and just as ugly, too. I leapt backward in time to see them crash into each other. Another pair of hands seized hold of me, a horrible face opening up to take a bite of my dragon arm. I ripped my arm from its grasp and punched it the jaw, drawing forth an eerie howl. They could still feel something, it seemed. Oh, and their bites. They can be quite deadly, so don't ever let them sink their teeth into you.

Brenwar slugged another one with his war-hammer, sending it careening into a tombstone.

"Quit holding back, Dragon! They're already dead!"

I'd become so accustomed to holding back in a fight, I'd forgotten what it was like to let loose. It had been a long time. And what Brenwar was suggesting sounded really good. But was he right, or was he wrong? I swiped another one in the leg. They were everywhere now. I ducked, dodged and dove. Struck, swung and stabbed. I crippled some, slowed most, but where one fell, another rose.

I huffed and panted. They were wearing me down, and my bum leg wasn't doing much good. A steady erosion, they came undeterred. A nick here, a cut there, and I was bleeding from just about everywhere.

"Nath!"

I couldn't even see Brenwar, just a mass of bodies where the voice came from.

"Nath! I've been bitten!"

NO! I had to get to Brenwar! Or else he might die. I shouldn't have been holding back. If I hadn't, my friend wouldn't be in dire straits right now. The next ghoul swarmed into my face and I swung, hard. The ghoul fell to the ground and moved no more. I started to fight my way toward Brenwar.

"Get off him, Vermin!"

They were fast and many. I was faster and angry. I swung hard and harder, but my arm began to tire. I was going to lose Brenwar if I stopped now, but I could barely lift my arm anymore. If it was made of lead, it would have felt lighter. I was surrounded; the ghouls came at me from all sides. One at a time, then two. I couldn't fight them off much longer.

"Hang on, Brenwar!" I yelled.

Desperate times call for drastic measures. I switched Fang into my dragon arm. *Oh my!*

Remember, I told you before that things happen when my dragon arm gets hold of Fang. Bad things for those who are not holding the blade.

Fang glowed with new life, throbbing red with power. I felt energy racing through my fingertips and toes. My entire body was becoming a new living thing. The ghouls stopped, shielding their eyes from my blade.

Three rushed.

Shing! Shing! Shing!

Three fell.

"YES!"

Fast. The word had a new meaning. I twisted around one ghoul and skewered another. Two fell at once from one mighty swing. I almost would have felt sorry for them if I didn't enjoy it so much. After all, the notion to run was not part of their being. Not when living blood was around.

Shing!

One came apart from the middle.

Shing!

Another clutched at its missing face.

Four came. Four died. Two came. Three died. The one behind me must have thought I didn't see it coming. Ah, the energy. I felt invincible. I could fight a hundred of these things.

Shing! Shing!

But there were no more. The fog lifted from the battlefield, and Fang's blade went dim. Only the picturesque morning in the Mountains of Nalzambor remained, with a litter of dead ghouls on the floor. I dropped to my knees. A wave of exhaustion assailed me. Blood and sweat dripped from my nose. My own blood, that is. I must have been cut to pieces, but I didn't care. I'd won.

Fang hummed one last time then quieted like a stone. Not a single notch, nick or drop of blood was on its keen blade. My dragon arm, well, it seemed blacker than ever in the morning light, but in my heart I felt I'd done no wrong. I just hoped Brenwar was right about killing ghouls not making me evil.

"Brenwar!"

I rushed to him.

He lay on the ground, banged up and stiff as a stone. His dark eyes were like marbles gazing into the bright sky. I put my head to his chest and sighed. His heart was beating like a heavy mallet. I patted him on the chest. "You'll be alright." *I hope.*

He had a nasty bite mark on his leg. It was deep, red and purple, and swollen. You couldn't wear armor everywhere. It would slow you down too much.

"Ah Brenwar, I apologize. I should have acted sooner. But you're still alive, and that's all that matters now." A thought struck me. "Huh … Did I just save your life?" I looked at my dragon arm. No changes. "Well, I'm sure even saving a dwarf counts for something. Don't worry; I'm sure the paralysis will wear off in a while. But if you don't snap out of it soon, I'm going in there without you."

He blinked. His lip almost curled.

"See, you're moving already. But it isn't much faster than before," I said, looking into his eyes, grinning.

The thought of me saving him would get him going, I hoped. I swore I heard a rumble in his throat.

I heard a rustle of feet. Something else began emerging from the tomb.

I grabbed my bow, Akron, and readied a special arrow, saying, "Not again."

CHAPTER

19

THE ARROW I DREW FROM my quiver was special. Magic, powerful and explosive enough to rock the entire mountaintop. I was going to take care of business with it. I drew the bowstring along my cheek and waited for the next ghoul to scurry from the tomb. *What?* Nothing came. Instead, I could hear tiny footsteps all over the grass. That's when I saw the first one. It was pink. It was fluffy. Not a ghoul. Instead, a cat-sized dandelion with rows of tiny feet and a mouth as wide as its body. A carrion caterpillar. I lowered my bow.

"Whew!"

It wasn't coming after me. No, it was coming after the dead ghouls, and it wasn't alone, either. Where there was one, there were two. Where there were three, there were ten. They came from all directions, bright pinks, pale blue and canary yellow, marching over the ghoul bodies and coating them one by one with strands of a wispy white fiber. Sure, it was creepy: giant caterpillars with teeth and a coat of brilliant and fuzzy colors, but just you wait. Those caterpillars would become the most beautiful butterflies in the world one day. And not just any butterflies, either, but a very special sort.

"Fortune's found us, it seems."

Brenwar didn't respond as I dragged him over to a tombstone and propped him up.

"I know, I know," I said. "Nobody drags a dwarf without permission." I felt a hundred tiny feet on my back as a lime green caterpillar climbed over my shoulder. Weird. "See that, a good sign, isn't it?"

He didn't respond, but his eyes were glaring at me.

"I'll take that as a yes."

It was a good sign. The Carrion Caterpillars, strange and dutiful, were often spotted on battlefields, coating the bodies of those who were not buried. The farmers said they made the best fertilizer in the world, though I found it hard to imagine anything good could grow from such evil things.

"I'm going in."

There was another thing about the Caterpillars: they didn't come out until the danger was gone. I put my arrow in the quiver and folded up the bow. Fang's light was a torch when I drew it, and down into the darkness I went, two steps at a time.

Musty and cold. Typical of all the dead spaces underground. But there were plenty of good things underground, too. Just go to any dwarven city. Still, a tomb full of ghouls was disturbing. Whatever was buried down here needed a great deal of protection, and I couldn't help but think that the ghouls were only the first wave. After all, guardians came in many shapes and forms, but at least the ghouls were out of the way. I'd have thought Corzan could have handled the ghouls, though, with the help of his goblin horde. But why risk it if you didn't have to?

The stairs stopped about thirty feet below ground. Above me, I could still see the dawn's light creeping in, but it was awfully distant. The room I stood in was part tomb, part temple. Rows of ancient stone pillars held the ground up, and behind them on either side of the wall were shelves for bodies, some vacant and some occupied.

I shoved one, a weathered husk wrapped in deteriorating cloth. Its head rolled off and cracked on the ground. It was a man. The body above it wasn't human, however. Its jaw had a row of canine teeth jutting out at the bottom, and the face was shaped like a dog. A gnoll, perhaps. There were lizard men, halflings, orcs, and many other faces of the races, all shriveled and shrunken.

I couldn't imagine why so many different people would be buried together. Their bodies all at rest. Was it possible there was a time when all the races got along together? *Be wary of the dead,* my father always said. Perhaps all these people were evil, a common bond that served the same cause. I wondered if they all shared the language I couldn't read on the stones above.

I treaded lightly, making sure my feet didn't land on any strange patterns or layouts. Tombs that held something of value would have booby traps.

"Perhaps I should have waited on Brenwar," I muttered to myself, wiping the cobwebs from my face and eyes. So many cobwebs, but I didn't see any spiders anywhere. I looked up. Nothing. Thank goodness.

So many bodies. Two dozen by the looks of things. Twelve on one side, twelve on the other, but a couple of shelves were missing bodies.

"Oh, there you are."

A pair of tarantulas crawled past my toes. I wondered what the spiders fed on down here. I couldn't shake the feeling that one if not all those bodies would reanimate and attack at any moment. The undead often did that. *Find the stone. Find the stone. Find the stone.*

The sad thing was, the Thunderstone might not even be down here. It could be anywhere on the mountain. I thought of the dragon, the blue razor. *Hurry.* I had to find the stone, make the deal, and free the dragon. My heart started to race. I didn't have time to waste.

I rested Fang on my shoulder.

"What do you think? Is it in here or not?"

I often talked to Fang when no one else was around. He was a good listener, and when he wanted he could help, too.

Thrum.

Fang pulsated with life, a single burst of energy. I held him out before my eyes and made my way around the room. There was only one way in, and one way out. The wall adjacent to the entrance was nothing more than a slab cut from the stone. The last thing I wanted to do was search all the long dead bodies. It was a great place to hide things, but disturbing the dead was never a good idea. Bad things could happen and often did.

I ran my dragon arm along the pillars. The shelves. The barren pieces of wall. My sense of touch was extraordinary. With my eyes shut, I could feel the imperfections as if I could see them. Still, nothing remarkable. Just an old tomb, filled with corpses that once housed a horde of ghouls.

"Fang, they must have been protecting something," I said, circling the room. "And they couldn't have survived down here in this small a room very long, could they have? Perhaps, I just need to wait for Brenwar."

Thrum!

Fang flared again, its tip a red hot glow, pointing down at the tiles in the floor. I scratched the back of my head. "Huh? I guess I should have looked there before." I cleared some of the dust and dirt away with my boot. A colorful mosaic was underneath. On my hands and knees, I set Fang down and brushed and blew more dust away until I could make out a face of sorts. Perhaps an animal. Maybe a lycanthrope.

I found finger holds around the edges of the stone, and my heart started to race. The floor was always a good place to bury things. And the face on the floor, well, so far as I could tell, it was a guardian. Something very important must lie underneath. Like a Thunderstone.

"What do you think, Fang? Should I wait for Brenwar?"

My sword glowed softly but said nothing.

"I'll take your silence as a *no.*"

It was always easy for me to justify my actions with Fang, especially when his silence could easily be construed at will between *yes* or *no.*

I placed my hands on either side of the mosaic face, squatted down, and pulled. It didn't budge. I tried again, putting my legs into it, straining.

"*Hurk!*"

Nothing. I sat down, trying to catch my breath, shaking my aching fingers.

"I hope this isn't one of those wizard locks. I hate those."

Every so often, it was good to travel with a magic user. As crafty as they liked to be, they loved to be challenged by magically sealed things. All things magical, really. But I didn't have one with me. I didn't sense any magic in the cover stone, either. This time, it was going to have to be my flesh versus the stone. I stared down at the odd animal face in the mosaic and said, "You will not beat me."

I hunkered down over it, got my grip, and threw all of my legs, arms and back into it. I'm a big man, and a strong one at that. I pulled. Nothing. I groaned. Nothing. I shouted out loud like an angry giant.

"HAARRR!"

Stone began to scrape against stone. My fingers ached; my back burned, but I kept on pulling. I could feel my veins thicken like cords in my neck, and my knees cracked, but I was pulling it upward. Inch by inch. How thick was this stone!

"RRRRRRR-RAAAAAAAH!"

I slipped free, toppling the stone over to the side and falling to my knees, panting for breath. It must have been the biggest stone I ever lifted because I didn't make a habit out of lifting anything heavy if I didn't have to. I had Brenwar for that. A gaping square hole greeted me now. A trophy of my achievement. A blue hew glowed from within.

"It better … gasp … be in there."

I sucked in a deep breath, exhaled, and peeked inside.

A Thunderstone! Well, it was a stone, big enough to barely fit in my hand, smooth as marble, with jagged brilliant blue markings. I couldn't imagine it being anything else. The question was… Was it safe to grab that thing? I ran my tongue across my lips. I wanted to grab it. Feel the power and magic within it. Perhaps it could even help reverse the effects of my dragon arm. Or it could make it worse. Father told me long ago of such things in the world that could help, help with anything, but you had to be very careful.

Eyes wide as saucers, I stared. Tempted. Tried. A struggle boiling within. How much easier would it be to save more dragons if I had greater power? I could wipe out the clerics of Barnabus. Maybe destroy an entire temple. What kind of power was within that stone? I had to know.

"What do you think, Fang? A little touch couldn't be too bad."

Silence.

I rubbed my dragon finger under my chin. "Hmmm … I ought to see what kind of power Corzan would be dealing with."

My golden eyes glimmered in the blue light. I grabbed the Thunderstone in my dragon claws. It was cold, and its markings were dim. Nothing. Nothing happened at all, and it felt just the same as before. I could only assume a mage could unlock the magic within. Disappointed, I flipped it up in the air and let it fall into my pack.

"Well, I guess that's it," I said, picking up Fang. "It's time to go."

To the stair case I went, limping as fast as I could. I'd spent enough time beneath the ground the past day.

Crack!

The floor groaned, rumbled and shook.

"Oh no!"

The bodies fell from their beds on the shelves, and the pillars popped with ear shattering splits. The entire tomb was caving in. I dashed up the stair case, five steps at a time. The dirt from the opening above was pouring all over me.

Crash!

The staircase busted beneath my feet, and I tumbled back to the bottom. As the earth spilled inside my grave, I realized I was seconds away from my death. I leapt back to my feet and bounded up what was left of the steps, fighting my way through the dirt and sand that was spilling all over me. The tomb was filling fast, and all the dirt and dust was choking me.

I stuffed Fang back in the sheath and renewed my climb. Stepping. Digging. Clawing for whatever foothold I could find. I couldn't see the top anymore. The falling dirt replaced the daylight with pitch black. I pushed upward, head down, fighting for every step, only to be knocked down again.

I couldn't believe I was going to die like this. Choking on a mouthful of dirt, of all things. I yelled out, "*BRENWAR!*" but he was paralyzed. I had to make it, though. I was going up, up, slowly. I could beat this catastrophe. I was Nath Dragon: I could be anything. I would not be buried alive! I would not die like this!

My fingers found another lip of the stair. *Ah, the top set, finally!* Freedom would be mine in a moment.

Crack!

Again, the earth shattered and rocked. I lost my grip and fell.

Down I went.

My final resting place, on a lonely mountain barely known to the rest of the world, of all places. A tomb of dirt and bones.

CHAPTER
20

FINNIUS STOOD INSIDE A LARGE circular stone chamber filled with many strange devices: cutting tools, bottles, knives, tables laden with power jars and odd glass contraptions. Shackles and chains lined the walls, but no person hung there now. He imagined men had, not so long ago. It was just another strange place, one of the many secrets beneath the Temple of Barnabus.

"This is it, Finnius," Selene the High Priestess said. "My special chamber of horrors."

Finnius swallowed. Despite his evil nature, a wave of concern for his own personal safety settled in.

"It's alright, Finnius. I wouldn't have brought you down here if I didn't want you alive. If I wanted you dead or tormented, my guards would have done that." She smiled, creepy, yet beautiful. "And as you can see, business has been slow for a while. Now, come. I've something to share."

He followed, now more honored than scared. Selene stood before a vat, rectangular in shape, big enough for the frame of a man, a large one at that. Inside it, a thick waxy liquid bubbled, a little red, a little orange, a little blue, and all swirling together. It looked like a boiling cauldron, but it did not burn hot.

"Blood. Dragon blood," she said.

Finnius the cleric had never seen so much before.

"Well, dragon blood, and many other ingredients, but years of magic worked in and something else."

Finnius's mouth was dry, but his fascination got the better of him.

"What else?"

"Dragon teeth, bones, scales and talons infused with another body."

"A man?"

"In some cases. See for yourself." Selene pulled her sleeve up over her elbow and reached inside the bubbling cauldron. Her lips twitched and curled as an ancient arcane language came forth. All of the strange waters stirred before draining into the husk within. She released a small lever on the inside of the tub.

A man, or something like a man with a dragon-like face, lay within, eyes closed.

Finnius looked at her, then back at the figure in the vat.

She said, "A soldier. A creation of my own. I call it a draykis: Part dragon. Part dead. Part hunter. Do you like him?"

"Fascinating."

"Awaken!" Selene said.

The draykis's eyes snapped open. They were yellow and slit like a snake's. It rose up and stepped out of the vat. A variety of dragon scales glittered all over its body. Whoever it was, was human once, now turned into a dragon abomination. A defiance of the laws of nature. A hulking man combined with the finer parts of a dragon. A work of arcane art come to life.

Finnius admired it, a lot.

"He's magnificent," he said, stepping forward and back. "Tell me more, High Priestess."

She stroked the arm of the draykis and said, "In the case of this one, it's a man fused with the parts and blood of a dragon. He has the unrelenting strength of a zombie, combined with the armor and weapons of a dragon. The mind of a man keeps it all working together along with all the mystic spells."

Finnius held his finger up and asked, "You said, 'one'?"

She patted him on the cheek and said, "Clever, Finnius, very good."

She clapped her hands together.

Four figures leapt from a concealed ledge above and landed on the ground.

Oh my!

Finnius stepped closer to Selene as four more draykis approached. They were awesome things: cloaked, with hoods drawn back revealing the scales and sharp teeth on their faces. Each moved with ease, but their stout frames suggested power, like the lizard men, but more agile and cunning. Finnius wondered how much they could think for themselves.

"They are at my command, but soon they will be yours to command, Finnius."

"It would be an honor, High Priestess." He was wringing his hands. Anything that gave him power felt good. "Are we to hunt more dragons?"

"No, you are to hunt Nath Dragon."

Finnius rubbed his hand over his skull. He'd tried taking the man down with lizard men before and hadn't fared too well. But these draykis he was confident would do better.

"I see a hint of worry in your eye, Finnius. If you are not up to this…"

"Nay, High Priestess. I'm honored. With this brood, I cannot fail."

"Don't be so sure, Finnius. But, the draykis will be well armed. And you'll be taking more than enough reinforcements. They'll be of great help. Questions?"

"Just one, High Priestess," he offered a smile. "Do you want him alive, or do you want him dead?"

CHAPTER

21

I WAS COVERED IN DARKNESS. SUFFOCATING. I could barely move my arms and legs under all the weight. I'd faced death before. Fought my enemies. Beat them with cunning and steel. But now I was in the fight of my life against the elements. My foe was vast and undeterred. The very earth itself. I tried to scream again, but the dirt choked off my words. I had undone myself.

I thought of my father. I wondered how long it would take him to realize that I was gone forever. Even worse, I had failed him altogether. I would die of shame. Without honor. Failing my charge.

NO!

I could not let that happen. I had to hang on. I just had to! I took one last gasp and counted.

One… Five… Eleven… Twenty… Thirty… Sixty… It seemed this was it. None could save me. My face must be turning purple now. *Good bye, Nalzambor.*

"WAKE UP!"

I wasn't sure if I heard that or not.

"WAKE UP!"

I felt myself being pulled from my grave.

"NATH! BREATHE!"

I could hear.

"BREATHE!"

It was Brenwar. Or someone that sounded very much like him.

"This ought to help," he said, putting the weight of the world on my chest.

"ULP!" *gasp* "URK!"

I felt that. Hunks of dirt flew from my mouth as I spat, rolling back and forth on the ground. I coughed and hacked until my face became numb.

I'm ALIVE!

I managed to wipe the dirt from my eyes. The sunlight was, well, like sunlight on my face, but it never felt so good before. The next thing, I saw Brenwar, his bulging arm outstretched, helping me to my feet.

"I hope you found what you were looking for," he said. "And I think we're even. Well, I'm pretty sure I'm still ahead, that is."

I shook the dirt out of my hair. Fang was still in his sheath. Thank goodness I had not lost him. I slung my pack from my back and reached inside. The orb was still secure.

"Well, if I'd died I would have expected you to use this to free the blue razor." I managed a smile. "Thank you, Brenwar."

"Ah, it's nothing."

He stepped back as I opened my arms wide. "Stop that, Dragon. I said stop—"

I picked Brenwar up off his feet, hugged him like a bear, and swung him around. I felt joy. The joy of being alive. The joy of being able to fight for the cause of good once more. Being an adventurer, a hero, someone that does right instead of wrong doesn't mean you won't be put in the thick of danger. If anything, you'll find yourself in the middle.

"PUT ME DOWN, NATH DRAGON!"

I dropped him.

"Sorry. I couldn't contain myself."

"You ever do that again," he shook his fist at me, "and I'll kill you myself."

"I know. But right now, I'm so happy to be alive I don't care. Here." I extended my arm.

We bumped forearms, inside then out. "Better?"

"Better."

I held out the stone, letting Brenwar take a closer look.

"What do you think?"

"Dwarven made. Definitely."

I shook my head. But I wasn't going to disagree with the person who just saved my life. I'd do that later.

"Seems we have plenty of time to make it back, but I still don't understand why Corzan didn't think he could handle that. A magic user, even one not so powerful, should have been able to outwit a horde of ghouls. And the trap? A well prepared magic user could handle that as well. Not much of a guardian, if you ask me. At least not to protect a Thunderstone."

Brenwar stretched his short limbs and yawned.

"What? I was paralyzed, you know."

"How's the wound?" I said, looking at the ghoul's bite.

"Wound? That's not a wound," Brenwar scoffed. "Now let's get going down the mountain. I've had enough of these ghouls, tombs and fluffy caterpillars."

I raked the dirt from my hair and dusted off my clothes. I must look terrible.

"Say, where'd all the caterpillars go? They usually stick around for hours."

"Who cares?" Brenwar said, stomping away.

Not a blotch of pink, blue, yellow or purple remained. I actually enjoyed watching them walk around on their tiny little feet. But their job was far from over. The ghouls lay dead, some covered, some not. The caterpillars never left their work until it was finished, unless there was danger.

"Brenwar ... something's wrong."

I could feel the hair on my chin tingling when a black shadow blotted out the entire sun. A heavy wind stirred about me.

"You got that right," Brenwar said, eyes up, jaw down.

WHUMP! WHUMP! WHUMP! WOMP!

Oh no! There it was. Big. Monster big. Perhaps this was the Guardian Corzan spoke about. Clearly, it was not something he could deal with.

"That's one big dragon," Brenwar said.

The dragon blotted out the sun as it loomed over us like a gargantuan bird of prey. His steel scales were like hammered metal. His nostrils flared with open fire. His claws were bigger and sharper than the deadliest spears. His horns, one broken, were as long as me. His tail was like a great serpent, swishing back and forth, shattering tombstones like twigs. Perhaps this was what I'd seen in the moonlight the night before. It had been so distant then.

I backed away. He snorted. His hot breath was like a furnace, his eyes, ancient as the stones, bore down on me like I was an insect as he approached. My father was far bigger, but I was used to him. This dragon was bigger than most I encountered. Much bigger. Bigger than rhinos, elephants or a team of horses.

I drew my blade and swung it in front of me.

The dragon didn't blink.

I was scared.

"Nath," Brenwar said, "what do we do?"

I didn't have an answer to that question. In most cases, I rescued dragons; I didn't confront them. Even in my youth, the dragons avoided me, both inside and outside the Mountain of Doom, or Dragon Home. It was lonely. That much I easily remembered. Being born of dragons but still not one of them. Oh, I still had dragon friends, not many—and family, too many—but over time, we'd gone our separate ways. I'd even had dragon teachers, too, but none of them prepared me for this. Not even my father, I think.

I raised my arm up.

His teeth snapped together in a clashing chomp that could have taken my arm off.

I moved away, but he cut off my path with a massive head that swung from one side to the other. I wasn't going anywhere. Not if he didn't want me to, that is.

"Just stay back, Brenwar. I'm not sure if he's for or against us."

I usually was big, fast, and strong, but not with this one. Right now, I was little more than a meal, shiny toothpick included. I mustered my courage, or what was left, anyway. The truth was I wanted to run for it, but instead I locked with his gaze.

Inside, I was trembling like a leaf. Before me, a steel dragon. A fighter. A warrior. A soldier. I could tell by the scars on his body and the tears in his wings. A remnant of the Great Dragon War, he had to be. Yet there was another remarkable thing. The markings. Bright spots, green, orange and yellow mixed with blue adorned his frame, aglow with what looked to be arcane symbols. I'd never seen a dragon marked in such a way before. Perhaps he was enslaved, or cursed.

Arms up, sword pointed down, I displayed the sign of surrender, trying to back away. I wasn't about to strike if he didn't strike first. I felt his tongue whip past my cheek then back again.

"What do you want me to do, Dragon?" Brenwar said, tucked behind a tombstone.

"Be still!"

I stopped. I couldn't just back down. All I needed to do was get back off this mountain. He came closer, massive head inches from my face, his hot breath ruffling my auburn hair. I opened my mouth to speak. He bumped me with his snout, knocking to the ground like a toddler. I was in trouble now. He pinned me to the ground with his nose.

"Dragon!"

"Be still, Brenwar!"

Now, I could stab the dragon, maybe put out his eye or scar his nose. They didn't like to be hit in the nose or poked in the eye, for that matter. But, that tends to make one mad. And I've told you before about dragon breath. Small dragons don't hold so much, but a big steel dragon like this? Well, it could turn the entire mountaintop to flame. I put my dragon hand on the top of his nose.

"Peace and Home," I said.

You may have been wondering whether or not I can speak Dragonese. After all, I am a dragon, and I should be able to speak Dragonese—and I can. But, just because I can speak to them, doesn't mean they will speak to me. I was a very talkative and lonely boy growing up, but sometimes a speaking dragon gave me more than I wanted. When they did talk, it might take hours or days. And right now I didn't have time for a long conversation. But, I said it again, in Dragonese, anyway.

"Peace and Home."

He snorted hot smoke, keeping the pressure on my chest.

Now it was time to worry, not that I wasn't already. Dragons were like most people: sometimes it was very difficult to tell if they were good or evil. This dragon, so far, was not giving me the friendly vibes that I was hoping for. The more pressure and uncertainty rose within me, the more I wanted to strike. For all I knew, his mind was battle damaged. His connection to his own kind lost. His eyes were heavy upon me. Any wrong moves and he was going to incinerate me. I tried to keep perfectly still.

"Peace and Home."

Who are you?

He spoke. It was a jolt, rocking my mind. Not vocal ... mental. This was good.

"The Son of Dragon Home," I said.

You are a man, but you smell like a dragon. Another wizard come to deceive me!

It pushed me across the grass.

"No! Not a wizard, a dragon! Son of Halz—"

Whack! The dragon reared up on his legs with a roar so loud it shook the very mountain top.

"Brenwar!" I yelled. "What did you hit him for!"

The dragon filled his lungs with a big gust of air, and all I could think was *RUN*!

CHAPTER

22

A DWARF, EITHER OVERPROTECTIVE OR OVEREAGER to fight, had started all this. I didn't have time to think about that, though. I ran. Fast. The sound of a roaring flame erupted in my ears. I dove behind the nearest tombstone. A bath of fire surrounded me, hotter than the hottest thing I'd ever known. I swear I could feel my blood beginning to boil beneath my skin.

Dragon breath didn't last long. It didn't need to, and I felt nothing but relief when it stopped. The air, once as hot as a stove, was now smoky and chilly. One extreme to the other. The green grass, once fertile, now was brown and smoking.

"Take that, Steely Beast!" Brenwar yelled.

The dragon's roar was like a thunderstorm. Brenwar swung another mighty blow into the dragon, who stomped the earth, huffed fire through brandished teeth, and turned on Brenwar.

SWHACK!

The steel-colored tail licked out, whipped across Brenwar's chest like a striking snake, and sent him spinning head over heels, over both my head and the mountaintop's edge. Brenwar wouldn't like that. It was the second time in two days he'd been flung through the air like a toy, but there wasn't much to be done about it now. And I had myself to worry about.

It left me alone with the dragon. An angry one at that. I could fight or try to surrender, but my gut told me he wouldn't want any part of my surrender. I remained with my back pressed against the tombstone and got Fang ready. If he came after me, I'd only get one shot. A kill shot, possibly. But I wouldn't kill a dragon! I just had to stop him. But how could I do that before he killed me?

I could hear him crushing the stones beneath his heavy feet as he made his way towards me. His head, long neck and horns emerged before me. I fought the urge to thrust Fang down on his nose. It would hurt, but it wouldn't kill or subdue. I tried the only thing I could think to do.

"Peace and Home!" I yelled. "I am one of you!"

He eyed me. Like a cat eyes a mouse before dinner.

I could only feel his anger. His curiosity from earlier was long gone. Only the hardened soldier from the dragon wars remained. His final mission, to protect this mountain. Protect the Thunderstone from invaders like me.

If I could presume such a thing, but I couldn't think. I could only feel right now. Fear. It stiffened the joints in my bones. Real fear was not something I was accustomed to. *Move. Move. Move.* I was too late.

A geyser of flame spewed from his mouth.

I was coated from head to toe in blistering heat. Agony. Pain. Fear. I stabbed Fang through the flames and into the soft flesh in his mouth.

The flames stopped as he cried out, recoiling on his paws, eyeing me with great suspicion now.

I patted out the flames on my shoulder. What had happened? Why wasn't I burned alive? I should be dead now. I could sense his surprise as well as mine.

He snorted. Shook his massive head. Tore a mausoleum from the ground with his great horn and stepped back. Perhaps he was willing to listen now.

I stroked my hair. It was still thick and warm in my fingers. How had I survived those flames? "Will you listen now, Mighty One!" I was trying Dragonese once again. "I'm not here for harm. For good."

You!

I could hear him in my mind. Ancient. Irritated. Potent. This dragon hadn't even gotten warmed up yet. But I'd earned some respect.

The Thunderstone is my charge. My ward. My duty. My fate. My curse. Give it to me. Or die, Little Dragon.

Dialogue is a good thing. And I certainly had a better advantage than fighting. I liked these odds. I lowered my sword, and I chose my next words with care.

"You are a Great One. As big as I've ever seen. As powerful as they come. How has this stone entrapped you? Perhaps I can help—"

GIVE IT TO ME... OR DIE!

My head ached. This dragon was holding back something. I could sense it. As intimidating as he was, he was desperate. I'd learned a few things about curses, too. I had a feeling the Thunderstone was protecting me, warding me from him. He needed it, though. I tried bargaining.

"The Thunderstone is mine. But I'd be willing to show it to you if you tell me your story, Mighty One with scales as strong as iron." Flattery always helps, no matter how big and bad a dragon might be.

SHOW ME FIRST... OR DIE!

I opened my mouth to speak—

OR DIE... AND REMEMBER, I'VE NOTHING TO LOSE. NOT LIFE. NOT TIME.

Now he was letting me know in a nice way that he was being patient. I saw no harm in it. If I wanted to get off this mountain alive and save the blue razor, I'd have to give a little. I removed the stone from my belt pouch and revealed it's smoothness from the cloth. It ebbed, a warm glow from the blue marking on the stone.

AH... MY TORMENTER. MY JAILER! MY LIBERATOR! GIVE... IT... TO... ME!

Ah, now I understood the curse. The dragon could not take what was not freely given. A common curse, but a strong one. Bonding, in some cases, forever and ever.

"The story, Mighty One. I'll have that."

A growl rumbled in his throat. He shook his neck and fluffed his wings, stirring the air.

So be it, Little Dragon. A wizard, vile and despicable, duped me into service. Powerful he was, the Thunderstone the greatest source of his power. So envious was he of other wizards, he refused to relent his power. Mortality. The shortcoming of man. They thirst for such power, only to acquire it quickly and see it fade just as fast. The wizard did not want to share his power when he passed. He bonded me. Cursed me. Tricked me. I'm to protect the stone upon his death. I have been for centuries, sometimes flying far from the mountain—only to be drawn back.

I pitied him. I pitied all dragons in danger or exile. And had I not sworn to save them? Save them one and all. Those who would let me, that is. Some didn't want saved. They just wanted left alone.

"How can I help, Mighty One?"

Give me the stone.

"Why do you need the stone? I thought you only needed to protect it. Why didn't you just dig it out and take it yourself?" I couldn't assume the dragon was telling me everything.

I can only take what is freely given. The wizard promised to return and give it to me long after his death. A lich, he said he'd be. I must possess the stone to be free. I can take it with me wherever I go and protect it. Give it to me. My patience thins. He looked up into the sun. A sad look came to his hardened eyes. A longing for the sky and the freedom it offered.

"Perhaps we can break the curse."

He slammed his clawed fist into the ground. *NOT POSSIBLE! GIVE ME THE STONE!*

No. I needed the stone to free the blue razor. And in case you're wondering why I didn't just tell him so, this steel dragon, he couldn't have cared less about the blue razor. I just knew. But, perhaps I could free them both.

"I'll make you a deal, Mighty One!"

A DEAL? THERE WILL BE NO DEAL! DEATH YES! DEAL—NO!

"If I die, you remain cursed. Stuck on this mountain, staring at a stone that you cannot touch. I can help you."

He shook his head and neck. Bared his fangs and teeth and snapped in my face.

I cannot burn you, but I can eat you.

Apparently, the curse prevented him from eating me so long as I had the stone. His mouth stopped inches from my head, and he got a sad look in his eyes. I held my arms out.

"Just hear me out, Great One. Give me one day. I must take the stone to free a friend. Once I've done that, I'll bring it back and give it to you. If I don't return, well, you can come after me and kill me. I am a man of my word."

HA! HA! HA!

Of all the fearful things the dragon possessed—his claws, his tail, his breath—it was his laughter that scared me most.

You take the stone to the wizard in the mountain, Corzan? You're a fool, Little Dragon. Did you think I did not know about all in the mountain? I know every creature and every tree. HA! HA! HA! Go then, Fool. You will give it to me in a day. If not, I will destroy you, your friend the dragon, Corzan, and all of his rotten goblins. I know the secrets of the stone. You and he do not. Be wary, Fool Dragon. But you entertain me. I shall wait. Sit. Watch. Death comes quick to the fools who seek it.

CHAPTER
23

I CAUGHT UP WITH BRENWAR ANOTHER hundred feet down the mountain, and he wasn't in much of a talking mood. It didn't help that I had to help him out of the tree he'd been stuck in, either, and he made me swear I'd never tell. His cheeks were flushed red behind his beard, so I didn't bother to tell him that it was all his fault. He should have waited, and he's lucky he wasn't dead. His impulsiveness could have killed us both. But, I bit my tongue, forgave him inwardly, and moved on.

Down the mountain we went, and for some reason, the Thunderstone seemed heavy, as heavy as ten. I had a feeling it didn't like being moved around, but I had to take care of my mission. My own thoughts were filled with worry. The steel dragon had mentioned that he knew the secrets of the stone and then hadn't offered any more information. He was desperate, though. I could feel it in his thoughts. If things didn't work out, I was certain, he'd wipe out everything on the mountain.

Corzan was another problem. Just as the steel dragon was tricked by a wizard before, another magic-user was trying to trick me. I had to stay focused. All I needed to do was get the blue razor free and hope the rest would take care of itself. Even though my goals sounded simple, they would be much harder than they looked.

"We're almost there," I said. The sun was setting, the mountain becoming a black face in the night. I could hear the waterfalls in the distance. I jumped from one ledge to the other, reached out, and helped my friend over. "Any advice, Brenwar?"

It was always good to have a backup plan, but at this time I had none. I would have to convince Corzan to free the dragon before I gave him the stone. If he would not relent, well, I had no idea what I would do.

"Just free the dragon. Don't worry about the stone," Brenwar huffed, crawling down a ledge.

"What about the steel dragon? I gave my word I'd help him."

"You gave him your word he could eat you, not me."

"Brenwar," I said, alarmed "he wouldn't eat you anyway. Dwarves are too chewy and sour, they say."

Brenwar shot me a look and said, "Lucky for me, not so lucky for you."

Well, it seemed my dearest friend didn't have a backup plan, either.

"Thanks," I muttered.

Down we went, my back beginning to ache from the load of the stone, and my leg was still agitated from days before. I should have been healed up by now.

Goblin guards, yellow-eyed with pointed ears and stiff jaws, greeted us with spears at the entrance of the burrow goblin home.

"Leave your weapons," one said, lowering his spear towards Brenwar's nose.

He ripped the spear from its hands and whacked it in the head. I clocked the other one in the face, busting his nose. I was tired. I wouldn't be playing any more games today.

My feet were dragging by the time I got there. The stone as heavy as a small boulder now. The sight of Corzan the Necromancer irritated me. The devilish faced man sat with a smug look on his coarse face, hairy hands folded over his robed lap. Meanwhile, I felt like a mouse that had just stepped into a trap.

"Ah … the son of the Dragon King has returned. And an hour not too late. I'm impressed," Corzan said. "Do you have it?"

I stretched my arms and shoulders. I was all too ready to get rid of it now. I should have given it to Brenwar.

"I have it," I said, folding my arms across my chest. This was it. It was time for Corzan to play his final cards. "Let the dragon go, and it's all yours."

Corzan chuckled. The great hall full of goblins, over thirty of them, chuckled as well.

Leaning forward, Corzan said, "Show it to me first."

His eyes were like dark moons when I removed the Thunderstone from my pack, and a collective gasp filled the air. The orb's arcane markings shone a brilliant blue in the dimness of the cave. Corzan rose from his chair, hands outstretched as he approached.

"Give it to me," he hissed. "Now!"

This was it. The moment of truth. The moment we'd all been waiting for.

"Free the dragon first," I replied, cradling the Thunderstone at my side. He wasn't going to push me around.

Corzan flicked his fingers. A shower of sparks hit the dragon cage, drawing forth a painful hiss from the dragon.

"Give me the stone, Nath Dragon! Or my next spell will kill the dragon."

My anger started to rise. Brenwar bristled at my side, war hammer white knuckled in his grip. It was time to be rid of Corzan, the goblins—all of them. But the necromancer had the edge. He held the dragon's life in the balance.

Holding the stone out in front of his eyes, I said, "It is my stone to give, and I give it to you freely, Corzan."

"What!" Brenwar started.

Corzan licked his lips. A smile as broad as a river formed on his hardened face as he reached for it.

I tossed it into the dragon cage.

"You'll just have to get it."

The stone rolled into the cage, and the blue razor coiled over it.

Corzan's hands burst into flames.

"You FOOL! You'll die for this! Kill them! Kill them both!"

CHAPTER

24

THE GOBLINS SURGED. CORZAN DISAPPEARED. Brenwar threw himself into the entire force, war hammer swinging, goblins flying. Me, I had another idea.

I ripped Fang from his sheath. "Don't fail me now," I said.

Bang!

I struck the sword tip on the stone floor.

Fang vibrated with life in my hand and began to sing a terrible song. Terrible if you were a goblin, that is.

The sound echoed in the chamber, shaking the debris from the rocky ledges and ceiling. The goblins in the path of the sword fell to their knees, fingers plugging their ears, crying out in anguish, pain and uncertainty. Half of them fled. Others cried and begged.

Whop! Whop! Whop!

Brenwar took them out, one by one, rattling bones and cracking their ribs.

I was elated. When Fang sung, it sang a beautiful song that repelled evil like baths repel goblins. A tuning fork gone berserk. The great hall, once a fortress full of many enemies, was now under my full control. I muttered a quick thanks to my father for crafting such a fine and magical sword, for me.

Fang sang for another few seconds or so, and we found ourselves surrounded by a heap of broken, passed out or cringing goblins and a lone dragon in the cage.

"Corzan!" I yelled, my words echoing from corner to corner. "Come out! Surrender the dragon before it's too late!"

"He won't come," Brenwar said, kicking a goblin in his path. "The cowards run. They always do." A goblin burst from the floor and dashed away from the pack. "See! I'm going after it!"

"No, Brenwar!"

Too late. He ran into the tunnels and out of my sight.

Beside me, the blue razor remained huddling in the cage, eyes open, unmoving. She was unafraid. I kneeled alongside the cage and said, "I'll have you free soon, Sister. Just don't let go of that stone." I reached my fingers inside the cage.

"I wouldn't do that if I were you!"

It was Corzan, but from where I didn't know.

"Oh, Nath Dragon, you have infuriated me! Do you think you've defeated me, Corzan the Necromancer? NEVER!"

I could sense the man. He was hidden, but not invisible. "Corzan, free the dragon and the stone is yours."

An arc of light shot across the room and slammed into the cage. The blue razor roared.

"STOP IT!" I yelled.

The dragon's scales began to smolder. My temper did as well.

"Fetch the stone, Nath Dragon. Give it to me, or the dragon shall suffer more agony than you can imagine!"

I couldn't stand the thought of her suffering any more, but I couldn't give in right now. I had to try something else. The Throne. The arc of light had come from behind it, and I could see the edges of Corzan's robes at the bottom. I stepped between the throne and the cage and made my offer.

"Last chance, Corzan. Free the dragon now, or else I'm coming after you. Nothing can stop a dragon!"

Corzan stepped from behind the throne, arms raised over his head, hands burning with fire. "You and the dragon both shall die, Fool!"

"Last chance, Corzan!"

Another arc of light erupted from his hands. I swung Fang right into it.

KRYSAA—AK!

A shower of flame lit up the chamber. Corzan howled in rage.

The blow knocked me from my feet, and Fang flew from my grip. My vision was spotted, the wind knocked from me as I fought to stay conscious. *Where is he?*

I could see his face now. His eyes narrowed. His mouth snarled. His fists balled up at his sides.

"NO!" I shouted.

Hands like burning torches, he rushed for the cage. I could see the murder in his eyes. He'd have to kill the dragon to get the stone.

I struggled to rise, but my aching muscles were like lead.

Corzan's flaming hands reached for the cage.

Move, Dragon!

I lunged for his legs.

Corzan side stepped me. He kicked me in the face, and I saw spots again.

I caught his robes by the hem and jerked him down to the ground.

Whack! Whack!

Two flaming punches burned into my face. It was like getting hit with a hot frying pan, but I held on. I'd been in a scrap before. But I'd never brawled with a magic user before. This one had a lot of fight in him. Anger, too.

"Let the dragon go, Corzan! I'm warning you!"

We rolled over the floor, back and forth, my human arm wrapped around his forearms, fighting to keep his flaming hands from my face.

He kneed me in the groin.

"Oof!"

A mage fighter, a dirty fighter, too.

"That's it!"

Pow!

I punched him in the chest with my dragon arm.

It took the wind from him. He sagged within his robes as the fires extinguished from his hands. I put my forearm on his neck, and pinned him to the ground.

"Let the dragon go, Corzan!"

"Heh-heh. You won't hurt me, Nath Dragon." Corzan coughed and gasped. "I know that much about you."

He was right. I'm not sure how I could convince him otherwise, not without Brenwar, anyway. Why'd that dwarf have to run off? Still, that didn't prevent me from roughing him up a little. I walloped him in the stomach.

"Oof!"

"Let her go!"

Corzan grunted, but he did nothing else.

I tried it again. *Whop!* Same result, a more painful expression. I drew my fist back one more time.

"All right!" Corzan finally said. "But you must promise me the stone."

"I already have." I dragged him over to the cage. "Do it, already!"

Corzan pulled himself onto his knees, put his hands together, closed his eyes, and began to murmur. I kept the pressure on his neck with my dragon hand the entire time.

The metal cage warbled like a living thing, popped, cracked and slowly fizzled from sight.

The blue razor reared up, stretched her long metal blue neck and black wings, and batted her lashes at me. I smiled.

Zing!

Like a streak of lightning, she was gone. Not much of a thank-you, either, but I'd come to expect that. A shame, I'd like to have gotten to know her, a little bit at least.

Relief assailed me. I'd accomplished at least one good deed today. Now it was just me, Corzan, a bunch of roughed up goblins and the Thunderstone in the chamber. That, and of course —My Word.

Corzan went for the stone. I went for my sword. I know you are wondering why I let him have the stone. I'm sure you think I'm crazy. But, I gave him my word. If my word's not good, then I'm no good at all.

We squared off. Corzan held the stone as if he had all the wealth and power in Nalzambor in his own hand. I could feel the scales shift heavily in his favor.

"So, what's it going to be now, Corzan?"

He didn't say anything. He just stared at the orb, its blue markings radiant with life.

"I've got what I want, and you have what you want. Can we go in peace or not?"

Of course, I still had to get the stone back, but I needed to buy more time. I needed to know what he was thinking first.

"Well?"

Corzan stroked his fingers of the orb. "Such power," he hissed. "I can feel it in my very bones. It strengthens me." His voice rose. "Like ten necromancers in one."

I stepped back. Corzan's robes blustered behind a radiant swirl that circled him from head to toe. I could barely make out his face now, but it was changing, transforming, stretching unnaturally. The necromancer had been formidable enough before, but there was no telling what he had inside him now. I had a feeling that I only had a few seconds of life left—or possibly some arcane form of lifetime imprisonment. I didn't want either of those things to happen, so I did what any reasonable fighter would do. I raised Fang up over my head and attacked.

CHAPTER
25

"DRAGON! DRAGON!" Shouting out my battle cry, I crossed the distance between me and Corzan as fast as I could. I was fast. Thought was faster. One second Fang's tip licked inches from his face, the next I was sailing from one side of the room to the other.

"OOF!"

I slammed hard into one of the support columns and crumpled breathless to the ground.

"HAH!" Corzan shouted from the other side of the room. "I'm invincible now!"

Somehow, I rose to my feet. I wasn't going to die on my back.

"No one is invincible," I managed, wiping the blood from my mouth and coughing.

Corzan's smile was broad as a river, his evil deep as a gorge. His expression intelligent, cunning, omnipotent. He was the wolf; I was the sheep.

"Your time has come, Nath Dragon. Say your farewells."

That's when I noticed the change. His arms were no longer hairy, and his face was more man, less goblin. He noticed me eyeing him.

"What? What do you see?"

I little honesty wouldn't hurt at this point, and it would buy me more time as well.

"You look more like a man than a goblin now."

Corzan inspected his fingers. The long jagged fingernails were gone, the coarse hair over his hands and wrists removed. "Finally," he gasped. "The curse is controlled, if not removed." He returned his focus on me. "Heh, I bet you think I'll thank you, don't you, Nath Dragon?" He laughed. "The truth is, I'd consider it if I weren't so evil and you weren't so good. Can't have troublemakers like you sticking around." He pointed his finger at me.

Whap!

I punched myself in the face with my dragon fist.

Whap!

I almost knocked myself out cold.

Corzan had his fingers on the necklace of dragon scales and claws. I'd forgotten all about that. I should have ripped it off of him when I had the chance.

"I've total control over you now, Dragon. As a matter of fact, I can make you do whatever I want."

He was right. Unlike the last time he controlled my arm, I was completely at a loss to fight back this time. If I couldn't use my muscles, I'd have to use my mind. *Buy time!*

"So, you couldn't control the guardian dragon before. He was too strong. But, I'd say you have enough power to defeat the guardian dragon now, and all of the other wonders he protects."

Corzan stopped.

"What other wonders?"

This was the tricky part. I wasn't going to lie. But I could bluff. Besides, I didn't really know there weren't any other treasures.

"I didn't see any, but where there are dragons so big, there are hoards as well. Just think, Corzan, everything in the mountain could be yours."

"Am I to understand that the guardian dragon still lives?"

"Yes."

"How did you get the stone, then?"

Now was another time when I could tell the truth or lie. I didn't need to lie, though. There was still another weapon in my arsenal. Silence.

"I'll never tell."

Whap! Whap! Whap!

I dropped to the floor. I could feel my eye swelling. Nothing could really describe what it was like to give yourself a black eye.

"Is that all you got?" I said, not sure if I was talking to myself or to Corzan.

Whap!

"You are a fool, Dragon, to think that you can trick me into a fight with the guardian. But, I'd be lying if I wasn't curious as to what happened up there. I can only assume you struck a bargain of some kind with him. After all, you animals have a way of sticking together in the herd."

With a motion of his arms, Fang was ripped free of my grasp and into his.

"A fine sword. Magic. Dragon magic. Hmmm. I could make use of this."

I needed to move. Far and fast. He was strengthening, and I was weakening. I could feel it. And I hoped Brenwar wouldn't come back, either. He'd be killed if he did. I had to have another trick up my sleeve.

With the stone in one hand and my sword in the other, Corzan was frightening. Tall, gaunt, and indestructible.

Well, at least I saved one dragon, but now I was worried about the other as well. What if Corzan could control him, too? The ancient wizard had done so. It was up to the steel dragon to beat him in battle, but it didn't seem likely right now. Not with the necklace Corzan wore and his knowledge of the dragons.

"Now what, Corzan? You have me defeated. Should I expect an unpleasant death?" I had to keep talking, at least long enough to figure out something.

"Be still," he said, holding the Thunderstone toward me.

Three purplish rings of magic appeared around me and squeezed. It felt like I was in the grip of an iron giant. I struggled, but all I could do was breathe, and that was difficult.

"I think I have a better use for you alive." He tossed my sword aside, its hard metal echoing on the hard stone floor. "Remember, the Clerics of Barnabus will be here soon, and I am without the dragon they came for. But, I think I have something much better to offer them. Their greatest nemesis, Nath Dragon, alive and well."

I hadn't even entertained that notion. The truth was, the Clerics of Barnabus hadn't even entered my mind.

"I thought you said you would be able to handle them with the Thunderstone now. Why don't you just test your powers and take them out?" I suggested.

"Living alliances will serve me much better than dead ones. You know that."

"You realize that once they find out you have the stone, they'll try to take it from you."

Raising the stone over his head, he laughed when it began to crackle with white energy.

KA-CHOW!

A bolt of lightning shot from it. The balcony above exploded into shards of rock.

KA-CHOW!

A large wooden door across the way was no more. Only smoke and splinters remained.

"No, they won't be taking anything from me. I can do this all day if I like." He looked around. "I wonder where that dwarf is. I'd like to test it out on that armor of his."

My heart sank. I'd never seen a man wield such raw power before. I could barely speak, but I managed spit out in vain, "You'll never find him! He's long gone by now. But if you follow the trail of goblin corpses you might get close."

Corzan laughed as he resumed his place on the throne, dragging me in my bonds before him.

"He'll be dead by dawn. I assure you of that."

CHAPTER

26

I DIDN'T KNOW WHAT HAD HAPPENED to Brenwar, but the longer he was gone, the better. *Buy time.*

"So, tell me about this curse of yours."

It was an unpleasant look he gave me, but he still opened his mouth and spoke.

"A goblin bite. It doesn't happen very often, but it does happen. The bite turns one from man to goblin. You didn't know that, did you?"

I shook my head. I hoped orcs couldn't do the same. Imagine getting bit by an orc only to become one.

"I'll elaborate. A goblin witch bit me. A curse it was, turning me from man to minion. In most cases, the witch can remove the curse for a price, but I ran out of patience and killed her. I set her horrid face on fire and watched her burn until she was dead." He shook his head. "I had a bad temper back them. Looking back, I could have been more gentle." He held the stone out and admired it. "But, that's where this came in. Ancient, powerful magic such as this can cure most things, with a little help, that is."

I looked at my arm. Was it possible it could cure me? Remove the evil from my scales and lead me back to home? Father had told me that there were many secrets in Nalzambor that could heal anything.

"So, how will you truly know if you are cured unless the stone isn't in your possession? I could hold it for you." Planting some doubt in his mind wouldn't hurt anything. There was a rustle behind me. The goblins I'd stunned with Fang's humming had started to stir. "Will they still follow?"

"My, so clever you think you are," Corzan said. "A dragon above, doubt below. Do you think I'm so easily fooled?"

"Either way, you'll still have to deal with them both," I said, smiling. "Just trying to help out."

"I'm getting the feeling the longer I keep you around, the more trouble you will be." He got up from his seat and thrust the stone at my chest, sending me skipping across the floor. There I lay, in the middle, where the dragon cage had earlier been, alone and unable to defend myself.

"The Clerics of Barnabus will have to settle for your corpse instead."

Defiant, I struggled back to my feet. If I was going to die, I would die on my feet. I'd had enough of him.

"Give it your best then, Goblin!"

His lip curled over his white teeth as he held the Thunderstone over his head. It became a whirling white sun of energy.

"Let him alone, Goblin!"

Brenwar rushed into the room, war hammer high over his head. The awoken goblins rushed him, and a few more were on his heels. He slammed the hammer into the floor.

KRANG!

The stone floor erupted. The goblins fell between the busted stone, others lost their footing.

Corzan laughed. Lightning sailed. Brenwar was lit up as he went spinning across the floor in a smoking heap and lay still.

"NOOOOOOOOO!" I screamed, stumbling forward.

Corzan was laughing, again.

"Now that I've seen what I can do to dwarves, let's see what I can do to half-dragons."

The Thunderstone charged up again, its blue light brilliant in my eyes. I was so angry, I couldn't even think. Let him hit me with all he had. I deserved nothing less. After all, I'd just gotten my best friend killed.

Wild with power, Thunderstone in hand, Corzan charged. Hungry. Angry. Unrelenting.

I could see it consume him. I didn't think he was going to leave anything of me for the Clerics of Barnabus now. I clenched my jaw and braced myself.

Snatch!

The bright light faded. The stone was gone from Corzan's grip.

"What!" he cried.

My bonds disappeared.

Above, the blue razor darted through the chambers, the Thunderstone in her back talons.

I couldn't believe my eyes. She came back. *She came back!*

She hovered over me, winked her beautiful eye, and dropped the stone in my hands. And with a crack of thunder, she was gone.

Corzan's faced was contorted with rage as he said, "Give it to me! You cannot handle its power, Animal!"

The stone was still heavy, even in my dragon hand, bewitched somehow. That didn't matter. What mattered was my friend lying still in the corner. Corzan would pay for that. He'd pay for it now.

His eyes widened as I rushed forward. My dragon arm popped me in the head with the rock.

"Ouch!" I cried, stumbling to the floor.

"Fool!" Corzan cried, grasping his necklace. "I control your arm."

Blood dripped into my eyes. I wasn't going to be controlled by anyone anymore, certainly not him. My dragon hand struck again, but I stopped it with my other hand. I wasn't going to be responsible for beating my own self to death. *Dig deep, Dragon! Fight it with all you can!*

"Give it up, Dragon! You have given the stone to me; it's mine, not yours. You cannot control its powers."

I could feel my dragon fingers peeling away from the stone. I fought it for a moment and let it go. The stone slipped free of my hand and into my other. It weighed like an anvil on my arm.

Whack!

The dragon arm hit me once, then tried again. I stopped it. The black scales on my arm trembled. My heart thundered in my chest. I would not surrender to Corzan anymore. It was my will against his. Shaking with every movement, I forged up the steps. Every fiber of my being was tested.

Corzan gasped as I took the first step. "NO! It's not possible!"

Sweat cascaded down his face and dripped onto the floor as he clutched the necklace of dragon scales and bones in his hand. He transformed as well. The coarse hairs on his hands returned, and his ears grew to points on the back. He reverted to more goblin than man. "The curse, it's back! You must give me the stone, Nath Dragon!"

I fought my way up two more steps.

"I'm going to give you something, alright," I said through clenched teeth. My heart was bursting in my chest. But it was my life or his. Fighting my own arm and carrying the stone was like dragging two anchors over the harbor.

"You cannot beat me!" he screamed.

I fought against belting myself again. Gritted my teeth and jumped up the last few steps. I could barely move. I gasped for my breath.

Corzan's hands burst into flames and reached for my throat.

"It's too late, Fool! You shall burn alive this day!"

I looked at him and then at my dragon hand, eyed him again, and said, "No I won't!"

All of my muscles fought against me, but they were my muscles, after all. They served my will, not his.

Whack!

I punched him in the face with my dragon arm.

BOOM!

I popped him in the belly with the Thunderstone. Corzan's body slammed into his throne. He sagged into his chair and moved no more.

"Yes!"

I ripped the dragon necklace from Corzan's limp fingers and put it around my neck. The only thing controlling me was going to be me from now on. The Thunderstone had lightened now, the glowing runes now dim, its energy spent. Why it was so heavy before and light now, I didn't know, but I could try to understand that later. I jumped at the sound of a rustle behind me. *Brenwar!*

I turned in time to see him sitting up, holding his head. I rushed over and helped him to his feet. He smelled like a saddle that had sat in the sun too long.

"Are you well?"

He blinked, cocked his head, and said, "Ale."

The goblins, what was left of them, gathered around me.

Brenwar growled at my side.

I held the stone up. "Who wants to be the first to die?"

They gawped, shuffled back, and disappeared from sight. Without their leader, they didn't have much fight left in them.

But what was I going to do about Corzan the Necromancer? Groggy and defeated, he didn't put up much of a fight, but I still had a problem. He was still alive. And that was one of the tough things about being good. Sometimes, you had to let your enemies live, and I figured Corzan would hold a grudge against me for a long time. So what did I do to keep him out of my hair in the meantime?

"This ought to hold you until your guests arrive," I said.

From his throne, Corzan looked up at me with blurry red eyes.

"What have you done to me?" he said, struggling in his bonds.

I continued to wrap the spool of copper twine around his wrists and legs. It was elven made twine, called *Elotween*, inescapable when applied, but temporary. In a few days, it would disappear, but nothing could untie it or cut it, not without magic, anyway. It would have to do for now.

"Now, don't struggle too much; it'll constrict and might cut your wrists off," I warned.

"Fool, I can escape these — *mrph*!"

I stuffed a rag in his mouth. I'd had enough of his talk.

I waggled the stone in front of his face and said, "Have fun explaining to the Clerics of Barnabus why you don't have them a dragon."

Corzan's eyes were as big as saucers.

"I'm sure they will be very eager to hear your tale."

If you can't dispel evil yourself, let evil do it for you. Leave evil to its own.

CHAPTER

27

TRAVELING BACK UP THE MOUNTAIN was even worse than the first time. The heavy rains splattered all over my armor, and rivulets of water slicked all the footholds. This trip seemed twice as long as the last. It wouldn't have been so bad if Brenwar stayed back, but he insisted.

"Brenwar, there's a cave near," I pointed to the mouth of a jagged edge. "Why don't you wait there until I come back?"

"No," he grumbled, shaking his head and beard like a black sheep dog. "You go; I go."

You'd think the lightning jolt he took would have eased him, but all it did was make him tougher. The more punishment they survived, the more stubborn they'd become. Brenwar had already survived enough battles to convince him he could handle anything, but often enough I'd seen otherwise. At least three times on this trip, anyway.

I pulled him up by rope, bringing him to the ledge along my side. Thirsty, I caught some rain water in my mouth from off the edge of the rocks and drank until it filled me. I felt like I'd been beaten up by an ogre. My face and lips were swollen. The gash in my head ached, and my leg was as bad as it'd ever been. For all of my dragon's constitution, I was tired. And now, I had to go and face a steel dragon, or at least catch up with him before he came after me. I had a feeling all of his patience had run out. It was time someone paid for all of his suffering.

I patted the Thunderstone tucked beneath my chest plate. It was warmer and heavier than when we started. If it got any heavier, I'd have to stop climbing. What was with this thing?

"Bloody dragon can have the thing," I said, rubbing my hands together. "Getting cold again, too."

"What?" Brenwar said in the pouring rain.

I pointed at the cave.

"No!"

We weren't so far from the top, but I was still pressed for time. I couldn't leave Brenwar alone, on second thought. He always stuck by my side, so I'd stick by his. I just hoped he wouldn't attack the dragon again.

I tugged at the rope around his waist and almost jerked him from his boots, saying, "Let's go, then."

"Listen, Dragon," he wagged his finger at me, "nobody—"

"Tugs a dwarf!" I finished. "I know!"

We practically crawled up the mountain over the next few hours. If Brenwar wasn't slipping, he was falling, all the time blaming the giants for the rain. He wasn't a horrible climber, not by your typical standard, but by mine, he was pretty slow.

"Come on, you legless goat!" I said, pointing, "We're almost there."

"Legless what?"

We reached the top an hour later, and the rain was a steady down pour. And it wasn't your typical rain, but high in the mountain rain, ice cold rain, one step from ice and snow. The clouds above were dark, full of thunder and flashing light. It was the perfect weather for a funeral. Mine.

The graveyard hadn't changed since we left, which was no surprise, but all the ghoul bodies were gone.

"You know," Brenwar started, "if you give him that stone, he might still kill you."

"I know."

Of course, if I didn't give him the stone, he was going to try and kill me anyway. And I'd been thinking that exact same thing for the entire trip. At least we made it back in time. I withdrew Fang. Brenwar clutched his war hammer in his meaty hands.

"A great morning for a battle," he said.

Do you have it?

The dragon's voice startled my mind. If he was near, I couldn't see him.

"I wouldn't be here if I didn't," I replied.

Brenwar cocked his head at me and said, "What?"

Let me see it!

The dragon's voice was demanding, unpleasant.

I removed the Thunderstone from beneath my chest plate and extended it in my clawed hand. The radiant blue runes illuminated my hand like a torch. I hated to give up so valuable an item. For all I knew, it could cure the evil in my dragon arm as well as many other things. But it was almost too heavy to hold.

"Here it is," I said.

A great shadow dropped from the sky and landed, shaking the ground beneath me. He seemed bigger, more sinister, and as powerful as ever. The heavy drops of rain on his scaled frame looked like nothing but drizzle compared to him. The bright markings on his body grew brighter at every flash of lightening.

Have you come to kill me? he said in my mind, eyeing my sword.

"Just a precaution," I said, twirling it in my hand.

The dragon snorted a puff of smoke from his nose and flashed a row of his teeth.

A fine blade it is. I've seen it before; you should know.

I looked at the blade and back and him.

"How'd you—"

THE STONE, PLEASE. MY PATIENCE IS AT END.

He extended his clawed hand that was big enough for me to have a seat in.

"From me to you, this Thunderstone I give."

I dropped it in his hand. It looked like little more than a tiny egg. I swore the dragon smiled when he had it.

I started to ask, "What are you going to do with it now?"

The dragon tossed it in his mouth.

"What did you do that for?"

The dragon showed his teeth.

"Get back," Brenwar said, tugging on my arm.

The dragon's luminous spots pulsated with life, swirling over the dragon's body, a living thing of its own free will. I'd never seen markings move on a creature before.

The dragon roared. I covered my ears as it went on and on. His head was filled with many colors now: blue, purple, yellow, green and orange, wrapping around his teeth and horns. The dragon shook and growled like an attacking dog. I retreated farther. He roared again and stretched his neck up high. Fire in all the colors of a rainbow came out shooting from his mouth. A hundred feet high it went, creating a cloud of many colors.

"Let's go!" Brenwar said.

I kept my ground, looking skyward. A creature formed above, part man, part bird, an apparition of many colors. Its eyes were black, evil, beauty twisted into a terrible thing. It hissed, spat and cursed something ancient and foul, its form dissipating and blowing away.

Brenwar's jaw was hanging when I asked, "What was that?"

He just shook his head.

A Weevilin. A spirit of evil that lives within. My tormentor, the lich, left me with that.

The dragon was face to face with me now. No longer dark or dreary, but with scales that shined brightly like a new coat of armor. Polished armor, like the ones the Knights of Quintuklen wore. I had the steel dragon all wrong. He was one of the most beautiful things I ever saw.

"What happened to the wizard who cursed you?" I asked. "I did not see any sign of him in the tomb below. Is he dead, or does he live in some other shape or form?"

So nice of you to ask, Nath Dragon. And for your service, I shall tell you. The wizard died and returned a lich, yet he refused to free me. So I refused him the stone. We fought long hours for many days, but I won out. He is no more, but the evil spirit I was cursed with remained. Only the Thunderstone, freely given, could send it away.

"So," I eyed his great belly, "is the stone destroyed?"

It's safe.

As the rain stopped and the clouds parted, all I could do was gawp at the wonderful beast beating his wings and flying off. And just like that he was gone. I stood there, numb, as if I'd lost.

That sword you have, Little Dragon ... you should get to know it better ... that day your father forged it, I was there ... tell him hello ... and thank you.

CHAPTER
28

IT WAS A QUIET TRIP down the mountain, through the forest and across where the small river went into the Shale Hills. I was frustrated. My arm was still as black as coal, and saving the dragons had given me little comfort at all. I felt empty, left out, and as confused as ever. Even Brenwar seemed perplexed.

Dragons! I'd saved a steel dragon, and all the thanks he'd given me was advice to talk to Fang. The fact that he knew my father—well, I presumed, seeing how they shared a forge—bothered me most. Certainly, he could give me a little more advice now that the curse was lifted. And what did he need the Thunderstone for, anyway? It had helped him. Maybe it could have helped me, too. I punched a tree.

"What's the matter with you?" Brenwar said.

I took a seat on a fallen log.

"All this work, and for what? My arm's no different than when I started." I held it out. "See!"

Brenwar took a step closer, squinting.

"What are you doing?"

"Looking," he said, "I haven't really taken a good look at it." He rubbed his chin. "I thought you said it was all black."

"It is," I said, eyeing my forearm and wrist. "What other color do you see?"

"White."

I fanned out my clawed fingers and turned my hand in the sunlight, saying, "Where?"

"In the middle of your palm."

"It's just the sun's reflection off the scales, I don't see a th—"

My lips froze. My heart stopped. A small group of scales in the middle of my palm had turned white. A thrill went through me, like the first time I flew on my father's great back as a child.

"Brenwar!" I exclaimed. "Can it be I'm on the higher road of doing good things!"

He didn't say anything, but he was smiling, in a dwarven way, a broad smirk, if anything.

I pumped my dragon fist in the air, jumped high, and shouted with joy! I couldn't remember the last time I'd felt so good in my life. I was finally getting somewhere.

"Maybe it's spreading, Brenwar?" I gave my hand a closer look. "My hand might be completely white by tomorrow, you think?"

He shrugged and said, "I hope so." He slapped me on the back. "You've done well, Dragon. But I still think you've got many good deeds to go."

I felt in my heart that saving the blue razor and helping the steel dragon got me over the hump. I'd saved many dragons of late, but those two were different, the circumstances more tough. Perhaps I wasn't challenging myself enough. I needed to investigate further the whereabouts of more dragons. I knew there were more out there.

"I'm coming home soon, Father!"

I had a spring in my step, and my wounded leg was less bothersome as we traversed the black shale. I had two things on my mind: my dragon arm and the Roaming Rangers, Shum and Hoven. It had only been a few days, but I wondered if they'd had any luck finding the winged ape. I wanted to track it. Fight it. Defeat it. I couldn't explain why, but I did. It was just another menace that needed to die before someone else did.

"Where are you going?" Brenwar asked, wiping his sweating head on his forearm.

I pointed with my dragon arm toward the hill where we'd last seen the elves. I felt more comfortable using it now. A bad thing had turned good in my eyes, and I loved it all the more.

"Just checking on those—"

"No! You need to focus on the dragons. The elves can solve their own problems, and the men can as well. Come now, I thirst for Dwarven Ale."

"But—"

"Come!" Brenwar said, marching off with determination.

I didn't have to follow him, and he didn't have to follow me—unless my father had told him to, but Brenwar never said. I eyed the hill where the elves were holed up and some of their traps were set. I was dying to see them again. I had never seen elves like that. Pot bellies on elves. Hah! Who'd have imagined such a thing?

"Alright," I said, heading after Brenwar. We walked on mile after mile until the sun began to set in our sight. "You hungry? I could use some good meat about now."

"I'll find a spot and start a fire."

I unslung Akron.

Snap. Clatch. Snap.

It was ready

"I'll fetch the meat."

I hadn't made it a mile from camp when I heard a muffled cry. A struggle was ahead, and without thinking, I rushed for the danger. Darting in and out of the trees like the swiftest of deer, I emerged in a clearing. Shum and Hoven, the Wilder elves, were interlocked in battle with the winged ape. It was hairy and blue-black with a slight blue sheen, roaring into the face of Shum, its mighty long fingers wrapped around the neck of another ranger I'd not seen before.

Twang!

My first arrow hit it square in the back, and it let out a roar.

It turned.

I reloaded.

Brawny muscles, black claws and dripping fangs charged me, faster than the fastest bull I'd ever seen.

Twang!

It ducked.

But my aim was low, intentionally, and the arrow exploded into its shoulder.

The winged-ape crashed to the ground.

I ripped out Fang and charged.

"Dragon! Dragon!"

I couldn't let the evil beast hurt or kill another thing. I chopped at its stomach.

It rolled away, bounced up, and swatted me in the face. It was fast. Like a striking cobra.

I stabbed.

It turned.

I slashed, grazing its arm.

It swung its big paw at me, nails nicking my face.

I countered and clipped its legs, drawing blood.

It backed away.

"Come on," I said, taunting it with Fang's glowing blade. I was ready for it. I was ready for anything.

It eyed me, two red coals gleaming under its heavy brow. It was smart, thinking about its next move. But I was ready.

"You heard me! Come on, Monster!"

It pounded its chest, lowered its shoulders, stretched out its mighty thewed arms, ready to scoop me up, and charged.

It came.

I swung.

It leapt high in the air and left me gawping before dropping on me like a load of stones. The eight hundred pound ape drove me hard into the ground.

Fang fell from my grasp.

It pinned my neck to the ground and roared in my face. It was strong, like oxen.

I kicked its stomach, twisted my wrist free, then clawed at its eyes.

It punched and punched me like a boxer. I found this odd, even in the midst of my face being punched in. It was bigger, stronger, but it was a beast; I was a dragon.

I drew back and punched it in the nose with my fist. I swore I heard it laughing as it shrugged it off and hit me back. Stars exploded in my eyes. I was getting beaten like a dusty rug.

A Wilder Elf jumped on its back, which one I couldn't tell.

With one arm, the winged ape flung him away.

I pulled my knees to my chest and kicked it in the stomach with all I had. To my surprise, it tumbled to the ground. Gasping, I rolled left and grabbed my sword.

Two more elves dove at the winged ape. They both fought hard before it slung them off like water. Another pair, from where they came I don't know, threw a large net at the beast. The net sailed beneath its feet as it jumped high in the air. How many of these elves were there, anyway?

I saw my chance. The ape had the elves in sight, not me. I lowered my sword, rushed in, and stabbed at its belly. It twisted a split second before I got there, but I struck a blow. The beast let out an odd cry, almost elvish, as its massive shoulders dipped to the ground. I had it where I wanted it now. Fang gleamed as I rose him above my head for the final strike.

"No!" someone screamed.

A Roaming Ranger slammed into me, knocking me to the ground. Another jumped on top of me, followed by another.

"What are you doing!" I screamed at them.

The winged ape groaned, holding its wounded side as it lifted its chin to the sky. Its black wings fanned out, flapped a few times, lifting it into the air, above the tree lines and out of sight.

"Get off of me!" I said, kicking one of the elves in the gut. I was mad now. Why did the elves mess things up?

"Nath Dragon!" one of the rangers said, extending his hand to me. It was Shum. "We do not want him dead! We want him alive, and you've fouled things up."

"Fouled things up? Are you jesting? It was beating the tar out of all of you. Why wouldn't you want that beast dead, anyway? It's a killer!" I shoved his hand away.

"It's our king," Shum said, glumly.

"Your what?" I said, eyeing the others.

There were five of them now. One just as tall and heavy as the other.

"Our king, Sansla Lybor."

"Let me guess..." I hated to say it, but I did "...he's cursed."

Not long after that, Brenwar arrived, huffing and puffing. Shum and Hoven had finished the tale of their cursed king. I felt for them. For more than a decade, they'd tried to trap him, and this was as close as they'd been in a while. I wasn't sure if I'd messed things up or not, but I only meant well. But as they left, I sensed their disappointment.

Shum said to me as he left, "You stick to your own, Nath Dragon. We'll stick to ours. And remember, Sansla Lybor is little more than a shadow of his glorious self now, but the curse within him is vengeful. He'll not forget that wound you gave him, but perhaps we'll find him before he finds you. Watch the skies. Farewell."

One thing was for certain: there were too many curses in this world! I had enough of my own problems to worry about. I eyed the white spot on my hand. It was a start. A dozen dragons freed, dozens more to go. One dragon at a time, Nath Dragon, one at a time.

"Come on, Brenwar. I think I'm ready for the dwarven home, Morgdon, for now."

Terror at the Temple

-BOOK 3-

CRAIG HALLORAN

PROLOGUE

THE DRAYKIS. BIG. SILENT. DEADLY. Finnius the acolyte of Barnabus had never seen or imagined anything like them. Men, with dragon parts grafted onto their bodies by magi: scales, talons, and another one with wings. Not just any men, but fighting men, men of skill and cunning. And they had something cornered, a dragon of all things.

They'd trapped a yellow streak dragon inside the mouth of a large cave. It was bigger than any one man, slender and about fifteen feet in length. Its spiked tail whipped out like the head of a snake, taking out one draykis's legs. In an instant, the draykis was back on its feet, charging. The dragon breathed a plume of white ash, engulfing the dragon man. The draykis turned stiff as stone where he stood.

Whack!

A draykis caught the dragon across the nose with his club as another draykis jumped onto its neck. Only a fool would wrestle a dragon, but the draykis were unrelenting, fearless. The yellow streak dragon bit one on the arm, clawed another on the face, but he was young and confined to a tight space. The fourth draykis appeared, the one with dark wings and a red scaled face, swinging a club. As the dragon men held the yellow dragon down, the winged draykis beat it until it fought no more. Finnius had never seen men take a dragon so quickly before. Nor with such brutality, either.

"What would you have us do now, Acolyte Finnius?" the winged draykis said.

Finnius watched as the other two bound the defenseless dragon's mouth and wings. He could see the look in the dragon's eyes, drained, defeated. That look thrilled him as he walked over and stroked the dragon's dark yellow belly. *Quite the catch. Quite the catch, indeed. High Priestess Selene will be pleased with this one.*

"Fetch a cart while this one thaws," he said, pointing his finger at a draykis that was coated in white and perfectly stiff. "And don't touch him—"

At that moment, a draykis touched the coated draykis and started to freeze.

"Either!" Finnius grunted as he turned back towards the draykis leader. "Fetch the cart while we wait for them both to thaw out." He shook his head. "Did I tell any of you to touch one another? Hmm? Did I? No! You follow orders. Explicit orders. Now fetch that cart and the rest of the acolytes, Dragon Man."

"As you command," the Draykis said, ruffling his wings before heading outside of the cave.

"You," he pointed at the last one, "stay with the dragon. We cannot afford to lose our bait for capturing Nath Dragon."

CHAPTER

1

MORGDON. HOME OF THE DWARVES. I was a captive here.

"Come on, Brenwar," I pleaded. "I'm ready to go. It's been three weeks already."

"Ah, but the Festival of Iron has just started. We can't leave now: you haven't even seen the best part yet," he replied, marching down a crowded street.

The opening parade had begun a week ago, and it hadn't finished yet. The dwarves only celebrated the Festival of Iron once in a decade, and they put a lot of effort into it. I stopped to watch as a regiment of dwarves marched by in full plate armor, with only their beards and weapons hanging out. They were in perfect cadence, every booted foot in step, not one out of a thousand dwarves out of line.

"How many soldiers are there, anyway?" I asked, looking over Brenwar's head. I was the tallest person in the entire city, at the moment, anyway.

"Oh, I can't tell you that, but I might entertain a guess."

I'd been asking questions every day for weeks. It helped pass the time. A certain question in particular always came to mind: "When are we leaving?" Still, I had to respect my host.

"One Hundred Thousand?" I said.

"No."

"Fifty Thousand?"

"No."

"Can you give me a hint?"

A tiny dwarven boy was standing on the shoulders of his father, smiling at me and holding nine fingers up.

"Ninety…" I said.

The dwarven boy, whose beard had not started yet, showed six fingers.

"—Six thousand?"

Brenwar turned. I could see the surprise in his stony face. His eyes flitted from me to the boy and back to me when he said, "Humph… close enough." He eyed the boy again, stroking his beard, and said, "Ye should mind your own business."

I put my arm over Brenwar and walked him away, saying, "Ah. It's no wonder you all look so grumpy all the time. You don't encourage fun when you're young."

"Fun is for the foolish. A dwarf's work is never done. We don't run around looking for things to smile about all the time."

"You would if you could smile like me," I grinned.

He shook his head, saying, "That smile would be much prettier accompanied by a nice long beard."

I rubbed my clean-shaven face. I was the only beardless man in the Morgdon, aside from the women and children. Of course, many of the women did have beards, and I never got used to that. It just didn't seem natural, a fuzzy-faced woman, but they could all cook a delicious feast. I'd give them that.

"Brenwar, honestly, when can we leave?"

I was restless. Now that I had a white spot on my dragon hand, I wanted to save the Dragons more than ever. I felt like a piece of me was back, like my honor had returned. I wasn't motivated before, but now I was more motivated than ever. And I couldn't help but wonder: *What do the white scales mean?*

"Soon, Dragon. Come now," he said, reaching over and grabbing a tankard of ale from the booth of a dwarven Ale Master. He quaffed it down in one gulp and belched like a man-sized bullfrog. He patted his belly and grabbed another round and thrust it in my face. "Drink and be merry. Be merry and drink."

"I'm fine, thanks. Now, Brenwar, let's go," I groaned. "You know I have Dragons to fetch."

"Wait until the song's over," he said with a wink.

"What song?" I said. "There's no one singing."

That's when I saw a smile from behind his beard as he raised his booming voice to the clouds and sang:

"HOOOOOOOOOOOOOOOOOOOO…"

Instantly, thousands of dwarves joined in.

"Home of the dwarves! Morgdon! Home of the dwarves! Morgdon!

We make the finest steel and ale. Morgdon! In battle, we never fail! Morgdon!

Home of the dwarves! Morgdon! Home of the dwarves! Morgdon..."

The singing went on and on, and I'd be lying if I said I didn't enjoy it. As much as I didn't want to sing, I couldn't help but do just that. The robust dwarves put everything they had into the moment. They jumped, swung, tapped, drank and sang all at the same time. I'd never seen so many happy dwarves before, and it made me happy, too. There was no better army in all Nalzambor than an army of dwarves. They'd fight until their hearts were black and blue.

"Home of the dwarves! Morgdon! Home of the dwarves! Morgdon!

We make the toughest armor and ale. Morgdon! In battle, we never turn tail! Morgdon!

Home of the dwarves! Morgdon! Home of the dwarves! Morgdon..."

When it ended, I was fulfilled. The dwarves were ready for anything. I was ready for anything.

Brenwar slapped me on the back and said, "What did you think of that?"

"I liked it!"

I decided I should make the most of it. You just couldn't let every day of your life be filled with worry. "Trust in the greater good instead," my Father would say. So I did. After all, Morgdon was a fantastic city with the boldest architecture I ever saw. A suspension bridge crossed from one side of Morgdon to another. The buildings and towers were all square-cut stone, but not just any stone: many stones of many colors, not bright, but not all dull, either. Where you didn't see stone, you saw metal. Burnished, hammered, polished or riveted, it adorned their bodies, faces, buildings and all places.

"Look at this, Dragon! Ho! You are in for a treat!" Brenwar pointed.

The parade was still going strong. The regiment of dwarves had marched on, but I could still hear their heavy boots pounding the ground like a steady heartbeat. I followed Brenwar's arm that pointed upward. A group of dwarven men were sitting in the sky.

"How are they doing that?"

They each sat in a tiny seat at the top of a pole that was ten stories tall, four of them in all. Beneath them, big dwarves with broad chests held them up on shafts of iron, eyes straight forward as they marched along. Every eye was filled with wild wonder as the dwarves stood high atop their perches and bowed.

"Are they crazy! What are they going to do?"

"Just watch, Dragon!"

A wild dragon couldn't tear my eyes away as one dwarf saluted, teetered backward, and fell.

CHAPTER

2

THE CROWD GASPED AS ONE dwarf fell, followed by another and another until the fourth one fell. My heart jumped in my chest as they plummeted to the ground amid the frightened streams. Certainly, there was a net, a magic spell or something to save them from breaking their necks? As much as I wanted to be, even I wasn't fast enough or close enough to catch any of them.

"Brenwar, they're going to—"

The first dwarf was caught by two others.

The second was caught by two more, and so on, and so on. The crowd erupted in cheers as the falling dwarves bowed and raced back up the poles to the delight of the crowd.

Brenwar elbowed me in the gut, saying, "Had you fooled, didn't they? Wouldn't you say?"

I didn't know what to say, actually. It didn't seem possible for a dwarf to be caught from a ten story fall, and it even seemed less likely for one to shimmy like a spider monkey up an iron bean poll. *Maybe I should take a dwarven acrobat with me on my next adventure. Such agility would move things quicker.*

"That was incredible, Brenwar! I'd like to meet—"

"Hah!" He waggled his finger at me. "I know what you're thinking about them dwarves. They might be acrobatic, but they can't fight worth a hoot. Humph."

"Is that so?" I said, surprised. "I thought all dwarves could fight."

"They can," Brenwar grabbed a loaf of bread stuffed with pepperoni and took a bite, "better than men, orcs and elves that is. But they're not dwarven soldiers. Dwarven acrobats is all, the best acrobats in all of Nalzambor!"

"Certainly."

The next few hours, I allowed myself to unwind and take in more of the city of Morgdon and all its rugged exteriors. They could hammer iron so thin that you could see right through it. An entire building was windowed with it. "No rock or arrow could shatter that iron glass," Brenwar boasted. There were so many objects and artifices of iron that it was just incredible, but as the sun began to set and the fervor of the festival renewed its rise, I realized it was time to go.

"Brenwar, I think I'm going to head back to your place and take a break," I said, walking away.

"What? But the festival has just begun!" he said, not looking at me but chewing his pepperoni loaf and watching the acrobats instead. "Just stay and watch a few hours more."

I could see he was enjoying himself, but frankly, I'd had my fill. And the white spot inside my dragon palm looked a tad smaller. I had to save more Dragons; I just had to.

"I'll see you later, Brenwar," I said, waving.

"Wait a moment, Dragon!" he said, stopping me in my tracks. "Remember, you cannot leave Morgdon without me, and every dwarf in the city knows that. So you go rest and stay put. I've a few ceremonies to attend to."

I nodded.

He eyed me.

"What?" I said. I could see he wanted confirmation from me, a promise that I would not leave, but I wasn't going to give him that. Never make a promise you can't keep. Just let them think it's a promise.

"Give me your word, Dragon."

I shook my head, saying, "Why bother? I can't leave anyway. A thousand eyes are on me. My Brenwar, I'm as much a prisoner as a guest."

"Prisoner?" he stroked his beard. "That's not polite, and you know it!" He combed his fingers through his beard and muttered under his breath. "Better be no pixies in there." Then he looked at me. "As for you, a prisoner? Pah! I'm looking out for you. That's all. Don't be hasty, Dragon."

"Every day we stay, the graver the danger gets for the dragons."

"You can't save them all, try as you might."

I glared at him.

"What if it were dwarves we were going to rescue? Would you wait then?"

"Ho! A dwarf needing rescued!" Brenwar laughed. "I've never seen such a thing. Nobody poaches dwarves. Not if they know what's good for them."

"Well, nobody poaches orcs, either!" I said, storming away.

"What!" Brenwar yelled at me. "You take that back, Dragon!"

I kept going.

He kept yelling.

"And don't you dare try to leave without me!"

Brenwar's home was small and quiet. His children were grown, and his wife was working at the festival. Such a fine cook she was, one of the finest I'd ever known. Still, it was good to be alone with my thoughts. If I wanted to pout, I'd pout alone. I pulled up a stool on the balcony overlooking the vast and colorful city. It seemed like every torch and pyre was alive with yellow, green, red, orange and even pink fires. The air smelled of roasted everything good, too, and I hungered.

"I can't wait any longer," I mumbled. I wanted to pass over the great wall that held Morgdon, dash over the plains below, and save the dragons. Holding my dragon hand before me, I studied it with intent. Was I getting close? Could I remove the evil curse on my own? But part of me wondered what would happen without my dragon arm. Making two fists, I punched one into the other. I could feel that extra power within me. Something great. It was part of me—the strongest part—and I didn't want to do without it.

Rubbing the white scales of my hand, I said to myself, "I wonder if the white are as strong as the black?" Standing up, I leaned over the balcony and looked as far out as I could see. There were dragons out there who needed me. And I needed them as well. But how could I get out of Morgdon without anyone finding out?

As the bats darted in and out of the night sky snatching the fireflies in their mouths, I snapped my fingers.

"That's a great idea, Dragon! A great one!"

I dashed inside Brenwar's place, found my pack and his, and tossed them both on my bed along with my longsword Fang and my bow Akron. I wouldn't be going anywhere without them. I counted the arrows in my quiver. I had hunting arrows, Moorite tipped arrows, and magic arrows for extraneous circumstances, plus one that I wasn't certain at all what it would do, but supposedly it would do what I told it to do. "Can't wait to use you," I said, taking it out and stroking its bright red feathers before sticking it back in. "Now what?"

I dug into Brenwar's pack. He'd kill me if he knew I was doing that, especially because he liked to keep things tidy, and I was not tidy, not by a dwarf's standards, not even close. I found a jeweled case trimmed in gold with a dragon-faced hasp. It was just what I was looking for. Opening it, I found two dozen vials filled with colorful liquids. Potions. And not just any potions, magic potions. I plucked three of them out. One of them was light blue, a healer. If I was leaving without Brenwar, I'd need to be more careful. The second, dark blue, a concealer. The third I shook in front of my face. The yellow colors swirled with white. "I hope this is it," I said as I closed the lid and put the jeweled case back in his pack as neatly as I could.

"I'd take the whole thing with me if I could," I said to myself.

It was heavy though, like a hundred stones. I could barely carry it, but Brenwar had little trouble at all with his pack. It was my father's design, no doubt about that, filled with all kinds of magic from my father's trove. I was blessed, that much was certain, that my father allowed Brenwar to take the pack and be its guardian.

I slipped into my chest plate armor, strapped my sword on my waist, then snapped my bow in place. Slinging my pack over my shoulder, I was ready to go now. I pulled the cork out of the yellow vial, stepped out onto the balcony, and started to drink.

"Oh wait," I said.

I left Brenwar a note.

Dear Brenwar,

The dragons can't wait, and I can't either.

Forgive me,

Nath Dragon

He would be furious, but I couldn't wait a moment longer. I yearned for freedom, not just mine, but for the dragons. They needed me. I put the vial to my lips and took the first sip. It tasted like berries and honey.

"Mmmmm' I said, smacking my lips.

A moment later, I pitched forward and fell to my knees as my mind turned to mud.

CHAPTER

3

EVERYTHING TURNED BLACK. SOMETHING WAS wrong. Terribly wrong. I couldn't see a thing, but my ears were just fine. I could hear everything in the street below but much louder this time. *What do I do! What have I done! That potion has me undone!*

My plan was simple: take the potion of polymorph and turn myself into something else. I stretched out and fluttered on the floor. This shouldn't have been so hard; I'd done it before. But, I'd never turned myself into a bat.

"Eek!" I screamed, but it came out a high pitched shriek.

Bats are blind, you idiot!

What was I thinking? Oh, now I remember. I was going to blend in with the bats and fly away. None of the keen eyed dwarfs would pay attention to such a thing.

Think! Take a breath, Dragon. You can figure this out.

I flapped my wings. Nothing. I rose on my tiny clawed feet and flapped once more. I lifted from the ground. *Yes!* I banged into a wall and plummeted back to the floor. *Ow!*

At least, I thought it was a wall; I couldn't see it. Head aching, I made my next attempt.

Up, Dragon!

Whop!

I hit something else and dove nose first into the floor. *Think, Dragon. Think!*

Morphing into a new body took some getting used to, and it didn't help that I was blind to boot, and—fair enough—I was stupid, too. I should have just turned into a bird. I rubbed my nose with the tiny fingers at the end of my wing and sniffed the air. Not only could I hear everything, I could smell everything as well. Pretty amazing. What I lacked in sight, I made up with everything else.

What else could bats do that I didn't know about? I had to think on that. Then I remembered they had a sonic power that helped them out.

"Eek!"

That wasn't it. I tried something else. A whisper of sorts. Soon after I let it out, an echo came back. *Ah! I get it now!*

I lifted my head up and sounded out towards the smells and sounds below. In my mind, I saw the shape of the balcony now. Gathering myself, I fluttered to the ledge. *Made it!* Then I took a deep breath. Well, as big a breath as I could, that is. I certainly felt like I was in a very small body. I sent out a signal. The bats and bugs were still there, but the rest of my path from Morgdon was all clear. *Here we go... Bat Dragon!*

I slipped from the ledge, spread my wings, and *whoosh*—I was flying! Everything in my body was tingling, making me all the more eager to become a dragon one day. Then a thought struck me. Not all dragons can fly. What if I was one of those? No, I must perish such thoughts; it shouldn't matter either way. Right now, I needed to enjoy that I was free!

I let out a signal. Moths and fireflies fluttered in the air, and a strange hunger came over me. I signaled again, and like a beacon, I knew where the firefly was. I zoomed in and snatched it in my mouth. That was fast! I liked that. *Yech!* It left an odd taste in my mouth, *but* I crunched it up anyway.

Time to move on, Dragon! The sooner you go the better. No telling when the potion's magic would wear off, and I didn't want to be in the air when that happened, either. I let out a new signal. The mountain was behind, but the open plains of Nalzambor were below. That's where I went, where the goat herders go.

Flap! Flap! Flap!

Something soared past me. What was that? I ducked and dove before I got a good look around. The other bats were attacking me. One after the other they came, nipping and clawing at me. What were they attacking me for? All I ate was one lousy firefly. It wasn't like there weren't plenty of them left out there, you know. But in full assault they came. I was in trouble now.

I shrieked. It didn't help. I dodged.

They struck.

I dove.

They bit. They were going to drive me from the sky.

I wanted to say something, but I don't think bats talked; they shrieked. *What would happen if they got me on the ground?* I was certain they'd tear me to shreds.

Ouch!

One of them got a piece of my leathery wing, sending me spiraling downward. I wanted to swing my sword, but it was part of me now, as well as all those other things. I regained my balance and dove into the alley of the city. Perhaps I could shake them from my trail; I understood things about the city that they did not. Maybe that would help. I flapped hard and fast, weaving into alleys and underneath bridges, drawing some cries from the crowds. I don't think the dwarves had ever seen bats chasing bats before. This might not be such a good idea, after all.

Clack. Clack. Clack.

Too late. Stones were clattering off the walls. The children were throwing stones now. Accurate ones, too. I flew under one and over another, one stone clipping the wing on a pursuer. It bought me time. Up I went. Down I came to find the bats in front of me. I was chasing them now. I sent out a signal. The one in the back, bigger than the rest, was driving the colony of bats. I knew what I had to do. I had to stop him, else they'd wear me down. I let out an awful screech. A challenge was my intent. Up, up, up! The big bat came after me.

Bat or man, I knew how to fight, and I'd fight anything anywhere. I wasn't sure how bat fights went, but I think the leader got the message. I circled him, and he circled me, then in rush he came right at me.

Whop!

We clocked heads. Blind, I saw stars, and I realized his head was much bigger and harder than mine. *I swear; with one gulp, he could eat me. What kind of bat did I turn myself into, anyway?* The more I flapped, the more my wings began to tire. Flying all the time could be very exhausting.

I sucked it up, flying straight upward as he barreled straight downward. At the last second, I dodged, and the others were upon me, clipping and biting at me. It seemed either I fought one of them head on, or I fought them all at once. The leader and I darted up and down in a wide circle. This was it: him and me, head to head for all the glory of the nighttime bug eating. I let out my final signal. He let out his.

He charged. I charged and let out my 'Dragon! Dragon!' screech. There was no need to close my eyes, but I think I did.

CHAPTER

4

FELT SOMETHING BURNING IN MY stomach and projecting from my mouth. The big bat screeched in the sky. I let out a sonic signal. The big bat was engulfed in flames and plummeting toward the ground. I could smell it burning—its hair, its wings—as I dove after it. *Where did that flame come from? Did it come from me?*

My mouth was hot, and I could taste the bitterness of sulfur on my tongue. Below me, the burning bat crashed into a rooftop. *Yes! What kind of bat am I, anyway?* I'd never seen a fire-breathing bat before. I swooped up into the sky where the other bats waited and let out a screech of triumph. I felt another streak of flames shoot from my mouth into the sky. I sent out another sonic signal, and all the bats were gone. I'd won.

I could hear shouts and cries from bellow and had visions of stubby fingers pointing in the sky. I flapped my way past the walls of Morgdon over and beyond where the green grass grows and flew through the night, exhausted, until I could fly no more.

I awoke to find myself in a very cramped cave with the new day's light creeping in.

"Sunken Sulfur! Where am I? Where are my arms and legs?"

I could see again, but I couldn't move a thing. It was as if I'd been nailed inside a coffin. I struggled and strained, wiggling my shoulder loose, then my arm and leg.

"Ah… I'm whole again," I said, crawling out of the cramped cave. "Whoa!" I tumbled down a rocky hillside and went crashing into the hard ground below. "Stupid!" *What was I thinking, turning into a bat? I almost got myself killed. And being blind wasn't any fun at all.* Next time I changed, it would be into something else, but I had to admit: all the flying was incredible.

I dusted myself off, and to my relief, everything was intact: my sword, my bow, and even my pack. You have to like magic like that, which transforms not only you, but everything you carry as well. "Thank goodness."

Above me, the sun was rising, and Morgdon was nowhere in sight. The last thing I remembered was flying as far and fast as I could, putting the Festival of Iron far behind. Guilt crept into me, however, about leaving Brenwar behind. I knew he'd be mad, but I also knew that he didn't understand. He was a dwarf; I was part dragon, part man. He'd just have to understand.

I coughed. The inside of my stomach churned like a pot of boiling lava, and the taste of sulfur was still inside my mouth.

Smacking my lips, I said, "That tastes horrible." I stuck a finger in my mouth, feeling around, certain I'd find a piece of charred wood inside there. What happened, anyway? Could bats breathe fire? Impossible.

I coughed again. No smoke. No fire. Doing my best impression of a dragon, I forced out a roar of air. Nothing came out.

"Hmmm… perhaps it was a side of effect of the potion," I said to myself. That happens, you know. I shrugged it off. It was time to go, but where to? I stretched my arms and limbs and raked my fingers through my hair.

"Freedom!" I yelled, stirring the birds in the trees. "Ha-Ha-Ha-Ha!"

I ran! Long legs cutting through the woodland like a wild stag's, I ran hard and long, with nowhere in mind to go. I was free. Not that I'd been a slave, but without Brenwar tagging along, I was liberated. Too often, he'd slow me down and nag.

"Quit looking at your arm."

"Focus, Dragon. Focus."

"Slow down."

"I need ale."

"Did I ever tell you about the time I killed an ettin?"

It wasn't all that bad, most of the time, but there was nothing like being alone without anyone to answer to. I could do what I wanted now, and I was going to. This time, I was going to rescue many dragons on my own. *I think that might better help my cause.*

I ran several leagues before I came to a stop beneath a shady tree and took a seat. Wind in my hair, civilization long from sight, I had all the peace and quiet I ever wanted.

"Ah, now this is the life!"

Finger on the white scaled spot in the middle of my dragon hand, I found relief.

"I guess it's alright to kill bats, then." And why wouldn't it be? After all, that bat was picking on me. I tapped my fist on my chest as another fit of coughing began, but the taste of sulfur in my mouth was gone. "Finally! That's much better." I took a pull from the canteen in my pack.

It was midday now, and I had a lot on my mind. Where was I going to go to find the dragons? And I didn't want to find just one. I wanted to find several at a time. I knew they were out there and that the most likely spot was one of the Clerics of Barnabus temples that were scattered and hidden throughout the world.

"Not a good idea," I said, rubbing my scales on my dragon arm. Such a fascinating thing, it was. I tried to imagine what it would look like in white. "If I was a careless dragon, where would I go? Hmmmm." I also wanted to get as much distance between me and Morgdon as possible, and I had to think about that as well. *If Brenwar came after me, where would he think I'd go?* Nalzambor is a very large place with each major city several hundred leagues from the other.

The Free City of Narnum was the closest and filled with the most trouble, the kind I like, that is. Pretty faces from all the other places gather there in celebration.

The Home of the Elves, Elomehorrahahn, or Elome for short, is a fantastic place hidden in the mist and trees. Their surrounding forests are well guarded as they like their privacy, and as far as I knew, they didn't meddle with dragons. They were jealous is what I always figured.

Thraag, or Thraagramoor, the home of the orcs, is simply too smelly to go near. I'd had my fill for a while in Orcen Hold.

That left Morgdon, that I had to avoid, and Quintuklen, where I hadn't been for a while. The humans lived there, and I'd had some friends there. Perhaps it was time I checked with some. I missed their colorful ways and wonderful things. The humans had the most zeal for life compared to all the others, simply put: because they didn't live so long. They gave "living life to the fullest" new meaning, and I could relate to them better than the rest. Especially now, when I had a sense of urgency within me.

But, Quintuklen was a long way off, and I could probably rescue a dozen dragons by the time I got there. But, there were many men and women in that city that knew an awful lot about dragons. Humans had poachers as well. Wizards, clerics, sages—many of them with questionable character—wanted the dragons, our magic and the secrets that we held.

I could hear Brenwar's voice in my head as if he was here saying, "There's nothing but troubles and temptation for you in the cities." I sighed. I was focused. I could handle those distractions now if need be.

And of course, there were still all the small cities, towns and villages spread out and in between. I would just head that way first.

"Perhaps I should buy a horse."

I had a long, long way to go.

By nightfall, I'd made it to a small town called Quinley, a thriving farming community. The buildings were well constructed, the people amiable but wary. I respected their hard-working kind, but I was certain they didn't care for a stranger like me. I fit in like a shiny button on a potato sack shirt. Not that they were dirty, but grubby from all their hard work. I almost opted to remain outside to avoid the stares, but the steady rain convinced me otherwise, so I entered. My coins were as good as any, and I was certain they wouldn't mind my business, so inside the nearest establishment I went.

My stomach growled as the scent of hot food aroused my senses. I could taste the roasted lamb and baked rolls in my mouth already. One thing about the well-fed people in the countryside: nobody made better buttered bread—and the vegetables were always fresh and delicious. Patting my tummy, I smiled as I walked in, keeping my dragon arm concealed under my cloak.

"Can I help you, er, Sir?" the innkeeper asked. He was tall and lean with a nice head of brown hair, for a man. He wore overalls underneath his apron and had a white scar on his clean-shaven chin. It was probably from some sort of farming accident as a child. He seemed alright, but his eyes were busy.

"I need food and a room for the night," I said.

"Eh," he started, wiping his greasy fingers on his apron, "we don't have any more rooms."

He was lying. There was no one else on the floor except me, him and a table where a young couple sat. A pair of passersby like me, judging by their traveling cloaks and boots. They eyed me. I eyed them back until they turned away. I looked the innkeeper square in the eyes.

"Are you sure you don't have any rooms? I'd hate to think I came all this way, to the wonderful town of Quinley, home of the finest carrots and heifers, only to find they don't have any rooms. Perish the thought!"

The innkeeper showed me a toothy smile as he leaned back and I leaned forward.

"Er... it's true."

The innkeeper jumped as I rapped my knuckles on the bar.

"Well that's just horrible!" I said. And it really was, for him, because I was starting to get mad. I didn't like it when people lied, and it was even worse when they did it without batting an eye. Something strange, very strange was going on in Quinley. But, that wasn't any of my business. Getting some hot food and a dry room was. I continued.

"And I suppose you are out of *food*, too?"

The innkeeper nodded his head.

A comely older woman emerged from the kitchen with two plates full of hot food. She stumbled as she saw me, eyes blinking, as she plopped the meals onto the couple's table. The woman turned towards me, pushed her hair back, straightened her shoulders, and smiled before casually making her way back to the kitchen. I smiled back and waved. Then I turned my attention back to the innkeeper.

"I suppose that was your last meal… eh, Innkeeper?"

Palms up, he shrugged, smiled and said, "Y-Yes."

LIAR!

Now, I was hungry. Really, really hungry. And tired. I wanted food, and a room, and they were going to give it to me. *Liar, Liar, Britches on fire!* And all those years, I'd thought the country folk were nice.

"What are you eating over here?" I said, walking over to the other travelers. "Smells good!" Something was wrong here. Why would they serve this ordinary man and woman, but not me? Sure, I had beautiful gold eyes and a wonderful mane of auburn hair, on the frame of an extraordinary man, but that's no reason to exempt me. Is it?

"Go away," the man said, hand falling to a small dagger at his side. "Just passing through, and we don't want any trouble."

"I don't want any trouble either, my friends. But I really don't want to sleep in the rain." I turned back to the Innkeeper. "Or on an empty stomach!"

A silence fell over the room. I could sense the Innkeeper didn't want any trouble, but I was certain he'd seen stranger men than me before. There were many other races that had come into this place. I could tell by all the unique objects that decorated the walls: elven shoes, a dwarven shovel and even the two-pronged forks of the orcs.

The waitress returned, a swagger in her hips, a smile on her lips, and a bowl of soup with a biscuit in her hands.

"Jane, no," the innkeeper warned, reaching for her.

Dipping her shoulder and shuffling over to me, she nodded and said, "Take this quick, and go."

I took the bowl from her and said, "Thank you, but why?"

She stared up at me and said nothing as she licked her lips.

That happens sometimes.

"Jane is it?" I said. "That's a pretty blouse you're wearing, and your eyes and ears, so pretty. Are you part-elven?"

She blushed.

"No, none at all."

"Jane! Get back in the kitchen! You're causing trou—"

Two large men pushed through the door, each soaked from head to toe. One cursed the rain, the other shouted out loud.

"Ale! Food! Now, Innkeeper. It's a lousy night, so it better be good. And none of that watered-down brew you have, either."

"You should have gone," Jane whispered. "It's not safe here." She scurried back to the kitchen.

Behind me, the couple were taut as bowstrings, heads down, chewing quietly.

I had the feeling they weren't expecting these men's company.

"As you wish, Enforcers," The innkeeper said, fixing two tankards. "Right away!"

The men tossed their cloaks on a rack in the corner. Thick-shouldered and heavy, each wore steel on his hip: sword and dagger. Strong chinned, beady eyed and rugged, they had the look of Enforcers. It seemed the friendly farm city of Quinley was under control of an unfriendly element. They were the kind that riled me.

Sluuuu-urp!

"Mmmm… that's good soup," I said. "You should try some, fellas."

Both men perked up, big hands falling to their swords. I don't think they were accustomed to anyone else's voice in the room, especially one as deep and rich as mine. They looked at each other and then the innkeeper, and one said, "I told you not to welcome any strangers."

The innkeeper set the tankards down and said, "I d-didn't, Sir. I told him we had no food and no rooms, but he's persistent."

One enforcer slid back out the door. The taller one's eyes drifted to my sword Fang that hung from the scabbard. He swallowed first before he said, "This inn is closed, Traveler. Set your soup down and be gone." He nodded at the door.

"But it's raining," I said, "And I'm really tired and hungry. So, I don't think I'll be leaving right away. But, maybe tomorrow."

"Don't be a fool, Traveler. You don't know who you're tangling with."

I wanted to laugh, but I slurped another spoonful instead. The big man's eyes started to twitch. I don't think he was accustomed to anyone standing up to him. *I should be worried about who I'm tangling with? He's the one who should be worried.*

"Tell you what," I said, digging my spoon deeper into my bowl. "How about you leave, ugly face and all, and come back tomorrow when I'm well rested and gone?"

"What!"

The innkeeper ducked behind the counter. The couple behind me got up from their table, heads down, and darted up the stairs.

"I'm sorry," I said much louder this time, "I didn't realize you had trouble hearing. I SAID—"

A half-dozen well-armed men burst through the entrance—and one of them was bigger than two put together.

CHAPTER

5

Inside the pillars of an old temple ruin, Finnius the Cleric of Barnabus was brewing something. Trouble.

"In order to catch a dragon, you have to have a dragon," he muttered, adding some ingredients to a mystic pot of stew. "Shaved scales and ogre nails. Blood from a vorpal snail." He sniffed the bubbling cauldron. "Yech. I never really did like this part." He covered his nose with the sleeve of his robes, saying, "Anything for High Priestess Selene." On he went, one more defiling component after another as the smell and activity of the cauldron became stronger and stronger.

"One more thing is all," he said, wiping the sweat from his head, then wringing his hands. He produced a tiny vial of blood Selene had given him. She told him it was the key ingredient of the spell. He dumped it in, and the entire cauldron lurched, smoked, sparked with gold fire, then bubbled and dimmed.

"Acolytes, bring me the prisoner." He smiled. "It's ready."

Yes, catching the bait, the yellow streak dragon, was one step. Luring Nath Dragon was the next, and it would be awfully hard to lure someone with bait when you didn't know where he was. The last he had heard, Nath Dragon had been in the Shale Hills. Many of the clerics had reported this, but that was weeks ago, and Nath Dragon hadn't been heard from since.

"Must find him. Must find him soon," he said.

The High Priestess was very clear about that. She wanted results. She had expectations, or she'd have his head. The fact that she'd taken a shine to him was odd, but he knew he had skills that others did not. He figured at some point she must have noticed.

"Ah, here you come," he said, taking a seat on a stone bench.

Two acolytes approached, robed from head to toe in dark purple with silver trim. Their heads were bald, and the tattoos on them were very little. They were expendable at this point. They each carried what looked to be a large covered bird cage with them. Bowing, they set it down.

Finnius crossed his legs and draped his locked fingers over his knee.

"Hmmmm."

The truth was: he wasn't so certain if this would work or not, but he didn't have any other ideas, either. Typically, when Nath Dragon entered one of the larger cities, he knew about it immediately. The Clerics of Barnabus were thick in those places, and the man was about as discreet in his activities as a weasel in a hen house. But of late, Nath Dragon had been laying low, and that complicated things. Selene's expectations must be met. He wasn't about to disappoint *her*.

He lifted the cloth cover from the first cage. A man, standing about one foot tall, stood inside, tiny arms crossed over his little chest. He had two wings. Like a humming bird's, they buzzed on and off behind him. He was a pixlyn: rare, and almost impossible to catch unless you had honey from the trees where the stump giants sat.

"The time has come to earn your freedom, little pixlyn."

It turned away.

"Oh, come now. It won't be so bad," Finnius said, digging a large spoon into the bubbling cauldron. "Besides, failure to carry out my order will result in certain death."

The pixlyn shrugged. He was a handsome and obstinate little thing whose eyes glowed with a faint blue fire.

Finnius snorted as he approached, holding the spoon of bubbling goo up to the bars.

The pixlyn held his nose.

"Oh, I suggest you reconsider," Finnius said, nodding to the other acolyte. "Especially since it's not you I'm threatening.

The man removed the cloth from the other cage.

"It's her."

The pixlyn man let out a tiny cry of alarm. A beautiful pixlyn woman with radiant pink eyes and bee's wings shivered inside her cage. The pixlyn man's hummingbird wings made an angry buzz as he zipped back and forth in his cage, slamming into one barred side and then the other.

Finnius laughed. He loved seeing good creatures suffer, and it was especially salivating when it was the suffering of one loved one for another.

"Settle down now, Pixlyn. All you have to do is seek, find and report. Of course, what you'll be searching for could be anywhere in all of Nalzambor. Now, take a sip, a big one that will fill your little gut, and on your way you shall go."

The tiny little woman rose up in her cage, her squeaky little voice objecting in a language only the pixie-kind could speak. Both their tiny little hands grabbed the bars as they faced each other. Tears went down the little woman's cheeks.

"How adorable," Finnius said. "Now drink!" He banged the cage with his hand. "Or I'll kill you both right now!"

Dejected, the little pixlyn man grabbed the spoon, gulped it down and wiped his mouth.

"Good… Good-Good-Good. That will make you strong and help you find Nath Dragon's trail." He opened the bird cage door. "Go now, go! The longer it takes, the less likely she lives."

The pixlyn grabbed her tiny hands on the bars, kissed them each and with the speed of an arrow, disappeared.

As the tiny woman sobbed in her prison, Finnius tossed one of his men an empty vial and said, "Get me those tears."

CHAPTER

6

NOW THERE WERE SIX OF them and one of me. They had leather armor and swords, and even helmets on, too. Not the kind of odds I expected in a small town like this. And to think, all I wanted was a room for the night and some food.

"Sorry fellas, but I think I just finished the last bit of food," I said, setting the bowl on the table. I patted my belly and burped. "Pretty tasty though, worth the wait until tomorrow. Say, any of you ugly men happen to have a toothpick on you?"

"Shut your mouth," the one who'd hung back in the room said. He came closer, the rest of the enforcers at his sides and spreading out except one, the big one, abnormally large, who looked like he had part giant in him. He was almost eight feet tall, and his big and meaty arms were crossed over his barrel chest as he blocked the exit.

I backed up until I bumped into the table. What was I going to do now? I couldn't fight them all, or could I? They came closer, wary, weathered and scarred, one just as mean looking as the other. A well-trained bunch of goons, mercenary and ex-soldiers types, men for hire judging by the steel jangling on their hips. They were the kind of men who wouldn't hesitate to hurt or kill.

I put my hands out in front of me.

"Perhaps, I should be going. I don't think a little bit of rain ever hurt anyone, eh?"

When facing a conflict of superior enemies, play nice before the first dagger strikes.

"Oh, ho-ho," the leader said, swinging his sword up on his shoulder. "So you want to play nice now, do you, Smart Fella? What's the matter? Are we too ugly for you?"

"As a matter of fact, yes, but that's not the reason I'm willing to leave."

The enforcers snickered as they drew their daggers.

"It's nothing personal," I said, "I mean, yes you are ugly, not like an orc, well except you," I pointed at one with the turned-up nose, "and you."

"Be silent, you fool! You've crossed the line, Big Mouth. And to think, all you had to do was walk out when I said, but now you'll have to pay. Possibly with your life, you golden eyed-freak!"

A heavy thumping pounded inside my chest. They meant business. I slid between the table and the wall. They came closer. I didn't need this kind of trouble.

"Tell you what, uh, what do you call yourselves?"

"Enforcers, Fool!"

"So it is, Enforcers Fool. Very catchy. Now here is what I offer. Leave me be, and I'll see to it that you can walk out of here, not crawl... or die."

They snickered.

"You've got a death wish, do you! So be it! Enforcers, take him!"

I stuck out my dragon arm.

They hesitated, eyes going back and forth between each other.

"What's the matter? Never seen a dragon's arm on a man before?"

Even the big one gawped and scratched his balding head.

I had them now. I had them right where I wanted them. I shoved the table aside, stepped forward, and towered over them, except the one in the back of course.

"Men! What are you waiting for? We've taken down plenty of stranger things before, but never one with a mouth so big. And do I have to remind you who your lord is? The Jackal will not be pleased if you fail him in this. Now, don't make me tell you again, Enforcers. Attack!"

They surged forward, striking high and low.

I leapt into the rafters. This isn't what I wanted. Not at all. These men were killers, and they wanted me dead. I couldn't stay up here forever. There was only one rafter and nowhere to go.

"Brock! Get over there and jerk that bird out of those rafters!"

The over-sized man made it across the room in three strides, reaching up my way. His big fingers reached at my feet as I kicked them away.

"Go away, Brock!"

He was big and ugly, but not stupid. He laughed.

"Get him, Brock!"

"Snap his neck like a chicken's!"

"I've got dibs on his pretty hair!"

I kicked Brock in the nose, drawing a painful howl. That last comment lit a fire in me. My problem was they could kill and seemed perfectly willing to, but I could not. Problem.

Brock threw his shoulder into the post. The entire building shook.

The innkeeper was screaming, "Stop it! Stop it!"

The leader shoved him to the ground.

It seemed these enforcers had a point to make. Something weird was going on here, and The Jackal, whoever that was, was behind it all. It was time for me to move.

Brock hit the post again, cracking it and shaking the room.

I dropped on his shoulders and blinded him with my hands.

"Easy, Brock," I said. "What you can't see, you can't hit!"

"Get off of me, Rodent!"

He reached for my hands.

I slapped him on his bald head.

"That will leave a mark. Woo! My, it's hot up here."

The leader shouted out, "Brock, kneel down so we can get a lick at him!"

The fun was over. Brock dropped to a knee.

I jumped from his shoulders to one table and then another. I had to get as far away from Brock as possible. He could crush me. Jumping, ducking, diving and dodging, I got a few punches in as they chased me around the room.

"Blast it! You fools!" The leader said. "Do I have to do everything myself! Brock, guard the door! We can't let him get away."

They seemed pretty persistent about not letting me go, for some reason. Perhaps they didn't want word getting out about their indiscretions. I jumped left, right, then found myself cornered, two daggers and a sword at my throat.

"Now we've got you!"

CHAPTER

7

"GIVE IT UP, OR I'LL cut your throat!"

I wouldn't yield. Not to them. Not to men lacking character. And my pride wouldn't let me give in to an inferior but skilled and well-armed force, despite the numbers.

I started to speak.

The leader cut me off. "Save it! Your tongue's caused you enough trouble. Keep your peace and get ready to die, Freak!"

I was tired and no longer hungry but agitated now. I didn't like that word, Freak. I would not yield. Not to this scum. Not now. Not no-how. Especially when I was fast. Faster than them all. I could draw Fang faster than they could swing. I told myself to do it. I willed myself to do it. But I did not. I couldn't risk killing, evil men or not. There had to be a better way; there always was, my father said.

I locked my eyes on his and summoned my magic within. Dragon magic, ancient, wonderful, accessible. I could see my reflection in the man's eyes. His hardened features slackened at the sound of my thoughts.

Lower your sword, I suggested.

"Huh," he said, shaking his head, "what did you say?"

It wasn't working. I summoned all I had within, my gold eyes glowing.

"What is that?" one said.

"A demon!" cried another.

I made my suggestion again, putting all my mental strength behind it this time.

Drop your sword!

The leader's blade clattered to the ground.

"What did you do that for?" the enforcers said.

"He's a demon, I tell you!"

Whack!

I punched the man in the jaw, dropping him like a stone.

"I'm…"

Whack!

I knocked another's helmet off.

"Not!"

Twist! Crack! Boom! Twist!

I disarmed and disabled the leader.

"A demon!"

One rushed.

I had room to move now. I dipped and struck. My dragon arm's jabs were like black lightning.

The leader struggled back to his feet.

I booted him in the ribs, lifting him from his knees. Evil men calling me a demon, such gall!

One dove on my back; another climbed on my legs.

I slung one crashing into a table and drove the other's head into the hard floor.

I was dusting my hands off and saying, "That should to it," when a large shadow fell over me. Big Brock was back.

Whop!

I crashed into the nearest wall, wondering, *how did I forget about him!*

Have you ever been hit by a log before? Me either, but I was pretty sure I knew what that felt like now. Brock was quick for a big man, not as quick as me, but as quick as an eight-foot tall man could be. And when he punched, you could feel it from one side to the other.

Bam!

My head!

Bam!

My gut!

I struggled back to my feet and raised up my fist, saying, "You want some more of this?"

Bam!

He knocked me off my feet and on my butt.

Gasping for air, I held my hands out, saying, "You don't hit very hard for a big fellow."

"What did you say?" Brock said, his voice as loud as distant thunder.

I held my nose. It was all I could do. I felt like the only thing holding my body together was my armor. "What did you say?" I mocked back. I don't know why I did that. I guess it was a character flaw that exposed itself in moments of desperation.

Brock grabbed me by my collar and with two hands, threw me across the room and into the bar. He was strong, very strong, and he hit as hard as an ogre. He came back.

I snatched Dragon Claw from Fang's hilt and stabbed him in the leg.

"Ouch."

That's all he said, "Ouch," as if I'd pricked him with a pin.

He swatted the small dagger from my hand, sending it spinning across the floor.

I was defenseless now. I was rattled. I couldn't understand why I couldn't handle this big man. I reached for the sword along my belt.

He stopped me.

"No! No! No! Demon!"

I'm not a demon!

He wrapped his arms around me as he lifted me from the ground. My feet dangled from the floor as he squeezed the life out of me.

"How's that feel!"

I managed to say, "Great! I haven't had my back cracked in forever."

He squeezed harder. I flexed my muscles. The harder he squeezed, the more I flexed. I just hoped my bones didn't crack. The pressure was becoming unbearable.

"Give up, Demon! I've cracked bones thicker than yours before. Dwarfs, orcs, elves, I've broke them all."

Who was this man, and what was he doing in this farm village?

I snapped my head back into his chin and saw stars as he laughed.

"Any moment, you will die," he said in my ear.

He might be right. I couldn't move. I couldn't breathe. And I didn't have an ounce of magic left inside me. Maybe venturing without Brenwar was a bad idea, after all. One thing was for certain, if it wasn't for the dwarven armor I wore, I'd have been cracked like an egg already. I had to do something. Anything.

"You ate it, didn't you?" I said.

"Ate what?"

"All the food."

Wham!

He slammed me to the floor as hard as he could.

Breathless, I tried to speak, but couldn't form the words.

Brock grabbed me by the hair, jerked my head back, and wrapped his arms round my neck and throat and squeezed.

Oh no! This was bad. Very bad. Brock the giant man had me in a sleeper hold. My fingers clutched for the door, the only way of escape. I expected Brenwar to burst through at any moment, but darkness came instead.

CHAPTER

8

I WOKE UP TO THE SOUND of rattling chains. When I opened my eyes, I noticed they were mine.

"What is this! Ow!"

I clutched at my chest. My ribs were broken. The big man had gotten the best of me. It got even worse. I was inside a metal cage, very much like the ones that held dragons.

"No!" I cried.

But no one answered. Groggy and dizzy, I rubbed a strange bump on my neck. I'd been injected with something. Possibly stabbed with a tainted stick, like the savages like to use.

Two lanterns illuminated the exterior walls of what looked to be an old barn. I could hear the heavy drops of rain pounding on the ceiling above me. Large drops of water splashed on my face and back. The chains rattled as I wiped the water from my face and scooted into the corner.

"I can't believe this," I muttered to myself.

I was caged like an animal in a barn that smelled like livestock, manure and hay. I pounded my head on the bars. It hurt. But I deserved it. I'd been stupid and careless, I guess. But it wasn't as if I was looking for any trouble, either. If anything, I'd tried to avoid it. I sighed. I should have been happy that I was still alive. After all, the enforcers made it clear that they wanted me dead. And Brock, that giant of a man, could have killed me easily with his own bare hands.

Cold, tired and still hungry, I collected my thoughts. It seemed I'd have to think my way out of this. And who was my captor? Was it some sinister bunch of village folk, or the character the lead enforcer mentioned, The Jackal? How could I get into this much trouble at some silly little farm? That was when a river of ice raced down my spine.

"Fang! Akron!"

I grabbed my head and tugged at my hair. I'd lost them. And not just that, but my pack with all my supplies. No not only did my chest and neck ache, but my head did as well. And how long had I been knocked out cold? That'd only happened one time before.

I grabbed the bars and tugged.

"Hurk!"

They didn't budge. I dug my heels in.

"HURK!"

A bubble of snot formed in my nose and burst. The bars bent a little, but didn't budge from my disgusting effort. I labored for breath as I said, "Ew."

I kicked the bars. I hit the bars. I raked my dragon claws against the bars, but nothing happened. I was helpless in my cage.

And there I sat: friendless, weaponless, and helpless while the water from the roof dripped, dripped, dripped. I moved from one spot to the other, only to catch a new drip from another hole in the roof again. The barn creaked and groaned from the weight of the wind, but little stirred. No animals, no rats, no cats, no birds, which seemed strange for a place meant to keep animals. But there was something else different and unique: the smell of decay and death. On one wall were more chains, and some digging tools: spades, shovels and picks. A few work tables were spread out with hammers, anvils and saws. My eyes were good, even in the poor light, but I swore there were bloodstains.

"Not good," I said, cradling my dragon arm. What if they were going to cut it off? Perhaps they really thought I was a demon. I wasn't a demon. What an insult! I was a dragon! Well, I was part of a dragon—and any fool could see that. Perhaps it was my gold-flecked eyes that freaked them out.

"I've got to get out of here."

Grabbing the nearest bar with my dragon arm, I tugged. The iron of the cage was at least a half inch thick. The metal groaned. I could feel my black arm growing with strength. What it would not do before, it was doing now.

"Come, Dragon," I said through gritted teeth. "You can do it!"

It moved no more.

"Sultans of Sulfur!"

I collapsed against the bars.

Now my head was pounding, and my entire body was sore all over. I felt like a bruised apple from head to toe, and I could feel my face was swollen as well. On the bright side, I guess whoever it was wanted me alive. On the dark side of things, I had no idea how long it would be until I found out who that was. Cold, sore, hungry and held against my will, in pain I waited.

CHAPTER

9

"How could I be so careless!" Brenwar yelled.

A dozen well-armed dwarves stood nearby, awaiting orders.

Nath Dragon had escaped. How he escaped, Brenwar could not figure. Every dwarf in all of Morgdon knew who he was. Every dwarf in Morgdon knew that he was not supposed to leave. Every dwarf was to keep an eye on him when another wasn't. But like a ghost, he'd vanished.

Brenwar rammed his head into a stone wall.

"I can't believe it!"

He rammed it again.

"Knock some sense into yourself!" he said.

The other dwarves did the same.

Clonk. Clonk. Clonk...

"Stop it, dwarves! We don't all need our melons damaged. We'll be needing all of our wits to track him down." He tugged at two fistfuls of beard.

Brenwar had thought he had it all under control, but he'd miscalculated. Nath had gotten into his sack and taken some potion. What they did, Brenwar didn't know, but one of them had to be the cause of all this. His investigation revealed a few other things. A small fire breathing bat was said to have been seen. Another one, as big as a large cat, was found burnt to a crisp. It had to have been Nath because no one had ever seen a fire breathing bat before. But with the Festival of Iron anything could happen. But that wasn't what haunted him most. It was what Nath's father, the grandest creature he'd ever seen, said the last time he saw him.

"I'll keep him alive, your Majesty," Brenwar had promised.

Nath's father had replied, "I'm not worried about him dying. I'm worried he'll turn evil."

Nath turning evil? It didn't seem possible, but the Dragon King's words had shaken his very core.

"Get your horses, dwarves! Get your horns as well. He's got a three-day start and could be anywhere in the world. The one that finds him gets a trunk full of gold!"

Brenwar was the last one out of the gate as they all exited with dwarven song and cheer. Brenwar took a deep breath as he watched them go, remembering another thing Nath's father had said. "If we lose him, it will begin another Dragon War."

CHAPTER

10

THE SOUND OF A BARN door opening jostled me from my sleep.

I wiped the water from my eyes and watched three figures stroll in. One was Brock, the big man, lumbering my way with the leader of the Enforcers at his side. The other man, I didn't recognize. He was lean, blond-haired and blue-eyed with my sword, Fang, hanging at his side. I would have stood up, but the cage wouldn't allow it. I sat up, and I crossed my legs as they approached.

"That's my sword," I said, glowering.

The man, light eyes intent on my arm, didn't even acknowledge me.

Rubbing his hairless chin, he said, "Peculiar, Barlow, but I don't think he's a demon. No, looks like a curse of some sort."

Barlow, an enforcer, looked at my eyes and then said to the other man, "But his eyes glowed. All my thoughts left me, and I dropped my sword. He doesn't even have a spellbook, Jackal."

The Jackal made his way around the cage and stopped alongside the bar I'd bent.

"Too strong to be a wizard. Hmmmm. Brock, get over here and fix this. Hm, he must have done this. It's practically a new cage."

Brock lumbered over and grabbed the bar. The metal groaned as he pulled it back into position. He grunted at me as he returned to his friend.

The Jackal said, "Well, you are pretty strong. I'll give you that. Probably a good thing Renny doped you."

The leader, Renny, nodded as he folded his arms across his chest and smiled.

"Care to tell me what this is all about, Jackal?" I asked.

The Jackal wasn't a bad looking man, but there was darkness behind his beady eyes. There was something primitive about him. The way he moved was dangerous. He withdrew my sword and cut it through the air a few times.

"This," the Jackal said fingering the blade, "is amazing! Tell me where you got it. Who made it?"

Good. He wants something from me. I can use that.

"The Mountain of Doom," I said.

Fingering the dragon-head pommels on the hilt, he said, "You jest! Am I to believe you stole it from there? No one goes into the Mountain and lives."

"That's where it's from, and that's all I know."

"So you were told," he shot back.

I shrugged. *Let him think what he wants.*

He stuffed Fang back inside the scabbard and said to his men, "You two would be dead if he had drawn this sword." Then he turned his attention back to be. "Why didn't you draw and cut them down? I would have."

"I didn't need it."

"It seems you did."

"The big fellow was fortunate, is all. Next time, I won't go so easy."

Brock and Renny laughed.

"I wish I could have been there, but perhaps I can set up another encounter."

"Why don't you set it up now?" I demanded.

Brock smacked his fist into his hand. It sounded like a clap of thunder.

"Fine by me," Brock growled.

The Jackal's eyes lit up. He liked the idea.

Good. All I have to do is get out of this cage.

"No, there will be plenty of time for that later. I need him still breathing tonight."

I don't like how he said that.

"What's the matter?" I said. "Are you afraid of Brock getting hurt?"

Brock's fist slammed into the cage.

"I'll break your neck!"

"Hah! You couldn't break a chicken leg, you oaf!"

"I'll show you!" he roared, reaching through the bars for my leg.

"BROCK, STOP IT!" Renny yelled, trying to pull the big man away.

I jammed the nail of my dragon thumb into his forearm.

Brock's howl shook the roof.

I laughed at him as Renny pulled him back.

"You're going to pay for that!" he said, shaking his fist at me.

The Jackal applauded saying, "Perfect. Just perfect... eh, sorry, I didn't get your name?"

"I didn't give it."

He waved me off, saying, "No matter. We'll think of something by tonight. Come on, men."

"What's tonight?" I said, pulling on the bars to my cage.

Renny and Brock both flashed sinister grins as they slid the barn door shut behind them.

I stomped my feet and punched the roof of the cage.

"DRAT! DRAT! DOUBLE DRAT!"

Again I was alone. To make matters worse, it seemed they had a short term plan for me: death.

I yawned. Whatever poison they stuck me with wasn't wearing off. I spit a gummy salty substance from my mouth, leaned back, and sat down. Now was not the time to panic. It was time to think.

"Excellent, Dragon. Look what you've gotten yourself into," I said, tossing my hair over my shoulder. At least the rain had stopped. But now I was thirsty.

An hour passed.

My stomach growled. My head swam. And I was seeing black spots from time to time.

Another hour passed.

Nausea set in and cold sweat as well, and I began to shake with chills.

What did they stick me with?

I wrapped my arms around my knees and huddled in the cage. And there I lay, spinning and spinning and spinning.

CHAPTER

11

AD PEOPLE DO BAD THINGS.

A ray of sunlight warmed my face, but it didn't stop the shivers. Time was lost to me, the minutes agony, but from the fading light coming through the cracks in the barn door, it seemed the sun was setting. I remembered the Jackal saying something about the night. Something bad was going to happen. As if it hadn't happened already.

I heard wood rubbing against metal, a horrible sound in my distorted ears. Light flooded the barn as the door was slid open. Enforcers. I couldn't see how many. The squeak of older wagon wheels felt like jamming nails in my ears.

"Hurry up and get them in there," one enforcer said. "And double check those locks. We can't have any escaping. Remember the last time. Jorkan's dead. The Jackal saw to that. And I'll not be losing my head over some busted locks!"

"You check them then!" one said.

"What? Who said that? Osclar, did you say that?"

"Yes!"

"Why you little toad eater! Get over there and check those locks, those bars, that door—or it's going to be the stockade for you! Understand!"

"Certainly, Harvey. Certainly!"

I heard the one I believed to be Harvey grunt, and I started my wait. I closed my eyes and let the shivers take over.

"What have we got here?" Harvey said. "Not feeling so spry now are you, Demon?"

"He's not a demon." I heard one say.

"What!"

"He's not a demon; that's was the Jackal said. He's cursed."

I heard Harvey chuckle.

"Oh, he's cursed alright. He probably just didn't know it till now. That Uken poison Renny stuck him with'll have him feeling and seeing all kinds of crazy things." Harvey checked the lock on the cage. "Tonight's going to really be something. You got those cages secured, Oscar!"

"Nope!" Oscar said, giggling.

Harvey grunted again.

"Shaddap and let's go; I'm hungry."

"Say, Harvey, how long do you think he'll last?"

"Shut your mouth, Oscar. The boss says no talking."

Oh, talk. Please talk.

"I don't see why not. It's not like it matters if they know what's coming or not."

"He likes the looks of surprise on their faces."

"Me too," the 3rd enforcer said.

"Let's go, chatter mouths."

My tongue clove to the roof of my mouth. *Say something, Dragon!* My quivering lips stayed sealed.

"Huh," Harvey said, "looks like this man is done already."

"He got some good licks on Big Brock, though. Never seen anyone hurt Brock before."

"Me neither."

"Shaddap you two! LET'S GO!"

Harvey's loud voice sounded like an explosion in my ears. I couldn't even open my eyes to see as I heard them walk out and slide the barn door closed.

Idiot. All I had learned was things were not only as bad as before but worse.

I shivered and shivered. I needed the Uken poison to wear off. *Fight it, Dragon! Fight!* The darkness came, leaving me alone in the barn with two torches and two new cages. I managed to open my eyes to see. Two forms huddled, one in each cage. Perhaps they could tell me something. I opened my mouth, but no words came.

"Father?"

It was the voice of a young man speaking to the other.

"Sssssh, be silent, Son. Else they'll whip us."

Silence came. A little rustling around followed.

"Are they going to kill us, Father?" the young man asked.

"No, now be silent!" the father said, forcefully, but quiet.

I heard the fear in both their voices. Innocent men. I could tell.

"Why did they pick us, Father?"

The father sighed, shaking his head as he said, "I don't know; they just did."

"But we were good farmers, Father. Good miners, too. I didn't steal any of the golden ore; I swear," the young man sobbed.

His father's silence told it all. The father had stolen; the boy had not.

My heart swelled. These men needed my help. Things came together.

Golden ore!

It explained all the secrets in the small town. Someone, a farmer most likely, had found a vein of it. The Jackal and his enforcers got word of it and took over the town. It wasn't the first time such things had happened, and it wouldn't be the last, either. Golden ore, however, wasn't gold, and it wasn't ore. It was a vein of mystic dirt that had a goldish hue to it.

"I'm hungry, Father. Do you think we'll eat again?"

Pitiful. I could make out the young man's face pressed against the bars. He was rawboned and lanky. Looked like he'd missed one too many meals already. It infuriated me, but the thought of action just made me sicker.

"Sure, Son. Sure we will," the father lied.

Don't think about it. Think of a way out. I allowed my thoughts to drift to the Golden Ore.

Farming was a big deal in Nalzambor. The land was rich, full, lustrous in many places. But working the land was still hard. It took time and a lot of work. And, in the case of hard work, many peoples and races were lacking. That's where the Golden Ore came in. Or, more simply called, Magic Dirt. A few pounds of it would turn a square mile of desert into a garden of vegetables. It was a pricey commodity, and it seemed the Enforcers had happened upon it.

But what did they want with me and these two men?

My voice was dry and raspy, but I managed to say, "I can get you out of here."

Both men stiffened and huddled down.

"I said, I can get you out of here."

The young man started to speak.

"Don't talk to him, Son. He might be that demon the innkeeper spoke of."

"I'm not a demon; I'm a man, same as the two of you," I said. *Sort of...* "Now, do you want help or not? Ugh!" I slunk onto the cage floor. My stomach was killing me. I needed healing.

"What happened?" the young man asked, pressing his face against the bars.

"Son, be quiet!"

"No." The young man was adamant. "I won't be. Sorry, Father. That man over there is offering help, and we need it!"

"But, I just—"

"I'm a man as well as you, Father. I'll live with the consequences of my actions."

I made it back to my knees and said, "Good for you. Now, tell me, how many of these enforcers are there?"

"I'm not sure, but there's a lot of them."

"Thirty-Seven," the father said.

He'd turned to face me now. Unlike his son, he was a barrel-chested man. The torchlight reflected dimly from the top of his head.

"How many of you in the village?"

"Almost a thousand," the father said.

Accounting for women and children, that didn't leave enough men to fight off a group of well-armed men. Fear doesn't wait long to rule.

"How long have they been here?"

"A few months. They showed up two days after we found the vein of Golden Ore. All the celebrating would have woke the dragons up. It's no wonder they showed up so fast with all the blabber mouths in this village."

I'd seen it happen before. If you didn't hire a well-armed force, the goons would quickly take over. Greed and treachery grew like weeds in Nalzambor. Better act quickly, before the roots got deep.

"And the Jackal? Where does he stay?"

I needed to find out where my gear was. It was the only way.

"He lords it over everyone in the day and diminishes in the night. He's wicked."

"He's crafty," the father added. "Dangerous. Something very strange about that fellow."

I'd sensed it, too. Something behind the man's eyes was raw, primeval.

The men jerked in their cages as the barn door slid open. Renny and Brock stepped inside, along with some of the other enforcers.

"Cover them cages," Renny said.

"What if they scream?" Harvey said.

"Oh yes, we can't have that, can we? Alright, gag these two, but the demon over there, he'll need more of the poison. Shoot him up, Brock!"

I could barely move already when Brock came, a sharp stick in one hand, a vial of Uken poison in the other. He dipped the stick in the ointment, laughing.

"Be still, Freak! Else I'll poke it in your eye."

I remained still. He stabbed through the bars. I tried to dodge, but caught the full force in my dragon arm.

"Did you stick him good?" Renny said.

"Real good."

I didn't hear anything else after that as my imprisoned world faded away.

CHAPTER

12

THE WAGON LURCHED TO A stop, and I awoke. It was still dark, but I knew I was outside because the breeze rustled the cover over my cage. Depressed and sick, I had a good idea how my brethren dragons felt. I had to escape, but I needed help.

"Almost time."

It was Renny, the leader of the Enforcers. Footsteps were all around, and I could also hear footsteps going up and down.

"Take the covers off. The Jackal will be here any moment, with company. Look sharp! Especially you, Osclar!"

Where was I? I felt the bump on my arm where Brock had jabbed me. It wasn't as bad as the one on my neck. I think the dragon scales had something to do with that. It had been more of a reflex than anything else when I made him hit my dragon arm. I hadn't meant for that, but maybe my arm had. And my head was a little more clear than before.

"Get over here, Harvey! Let's take this cover off and get started. Heh-Heh! Won't be long now before the fun starts."

Fun for him, maybe. Fun for me? I didn't think so.

"Sure thing, Boss. Sure thing."

The first thing I saw was the moon peeking through the clouds. Then I could smell the Enforcers' rancid breath.

"Huh, he's awake," Renny said, rubbing his chin. "Not sure the Jackal will like that. Harvey, let him know."

"Alright," Harvey said, strolling off.

I was inside a wooden fort, but I had a feeling it was designed to keep people in rather than out. Catwalks ran twelve feet high from one corner to the other. Enforcers with spears and swords guarded every corner and the space in between.

"Welcome to our Arena, Demon," Renny said. "The final resting place for you and many others on Nalzambor."

I locked my eyes on Renny and said, "And possibly yours as well."

He stiffened, said, "We'll see about that," and walked away, casting one glance back.

Entertainment! That's what I was. I remembered the blazed ruffie battling the trolls. It turned my stomach, the cruelty of men.

"Go ahead and take those other two out," Renny ordered his men.

The farmers were pulled from their cages and the cages pulled away.

"Alright everyone. Get up on the wall. It's time for the battle to begin."

The father and son shook at each other's side.

"Please! Mercy enforcers! At least spare my son. I'm the guilty one!" the father begged.

The son looked at his father, a sad look in his eyes as he said, "You stole, Father?"

The father shook his head and replied, "Son, they stole from us. It's our land and our Golden Ore. These vultures have no right to take what is ours."

The Enforcers tossed down two shields and two clubs.

"I don't know how to fight, Father."

"Neither do I, Son." He hugged his boy. "I guess we'll have our first and last one together," the father said, picking the weapons up.

"Together then."

Renny shouted from above.

"That's the spirit!"

"Here he comes, Renny," Harvey said, looking over the backside of the wall.

The Jackal emerged from behind a wall and stepped onto the catwalk. My sword Fang hung at his hip. My breast plate armor adorned his chest. My bow. My quiver and my pack. Infuriated, my heart thundered in my chest.

But he was different. His face was no longer that of a man, but an animal's. A Jackal's.

"I see everything is in order," The Jackal said, yellow eyes glowering at me. "I see our guest is bright eyed and bushy tailed. No matter." He fingered his claws over my sword. "Nothing I can't handle if need be."

A were-jackal. Another cursed man, like myself, but more like Corzan: corrupted by the evil. I felt a sliver of fear inside as I wondered if they'd both been good men once. I wondered what was in store for me. I rubbed the white spot of scales on my hand and vowed to do more good, given the chance.

"Farmers!" the Jackal yelled, the moonlight shining brightly on his face, "the time has come that you paid for your deceit. I told you when I came: what's yours is mine and mine alone, yet you stole. You sought to warn my enemies. And now you must pay."

The father and son trembled. Nalzambor was full of wonders, but I was certain they'd never seen a were-jackal before. Lycanthropes were evil. And there were plenty of stories and legends about them tearing people limb from limb. I could only imagine what was going through their minds at this moment.

"It's not much sport, is it?" I managed to say.

All eyes were on me. *Good.*

"But, I guess this is how cowards play," I added.

The Jackal leaned on the rail and smiled, his sharp teeth dripping in the moonlight.

"Oh, the do-gooder speaks. Interesting. And I can only assume you are going to talk and talk until it's over. Well then, I'll let the games begin. Enforcers, have at them."

Renny, Harvey and Osclar climbed down the ladders, while two more posted themselves at the top. The farmers readied themselves as more clubs and shields were tossed down from above.

Renny picked up his club and twirled it in the air.

"This won't take long. Watch my back, fellas."

The farmers shuffled back.

"Come on; take a swing," Renny said, sticking his chin out. "I'll give you a free shot."

The father's swing sailed over Renny's head.

Renny walloped him in the stomach, doubling him over.

The son caught Renny in the shoulder.

"Ow! You two idiots! I said to watch my back!"

Harvey and Osclar attacked, swinging hard and fast at that young man. The son gathered himself behind his shield, but they beat it down.

Wham! Wham! Wham!

The son folded like a tent.

Rushing to his son's aid, the father screamed, "NOOOOOO!" He huddled over his son, but the blows kept coming. I felt sick in my stomach when the men stopped, laughed, and walked off. There was nothing worse than seeing the work of evil first hand.

"Excellent, men!" the Jackal said. "Now that the warm-up is over, it's time for the real fight to begin. It's time to see how tough our visitor truly is. Let him out!"

CHAPTER
13

RUN! THAT'S WHAT I NEEDED to do. But not without my gear. And I couldn't abandon these people. I had to do what I had to do: stand up and fight for what's right.

I took my time getting out of the cage. My limbs were sluggish, and my head was full of mud.

But I could move at last, and maybe I had my dragon heart to thank for that. Father had said it could do wonderful things.

Above, the Jackal stood, arms folded over his chest, all of my gear in place. It made me wonder if I was looking in a mirror. If that was what I would become if I didn't get my act together, then I had better try, and fast. Dark, primal, animal. That's what Corzan had called me, an animal. The Enforcers had said I was a freak and a demon. Sorrow and anger mixed in my stomach as I reflected on all I'd done wrong over the years. Holding my stomach, I shuffled forward and glowered up at him.

"I'll be needing my gear back, Lycan!" I said.

He sneered at me. They didn't' like that word, Lycan. But I didn't like the words Demon, Freak or Animal.

"I didn't come here to entertain your talk," he barked. "I came to watch you die. Take him!"

Clubs raised, Renny, Harvey and Osclar came at me.

Stomach in knots, weaponless, and with a dizzy head, I forged into battle.

I jumped over the three of them and darted for the farmers. They breathed, barely. I wrapped my fingers around both of their clubs, banged them together, and said, "Come and get me!"

They stopped, eyes wary.

"Fools! Take him!"

They screamed as they charged.

I cracked Renny in the jaw. Osclar in the head. Harvey in the knee.

Three down. Ten to go.

I smacked the clubs together and said, "Who's next!"

A wave of nausea assailed me, and I sank to my knee. The more active I was, the more the poison attacked my system. *Drat!* I had to fight it. I had to make my body do what it did not want to, or I was going to die.

I rose to my feet.

"Get the swords!" the Jackal yelled. "And get in there. You. You. You and You!" All the enforcers eyed the Jackal.

I smiled. All I needed was a blade. I could cut them to ribbons. They knew it.

"No! Just use clubs. And more men. You! You! You!"

They scrambled down, clubs and bucklers ready. That battle with the first three had taken a lot out of me. *Suck it up, Dragon!*

They came.

I swung.

They swung.

Back and forth we went, them chasing me from one side of the fort to another. I dodged, poked and parried. Where one fell, another popped up. A hard shot on my back knocked me to my knees. I ducked under the next swing, clubbed one in the chest, another in the knee.

Hard wood cracked. Shields smacked. Alarm and pain cried out.

I took a shot in the back of my head and pitched forward.

Whop! Whop! Whop! Whop! Whop!

They beat me like a drum.

I roared out.

"His eyes!" one said, backing off.

"He's a demon!"

A spark. A fire. An inferno came. My head cleared. My muscles loosened. I could see my reflection in the nearest man's eyes. My own eyes flared briefly with life. The effects of the poison fizzled out.

I cracked the clubs together.

"Let's try this again."

They ran. I pummeled.

I caught one in the chin. One in the nose. One in the jaw.

I laughed. It felt good to laugh and swing. Torment those crueler things. A minute later, not one man stood except me.

I looked up at the Jackal and said, "So, what happens when you run out of men?"

"I'm not concerned about that. Get in there, Brock!"

Brock, all eight feet of him, hopped down into the arena like a big ape. Well armored, he carried a spiked mace with a round head in one hand and a heavy chain in the other. When he stretched his arms out, it looked like they stretched from one side of the fort to the other.

"I see you've grown since we last talked," I said.

His lip curled over his teeth as he came forward.

"My, what an awfully long stride you have. Have you been eating Golden Ore? It's dirt you know. Is that why you grew so big?"

Swack!

I ducked as the chain licked out over my head.

His mace rose up.

His mace came down.

I dove away.

"I'm going to turn you into a mud hole," Brock said.

The mace and chain were like toys that he wielded like a child. A vicious child. The kind who plucks the wings off fairies.

He charged. I ran. He swung. I dodged. I ducked. I dived.

I could hear the Jackal's high-pitched laugh. Evil, condescending. I cast him a quick glance. He was twirling one of my Moorite arrows in his clawed fingers.

Brock's chain whipped around my legs and jerked me from my feet. I rolled as his spiked mace came down, clipping my arm.

"You're as big as you are inaccurate—Goon!" I said, whacking him in the hand.

He roared, releasing the chain. His mace came down, and rolling over the ground I went, kicking the chain from my feet.

"You are going to die!"

Brock swung.

I blocked. The impact of his hit jolted my elbows and ripped one club from my hand. The next blow was fast. I ducked. Brock knocked a small hole in the wall.

"What!" he cried out. The mace was stuck in the wall.

I swung the club full force into his elbow.

Brock howled like a banshee. I cracked one of his knees, then the other. Down on his knees he went. Tears filled his eyes as he screamed.

"Stop! Please stop it!"

I did not. Evil never showed me any mercy, so why should I show it?

I struck fast.

Whack!

Hard.

Whack!

On the final blow, I used both arms.

CRACK!

Brock fell face first into the ground. A red lump on his bald spot quickly formed.

Chest heavy, I said, "How's that treat you, Knothead!"

Above, the remaining enforcers gawked.

"Who's next?" I said, twirling my club around my back and front.

Every hair on my body lurched. *Move, Dragon!*

I felt my back catch fire as I spun to the ground, wounded, bleeding.

The Jackal loomed above me. Fang glimmered in his hand.

"You fight well against mortals. But you'll die against the power of the supernatural!"

CHAPTER

14

A PREDATOR. A TORMENTOR. THE JACKAL was a towering figure. Broad shouldered, strong and supple. An animal with the cunning of a man, the killer instinct of an animal. And Fang dangled in his evil grip. I never would have imagined I'd die on my own sword's blade. Backpedaling, I danced, and the lycan's swift strokes licked at my skin.

"You are fast for a big man," the Jackal said. "But, not as fast as me. I have supernatural speed. Skill. I'm your superior in battle!"

I laughed.

"You call this a battle? You wield a fine sword, and I use a club. Ha! You're letting my weapon and my armor do all of your dirty work, you over-sized rodent!"

"There is no honor among jackals!" he said, talking a swipe at my gut.

I jumped away.

"Or lycans, for that matter."

The walls of the fort were closing in, and the Jackal was quite a sight as four feet of razor sharp steel hung in his fist. My steel that is.

"It's sad to see your men are so much braver than you. At least they had the courage to fight with what they had, not with what the enemy had given them."

Fang sliced the top off my club. *Drat!*

I snatched a shield from the ground.

Wang!

The Jackal struck, jarring my bones. Again and again he tore at my shield, making pieces of metal and wood scatter all over.

"Coward!" I yelled. "Fight fair! What are you scared of?"

Krang!

"Your men are watching you. When the day comes, what will they think of you?"

Chop!

Only the straps and a small strip of wood remained. "Will they respect you? Will they follow?"

The Jackal stopped. I fought for my breath. He was little winded.

"I tire of your mouth. Perhaps it's best that I tear your throat out."

With a flick of his wrist, he tossed Fang to the other side of the fort. He stretched out his arms and extended the long nails on his fingers. I'd never fought a lycan, but I once saw one break the neck of a dwarf with his bare hands before. And there wasn't much that would kill a lycan except the pierce of silver or magic. I'd bought some time, but I was still a dead man without Fang.

"You'll wish I used the sword soon enough, Fool," he growled at me. "Now I'm going to tear you to pieces!"

Claws and teeth bared, he sprang. I dropped on my back, jammed my boots in his gut, and launched him head over heel. He crashed to the ground and howled. Not like I would, but with the strange high-pitched howl of a jackal.

He gathered himself, eyes filled with rage, and came again. Legs and arms ripping up the ground like an animal. I braced myself.

Slam!

I gave it all I had. I punched, kicked and clawed.

He bit, ripped and howled.

Blood was in my face. My blood, not his; I was sure of it. I walloped him in the jaw with my dragon fist, snapping his head back. I drove the heel of my other palm in his gut.

He backed off, smiled, and spit a tooth from his mouth.

"That's a first. But you bleed. I do not. I cannot."

I'd hit him with all I had with that punch. A dragon punch, at that—to no effect. That was the problem with the supernatural. Only the supernatural could stop it or kill it.

"You sure you just don't want to talk about this, Perhaps?"

He jumped again, his full weight landing on me. He rammed my face in the dirt and jammed a claw in my leg.

I thrashed. Drove an elbow in his ribs and rammed my head under his chin, crawling out from under him.

He shook it off like water and punched me in the face. My nose started to bleed. It might have been broken.

"I can do this all day," I said.

"Do what? Bleed? WHHHHHHEEEEEEEEEEOOOOOOO!" he howled like a tormented banshee. "We'll see about that!"

I had to fight smarter. Fight harder. Or else I'd be dead in the next minute. I gasped for breath. *Think, Dragon! Think! How do you beat something that is indestructible?*

I balled up my dragon fist and said, "Come on. What are you waiting for?"

He came after me, claws striking like snakes.

Jab! Jab!

I hit him in the nose.

Jab! Jab!

I hit him in the face.

He was fast, but my jabs were must faster. I was the dragon. He was the animal, not me.

He broke it off.

"What are you doing, Fool! You're can't hurt me!"

"Stings, don't it?" I shook my fist. "You might as well surrender. I can do this all night, remember."

I was exhausted, and my knuckles ached. The Jackal was like hitting a statue, but at least I had him aggravated.

Balling up his fists, he circled me.

"So it's a fist fight you want?" He smacked his together. "Then it's a fist fight you'll have."

He lunged.

I jabbed.

He snared my wrist in his hands.

"Gotcha!"

He jerked me to the ground and drove his elbow into my gut.

All my wind left me. The Jackal had outsmarted me. Pinned to the ground, I couldn't move. I couldn't breathe.

He opened his jaws.

I could see a tunnel of fangs in his mouth. I tucked my chin down as he went for my neck. *NO!* My mind screamed, but I knew it was over.

An inch from my face, the Jackal stiffened. His grip loosened. His jaw fell open. I noticed the tip of a sword sticking out of his chest as I crawled out from underneath him. His eyes rolled up in his head as he fell over.

Fang hung in the farmer's son's grip.

I scurried to my feet and watched the Jackal transform from lycan to man, dead.

The farmer's son stood there, trembling, with blood on his hands. I didn't know what to say, but the remaining Enforcers did.

"Kill them!"

CHAPTER
15

"LET ME HAVE THAT," I said, holding out my hand.

"Oh," the son said, handing Fang over.

The metal was warm, welcoming, an old friend returned from a long trip.

The enforcers, five of them in all, surrounded us. A few others I'd knocked down before began to stir.

"I'll handle this," I said, twirling Fang around my body. Fang's radiant blade flared with light, a mix of many hues.

All the Enforcers gaped, eyes filled with wonder and fear.

"The Jackal is dead. Your leader's defeated. Do you want to be the first to taste my steel?" I said, pointing Fang at the nearest one. He cringed. "Would you rather die, or surrender?"

All the enforcers looked at one another and dropped their arms.

"Excellent. You soft bellies are not as stupid as you look. Now get in those cages."

They hesitated.

"Now!"

"We're going. We're going. We just weren't sure which one," one said, with shifty eyes and a black bandana on his head.

I gathered my pack, grabbed a healing vial, and applied a few drops to the young man's father's lips. He was barely breathing, but he coughed and sputtered.

"He's going to be alright," I said, extending my hand to the young man. "And I thank you. I owe you my life. That was a brave thing you did, you know?"

His chest swelled, and he couldn't help but smile as he grabbed my hand and squeezed it. He had a strong grip for a skinny fellow.

"I don't know what came over me. I didn't even think. I saw the Jackal tearing into you. The sword caught my eye, and I was moving." There was a watery twinkle in his eyes. "I've never wanted to kill anything before. Except food that is. But, I-I killed a man." He cast a look where the Jackal lay.

I squeezed his shoulder and said, "No, you killed a monster. You saved me. Your father. Yourself—and freed your village. One single act of bravery can yield great things."

Tears streamed down his cheeks as he helped his father to his feet.

"S-Son, what happened here?" the father said, looking around, a bewildered look in his weary eyes.

"Come on, Father. I'll tell you all about it on the way home." He stopped and looked at me, saying, "What is your name?"

"Call me Nath. Nath Dragon."

"Odd name, but memorable."

I smiled and asked, "What's yours."

"Ben."

"A fine name, Ben. A warrior's name."

"I'll be back with help."

I gathered my armor from the Jackal's corpse. All the stitching and buckles were fine, but Fang's tip had gone straight through the armor. A normal blade couldn't have done such a thing. It would be a little something for Brenwar to stitch up. *I bet he's ready to kill me.*

Gathering all my gear, I made my way up the ladders and onto the catwalk. I had no idea where I was. Horses nickered along the wall, a good sign. The fort was erected on fertile land, between the rolling hills that stretched out mile after mile. Ben and his father traveled on horseback on a faint road that winded out of sight. I had a feeling it would be hours before I saw anyone else again, which left me and my prisoners, the Enforcers.

I looked at the men crammed in the cages. They were rotten. Every last one of them. How many people had they terrorized? How many had they killed? If I could have killed them in battle, I would have.

"And to think, all I wanted was a good meal and a warm night's sleep. Now what?"

I would be hours before anyone else came around, and I wasn't going to wait. I had dragons to save.

I said to Fang, "I guess it's me, you and the outdoors from now on." I slid him back in the sheath and hopped off the catwalk onto the ground.

"Let us go, Demon."

It was the leader, Renny, who spoke.

"We'll ride out of here and never look back. I promise."

Ignoring him, I grabbed the cloth and threw it over the cage.

"We can't see! You can't do that! It'll get too hot in here."

"And you will all begin to stink really bad, too. You better hope the gnolls and orcs don't get wind of you."

I covered the other two cages as well, laughing at all their colorful complaints.

"It smells like an orcen bathhouse in here!"

"Please don't leave us!"

"We're sorry! We won't raid any villages no more!"

"Oh no!" one moaned, "Brock just farted."

I was bound for Quintuklen. And I wasn't alone this time, either. I took the finest horse the Enforcers had, a big brown beauty. I rubbed his neck.

"No hurry, Boy. No hurry."

I found horses the most fascinating and noble of all the animals. Noble, strong and reliable. If you ever get a chance to know one or ride one, I suggest you do.

North I rode. Past the trees, through the ferns, over the streams from sun up until almost sun down.

"Wait!"

I heard someone crying out in the distance. Behind me, a man galloped waving a rag shirt or something in the air. It was Ben. Something must be wrong.

He came along side me, panting for breath.

"Your horse should be panting, not you." I said. "What's going on? Did the enforcers escape?"

"No, no!" he managed. "That's fine. The legionnaires are coming to haul them off."

"And you rode all this way to tell me that?"

He looked at me funny.

"No. I'm here because I'm coming with you!"

CHAPTER

16

"No, you aren't coming with me!" I said.

"Why not?" he said, grinning ear to ear.

Now it was my turn to gape. The young man was bruised from head to toe with a big knot on his head. He'd almost died hours ago, and now he wanted to follow me to a certain death.

"Because you'll die."

There, I'd said it. He'd just have to get over it.

He frowned.

"Ben, be realistic. You stabbed a monster in the back. It died. And you have my sword to thank for that, else you'd never have scratched his hide."

He brushed his black hair behind his ear and said, "I never really thought about it."

"What you did was as I said. Brave. 'Bravery is for the foolish', some say. But fortunate as well. Why don't you just go home and enjoy your days being the hero of the village? The man that saved the town. I'm sure the milk maids would love for you to stick around."

A pleasant smile formed on his face.

"I hadn't' thought about that, either. Do you really think they'll like me?"

"A handsome young hero like you? Hah! They'll swoon as soon as you enter the room."

He was eyeing the sky and rubbing his chin. I knew I had him thinking now. With excitement in his voice, he said, "No! I want to go with you, Nath Dragon."

I shook my head. *What has possessed this young man?*

"No, and I don't have a shovel with me, either."

"A shovel? What do you need a shovel for?"

I turned my steed and trotted away, saying, "To dig your grave. Goodbye, Ben. And tell the milk maids hello."

The clopping of horse feet were catching up. I turned.

"Ben, go home. I mean it!"

"But you owe me!"

"Owe you? For what?"

"You said, 'I owe you my life'. You can pay me back now."

Great! Ben had a point. I owed him my life.

Irritated, I said, "What do you want?"

"Uh, well, er... I just want to go with you. See the world. Travel Nalzambor."

Ben looked about as fit for travel as a one-legged horse. His trousers were held up by a rope belt, and the leather armor that he must have taken from an Enforcer was too big. His arms jutted out from under the shoulder plates like sticks, and the sword strapped to his waist looked like it would pull him from the saddle. He would have been the most pathetic enforcer I ever saw.

"Are you certain you want to do this, Ben?" I smiled.

Reason with him. Talk him out of it.

"Absolutely. More than anything. I don't want to work on the farm anymore. It's boring. I want to see the world."

"And you want to face all the dangers therein?"

"Well, I guess."

"You ever seen an ogre pull a man's arms off?"

"No."

"Have you seen a Chimera swallow a gnoll?"

"What's a Chimera?"

I rolled my eyes.

"Do you know there are goblins that eat people?"

"No."

"Orcs that enslave people?"

He shook his head.

"Fierce dragons that burn the living to a crisp?"

His eyes fluttered in his head. Then he said, "Oh... I'd love to see that!"

"Really?"

"Well, not good people. Just ones like the enforcers and all."

I could see a dangerous look in his eyes. A fire. A twinkle. A zeal. Ben wasn't going home. He was coming with me, on an adventure.

I sighed.

"Come on then. But I'll not feed you, clothe you or baby you. So, you better keep up."

His long face lit up like a halfling parade. "Really? You'll let me come!"

"It's your life to throw away, not mine."

"So it is," he said, grinning ear to ear. "Let's go!"

I led. He followed. Over the faintest of trails we went.

As the minutes passed and the sun set, Ben finally asked, "Er... Nath?"

"Call me Dragon," I scowled.

"Er... Dragon, where are we going?"

CHAPTER

17

"**Q**UINTUKLEN, WHERE THE BUILDINGS ARE as tall as the Red Oak trees," I said. "But it's a long, long ride."

"I'm in no hurry," Ben replied, yawning.

Skinny as the young man might be, he had some grit to him. Underneath all the bruises, he probably wasn't a half-bad looking lad, either. He just needed to eat more. Dark-complexioned and tall, he was at ease in the saddle. His light eyes followed all the sights and sounds. And unlike Brenwar, he smiled and talked a good bit.

"Tired, Ben?"

"A good bit, actually. I haven't rested since being hauled off in that cage. Shouldn't we be making camp already? I can make a fire."

"What do you need a fire for? Didn't you bring a blanket?"

"No."

I shook my head.

"But I meant I could do some cooking. I'm a good hunter and trapper."

"I thought you were a farmer."

"Well, you can't survive in the country if you can't hunt or fish. You'll starve eventually."

As soon as the white owls began to hoot, I stopped in a grove and made camp, which consisted of little more than two horses and two men with a rough patch of ground to lie on. Ben yawned the whole time as he gathered twigs and started a fire. He did well. After a few minutes, the orange glow burst to life and the warmth came.

"Outstanding, Ben. You are pretty handy, are you not?"

Covering his yawn, he said, "I told you."

"Good, now you can take the first watch. Wake me up when the moon dips."

Ben had a blank look in his eyes.

"And keep your ears open. They'll serve you better than your eyes at night," I said, closing my eyes. I could feel Ben's eyes on my back as rubbed his hands on the fire.

"I'll stay awake, Dragon. All night if I have to."

I lay and listened. Chirps of critters and crickets filled my ears. All those little things that crept and crawled in the night had come to life. A burning fire offered sanctuary, but it could attract the unwanted. Good thing I was a light sleeper. And I had a sixth sense for danger. The Dragon's Gut, I called it. An awareness I had when I slept, though I didn't sleep much. As I drifted off to sleep, the soft snoring of Ben drifted into my ears.

"Oh great," I said, sitting up.

He lay alongside the fire, curled up in his armor.

"Looks like I have the first and the second watch."

The pixlyn flew as fast as he could fly, covering a mile a minute. Hummingbird wings buzzing as fast as they ever buzzed before. Over the tree tops he went, scattering insects and small birds. Little noticed him. Little could see him.

In a day, he'd covered the northern part of Nalzambor. He'd seen many faces in that day: dwarves, elves, orcs, giants and dragons, some hard at work or mischief, others at play. But there was yet to be a sign of the man he sought. Nath Dragon. He rubbed his belly, panting. The potion Finnius had given him was a nasty thing, like rotten stew boiling. It gave him strength somehow. A sense of direction, too. The man must be close. He could feel it.

He thought of his companion, the pink-eyed pixlyn he'd been with all his life. Find the man, save her. He couldn't bear the thought of horrible things happening to her. He took a deep breath in his tiny mouth, stuck out his chest and buzzed into the sky.

A streak of red came at him. He rolled away, hovering in the sky. There were three of them. Each was as big as him, red-scaled and black-winged, tiny dragons called firebites. They circled, snorted puffs of fire, and dove.

The pixlyn shot through the sky, three dangerous dragons nipping at his toes. Firebites didn't play with pixies and fairies. They roasted them and ate them whole.

The pouring rain didn't bother him. Nor the stubborn horse between his legs. No, as Brenwar trotted along the road, he was consumed with something else. Guilt.

"I should have listened to him," he growled, wringing the water from his beard.

He had known Nath wanted to leave Morgdon, and Brenwar should have gone. Instead, being stubborn, persistent and consumed with the Festival of Iron, he might end up losing his best friend. And it might end up starting another war. Not that Brenwar would mind that. But he had to catch him. And catching Nath wouldn't be easy. Not if he didn't want to be found.

Another Dragon War, Nath's father had warned. That's what evil wanted. Another shot at the throne of Nalzambor. Nath's father, the Dragon King, wasn't the same as he had been of old. Not after the last war. He was ancient, but not immortal. Brenwar sensed that the Dragon King's time on Nalzambor was coming to an end. And who would keep the peace without him there? It was either Nath Dragon or no one.

The horse nickered and stopped.

"What is it now?" Brenwar said, rubbing its neck.

A group of figures approached, cloaked from head to toe. Men, by the looks of them.

"Hail and well met," one said, fingers itching at the sword on his hip.

"Agreed," said another who stepped behind Brenwar's back.

As easy as a fish swims in water, they had him surrounded.

Brenwar stiffened as the next one said, "That's a fine horse you have there, Little Dwarf."

Whop!

Brenwar knocked him out of his boots with his war hammer.

"Little! I'll show you brigands little!"

Brenwar slid from his horse to the ground.

"Take him down!" one ordered, drawing his sword.

Two rushed forward. Brenwar busted one in the chest, dropping him in the mud. The other stabbed a dagger into his armored chest, snapping it at the hilt.

"Fool! This armor's dwarven made!"

"Drag him into the mud!" one of the brigands said.

Brenwar took in a loud draw through his nose.

"Ah, I smell an orc, a part of one at least."

Brenwar knocked a curved sword from one's hand. Kicked in the knee of another. He was a machine. A black bearded typhoon in the rain.

A man screamed as he busted his hand. Another fell as his knee gave out. One caught Brenwar in the back of his leg with a knife.

"You should not have done that!" he said, swinging his war hammer.

Pow!

He lifted the man's feet from the ground.

The rain poured. The brigands tumbled down. No group of Brigands stood a chance against a dwarven soldier with centuries of fighting under his belt.

Brenwar grabbed the fallen half-orc by its head of hair and said, "Happen to see a man with long auburn hair and golden eyes pass through here, Wart Face?"

"I wouldn't say if I did, Halfling. Heh-heh!"

"Why is it the ugly ones always have the smartest mouths!"

"Because—"

Brenwar clonked his head into the orc's, knocking him out.

"That was a statement, not a question. Now, what about the rest of you?"

"Mercy, Sir," one said, clutching his broken arm. "Never seen such a man. If I did, I'd tell you. I swear."

"Sure you would," Brenwar said, hoisting himself back on his horse. "If I ever see any of you again, I'll break every bone in ya!" He snapped the reigns. "Yah!"

Aggravated, Brenwar felt he wasn't any closer to finding Nath Dragon than when he started. But he was certain time was running out.

CHAPTER

18

"SLEEP WELL?" I SAID.

Ben stretched out his arms and yawned.

"What happened!" he said, covering his eyes. "Where'd all this daylight come from?"

"I'm pretty sure it's from the sun," I said, roasting a rodent on a spit. "It does that most days, you know."

"I'm sorry. I didn't mean to fall asleep. I felt just fine, then I was out." Ben's stomach growled. "What's that you're cooking? Smells good."

"Just a little white-eared rabbit."

"Really? How'd you snare it? We can never keep them out of the garden. Too smart for snares, too fast to shoot."

I held out another rabbit on the end of my arrow.

"I shot this one, too," I said.

"Nobody's that good a shot," Ben objected. "Not even my uncle. He's a Legionnaire bowman, you know. He told me they could hear me pulling the string back before I shot." He tore a hunk of meat off the stick. "Hmmm... this is good. Really good!"

"Well, I'm sure your uncle is a fine shot. And the white-ears are impossible targets. You just have to know where to shoot before they go. It's called 'anticipation'. And, I had a little help, too."

I held Akron out.

"What is that?"

Snap-Clatch-Snap!

"Whoa," he said when the bowstring coiled along the bow and into place. "Is that magic?"

"No, all bows do that."

"Really?"

"Of course not. This is Akron. A gift from my father. Elven made. Elven magic. Can you shoot?"

"Can I shoot? You bet I can shoot. My uncle started teaching me when I was just a boy. I once shot a sparrow in the sky. I feathered a boar, too. Right between the eyes. It was him or me, that time." He licked the rabbit meat from his fingers. "Can I try?"

Ben rose up, twisted and cracked his back. His eyes were alert, and the rangy muscles throughout his body were supple, not stiff. If he had some armor that fit, he'd actually look like a soldier, and the fact that his uncle was a Legionnaire archer left me a little more comfortable. I handed over the bow and an arrow.

"*If*," I emphasized, "you can pull the string back, let it fly." I pointed. "That oak tree will do."

Ben took the grip in his hand, loaded the shaft on the shelf, and nocked it back like a seasoned soldier. Arms quivering, he pulled the fletching to his cheek.

"Hold it steady, Ben."

He took a small breath, held it, steadied his aim, and released.

Twang!

The arrow sailed with speed and accuracy.

Thunk!

"Yes!" Ben pumped his arm. "This bow is amazing!"

"That's a great shot, Ben. You're pretty strong for a scrawny man," I said, taking my bow back. "You were a little low, however."

The tree was thirty yards off, but I couldn't have him getting cocky.

"I don't think many men could do much better."

I loaded Akron, pulled the string back, and let one arrow fly after the other.

Twang! Thunk!

Twang! Thunk!

Twang! Crack!

The first hit above Ben's, the second below. The third went right through his shaft.

"Uh, that was amazing!"

"Of course it was," I said handing him my bow.

"Can you teach me to do that?"

"Probably not, but..." I eyed the heavy sword on his belt, thinking. "Ever swing a sword before?"

"Just the once. My mother didn't like weapons, and my father didn't care for them much, either."

"Well, if you have to use it, better try it two-handed. I'll show you a few things later. Now run down there and fetch those arrows."

Ben started walking towards the tree.

"I said *Run*!"

He sprinted for the tree. *At least he's fleet.*

Looking backward, the pixlyn wiped the sweat from his brow. The skies were empty. His pursuers gone. The firebites, who in comparison to him, for all intents and purposes, might as well have been full-sized dragons, had chased him until it felt like his wings would fall off. He zipped down into the trees and took a seat on a branch behind the leaves. He'd never flown so much in one day before.

Chest heaving, he frowned as he thought of his companion: her beautiful pink eyes and sweet smile. Even if he returned with what the evil man wanted, he knew they were both still dead. But it was better they died together, rather than separate. They'd lived for one another. They'd die for one another. That's what love is.

He shuddered as he thought of the firebites. He could only guess they had tired out or found the scent of easier prey. As for the rest of the journey, he'd have to be more careful. No doubt they would pursue if they found the scent again. He shivered, mumbling in Pixlyn to himself. He rubbed his belly. The strange aching had grown stronger. He could sense the man he'd been sent to track was getting closer. His toes lifted off the branch as his wings hummed to life, and he darted off. His neck whipped around at the sound of tiny dragons roaring.

Zip!

Into the night, he was gone.

CHAPTER

19

THE NEXT COUPLE OF DAYS occurred without incident, and I was relieved. Ben had a strong core, and after a few lessons, he could swing his sword like a weapon. He was pretty adept for a long-leg with skinny arms, but working on the farm will do that to you. The problem with most farmers being soldiers was the only weapons they wielded were pitchforks, hoes and buckets of slop.

"Slash, Ben!" I said, banging his sword away. "Don't poke. Don't stab. That sword's not made for that. You need a light, smaller sword if you want to stab. And a quick opponent will roll right past you and slash your arm off. Have you ever seen a man poke a man's arm off before?"

Ben shook his head.

"If you poke them, they might bleed, but slash a part off, and they'll run."

Ben's face tightened.

"Hard to imagine such a thing, but when you fight, these things happen. They can happen to you just the same." I slapped him on the shoulder. "But this *is* what *you* wanted, isn't it?"

He looked a little green as he shook his head yes.

"But stabbing's how I killed the Jackal," he said, thumbing notches on his blade's edge.

"True, but the Jackal wasn't looking—and you had a magic sword, to boot." I twirled Fang with my wrist. "He's a fine thing, isn't he?" I rubbed the dragon heads on the pommel then jerked Dragon Claw out for display. "Now, if you want to poke somebody, you need one of these."

"Whoa! I never would have imagined such a thing," he said, eyeing it with fascination.

"This is Dragon Claw, and he's helped me out of more than one jam or two. When we get closer to town, we'll find you a dagger for your boot." I tugged at his girdle. "Hmmm, probably can fit a nice one in there, as well. You can never be too careful."

As Ben rubbed the back of his neck, I could see the uncertainty build in his eyes. *Good. A young man like that needs to know what he's in for.* But I was going easy on him, for now.

"I'm hungry."

"I'll check the fish traps," Ben said, sliding the broad sword into his belt.

"And I'll start the fire," I said.

I liked Ben. He was good company, and other than a few glances, he hadn't even asked about my arm, which I found extraordinary. But, country folk always did have the best manners.

After gathering a few twigs and skinning down some branches, I had a fire going in no time. It wasn't long after when Ben returned with a string of fish.

"Pretty nice catch you have there," I said.

He grinned from ear to ear.

"That stream is full of them. I could fish here all week."

I cooked; he skinned, and not long after I lay on my back and watched the wind blowing the black silhouettes of the leaves.

"Think you can stay up this time?" I said.

Ben covered his mouth, yawning.

"Oh, I'm feeling spry tonight." He grabbed a stone and ran it along the edge of his sword. "Dragon, I was wondering. What do you do, exactly? Do you hunt treasure? Where are you from? I've never seen a man like you before. And when I left, all the people were talking about you."

I sat up.

"Really, what did they say?"

"My cousin said you were one of those dragon poachers."

"Really," I held up my hand, "with an arm like this?"

He scratched his neck and said, "It is peculiar, but I've seen strange travelers before." He perked up. "I even saw some elves once. They didn't talk, but they had the most beautiful armor."

"Listen, Ben. If you're going to ride with me, and you might just die with me, you might as well know."

He leaned forward.

"Know what?"

"I'm looking for dragons."

His eyes brightened.

"You're a hunter?"

I shook my head.

He snapped his fingers.

"A poacher then? I've heard about them. Uh…" He shrank back. "…but aren't they… evil?"

"Yes, but I am neither. I don't hunt dragons. I don't kill them. I rescue them."

He scratched his head and asked, "Why would a dragon need rescued?"

"What do you know about the dragons, Ben?"

He shrugged.

"They have fiery breath and scales as hard as steel. Some are as big as horses and others as small as a goat." His face drew up. "Will you take me with you? To rescue one? Oh, they have treasure, too. Wagon loads of it, I hear. And… and there are thousands of them in the Mountain of Doom. They say there's one so large there he can swallow an elephant whole."

There was only one who could, that I knew of.

"Where'd you hear that?"

"A troubadour who was passing through one day sang about it. She was a pretty young thing. Half-elven she said she was, with honey-brown hair and lips the color of wine."

"And she sang no songs of auburn-haired fellows with eyes as gold as the sun?"

"No."

"Are you certain?"

"I'd have remembered for sure. We don't get many bards where I come from."

I rose to a knee, hand instinctively falling to my hilt.

"What is it?" Ben said.

I put my finger to my lips.

He cupped his ear.

What I heard was flapping. And not the common kind of the night air. Not birds, not owls, nor any other common thing, but something vastly rare.

The horses nickered. Their hooves stomped and stammered.

"Stay with the horses!" I said, pulling my bow out. "Something bad is coming."

CHAPTER

20

IT WAS BAD, ALRIGHT. THREE times as bad as I thought it would be.

"Firebites! What in Narnum are they doing here!"

Yes, they're dragons. No, they aren't good. Not evil, but not good. They're also known in the Dragon Home as firebrats.

I ducked.

A small creature zinged over my head. A pixlyn. A small fairy-like man with wings. A firebite was on his tail, chasing him into the sky, darting in and out of the trees. I could see two more waiting above as their brother flushed the pixlyn out.

"Ben! Don't leave those horses, do you hear?"

Firebites are small, little bigger than my foot, but they're all dragon. Nasty dragons, red-scaled, black-winged, more than capable of handling their own in the big, big world.

"What did you say?" Ben shouted back. "What are those things, anyway?"

"Stay with the horses, Ben!"

I nocked an arrow. Not moorite. Not magic. Just one I used for hunting. The pixlyn came again. I shot. He dove. The arrow splintered off the pursuing firebite's nose. It howled a split second before it crashed into a tree.

"Excellent shot, Dragon!"

"Get to the horses, Ben!"

In a blink, I reloaded, eyeing the sky. Down the next two came.

"Always have to do it the hard way, don't you fellas?" I said, aiming.

Twang!

The arrow split on its face. A normal arrow wouldn't harm it, but it would sting. I stepped out of the way as it crashed to the ground.

A stream of flame shot from the third one's mouth.

"What are you doing, Fire Brat?" I said, jumping away. The tree behind me burst into flame. If I didn't calm them down, they'd set the entire forest on fire. The next thing I knew, they had me surrounded. Vicious little lizards, tongues licking around their red hot mouths, snorting smoke and flames from their nostrils.

"Why are you attacking me?"

I felt something brush against my hair.

"Sultans of Sulfur!" I had a pixlyn on my head. "Get off me!"

The dragons' razor-sharp teeth nipped at my boots as they circled.

I could feel the white-hot heat coming out of their mouths. They could fry me in an instant if they wanted. I could see the fury in their eyes. They wanted that pixlyn.

I tried some Dragonese, saying, "Go away. The hunt is over."

They stopped and cocked their heads like little red dogs.

"Peace and Home," I said, and repeated.

Firebites are rebels. They come and go as they please. And they're harder to catch than most dragons. They don't have the weakness for gems or gold. It's the hunt and torment of all creatures inferior that they live for.

Sitting back on their haunches, they growled a little. Behind me, the burning tree was beginning to crackle.

"That's more like it," I said, reaching my dragon arm out to the nearest. It growled, bloodstone eyes fixed on my shoulder. There, the pixlyn sat, huffing for breath, a worried expression on his tiny face. The poor creature was exhausted. "You better stay back," I said. I felt it conceal itself in my locks.

"I'll help you, Dragon!"

From out of nowhere, Ben came swinging his sword.

"No, Ben! Stop!"

It was too late.

"EEE-YAH!"

Ben swung hard, hitting a firebite, sending it skipping across the ground.

"Fool! I told you to stay with the horses! Now we'll—"

A stream of flames shot from two dragons' mouths.

I leaped, knocking Ben out of the way.

"Stay behind me!" I said, locking my bow on my back. *Shing!* Fang was secure in my grip.

"Are those dragons?" Ben said, behind my ears.

"No, fool! Those are angry dragons! Very angry!"

"You sound angry," Ben said, worried. "Are you?"

I didn't say anything. Ben only meant well, but good intentions were often a brave man's undoing.

Puff! Puff! Puff!

Three balls of fire shot my way. I swatted them away with my sword, the splatter burning my fingertips and arms.

"Ow! That burns!" Ben said behind me.

Whatever connection I'd had with the firebites was gone now. Not only did they want the pixlyn, they now wanted Ben and me, as well. And these firebites were fully grown; their fire, though small, would last much longer than others'.

"What do we do?" Ben said. "I don't want to be burned alive."

I could feel Ben sliding away from me.

"Don't you dare run," I growled. "They'll turn you into char before you get within a dozen yards of a horse. Stand your ground and live. Give ground and die."

Nervous, Ben said, "That's what my uncle the Legionnaire says."

I didn't see any way out of this. They were going to hurt us, fry us, burn us. The intent was there as their tails snapped back and forth. They'd burn the entire forest down if they wanted to. I'd have to use Fang. I'd have to be quicker than them.

"Fang, if you have any advice, I could use it now."

"What?" Ben said.

"Nothing," I said. "Prepare yourself."

As Ben and I stood side by side, I saw the firebites' tiny chests swell. A torrent of flame shot out.

CHAPTER
21

INSTANTLY, A WALL OF ICE formed before me. Fang's blade radiated an icy blue color, the like I'd never seen on the metal before.

"Whoa!"

On the other side, the dragon flames crackled against the ice, causing the sheet to melt. With Fang glowing like a blue star in my hand, I seized the moment.

"Stay behind this wall," I ordered Ben.

Fang was pulsating with power. It was intoxicating. I stepped around the wall and faced the tiny dragons. In Dragonese, I spoke.

"That's enough! Be gone, firebites!" I said, pointing at them with my sword.

Fireballs shot from each mouth, pelting me with fire.

"Argh!" I screamed. It hurt, but just like when the steel dragon breathed fire on me, it didn't destroy me.

Fang moaned, angry, and blasted shards of ice into all of them.

Defiant, they let out with tiny roars, mouths shooting with fire.

Fang hit them again, coating them with frost from head to toe.

Growling, shivering, they backed away.

I willed Fang to shoot them again. The fire brats deserved it.

"Get out of here while you can!"

Wings pinned to their sides, one by one, they scampered away. The last one, looking back, shot another blast of fire my way. I ducked, and when I looked back, it was gone.

Still filled with power, I shot another blast into the burning tree. The ice smothered the flames out. Admiring Fang, I said, "That was incredible."

Fang flared and moaned, then returned back to his shiny coat of steel.

"Well done, Fang. And thank you," I said, sliding him back into his sheath.

I remembered what the steel dragon had said. *That sword you have, Little Dragon... you should get to know it better... that day your father forged it, I was there... tell him hello... and thank you.*

There was certainly much more to that than I expected.

"You talk to your sword," Ben said, stepping from behind the wall of ice, "And it makes snow?"

I fought the urge to slap him.

"Ben! You almost got us killed. Do you understand that?"

He stood there, blinking.

"Do you want to continue this journey with me?" I said, patting out a patch of flame on my armor. I had burn marks all over me, and a nasty boil popped up on my arm.

He nodded.

"Then, follow my orders from now on!" I punched him in the arm. "Got it!"

He grimaced, holding his shoulder.

I shrugged. That's what Brenwar would have done if I'd acted so foolish. I felt Ben eyeing my back.

"Were those dragons? They were so small."

"Yes, those were dragons. And as you can see, just because something is small, doesn't mean it's not dangerous. Take a moment to think: what would have happened if they came after you without me? You'd be a Human Roast, right? And they have our scent now. They might come back, you know. Burn us in our sleep."

Eyes like saucers, tone somber, he nodded and said, "I'm sorry, Dragon. I guess we're even, huh?"

"I guess—say what?" Something rustled in my hair. I'd forgotten about the pixlyn.

Snatch!

I had him in my dragon claws.

"What is that!" exclaimed Ben.

The pixlyn struggled in my grip, but I wasn't hurting him. I wasn't letting him go, either.

"A pixlyn, part of the fairy race."

Ben came closer, gaping, and said, "I heard they granted wishes."

I laughed but not out loud. *This should be good.*

"Go ahead, make a wish then," I suggested.

"Well, why don't you make a wish, then?"

I closed my eyes, thinking, and said, "Hmmm... well, I didn't really have one in mind, but if you're not interested, I could think of one; I guess. I'm hungry: maybe some food."

"No! Do something bigger than that."

"What would you wish for, Ben?"

This should be interesting. You could learn a lot about a person if you knew what they wished for.

Scratching the side of his cheek, looking between me and the fairy, Ben said, "I'd wish for peace in all Nalzambor."

Well, that was touching. Naïve, but at least his heart was in the right spot. *He'll make a fine hero yet.*

"Impressive, but pretty big, Ben. Their magic is limited, so you might as well ask for something smaller."

"Can I save it?"

"Sure, you can do whatever you want."

He glanced at me and said, "He can't really grant wishes, can he?"

"I can neither confirm nor deny that.

The pixlyn chattered at me, but I had no idea what he said. I imagine it was "Let me go!"

"What are you going to do with him?"

The pixlyn was an exotic and handsome little thing. His skin was the color of pollen, his eyes like tiny gems. A perfect figurine of a man. Still, it was strange to find a pixlyn so far from the high mountains. And I found it hard to believe the firebites rousted him out from there. And the creature, though defiant in my grasp, seemed sad, almost worried.

"What is wrong—"

A puff of blue smoke shot from his mouth and into my face, my mouth, my eyes.

Oh no! The lights went out, and my memories began to fade.

CHAPTER
22

AWOKE WITH THE SUN IN my eyes and a headache.

"Ugh... what hit me?"

"Nothing," Ben said. "That fairy or pixie thing just spat on you."

I rolled over. There was Ben, glum-faced and dark-eyed. He looked like he hadn't slept in a week.

"You been up all night?"

He rubbed his eyes, yawning.

"Yep. I couldn't sleep if I had to. I swore I heard those little dragons prowling around all night." He huffed out a breath. "I'm really glad you're awake because I couldn't wake you, and I tried. Oy, did I try."

I sat up, looking around, rubbing my head. There was a lump on it.

"Sultans of Sulfur, Ben! Couldn't' you catch me when I fell? What did I land on, a stone?"

"Sorry, but I was watching that pix... er—"

"Pixlyn!" I growled. "So, I guess it's long gone by now. Hope you got your wish in. Now get the gear and the horses; let's go!"

I was agitated. It wasn't all Ben's fault, but having him around didn't help. It just slowed me down. I had dragons to save, and the only thing I was saving was myself and him. It was time to get him to the city and settle him in. I had things to do.

I saddled up as soon as Ben led the horses over.

"You get everything?" I asked.

"Certainly. Eh, Dragon?"

"What?"

"That blister on your arm, it looks painful. I could lance it for you. I saw my mother lance one on my father once. He burned himself really bad at the forge. A hot horse caught him."

The blister was as big as an egg and throbbed with a life of its own. A chronic reminder of my carelessness.

"Do I look like someone who's worried about a little blister on my arm?" I said, scowling. I didn't smile all the time, unless ladies were around.

"No."

I slit it open with my dragon thumb.

Ben looked like he'd swallowed a scorpion as the puss drained out.

"There, Ben. You don't have to worry about me anymore." I snapped the reigns. "Yah!"

Quintuklen. A monolithic marvel against the northern skies.

"What do you think?" I said.

Ben stared, saying, "I never imagined it was so big."

It was big. The biggest city in Nalzambor, which I always found odd, because humans didn't stick around as long as the rest of us. But they were an ambitions lot.

"How tall are those... those things?" Ben pointed.

"Those are called *buildings,* and they're the tallest structures in the world. Excluding the Mountains of course. Naturally."

Even I admired them. It was a fascinating view, from the top of one to the streets below. The people seemed so tiny. It made me long for flying once more.

We trotted along a road heading towards the city, which was still miles in the distance.

"Uh, Dragon?"

"Yes."

"I'm, well, I'm..."

I saw the lump in his throat roll up and down.

"Scared, I'd imagine."

He nodded.

"Don't worry, Ben. It's normal. And once we get in there and see all the people, those fears will trickle away. Just don't buy anything or talk to the painted ladies. The merchants have a name for newcomers like you."

"A name? What kind of name?"

"Lilly pad. People will be nice, but too nice can be deadly."

He blanched.

"And if you have any money, keep it in your boots. There are pick pockets all over. Are you listening?"

"Oh... sorry, it's just those buildings. So big. I never could have imagined it."

"You'll get used to it. Now, stay close to me and don't smile. That only invites unwanted attention."

"Alright, Dragon."

The city, like all the rest aside from the Free City of Narnum, was fortified. A stone wall just over six feet tall was the first line of defense, but there were no gates or guards, just gaps spaced out every half mile or so. A hundred yards farther in, we came to the second wall: about twelve feet high with soldiers marching back and forth on the catwalks.

Looking around, I said, "Hold on." Reaching into my pack, I grabbed the Vial of concealment and dripped two drops on my dragon arm.

"What's that?" Ben said.

"Watch."

I thought of what I wanted. My black scales faded, and only my skin and fingers remained. I wasn't so sure I liked it, but I didn't want any attention, either.

"Whoa!" Ben said. "Can that make me look different, too?"

Does he think potions grow on trees? "No," I lied, "It just conceals my scales. That's all I wanted. Come on, now."

Two massive wooden doors remained open, and we passed through with a throng of merchants and travelers, maybe an adventurer or two.

"Follow me," I said, "And don't stare at anybody."

Through a gap in the wall we went; into the city we came. Ben gasped from behind me. There were people everywhere. Women draped the windows of tiny apartments: whistling, smiling and carrying on. Pushy merchants shoved sticks of cooked meat in our faces.

"Try some. The best. Make you strong warriors!" an elder one said, flashing his gums.

"Stop that!" Ben cried.

A half dozen little children were pulling at his boots. He shoved one down and into the ground. All the children screamed and cried, "Soldiers! Soldiers!"

"Stick your boots in the stirrups and ride on, Ben," I said through my teeth. "Let's go."

"Halt!"

A group of well-armed soldiers were coming our way.

CHAPTER

23

EVIL GLEE ON HIS FACE, Finnius the Cleric slapped his hands together. "Headed towards Quintuklen! My, that's perfect, maybe too perfect, but I'll take my chances. You've done well, Pixlyn, very well indeed."

The pixlyn stood back inside his cage, tiny hands wrapped around the bars, speaking shrill words of fairy kind. Along his side in her own cage, the female pixlyn sat, knees folded up in her arms.

"Certainly, I'll let you go," Finnius said, leering down at the cage. "I'll let you both go, just as soon as I'm... FINISHED WITH YOU!" He motioned for one of the acolytes. "Cover them both. I've no need of them at this moment."

The acolytes each dropped a heavy dark cloth over a cage and bowed their bald heads at Finnius. He nodded. It wasn't so long ago that he was one of them. A lowly cleric, given a simple task of confronting Nath Dragon. He had a limp to show for it, but that was all it had taken. Selene was pleased with his success. He'd earned her trust, which was no small matter. Now he had the tattoos and greater power to show for it.

"Follow me," he said, leaving one chamber for another.

The temple rooms were an excellent sanctuary for evil. Tucked in the rocky folds of the hills east of Quintuklen, they didn't get many trespassers in the long-abandoned temple. It was easy to keep secrets that way. And the constant howl of the winds kept the staunchest adventurers away.

"Nath Dragon," he said, laughing a little, "falling right into our hands. The High Priestess will be pleased, pleased indeed."

Down a short set of stone steps he went, torches bristling in the stiff wind, leading them into a chamber of worship. The draykis hissed as he entered. The accompanying lizardmen stood at attention, spears crossed over their chests.

"At ease; I've news to share," he said, walking over to the cage of the yellow dragon they'd caught days earlier and squatting down. Eyes closed, it didn't budge an inch. "It seems our game is close. Close indeed, and if we plan and stay prepared, we can lead our prey right here."

"Just tell us where he is, Finnius," the winged draykis said. "We shall go and kill him."

The draykis towered over him, fists clenched at its sides, fiery eyes boring down on him.

Finnius's hand fell to the symbol of Barnabus that hung from his neck.

"Back up," he said, "and mind your distance, Creature."

"Hah, Mortal, don't be so certain that amulet will protect you. It's you who should show respect," it said, clutching the long claws on its fingers.

Unruly. The dead are so unruly. Finnius squeezed the amulet tight.

"Barnabus!"

A wave of dark and eerie light burst forth, knocking the draykis from their feet. The amulet shimmered, ebbed, then returned to form: two bronze dragon heads facing outward. Each different; both evil.

"I've been dying to do that," he said. "Now, as you can see, we have many prisoners that need protection."

Scowling, the draykis rose back to their feet, looking around.

Four cages were lined up along the walls of the worship chamber. The yellow streak, as big as a man, and three small dragons, each in a cage of his own. One White, the size of a cat, and two greens as big as dogs. The draykis made catching the dragons easy, and Finnius was astounded by their success.

"Finnius," one of the acolytes spoke up, a younger man in oversized robes, "the cages' enchantment ebbs. Shall I fetch the elements?"

"Certainly," Finnius said. "And you may handle it yourself. I can't have the dragons getting out, and a little more deterrent will help."

One dragon, a purple tail, had chewed through the bars and escaped. It had been an error on Finnius's part, and a costly one. Two lizardmen were dead and one acolyte. High Priestess Selene would have been furious if she knew. Now, the draykis remained on guard as well. They could handle the dragons, but some cleric magic was needed as well.

One acolyte sprinkled the cages with a mix of colorful powder. The dragons snorted and scooted away as he dusted. The elements adhered to the bars, glowing at the sound of the acolytes' words of power and spreading with a dark blue glow up and down the bars. From one cage to the other they went, one sprinkling and the others chanting, until all were finished.

"Very well executed," Finnius said, "and now I have another mission for you."

They bowed.

"Anything, Finnius."

"You, get word to our brethren in Quintuklen. See to it rumor of this temple finds the ears of Nath Dragon. And you, send word to the High Priestess Selene. Tell her that the trap is set. Go!"

Finnius took a seat on the stone bench and wiped his sweaty palms on his robes. Capturing Nath Dragon wouldn't be easy. He'd seen the man in action before. He eyed the draykis.

"He's faster than you. That sword of his can split an anvil in two."

The lead draykis folded his arms over his chest and said, "Do not underestimate us. We are many; he is one. He may be fast," The draykis flexed the thick scaled cords in his arm, "but we are strong."

"Certainly," Finnius dabbed the sweat from his head with a satin cloth. *They are a cocky lot. But they'll have to do.*

CHAPTER

24

"**B**EN, HAVE YOU EVER SLEPT in a dungeon before?"

"No," Ben said, confused.

"It's the worst food you'll ever eat and the worst company you'll ever keep. But, as they say, 'What doesn't kill you makes you wish you'd died anyway'.

Ben gulped as the soldiers, each brandishing a long spear, approached.

"What's going on here? Are you harassing our citizens?" one said, helping the fallen child up.

Trouble with the local authorities was the last thing I wanted in Quintuklen. They kept things in order, and they had more dungeons here than in all the rest of Nalzambor. I'd been in their dungeons, and they were the last place in the world you'd ever want to go.

"The funny looking one kicked me," the boy said, pointing. "Said he'd kill me if I didn't move."

"Liar!" Ben exclaimed. "I did no such thing. He tried to steal my boots. They all did."

The soldiers weren't much better than children in some cases. They'd rob you blind as well. I could see it in their eyes; they knew Ben was new to the city.

"Where'd you get that armor? It's not a very good fit," one soldier spoke up. "It looks stolen to me."

Ah great. I could see the dungeon doors closing on me now. I hadn't been back in the city five minutes, and I was about to be arrested. I had to do something, fast.

"Soldiers of Quintuklen, may I address?"

They turned and stared.

I leaned forward on my saddle horn and said, "We're just passing through. Supplies for us, food for the horses, one night's rest, and maybe a trip to Dragon Pond out west. My friend's never been to the city, either. He's from the country; can't you tell? But, his uncle…" I eyed Ben.

"Louis of Quinley," he sputtered out.

"Yes, Louis told us to stop in at the Garrison and say hello." I crossed my arms over my chest and shot each man a discerning look.

They glanced at one another, and a moment later the leader said, "Move on!"

"But what about my justice, Soldier?" one of the children said.

"Shaddap, you lazy little rodent, before I whip you." He swatted at one. They scattered. "Troublemakers, the lot of you!"

"Are we really going to the Garrison *and* Dragon Pond?"

"Maybe," I said. Well, now I'd possibly told a lie. I didn't have any plans to take Ben anywhere else with me; I just wanted to get him settled in and go. And with any luck, his Uncle Louis could take him in for a spell.

The farther into the city we went, the less commotion occurred. Quintuklen was well laid out and organized. Gardens, fountains, colorful storefronts and banners could be seen all along the way. The streets were cobbled, and lanterns were lit by magic at every turn of a corner. In the good parts, at least.

"Dragon, can I stay with you one last night? I know you're wanting to get rid of me, and I can only guess you're going to set me up with my uncle," he said atop his horse, dejected.

I felt bad now. I liked having Ben around. He was like a younger brother, and none of my dragon family ever hung around much. Ben had saved my life… and he'd almost gotten me killed. I had things to do.

"Tell you what, Ben. I've got a few things to do around town, and I guess you can follow if you like. But, I've got business. Serious business. Dangerous, sometimes. You follow my lead. Any more foul ups, I'm leaving you lost in this city."

He shot up in his saddle, showing all of his teeth.

"Thank you!"

"Don't foul up. I mean it!"

He frowned again.

"Come on; let's get inside some walls and have a tasty meal. I guess I'm feeling a little cranky."

Horses clopping over the cobblestones, we made our way down the street. It was dark, but the lanterns made for ample light, but I didn't like that. I liked places that were more discreet. Not where the merchants went, but where the adventurers, soldiers and troublemakers went. They always had the most interesting stories to tell. We stopped in front of a stable.

"This is good," I said.

A young girl came out. She had a button nose and her hair was pulled back in a ponytail. Her eyes lit up when she saw me.

I smiled and flipped her two coins.

"One night, Pretty Thing. A meal bag for each as well."

I slid off my horse, and Ben followed suit.

"Anything you wish, Traveler." She grabbed the reigns and said, "I'll brush them both and check their shoes. Just let me know anything else I can do."

"Thank you," I said, rubbing her head. "That will be fine."

"Yes, thank you, Little Miss," Ben added, reaching out.

She ducked under his hand and moved on, taking a glance or two back at me before she was gone.

"You don't have to do that, Ben."

"Do what?"

"What I do. Just stay close. Look. Learn. Listen, Lilly pad."

His face scrunched up as he said, "Look. Learn. And Listen."

He'll figure it out.

A tavern sign hung nearby, and Ben squinted as he read the words above and said, "Hogfarts?" He grabbed his nose and shook his head.

"They have the worst ale in town, Ben. Let's keep going."

The next sign, another block down, seemed more appealing: The Ettin's Toe. A small crowd of men and women, a hard looking bunch, were full of life on the balcony above.

"This will do," I said, stepping up onto the porch.

Two figures came crashing through the door. A very large, bearded man was entangled with a half-orc: soldiers by the looks of their armor. The man bashed the half-orc in the gut. The half-orc walloped the man in the jaw. As the crowd came out jeering, we went in. Ben was pale when we sat down.

"Relax, Ben. It's best you see the best and worst of what the city offers. And, believe it or not, places like this have the best food to eat." I winked. "Trust me."

Wide-eyed, Ben couldn't help but look around. And I couldn't blame him. There were all sorts of people, which was a big part of what I liked about this town. Small torches lit up all the walls but not the corners. Two men as big as ogres sat at the bar with shoulders bulging up to their necks. A squad of bowmen sat in the middle of the room, joking and jesting of high times. Robed women with dark eyes and painted hands read the palms and heads of others in the room. One woman squealed as she sat on the lap of a man in full plate armor, who was tickling her knee. I smiled. There was nothing more entertaining than people. Especially the human ones.

"What can I get you, Handsome?" the barmaid asked. She was a short buxom woman with blonde curls all over her head. "I recommend the roast and biscuits. We have some chicken and egg soup, too."

"Is it hot?"

She fanned her sweaty neck and winked, saying, "Everything is hot in here."

"Then that will do. Oh, and a small bottle of wine as well, Pretty Thing."

"And a glass milk as well, Pretty Thing," Ben said.

The barmaid cackled like a hyena as she walked away.

"Ben, I don't think they have milk in here."

"But that's all I've ever drunk. Well, that and water."

I rolled my eyes. The two big goons at the bar were eyeing us now, and word was spreading.

"Did somebody order a cow over there?" one of the bowmen shouted our way.

The guffaws followed.

"What, what's he mean by that?"

"Next time, just ask for Honey Brown," I said. Honey Brown was ale, but it wasn't fermented. "It won't get you drunk, and your tongue won't take over your mouth, either."

The barmaid returned with two plates full of steaming food in one hand, a bottle of wine and a pitcher in the other. Setting them down, she said, "Sorry, Young Fella, we're all out of milk, but this should hold you over." She tussled the hair on his head.

"Thank you," I said, placing coins in her hand. "And a room is needed as well."

"I'll fluff your pillows myself, Handsome. My, where did you get eyes like that?" she said.

"From my father."

"Mmmm. Mmmm. Mmmmm. He must be something special as well."

"He is." I looked at our hands. "You can let go now."

"Oh," she blushed, walking away with a swing in her hips.

Ben was stuffing his face full of food.

"I'm starving," he raised the tankard to his lips.

I stopped him.

"Let me see that." I sniffed it. "Honey Brown. You're in good shape. Enjoy."

You couldn't be too careful in a place like this. I'd seen more than one man the night before his first adventure who'd never make it out of the tavern. People would do all sorts of rotten things to one another when you weren't careful.

I sawed up a bite of food and stuffed the meat in my mouth. *Tender and greasy, just how I like it.* And the biscuits, almost more butter than bread, were delicious. I never got to eat things like this in Dragon Home.

"Honey Brown, is it?" Ben said, gulping it down. "Tasty like a thousand honey suckles." He looked over his shoulder. "What are we in a place like this for? What are you looking for?"

"Dragons."

"In here?"

The tavern door slammed open, causing Ben to jump in his chair.

"TORMAC WINS!"

The large man who'd been fighting outside moments earlier sauntered in, dusting off his hands. His beefy forearms were scraped up, and his beard reminded me of an oversized dwarf.

"Does anyone else want to tangle with Tormac?" he said, walking over and slapping the two goons sitting at the bar on the shoulder. "Anyone?"

Heads down, they shook their heads. They were big men, hardy, but not as big as Tormac.

Ben, chewing a mouthful of food, was all eyes as he gawped at Tormac.

"Ben," I said, snapping my finger, "eyes over here!"

He didn't budge.

The crowd fell silent when the leering Tormac said, "What are you looking at, Bug Eyes?"

CHAPTER

25

TURNING PALE, BEN CHEWED ONCE and stopped.

Tormac was a warrior. He had the scars to show for it. The steel on his wide hips was heavy, and the dark eyes over his big flat nose made him all the more menacing. This was not what I needed.

"Well, Bug Eyes?" Tormac said in a grizzly voice, smashing his fist into his hands. "What are you staring at?"

"Don't hurt him, Tormac! He hasn't had his milk yet!" someone shouted.

The tavern erupted in laughter. Ben's cheeks turned red.

Tormac chuckled as he pawed at his beard.

"What's the matter, Bug Eyes? Did you leave your cow at the farm?"

More laughter.

Ben looked at me. Tormac looked at me. All eyes were on me.

I hitched my arm over the back of my chair, leaned back, tossed my hair over my shoulder, and said, "What are you looking at... Ogre Nose?"

It got so quiet I could hear Tormac blink. I continued.

"The last time I saw nostrils that big, dwarves were mining copper out of them."

Somebody laughed, somewhere. I think it was the barmaid.

"What!" Tormac said, hand falling to his blade.

"Ah, good idea. Get your nose picker out. I think I see a boulder... er... I mean a booger in there."

Chuckling ensued. Tormac leered around, bringing the chuckles to an abrupt stop.

"Or is that a toothpick? You could use it; I can see a halfling wedged in that gap between your teeth."

The entire room erupted.

"BRAHHHH—HA-HA-HA-HA!"

My chair clacked on the floor as I teetered forward and stood up, smiling.

Tormac's face was as red as his beard.

"You're going to die," he said through clenched teeth.

I fanned my hand in front of my face and said, "What happened with you and that half-orc out there? Did you eat him?"

Food fell from Ben's mouth. The entire tavern was doubled over now, except Tormac.

He swung.

I ducked.

"Let's settle this at the table," I said, dodging another swing. "My arm against yours."

Tormac stopped. An ugly smile started on his face. He was taller than me and as thick as an anvil, an over-sized man with the girth of a dwarf. I was strong. As strong as any man, but Tormac was more than that. He was a mountain. He pulled out a chair and sat down.

To the cry of cheers, I joined him. I looked at my right arm, my dragon arm. It was still well concealed. And Tormac, I'd known he was right handed when he reached for his sword. Of course, you could always tell by which side of the hip it rested on.

We locked hands.

"I win, you leave. You win, I leave." I scanned the crowd. Hope filled the eyes of some. "For good."

"Hah!" He nodded. "You'll be leaving alright," he growled, "in pieces. Your friend, too."

The barkeep raised his arms, hushing the crowd, then wrapped both hands around our knuckles. "That's odd," the barkeep said, looking at me, "you have very rugged skin."

"Get on with it," Tormac said, sneering. "I broke that last man's arm at the elbow, and I'm going to do worse to yours." He spat juice on the floor.

I winked.

His knuckles turned white as he began squeezing my hand. I'd never arm wrestled such a big, big man.

"Ready," the barkeeper started, "Set... Wrestle."

Tormac put his shoulder into it, shoving my arm down. The crowd roared as my arm bent towards the table. He was strong. Every bit as strong as he looked. A real brute who knew what he was doing.

"Come on, Dragon!" Ben shouted.

I stopped the descent inches from the table and heaved back. Tormac's eyes widened as I began pushing his arm back.

The lively crowd found new life.

"He's pushing Tormac back!"

"Impossible!" someone said.

I loved the attention. I put more dragon muscle into it.

"Hurk!"

I forced Tormac's arm past the starting point and back.

"Golden eyes is winning!"

Sweat dripped from Tormac's forehead and down his nose. The salty taste of my own sweat stung my eyes. I pushed his arm downward little by little.

"NO!" Tormac yelled. "No one beats me!"

The big man snorted in fury, shoving me back, up, up, to the starting point and backward. The entire tavern exploded with shouts of cheers and triumph.

I felt my own ears redden now. My dragon arm was aching. It was fast, but how strong was it, actually?

"Hang on, Dragon!" Ben shouted.

I was, barely. I fought back with everything I had, shoving the brute's arm back. We teetered from the starting point, back and forth. Part of the crowd was chanting...

"Tormac! Tormac! Tormac!"

The other part chanted...

"Dragon! Dragon! Dragon!"

I liked that, but it wasn't helping. Tormac shoved my arm back down, my knuckles barely an inch from the table.

Tormac was huffing and puffing. I held on. Arm throbbing, head aching, I fought on. I didn't care who you were, or what you did, I wasn't going to lose to anyone. Not while I lived. I shoved back with everything I had.

Tormac's eyes were full of triumph as he said, "You're finished!"

Something in the man's face angered me. An evil menace lurked there. A bully. A man of violence. A troublemaker. A thug for hire. A kidnapper. Maybe a murderer. I could see the truth. This man had preyed on the weak all his life. Used his gifts for evil, not good. My inner furnace was stoked.

"No, Tormac," I growled, "You're finished, not I!"

I shoved his arm upward. My dragon arm may not have been stronger, but it hadn't tired.

"No!" Tormac snarled.

Our wrists reached the starting point, and Tormac's arm when down.

The roaring crowd were jumping to their feet!

"Dragon! Dragon! Dragon!"

Tormac was shaking his head. Desperation filled his eyes. I took a quick deep breath and shoved everything into it.

"Nooooooo!" Tormac pleaded.

Wham!

I slammed his knuckles onto the table.

Chest heaving, I managed to say, "Time to go, Tormac!"

The crowd was all smiles as they helped the exhausted man out of his chair. His eyes were weak as he held his arm and was shoved towards the door with the crowd turning on him.

"Get out of here, Tormac! You stink the place up."

"Be a stranger!"

"Your mother's a bugbear!"

Raising my arm in the air and waving, I said, "That's enough, everyone. It's time to celebrate that he's gone."

The room fell silent.

I had a very bad feeling.

Someone gasped.

Others pointed.

Ben was pointing to his arm.

I looked at mine. My dragon arm had returned. Black as the night. Strong as steel. Beautiful as a black pearl. "Welcome back," I said.

"What manner of trickery is this!"

"He's a changeling!"

"A demon!"

"Fiend!"

I shot Ben a look and mouthed the words, "Get to the horses!"

Something as big as a ham and hard as a rock smacked into my face.

CHAPTER

26

TORMAC LEERED OVER ME WITH a face filled with fury. The man, I hated to admit, punched like an ogre. I could only imagine his booted heel descending towards my head would be twice as bad. Seeing spots, I rolled, gathered my feet, and sprung away. All the people who'd cheered me on moments before now screamed for my head.

"Cheater!"

"Changeling!"

"Kill him!"

"Bash his face in, Tormac!"

My, the tides change fast here.

A wooden tankard zinged past my head.

"Hold on!" I shouted, holding my arms up. "No one stated any rules! I've deceived no one. All I did was make a challenge to arm wrestle. Tormac Agreed! He lost. I won. Now back away!" I said, shaking my fist.

No one moved. I had a way of capturing people's attention like that.

One woman in the back, dressed in a black vest of leather armor, spoke up.

"Men in disguises can't be trusted! Get him!"

"But—"

The two big goons who sat at the bar seized my arms, locking them behind my back. By the look and smell of them, they were ugly brothers. And not just any type of brothers, but wrestlers, judging by their tattoos and scars and how they locked up my arms.

"Them's scales on his arms," one said.

"Never seen anything like that," said the other. "He's a monster of some sort!"

"A changeling! They're Evil; Burn him!" A woman shouted.

"He's a Demon! No one has gold eyes like that!"

"Hold him still!" Tormac said, rolling the sleeves up on his bulging arms.

"Tormac," I said, "you don't want to do—*oof*!"

The belly blow lifted me off my feet. I groaned.

"That..."

"Hit him once for me, Tormac!"

This can't be happening.

Whop!

I couldn't speak or breathe, and I swore my stomach was screaming from the other side of my back.

"Let's see if we can't take care of that smart mouth of yours."

He swung at me.

I jerked back, letting Tormac's fist hit one of the goons in the face.

"Watch it!" the goon said.

"Don't hit him in the face; he's too handsome!" one lady said, standing on a table wearing a helmet of lit candles on her head.

"Thank you!"

"No, hit him in the face!" one of the bowmen said.

"What is wrong with you people!"

Whop!

Tormac belted me in the stomach again, draining my strength from my head to my toes. I tried to fight, but the goons held me tight. They were like two pythons around my arms.

Whop! Whop!

Tormac laughed. "I told you you'd leave in pieces. *Pow!*

My teeth clattered in my face. *I have no business being here without Brenwar.* I'd settled for Ben the Lilly Pad, instead.

"Get him out of here!"

My body was moving, but not by a will of its own. I could hear the jeers as my knees were dragged across the floor.

"One!"

I felt the wind rushing past my ears.

"Two!"

My stomach was teetering inside my belly.

"Three!"

I was flying.

Crash!

Through a window I went, skipping over the cobblestone road. Struggling, I rolled onto my elbows, groaning when I touched my bleeding lip.

Everyone else spilled out of the doors or were gawping out the broken window.

I waved, saying, "Never let it be said The Ettin's Toe isn't full of charming hospitality."

Someone grabbed me by my shoulders and began pulling me up to my feet.

"Come on, Dragon."

Thankfully, it was Ben.

"Ah look, Bug Eyes has come to help his Demon friend."

"I'm not a Demon!" I said, grabbing my saddle. My leg wobbled in the stirrup as Ben shoved me up into the saddle.

It sounded like the entire city burst into laughter.

"Soldiers!" someone said, pointing.

"Tell them we've found a demon!"

I'd had enough already. I wasn't about to spend the night in jail. Even worse, I didn't need to be accused of being a demon by soldiers.

"Follow me, Ben!" I said, snapping my reigns.

Tormac waved and laughed as we galloped away.

From one side of the city to the other we'd gone when I came to a stop. Tired, aching and weary, I slid from my saddle and took a seat on a stone bench in a long-forgotten park. It was the Garrows. An old part of the city: quiet, discreet, creepy.

"I don't like this place," Ben said, eyes flitting around.

"It's not so bad in the daytime. See," I pointed.

Statues, fountains and gardens were everywhere, but shaded in grey and black, leaving an eerie feeling in the air.

"Come on, I've a friend I was going to check on anyway. Now's as good a time as any," I said, clutching my side.

"You alright?"

"Just a couple of broken ribs," I said through my teeth. They hurt. How many more beatings was I going to take over Ben? Everywhere he was came trouble.

"Sorry, Dragon. I know it's my fault. I should have stayed in the country."

Yes! Yes, you should have!

I didn't say it, however. It was his life. He had the right to do what he wanted. *But I think he'd start to think first more often if his ribs got busted, not mine.*

"This is it," I said, wrapping my reigns around a lantern post.

A single building, no wider than ten feet, stood in stark contrast to the larger buildings at its sides. There were no windows, only an open doorway with stairs leading up.

"You first," I said.

"What about the horses? We can't leave them here."

"Do you see any people?"

He looked around and shook his head.

"No."

"They'll be fine then. Trust me."

Standing at the bottom and looking up, a stairwell lit with small gemstone lights led to a doorway at the top.

"Is that?" Ben squinted, leaning forward, "a door?"

"Yes."

"It looks like it's a hundred yards away, more maybe."

"Then we better get started."

"But?"

I grabbed him by the collar and shoved him forward, saying, "Trust your feet, not your eyes this time."

Up the steps we went. One flight. Two Flights. Three Flights. Ten flights. My body ached with every step. Ben was huffing in front of me, eyes wide as saucers as he kept staring back.

"Keep going."

Twenty flights. Thirty flights. Ben stopped, hands on his knees, scrawny chest heaving, looking back.

"Dragon, what is going on? We aren't going anywhere!"

I cast a look over my shoulder. We were only one flight up from where we started, and I could see the tail of one horse swaying at the bottom.

I smiled. "We're almost there, Ben. Keep going."

Forty Flights.

"You did good back there, Ben."

"I did? How?" he said, wheezing.

I took a breath.

"You got the horses as you were told. You got out of harm's way like I said. If you hadn't, you might be dead, but you'd have been beaten up pretty bad still."

"But you got hurt."

"True, but I'm used to it." I squeezed his shoulder. "Up. We're almost there."

Fifty Flights.

Sweating like orcs, we both let out sighs of relief as we placed our feet on the landing at the top. It was marble, checkered in red and green, with the pattern of a mage on the bottom.

Both of us looked back. We still weren't any farther than when we started.

"I don't understand," Ben said, blinking.

"And you probably never will."

I reached past him and grabbed the ring of a gargoyle faced knocker.

Bang! Bang! Bang!

It echoed like thunder.

Ben stuck his fingers inside his ears.

"Who lives here?" he asked.

"Bay—*ulp*!"

The marble floor disappeared beneath our feet, and into the black we went.

CHAPTER

27

BRENWAR INSPECTED THE HORN HE had strapped around his shoulders. It was a horn carved from bone and gilded with brass and iron. It had two purposes. One was to make noise that was privy to dwarven ears. The other was to listen.

He took the small end and held it in his ear.

From a hilltop, he looked down on a small village. A few hundred residents lived there, and he knew that they, like most small towns, weren't welcoming to dwarves. He could hear voices, talking, and laughter, all of it as clear as a bell. After an hour of listening, he huffed. There were not sounds nor any talk of Nath Dragon. He slung the Dwarven Horn back over his shoulder.

"Two-Hundred years old and he still acts like a boy." He huffed. "And to think: he might live another thousand years."

Steady through the night he went, down the hill, through the trees. The sun and the rain and the days without sleep did not slow him. His brethren had been scattered towards all of the major cities, seeking for signs, yet none of them had sent word. The Dwarven Horn could send a sound over the air that only the dwarves with other horns could hear. It was dwarven magic, rare and ancient, more pertaining to their craft. One horn linked to another, forming a network of dwarven logic and mystic bounds. Normally, they were used in times of war.

"We should have found him by now," he muttered under his beard.

He knew Nath would be looking for dragons. His friend could be anywhere in the world. But it would be easier to find a needle in a haystack if that's what Nath wanted.

He combed his stubby fingers through his black beard, eyeing it.

"There better not be any pixies in there," he warned. "Hmmm... perhaps my thinking is wrong.

Should I be searching for Nath, or searching for dragons?" One would certainly lead to the other. "Perhaps the Clerics of Barnabus?"

What if the clerics had already trapped the man? Nath's father had said, "Keep him from the hands of Barnabus."

Many of the people in Nalzambor thought the clerics protected people from the dragons, unaware it was the other way around. But the clerics were a devious lot. Doing good deeds in the day and dark things in the night. Many were fooled by that, and many were not. Barnabus had been a great warrior who fought alongside the dragons long ago, but now his memory had been turned into something else. No longer a dragon warrior, as the seers said, but a dragon hunter.

Just thinking about it made Brenwar want to pull his beard out.

"If men were as honest as dwarves, we'd never have all these problems."

Miles from the next settlement, he put the horn to his ear and listened hour after hour in the pouring rain.

"Nothing," he grumbled, then traveled on.

CHAPTER

28

"Baaaaaaaaaaaaay-Zog!" I screamed as I fell. I couldn't even see Ben, but I could hear him in the darkness.

"HEEEEELP MEEEEEEEE!"

There was light.

Thud!

Pain.

Thud!

And Ben landing on top of me. Whatever hadn't hurt before hurt now, and everything else was worse. I pushed Ben's groaning body off of me and rose to my feet.

The room was filled with brilliant lights, colorful cushions and silk drapes. The incense was so strong I could almost taste it.

"Whew! What is that?" Ben said, fanning his face.

I jerked him up to his feet.

"Just relax, Ben. He'll be offended if you don't."

"Who?" he said, pinching his nose.

Shuffling towards the center of the room, I said, "Bayzog, I know you wish to greet, else I would have landed on a harder floor."

"How big is this place?" Ben said, spinning around. "It was just a tiny building."

It was a huge room, like the ballrooms in the castles. A large sphere of square cut crystals twinkled above. The floor was hardwood, the room a rectangle, with a fireplace of burning logs in every corner. Huge cushions were scattered all over the room, and in the middle was a large square table, waist high and no chairs. Bayzog stood there, staring down into a book the size of ten. He turned and spoke in a strong dark voice.

"If I'd known you were coming, I'd have left a pillow out... maybe." He bowed. "Unwelcome, Nath Dragon."

"Not glad to be here," I replied.

Bayzog was black-haired, small-framed, but sturdy. He wore a red wizard's tunic embroidered with arcane signs and symbols. Everything was impeccable about his character, and his violet eyes were bright, deep, probing. He was part-elven, rich and full of mystery.

I extended my dragon hand.

"My, how eerie are those? He grabbed my arm and started needling it with his fingers. "Nath, I've never seen black dragon scales before. But I've heard about them."

"You have?"

He grabbed a clear glass lens the size of a fist off of his table and took a closer look.

"Certainly."

"Sorry, of course you have." I said. "What can you tell me about them?"

"Hold on," he said, glancing over Ben. "Hmmm… I see you've replaced Brenwar… obviously a good choice." He grabbed Ben's hand, blinking.

"Nath," Ben said, pulling away, but Bayzog held him fast, "what is he doing?"

"Just be still, Ben. If he wanted to harm you, you'd know already."

Studying Ben though, Bayzog said, "My, this one's nothing but trouble, isn't he?"

"Er… what do you mean? I'm not trouble." Ben looked at me. "Am I?"

I shrugged.

Ben tried to pull away again, but Bayzog closed his eyes and held him fast.

"Hmmm… could be good… could be bad." He released Ben. "He needs more time, Dragon." Opening his eyes, Bayzog said, "And some polishing up will do. Sasha!"

A lovely woman, all human, appeared in white robes.

"Sasha," I said, unable to contain my smile, "It's been too long."

She brushed her auburn locks of hair from her blue eyes and said, "It's good to see you, too, Dragon." She took Ben by the hand and said, "Come along."

Ben, stupefied, said nothing as she led him, smiling, out of the room. I felt like a boulder had rolled off my chest.

"Unthank you, Bayzog."

"Unwelcome, and don't worry; she'll find suitable stitchings, but you'll have to do the rest," Bayzog said.

"I'm not doing anything. I agreed to bring him to the city. Promised him a meal and good rest. He's off to the Legionnaires after this."

"No he isn't," Bayzog said, thumbing through the book's huge pages.

"Yes he is," I objected. "And if you like him so much, he can stay with you."

"Did you come here to argue with me, or did you come for my help?"

I came to get answers. When it came to dragons, Bayzog could deliver. He knew almost as much about dragons as I did.

"Alright, what's in that big book of yours?"

Somehow, Bayzog had everything he ever learned in one book. The Book of Many Pages. It was one big book, or tome rather, on one big table, accompanied with magic ink and quill.

"You know, I have many things in this book. Stories, legends, maps, spells, histories. Everything I've ever learned or heard is right here."

"How do you add more pages?"

His cheerless face brightened a little.

"It can add as many as I need. That's why I made the book."

Looking at it, I said, "That's a lot of pages. How do you know where to look for something? Where do you start?"

"Book, black dragon scales."

The pages came to life, stirring the air, ruffling my hair before they came to a stop.

"Impressive." I squinted. The words would shift and move as I read. I leaned away, pinching the bridge of my nose, and stepped back. "How do you read that? It hurts my eyes."

He showed a wry smile.

"Right. I understand, Wizard. So, what does it say?"

"The color of scales on black dragons," he said, running his finger down the page. "Rare. No black dragons seen since the last dragon war."

He closed the book and stepped away.

"What did you do that for?"

"Nath, tell me what happened. How did you get that arm? You're supposed to get scales, but black ones?"

I'd been friends with Bayzog over a hundred years, and he knew my story and who my father was. He was fascinated by dragons, but in a good way. So, I told him about the people I killed in Orcen Hold and the last conversation I had with my father.

"But," I showed him the white spot on my hand, "I think I'm turning things around. I even saved a steel dragon and found a Thunderstone."

Bayzog's eyes lit up.

"Do you still have it?"

"No, the steel dragon swallowed it."

Pacing back and forth, Bayzog said, "That's a shame."

"Losing the Thunderstone?"

"Yes to that. No," Bayzog frowned, "to never going home again. I know how that feels."

The brief moment of emptiness in his eyes left me feeling empty again as well.

"So, Dragon, what is your plan?"

"I want to rescue dragons. Many of them at once. That will do it! I know the more I free, the more I can be cured. I know you can help me find them. I need to find a flock of dragons!" I grabbed his shoulder. "You have to help me, Bayzog."

"Ahem."

Sasha, now wearing loose fitting robes, re-entered the room with a pleasant smile on her face.

"Where's Ben?" I asked.

"He's taking a nap," she said, drifting to Bayzog's side.

"A Nap?"

"The young man is tired, Dragon." Her blue eyes flared at me. "And *you* should do the same."

Suddenly, my lids became heavy, and I couldn't fight the yawn.

"Ah Sasha," Bayzog wrapped his arm around her waist and smiled, "always trying to comfort her guests."

Covering my yawn, I fought back and said, "No, not this time, Sasha. Last time, you put me down for two days. I appreciate your concern, but your efforts won't work on me this time. I'm ready."

"Ah Dragon, you know she can't help herself. She knows what's best for you, you know. And you look tired. I've never seen a tired dragon before."

I felt tired. My jaw ached, and my face felt swollen. And with every little movement I felt my cracked ribs inside. *And I remember the last time I took a long nap and what happened when I woke up.*

"Come on, Dragon," Sasha pleaded.

A chair slid across the room and stopped beside me.

Magi didn't get guests very often, so when you came, they expected you to stay awhile.

"I'll sit, but you, Bayzog, need to tell me what you know. I saw that look in your eyes before your book closed."

Sasha looked at him and said, "What is it, Bayzog? You can't keep secrets from our friend."

"Please, Dear," he said. "It's a delicate matter. "

She pulled away, fists dropping to her hips.

"Too delicate for my ears?"

Bayzog's hand recoiled to his chest as he pleaded.

"Certainly not, My Love."

I liked Sasha. She was all about the truth, which was uncommon for a wizard. And as I've said, wizards, magic users, and necromancers could not be trusted. Not even an old friend like Bayzog. When it came to power, they had their weaknesses. Sasha, however, wasn't like that. What she lacked in Bayzog's power, she made up for with integrity.

"Well?" she said, tapping her bare foot on the floor.

Bayzog flittered his fingers and muttered the strangest words.

Where one fireplace blazed in the corner, cushioned chairs and a sofa accompanied it now.

"Shall we?" he said, arm extended to the corner.

I limped over and slumped into the furniture.

"It would have been nice if I'd landed on this sofa, rather than your hard floor."

Sasha readied me a drink from the serving station.

"Coffee, Tea or—"

"Wizard's Water would be fine."

She smiled, saying, "Excellent choice."

She poured a red melon-colored drink in a crystal glass and served us all.

Bayzog hoisted up his glass and said, "To old friends."

"And dead enemies," I added.

I drank. Smooth, bitter and invigorating, I felt my mind and body begin to rest. Tea, Coffee, wine, Ale did little for me, but the wizard's magic elixir did much. It filled me, refreshed me and cleared my senses.

"Ah… I needed that." I clopped my glass on the table and leaned towards Bayzog. "So, tell me what you saw, Wizard."

Sasha leaned his way as well, her beautiful eyes intent on his face.

"Dragon, listen, it's not something that I think is worth mentioning. I can't confirm any of it."

"Bayzog, tell him!"

Bayzog, the epitome of poise, slumped back in his chair, face drawn up with worry.

Sasha gasped, "Bayzog, where are your manners?"

He sighed, one eye open, one on my arm.

"Dragon, your arm, its curse is much worse than suspected."

"How much worse can it be?" I said. "And besides," I showed him the white scales in the palm of my hand, "I think it's getting better."

Sasha took my hand in hers and traced her fingers over it.

"I've never felt live dragon scales before, at least not on a man," she said. "They're beautiful."

That made me feel good. After all, how could something beautiful be bad? I knew I was good.

"Sasha, please, can't you tell he's enough in love with himself already?" He paused, looking at me. "You like it, Dragon. Don't you? The raw power it contains."

I reached over, refilling my glass of Wizard's Water.

"Wouldn't you, Bayzog?"

"Power, yes. Cursed power… no. Listen, have you ever seen a black dragon before?"

I shook my head.

"There's a reason for that," he said, sitting back up in his chair. "They're all dead. They all died in the last dragon war."

"So?" I shrugged. "I'm sure many dragons died off in the last dragon war."

Rising to his feet, Bayzog walked over to the fire, rubbing his hands.

"How much did your father tell you about the Great Dragon War?"

I had to think about that. My father had told me many things, but he never spoke about the dragon wars, and I'd never really given them much thought until now.

"I see," Bayzog continued. "Just so you know, legends say that it was the black dragons that started the Great Dragon War."

I fell back in the sofa, glancing at Sasha's eyes. I could see she was worried.

"And my father killed them?" I asked.

Bayzog shook his head slightly, saying, "We don't know that _he_ killed them. Any of the dragons could have killed them. But, they were the cause. They were the solution."

I pulled my arm from Sasha. It was no wonder my father was so furious with me. Black dragon's scales. A reminder of the war. But why did I have them? I was good, after all.

"Bayzog, how come I've never heard of this: the black dragons, the war? You'd think I would have crossed paths with it by now."

"There are legends and histories, some true, some not, in some cases neither, others both."

"That's not really an answer."

"Well, the Great Dragon War might be over, but the evil remains. Much of it is hidden from our eyes, but some of it is right in front of us, mixing the truth with lies."

I took another drink because I was feeling weary again.

"Like the Clerics of Barnabus?" I sighed.

"Do you know the legend of Barnabus, Dragon?" Sasha said.

"Well enough, I suppose."

"Oh, show him, Bayzog. Show him how the story unfolded." She batted her eyes at him. "Please."

He frowned at first and then smiled, saying, "You know I can never tell you no."

She huffed. "You tell me no all the time."

"Only when I study."

She whispered in my ear.

"That's all the time."

He brushed his black hair past the point of his elven ear and said, "I heard that."

Then with a twitch of his fingers, the flames swirled into a sea of color. In the flames, the image of a mighty man appeared, fully armored, carrying a great sword over his shoulder.

"Barnabus," Bayzog said. "One of the few Legionnaires who aided the good dragons in battle."

The image of Barnabus was doused in flames as a dragon appeared from behind.

"I love this part," Sasha said, hugging my arm.

Barnabus turned and ran his sword right through its heart. The flames roared out, and only Barnabus remained. You could see nothing of the man, only his armored metal shell.

"Barnabus, the histories say, killed the last black dragon. It was his bravery and his sword, Stryker, that ended the war. But the Clerics of Barnabus would have Nalzambor believe differently. Under his name, they claim to protect us from all kinds of dragons, claiming they are evil, dangerous. We know better, but most people don't. They fear the dragons. They loathe them. They capture them and sell them from the temples of Barnabus."

"Oh, I hate those clerics!" Sasha said, reddening. "I'd kill them all if you'd let me."

"It's not our fight, Dearest."

I eyed Bayzog, saying, "What's that supposed to mean?"

Holding his hands up, he added, "At least not yet. Dragon, I'm fascinated by you and your kind, but it's the people I protect, not dragons. That's your charge. But," he bowed, "I'll help you with whatever you can do."

I felt that Bayzog was holding back. Wizards always did.

"Tell me where the dragons are?"

"I can't help much there, Dragon. They're hiding. The Clerics have their ears, and they have been as thick as wolves' fur out there. And then you, you of all people, come strolling into this city, knowing full well they've a bounty on you."

I jumped to my feet.

"How did you know that?"

He rolled his eyes.

I threw my arms up.

"Of course! Of course you knew! Alright Bayzog, if you don't want to help, just say so."

I slammed my glass down on the table.

Sasha grabbed me, saying, "Dragon, behave yourself. You know Bayzog means well."

"Does he? Sorry Sasha, but I don't have time for games. I took the risk coming here certain you would help me out. But all you offer is fairy tales and water." I glared at Bayzog. "Let me out of this crazy place." I scoured the room but saw no door.

"Calm yourself, Dragon," Bayzog demanded. "You need rest, and your fresh wounds need to be healed. Have a few hours of peace. I'll see if I can find something, and you can leave when I do."

"Let me out now, Wizard!"

"You're a guest; you can leave whenever you wish. But what about your friend, Ben? Will you abandon him as well?"

I'd forgotten about Ben, but I didn't care. I just wanted out of there.

"Yes. Goodbye, Sasha. I hope you stay well."

She kissed me on the cheek and said, "Be careful."

I shot Bayzog another look, and then I closed my eyes. Remembering how this went, I thought of the front door. I opened my eyes and saw the gargoyle knocker. Behind me, the stairs. Maybe I'd been hasty. Maybe I'd been rude, but I had things to do.

I stomped down the stairs.

"I don't need your help anyway."

"Bayzog! What is wrong with you?" Sasha said. "Dragon is our friend, and he needs us."

He sighed as he took her by the hands and said, "Yes, he does need us, but we cannot help him. Only he can help himself. If he can't … we'll all need help."

"What do you mean?"

Bayzog strolled over to his massive table and opened his book.

"I read something that I can only assume is true."

Sasha gathered beside him, eyes intent of the pages.

"What does it say? You know I can't read it yet."

He said nothing.

"Bayzog, what does it say!" she demanded.

He cleared his throat.

"The ancient scribes say…

And the black dragons were vanquished, and peace was on Nalzambor until the black dragons returned. So it was. So it has been. A Circle. And the last black dragon shall envelope the world forever.

He closed the book and finished, "… this is much bigger than us. I feel for his father. I feel for the world."

CHAPTER

30

"**B**LASTED WIZARDS!"

I wasn't happy. I wasn't mad, but I wasn't happy. Bayzog hadn't really done anything wrong, other than disappoint me. He was holding something back, something big, something bad—about me; I could feel it in my bones. So I wandered, alone on horseback, through the streets from one side of the city to the other.

"What to do?" I mumbled, drawing a few stares from passersby.

The night wasn't much different than the day in Quintuklen, just darker and quieter. I didn't care for it. I liked watching the people, but tonight, I wanted to be alone. I wanted to sulk. But I knew better. Instead, I headed for the wall, near where we came in.

"Should I go or not?" I said. I hated to leave empty handed. I came here to find out about the dragons, and I couldn't leave without something.

Above, the moon was full like a brilliant pearl, casting dark shadows in every corner. I had an idea. I just needed to find the Clerics of Barnabus. Like Brenwar would say, "Face the problem axe up and head on!"

The Clerics of Barnabus were the problem. Find them; find the dragons. They'd been looking; I'd been hiding. I decided to take my problem straight to them.

"If I were a cleric, where would I be?" I was gazing up at the moon when it hit me. "The Sanctuary." There were always clerics there.

It was early morning when I arrived at the bubbling fountains just outside The Sanctuary's gates. Within, monuments and statues were covered with dew, and clerics in a colorful variety of robes were milling about. The Clerics of Barnabus were easy to spot, and within seconds I spotted a few tattooed foreheads. My first urge was to gallop over there, snatch one, ride off, and beat the information out of him. But, I donned my cloak and pulled my hood over my head. Leaving my horse, I moved in.

About twenty feet away from them, I took a seat on a bench, head down and listening. There was no loud talking in The Sanctuary, but there was a lot of whispering. And much of it was in a language you couldn't understand. The Clerics had their ancient dialects in which they spoke, but I'd picked up on Barnabus words over the years, sort of. But it was Common I heard.

"We've many to sell. Small ones. Dead or alive, as you will," one Cleric of Barnabus said, speaking to a Cleric in stone-colored robes. I could feel my blood run hot. The Stone Clerics drew their power from the rock, and they weren't noble. According to them, the stone was neither good nor bad, only the one who threw it.

"I've no need of such things."

"Any word on dragons?" the Cleric of Barnabus asked. "We aim to keep the world safe from the menace. Keep them under control we must."

"You can tell those tales to the regular folk, but I know better. Most dragons are as good as you are evil. Be gone with you, I say."

"Pardons and Blessings, Stone Wielder." The Cleric bowed and slowly backed away.

Good for him. I'd have to remember that. The Clerics of Stone were neutral, but they weren't fools. It was good to know.

The Clerics of Barnabus split up, spreading the word about dragons from one group to the other. One of them had the attention of a small group in gold lace with heads hidden under their purple hoods. I didn't recognize the order, but there must have been a hundred different ones in Quintuklen. I got up, stooped down, and picked my way through the people. It was getting crowded.

Ten feet away, back turned, I was leaning on a monument when an odd feeling overcame me. Peering around, I caught the eyes of another cleric of Barnabus who quickly glanced away. They couldn't have seen me, could they? I didn't exactly fit in, but there were all sorts of robed figures and cloaked characters in the Sanctuary. I turned away, took a moment, and glanced back. He was gone.

"We have a Yellow Belly, with pollen breath that turns one to stone," I overheard one cleric say. "Some of the dragon tykes that don't have breath yet, they make fine pets, when broken."

I bunched up my fist and fought the urge to walk over there and punch him in the face. I could barely stand it. *Patience. Look. Listen. Learn.* I might explode first.

"Where do we meet?" the cleric in the purple said.

"Five leagues west, in the Crane's Neck. After the sun sets tomorrow. Gold only."

"Agreed."

That's all I needed to hear. As I turned to head back to my horse, it felt like a bucket of ice water hit me when someone said, "Dragon!"

CHAPTER
31

"DELICIOUS, SIMPLY DIVINE," FINNIUS SAID, wiping his mouth with a cloth napkin.

Good food was hard to come by in the Temple ruins, but the lizardmen were excellent hunters, and the acolytes, when prompted, were decent cooks.

Thumping his fist on his chest, he burped as an acolyte refilled his goblet with wine.

"At least the cellar kept the bottles in order all these centuries, and it would be a shame for it all to go to waste, wouldn't it?" he said, eyeing the cage that sat on the small table.

The pixlyn woman was there: tiny, pink, knees drawn up, head down.

"Oh, you can speak to me, little faerie. As a matter of fact, I'd like to hear you sing. They say the song of the faeries is a beautiful and magical thing, but I've never heard it."

Finnius pulled the cage closer and peered in.

"What do you say?"

She didn't budge.

He slammed his fist on the table.

"SING!"

She flinched, then rubbed her tiny fists in her eyes, sniffling.

"Oh, how adorable." He tapped the cage. "Little Pixlyn, sing for me, else I'll pluck your husband's wings off when he arrives."

Her bee wings buzzed as she hovered up, nodding her head.

"Oh, I have your attention now, don't I? Sing, Little One. I want to feel the mystic words you hold. Sing to me," he beckoned, "share your powers... or die."

Her tiny little mouth opened up, and beautiful words flowed out. Not words men could recognize, but a beautiful, ancient language. Harmonious and Delightful.

Finnius sat back and sighed, letting the music fill him from head to toe.

"Wonderful," he muttered. He'd been weary, but no more. His once spent energies from his mission now recharged. His mind refreshed and cleared.

"Excellent," he muttered, slumping back, tears forming in his eyes. *So pure, so good, so amazing.* It was nothing like he'd felt before.

Something banged into the pixlyn cage.

Finnius lurched up, rubbing his watery eyes.

"What?"

The male pixlyn was back.

Finnius shook his head, saying, "What is the meaning of this, Pixlyn?"

The little man's tiny mouth was a buzz of words.

"I see. Hmm... Excellent, I see. Nath Dragon is on his way already." He clapped his hands together. "My, won't the High Priestess be pleased. Tell me. Tell me about it all."

Finnius muttered a spell and sprinkled powder over the pixlyn.

The words of the pixlyn were high and garbled momentarily, and then a sound of man came forth.

"It took me no time to find the man. I told your men who he was and where to go. Your men spread word as I watched. The man overheard the conversation about the dragons. Your men spoke to your men in disguise. The man you want believed it. He and them travel this way now."

"Hah!" He slapped his knee. "Keep me posted then, Pixlyn! Go! Spy!"

The tiny winged man flew into his face and said, "My mate?"

"Yes, well, she'll be quite alright," Finnius flashed a wicked smile, "assuming she keeps her wings, assuming you do as you are told and I don't have to clip her wings. Now go!"

CHAPTER
32

BRENWAR'S STOMACH GROWLED. HE COULDN'T remember the last time he was so hungry. His horse bent its neck towards the stream water and began to drink. His stomach growled again.

"Ah, be quiet, will you?" he said, reaching into his pack and withdrawing peppers and bread. He took a bite. "That might hold you, until we find Dragon, that is."

He hadn't eaten since he left, or slept either. He rubbed his mount's neck, watching the trout swimming upstream. He'd like to fish, but he didn't have time.

"It's a shame you horses don't eat fish," he said. "You don't know what you're missing."

The horse nickered, raising its neck. Brenwar got a sour apple from his saddle bag and fed the horse. At some point, the horse would need rest; he knew. And stopping in the next village might be in order.

"I hate stopping," he grumbled.

"Me too," a deep voice responded from the nearby trees.

Brenwar jumped from his horse and rolled over the ground, rising up with his war hammer ready.

"Who said that?"

The woods were tall, green and quiet. Only the wind and rippling waters hit his ears.

"Easy, Dwarf," a tall figure said, stepping from behind the trees. "Remember me?"

Brenwar squinted his eyes beneath his bushy black brows.

"Bah! You're one of those fat bellied elves."

"And you're one of those short-legged orcs," the Wilder Elf replied.

"I see you've got a death wish, don't ya?" Brenwar said, pointing his weapon. "Come then, I'll make a fine grave for you!"

Eyes twinkling in the light, Shum laughed, like a man laughs at a child. With the grace of the elves and girth of a large man, he approached, swords silent on his hips. He clasped his hands over his belly and said, "I mean you no harm, Dwarf."

"That may well be, but I can't say the same."

Brenwar moved in, taking a chop at Shum of the Roaming Rangers' legs.

The elf sprang away.

"Stop!" Shum held out his arms. "I'm not here to fight, as much as I'd like to teach you a lesson."

"A lesson!" Brenwar rushed.

Shum jumped back, Brenwar's axe clipping his cloak.

Brenwar would fight anyone, any place, any time. Especially an elf. They bothered him. Not so much as orcs and giants, but still, they were elves. Dwarves and elves: both on the side of good, but unable to get along since the days their races were young.

"You would strike me down when I'm not even defending myself," Shum said, aghast.

Brenwar swung.

Shum dived.

"I would."

He chopped.

Shum rolled.

Brenwar kept coming, swinging, chopping.

Shum was off balance as he waded into the waters.

"Stop it, Dwarf! I apologize," he said, holding his arms out.

Brenwar swung his war-axe into water-laden log where Shum's toe had been.

"For what!"

"Calling you a 'short-legged' orc?"

Brenwar stopped and pointed at him.

"No one calls a dwarf an orc and lives."

"Well, you shouldn't call me a fat bellied elf."

Brenwar's black eyebrows cocked over his eyes.

"But you *are* a fat-bellied elf."

Shum huffed, dragging himself out of the water, towering over Brenwar, and replied, "And proud of it." He extended his arm. "Can you talk, Brenwar?"

They bumped forearms, outside, then inside.

"Aye," Brenwar said, "what is it you want?"

"Nath Dragon."

Brenwar walked over to his horse and fed it another apple.

"Why?"

Shum's jaw tightened.

"I think we need his help finding our King again."

Brenwar pulled himself up onto his horse.

"I don't know where he is."

"But you're looking for him; I know. I've been following you since you left Morgdon. I was waiting for him, but he never came, only you. I've been trying to figure out what was going on, but I didn't realize you'd lost him until now."

Brenwar stiffened in his saddle, saying, "What do you mean, days? I got attacked by brigands, and you didn't help!"

"And you handled them quite well. I respect your skills, Brenwar, and I'd have aided if needed."

"Humph! What makes you think Dragon can help you find your king? You're the best trackers in the land, aren't you? Why would you need Nath?"

Shum ran his long finger back and forth on his chin and said, "It's just a theory really, but we think they are linked. They have the same needs."

"Pah," Brenwar started leading his horse away. "They aren't linked. He's an elf or an ape, and Dragon is a man, or a dragon. He shall tend to his affairs, the dragons; you attend to yours, the elves or... er the apes."

"We're all linked whether we admit it or not. Dragon has a curse. My King is cursed. It's a common evil they share."

"It's your king, not mine, not his. And, Nath is not evil, and I can't say the same for your king." Brenwar waved as he galloped off. "Goodbye, Fat Bellied Elf!"

Shum shook his head, watching him go as he said, "I can walk faster than that little horse can run." He took off at a trot. "You're getting my help whether you want it or not, Dwarf. Too many lives depend on it."

CHAPTER
33

"**D**RAGON!"

I whirled, knocking a man over. It was Ben. Despite the bewildered look on his face, I could have killed him.

"What are you doing here?" I exclaimed under my breath, lifting him up and with haste guiding him away.

"Bayzog—"

"Keep it down, you idiot," I hissed through my teeth.

Every eye in the sanctuary was looking.

"Sorry, Drag—"

I squeezed his arm.

"Quiet, will you?"

"Ow," he whined as I dragged him to where my horse was, as discreetly as I could.

His horse was next to mine.

"How did you do that?" I said, grabbing the reigns and getting out of The Sanctuary.

"Bayzog did it, how I don't know. I was talking to him, and he said you'd be here, and I said, 'Where?' and poof, here I was. He said you needed to come back, that he had some information for you that could help." He rubbed the back of his head. "Sorry, Dragon, did I do wrong again?"

"Get on your horse," I ordered.

I was angry. If Ben had shown up seconds earlier, it could have ruined everything, and I wasn't so sure it hadn't. When I glanced back, all the bald heads and purple robes were gone.

"Great."

I led; Ben followed.

"Are we going back to Bayzog's?"

"No."

"He said you'd say that, but he also said, um…" he looked up into the sky, "It's your burial, not mine."

"Figures." *Lousy wizard!* "Listen Ben, you didn't do wrong, but you aren't coming along, either. I'm taking you to the Legionnaires to be with your uncle."

Ben shook his head.

"No! I don't want to go. Please, I want to stay with you! I'm ready, see?" He pulled his cloak open, revealing a well-fitted tunic of leather armor. A nice sword and dagger were belted at his sides. I could tell by the pommels they were elven made. He even had boots to go with it.

"So, you think if you get some armor that fits and sharp and shiny blades that makes you a soldier? You haven't even had any training, Ben. You almost died once on the way up here, and now I'm heading into the mouth of danger. You think you're ready for that? Do you?"

Biting his lip, he fingered the pommel on his sword.

"We'll just go back and see what Bayzog says. It was important."

"No, Ben. I'm on my own from here. Now don't follow me anymore."

Good luck or bad luck Ben was, according to Bayzog. The part-elven wizard had a way of reading people.

"Bayzog said I should come, no matter what."

I stopped my mount.

"Really Ben, how well do you know Bayzog? You barely spent a minute with him in there."

"Well, it's not him so much as," he smiled, "Sasha. Ooh … She is so beautiful."

"And troublesome, Ben." I got closer and checked his blades. "Fine steel for a wizard to keep. What else did they give you?" I reached into his belt pouch. Two potion vials were within. "What do these do?"

"He said I'd know when to take them."

I slapped Ben upside the head.

"Ow!"

"You don't know when to do anything!"

I'd had enough and headed for the wall. It was time to make way for the Crane's Neck, and I didn't care whether or not Ben followed.

"So be it, Ben. It's only your life."

The trip was long. Not because it was far, but because my tongue was tired from trying to convince Ben not to go. He wouldn't have any part of it, however.

"It's my life; I'll do what I want with it," he'd decided, saying it over and over, with his chin up.

Oddly, he was starting to remind me of Brenwar—aside from his shivering in the rain.

The Crane's Neck wasn't hard to find. It was a valley of enormous rocks, some of which looked to be left over from a battle between the giants. I followed a faint trail over the brush and climbed up a rocky cleft that overlooked the Crane's Neck. It was a rock, stretching fifty feet in height, shaped like a long flowing neck. The setting sun peeked from behind the dark clouds, shining on the beak-like peak at the top.

"Lie down. Be quiet. Don't move." I said to Ben, lying down myself.

Ben did. I actually wanted to thank him. It wasn't very often that he did what I said.

"It'll be a few hours before dusk, so we'll just lie low for now. Got anything to eat?"

Ben shook his head.

"Great. I'm surprised Bayzog didn't prepare you better. Are you sure one of those vials isn't a bottle of Tasty Wonders?"

He scrunched up his face, shook his head and said, "I don't think so."

"Well, that's too bad. Those are pretty good, and they can hold you over for days. Stupid wizard. You'd think he'd have better prepared you." I looked at him. "Right?"

He nodded, his eyes focused on the Crane's Neck, lying on his belly sopping wet. The rain would start and stop, between drizzle and heavy drops. He shivered, even though it wasn't that cold. At least he was quiet. At least he obeyed for once, and that was a comforting thought.

Rain pelting my face, I sat alongside him thinking. How many dragons did the clerics have? They'd spoken of at least three, but there could be more. I rubbed my dragon arm, imagining if my scales might turn white after I freed them. I could go home then. I wanted to see my father more now than ever, and I couldn't remember ever wanting to see his giant dragon's head so much before. I pulled my hood over my head, sat down, and waited.

A few paths led past the Crane's Neck, some narrow and some wide, between the rocks and ridges. There wasn't much else in the valley, either, just a small variety of trees and bushes, enough to be hospitable to the critters. Another hour had passed when I heard Ben's stomach growl.

"Still glad you came?"

He didn't say anything.

It was getting annoying.

"Alright Ben, you've made your point: you can be quiet."

He rolled over and smiled, saying, "See, I told you I could be a good soldier."

"Indeed," I said, rolling my eyes. "Well, there's no sense in having your ravenous stomach give us away. It could wake up a drunk bugbear. Run down to the horses and fetch the rations hanging from my saddle."

He quickly ambled over the rocks, down and out of sight. I had to admit: I was hungry, too. I rubbed my ribs. Tormac had given me a good walloping, and my jaw still felt loose. It was a shame; he'd be a good ally if he wasn't such a bad man. The world was full of men like him, but there was always something worse. The orcs. The ogres. The goblins. The bugbears and gnolls. You'd think men would act better than them, but often—too many times—they disappointed me. Their short lives made them particularly greedy.

Ben shuffled back over the rocks and fell to his knees.

"Here you go, Dragon," he said, holding out a small sack.

"Eat, Ben."

He reached in the bag and dug in. I grabbed a bite as well.

Ben shook a canteen in my face.

I took it and drank, handed it back, and said, "Drink, that dwarven bread is hard to get down sometimes."

"Kind of bitter," he said, talking a swallow. "But I feel full already."

"Brenwar would kill me if he knew what I was doing."

"Who?" Ben said, looking up at me.

"Oh, sorry Ben, just a friend of mine, a dwarf. He's usually with me on days like this, telling me what I can and cannot do. Or what I should, or should not do."

"Kind of like you do me, huh?"

I felt like I'd swallowed a bug. I was nothing like Brenwar.

"Just eat."

Down in the valley, about an hour later, I noticed a small group of figures coming from behind the Crane's Nest.

"Get down, Ben!"

From our bellies, we could see the Clerics of Barnabus, five of them in all, and a small cage. I had a pretty good idea who was in that cage, too. A dragon. Two broader figures emerged with spears and armor. Lizardmen. I could feel Ben tense up at my side.

"It'll be alright. Don't move, Ben. Don't make a sound."

The five Clerics faced the path leading from the east. The lizardmen began searching the nooks and crevices in the area. The rain became a steady pour, and I lost sight of the lizardmen.

"Not good, Ben. Not good."

CHAPTER

34

INSTINCT. SOMETIMES IT WAS THE only explanation as to why some men lived while others died. My own had bailed me out many times, but I wasn't sure about Ben as he kept looking over at me. It takes time to develop instincts in some; others it's quite natural. Some don't get it at all.

Keeping my voice low, I said, "What are you thinking?"

"There's probably more of them, isn't there?"

"Good." I was reassured. He wasn't stupid; he had some savvy to him. "Maybe a couple, just keep an eye out."

I rose up to my knee and readied Akron.

Snap. Clatch. Snap.

"You going to shoot them?" Ben asked.

"Hopefully at some point in time, but right now I'm just being prepared."

"Oh."

I wasn't really sure why I readied my bow. I just did. Something bothered me. Tired, swollen, and stubborn, I felt a little off, and there was a nagging warning bell behind my eyes. Peering through the rain, I looked for any sign, anything odd.

"Can they smell us?" Ben asked.

It was a good question. *Good for him.*

"They're pretty good trackers, but not like most hunters, and their snouts are so, so. It's the orcs you have to watch out for. But, this rain keeps our scent down, plus we're downwind. So, I'd say we're safe for now."

The farther the sun dipped, the colder it seemed as we waited. The lizardmen reappeared about an hour later and gathered near the clerics.

"Dragon, I see something coming," Ben pointed.

I could barely make out the purple through all the rain, but it was the clerics from Quintuklen, riding on horseback.

My heart raced as they greeted one another and revealed the covered cage.

"What is it?" Ben asked.

Despite the heavy rain, I could make out a small white dragon inside. Not just any white dragon, but a long-tailed white. They weren't very big dragons either, but one of the smaller breeds.

"A dragon. A powerful one at that."

Below, I could see no coins were exchanged, and the talk had stopped. The Clerics of Barnabus led, and The Clerics from Quintuklen followed.

"Are we going to rescue it?"

"Don't you worry about that," I said, grabbing his shoulders. "Now listen to me Ben, and listen good."

He was all ears.

"Stay with the horses. There's plenty of food with them. If I'm not back in two days, go back to Quintuklen and see Bayzog and Sasha. Just tell them what you know, not that it will matter."

"But, I want to go."

I squeezed his shoulders until he grimaced.

"I'm counting on you. We can't follow those men on the horses. They'll catch us. We can't leave the horses now either, can we?"

He shook his head, eyes down saying, "No."

"What you are doing might not seem important, Ben, but it is. It is to me and to the horses. This is what a good soldier does."

He frowned, saying, "But Bayzog gave me these weapons, and potions too." He unsheathed his dagger and stuck it in my face. "See?"

In a single motion, I twisted it away and jammed it back in his sheath.

"Yes, Ben. Perfect weapons and potions to protect yourself and the horses with." I slapped him on the shoulder. "Remember what I said, and take care, Ben."

As he started to object, I turned and leapt off the ridge, hopping down from one boulder to the other like a Mountain Cat. When I made it to the bottom, I looked up and waved.

He was gaping.

"Sorry Ben, I can't have you following me, now can I?"

Off into the rain I went. I had monsters to stop and dragons to save.

The sun had set by the time I traveled the first league, and the trail was already faint. Ahead, I could see one lizardman had drifted back, waiting. It was a common tactic.

The lizardmen made good guards and soldiers, ferocious soldiers, but not as loyal as hounds. They were known to take bribes now and again. No, the lizardmen were the orcs of reptiles, a blasphemous creation and insult to dragonkind, in my opinion.

I crouched into the bushes, waiting. "Come on," I said to myself, "get going, will you?"

He stood like a statue alongside the path, a dark statue. Five minutes passed, then ten, then twenty.

I heard him chew on something, swallow, spit, then begin to tread up the path.

Finally!

I had followed him another league when he stopped and waited again. Ahead, I could see a series of hills forming into the perfect place to hide in. "There are always secrets in the hills," the seers said. I hunkered down. *What to do?*

The lizardman was making sure no one followed. But how did I know he was following them, and not leading me somewhere else? With the time all his breaks took, they could have gone anywhere by now. The heavy rain would easily wash away their tracks.

"Drat!" I cursed under my breath.

Maybe they knew I was onto them already.

Frustrated, I ambled down the path.

Twenty paces away, the lizardman stepped full into the path, spear lowered.

I unleashed Akron's arrow into his scaly green thigh.

Thwack!

The lizardman pitched forward, hitting the ground with a painful hiss.

Lizard men don't scream, but they hiss something awful when you shoot them in the leg.

It took a stab at me as I walked over. I sidestepped, then ripped the spear from its hand and broke that over its head.

"I can't have you following me now, can I?"

I slugged it in the jaw, and its eyes rolled up in its head.

"I hope they weren't expecting you. You'll be awfully late with that arrow in your leg," I said. *Got to move, Dragon.* I didn't have much patience left, and the disturbing thought of caged dragons infuriated me. I hooked Akron on my back and jogged up the path. *It shouldn't be that hard to catch up with a bunch of clerics, even if they do know the terrain better than I.* An hour later, I stopped and kneeled down. I ran my fingers over some muddy footprints in the path. *Excellent!* Through the slop, I forged ahead.

Two more leagues I had followed the trail when the rain let up. The bright stars peeked over the trees, and the waters rushed over the hillside while I heard the sound of people shuffling up ahead. I crept up until I could see them. It was them, a small band of clerics accompanied by one lizardman that guarded the rear.

The path winded up the hill, through the trees and alongside a gulch. That's when I got my first look at it. A temple jutted out in stark contrast to the woods. The exterior wall was overgrown in vines and withered with decay, and many of the stone columns behind it had fallen. The party of men filed through a gap in the wall and disappeared from sight. The lizardman hung back at the gate. I remained behind the trees.

Great.

The temple wall, or what was left of it, was a hundred feet long and fifteen feet high. It ran from hillside to hillside. On the wall, a few lizardmen stood watch, and for all I knew, the place was full of them. Now, I could handle a few lizardmen, but ten or twenty? That would be something.

What to do, Dragon? What to do? Sneak inside, or bust them all in the face?

I unhitched Akron.

Snap. Clatch. Snap.

The string coiled into place.

Clerics. Lizardmen, whoever else. No one was going anywhere until I freed those dragons. I had them trapped.

I whipped out an arrow and rubbed spit on its tip. It twinkled with life. My dragon heart began to thunder inside my chest. I knew the dragons were in there, but not for long. The time to fight had come.

"Show evil no mercy," I said through gritted teeth.

I took a deep breath, nocked the arrow, pulled back, aimed, and let it fly.

CHAPTER

35

T HE ARROW SAILED TRUE TO its mark, smacking into the temple.

KA-BOOM!

My blood coursed through my veins with new energy. Explosive action. That's what I liked. The lizardmen on top went flying up in the air with a shower of rock before crashing to the ground. I don't know if that killed them, but it wouldn't hurt my feelings if it did.

The lizardman at the gate stood gaping at the hole in the temple wall, waiting, uncertain.

Still hidden from sight, I nocked another arrow, waiting. *One. Two. Three...*

Lizardmen poured from the gate, and even more of the reptilian heads popped up over the wall again. *I knew it!* I let another arrow fly. It juttered at the feet of the lizardman at the gate, drawing grunts and cries. I stepped into the clear and waved at them as they raised their weapons at me.

"Wait for it, Snake-Face!" I yelled.

KA-BOOM!

A half-dozen lizardmen filled the sky with green.

A crossbow bolt zinged past my head. Nocking another arrow, I charged the gate. Three reptilian faces peeked over the wall, crossbows pointed at my chest. The crossbows rocked into action as I tried to dodge. A bolt skipped off my chest plate as I let the other arrow fly.

KA-BOOM!

Shards of rock flew everywhere. The top of the wall where the lizardmen stood was a smoking ruin as I scrambled over the rubble and through the smoky hole. I heard the lizardmen hissing and moaning nearby. I put a normal arrow in my teeth and loaded another in my bow. I aimed through the dust and smoke.

Twang!

I caught one in the thigh.

Twang!

Another in the shoulder.

Their loud hisses caused another alarm. I let my other senses guide me through the ruins and dust as another throng of lizardmen came on. I didn't care.

Twang! Twang! Twang! Twang! Twang!

I had plenty of arrows.

Twang! Twang! Twang!

Hisses and smoke were all I heard, and the lizardmen weren't going anywhere without severe limps.

Locating one, I kicked the crossbow out of its hands, wrapped my dragon arm around its neck, and squeezed.

"Where are the dragons?"

Lizardmen could speak; they just didn't speak much.

It shook its head, hissing.

I cranked up the pressure.

"Where are the dragons?"

He pointed his scaly finger as he choked out the word, "There."

Two columns led the way from the courtyard into a narrow tunnel.

"How many more?" I demanded.

"Many clerics. No more Lizard—", it started as a shadow fell over me.

I jerked away.

Clonk!

Something clipped the back of my head, drawing spots in my eyes. It was a lizardman, a big one with brawny arms and shoulders. It reminded me of Tormac, but with scales and not as ugly.

It swung its club into my shoulder, almost breaking my arm as I dove to the ground.

I rolled onto my back, pushed off, and landed on my feet, ripping Fang from his sheath.

Shing!

The bullish lizardman charged, club high, swinging down.

Fang sheared its club in two.

The slits inside the lizardman's skull widened as it stared at what was left of its club. Shielding its eyes from Fang's glow, it backed away.

"Run," I said. "Or die," I warned. "It matters not to me."

Tongue flicking from its mouth, it eyed me and my sword.

Poised to strike, I took another step forward.

It turned, ran towards the gate, and was gone, leaving me alone with a bunch of groaning lizards.

It took everything I had not to kill that big lizardman, and if he had attacked, I'm not so sure I could have held back. I'd had enough of clerics, lizardmen, dragon poachers, orcs … the whole lot of them.

"You should follow your comrade if you know what's good for you," I said as I headed for the entrance, waggling my sword under the nose of one lizardman as I passed. "You better not be here when I come back, or I'll slice every bit of Lizard from your skin."

Hissing and crawling, they slowly made their way towards what was left of the entrance.

"Good."

Still, my anger rose as I made my way inside the tunnel. I told myself it was the heat of battle, but I loved to battle. I just had to exercise control.

"Just free the dragons, Nath," I said to myself. "Knock all the clerics out if you have to."

Into the darkness I went, following a stone corridor where no torches were lit. My keen eyes could barely make out the faint lines of the corridor I traveled, but I could smell them. The men, the sweat, the evil, and something else.

"Hmmm... Be ready, Fang," I whispered.

His razor-sharp edge hummed in reply, flaring once then winking out.

The air was still: quiet, like a tomb of the dead. Using caution, I planted one foot after the other until I found myself at a crossroads. Three tunnels opened like mouths. There was no telling how far this temple went back into the mountain.

"What do you think, Fang?"

The cold steel didn't sing.

"Thanks." Peering down the middle tunnel, I inhaled. Decay, men, incense and dragons. If I got close enough, I could smell their blood. "A little light would be nice. Besides, I'm sure they know I'm coming—unless of course they are deaf acolytes."

Fang's hum added a soft white light.

"Thanks," I said, making my way down the middle tunnel. That's what Brenwar would have done, I figured. "Take the direct approach," I said in my best Brenwar voice.

Ancient markings—carvings and paintings long worn and faded—lined the walls. It was hard to tell what race of people lived here so long ago because it was another ancient language I did not recognize. A door greeted me at the end, or at least what was left of one. I heard something on the other side and pressed my ear along the door. Beautiful humming or singing grabbed me by the ears and pulled me through.

It was wonderful, sweet, and melodious as a waterfall of honey, removing all the anger and pain from my body. Fearless and care free, I went forward, a smile stretching across my face, ignoring Fang throbbing in my hand.

"It's alright, Friend," I said, sliding him into his sheath.

Drunk with elation, I hummed and twirled my way down the ancient corridor, its pictures and traces now colorful, vibrant and real. I hadn't felt this way in years. I laughed, a hundred laughs in one, following the music.

"Oh dragons," I half sang, half said, "Where are you, little dragons? Come and play with your brother. You cannot hide from me."

The warm glow of a fire was in the distance, and my compulsion drove me onward. Up there must be the most wonderful place in all of Nalzambor. *The dragons*, I thought as I drifted forward, *they aren't prisoners at all, but instead the luckiest dragons in the world.* And somewhere they were being sung to by the most beautiful woman in the world. I couldn't wait to see her as I passed from one room to the other. There she was, simply captivating.

"My, you are so beautiful."

CHAPTER

36

SHE WAS EVERYTHING I IMAGINED. The kind of woman so magnificent, the entire room lights up in her glory. And it did. Fires burned with vibrant life, and many robed men sang praises to her along the walls. Every face was happy, joyous, elated, and my heart cried out in my chest as I longed to be with her. To hold her. To kiss her. To love her like no other.

"Who are you?" I said, stretching out my hands.

Her face was gorgeous: part-human, part-elf, part-dragon, a combination of all the most beautiful faces I'd ever seen.

"Relax, Nath Dragon. Sing." She poured me a goblet of wine. "Drink. You look thirsty."

I took it as her hands caressed my face, and she unbuckled my sword belt and tossed it aside. I didn't even notice the singing acolyte lifting my quiver and bow from my shoulder. No, I was too infatuated with her dark gossamer robes blended in with her lustrous hair and how her toes did not show as she floated over.

"We've been expecting you," she said, draping her long sensuous arm over my shoulder. "Come, sit, rest." She led me towards a magnificent chair and sat me down. "Comfortable?"

My tongue clove to the roof of my mouth, and my mind swirled. I wanted to be with her so bad. I'd do anything she said. But why, the recesses of my mind asked, did she smell so bad? I had to ask.

"You are so amazing, but why do you smell... er... smell so funny?"

Her beautiful face suddenly turned dark as the music stopped.

I shook my head saying, "What's happening?"

Whop!

A fist made of dragon scales lashed out, striking me in the chest. She howled in triumph, her face contorting with rage as she struck again.

Whop!

My neck snapped back, slamming me into the chair.

"What in Nalzambor are you?" I said, holding my busted face.

She growled. Part-animal. Part Something Else.

All the colorful images began to fade, the beauty of the ancient sanctuary melting away, leaving only the fires (which were just torches) and the clerics (some bald as eagles, the others draped like purple curtains).

Behind me, the chair came to life, arms as strong as iron wrapping around me, crushing me.

My dream had become a nightmare, and it was just beginning.

The woman changed as well, her lustrous face and figure drifting like smoke and forming something else. A horrible, hulking abomination loomed over me, almost seven feet of meat, muscles and bone. It was built like a man, and armored, with a face like a dragon and scales, too.

It curled up its clawed hand as big as my face, drew back, and punched me again.

I groaned in pain. I'd thought it was over with the lizardmen.

A human voice cackled as whatever it was that held me slammed me into the ground. I couldn't move. I couldn't breathe. I could feel though. I felt like a pane of glass catching a giant stone.

"Ugh..."

"Welcome to your party, Nath Dragon. I hope you like your surprise," said a robed man with a slight limp in his step.

I looked up, face bleeding, getting a glimpse of the source of the familiar voice through my swelling eye.

"You, I know you," I managed. It was the Cleric from Narnum, the one who ratted out the Orcen Hold, where the Blazed ruffie was freed. The one I saw the day before my arm turned black. I tried to smile. "Tell you what: if you let the dragons free, I'll go easy on you. It won't be nearly as easy walking with two limps instead of one."

Finnius nodded at his dragonian goons.

One kicked me in the ribs, then the other wrapped his monstrous arm around my neck.

"Easy, Draykis, we need something left of him before dinner." Finnius squatted down beside me. "Tsk. Tsk. Catching you was so much easier than I'd thought it would be, Nath Dragon. Look around.

The best plan is a well-executed one. See?" He motioned to the clerics in purple behind him. They pulled back their hoods, revealing the same bald heads with tattooed signs that I had seen in the garden.

I felt like a fool. They'd known I was coming all along. *Ben!*

"Oh, what is wrong, Nath?"

"It's Lord Dragon to you," I said, shifting his focus. Maybe he didn't know about Ben.

He shoved my face into the dirty floor saying, "Fool!"

"Don't touch my hair, you little worm," I warned. "Ow!" I felt a dragon claw poking into my leg. "What are these things... uh... what is your lowly name anyway? Ow!"

He rose, wrapping his hands behind his back, and said, "Finnius. Hah. And even you should know that it only takes a little worm to catch a big fish. A big bald fish once this day is over." Some of the acolytes chuckled as he paced the sanctuary. "Perhaps some of the draykis would be more appealing with some of your locks attached. Or maybe I can fetch a fine price for your hair in the cities."

"It would certainly do wonders for that bald head of yours, but these," I stared over my shoulder, "Draykis are well past ugly. I don't think hair would help. What in Nalzambor are they?"

"Men fused with dragon skin, dragon blood and magic," he said, stepping on my dragon hand. "A glimpse into your future." Looking at my hand under his boot, he went on. "My, what have we here? It seems there is part draykis in you. This is a fortunate day for you indeed, the day you get to see what you are about to become. Dragon? Draykis? Or one and the same."

My stomach knotted. What he said didn't so much anger me as worry me. But, there was a ring of truth to it. I was a man with dragon blood and magic, and there was no telling what I might become.

"So, Finnius the Worm, now that you have me, what is in store for me? Death? Collect a bounty? Sell me off with the other dragons?"

"Oh Nath, as much as the Clerics of Barnabus despise you and your heroic doings, we have no intention of killing you. You see, I follow orders whether I like them or not. It's why I have this limp." He tapped his thigh. "These signs." He fingered the patterns on his head. "And more to command. More power. Why, I even control these powerful draykis." He grabbed a torch off the wall and held it to the standing draykis's mouth. "Eat."

The draykis snatched the torch from his hand and stuffed it inside its mouth, chomping it to splinters and swallowing it whole. It burped a puff of smoke.

"Charming." I struggled to get out. "Show me some more tricks. Can it eat worms, too?"

Finnius bent over, picked up my sword belt and scabbard, and handed it to one of the acolytes. He tossed another one my bow and quiver.

"Take these away," he said.

The bald men disappeared through the door that I came in.

Finnius clapped his hands together. "Now the festivities shall begin."

"You mean ole torch eater has more tricks?"

A wry smile formed on Finnius's face, sending a chill down through my bones.

"I'm not supposed to kill you, Nath Dragon, but the High Priestess didn't tell me how alive she needed you, either."

Finnius almost pinched his fingers together when he said, "Almost dead will do." He waved his arms over his head. "Algorzalahn!"

Finnius disappeared in a puff of smoke, leaving me sealed in the room with the draykis.

"This is going to hurt, Nath Dragon," one said, tugging on my hair.

CHAPTER
37

THE ONE DRAYKIS, OR WHATEVER type of evil it was called, released me as the other watched me rise to my feet.

"So, are you monsters going to teach me a lesson?" I said, woozy.

Both were taller than me, framed like big men, coated in assorted dragon scales. One smiled, showing an extra row of teeth as it continued to smack its man's fist into its hand. The other wasn't much different, aside from two horns, and both wore a mish-mash of metal armor. I couldn't imagine what they needed that for. Their eyes were bright yellow dots of evil that glowered at me like a last meal.

"Aren't you going to introduce yourselves?"

Circling me, both creatures howled and gnashed their teeth, their bare arms grasping the air.

One said, "Pain."

The other said, "Destruction."

"You," one said in a growl as it waved me forward, "come fight. Come."

"So many words you know; good for you. I imagine that's no small chore with all those rotten teeth in your mouth." I stepped up, squared up, and raised my fists at it approached.

It chuckled.

"Have it your way then," I said, jabbing my hand into its rock-hard chin.

I danced back, shaking my human hand. Now my hand would be as swollen as my face.

"Use your other arm, Idiot! Sultans of Sulfur!"

I ducked under one blow and sidestepped another. It was fast, but I was faster. I launched my dragon fist into its face, rocking its head back with a smack.

It staggered back, hissing and shaking its head, eyes narrowing.

"Rooooar!"

The other came, hard and fast, almost bowling me over as I leapt over the top of it.

"You're fast for such a big and ugly thing. I'm impressed, but I can do this all day."

No, I couldn't do it all day. My body felt like it had been shot out of a catapult, and my strength was fading.

Roaring, they both charged again. I swept the legs out from under one and kicked the other in the gut, doubling it over. Shrugging off my blows, they snarled.

Great! Every monster, no matter how big or strong, has a weak spot. I just had to find it before they found mine—which was probably any place on my body right then.

I caught the charging draykis by its horn, swung onto its back, and slugged it in the ear. It shook its head like an angry bull. Like a gorilla, the other one pounced on my back and dragged me to the ground. I rammed my knee in its ribs. I drove my boot heel in its crotch. Nothing. And that move almost always worked.

"Sultans of Sulfur! What are you things made of!"

The draykis tore into me, claws tearing into my legs and arms, shredding my clothes until I could see my blood dripping on the stone floor. Quicker, I wrestled out from underneath it and made a dash for the wall. Chest heaving, I stuck my arm out and said, "A moment... *gasp*... Please."

Dragons are fast, and these dragon abominations were fast as well. I could outsmart them or out-quick them, but I didn't have anywhere to go. It was like two big cats chasing a bird in a cage. Scanning the room, I saw no other doors or windows. Just columns, stone benches and ancient symbols. *Drat!* I needed another plan. Fast.

Find a weakness. Save the dragons!

Catching my breath, I stepped out from behind the column. The two monsters stood tall, mouths snapping, claws bared, dripping my blood. They were fiends. Men turned into monsters against their wills. Like me. My arm, I saw, wasn't so much different than theirs. But, mine was perfect: black and shiny, a glorious work of art. Their scales were drab. They, unlike me, were monsters. Stone-cold killers. Heartless and cruel. I hated evil! A cauldron erupted inside me. A flood of energy came as I charged.

I struck like a viper—*pow!*—driving my fist into the nearest draykis's jaw. It wobbled on its knees.

"I AM!"

I dunked under the other's fist and shoved my elbow into its ribs. *Crack!*

"NOT!"

Like a tornado, I hit them with everything I could.

Whap! Whap! Whap! Pow! Pow! Pow! Boom!

"A DEMON!"

One fell face first to the mosaic floor.

"A FIEND!"

I hoisted the other one over my head and slammed him through a stone bench.

"OR A MONSTER LIKE YOU!"

Neither draykis moved while I fell to my knees, clutching my sides, shaking. *I did it. I defeated them, but now what?* I was still trapped.

"Impossible!" Somewhere, Finnius raged, his voice echoing throughout the chamber.

I brushed my hair from my eyes and spit the taste of blood and dirt from my mouth.

"Where are you, Worm?"

Stone scraped against stone somewhere as a secret passage opened.

"Come, Nath Dragon. You've earned the right to live," Finnius said from somewhere beyond, "but I'm not sure about your friend."

I dashed into the tunnel as I heard the voice of a man, screaming.

"Ben!"

CHAPTER

38

INSIDE HIS CAGE, THE MALE pixlyn fought against the bars. His mate sang encouraging words that filled him with power. With him straining, the bars began to bend. Exhausted, the pixlyn squeezed free. He flew over and grabbed a ring of keys that hung from a peg on the wall. Seconds later, he unlocked his mate's cage, and they were free. Tossing the keys on the floor, neither looked back, and they were gone. From a lone cage in the corner, a little white dragon saw it all.

The temple was a series of catacombs that wound from one room or corridor to the next. I passed shelves, tombs, and altars but nothing undead. In pain, I trudged forward as fast as I could, worried, exhausted.

"Nath!" a voice cried from out of nowhere. Stopping, I turned and saw a familiar face in an ancient mirror bigger than me. It was Ben, bleeding and beaten. "Help me, Nath!"

All my hairs stood up on end as the haunting voice faded and the image disappeared.

I stood staring at the mirror and gawped at myself. I'd never looked so bad before. My face was swollen, my nose broken, and my ribs felt like scattered pieces from a dwarven puzzle. "Ben," I muttered, touching the glass. I had to save him. I had to find him fast.

I turned my back to the mirror and yelled.

"Enough, Finnius Worm, show yourself!"

Nothing.

I decided to renew my search, and I was heading toward another tunnel when I heard Finnius say, "So close yet so far, Fool."

Now Finnius's image was inside the large oval mirror, taunting me, mocking me. "You'll never find your friend in time, but I thank you. He'll make a fine meal for the draykis. Even monsters get hungry."

Finnius's words went straight through me.

"Noooooo!"

I charged across the chamber in two leaps, lowering my shoulder as I crashed through the mirror.

Glass shattered as I passed from one side to the other and kept going. Fear assailed me. I spiraled downward, free falling through the darkness before hitting the hard ground with a thud. I could have sworn I broke every bone in my body when I tried to rise to my feet.

"Welcome, Nath Dragon. How fine of you it was to join us."

Finnius stood on the other side of thick metal bars, gloating.

"My, I never imagined you would have fallen for that one. You actually ran through the mirror and fell into the pit. It's one of the stupidest things I've ever seen. And coming from you, Nath Dragon, one of the greatest warriors of all. Tsk. Tsk. I can't begin to express how disappointed and elated I am." He drummed his chin with his fingers. "Then again, maybe I'm just, oh, I almost hate to say it… Brilliant!"

My prison was solid steel, corroded, but solid nonetheless. High above me, a trap door was being pulled up and into place. I wasn't going anywhere, not without help.

"Where's Ben?"

"Oh, the young man whom you have doomed? Why, he's over there, dying," Finnius said, pointing.

I felt my heart stop in my chest. Ben spun in midair, surrounded by acolytes muttering a spell. Ben's eyes were watery with terror as his unmoving lips seemed to cry out for me. We locked eyes, but he couldn't even blink.

"What are you doing to him, Finnius!" I shouted through the bars.

Finnius lifted his finger up and said, "Ah, well you are going to like this, really. You see, when the High Priestess arrives, she is going to teach me how to create a draykis. You see Nath, all we have to do is add dragon parts." He pointed farther back in the room. "And dragon blood."

I could see several cages with coiled up dragons inside. One was a yellow streak, the other two evergreens inside eerie glowing cages.

"That's not going to happen, Worm. I'll see to that."

Finnius let out a creepy bubbly laugh as he walked over and grabbed my sword from one of his acolytes.

"I wouldn't draw that blade, if I were you."

"What is the matter, Dragon? Are you afraid I'll kill you with it?"

"It doesn't like evil," I said, pulling myself up by the bars. "You'd best let go of that."

"Hah. Nice try, Dragon. But, I believe I'll be alright. Oh, and don't worry: as I said, I'm not going to kill you. The High Priestess will do that. But, I will at some point, have to kill your young friend, Ben. And won't it be agonizing to watch him die by your own blade? Hmmmm?"

"He dies, you die, Worm."

Holding Fang by the scabbard, Finnius eyed me then the sword and said, "Acolyte, withdraw this blade."

"Again, Finnius, I wouldn't do that unless you want another man dead," I warned.

The acolyte's fingers stopped inches from Fang's hilt. He widened his eyes on me.

"Withdraw it, Servant, or die anyway! Draykis!"

Several hulking figures stepped out of the shadows, two of which limped and had busted faces. It seemed all of my valiant efforts from earlier had been deflated. One stepped over the acolyte and wrapped its clawed fingers around his neck.

Sweating profusely, the acolyte wrapped his trembling hands around the hilt. Taking a sharp breath, he slid Fang out from the sheath, holding my sword out in his robed arms. Fang's steel flickered with life in the lantern light, but was otherwise dim. I sagged. I hadn't really expected Fang to do anything, but you never know with him.

"Huh, I see your bluff has failed you, Dragon. Perhaps you should have stayed in bed. You look awfully tired. Maybe you should just sit down and rest." Finnius jerked the sword away from the acolyte and pointed it in the acolyte's face. He clipped one cheek, then the other. "Next time, it will be your neck with a large hole in it." Finnius whirled towards the others and said, "Lower him."

Ben's body slowly drifted over next to a large stone altar, where he sat upright, listless and catatonic. They had done something to him. His eyes flickered between me, the draykis and the ceiling.

"Don't give up, Ben. I'll save you!"

"No Dragon, no you won't," Finnius said, stepping over towards Ben and stabbing him in the chest. "NOOOOOOOOOOOOOO!"

CHAPTER
39

I DIDN'T FEEL A THING WHEN my buttocks landed on the cold stone floor. I was dead inside. Worse, Ben was dead! The only thought racing through my head was, 'It's your life to throw away, not mine.' I'd tried to warn him, yet guilt overwhelmed me. It mixed with something else: anger. It was all my fault. I had failed.

"Good, Dragon," Finnius started, "you should rest as you look absolutely horrible. I hope the High Priestess doesn't mind when she arrives any minute now." He clapped his hands. "Acolytes, begin the summons."

Listless, I watched the Clerics of Barnabus gather around an archway off center in the chamber and begin their moans and mumbles. I felt my heart explode in my chest when the draykis hoisted Ben's body up onto the slab altar.

"I'll kill you, Finnius," I muttered.

Finnius cupped his ear, saying, "What's that?" He jabbed Fang into the stone floor by the altar. "A fine weapon, a fine-fine piece of steel. Is it made of Jaxite? I didn't even feel it go in or slide out." He turned his attention to the archway and looked back at me. "Won't be long now, Dragon. And I can't wait to see what the High Priestess has in store for you."

Smoke of many colors swirled inside the archway, pulsating with life and energy. The sound of the acolytes chanting increased in volume and tempo. I didn't care. Whoever the High Priestess was and whatever they wanted to do with me didn't matter. I'd failed. I'd abandoned one friend, only to see another one dead. Huffing for air, I rose to my feet. I wrapped my hands around the metal.

"I'm going to kill you, Finnius!"

I wasn't supposed to kill anybody, unless it was life or death. *What about Finnius's death for Ben's life?* It was more than fair.

Finnius leered at me, wringing his dirty hands together and saying, "Not even in your wildest nightmares. It's over for you, Nath Dragon."

The draykis, no longer two but ten, sprang into action as something small and white skittered across the floor.

"What is it!" Finnius cried out as a small white dragon leaped past his face and into the corner. "Who let it out! I'll kill one of you! Acolyte, get me those Pixlyn!" One broke from the group and dashed off. "Draykis, capture that dragon!"

It was a long-tailed white, the same one I'd seen in the cage on my way in here. Quick and fierce, the draykis were no match for it. One sealed off the other way out as the other three chased it around the room. It scurried, hissed, snapped and slipped through the claws of one then the other.

"Get it, Draykis! Kill it!" Finnius screamed. "It doesn't matter how!"

I jumped to my feet, pulling at the bars, fuming.

"I'll not see any more of your murders, Finnius."

"You'll see many more before this day is over, I assure you."

The acolyte rushed back into the room.

"Well?" Finnius snapped.

"Gone, Cleric Finnius."

Finnius wrung his hands and tugged at his robes, screaming at the draykis, "You idiots! Why did you abandon those cages!"

The draykis at the door replied, "We did as you requested."

The long-tailed white flew from one side of the room to the other.

Finnius stomped his feet.

"Catch it! NOW!"

The long-tailed white locked eyes with me, and I felt a connection. It wanted the dragons free, and so did I.

Finnius howled. He saw us.

The dragon darted across the room towards me.

"Stop it!" Finnius yelled.

Lunging, two draykis collided with each other, but a third caught the end of the dragon's long tail and jerked it to the ground. The dragon screeched, tiny claws digging into the stone floor, straining towards me. I reached through the bars, my arm inches away.

"NO!" I screamed as another draykis, wielding a sword, rushed over, swinging it.

"Kill it!" Finnius shouted. "Kill it!"

CHAPTER
40

THE WHITE DRAGON'S EYES GLOWED with green fire as the draykis swung the sword. A jet of white smoke shot out of its mouth, filling the room in an instant. I couldn't see a thing, but I heard a blade chopping into flesh and stone. Something let out a nasty grunt, and I could hear Finnius hack and cough while I tried to fan the smoke away. As the smoke dissipated, I could hear him scream.

"Did you kill it? Where is it? Find it!"

Through the thinning smoke, a draykis rose from the floor, staring at the stump of his arm. The other with the sword was looking around, and that's when I felt it. The tiny dragon had squeezed through the bars and was crawling up my back and onto my shoulder. His extra-long tail coiled along my waist and arm.

"Ahem," I said.

Finnius turned my way. His face reddened and his chin quivered when he said, "Give me that long-tailed white, Dragon. Or I'll kill the rest of them."

"If you want this dragon, Worm, why don't you come and get it?"

The dragon's tail tightened around my arm and waist. A surge of power raced through me like never before. Every muscle in my being pulsated as the purring dragon filled me with awesome power. I wasn't a man any more. I felt the strength of a full-grown dragon. I grabbed the bars, and the metal groaned as I pulled them apart like noodles. Finnius's jaw dropped to the floor when I stepped through the gap I'd just made.

"Unless you can bring my friend back to life, it's time to die, Finnius!"

I knocked the first draykis that came at me from one side of the room to the other. I ducked under another blade that almost took my head from my shoulders. I was fast. Faster than ever before. Stronger than ever before. The power the little dragon gave me was unbelievable!

"You're dead!" I said, rushing Finnius.

He had turned to run before I closed in when two armed draykis jumped into my path. A sharp blade tore past my stomach, and a large hammer ripped an inch away from my head. I was faster and stronger, but I wasn't impervious to metal. I did a back flip towards the altar and landed in front of Fang. I ripped him free.

"Now it's even, uglies," I said. I could feel the dragon's power flowing from my shins to my neck. Fang's blade hummed with life. "Who's the first to pay for the life of my friend!"

"You cannot kill us," said one draykis, holding a sword. "We are already dead."

"We'll see about that," I boasted, knowing full well the odds were against me. I'd never faced such a formidable force of warriors before. So be it. I felt like I could fight an entire army now. I felt even better than when the crowd had cheered me on, "Dragon! Dragon!"

Faster than sight, I drove Fang into the nearest one's chest, drawing forth a groan as it fell. I chopped another one in the arm and kicked another one in the face. Another parried my strike and countered with a deep cut across my leg. On they came at me with the skill and precision of hardened soldiers, forcing me backward to parry again and again.

"NO!"

I knocked a blade free from one and stabbed another in the shoulder. Another fell as I hacked through its knee. Fang cut through the air like a living thing. Cutting, blocking, and chopping. But all my strength and speed didn't stop them from coming. Limping, snarling, and slashing, they pressed.

"Gah!"

One ripped its claws through my arm. Little dragon or not, I couldn't keep this up much longer, and if I died, the dragons would all die as well.

Without thinking, I said, "Fang! Do something!"

Fang flared with brilliant icy light.

Striking like a snake, I jabbed a draykis that wielded a sword.

It stopped in its tracks, its scaled body turned to ice. I struck another draykis and one more. Instant statues of ice they'd become. I cut one in the arm and another in the leg with the same effect. Weapons poised high over their heads, the last two charged.

Slice! Slice!

They crystalized into pure ice.

There I stood among eight frozen horrors, feeling almost as astounded as they looked. Fang throbbed in my hand.

"What's that, Fang?" I saw the tip flare up. "Ah, I see."

I struck Fang's tip on the stone floor.

KRAAAAAAAAAAANG!

The perfect metal resonated through the chamber like a giant tuning fork.

One by one, the icy figures of the draykis exploded into a thousand shards of ice.

"NOOOOOOOOOOOOOO!" Finnius screamed from right behind me.

I whirled just in time to catch a long dagger plunging at my chest. I twisted it free from his wrist, punched him in the face, and sent him sprawling to the floor.

"You're going to pay, Worm!"

Crawling backward, he shouted back, "It's too late, Dragon. She comes."

The mystic smoke in the archway was filling the room, but all the clerics but Finnius were gone. Eeriness covered me like a blanket. I shook it off.

"Great, then she'll be here just in time to make arrangements for your funeral." I raised my sword and closed in. I didn't ever want to see this man alive again. "But there might not be much left to bury once I'm done with you."

"Go ahead! Kill me! My High Priestess will just bring me back," Finnius said, chuckling. "But that's much more than I can say for your friend." His eyes twinkled with darkness as his lips curled in a smile. "Come Dragon, Avenge your friend."

"I'll do more than that!"

The dragon on my shoulder hissed out a warning.

Crack!

It felt like a large mallet collided with my skull, knocking me to my knees. Finnius seized my wrists and shouted.

"AZZRHEEM-KAH!

It felt like lightning exploded inside me as I lay on the ground, hair smoking, every fiber of my being throbbing in pain. My eyelids hurt as I opened my eyes to witness a winged draykis reaching for me. Bigger than the rest, it scooped me off the floor like a doll and crushed me in its arms.

"Break his back!" Finnius yelled from somewhere. "I want to hear it snap, Draykis!"

It didn't have lips, but it smiled.

"Certainly, my Lord."

CHAPTER

41

ALL MY STRENGTH FLED WHEN I gazed at the small white dragon lying still on the floor. Completely drained, I fought on, legs kicking, but the monster had its mighty paws locked behind my back.

"That's it!" Finnius said with glee. "Ooh! Your face is awfully red, Dragon, but I think it will look even better in a nice dark shade of purple." Finnius limped over, leering up at me, triumphant.

I felt it. I was defeated. I'd failed. Any moment, the winged draykis would crush all my bones, leaving me living but an invalid.

"Worm!" I managed to spit out.

My spit sizzled through his robes.

"Eh... What is this?" Finnius asked, fingering the hole in his robes. My stomach churned with fire, and the taste of brimstone charged inside my mouth.

The draykis licked its lips, said, "I'm hungry," and squeezed me with all its might.

I felt something snap as hot smoke burst from my nose.

Eyes filled with horror, Finnius backed away. "NO! What are you doing, Dragon? Stop that! Make him stop, Draykis. NOW!"

The draykis, jaws filled with long sharp teeth, opened wide.

I tried to scream, but a jet of flaming hot liquid erupted instead.

One second the draykis's horrible face was about to eat me, in the next it was a ball of fire. There was nothing left of its face but bone as it released me and fell to the ground.

I jumped up from the floor to chase Finnius down.

He slipped on the shards of ice and fell hard to the ground on his knees, saying, "Mercy, Dragon! Mercy!"

Evil shows no mercy. No mercy shall it receive.

"Where was your mercy when you killed my friend, Worm?"

"Mercy! I'll do anything! Please!"

I wanted to stop it, but I couldn't. A geyser of flame shot from my mouth, coating Finnius from head to toe. In an instant, he was burnt to a crisp.

A new rush of power assailed me as I chased the other acolytes down. Some burned, some escaped, and some died before it was over.

The only ones left were me and the dragons. One by one, I freed them from their cages, and one by one they were gone. The long-tailed white as well. Exhausted, I fell to my knees and fought the tears coming from my eyes.

"Ben," I moaned as I crawled over to the altar.

There he lay on the granite slab altar, pale as a ghost. His energetic face, once full of life, now as stiff as stone. I'd saved the dragons but at what cost?

I brushed the hair from his eyes and said, "Ben. I'm so sorry, Ben."

"For what?" he said, blinking.

I stiffened.

"Huh? Ben?"

He yawned, stretched out his arms and asked again, "For what?"

I stumbled backward, clutching my heart.

"BEN! You're alive!"

"That seems to be the case," he said, fanning the eerie smoke from his face. "Is that your breath that I smell? It's awful."

"I guess that's why they call it dragon breath."

Sitting on the altar, Ben said, "Is this place shaking?"

Shards of rock and debris fell on my head and his. The High Priestess. Was she still coming? I rushed over and grabbed Fang. But where was Akron—and the rest of my things?

"We need to get out of here, Ben."

Something was coming through the portal, something big.

"Ben, do you see my bow?"

I swung Fang into the archway, splintering rock, but it held. I felt the urge to hew the thing down. I felt evil as great as I'd ever felt before.

"Found it!" Ben said, hoisting it over his head.

"Bring it over here."

I snatched Akron from his hands and nocked it with a powerful arrow. I rubbed my spit in the tip and watched it glow.

Holding his ears, Ben shouted, "What are you doing?"

"I don't know," I said as I let the arrow fly. It disappeared into the smoky archway. A split second later, a roar came out that shook the entire temple. I grabbed Ben by the arm and led us dashing through the corridors. The floors wobbled and the walls warbled as we rushed past the dust and debris through one winding corridor and another until we arrived outside in the courtyard. The night air was like ice in my breath.

"We made it," I said, leaning over and grabbing my knees.

Ben was lying on the courtyard grass, wheezing.

From inside the ruins of the temple came a mighty thud like someone closing the lid on a giant sarcophagus. I fell to my knees, rain pelting my face, and scanned the area. No acolytes, lizardmen or draykis. It was over.

For a moment, I took it all in. I was alive, but more importantly so was Ben.

"Look," Ben said pointing.

A group of small dragons flew across the moonlit clouds in the sky.

I wanted to hug Ben but didn't. Smiling, I squeezed his shoulder instead and said, "Ben, why aren't you dead?"

He shrugged.

"I think Bayzog's potion did it."

"How so?"

"Well, he said that I would know when it was time to take it, so I did."

"And when was that?"

"Well, I was with the horses, like you said, guarding them like you told me. After you'd been gone a little while, the horses started whining."

"Whining?"

"Yes, I've never seen such nervous horses before. And that's when I noticed it." He stopped, thinking.

"Noticed what?"

"A giant shadow circling in the sky." He shivered. "I'd never been so scared in all of my life. And I knew, instantly, that it was coming for me. That thing, those eyes, locked on mine, and I knew I was dead. I grabbed that vial and swallowed the entire bottle full. The horses galloped off, and the next thing I knew I was face to face with it. I'm embarrassed, but I think I fainted in its arms. I awoke, and I was sailing across the sky like a bird. That monster was carrying me. That's when I blacked out again. Next time I awoke, I was spinning in that room, surrounded by those clerics and beastly things. Then that man took your sword and stabbed me."

He pulled off his leather armor, which was cut clean through. He ran his finger along the white scar on his chest. He shook his head. "It was cold, the blade going in. As if someone shoved ice in my chest. But I didn't die; I felt strange, outside of myself. I just closed my eyes and played possum." He put his armor back on. "What was in that vial, Dragon?"

"Let's get out of here," I said, grimacing.

I headed for the forest—limping, bleeding and aching all over. I'd had enough of these temples.

"Well, what was it?"

"I can't say for sure, because you can never tell with Bayzog, or any other wizard, for that matter, but I'd say what he gave you was Moments of Immortality. And that's very potent magic."

"Whoa... How many moments do you think I have?"

I socked him in the arm.

"Ow! Why'd you do that?"

"Do you feel Immortal?"

"No," he said, rubbing his arm.

"Then I'd say your moments ran out. Now come on: maybe we can track down the horses by dawn if we run."

"Run?"

I took off, but not as fast as I would have liked. My joints ached. My body was swollen like a watered down log. I'd taken a pretty heavy beating those last couple of days. But Ben, despite his huffing, tried to keep up. I had to let him catch up.

"There should be a potion to make this running easier," he wheezed.

"There is. Come on."

We arrived back at the Crane's Neck as dawn broke and began the search for the horses. Starting from where Ben left them, I spotted the hoof prints in the dirt.

Kneeling down and pointing, I said, "See these horseshoe prints, Ben? They left deep impressions after the rain, so they shouldn't be hard to follow—unless another storm hits. And they won't take off more than a mile. With any luck, they're grazing somewhere. Why don't you see if you can track them?"

His face lit up.

"Really, me?"

"Now's as good a time to practice as any."

"Alright then," he replied, giving me a funny look. "Well, uh, Dragon, do you feel alright?"

"I'm fine. I've been in plenty of bad scrapes before. Why do aaaaa—?"

I forgot what I was saying. My lids became heavy as Ben's eyes filled with alarm. His mouth twisted like a pinwheel as he yelled, and his fingers stretched out like worms. *What's happening?* The light of the dawn faded to black.

Inside the temple ruins, a magnificent woman surveyed the chamber where the battle had taken place. It was High Priestess Selena.

"Interesting."

Hours earlier, she had been attempting to enter the portal when a magic arrow sailed through the smoke, struck a draykis, and blew it and another to pieces. Her chamber room was half destroyed, and her roar wiped out most of what wasn't already. She'd gotten over it. Not all plans were perfectly executed, but the execution still had its rewards.

She stepped through a puddle of water, kneeled along the charred corpse of Finnius, and said, "The best pawns end up being dead pawns." She grabbed the magic amulet from around his neck and pulled it free of his charred remains. "Here," she said, tossing it to a man among the draykis. He was big and armored, with many colorful tattoos on his head. A cruel looking warrior's mace hung from his belt.

"Clearly, this was a job for a High Cleric, but..." She waded past the other burnt and broken bodies in the room. "I still think it will bear the results that I was hoping for. Humph. Nath Dragon evades traps with the cunning of a snake, but he'll never escape the biggest trap of all."

"And that is?" the deep voiced warrior cleric said.

"Himself."

Before she stepped through the smoke in the archway, she commanded one more thing.

"And bring along all the corpses of the acolytes. The dead tell the most accurate tales."

Clutch of the Cleric

-Book 4-

Craig Halloran

PRELUDE

A FLUTE-LIKE SOUND DRIFTED INTO MY ears.

My head started spinning. My fingers turned numb. Limp.

Brenwar's eyelids fluttered. His meaty hands clamped over his ears. "No!" he growled.

I couldn't say anything. My tongue felt like water. But I could see. Both of them. Shadows in the forest coming out of the darkness. One was male, the other female. Each pressed a set of small pipes to their lips. Tiny horns protruded from their heads. They stood on stout legs with the hooves of mountain goats.

Satyrs. Crafty and Merciless.

The music tore at my mind.

I screamed, but I couldn't hear myself. I had to move. Had to escape. Run. Flee. I knew the stories. I knew the tales. Whatever the satyrs captured they kept. Never to be seen again.

CHAPTER

1

I FELT LIKE I'D GONE DAYS without water when I opened my eyes up. A soft soothing light was in my eyes, but I still felt weary.

"Uh… where am I? Ben?"

The smell of sweet ginger filled my nostrils, and someone placed a cold damp cloth on my head.

"Sssssh. Rest, Dragon."

The warm face of Sasha greeted me with a smile as she reached over and touched my face.

"Bayzog, he awakens again."

Again? I didn't remember waking the last time.

"It's not time yet, Sasha," Bayzog said. A faint image of him in his red wizard tunic caught my eye.

Her perfect lips started singing; the gentle, mystic words of an ancient lullaby churned in my ears.

"No, don't do thaaaaaa—"

The soft lights turned dark again.

"Wake him up!"

Slowly, I opened my eyes, the thirst I remembered now gone. Then I saw Brenwar, as angry as I ever saw him before.

"What are you yelling for?" I said, shielding my eyes, squinting.

He whirled on me, so angry I could see the red behind his beard.

"WHAT AM I YELLING FOR?"

A large figure stepped between us. It was one of those Roaming Rangers.

"Shum?"

"Get out of my way, Elf," Brenwar growled.

"Brenwar," Bayzog intervened, "now is not the time."

"Oh, it's the time, alright!"

Brenwar shoved past Shum, stuck his stubby finger in my face, and said, "Why did you leave me, Nath Dragon!" His voice cracked. "Why did you do that?"

I didn't know what to say. I was feeling great, but I had the feeling I shouldn't be.

"Why is everyone looking at me like that? Where's Ben? Is he alright? And how did I get here?"

Brenwar stood frowning and tapping his foot, Shum unmoving, Bayzog muttering and Sasha twitching her nose.

"What?" I said.

Bayzog took a seat beside me and said, "I'll catch you up. Ben led you back here on the horses after you fainted."

"Ah good, I knew Ben had it in him. I guess my wounds were much worse than I thought. So, where is he?"

"He's with the Legionnaires, on a mission."

"Huh, a mission. He couldn't be on a mission already. Could he? Don't they have to go through training?"

Brenwar stormed forward.

"Fool! He could have been on twenty missions already. He's been gone for weeks. You've been asleep for weeks. I've been looking for you; my men have been looking for you, and we might never have found you if we hadn't come across that temple. And we might not have ever known you were there if we hadn't found this!" He held out a black dragon scale. "And this led us here."

I grabbed the scale with my left hand and pinched it in my fingers. My black dragon fingers. I jumped off the couch.

"SULTANS OF SULFUR! I have two dragon arms!"

"You can say that again!" Brenwar shot back. "You foolish dragon!"

I touched my toes, my shins, my thighs, chest and face.

"Am I?"

"Just the arms, Dragon," Sasha said. "You'll be alright."

"No, he won't! He'd have been alright if he'd done as he was told. Dragon! What have you done?" Brenwar exclaimed.

"I saved dragons!" I yelled back. "And if I'd waited on you, they'd probably be dead!"

I gazed at my scales, my hands, my claws. A thrill went through me. I felt unstoppable! But there was something else. The white spot of scales was on both palms in the middle.

Brenwar poked me in the chest, saying, "I was at the temple. I saw what you did. And your new friend, Ben, confirmed it. You killed again! Now look at you!"

"You started it!" I said, pointing at Brenwar.

"You did this, not I, Dragon! You ran off on your own, like a fool, and now you have twice the problem!"

"Don't call me a fool again, Brenwar," I said, glowering down on him. I was ready to rip his beard off.

He rose up on his toes and said, "What are you going to do, breathe on me? Fool!"

I took a deep breath.

He laughed at me.

Sasha's vibrant form stepped between us. "Please, everyone, stop yelling. You aren't children; you're men," Sasha said, gentle hands pushing me into the sofa.

Calmness fell over me. "We have to work together on this." She said, eyeing all of us. "It's that important. Bayzog, tell him."

I slumped into the sofa, feeling incredibly angry and guilty, but I let Sasha's charm calm me.

"Yes, Bayzog, Ben mentioned there was something you wanted to tell me. What is it?" I said, noticing my beard. "Ugh! Really?"

Bayzog gave me a funny look.

I shook my head, which was beginning to ache, saying, "Go on then."

"Dragon, I can't say that I, or anyone in the world, for that matter, can understand your unique constitution—well, excluding your father, of course."

My head started aching. What would my father think?

"I don't think things are as bad as they look, however. I would venture that it was inevitable that you would start turning into a dragon eventually, and your scales, well, they aren't a true reflection of your nature. Nath, we all know that you are good, as good a man as we all know, but there is darkness in all of us. No one person is perfect or without blemish; most just hide it better on the outside. That's why it is difficult to tell the good people from the evil sometimes."

"This isn't helping, Bayzog," I said, holding my head in my hands, irritated.

"Our deeds are what define us. Our actions. Our words. Not our garments, not our looks. What is inside a man, in his heart—his dragon heart—is what counts. Keep doing what you are doing."

"But I want to get rid of it." *Sort of.*

"And what if you can't? Will you stop being good altogether then? Will you join the Clerics of Barnabus?"

"NO!"

"So stop whining then," Bayzog said.

"I'm not whining."

"You are whining," Brenwar added, folding his arms across his chest. "Like a baby orc."

"Fine, I'm whining, but I'm sure all of you would do the same if you had these." I lifted my arms. "I'm not going to be wooing the ladies like I used to; that's for sure. But, I imagine I could be used in a carnival to frighten children."

Brenwar harrumphed.

"I like them," Sasha said, rubbing my scales, smiling. "I think they are marvelous."

Her sweet words made me feel better; they really did. I guess I was just going to have to get used to it, but I really needed to fix it.

"Bayzog, my father says there are many things in this world that can heal. Perhaps you can help me find some of those things. Maybe I just need a different Thunderstone or something."

Bayzog walked over to his large table, opened his tome, thumbed through the pages, and threw his hands out. When he twitched his fingers, an image of a mystic amulet formed and hung in the air, gold and silver with a bright green gemstone in the middle.

"The Ocular of Orray. The legend says that it can bring health, peace and prosperity. Its powers have been known to cure lycanthropes and liches, and to restore the undead. Perhaps it can help."

"So, where is it?"

Bayzog flicked his fingers. The amulet broke into several pieces.

"It was stolen from the elves in Elome a century after the last Dragon War, never to be seen again. According to the lore, the thieves broke it up into many pieces and spread them all over Nalzambor, for the Ocular cannot be destroyed."

"So, who stole it? Who can go into Elome and steal anything?" Nath sighed. "It's a fortress."

"We'd have to ask the elves that," he said, closing the book.

"So, I'm supposed to search the entire world for this Ocular? I'd rather just save the dragons." I looked at Shum. "And what are you doing here?"

"I have an interest in the power of the Ocular as well. Remember my King? He needs the healing, too."

"I see. And what about the dragons? I'm not going to abandon them for this quest."

Brenwar shoved my sword and scabbard in my chest.

"We won't!"

Bayzog and Sasha donned their traveling cloaks.

"Where are you going?"

"With you," Sasha said, tying the neck with the magic of her fingers. "I've been needing to stretch my legs. Bayzog has kept me cooped up in here too long."

It seemed everybody was ready for a trip but me as I shook my head and rose to my feet.

"So, now I need supervision everywhere I go?"

"And then some," Brenwar huffed. "Let's go!"

"Fine," I said, buckling my sword around my waist as Sasha draped my quiver over my shoulder and handed me Akron. I was ready for anything. But before I closed my eyes, I said one last thing. "But I'm going to save whoever and whatever I want to. Agreed?"

Everyone shook their heads except Brenwar, who laughed.

"Well, let it never be said I didn't consort with highly unreasonable people."

As soon as I closed my eyes, the adventure began.

CHAPTER
2

HIGH PRIESTESS SELENE SAT ON her throne. Dark. Cold. Cunning. She was beautiful. Dark-eyed and raven headed. Her hair was pulled back behind her shoulders as she shifted in her chair, eyes intent and focused on the great doors on the other side of the room.

Nath Dragon. She looked forward to the day he was dragged to her on hands and knees, bound and broken. *I shall have him. I shall have him and all the world of Nalzambor.*

Something fluttered above. A dark bird-like creature landed on her shoulder. It had a mix of dark green and red feathers, but it was not a bird. It had the face and mouth of a dragon. Its tongue licked her ear and its feathers shuddered when it roared with little sound.

She patted its head. "Ah, my little Drulture. Such a caring and endearing pet," she said. "Are you worried about me?"

It stretched its neck, feathers ruffling on its wings, and let out another tiny roar.

Her black lips pecked its cat-sized head. The Drulture was her companion when no one else was about. So she sat alone in her thoughts in the grand room. She liked the open space. The quiet. She needed time to plan. Nathan Dragon had escaped her clutches again.

"Are you hungry?" she said.

The Drulture bobbed its head.

"I see," she said. "Just give me another moment." She snapped her fingers. *Pop!*

The great doors across from her opened and a pair of lizardmen stepped inside and kneeled.

"It's feeding time," she said.

The pair departed and returned less than a minute later carrying a barred cage between them. A spotted bobcat, every bit of thirty pounds, was inside, its eyes and ears alert.

"Leave us," Selene said, "and seal the door behind you."

The lizardmen departed, leaving her, the Drulture and the bobcat all alone.

"He's a big one," she said, "bigger than the last. I hope you won't have any trouble."

The Drulture let out a tiny roar and hopped to the ground. The dragon-bird was less than half the size of the bobcat. It strutted around on two legs, making a chirp-like sound. The bobcat licked its lips. Its cat eyes narrowed.

Selene tapped her fingers together. She liked games like this. Who is the hunter and who is the hunted. She'd tried to trap Nath Dragon in a similar way before. Letting him think he was freeing a dragon when in all reality the dragon bait was trapping him. It had almost worked a couple of times, but Nath had come out on top again. It had been costly too. She'd lost many of her draykis, and one of her temples had been wrecked. She clenched her fists.

"I'm going to break him," she said. "Soon." With a wave of her hand the metal cage opened.

The bobcat jumped out and gave chase after the Drulture. The bobcat pounced. The Drulture flapped and soared into the air and began circling the bobcat. Once. Twice. Three times and dove.

Swish!

It snatched the bobcat by the back and lifted it high in the air. The bobcat hung by the scruff of its neck, clawing, scratching and growling. Higher they went, towards the domed ceiling. The drulture dropped the bobcat. The big cat plummeted fifty feet towards the ground.

The drulture dove, snatching it inches from the ground. Then swooped up to the rafters once more. Drop. Dive. Catch. Drop. Dive. Catch.

Three times it happened. The bobcat fought and clawed until its strength was out. The fourth time, it hung limp in the talons of the dragon-bird and fought no more. Circling thirty feet high in the air, the drulture swung the bobcat up into the air and opened its jaws wide. They became wider and wider.

Gulp!

It swallowed the bobcat whole and landed softly on the floor. Its belly bulged. It waddled around like an overstuffed chicken for about a minute, burped an awful sound, and returned back to normal.

"Now there's an idea," Selene said. She patted the drulture when it returned to her shoulder. It purred. She snapped her fingers. The grand doors opened and the lizardmen came forward and bowed.

"I need the High Cleric," she said, "and take the cage and fill it with something bigger. A halfling or gnome perhaps."

The dragon-bird purred and batted its eyelashes.

Selene smiled. "You've given me an idea. If it works, my master will be pleased. If I can't beat Nath Dragon as he is, then perhaps I should wear him down first."

CHAPTER

3

"ARE YOU POUTING?" BRENWAR SAID.

"No," I said.

"Don't lie, Dragon. I can see your brows buckling. Straighten up."

The ride from Quintuklen wasn't so bad the first day. It was good being in the company of Bayzog the part-elf, Sasha his apprentice and mate, and Shum, one of the Elven Roaming Rangers. It had been a long time since I'd spent time with so many people. Usually it was just me and Brenwar.

I kicked my steed and rode ahead of the party, leaving Brenwar in the rear. The day was dreary, a little chilling and nothing but rolling greens hills and wild flowers ahead.

"Don't leave my sight!" Brenwar said.

I didn't even look back. Instead, I rode farther out. Far enough until I got the feeling I was alone. As I said, it was nice catching up with everyone, but their chronic presence was disturbing. Every eye seemed to watch everything I was doing and Brenwar kept commenting on what he thought I was thinking.

"Don't think you're gonna sneak off!"

"Stay on this side of the river."

"Shum, go with him."

"Bayzog, can you cast a spell that can track him?"

It got old. It was aggravating. I was a man. I was becoming a dragon, and I didn't need anyone's protection. Especially now. Now I had two dragon arms, not just one, and I was itching to see what I could do with both of them. I massaged my arms. I loved the slickness and toughness of my scales. And my claws—mostly yellow, but a little gold—came in handy when I gutted fish for dinner. I clicked them together. I loved the sound they made.

Burp.

A white puff of smoke came out my mouth. My nostrils steamed. I tapped my fist into my chest.

I guessed I'd had too many fish earlier, but I was still hungry. Hungrier than ever. Nowadays I was even eating more than Brenwar, and he always ate a week's worth.

I fanned the smoke. I didn't want Brenwar to see. He'd say 'Smoking's bad' or something silly like that.

I had been able to burp smoke a few times when no one was looking, but I hadn't summoned anymore fire yet. I wasn't certain how I'd done it the last time, but I knew it was in me, brewing. A volcano ready to burst. Remembering the cleric Finnius whom I'd turned into a human roast bothered me, but not as much as it should have probably.

Well, remembering the smell did make me grimace. A little.

I heard horse hooves trotting up behind me. *Oh great.* I hadn't even been alone for a few minutes and already—still well within eye shot—I had company.

I turned and yelled, "Will you leave me alone!" *Gulp.*

It was Sasha. She sat tall and splendid in the saddle. Her blue eyes were bright and her auburn hair was lustrous. Her apprentice robes hung loosely over her elegant form. She was one of the prettiest women I'd ever seen. And she was smiling.

"No," she said, smiling bigger.

"What?" I said. "Oh. Well, I'm glad you aren't Brenwar and I'm sorry that I yelled, Sasha. I'm just not used to having all of this bossing around."

She rode alongside me, giggling.

"I understand, Nath," she said. "Even Bayzog is demanding from time to time."

She called me Nath and that was fine by me, but I didn't like it so much when others called me that. Nath was just the beginning of my long name. Longer than a hundred men's strung together, and whenever I heard Nath, my mind would start running through it.

"I believe you do know what I'm talking about. Bayzog's rigid as a dwarf sometimes." I winked at her. "But don't tell him I said that."

"I won't," she said. "So, Nath, tell me. What's it like having two dragon arms?"

She caught me off guard with that one. I figured she was going to ask how I was feeling or in her own polite way offer some advice. And I'd hate to tell her I'd had all the advice I could swallow. My father was bad enough, but Brenwar was worse.

"Uh …," I said, glancing over my shoulder, then back at her, "can you keep a secret, Sasha?"

"So long as it doesn't place me in conflict with the others," she said, nodding.

I hesitated. I could see her point, but I didn't think what I was about to tell her would create a conflict.

"Alright … It's wonderful, Sasha. I feel like I can do things I could never do before. I feel faster. Stronger." I held my hands out in front of me and gazed at the black scales that shined like black sheets of ice in the sun. "I feel like I could fight anyone, anywhere, and win." I flexed them. "I was strong before, but now, well, I just want to test them out."

"Whoa," she said, "you really are infatuated with yourself, aren't you?"

"Well, no, it's not like that. I'm just amazed."

She giggled. "I'm just teasing you, Nath. I really like them too…"

She trailed off, her light eyes glancing away.

"But?" I said.

She reached over and rubbed my arm. Her eyes brightened when she did it.

"Oh, but nothing, Nath. I trust you and I'm thrilled for you. Who wouldn't want to be a dragon anyway? And Nath, you know I think the world of you. I always have. You're a hero. You've done great things and you'll do more…"

She did it again. Trailed off and glanced away.

"But?" I said.

"As long as you stay on the right path. Let us help with that, Nath. Why do you rebel?"

"Because I'm a rebel," I said, laughing a little. But it wasn't very convincing. Not to me or her.

"Oh Nath," she said, "you just have to be careful. This world, Nalzambor, it has a way of changing people who aren't careful. I lost some family because of that. I don't want to lose you too." Her eyes watered up and she was looking right at me.

It got me, right in the heart, the dragon heart. And I felt guilty. Unlike the others, Sasha had a way of saying things in a manner that I would listen.

I think it helped that she was pretty and her soft voice gave me chills.

I cleared my throat. There was a lump in it still. I did it again.

"Sasha," I said, touching her hand, "you don't really think anything will happen to me, do you? I'm a good dragon, remember. I'll never turn evil." I said it as if I was trying to convince myself. That bothered me. "Look, I know I have to be careful and that I can't run off on my own like I did before. But, what if it happens anyway? Didn't you say something about it mattering more what's on the inside that on the out?"

She nodded.

I went on. "And, we don't know that black dragons were all evil. Maybe just some of them. Aw … I don't know, Sasha." I shook my head and ran my fingers through my mane of hair.

I blew a puff of smoke.

"Wow!" she said, "I'm impressed. When did you learn to do that?"

"I've been practicing when no one is looking—what now?"

I glanced back. Brenwar, Shum and Bayzog were galloping towards me. "Aw, here comes another lecture." I started to fan the smoke away, but thought better of it. "Alright, there's nothing I can do about … what's going on?"

They galloped right past us and Brenwar was yelling.

"Are you coming or not, Dragon?"

Sasha and I looked at each other and then our eyes followed them.

Up ahead, miles distant, was a giant black plume of smoke.

I might get to test my arms out after all. Whatever it is, I hope it's big. Dangerous. Because if it is, I've got a surprise for it.

"Let's ride, Sasha! Yah!"

CHAPTER
4

SELENE SAT WITH HER SCALED black tail coiled around her, petting her drulture as the great doors opened. The lizardmen led a large man inside. He wore dark crimson and purple robes and was accompanied by two dragon-like men. The draykis.

The man stopped at the edge of her throne's dais, kneeled, and bowed his big shoulders. The draykis kneeled at his side.

"I come as you wish, High Priestess," the man said. His voice was dark and cheerless. "My life is yours."

It warmed her cold heart whenever he said that.

"Arise, High Cleric," she said, "and tell me what you know."

He nodded, rose and pulled back his hood. The High Cleric's bald head was covered in colorful tattoos. They moved, shifted and changed. Different shades. Different hues. The man's face was hard. Not old. Eyes dark and mean. His hands were thick and calloused. A heavy war mace hung by a strap over his broad shoulders. He looked more like a warrior than a cleric. A destroyer, not a healer.

"The draykis are excellent soldiers. Hunters as well." He ran his hand over the amulet that controlled them. "Nine dragons have been captured in the last month. Our poachers are in good order."

"Any unusual run-ins, Kryzak?" she said.

"No, Selene," he said, "not as I'd hoped to report, I'm afraid."

"Selene?" she said, leaning forward.

Kryzak shrugged. "You know how deep my love is for you, Selene." His eyes sparkled and flared. "I've died once for you. I'll do it again."

She eased back into her chair. Kryzak was the only man who spoke to her so informally. He'd earned it. He used it. She liked that about him. Cold. Confident. Fearless.

"Of course, Kryzak, but mind your tongue. You might lose a soldier if he followed your insubordination."

"Certainly," he said, nodding, "And if he did, I'd kill him myself."

He stood still, chin up, arms folded behind his back, waiting.

She sat, quiet, thinking. Nath Dragon had disappeared once more. But he would show up. He always did. Even Finnius the acolyte had tracked him down, but the High Cleric Kryzak could do better. He never failed any charge. Not once. Not ever. The man was on a mission. Her mission. The mission of Barnabus. Capture the dragons. Sell the ones that could be sold. Kill or turn them. But most importantly, stop Nath Dragon. Run the world.

"Find him, Kryzak," she said. "Grind him down. Torment his friends. His allies. No mercy. I want him weak. His purpose meaningless. His focus frayed."

Kryzak caressed the long wooden handle of his war-mace. The wood was weathered. The flanges of the head a dark iron metal. He nodded. "Our spies are everywhere. As soon as he shows, I'll know. Track him. Trip him. Snare him. Bust him up. Break him. It will be a pleasure."

"Don't get too carried away, Kryzak," she said, "I want him alive, but his friends, his allies—do with them what you wish."

He patted the head of his mace.

"Then his friends and allies," he said, glowering, "will be dead. Or horribly mutilated."

Her black tail uncoiled from her body, stretched out, and brushed his rugged face.

"My resources are yours," she said. "I have many. Be sure you keep me informed."

"As you wish, Selene," he said, closing his eyes. "You touch inspires me." He smiled and stroked her scales.

Her tail coiled around his neck and squeezed.

"Do not fail me, Kryzak."

"Ah," he moaned, "Your touch is divine and I won't fail. When Nath Dragon is in my clutches," he said, "You'll be the first to know."

Her tail slid away and draped over her shoulder.

"You're dismissed, Kryzak," she said.

Kryzak bowed, turned, and walked away. The draykis followed. The great doors closed behind them, leaving her and the drulture all alone once more.

Selene let out a sigh and patted the creature's head.

"I don't know who to feel worse for: Nath Dragon, or his friends."

The drulture flicked out its tongue and let out a tiny roar.

Selene chuckled.

"No, of course I don't feel for them. It's just an expression." She got up from her throne and walked down the steps. Her tail swished left and right from behind. "Stay, my pet. I have a grave meeting to attend."

It chirped and growled.

"No, you can't come," she said, headed for a concealed exit in the back. "I fear my Master might eat you. He's eaten too many of my pets in the past."

CHAPTER

5

WE RODE HARD THE NEXT few miles. Ahead, a small village was smoking and in tatters. Men labored. Children scurried back and forth and some cried. It must have happened days ago. Beyond the village, the smoke was coming from somewhere else.

"By Guzan," Brenwar said, "who'd do such a thing?"

"Who, or what?" Bayzog said, pulling a spyglass from his robes.

I hopped off my horse.

Sasha followed me down into the disaster-struck village.

The charred remains of houses and storefronts still smoldered. The farmers, tanners, bakers, herders and blacksmiths were dirty and drained. Milling about and scraping up what was left of their homes. Their memories. Heirlooms and such things. It tugged at my heart. Their peaceful lives had been destroyed.

A farmer, covered in dirt and soot, picked up pieces of a fence and stacked them nearby. A little boy, maybe twelve with tawny hair, wiped his eyes and stared.

"Sir," I said, "what happened? Who did this?"

The man didn't even turn. He kept working and told his son to look away.

"Sir," I said again. I didn't like to be ignored. I was only trying to help.

Sasha put her hand on my arm and led me away. "They are still grieving," she said. "And I don't see the mother. Seeing how they've lost a home, you'd think the mother would be near."

Scanning the village of broken wood and busted storehouses, I noticed something else. I didn't see a single woman. Dread filled my chest.

"Sasha," I said, "I don't see any women at all."

She pinched her lips with her fingers. "Oh dear." A crease deepened in her brow. "Perhaps one of them can help," she said, gesturing towards an organized-looking group of men.

The Legionnaires were a welcome sight. Two soldiers approached on foot, the City of Quintuklen colors and insignia emblazoned over their breast plates matching a small plume on their open faced helmets.

"Dragon! Is that you! Draaagon!" a man yelled at the top of his lungs.

It was Ben. He ran up to me and gave me a firm embrace.

"Easy, Ben."

"Oh," he said, patting my arms, "I'm sorry, I'm just so glad to see you. I was worried." He gasped, eyes widening. "You've got two dragon arms now. That's incredible!"

"Ahem," Sasha said.

Ben lost his breath. "Up … er …" He swallowed a lump, took off his helmet, and bowed a little. "So nice to see you again, Sasha. You are even more beautiful than I recall."

Sasha giggled. "Thank you. It's good to see you too."

"Why Ben," I said, "you really are a soldier, aren't you?" I patted his armored shoulder. "Complimenting a lady and everything. I'm impressed."

Ben stuck his chin out and grinned. He'd changed. His armor fit well. He'd thickened up in his chest and shoulders. He looked good. Like a soldier. He was no longer a lanky son of a farmer, but a strapping young man with some grizzle on his chin.

"Nice bow you have there," I said.

Ben had a full quiver of black-feathered arrows and a short bow. He beamed at me. "It's not Akron," he said, "but it's a good one. I strung it myself. Dragon, I'm actually one of the top marksmen on account of my training and all. The Commander says I'll get to train new recruits in the future."

"That's great, Ben." I tuned my gaze to the soldier beside him. He was stout and short-bearded, with a heavy axe on his belt. "And who's your friend?"

"Oh, forgive me," Ben said. "This is Garrison. He's my comrade."

I nodded and said, "Nice to meet you, Garrison."

"Aye," Garrison said. Head down.

"Don't worry about him, Dragon," Ben said. "He's not the talker that I am. But he's a fine fighter and wrestler. I've seen him pin a goblin and an orc. One right after the other."

"Impressive."

Sasha nudged me.

"Huh? Oh," I said. "Ben, what is—"

"No, Dragon, you owe him something else," she said.

"I do?" I said, looking at her. I didn't take her meaning right away, but then it hit me. "Oh, I do. I, uh, certainly do."

But what I owed him didn't come easy. It was Ben who had dragged me back to the city of Quintuklen after I blacked out. He'd secured the horses as I ordered. Ridden me back to safety. He'd done everything by himself. Done it right. But saying thanks didn't come easy.

He wasn't supposed save me. I was supposed to save him.

I rubbed the back of my neck and said to Ben's friend Garrison, "Did Ben tell you how he saved my life?"

Garrison nodded.

Ben was beaming.

"Ben," I said, extending my hand, "thanks for taking care of me."

He accepted my hand. "Well, you taught me. Told me all about adventuring and responsibility. It was easy."

"Oh, is that so?" Sasha said. "My, you sound like someone I know."

"Don't say it," I said.

"I won't," she said.

Ben tried to hug me again but I stopped him. "That's enough of that. Now tell us, what is going on?"

"Ettins, Dragon! Ettins are doing this!" he said.

Sasha looked at me with a funny look on her face. "Ettins are awfully rare. It doesn't seem likely that ettins are about."

I had only seen one once before, and I'd gotten little more than a glimpse. "Really, Ben? How can you be sure? Did you see them?"

He shook his head yes with vigor. "I swear it, Dragon! I even shot at one with my bow. My arrow skipped right off it, like its eyelid was made of stone."

"I don't know. Ettins are pretty big and slow," I said. "You only got one shot off? Not at least three or four?"

"Oh, it's big alright. At least thirty feet tall." Ben stretched his arms up and held them wide. "And I only got one shot off because I had to run for my life."

"Why?"

"They're like rolling boulders when they run! They would have crushed us," he said, "so Garrison and I ran. We hid!"

It seemed a stretch. The ettin I'd seen was only twenty feet in height, if that. Maybe just fifteen. "Thirty feet tall?" I said.

Both Ben and Garrison nodded their heads yes vigorously.

Ben went on in a high-pitched, fast rush. "And it has two heads! Ugly as an orc. Well, kinda. Scary though. Really scary. It ate a man whole!"

"And they kidnapped the women?"

Again, they nodded yes.

Ben said, "You believe me don't you, Dragon?"

"Sure he does," Sasha said, "and I believe you too."

"So," I said, "where is the ettin you shot at now?"

Ben pointed toward the smoke over the next hill.

"The Legionnaires followed him that way. The Commander ordered us to stay put at this village and help out. This isn't the only village to fall. Another burns. They like setting things on fire. Why do they do that?"

I exchanged another odd look with Sasha. "Have you ever heard of an ettin raiding a village or stealing women?"

"No," she said. "That makes no sense. Not one bit."

"What does it look like, Ben?"

"Well, like I said, it's really tall. Has two heads… "

"We've established that, Ben. Can you tell me a little more? Does it have skin, scales, or fur? A tail? We can't be sure it's an ettin."

"Uh …, uh …," Ben's eyes were growing.

Garrison stepped behind me.

"Dragon!" Brenwar yelled from out of nowhere.

The ground shook under my feet.

Thoom! Thoom!

I whipped my head around. Lumbering downhill it came. Two-heads. Thirty feet tall. It had a squirming Legionnaire in one hand and a club the size of a whole tree in the other. It skipped the soldier over the ground like a stone.

"There be an ettin!" Brenwar said. He hoisted his war hammer over his head. "Battle Ho!"

CHAPTER

6

IT WAS AN ETTIN. Two heads of matted brown hair. Thick skin covering hard packs of muscle. It towered even more than thirty feet in height. Its massive legs shook the ground.

Sasha wrapped her arms around my waist. She was trembling.

"Dragon!" she said. "Can you stop that … that monster?"

"I told you he was big," Ben said, nocking an arrow.

I jumped on my horse.

"Stay here!" I said. "Ben. Garrison. Keep an eye on Sasha!"

Thoom!

Thoom!

Thoom!

The ettin's club went up and down, pulverizing everything in sight. A host of Legionnaires scrambled. Others fell. Horses bucked and whined.

Brenwar, Bayzog, and Shum had galloped towards the monster, obstructing its path. I sped after them.

"Yah!"

Brenwar was the giant expert. Not me. But he'd told me stories about how the dwarves fought the giants. And best as I could recall, and I recalled plenty, it took many, many dwarves. Today we only had one. I could hear Brenwar's thunderous bellows. He was fighting mad. But he was happy.

A blue ball of fire erupted from Bayzog's fingers, shooting across the sky and into the ettin's face.

It roared and shook its thick neck. Face smoking, it turned on its attacker, roared again and charged.

"Bayzog!" I yelled.

He couldn't hear me. There was too much noise. The Legionaries galloped by, hurling spears into its legs. Arrows ricocheted off its faces. Just like Ben said.

"Bayzog!" I said. "Get out of the way!"

The ettin loomed over them and raised its crude club.

Brenwar attacked its ankles with his war hammer.

Its great club came down. Bayzog was right underneath it.

Boom!

"Noooooo!" I screamed.

Bayzog was down.

I snapped the reins. "Monster!" I galloped up the hill at full speed.

A man was standing in my path. Waving.

"Huh?"

It was Bayzog. I'd almost run over him.

I jerked back the reins and stopped.

"Pretty fine sorcery, eh, Dragon?" he said, lifting his black brows.

"You trickster you!" I said. "Get on, will you?"

Bayzog shook his head. "I do my best work from a distance. That illusion was just a test. He's strong, Dragon. Resistant to normal weapons—and to some magic too. That ball I sent was no illusion. It should have knocked one head out."

"What do you suggest, Bayzog?"

He lifted one brow. Everyone else was fighting, and he was thinking.

I didn't have time to wait. I pulled Fang from his sheath and charged onward. Behind me I heard Bayzog shout something, but the wind carried it away.

"Dragon! Dragon!"

Fang flared with blue life.

Chaos surrounded the ettin. A score of soldiers attacked from all directions. Shum was nowhere to be seen. I searched for Brenwar. *Where are you, Dwarf?* The heavy head of his war hammer flashing in the air caught the corner of my eye.

KaRoom!

Brenwar smashed the bones in the ettin's ankle.

The ettin screamed like the world was going to end. *Good!*

Thoom!

Thoom!

Thoom!

It hopped up and down on one foot. The club swiped over the ground. Brenwar ducked beneath it. Soldiers and horses skipped over the ground.

I dug my heels into my steed. I had to stop this monster before it killed or hurt anyone else.

KaRoom!

Brenwar hit it again.

The ettin toppled forward.

"Nooooo!" I yelled.

It landed on top of Brenwar.

"Great Guzan!"

I was almost there. The Legionnaires piled on the monster. They pinned it down with weighted nets and ropes. Bound its arms and legs.

Shum appeared on the ettin's great chest. Agile. Graceful. The Elven Ranger flung a sparkling dust in the eyes of one of its heads.

The ettin thrashed and rolled. The soldiers holding the ropes were flung into one another and scattered. Its huge fists came down. Crushing one soldier. Crippling another. Its powerful legs snapped the ropes that bound it. It ripped them from its body like threads.

It was going to take a lot more than plain ole' manpower to take this monster down. I readied my sword.

"Fang," I said, "don't let me down."

I held onto Fang with both my dragon arms and swung into its knee like I was chopping into a tree. I got halfway through in one swing.

Both heads cried out.

White-blue energy erupted from the blade. Ice formed. Spread above and below the knee.

"Brenwar!"

The dwarf lay smashed face-first in the ground.

I jumped off my horse and pulled him up. His full body impression remained in the grass.

"Are you alright?"

He was moving. His voice was muffled. "Blecht!" He spit out grass, wildflowers and dirt. "Bloody ettin sat on me," he said. "Don't you dare tell anyone, Dragon. No one sits on a dwarf and lives to tell about it." He picked up his hammer. "Where is it?"

I pointed.

The ettin was standing again, right behind us. Its legs were stuck together. The ice had frozen everything between its knees and ankles. Its ugly heads bickered at each other, speaking in Ettish. One hand rubbed at the dust in one of its head's eyes. Arrows and spears zinged off its bare chest. Spears dangled in its other arm, which swung wildly, pounding at the ice.

Brenwar huffed. "It's a tough one, it is!"

"I agree. So, you're the giant killer. What do we do now, Brenwar?"

He shrugged. "Keep fighting. We'll wear it down!"

"That's it? Five hundred years of dwarven wisdom and it narrows down to 'Keep fighting. We'll wear it down?'" I said.

"Don't have time for a longer answer," Brenwar said. He slammed his war hammer into one toe, then another.

The giant's club swept over the grass, with Brenwar right in its path.

I jumped and knocked Brenwar out of the way.

Wok!

The club hit me square in the chest. Head over heels I crashed. I saw spots. I was dizzy. My chest felt like busted glass. I couldn't catch my breath. I made it back to my feet, and fell again.

Ahead, the ettin whacked at the ice, but it held.

Somehow, Shum managed to lasso the ettin's necks.

The Legionnaires tied the ropes off with a team of horses. They snorted. Dug their hooves in. Tried to pull it down.

The ettin wasn't going down. Not for anyone. It fought. It yelled. Then, one head yawned. The one Shum had dumped the dust on. The monstrous body quavered. One head looked dreamy eyes at the other. Then one head shouted at itself. It clonked itself on the sleepy head with its club, but the head dipped into its chest. One side of its body went slack. The horses heaved one more time.

Down it went.

Boom!

So did I.

CHAPTER

7

"WAKE UP, DRAGON! WAKE UP!" I heard Brenwar say.

Oh no! I thought. *Not again.* I opened my eyes.

Brenwar held a hard stare on me. Shum, Bayzog, and Sasha looked concerned. Even Ben was there. Kneeling along my side, fanning me with a shield.

"How long have I been out?" I said, looking at my hands.

"Ho! How long! What do you ask that for?" Brenwar said, fists on hips. "Afraid ye might wake up with a tail?" He held out his arm and pulled me up. Checked my behind. "All clear."

The others laughed.

"Are you alright, Dragon?" Sasha said. "You've only been down a few minutes. Were you worried that you might have changed again?"

"No," I said, clutching my chest. It ached, and yes, I had been worried. But now I was relieved. Same day. Same me. A good thing. I rubbed my chest. "Great Guzan, that was quite a walloping. I don't think I've ever blacked out before from a hit. Ugh. Still hurts."

"Good thing you had dwarven breastplate on," Brenwar said. "Else yer stomach be on the other side of the village. Hah."

A good thing indeed. But something troubled me.

"I took that blow for you, Brenwar. If you weren't so slow—"

"Slow!" His beard bristled. He shook his hammer in my face. "I'll show you slow, Dragon. On yer feet! I'll put another bump on yer head."

Shum stepped between us. "Let's focus on the wounded. We're all fine. For now, that is."

"What do you mean by that?" I said.

"Can you walk?" Shum said.

"Of course I can." I started to stand. "Oof!" Sweat beaded on my head.

"Let me help you, Dragon," Ben said, offering his hand.

"No, I'm alright." I eyed Brenwar. "I'll just be more careful who I decide to save next time."

"Pah!" Brenwar said, walking away.

Shum stood and waited. Fingers locked over his pot belly. Bayzog was beside him.

My eyes rested on them a moment, thinking how both were elves, but different. Shum, dressed in worn leathers, was tall, broad, relaxed and thick wristed. Bayzog's dark robes were elegant, his features stern, his movements purposeful, even for a part-elf. They were the kind of people I liked to be around. Different. Like me.

"Where we going?" I said, following.

Shum pointed.

The ettin. It was right where they left it. Sitting up. Coiled in ropes, chains and mystic banding that sparkled. One head snored. The other was silent. Searching. It locked eyes on me. I felt a chill. Most giants were ornery and stupid. This one was pure evil.

"What are the Legionnaires doing?" I said.

"Building a fire," Shum said. His brows perched. "A big one."

"For what?" I said.

"Burn it!" a farmer yelled. He brandished a hoe in his hands, and tears fell from is eyes. "It took my wife. It killed my friends! Burn it!"

A crowd of villagers gathered around. Several threw rocks and stones at the ettin.

It laughed.

"Garrison," I said. "Who is in charge here?"

"Commander Wuzlin. Why?"

"Make sure he realizes that ettins don't burn. And if we kill the ettin, how are we supposed to find the women?"

"But," Ben said.

"Just go! Make haste, Garrison, before they burn down everything."

Garrison scurried away. Ben frowned and watched his friend go.

Sasha patted Ben's back, and he smiled, just a little.

I shook my head and spoke kindly to Ben. "These villagers are angry. Scared. Being unreasonable will follow. They want justice. They want blood. But I want answers." I turned to the rest of my friends. "Come on. Any of you speak ettin?"

"Perhaps he speaks Common," Ben said.

"I can speak a little giant," Shum said, "and ogre. He might understand that."

Bayzog stepped between Ben and Sasha and took Sasha's hand. "Even if the ettin understands what we say, why would he acknowledge it? Ettins, like all giants, are as stubborn as they are big."

I thought that unfortunately, Bayzog was probably right.

And this ettin, he was massive. A thick slab of hair and skin slapped over solid muscle. One head had a nose ring, the other two hooped earrings.

I couldn't help but wonder who had made them such things. Did ettins have blacksmiths?

I hopped up on its ice-coated knee, walked over its leg, and poked Fang into one of its noses.

"OW!" it said, shaking its awake head, looking away. "Don't do that again."

I understood it. It was a rugged language. But not ancient. Clear enough to make out.

"Ettin. Where are the women?"

One head snored. Drooled. The other turned back to face me and breathed.

"Ew!" I covered my face with my arm. It was foul. Beyond words.

"Heh-heh-heh!" it said. "Like that, do you? The smell of many men I ate."

I poked its nose again.

"Ow!"

"I'm not playing games, Ettin. Where are the women?"

It shook its shaggy head. "Hah! You'll never know!"

A rock pelted me in the head.

"What are you doing?" I turned and locked eyes with a villager who stood there wide-eyed.

A moment later Ben tackled him. "I got him, Dragon. What shall I do with him?"

Knock some sense into him. I wanted to say that. I really did. "Take his rocks and send him home!"

"Burn it!" someone said.

"Burn it! Burn it! Burn it!" They started to chant.

The bonfire was getting bigger and bigger. Flames went up and black smoke rolled over the hills. If I was going to get an answer, I would have to get it quick.

"Alright, Ettin," I said, "Tell me this. Why did you take the women? Why did you attack the village?" I tapped the flat blade of Fang on its nose. "Hmmm?"

Its voice was gruff. Harsh. A deep tunnel when it spoke. "Why not!" it said. Quick. Angry.

"I see. So, you just like picking on little things. Perhaps where you're from they pick on you? You are a bit small for an ettin."

"Gggggrrrrrrlll!" Its brows buckled. The other head started to wake up.

"Dragon!" Brenwar said. Shum was helping him up on the ettin's leg. "Let me at him! I'll make him tell us where the women are!" He raised his hammer over the ettin's icy knee. "Answer up, Ettin!" Brenwar yelled.

"Hold up, Brenwar! Give me a few minutes at least," I said.

"Hah! Stupid dwarf can't hurt me!" The ettin laughed. "Little bearded hogs. That's what we call them."

Brenwar brought that hammer down.

Whack!

Both of the ettin's heads let out ear-splitting howls.

Ears covered, the villagers fled, screaming.

I yelled at Brenwar. "Did you have to do that?"

"Aye!" Brenwar said, raising his hammer again.

"Stop it, will you!" I said.

I watched the villagers. They sprinted. Panicked. It didn't make sense to me. The ettin, loud as it might be, wasn't going anywhere. But I'd had enough of their lousy rock throwing already. How could you miss an ettin at close range?

"Nath!"

"What!" I said, looking around.

Shum and Bayzog, standing on the ground, were waving their hands at me.

I shrugged. "Really, what is it?"

The sound of a Legionnaire's War Horn blasted through the air. Briefly, I thought, *What is taking Garrison so long?*

Then the elves pointed towards the smoke over the horizon.

I turned.

Thoom!

Another ettin cleared the hill.

"HA! HA! HA!" My ettin prisoner laughed. "My brother is here!"

CHAPTER

8

ONE ETTIN ENCOUNTER IN A day was enough to last you a lifetime, but two? That seemed impossible. I shook my head and looked at Brenwar.

He had an expression I'd never seen before. His brows were lifted. His mouth was open. The grumbler was puzzled.

"Nath," Bayzog said, "Suggestions?"

Thoom! Thoom! Thoom!

The second ettin strode past the tall trees. Head higher than the branches. A heavy chain was draped over his neck with a massive anchor on the end of it. He uprooted trees from the ground like pulling carrots, and he slung them across the land. He was bigger than his brother. Dark bearded. Terrible. Mean. Cruel expression. Heavy muscles over a solid round belly.

"You die now, Dragon Man," the first ettin said.

The other head shook. Blinked its blurry eyes. Snorted. "What happened?"

"Quiet! I'm in charge of this."

The other head snorted. "No, I'm the oldest." It whipped around. "Say, who tied me up!"

Thoom! Thoom! Thoom!

"Dragon!" Bayzog said. "Time to act!"

"Hold yer ground, Dragon," Brenwar said. He raised his hammer. "We've got a prisoner."

I nodded. Watched.

The Legionnaires lined in rank, making a wall between our prisoner and the brother ettin. The bright plumes on their helmets billowed in the wind. They lowered their lances. The ettin heads stopped and bickered. The War Horn sounded again. The Knights of Quintuklen charged. They were brave men. Some of the bravest men I ever saw.

The first ettin laughed in my face. Low. Wicked.

Hooves thundered up the hillside. Shiny armor gleamed in the sunlight. It was a glorious sight. Brave men riding into battle. Doing what was right. Fighting evil.

The second ettin lifted the chain from his neck and roared. The anchor circled like a lasso over its heads. A fierce grin crossed its faces.

SWOOSH!

The ettin struck, scattering horses and riders all over the ground.

I yelled, "Nooooo!"

The bound-up ettin laughed.

More people would die if I didn't stop this.

A white streak of power slammed into the second ettin's face. It howled and dropped the anchor on its toe. One face was smoking. Angry.

The Legionnaires struck again. Their volley of arrows skipped off its face. Lances shattered on its limbs.

It swatted them away. Knocking men into men. Horse toppled riders.

"Retreat!" I yelled.

It picked up its anchor and came right at us. Angry eyes locked on Bayzog.

I could see Bayzog's eyes were drained. Weary.

"Shum!" I said, "Get Bayzog and Sasha to safety. I'll handle this."

Shum scooped his hands behind them and scurried them away.

Thoom! Thoom! Thoom!

"YOU GONNA GET IT NOW, DRAGON MAN!"

"Be quiet," Brenwar said, shaking his war hammer in the first ettin's face.

I reached over my back and grabbed Akron.

Snap. Clatch. Snap.

The ettin brother would overtake us in two more steps.

I loaded a Moorite Arrow and pulled the bow with my two dragon arms.

Twang!

The arrow buried in its knee.

The second ettin roared and turned on me.

I reloaded. A different arrow this time. I rubbed some spit on the tip and it glowed white hot. I pointed it at one face of the ettin prisoner, whose chest I stood upon.

Towering over me and the others, the ettin brother swung his anchor and chain.

"LET MY BROTHER GO!" it said.

I pulled back on the arrow and pointed right at one of the ettin prisoner's eyes. They all widened. The tip of my arrow was still white hot. I took my aim back and forth from face to face. Eye to eye.

"You better tell your big brother to back off," I said. "You don't you want any part of an exploding arrow, do you?"

"No!" one head said.

"No! No! No!" said the other head.

I touched the tip of the arrow on one of the ettin's noses. It sizzled.

"Tell your brother to back away then," I said.

Tears formed in the eyes of one. A grunt came for the other.

"Don't do it," one said.

"No! I don't want my head exploded," said the other.

"Oh, don't worry," I said. "I have plenty of arrows for the both of you."

Lumps rolled up and down their throats. They shouted.

"Brother! Back off!"

The ettin swinging the chain did no such thing. He stomped his foot, shaking the ground. He growled.

The Legionnaires continued their attacks. Some spears and arrows stuck in the ettin's hide. Others broke. The ettin didn't seem to notice.

A spear zinged by my head.

An arrow splintered on Brenwar's chest. "Who shot that!" he said.

"Ben!" I said. "Find the commander. Tell them to back off!"

"Alright, Dragon!" Ben dashed away.

I stood on the ettin's chest, thinking. *Why the sudden attack on a small village? I have to find the women. Get them released.* But the Legionnaires would want to avenge their casualties. The villagers would want payment for the lost.

"Dragon," Brenwar said, "you can't trust what they say."

Crack!

Another arrow shattered on his armored chest.

"That's enough of that, I say!"

The ettin turned. Swung his anchor into the ranks, scattered the soldiers like leaves.

"Ettin!" I yelled. "Don't do that again! Else, your brother's going to have one head, not two!"

It turned and lowered its big eyes. Its hairy brows buckled like giant caterpillars and one head licked its lips. It stopped swinging and draped the chain and anchor around its neck like jewelry. What was taking place was just not normal.

"Let me hit him in the knee again," Brenwar said.

"No, just give it a moment."

The War Horn sounded. The Legionnaires, on horse and foot, made another formation and trotted back up the hill, leaving me, Brenwar and two ettins all by ourselves.

"Can we talk now?" I yelled up to him.

His words were loud. Slow. Deep.

"FREE MY BROTHER. OR DIE!" Its ugly faces smiled. "I CAN KILL ALL OF YOU. I WILL KILL ALL OF YOU IF YOU HARM MY BROTHER!"

Great Guzan! I hadn't thought of that. Supposing I did kill the ettin—which even though it was evil, I shouldn't—what was to stop its brother from going on a rampage and killing more people?

"You won't be killing me," Brenwar said, "you smelly animal. I've taken down giants bigger than you!"

"GO BACK TO MORGON," one head said.

"YOU BEARDED HALFLING," said the other.

"Bearded what!" Brenwar started to bring his hammer down.

"Don't!" I said. "Brenwar, let me handle this."

Delay him, Nath, a voice said in my mind. It was Bayzog. *We search for the women as you speak.*

"You better make it fast," I said.

"Make what fast?" Brenwar said. "Hitting the ettin?"

"No," I said, "I was … never mind. Just be still."

I didn't want to tip the ettins off. They weren't the smartest of the giants, but they weren't stupid as orcs either. Well, maybe.

"Listen, Ettin," I said, "No one has to die. Not me. Not you. Not your brother. Let's just trade. Your brother for the women. Even is even."

"It's a good idea, Brother," the ettin prisoner said.

"THERE CAN BE NO DEAL." Both of the free ettin's heads shook as they said it.

Something about the way it said that ran a chill right through me.

"Of course there can be," I said. I didn't want to say the next thought I had in my mind, but I did. "Unless something has happened to the women."

"HA, HA, HA," it laughed. "THEY ARE ALL DEAD."

CHAPTER

9

"THIS IS PERFECT. DELICIOUS. SALIVATING." Kryzak wiped the sweat from his colorful head.

Before him, a small image of a man shimmered inside his grand tent. Speaking on a bright carpet.

"It's going well, High Cleric," the man said in Common. "Nath Dragon battles the ettins as we speak. Others have split up. I must go now." The gray image bowed.

He snapped his fingers. The image faded away.

"I wish I could see it," Kryzak said, wringing his hands. He walked over and sat in a plush chair.

Two draykis were on each side. Four acolytes in grey robes and with single tattooed rings on their bald heads stood inside the tent as well.

He snapped his fingers.

One acolyte readied a goblet. The other poured.

Kryzak took the goblet and drank.

For years he'd been hunting dragons. Now he was hunting the most valuable one of all. Nath Dragon. He had longed for this day. Longed for the day he could prove himself to be the one, the only one for High Priestess Selene.

"I want to be alone now," he said.

The acolytes departed, ducking through the tent flap one by one. Behind him, the draykis, nearly seven feet of brawn and scales, stiff as statues, remained. He liked them. Commanding things so big and powerful gave him a thrill.

He patted the bright tattoos on his head with a satin cloth.

"Nath Dragon," he muttered. "So far, so easy… "

The Clerics of Barnabus were a crafty lot. Their eyes and ears were everywhere. In cities, large and small. In villages, but not all.

He slumped back in his chair and closed his eyes. He smiled.

"No one can evade Barnabus."

Nath Dragon and his party had been caught leaving Quintuklen. It was the last place he'd been seen since they trapped him at the temple. That's where the Drultures came in. Flying notes back and forth faster than eagles. They tracked his every move southeast, towards Narnum.

Kryzak's guess at Nath Dragon's destination was the elven city of Elome, judging by the direction of his travel and the company he kept. An elven wizard. A Roaming Ranger. Why there he didn't know, so he kept his distance. He had to work fast though. Find any help he could get.

That's how he'd found Ettin Cove. The giant brutes had taken some convincing, but in the end, they had agreed. Kryzak had his ways. Now, the ettins laid into one small village after the other. There was no way Nath Dragon and his party would miss them. No way the cries and despair of the voices wouldn't lure him.

Especially when Kryzak had spies within the ranks of the Legionnaires.

"I wish I could see it." He mumbled some words, and smoke billowed from his mouth and nose, filling the tent in thick layer of gloom. "But we'll see how it goes."

CHAPTER
10

ON HORSEBACK, SHUM AND BAYZOG made their way from the village. Shum the Roaming Ranger was leading the way, following the trail of the ettins, when he pulled his horse to a stop. The big-boned elf slid off his horse, stepped into one of the giant foot impressions in the tall grass, and kneeled.

Bayzog, a bit weary, prepared a spell on his lips. He didn't feel comfortable. He wasn't ready. Over the decades he'd spent most of his time indoors. Studying. Crafting. And it had been a decade since he last ventured into the wilderness. He was a little unsettled. He sneezed.

Shum looked up at him with a funny look on his face.

"What?" Bayzog said, "Nothing to worry about. Probably from the excitement."

Shum shook his head and sniffed the air. The smoke in the distance was dying down.

"I could smell them before," Shum said, pushing his long hair from his face, "but the wind has changed. The tracks however, hmmm, well, they come from separate directions."

Bayzog coughed a little. Tapped his chest with his fist. He'd been uncomfortable since they left. Not so much about the woodland, but about heading back home. To Elome. He was an outsider. Part elf. Part human. His human side didn't fight off the elements like the elven blood did. It bothered him. It always had. Shum was different too, but a pure elf. One born in the harsh outdoors, living among the beasts and the monsters. A part of nature itself. The big elf stood in the footprint as tall as him, staring over the horizon. Bayzog wondered if Shum felt the same.

"I say we follow the bigger one. Away from the smoke." Shum swung himself into his saddle. "Their lair can't be too far." Shum looked at him. Waiting.

"After you," Bayzog said.

They rode until the hills became steep and the terrain rugged. Moss over rock-covered ground. This was the part Bayzog didn't like. The sudden changes. The air. The wind. The setting sun. No roof over his head. He wasn't sure if it was the man or the elf that preferred the indoors over the out. Elves, by nature, liked open spaces. The comfort of greenery, blended with stone and tree trunks.

Shum slowed. Hooves splashed over a creek bed into a denser patch of woods. He looked over his shoulder at Bayzog with narrow eyes.

Bayzog felt it too. A shift. A darkness. The fine hairs on his arms tingled. That was the elf in him. He was certain. He still had the instincts, just a little dormant. He thought of Sasha. He hated not having her by his side. She gave him comfort. Security. She understood his nervousness and the edginess he fought so hard to hide. He made a sound in Elvish. A hoot of sorts.

Shum let him catch up.

"I should check in with Dragon. It's been awhile," he said. "And if we go too far, I can't connect."

"Do as you will, Wizard. I'll scout ahead."

"No," Bayzog said.

"Beg pardon?"

"Oh, nothing," he said, scanning the area. "Don't let me hold you up. I'll be fine."

Shum and his horse blended into the brush and out of sight.

Bayzog took a deep breath. It was still day, but dark under the heavier foliage. The trees seemed foreboding. The sounds of nature—the trickle of the creek, the buzzing wings—did little to soothe him. He was alone and anything could happen. Like running into an ettin. He shuddered. They were some of the most fearsome things he'd ever seen. So big. Strong. Unpleasant.

"Ease yourself, Bayzog," he said to himself. "Check in with Dragon and Sasha."

He started the incantation for the communication spell, and magic filled his body. His mind became a spring of energy.

Thoom.

The ground shook. He lost his concentration.

Thoom.

His horse stammered and snorted. He clutched at the reins. Heart pounding.

"Alright, Shum, where are you?"

CHAPTER

11

THE VILLAGERS. THE LEGIONNAIRES. SASHA and Brenwar. They all fell silent.

The ettin had said, in words all could understand, "The women are all dead."

Children sobbed. Tears watered in men's eyes. The hardened soldiers' faces were creased in worry. And there stood the second ettin. Arms folded over its chest. Gloating.

"NO WOMEN TO TRADE." All four of its brows lifted. "BUT, LET MY BROTHER GO, NO MORE HARM. NO MORE DEATH ... SCALY ONE."

"You lie!" I said.

I've said it before. I'm good at telling the truth from a lie. And Brenwar had already told me a thousand times that giants are liars.

But the villagers. They didn't know that. The soldiers didn't either.

I searched for Sasha. She was tending to the wounded in the field. I hoped maybe she could contact

Bayzog. Tell him to hurry. At the moment, we were at a standstill. I had to buy time. I had to calm the villagers.

"Ben!"

He ran over to me. Marveled at the ettins, then turned to me.

"Yes, Dragon?"

"He's lying. The women aren't dead. Spread the word around."

He started to run off.

"And be convincing!"

The villagers wouldn't stand for this much longer. They'd attack. So would the soldiers, and more of them would die. I couldn't let that happen.

"I'm losing my patience, Ettin." I turned my bow on the second ettin. "Perhaps it's you that would be better off without one head. Perhaps one doesn't agree so much with the other."

The ettins scratched their heads. Turned to one another and whispered in Ettish.

I could understand it.

I whispered to Brenwar. "Get your chest."

"Why?" he said.

"Just do it."

"And what?"

"I don't know. Think of something. Ask Sasha."

Brenwar looked at me and the ettin's knee.

"Just one more lick, ay?" He lifted his bushy black brows.

"Go!"

"Alright then." He hopped down and marched off.

The ettins turned back to me. The second one scratched one of its heads. The first one looked worried. At least I had them thinking.

"YOU WON'T SHOOT. YOU SHOOT. WE SMASH PEOPLE."

"I shoot, one of you won't be smashing anything. And need I remind you I have plenty of arrows?"

I knew one of my arrows would hurt them. But kill them? Maybe. And I wasn't so sure it was alright to kill an ettin. Even if it had killed many innocent people. It was all confusing. But, I should be able to outsmart an ettin.

Twang!

The ettin ducked. My arrow sailed high over its head.

"HA! YOU MISSED!"

"No, no I didn't. Take a look behind you," I said.

The ettin's heads turned.

KABOOM!

The ettin flinched and covered its eyes.

Everyone screamed.

Less than a hundred yards past the second ettin, a hundred-foot-tall oak cracked and groaned. Its trunk was bigger than the ettin's hairy legs. It wavered. Teetered and toppled and crashed to the ground.

The second ettin turned to me, grunting. Scratching its heads. A worried look grew on its faces.

I had another arrow aimed right at it.

"HMRPH," it said. "We think about this."

"You do that, Ettin. In the meantime," I said, pointing my bow at its brother, "I'll keep a close eye, a very close one, on your brother."

"No shoot!" It said. "No shoot!"

Its chest rose up and down under my feet. I could feel its heart beating in my toes. Heavy rapid thumps. It was worried. The more worried the better. It gave me control.

For some reason, I was thirsty. I felt really hot and uncomfortable, not to mention the ettin's hot breath was so foul and nasty. It took away my appetite. Still, something else was gnawing at my stomach.

Earlier, I'd felt great. I had two dragon arms. I was bigger, faster, and stronger. Now, I felt so small and ineffective. I wasn't sure how to fight a monster over thirty feet tall. Its hands were so big that it could squeeze my head off. Snap me like a twig. Perhaps I wasn't such a big deal in Nalzambor after all.

The second ettin turned and took a knee, facing me and its brother. It spoke quieter.

"Let my brother go and we'll bring back your women," the head on the left said.

"I thought you said they were all dead?"

"I didn't say they were alive," he head on the right said, "but at least you could bury them." It chuckled and showed a toothy grin.

Now I had to wonder, did one head lie? Did the other head tell the truth? It was best to assume they both lied. But it angered me. It was a horrible thought, them killing innocent women. I adjusted my bow. Drew it tight. Aimed at the last head that had spoken.

"I've had enough! Take us to the women or your brother will suffer."

"Alright! Alright!" It said. "We'll take you. Just, please, put down your bow. We don't want to lose a head. We don't want to have a hole in us." It leaned back. "You win, Dragon Man."

"That's better." I un-nocked my arrow. "Now, tell me where—"

"*ACHOO!*"

The first ettin sneezed. My footing shifted, and I dropped to my seat. The disgusting spray was all over me.

"Yuck!" I said, slinging my hands and wiping my face.

Snap! Snap! Snap!

The first ettin's bindings were breaking. A howl of villagers and soldiers went up in the air.

"What is going—"

Whap!

A big hand swatted me from its chest. I tumbled to the ground and Akron fell from my grasp. Above me, the second ettin was cutting the cords with a stone knife I hadn't noticed earlier. I dove for my bow. The first ettin slapped its hand over it.

"No 'Boom Boom' for you, Dragon Man!"

They had me surrounded. A pair of great hands clutched after me. I ducked under a swinging fist and hopped over a clutching hand. They were quick for being so big. Their size negated my speed.

Wham! Wham! Wham!

Fists bigger than barrels shook the ground. Big fingers grasped for me. I went for my sword.

Swat!

The second ettin back handed me and flattened me to the ground. The first ettin scooped me up in both hands, pinning my arms to my sides.

I flexed my dragon arms. I tried to kick. But I could only move my toes.

The ettins chuckled.

"Look what we have here, Big Brother," the first ettin said. "We got us a dragon man. Let's take him, throw him in a pot, and turn him to stew like the others."

CHAPTER

12

THE GROUND SHOOK. BAYZOG SHUDDERED. Pictures of angry ettins danced in his head. He had to run. Hide. Do something. He muttered a protection spell. A mystic surge coursed through his blood. Calmness and security followed.

He sighed.

"That's better."

Thoom.

The footsteps were distant and he didn't have to be an elven ranger to know that. But how close was too close?

Something else caught his ears and he hunkered down in his saddle, eyes searching. The rustling foliage. Darting. Jumping. It was fast and coming right at him. He dove to the ground and covered his head. A herd of gazelle burst across the path, leapt over him and disappeared. His spooked horse trotted out of sight.

"Oh great," he said, rising and dusting off his robes. "Shum would laugh, maybe, if he saw that. Every elf in Nalzambor would. Shameful."

He ambled down the path—tripping over his robes before pulling them up—and went after the horse. The beast was well trained and wouldn't run far unless it was really spooked. He figured on the worst-case scenario for Shum. *Probably being eaten by an ettin by now.* He forged ahead, pushing branch after branch from his face. He caught his robes on one, jerked it free and tore it.

"Drat it all," he said, under his breath. He wiped the sweat from his forehead.

Thoom.

His heart skipped and beat faster.

"Thank goodness for protection spells. Otherwise I'd be on the other side of the creek by now."

He moved on.

Thoom.

He stopped.

Breathe, Bayzog. Breathe.

The points on his ears bent a little. Something else was running towards him.

He grabbed a stick and waited. *I'm not getting my robes dirty this time.*

A woman's voice cried out.

"Aiiyee!"

He ran towards the sound of her voice.

She screamed again.

He jumped over a log, smashed through the branches, and ran right into her. They both tumbled to the ground. The woman was distraught and her clothes were in tatters. She had to be one of the villagers.

"Woman," he said, "it's alright. You are safe now."

Her eyes were wide, darting and glossy. Her entire body trembled. Bayzog brushed her dark hair from her scraped-up face. She just blinked at him like he wasn't there.

"Did the ettins have you?"

She nodded.

Thoom!

She grabbed his robes and said, "Please! Please! Take me home! Get me away from here!"

"Easy," he said. "We'll get you home—"

Thoom!

She tore away from him and dashed into the woods.

"Wait!" he said, jumping after her.

"Aiiyee!" she said.

Bayzog ran after her, darted behind the trees and stopped. Someone had a hold of the woman and she beat and clawed at his chest. It was Shum. The big elf grabbed her by the back of the neck and squeezed. The woman collapsed in his arms.

"Is she alright?" Bayzog said.

"She'll be fine."

"What happened? Is she hurt?"

Shum showed a little teeth and said, "No, just a little Roaming Ranger trick."

Thoom!

"That thing's getting closer," Bayzog said. "Is it an ettin?"

"I suppose. And looking for her no doubt. Come on."

They weaved in and out of the trees. Shum carried the woman in his arms like a baby. Seconds later they found both horses.

"Ah, good," Bayzog said, "I thought he was lost."

"No worries," Shum said, "can you ride with her?"

"Me? Why not you?"

"I'm not going back," Shum said, "you are."

"What are you going to do?"

"What I always do," Shum said, "find the missing."

Bayzog swung himself up on the horse. Shum handed up the woman and draped her over the saddle. Then, Shum whispered in the horse's ear.

"Can you speak Horse?"

Shum nodded.

"What did you tell it?"

"To ride you right back to where we came from," Shum said, guiding the horse away.

Thoom!

The trees shook and birds scattered. Several critters dashed under the horses.

Bayzog was saying, "I'll come back with the others—"

When Shum whacked the horse on the rear and the horse leapt forward.

Bayzog surged ahead, glancing back over his shoulder.

Shum leapt on his horse and disappeared.

A tree crashed down right behind Shum, followed by a loud yell.

"WHERE ARE YOU?"

An ettin emerged. It stood as tall as the trees. Its dark eyes found Bayzog.

"Oh no!" he said, snapping the reins.

Thoom! Thoom! Thoom! Thoom!

The ettin ran right after him.

Shum realized his error. He had assumed the ettin would come for him, not Bayzog. That had been his plan, but plans change. He turned his horse and galloped after the ettin.

Ahead, two big heads bobbed up and down. Massive arms swung at its sides like hammers. The ettin's giant strides covered the ground as fast as a horse. He dug his heels into his steed.

"Yah!"

The horse thundered ahead. Shum's horse wasn't just any horse, but a special one bred by the Roaming Rangers. Big and sleek, the Roamer Stallions were the rarest horse breed in the land. This was one of the fastest creatures on four hooves. In seconds, the chestnut mare was on the heels of the ettin, but Shum rode right by with the wind whistling in his long pointed ears.

Ahead, Bayzog was doing little to distance himself from the ettin, despite his mare's efforts.

Shum ran out in front of the ettin and angled the other way. The ettin didn't follow. It kept after Bayzog. It wanted the woman. *Time for plan two.*

Shum's long fingers wrapped around the shaft of a short spear that was hooked to the saddle. Its tip was intricate. Elven crafted. Only two feet long. He charged after the ettin. Its big steps would close in on Bayzog at any moment. Shum caught the worried look in Bayzog's eyes.

He pressed the spear to his lips and spoke in Ancient Elvish.

The spear extended. *Snap.* Three feet. *Snap.* Four feet. *Snap.* Six feet. The spearhead grew, widened, and brightened. Shum hopped up in the saddle and stood tall. He readied his spear over his head. He closed in. Five horse lengths. Three horse lengths. He dove at the ettin.

Ettins aren't as slow and stupid as they look!

Bayzog's protective spell did little to calm the fear in his belly now. Instead, he was riding for his life. A monstrosity of hair, heads and yellow eyes followed behind him. Feet almost as big as his horse ready to crush him. *I'll never leave home again.*

Shum appeared. Riding hard. Eyes narrowed. Right on the giant's heels.

Yes! Follow him, Ettin!

He glanced forward. The open plains to freedom waited. He glanced back over his shoulder.

No!

The ettin was still coming. Closer. One world-shaking foot after the other. He tried to think of a spell. Anything. *I can't ride and cast.*

The ettin's long arms stretched towards him and touched the horse's tail.

"Shum!" he yelled. *Where did he go?*

The ettin roared and said, "I HAVE YOU NOW!"

Bayzog cracked the reins.

"No!"

Shum reappeared. Standing on the saddle. A spear as tall as a man glimmering in his hands. He was heading right for the ettin. One ettin head turned his way. The ettin stopped, whirled, and braced itself for impact. Shum leapt off his horse with his spear high over his head.

The ettin swung both fists at the same time. They came together like a clap of thunder. The elf and ettin tumbled to the ground. Shum disappeared under its bulk.

"No!" Bayzog yelled, pulling on the reins. The horse kept galloping. He pulled harder but the horse kept going. The ettin's form disappeared behind the dale and out of sight.

"What do I do?"

CHAPTER

13

PAIN. I WAS FAMILIAR WITH it. I'd been in pain before. But not like this. The first ettin was squeezing me to death with both hands.

I tried to yell, but I couldn't get enough air. It came out like a frog's croak. "Brenwar ..."

All four ettin heads laughed.

"Dragon man hard to squish," the first ettin's one head said. Then its other head said, "I likes a challenge."

"Let's just eat him," the second ettin's one head said. His other head said, "My belly groans." Both of its heads smacked their lips.

The first ettin's mouths both watered, dripping spit all over me. "Wonder if he tastes like fish, with those scales."

Eaten! I can't let this happen.

I flexed my dragon arms as hard as I could, pushing out with my elbows.

My dragon arms pushed back the first ettin's grip on me just enough that I could gulp in some air. I yelled, "Brenwar!"

The second ettin came closer. Its one head said, "He's loud." Its other head said, "I don't like that!"

"SILENCE!" all four ettin heads yelled.

My ears were ringing. It made me dizzy, they yelled so loud.

"You!" Brenwar yelled from somewhere.

I gazed all around. The ettins did as well.

"What do you want?" the second ettin said.

I spotted Brenwar. A vial of bright liquid in his hands. He tipped it up and drank it down. Eyed the ettin and yelled back up.

"I bet your rotten teeth can't gnaw through dwarven hide," Brenwar said. "I bet my beard you can't even catch me." He teetered back and forth on his feet. "Stupid giants!"

I had no idea which potion Brenwar drank. Perhaps it made him fast, like me. Well, maybe not that fast. Or hard as stone. Invisible, maybe.

But nothing happened.

The second ettin reached for Brenwar.

"Move, you stubborn dwarf!" I yelled.

My dragon arms weren't even getting tired. I could breathe just fine now. I wriggled, but I still couldn't get out of the first ettin's hands. If I stopped pushing out with my elbows, I would suffocate. I was stuck.

Brenwar just stood there. Shaking his first. Screaming at the giant. He was going to die. I was going to die. I could feel it.

The second ettin reached down and snatched Brenwar up from the ground.

"TIME TO SQUISH DWARF!" its one head said. It started to squeeze, and both of its heads groaned, "*HURK!*"

I almost turned my head. I yelled instead. "Put him down!"

The first ettin, the one who held me, the one whose spit was all over me, was laughing now with both heads. Low. Loud. Evil. "Hum, hum, hum, hum, HUM!"

Brenwar didn't even flinch. Instead, his beard got bigger. So did his head.

"WHAT!" both the second ettin's heads said together.

Brenwar was laughing. Growing. Six Feet. Ten feet tall.

The second ettin dropped him on the ground.

Brenwar kept growing. Fifteen feet. Twenty. He was the biggest dwarf in Nalzambor. A bearded mountain.

The second ettin stepped back, gaping.

Brenwar closed in on him. Socked him in the gut with a fist as big as a boulder.

WHOP!

The ettin buckled over. A chorus of cheers went up from villagers and soldiers.

Brenwar grabbed the second ettin by the shaggy hair on its two heads and clonked them together. The ettin staggered back. Fell.

"Make him stop!" the first head of the ettin holding me said. Its other head said, "Stop him, or I'll crush you like a bug!"

"Crush me," I said, "and you'll make him mad. And you don't want to see him mad."

All four eyes blinked. Drifting between me, Brenwar and its brother.

"Maybe you should help your brother," I suggested.

"Quiet, Dragon Man!" it said with both mouths, narrowing all four eyes at me. It was getting mad. Thinking.

I struggled.

Its grip was like iron bars around me.

Brenwar and the ettin thrashed over the ground. Rolling. Punching. Cursing at each other. I didn't know how long the potion would last, but I didn't think it would last long.

POW!

Brenwar took a solid shot in the jaw. Shrugged it off. Punched into the ettin's ribs. Quick. Powerful blows. One right after the other.

BAP! BAP! BAP! BAP! BAP!

"Stop it, Dwarf!" the first ettin's one head cried. His other head said, "Or I'll kill your friend."

Brenwar paused. Looked over. Giant drops of sweat beaded on his head. Broad chest heaving.

"NO!" he said. Then he socked the ettin again.

"What!" I said.

The angry first ettin squeezed harder.

My dragon arms gave in. My eyes bulged out of my head.

Zzzzzap!

The hairs stood up on both of the first ettin's heads. Its grip fell open. I dropped to the ground. Sasha was there. Delicate hands glowing with flecks of energy.

Withdrawing Fang, I croaked in my frog voice, "Thanks, Sasha, but you better get out of here."

I blushed at how funny I sounded, and gulped in some air. Whew!

The first ettin roared, "RRRRRAAAAHHHH!" It looked down and boomed, "WHO DARES!"

"Fast!" I said.

Sasha ran.

"You better help me," I said to Fang.

I banged the blade on the ground. Nothing!

"Drat it, Fang! I need you!"

The blade shimmered with blue light. Almost mocking me. I shook my red mane. I was getting frustrated. But I had a bigger problem to deal with. The first ettin.

Both its fists came down.

I jumped out of the way.

"Fine then," I said to Fang. "I'll do it the hard way!"

I darted between the ettin's legs. Chopped halfway through the back of its foot with Fang and my dragon arms.

It howled. Hopped after me. Fingers stretching for my neck.

But I was fast. Angry. Stronger now than ever. My blood was up too. And I could breathe. I'd had enough of this. I pocked its hand. It howled again. I ducked under a fist. Hopped back from a kicking toe. Stabbed Fang into its other big toe.

"Stop it!" "Stop it!" both of its heads yelled. It was hopping up and down on the foot with the bleeding big toe.

I did no such thing. I struck out at its legs. Hit one. Then the other. I wanted to punish it.

It wailed. It begged. Finally it fell.

"No more, Dragon Man!" "Stop now!" It waved its bleeding hand in my face.

I cut off a finger.

It howled and rolled.

"Dragon!" Brenwar yelled. He towered over me. Hands on hips. "Get ahold of yourself."

"Would it show mercy to me?" I said, raising the sword over my head. "To the people it's hurt? Killed?"

"No," Brenwar said, "but it's Evil. You're good." He nodded to the ettin that was out cold behind him. "Besides, I think they'll tell us what we want to know, now."

I took a deep breath. I was shaking.

The ettin was bleeding. Badly.

I didn't feel bad. I felt frustrated.

"This is your fault, Fang." I slammed him in the sheath. "Well, start the interrogation then, Giant Beard!"

"Don't you dare call me a giant ever again!" Brenwar poked me in the chest with his oversized finger. "And settle yourself down, Dragon."

I walked away, clutching my ribs that ached from the first ettin's grip.

"Dragon."

It was Sasha, coming after me.

"Just go away," I said.

She stopped, a sad look on her face, and turned away.

I just wanted to be alone. *How can I fight evil when I can't kill it?*

CHAPTER

14

"Urk!"

All four eyes of the ettin widened. Shum got it. Right in the heart. The great elven spear jutted from its chest.

"Ugh," he said, removing his spear.

Shum had been fighting for hundreds of years. He'd killed and hunted many beasts, some mystical, some natural. Killing didn't bother him. It was survival. Him or them. Such was the Roaming Rangers way.

He closed the ettin's eyes and muttered in Roamer, "May Nalzambor make good soil from your wicked bones."

He called for his horse.

It trotted over.

Shum hopped on, muttered a word.

The spear collapsed to little more than a pointed rod that he tethered to the saddle.

He looked for Bayzog.

The wizard was gone. Safe now, he hoped.

"Good," he said. He patted his horse on the neck. "Let's go."

Over the plains, across the creek and into the forest he went, picking up the trail where he left off. The ettin had made it easy. Branches were broken or crushed on the forest floor. It had been sloppy, trying to find the woman.

Even an ettin can be cautious. It must have been in a hurry.

His horse nickered.

Shum stopped. Cupped his ears and closed his eyes. His nose crinkled.

The sweat of ettins caught his nose. Pungent. Like a rotting rain.

"Ah," he said, "more mystery, it seems."

The scent and trail led him to a crater. Not one of the small ones that littered the hot lands in the south, but a huge crater a mile across, filled with rocks and greens. It was the biggest crater he'd ever seen. An inverted mountain. Its sides were lined with caves, clefts and other openings.

"You better wait here," he said to his horse.

This crater was different. Ancient. Mysterious and out of place. Maybe it was carved out by the giants or dwarves at one time. Maybe it led to the mines. His keen eyes scanned it from one rim to the other.

"Ah," he said. He hopped over the lip and—nimble as a spider—climbed down the wall.

It was deep. A hundred feet down, maybe two in some places. The farther down he went, the more he heard. He pulled his cloak over him and covered his head. The fine hairs on his arms stood on end. His hand fell to his sword. He sniffed. Shook his head.

Not good.

The bottom of the grade was a forest of rocks and trees. Birds, dark and black with yellow eyes, darted in and out of the tree tops. The sunlight was blocked by the rim, bringing darkness early. Shum could see the warm patterns of the creatures that scurried.

The smell became stronger the farther towards the middle he went. On cat's feet he moved. Swift and quiet. He could hear them better now.

Voices. Harsh. Unfriendly. Threats were made. Whips were cracking.

Women sobbed and cried.

He climbed a tree. Fingers digging into the thick wood and knotted branches. Up he went. Across a branch towards the sounds. He hunched down and narrowed his eyes.

Goblins.

Wolf faced, hairy, and ugly.

Gnolls.

Thick skinned yellow eyed minions.

Village women.

Dozens of them sat in barren clearing. A camp. Sewing nets similar to what he used for fishing. Hunting. Trapping.

It was a surprise. Why would poachers be aligned with giants? Shum made a quick head count. Five gnolls. Nine goblins that he could see. It would take hours of scouting to cover the rest of the crater. He watched. Waited. The goblins stood guard, hand axes on their belts or in their hands. The gnolls ate slabs of meat and barked out orders. Every so often, a gnoll would come and go out of sight, but no others returned. *Manageable.*

The women's fingers worked hard at the nets. He could see they were frightened, hungry, and thirsty.

"Water, please," one said. She held her hands out.

A goblin walked over, held out a jug, tipped it to its lips, and gulped it down. He wiped his mouth and shook the jug in her face, the water swishing around.

She clutched for it. The goblin jerked it away. Swatted her in the face with his other hand. The goblins laughed. Holding their little pot bellies. Mocking the cries and tears of the women.

Shum had seen enough of that. His blood stirred. The muscles in his jaw tightened. Roaming Rangers weren't the aloof clan the other races made them out to be. They believed in doing right wherever there was wrong. Slavery was wrong. Goblins were wrong. Gnolls were wrong. He slid his sword from his scabbard. It was time to make it right.

He hopped out of the tree. Strode right into the camp, sword resting on his shoulder.

The goblins froze. The women stopped working. Silence fell among them. The gnolls didn't even notice.

"Let the women go," Shum said, looking down at the goblins.

"Huh?" A goblin said, turning his way.

"What!" A gnoll dropped his bowl on the ground and snatched up his flail.

The others jumped to his side, reaching for weapons. "You dare!"

The gnolls were big. Bigger than orcs. Bigger than Shum. He wasn't much of a threat to them at first glance.

"Kill him, the trespassing elf, goblins!" the tallest of the goblins ordered.

No hesitation. No fear. The goblins raised their axes and charged.

Swish! Swish!

The women screamed.

Two goblins fell dead at Shum's feet. The other goblins stopped. Blinking.

The lead gnoll's lip curled over his long canine teeth. Fear was in his eyes. He looked like he might consider talking.

Shum decided to give it another try.

"Let the women go," Shum said, "and no harm will come to you."

The goblins, the remaining seven, had him surrounded now. Axes poised to attack him from all directions.

"Come any closer, little minions," Shum said, "and I'll finish the rest of you."

They backed off a step, maybe two. Eyes darting between him and the gnolls.

"I know what you are," the gnoll leader said. "You're one of those rangers. A Roamer. Is that so?"

The gnolls' eyes were all intent on him. Reputation alone could win battles, stop wars.

"I am."

The lead gnoll started laughing. The others followed suit, weapons jangling with their armor.

"Does something amuse you?" Shum said.

"Hah!" The gnoll hitched his foot up on a log and slapped his knee. "You really do have a big belly. Kinda like an orc."

"Your insults won't grant you any mercy," Shum said, "and my patience thins. Let the women go. I won't ask again."

It coughed a laugh.

"There's more of us in this crater than you know, Ranger. I think you better surrender." It picked its slab of meat back up and tore off a chunk with its teeth. "Might even have you for dinner."

If there were more, he hadn't seen or heard them. But the tactic was sound. Even for a gnoll.

"Well," Shum said, "I hope you have enough for all of us?"

The gnoll stopped chewing. Looked around.

"All of who?"

"Surely you didn't think I came alone. A half dozen arrows are pointed right at you." Shum held his hand straight up. "Awaiting my signal."

Every pair of eyes shifted from tree to tree. But Shum's gaze was steady. Right on the gnoll. Not blinking.

It raised its arm and smiled.

"I've got a dozen in the trees," the gnoll said, "and they're all pointed at you. Your bluff has been called, Ranger."

"I don't think so," Shum said.

"I do," the gnoll grinned. The leader dropped his arm.

Clatch zip!

Clatch zip!

Shum spun away from the first bolt that found a home in a gnoll. The next bolt ripped into his thigh, sticking through one side to the other. He dropped to a knee.

"Argh!" he said.

The village women cried out.

"Didn't see that coming, did you, Ranger?" the gnoll said. "Kill him!"

<h1 style="text-align:center">CHAPTER 15</h1>

WE HAD THEM. TWO ETTINS slugged along over the grassy knolls with their four chins down. Arms shackled behind their backs, they led the way, one heavy footstep after the other. A host of Legionnaire riders accompanied us along with Ben and Garrison, who ran along on foot.

"Dragon," Ben said. "Can I ride with you? My legs are tired."

"No, Ben," I said. "Commander's orders."

"But—"

"None of that now. Why don't you scout ahead or something?"

"Aw," Ben said, drifting back with a frown.

Sasha rode alongside me.

"Are you feeling better now?" she said.

I felt ashamed. How I'd shunned her earlier was wrong. Even worse, I'd have to admit it. I couldn't treat her like Brenwar treated me and hold a grudge for days, weeks, or months.

"I'm sorry, Sasha." I didn't look at her. "I really am. It's just—"

"Don't explain yourself," she said. "I understand. After all, you just came out of a battle. Men are different when their blood runs hot. I wish Bayzog would get upset every once in a while. I don't think I've ever seen his cheeks flush."

I looked at her, smiling a little.

"Well, maybe he doesn't have any blood?"

"Dragon!"

"Sorry," I said.

She giggled.

"No, that was funny. I think we needed it, but I am a bit worried. Do you think he's alright with Shum? I don't know anything about him."

I reached over and patted her arm.

She didn't flinch or pull away, which surprised me.

I said, "I'm sure he's alright. The Roamers are the greatest Rangers in Nalzambor. He couldn't be any safer if he was with me." I squeezed her arm. "And thank you."

"For what?" she said, staring at my arm, stroking it with gentle fingers.

"Er … well, saving me, Sasha. That ettin nearly popped my head off."

"Oh, ho ho, don't sound so surprised, Nath. Did you think I was just going to stand there and let you get all the glory?"

"Well, uh…" I rubbed the back of my head. "It's just, I wouldn't want you to endanger yourself on my account."

She rolled her eyes. "You men wouldn't make it through the day without us women," she said. "How old are you?"

"Old enough to know that."

She didn't say anything for a moment. "Nath," she said, still rubbing my arm.

She was trembling inside. I could feel it.

"Truth is…" She swallowed, looked me in the eyes. "I was terrified. I don't know how I did it. I just did." She squeezed my arm. "My heart starts beating like a rabbit just thinking about that. Did I really do that, Dragon?" She looked forward at the ettins. "Those things are huge."

Now I was laughing.

"What are you laughing about?"

"Nothing," I said.

"Tell me, Dragon."

"Alright, it's just an old saying, is all."

"And the saying is?"

I took a breath. "Little women make big men stumble."

"That's it?" she said. "That's not so bad."

"Well, that's not all of it, but that's all that applies in this case," I said, trying to pull my dragon arm away.

She held firm. "I want to hear the rest of it."

"Loud women make a boastful man grumble. Pretty women make all men bumble. Wise women make a proud man humble."

"Hmmm," she started, "I think I like the last part best. Is that a song?"

I nodded.

Her eyes brightened. "Can you sing, Dragon?"

I shrugged.

"Really," she said, "please sing for me. I love singing. I sing all the time but sometimes Bayzog has to quiet me down."

"Why don't you sing then?" I suggested.

"You first," she said.

"Well, it's been a while, but I think I can remember a few verses."

Yes, I could sing. Dragon music was the oldest in Nalzambor, and I knew many songs. Long as rivers. Ancient as the oldest forest. Songs men and women had never heard and never would hear. It had been so long I wasn't sure I could do it anymore. I could try something in Common at least. I cleared my throat.

Sasha's eyes brightened.

"In the meadow, the dragons play, their scales sparkle—huh?"

"Why'd you stop, it sounded so—"

"Sssssh," I said. I could hear something. Horse hooves coming our way.

"What is it?"

"Not what, but who. Yah!" I galloped off.

"Where do you think you're going, Dragon?" Brenwar said.

I kept going. Racing up the hill, leaving the Legionnaires and ettins far behind.

A lone figure on a horse rode over the crest. It was Bayzog, with a woman draped over his horse, sleeping, I hoped. "Dragon! Thank goodness I've found you!"

Brenwar had come too. We rode right up to one another. Formed a triangle of horses.

"Are you alright, Elf?" Brenwar said. "Where's the big belly?"

Bayzog took a breath. "He's a couple leagues back. Dragon, I'm sorry. He was fighting with an ettin."

"Who is she?" Brenwar said.

"One of the villagers, I assume. We were close. She escaped and the ettin came after her."

"Bayzog!" Sasha said, riding right up to him. "Are you alright?"

"I'm fine, Dear. It's Shum I'm worried about." Bayzog's stern face was wracked with grief. "I left him. The horse wouldn't stop and I, I couldn't leave the woman."

"Shum can handle himself, I'm sure, Bayzog. Come on, Brenwar," I said.

"Come on? Hah, I'm already going, Yah!"

"Bayzog. Sasha. Stay with the Legionnaires. Help them keep an eye on those ettins." I snapped my reins and off I went.

There'd been a battle alright. An ettin was face first in the ground, dead as a stone. There was no sign of Shum.

"Took an ettin all by himself," I said, looking at Brenwar. "Pretty impressive, you have to admit."

Brenwar kept his arms folded across his chest. "Humph. It probably died laughing at his belly."

"Brenwar," I said, "would it kill you to give an elf some credit?"

"Don't know. I've never done it before. But it just might, so I'll not chance it. Ever! Humph. Luck. Elves have lots of it. Even the big bellied ones."

"Let's go," I said. "It's getting dark."

"So?" Brenwar said. "Monsters die in the night as easy as in the day."

We followed the hoof prints.

I couldn't get the image of the dead ettin out of my mind. It was now a lifeless clump of hard bone and muscle. Soon to be sweet soil for the world. But it ate at me.

Shum was good. Very good. And he'd killed it.

Why couldn't I do that? If it came down to me and an ettin, what was I supposed to do, knock it out? It wasn't possible.

"Outsmart it," Brenwar said.

"What?" I said. "What're you talking about?"

"I can see the look in your eyes, Dragon," he said. "You want to know why Shum can kill an ettin and you can't. How you fight evil without killing."

"I wasn't thinking that."

"Yes you were."

I hated it when Brenwar was right. Crusty old dwarf.

"No I wasn't!"

"If you say so," he said, "but I can answer you this. You can outsmart an ettin. That's how you beat it. But can you outwit Evil? That's the question."

"Put a sword through it," I said, riding off up ahead.

Dwarves don't know everything anyway. They just think they do.

But the question gnawed at me.

Outwit evil. My father had said that. Many times. In hours-long form. And it had never sunk in until now. How do you outwit something that kills and destroys? Shows no mercy or compassion?

We navigated into the forest. It was dark, but my eyes didn't have a problem with that. The horses had little trouble navigating either. They were well trained. Accustomed to hard travel and treacherous terrain.

"Whoa," I said.

"What is it?"

I motioned up ahead. Something was moving. And it wasn't a small creature that scurried, but something much bigger.

"Wait here."

Brenwar started to object but I was already gone. A shadow slipping through the foliage. Not bad for a dragon. My ears caught more rustling. I hunched down. Something was coming right at me.

Clop. Clop. Clop.

Shum's horse emerged. It stopped, dark eyes looking right at me. I made my way over. Grabbed the reins. Felt the saddle.

"Where's Shum?" I said.

The horse pulled away as if saying, "Follow me."

A rustle caught my ears. I whirled around. It was Brenwar fighting through the pine branches.

"Stay with the horses," I said.

"The horses can stay with themselves," he said, "besides, I smell something as well." He snorted. "Ettins and something else."

"Just come on," I said.

Shum's horse led. I followed, Brenwar huffing right behind. I wasn't sure what Brenwar smelled, but there was something in the air. It didn't blend with the smells of the forest.

The horse stopped. Nickered a little.

"What have we here?" I said. It was a crater. Strange to see. Like a gargantuan spoon dug it all out. The rising moonlight lit up the trees of the thick forest down below. "What do you make of it, Brenwar?"

He peered over the side, glancing back and forth, squinting his eyes. He shrugged.

"Let's go."

"That's pretty steep, Brenwar," I said.

"It's just a hole in the ground," he said, shuffling over the edge. "It's not a cli—*ulp!*"

"Brenwar!" I jumped out, reaching for him.

He disappeared over the rim. I heard him tumble and complain. I followed his dark sharp rolling.

Heard his grumbling. Then nothing. My keen eyes searched for a sign. Anything. He was gone. This crater was deeper than I thought. I started after him.

"Should have tied a rope to him," I said, climbing.

"Dragon!"

I heard a voice. It was faint, but it was Brenwar.

"What!" I yelled back down.

"Watch out for—"

There was a rustle. Then nothing.

Brenwar!

CHAPTER

16

ELVEN STEEL SANG. GOBLINS DIED. One. Then two. Shum, hobbled, a bolt in his leg, was all over them.

The third goblin chopped its crude axe at his mid-section, glancing off his leather armor.

Shum popped it between the eyes with his sword hilt.

It cried out and flailed.

Clatch-zip!

Shum dove onto the ground.

The bolt sank into the dirt by his face.

He rolled. The bolt in his leg snagged, drawing tears in his eyes.

The goblin swung wild after him.

Clatch-zip!

The goblin stopped. Fell face first to the ground. A bolt stuck in its back.

Shum scrambled for cover. He pressed his back to a boulder and took a breath. The Roaming Ranger was calm. Collected. He'd been in plenty of fights before. He slid his dagger from his belt. Both hands were filled with sharp elven steel.

Clatch zip!

The bolt whizzed high over his head. It was a good thing. The shooter wasn't the best shot, but he had him pinned down. Crossbows took more time to reload than bows, too. He could take advantage of that. He was fast, but not as fast as he'd been. Not with a bolt stuck in his leg. He grabbed the shaft and yanked it out.

The women screamed. Running every which way.

One of the gnolls barked and chased after them.

The others, the leader particularly, he'd lost sight of.

"Ranger!" the gnoll leader growled. "Come out!"

Shum tied a bandage over his calf. Lifted his hand over his head. Waited.

"Are you surrendering then?" the gnoll said.

He didn't reply.

Clatch zip!

Another bolt shot high and to the left of his fingers. Gritting his teeth, blocking the pain in his leg, he charged from behind the boulder.

The gnolls were waiting. Three of them. One lowered its spear at his chest.

Shum swept it away with the flat of his sword and plunged his elven dagger into its chest.

The gnoll leader roared. Its spiked flail whirled like the wind. Lashed out like a snake's tongue, catching Shum in the chest.

He doubled over. Tumbled to the ground.

Clatch-Zip!

The bolt whizzed past his head and stuck in the ground between the gnoll's legs. Its eyes widened. "Stop shooting, fools!" The gnoll twirled the spiked ball of steel over his head and brought it down again.

Shum rolled left.

Up it went. Down it came.

He rolled right.

Bang!

The flail got him in the thigh.

"Hah!" the gnoll said. "Not so tough for a Ranger, are you?"

Shum pushed himself back over the dirt, chopping back and forth with his longsword, keeping the gnoll at bay. His sword was a superior weapon to the crude flail, but the gnoll swung with fury. Power. Juttering his arms with every blow. It didn't help that his leg was banged up. Bleeding. Shum was concerned. Was he over-confident? Foolish? He'd just killed an ettin, after all. Couldn't he handle a handful of gnolls and goblins?

An elven proverb danced is his head. *Death comes from any corner.*

The gnoll kept swinging. Harder and harder. Every blow fast and heavy.

Shum dropped his dagger. Wrapped both hands around his sword.

Clang!

The flail chain wrapped around his blade. Locked the weapon up. The gnoll heaved, ripping Shum's sword from his hand. The gnoll's dog face let out a howl. It tossed its weapons aside, bared its claws, and pounced on Shum.

My dragon claws dug into the rocky dirt of the crater wall, making it easy to climb down. I caught myself wondering if I could scale city walls with them, and then I forced myself to concentrate on finding my friend.

"Brenwar!"

Still, I heard nothing. I hopped from one foothold to another. Traversed gaps and ledges like a critter. I had to admit, I was getting used to this climbing. Having two clawed hands made it much easier.

A hundred feet I descended. It was dark above and below me now. All I could make out were the outlines of the crater rim and the treetops below it.

"Brenwar!"

Great Guzan! I couldn't believe I'd lost him. The climb wasn't so risky, but Brenwar wasn't the best climber. The last time we'd climbed, I'd tied a rope around him.

He must be getting old or something.

Straight down I went, sliding on the steepness of the crater the final fifty feet. There was no sign of Brenwar. I sniffed the air.

There was that smell again. The one from earlier. The one Brenwar mentioned. What was it? Not as bad as orcs, but bad. *Ew!* I felt as if I should know, but I'd forgotten somehow.

I scanned the ground. The trees. Looking for heat. Anything. I could see small creatures nesting. Some scurrying through the night, but not much of anything else. I ran my hands over the ground. My touch was sensitive. So sensitive I felt like I could almost taste the ground with it.

"Come now," I said, "a crusty old dwarf couldn't have gotten too far."

On hands and knees, I searched. I sniffed. I was an excellent tracker. But it took a while when I was dealing with new terrain. The out of the ordinary wouldn't be as plain.

"Ah, there it is. There it is, indeed."

Whatever it was had tossed a net over Brenwar and dragged him away. But what? That was the question. I looked for prints. I found them, and they weren't at all what I expected.

"Oh no," I said. I readied my bow. *Snap. Clatch. Snap.* And darted along the trail. Brenwar was in trouble.

CHAPTER
17

"ARE YOU ALRIGHT?" SASHA SAID.

Bayzog nodded, but his face was drawn up tight. His dark eyes looked through her, up ahead, past the ettins. He was worried. Sasha could feel it. It left her unsettled. Her stomach fluttered. She'd never seen Bayzog out of sorts before.

She brushed his hair out if his eyes and held out a canteen of Wizard's Water.

He pushed it aside, gently. "No," he said, "It doesn't seem right. Not with them out there at risk. And here I am, doing nothing." He looked at her, then looked away, fists balled up at his sides.

Anyone who didn't know Bayzog would see nothing but a part-man, part-elf who oozed with confidence. Chin high. Speech polished. Impeccable in character. But he was rattled.

"You saved the woman, Bayzog. You've battled ettins. We guard them as we speak. We march them over the plains, our prisoners." She tried to sound reassuring. "You've done well. The others, they can take care of themselves."

He kept riding. Focused.

Up ahead, the ettins lumbered over the ground. Their four heads glanced back, then muttered to themselves.

They were up to something. Sasha could feel it. But surely they could not break the bonds that Bayzog had cast on them. Bright green shackles bound their wrists behind their backs.

Sasha didn't know if she felt good or bad. She didn't know how to feel actually. It was thrilling and dangerous all at the same time. What was to be a simple trek south towards the elven lands had become a full blown adventure. And it had all happened in moments. She didn't know whether she should fell proud, or scared to death.

"Sasha," Bayzog said, looking back at her, "come."

She caught up. "Yes?"

"I'm sorry." He caressed her cheek with the back of his palm. "I didn't even take the time to ask you how you were. Are you alright?"

"Just a little edgy." He eyes drifted to the ettins. "Do you think they can get free?"

"No, no, my dear. Ten ettins couldn't break those bonds. And if they try," he said, offering a grin, "they'll be in for a shock."

"I hope they struggle then," she said, glowering.

"Sasha!"

"Well, it's true. They're evil. I can feel it. I get chills looking at them. And those eyes. So big and dark." She tore her stare away and looked at him. "I hate them."

"Strong words, my dear." He cleared his throat, lifted his brow. "Try to ignore them. They're ignorant of their actions. Born that way. It's a shame. I used to think there was good in everyone, but over the centuries, I've come to know better." He squeezed her hand. "But what I have learned is even worse."

"What's that, Bayzog?"

"I've learned about the evil that resides in all of us. The evil that lurks beneath the surface of love and hate. The good roots without the strength to grow out. How it's so much easier to do the wrong thing instead of the right. I worry, Sasha." He looked up to the clouds. A frown forming on his face.

"About me?" she said, following his gaze.

Night was almost upon them. The clouds that drifted were black and the stars behind them gone. A strange fog rolled over the grass. What was earlier a blustering day in the sun had become a land more sinister. A distant flash of lightning caught her eye.

"Yes, of course I worry about you," he said. "I sometimes wish you hadn't come. I want you safe. I fear I can't always protect you."

"I don't expect you to. I have to learn how to protect myself."

"And you've done well with that," he said, "but I wanted you here with me, Sasha. I needed you here with me."

A chill went through her. Bayzog never needed anything from anybody.

"Why?"

He looked her straight in the eye.

"In case none of us make it back."

Her heart stopped. Then started again. At least it felt like it did. What was he saying? What did he mean?

"Bayzog, I'm certain we'll make it through this. We'll find the Ocular of Orray, heal Dragon, and then things will be the same."

He shook his head.

"The climate changes. Even though my elven instincts aren't as sharp as they used to be, I know. That's why I wanted to have you with me. I wanted you by my side, selfishly, just in case."

"Just in case what?"

She could see her reflection in his violet eyes when he said it.

"Just in case we're near the end of this world."

CHAPTER

18

SHUM PULLED HIS KNEES UP and caught the full force of the gnoll's greater weight on his chest. He locked his hands around the creature's wrists and hung on. Shum was centuries hardened by training and battle. His muscles as taut as steel. But he was no match for the raw strength of the gnoll. Its thews were thick. Savage. More animal than man. Its dog face snapping at his neck. He turned his face away. Hung on with all the strength he had in him.

"Time to die, Ranger!" Saliva dripped from its mouth. "I've never tasted a Roamer before." It snapped at him.

Shum shoved it back. Still lithe, he got one foot underneath the gnoll's hard belly. "Not today, Gnoll!" He thrust. Lifted the gnoll up and over the top of his head.

It let out a howl, crashing into the dirt.

Shum dove for his sword.

The gnoll regained its feet and pounced right onto his back. Its claws tore into him.

His elven leather kept him from being torn to shreds.

They thrashed back and forth over the dirt.

Whop!

The gnoll punched him in the face, drawing spots.

Jab! Jab! Crack!

The gnoll howled. Jumped off, holding its nose.

The creature might be bigger, meaner, stronger, but Shum was smarter, faster and tougher. And he knew the weak spots of all the races. He spotted his sword. Limped over and snatched it up. "One more step, Gnoll, and it will be the end of you," he said, shuffling forward.

The gnoll backed away. Eyes darting from side to side.

The women and other gnolls were gone. Hiding. Leaving the two of them in the darkness. The only light the small campfires glows.

"Surrender, Gnoll, or meet your—"

Clatch-zip!

Shum's sword fell from his grip.

The gnoll let out a triumphant howl and charged.

I was on alert. Eyes peeled. Ears sharp.

That smell. That smell in the air. I knew what it was. The prints on the ground gave me a good idea. Trouble. The kind of trouble wise people sought to avoid. The kind of trouble that was hard to get out of.

I hurried along. They could move fast, even with Brenwar. Possibly faster than me. One mistake on the trail and I myself could be in jeopardy.

I stopped. Looked. Listened.

Something rustled over the ground. Yards ahead. I could've sworn I heard Brenwar grumbling under his beard.

I nocked an arrow, a normal one, and sped after him. I jumped along. Winding through the trees. My footfalls light as feathers.

There he was. A clumped dwarf fighting in a net surrounded by pines and a floor of pine needles. I didn't see anyone else. Still, I remained hidden.

"Dragon!" Brenwar said. His voice a loud hush. "They're gone. Get me out of this net!"

I peeked at him.

His dark eyes were right on me.

I wasn't sure how Brenwar could see me, but he could always find me when I was close. I never knew for sure if it was my scent or his vision, but the only way to escape him was to outdistance him.

I crept over, withdrew a dagger, and quickly cut at the net.

"Hurry, will you!" he said.

"Stop struggling, will you!"

"You're not the one in the net."

I laughed.

"Stop laughing and hurry. You spooked them, but they'll be back. They always come back."

I cut at the cords. It wasn't easy.

"Use your claws, Dragon!"

"Oh, good idea." I cut. One. Two. Three at a time. "Nice."

"How many of them?" I asked.

"Two."

"Two that we know of." I sawed away. Brenwar was almost free.

Clop. Clop.

Clop. Clop.

I wanted to stop, but I didn't. I ignored the sound. Kept cutting.

"Hurry!" Brenwar said.

A flute-like sound drifted into my ears.

My head started spinning. My fingers turned numb. Limp.

Brenwar's eyelids fluttered. His meaty hands clamped over his ears. "No!" he growled.

I couldn't say anything. My tongue felt like water. But I could see. Both of them. Shadows in the forest coming out of the darkness. One was male, the other female. Each pressed a set of small pipes to their lips. Tiny horns protruded from their heads. They stood on stout legs with the hooves of mountain goats.

Satyrs. Crafty and Merciless.

The music tore at my mind.

I screamed, but I couldn't hear myself. I had to move. Had to escape. Run. Flee. I knew the stories. I knew the tales. Whatever the satyrs captured they kept. Never to be seen again.

Shum lay still. Eyes closed. A mouthful of pine needles. A crossbow bolt sticking through his back. Bleeding. Over him, the gnoll leader gloated.

"Great shot!" he said. "Now get down here. It's time to skin him."

Shum remained. Ears picking up his surroundings. The gnoll leader kicked him hard in the ribs. He didn't move. Didn't flinch. The gnoll walked away, footsteps crunching over the ground, and picked up his flail. The air whistled as it twirled around. Another pair of footsteps approached. Followed by another. There were three of them.

"Get those bows ready. If he moves so much as a hair, shoot him."

"Isn't he dead?" one said, cranking back his string.

"If he's dead, he won't feel it," the leader said. "Of course, he's a Ranger, so you can't be too cautious. Humph. Go ahead. Put another in him. Right in the heart. Maybe between the ears. That'd be a funny trophy now, wouldn't it?"

They snickered a howling sort of sound and stretched their strings.

Shum had been in tight spots before, but this was ridiculous. *Death comes from any corner. The darkness sings.* Hands under his belly, he scratched at the dirt. Tapped the world's power. He was an elf. Attuned to nature and magic. Using it when needed to save others. To save himself. He focused. Concentrated. Stretched out the powers he summoned.

"What is this?" one of the gnolls said. Its crossbow trembled in its hand. The wood creaked and groaned.

"It's cursed!" said the other. The crossbow in its hand warped too. It let out a cry.

Both crossbows were now twisted like roots. The strings snapped. The gnoll leader let out an angry cry.

"It's the Ranger, you fools!" He jumped forward, swinging his mace. "Draw your blades! Have at him before he escapes."

Shum felt the flail coming down. In a blink he dove into the gnoll's legs, toppling it over. He kept on going. Blocking out the blinding pain in his legs and his back. He had to free himself.

The gnoll snatched his leg.

He kicked it in the face. He was free.

The other two were coming. Drawing their weapons. Still gawking at the twisted crossbow and bolts that writhed on the ground.

Shum went for his sword, snatching it from the ground. He wished he could keep running. Into the forest. Lose them. Survive. Fight later. He was bleeding too badly, though. It was fight now or never. He stopped. Turned.

They swarmed him.

The first one was big, clumsy.

Slash!

It died.

The next lunged. A big axe in its hands. Shum side stepped.

Crack!

Drove the pommel of his sword into the back of its head. It was out.

"You're good, Ranger," the leader said. "But yer bleedin' to death too. I think I'll watch. Wait for the reinforcements to arrive."

"Trust me, Gnoll, you'll be dead cold before they get here."

"Is that so?" it said. "How you figure?"

Shum swayed. A wave of nausea hit him. His chin dipped. His knees buckled.

The gnoll barked at him. "You've got nothing left. I'm taking you out." It came at him. Savage. Powerful. Flail spinning like stars in the air. Its eyes widened. It caught the steely eyes in the elf. It tried to stop, but couldn't.

Shum struck like a cobra. The blade went in one side and out the other.

The leader died, mouth wide open.

"They always fall for that," Shum said, removing his blade and fetching his dagger. Still ailing, he hobbled after the women.

CHAPTER
19

I T WAS STRANGE. THE MUSIC the satyrs summoned bent my knees, my ears, even the trees right before my eyes.

The little beady-eyed horn-heads were full of surprises. Deceivers. Stealers. Enslavers. And dragon poachers. They loved dragon charms, bones, teeth and scales, more than gold itself.

I fought for my focus. Locking my eyes on their twisting and distorted faces, I yelled. At least I think I did.

I could see my bow, Akron, in my hand that I could not feel. An arrow was stuck between my numb fingers. I fought against the music. The horror. The carnival erupting in my mind.

Come on, Dragon! Do it! Do it or you're done for!

Muscles straining, I forced my dragon hands to respond. Shaking, I nocked the arrow. I rolled on my back. I think I did anyway. I couldn't feel anything. It was like I was watching someone else's hands draw back the string. An out of body experience of sorts. I took aim at the nearest obscured image before me and let the arrow fly.

The snapping string cracked in my ear. Not tight, but slow. The arrow sped away from me at an agonizing pace. Even an ettin could have dodged that slow arrow.

I felt my breath thinning. Drops of sweat fell in front of my eyes. All I wanted to do was escape the madness. Sleep. Find my legs and run. But at the moment, I could do nothing. Just suffer the insufferable sound of the pipe-playing satyrs.

"Uh!"

The music shifted. Stopped.

My head pounded like a drum but my vision began to clear.

The male satyr clutched at its belly. Its pipes no longer pressed to its lips, but on the ground.

The woman dashed over on her hooves. Distraught and full of worry. She leaned her mate back in her arms. Tears swelled in her eyes.

The male gasped for breath. Clutched its side. Looked right at me. Then at my dragon arms. Its eyes widened, and it whispered to the female satyr.

I gathered my feet under me and stumbled over. I didn't want to see him die.

Brenwar beat me there.

Crack!

He walloped the female in the back of the head with a leaden bag called a Dwarven Sap.

She pitched forward. Knocked out cold in her mate's lap.

"Brenwar," I said, "did you have to be so gruff. She's a—"

"She's no she. It's a satyr. A monster. About to kill us both."

Crack!

He stomped her set of pipes under his boot. Crushed them into the ground.

The male satyr let out a whine. Like a goat.

Pop!

Brenwar slugged it in the jaw. It fell over. He snatched its pipes off the ground and crushed them in his hands.

"What about his wounds?" I said.

"It will live."

We grabbed the net and bound them up. Satyrs—little taller than dwarves, not as wide—weren't very formidable without their pipes.

Still, I was a little surprised Brenwar hadn't killed them.

"So, you think they won't come after us again?" I said. "There could be more, you know. Maybe an entire herd of them lurks in this crater."

"Then I suggest we get out of here before they get out of this," he said, storming off.

I guessed it was my turn to follow. I gave the satyrs one last look. They never looked as bad as they seemed. They looked almost peaceful. Their faces calm and expressionless. I just hoped I'd never hear those pipes playing again. After Brenwar I went.

We found a camp.

"Look at this," Brenwar said. He was kneeling down beside some dead goblins. "Look at how clean that cut is. That's elven steel. Shum must be close by."

I inspected the gnolls. Three of them were dead. Big ones too. All bigger than Shum. I could tell by the dirt it had been a hard fought battle. A nasty one, judging by the blood.

"Looks like he went this way," I said, "but I don't think he was followed."

"Hmmm," Brenwar said, "look at this." He held out what looked like a crossbow, but the wood was twisted.

I picked up a bent bolt. "Now this is something. Pretty impressive." I waggled it in Brenwar's face. "Wouldn't you say?"

"Pretty sad if you ask me. Pot Belly must not be much of a fighter if he can't get the upper hand on the likes of these. Using magic. Pah!"

"Of course," I said, rolling my eyes behind his back. "What was I thinking? Let's go."

I took the lead this time. My keen eye picked up drops of blood on the ground, the needles, and the stones. There were footprints now. Many. I could smell the women. Some of them still touched by the natural fragrances of the flower and vegetable gardens of the village.

"Brenwar," I stopped. Hunched down. Something was coming.

Brenwar leaned over my shoulder. Farther down the crater a large group of people was coming. We waited. Closer and closer they came. The silhouettes became familiar. One, taller than the rest, was limping. Wheezing a little.

"Shum!" I said, dashing up to him.

Two women were holding him up. His long arms draped over their shoulders.

"He saved us," one woman said. "Saved us all. Killed all those nasty dogs and goblins!"

Indeed, he had saved them all. Every last one by the looks of it. The women all chattered among themselves. Excited. Free.

"Shum," I said, bracing him over my shoulder. "Are you alright? Can you make it?"

"Just," he said, wheezing. "Just get me out of here, Dragon. Take me to my horse."

"Pah!" Brenwar said, rolling his eyes at me. "I bet he wants us to carry him, too."

The brisk wind picked up, chilling Bayzog's bones. The warmth from the Legionnaire fire looked good right now, but he remained back. In the dark, peering towards the crater.

"Come, Bayzog," Sasha said, taking his arm. "You need some food. The soldiers have plenty and their tales are very exciting."

He turned his eyes towards the ettins that now sat on the edge of the camp. They kept looking into the sky. What they were looking for, he couldn't imagine.

"I appreciate it," he said. "I really do. Perhaps you can bring me something."

"As you wish, Bayzog." She pecked him on the cheek. "I'll be right back."

Being around men left Bayzog a little uncomfortable. He was more elf than man, and never felt his human part was well received. And he didn't have the color of the humans either, at least not in terms of personality. He was resolved. They were vibrant. Most of them anyway.

Staring into the sky, he noticed the dark clouds seemed to lower. Like a fog that fell rather than lifted.

"That's odd."

It wasn't uncommon for the night air to become misty but not so early in the night. Over by the campfires a haze was dropping over the men's heads. But they kept talking, eating, and many of them were smoking pipes. His nose crinkled.

He looked at the ettins. They were fifteen feet high sitting. But he could see their heads no more.

"Bayzog," a man said, approaching from the camp. "Have you have seen such a fog before?" It was Ben, trying to fan the haze from his face.

"No, have you?"

"Great Guzan!" a soldier said. "I can't even see my roll-up. Stop smoking, will you!"

"That's not my smoke," another soldier exclaimed. "It's this infernal fog. It's thicker than a mud hole!"

"Get out of my way!"

A chill went right through Bayzog. Suddenly he couldn't see a hand in front of his face.

"Sasha! Sasha! Where are you?"

It didn't do him any good. Everyone was yelling. Shouting. Ordering.

"Ben! Ben!" he said. "Can you hear me?"

"I'm right here," Ben said. "I think I am anyway. What do you want me to do?"

"Be still. Don't move!"

Bayzog muttered. Incanted. The magic within him came to life. Raising his arms over his head he summoned the wind.

At first nothing happened.

He focused. Concentrated.

Then it came. Up the hill, flattening the grasses it pushed through the camp to the astonishment of many voices. It was a strong wind. Not a storm. Not a gale. Strong and steady like right before a storm. It whisked the fog away. Scattered it into the sky. Carried it far away and beyond.

When he opened his eyes, Ben was standing there. Fixing his hair. Gaping at him. Sasha rushed up towards him and wrapped her arms around him. He was relieved.

"Great Guzan!" another soldier shouted.

"What now?" someone said.

"The ettins are gone!"

CHAPTER
20

IT WAS EARLY MORNING WHEN we ran into Bayzog, Sasha, Ben and the Legionnaires. Bayzog explained everything that occurred the night before. I listened intently while Sasha tended to Shum's wounds.

"What do you make of it, Bayzog?" I asked.

Bayzog's face was calm but his voice was intense.

"I never figured the ettins to wield magic," he said, "and the fog. It came from nowhere. Unnatural. Dragon, it takes a lot to summon the weather and make such big monsters disappear. Someone powerful had to have done it."

"Or several someones," I said.

There was no sign of anything. No tracks. No scent. Nothing. Even Brenwar and Shum seemed astounded.

"What do we do now, Dragon?" Ben said. "What if the ettins come back? And why did they take the women?"

I hated to admit it, but it was perplexing. Why did they take the women, indeed? And why were they aligned with dragon poachers? Even though it was night, I'd still gotten a close enough look at things at the camp in the crater. The goblins and gnolls were poachers, no doubt about it. They had the tools, traps and snares. And the women, they had them working on nets. Dragon nets. The kind that pinned dragons' wings together or to their backs. The mere sight of such tools infuriated me. There'd been no signs of dragons, which was good. But Shum said there were caves. That was bad. There was no time to search them. What was important was getting the women to safety.

"Easier to control," Shum said. "Easier to scare. Men are rebellious and children can be difficult to keep track of. Plus, the women from these villages are good menders. Quick hands. Hard workers." Shum rose up to his full height, put some weight on his leg and grimaced.

"Take it easy," Sasha said. "It'll take some time for those wounds to mend."

Shum looked down at her and showed his dashing elven teeth.

"You've done well." He helped her up and kissed her hand. "You've got excellent hands. A soothing touch."

Sasha's pale cheeks turned pink and she tossed her hair.

"You've found a special partner, Bayzog. An honor for any elf."

"I know," Bayzog said. He walked over, grabbed Sasha's other hand, and led her away.

"Hmmm," I said, looking at Shum. He was watching them go. "So," I said, "maybe we should check on that ettin you killed. Perhaps it's gone as well."

Shum pulled himself into his saddle. "Makes you wonder if any of it happened at all, doesn't it?"

I got on my horse and spent the next couple of hours leading the women back to their village. The men and children were overjoyed, and for the first time in a long while I felt like I'd done something positive, right.

"Does the heart good, doesn't it?" Sasha said.

"Indeed it does," I replied. "Seeing such joy come from tragedy is an amazing thing."

"Do you think they'll be alright?" she asked.

I looked at her seriously. "Sometimes people just have to fend for themselves. If they felt the need to leave, they'd leave. This is their home. I wouldn't leave if I didn't want to, either."

She gave me a weak smile.

Ben and Garrison rode up to us.

"Well," I said, "what did the commander say, Ben?"

"They're going to stay. Help the villagers settle themselves and send for more help from Quintuklen." He was grinning from ear to ear.

"Well, you seem pretty excited about that. Are you looking forward to helping out or maybe getting a quick trip back to the city?"

"No-no-no," he said, waving his hands. "I've got even better news than that."

"Really, and what might that be?"

"The Commander. He says Garrison and I can go with you!"

I looked at Sasha.

She shrugged.

"Go with me where?" I said.

"To Elome The Elven City, of course. The Commander says we can go!" He hoisted his helmet up in the air. "YEEHEE!"

I didn't have any reason to bring Ben. There were plenty of us already. But a part of me liked his enthusiasm. People liked Ben. Having him around. And he'd proven he could take care of himself. He was a legionnaire, after all. Even looked formidable in his well fitted armor.

Still.

"Come on, Dragon," he said, voice excited. "Don't tell me no. You know I want to see the world, and this is my chance. Just another journey. After this trip, I'll do whatever you say. I'll head right back to Quintuklen. Plus, I have to be back in a month anyway."

"A month!" I said. "We won't be there a month, Ben. Did you plan on starting a family while we were there?"

"Uh," he said, scratching his head, "no."

Sasha was laughing. Bayzog sat in is saddle, silent, distant.

"Garrison, do you want to do this?" I asked. The man wasn't much of a talker. Hard to read.

He shrugged and said, "I wouldn't mind seeing the home of the elves. Sounds interesting."

"Interesting, indeed," I said. "Alright, gather your things. Let's go." I scanned the hills and what was left of the village.

The people were hard at it already. Hammers and saws were working, and the women—some of them and the children were singing.

"Say," I said, "shouldn't Brenwar and Shum be here by now?"

They'd gone to check on the third ettin. To see if it was still there or not. My scales tingled at the thought of it. The thought of all of it. Everything was out of place. Unordinary. Villagers. Ettins. Dragon poachers and craters, not to mention the satyrs. I hadn't even mentioned them to Sasha and Bayzog yet. But something was amiss. I wanted to go back to the crater. Take a closer look. For all I knew, there were dragons there. It bothered me.

"Here they come," Sasha said, waving.

The pair bounced in their saddles at a trot and came to a stop.

Brenwar propped his hands on his hips. "Seems the elf didn't kill that ettin after all. It's gone." He slapped his knee. "Ha!"

"Any signs?" I said.

"None," Shum replied.

Something was wrong. I could feel it in the tips of my claws. It ate at my stomach. I was missing something. We were all missing something.

"Let's go, Dragon," Bayzog said. "We've done all we can do here. We should ride to Elome, before things get any more weird."

CHAPTER

21

KRYZAK STOOD IN THE CENTER of the dragon poacher camp, inspecting the carnage. The gnolls were dead. The goblins were dead. But that was not all. One ettin out of three was dead, another's hand maimed. The two that lived now roamed the woods in the crater, awaiting his call. He picked up the flail of the gnoll leader. Eyed it.

"Interesting," he said, running his finger over the blood on the metal. "I can make use of that." He motioned for one of the draykis. Its hulking frame made its way over, silently as a cat. He handed the draykis the flail. "Keep this. It may have more uses."

Making his way around the camp, Kryzak reenacted the battle in his mind. A Roaming Ranger. That made him curious. Why would a Roaming Ranger be with Nath Dragon? It bothered him. Ranger Elves he'd just as soon avoid. They were a formidable bunch. Strange and deadly. And he didn't like to take on things he didn't understand.

He picked up one of the gnarled crossbows, grunted, and tossed it aside.

He took a seat on a log near the extinguished campfire, pulled his hood down, and let the sunlight warm his head. His tattoos sparkled in the bright light. He rubbed the sweat that glistened on his head away with a dark cloth and tucked it back inside is robes.

"It's a great day."

He grabbed his canteen, took a drink and closed his eyes. Bounced his war mace on his heavy shoulders. Ground his teeth a little.

Kryzak liked to fight. He was a warrior just as much as a cleric. He hated missing the melee and combat that had occurred over the past couple of days.

But he was a planner too. Strategic. Cunning. He'd set a trap. A test. He had to get some idea of what his was dealing with in Nath Dragon and his companions.

The encounter with the ettins had told a lot. Nath and his companions were strong. Powerful. An efficient team. They trusted one another. It surprised him. He'd figured the ettins a match for them.

But he'd been wrong.

He smashed his mace into the ground. Again and again. It was a big thing. Heavy. Meant to be wielded by a big man such as himself. He could cave plate armor in with it. Bash the locks on heavy doors. He'd killed a giant with a single blow to the head once. And he was itching to use it again.

"Barnabus!" Kryzak cursed. "I need a fight."

He would get it too. But not before he was ready. He needed to know more.

His spy would have to fill in the details. His spy had earlier filled him in on everything that had happened. The giant-sized dwarf. The magic the part-elven wizard used. The female wizard as well. Not to mention the arrows and sword that Nath Dragon could wield.

Even with the help of ettins and draykis, Kryzak would be hard pressed to defeat Nath's party. He'd have to separate them. Maybe kill them off in pieces. He grinned.

"I like the way I think."

He clapped his calloused hands and muttered a mystic word.

The blackened logs in the pit burst into flames.

He liked the fire. It had magic, warmth and power. It could do good or bad. Destroy life or save it.

He poured out his canteen into a pool of water on the ground. Muttered some mystic words and watched the water take form. Then the fire.

Two tiny elementals, each less than a foot tall, started to battle. Like gladiators that hated each other.

He laughed, watching them fling tiny balls of fire and water at each other.

Ssssz. Ssssz. Ssssz.

They locked up. Wrestled like Minotaurs until they extinguished one another. It made him wonder if evil could truly defeat good. Where would all the excitement be?

He rubbed the amulet around his neck.

A draykis came forward. Towering over him. "Do we hunt?"

"No, not yet. We'll wait until they depart the elven lands," he said.

"And then what? Care to let me in?"

Kryzak scoffed. The draykis weren't mindless things. They were the best dragon hunters he'd ever used. They made typical poachers—gnolls, goblins and orcs—look like halflings and gnomes. They were fearless. Never rattled. And if it weren't for his amulet, he was pretty sure they'd rip him to pieces.

Kryzak respected them. He had to make sure they respected him.

"You heard what the spy said. Now we wait until he reports more," he said, rising to his feet. The pair were almost eye to eye know. He dangled the amulet between his fingers and slung his mace over his shoulder. "I want to know what they are after. And I don't want to fool with the elves. Come."

The Crater made for an interesting hideout. Filled with dangerous predators and excellent places for monsters such as giants to conceal themselves. Even dragons. For years poachers had roamed this location, and now Kryzak had taken it over.

And no one had challenged him.

There was no need now that word was getting out.

Another war was coming.

Maneuvering through the woods, he came across a hole over a dozen feet wide that led into the ground and formed a tunnel. It was pitch black, but the eyes of the draykis and the tattoos on his head both gave off a soft glow of light. Damp and cold, a hundred steps down the steep incline he came to a stop.

He muttered, "*Shompin.*"

Torches lit up a large cavern. Inside were many cages. Some big enough for an ettin, others small as a cat. Many of them were filled with dragons.

Two more draykis emerged from the dark corners, followed by something else. A dragon, dark scaled, bigger than a horse, wingless, with bright yellow cat-like eyes. The feline fury. Its long whiskers touched the floor. He stroked its face. Its purr was like thunder.

"Ah, my favorite," Kryzak said.

The feline fury had been instrumental in capturing other dragons. It was an excellent hunter. It and the draykis had become the most effective poachers of all. The captured dragons lay curled up in their cages, eyes closed, unmoving. The biggest was a red-belly dragon. It was male, dark yellow scales on top, dark red on the bottom. A fire breather and hot land dweller. Smelled like sulfur all the time. Not much of a flyer. It would fetch a great price in the market. Its parts, that is. It was too big to keep alive. Too dangerous.

The others—most as big as tigers—would make pets or catalysts to magic. The wizards preferred them. They were all fantastic creatures. Beautiful in some cases. Metallic in color, some pastel, others with chameleon-like powers. All in all, the dragons were worth a fortune.

"Almost a shame to put an end to them," he said, stroking the whiskers of The Fury. "Of course, like you, maybe some of them can be turned to our service."

CHAPTER

22

WE MADE IT TO THE Elven Lands without any more trouble. Shum and the rest of us were in good shape. Even Brenwar had loosened up. I spent most of my time hunting and fishing with Ben and Garrison when were weren't riding. They were good company, especially Ben. I was amazed at how much he had changed in a matter of months. A boy to a man.

It almost made me feel ashamed of myself, for some reason.

But my sense of guilt and worry started to subside in the Elven Lands. They were well protected and monitored. Filled with wild animals of incredibly rare sorts. They said unicorns were seen from time to time. But the elves kept a close watch on such things—assuming of course they could find them.

One thing was for sure: there wasn't much to do with evil. At least not that they knew of.

The Elven Lands weren't so different, just more lush and colorful. The water sparkled in the streams and ponds. There were roads, farms and villages—and so long as you traveled with elves or weren't suspicious, they didn't seem to notice you.

Slighter in build than men, the elves didn't care to answer questions and would just wave and offer smiles. Elves were pleasant, laid back, easy going, at least in the country. It was the serious ones that kept things in order. And they were in the main city, Elome, which was right where we were going.

"What's that?" Ben said, pointing ahead.

"That's Elome, Ben," I said.

He squinted. Held his hand over his eyes.

"Are those trees? Or buildings? They're touching the clouds, whatever they are"

"You'll see," I said. "You'll see."

We were miles away, but the object in Ben's eyes, all our eyes, was miles long. Everyone was solemn. Bayzog's face was tight. Sasha's eyes were saucers. Shum and Brenwar didn't look any different than they normally would, but I was sure Brenwar would have something contrary to say about it.

We took our time too. The horses clopping over the road at a normal pace. Things seemed to go much slower in the Elven Woods. There wasn't a great deal of business about them. It was different. Calm. Serene.

"I don't think we're getting any closer, Dragon," Ben said.

"We'll get there when we get there, Ben," I said, raking my hair out of my face. "Enjoy it. It's not the same going as it is coming."

Onward we went, one mile, then two, three and four. As we got closer, the city widened, impossibly so. The trees that reached for the clouds weren't all trees but a network of stonework, cut blocks and polished stones that looked as natural as nature itself. There were no city walls, not like Quintuklen, nor steep mountain ridges like Morgdon. It was the imagination and cultivation of elven kind and nature working as one. Fantastic. Almost magical.

"By the Sultans," Sasha said, "it's absolutely beautiful."

"To you, maybe," I heard Brenwar mutter under is beard.

We made our way through one of the massive arches that led into the city. Elven soldiers were spaced throughout the structures but hardly noticeable. The elves went about their business—trading, selling, buying—the same as other people, just talking in Elvish. The men were slender and purposed. The women elegant, pretty, even exotic in some cases. But not a one batted an eyelash at me, which was disappointing. But on the other side of things, they didn't gawk at my arms either.

"Dragon," Ben said, trying to look everywhere at once, "this place is fantastic. Not anything I ever imagined."

It was true. The buildings were of all sorts and sizes. Some carved from stone, others wood. Soft mosses—blue, green, even yellow—coated many places like paint, and the roads were laid out in pale red stone. Children ran through the streets, darting in and out of wicker hoops. Others chased after one another, filling the air with laughter and giggles here and there.

"Smells good," Ben said, rubbing his stomach. "I've never had elven food before."

"Pah," Brenwar said, "you won't like the taste."

"I won't? Why not?" Ben said.

"Well, do you like meat?"

"Sure, everyone does," Ben said, "Don't they?"

"Well, their meat tastes like fruit and gardens, Farmboy. And their ale tastes like honey. Do you like honey, Boy?"

"Uh," Ben said, scratching his head.

"Well?"

Ben rode up to me and said, "Brenwar scares me."

"Ho! Ho! Ho!" Brenwar said from behind.

"Take it easy, Ben. Brenwar's set in his ways, you know."

"Does their meat really taste like vegetables?"

"Don't worry, you'll like it," I said. "I always do."

Well, I mostly did. The elves didn't eat much meat. Not much of any at all. As a matter of fact, they ate very little.

That was one of things that was different about Elome. There weren't taverns like the other cities. Whatever they needed, they just plucked it from the vines that cropped up everywhere.

The elves nurtured.

The plant life fed.

I plucked a fruit from a vine we passed and tossed one to Ben and another to Garrison.

"Eat," I said. "There's plenty."

Brenwar was scoffing in the back. I tossed him a fruit. He snatched it from the air. Eyes filled with venom.

"What's this for?" Brenwar said.

"To eat," I said. "It won't kill you."

"Dwarves don't eat fruit! We eat beast. We eat stew!" He chucked it at one of the children.

The light headed boy snatched it with his hand, nodded and took a bite out of it.

"Next time I'll toss him a rock to eat."

"Come," Bayzog said, taking the lead. "I'll take us to the Place of Meets."

The Place of Meets was marvelous. A gathering space a mile long and a mile high. We weren't so unique there. Men and elves consulted. Halflings and gnomes appeared, shuffling by with smiles and intense conversations. Brenwar, arms folded over his breast plate, made it a point to scowl at each and every one of them. He took pride in being part of the tallest of the short races and didn't hesitate to make it known.

"Sit, everyone." Bayzog took his place on a sofa carved in a tree with violet covered moss cushions.

Sasha sat close beside him.

"Sit, everyone," he said again. "Relax. They won't be with us anytime soon."

"You can say that again," Brenwar said.

Ben hopped from spot to spot. Sampling the foods. Tasting the drinks the elven servants laid out. Finally he stretched out on a padded lounge and stuffed fruits and cheeses in his mouth.

"Sit!" he said. "How about live? This room is the most wondrous thing I've ever seen. I could live here!" He thumped his arms on his furniture. "Right here. This spot! Never move again."

An elven maiden with pale violet hair and green eyes sauntered in with another tray. She was petite, pretty, eyes engaging.

Ben choked. Thumped his chest with his fist. Took a drink. "Hello," he managed to spit out. "My name's Ben."

She nodded and walked away.

"Ah!" Ben said. "Did you see that, Dragon? The way she looked at me? I think she likes me!"

"I think you need to ease up on the elven fruit juice, Ben. It's pretty potent."

Sasha and Garrison chuckled along with me.

Everyone else was quite serious.

"What?" Ben said. "I swear she liked me. She really did."

After an hour, everyone had settled in. Chatting openly with one another. The elven juice often did that to you.

Brenwar groaned when he took a seat. "I'm sitting, but I swear I won't be comfortable." He combed his beard with his fingers. Grumbled. "Better not be no pixies."

Now came the wait.

The waits weren't so bad for the likes of me, Brenwar, Shum or Bayzog. But to humans like Sasha, Ben and Garrison, it could be agonizing. It was one of the reasons men didn't mingle with the elves so much. Elven things took a long time. A simple meeting might not start for days, maybe weeks, unless you planned it out well in advance. In the case of us, our business was unexpected. There was no telling when they'd officially greet us.

I took a chair near Bayzog and Sasha. Tried to enjoy the tunes of the elven bards who strummed and strolled along. I was uncomfortable though.

Waiting, which really wasn't much of an issue with dragons, made me think of my father. He always made me wait. Well, maybe not wait as much as dragon things just taking a long time. But right now, I wouldn't mind *waiting* to see him again as opposed to maybe never seeing him again at all.

I set down my goblet of elven juice. I needed to focus.

"Thanks for bringing me here," Sasha said to Bayzog. "I've always wanted to come."

Bayzog sat with his arm on her knee, poised but not relaxed.

I could feel the tension in him. I understood it. I could relate. But I had to wonder what he was thinking. I didn't know much about Bayzog and his family.

Sasha gently turned Bayzog's chin with her fingers, to face her.

"Why don't you go see them while we wait? I'm sure they miss you."

I saw a little fire ignite in Bayzog's violet eyes. But that fire was met with Sasha's sweet determination. *Good for her*, I thought.

"Perhaps," Bayzog said.

The night came. The leaves on some of the trees glowed, and all the humans in our party fell asleep. The rest of us sat in the quiet. Alone in our thoughts. Contemplating the next step in the journey. Would the elves help? Or would they shun our efforts?

There was only one way to find out.

Wait.

CHAPTER

23

HIGH PRIESTESS SELENE, ACCOMPANIED BY a dozen acolytes and lizardmen, had finished her journey west towards the Ruins of Barnabus. It was there her lord lived. Hidden from prying eyes deep inside the belly of the mountainous terrain. They rode on horseback, traversing the narrow trails until they stopped at a cave mouth. It resembled a maw, dragon-like, over forty feet tall. Standing just outside the entrance, she rubbed her shoulder. It was cold in there. Dark. Vast. She could feel eyes all over her.

"Stay here," she said. "And make no sudden moves." She pointed at the ledges of the cave's entrance.

Several carved dragons blended in with the stones and vegetation. As big as men, some bigger. They were breathing. Their eyes sparkled like gems.

"You don't want those guardians to greet you. One bite and it's over."

Inside she went, heavy dark robes dragging over the ground, tail swishing back and forth. She felt cold. Nervous. She was the High Priestess of Barnabus, so she shouldn't fear anything. Yet she did. Her breath showed. Her heart beat faster. It smelled of death. Decay. A tomb of sorts.

Straight she went. Down a gentle grade until a distant light shone. Torches. The fires green and blue ignited by magic.

A massive stone archway adorned in gargoyle heads and dragons looked down at her.

She kneeled. Bowed. "High Priestess Selene comes to see the master of all masters. The priest of all priests. The one true Lord of Nalzambor."

On the other side of the archway, two stone urns flared with icy burning light. In between it a throne made for someone ten times her size waited. Empty.

"COME."

The voice was deep as a canyon. Powerful as a stormy wind.

Selene made her way inside. Stopped at the marble step as high as her head and bowed.

She felt small. Insignificant. Her hands went cold. She waited what seemed to her a long time.

"YOU TREMBLE. WHY, SELENE?"

She swallowed. Words were stuck in her throat. She trembled.

"HAVE YOU NO GOOD NEWS TO BRING?"

"I-I do."

"LOOK AT ME!"

She snapped her chin up. A presence sat. Huge. Ominous. A dragon-like being of shadows and scales. His eyes were black pits with burning stars in the middle. A crown of thorns adorned his head. He sat like a man. Shoulders like a Titan's. But all dragon.

"THAT'S BETTER … DAUGHTER. WHAT NEWS DO YOU HAVE FOR ME?"

She yelled, even though she didn't have to, her voice echoing.

"Nath Dragon has black scales, Father."

"HEH … HEH. SOON NALZAMBOR WILL BE OURS. BUT I GROW IMPATIENT." He reached down his hand. "COME."

She stepped onto the center of his hand.

He lifted her like a doll and set her on the arm of the chair.

Still looking up at him, she waited. The dragon was her father so far as she knew. She'd never known any other parents other than the family of Barnabus.

Unknown to her, this was a lie. Barnabus had been a hero in the first dragon wars. His legend had been twisted into something else. His good name used to spread evil. It had all been the idea of Gorm Grattak, the Dragon Lord on the throne. King of the evil dragons. One of a few survivors of the last Dragon War.

"TELL ME MORE, CHILD."

The tightness in her chest eased. Her confidence returned. She'd made it this far. She'd live.

She said, "We capture dragons by the dozens now. We've turned the world against them. For every one Nath Dragon saves, we take ten. Extinguish them. Sell them. Or bring the willing ones here. As you wish, Father.

"We watch Nath Dragon. Wear him down. Hunt and destroy his friends. His allies. He's still attached to this world. Banished from the Dragon Home. A wayward one, trying to redeem himself."

Again, Selene waited what seemed to her a long time.

"HIS REDEMPTION MUST NEVER HAPPEN," Gorm Grattak said. "SEE TO THAT PERSONALLY, IF YOU MUST."

"Yes, Father."

"I CANNOT LEAVE, DAUGHTER. ELSE I BE DISCOVERED. I FEEL MY STRENGTH GROWING. MY ARMY BUILDS."

He waved his arm across the air. The entire chamber lit up. Bones, treasures and tributes covered the edges of the room. A mural spanned the entire back wall filled with dragons battling in a storm. There were hundreds of them. No two alike. They moved. They hissed. Trying to escape one world for the other.

"THEY ARE READY TO FIGHT. THEIR BANISHMENT ALMOST OVER. SOON WE WILL RUN THIS WORLD OVER." He lifted her chin with his clawed finger. "THE TURNING OR DEATH OF NATH DRAGON WILL MAKE IT CERTAIN. I PREFER HIM TURNED." He snorted. Smoke billowed from his nose like icy air. "GO NOW, DAUGHTER. RETURN ONLY WHEN YOU HAVE SUCCEEDED." He set her down.

The room went black.

She didn't turn. Just walked away. Though she had no aversion to darkness, she welcomed the light of the sun that greeted her at the end. She would do things right or else she would be dead.

Clearing the mouth of the cave, her heart stopped.

She gasped.

All of the lizardmen and acolytes were dead. Devoured in most cases. Even all the horses, but one. She got in the saddle and eyed the guardians above the mouth of the cave. The statues didn't move or blink, but their bellies bulged where'd they'd been flat before.

Her eyes narrowed.

Her jaw set.

Nath Dragon will be mine one way or the other. "Yah!"

CHAPTER

24

THREE DAYS LATER THE ELVES came. It was a good thing too. Ben and Garrison were getting antsy. Pestering the elves. Almost stalking them.

I didn't have the patience to explain elven etiquette to them. Don't touch. Don't stare. Eat and sleep until they get here.

Brenwar grumbled every half day or so. Hadn't eaten a thing.

Sasha lay on the sofa, legs over Bayzog's lap. She slept most of the time.

Shum sat by himself. Eyes closed the entire time. But I could tell he saw everything through his ears. He was the first one to rise moments before the elven delegation appeared.

There were eight of them in all. Light and dark headed. Fair skinned and tanned. Adorned in soft and intricate robes. The tallest was half a foot shorter than me, the shortest half a head taller than Brenwar. Their expressions were stern, but friendly.

I knew two of them and nodded.

They led us to another open room with a large oval table. It looked more like it was grown than carved.

"Dragon Son, it's good to have you among us again," one said. "I see Akron is still honored in your possession."

"Yes, Laedorn," I said. "Your excellent gift has never failed. Put a lot of new holes in orcs, I'll say."

He chuckled. "Those were the days," he said. "So, Nath, I see you've changed since last we met? Is that what brings you here? I understand you seek the Ocular of Orray?"

I wanted to shrug. I in this by the prompting of my friends and for the benefit of Shum and his King. I felt great.

"Yes," I said, "my friend Bayzog believes it might heal me."

Laedorn's eyes drifted between Shum and Bayzog. The other elves' eyes did as well. I could feel the tension among them. Something old. Unsettled.

Laedorn rested his eyes on Bayzog. Smiled briefly at Sasha.

"Bayzog, you should visit with your family. They miss you. But they respect your privacy. They don't anticipate your arrival, but that's up to you."

"Tell them I'll return when the time is right," Bayzog said, "but that time is not now. Certainly the elves are aware that damp winds have begun to prevail. The seasons change. Rapidly."

"We know this. The evil races are emboldened. Their skirmishes increase. They've crossed our lands and hunted our game. Testing us day in and day out." Laedorn's brow furrowed. "Tell me what you have learned of the Ocular of Orray?"

Bayzog furrowed his own brow. "It can heal anything. Curses. Lycanthropy. Disease. I've even read it can take you from one time to another. Perhaps it can return Dragon back to form. Take him back to before the trouble started."

"Possibly."

"But," Bayzog said, "it's been taken. Stolen. Scattered in six pieces all over this world. Taken from right underneath the elves' noses. A hundred years after the last war."

"You suppose," Laedorn said. "But you do not know for certain."

"And you do, Laedorn? Are the histories wrong? My sources polluted?"

The elves at the table muttered in elven among themselves. There weren't speaking thoughts so much as grumbling at one another. I spoke elven and many other things, but they muttered with uncertainty.

"Enough," Laedorn said. He turned his focus to Shum. "And what is your interest in all of this, Roamer Shum?"

"I'm in it for my King, Sansla Libor," Shum said.

The elves stirred.

"There is no king but the one Elven King," Laedorn said. His eyes narrowed. "Mind your manners."

"Your king is here, in these lands. The Roamers have one King and one alone. Sansla Libor is the King of the Roamers." Shum said it matter-of-factly with a bow. "Always has been; always will be."

"Your *king*," Laedorn said, voice hardening, "is wanted for murder, Shum. Over a dozen elves died by his hands. There's blood on that winged monster's claws. You know this. All of the elves know this."

"He's cursed!" Shum said, slamming his fist on the table.

All the humans jumped in their seats.

Shum went on. "He cannot be blamed."

Laedorn said, "Curse or no curse, the blood is on his hands, not someone else's, Roamer. We hunt him, yet you protect him."

"You don't seek to cure him," Shum said. "You seek to destroy him."

"He needs to stand trial. He must answer. He must be stopped. He kills, Shum. You've seen it. He'll kill today. Kill tomorrow." Laedorn tapped his fingers together. "So I presume you want the Ocular to cure your King?"

"You would do the same thing for your king, wouldn't you?" Shum leaned forward on the table. "Isn't that what this Ocular if for, healing?"

"Healing the sick. Not murderers!"

"Alright, everyone," I cut in. "Let's back up. About the Ocular, Laedorn. We want to help find it. Will you let us do that at least?"

The elves went stone cold silent. Expressionless. One and all. They had secrets deeper than the world. They guarded them well.

All eyes were on Laedorn. Except Brenwar's. His eyes were closed. Head was back. Snoring softly.

Laedorn sighed. "Dragon, I need you to come with us. As well as Bayzog and Shum."

"Why?"

"It has been required of me. You see Dragon, as soon as you showed up, we met. Our full council, not just these elves. Even the King. The decision has been made."

"What decision?" I said, easing my way out of my chair.

"I need you to leave your weapons and come with us," Laedorn said, "Now."

Elven Guards sealed the room. Leaf-shaped helmets on their heads. Elven steel on hips and spearheads. There must have been thirty of them.

Sasha clutched at Bayzog's arm. "What is going on? Laedorn, is this how you treat your guests?"

"I'm sorry, Lovely Lady, but you'll just have to trust me. Dragon, must I ask again?"

I unhitched Akron, unbuckled Fang, and dropped them on the table. "Lead the way."

After all, I still had my claws.

Not to mention my breath.

CHAPTER

25

THE ELVEN GUARD LED US on a casual march through the city. Not a single eye batted. It was as if strangers and armed guards strolled through the city all the time. The three of us were side by side, Bayzog in the middle, the elven greeters in front and behind us, with Laedorn close by.

"I wasn't expecting this, Laedorn," I said, not hiding the irritation in my voice. "Didn't you forget to shackle us?"

He said nothing.

We kept going, following a deck roadway that led up and around the trunk of a tree. We came to a tunnel concealed behind the woodland. I'd never heard of an elven dungeon before, but this had to be one.

The hair on my neck stood up.

"Where is this?" I whispered over to Bayzog.

"I don't know," he whispered back.

We stopped. Dark hoods were placed over our heads.

I said, "You can't be serious, Laedorn."

He said nothing.

We were prodded along. Prisoners. Our footsteps silent through every twist and turn.

I couldn't keep track of where we were going. I was disoriented. And I had to wonder if it was the structure or the hood.

It tingled on my head. Muffled sounds. At times it seemed to guide me.

I lost track of time. Seconds. Minutes. Or hours. But my legs didn't tire.

KaRoom!

It was the first notable sound I heard. A large metal door closing. The stuffiness of an enclosed room. Like a tomb.

My hood was lifted. Laedorn and many others stood before me.

"We're here," he said.

"Where?" I said. "Our prison?"

"Sort of," he said. "It's a place more secure that a prison, Dragon. It's a vault."

My eyes adjusted quickly. The room was ornate, metal, completely sealed with one door going in and out. Lit by mystic Lapis Lazuli that hung from chains on the ceiling. Behind Laedorn, the other elves stood on a dais the color of pearl. The Elven Guard were gone.

"A vault for what?"

"Ha! For centuries we've been searching. Redeeming ourselves for what we lost. We scoured Nalzambor from one corner to the other. Sailed the waters. Crossed the lava. Tunneled where no elf had been before." He smiled at me. "And now we have it." He stepped aside. The other elves parted in the middle. "Dragon, behold The Ocular of Orray."

A cluster of diamonds in the middle were brilliant like stars. Encased in the purest gold and platinum, the Ocular was spectacular.

Bayzog's violet eyes were wider than I'd ever seen.

Shum's narrow eyes were circles.

I found myself swallowing a lump in my throat. It was as great a treasure as any in my father's throne room.

"How long," I said, squinting my gold eyes a little, "have you had it?"

"Not long. Little over a decade," Laedorn said.

"Have you used it?" Bayzog asked.

"Once," Laedorn replied.

Bayzog stepped forward, eyes on the pendant.

"Did it work?"

"Of course."

"And, what did you heal?" Bayzog said. "Or let me guess, you won't reveal?"

"You are wise, Bayzog," Laedorn said, shifting his feet a little, "but it's not anything you should concern yourselves with. It is Dragon and Sansla Libor that you are concerned with." He looked at me, my dragon arms. Waiting. Studying. "Well, Dragon. Is this what you want? Are you ready?"

All eyes were on me.

I wasn't ready. Not at all. If anything, I'd just gotten used to my dragon arms. My stomach quivered. Knotted a little. What if the Ocular did cure me? I looked at my scaly hands and sharp golden-yellow claws. I would miss them. I could do more good with them. Could I do as much good without them?

"Dragon," Bayzog said.

"Huh?" I replied, shaking the fog from my head. "Oh, well, will it heal me, or send me back in time before the trouble started?" I was buying time now. But I had to be smooth. Make certain no one suspected it.

"The Ocular heals, that much is certain. But the other effects of the artifact are unpredictable," Laedorn said.

The tightness in my chest began to unravel.

"Well now, that's the trick, isn't it? You can't really guarantee what will happen, good or bad." I folded my arms over my chest, held my chin in my hand. "I've a great deal of thinking to do. Weighing the consequences of this action."

"Dragon!" Bayzog stomped his foot. "This is a great honor and opportunity the elves are offering you! This is what we came for. We don't even have to risk our necks. The gift is there. Your only thought should be to take it!"

I'd never seen Bayzog angry before. There was fury under his creaseless brown skin that was now crinkled. Fists balled at his sides. His human part had come out. If I hadn't known him better, I'd have supposed he'd strike me.

"Easy, Bayzog," I said. "I'm a dragon. I don't rush into things."

"You rush into everything! That's what got you here in the first place!" Bayzog said, getting right in my face. "Don't be a fool, Dragon!"

My belly caught fire. My eyes narrowed on Bayzog.

"What did you—"

"I said what Brenwar would say. What your father would say!"

"It's not your decision, Elf." I poked him in the chest. "It's mine and mine alone." I stepped away from Bayzog's glare. Faced Laedorn. "What about Sansla Libor?"

"We've discussed this already," Laedorn said, "and we agree to the following." He faced Shum and looked up into his eyes.

Shum stood still, hands crossed over his belly.

Laedorn said to Shum, "Capture Sansla Libor and bring him to us, and we promise we'll use the Ocular on him before he stands trial and judgment is delivered."

"How can he stand trial for something he'll have no recollection of?" Shum said, leaning forward.

"You don't know that, Shum," Laedorn said.

"And if he's not healed, how do you try him them?"

"The same as we try any other murderer and monster in our lands," Laedorn said. "I'm sorry, Shum, but the elves won't budge on this. I won't either. Justice must be delivered."

Shum's face drew tight. Conflicted. His loyalty to his king was unquestionable. He'd give his life for Sansla Libor.

I felt for him. I really did. "Shum," I said, "what would Sansla Libor do if he were in your boots?"

"Well said, Dragon," Laedorn said.

Shum's steely eyes drifted onto me. There was sadness mixed with determination. "Are you going to help me find him, Dragon?"

"I give you my pledge."

"I too," Bayzog said.

Shum extended his crossed arms to Laedorn and stretched out his hands.

Laedorn took them in his and nodded. "Agreed then."

"Now, Dragon," Laedorn said, "what is your decision? Sometimes opportunity such as this only comes once in a lifetime."

"Give me a moment," I said, stepping away. I pinched the bridge of my nose. Rubbed my eyes. Raked my claws through my hair. A hundred thoughts simultaneously raced through my head. I felt the greatest decision in my life pressing upon me. At times like this, I would make a mental list. The good side and the bad side of my consequences.

"Dragon," Bayzog said, "the elves are offering you a gift. Don't test their patience."

"Another moment, please," I said, spite in my voice. "What seems so easy to you might not be so easy to me. There are consequences to everything. And Laedorn clearly noted there could be side effects. Did your pointed ears not note that? Because I'm pretty sure everyone else heard."

I moved farther towards the corner. I thought of Brenwar.

If he were here, he'd shove the Ocular down my throat.

And what would Brenwar say once I left and told him I received an offer of healing and didn't take it? I'd never hear the end of it.

And my father. Should I not do it for him? I could be healed and go back to Dragon Home again. I could clean my slate. Start all over again.

But I wouldn't be as powerful.

I flexed my arms. Felt the tough but pliable scales over layers of hardened muscles. It felt amazing. I snorted a puff of smoke from my nose. I would lose that. The fire in my belly that could melt metal bars. I was twice as powerful now as I'd ever been before.

It was my choice.

Mine alone.

I could save more dragons with my black scales than without them.

I turned. Faced them. Shook my head.

"I'm not doing this."

CHAPTER

26

THE ELVES IN THE ROOM had resolve. They weren't easily rattled or surprised. They weren't without passion or personality either, but they were quick minded.

Brows lifted. Mouths sighed. The expressions on their faces were unforgettable.

Bayzog sat on the dais, holding his head.

Shum was the only one who didn't change at all.

"Are you certain about this?" Laedorn said, frowning.

It bothered me. Laedorn always featured a pleasant smile. Nothing ever bothered him. Not a hundred charging orcs. Not a thousand. But this did.

I stared at the Ocular of Orray.

It was brilliant. Beautiful. Pure as the face of an elven maiden. It hummed. Twinkled. Stirred the bones under my scales.

My dragon heart thumped in my chest. "No," I said. "I'm not."

I stepped onto the dais alongside Bayzog and patted his shoulder.

His eyes looked up at me. Pleading. *Do it, Dragon. Do it.*

I could feel the warmth of the Ocular.

Its glow caressed my scales. Warm. Inviting. A mother. An old friend.

My eyes began to water. The closer I went, the more my stomach turned. A struggle brewed within me. Pride. Vanity. Arrogance. Power. They clashed with all that was right within me. What was left?

An image of my father formed in my mind. Patient. Powerful. Kind.

"Do it," I said.

The elves encircled me. One twitched his slender fingers. The pendant floated from its station and dropped over my neck. Someone was holding my hands. My arms. Others muttered incantations. Soft. Strong. Melodious chanting.

I closed my eyes. Exhaled. Let go.

Warmth coated me from head to toe. Every hair tingled on my head. My legs. My arms. My chest. The mystic power soaked in. Washing me from the inside out. I squeezed my eyes shut.

The light was blinding through my lids.

I heard voices. Ancient. Wise. In languages no man had ever heard.

Cleansing energy raced between my feet and my heart. My heart thundered in my chest. Something deep inside me was being dug out. Strong. Dark. Like a tick made of moorite.

I started to shake.

"What's happening?" Bayzog cried out.

I slung one elf from my arm. Then another. I let out an ear splitting roar.

Zzzzzzt!

The light of the Ocular died. It floated from my neck, back onto the pedestal.

I fell to my knees. A shaking leaf. A snake's rattle. My mind a cloud in the air. Time passed. Faces drifted in and out.

"Dragon, Dragon," Laedorn said, jostling my shoulder. "Can you hear me?"

"Huh?" I had a funny taste in my mouth. Unpleasant was more like it. "Yes, yes, Laedorn. I can hear just fine."

They were tending the elves I'd slung into the wall.

Bayzog stood alongside Shum, staring.

I stood up, gently pushed Laedorn aside and extended my arms. My black dragon arms were as beautiful as ever. Claws still as sharp as knives. I felt my face.

"Anything happen?" I asked.

Laedorn eyed me from head to toe. "Nothing at all that I can see. It seems either you're still cursed or you were never cursed at all. I believe it's the latter, Nath Dragon."

I hid my smile. I was elated. But what should I say?

"I felt something, though. Old wounds being mended." I feigned a sigh. "I am disappointed. I really thought this would work. Even though—and don't tell Brenwar this—I was scared at first." I patted Laedorn on the shoulder. "I don't think I'm cursed. I think I am the cure. Thank you for trying, Laedorn."

With a thoughtful expression on his face, he squeezed my hand that rested on his shoulder.

"It was our pleasure, Dragon. And I wouldn't speak of this to the others," Laedorn said to everyone. "We prefer that the rumors of the Ocular of Orray being lost remain so. It is a closely guarded secret. Come, they'll show you out."

I shuffled by Shum and Bayzog, head down, hiding the golden glimmer in my eyes.

Back at the Place of Meet, Bayzog separated himself from the others in his mind.

The others talked, partially explaining where they'd been. But it was clear enough. They planned their trek to find Sansla Libor the Roamer King.

The Ocular of Orray wasn't mentioned. It bothered him that he couldn't speak of it to Sasha. What if she asked? What would he say? Wizards were masters of the partly true story. But he couldn't deceive the one he loved.

"Bayzog." Laedorn approached, alone. A solemn look in his eyes. "What do you think?"

Bayzog said, "I think Dragon is glad he isn't cured. I think he wanted it that way."

Laedorn looked over his shoulder where the others gathered. Dragon was laughing. Joking. All eyes were upon him. Even the elven troubadours and maidens.

"I share your thoughts, Bayzog. And I wonder if the Ocular could cure him and he didn't let it. The council certainly hoped that it would. This news that it didn't will be dreadful." Laedorn shook his head. "Dreadful, indeed."

"Why do you say so? What do they know? What do they suspect?"

"Some of us were still around for the last dragon war. I was younger then. But many saw the black dragons. Nath makes them uneasy. Nalzambor is in unrest. We were hoping to prevent something that might not be preventable."

"Are you saying war is inevitable?" Bayzog said.

"You are as much a great historian as you are a wizard. What do you think?"

"I think I'd better keep a close eye on him."

Laedorn looked hard in his eyes. "I think we all better do that." Laedorn slipped a bracelet over Bayzog's wrist.

"What this for?"

"Keep me posted, Bayzog." Laedorn turned to walk away. "I wish you all the fortune in Nalzambor."

CHAPTER

27

THE RIDE OUT OF THE Elven Lands was quiet. Steady. A soft rain accompanied us after the Elven Guard departed. For some reason I felt happy, but the others' expressions weren't so bright.

Shum was determined to find Sansla Libor.

Bayzog, I could clearly see, was disappointed. He hardly even spoke to me.

Up ahead, Brenwar slowed. Allowed me to catch up. Wrung the water out of his beard.

"What's the plan?" Brenwar asked. "We taking the boys back north or do we follow Shum, after Sansla Libor?" Brenwar's brown eyes narrowed. Gazing after the big boned elf. "What happened with those elves, anyway? Back in Elome. No one's talking. And I'm not stupid, Dragon. You're holding back something."

He looked me in the eye. His stare hard. Penetrating.

I couldn't lie to Brenwar. But I could keep a secret. I could tell part of the truth. Not all.

"I've agreed to help Shum find his king for now. Bring him back to the elves for trial." I looked away and rode on. "My problems will just have to wait until later."

Brenwar came right after me. "Am I to understand we no longer search for this Ocular? That's all we talked about on the way here!"

"Plans change," I said. "It can't be all about me, you know. Now keep your voice down."

Brenwar harrumphed. "What do ye mean, keep my voice down?"

"Just do. I don't want to have a group discussion about it, if you don't mind. I just want to ride. Find Sansla. Save some dragons along the way. It's bound to be a long journey."

"Most journeys are—pah—when you don't know where you're going," he said. "And you, Dragon, don't know where you're going. And I know yer hiding something. I can feel it in my bones." He rode off. Towards Shum. Far enough ahead where I could barely see him with the fog. The rolling mist.

Ben and Garrison rode up alongside me. Excited looks on their faces.

"Look at this, Dragon," Ben said. He had a horned rabbit skewered on a stick. "Snared the both of them we did. Just like you taught me. Like I taught Garrison."

Garrison had another one.

"Somebody's going to eat well tonight," I said, "and those pelts are worth a week's pay, I bet. Each I'd say."

"Told you," Garrison said. "Say, what's wrong with Brenwar? Does he always get mad at everything you say?"

I laughed. "That's a good observation, Garrison, but you'll get used to it."

"Are all dwarves like that?" Garrison asked.

"Some more so," I said, "but most not nearly so bad."

Garrison shifted in his saddle. Eyeing me. Catching my eyes, then looking away.

"Is there something else you wanted to ask?"

The young legionnaire brushed his bangs from his forehead. Wiped the water from his face.

"Who's Sansla Libor?"

"Yes, Dragon," Ben said. "Tell us about that?"

I didn't see the harm in telling Ben and Garrison about it. They'd need to be prepared for such things in case he showed up again. But I wasn't going to tell them the part about him being the Roamer King.

"He's a monster."

"What kind of monster?" Ben said.

"Give me a moment. I just started."

Garrison hit Ben in the shoulder. Motioned for me to continue.

"Ahem. A winged ape. Bigger than me. Fast as a cat and powerful as an ogre," I said. "It drops out of the sky as quiet as rain. Snatches its prey up like an eagle does. Sweeps them away, never to be seen again. I faced it twice. Took my lumps, I did. But the next time I face it." I held out my claws. "I'll break it."

We rode on. The rain was a drizzle now. Silent until someone spoke again. It was Garrison.

"What do the elves want it for?"

"Murder," I said.

"It killed elves?" Ben said.

"That and other things. And we have to stop it before it kills again."

"Well, I'm ready," Ben said, sticking out his chest.

"You're going home," I said, bothered. "It's back to the Legionnaires where you belong, Ben. This mission's dangerous enough already."

"What? Really?" Ben said. "It's only been a week. I have a month and I can handle myself just fine already. Think about it, Dragon. I've survived fights with both draykis and ettins."

"And horned rabbits," I said, laughing.

"Draykis," Garrison said. "What's a draykis?"

"Sort of like a lizardman, but more like a dragon," Ben said. "Right, Dragon?"

"Close enough," I said. Ben and Garrison were starting to bother me. I didn't want them around but it was going to take some convincing. "But honestly, Ben, this journey might take months, years maybe. You might be an old man before we even find him. If we find him."

"But I want to stay with you, Dragon. I want to travel. Adventure. I'm ready. You know I am."

He was ready. But he still wasn't coming.

"Oh," Garrison said, turning his horse around.

"Where you going?" Ben asked.

"There's another snare I forgot to check back there. I'll be right back," he said, riding off.

"Want me to come along?" Ben yelled after his friend.

I grabbed his shoulder. "He'll be fine. Let him go. Besides, I need to work on that hard head of yours. You're going back, Ben. No choice."

"But what about Sasha?" he said. "She's human too."

He made a good point, but Sasha wasn't my problem. Not that she was a problem, but that was up to Bayzog. I did find it strange that he let her travel with him at all. Especially as protective as he was.

"She a sorceress, Ben. She can live longer. You can't do that, can you?"

He frowned. "No."

"And she not a legionnaire either, is she?"

Still frowning, head down, he rode away.

I felt bad for him. I really did. But it was the right thing.

Garrison drifted back, out of sight, taking a spot in a sparse grove of turning trees and falling leaves. He hopped out of his saddle, checked his surroundings, and procured a small figurine from one of his pouches.

It was a robed, bald man carved out of wood. An evil look in its eyes.

He rubbed it between his hands, faster and faster. His hands glowed. Became hot. He dropped it to the ground.

"Sheesh!" He rubbed his smoking hands in the dirt. Gritted his teeth. "Hate doing this."

An image formed over the figurine. A man-sized shadow. Almost as real as his nose. Dark eyes encircled pupils that burned like fire.

Garrison kneeled down. Bowed. Rose up a hair.

"High Cleric Kryzak," he said, "I have news."

The image wavered in the wind, then stiffened. The voice was strong. He could feel it.

"Share, Soldier, share," Kryzak said, "What business had they in the Elven Lands? We could not communicate with you there."

"My Lord, they sought aid to find Sansla Libor. He's cursed and seeks a cure. Nath Dragon does too."

"Are you certain of what you report?" Kryzak said, his image coming closer.

Garrison broke into a cold sweat. He'd seen what the war cleric did to those who failed.

"I'm certain," he said. "I've picked up on what they've tried to keep hidden. My ears," he said, rubbing a small metal earring on his lobe, "are picking up lots of things thanks to this enchanted jewel."

"Tell me more," the dark voice said.

"They sought an item. The Ocular of Orray. It heals. Removes curses and disease they say. The elves search for a winged ape. White. Powerful. He is the Roamer King, Sansla Libor. Nath Dragon sought to remove his black scales, but does not talk of it now." He caught his breath. "He seems content."

"I see," the shadow said, rubbing his chin. "And what of you, Soldier?"

"He sends us back towards Quintuklen."

"Hmmm," Kryzak said, "journey back to where you started. Convince Nath Dragon to follow. If needed I will assist you. Worry naught about the others. I'll take care of them when the time comes."

Garrison bowed again. "As you wish, my lord. I'll not let the Clerics of Barnabus down."

The image faded. The glow of the figurine went out.

He picked it up and stuffed it in his pouch. Stuck his boot in the stirrup and boosted himself up. "This will be interesting."

He wondered what Kryzak had in mind for Dragon. *Death. Torture. Mutilation.* He'd heard about Nath Dragon much in his life. His parents were servants of Barnabus. It was all he'd ever known. He was raised to hate the dragons. But he hid it well. Unlike his parents he wasn't deft in magic, but he had a clever tongue. A simplistic, non-threatening demeanor. It made for an excellent spy, and he liked it. *How I enjoy messing with people. Pulling rugs and dragons out from underneath them.*

He rode with a sly smile under his nose until he got there. This was the greatest mission ever.

CHAPTER
28

"DRAGON, COME," SHUM SAID.

I followed him on horseback, leaving the others behind.

We were another day into our journey. Garrison had pleaded we escort them back to the village the ettins attacked, to see that everything was alright. Shum and Brenwar saw no problem with it, seeing how the last time we saw Sansla Libor it was in the north and it was the most likely place to head anyway. Personally, I didn't mind. I wanted to get a look at that crater again anyway. Something ate at me about it.

Shum hopped off his horse and I followed suit. The big elf had been scouting ahead the whole time, keeping out of sight until night sometimes. His movements were purposed. His gestures quick.

I followed along. Up a faded path, past the naked branches and stopped behind the bushes that overlooked a cliff.

"Smell that," he said.

My nose crinkled. It was offended. "Orcs!" I whispered, my blood charged.

Shum nodded. Battle awakening in his eyes.

If there was one time when dwarves, elves, and men got along, it was against orcs. We all hated them and they hated all of us.

Shum stuck his long finger out. There must have been two dozen of them camping, that I could see.

"Pretty close to the Elven Lands," I said. "They are getting braver, just like Laedorn said."

"We can go around," Shum said, "but I figured you'd want to get a look. You've tangled more with them than I have recently."

I flexed my arms. Clenched my claws. What an opportunity! Turn loose both my arms and my breath on the orcs. Sure, I couldn't kill them. But I could hurt them. Maim them. Frighten the hair off their backs.

We hunched down. Watched. Waited. Shum was right. No sense in endangering ourselves or the rest of the party on account of orcs.

The breed below were wild ones. Some had small tusks under their noses. Some hard flat bellies while others' bulged over their belts.

I just wanted to punch them out. Break some bones. Leave some with a limp for life maybe.

They tussled, grunted, and poked fun at one another, making coarse sounds and jokes.

"I suppose we should go," I said, "but do you think it necessary to send word to the elves?"

"No," Shum replied, "they've doubled patrols already on the borderland. Perhaps these are some of the ones that have been hunting game on their land."

"I wonder what kind of game they're after," I said, watching one of the orcs.

It was stirring up a commotion. Beating its chest about something. It waved another orc over with a face filled with metal and rings. It had a leash.

It has a dragon on that leash!

My blood turned white hot.

Shum grabbed my shoulder. "Don't react, Dragon. Plan, then attack," he said in my ear.

I took a sharp breath.

They had two dragons, not one. Each the size of a large goat. They were golden flowers. Canary yellow scales sparkled with pale bellies. My keen eyes picked up the long lashes on their eyes. Two girls. Sisters, probably. Beautiful and sleek. Hissing and slashing their tales while the orcs stood by laughing. Jerking the collars on their necks.

I tore out of Shum's grasp.

"Dragon!" he half-yelled. "Let's get the others!"

As I dashed down the hill, the wind whistled through my ears. My auburn hair flowed around me.

An orc pointed my way. Sounded the alarm.

I kept on going.

They formed a row at the bottom. Weapons ready to greet me. Axes, hammers and flails, wielded in handfuls of ugly.

I leapt over the tops of their heads—leaving them to their cries of astonishment—and made a bead for the dragons.

A big orc, rock solid and black-haired, charged after me.

I struck. Snapped his head back. Knocked him out.

One dove at my legs.

Another swung a cleaver at my head. The blade skipped off my scaled arm as I jumped up.

I tore a hunk of its chest armor out. Twisted the blade from its grasp and hoisted the orc over my head.

Three orcs with wet pig noses closed in.

I gave them a gift. Hurled their pig-faced brother right into them.

Wham!

They rocked and reeled.

I kept moving.

The orcs were dragging the golden flowers away. Jerking at the ropes.

I yelled something. I don't know what, maybe "Stop!"

They didn't listen. They should have.

My black arm flashed into the nearest orc's chin.

Crack!

It wobbled to the ground.

Slit!

I cut the leash from the first dragon's neck with my claws and went after the rest of the orcs.

The metal-faced orc greeted me with long sharp steel in hand.

I chopped. I blocked.

Its blade skipped off my scales.

I didn't feel a thing. But the orc did.

Crunch!

I drove my knee into its crotch.

Its eyes exploded in their sockets. At least I could slow the orc breeding process.

Whop!

I knocked it out with another punch. Grabbed the second leash and sliced if off with my claws.

Two yellow dragons scurried over the ground, squawking like birds.

Orcs dove after them from all directions.

They spread their wings and darted into the air like shooting stars.

Crack!

Someone clubbed me in the back of the head. Stars circled. The orcs piled on.

Shum hesitated. Didn't move. Watched Dragon dash down the hill. There were too many orcs, way too many to take on at once. They'd need help. At least Brenwar to even things out.

"Probably dead if I do, dead if I don't," he said, pulling out his sword.

He kept his eyes fixed on Dragon. The man was fast. Fluid. Strong. He cleared the first wave of orcs in a single bound. Assaulted the others with the fury of a storm. Dragon disappeared under a wave of orcs when he hit the bottom of the hill. He stabbed the nearest orc.

Krang!

He clocked the helmet off another. The orcs responded. Their forces divided. Coming after him and Dragon.

"Har! It's an elf," one yelled. It was a big orc. Heavy and gusty. A heavy sword in both hands. "A big one at that. I'll have his head."

Swish!

Shum ducked under the orc's swing and countered. *Slice!* The orc fell to the ground with his head missing.

"No, I'll have yours."

A fervor rose among the orcs. A cry of alarm.

Dragon rose from the pile with two orcs by the necks. He slammed their heads together and let out an inhuman growl.

The orcs stabbed and chopped.

Dragon brushed them away. Dragon's eyes were wild. Golden flares.

Shum sliced, dodged and parried. Kept the orcs at bay with the sword and dagger both quicker than snakes. "Dragon!" Shum yelled, "Make a run for it. The dragons are free. We've no quarrel left with them."

Whop!

Dragon upper-cutted one in the belly, lifting it off its feet.

Shum had seen Dragon fight before. Against the winged ape, Sansla Libor. Dragon had been strong then, but he was stronger now. Quicker. Dragon's claws were cutting the orcs to ribbons.

"Don't lose control, Dragon!" he said. "Run! I'll hold them off!"

If only the orcs were wiser, they'd run from the danger. But they were stubborn. Stupid.

For a moment, Shum wasn't sure if he was saving Dragon from the orcs or the orcs from Dragon.

And there were still twenty of them. Slow. Angry. Strong. Coming at him three, four, five at a time. Shum killed some, wounded others, but they kept coming. Their crude weapons nicked him up. Drew his blood.

I've got to get us out of this.

Shum was yelling, "Run!"

I wasn't running anywhere. I laid into the orcs with no mercy. Left them alive, but bleeding. Limping. Crawling. I was Dragon. And I hated orcs!

An orc took a wild chop at my head.

I caught the blade in my hand and yelled. My scales were as tough as steel. I laid that orc out. Tore into the others. I was faster. Stronger. Tougher than they were.

And the thought of them capturing dragons! I would make them pay. Punish them. Hurt them.

Whop! Crack! Bang! Slice! Slam!

They cried out.

I laughed.

Someone was saying something. Yelling again. Perhaps Shum was in danger, but I didn't see him.

BOOOOORANNNNG!!!

The ground beneath me burst open. Rocks and dirt flew everywhere. The orcs fell and tumbled all over. I stumbled but didn't fall. My ears rang. Orcs snorted and started to flee. I was going after the nearest when someone pounced on my legs. I took a swing. Landed a hard shot cracking its ribs. Drew back again.

"Dragon!" a voice bellowed. "STOP!"

I hesitated. Looked down at my victim. It was Ben. My hot blood turned cold.

CHAPTER

29

"I CAN'T BELIEVE IT," BRENWAR SAID, grumbling from his saddle. "Fighting orcs without me. Bloody elf. You could have gotten yerself killed. Would've if I hadn't come along and dropped down my War Hammer!"

The orcs had fled, and that had been over a day ago. I'd apologized to Ben several times since. I'd busted his ribs. Put a dent in his armor. I'll never forget the look in his eyes when I realized it was him.

Fear. Pain.

I couldn't believe I'd done that to him. I just wanted to crawl into a pit. Bury myself. I'd lost control again.

"And you, Dragon!" Brenwar said, "Like a fool you run off. No plan. No backup. Not only did you hurt yourself, you hurt your friend. I saw that look in your eyes." He shook his head and stroked his beard. "You could've killed him."

My mane dangled over my eyes. I couldn't even look at Brenwar. He was right. He could chew me out all he wanted. All the way back to the village. Back to Quintuklen. I deserved it.

Brenwar rode along my side, the others much farther ahead. No one was saying much of anything, at least not to me. Shum had spoken to Bayzog and Sasha separately, and I saw worried expressions whenever they turned to me.

I'd freed two dragons, but I felt like I'd let everyone down somehow.

"You can't be running off on your own, Dragon. We've got to stay together." Brenwar poked his stubby finger at me. I hated that. He continued. "And don't you ever, and I mean ever, fight orcs without me. Ole' Pot Belly ended up taking more of them down than me." He growled. "Never again."

He went on and on. A thorn in my side. A nagging companion I wouldn't shed. A burr in my saddle.

I kept my eyes open and my mouth closed. I paid no attention to the wonderful terrain and babbling brooks we passed. I didn't fish in the streams. I didn't eat a thing. Mile after mile. League after league. I just wanted to get Ben back to safety.

He told me he was alright and there was nothing to forgive.

But I couldn't forgive myself. I'd hurt a friend. *Never again*, I recounted in my head, *never again.*

Garrison kept busy tending to Ben and the others. He helped hunt, cook, and gather the wood. All the time he listened to their whispers. Their worries. He rubbed the mystic earring. It was perfect.

"How are you feeling, Friend?" he said, helping Ben off his horse.

The wiry country boy held his ribs and groaned. "I'm getting better. That potion Sasha fed me really mended me, but I'm still sore." Ben looked around. "Say, where're Dragon and Brenwar?"

"They're coming," Garrison said. "I think Brenwar's still lecturing him. I didn't think dwarves talked so much, but when they start they get on a roll." He helped Ben sit down. "I'll fetch you some fresh water."

"No need," Ben said, looking around. "I wish Brenwar wouldn't do that. I'm alright. Dragon is alright too. He seems sad. I don't like seeing him so sad."

"Well, I'm sorry too, Ben," Garrison said, shaking his head.

"For what?"

"I never should have told you to grab him. But I thought that's what they wanted. Everyone was yelling at him." Garrison sighed. "It should have been me, not you."

"Oh," Ben said, "you know I'm faster than you." He turned away, eyes searching for Dragon.

"I know you are," Garrison said, a sneaky smile parting his lips.

I was counting on it. Kryzak will be pleased.

"What is it, Darling?" Sasha said. "Are you still worried?"

Bayzog *was* worried. He was worried about Sasha, Dragon, all of Nalzambor. The encounter with the orcs filled him with fear. Dragon's eyes had been wild. Filled with lust and power. Dragon had almost killed Ben—and there was something else that he and the rest of the party had allowed to escape Dragon's attention. He'd killed some orcs.

Bayzog shifted in his saddle. Long rides he'd never gotten used to, but it was better than walking. He replaced his long face with a smile. "That obvious, is it?"

"You can't fool me," she said, smiling back at him. "Dragon will be alright, Bayzog. He's good."

"He's lucky," he replied, glancing over his shoulder. The party was spread out, but closing in on the village border. "And dangerous."

"Bayzog, they were orcs. Since when are you so compassionate about orcs? You've told me countless horrors about them. Why can't Dragon take them out? The best way to stop evil is to kill it." Her jaw tightened. "I hate evil and so do you. It causes all the terrible things. Good for him, I say."

"Sasha!" he said, neat brows lifted. "Watch what you say!"

"Well," she said, flipping her hair. "Shum and Brenwar killed some of them, and you would have too if you were there. Why can't Dragon?"

"He's not like us," Bayzog said with a sigh. "He's different. He's a dragon. The son of the King Dragon, and his standards are not ours. It's complicated. But as I understand it, the more Dragon kills, the more danger for the world."

"Well, I think it's ridiculous. He's so young and that's too much responsibility."

"He's over two hundred years old, Sasha. He has to do what dragons do."

Sasha's eyes got big at hearing how old Nath was, but she tried to cover up her surprise. "Dragons kill, don't they?" she said. "I really want to see them. Those two yellow ones were so magnificent. I only got a glimpse of them. What were they called?"

Bayzog wasn't fooled, but he let it go. "Golden flowers," he said, "and, yes, dragons kill, I suppose. But Nath is not like other dragons. He's a dragon born a man. He's special. We have to guide him. You understand that, don't you?"

"Uh," she said, mouth open, her smile gone, "of course I do. I'm just talking to you, Bayzog. I'm not a fool."

"Sasha, you know that's not what I—"

She rode way, auburn hair bouncing on her head.

"—meant. Great Guzan."

His Sasha was miffed. It happened, just not often, but when she was angry, she stayed that way awhile. He let her go. She'd be back to give him an earful. But if she didn't come back within a reasonable time, then he'd better go after her or she might get even madder.

The drizzle turned into rain and splashed off his robes.

He sighed. "If I ever understand women I'll be the world's most powerful wizard."

Everyone needed to be on the same page. Everyone had to keep an eye on Dragon. He was changing. For all Bayzog knew, Dragon might be transcending into another age. From a young dragon into a mature one.

And Bayzog had already shared the secret about the Ocular. He'd told Sasha and Brenwar. If they were going to work together, they'd have to trust each other.

But they didn't tell Dragon they were working together to keep an eye on him. They didn't tell Ben and Garrison either. What they didn't know wouldn't hurt them. They'd be leaving the company soon anyway.

He'd ridden onward alone for another hour and Sasha hadn't returned.

A strange feeling overcame him. The plains were open, but no one was in sight. Lost in his thoughts he must have fallen behind. "I better go after her," he said to himself. He snapped the reins.

Another mile into his ride, the rain came down so hard it stung his face. Horse hooves splashed through the water. He couldn't see a thing.

CHAPTER
30

Sasha's horse nickered and they came to a stop. A heavy rain was coming and the distant trees were bending.

"Oh great." She tugged on the reins to turn around. Those cool rain drops might extinguish her temper. She rubbed her horse's neck and spoke to it. "It's not like me to get so upset. I'm sorry, but I'm glad you're here. Us women need to stick together."

Her horse snorted and wriggled its long neck.

Sasha laughed a little. "Good to know someone understands."

She felt a bit guilty. After all, Bayzog wasn't the best communicator. She knew that. What he'd said wasn't that bad. She'd just overreacted.

"He must think I'm a witch."

Bayzog was normally calm, in control, intent on his studies. But now he was worried. And that worried her. It scared her.

She sniffed. Took out a handkerchief and blew her nose. "Dratted weather, always does this."

Two riders approached, side by side. She smiled. It was Ben and Garrison. Ben was waving, hand high in the air.

"Sasha! Sasha! Storm's coming!"

"I know," she said, "Did Bayzog send you for me?"

Ben and Garrison looked at each other, then back at her.

"No," Ben said, "we just saw you riding alone and thought you might want some company. Besides, we humans need to stick together. We don't live forever like the others."

Sasha giggled. Ben had a strange charm in how he said things. And he was right. The others tended to take their time about things.

She brushed her hair from her eyes and yawned. "I don't guess there's any way around this storm," she said. "Do you think we can make a ride to town? Where are the others?"

"I hate storms. I hate being wet," Ben said. "You'd think you'd get used to it, but the legionnaires insist on sleeping out in the rain. They say it makes you tougher. I say it's stupid. Why would you be wet or cold if you didn't have to be?"

"I agree, Ben," she said. "And what's your opinion on all this, Garrison?"

He shrugged. "It's not so bad I guess. Ben just complains too much."

"I do not!"

"Do too!"

"Alright," Sasha said, "let's find the others. Maybe they have a plan. They couldn't be too far, right?"

"Shum said to just whistle and he'll find us," Ben said, putting his fingers between his lips.

Garrison pushed his hands down.

"We're almost to the village. Let's just ride through the rain and find shelter. They'll catch up with us there. Come on, it's less than a league away."

"What do you think, Sasha?" Ben said.

She squinted her eyes and looked around. There was no sign of Bayzog. It riled her anger up again. *He should have come after me by now.*

Ben looked at her kindly. "I think there's no chance of avoiding the rain either way." He patted his stomach. "And I have a feeling there'll be some warm food cooking. And I'm ready to eat. The elven bread's tasteless. Needs some salt and pepper. I'm sick of it."

"Come on," Garrison said, waving after them. "Let's ride right through it. We'll be safe together. After all, we're Legionnaires."

Ben lifted his eyebrows at Sasha. "He's right you know. I say we go."

"And I say," Sasha said, "last one to the village is buying our meals!" She dug her boots in. Snapped the reins. "Yah!"

They'd raced the first mile when the hard rain hit. It soaked Sasha to the bone, but she liked it. She'd been indoors so much she'd forgotten how much fun the outside could be.

"You alright, Sasha?" Ben called out.

"I'm fine, just stay close. How about you, Garrison?"

The young man motioned with his hand from up ahead.

She squinted to see him. "Lead the way, Garrison."

They moved at a trot. The rain was heavy to ride through and they didn't want to slip on the rugged spots. Besides there was no hurry. They'd see the warm torchlight of the village at any moment.

"Well, we'll make it before dark anyway," Ben said.

"It's pretty dark now," Sasha said. "I wonder how long this rain will last? Seems like it's been raining forever."

"Like I said, you never get used to it."

"If you were a rock maybe," she said.

"Or a river?"

"A pond," she said.

"A fish."

"A Kraken."

"A dwarf," Ben said. "I bet Brenwar is just fine with it." He cupped his ear. "I think I can hear him singing a cheerful song right now." He started to work his elbow and sing:

Dwarves smell bad—Hoy! Dwarves smell bad— Hoy!

We like to stay mad—Hoy! We like to stay mad—Hoy!

Being sad makes us glad—Hoy! Being sad makes us glad—Hoy!"

"Hahaha," Sasha said, holding her belly. "Ben, only you could find humor in this rain."

"Well, it's just part of soldiering, is all. Making up silly songs to lighten the mundane," he said, beaming. "But I thought of that one myself."

"Well, you have a gift for it," she said. "Whoa!" Her horse nickered and stopped. "What is it, Girl?" Both horses stomped their hooves and nickered again. "Ben, do you see Garrison?"

"No," he said.

The heavy rain started to feel like ice, and Sasha's nose tingled.

"Stay close to me, Ben. I'm going to cast a little spell," she said. "I think we need some more light in the darkness."

Ben's horse reared up and neighed. A dark hulking form emerged from the rain. It was bigger than a man. Black wings spread over its back.

"Sasha, get behind me," Ben said, ripping out his sword.

Sasha's words froze in her mouth.

Ben struck. The creature was faster and ripped Ben out of the saddle. It tossed him through the rain and out of sight.

Sasha fumbled with the locket on her neck and tried to speak, but her tongue was tied.

Thunder cracked.

The monster spread out its thick arms and snatched her up. Smothering her in its powerful arms, it leaped from the ground and flew up, up, up.

Helpless and tongue-tied, she couldn't even scream. Arms pinned at her sides, she couldn't do a thing.

CHAPTER
31

THE VILLAGE HALL WAS REBUILT, but not finished. Water dripped through the cracks in the incomplete roof and soaked the rafters of the wooden structure. Several lanterns gave them all the illumination they needed but it was still dim.

Inside, Bayzog paced back and forth. A dozen villagers dwelled there for now, riding out the storm, still eager to finish their own homes. Their offers of food brought him no comfort. Ben, Garrison and—most importantly—Sasha, were missing, or perhaps lost. Back and forth he went, hands locked together, thumbs circling one another. *This is my fault.*

Dragon, Shum, and Brenwar had been with him when they entered the village just before dark. They'd waited almost an hour for the others to arrive. Every minute of that hour had become more miserable than the previous.

"I must go look for her," Bayzog had said. "Something is wrong, I know it."

Dragon's voice had been so reassuring. "They're fine, Bayzog. I'm certain they're just waiting out the storm. Probably found shelter somewhere close. They might be here in one of the homes. I'll send one of the villagers out."

"Do as you wish," Bayzog had said, "but I'm heading back out."

"Tell you what," Dragon had suggested, "let the three of us go. We'll find them."

"No, I insist. I wouldn't feel right not searching for Sasha myself," Bayzog had said, "and my magic can be of assistance."

Dragon had put his hand on Bayzog's shoulder and smiled. Nath had a soothing way about him when he wanted to. He voice was convincing. Smooth. "You need to be here when she shows up and we're still out searching, getting our boots full of mud. Things like this always work out that way. Trust me."

Bayzog had reluctantly agreed. Over two hours ago. He'd been in torment ever since.

I should've gone. I should've gone. I should've gone.

"Please, Elven One," a village man said. He was older, salt & pepper haired with big brown eyes, "have some Honey Tea. It will soothe your worries. I promise." The man held a mug out to him, his hand shaking a little.

"Why do you tremble?"

"Er, well … you're a wizard and an elf. We're not so used to that. We fear that if you get too upset, things will explode."

Bayzog sighed and took the mug in hand. "Is it that obvious?"

The man nodded.

Bayzog took a sip. It was good, soothing like the man said. He had a seat on a bench and leaned back. "Perhaps I am overreacting," he said.

The man sat along his side. Another man pulled out a small set of pipes and played. It was upbeat, but not fast. The children clapped. The women and men swung arm in arm and danced.

"I must admit," Bayzog said, "you people certainly have a way to overcome dreariness. Such a great spirit among you." He drank the rest of the cup. "Refreshing actually."

"We're used to hard times," the older man said. "Life's filled with the good and the bad. You just have to deal with it. The rainbows will come again. The crops will grow. They always do."

The front door banged open. The room jumped and gasped. A large cloaked figure filled the doorway and stepped inside. A man was in his arms. It was Ben. Bayzog jumped to his feet when the figure removed his hood. It was Dragon.

"Is he—" Bayzog started, but he didn't want to say.

"He's wounded, but he lives," Dragon said, laying him down on a table. "Find something for him to drink."

Ben's face had a nasty gash and there was a large purple knot on his head.

"What happened?" Bayzog said. "What about Sasha? Did you find her?"

Dragon shook his head and held out something in his hand. It was her locket. The chain was snapped.

"Nooooo!" Bayzog slumped to his knees. He punched Dragon in the arm. "What happened?"

Two more figures made it inside and shook off the rain. Brenwar and Garrison.

Garrison's arm dangled at his side. His face was pale, and he shivered.

"Get him something to drink," Brenwar ordered.

The villagers did so. Someone threw a blanket over the young soldier.

"Thank you," Garrison said, taking the first hot sip, wincing. "My arm hurts."

"Dragon," Bayzog said, "what is going on? What happened out there? Where is Shum?"

"I'm here," Shum said, stepped through the door and closing it behind him.

"Anything?" Dragon asked.

Shum shook his head. "All the tracks are washed away. Assuming there were any."

"What do you mean by that?" Bayzog demanded, rising to his feet.

"Tell him what you told us, Garrison," Dragon said. "Recount it all again."

Bayzog's mind raced. *Maybe the ettins came back. Or the orcs followed. What in the world could it be?*

Shivering, Garrison said, "We decided to make for the village. Slog through the rain. I was leading when the horses stammered and screamed." He winced. Adjusted his arm. "Something knocked me from my horse and I landed hard on my shoulder. I couldn't see much in the rain, but I heard Ben scream, 'Sasha, get behind me!' That's when I saw it. It grabbed Ben and flung him like a doll out of sight. It grabbed Sasha ..." He swallowed and his eyes watered.

"Go ahead, Garrison," Dragon said. "You're doing well."

He sniffled. "It was horrible. Fanged. The wings spread out and it just scooped Sasha up and leapt into the night. I-I-I was terrified." He looked right at Bayzog. "I'm sorry. I wanted to help, but I was too slow. And I was scared. That thing's eyes were pure evil."

"Sansla Libor did this!" Bayzog said, pointing at Shum. "You know it!"

"We don't know that," Shum said.

"Don't you dare defend him!" Bayzog shouted. "He's a murderer. And knowing you and your Roamer kin, you probably had some idea he was near. Well I'm going after her." He bumped past Shum and slammed open the door. "No thanks to you!"

Brenwar wrung out his beard and said, "Now that's my kind of elf. Humph."

I'd never seen such emotion from the elf, but I reminded myself that Bayzog was part human. And even though my friend was angry, it was good to see a little color in his cheeks. I checked the wound on Ben's head. It was ghastly but not fatal.

I sighed. Ben had been through much since coming to know me. The young man had fought a Jackal-were, even killed it. Almost been sacrificed by the Clerics of Barnabus. Battled ettins. Been punched out by me, and now this. Flung over the rocks by the winged ape.

"Sometimes, Ben, I wish we'd never met," I whispered, handing a vial to one of the village women. "Rub a couple drops in his wounds every hour or so." I put my clawed hand on Garrison's head. "You, take care of that shoulder."

"Wait, where are you going?"

"After Bayzog and after Sasha."

"But I want to go. I can help. I've seen the monster."

"And lived to tell about it," I said, walking away. "Live storytellers are better than dead ones. Share this adventure with your fellow soldiers."

Garrison watched the dragon, elf and dwarf depart and hissed in relief. He'd fooled them. There'd been a moment when he doubted himself. When Dragon looked at him. His eyes. Those golden eyes he swore saw right through him. But as he'd been taught, it's easy to hide a lie with a layer of truth.

He drank his Honey Tea and closed his eyes.

Garrison hadn't lied about one thing. The winged monster *had* terrified him. He'd rather face the ettins than face it again. It was evil. And even though he'd known it was coming and had led them right into the trap, he still hadn't been ready for what he'd seen.

It wasn't Sansla Libor.

It was a winged draykis.

What they don't know might kill them. Heh. Heh.

He dabbed a damp cloth on Ben's head. He felt bad for him. For the second time he'd almost gotten the young man killed. Once by Dragon, again by the monster, yet Ben still lived.

"You're different," Garrison said. "Lucky and unlucky. But it'll catch up with you sooner or later."

He thought about Bayzog. The look on the elven wizard's face when he told them about the winged-ape. *Almost made that elf cry. Now that was a performance.* He checked the figurine in his pocket. It was time he sent word to his master. The last trap was about to be sprung. He just wished he would be there to see it.

CHAPTER

32

THERE WAS NO STOPPING BAYZOG. He insisted we take him to where Sasha was abducted, which we did. He scoured the spot where the necklace was found, holding a small rod in his hand. It glowed like a lantern but was fueled by something else. Magic. It formed a wide beam of light, illuminating the ground.

"That's not going to help," Shum said. "Even with a full day of light, the water washed all signs and tracks out. I can't make out one single hoof print."

Bayzog kept going about his business. On his knees, he rubbed his hands in the dirt where the locket was found.

The rest of us did our best to assist him. Even Brenwar dug around.

After hours of stumbling around, the rain came to a stop and dawn began to break. Birds chirped and the distant sound of a rooster's crow caught my ears.

"We can broaden the search now," Shum suggested.

"Oh, can we now, Ranger?" Bayzog said. "Perhaps you can lead us right to him, unless you're protecting him."

"You know better," Shum said.

"Shum, I hardly know you at all, or your kind. You're practically shunned by the rest of elven kind, and now I'm supposed to trust you?" Bayzog extinguished his rod with a word and stuffed it in his robes. "Your king snatches women and children. Is accused of murder. Is cursed. A monster. And now he has Sasha!"

"We don't know that for certain," I said, stepping between them.

Bayzog turned on me with his fists bunched up. "What?"

"We only know what Garrison said he saw," I said, "and I don't fully trust Garrison. Maybe Ben saw something else. It was dark."

"I don't follow," Brenwar said. "What is it you sense with Garrison, Dragon?"

I smiled grimly at Brenwar. He knew the sense I had. A detection. I could tell the truth from a lie most of the time. "I'm certain Garrison is holding something back from us. Maybe from fear, or maybe from embarrassment."

Bayzog swung himself up into his saddle.

"Where are you going?" I said.

"Wherever I have to go to find Sasha."

He trotted off, leaving the three of us looking at each other.

"Let's just follow him," I said. "I'm certain he has his own way of tracking her."

We spent the next few hours scouring the plains. Bayzog cast detection spells here and there and kept his eyes up often.

Shum rode along my side, talking. "It's possible it is indeed Sansla Libor, Dragon," he said.

"Why do you say that?"

"As I've said before, I think you two were connected when the both of you met. He searched you out, remember?"

"Of course," I said, "but why would he take Sasha? Why not come right after me? Besides, we were far north the last time."

"Anything can happen," Shum said, riding his horse away.

"Look!" Bayzog cried out from afar, pointing into the sky.

There are many things that fly, particularly birds and dragons. But this was neither. Whatever it was, it was shaped more like a man. A big man.

Bayzog was already at a full gallop. Everyone else was riding behind.

The creature was high in the air and seemed to hover at times, but I couldn't tell. It wasn't getting any farther away and we weren't getting any closer. Bayzog wasn't going to stop and we weren't either.

All my doubts about Sansla Libor faded away. *It must be him. What else could it be?* And I'd expected a lengthy search, weeks if not months to find the Elf King turned monster. And now there he was, flying high above us.

It seemed Garrison had been right after all.

We'd kept pace for a few more miles when it finally dipped and dove into the mouth of the crater. Bayzog stopped and looked back at me. He wasn't the only one. Shum and Brenwar's eyes were intent on me as well. In a world full of monsters I shouldn't have been surprised. Perhaps all along the winged-ape had been hiding in the crater. Back in the caves that I wanted to search through earlier. Now, it must have sniffed me out. Been waiting. Perhaps luring me within. It wanted me for some reason. Perhaps another fight like the last time, but this time I'd be ready.

"I suggest we leave the horses," I said. "They'll be alright."

Shum swung his long leg out of his saddle and hopped to the ground. He whispered in his great stallion's ear and turned to face us.

"Aaryn will keep them safe," the ranger said, slipping his small spear from the saddle and hooking in behind his back. "He'll lead them out of danger if need be."

Brenwar unhitched his small chest from his horse and dropped it to the ground.

"Brenwar," I said, "Careful, there are potions in there."

"So?" he said, unhitching the catches and opening it up. Rows of color-filled vials popped up. "See anything you need, Dragon? Wizard?"

Bayzog came and leaned over.

The bottom of the chest was filled with trinkets and other items I hadn't noticed before.

Bayzog slipped his fingers around two of the vials.

Brenwar grabbed a strange metal horn and stuffed it in one of his pouches.

The chest made me think of my father and his throne. When he banished me he didn't let me take a thing. But he let Brenwar take what he thought would be needed. I reached inside and wrapped my fingers around a large bright marble. It was a dragon's eye. Not a real one of course, but it might aid us on our search.

"Got everything ye need?" Brenwar said. We shook our heads yes. He grabbed the Cloth of Concealment, sealed the chest shut, carried it to the edge of the woods, and covered it up.

"You sure that's safe?" Shum asked.

"You sure you're an elf?" Brenwar grunted and headed into the woods.

But it was Shum who led us to the lip of the crater. "There's a path up ahead," he said, "that took us out of here before. I don't advise that we take it back down again."

"I say we go in right here," Bayzog said, twisting a ring on his finger. "Stay close." He jumped off the edge and floated down. "Hurry!"

"Dwarves don't float," Brenwar said.

Shum and I grabbed him by the arms and jumped after the wizard.

"You dare!" Brenwar said. That, and a few other things, all the way down.

We landed soft as a feather and trekked into the woods on quiet feet before stopping briefly to speak.

"I say we search the caves first," I suggested.

Bayzog disagreed. "We should split up. Cover more ground."

I looked him in the eye and said, "This needs to be a united effort. We stay together."

Bayzog glared at me. It was a new look. I'd never even seen the elf rattled, for that matter, but now he was.

I didn't blame him. I put my hand on his shoulder. "We will find Sasha."

Bayzog nodded, kept his chin down and said, "Agreed."

The leaves on the trees started to shake.

Thoom. Thoom.

CHAPTER

33

RENWAR'S BROWS BUCKLED. "GOOD, ANOTHER giant."

"No," I said, keeping my voice down. "We aren't taking this one head on."

"Why not?" he said.

"We're here for Sasha," I said. "We won't be fighting anything if we can avoid it."

"Says you," Brenwar said, smacking his war hammer into his hand.

Thoom.

"I'll take us around," Shum said, "and let's hope there aren't many more around."

"I might not be a giant anyway," I said.

"Oh, it's a giant alright," Brenwar added, following along after Shum and Bayzog.

I took up the rear. I didn't want any of us to get separated.

Ahead, Shum led us away from the heavy steps of the ettin, giant, or whatever it was. Fighting that would let the entire crater know we were there. We just needed to get in and out. Be quick about it.

Navigating the forest wasn't difficult. The dwarf and the elf both had keen vision, as did I. But satyrs did too, so we had to be careful. They were dangerous and known to be vengeful.

Shum stopped and held up his hand.

The heavy giant steps had faded away, but something howled. A predator. Wolves, I believed. The crickets and bugs still chirped, however. That was a good thing. If danger or evil were near, they'd fall silent.

Shum signaled back to me with his fingers flashing in the air.

I'll be right back.

I signaled a reply.

Wait!

He was gone as if he'd never been there at all.

Brenwar slung his hammer over his shoulder, shaking his head.

Bayzog stood with a frown.

I trusted Shum, but in truth I didn't know him that well. Not like Brenwar and Bayzog, both of whom I trusted with my life. I brushed my hair out of my eyes and sat down. Shum didn't have any business running off like that. Not at a time like this.

I could feel Brenwar's eyes on me. He was saying something. Nodding a little.

I looked away from him. I got it. I just didn't want to admit it. The feeling you get when someone runs off without your permission. It makes you worry a little.

Minutes later Shum emerged and we gathered around.

"The gnolls and goblins are gone. Disappeared. No tracks," he said.

That was odd. There had to be tracks of something.

"Did you notice anything else?" I asked.

"Just the entrance to the tunnels. Wide open."

"Tunnels, you say?" Brenwar said. "Guess I'll be leading then."

"Hold still, will you?" I said. I pulled out the marble. The Dragon Eye.

The tunnels were many. Some goblin-sized. Others large enough to ride a horse inside. We needed to choose one out of the many.

Brenwar kneeled at the mouth of one, tasted a handful of dirt and spit it out.

"What do you think, Brenwar?"

"It's dirty."

"Well, yes," I said, "I think that's obvious."

"No," he said raising to full height. "Evil dirty. Bad something in there. Real bad."

"Shum," I said, "don't you find it odd that Sansla would live in a cave?"

"No," he said, "we use caves for shelter and hide outs all the time. It's not uncommon, not for us anyway."

"I'm going in," Bayzog said. "Brenwar, will you lead the way?"

"Certainly," Brenwar said, marching inside.

"A little caution please," I said, holding out the Dragon Eye. "Let this be our guide. No offense, Brenwar."

He turned his cheek and harrumphed.

I flicked the marble into the tunnel. It glowed a pale green like a lantern bug and hovered forward into the darkness until it disappeared.

"Lead the way," I said, gesturing to Brenwar.

"I thought we were following your little bauble," he said, marching along with Bayzog right in step behind him. "What's that thing do anyway?"

"Sees what we cannot. Warns us of any danger," I said.

"Good, then I guess we don't have anything to worry about now, do we?" Brenwar said, marching off.

The tunnels led from one to another. It only made sense to head through the openings big enough for a large ape to manage.

"Look," Brenwar said.

In a cave nook were some gnawed up bones and other remains. Cloth, ashes and embers from a fire. We kept going, seeing traces of life here and there. It made me think of the goblin hideout we had ventured through before.

"Hmmm," Brenwar said, stopping and pulling at is beard. He eyed a cave wall and ran his hands over the rock. "Seems there have been some civilized settlements here after all. Sloppy work. Probably from orcs or some other beast that's not smarter than the pick it swings."

I checked with Shum behind me. "Anything?"

"No," he said. "But these tunnels probably go for miles."

Bayzog was silent at my side, a faint glow on his fingertips.

"We're going to find her," I said.

"I know we are," Bayzog said. "We have to."

We spent the next hour following Brenwar and I only assumed the Dragon Eye was still ahead. I grew more and more puzzled. We saw fewer and fewer signs of life.

Finally, Brenwar put his hand out and gestured, touching his nose. *Something ahead.*

I could smell it myself. Life. Blood. We kept moving.

From the way the air moved, I knew the tunnel had opened into a large cave. But it was pitch black and I couldn't see from one side to the other. There were no outlines. No nothing. We crept inside, keeping close to one another.

Something shuffled in the dark. Its breath was heavy and it grunted a little.

My fingertips tingled beneath my claws, and my heat-sensitive eyes adjusted a little to the darkness.

A warm figure was huddled on the floor, trembling.

Sasha! That was my first thought. I wondered if Bayzog saw her as well. Her fragrance filled my nostrils. It was her! I reached for Bayzog. We had to be careful. Take it easy. Slow. I touched his shoulder and pointed towards her.

Bayzog's body stiffened.

I waved my finger in front of his face. *Hold.*

The Dragon Eye hadn't alerted me, so perhaps there wasn't any danger. Maybe the winged ape had left her and taken off.

But I heard something else breathing in here. Something big.

I picked up a stone and chucked it over the room. Something bounded after it. Heavy and powerful.

Bayzog dashed towards the figure of Sasha.

Brenwar and I stood guard, waiting for the creature to return. It was coming back.

"Why can't I see it?" I said.

"Perhaps you need more light," an unfamiliar voice replied.

Pop!

Fire pits erupted throughout the cavern in orange green flames

"Is that better, Nath Dragon?" the dark voice said.

I tore Fang out and faced the sound of the voice.

Shing.

"Who are you?" Brenwar came along my side, with Shum right behind us. Bayzog held Sasha in his arms. "What is this?"

"Well," the voice said, emerging from a darkened cove. It was a large hooded man in deep purple robes. In his hand it tossed my Dragon Eye up and down. "It's called a trap. Certainly you know that." He tossed the marble to the floor and it stopped between my feet. "This might have worked if I weren't expecting you."

"Told you, can't always count on magic," Brenwar said, crossing his arms.

"Your little friend is right, Nath Dragon," the man said. "You can't always trust what you see or hear, either."

A large winged figure came forward.

"What in Nalzambor is that?" Brenwar said.

"A draykis," I replied.

"You didn't tell me they were that ugly."

"You didn't ask," I said.

"Dragon," Shum's voice warned.

The walls and rocky floor started to move. More draykis popped up all over. Over a dozen of them.

"Bayzog, get Sasha out of here," I said. "We can hold them off."

"No, we stay together."

"Don't be a fool," I said.

The tunnel we came through began to fill with goblins and gnolls.

"Ah, too late now," the robed man said.

"So, this is another ploy of the Clerics of Barnabus? An effort to what, capture and kill me? And just who might you be?"

"Kryzak," he said, swinging a war mace over his shoulder, "and I think my effort to capture you has succeeded. I even have your friends. Now the question is, do I kill you all, or let some of you live?"

CHAPTER

34

WE WERE TRAPPED. FLATFOOTED. DOOMED maybe. My head was racing. Kryzak had been ten steps ahead of us the entire time, and that meant only one thing. Garrison was a spy. Which led to another problem. Ben was in danger. Perhaps the entire village was.

Brenwar set his war hammer down, spit in his hands, rubbed them together and let out a gusty laugh before picking it up again. "It is you who are mistaken. I'm no man's prisoner, but you are mine."

Brenwar hurled his hammer into the winged draykis. *Crack!* Sent it reeling, head over heels.

I banged Fang's tip on the ground. Nothing. "Fang!" I launched myself towards the Cleric Kryzak.

Three draykis cut off my path, swinging heavy swords and axes at me.

I ducked.

Swish.

Rolled.

Clang.

Kicked one in the chin.

The brutes were fast and strong, raining down one pulverizing blow after the other.

I parried and swatted.

Slice!

Caught one in the leg.

Stab!

Hit another in the shoulder. "Blast, Fang!" I said. "Freeze them or something."

They'd beaten the snot out me the first time I encountered them, but I hadn't had my sword that time either. Now it was a little more even. I was still quicker. And now two of them were slower, but I lost sight of one of them.

"Ulf!"

It bear hugged me from behind.

Not this again! I wheezed for breath.

The other two came at me.

I kicked one in the nose, drawing a roar.

The other one slugged me in the face. Walloped me in the belly.

The stars I saw made my aching stomach queasy.

"No!" I tried to yell, but I couldn't breathe. Again.

Snatching up his war hammer, Brenwar slammed in into the toe of the reeling winged draykis. "That'll teach you." He didn't stop there.

Wham! Wham!

The monster's howl was desperate. Angry. It ripped at Brenwar with its claws.

Wham!

Brenwar broke its hand, drawing forth a howl. He raised his hammer for a final blow. "Yer one of the ugliest things I ever … eh?"

Swack!

A tail licked out, sending him tumbling over the cavern floor. A second later something pounced on top of him, pinning Brenwar down under its greater weight. A round dragon face with long whiskers peered down at him with bright yellow cat eyes. Its purr was a rumble.

"Get off me, you scaly cat!"

It dug its claws into his shoulder.

"Ow!" Brenwar said. "Ya poked a hole in my armor. Yer gonna pay for that!"

Streams of smoke drifted out of the cat's nose.

Brenwar's eyes became heavy. "Ye better not eat me," he said, dozing off, "Dwarves make lousy mealzzzz …"

Shum, short spear ready, braced himself.

A draykis with a large iron club charged.

Shum muttered a word in Elvish.

Shtikt! Shtikt! Shtikt!

The spear grew from two feet to six, piercing the draykis in the middle of the chest.

Its club clanged off the cave floor. It was dead.

Shum went after the next one.

Bullish and scaled, it wore a helmet with metal horns.

Shum jabbed at it.

It backed away, swinging a pole axe from side to side with the skill of a veteran soldier, but more power.

Make it quick!

The cavern had erupted in chaos. Bright flashes and bursts of energy brightened the room. Howls and screams followed. It all happened fast. Sometimes fast is good. Sometimes fast is bad.

Shum swatted his spear into the pole axe of the draykis, jarring his arms.

The part man, part dragon monster was formidable. Fast. Strong. Vicious. A lethal blow ripped over Shum's head.

He bounded back.

The draykis kept coming. Swinging hard. Chipping the stone from the ground. Making sparks.

Shum ran his spear through its side.

It roared and twisted away, ripping the spear from Shum's grip.

He went for his sword and dagger.

Two goblins dove into him. Drove him into the ground. One stuck a dagger in his leg. The other punched him in the face.

Pinned down, he somehow wriggled free. Bounced to his feet and freed his elven steel, leg throbbing.

Goblin after goblin fell. The gnolls barked and howled. Swords and axes ready. The draykis pulled the spear from its side and came back after him. They had him surrounded.

Bayzog sent an arc of blue energy into the oncoming goblins and gnolls, throwing them back into the tunnel. He'd had it. They'd taken Sasha and she wouldn't wake up. But she was breathing.

Around him, everything happened at once. Brenwar threw his hammer and everyone burst into action. Including him. The gnolls and goblins scrambled back to their feet and scurried into the room, breaking off in all directions.

Bayzog tipped a vial full of pale red liquid to his lips and drank. His mind became sharp. Focused. Everyone in the cavern slowed down. Either that or his mind sped up. *I like it.* He pulled out a small wand and let them have it.

Bwing! Bwing! Bwing!

Purple hornets of energy showered the horde. Small explosions erupted all over them. They hopped and screamed, danced around, swatting at the balls that danced off their heads.

A gnoll broke through and came at him. But it was slow.

Bayzog muttered a quick word and sent the creature hurling through the air into the others.

They kept coming at half speed. But there we so many. He and his party were outnumbered greatly.

Perhaps I should get Sasha out of here while I have the time and energy.

Bwing! Bwing! Bwing!

He sent the purple hornets back into the horde, then gathered Sasha in his arms.

"Wake up," he said, shaking her.

She remained still. In a deep sleep.

That cleric, Kryzak, must have done something to her. He searched the room for the man. He'd take out the leader and put an end to this. "Where are you?"

"Right behind you," a dark voice said.

Bayzog whirled around and faced the tormenter.

Impossible!

Kryzak towered over him with his arms over his chest. "You have no power over me here, Elf. I was expecting you."

Bayzog cast the wand right at the man.

It sizzled out.

"Seems you're empty," Kryzak said.

"My wand maybe, but not the rest of me."

He raised his arms over his head and summoned sunbursts of energy forth, blasting Kryzak full in the chest and skipping him over the floor.

The cleric rose in his smoky robes. Laughing over the chaos.

Bayzog sent another blast.

Kryzak swatted it away with one hand. "You have no power over me, Elf, but I have power over you."

Bayzog felt the hairs rise on his neck. The shadows of the gnolls and goblins took a life of their own and slithered towards him.

He summoned his words, but no sound came out. The cleric had silenced him.

The shadows slithered around his ankles, his waist, his chest and neck—and dragged him to the ground.

CHAPTER

35

MY SWORD CLATTERED ON THE stone floor. Pinned in the bear hug of one draykis, I took a shot in the stomach from another. Smoke erupted from my nose and that wasn't all. My blood boiled. My temper flared.

The draykis drew back to punch me again.

I opened my mouth.

A geyser of flames shot out, coating the monster from head to toe.

It shrieked. Engulfed in flames, it sputtered around, igniting others in its path.

I wasn't finished either. I kept on breathing.

The gnolls and goblins ran from the flames. Still the draykis held me tight. But noting could hold me now. No draykis. No ettin.

I flexed. I heaved. I roared.

The bats above scattered. The draykis lost its grip.

"Now you've had it!" I spun away and slugged it in the face. We exchanged blows.

Whop! Crack! Jab! Jab!

I was faster. Madder. Furious. I was Dragon! I pounced on its chest. Drove it to the ground and beat it into submission. Chest heaving, I looked for my friends. Flames were scattered everywhere. Thick smoke was rolling.

"Dragon," a voice shot out.

I found Shum. Goblins and gnolls had dragged the elf to the ground. I dove into the fray. Grabbed hair, arms, and legs and slung them away.

Shum clutched at his side and bled from many wounds.

I helped him to his feet. "Can you still fight?" I said.

"Certainly," he said.

Back to back, we faced the horde. Surrounded by barking faces and cautious eyes. Then I caught sight of something else. A dragon almost as big as a horse. Below it, an unmoving Brenwar.

"No!" I cried out. I didn't think. I reacted. Grabbed Akron from my back.

Snap. Clatch. Snap.

I whipped out an explosive arrow from my quiver and nocked it.

"Better duck if you want to live, Vermin!"

They dove.

I unloosed.

Kaboom!

The dragon the likes I'd never seen leapt screeching like a cat jumping out of water. Wingless, cat-like and serpentine, it landed on all fours facing me, whiskers dragging on the floor. Part of its back smoking.

I nocked another. "Great Guzan!"

The arrow should have slowed it, maybe even killed it.

But it was a dragon. A powerful one.

I spoke at it in Dragonese. "Better back away, Feline Fury." Normally, I wouldn't attack another dragon for anything.

But this wasn't an ordinary dragon. It was a mean one. And it had done something to Brenwar. It flashed its razor-like claws and narrowed its eyes.

I fired.

It jumped.

The arrow zinged by it. *That was fast!*

Kaboom! The cavern shook.

The feline fury pounced right at me.

I jumped over its head and onto its back.

It twisted beneath me.

I fell to the ground but jumped right to my feet.

Its claws slashed, clipped my chest armor and spun me around.

I struck back, clipping its nose.

It bounced back.

Dragons hated that. Still, I had to find its weakness before it tore me to pieces.

The feline fury was much bigger and far stronger than me. It was a beast. It'd take more than my claws and speed to stop it.

I dashed for my sword, Fang. Dove and wrapped my hands around the pommel.

The feline fury crashed on top of my back.

Fang skittered from my grip.

"No!" I elbowed it in the nose.

It slammed my face into the dirt with its paw. A cat toying with a mouse.

I wriggled and squirmed. Found myself on my back, pinned down. I struggled and strained.

The foul beast had me. Smoke billowed from its nostrils.

I opened my mouth and breathed, bathing its face in fire.

It sprung away, shaking its flaming head. Mewling, it roared and disappeared into the caves.

Fang's shiny blade caught my eye.

I crawled over, picked it up and rose.

Goblins, gnolls and draykis were all around me. Some living, some smoking, some dead. Where were my friends, though?

Clap! Clap! Clap! Clap!

"Well done, Dragon," the cleric said. "But I suggest you put your weapon down. It's time to surrender now."

That's when I saw. A cool chill went through me, dousing the flame in my veins within. Shum was in a gnoll's stranglehold with two blades on his belly. Brenwar's arms were bound behind his back. A draykis tossed his snoring form over its shoulder. Bayzog and Sasha's limp forms lay at Kryzak's feet, unmoving.

"They better not be dead," I said, pointing with my sword.

"They all still live at the moment," Kryzak said. His voice was deep and rough. Merciless. "But my word can be the death of them all."

The draykis dropped Brenwar to the floor. The goblins bound and gagged all of them.

"Drop your weapons," Kryzak said.

"What is it you want?" I said. *Keep him talking. Think of something.*

Kryzak reached down, grabbed Sasha by the hair and pulled her to his chest. "Such a pretty lady," he said, "I'd hate to hurt her. Of course, I could leave her with the goblins and gnolls maybe. They appreciate a pretty face more than I do."

The goblins howled and panted. Beat their chests. Danced back and forth on their feet.

"Enough!" Kryzak shouted.

They fell silent.

"What will it be, Dragon?"

"Are you exchanging their freedom for me?" I said.

Kryzak nodded. "Certainly."

I stuck Fang's tip in the floor. Nothing.

CHAPTER

36

SURRENDERED. IT ATE AT ME.

Above was an opening and rain was pouring down from on high. I'd been moved, shackled with mystic bounds to some sort of sacrificial rock marked in bright colors. My friends, every last one, were gone.

Kryzak stood before me. Hooded. Shaded face gloating.

Testing my bonds, I said, "How do I know my friends are free?" The harder I tugged, the more they bit into me. "Argh!"

"You're a strong one, Dragon. I can feel it," he said. Purple energy raced around his hands and wrists. "Such raw power. Incredible." He removed his hood. His face was big and scarred. His bald head tattooed with many bright colors. Shoulders broad and thick. Not the typical cleric, but a warrior. Seasoned. Formidable. "They are almost free," he said. "For now."

"What!"

He tapped his war mace on his shoulder. It was crude and ugly with a twinkle to its dark metal. "You'll see, in a moment." He came closer. Eyeing me up and down.

Smoke steamed from my mouth. "What game are you playing, Kryzak?"

A twisted smile formed on his lips. He said, "Game? I thought you liked games, Dragon. Games where you show off your speed, skill and underwhelming intellect." He didn't get any closer. "And that breath of yours, really something. A surprise I wasn't expecting. But don't use it on me. You might need it for later, Dragon."

He's a strange man.

He was cold. Familiar. He pretended like I should know him. And he liked to play games it seemed.

So, I played along. "Hmmm … So, you have me. And I guess you went to all this trouble so I could play a game with you? What did you have in mind? Unhitch me—fiend—and we can play all the games you like. You look like you might be really good at painting eggs or something."

"Heh. Heh. Also a fast tongue, haven't you Dragon," he said. "Generally fast. You'll find out how fast you really are, soon."

He seemed to know me, and I wasn't without my enemies. After all, I'd been roaming Nalzambor for over 100 years. I'd crossed paths with many men once or twice. But the Clerics of Barnabus? I had no friends among them. I was getting antsy though. Where were Brenwar, Shum, Bayzog and Sasha? Had I surrendered for nothing? Should I have fought to the end?

"You seem bitter," I said. "Perhaps it's that ugly face of—*umph!*"

He slugged a mallet-like fist into my belly.

I grimaced and groaned.

"You always talked too much. Never shut up. And all the women seemed to love your meaningless words," he said through clenched teeth.

"And don't forget my hair," I said. "They love the hair just as mu—*oomph!*"

My eyes watered. I had that coming. Well, from evil anyway. I knew the Clerics of Barnabus hated me. Hunted me. But what grudge did this man have with me?

Smoke steamed out of my nose.

Kryzak stepped aside.

Two gnolls walked over and set down two man-sized mirrors in iron frames in front of me.

I finally caught my breath. "I appreciate it, but I can't reach my comb at the moment," I said. "And why two? I don't need to remind myself I look twice as good as any of you."

Kryzak stood off to the side with his thick forearms crossed over his chest. "Just keep watching," he said. He made a cup with his hands that quickly filled with rain water. "During the long rainfalls the deepest tunnels quickly fill with water. If one's not careful, one might drown. Lots of bones down there to be found when it dries out."

My heart skipped a beat.

Colors shimmered in the mirrors and images formed.

Shum and Brenwar were in one mirror. Bayzog and Sasha in the other. Water was pouring around them. Rising over their waists. They were chained to something. Soaked. Eyes darting up and down. Sasha was yelling or screaming, but I couldn't hear a thing.

"What are you doing?" I yelled. "You said you would free them!"

"And I will. Free them from life that is," he said. "But, Dragon, there is hope. You're fast, remember? You can do things most men can't do. Can't you?"

I fought my restraints.

Kryzak laughed. "Save your energy. I'm going to allow you to save one a pair of them, assuming you can find them inside these caves. But who do you save? Who is closest? I am confident you'll find one pair, but I'm not so sure about the other. Then again, they all might just die if you're not careful."

"I'll make you pay for this!" I yelled. "I'll kill you if anything happens to them!"

I was coming unloosed. My temper unhitched. I didn't know what to do. I needed to think. Concentrate. Settle down.

"No doubt you'll try, Hot Head," he said, moving away. "But you better save your efforts for what awaits. Plenty of obstacles will be in your path. It will be interesting to see how you handle them, Dragon."

"Why! Why are you doing this! Why take my friends?"

"Good for evil, evil for good. That's the way it is in this world." He turned and started walking away. "Your bonds will fade soon. When they do I'll be long gone. See you around, Nath Dragon." He stopped and turned. "Next time I see you, I'm sure you'll have more wonderful stories to tell. It's always fun to talk about the dead."

The Chronicles of Dragon

Hunt for the Hero

-Book 5-

Craig Halloran

CHAPTER
1

Heavy raindrops splattered off me, the ground, and the mirrors, distorting the images. I was alone. The water rose faster. Up to Brenwar's chin and Shum's belly.

I couldn't hear Sasha's screams, but I could feel them. Through my scales. Into my bones. The panic in her face surrounded by the cold surface of the iron mirror's frame made my spine chill. I fought at my bonds. The purple bands pinched into my wrists but not as much as they had. Either I was getting stronger or the magic was fading, just as Kryzak had said it would.

"Brenwar!" I yelled. The thought of him perishing had never occurred to me before. But he'd be the first to drown. He was the shortest. "I'll have you, Kryzak!"

The rain overpowered my voice. I was alone in another room of the cavern where a pair of ember urns burned dimly. Kryzak and his brood had long since departed. I still heard the chuckles of the goblins and gnolls in my ears. Helplessly, I watched my friends struggle for life. Dying in some cruel game because of me. What were the Clerics of Barnabus trying to do to me? Why not just kill me and be done with it? Why did my friends have to suffer as well?

Scaly arms bulging, I tore at my bonds. The cuffs bit deep, like burning razors. I screamed. My mind was racing. What if Kryzak had lied? What if the bonds weren't going to fade? Maybe it was just another part of his twisted game. Watching my friends die. Drown slowly. He must have lied. Why wouldn't he? He was evil.

"I can't let this happen!" I pulled. It felt like my wrists would snap off. "I won't let this happen!" I braced my feet against the stone behind me. I had to break free and break free now. I needed to buy all the time that I could.

"*Hurk!*"

The bonds crackled. Bit. Burned. I put everything into it and roared.

Snap!

I pitched forward and crashed into the mirrors. They toppled and the glass shattered.

"No!"

On my knees I picked up one of the large pieces and thought I saw Sasha's pretty eyes before the image faded. I was alone. Worried. Stomach turning. I dashed into the nearest tunnel with my heart thundering inside my chest. My dragon eyes could make out the faint outlines of the tunnels. The entire time I was shackled I'd been thinking what I was going to do. I'd have to figure out how I would find them.

I rubbed my wrists. They were warm and wet. I'd bled. I was seeing red when I came to the first fork in the tunnels. I stopped.

Settle down, Nath. Think. What's the plan?

I'd had a plan a minute ago. A sound one, but it was lost at the moment. What was it? Assuming what Kryzak had said was true, I could save one pair, not the other. And if I had my choice, who would I save? In my mind it would be Sasha. That's what the others would do. It was an unspoken code among men: save the women and children. Then the men can save themselves. But Brenwar. The thought of not hearing his voice again haunted me already. I couldn't imagine it. Couldn't think it.

I tore a hunk of rock out of the wall.

"Guzan! What do I do!"

The only reply was my echoing voice. I didn't have a choice it seemed. Whoever I found first would live. Whoever I didn't find would die. Unless I was fast enough.

Quit wasting time or they'll all die.

CHAPTER

2

I DASHED INTO THE TUNNEL ON the right. Right always seemed to be the better path. My natural inclination at crossroads time and again.

The tunnel twisted and turned and branched off again.

I stopped. Fury built inside me. I needed to clear my head and my mind. Use my wits and instincts. I closed my eyes and sniffed the air. I wasn't a bloodhound, but my dragon nose was pretty good. I could smell gnoll and goblin sweat. Their stink. The dirt from their matted hair. I just needed to find some of them and wring the location of my friends from their greasy necks.

I trotted right again, following the stench. My eye caught water flowing downward in the sloped tunnel. A good sign.

If Brenwar were here, he'd know exactly where to go.

I followed the cave wall and stopped at the edge of an alcove naturally concealed off the path. Heavy breathing caught my ears. Several pairs of feet shifted on the ground and weapons and armor creaked a little.

"Be still, will you?" a gnoll whispered. His voice was gruff and throaty.

Another good sign. They expected me. My clawed fingers drifted to my waist. Fang was gone. What was I thinking? I had no armor or weapons aside from my scales and claws.

I might not see Fang or Akron ever again!

I didn't have time to worry about that though. I needed to act!

Gnolls and goblins saw well in the dark, but their vision wasn't better than mine. So they waited to ambush me, but it was I who would ambush them.

I peered around the corner.

Clatch-zip!

I jerked back. A crossbow bolt zinged past my eye and clattered off the stone.

"He's here! Kill him!" a gnoll ordered.

A mass of warm bodies swarmed me. I launched myself into them. Reckless. Wild. I'd had enough of evil.

Whap! Whap! Whap!

I hit a gnoll so hard its teeth shattered. Two goblins wheezed from broken ribs.

Crack! Crack! Crack!

They cried out. Cursed.

I poured it on. My speed and power were unmatched. Relentless. I punched and kicked until none of them moved anymore … except one. I clenched a goblin in the nook of my arm, suffocating.

"Where are they?" I said in his hairy ear.

He said nothing and opted to try and dig his thick nails into the scales of my arm. Stupid goblin.

I shook him, rattling the bones on his necklace.

"I'll ask one more time … WHERE ARE THEY!"

His fingers no longer clutched at me. They tapped my arm a little. I released him.

He fell on all fours, coughing and sputtering.

I kicked him in the ribs.

"Oof!" he said.

"*Oof* better be a place," I said, squatting down, "and my friends better be there when you take me there."

He shook his ugly head. "No, don't know. Don't know. Don't—*ulp*!"

I slung him into the wall.

A sad thing. I needed Brenwar to find Brenwar. He had no difficulty beating information out of these things. My higher standards prohibited me, but what was I supposed to do in this kind of an emergency? I had to convince him. Now!

I tore a spear from a gnoll's grasp and poked the tip in the goblin's leg, drawing blood.

"Ack!" it said, pushing itself against the wall.

Goblins could inflict pain but they couldn't take it. They were weak like that.

I rested the spear tip on its nose. "I might not kill you, but I have no issues poking tiny holes in you," I said, watching the yellows of its eyes darting back and forth.

"Come," it said. "Come. I show. Just poke no more holes."

I backed off. "Lead the way."

Limping, the goblin traversed the tunnels with my spear at its back.

We were going deeper. I noticed something else. I was limping a little as well. My side and legs were wounded. Seems the goblins and gnolls got a piece of me after all. The scary thing was I hadn't felt it before. Burning. Throbbing. *Blast!*

Ahead, the sound of rushing water became louder.

I jabbed the spear in its back.

It screeched.

"Move faster!"

Its short figure half scurried, half limped along. I could see the hoop earrings dangling from its ears. The bones and armor rattled when it moved. Noisy.

I didn't have time to worry about another trap, however. I just had to hope this was the right direction. Hope that the goblin was more scared of me than of its master.

It slowed again.

I pressed the spear into its back, lifting it up to its tip toes.

It whispered and pointed. "Up ahead. Up ahead."

There was light. Wavering. From a lantern or torch. Water was splashing.

"You go first," I said.

The goblin looked back at me with its bottom lip drooping.

"But… "

I glared at it.

Forward it limped with its hands up a little.

I stayed a few feet back and I could feel the hairs rising on my neck.

The goblin glanced back over its shoulder, flashed a toothy grin, and bustled around the corner.

I started after and stopped. Something was wrong.

"No! No!" I heard the goblin say. He stepped back into my sight with his arms up and pleading.

A sword flashed.

Slice!

The goblin's head fell from its shoulders.

The brawny body of a draykis blocked the exit of the tunnel. Its big scaly hands were holding a dripping sword.

"Fang!"

The monster had my sword.

I flung the spear at its face.

It batted the spear away, bringing Fang down in a flash.

I jumped aside.

Swish!

"Fang!"

Death by Fang was never a thought that had occurred to me. In most cases Fang wouldn't even let another creature pick it up. The hilt would burn hot as fire. But maybe that was a dragon thing and the draykis's scales confused it.

Of course, I didn't know what Fang thought about anything.

I ducked. Twisted. Turned.

Swish. Clang. Swish.

"Nath!"

"Huh?" I said, looking around.

It was Bayzog. Far away. The water was over his neck and almost to Sasha's lips. Water poured in from above, filling the pool. Sasha's chin was covered in water. Her lips fought for gulps of air.

"Hurry!"

I ducked under the next swing and dove into the pool of rising water. Something powerful jumped on top of me and dragged me into the depths of the pool.

CHAPTER

3

THE DRAYKIS LOCKED HIS ARM around my neck and dragged me down. Now I was drowning. Maybe. I could hold my breath for a long time compared to others. But in this case I was choking and I didn't have a good breath from the start.

I drove my elbow into its ribs. Jammed my head under its chin.

Its grip slacked.

I twisted away, swam to the surface, burst from the waters, and sucked in more air.

"Urp!"

The draykis dragged me back under. Its huge arms were wrapped around my legs and its great weight was pulling me down into the black depths.

I grabbed its face and pushed my thumbs into its eyes.

It let go.

I kicked it in the face. Then I slipped behind it and locked my arms behind its neck and squeezed with all my might.

It rocked and reeled in the water. I held on. I wasn't sure if these things needed to breathe. They were strange. Living but dead somehow. Life reincarnated in an evil form. I squeezed harder.

Crack!

Its body went limp. I released it and was watching it float towards the bottom when I noticed something twitching in the waters above.

Sasha! Bayzog!

I could see their feet chained at the deep pool's edge to a ring hooked at the bottom. Bones were layered on the bottom. Skulls and whole skeletons. I cut through the water and popped up right beside them. Sasha's eyes were widened and her mouth was filling with water.

"Hang on!" I said.

"Nath, there is no key," Bayzog said. "You'll have to break them."

I dipped below the surface, wrapped my hands around the chains and braced my feet on the bottom. I put every ounce of energy I had into it.

The metal groaned. My bones popped and cracked in the water. *Come on, Nath! Do it!*

The chains held fast. Sasha swam down beside me and Bayzog did as well. I could see their eyes. They weren't pleading. They weren't helpful. They were forgiving. They placed their arms on my shoulders and grabbed each other's hands. Sasha smiled a little as if saying, 'It's all right. You tried your best.'

Noooooooo! Pull, Nath, pull!

My dragon heart pumped. My energy surged. I put everything I had left into it.

The chain snapped.

I pushed them up out of the water and onto the ledge, where we all lay coughing and gasping. I was the first to gather my breath.

"Brenwar and Shum!"

"Let us help, Nath," Bayzog said, coughing and trying to stand.

"Do you have any idea where they are?"

There was a blank look in his violet eyes. He shook his head.

I dove back into the pool and swam across.

Fang lay on the ground, and I snatched him up.

"Wait!" Sasha said. She pushed her soaked hair out of her face. "I have a spell that might help."

"You can't cast through those iron shackles," Bayzog said, showing the heavy cuffs on his wrists.

But good wizards always have something up their sleeves.

"Hurry!" I said.

Bayzog led Sasha along the rim of the pool and stopped in front of me.

"What do you have in mind?" Bayzog said.

"I created a spell that I've kept on my tongue since I was a girl who feared getting lost." She kneeled down. "And if I ever got lost, I'd summon a pathfinder to lead towards something good. There's nothing good in these caves, I figure, save us."

"Do as you will," Bayzog said, taking a place along her side. He placed his hand on her shoulder and nodded.

Sasha closed her eyes. Her lips didn't move, but sound came out. Sweet. Peaceful. A humming from her throat.

I was tapping my foot.

Wizards take a long time to cast spells in many cases. I just hoped this wasn't one of them.

Her body quivered. Her tear-drop face tightened.

Ping!

A spark of light appeared from nowhere and hovered before her. It grew and glowed into a small sphere of light a little smaller than my hand. Its light was pink and yellow and it pulsated. Sasha opened her eyes and held out her hand. It dropped on her palm like a colorful dandelion.

"Find anything good but us," Sasha whispered to it, "quickly, Pathfinder."

It lifted up and darted away back through the tunnel I'd come through and disappeared.

I was looking at Sasha and she said, "What are you waiting for? Get after it! We're right behind you."

Pathfinder moved fast. My legs churned, winding in and out of the slick corridors.

Behind me, Bayzog and Sasha puffed for air.

"Can you keep up?" I said.

"Just go, Nath," Bayzog said. He was holding his side and Sasha was too. "We'll catch up. Save the others."

It tugged at me. I didn't want to leave them again. They were practically defenseless.

"Protect yourselves," I said. "There are draykis about."

Either Pathfinder was getting faster or I was getting slower because it was hard to keep up along the caves that sloped up and down. Water rushed over my toes in some places. It was bone dry in others. Every step I expected something to pop. A draykis, goblin, gnoll or something else.

The seconds became minutes, the tunnels endless catacombs. The small orb of bright color might as well have been lost for all I knew.

"Where are you going?"

My voice only echoed.

My heart thundered in my ears. My friends were dying, drowning somewhere.

Pathfinder slowed.

I found myself trudging through ankle-deep water and into another cavern where torches hung on the walls. A large pool of water greeted me and water cascaded down from above. Pathfinder dipped into the waters and burned with bright light.

Two figures stood, heads below the waters, chained to the bottom—and not moving.

My heart stopped. My jaw dropped open.

"Brenwar!"

CHAPTER

4

BEN SAUNTERED IN AND OUT of the hard-working men and women of the village with a long face. Hammers and saws pounded and grinded the wood. Men shouted back and forth to one another. Ropes hoisted up walls. Logs were brought in by horse-drawn carts, and the Legionnaires stood guard. Everyone was working but him this morning it seemed.

His head ached and his face was swollen. Every step was difficult. He had bruises and scrapes all over him like he'd been skipped over a gravel road. Whatever had slammed him into the ground was a nasty thing. Strong. Powerful. Familiar. And there had been a smell. It bothered him.

A pair of boys dashed back and forth, rattling their sticks like swords with one another. They stopped and stared at him, blocking his path. One's hair hung over his eyes and the other's was closely trimmed.

"We're going to be Legionnaires," one said.

"Can you teach us how to kill ettins?" said the other, blowing the hair from his eyes.

Ben rubbed their heads and smiled.

"Not now, but maybe later."

One kicked at the dirt.

"Ah! I want to learn now."

Ben squatted down.

"A Legionnaire has to be patient and able to follow orders." He looked into their eyes. "Can you do that?"

One nodded, but the long-haired one said, "My mother's always giving me orders. 'Fill the bucket.' 'Sheer the sheep.' 'Pluck the chickens.' 'Skin the rabbits.' 'String the beans.' Blah! I want to get out of this place."

Ben stuck his chin out a little and bobbed his head. He understood. He'd been done all those things hundreds of times if not thousands. His home village of Quinley was a little bigger than this one, but the work was still the same. He didn't hate being a farmer, but he didn't love it either. If anything, it had prepared him for the Legionnaires. The training was tough, but his body and mind were already used to the work. He'd succeeded where many failed.

"I used to love plucking chickens," he said to them.

The boy's eyes widened.

"You plucked chickens?" the long-hair said.

The other teetered on his toes.

Ben smiled.

"I was the fastest feather-plucker in the village and I just loved stringing those beans. You want to know a secret?"

They nodded their heads yes.

Ben looked around and lowered is voice. "Farm boys make the best Legionnaires. My commander told me so." He winked. "And I'm a pretty good one you know."

"I'm going to be the fastest feather-plucker in my village!"

"No, I am!"

They took off running, tackling and bumping each other all the way back home.

Ben stood up, stretched his back and smiled. Then he frowned. Giving advice to children made him feel old. And he'd never worried before, but now he was worried about Sasha. He felt responsible, and it left his stomach a little sick. He shuffled along, rubbing the knot on his head.

"I should have gone with them," he said to himself. "I should be the one to find her. Dragon's probably mad." He adjusted his sword belt on his hips. "I can't fail again."

He rubbed the bump on his head. It felt like a tomato was growing under his skin. Garrison said it was the winged ape that had grabbed him and tossed him like a fish. But Ben wasn't so sure. There was something about Garrison that didn't seem right. Ben had asked his friend several times what he'd seen and what had happened, but the story seemed to go back and forth.

"I'm not sure."

"It was an ape, like they said."

Ben knew Garrison wasn't telling him everything. Dragon had taught him a bit about liars. 'Just watch their eyes,' Dragon had said. 'Their hands. Sometimes they fidget a little. And sometimes, if you're wise, you can just tell. Your gut will tell you.'

Garrison's story, though a bit inconsistent, did seem sincere. His eyes and hands were steady. Maybe too steady. But what would Garrison have to hide?

Ben's stomach rumbled. He decided to head back to the lodge room and dig up a biscuit. He could smell them better in the air the closer he came. Hot. Buttery. Village or no village, these people were gonna make their biscuits. He patted his tummy. "Well not all of my body has to be unhappy."

Walking along he noticed a man making his way through the tall grasses in the distance. It was Garrison.

"Say, where's he going?" He rubbed his chin. He was hungry, but more curious. Something about the way Garrison moved bothered him. His friend checked over his shoulder a couple of times and disappeared over the dale. "I've a feeling I'd better find out."

CHAPTER

5

I DOVE INTO THE POOL, CUT through the water and grabbed the chains. I didn't look at either of them. I couldn't. Brenwar and Shum's chains ran through a metal ring in heavy stone and the pool was littered with bones at the bottom. I pulled at the chains. They were thicker. The stone bigger. I don't think Kryzak had any plans for them to survive at all. I dug my feet in and pulled again. The metal didn't groan or twist. The ring in the stone didn't loosen.

Nooooooo!

I felt a hand tapping me on the shoulder. I jerked in the water and faced Brenwar. He was still alive. He slid Dragon Claw out of Fang's hilt, stuck it between the links and twisted. I slid Fang between the links as well. Its steel was unbreakable. I was turning the blade, twisting the links in the metal, when something else happened. The chains crystalized like ice, stretching from one link to the other. *Yes!* I kept twisting. So did Brenwar.

Snap. Snap. Snap.

The metal links busted away. I grabbed Shum, pushed him to the surface, and swam for the edge. Brenwar crawled out of the water, gasping for air.

"Dwarves can hold their breath longer than any mortal race, but that was pushing it."

The Ranger was limp in my arms. Lips pale blue. His eyes were closed and his body was cold.

"Shum," I said, slapping his face. "Shum, wake up!" I pushed on his chest.

Brenwar stood over me as I sat on the pool edge and squeezed my shoulder.

"He's gone, Nath. He's gone."

"No," I said, looking up, "he can't be."

I'd seen Brenwar's mad face plenty of times in my life, but never his sad one. Beard dripping, his expression was long, eyes wet. He rubbed his nose and sniffed.

"I tried everything to save him," he said. "But those chains would not give. I've never seen anyone die like that before. Such evil, Nath. Such evil."

I hit the wall.

"Noooooo!"

Bayzog and Sasha appeared on the other side of the pool, mouths gaping. I could hear what they were saying without the words. "Is he?"

I just shook my head and wiped the hair from his face. Our friend, Shum, had died.

I lifted him up in my arms and headed back for the tunnel. Everyone stepped aside with long faces and followed.

"Let's get out of here," I said with determination.

Tears streamed down Sasha's face. "Pathfinder will lead us out."

I followed the light. Numb. Angry. This was my fault. My friends were pawns set up to torture me and now one was dead. It could have been all of them. They insisted on protecting me, but I couldn't protect them. I sniffed and my eyes watered. I wanted to cry. I wanted to kill. I felt cold.

There was evil here. Death and decay, but there was something else. Something I'd missed before. Dragons.

Somewhere. Caged. I could feel them. Smoke rolled from my nostrils. This wasn't over yet.

Unmolested, we made it out of the tunnels and into the pouring rain. An evil echo of laughter followed us out. We all looked back, then at one another. I kept peering down the tunnel.

"We stay together, Nath," Brenwar said, "We can go back in later. We should head back to the village and give a proper burial." Brenwar sniffed. "He'd want that."

Jaw clenched, tears in my eyes, I whirled.

"I'll do what I have to do!"

"One of us is dead," he barked back, "do you want to see another? We came for Sasha. Our lives for hers. Shum knew that. He died with honor. Now don't dishonor him and get more of us killed. That fiend has you rattled, Nath." He tossed Dragon Claw into the dirt at my feet. "We can get him later. We need a plan."

He was right, but I didn't care. I plucked Dragon Claw out of the ground and stuffed him back in Fang's hilt.

"Then you can stay here," I said, stepping towards the tunnel.

Thoom! Thoom! Crack!

An ettin pushed through the trees, uprooting them. Both heads showed ugly sneers. It wore an anchor and chain around its neck.

"Time to eat," one head said, looking at the other, patting its belly.

"Ah," the other head said, "it seems they've prepared an elf for us. Mmmm-mmmm-mmm. They're the most delicious."

It stepped closer.

Brenwar, Shum and Sasha were still shackled and weaponless. I moved in front of them.

"One step closer, ettin, and you're dead," I said, holding out Fang.

The ettin towered over us, hands on hips, laughing.

"HA! HA! HA!"

Smoke rolled from my mouth. I bent over and took a swing, sinking Fang into its wrist.

The ettin howled.

I struck again, dodged and sprinted through its legs and chopped into the back of its heel.

It roared, teetered, screamed, and brought down the anchor.

I dove out of the way.

Smash!

It tore out a clump of boulders and scattered them like ninepins.

I dashed under its thigh and stabbed it behind the knee. *Come on, Fang!*

Glitch!

I hoped it would freeze or something.

But the ettin only screamed and brought the anchor down again.

Crash!

It missed.

"YOU'RE FAST! BUT YOUR FRIENDS ARE NOT!"

It stomped after them.

Brenwar, Bayzog and Sasha scattered.

"THEY RUN LIKE CHICKENS! SLOW ONES!"

"Over here, Ugly!" Brenwar yelled, waving his hands over his head.

It went after Sasha. She'd disappeared behind a large rock. The ettin picked it up like an egg.

She screamed.

It laughed, looked over its shoulder and hurled the boulder at Brenwar, hitting the stone he hid behind. The ettin reached down for Sasha. Fingers clutching at her tiny frame.

Something exploded inside me.

Slice! Slash! Slash! Stab!

I ripped into the back of its leg.

It arched its back, arms wide and started howling in fury.

Slash! Slash! Stab!

Bayzog appeared. He swept Sasha up in his arms and scurried her away.

The ettin's arms flailed for balance and it toppled to the ground like a great tree.

I jumped on its chest and raised Fang over my head with two hands.

"Nath, no!" Brenwar yelled, rushing toward me.

I drove Fang into its heart.

All four eyes popped open and the beating under my feet came to a sudden stop. Its anguished stare was frozen and its arms fell limp at its sides.

Silence and rain filled the crater.

I sheathed my sword and hopped down.

"Ye didn't have to do that," Brenwar said, limping over, "I could've you know."

I headed for the tunnel.

"Where do you think yer goin'?"

I didn't reply. I didn't stop either.

CHAPTER

6

"Brenwar," Bayzog said, "shouldn't we go after him?"

The dwarf stood like a tree stump, thick fingers clutching at his sides, brows buckled.

"No," he said under his beard. "We've lost enough already. Nath should know better." He turned back towards them. "I'm afraid we can't help him any right now. He's temperamental."

Bayzog's hand wrapped around Sasha's. It was cold and she was shivering.

He looked up, hand over his eyes and said, "Let's get shelter. Perhaps under those trees."

"What about Shum?" she said.

The elf lay on the ground with a layer of wet dirt and rain muddying his armor.

Brenwar tended to him. Picked him up, moved him, and set him down somewhere more suitable. He crossed Shum's arms over his chest, took a knee, closed his eyes and bowed his head. Placing his hand over Shum, he began to sing in Dwarven. A throaty melody. Pleasant and strong.

Bayzog held Sasha tight, but her sobs shook both their bodies.

Brenwar finished.

"That was beautiful," Sasha said.

Brenwar nodded.

The rain splashed on Shum's face, bringing life to it a little. Everyone stood and stared, but Sasha was still crying. Bayzog's stomach twisted and turned.

"I-I feel so guilty," Sasha said. "He shouldn't have died over me."

"He'd have died a hundred times for all of us," Bayzog said, "That's what good does. Gives its life so others may live."

"The Roamers say 'Act or evil takes the reins.' He told me that once in our travels," Brenwar said.

The rain slowed and the clouds began to part. The sun was warm but Sasha felt cold. Nath was gone. Buried in a well of darkness. They'd barely made it out the last time and now he had to make it out alone. It didn't seem right. She felt helpless.

"Sasha," Bayzog said, "Your spell. It saved us too you know. And Brenwar. You did well." He kissed her on the head. "Shum would be proud."

"Aye," Brenwar said, stepping over and patting her hands. "I'm grateful to you, Lady Sasha. I'm pretty sure I only had a few more seconds at most in me."

His kind words did little to lighten her spirits. But she was glad she lived. Just miserable.

"I think I need to sit down," she said. She sat where she stood, folded her arms over her chest and watched the tunnel. It was dark. Foreboding. She never wanted to go in there again.

"If I can find some metal," Brenwar said. "I can get these cuffs off. Maybe you can then cast a spell to warm yerselves." He sauntered away.

Bayzog sat down and draped his arm over her shoulder.

"Did you see Nath's eyes?" she said. "When he killed that thing?" She nodded back towards the ettin. "And when he left into the tunnel?"

"Yes, Dear."

"I think I was more scared of him at that moment than I was of the ettin. His eyes were like fire. I almost felt bad for the ettin," she said. "Is that wrong?"

"I don't think it's wrong at all. There's light in all creatures, Sasha, but many prefer the darkness."

"Why?" she said, scratching her head. "Why do they do such things?"

"Doing right is never as easy as doing wrong," he said. "And I fear our friend, Nath, is doing wrong now."

She rested her head into Bayzog's chest and stared down into the tunnel. "Me too," she whispered.

CHAPTER
7

I DIDN'T NEED THE LIGHT. FANG provided that. A sheer a pale blue light adorned the blade. I didn't need an orb to follow either. Now that I knew where the dragons were, dark or light, I'd never forget. No twist or turn would fool me.

I didn't run. I didn't trot. I dared anything to cross me.

Two gnolls did.

Two gnolls died.

No one would harm any of my friends again. No one from this tunnel anyway. Not ever again!

I wasn't far from the large cavern with the urns of light where I'd met Kryzak the first time when another draykis greeted me in the large tunnel.

It held Brenwar's War Hammer in its hands and smiled.

"Put that down," I said.

"Take it," it hissed.

I didn't realize they could talk so well. It surprised me.

We charged. Our weapons clashed.

Krang!

It sounded like the world exploded.

Fang kept humming.

The draykis kept swinging, hammering away at the sword in my arms.

Fang's humming got louder and louder. The ringing rose.

The draykis dropped to its knees. The War Hammer fell from its fingers.

I struck it down with a single blow.

Its head rolled away.

Fang's humming stopped and the blade's light went cold.

Laughter echoed in the chamber. I picked up Brenwar's War Hammer, stepped over the draykis, and strode into the light of the cavern.

Twang! Zip!

An arrow buried itself in my scaled shoulder.

"Welcome back, Nath Dragon," Kryzak said. He was holding Akron and nocking another arrow. "I sure like these Moorite arrows. They'll put a hole through anything. Extra light and fast too."

"Shoot all the arrows you want," I said, yanking the arrow from my arm and tossing it. "They won't prevent your eminent death. I'll avenge my friend."

"Friend?" Kryzak said, cocking his head. "Are you certain about that, Nath Dragon? Perhaps I did you a favor."

The words struck me funny. Cooled my inferno. My stance softened. What was he talking about?

Kryzak lowered the arrow tip towards my chest. He was alone. I sensed no more draykis, gnolls, or Goblins. But, certainly the feline fury was near, ready to pounce from anywhere? I scanned the nooks and crannies. But it was only the two of us and the flames. Where was everyone else? What game was he playing?

Shoulder aching, I switched Fang into my good arm and stepped forward.

"I think it's time to close that mouth of yours, permanently."

"Ah, yes, you never were one to let others do the talking, now were you?"

Again, what was he talking about? How did he know me?

"No," I said, "I always found the conversation of others quite boring, just like the one we're having now." I continued forward.

Kryzak closed one eye and took a half breath.

Twang!

Cling!

The arrow ricocheted off Fang's blade. I bolted towards Kryzak and swung.

Swish!

Like a phantom, he faded and was gone.

"Ah-ah-ah-ah," he laughed, his voice echoing. "Awfully hard to hit what you can't touch." He was distant now, on the other side of the cavern, standing by one of the urns. He lowered Akron to the ground and held up a finger. "A moment, Nath Dragon. Then you may have at me with all your fury."

My blood raced. His tone and demeanor irked me. He slid his deep purple robes from his big frame, revealing a thick leather chestplate of armor. His long arms bulged with hard muscle and tattoos. He wiped the sweat from his tattooed head, rubbed it into his hands, and slid one mailed gauntlet on over the other. He reached down and wrapped his meaty hand around his crude looking war mace and nodded, closing his eyes and murmuring.

I didn't attack until he was ready. This was a challenge fight. All of me against all of him. So be it then. No one ever stood against me, one on one. I didn't care what weapon he had. I had two dragon arms.

He opened his eyes. "I'm ready now." He banged his mace on the floor. It started to glow. "Prepare to feel my power."

"No, prepare to feel mine!"

I raced across the cavern floor, Fang high over my head in one dragon hand and Brenwar's War Hammer in the other. I leapt.

He swung. His mace exploded into my chest like a crack of thunder. It hurled me backward and slammed me across the floor.

That was fast. That was powerful. Like a giant.

"I've been dying to do that," he said.

I could barely breathe. *Not again!* I gasped and coughed and rose to my feet. "Why is that?" I said, walking back over.

He didn't say. He swung instead.

Krang!

Bang!

Clang!

I blocked and shuffled.

Kryzak hammered at me, each strike getting faster than the other. Every blow juttered my arms at the elbows and buckled my knees.

Magic!

He was using magic, and a great deal of it, at that. Speed. Strength. You name it, he had it. No mortal was that strong or that fast. His head glowed with bright colors and his eyes were like fire.

"What's the matter, Nath Dragon?" he said, "Nothing smart to say?"

I drove my fist into his mouth. It felt like hitting a rock.

He drove a mailed fist into my belly.

"Woomph!"

Steel clashing against steel.

I struck.

He parried.

He struck.

I countered.

We banged back and forth for another minute.

"Tell me how you know me," I said, shoving him back. I backed up and rubbed my aching shoulder. My chest burned and heaved.

"Ah," he said, "so now it matters what I think, does it? Well, after I've beaten you into submission, perhaps I'll tell. Assuming you survive."

"Oh, I'll live alright," I said, "I just wanted to give you a chance to talk, before you die. You see, Kryzak, I'm not holding back anymore."

"Is that so?" he said.

"Absolutely."

I sheathed Fang and pulled Dragon Claw out. Its blade shimmered and shined.

Kryzak narrowed his eyes. "Have at it then, Nath Dragon."

I puffed smoke and let the dragon out.

Kryzak was a skilled soldier, but his technique was flawed. It was all strength and no finesse.

I ducked under the war mace ripping over my head and drove Dragon Claw into his shoulder. "Argh!"

I busted his iron chin with Dragon Claw's hilt.

Kryzak's knees wobbled. He was fast, but not the fastest thing I'd ever seen. Dragons were faster. He wasn't a dragon. I was.

Bang! Bang! Bang!

I busted his wrist with one blow after the other.

"What are you doing?" he said, wrapping two hands around his weapon.

"Picking you apart," I said, laughing.

Stab!

Dragon Claw dug into his leg.

Kryzak busted me in the arm and Dragon Claw slipped from my grasp. He punched me in the face and rocked my head back. I punched him back. We locked up.

"Drop yours and I'll drop mine," he said, staring into my eyes.

"Gladly," I said.

I broke it off and tossed Brenwar's War Hammer and Fang to the ground.

He dropped his mace.

Kryzak was bleeding bad and limping. He didn't stand a chance. He wiped the blood from his mouth and spat. My shoulder burned, but I could still take him. One dragon arm was better than two man arms, magic or not. I would make him pay for what he'd done to Shum. But I wanted answers to my questions. Why was he doing this? Who was behind it all? I was going to pin him down and squeeze his neck until I found out. I balled up my fists and took a step forward.

He raised his mailed fists, said, "Next time, Nath Dragon," and bumped them together.

Boom.

The cavern shook and started to cave in. I jumped out from under a falling boulder. When I looked up, Kryzak was gone. His war mace as well.

"Guzan!" I said. But I wasn't alone. Goblins and gnolls spilled into the room, weapons raised and mouths crying for my blood. I snatched up Fang and War Hammer and faced the horde that came at me. A furnace erupted inside me.

I yelled out my new battle cry.

"Dragon! Dragon!"

CHAPTER

8

THE RAIN HAD STOPPED. A foggy mist remained over the grasses but Ben kept Garrison in his sights. He stayed back far enough, looking like little more than a squirrel in the distance, and trudged after him.

"What is he up to?" he said, wiping the rain from his face. "Ah, I've had enough of this already."

Garrison had been wandering off plenty over the past few days. He'd had a zeal for snaring and trapping lately and he'd wanted to hone his skill. He'd sell the pelts for extra coin, but his business wasn't very good. Rabbit pelts didn't go for much, unless you caught a bunch of them. Garrison hadn't.

Ben stopped and squatted into the grasses. Garrison's head was over his shoulder and he spun around. Ben's heart pounded in his chest. *Oh great, he must have seen me.* He kept down and waited. When he peered up again, Garrison was gone.

"By Guzan! How'd he do that?"

Following the path in the tall grasses, Ben trotted after him, heading in a direction he'd never been before.

Trees were ahead. Tall pines, oaks, and birch that stretched over a mile in each direction. It would've been as good a place to set snares as any, but plenty of dangers lurked in the woods. It was safer in the open plains. Easier to spot people or things. Easier to spot anything. At worst a herd of deer or gazelle might pass or you might spook a flock of birds.

He stopped a dozen feet from the woodland's edge and fingered the pommel of his sword.

"What are you up to now, Garrison?" he whispered. His heart pounded behind his ears.

Maybe I should go back? No, maybe he's in danger.

He looked over his shoulder. The rolling hills offered safety. The forest offered another element. Danger. Chill bumps raised on his arms.

"Better be no ettins in there," Ben said, moving on.

He pressed through the branches. The ground was covered in needles and leaves. He kneeled down and picked Garrison's trail back up. Garrison didn't bother to cover his tracks and Ben had a keen eye for them. Dragon had taught him that.

Taking his time, he picked his way through the forest and stopped. Garrison's voice caught his ears. Ben crept towards the sound and pressed his body against a tree, then peered around.

Garrison kneeled in a clearing, rocking back and forth, rubbing something in his hands. He wasn't alone. Ben froze and his chill bumps got more bumps.

Who is he talking to?

Garrison was talking to someone or something. A shadow or a shade.

And it was talking back.

"Well done, Garrison," it said. Its voice was deep and creepy. "Keep me informed."

"As you wish," Garrison said, bowing. "All hail Barnabus."

What did he say?

"All hail indeed," said the shade. The image shimmered and faded away.

Ben remained hooked to the tree. *What was that? Who was that? Barnabus?*

Here was the itch that Ben had needed scratched. Ben could feel it in his gut now.

Garrison's a spy! A traitor.

He stepped out from behind the tree and drew his sword.

Garrison jumped.

"A ... Ben, what are you doing here?" Garrison said.

"No, Garrison, What are you doing here?" He took a step closer. "Traitor!"

Garrison stepped back and lifted his hands, palms up.

"I'm just checking the snares, Ben. You know that." He eyed the lump on Ben's head. "Say, you aren't feeling so well, are you? And that bump's looking worse. Let's get you back to the camp."

"Checking snares my behind, Garrison," Ben said. "You work for Barnabus. You know about Sasha, don't you! Where is she!"

Garrison's smile was like a fox's. Ben had never seen that look before. All these months his friend had been quiet and agreeable, even dull, but now he was different.

"Ben, really, whatever it is you think you saw, I can explain," Garrison said. "Listen, let's get out of this rain. There's a spot nearby where we can talk."

"Here is just fine," Ben said. "I'm all ears."

"You're trembling, Ben. Are you afraid of something?"

Ben swallowed. He'd never been in this sort of confrontation before. He was alone. No back-up. His eyes slid through the trees. *Maybe he's not alone.*

"Out with it, Garrison!" Ben said. "I want to know everything."

Garrison shrugged his broad shoulders. He had about thirty pounds over Ben and was strong as a black bear. He took a step forward.

"You going to kill me, Ben? With your little sword?" Garrison rubbed his chin. "I don't think you have it in you. Killing a man. Your friend. A fellow soldier? How are you going to explain that, Ben? Murdering a Legionnaire. Over what? They'll hang you for certain."

"I'm sure they'll figure it out," Ben said. "I'm an honest man."

"You aren't going to stab a man whose sword is snug in the scabbard, are you, Ben? Tsk, tsk. No, I don't think so." He kept his hands up and offered a smile. "Listen, Ben, no one else has to get hurt. Not me, and not you. And do you really think I'd be doing this if I didn't have to? I don't have a choice, Ben. The Clerics of Barnabus ... they have my family."

"Say again."

Garrison's eyes drifted left.

"They have my family."

"Liar," Ben said. "I know it, and you know it. Now, you're coming with me. Keep those hands up."

"What?"

"Clasp your fingers together on your head," Ben said. "You know that drill. Don't play stupid with me, Garrison."

"Oh, with you never, Ben." Garrison rolled his eyes. "Never at all." He locked his fingers over his head. "Alright then, it this better?"

Ben stepped around behind him and poked his sword in his back.

"Go!"

"Do you want to march me back or can I walk normal? Ow!"

"Waddle like a duck for all I care, Garrison. Just get moving."

Garrison waddled forward and started making quacking sounds.

"Stop it!"

Garrison kept at it.

All these months I never suspected a thing!

Garrison had been quiet, but not too quiet. He'd worked hard, trained hard and fought hard. He'd always had a steely quality about him, but Ben had put that down to his being a soldier. Now Garrison was a different person. Sly and confident. Speaking with another level of intelligence.

Ben wiped his sweaty palm on his trousers and swallowed.

"So Ben," Garrison spoke up as they cleared the forest. "What are you going to tell the Legionnaires? There's only a few of them. And the sergeant in charge isn't so bright. The villagers won't know who to believe. Are you going to tell them I'm a spy? Where's your proof?"

"I'll figure it out when we get there," Ben said. "Just keep quiet."

"Certainly, Ben. I wouldn't want to interrupt your thoughts. After all, you've much thinking to do. Very much indeed." Garrison shrugged and barked a laugh. "Let me know if you need any help with that."

Ben didn't know what do to. He knew that Garrison had information that would help him find Sasha. But his gut told him something else. Garrison was dangerous. Evil.

Maybe now is the best time to stop him.

He poked Garrison in the back again.

"Ow!" Garrison whirled. "There's no need of that, Ben!"

Ben clipped his thigh, drawing blood.

"Ben! Cut that out!"

"You want me to stop, Garrison? Draw your sword!"

"You can't be serious. Ow! Stop doing that!"

Ben was seething. "Stop me."

Garrison backed up and withdrew his sword. "I'm much better than you." Garrison smiled. "You know that."

Rain splattered off steel.

Ben said, "Prove it."

CHAPTER

9

GASHED FROM HEAD TO TOE, I trudged back to the mouth of the cave and out into the rain.

Sasha was the first person I saw, huddled down out of the rain under a dead tree. Her blue eyes widened and she gasped. Froze.

"N-Nath," she said, slowly rising to her feet.

"Aye," I said. "What's left of me."

"What-what happened to you?" she said, running up to me. She hooked my arm over her shoulder and helped me along.

"Nothing I care to talk about," I said, "but this is over, for now." I tossed the bundle under my arm to the ground.

That's when Bayzog and Brenwar appeared.

"You're all bloody," Brenwar said. "What did you do?"

"It's good to see you too, Brenwar." I kicked the bundle open. "I brought you gifts."

Brenwar's War Hammer lay there along with Shum's sword and Bayzog's baubles. I'd even put my armor back on.

Brenwar crossed his thick arms over his barrel chest. "Did you kill him?"

Kryzak. I wished he was dead, more than anything. He'd killed Shum. And now he'd escaped. It really burned me. I shook my head no.

"Give him a moment, Brenwar," Sasha said, "he can barely walk and he's wheezing."

"So?" Brenwar said.

I eyed him. "Kryzak escaped," I said.

"What about the rest?" Brenwar said.

I shrugged. "Maybe dead," I said, "except them."

"Them, who?" Bayzog said, his violet eyes like saucers. He looked at me like I'd turned into an ogre or something. It made wonder. *Have I changed again?* I swung myself and Sasha back towards the mouth of the cave.

"Them," I said, pointing.

Sasha let out a sharp gasp. The first dragon appeared. She was bigger than a dog, with bright yellow scales and white stripes. Dark-eyed and winged, she batted her long lashes at me and brushed past my leg.

Sasha started saying, "He's so—"

"She," Bayzog said, kneeling down and holding out the back of his hand.

The yellow dragon, a golden flower, lifted her nose and snorted past. She then spread her wings and rose into the sky.

Another came, big as a man and long necked.

"A purple tail," Bayzog said.

Its clawed feet splashed into the mud and the rain splattered off its dark violet scales. It showed a row of sharp teeth six inches long, dragged its belly over the stones, and disappeared into the woods. Good thing, too. The wingless ones were ill-tempered and harsh. Their heavy tails could shatter bones and rock.

The others came out. Some on two legs, most on four. All splashed with vibrant colors. Most of them were little taller than my knee. They were rubies, diamonds and emeralds in the muddy rain.

"I want to hold one," Sasha said, kneeling down.

"No you don't," I replied, pulling her up. "And don't ever try it. If they want to be held, they'll come to you."

"They're just so," she clasped her hands, "magnificent."

One by one they darted into the sky. Only one out of the many thanked me. Barely.

"That," Sasha said, gawping as they went, "was incredible." She looked me in the eye. "You saved them all, Nath. You did something good."

I groaned and shuffled to a log and sat. Sure, I'd done some good, but I'd also done an awful lot of killing.

Was that bad?

I watched the rain wash my blood off into a puddle between my feet. My blood and theirs. It would take more than the rain to cleanse what I had done. Those goblins and gnolls, they were dead. But it had been them or me.

Brenwar picked up his War Hammer and slung it onto his shoulder.

"Let's go," he snorted. "We've got a friend to bury."

Brenwar had a stretcher made, but despite my wounds, I carried Shum's body out of the crater. Unlike most elves that were lither in frame and lighter in weight than men, the Elven Ranger was heavy. I didn't complain. His death was my burden and mine alone. I'd walk him all the way back to Elome if I had to.

Silently, we picked our way through the woods and back to the plains. It had stopped raining and the sun began to set. The horses awaited us there. Shum's Roamer Stallion stood taller than the rest and I lay Shum down before him. The horse nickered, stammered its hooves, and snorted. I grabbed the reins and patted its nose.

"I'm sorry, Boy. I'm sorry."

I probably knew more about the Roamers than anyone except them, but that was still very little. They were a discreet bunch. Always moving through the lands and keeping to themselves.

"What do we do?" Sasha said. "Do we bury him here or do we take him somewhere else?"

I looked to Bayzog.

He shrugged with his eyes. "It's not good to keep the dead above the ground for more than a day." He shook his beard. "Not good at all."

"They're a private people," I said. "I suppose a modest burial will do."

"I think he'd like that," Sasha said, picking at her lips. "I'll pick some flowers."

"I'll help."

Shum's stallion nudged me, almost knocking me over.

"What is it?"

It dug its hoof by Shum and slung its head over its shoulder.

"Huh?"

It did it again.

"I think Shum's horse wants to take him," Sasha said.

"Is that what you want?" I said in its ear. "You want to take Shum?"

It nodded its head and neighed.

I looked at the others. "I suppose we can follow him. What do you—"

A black shadow crossed the sun and dropped into the grass.

Sasha screamed.

It was Sansla Libor.

CHAPTER

10

Sansla Libor stood with his black wings spread and his knuckles on the ground. He was a towering figure, the breadth of two men, and the muscles of a savage beast rippled under his fur. He beat his chest with one mighty fist and bared his fangs. He grunted.

"Get behind us," Brenwar said to Sasha and Bayzog.

He brought his War Hammer to the ready. I went for Fang.

Sansla's wings collapsed behind his back and his arms spread wide. His eyes grazed over all of us and rested on Shum's body. He barked and shuffled back and forth.

"You think he wants Shum?" Sasha said.

"Well he ain't getting him," Brenwar said, storming forward. "Get out of here, you ape! I'll put a dent in your head as big as that crater. Do ye think I forgot what you did to me?"

My blood charged. I remembered the last scrape I'd been in with the ape. I could barely handle him then, but now, with my two dragon arms, his timing couldn't have been better. I limped after Brenwar. I couldn't hide my limp, and I didn't care.

"Let's do this for Shum," I said.

We flanked the ape. Brenwar was left and I was right.

The ape didn't glance at either of us but headed towards the others.

Brenwar charged. "No you don't!"

I followed suit.

Sansla sprang over the top of Brenwar and swatted him in the back. Brenwar's boots flew over his head, like a child had flung a doll.

"Now you've done it," I said. I brought Fang down.

Sansla snatched my wrist and twisted.

"Argh!"

Fang fell from my fingers. I punched Sansla in the face. Then the gut.

The winged ape winced and slammed me into the ground. It was bigger and stronger. Just as fast. It twisted me around and stuffed my face in the grass, putting its full weight upon me.

I don't remember it being so big or powerful!

Whop!

Its body shook and it let out a howl.

"Get off him, you hairy beast!" Brenwar yelled.

It pounced off my back and onto Brenwar.

The dwarf disappeared under its girth, only to reappear hanging in Sansla's grip by his beard.

Sansla slung Brenwar right at me.

I caught Brenwar in my chest and we tumbled head over heels before we pushed off one another.

"Not a word about this," Brenwar said.

"I think I've had enough of this myself," I said, rising to my feet. I stuck Fang in the ground and clicked my claws.

I narrowed my eyes at Sansla. "I'm going to rip your wings off."

Brenwar was already moving.

I passed him in a blink.

Sansla met me halfway and we tore into one another.

I pounded into his ribs.

He socked me in the belly and slung me to the ground.

I jumped up and busted him in the face. The chin. The belly.

His hairy arms flailed me with savage fury.

I got my fingers around his neck.

He wrapped his big paws around mine.

I squeezed with all my might, feeling my eyes bulge from my head.

"You've met your match, Sansla," I managed to say.

Sansla dropped a knee into my chest, kicked me off him, and grabbed his bleeding neck.

I grabbed mine and rose to my feet again.

Brenwar stepped in between.

"You've met double your match, Beast!"

Sansla Libor held out his oversized palm and said, "Stop."

I froze.

Brenwar huffed and looked back at me. "Did it speak?"

I nodded, cocked my head—chest heaving—and cupped my ear. "Say again?"

"Stop," Sansla said. "I can speak, but not for long. The curse. The curse will take over."

Sansla Libor kneeled alongside Shum's body with a sad look in his eyes. It was the first time I got a close look at him. His eyes, a rich brown, were flecked with blue and distinctly elven. There was a sleekness to his face, and his expressions were elven. There was even a notable point to his ears, and his husky and powerful body moved with an agile quality about it.

He leaned over Shum, brushed his face with his paw, and closed his eyes. A savage beast turned inside out. He opened his eyes and studied the four of us. I couldn't tell if he was angry or not, but something bothered him.

"How did you know?" I said.

"I'm the King." His voice was throaty but still elven. "I know of such things." He shook his head. "Who is responsible for this?"

"I am," I said.

Sansla rose to his full height. His face twitched and he squinted his eyes. His paws clutched into fists. He shook it off and sighed. "No, it was not you that killed him. Who was it?"

I explained.

When it was over, he said, "I see." He scratched his chin. "Times are dangerous. Beware. Anything can happen." He pointed at me. "Especially to you. Your curse can mislead you. It gives you power but takes control."

My breath left me. Coldness filled my belly.

Sansla twitched again. His face contorted and turned. Mean and ugly. He gasped.

Brenwar's knuckles were white on his War Hammer.

My hand fell to my hilt.

"I've not much time," Sansla said, forcing the words out. "I must take him."

"Hold on, Sansla," I said, "Where did you have in mind?"

"Home," he said. His voice thickened.

"Come with us," Sasha blurted out. "The Ocular of Orray can heal you, the elves say. That's what Shum was here for. He was trying to find you. He wanted to help you."

Sansla shook his great head. Pain filled his eyes. "Do they have the Ocular?"

Bayzog and I met eyes for a moment.

Brenwar's brows buckled as he looked at me. "Why, you liar!" He stormed away.

I hadn't told Brenwar that the elves had the Ocular of Orray because I simply didn't think we'd find Sansla so quickly. Plus, I didn't want him to know that it had failed on me.

But I had lied to my Best Friend, and that was as bad as it got. I'd have to try and settle up with Brenwar later.

"Did you try the Ocular?" Sansla said to me.

"It failed," I said. "But I might not be cursed. This might just be me." I showed my arms. "I am a dragon, after all. You're an elf. You're not supposed to be a monster."

"Nath!" Sasha said, eyeing me. "He's not a monster."

"Sorry," I said, "but I'm not cursed and he is. Sansla, you need to come with us and take your chances with the Ocular. I'm certain it will heal you."

He stepped forward and looked down on my snorting face.

"We are cursed, Nath. Evil grows within the two of us. I can sense it in you. I could smell the blood on your hands from miles away. Death and decay surround you now. A cloak you cannot shed." His thick neck twitched and strained. "You should mind your friends better."

I balled up my fists. "I'm not cursed! I'm a dragon!"

"I can't stop what is happening to me," Sansla said, "But you can." He turned his back on me and picked up Shum. "The Elome elves would kill me," he said. "They won't trust me. I must control the darkness that consumes me. There are other ways. Shum's death awakened the good within me, but the curse takes hold again."

"Let us try," I said.

Sansla placed Shum on his horse. "Secure him." He rubbed the Roamer Stallion between the eyes. "He knows where to go."

"But—" I said.

Sansla stepped back and spread his wings. "We'll meet again, Nath Dragon," he said. "Next time, I might have to kill you or you kill me." Sansla jumped into the air, batted his wings and soared into the sun and out of sight.

CHAPTER

11

BACK IN THE SADDLE, HORSES walking through the grass, we headed for the village. We'd talked, all of us except Brenwar, about what had happened.

I wasn't so sure what Sansla Libor meant about meeting me again and fighting to the death. Did he mean he should die because he was cursed or that I should die because I was?

Am I cursed?

I didn't know. All I knew was that I was beaten, angry and had unanswered questions. But something else ate at me. There'd been more unneeded deaths.

Bayzog and Sasha rode up along either side of me. Sasha was smiling. Bayzog showed a bit of a smile over his slender chin.

"What?" I said.

"Are you wanting to pursue Kryzak?" Bayzog asked. "We're with you."

It irritated me. They'd almost died because of some twisted test and now they wanted to tag along again. I couldn't have it. I might not be able to shake Brenwar, but I could at least shake them.

"Come now, Bayzog. You know I can't have that." I shifted in my saddle. "I think you'd be safer in Quintuklen. After all, we found the Ocular of Orray like we set out to. Sansla Libor found us, and he seems to be faring better than me." I shook my head. "I'm going to the village to make my goodbyes to Ben and move on."

The both of them frowned.

I frowned too. Our quest was over and now all I wanted to do was get back to saving dragons. I'd hunt down Kryzak later if I had to.

"So," Sasha said, "you don't want to track down the fiend that almost killed all of us? You're just going to ride the opposite way?"

"Sasha," Bayzog intervened, "vengeance isn't always the answer. I think Nath is wise with what he speaks. There's been enough death already, hasn't there? And what was gained for it?"

"I'll tell you what was gained," she said. "We took down more of them than they took down of us." Her knuckles were white on the reins and her cheeks reddened. "I say we hunt them down and take it to them."

Bayzog and I locked eyes.

I wanted to smile.

He continued his frown. "Let's reassess when we get back to the village."

Sasha huffed and trotted up ahead.

Bayzog followed right after.

My eyes drifted onto Brenwar. Rigid in the saddle, he kept his eyes forward. *I should be glad.* He might not have meant to speak to me ever again, but I was certain he couldn't contain himself. I was confident that he'd yell at me at some point. Something tugged inside my chest. A notion. A feeling.

Sorry. I should just ride up there and say, Sorry.

I didn't.

Ben could feel his heart pounding inside his chest and the blood rushing behind his ears. Garrison stood, stout and formidable with cold steel ready. Ben swallowed. He knew he had to stop the man. Put him down before more people died. Wait, the ettins. Had Garrison been in on the ettins, too? A dozen thoughts rushed through Ben's head. He locked his eyes, readied his stance, and nodded his chin.

Garrison charged.

Ben's knees locked.

Garrison chopped right at him.

In an instant, Ben dove away. He scrambled back up to his feet and regained his stance. Shaking. Heart beating like a rabbit's.

"Hah!" Garrison said, chopping his sword into the grass. "This will be over in seconds. Sorry, Ben. I hate to kill you."

Fight, Ben. Fight!

Garrison closed the gap between them and swung hard.

Ben's lanky sword arm snapped up.

Clang!

He winced.

"Yes, Ben. We aren't practicing anymore." Garrison chopped.

Ben parried.

"Rattles the joints doesn't it, Farm Boy?"

Clang. Clang. Clang.

Ben's hands ached and fear blossomed inside his chest.

Slit!

Garrison cut his thigh open.

Stab!

Poked the other.

"Hurts, doesn't it, Ben? Now we're even though. I just wanted to see you bleed before you died. I might even poke extra holes in you after you die."

Garrison struck harder and faster.

Bang. Bang. Bang.

Ben blocked and parried every strike.

"Stop doing that and die, will you!" Garrison said, spitting blood from his mouth.

Ben saved his breath. *He can't hit me. Just hit him!*

Garrison was stronger, but his technique was routine. They'd sparred dozens of times.

Ben knew every move, but did Garrison know his? Did he even have a move?

Think of something, Ben!

Garrison backed away, chest heaving.

"I'm not—*gasp*—going to hold back any longer."

Ben took a deep draw in through his nose. He wasn't tired. He was loose. A spring of energy was inside him.

"I'm not holding back either," Ben said. He darted in and struck with all his speed.

Bang! Bang! Bang!

"Stop it, Ben!"

Bang! Bang! Bang!

Garrison fought him off with two hands on his sword. Desperation crept onto his face.

"Stop, Ben!" Garrison said, sucking for breath.

Bang!

Garrison's sword flew from his hands. He collapsed to his knees with his head down.

"You win," Garrison said, still huffing for breath. "Go ahead—*gasp*—kill me."

Ben inched closer and raised his sword over his head.

Garrison slowly shook his head back and forth.

"Go—*gasp*—ahead, Ben. I deserve it."

"Yes you do," Ben yelled. "You're evil. You hurt people and you'll hurt more people."

Garrison's head rose. Laboring for breath, the man offered a sheepish smile behind his short beard. "I know," he said. "Might as well continue the trend with you."

"Huh?"

A small dagger appeared in Garrison's hand. "For Barnabus!" In a flash, he struck Ben in the belly.

Ben's eyes widened, and then narrowed.

"NO!"

He brought his blade down on Garrison's head.

We'd made our return back to the village only to find both Garrison and Ben missing. Garrison worried me. When Sasha was abducted, Garrison's eyes had drifted and his voice had trembled a little. He was either a good liar or really confused, but I'd given him the benefit of the doubt.

None of the villagers or Legionaries had seen them coming or going, either. It made me wonder if Ben had come after us or if maybe something bad had happened to them.

"Look!" a villager yelled, pointing.

A man staggered down the path of a grassy gnoll. It was Ben, and he was clutching his belly. I ran to him and caught him in my arms when he collapsed. His eyes were weak and his hands were bloody.

"Ben," I said. "What happened? Who did this?"

"G-Garrison," he sputtered out.

He pushed his hand into mine and handed me something. It was a small totem. A figurine.

"Barnabus," Ben said. "He spied for Barnabus. Set us all …" his body shook, "u-up." His eyes rolled into his head.

I screamed.

CHAPTER

12

LEAGUES AWAY, KRYZAK WAITED IN a strange grove in the woods. The trees stood, but they had no leaves. Reptiles and bugs crawled over the dirt. A draykis carried stones as big as skulls and placed them on the ground, completing a full circle. It was big enough for a man to lie down in.

"That will do," Kryzak said.

He reached inside a pouch and tossed a colorful powder inside the ring, adding some small dragon bones and dragon claws. He clutched a large dragon tooth inside his hand and squeezed.

The time to report to Selene had come.

He took a deep breath.

Selene. As much as he adored her, he feared her. Perhaps that was what drew him to her. He'd never seen anyone so beautiful and evil before.

She didn't tolerate failure, however. She'd kill him at the slightest sign of weakness.

The draykis concerned him. They weren't pawns the likes of lizardmen, gnolls, goblins and acolytes. They were powerful weapons, and many of them had died. He wasn't happy with that. So why should she be.

He stretched his fist over the circle and squeezed the tooth, breaking his own skin. Blood dripped through his fingers and to the ground. Then he chanted an incantation, stepped back, and watched.

The dust inside the circle stirred and a tiny vortex of mystic colors formed. A woman's figure took shape. It was Selene, standing with her arms folded across her chest. The image twinkled with tiny sparks, filling it with color.

Kryzak's fingers stretched out.

"Don't you dare, Kryzak," she said.

He withdrew his hand.

"My," she said, "so eager to see me again, are we?"

He bowed.

"As always, but now more than ever."

"Your flattery is charming, but it won't compensate for your failure," she said, her colorful image darkening. "What is the situation of Nath Dragon?"

"He lives, but his company is smaller."

"Go on."

Kryzak told her everything. How he had incorporated the ettins and enlisted the aid of the dragon poachers. How he had trapped them in the tunnels and almost drowned them all. About his spies and Nath's search for the Ocular of Orray and about the cursed Wilder Elf, Sansla Libor.

Selene's tail brushed back and disappeared where it crossed the rocks. Her face was a mask of concentration.

Kryzak's hand fell to the wooden grip on his war mace. It gave him little comfort.

"How many did Nath Dragon kill when he came back?" she asked.

"The tunnels were filled with death."

"And Nath Dragon," she said, toying with her robes, "what was his condition?"

"He was distraught. Confused. A storm trying to hold back its anger."

"And you saw the Roamer die?"

He nodded.

"Interesting," she paced inside the circle and folded her arms behind her back, "And what of *my* draykis? Are they all dead as well?"

"Save one," Kryzak said, his head beading with sweat.

"And the dragons you mentioned," she said. "I assume you still have them captured?"

"It was me or them, but the Fury still remains."

"What!" she screamed. The dust exploded around her feet. "How many!"

"Nine," he said. "I'll capture eighteen—"

"With what, you fool! You have one draykis!" Her eyes blazed like fire. "It will take months at least. You have failed me, Kryzak! Perhaps you are helping Nath Dragon save the dragons now!"

"Never, High Priestess! I erred, that is all! I misjudged him!" He pleaded. "It was me or them!"

Selene's face was a mask of fury.

"Do you value your pathetic human life above that of dragons?"

"I-I—certainly not, High Priestess!"

"Close your eyes," she commanded.

"Er," Kryzak swallowed, "as you wish." He shut is eyes.

"Draykis," she said.

It stepped alongside Kryzak.

"Strike him."

Its long tongue licked out its mouth and along its teeth. "With pleasure," it said, balling up its clawed fist.

Whop!

It flattened Kryzak to the ground.

Kryzak could feel his face swelling already.

"Find my dragons!" she yelled. "And don't lose Nath Dragon either! And if you don't have better news to report soon, you'll be dead."

When Kryzak opened his eyes, she was gone. The one remaining draykis stood over him with a grin on its face. Kryzak dangled the purple amulet and said, "Looks like you're going to be the next one to face Nath Dragon."

Selene sat on her throne with a smile on her face, petting the drulture on her shoulder. Kryzak had done well. Even better than expected.

"I have to hand it to him: he's very creative."

The drulture let out a tiny roar and its feathers ruffled.

"Oh, not as creative as you, my pet, but he's awfully good for a man."

Yes, Kryzak had exceeded expectations, but letting him know that wasn't a good motivator.

"I have to keep him on his toes."

And it seemed Nath Dragon was wearing down. The evil within was growing. He couldn't fight it forever. Not when his friends died or when dragons were captured. He'd meet with failure after failure. She almost felt sorry for him. He was naive. His head was filled with a standard that was impossible to live up to, set by his father.

"Not killing anyone. In this world. Hah!"

Gorn Grattack had told her about the high standards set by the Dragon King, Nath's father, and they'd both laughed. No, it was so much easier to do evil than good, and Nath would learn that. And why wouldn't he want to learn? Why wouldn't he want to rule Nalzambor and do whatever he wanted? He didn't need his father. His father needed him. She'd show him that.

"Are you hungry?" she said to the drulture.

It offered a growl.

She clapped her hands.

The great doors opened and the lizardman soldiers stepped inside and kneeled.

"Feeding time," she said.

Moments later they returned with a cage. Inside it something wide-eyed trembled.

"Think you can handle it?"

The drulture's eyes narrowed. It hopped onto the back of her throne, spread its wings and growled.

CHAPTER

13

"NATH," A SOFT VOICE SAID. Someone shook my shoulder. "Nath, he's going to be fine."

I looked up and found Sasha's soft eyes. She sounded confident, but I wasn't so sure. Ben had looked gaunt and pasty when I left. I'd wanted to stay by his side, but Bayzog and Brenwar had insisted that I go. Said they had it under control. At least someone did.

"He's breathing well now, Nath."

"And the fever?" I said.

"It will break," she said, taking a seat on a stone bench beside me.

It was late in the night. The clouds covered the moon, and the villagers' lanterns twinkled from inside their homes. It was a peaceful setting.

"Sasha," I said, "I-I just couldn't forgive myself if Ben died. And I'm far from over Shum being gone."

The stiff wind blew her hair into her face, and she pushed it away and offered the sweetest smile.

"You can't control everything, Nath. You can only control yourself. You can't protect everyone. Not your friends or the dragons. You just have to do your best with what you have."

I shook my head.

"That's not helping, Sasha. Sorry."

"Oh, Nath …" She looked away up the hill and sighed.

I sat there pondering all that had taken place, searching for answers. The Clerics of Barnabus were either trying to kill me or to scare me. The question was why? Did they think I would give up? That I would quit trying to save the dragons?

"Why didn't they just kill me when they had me, Sasha? Why go after my friends instead?"

"Evil has a twisted way of doing things." She pulled her robes tighter and scooted closer. "They must know something we don't."

I stiffened.

"I don't like that."

"I don't either," she said, looking back at me. "I think we should go after them, Nath. Find answers to your questions. They hunt you. Perhaps you should start hunting them. We'll find that Kryzak and put an end to him."

"Sasha! I like the way you think."

Her eyes were bright sapphires. Her voice was excited.

"Well, I can't help it, Nath. I think it's too much that you can't kill those who try to kill you. If it's me or them, it's going to be them." A spark of energy burst from her hand into the ground. "Oops."

"Well, I can kill, but only as a last resort. I'm not supposed to seek it out. I'm supposed to find another way."

"It seems the other way will get you killed."

"It hasn't killed me yet and plenty of dragons have been saved. Perhaps I should focus on that again." I sighed. "Maybe Brenwar and my father are right. Maybe I need to focus on saving the dragons and not dally with all the problems of the rest of the world. Sorry, Sasha, but I really need to be more careful."

I couldn't believe I'd said that.

"Perhaps you're right," she said.

I caught her trying to hide a smile.

"Hold on," I said. "Are you toying with me, Sasha?"

"I don't follow."

I stood up and glared at her.

"Yes you do," I said. "You're doing that thing."

"What thing?" she said, touching her chest.

"That thing. That thing Bayzog does. Whenever I want to do something he doesn't like, he'll go along with it and for some reason I talk myself out of it." I pointed at her. "It's deceitful."

"No, it's thoughtful," she said, standing up. "And you found the right path on your own. Vengeance is not the way. You need to do what your father told you to."

Now I was mad. Seething. It seemed everyone was against me.

"No Sasha, I like your suggestion. I think I should go after them and put an end to them. Who's to stop me?"

I turned to walk away. She grabbed my arm and pulled me back.

"Nath! When you came out of those tunnels ..." her voice trailed off.

"What?"

"I ..."

I could see more than worry in her eyes. There was fear, real fear. But for what?

"Just say it, I won't tell anyone."

"You scared me, Nath." Her voice trembled. "You weren't yourself, but something else. Savage and unpredictable. And when you killed that ettin?" She paused. "I didn't know you."

My heart dropped into my toes.

"I'd never hurt you, Sasha, or any of my friends." I touched her cheek and brushed her hair from her eyes. "That couldn't ever, ever happen. I swear it."

She grabbed my hand and held it to her face. She started crying.

"Don't do that, Nath. Don't swear anything. It's better that way."

I'd never felt smaller. How could this woman be scared of me? I was her protector. I slumped back down on the bench and buried my head in my claws. I couldn't believe what I was hearing.

"I'm going to go check on Ben," she said, wiping her eyes. "And then I'm going to get some sleep. Perhaps you should do the same."

I didn't wave or do anything, but I heard her walking away. Each step left me emptier inside until I was all alone.

CHAPTER

14

"I'M ALRIGHT, DRAGON, REALLY," BEN said. He swung himself up on his horse and groaned.

"You don't need to be riding, Ben," I said. "It'll shake your guts out. Just give it another day or so." I grabbed his horse by the reins. "Get off. Go rest. That's an order."

"I'll not do it," Ben said. "No offense, Dragon, but I know when I'm ready."

It had been almost a week and in that time Ben's fever had broken and his belly had mostly healed. I still hadn't spoken with Brenwar and had said very little to Bayzog or Sasha. But I'd made my intentions clear. I was going after Kryzak.

But now Ben wanted to come along.

Everyone gathered around. Bayzog, Sasha, Brenwar and I sat on our horses watching Ben. He was tormented. Garrison was dead. A man who'd pretended to be our friend had betrayed us, and it had almost cost Ben his life.

Ben's face became long and downcast.

"I should have just let him be," he said. "I should have walked away, but he was just, so… "

"Evil," Sasha said.

Ben nodded.

I felt sorry for him. I think we all did. He'd killed a man whom he'd come to trust as a friend—only to be betrayed.

"You did the right thing," Sasha said. "His deception led to Shum's death. Ben, more people could have died if you hadn't stopped him." She rode over and patted his back. "I'm grateful."

Ben didn't even look at her.

"The Legionnaires were going to hang me!"

It was true. The Legionnaires were a brotherhood, sworn to give their lives to one another and never to harm one another.

Ben had known that, but he'd gone after Garrison anyway. It was a brave thing. Risky too.

Given Sasha's abduction and Garrison's evil magic totem, Ben had been spared. But humiliation followed. His helmet, sword and armor were gone. His bow and arrows as well. He was an outcast like me now.

"Ben," I said, releasing his reins. "Let's go, shall we?"

He sat up in his saddle. "You're letting me go with you after Kryzak?"

"No, I'm letting you go as far as I let you."

Brenwar harrumphed and took the lead.

I knew I needed to talk with him, but there would be plenty of time along the way. Plus, I needed to find the right words to say. It would have to wait.

It was morning when we left, and Brenwar led us in a zigzag north of the village.

Bayzog made his way along my side for a chat. His violet eyes were tired for a change, and I knew the loss of Shum had shaken him.

"You look like you might yawn," I said.

"Me? Not ever," he said, offering a smile. "How are you feeling, Nath?"

"Well enough. And you?"

"I'm not sure what we're doing?" Bayzog said.

"We're looking for Kryzak," I said. "And the best way to find him is to find the poachers. At least now we have the advantage of knowing who is in charge of all this." I gave him a hard look. "You don't have to come along, Bayzog. I think you, Sasha and Ben should go back to Quintuklen. Brenwar and I can handle this."

"You and Brenwar aren't even speaking."

I smiled.

"I don't miss the nagging. You don't plan to fill in for him, do you?"

"Come now, Nath," Bayzog said. "Do you know so little of me? We've all been through much the past few days. I think it's time we stopped and talked things out for a change. Right now I'm not so sure what we're doing—or rather, if what we're doing is best."

"It's best for me," I said. "That's all that matters. I need to save dragons. You need to save yourself from me."

"You need us, Nath."

"You mean what's left of us? Shum died, remember. Ben almost died and so did you and Sasha. Not to mention Brenwar. What would you have me do?"

He grabbed my arm, narrowed his eyes and spoke through his teeth.

"Slow down and think, will you? Perhaps they set another trap. An ambush perhaps. We need more caution and less action. We need council."

Council. Elves loved councils and long meetings. So did dwarves, for that matter, but I wasn't going to bite on any of it. No, all he wanted to do was talk me out of doing what I wanted. I was going to save the dragons, and in order to do that I was going to stop the poachers that captured them.

"Here is my counsel for you, Bayzog. Go home and leave my life to me."

Bayzog led his horse away, saying, "You're as stubborn as Brenwar."

I had to admit: that stung a little.

CHAPTER

15

WE SCOURED THE COUNTRYSIDE OVER the next few days, taking our time on the journey. No one was saying much of anything and we hadn't sat down for council. They had offered, but I'd refused. For the most part they were all just tagging along and that was fine by me. Eventually we'd be close enough to Quintuklen and they'd head home. That was my plan anyway.

"So, Dragon," Ben said. "How do we go about tracking down someone when the world's so big?"

It was a good question. I waded into a nearby river and acted like I didn't hear him. I was getting hungry and I had an appetite for fish. The cold water rushed past my knees as I searched for signs of life. The sun was bright and the water was clear, and I could see my reflection shimmering in it. My mane of auburn hair looked fine. Of course, it always did.

A fish darted through my feet, followed by another. Moments later one of them settled.

I readied my claws and licked my lips. I could taste the meat already. I slipped my hands into the water.

Ben sloshed up behind me.

The fish squirted between my fingers.

"Ben!" I cried. "Quit scaring the fish. I've taught you better than that." I frowned and shook my head at him.

"Then you stop ignoring me," he said. "You've been ignoring everyone, and I'm getting tired of it."

"They you should go home," I said.

"To what?" he said. "I don't have anyone anymore. Just you, Dragon."

"I'm sure Quinley could use you in the cornfields," I said. "And you're a better bowman than you were. You'd be the best shot for miles around." I sloshed away, eyeing the water.

"What's wrong with you, Dragon?" he said. "You didn't used to be like this. You used to be nice. Now you're just—"

I turned and faced him with my hands on my hips.

"I'm just what, Ben? Mean?"

"I wasn't going to say that," he said.

His eyes drifted to the left.

"You were going to say that," I said. "And guess what, Ben? I don't care. I'm being mean because I don't want you here, and I've told you that. I've told all of you that, but none of you listen."

"You need us," he said.

I laughed.

"For what, Ben? You don't even have a sword or bow. What are you going to fight with, your hands?"

I took a jab at another fish and missed.

"Blast it!"

My stomach was growling. I was growling. Why wouldn't they leave me alone?

"UGH!" Ben said. He threw up his arms and sloshed away in the waters.

"Goodbye, Ben," I said.

He stopped and turned. His pleasant face was turning red and his fists were balled up at his sides.

"You know, Dragon, there's a saying in Quinley. *You can tell a lot about a man by the friends he keeps.*"

I shrugged and said, "So, I've heard that one before and you didn't say it quite right."

"I'm don't care if it sounds right or not because I've got a better saying. *You can tell a lot more about a man who doesn't have any friends.*" He pointed at me. "That's for you, Dragon!" He stormed through the waters, fell, and completely soaked himself.

I started laughing and holding my belly.

Soaked, Ben shook his fist at me and stormed away. As he was leaving, Brenwar, Bayzog and Sasha were coming up along the sandy riverbank. I rolled my eyes.

"What's the matter, Ben?" I heard Sasha say.

"Nothing!"

They all stood there gawping at me, except Brenwar. He was glaring. I didn't care though. I just wanted to eat some fish and be left alone. I made my way down river a ways and when I looked back they were gone. Good.

I readied my hands, spread my feet in the river bed and waited for the next fish to pass. A fat bellied bass swam by. My hands splashed into the waters and dug into its scales. I got him! A big one. He wriggled in my hands, tail flopping back and forth with his wide mouth gawping.

"You look like some people I know," I said.

My belly groaned again. I was hungry. I made my way out of the water, sat down and gutted the fish and scaled it with my claws. I could feel my fire in my belly.

"Hmmm," I said to myself, "I have an idea."

I tried to summon my fire. Just a little bit. Only enough to roast the fish whole. Who needs a fire when the fire's in you already? Gently, I exhaled. Nothing came forth. I put a little more wind and belly behind my next breath. A whoosh of flame rushed out.

The fish charred and crumbled in my hands.

"Sultans of Sulfur!"

I stormed back into the waters. A minute later I found my next fish. It was bigger than the last, green scaled and speckled. I licked my lips. The Speckled Bass were the best. I wasn't going to waste this one.

I plunged my hands in and snatched him up.

"Woohoo—*ulp!*"

Something wrapped around my neck and jerked me under the waters. I couldn't breathe. I clutched at the creature that coiled itself around my neck. I didn't know what it was. I ripped at it with my claws. It dragged me to the middle of the river and down towards a dark hole.

"Brenwar! Ben! Help!" I said in my frog voice.

No one could hear me.

No one would even know.

CHAPTER
16

I WAS PULLED DEEPER INTO THE waters and the surface receded, way above my head. Below waited a darkness surrounded by wriggling things. Tentacles! They stretched out and grabbed me by the ankles and bound my hands. I jerked at my bonds but I was helpless. It pulled me down towards a mouth big enough to eat a horse. The tentacles, like tongues and snakes, were pulling me inside. I wanted to scream! I wanted to breathe! That mouth full of teeth chomped at my feet.

All I could think of was how bad I'd been to my friends.

Those last few moments ... I'd like to have them back again.

I stretched out my arms with all my strength. I could see the sun wavering in the waters above me. I fought against my bonds, but nothing helped.

A splash of water erupted above me. Ben swam at me with a glowing dagger between his teeth. Dragon Claw. He cut the first tentacles and freed my arms. The creature jerked and made an eerie underwater whine. Ben sawed at another tentacle that was wrapped around my neck. The River Monster reeled again. The tentacles released me. I swam for the surface and busted out of the waters gasping.

"Ah!" I gulped in mouthfuls of air. I wanted to kiss the river bank. Wait.

"Ben?"

He'd disappeared.

I ducked back under the waters.

The River Monster had Ben wrapped up in tentacles. He was snared by the wrists and being pulled down into the mouth.

I swam after him.

More tentacles burst out.

I saw Dragon Claw fall from Ben's fingers and sink towards the maw. I snatched it with my fingertips and started cutting. There were too many of them. Dozens of the sticky things. *Enough of this! I'm a dragon!*

I swam straight into the monster's mouth and started stabbing. I looked up and saw Ben free and heading for the surface. Then, the massive jaws closed upon me.

Ben treaded water in the river, yelling, "Dragon! Dragon!"

He coughed, fought for his breath and ducked his head into the water. He didn't see Dragon or the monster. Even the tendrils were gone. He swam deeper, eyes searching, but everything was blurry.

What happened to you, Dragon?

He dove deeper and found nothing. Chest burning, he swam back to the top and gasped for air.

"What is going on?" a voice said from the river bank. It was Brenwar. Bayzog and Sasha were right beside the dwarf, and their faces were filled with worry.

Ben fought to tread water. His arms and legs were exhausted from fighting the current. His face dipped up and down in the water.

"It's..." He gasped. "It's Dragon. He's -*gasp*- gone under. A monster got him!"

Brenwar and Bayzog waded into the waters and reached out for him.

"Swim back here, will you?" Brenwar said, gesturing with his arms.

Bayzog slid out of his robes and swam towards him. The wizard hooked his arms beneath Ben's chest and swam him back to the bank. Huffing for breath, they both sat waist deep in the bristling water.

"He went down over there," Ben said, pointing. "It had tendrils like snakes and was stronger than iron. I cut them and freed Dragon, then they got me. Dragon saved me and when I swam up I looked down and he was gone."

Bayzog patted Ben's back with his slender arm and Brenwar studied him with a cocked eyebrow. The black-bearded dwarf pointed at him.

"You say he's in there?" Brenwar pointed in the water. "That way?"

Ben nodded.

Brenwar, in full armor, marched into the river, one step at a time until his head disappeared.

"What's he doing?" Ben said, looking at Bayzog.

The wizard shrugged.

"Come on Ben, let's get back out of this. The water might still be dangerous. And I need to think of a spell that I can cast." His face was filled with anguish. "I hate to admit it, but I'm not very prepared for dealing with water. I'm surprised I could still swim."

Ben, exhausted, remained in place.

"I've got to go after him," he said. "I'll just make one more dive."

Bayzog held his arm tight. "I've thought of a spell that might help. But I need to be on shore to cast it. Come, we must hurry."

Ben slowly backed towards the bank, frowning.

"Sasha!" Bayzog yelled. "Get my pack. I need my components. And fetch Brenwar's chest. That might help as well."

Ben stood ankle deep in the waters, watching. Every second felt like a minute. It was torture. Bayzog and Sasha worked behind him, trying to get something ready that would help. He had a feeling that whatever it was they came up with would be too late.

"Is it ready?" he said, turning his head, but not taking his eyes from the water. "I need to get back in there!"

"A moment, Ben. A moment!" Bayzog said.

Life begins and ends in moments. His father had told him so. *The important thing is to make the moments you have count.*

Ben waded back into the waters.

"Ben, hold on!" Sasha said. "Don't be foolish."

"I'll be fine," Ben said, waving his hand. "And if I don't make it back—"

Splash!

Nath's head burst out of the water.

"Dragon!"

A clawed hand waved at him.

Ben swam for him. He grabbed Dragon and guided him onto the bank.

Dragon was covered in river muck and tendrils, gasping for air. Dragon Claw glowed in his hand. He had cuts and scrapes all over him.

"You made it!" Ben said.

Dragon nodded.

"What about Brenwar?" Ben asked.

CHAPTER

17

DRAGON LOOKED AT BEN, THEN back in the waters. There was no sign of Brenwar.

"He's coming, I think." Dragon started to wade back in. "He was right behind me."

At last Brenwar's head popped out of the water, and foot by foot he walked up the bank. He looked at Dragon and kept going.

"Did he save you?" Ben said.

"I was fine," Dragon said, coughing. He slung some purple tendrils off his shoulders. "He showed up right after I didn't need him."

"What happened? What was that thing?" Ben said.

"I've no idea what it was," Dragon said, "but it was nasty. It swallowed me whole. I couldn't see a thing." He dangled Dragon Claw in front of his face. "I jammed Dragon Claw into anything it could bite and finally the mouth opened up again. I swam out as fast as I could."

"Is it dead?" Ben said.

Dragon's golden eyes drifted over the waters.

"I think so."

Growl.

"Was that you, Dragon?"

Dragon stood up, slinging his hair from his eyes and rubbing his belly.

"It's my stomach. I'm famished." He marched towards Bayzog and Sasha. "Say wizards, do you have any of that water? I need something to hold me over. I'm so hungry I could eat goat horns."

"Certainly," Sasha said. "We have other things we can procure as well, but it will take some time."

"It's got to be better than hunting," Dragon said, stretching out his great scaled arms and yawning. "I think I've done enough of that today. Tried to catch a fish and almost caught my death." He climbed up the bank, took a seat on the grass, and motioned for Ben to come over.

Ben took a seat beside him.

Dragon patted him on the back.

"How did you know, Ben?"

"Know what?"

"That I needed help?" Dragon's face was puzzled.

"Well, I don't know," he said. "I just knew. And Brenwar, well, he knew too, because he came over right at the same time I did."

Dragon shook his head and huffed a little laugh.

"You know, Ben, you're right. I need my friends. Without them, I would have died."

Ben patted Dragon's knee. "We need you too."

"Well, you deserve better than me," Nath said. "And I promise to do better. Honestly Ben, I just don't want to put anyone in danger." Nath's voice was solemn and humble. "Shum died because of me. Almost everyone did. That's not easy to live with. I just want those evil doers dead." He jammed Dragon Claw in the ground.

"Me too," Ben said, nodding. "Me too."

They didn't speak after that. Ben watched Bayzog and Sasha do their thing, and Dragon kept his eyes on the river. Ben glanced back at him from time to time, but Dragon didn't seem to notice. He sat there like a statue. A large muscular man with black scales that stretched across his arms to his shoulders. His features were chiseled and his face was like polished stone. The wind whipping through his red hair was the only thing that seemed real about him.

Dragon sniffed the air. "Mmmm, something smells good." He patted his stomach and headed towards Bayzog and Sasha.

Ben fell in step right behind him.

A sand bar lay along the river bank and Brenwar had stacked up some wood and begun a fire.

Bayzog and Sasha bowed when they arrived.

"I hope you like!" Sasha grabbed both of them by the arms and led them down the riverbank.

Ben's jaw dropped open. Dragon's eyes were golden plates.

"How did you ...?" Ben started to say, but he had to swallow the water in his mouth. "And where did the ...?"

Sasha giggled and Bayzog laughed.

A table and eight chairs sat in the sand, loaded with every dish he could imagine. A roasted hog stuffed with an apple, a turkey as big as a pig, steaming potatoes, vegetables, pies, and jugs of water and wine. Silverware sparkled in the setting sun with cloth napkins laid along the sides. It was a feast.

"I've, well, we've," Bayzog said, "never cast this spell before and we didn't know what to expect. I assume it was meant for a larger gathering."

"Is it real?" Ben asked.

Brenwar ripped off a leg of turkey and tore a hunk off with his teeth.

"Mmmm," he grumbled, "It's as real as my beard."

Ben stuffed a handful of meat into his mouth, chewed it up and washed it down with some sort of delicious wine. Sasha gently carved small bits of food on her plate and Bayzog did the same. Brenwar bit into chunks of ham that were poised on his knife. He grunted and his brows lifted up and down with a dwarven sort of praise. He did have one complaint.

"No ale?" he said, eyeing the bottom of a jug he had drained.

"Sorry," Bayzog said, "but I didn't know what to expect."

Nath stuffed the feast in his mouth with his claws and a heaping spoon. He smiled a lot and talked little and ate as fast as Brenwar. He was putting food down like he'd never eaten it before. The pair kept eating long after the others finished and most of the food was gone.

Ben stood up at the end of the table and cleared his throat.

"Ahem."

Sasha and Bayzog stopped, but Nath and Brenwar were still chewing.

"I just wanted to say something," Ben said, picking up his goblet.

"What is it, Ben?" Sasha said, "Please speak."

"Well, where I'm from, we always thank the preparers. To the both of you, Sasha and Bayzog, I want to express my thanks. This has been wonderful. And to all of you," He raised his goblet, "I'm honored to be among you. I'm honored to be your friend. Thank you all."

"Well said." Nath halted in tipping his goblet to his lips. "Well said."

"Agreed," said Brenwar, "now pass that cheese."

"Brenwar!" Sasha said.

"Oh, sorry," Brenwar said. He straightened himself up in his chair. "Please pass the cheese."

"Hahahaha! That's not what I meant," Sasha said, holding her belly.

"What? I just want the cheese. What's the humor in it?"

Everyone started laughing. Everyone but Dragon.

"Dragon," Ben said, "Lighten up, will you? You're as stone faced as Brenwar."

Dragon didn't move. He sat stiff as a board with his eyes closed.

"Nath," Sasha said, worried. She rose from her seat and gasped.

Nath fell face first into his plate of food.

CHAPTER

18

"WHAT'S WRONG WITH HIM?" BEN said. "Is he breathing?"

Dragon lay stretched out on the table with Bayzog's pointed ear on his chest.

"The heart beats," Bayzog said, "but slowly."

Brenwar punched Nath in the arm and said, "Wake up!"

"Easy," Bayzog said.

"Easy nothing," Brenwar said. He pinched Nath's thigh. Nothing happened.

"Why don't you tickle him or something?" Ben said.

Brenwar eyed him.

Ben shrugged.

Sasha dripped some water over Nath's lips.

Nothing moved. Nothing twitched.

"I think he's changing again," she said. She held her fingers over his lips. "He breathes, same as the last time. Barely."

"I agree," Bayzog said. "Brenwar, what do you think? You were with him the first time this happened, were you not?"

"Aye," Brenwar growled, "And I had to haul his carcass all over until he came to."

"So did I," said Ben. "And he was out months the last time. Do you think it will be months again?"

"What if it gets longer every time?" Sasha said.

Silence fell and all eyes were on Nath. He was the reason they were gathered. He was the future, and now he lay still as a stone.

"What do we do, Bayzog?" Sasha said, brushing Nath's hair away from his stony face. "Do we take him back to Quintuklen?"

"I say Morgdon," Brenwar said. "Let the dwarves keep him safe."

Bayzog clasped his fingers behind his back and began walking around the table. They had all pledged to look after Nath, but he was their leader, and he was down. So the question was, who did they follow now?

"They are both good suggestions, but Quintuklen is closer," Bayzog said.

"And full of the Clerics of Barnabus," Brenwar said. "I say we take him to the hills. He'll be safe there. We don't have the foulness of the races up there."

"You don't have the security of my home there either," Bayzog said.

Brenwar bristled.

"Security! No one's ever penetrated Morgdon. Not once. Not ever." Brenwar rapped his fist on the table. "He's my charge by the Dragon King himself, not yours, Elf. I'll decide what's best for him."

"This could go on for months again, maybe a year," Bayzog said. "I don't want to wait in Morgdon that long. Not when I can do research and seek other help. There are other things we need to prepare for, Brenwar. What happens when he wakes up? What if he changes even more? Will you be ready for that?"

"As much as you, Elf!" Brenwar thumbed his bearded chest. "He comes with me."

Bayzog made his way back to Brenwar and looked right down at him.

"I disagree."

Brenwar poked him in the chest three times with his stubby fingers. "I—Don't—Care."

"Are you the only two that have a say in this?" Sasha said with her arms folded across her chest. "I think I can offer some direction."

Ben pulled back his shoulders and said, "Me too."

"Pah, this is ridiculous. I'll not be taking orders from the likes of you three. No! Nath comes with me."

"Who do you think you are?" Sasha said, approaching the dwarf.

"I'm under the charge of the Dragon King, Lady. Who do you think you be?"

Bayzog stepped in front of her and held her back.

"Alright, let's not feud with each other. We all want what's best," he said. He walked back over to Nath and put his hand on his chest. "I have an idea."

"I don't care," Brenwar said. He tapped his foot on the ground and combed his fingers through his beard.

"Just hear me out," Bayzog said. "We'll take a vote."

"No," Brenwar said, crossing his arms over his chest. "And with that we'll be leaving." He grabbed Nath by the ankle and dragged him off the table. Nath's head bounced off the ground with a thud. Brenwar kept going.

"Brenwar!" Sasha said, "What in Nalzambor are you doing? He's not hunted meat to be dragged. How disrespectful!" She grabbed Nath's arms and pulled back.

Brenwar pulled both of them forward without looking back.

"Will you stop it, you bearded child!"

Bayzog spread his arms wide, exasperated. "Alright, Brenwar! You win!" He practically yelled. And Bayzog never yelled. "We'll head to Morgdon first."

Brenwar stopped and looked back over his shoulder.

"You don't need to come."

"Well, we're coming anyway," Bayzog said. "Just show a little more respect for our friend."

Brenwar dropped Nath's booted leg.

"Pah ... His head's harder than mine."

After dawn broke the next day, Brenwar, Ben, Bayzog and Sasha rode the horses south towards the Mountains of Morgdon. Nath Dragon lay on a stretcher Brenwar and Ben had hewn from the woodland and was towed behind Brenwar's horse. Brenwar led and the others followed, all quiet and resolute.

"What about the table and all the food?" Ben had asked Bayzog.

"What you had, you have. All the rest will pass," the part-elf said. "I'm sure some creature will finish it off for us. Don't worry, Ben."

"Well, I just hate to see it go to waste."

"It won't. I'm sure of it."

Following the river south, the company disappeared from the view back towards the table. A small head popped up from the tall grasses before the trees and crept up to the table on the legs of a goat. Another one popped out from behind the trees and followed. The pair stomped around the table, sniffed the bouquet of food that was left, and took seats. They nodded at one another and stuffed food into their horned faces. One burped. The other guzzled. Then, the satyrs began their conversation. Their voices were low and evil.

"We'll have them now, aye my dear," the male said.

"Yes, all of them," the female said, "and to think they even left a fine meal for us. It won't be our last, but it just might be theirs." She sucked down a pitcher of wine and wiped her lips with her forearm. "And that dwarf who busted my pipes and clocked me in the head … I can't wait to get back at him. I think I'm going to shave every hair from him and stand him before a mirror before I cook him."

The male laughed. It was loud. Part goat and part man.

"And that elf," he said. "What would you do to him?"

"Oh, I'll shove the dwarf's beard into the spellcaster's mouth and then I'll nibble on his fingers and toes."

"And the man?" he asked.

"I'll make him chop the wood and start the fires." She pulled out her new set of pipes from under her vest. "And make him smile as he does it."

"And the woman?" he said, stuffing some leftover cherry pie in his mouth.

She grabbed a goblet and lifted it to the sun.

"I'll drink her tears and bring her greatest fears to life."

He swung his hairy legs up on the table and drummed his hooves on the wood.

"You are so terrible," he said. His teeth were covered in cherries. "We are only allowed to spy on them. We aren't supposed to eat them. Kryzak won't allow that."

She pulled her long dark hair over her head and tied it in a knot. She was pleasant looking. All woman from the waist up, fluid in her motions and stout in frame. Leathers and skins covered her chest and formed a short kind of dress. Her smile was pretty but wicked.

"He just wants the dragon man," she said. "He didn't say anything about the others. And now it seems the dragon man sleeps and he'll be down for quite some time."

"What are you thinking?" he said. "We must tell Kryzak this news. There will be a great reward in it."

She pulled the apple from the pig's mouth, hitched one arm over the chair, and said, "I think the sooner he knows, the better." She bit into the apple, chewed it up and spit the seeds out. "And the sooner he knows, the sooner we avenge ourselves. The only question is, who follows them and who tells Kryzak what we know?"

"I could use the run," he said. "Hiding in the woods has started to make my legs stiff as stone."

"Fare thee well," she said, winking. "You run, and I'll hunt."

He hopped on the table and his hooves became a blur, shaking everything off. He pounced through the air and dashed up the river faster than the fleetest deer. He paused, waved, sped along and disappeared into the woods.

"He makes a fine ally of evil … *burp*," she said, tossing the core away, "but never as fine as me."

CHAPTER
19

KRYZAK STOOD ALONGSIDE A STONE hewn doorway in the midst of a temple ruin. Columns and rubble scored the grounds of what was once a fine work of man. Such ruins were scattered over the land of Nalzambor. Many of them served as hideouts for the Clerics of Barnabus and many of them had secrets. Catacombs and caves lay below the surface of some and others were portals from one to another. It was powerful and ancient magic the Clerics of Barnabus had harnessed long ago to serve their will. To spread their destructive ways.

"And there are only the four of them guarding Nath Dragon?" Kryzak said.

The young satyr nodded his head.

"That is all, High Cleric. Only a few leagues away and heading south towards Morgdon," it said, raking its hoof over the ground. "I can take you straight to them. We can stop them and capture them. But there is a price for our services."

Kryzak swung his war mace over his broad shoulder with one arm and took two steps forward. The satyr looked up at the man twice the size of him and swallowed.

"What is your name?" Kryzak said.

"Finlin."

"And this price, little hooved one," he said. "What did you have in mind?"

The satyr's thumbs rolled between his clasped fingers and his eyes bounced back and forth.

"The dwarf, elf, woman and a small dragon would suffice."

"Hah! You think too much of yourself, Horned Rodent. What would you do with them?"

"We shall make a feast of them," it said. "A fine dining—"

Kryzak slung his mace into the dirt.

The satyr hopped back.

"Don't jest with me, Satyr! Your legends only frighten children, not the likes of me." Kryzak poked the satyr with his mace. "What will you do with them?"

The satyr cringed and said, "High Priest, do you really care what we do with them?"

Kryzak moved his head from side to side and his thick neck cracked. He showed a toothy grin and jutted his chin out.

"Gutsy. Foolish, but shrewd. Fine, make a legendary pot of stew with them, but you aren't getting a dragon," Kryzak said. He then ran his mailed fist over the stone archway and muttered something.

The satyr looked around. There was only Kryzak, him and the moss coated ruins.

"Who are you talking to?" the satyr asked.

"Stand back and you will see."

Kryzak backed up from the stone doorway. Two huge slabs of stone jutted from the ground standing twelve feet tall and another stone cut in a semi-circle was laid over the tops of them, perfectly aligned. Kryzak slipped his gauntlets from his hands and dropped them to the ground. He rubbed his fingers together, kneeled and stretched his arms out wide. Chin up, eyes closed, an incantation spewed from his lips.

"*Oleenapaaaawwwwn... Oleenapaaaawwwwn... Oleenapaaaawwwwn...*"

The tattoos on his bald head pulsated with life.

The satyr stepped back, biting his nails.

A swirl of dark colors filled the archway and a grey mist rolled out and covered the grasses and the ground.

The satyr couldn't see his hooves. His heart beat faster. His tiny horns tingled. He couldn't take his eyes from the archway. And time seemed to stop.

A woman stepped through. She was tall, dark and raven-haired. Her eyes were like black pearls.

Kryzak didn't move but his eyes popped open. A crease formed on his brow.

The satyr fell to his knees. His gaze remained on the woman. Her eyes glossed over him, bringing a chill, before falling on Kryzak.

"Rise, Kryzak," she said. Her voice was polished and commanding.

Kryzak rose. His fingers twitched at his sides.

"High Priestess! I was not expecting your audience." His strong voice trembled a little, shaken. "It was not my desire to disturb you."

She sauntered through the mist, looking around with her arms folded over her robes. She was graceful and purposed when she moved.

Finlin felt his heart flutter. He feared her yet was drawn to her.

"You've summoned much without my consultation, Kryzak. Did you think it would not escape my notice?" she said. "You must have tracked down many dragons. And so soon?"

His feet didn't move but he turned the best he could to face her.

"I have the greatest dragon of all in my grasp," he said.

"Oh," she said. She stepped in front of Finlin and rubbed the hair between the horns on his head. His hoof pounded the ground. "And how is that?"

"Nath Dragon," he said. "He sleeps."

Her fingers stopped and she turned.

"Tell me more," she said, stepping away.

Finlin felt his heart sink. His fingers stretched through the mist and after her. *Oh, my Queen!*

"This satyr is my spy and he's trailed them and heard their speech. Nath Dragon slept months the last time. They suspect he'll sleep just as long again. He'll change. They fear the change is bad for him. I suspect that is good for us."

A black tail rose out of the mist and struck Kryzak across the face. He was lifted from his feet and disappeared into the mist. The tail slithered under the fog and jerked Kryzak back to his feet by the neck. His face was red.

Finlin trembled, eyes searching the mist, backing away. *What is that thing?*

"Satyr," she said.

"Yes!" Finlin blurted out.

"Are you certain of this?" Her eyes probed his. He could feel it in his bones. "Every bit of it?"

"As certain as I am of my hooved feet," he said, bowing. "I can take you right to him. Anything you please."

The black serpent tail lifted Kryzak farther from the ground. His feet dangled over the mist and his fingers dug at the scales. He tried to speak but couldn't. He was choking.

"I feel you've done well, Kryzak," she said. "Possibly better than I hoped. Nath Dragon is changing even sooner than expected." She lowered him down and faced him eye to eye. "Would you still die for me, Kryzak?"

His hard face dipped up and down.

"Good," she said, smiling a little. She gave his forehead a kiss.

The tail squeezed his neck until his big body went limp. She flipped the body through the air and it disappeared through the swirling portal.

Finlin shook without control when she turned and faced him.

"What are you shaking for, Fawnish Man?"

"Why-Why d-did you d-do that?" he said. "You said he'd d-done well?"

Her tail petted the hair between his horns and she showed him an icy smile.

"And he had done well, but his part is over." She coiled her tail around his waist and lifted him up to face her. "No one is indispensable." She checked her colorful nails. "And I tired of him. Will you still help me?"

Finlin nodded vigorously. "What would you have me do?"

She set him down. The tail patted his horned head. "I want you to lead my servants. Do well and reap the rewards. Fail and suffer my disappointment."

"Will do. Will do. Will do," he nodded fast. "Will do."

She walked away and stepped into the portal, but before she disappeared she said, "Come."

A big creature, like a man but with scales and black wings, followed.

Finlin gasped. He hadn't seen it there before.

"Eep!"

Something scaly and big as a pony brushed by Finlin's feet. He jumped four feet off the ground. A big face with long whiskers turned at him with bright cat eyes. It licked its lips and bared its fangs.

Finlin froze.

The feline fury followed Selene into the archway and they disappeared from sight.

He couldn't tell if he was thrilled or scared. His heart pumped like a racing horse's. He waited, pacing back and forth before the swirling archway. What was going to come through there next?

What do I do? What do I do?

A large figure stepped out of the archway and waded into the mist.

Finlin stopped pacing.

The figure wore crimson cloth robes. Thick thewed arms emerged from the sleeves. A great scepter of dark metal was clutched in one hand. A horned metal helmet in the image of an angry bull covered his face. His eyes were dark behind the eyelets.

Finlin looked up at him and stepped backward. "Who are you?"

Something snorted behind the mask.

Finlin stepped aside as the figure marched right past him.

More figures emerged. Lizardmen with spears and swords led small gray-scaled dragons on leashes. There were a dozen of them, sleek and black-winged. Bald-headed men with tattooed heads followed. Their robes were simple. Their faces grim and hard. They carried clubs, maces and flails. All in all there were over a score of lizardmen and acolytes. They formed ranks on both sides of the arches.

The man in the bull mask stood at the end, leaving Finlin alone facing the archway.

"Awkward," he muttered. He turned in time to see a great shadow emerge and swirl off the arch and come forward. He darted to the man in the bull mask.

A dragon, bigger than him, appeared. Its long neck was dark copper, and streaks of black stretched all over its body. Its eyes were like fire and its breath smelled of acid. It lumbered forward on soft feet, bigger than two horses. A great terrifying beast. A lone figure sat saddled on its wingless back. A petite young woman with a row of long white hair flowing from a mostly bald head. Jewels adorned her robes, which enhanced her figure. She sat perched high in the saddle with her arms folded on her waist.

My, she's pretty. He combed the hair between his horns with his fingers.

Her light eyes found his.

"I am Marlay, a priestess of Barnabus," she said. "And you are?"

"Finlin," he said, stepping from behind the warrior.

"Lead the way, Finlin," she said, chin up and eyes forward. "We have a sleeping dragon to catch."

CHAPTER

20

"I WAS SCARED," SASHA SAID TO Bayzog. "I, I'm so sorry."

"Darling, it is alright. I understand." His voice was soothing and he reached out and held her hands. "Please let it go. It will pass. It happens to all of us."

"What if it doesn't pass?" she said, hugging him. Sobbing.

They were two days into their journey to Morgdon and still had days to go. Sasha had been very quiet, strangely so, and it had irritated Bayzog. So he had pressed. Slowly. Gradually. Politely. Until she broke. A flood of tears had come.

"If it doesn't, it doesn't," he said. "We'll just be cautious."

She looked right into his face. Her beautiful features were contorted with deep fear and worry. He'd never seen her so. Not ever.

"I was so scared. I just stood there, helpless and frozen. Watching and doing nothing. You have to be able to count on me, Bayzog, and you can't now. Not ever." She looked away and started to walk away. "Ever again."

They'd stopped traveling for the day, but Brenwar and Ben were gone gathering food and making camp. He hadn't left her side since.

"Sasha, come back," he said. "Let's talk about this."

"There's nothing to talk about!"

He let her go. The river. The river where Nath Dragon almost drowned had triggered it all. Sasha, after almost drowning herself deep in the tunnels of the crater, had become terrified of drowning again. Bayzog had wondered what happened in that moment he swam in and helped Nath and Ben in the water. Sasha wasn't there and she'd loved water. She was even a better swimmer than him, though they didn't go swimming often. But they did travel the lands from time to time and had been to the Dragon Pond several times. She had loved it there.

He tossed a rough sack on the ground and snapped his fingers. Slowly a tent took form. He slipped inside and waited. It was best to leave her alone at times like this. He didn't like her being out there alone, not after he'd lost her once, but he'd take his chances.

He pulled a golden locket out from his robes, opened it up and muttered an incantation. A small image of Sasha formed. He could feel how close she was and feel her heart in his palm. He sighed. She was safe and he could sense Ben and Brenwar were nearby as well.

The peaks of the mountain ranges of the dwarven city of Morgdon could be seen if Bayzog squinted his keen eyes. He felt uncomfortable with the unfamiliar, particularly with being an elf in a dwarven land. But Brenwar hadn't seemed bothered in Elome, so why should Morgdon bother Bayzog?

Don't overthink it. You've still got days to go.

He searched for Sasha. She rode in the front, not far from where Brenwar led, towing Nath on his stretcher. They had hardly spoken since last night.

Despite the dry weather his elven bones felt cold. He wished Shum were still here. The Roaming Ranger had brought him a great comfort. Shum had been older, at least by a few hundred years or so, and his wisdom was needed. Perhaps Shum could have convinced Brenwar that Nath would be better off elsewhere.

His eyes drifted back over Nath, and he sighed.

He wasn't sure if Nath being out was a good thing. It certainly left them vulnerable. In all truth, he was excited to see what happened. What kind of change would Nath go through? Would it make him stronger? More savage? It seemed the more Nath changed, the less control he had, but dragons weren't impulsive creatures.

He should have more control than he had. If he gets any more powerful, he might not listen to any of us at all.

He looked up to the clouds. They were dark, and even though it hadn't rained, he hadn't seen much sunshine the past few days. Something didn't seem right with the world. Not at all.

Be as prepared as you can be. Wise as a dragon. Slick as a snake.

It wasn't an elven saying, but he liked it, wherever it came from.

"Bayzog," Ben said, riding up to him, "may I join you?"

Bayzog nodded.

"Why certainly, Ben." Ben's typically loose and smiling face was drawn tight. "Is there something on your mind?"

Ben's eyes met Bayzog's and glanced away just before he said, "Evil."

Bayzog felt his tongue catch in his throat but he didn't show surprise. There were very few things that rattled him, but this word coming from this young man did. He offered a simple smile.

"Do you want to discuss it, or were you making a confession of sorts?"

"Well, uh," Ben said. His long face turned a little red. "I just don't understand how…" He reached back and scratched his head. "Ah, never mind."

"No, no," Bayzog said, "It's a good topic, Ben. Well, in the sense that it's much better to talk about it that ignore it. You see, the way I understand it, evil doesn't want us to discuss how to deal with it."

Ben blinked his light brown eyes, leaned forward in his saddle and said, "Go on, please."

"Alright then." Bayzog cleared his throat and tapped his chest. It felt good to talk about something like this. "Ben, let me see if maybe I understand some of your thoughts, and remember I'm no sage, but I am part human, and at some point I was a young human like you. So it's possible … well, actually, I'm certain I've asked the same question. What is evil? What is good?" He eyed Ben. "Am I on the right track?"

"I think so."

"Maybe, just maybe, you are wondering how we know whether our actions are good or evil. Right?"

Ben nodded

"And you want to be sure about that, don't you?"

"Absolutely."

"Ben, there is no easy way to explain it, but I offer this." Bayzog locked his violet eyes on Ben's. "There is evil in all of us."

Ben's eyes widened like saucers.

"Sounds really bad doesn't it?" Bayzog said.

Ben blinked a few times. "Yes, but does that mean there is good in all of us as well?"

"Certainly." Bayzog grabbed his canteen, pulled off the top and took a drink. He offered it to Ben.

The young man shook his head and one of the horses nickered.

A stiff breeze came and blew hair into Bayzog's eyes. "But it's often buried deep beneath the surface, choking, you might say."

Ahead, he noticed large birds dipping in and out of the distant tree tops. The bright leaves on the trees started to bend, and lightning flashed behind them. The hairs on his arms rose.

There's that feeling again.

"It sounds more confusing than it should be," Ben said.

"There is a fine line between the two, but a good heart will warn you."

"How do you know which is which?" Ben asked. "There are so many things to consider. I mean, I'm good, aren't I?"

Bayzog chuckled.

"Of that I have no doubt. Don't let your mistakes confuse you, Ben. Or guilt either," Bayzog said. "Those are traps evil prepares for you. It can distract you or immobilize you. Doubt and worry are deadly."

"Oh," Ben said. "But ..."

Bayzog interrupted.

"Listen, good wants you, all of us, to be free. Evil wants to enslave and control things. And when in doubt ask yourself this: which is easier? Doing the right thing or the wrong thing?"

Ben looked up at his brows and rubbed his chin. A moment later he said, "I don't know."

"Well, you're a farmer, right?"

"I was a farmer. Now I'm a soldier." Ben's brows buckled. "Aw, I'm not even that anymore."

"Sorry, Ben, but let me continue. Is it easier to steal the food from the farmer or farm the food yourself?"

"Steal it, I guess, but nobody better steal my food." He shook his fist. "They'll get busted up for that."

"So stealing's evil, right?"

Ben sat up in his saddle and nodded his head.

"Right!"

"What about what happened with the Golden Ore in your village? Those brigands could have bought it or bartered for it, but instead they stole it. What do you call that?"

"Evil."

"Would you ever do that?"

"No," Ben said, shaking his head.

"Nor would I."

Ben cocked an eyebrow and said, "Huh, now that I think about it, it's always tougher to do the right thing than the wrong thing."

"Doing right builds character. That much is certain."

"But," Ben said, "do you think they know it's wrong?"

"At one time, maybe they did, but over time, evil debases the mind."

"Hmmm," Ben said, "are you worried that can happen to Dragon?"

Several horse lengths in front of them, Nath's big body was being towed through the tall grasses. His body was covered in cloth and his head was wrapped up in a cowl, still leaving his face and jaw exposed.

"I shudder to think such a thing, Ben. Nath's been nothing but good, but those scales ... his moods ... they seem to be gaining control of him. The catacombs of evil are deep, and it's easy to get lost if you go too far. Many never return. Guilt, worry and power can consume you."

"This is bigger than just Dragon, isn't it?" Ben said. "But he has something to do with it."

The statement was a surprise, but Bayzog found relief in it. Ben had wisdom, and that could help them.

Still, Bayzog shrugged.

"What about wars and such things?" Ben asked. "How do we know when they are right or wrong?"

"We are allowed to defend ourselves, Ben. The important thing is that in the name of peace we don't compromise with evil."

"Why?" Ben said. "What if it saves more people?"

Bayzog looked right at him.

"Evil always does bad things, Ben. It never moves closer to doing good. Trying to compromise with evil only moves you closer to doing bad."

"I guess so," Ben said.

They kept riding and Ben finally drifted away. Bayzog figured he'd given him plenty to think about and even more for himself to consider.

What an interesting young man. The world could use more like him.

Still, Ben's questions plagued him more the farther they rode. Bayzog wasn't sure he'd made himself clear, but hopefully Ben had understood.

There were other examples he could have told, such as the stories of the elves and orcs. The Elvish strove to live by the highest standards, relishing in peace, knowledge, art, and beauty. Orcish standards were deplorable: fighting and wallowing in filth for power. That was evil to see.

But what about the evil that wasn't so easy to see? Beautiful, cunning and lethal. A beautiful flower whose leaves were poisoned. How did one prepare for that?

Ahead, Brenwar had stopped. Shifting in the saddle, the burley dwarf sniffed the air and combed his fingers through his beard.

Bayzog rode up to Brenwar's side, as did the others.

"Why are we stopping?" Sasha said. "Is that a bad storm ahead?"

"The storm isn't anything to worry about," Brenwar said in his gruff voice, "just water for the trees and the flowers. It's those birds." He pointed.

They were circling now, floating on their wings above the trees, but moving forward.

"Looks like vultures," Ben said. "Or other carrion eaters. I'd assume something's dead below. You aren't worried about birds, are you, Brenwar?"

Brenwar eyed Ben and then made a sound. His horse started forward.

"Are you ready for anything?" Brenwar unslung his War Hammer from his shoulder. "Because anything is coming."

"What do you mean?" Sasha said.

Bayzog placed his hand over his brows and scanned the sky.

"Those aren't birds," he said, squinting. "Those are dragons."

CHAPTER

21

"MAYBE THEY'RE GOOD DRAGONS," BEN said.

"Good dragons aren't so easily seen," Bayzog said. "Remember the last ones we saw at the crater? They scattered."

"Oh," Ben said.

Bayzog's heart pounded. Dragons were the most exciting things you'd ever see, but only because siting them was a rare thing. Like watching a flower bloom. This was different. Dragons flying in plain sight and coming right at them. Reason for concern.

"Brenwar," he said, "Perhaps we should venture on another course. There's no rush, after all, is there?"

Brenwar grunted. "Perhaps." He tugged at the reins, taking a more westward direction. The dragons, less than a mile away, stayed headed right for them.

This is not good.

Sasha came along Bayzog's side. "I can't tell if they're dragons or birds. They're just specks to me. Are you certain they're dragons?"

"I am," Bayzog said, reaching over and grabbing her palm. "Stay close, Sasha, and have a spell prepared."

"What kind of spell? Don't I need to know what kind of dragons they are?"

Every dragon had a weakness. It might be an element such as water or fire. It could be a sound, loud or soft. Different metals and different magic. If you didn't have what you needed in a battle of mortal versus dragon, they'd rip you apart with their teeth and claws. In most cases that was all they needed.

"I'm not sure. Not without a closer look. What do you think, Brenwar?"

"Yer eyes are better than mine, Elf," Brenwar said, squinting, "Tell me what you see?"

"Black wings and grey scales," he said, "and a smooth oval head. A little more color in the tail, a dark red."

"Oval head," Brenwar said, rubbing his beard. "Hmmm, what about the belly?"

"Dark grey, almost black, I'd say."

The dwarf made an ugly sound in his throat and pulled his horse to a stop. Brenwar had at least a few centuries on Bayzog, and he was certain the dwarf had more dragon encounters than him by far. Bayzog also knew that Brenwar had been inside the Mountain of Doom, where he'd probably seen things an elf could only dream of.

"Those," Brenwar said, "if they are as you say, then they are Grey Scalers."

"Why do they call them that?" Ben said. "Because they have grey scales?"

"It doesn't matter why they call them that!" Brenwar huffed. "What matters is what happens if they come after us." Brenwar eyed their surroundings.

The mountains were still distant. The closest forest was miles away. For now, it was just them, the dragons, and the plains.

"Do you know how to handle Grey Scalers?" Sasha said to Bayzog.

He shook his head.

All this time with Nath, and I've never bothered to ask him about all the different dragons. You always think you have more time than you have. What a fool I've been.

"Whatever you've got, Wizard, get it ready!" Brenwar hopped off his horse and slung his trunk on the ground. "Sorceress, see what you can find in there." He fumbled with Nath's wrappings and pulled out the bow and quiver. "You know how to use this?" he said to Ben.

Ben nodded his head yes.

Brenwar tossed it to him. "Load it up then. And use the Moorite." He started to walk away and stopped. "And aim for the belly when they ain't looking. And don't fire until I tell you."

"How powerful are those things?" Sasha said.

"Just pretend they're big scaly dogs with wings." He winked at her. "A few good licks and we might scare them off." He looked up at Ben. "Get off that horse, will you? And kneel down in the weeds. They come!"

CHAPTER
22

Snap. Clatch. Snap.

A circle of dragons, wings beating, screeching a terror, was coming right at them.

Ben wanted to plug his ears. Instead he took aim, but his arms were shaking.

"Don't shoot, Boy!" Brenwar growled from somewhere near.

Ben didn't take his eyes off the dragons.

They flew in a ring, stretching their long necks and screeching down. Their talons clutched in and out and clicked and clacked. Their jaws snapped in the air and their tails rattled.

Ben swallowed hard, closed one eye, and took aim. "You can do this, Ben," he muttered to himself. "Be brave. Not foolish."

A Gray Scale swooped down and snapped at Brenwar.

The dwarf swung and missed.

Another dragon came, snapped, and darted back into the ring.

"Keep coming, you ugly birds," Brenwar said, waving his hammer. "I'll show you!"

A gray scaler dove straight at Ben.

He hunkered down.

It clipped his helmet with its claws, screeched, and flew away.

Ben rose back to his feet with his heart pounding in between his ears. He couldn't breathe.

One by one, the dragons dove, dipped and snapped, like eagles snatching at fish in the river.

Ben heard Sasha scream. He whirled.

A dragon stood on its hind legs, facing her and snapping.

Brenwar charged it.

Twang!

When the first arrow embedded itself in the dragon's chest, the dragon screeched an awful sound and twisted in the grass.

"I got him!" Ben pumped his fist in the air and raised his knee up.

"Quit talking and start loading," Brenwar said. "Now they're all coming!"

Ben nocked another arrow and aimed at a diving dragon.

Twang!

It dipped under the arrow and barreled straight into his chest, driving him into the dirt.

"Get off me!" Ben yelled.

The dragon pinned him to the ground, biting and clawing at him. He felt his skin start to burn. It was like a big dog with a long neck. Strong and fierce. It bit Ben's leg.

He screamed.

"Let em' have it," Brenwar yelled. "All of them!"

A missile of blue light blasted through the wings of the dragon on top of Ben.

It shrieked and darted away.

Nearby, Bayzog's hands were bright with energy, sending one missile after the next.

Ben slipped an arrow from his quiver and nocked it. Kneeled down and searched the sky. His heart was racing. His breath was lost.

Dragons streaked through the sky from all directions, swooping, circling and diving.

"They're too fast!"

Twang!

The arrow sailed. The dragon rolled from its path and darted straight for him.

"Ben, look out!"

Brenwar swung his War Hammer. Bayzog fired his missiles.

Too late.

A dragon swooped behind Ben and knocked him to the ground, making Akron fall from his grasp.

He looked up in time to see a dragon wrap its talons around it. "No you don't!" Ben jumped on his bow.

The dragon's claws tore into his arm.

"Argh!"

The pain was blinding. Ben held on. He was bigger than the dragon by at least a hundred pounds but the smaller creature was stronger than him.

Swap!

The dragon's tail cracked him across the face.

Akron fell from his fingers. He hit the ground. There was blood in his eyes. Dizzy, he stumbled forward, chasing after the dragon.

It hissed and took flight with Akron gripped in its talons.

"Dragon's going to kill me," Ben said, dropping to his knees.

A bolt of light flashed over his head.

Ssssram!

The dragon exploded in the sky and spiraled to the ground. Akron dropped to the ground as well.

"Hurry, Ben!" Sasha said.

She was right behind him with her hands smoking.

He ran over, snatched up the bow, nocked an arrow and pulled the string back.

"There!" Sasha pointed.

Two gray scalers flanked Bayzog. The wizard had a long mystic shield up that only protected one side.

Twang! Twack!

The arrow struck the pressing Grey Scaler on its back between the wings. It fell to the ground and died.

"Look!" Brenwar yelled. "They flee!"

Less than a dozen of them took to the air, screeching and roaring, and disappeared.

Bayzog's shield winked out, and he jogged over to Sasha, who was dusting off her smoking hands. "Are you alright?" Bayzog said.

She swallowed hard. "Just a little faint, but I think I'm alright."

"You made that dragon explode!" Ben said. "Into pieces! How did you do that?"

"Yes," Bayzog said, "how did you do that? It was certainly impressive."

"I drank from this," she said. She held a sparkling vial that looked like lighting lived in it. "It was in Brenwar's chest."

Bayzog leaned over and kissed her forehead.

"Excellent choice. I think you saved us."

Brenwar walked over with a dragon in his arms. An arrow jutted from its back. "It was a good shot," Brenwar said.

Ben reached over and touched it. The creature didn't seem so deadly anymore. He wondered if Dragon would be upset.

"Well, what are you waiting for?" Brenwar said.

"What do you mean?" Ben said.

"Take the arrow out of it, Boy! Great Guzan! It's Moorite. Do I have to do it for you?"

"Uh ..."

Brenwar set the dragon down at his feet. "Whenever yer ready."

Ben stroked his neck and said to Bayzog, "Do you think it's evil? Maybe this was one that Dragon would have saved?"

Bayzog perched his eyebrows at Ben. "Do you think it would have killed us?"

"Ah," Ben said. "I see." Ben pulled the arrow free, cleaned it on the grass and slid it back into his quiver. "Do we just leave them? Won't the dragon skin be worth something?"

"Ben!" Sasha said. "What would Nath say if he heard you say that?"

"He wouldn't say anything," Ben said, grinning. "He'd just knock me out."

They laughed.

"Ben, chances are the dragons will come back for their own. I don't think any poachers will get them." Bayzog stretched out his fingers and ran them over the dragon scales and wings. "They are such magnificent creatures. It's hard to believe they can be evil."

"Get yer heads down!" Brenwar yelled.

Zip!

Something hit Bayzog and spun him to the ground.

"Bayzog!" Sasha yelled. A hail of arrows followed.

Zip! Zip! Zip! Zip! Zip...

Beads of energy showered everyone in a hail that came from the distance. Everyone was cut and scraped up already, but these magic missiles took things to another level.

"Get us some cover, wizards!" Brenwar yelled. "Return fire, Boy!"

"Where?" Ben said.

Brenwar pointed towards the mountains where the light was flashing.

"That way!"

Ben unslung an exploding arrow, nocked it and let it loose. It sailed through the sky in what seemed to take an age then disappeared into the ground.

Brenwar stormed back at Ben and said, "You got to be a dragon to fire those! Gimme that!" He spun Ben around, snatched another exploding arrow, stuck the tip in the Gray Scale's wet mouth, and handed it to Ben. The arrow tip glowed like fire.

"Stop staring and shoot it!"

Ben let the shaft fly.

A bright flash of light and the sound of an explosion followed.

Zip! Zip! Zip! Zip!

A green wave of missiles ripped into them. The sound of a thunder clap followed. A bolt streaked down from the sky and knocked Brenwar clear out of his boots.

Head ringing, bones aching, Ben crawled up on his knees.

"Brenwar! Bayzog!"

He couldn't hear himself yell. One of their horses darted by him, knocking him back down. Smoke was everywhere. When he looked up again he was surrounded by spears pointed at him. They were held by lizardmen.

CHAPTER

23

"CIRCLE NATH!" BRENWAR ORDERED ABOVE the commotion. He stood tall for a dwarf, waving his War Hammer back and forth. "Wizards, what are you doing?"

"Can you move?" Sasha said to Bayzog.

"I'm alright," he said, taking her hand. "It's you I'm worried about. Just get us over to Brenwar." He got up wincing and clutching his side. His robes had burning holes in them. Whatever had attacked them had rocked them, and he wasn't sure where he was. There was smoke everywhere and it burned his eyes. "Brenwar?"

"Get over here, wizards," Brenwar said. "Hurry!"

They stumbled through the smoke and almost ran right into Brenwar.

"Where's Ben?" Sasha said. "Ben!"

Bayzog didn't know who had hit them, but he could feel their energy now. It was dark and powerful. It had hurt him. Rattled him. He fine-tuned his thoughts and found something.

"They're not after us," he said. "They're after Nath."

"Who's after Nath?" Brenwar said.

An unnatural breeze started, bowing the grass and pushing away the smoke. The horse Nath's stretcher was harnessed to nickered and whined. The smoke cleared and Sasha gasped.

They were surrounded.

A group of lizardmen had Ben pinned down.

"I'll be," Brenwar said.

There were men in robes with rings on their bald heads, well over a dozen lizardmen and some with Grey Scalers on leashes. Two satyrs—one male, one female—stood with their arms crossed over their chests in front of a really big man wearing a metal bull head.

Bayzog felt Sasha wrap her arm around him and squeeze him tight.

Their attackers weren't here to bargain. They were here to take.

"What do you want?" Brenwar said. "And make it quick. I've got things to do."

No one said a thing. Instead they all stood ready, glowering. Ben struggled in his bonds and tried say something but he was gagged. A lizardman held Akron. Something snorted behind them. They all jumped around.

"Where in Narnum did you come from?" Brenwar said with wide eyes.

The dwarf looked startled and Sasha was distraught.

A tiny woman sat atop a wingless bronze dragon with a long black tail. She was pretty with a long strand of white hair flowing from her head. The rest of her head was tattooed like Kryzak's. Her dark robes were sleeveless and she had a gentle demeanor about her, but her bright eyes were penetrating and evil.

She leaned forward on the horn of her saddle. "I'll make this simple for you, Dwarf. I am here for Nath Dragon. Stay out of my way, you live. Get in my way, you die. Do you understand that, Bearded One?"

Brenwar huffed. "So it's just me that dies and not the rest of us." He rubbed his bearded chin. "I'll have to think about that."

"A witty dwarf," she said as her pleasant voice turned to venom. "Or a stupid one. Any fool would know I'm referring to all of you."

"Ah," Brenwar said, "so if we fight we die. Hmmm. But did you think to consider that when we fight, you will die?"

"Hahahahaha," she said. "I assure you there in no chance of that. But if you care to try, I'll see to it your young friend over there will be the first to die." Her eyes drifted to Ben.

Bayzog's mind raced to assess the situation while Brenwar delayed. The woman would be ready for anything thrown at her. He was certain of that. Just moments ago she appeared from nowhere and he could only assume she'd just as easily disappear. He wondered if that was her power or the dragon's. That left all the rest of their aggressors.

What can I do that wouldn't endanger Ben?

He had some spells ready but what help—if any—would they offer?

"Can I have a moment to think about it?" Brenwar said.

"I don't think there is much to think about, but why not?" the young woman said. "A moment then, but not a dwarven one. When I say it's done, it's done."

I hope Sasha remembers this.

He squeezed a series of signals into Sasha's arm, which was still hooked to his.

She squeezed back!

Good.

"My, you are a pretty lady," the young woman said. "What is your name?"

Sasha released his arm and stepped forward. "Sasha, and what is yours?"

"I am Marlay," she said, flipping her white hair back over her shoulder. "And I must admit I admire that hair of yours. It would be a shame to lose it, wouldn't it?"

"You seem to be doing well without it."

Bayzog grabbed her arm and pulled her back, whispering, "Sasha, please."

"You have a spirited woman, Part-Elf. It would be a shame to watch her die, wouldn't it?"

"Certainly," Bayzog said, locking eyes with Marlay. She seemed young, but powerful. Harmless, yet deadly.

Careful, Bayzog.

Marlay made a short smile. "Talk some sense into your friend the dwarf," she said, stroking her dragon mount's horns. "I've a feeling he's about to get all of you killed." She made a clicking sound and the bronze dragon opened its mouth. Its breath was repulsive and sour.

Bayzog covered his nose.

Sasha's knees buckled.

Marlay's dragon mount raked a hunk of ground out with its claws.

"My dragon hungers, and I don't think you want to see this pretty woman devoured, do you?"

"A parlay, perhaps?" Bayzog said. *Delay. Delay. Delay.*

"There's nothing to parlay about," Brenwar said. "We don't parlay with this brood!"

Marlay leaned back in the saddle and folded her arms over his chest.

"Interesting, Wizard, but my patience thins. I've no need to parlay." She pursed her dark lips before she spoke more. "Look around you. Dragons, acolytes, and lizardmen—not to mention my finest warrior, Kang. And those satyrs are something. Now, I know you've survived Kryzak—well, most of you—but you won't survive me. Walk away and you live. Stay and we will destroy you one piece at a time."

It was a moment. One that splintered Bayzog in two. His elven side would never give in to evil, but his human side was unpredictable. Half of him wanted to run and the other half wanted to fight, but there was so much to consider. Sasha was in danger. Nath was too. His gut told him if they lost Nath they'd lose everything. Sasha squeezed his arm again.

Bayzog stepped back and gestured towards the lizardmen who held Ben.

"Show some good faith, Marlay," he said, "and let loose our friend. There is nowhere for him to go."

She nodded.

The lizardmen cut Ben's bonds and shoved him forward. Ben fell to his knees, got up and ripped out his gag.

"Akron," Ben said to Marlay, looking at the bow. "I need Akron."

"Oh," she said, smiling a little, "about that. I can't have you leaving with your weapons, or your horses, for that matter. I'll need just about everything you have on you. After all, I have to pay my henchmen and make offerings to the temple."

"What?" Ben said, stepping forward.

Bayzog grabbed his arm.

"What is your life worth, Young Man?" she said. Her voice became louder and her eyes flickered with lightning. "Now, drop everything. We'll start with you, Dwarf."

Brenwar, stalwart as a tree stump, didn't blink. He just stood there with his hammer crossed behind his arms, eyeing her.

"It's a well-crafted war hammer, Dwarf. Perhaps it has a name?" she said.

"Aye," Brenwar said, "it has a name."

"And what might that be? My warrior Kang is in need of a new scepter, and I think that one will do." Brenwar tilted his head in the direction of Kang and snorted.

"I call my weapon War Hammer." He held it out with his arm. "And if he wants it, let him come and get it."

"There's no need for that," Marlay said. "Just drop it."

"So be it then." He lowered War Hammer down to the ground and set it down, head down, shaft up. His chin dipped into his chest.

Marlay cocked her head and her eyes narrowed. "I'm surprised. Now the rest of you."

"Bayzog? Brenwar? Are we really doing this?" Ben said, exasperated. "Is this a *compromise*?"

"What choice is there?" Bayzog said, loosening his robes. "It's this or death."

"What about Nath?" Ben said. His voice and eyes were filled with confusion.

"Mrrrruh…Muh…Muh…Mrruh…Muh…Muh," Brenwar muttered under his beard.

"What is that you say, Dwarf?" Marlay said. She snapped her fingers. All her servants started forward. "I can't hear you."

"It's Dwarven," Brenwar said, lifting his head, "For War Hammer. In Dwarven it's pronounced 'Mrrrummaah.'"

"Interesting," Marlay said, "and does that mean something?"

"Aye," Brenwar almost smiled, "in Dwarven it means War Hammer. We covered that already."

"I don't believe you, but if you say so."

"Mrrummaah!" Brenwar said. He looked at Kang, who was coming closer. "Don't forget it. Mrrummaah!"

Kang walked over in front of Brenwar and set his scepter down. He bent over and picked up the war hammer and tested its heft. The thick muscles in his forearms rippled with effort. He turned and nodded his bull head at Marlay.

She nodded.

Then Kang looked at Brenwar and said, "Mrrummaah."

In a flash, Kang twisted on his hips, rose his huge arms up and brought the hammer down.

Marlay shouted, "No!"

CHAPTER

24

A FLINCH. IT SAVED THE BRONZE dragon's skull from cracking like an egg. Kang's blow landed right between its eyes. The beast let out a roar so awful, Bayzog's knees buckled.

It was Marlay that screamed. Heaved from atop the dragon's back, she crashed to the ground and disappeared in the confusion.

Where did she go?

Bayzog set his first spell loose.

A circle of bright white and yellow light launched from his arm into the air, where it hung high above them. Its glow was mighty and blinding.

The lizardmen cringed, dropped everything, and fled.

The Grey Scalers ripped their leashes and flew away.

The satyrs disappeared in the grasses.

The acolytes fled, tripping over their robes.

The wounded dragon quickly backed off, snapping its maw.

Bang! Bang! Bang!

Kang kept hitting himself in the head with the hammer until Brenwar crawled up his body and ripped it free. The stunned man fell to his knees.

"Lay hands on my hammer, will you!"

Bang!

The bull helmet clanged off the man's face. Kang wavered on his knees, still taller than Brenwar, eyes blinking slowly.

"Huh…" Kang managed to say.

Brenwar brought a right cross through Kang's jaw, knocking him over. "That'll teach you!" Brenwar said. He shifted back and forth on his feet, eyeing his enemies. "Wizard, what is the plan?"

Bayzog held his arms up with outstretched hands, face straining. "I can ward off evil with this, but not for long. A few minutes at best." Sweat dripped into his eyes and over his face. "Sasha, see what you can find in Brenwar's chest. Find anything that can get us out of here."

Ben appeared at his side with Akron ready in his hands.

"Should I start shooting?" Ben said.

"Just hold," Bayzog said. "Save those arrows for when we really need them!"

All of their enemies had covered their eyes and scurried away to a certain point and then turned—hooting and gloating—little more than a couple dozen yards outside the circle. Once the spell faded there would be an all-out battle.

"Again, what's the plan?" Brenwar said, guarding Nath.

"Perhaps you should come up with one," Bayzog said, irritated. "I thought dwarves were masterful planners."

"We are when it comes to everything else but this magic stuff. Whisk us out of here or something."

"Easier said than done. Sasha, have you come up with anything?"

Sasha rummaged through Brenwar's chest, shaking her head. "No!"

Bayzog ground his teeth. There were the four of them to move, plus Nath, not to mention the horses—and they had nowhere to go. He had his own spells, but that wouldn't be enough, not to hold the horde that surrounded them.

At least one enemy was down, thanks to Brenwar.

"Perhaps you and I should take on Marlay and the dragon," Bayzog said. "Ben and Sasha will have to handle the rest."

Marlay reappeared alongside the bronze dragon, laughing.

"Hahahahaha! Such fools you are," she said. Her voice was taunting and exaggerated. "Now you all will die, but perhaps I'll let that woman of yours live, Wizard. Hah-ha. I might just convert her to an acolyte of Barnabus yet."

"No such thing will ever happen!" Bayzog said. "And lives will be lost on your end. Certainly yours!"

"Aye!" Brenwar said. "There be no mercy on the likes of you, Woman!"

Bayzog wondered if Brenwar meant that. Protecting women was one thing, but fighting them was quite another. The situation was new to him. Marlay seemed young, but more than formidable. The tattoos on her head were many, more than Kryzak had, which meant she wielded greater power. And that bothered him. Bayzog was far more than some adept of magic, but he wasn't a magic-user of the highest levels either. His powers were limited, but he couldn't let on with that.

Standing on the ground, Marlay patted the head of her dragon. The beast's tongue licked in and out of its mouth, and it chomped in the direction of Brenwar. It could easily swallow the dwarf in a single bite.

"My pet will make a fine meal of you," she said to Brenwar, "and all the rest of you as well."

The dragon's great tail swept back and forth, flattening the grass.

Bayzog didn't figure that even all four of them could take the beast if they tried. He reached behind Ben and pulled an arrow from the quiver. The tip sparkled in the light. It was Moorite.

"What do you want me to do?" Ben said. Despite his age, the young man seemed confident.

Above, the halo of the ward against evil wavered, its bright light winking in and out.

The hisses of the lizardmen became louder.

Bayzog's concentration was strong but his strength was fading. He motioned for Sasha. "Well?" he said.

"I casted a summons," she said, wiping his forehead. "But I've no idea what will come, if anything, or if it will offer assistance."

Bayzog wanted to roll his eyes. Summoning spells took time and weren't very effective. But Sasha liked them. The last time she'd cast one, a herd of deer had come, and some horned rabbits. "Alright then," he said with his voice quavering. He was sweating.

Sasha said, "You need assistance. Let me lend my strength to yours."

"No," he said. "Take Ben and do as I say." Bayzog whispered quickly in her ear.

Sasha said, "Come, Ben."

Marlay came closer, eyeing the Halo of Light. Her eyes and hands began to charge with a dark mystic purple power. An evil smile formed on her lips.

Beside her, the dragon's claws ripped up the dirt and its tail swished back and forth faster.

"This is it," Brenwar said. "What is the plan?"

"You know the plan."

"Aye."

CHAPTER

25

"WHAT IS THIS?" BEN SAID, standing over the chest.

"Just hand me those arrows," Sasha said.

One by one, Sasha coated the arrow tips with dark green liquid from a potion vial. The metal sucked it up and turned a little green.

"What will that do?" Ben said.

She shrugged. "Maybe something, maybe nothing. It's an experiment." She whispered the plan in his ear, finishing with "Good Luck, Ben."

Ben returned to Bayzog's side and faced the lizardmen with his bow and arrows ready. Sasha came and now they all stood in a half circle around Nath.

"On my signal," Bayzog said under his breath. "In only a few moments, the ward will go."

The Halo of Light winked in and out.

Bayzog wiped the sweat from his brow and eyes. *Here goes.* "Now," he whispered.

Brenwar charged at Marlay.

Sasha fanned out her fingers and shot forth streaks of light at the dragon, striking its eyes.

Bayzog held the Halo of Light a split second longer.

The lizardmen and acolytes came at them from the backside.

Ben turned towards the dragon and fired his first arrow.

Thwack!

The arrow struck the dragon in its hind quarters, drawing a roar.

Brenwar swung War Hammer into Marlay's shield, rocking her back.

A split second later she blasted him full in the chest with a handful of energy.

He fell to the ground.

The dragon lowered its horns and barreled towards them.

Ben fired another arrow.

Thwack!

A dozen yards away, the dragon levitated off the ground. Up and up it went, claws ripping at the air. It let out a confused and angry roar.

"Did I do that?" Ben said, incredulous.

"Yes!" Sasha said, "With a little help from a potion. But I don't think it will last long."

Bayzog gathered his thoughts and cast at Marlay.

The woman stood over Brenwar, slamming bolts of energy into him one at a time.

Bayzog's arc of light slammed into her, driving her back.

Brenwar popped up and charged again.

All over the field of battle, the rest of their enemies were coming. If there was ever a time they needed Nath, it was now, but Nath lay still as a corpse on the stretcher.

Ben fired another arrow at Marlay. It sailed high.

"Blast!" Ben said, whipping out another.

"Ben, watch out!"

Two lizardmen slammed him into the ground.

The acolytes formed a ring around them, wielding their flails and maces.

Bayzog pulled Sasha to him, unable to hide the disappointment in his face. "I'm sorry," he said.

"It's alright," she said. "You tried."

Bayzog's plan had been simple: bring down Marlay in one swift strike. With the leader down, chances were the others would flee.

He looked up.

The bronze dragon still drifted, a lone speck high in the sky, floating like a cloud. Its distant roars could still be heard and when the spell faded and the creature landed, no doubt it would come back to devour them. Perhaps it would be better if they were killed first.

I should have been better prepared.

The lizardmen prodded them forward and pushed them all to their knees before Marlay. The small woman stood with her boot on top of Brenwar's chest. The grizzled dwarf was bound up in mystic bindings that were corded around his arms and legs. There was even one around his mouth.

He still squirmed and struggled.

"Clever," Marlay said, "very clever, Part-Elf. You almost pulled something off here, but what it was I don't know." She checked her bright blue finger nails. "Ah, you at least managed to chip one of my nails. Of course, the penalty is death for that."

"What are you going to do with Nath Dragon?" Bayzog said. "I'd be curious to know before I die."

"Ah, well, if you must know, he'll come with us to the Great Temple of Barnabus. Selene, the High Priestess, will be the one to decide his fate."

Bayzog had a name at least and a location. If they survived somehow, they'd at least know who to look for, and where.

"I see," he said, head downcast.

Marlay turned, started to walk away and said, "Grab Nath Dragon and," she looked back at Bayzog, "bring the woman along."

"No!" Bayzog said, holding onto Sasha.

A lizardman ripped her out of his arms, picked her up and slung her over its shoulder.

"Let go of me!"

Something struck Bayzog hard in the head and he fell onto his face, seeing spots and blood. He rolled over onto his back and stretched out for Sasha, who was being hauled off.

A dark blot dashed over the sky.

"What was that?" Ben said, looking over at him.

"Ayyyyieeeeee!" someone screamed.

"Great Guzan!" Ben said. "Is that what I think I'm seeing?"

A great winged ape swooped out of the sky and snatched Marlay off the ground. He was holding her by her long white ponytail.

"Sansla Libor!" Bayzog exclaimed.

Everyone—man, elf, dwarf, and monster—stopped and watched.

High in the sky, energy crackled from Marlay's fingers. Tendrils of energy dug under the great winged ape's fur.

Sansla held on, his ape face in agony. Higher and higher he soared.

Marlay's face was filled with rage. Her screams shattered the air.

There was a bright light and an explosion. The two plummeted hard to the ground.

A long moment of silence followed.

Please be dead, Bayzog thought.

His heart stopped when the small lithe from rose up in the tall grass and staggered forward. There was a scowl on her lips and her eyes locked on Bayzog. He could read her lips.

"I broke another nail. You'll pay for this."

The acolytes ran to her aid.

Sansla Libor's large form rose up high above the grasses. He roared. Beat his chest with his great fists.

Marlay whirled around, screaming, "Noooooo!"

A blast of energy slammed into Sansla's chest.

He snarled.

Marlay blasted him again.

He charged right through the next blast. A second later he had the tiny woman in his great clutches.

"Let go of me, you beast!" she yelled. "Let go of me—"

Crack!

Marlay's life ended, and the acolytes froze until Sansla tossed her body aside like a doll.

Then they bolted away, afraid of him.

Sansla bounded right after them. He caught one in one hand and one in the other and smashed them together.

Bayzog cheered.

A lizardman shoved him into the ground.

"Ahem," another voice said, "Lizard Face."

Krang! Krang!

Brenwar knocked them down one right after the other. "Get off of my wizard!" The dwarf stretched out his hand and lifted Bayzog to his feet.

"Sasha!"

The lizardman whisked her away.

Sasha grabbed its back and yelled something.

Zzzzzrt!

The lizardman lurched, stiffened and teetered to the ground.

Sasha dusted the energy from her fingertips.

Bayzog ran up to her and caught her hands in his. "Are you alright?" he said.

"I'm woozy, but I'm well enough. How are you?"

Bayzog looked around. Brenwar had the lizardmen on the run and Sansla Libor was tossing acolytes around like dolls. The winged ape was fearsome.

After all evil had fled or died, Sansla stopped in front of the pair of them, nostrils flared, chest heaving. Sounding more ape than elf, he spoke to Sasha.

"I heard your summons. Strange, but I could not ignore." His dark face jerked a little. "Such desperation. Such evil. Grrrr. You … must … go." He turned his big frame around and glanced at Nath. "He lives?"

"Yes," Bayzog said, "And we're taking him to a safer place until he wakes."

Sansla moved away from them and pointed. "The bronze dragon comes." He looked back at Bayzog. "Get on your horses. I'll slow him down."

There was a terrible roar far away from them. It seemed the Potion of Floating had worn off and now the bronze dragon stormed their way.

"On the horses everyone!"

"What about Nath? We can't gallop with him behind us," Brenwar said.

"I can help," Sasha said. She slipped a vial out of her robes and held it out. "This is what is left from the Potion of Floating." She dabbed some on Nath and the stretcher and rubbed it in. "This should last a bit."

"Ben!"

The tall country boy lumbered over, shoulder sagging. He grabbed the reins of his horse and stuffed his boot in the stirrup.

"Let's get out of here," he said, exhausted.

Everyone mounted up and Brenwar eyed the stretcher behind him.

"Well?"

"It'll work! Just start moving," Sasha said.

They started at a trot and gradually the stretcher lifted Nath up from the ground. Bayzog looked back a Sansla Libor.

The big ape waved his huge arm. A second later they were galloping away until the battle field was long out of their sight.

"Sasha," Bayzog said with his hair whipping in his face. "You did well. Your summons spell, I believe—I know—saved us all."

She smiled. "I told you it was a great spell."

CHAPTER

26

THEY MADE IT AS FAR as the first run of forested hills and found shelter in the rocks. It was evening and the rain had come in a downpour. Over the rocks, Brenwar and Ben stretched a canopy that kept them dry. It wasn't an ordinary canopy either, but something Brenwar had kept rolled up on his saddle. Another treasure from Dragon Home.

"It'll keep you dry and warm, even cool during the hot seasons and such," Brenwar grumbled, wringing out his beard. "Made for man, not dwarf. The harsh elements are a dwarf's best friend. Well, that and ale."

"I'm thankful, Brenwar," Bayzog said. He cast a quick spell that made a small pile of rocks begin to glow red hot.

Sasha was dripping wet. She shivered and said, "Yes, many thanks."

"Me too," Ben said, nodding.

The ground dried out quickly, thanks to Bayzog's magic fire. As soon as it did, he sat down and leaned back against one of the warm rocks nearby.

Sasha sat next to Bayzog and leaned against his shoulder.

"That was a close one," Brenwar said. "You did well, all of you. I believe our friend Nath would be proud."

"It was close alright," Bayzog said, "but my concerns are far from over, Brenwar."

Brenwar grunted.

"They knew Nath was down and they wanted him this time. They sent a small army after him." He shook his head. "They'll still be coming after him. Wherever he goes, war will follow."

"He'll be safe in Morgdon," Brenwar said.

"But will Morgdon be safe from him?"

No one said anything, but at least Brenwar was thinking.

At the moment, there was peace in Nalzambor. No major wars were stirring. According to the Laedorn and the elves, the orcs had started to press and the atmosphere of the world was getting prickly. And now it seemed that the evil forces at work wanted Nath Dragon—alive, not dead.

Bayzog could imagine why. To spark the next Great Dragon War. He feared that Nath would be the prize of that war.

"They want to turn him, I fear," Bayzog said. "We can't let them have him. We don't need to risk an all-out war, either, and you know as well as I do, Brenwar, that the dwarves require little provocation. Our enemies are counting on that."

Brenwar huffed. "The dwarves won't overreact, and I assure you that he..." He pointed at Nath. "... and the rest of us will be plenty safe in Morgdon. We have plenty of places to hide him."

"Didn't you lose him the last time?" Bayzog said.

"No! Don't you worry. He's asleep now. He was plenty awake the last time." He pointed at Bayzog. "We'll keep a close eye on him."

Bayzog closed his eyes and rested his cheek on Sasha's head. She was sound asleep. Across from him, Ben was yawning and stretching out his long arms. Inside himself, Bayzog's human side felt a thousand years old.

Close calls with death will do that to you, I suppose.

Bayzog missed his home in the City of Quintuklen, the perfect sanctuary for study, rest and quality time with Sasha. She'd turned his dull lab of magic into a home, and her good spirits kept him entertained. Now, for reasons he didn't entirely understand himself, he sat in the harsh elements where the word 'relax' had no meaning.

He stroked Sasha's soft hair as her chest rose and fell gently on his. He felt guilty she was here, but she wouldn't want to be anywhere else in the world. She'd made that clear.

That's what people who love each other do. They stick together.

It was one of those things he'd learned to understand in his experience with the conflict between good and evil.

Love grows. Evil destroys.

His eyes drifted over to Nath, who lay still as a corpse. Without saying so, they'd all pledged to protect their friend from one end of Nalzambor to the other. And they probably weren't going to get much help, so they'd better take what they could get.

"To Morgdon on the morrow then," he said to Brenwar and closed his eyes. A moment later he slept.

Brenwar, eyes alert, huddled over Nath's deep sleeping form and brushed the hair from his face. "We're going to get you back to Dragon Home one day. I swear it."

Nearby, two forms huddled over the rocks with their horned necks craned: Finlin and Faylan, the satyrs. She tugged on his shoulder and led him away, their hooved feet gently passing over the rocks.

"Morgdon, pah," she spat, "I hate the dwarves and their city. I wish a gargantuan sink hole would swallow it up."

Finlin giggled.

She smacked him across the face.

Whap!

"Now is not the time for laughter. Now is the time to plan."

"Who do we tell?" he said. "Marlay is dead, and all of her followers have died or fled. Do you suppose that we can snatch the dragon man on our own? The reward would be great, would it not?"

She gored him in the head with her horns.

"Ow!" he said. "Stop that, will you?"

"Ow? Don't be such a fawnee boy, Finlin. You need to get tougher." She pushed past his shoulder and down the rocky slope. "I'll take the message to the clerics. You follow the dragon man. Be sure to leave a trail—and don't use your pipes unless you absolutely have to."

"As you say, as you say."

Whap!

"Ow!" Finlin said, rubbing his cheek. "Stop doing that."

She glowered at him.

Whap!

He started to speak but bit his tongue. He glowered back at her.

"That's better," she said.

CHAPTER

27

"Morgdon!" Selene slammed her first onto the arm of her throne. "Gorn Grattack will not be pleased!" She grabbed her golden goblet and slung it across the room. Not an acolyte nor a lizardman moved. The draykis remained tall, still and silent near her sides.

At the foot of the dais, the satyr woman, Faylan, kept her eyes and horns down.

Selene's tail slid over the marble floor, hooked around Faylan's leg, and dangled her upside down. "I am not pleased with this news, Little Fawn. How did this happen?"

Faylan crossed her arms over her chest and said, without trembling, "The winged ape showed up and ripped your servants apart. All the acolytes and lizardmen dropped like bleeding stones after that. Your lone remaining dragon, the bronze one, was negated. That winged ape diverted its path, but me and Finlin followed them all the way to the rocky cliffs of Morgdon."

Selene looked into the steely eyes of the satyr, trying to decide whether or not she should rip them out. The evil goat-legged woman was brassy, borderline sassy, and maybe a bit too much to swallow. However, Selene needed her for now, which bothered her. And the fact that Faylan knew it bothered her even more. But the satyrs had at least survived, and they were excellent spies. She dropped Faylan on her horned head.

"Morgdon, Morgdon, Morgdon," Selene hissed more than said. "I hate dwarves, so stalwart and strong. It will take an army to pry him loose from there."

Faylan backed away.

Selene smote Faylan with her tail and sent her spinning across the floor.

The satyr woman didn't move. Still as a possum.

"What to do," Selene said under her breath. "What to do."

Nath Dragon was in a deep sleep. Gorn Grattack had talked to her about that. Her Lord had told her to seize the opportunity. Nath might sleep for weeks, months, or even years. And it would be easier to turn him when he wasn't fighting against them. But even with Nath Dragon down and sleeping, his friends had foiled her plans and even killed her most precious servant, Marlay. That was what angered her most of all.

She resumed her seat on the throne and her drulture landed on the arm. She stroked its head and long neck. "Have you ever eaten a satyr before?"

The colorful drulture flashed its teeth in the direction of Faylan, stretched its neck, and hissed.

"Too big?" Selene said. "I could always feed you a piece at a time."

Faylan clenched where she lay.

Selene sighed.

She wanted to avenge Marlay. She had adored the dedicated and adorably evil woman who now was gone. Killed by a cursed elf, of all things. An elven monster, Sansla Libor, the Roamer King. Someone was going to pay for that. Pay dearly.

"Hmmm," she said, twisting her hand in her robes, "every dwarf, elf and good human that gets in my way is going to pay. And those dwarves will wish they'd never taken Nath Dragon in at Morgdon. Every village and every town within leagues of their mountains with cry for mercy. Because I'm going to ruin them."

She stood up and stepped down from the dais with fists at her sides. "We'll burn their crops! Ransack their homes! Soil their fertile land with innocent blood! They'll have to turn him over to me. That will be my ransom for peace!"

She straightened her robes down over her excellent figure.

"Get up, Goat Woman. I'm not finished using you yet."

CHAPTER

28

"Ugh," Nath said. "My head's killing me."

Slowly he sat up, squinting his eyes. The light was dim, blurry, and wavering but it felt like he was waking up to the dawn's bright light. Something covered his mouth and face. It was sticky. A thin layer of webbing. He peeled it away, swung his legs over the edge of the slab of stone he sat on, and rubbed his aching eyes.

"I have a bad feeling about this," he said. Opening his eyes for what seemed like the very first time, Nath Dragon took in a sharp breath. "Where am I?"

He sat on a slab of granite, like an altar, big enough to hold three men. The room was an octagon, with a lone candelabra flickering above. It was sparse, but the stonework was magnificent. Round columns were carved from the stone, and the floor was tiled in patterns he did not know. It made him think of the tomb in the Shale Hills where he and Brenwar had confronted the steel dragon with the Thunder Stone.

He slid off the slab and began walking around. He wobbled and stumbled.

"Guzan," he said, grimacing, "my legs are leaden."

The chamber was big enough to hold a hundred people if not more, and a single iron door straight across from him was the only exit.

"Where in Nalzambor is this?" he said. "Brenwar?"

There was no answer.

He shook his head and rolled his neck. It cracked and felt funny. He stretched out his great arms and locked them behind his neck, yawning a long yawn.

"How long have I been sleeping this time? Feels like months." He swallowed hard. "Oh no."

He held out his arms. His clawed hands jutted out of the heavy green robes that covered him. His fingers seemed the same as they had before, but the nails seemed a little longer and thicker. He reached back and rubbed his neck.

"What?"

He felt a series of bumps on his neck.

They felt like hard, rigid, protruding *scales*.

"No!"

He grabbed the heavy robes that covered his chest and tore them off.

His chest was covered in black scales that reflected the candlelight.

"No!"

Gaping, he stared at the long nails on his scaly toes and fell back against the granite altar. "This can't be," he said, grabbing his head and shaking it in his hands.

"My face!"

He ran his scaly fingers all over it and found long locks of his auburn hair. His chin was covered in a beard. He stormed through the room, looking for anything that might give him a reflection of his face. But only the door was there and it showed nothing.

Gently he traced his face with his fingers once more. "I think it's still the same." He gave himself a once over. Everything he could see was covered in scales. And they weren't smooth like a snake's either.

"What is this?" He ran his hand over the armor-like ridges on his arms. They were as hard as rock and metal. "I don't think I'll need Brenwar's breastplate anymore."

He combed his long hair though his fingers in front of his face and shook his head. "It's never been this long before. I wish I could see myself ... I bet I look magnificent." He sauntered through the chamber. "But first things first. Where in Nalzambor am I?"

The last thing he remembered was eating enough food to feed an army, sitting at that magic table down by the river with Brenwar, Bayzog, Sasha and Ben. Licking his lips, he could still taste the pie on his tongue...

His tummy rumbled. Worry crossed his features.

"I've got to get out of here," he said.

He walked over to the iron door, started to pound on it and stopped. He'd been assuming Brenwar must be on the other side, or another of his friends, but what if that wasn't the case?

What if he was captured?

If his enemies had him?

And his friends were dead?

The Clerics of Barnabus could easily be behind it. He pressed his ear to the great metal door and closed his eyes.

A minute passed, then two. Nothing.

"Hmmmm," he said, rubbing his chin and eyeing the torches high above him.

The flames didn't flicker or waver, and no wispy smoke billowed from them.

"Magic is behind this."

He ran his hands over the great columns with ancient carvings in them. He tested the tiles on the floor. He knocked on all the walls high and low, but the chamber was as solid as a mountain of stone.

He punched his fist into his hand. Grinded his teeth. Let out a puff of smoke. "I need out of this tomb." He took a deep breath and yelled at the top of his lungs, "BRENWAAAAAAAAAR!"

His voice fell flat. Not even an echo. Nath felt alone. Scared. Angry.

"No! Someone must know I'm in here!"

He punched the iron door over and over.

Bang! Bang! Bang! Bang! Bang...

He beat it until his knuckles ached and he couldn't hit it anymore. Chest heaving and sweat rolling down his eyes, he glared at the door with anger. He'd dented it, but the door was just as tight as ever in its ancient frame. Whatever was put in here was never meant to get out. That much was clear.

He rubbed the sore knuckles on his hand.

"This is bad."

Nath's mind started racing. Had they put him in here to protect him or to keep him? How long could he live inside the chamber without starving to death? Without water? Why was he even alive? All of that food he'd eaten must have lasted him.

He began pacing back and forth, angry and muttering under his breath.

What is going on? I can't die like this. I'll starve.

He hit the columns. He kicked the slab altar. He let out a roar. Smoke billowed out.

Hmmmm.

He felt his great chest fill with heat. He wanted nothing more than to let it out. He eyed the door.

How hot is my breath, anyway?

He squared up on the door. Inhaled a deep breath.

WHOOOSH!

A geyser of hot flames roared out. Nath poured it on. The entire chamber lit up in the red hot light. He breathed until he was out of breath.

Smoke was everywhere. The stink of charred metal filled his nose. He fanned the smoke from his eyes and saw a large hole of dripping iron metal greeting him like the mouth of a melting giant. He jumped right through it.

"Yes!"

It was dark on the other side, but the glowing metal gave him a little illumination. His keen sight came into focus. He stood at the bottom of a stone staircase that led up in a spiral. It wound along the inner sidewall that stretched into the fathomless darkness.

"Great Guzan!" he said, exasperated. "Where am I?"

He headed up the slowly winding steps, traversing what seemed to be the mouth of a volcano or geyser or something. It must have been a hundred feet from one side to the other. The rock walls were smooth, the steps wide as he traveled upward, minute after minute, hour after hour until he stopped and sat down.

He wasn't tired.

What madness is this?

He could see thirty feet up the steps and thirty feet back, but everything else was black as a moonless night. Below, the warm illumination of the torches gave him comfort. Above, uncertainty was wrinkling the thought of freedom.

"Perhaps I dream," he said to himself. "Perhaps I'm dead." He groaned. "On your feet, Nath Dragon. Even if you are dead, you can at least act like you're alive."

Running his hand along the wall, he ascended two steps at a time, sometimes three. Losing track of time, he moved onward, upward, higher and higher.

This is madness.

"Bayzog!"

CHAPTER

29

Nath's voice echoed in the cavern and fell flat. A brisk draft of cold air hit him like a stone.

"Perhaps I'm alive after all," he said, resuming his trek up the stairs.

The sensation of the moving air tingled his senses and up above, way in the distance, he swore he saw a wink of light.

That has to be a door. It has to be.

Minute after minute he continued his ascent up the stairs while the dot of light became bigger and bigger. He doubled his pace, taking five steps at the time, sometimes six. If he had to guess how far he had walked it must have been miles, maybe leagues. Oddly, this didn't make him impatient, only more determined.

"If the Clerics of Barnabus are behind this, I might kill them all," he said when he reached the top, where a small portal of light gleamed like a white star.

A large wooden door—girded in straps of iron with a ring for a handle—greeted him.

He reached for it, then pulled his hand back. "Better at least take a look first." Holding his clawed hand out, he felt a cold breeze blasting through the cracks around the door. He took a peek, popped backward, and shook his head.

"What in the world? This can't be." He grabbed the rung of the door and pulled it open.

Icy wind and snow blasted into him.

Forcing his way through the stiff winds, covering his eyes with his arms, he treaded into what looked like the icy mouth of a cave. Icicles dangled from above like great dragon teeth, and sunlight sparkled on the jagged tips. Drawn to the sunlight like to a hot bath on a cold day, Nath lumbered forward with his teeth chattering.

"Where in Nalzambor am I?" he said yet again, stepping through the cave and eyeing his unfamiliar surroundings. "Who brought me here and why?"

There he stood outside the mouth of the cave with icicles already forming on his eyebrows. He waded through knee-deep snow until he found himself peering from the overlook of a great mountain. Above him was more rock and mountain, and the bright sunlight was a ball of fire behind a misty and cloudy sky. Ahead and below him were more snow-covered peaks as far as the eye could see. The sight was both beautiful and terrifying. The bitter cold felt like a blanket of death. He had to get moving. But who put him up here and why?

"Did I just crawl out of my own tomb?" He stretched out his arms and yelled, "Where am I?"

A snow-covered crop of boulders nearby shifted and tiny balls of snow trickled off them.

Nath watched it with a keen eye as a renewed sense of danger coursed through his freezing blood.

The boulders started to move.

Nath's hand fell to his waist.

Fang wasn't there.

Like cracking eggs the snow split, and thick-thewed hairy monsters emerged, carrying razor sharp battle axes.

Nath backed towards the edge of the overlook.

They flanked him. Closed in, trudging through the snow. They were grisly, inhuman and bearded.

"Finally finish yer nap?" one spit out from a snow-covered beard.

Nath leaned forward, squinting his eyes. "Brenwar?"

The old dwarf shook the snow from his face and beard and nodded.

The rest of the dwarves dusted the snow from themselves and remained in their places.

"Of course it's me," Brenwar said, dusting off his shoulders. "Now come on, we have to get going."

"Wait a moment," Nath said, trudging through the snow towards him. "What are we doing up here to begin with?"

Brenwar looked Nath over, snorted, and started shaking his head.

"What?" Nath asked.

"What? I'll tell you *what*! Ye've changed again. It's even worse than I expected." Brenwar started to march away through the snow. "Now come on."

Nath grabbed Brenwar by the arm and stopped him. He looked him dead in the eye and said, "What am I doing up here?" He gestured toward the cave where the door was. "And what was I doing way down in there?"

Brenwar jerked his arm away. "We were hiding you."

"From who?"

"Who do you think?"

"Barnabus? All the way up here? That's crazy!"

"It's a crazy world," Brenwar said. "Why do you think we put you in there?"

Nath took a pause. He didn't like the way Brenwar had said that, not at all. There was something edgy about the dwarf's tone. Brenwar seemed to be in a hurry. *He's never in a hurry.*

"I'm just as ready to get off this mountain as you are," Nath said, starting after him, "but you could at least act like you're glad to see me."

Brenwar stopped, swung his War Hammer over his shoulder, and glared.

"I'm hungry! Can't you tell?" Brenwar said. "Me and my dwarves didn't get much food up here guarding you, and in case you didn't notice, there ain't no ale. No taverns or toasty fires either."

"Well, how long have I been asleep?"

"Long enough," Brenwar said, moving down an icy path that only the keenest eyes could make out.

Nath fell in behind him and the rest of the dwarven soldiers followed.

"Longer than the last time?"

"What do you think?"

"I think these icy peaks are warmer than you!"

"Good!"

Nath didn't have any trouble keeping up with Brenwar, but he was irritated. Once again he could tell that Brenwar was holding something back. Brenwar was normally very forthcoming with the truth.

And there was another thing that bothered him. If he'd been out for months like the last time, had Brenwar and the rest of the dwarves been guarding him all this time in this intolerable climate? Why hadn't they just kept him in Morgdon? No one could have gotten to him there.

Nath fought the urge to ask more questions, opting to keep his mouth shut until they returned to a more palatable climate. His cheeks were numb, but the rest of him didn't feel that bad. Even his clawed toes weren't cold. He puffed out a cloud of warm smoke and Brenwar caught it out of the corner of his eye.

"Don't do that," Brenwar said. "They're looking for you."

"I doubt anyone is looking up here. I have to say, I wouldn't follow anyone up here."

Brenwar huffed along through the dusk and until dawn before he finally came to a stop. The snow had stopped and there were green trees and tall grasses on level land that greeted the mountains.

Nath still didn't know where he was, but now that Brenwar had finally stopped, it was time to ask questions.

"How long was I asleep?"

"Long enough."

Nath grunted. He figured it couldn't have been much longer than the last time.

"Where are Bayzog, Ben and Sasha?"

Brenwar shrugged.

"Why didn't you just take me to Morgdon?"

"You didn't like it much the last time," Brenwar said, "Did you? You think I'd let you wake up and sneak out again? No, no, no."

"Where are we?"

"Between the Ruins and the Pool of the Dragon," Brenwar said. He combed some snow out of his beard and shook it.

"I think you missed some," Nath said, reaching out his taloned fingers. He stopped. "Is that white hair in your black beard?"

Brenwar pushed his hand away and turned his back.

Nath jerked him around. "Brenwar, how long did I sleep?"

Brenwar mumbled something that Nath heard just fine.

"Not long," he said, "for a dragon."

CHAPTER
30

NATH SAT SHAKING HIS HEAD with his eyes fixed on Brenwar. It seemed pretty clear he'd been asleep a couple of years, maybe more. The lines in Brenwar's face had gotten deeper and his scars were more.

"Come on," he urged. "Out with it."

Around him, mostly standing, were the rest of the dwarves. Though younger by maybe a century or two, they looked like they'd seen a lifetime of battle. Nath recognized some of them, but they'd changed. One was missing an arm, another a hand. One's face was badly acid burnt, and another one's hairless arms were scorched. In one way or another it was clear they all had suffered a loss of some sort, even Brenwar. His wounds might be less visible, but they were deep. Nath could tell.

"We kept you in Morgdon the first year, but the Dwarven High Council voted you out," Brenwar said. "And I agreed. The Clerics of Barnabus raised an army and the senseless slaughter began. They tore through every town and village they could, terrorizing women and children. There was only so much the dwarves could do to protect them, so they turned you over."

Nath popped forward. "You turned me over!"

Brenwar stuck out his hand. "Settle down. I'm not finished yet. We turned you over and rescued you. It was Bayzog's idea."

"Well that figures," Nath said. "Blasted wizards. So what happ—"

"I'm getting to that. Let me tell the story, will ya!"

Nath sat back, frowning, but motioned to continue.

"It was you, and it wasn't you," Brenwar said. "It fooled them anyway. It especially worked when we rescued it and you were taken away to be hidden. But a great many paid for it. A great many indeed. It was one of the bloodiest battles we'd ever been in. But it had to be convincing."

Nath's brows buckled. He hated to ask, but he did anyway.

"How many died, Brenwar?"

"It doesn't matter how many died. What matters is that you are safe."

"No," Nath said, crossing his arms over his knees, "I want to know how many, and I want to know their names. I can at least honor them. I'm grateful. I need to say thanks of some sort. It's hard to take that so many died on account of me. I have to do something. Just tell me."

"All the fallen are written on a wall in Morgdon and their heroics have been noted. You can take a look at them the next time you're there."

Nath looked around at his surroundings and everyone else. Sadness mixed with anger in his belly.

"Just tell me now. We don't seem to be going anywhere at the moment. I don't even know where we are. Just give me some names."

Brenwar put his hand on Nath's shoulder. "Let it go. We've got other things to do."

"Like what?" Nath rose to his feet and towered over Brenwar. "Finding more ways to not tell me anything?"

"More than a thousand, you black-scaled, red-headed step child!"

Nath whirled. "What?"

It had come from the smallest dwarf. He came forward, walking with a limp. His eye was missing and what was left of his brown beard was corded and braided. His eyes were bright and fiery.

"I'm Pilpin, and since you want to know so much, I'll tell you. My brothers, six of them, Chilptin, Kiltpin, Lilpin, Farpin, Stigpin, Zerpin are dead. My father Lanpinpin is dead from defending you too.

You see all these dwarves?" he said, flailing his arm their way. "They've got dead kin too and that's just the ones that were fighting. That's not counting the thousands that died in the towns and villages and that's just the ones that we know of. So sit down and I'll give you all the names you want! Harrumph!"

Nath grabbed his own head and dug his nails in. His blood stopped. Guilt set in. Thousands had died because of him? Why? He stepped backward, shaking his head.

No. How can this be?

Pilpin started prattling off names.

"That's enough," Brenwar growled. "He's got plenty to chew on now."

Nath offered Brenwar a blank look and took a hard swallow.

"Tell me more, Brenwar," he said, "I most know. Everything!"

"Alright then," Brenwar nodded. "So we rescued this pseudo version of you. And it's still alive."

Nath groaned. More guilt was setting in.

"After that we moved the real you from place to place, trying to hide you. We tried the Settlement, Borgash, and all the borders west and north. Morgdon would not have you. No, not after the losses. Every time we settled, we were found out." He cracked his thick neck. "Barnabus has spies everywhere. At every turn there was betrayal, but we did our best the first few years."

"Few years!" Nath said.

"Aye!" Brenwar shot back. "And dragging you around all those years wasn't no festival either! Hah! Nath, you be fortunate I had these volunteers to protect you. And thank Bayzog too. He did some mighty convincing that wasn't easy. That said, we finally found a safe place for you."

Brenwar peered up the mountain. "And you've been here ever since. We've been here ever since, fighting off anything that came and waiting for you to wake. We're about all you have left."

Nath shook his head. He wanted to hit something. He wanted to cry. Crawl back in that mountain and maybe die. He was supposed to saves lives, not lose them.

"How long was I in this mountain?" he said, patting a rock.

Brenwar just said, "Long enough for the entire world to change."

"Ah, blast it, Brenwar," Pilpin said, limping over. "I'll tell him." He stood in front of Nath and clapped his hands three times, saying. "Twen—Tee—Years!"

Nath blinked.

"Shall I say it again?" Pilpin said. "Twenty years! Twenty years! I've been freezing my fanny off for twenty years!"

Nath was numb. His mind scrambled.

How can this be?

"I ... I don't know what to ... Uh ... How did you survive up there in all that snow with no food?"

"We're tough," Pilpin said, poking him in the chest. "Tougher than sleeping dragons."

"Twenty years!" Nath said. "How do you know it was that long?"

"Because we counted the sun rising and falling, Stupid," Pilpin said.

"And I can tell by how much snow has fallen," said another that was missing an arm.

"Enough," Brenwar said. "We rotated. Are you satisfied now?"

"No," Nath said, rising to his feet. "I'm not satisfied. I'm not satisfied at all. And I won't be until all the Clerics of Barnabus are wiped out." He clenched his fists.

CHAPTER

31

"W E CAN'T JUST GO STORMING through the countryside," Brenwar growled. "Everyone is looking for you. Looking for us." He motioned to the others. "We're wanted dwarves, you know."

Ever since they made it to the bottom of the mountains, Nath had been determined to see what was going on. How much had the world really changed while he'd been asleep? It couldn't be that bad.

"Certainly not everyone is looking for us," Nath said. "There must be allies, and I find it hard to believe the Clerics of Barnabus have taken over everything. There's always been plenty more of us than them."

Brenwar stormed ahead, cutting through the forest and into the valleys, veering clear of any noticeable paths.

Nath didn't notice much of a difference in anything. The air was chill and the sky was cloudy, but the day wasn't any different than the last he remembered.

Brenwar stopped his march in a small clearing near at the bottom of the valley where a gentle stream trickled. Nath's old friend turned and faced him with a serious look in his eye.

"Let me explain this once again, Nath. All that is evil in Nalzambor is looking for you. There is a bounty on your head higher than those mountains. They want you. Alive. Wars are going on everywhere. The good fight and the good die, all because the evil want you." He scooped some water out of the stream and drank. "According to Bayzog, you are the catalyst for the next Dragon War. Perhaps the last war of all time."

"That would be a good thing," Nath said.

"Not if the other side wins. Not if we lose you. Everyone needs you."

"Why?" Nath said. His stomach growled. "I'm starving." He sloshed into the stream, hunkered down, and spread his arms over the waters that rushed past his legs. Fish, big and small, darted between his legs. "Ah, there's a meal."

Nath jabbed his hand into the waters and pulled out a large, wriggling, black-spotted fish. He gutted it, scaled it, torched it with his breath, and swallowed the rest down whole. He tapped his fist with his chest.

Buurrp!

One of the dwarves applauded.

"Pah!" Brenwar said. "Let's go. As for why they want you, I can only assume it is to turn you."

"It won't happen," Nath said through a clenched jaw. "Ever."

"Don't say that. Come on."

Nath snatched another fish and gutted, scaled, torched, and ate in on the way.

Hours later, dusk had returned when they happened upon a broken and overgrown village. He stopped, looking down at hundreds of stone markers. They were simple stones with names carved in them, noting all who had fallen but not been recovered. The layout of the village was familiar and Nath knew that he'd passed through here before, maybe a hundred years ago.

"It's like this all over," Pilpin said. "Some save themselves, some are saved by others, but we can't save all of them. The peace in the land is gone." He nudged Nath. "Come."

Pilpin led him to a half sunken stone building that looked like it was being consumed by the ground. Nath ducked under a doorway that was tall enough for a dwarf and followed him down into a tunnel.

All the dwarves funneled inside save for two, who remained outside with their battle axes crossed over their chests.

At the end of the tunnel they emerged into a large room, like a barracks, lit by smokeless torches. In the middle, a table large enough to feed twenty was stacked with bread cakes and littered with jars of jam and honey and slabs of dried meat. The dwarves sat and dug in, while a pair emerged from another entrance with an oaken barrel between them and set it on the table.

"Welcome," a dwarf with a white curly beard said, teetering in. "I see we have a visitor."

"No," Brenwar said, "we have *the* visitor, Gorlee." Brenwar made his way out of the room.

"Ah," Gorlee said, stroking his beard. He pulled out a chair. "Then I imagine he is hungry. Come, have a seat. Eat."

Gorlee might have been the most pleasant dwarf Nath ever encountered. He was rugged, but robed in grey, without a stich of metal showing. The rest of the dwarves were coated in steel, sharp and dull, and armored in thick leather and dull metal. They all ate like they'd never eaten before and guzzled down tankard after tankard.

"Help yourself," Gorlee said. "It won't be there forever."

Nath tore off a hunk of beef and grabbed a roll of bread. He stuffed it in his mouth. The dwarves weren't known for their cooking, but what they made sustained you.

Gorlee eyed him intently. The dwarf seemed to be counting each and every scale.

"How many are in here?"

"Forty eight," Gorlee said.

"And you've all been watching over me?" Nath said. "All these years?"

"It's what we're sworn to do."

"And now that I'm awake what will you do?"

"I don't know," Gorlee said, scratching his beard. "But now that you're awake things will be a lot more exciting around here." He clapped his hands and a jar of honey slid down the table. "Put some honey on that bread. It doesn't taste so good without it."

Nath waggled his hunk of bread in Gorlee's wizened face. "I wish more dwarves were like you."

Gorlee laughed a little. "Me too, but then I wouldn't be so special. You see, I'm not really a dwarf."

"You look like a dwarf to me," Nath said. "Even with all those teeth in your smile."

Gorlee laughed. "Watch this." The old dwarf began to stretch and thin.

Nath felt the scales on his arms tingle. A few seconds later he found himself staring at—himself.

Gorlee showed a mouthful of bright white teeth. "I'm a Chameleon."

CHAPTER
32

"THE HAIR'S WRONG," NATH SAID. "It's supposed to be parted in the middle, not the side." He rubbed his chin, staring the Gorlee version of himself in the face. "I've never seen myself bearded before. It's really handsome."

"Agreed," Gorlee said, helping himself to a tankard. "You might be the finest creature I've ever mimicked."

"But can you do this?" Nath said. He huffed out a ring of fire.

Gorlee's face bunched up and he shook his head. "No, but I can cast some wizard spells. Watch this," he said, pointing at a chair and twiddling his dragon claws. "Tweeedleee Ickle Steeeezzz!"

The chair turned into a goblin with wild and savage eyes, wielding a spear. Four dwarves pounced on it with their fists hammering and mouths yelling. One by one they popped up with a piece of wood in their hands or teeth.

"What's all the clamor?" Brenwar said, bursting back in the room. "Aw, cut it out, Gorlee, and quit looking like that, will you? One Nath is bad enough around here, let alone two. Blast my beard." He dropped onto a seat at the table.

Gorlee resumed his dwarven form and shrugged. "They don't' much like my other visages, so for the past two decades I've been mostly stuck in this one."

"That must be frustrating," Nath said.

"Well, I do get out sometimes. I'm the supplier. I can travel the world without notice. The dwarves can't go much of anywhere as they aren't very popular right now. Unless they're in Morgdon they aren't anywhere else. So I get the food and whatever other needs might be met. I also pick up any information that might be pertinent."

"Such as?"

Nath could sense that as friendly as the Chameleon seemed, he was nothing short of dangerous. Why Brenwar trusted him he'd have to ask later.

Gorlee said, "Dragons, Nath. The Clerics of Barnabus search for you and not the good dragons, but the bad ones. The turned ones. They aid Barnabus. Their frustration grows and they take it out on the weak." Gorlee dipped a piece of bread in the honey. "Sure, the cities and towns are getting by, but the pressure is great. The people no longer smile. They frown instead, as if waiting for the entire world to explode."

"I can't run and hide forever," Nath said, "and I won't. Before I slept, the plan was to take the fight straight at them and end them. Destroy the snake before it got too big." He looked at Brenwar.

"We tried that," Brenwar said, "but it turns out the snake was too big already."

"And now it's bigger?" Nath said.

"Much," Gorlee said.

"I want to see this," Nath said, rising from his chair.

"Sit down," Brenwar said, slapping the table. "We've got to wait for the wizard."

Nath made for the tunnel, but three dwarves barred his path.

"See?" Brenwar said to Gorlee. "I told you he'd try to run off again. He always does. Thinks he can fix the world by himself. Hah."

Gorlee nodded.

"I'm just going outside to get some fresh air," Nath said, hunching down under the low ceiling. "My wardens can come along. I'm not going to sit here until Bayzog shows. I've been asleep long enough already. I need to fill my lungs and stretch my limbs. I need to run."

Brenwar huffed and left the room, but no one else moved.

"Give it some time, Nath," Gorlee said. "After all, we've been waiting a score of years. You can at least give us a few days."

Nath folded his arms over his chest and plopped down in a chair.

"Fine."

Over the next few days Gorlee did his best to entertain Nath. He changed his appearance from one dwarf to another. He animated the food and made it dance while the dwarves sang merry songs.

But not too loud.

Brenwar wouldn't allow it. He swore eyes and ears were everywhere and he went outside now and again.

Gorlee said most of his kind were good, and that they'd chosen him to aid the dwarves and the elves when the world began to change. He said he was glad to do it, that he'd already known the stories about Nath Dragon as much as anyone. He said time wasn't a factor either, that the lifetime of a Chameleon was as long as a dwarf's or an elf's, maybe longer, but that he was young, the same as Nath.

"The dragons are turned or killed," Gorlee said. "And they change. Many have black stripes and tails. Some even take riders now."

"Riders?" Nath said. He thought back to his time as a boy, riding on his father's back. He hadn't flown since. Thinking on that, a great emptiness filled him.

"Just like the paintings you've certainly seen. Some of the dragons even perch on the spires of the cities, watching every little thing. It's scary," Gorlee said. "The people practically dart from one street to the other and the strange ones set up places of worship. The dragons that were once reviled are now being embraced."

"But the dragons were reviled for all the wrong reasons before," Nath said. "They were good and made out to be evil and now you're saying the evil ones are being made out to be good."

Gorlee shrugged. "I suppose."

Nath rapped his fist on the table. "That's sick." He clenched his teeth and rubbed his temples. "I have to stop this."

"*We*, we have to stop this."

"Huh?"

It wasn't Gorlee that spoke but someone else.

Nath turned.

There stood Bayzog. The part-elf wizard's black hair was streaked in white, and his violet eyes were hard. A white scar ran from his eye and over his lip to his chin, and his robes were in tatters. He held a gray staff of wood with a twisted metal tip at the end. He looked tired, but strong.

Nath clasped Bayzog's hands. The grip was much firmer than before.

"Then *we* need to get moving," Nath said. "I'll do anything to get out of this mole hole, and I'm more than ready to stop all this madness."

Brenwar bustled forward and looked up at Bayzog. "Is it safe to go out?"

"Yes, but the hunters are close." Bayzog released Nath's hands. "We need to get the jump on them."

"Why's that?" Brenwar said.

"Come."

Nath was all too happy to be outside again.

It was dusk, and the dwarves that guarded the door were not alone. They had company much taller than them, but they were also looking down at something.

Bayzog made his way over and they parted the way, revealing a small dragon, little bigger than a cat. It was white. On its wings were strange black streaks Nath had never seen before.

Nath pushed his way through and fell to his knees beside it. It wasn't breathing and something had pierced its side.

"Who did this?" Nath said, angry and eyeing the others.

"Nath," Bayzog said. "This dragon was a spy for Barnabus. It had to be put down. We're fortunate we got it before it disclosed our location—"

Nath rose up to his feet, towering over Bayzog and pushed him in the chest. "Who did this? Was it you?"

"Does it look like something I did?" Bayzog said. He held his ground. "Do you want to push me again?"

"I did it," a deep voice replied. A big man stepped forward. His face was short bearded, and his eyes were hard as stone. He had a bow slung over his shoulder and dwarven leather plate that covered his chest but not his sinewy arms. "Do you want to shove me too, Dragon?"

Nath balled up his fist. "No, I think I'm just going to punch a hole in you."

Brenwar stepped between the two. "Not through dwarven plate, you won't. Now settle yourself down, Nath. Can't you see who this is?"

The man didn't seem familiar at all. His features were hard and his body was scarred like that of a veteran soldier. His brown beard was salted with grey. A fine longsword hung on the man's hips and a pair of daggers too. He had the look of a seasoned fighter.

The man shook his head and turned towards Bayzog. "We don't have time for all this. We need to move. The Pool of the Dragons can't wait. But I'm not so sure we need to bring him." He eyed Nath. "Seeing how he's the one they're after."

"I don't think it matters now," Bayzog said. "The next stage has begun. Sooner or later they will know that he has awakened. In the meantime, we need to properly bury this dragon. No offense, Nath."

"Ben?" Nath said, taking a closer look at the man. "Are you Ben?"

Ben turned to face him. "Yes, do I look so different to you?"

"Well, yes," Nath said. "You have a beard and muscles like an old warrior now. It's strange to see you. What have you been doing?"

Ben huffed. His expression was agitated.

"What have I been doing? I've been protecting you."

CHAPTER

33

THEY SPENT THE NEXT SEVERAL days traipsing with discretion through the small towns and villages, making their way to the Pool of the Dragons. It was there that Bayzog said they had allies and information. They traveled on foot, but the dwarves towed a couple of pack mules. Nath spent the time catching up on things with Bayzog and Ben. Even Brenwar began to warm up to him. Gorlee played a big part in that.

"Many of the wild dragons have been turned," Gorlee had said. "The rest, I'm certain, are back in Dragon Home. The poachers no longer hunt them for profit. They turn them into soldiers. Well, the clerics do that."

The news got worse and worse. It gave Nath a headache, and the guilt consumed him. He should have been awake all this time. He could have saved many of them. Most of them.

"Sometimes they have to save themselves," Bayzog said.

But Nath couldn't live with that. Not another day longer, now that he was awake again and feeling stronger than ever. He wanted to sink his claws—or a blade—into something.

"Say, Brenwar, what happed to Akron and Fang?"

Brenwar growled in his throat and signaled to the rear.

Pilpin rummaged through the mule packs, brought over a rugged looking bag and dropped it at Nath's clawed feet. The little dwarf eyed him with suspicion and strutted away.

Nath reached into the bag and found the quiver.

"Some of the arrows are missing," he said. "Exploding ones at that? How did that happen?"

"Are you really worried about a missing arrow?" Brenwar said. "It's not like you made the thing."

"Well, I was just surprised is all," he said, slinging it over his shoulder. He took out the compact form of Akron.

Snap. Clatch. Snap.

The string coiled right into place. Nath stuck his chin out and smiled. He reached over his shoulder to hook it when he realized he no longer had the armor to latch it onto.

Brenwar rolled his eyes and walked away. "That's a problem."

Nath did have clothes on, however. A jerkin covered his chest and most of his arms, and a pair of trousers covered his legs. Bayzog said that was best in case any distant eyes were spying. The wizard had tried to get Nath to cover his head too, but he'd flat out refused. "One should never hide something as beautiful as this," he'd argued.

The last remaining item was Fang. The beautiful weapon with twin dragons on the hilt sent a charge of energy through him.

"Have you missed me, Old Friend?" he said, wrapping his clawed fingers around the hilt. "Ow!" He jerked his hand away.

Every eye in the party fell on him. Bayzog's expression filled with worry.

But Nath didn't pay attention.

"Fang, what's wrong with you? Do you not know me? It's Nath." Slowly, he wrapped his hand around the hilt once more and gently pulled the blade from the sheath. "That's better, Fang. It's me."

The mystic blade throbbed in his palm and was hot in his hand. Nath made sure he didn't grimace. *Stop it, Fang! It's me!* The hilt got hotter and a bead of sweat dripped from his forehead. *Fang! It's me, your master!*

"Problem, Nath?" Bayzog said.

"No," he shot back. The sword began to cool in his palm. "I just think Fang was a little uncertain." He pulled the great blade out to its full length, smiled, then slid it back in. "We're fine now." He buckled the blade over his shoulders. "Shouldn't we get moving?"

Troghlin the Harbor Town. It was one of dozens that circled the Pool of the Dragons, and it was under siege.

"Is this where you were taking me?" Nath said to Bayzog. "It doesn't look to be as safe as I presumed."

Bayzog stood silent, peering through a spy glass that Pilpin had handed him, shaking his head.

"No, we've another hideout, but this town is full of friends. I fear the worst; there's no doubt someone in there is bound to give us up." He shut the spy glass and handed it over to Ben. "We're going to have to find another place to hide. Again."

Nath's eyes were sharper than they'd ever been. He couldn't say for sure but he felt like he could see five times farther than he already could, and that was pretty far. Troghlin was burning in some places and the people that weren't fleeing were hiding in boarded up stores and apartments. The enemy marched prisoners through the streets and some were dead already. Nath's dragon heart pumped faster.

"I see that look in yer eye," Brenwar said. "Settle it down."

Nath ignored him. Troghlin was a wonderful little town that was more like an oversized fishing village with large piers connected by a series of storefronts and boardwalks. People from all over Nalzambor came to rest and enjoy food by the sea in hopes of observing the sea dragons that appeared now and again. Now it was in ruin.

Nath said to Bayzog, "Are those the hunters that you spoke of?"

"Indeed."

"Hmmm," Nath said. "Can I see that spy glass, Ben?"

"Sure," Ben said, handing it over.

There was a draykis leading the soldiers that consisted of robed clerics, gnolls, goblins and lizardmen. They pushed and shoved their way through the town, busting windows and bullying people. The lizardmen had two dragons with them that were wingless and black tailed. Their scales were maroon and their bellies were a darker color, almost black. They sniffed around more like dogs than dragons, with lizard tongues licking out of their snouts. They were burrowers and hunters called Red Rocks.

"Those dragons are awfully far from home," Nath said. "They like the lava in the south. It seems awfully strange to see them way up here. Hmmmm." *Snap. Clatch. Snap.* "I think they don't like it here."

"Oh no you don't," Brenwar said.

"Nath," Bayzog began, "Those hunters are looking for us. They're looking for you. We can't risk it."

"Risk what? Our hides, while those people's lives are on the line?" Nath whipped an arrow from his quiver and spit on the tip. "I'm not going to let anyone else suffer on account of me if I can help it. And I'd expect you to do the same."

"I'm with Dragon," Ben said, taking a place beside Nath. "We've been running too long. Sometimes you just have to stand and fight … for what's right."

"Agreed," said Pilpin. "I didn't stand years in the snow for nothing. I stood because I knew a big fight was coming. My beard's itching for it."

Brenwar looked at Bayzog and Bayzog back at him. They both nodded.

"We need to have a plan," Bayzog said.

"Don't worry," Nath said, "I've already got one. It's called…"

He drew the string back along his cheek and let the first arrow fly.

"… Surprise."

CHAPTER

34

THE ARROW'S FLIGHT SEEMED TO take forever with the tip winking at its zenith before descending.

"What are you doing?" Bayzog exclaimed. "Are you crazy?"

Over two hundred yards away the arrow finished its flight and buried itself in the shoulder of a draykis.

"Did you see that?" Pilpin said, holding the spy glass to his eye. "He hit it. Egad, but it still lives."

Nath could see it just fine. It was a perfect shot and the draykis's bewilderment was amusing.

"What happened?" Brenwar said, standing on his tip toes. "Shouldn't something be exploding?"

As the Hunters gathered around their ailing leader, the rest started to point right at Nath.

"You have to wait for it, Brenwar."

"Wait? I'm not waiting. Can't you see they're coming? A small army of them." He punched Nath in the arm. "All you did was waste an arrow and get our necks exposed."

Nath stood tall, eyeing the draykis in the distance. It wrapped its clawed hand around the arrow, barked a laugh and started to tug.

Nath's keen eyes picked up a click and a mystic whine. All the surrounding Hunters leaned in towards the sound.

KABOOM!

Bodies flew in the air and others were flung on the ground.

"Did you see that!" Pilpin said, jumping up and down. "I like that!"

The dwarves let out a gutsy cheer and raised their weapons high in the air.

Troghlin was shaken. Its captors were rocked.

Nath raised Akron over his head. "Time to finish what I started!"

In the distance, the lizardmen unleashed the pair of red rock dragons. They scurried over the ground. Fast for lizards. The Red Rocks covered the distance between them in seconds.

Nath blocked their advance, shouting in Dragonese, "Go home. Be free or suffer."

Their heads gazed between one another before turning back to Nath and his party. They opened their mouths like tunnels and a blast of hot air came out.

"Sultans of Sulfur!" Brenwar cried.

The intense heat dropped everyone to their knees. The dwarves backed away. Nath stood his ground. And someone else. A tall man he hadn't seen before stood at his side.

"Who?" Nath said.

"It's me, Gorlee," the Chameleon said. "I've thick skin." Gorlee dropped to a knee beside him and sucked a vial into his mouth. "Ah, perhaps this will help."

Nath nocked another arrow and spoke in Dragonese again. "I'll warn you no more. Go home or suffer."

The hot blast of breath kept pouring out.

Nath could barely keep his eyes open.

Twang!

The Moorite arrow buried in a dragon's side.

It lurched. Its breath stopped.

Nath loaded another arrow, pulled the string back, and fired at the other dragon.

Twang!

The Red Rock roared back. Both dragons eyed him. Tongues licked from their mouths. Jaws snapped open and closed.

I'm going to have to kill them.

The pair of dragons slowly came forward.

The dwarves jumped into their path and formed a blockade.

"No," Nath said, "Your weapons won't hurt them. Leave them to me!"

The rest of the Hunters were almost on top of them.

Gorlee grabbed Nath's shoulder. "I can handle these dragons." He pointed at the horde of draykis, goblins, gnolls and lizardmen. "You better take care of them."

"What can you do?" Nath said.

"You'll see," Gorlee said, pushing him onward. "What do dragons love more than anything?"

"Gold," Nath said.

"Aye," Gorlee said. But he had changed. His body was solid gold.

The Red Rocks drifted from Nath to Gorlee.

"I'll be fine," Gorlee said. He took off running. The dragons darted straight after the golden man.
Nath shook his head. *That was strange.*

"Nath!" Brenwar yelled. "Quit standing and start fighting."

He turned.

The Hunters and dwarves clashed, metal on metal. He dropped Akron on the ground. His hand went to his hilt and stopped. He clenched his fists and smiled.

Let's see what you can do on your own.

A shadow dropped out of the sky and punched him in the face.

Pop!

It was a draykis.

Ben stood flanked by two gnolls, being beat on with flails.

Bang! Clang!

Ben kept his shield up and his sword moving.

Wait for it...

The gnolls pounded at him. Heavy, furious blows that juttered his arms. They knocked down his sword and shield arm only to see them snap up again. Their strength was raw and relentless. Their jaws snapped and howled at him.

"Human meat," one said.

"Dead meat," said the other.

The gnolls stopped and backed away.

Ben lowered his guard.

"Tired," he said, huffing for breath.

"Fool!" one said.

Both gnolls struck at the same time.

Bang!

They tore his shield off his arm.

"Dead meat now, Human," one said, closing in.

The gnolls twirled their flails at their sides. Snapped and growled.

"He's got some meat on him."

"Bet he tastes good."

They struck high and hard.

Ben ducked and rolled. The gnolls' weapons slammed into each other.

Ben's sword was a stroke of lightening.

Slash! Slash!

The gnolls howled and fell dead to the ground.

Stupid gnolls. That must be over fifty.

Bayzog stood behind the melee with anger in his eyes. All of his plans were unraveling, no thanks to Nath.

Why do we guard a man who refuses to play it safe?

For the past twenty-five years they'd risked their lives to protect him and keep his whereabouts secret. Now, in a matter of seconds, all of Nalzambor would know where he was and that he lived.

Bayzog shook his head. His eyes glimmered with power.

The dwarves were knotted up with the goblins, gnolls and lizardmen led by Brenwar. Gorlee had distracted the dragons, and Nath was battling a draykis.

That left the Clerics of Barnabus that had not advanced. Some were dead from the explosion, and in the spy glass he counted only six remaining. He set it aside. Most of them stood their ground, watching from the edge of the lake town. Bayzog had no doubt they'd sent for reinforcements already, but how close were they?

Everyone is fighting but me it seems. He rested his staff over his shoulder and muttered an Elvish incantation. The staff glowed with life and Bayzog's feet lifted from the ground. He drifted over the fracas below and straight towards the town's edge, where with wide eyes the six robed acolytes waited. *All those bald headed fiends. I'll take care of that.*

Goblins were fierce. Gnolls were strong. Lizardmen were deadly. They all hated the dwarves.

And the dwarves hated them.

"A barrel of ale to whoever crushes the most!" Brenwar yelled.

Forming a wedge with Brenwar leading the way, the dwarves crashed right into the oncoming horde. Brenwar whopped the first lizardman he came across in the chest, dropping him dead. Pilpin rolled beneath the blades of goblins and cut into their legs with his axe. Another dwarf, the roundest and biggest of them all, bowled a gnoll over with his girth and cracked its head with a round mace.

"Powder their bones!" Brenwar yelled.

The horde of evil pressed, but the well-oiled dwarven squad hacked right back with centuries of skill and precision. The dwarves weren't as fast as their attackers, but they were stout as stumps and tough as kettles of iron in armor.

Brenwar's beard was clipped by a lizardman's sword.

"You dare, you lipless pair of boots!"

With both arms on the shaft of War Hammer, he brought it down with all his might on the lizardman's scaly foot.

Crunch!

It dropped its sword and started to hop and hiss.

Brenwar busted it in the knee.

It fell to the ground, raising its arms in defense a split second before Brenwar put an end to it.

Pow!

He checked his beard. A small portion was dangling off.

"Now I'm mad!"

He was surrounded by angry howls and cries of pain. His dwarves were busted and bleeding, but they didn't cry out. They cheered, snarled and fought back. But they were in trouble. The enemy wasn't falling fast enough.

"Blast my beard!"

Pilpin slipped to the ground and fell underneath four goblins.

Brenwar rushed over and starting swinging his hammer like a sickle. He knocked two aside with one blow. Dented the helmet of the third, cracking its skull.

"Pilpin!" Brenwar said.

The dwarf lay on his back, eyes wide, bleeding. A goblin lay on top of him, unmoving.

Brenwar shoved it off. Pilpin's dagger was in its chest, but its dagger had found a home in Pilpin's stomach.

"You'll have to finish the rest, Brenwar," Pilpin said. "It's been an honor…"

CHAPTER

35

NATH'S EYES WENT STRAIGHT TO the draykis. It towered near seven feet tall and its eyes were dark and beady with a glimmer of fire behind them. It pointed its clawed paw at Nath, flexed its brawny muscles under its scaly skin, and beckoned.

Nostrils flaring, Nath went right at it.

It took a swipe and its claws tore across Nath's scaly chest.

He laughed and punched it in the face.

Whap!

The draykis spit out a tooth and narrowed its eyes.

"It's not like you needed that," Nath said.

It popped him in the nose. Blood dripped onto Nath's chest.

His gold eyes flashed. Fury swelled inside him.

Back and forth they went. Punch for punch.

Bap! Bap!

Crack! Pop!

Pow! Pow! Boom!

Nath beat into it with reckless fury.

It fought back with power and cunning.

Duck, you fool!

The draykis threw a haymaker.

Nath dodged, shifted his head left and right, tucked his chin back, bobbed his head.

"Enough of this!"

Nath jacked it in the jaw with an uppercut, snapping its head back and shattering more of its teeth.

It shook it off with a shiver and pounced.

Nath caught it in midair and slammed it into the ground, pinning its wings. In Nath's mind, this triggered the memory of the winged ape and the kidnapping of Sasha. The image of Shum drowned and dead.

"You will die!"

Nath's fists were like metal gauntlets busting up rocks. They broke bones and busted teeth.

The draykis snapped up its forearms, protecting its face.

Nath pummeled its ribs and belly.

Whop! Whop! Whop!

The draykis gasped, flailed and kicked. Desperate, it wrapped its claws around Nath's hair and pulled him off. It scrambled to its knees, spread its wings and tried to jump away.

"No you don't!"

Nath jumped on its back. He wrapped his arms around its neck and squeezed.

The pair thrashed over the grass.

"You aren't going anywhere!"

Nath felt his strength growing. He squeezed harder and harder, hanging on with his dragon legs and choking it with his dragon arms.

The bulging muscles of the draykis started to slacken.

Crack!

Its neck broke.

Nath shoved it away, sucked for air, and wiped the blood off his face. "That's better."

Clonk!

His head exploded. Stars burst in his eyes. He took another shot to the chest and belly.

A gnoll loomed over him, raising a club high.

Nath caught it in his hands and ripped it loose. "You shouldn't have done that," he said, shaking the club.

The gnoll barked a warning.

Whack!

It barked no more.

A sea of lizardmen swarmed Nath and dragged him to the ground.

The Clerics of Barnabus fanned out and pointed at Bayzog while he sailed over the grass on legs of air. There were six of them in all—bald, robed and cunning.

He could see their lips moving and the air before them beginning to stir and the pendants on their chests beginning to glow. Bayzog readied his staff and touched the ground.

"I'm here to negotiate your surrender," he said.

The clerics huffed a laugh, but it was far from gutsy.

Bayzog could see the air shimmering before them.

"I see," he said. He muttered quick words in Elfish. His fingertips glowed with life and a streak of orange shot from his hand. It flicked over the grass and ricocheted off an invisible force, inches from the closest man's face.

The clerics flinched. Two began to mumble and mutter while the other four, wielding maces, flanked him. Two on each side.

I need to put a quick end to this. He opened his mouth to summon another spell but everything fell silent. His words were gone. The sounds of the battles behind him had disappeared. He was silenced. A chill went through him.

I should have seen this coming.

Bayzog started to back away.

The clerics had him surrounded now. Maces raised high, they closed in to deliver death blows.

Bayzog's heart raced. He had nowhere to go.

The lizardmen pinned Nath down. Five of them in all. The biggest one had his arms wrapped around Nath's neck and was squeezing. Another took its spear and jabbed it into his ribs. The metal tip skipped off his black scales.

"Nice try. Now get off me!" Nath said. He kicked one in the face.

The lizardmen kept poking at him. Their serpent eyes were wild and their long tongues licked out of their mouths.

Nath felt like a pin cushion.

They poked and poked and poked. One spear shaft broke. A lizardman slugged him in the jaw. Then the rest joined in and started to pummel him.

He didn't feel a thing until he caught a punch in the face again.

Saying, "That's enough of this! I am Dragon!" Nath gathered his knees under him, flung the lizardman off his neck, wiped his bloody nose, and laughed.

"You can't hurt me," Nath said. "But I can hurt you."

A lizardman hurled a spear at his chest.

In one smooth movement, Nath caught the spear in mid-air, snapped it in half, and then twirled both pieces in his hands, holding the lizardmen at bay with one of their own spears.

Their eyes slid over one another. Lizardmen were good soldiers, brave but not foolish like the orcs. The rushed him anyway.

Nath didn't hold back. He clawed and punched. Harder and faster. He slammed heads together. A dagger broke on his arm. Another spear snapped on his back.

"Is that all you have, Reptiles!"

Whap! Whop! Whomp!

He kept slugging.

The lizardmen piled up at his feet, busted or maimed.

"Dragon!" someone yelled.

Ben was hemmed in by three goblins, and four lay dead at his feet.

Nath dropped the lizardman he had in the nook of his arm.

"Hold on, Ben!" he said.

Ben's sword licked out.

Bang!

A goblin dropped its axe.

Slash!

Ben cut a streak across its chest.

Glitch!

The third died on the end of Ben's blade the moment Nath arrived.

"Ben," Nath said, wide eyed, "I thought you needed help."

Ben pushed the dead goblin off his sword with his boot. "No, I was seeing if you needed my help."

Bayzog's simmering anger was beginning to blossom. The man in him was no brawler, nor was the elf either, but fighting evil had a way of making you tougher and meaner, no matter how polished you tried to be. His violet eyes narrowed. He didn't like being muted.

How dare they!

He couldn't speak, and that limited him, but it did nothing to the staff he held in his hands. It was an Elderwood Staff that Bayzog had filled with wondrous powers. And it was time to let those powers loose. The metal on the top of the staff flared like a sunburst. Bayzog's entire self was soaked in its power. His feet again lifted from the ground.

The mystic smolder in his eyes stopped the clerics in their tracks. One of them started to turn.

A ball of light shot from the staff and socked the man in the back, knocking him face first into the dirt.

The others started to run.

Bayzog swept his staff over the ground and they all stumbled from their feet. He turned his attention to the two chanting clerics and pointed the Elderwood straight at them.

They raised their arms and another shield of transparent energy formed.

A dark ray of light burst from the staff.

Their shields shattered.

The Elderwood Staff blasted the two Clerics of Barnabus out of their sandals. They moved no more. Once more, sounds of life and battle filled his ears.

"That felt good," Bayzog said. He turned his attention to the three remaining Clerics.

Two were kneeling and begging for mercy. The third ran as fast as his feet would take him.

Bayzog choked back his urge to destroy them entirely, but then shrugged and let loose, blasting them apart. A ball of energy formed in his hand and he tossed it at the Cleric who ran.

"I don't take prisoners," Bayzog said.

The ball of energy glided over the grass and struck the man square in the back, lifting him from the ground. The man sailed through the air over the town where the people waited. He dropped the man in the middle of them. "But maybe they do."

Bayzog turned his attention back towards his friends, ready to unleash more of his fury on his enemies. He'd bottled up his frustrations long enough and he had plenty more to let out. But by the time he got there, the battle had been won.

Nath, Brenwar, Ben and the dwarves were all busted up and bleeding, but all the enemies looked to be dead, or at least almost dead.

"That was a fine show you put on, Bayzog," Nath said, holding a rag to his nose. "And not a scratch on you. Maybe you can teach me how to do— "

"If you didn't act like a child you wouldn't have to!"

Nath shrugged. "Sorry."

CHAPTER
36

"YOU COULD HAVE GRABBED SOME steel and start swinging, Gorlee," Brenwar said. "Fighting every once in a while wouldn't kill you."

Gorlee was still golden when he laughed and said, "Well, I suppose I could have, but how often do I get a chance to play with dragons?"

"We're not here to play. We're here to fight, and Pilpin's dead because of it."

"Well, more might have been dead if I'd not spared you from the dragons." Gorlee yawned and took the shape of Pilpin. "I think my strategy was sound."

"Are you mocking the dead?" Brenwar said, angry.

"Dead?" Gorlee said. "Who's dead?"

"Why you disrespectful..."

"Yes, who's dead?" someone behind Brenwar said. "Say, is that me?"

Brenwar turned and found himself facing Pilpin. He took a double take between Gorlee looking like Pilpin and Pilpin. There was a nasty wound in the real Pilpin's belly.

"Is this a trick?" Brenwar said, poking him.

"No," Pilpin said, "I'm quite alive. I couldn't let a mere goblin kill me. A dragon maybe, but a goblin? Never!" Pilpin teetered and clutched at Brenwar. "But its steel is a tad uncomfortable and my legs feel numb."

"Someone bring me a horn of dwarven ale!"

"We spent twenty-five years trying to hide you, and this is what you do? The whole world can hear you now! Is that what you want?" Bayzog said, tapping his staff on the ground.

Nath kept his back turned. He was busy with Gorlee, inspecting the red rock dragons. Both of the savage reptiles lay still and had burrowed half their bodies into the ground. Nath placed his fingers on one's back, where he could feel it breathing and the warmth of its life.

"What did you do to them?" he said to Gorlee the Chameleon.

"Well," Gorlee said, resuming his golden form, "after they chased me for a few minutes, they started to slow. I'd forgotten you'd sent those arrows into their bellies. I think that took the wind from them and they dropped and started hibernating."

"Hmmm," Nath said, rubbing his chin, "I can't believe I did that." He grabbed one of his arrows by its shaft and pulled it out.

"Are you certain you want to do that?" Bayzog said. "They'll come after us again."

"Agreed," Gorlee said.

"No," Nath said, "they'll burrow for days, if not longer." He put his ear on one's back. It was almost too hot to touch, but the thump thump of its heart was strong. "If they were near the lava pools they'd heal faster." He sighed. "They're usually much closer to Dragon Home. And these black stripes and the black tail ... that's far from normal."

Nath pushed the dragon's eyelid open with his fingers. Its eye was almost black as coal.

"Those eyes should be orange as amber," Bayzog said, kneeling at his side, "shouldn't they be?"

"Absolutely," Nath said. "They've been poisoned, or majicked, or something. I know some dragons are bad, but not the red rocks. They are being controlled."

Nath's nostrils flared and his breath became hot. He stretched back up to his full height. "We're going to find who is doing this and put an end to them." He eyed Bayzog.

The part-elf wizard parted his lips, shook his head, turned and walked away.

"Where are you going?" Nath said.

"Where I'm needed," Bayzog said.

"You're needed here."

"No, I'm needed where my counsel is considered. It can't penetrate that great stone between your ears."

The dwarves let out a gutsy chuckle.

Brenwar even smiled, sauntering with the others behind Bayzog.

Gorlee resumed human form. A pleasant and mild mannered man. "You might want to take some time to catch up on things," he said. "Bayzog's been an outstanding leader and has suffered many trials since you've been down. Much has changed. You need to become wise to the new season."

"Perhaps," Nath said, "but the Clerics of Barnabus are after me, not them."

"They're after all of us, Nath. And now you've led them right to us."

Wherever they'd been going before, they were going again. Nath chose to keep his mouth quiet and let Bayzog lead. He'd make his case later, after Bayzog's emotions settled. He'd never seen his friend so angry before, but the world had changed. His friends had changed.

A few strides ahead of him Ben walked. The cheerful country boy was gone, replaced by a thick thewed warrior with a steely gait.

Nath stretched his strides and caught up with him.

"You're a master of the steel I see," Nath said. "I like how you turned those goblins into Troll food. I envy you."

"Because I can kill?" Ben said.

"You could say that. Being able to fight without holding back must be exhilarating."

"I don't enjoy it, but it's me or them. I can't afford to think about it. If you think too much, you die."

Nath placed his scaly fingers on Ben's broad shoulders. "Ben, I'm glad you live."

Ben looked at him with his hard eyes and managed a smile.

"I'm glad you're back among us." He huffed a sigh. "I didn't think you'd ever wake up. I've never slept more than a day before, and that was only because I was wounded. As soon as the rooster crows, even if I don't hear it, I'm up and about."

The boyish charm started to return to Ben's voice. Nath felt the tautness in his jaw loosen.

Ben went on. "And traveling with dwarves and a moody Bayzog isn't the most fun either. It's hard on a fella. I feel like I'm the only one getting older."

The hard lines and scars on Ben's face told it all. Nath felt guilty. Ben had dedicated his life to protecting him.

"Have you no wife or children, Ben?"

Ben's bright expression dimmed. "I did."

Nath's heart sank. "What happened?"

"They died. All of them."

Nath felt empty. All this time, he'd only been thinking about himself, not appreciating the sacrifices others had made for him, for the world, in the battle against the evil forces that wanted to enslave them.

"Ben, I'm so—"

"It's alright, Dragon. That was long ago. Besides, it helps me empathize with Bayzog."

"Is Sasha dead too?" Nath said, grabbing Ben. His heart burst inside his chest.

"No, she lives, but Bayzog hasn't seen her in fifteen years. Nor his children either. I think that's why he's so moody. I miss my family too, but at least I know they're in a better place."

Ahead, Nath watched Bayzog lead. The wizard's long black hair whipped behind him and the stiff winds billowed his robes. The part-elf's shoulders seemed heavy, and he rested part of his lithe frame on his staff. If Nath were to guess, Bayzog was tired and he was probably angry too.

Nath decided to show a little more caution, but he still had to do what he had to do.

He's just going to have to get used to me being awake. I needed guarding while I slept, but now that I'm awake I'm not holding back and watching this world get destroyed.

With the Servants of Barnabus vanquished, the lake town of Troghlin welcomed the heroes. The finest food from the Northern Sea was unloaded from the docks on the gritty beaches, dumped onto the boardwalk planks, and fried, boiled, baked and sautéed. The people were happy. They danced and sang arm in arm and drank with the dwarves on top of the tables.

Even Bayzog's dour mood had lightened. He stood by the railing staring out over the great lake and holding a pleasant memory on his face. He thought of Sasha and his children and hoped they were well. Perhaps now that Nath had awakened, it was time to return to see them before anything else terrible happened.

Sitting outside the boardwalk tavern, most of the once grim faces smiled. Nath and Ben were stuffing their faces with fish meat and crab cakes while the town's women swooned over them. The dwarves, as hard as they were, seemed jolly as they showed their fresh wounds off to one another.

Perhaps Nath is right, Bayzog thought. *Perhaps now is the time to take it to them.*

He placed his palm over his mouth and yawned. Using magic always drained him, but using it felt so good. Blasting those acolytes had felt better than good. It had felt great. He finished off his goblet of wine, closed his eyes and enjoyed the sun. Troghlin was a fine place, for a human settlement anyway, and he could stand where he was for hours watching the birds glide over the waters in hopes of seeing a dragon snatch them in its jaws.

A wave crashed into the rocks and splashed heavy mist all over him.

Is that odd?

"That's odd," said a fisherman standing nearby. "We don't get tides so high." He looked at Bayzog and pointed. "You better move; here comes another."

A wave bigger than the last busted on the rocks and soaked him.

"Whoooweeee!" the fisherman said. "Never seen anything like that!" He squinted his eyes. "There's no storm over the sea either. Huh."

"Sheesh," Bayzog said, wringing out his robes.

"Braw-haha," one of the dwarves pointed and laughed. "The pond is welcoming you! Say hello back!"

One wave rolled in and crashed after the other. It doused beards and soaked the bread on the table. Almost everyone was wet now. The boats on the docks were rocking and creaking in their slips.

"What's going on?" Nath said, wringing out his long hair and scanning the waters. "There's no storm out there."

"Look!" the fisherman cried. "Something is floating in the waters. It looks like a rock."

Bayzog's violet eyes locked on the object. Closer and closer it came and a chill went through him.

"I've never seen a rock that could float," Brenwar said. "Nor a dwarf either."

"That's not a rock," Bayzog said.

A gargantuan spiked head emerged with bright blue glowing eyes.

"That's a dragon!"

CHAPTER

37

"GET EVERYONE OUT OF HERE!" Nath said.

The dragon rose up from the lake and let out a terrifying sound.

Troghlin shook. The townsfolk fell. Covering their ears, they ran screaming.

Nath rallied his men and dwarves.

"What kind of dragon is that?" Bayzog said.

It towered over thirty feet tall. Its body was armored in sharp horns and scales. Its footsteps were storms surging out of the waters. It was terror. It was power. It was evil.

"It's a hull," Nath said. His heart pounded inside his chest. "Part of the Titan race. I've never seen one before. They lurk in the belly of the sea, only surfacing every few centuries." He shook his head. "This is not good!"

Nath loaded his first arrow onto Akron's string.

"We need to lead it away," he said. "Ben! Get those people to safety. The same for your dwarves, Brenwar! Get them all out of harm's way! Hurry!"

The hull sloshed through the water. Walked through a pier and crushed it into pieces. Busted boats up like twigs. Picked them up and smashed them together. In three strides, the hull was on the beach. It drew a deep breath into its lungs.

"Move!" Nath yelled.

The enormous dragon's horned head and tail ignited with brilliant blue energy.

Nath fired.

Twang!

His arrow rocketed through the air into the dragon's face.

Ka-Boom!

Its blue breath shot out all over the sky. Bursts of blue lightning rained down, igniting everything it touched. The boardwalk was burning. The store roofs caught fire.

"Come on!" Nath yelled, waving his bow at the great beast. He fired again.

Boom!

The hull's head snapped back. Its nostrils flared. Its eyes narrowed on Nath.

"That's right. Here I am!" He back pedaled away. "Come and get me, you ugly beast!"

The hull let out another terrifying roar. Its great foot stomped the ground.

Nath's feet flew out from underneath him.

"Sultans of Sulfur!"

He licked and nocked a Moorite arrow and let it fly.

It sunk into the hull dragon's eyelid.

The hull reared up. The muscles in its neck bulged.

"KAAAAAAAAAAAABOOOOWWWWW!"

Nath fell to the ground, covering his ears. His legs turned to noodles.

A shadow covered him. The dragon's foot hung above him and started coming down.

Great Guzan!

Nath curled up into a ball and closed his eyes.

Stomp!

Nath didn't feel a thing.

That wasn't so painful.

He popped open his eyes.

The hull was twenty yards from him. He lay in the grasses on the bank.

"How'd I do that?"

You didn't, Bayzog's voice said in his head. *Now get moving. He sees you.*

The hull craned its neck from side to side. It checked under its foot and grunted.

"Ha-Ha! You missed me!" Nath yelled.

It roared and started running.

Nath ran away from the town, legs pumping.

The hull wasn't moving fast, but its long strides shook the ground and kept pace with him. Nath stretched his lead to a hundred yards. *He'll never catch me.*

A bright light caught the corner of his eye. He glanced over his shoulder. A blast of lightning blue fire was coming straight for him. He dove to the ground.

"Argh!" he screamed.

The fire danced over his arms and chest. It sizzled and danced on his scales. It was painful. Awful. He screamed again.

The hull stormed right towards him.

Nath scrambled up, grimacing, and ran.

Ahead, shelter was in the great rocks.

Faster, Nath! Faster!

He began to stretch his lead.

The hull was still coming.

The town became smaller. Safer with every stride.

Good!

He turned and started running backwards while loading another exploding arrow. If he could shoot into its mouth the next time it took a breath, he just might be able to stop it. Otherwise, he had no idea what the hull's weakness was.

The hull dragon slowed its pace and stopped. Its scales and horns lit up. Crackled with blue energy.

Nath stopped and drew the arrow along his cheek.

"Perfect!" he said. "Open wide!"

Its scales and tail twinkled and its blue eyes narrowed. It was there, evil and enormous.

SSSZZZRAT!

There was a blinding blue flash.

"What!"

Nath covered his eyes. Colorful spots were all over. He shook his head and rubbed his eyes. He felt dizzy. Finally, he reopened his eyes. The hull was gone entirely.

Bayzog kept his eyes fixed on Nath. The dragon man was moments from death. Curled up in a ball on the beach. Bayzog summoned the power of the Elderwood Staff. He reached out with an invisible hand, grabbed Nath and flung him from harm's path.

"That was close."

Smoke. Fire. Shouts and screams. The people of Troghlin formed a line on the beach and raced buckets up the shore. The fire was spreading fast. Brenwar had ordered his dwarves to assist, but their efforts so far were in vain. The dragon's fire spread too fast. Troghlin would perish.

"What is that fool doing?" Brenwar said, watching Nath run.

"Drawing the menace away," Bayzog said. "And it's working."

"He knows I can't keep up with him," Brenwar said, shaking his War Hammer. "That's cheating. He wants to kill it all by himself! Well, I ain't going to let that happen!"

Bayzog would never get used to the dwarven spirit of fighting anything anywhere. The hull dragon's roar was the most terrifying thing he'd ever heard. Not to mention what he'd seen. This was a monster in every sense of the word. Terrifying. He wanted to run. Hide. He had to act.

"What are you waiting on, Wizard?" Brenwar pointed. "Get us up there."

"What do you mean?" Bayzog said with a tremble in his voice.

"We've got to help Nath," Brenwar said. "Pilpin! Get the chest and make it quick!"

Bayzog's mind was scrambled. Fighting humanoids was one thing. A three-story dragon was another thing. It might be impossible to wound. He rubbed his smoke-stung eyes. The town was about to perish. He wasn't sure what to do. Save the town or his friend?

"I hope yer doing something, Wizard!" Brenwar said. "Because standing here isn't helping anything."

Bayzog shook his head and pointed his staff at the lake waters. He started an Elvish chant, twirling the staff in tight circles. A funnel spouted out of the waters.

"Get everyone clear," Bayzog yelled.

The tornado of water raced up the beach, over the boardwalk and into the town, washing every burning building in sight. The flames started to sizzle and extinguish. Smoke began to roll like a heavy fog.

"Let's hope that does it," Bayzog said, watching the tornado attack any flame in its path. "Let's go after Nath."

Bayzog and Brenwar raced after the hull. Nath was leading it away, toward the rocks, a good thing, but they were too far away to help. The beast was distant and Bayzog was already laboring for breath. Brenwar didn't move very fast on his short legs either.

The hull had slowed to a stop. There was a bright blue flash and the great dragon disappeared.

"By my beard! Did you see that?" Brenwar said. "It's gone. Nath better not have killed it!"

Bayzog could see Nath standing all alone in the field with his bow ready when another blinding flash hit. While Bayzog was blinking the stars from his eyes, the hull appeared again. It was right behind Nath.

Bayzog and Brenwar started waving their arms and yelling and pointing.

"Move! It's behind you."

Nath was staring at an empty field. Where a moment earlier a hull dragon the size of a large building had stood, was nothing. There was a strange smell of something burning that tickled his nose. Something flashed like lightning behind him. That's when Bayzog and Brenwar appeared far away and they were waving frantically. He felt a giant shadow over him. He turned. The hull was right over the top of him, clutching at his head.

"No!"

He fired into the hull's great belly. Point blank range.

Kaboom!

The blast blew him off his feet. He sailed head over heels. His limbs were numb. A lizard's foot the size of a horse rose up and came down.

"Not again!"

Nath balled up like a rock.

Thoom!

Pain erupted all over. Things cracked and squished in his body. He couldn't move. He'd only been awake a few days and now the thought of any more days was over.

Death lingered over Nath in the form of the ugliest dragon he'd ever seen. It leaned down and roared at him once more. He thought his ears would burst. He tried to cover them. His arms wouldn't move fast enough.

If I can move, I can fight.

He rolled up to one knee and reached for his bow. It lay in the grass a few feet away, but it might as well have been a mile. With every muscle in pain, he stretched out for it.

The hull sucked in another great breath and fixed its fiery blue eyes on him.

Shoot it, Nath! Shoot!

He was too late. Down came the fire. Down came the pain.

"Take hold of my staff, Brenwar!" Bayzog said.

"What fer?" the dwarf replied.

"Never mind then," Bayzog said. He started summoning his power. He needed to get to Nath, and get there quick.

Brenwar wrapped one paw around the staff and said, "Oh no you don't. You won't be fighting that dragon without me. Now hurry up will youuuuuuuuu—"

Bayzog fixed his eyes on Nath. Power surged in his veins. He envisioned himself moving instantly from where he was to where he needed to be. A portal opened. He stepped through time and space. A split second later he was under the hull's gaping mouth.

"You trying to get us killed, Wizard?" Brenwar yelled.

Bayzog jammed the Elderwood Staff into the ground and shouted.

"*Moooorentanglaheeen Loooores!*"

A geyser of blue fire erupted from the dragon's snout. Blue flames of lightening scattered everywhere.

Bayzog took a breath. His protective dome had formed.

It covered them all: Brenwar, himself, and Nath.

Nath fought his way back to his feet, shaking. He clutched his head and sides. He looked more dead than alive.

"Thanks," Nath managed to say.

The hull started pounding away at the mystic dome. It scratched, clawed and kicked. Its blows were thunder. Its eyes lightening.

"I can't hold it much longer!" Bayzog said, arms shaking. "We have to be ready to run!"

"Run?" Brenwar said. "There be no running. Take down that shield. Me and War Hammer be ready."

Bayzog's arms trembled and his knees started to bend. The hull was seconds away from overtaking them. All of them.

"Just give me a little more time, Bayzog!" Nath said.

The hull rammed his horns into the dome. It started cracking.

"I can't hold it any longer," Bayzog said. "If you're going to do something, do it now."

Nath had hunting arrows, Moorite arrows and exploding arrows, but he didn't think any of them could to the trick. Not alone. He laid his quiver down at his side and pulled his last three exploding arrows out and wet the tips. They glowed with red light. He nocked them all on Akron's string.

Taking a knee, he took aim. Stretching the bow string tight, his chest and shoulders burned like fire. Something inside him had broken, but he held his aim.

"Give me your best, Akron," he said.

The hull drew back its great arm, punched, and shattered the dome.

Bayzog collapsed in a heap of robes, bleeding at the nose.

The enormous hull dragon reared up and exposed its great neck.

"Cover Bayzog, Brenwar!"

Nath let the arrows fly.

Twang!

KABOOM!

The hull stumbled backwards and toppled like a stone.

Nath skipped across the burning grass.

Everything was hazing. Ringing. Quiet and smoking.

Somehow, Nath rolled to his knees.

Brenwar helped Bayzog to his feet and they stood there gaping.

The hull was slowly struggling to rise. It shook its great neck. It was angry. Worse. It was still living.

Nath's clawed hand fell on Fang's hilt.

"I need you now more than ever, Brother."

The hilt was hot, but not burning.

He unsheathed the blade. It was bright as the sun.

Nath raised it over his head and charged, yelling, "I am Dragon!"

Brenwar sped after him with his War Hammer ready.

Bayzog rushed with his staff.

Nath jabbed Fang into the hull's chest. Ice formed over its scales. It spread fast.

Bayzog encircled its legs with mystic energy.

Brenwar busted it in the snout.

Ka-Raaaaang!

The great beast writhed over the ground. It squirmed and hissed.

"Get out of here, Bayzog!" Nath yelled. "And watch out for its tail!"

The tail flicked with blue fire and struck Nath like a jolt of lightening.

"Aargh!"

Pain erupted in every inch of his body. He held on. He drove Fang deeper.

The great hull dragon roared.

Brenwar popped it in the snout again.

The tail licked out. Cracked like thunder and struck Brenwar in the chest, skipping him over the stones.

"Nooo," Nath yelled, yanking Fang free.

He gritted his teeth.

"Try that again!"

The tail flicked his way again, flashing like lightening.

Nath swung Fang with all his might.

Slice!

He clipped the end of the tail off.

The hull twisted and howled. The blue lights in its eyes went black. The crackling energy on its horns disappeared. Its tail swished back and forth like a headless snake.

Brenwar rose up from the rocks and charged over. He brought War Hammer down on the back of the hull dragon's skull.

The hull moved no more.

CHAPTER

38

THE BATTLE WAS WON. TROGHLIN was saved and everyone was celebrating. Everyone but Nath, Bayzog, Ben, Gorlee, Brenwar and the dwarves. They'd moved on, leaving the remains of the hull to the townsfolk of Troghlin to deal with.

"I don't suppose there is any turning back now," Bayzog said. His eyelids seemed heavy. "I agree. Now that you're awake, we might as well take it to them. But let's pursue with wisdom."

Nath groaned. Everything ached. His head. His toes. And the air tasted funny. Awful actually. Everything felt awful. Still, he limped along, just like the others, glad to be alive.

"I don't think a little caution ever hurt anyone," he said. "I'll do my best to heed your advice."

"Sure you will," Brenwar said. "And the day that happens I'll shave my beard. Har!"

They headed west along the lake for miles until they reached a series of huts stretched out over the waters. They were connected by a series of catwalks and piers and Bayzog took them inside one near the middle. It was larger on the inside than it looked on the outside and sparsely furnished.

"Remote enough to hide us for now," Bayzog said. "Let's rest our eyes and keep our ears peeled. Now that the hull is down, our enemies will hesitate before they come after us. We'll be long gone by then."

"Gone to where?" Nath said.

"Wherever you lead us," Bayzog said.

Nath eyed Bayzog. It was hard to believe that he really meant that.

"We're going after the Head of the Clerics of Barnabus," Nath said, "And there will be no fuss about it."

"This is your decision, not mine," Bayzog said. The wizard set down his staff and leaned back against the wall. His violet eyes seemed to glow. "I'm just here to advise you. It's up to you to lead." He looked over the room. "To lead all of us."

Nath felt all the eyes on him. He felt sacrifice. Courage. All the good in their hearts. There were plenty of people in Nalzambor just like them, suffering something dreadful. All because of him, and he still didn't understand why. War was coming. He felt it in his busted bones. It was time to make things right.

They'd just defeated a hull. If they could handle that, they should be able to handle anything. He forced a smile. His golden eyes flashed.

"Then *our* hunt begins tomorrow."

Siege at the Settlements

-BOOK 6-

CRAIG HALLORAN

CHAPTER

1

"IT DOESN'T SMELL RIGHT TO ME," Brenwar grumbled through his beard.

"What's it smell like?" Nath said, squinting his eyes and peering down below.

Brenwar snorted.

"Trap."

Nath huffed. "You said that the last two times, yet no surprises, except us."

"Trap," Brenwar said, glowering at him.

It had been almost a year since they defeated the hull dragon just outside of Troghlin. Nath and company had been running all over Nalzambor ever since. They had started with the smaller towns and villages, liberating them one at a time. Bringing hope and peace back to a devastated land. It was little, but better than nothing. It slowed the Clerics of Barnabus and the evil dragons from gaining a superior foothold on all the lands.

Nath raised up out of his crouch. "I'll go take a closer look."

Brenwar snatched his arm. "No you won't."

Nath twisted out of Brenwar's iron grip with ease. It seemed that not so long ago, he couldn't break it at all, but in reality, it was over twenty-five years ago.

"Take it easy, Brenwar. We can scout another day or so if you insist."

Nath hunkered back down into the dry woodland overlooking the settlement. It was once well known and thriving farming and trading community with a thousands of people that worked west of the Settlements. The land was still good there, or at least it had been. Much had changed since the last time Nath was here. The green forest and high grasses had lost their luster and many of the crops were bare. It happened in times of war, and war was everywhere now. Nath snorted a smoke ring.

"Will you stop doing that," Brenwar said, covering Nath's nose.

Nath leaned away. "They won't see anything. We're too far." He held out his scaled palm. Tiny drops of rain splattered on it. "Not to mention the fog that lowers like doom."

Brenwar turned from him. For another two hours, they sat like the stones their butts rested on.

Fog rolled down from the hilltops into the small town and stretched through the muddy road like a ghostly hand.

"You have a good count?" Nath said.

"Of course."

Nath had a good count too. Not just the headcount of the enemies that had captured the small town below, but something else. The grey hairs in Brenwar's black beard were many, the hard lines on his forehead no longer few. Brenwar had seen a lot while Nath slept, and Nath had a feeling it was more than he'd seen in his dwarven lifetime altogether. And there was more to come. He could feel that in his scales.

"What are you staring at?" Brenwar said. "No one stares at a dwarf and—"

"—ever stares again," Nath finished. "I know."

"It's true. Not even dragons." Brenwar turned from him.

Nath shook his head. He heard Bayzog's voice inside his head. *Focus, Nath. Focus.* He had to admit that Brenwar and Bayzog had made some progress with him. He was more willing to listen than he had been before. He wasn't sure if that was from guilt or wisdom, however. *Probably some magi mind trick.* He twiddled his thumbs. Scratched markings with his claws on rocks. Hummed a little tune.

"Will you stop that?" Brenwar's face was red.

Nath huffed. Rolled his eyes. He was bored. Very bored. They had been watching this village for two days and nothing had happened. The village kept up with its chores under the watchful eye of the Overseers of Barnabus. There were about twenty of them consisting of lizard men, orcs, and Clerics. They carried steel and cracked whips with heavy hands. The villagers gathered supplies for the caravan trains. They pushed carts dusk till dawn and dawn till dusk. The children no longer played. The women no longer sang happy tunes of the old, old world. Instead, they all worked their fingers raw to feed and equip their oppressors.

Nath grabbed Brenwar by the shoulder.

"Let's go down there and put a stop to this. The fog is a perfect cover." His golden eyes flashed. "They won't even know we're there."

"We wait," Brenwar said, combing his fingers through his beard. He eyed it. "Better be no pixie in there." He grunted. "Aye … we wait. Some supplies be going or suppliers be coming. And I don't like the smell of this place."

Nath wrapped his scaled arms around his knees. "You'd let Gorlee go."

"That's because he's a chameleon. You're a scaly man or a pale-faced dragon. Not sure which, but you're not going."

"Need I remind you that you aren't in charge?" Nath said, mindful of his tone. "And if I want to go, I'll go … and Brenwar, I think I should go."

Brenwar looked back at him with eyes as hard as coal. Brenwar's knuckles were white on War Hammer's shaft and the leather binding creaked.

The old dwarf said through clenched teeth, "You're insufferable. Just go. Scout. Be quick and report."

Nath's eyes widened. "Are you—"

"Go!"

Nath made it halfway down the mountain, stopped and looked back. It was the first mission Brenwar had let him go on without further planning and consultation. Even though Nath led, they still had input from the groups. They planned. They back-up planned. They backed up the back-up plan. And it worked. Thousands had been liberated. Hundreds defeated.

"Just do it right, Dragon," he said to himself, heading back down the hill. It didn't matter if there were ten, twenty or fifty Barnabus soldiers there. He'd take them all. He clenched his fist. "They can't stop me."

Near the bottom of the mountain, he stopped and waited within the edge of the trees. Night had fallen. He could see the fog rolling through a field of gravestones nearby. Mounds of dirt from the graves were only weeks old. *Roast the oppressors!*

The town was little more than a collection of small buildings used for commerce and storing goods. Small cabins spread out along the edges like mushrooms and beyond that, farms. It was common in Nalzambor. Farmland dotted with towns, each with a special uniqueness and craft of its own. Some towns farmed, and others mined, wove cloth, or made candles. Many raised acres of livestock.

The townspeople were hauling in the last of the day's work. Soldiers in dark armor inspected the goods. Some of the robed Clerics of Barnabus counted the goods while others counted the people. Nath could smell the evil in them. He could feel the fear in the people too. They were scared. Uncertain of what tomorrow might bring as they tried to live out another day. He donned the hood of his cloak and slipped into town, moving first from cabin to cabin and then from storehouse to storehouse. The people gathered their children, secured their doors and talked in low voices. Candles didn't even flicker inside the cabins.

Nath picked his way through the town, making a headcount of the soldiers.

Fourteen.

It seemed lean for a town of a few thousand people, but even though the people were superior in number, they weren't fighters. Their strongest men were probably those who filled the graveyard outside of town. He started to see the inside. *Scout. Report.*

He spent the next hour crouched alongside a small cabin on the edge of the town, watching the soldiers patrol back and forth. Lizard men's tails dragged over the muddy roads. Orcs snorted with harsh laughter. They weren't worried about anyone or anything. Maybe it was because this village wasn't that important. Maybe it was because … *They're stupid.*

Backing away along the side of the cabin and around the corner in the back, he turned and found himself face to face with a pair of orcs.

Sultans of Sulfur!

CHAPTER

2

BRENWAR'S STUBBY FINGERS CHECKED THE buckles on his Dwarven Armor and fingered the chain's heavy links one at a time.

"One thousand and one," he said to himself. "Dwarven … The finest armor and ale." His fingers started to fidget through the links again. "One, two, three, four … "

Below the mountain, the fog had become so thick he could barely make out the small town, and the darkness didn't help. Still, the small town nestled on the backside of the mountains didn't make much of a sound. Evil was a quiet business. A viper ready to strike in the night. That was what worried him.

Nath was down there, and he liked to make noise when he wanted to. The fact that nothing yet burned nor had any clamor risen left the tiniest of butterflies in Brenwar's stomach.

"It's been twenty-five years, 'bout time he grew up. Thirty-two. Thirty-three. Thirty-four."

He had to admit, Nath's character changes were a little more than surprising. Given his dragonly powers, he'd shown something new. Responsibility. This reborn young man or dragon listened. Took counsel. Made plans rather than just throwing himself right at it. And there was something else. Guilt behind Nath's golden eyes. And his shoulders hung heavy.

One hundred thirty, one hundred thirty one, one hundred thirty two.

Brenwar had been with Nath since he was a boy: always happy, brave, and somewhat unpredictable. Brenwar had guilt of his own. Though Nath was nothing close to a dwarf, he felt like Nath was one of his own. And he felt like he had failed him. Brenwar had reinforced all the rights and wrongs Nath's father had told him—if a dozen times, then a hundred—and still, they'd almost lost him. He might even yet be lost.

"Five hundred sixteen, five hundred seventeen … eh?"

The woodland behind him crackled.

Hidden deep in the shadows, he grabbed War Hammer and slowly turned his head.

Slow, soft steps came. He sniffed the air. Nothing. His beady eyes squinted in the dark, gazing left and right. He waited. No more footfalls came. Whatever or whoever it was had sniffed him out. He thought of the satyrs. He'd shaken them a hundred times over the years and still they came. Poking their little heads where they didn't belong. Playing music that turned his head inside out. If it was the satyrs, he'd end them right now.

"Come out of there," Brenwar growled.

Two dark figures drifted from behind the tall pines. Small, dark and horned.

"Brenwar," a familiar voice said, coming closer, "you hid quite well for a dwarf. Even a venerable one."

"Keep your voice down, Pilpin."

The little dwarf looked around. "Why?"

"I suppose no one can hear us," the other dwarf said, coming forward. It was Gorlee, still wearing light grey dwarven robes and sandals. "Where's Nath?"

Brenwar looked down the mountain. "Where do you think?"

"He slipped out on you, didn't he?" Pilpin said. The tiny dwarf marched forward with his breast plate stuck out. He slapped the head of his war mace in his hand. "I'll fetch him."

"Nay," Brenwar said, "I gave him my blessing."

Pilpin stopped and turned.

Gorlee's bushy eyebrows lifted. "You should have waited on me."

"I didn't know when you were coming. Besides, we can't keep Nath on a leash. At some point we have to trust him … again."

"He's come a long way, then," Gorlee said, eyeing Brenwar.

"He's further than he's ever been, and he hasn't let us down so far."

"So, you trust him?"

Brenwar shrugged.

"I trust him," Pilpin said. "Nath has never let us down. Not since I've known him. He's a friend. A good one."

"Aye." Brenwar slapped his hand on Pilpin's armored shoulder. "A good one. But I still think we should shuffle closer."

"Why's that?" Gorlee said.

"I think there's a trap down there."

"A trap?" Gorlee said, "Then why did you let him go?"

"I told him what I thought. Might as well let him prove me right or prove me wrong."

"I question your judgment on this matter," Gorlee said, taking the lead.

Pilpin looked at him and looked away.

Brenwar felt some guilt, but it wouldn't be the first time he had to bail Nath out. At some point, he had to trust him to do what needed to be done. After all, that's how dwarves did things. Plan all you want, but sometimes you just have to *do*. He'd made his decision. Nath had made his own. They were both men and willing to live with them.

They made to the bottom of the hill, cut through the fog, and stopped on the edge of the town. All was quiet. Ghostly. The rustle of patrolling soldiers' armor caught his ears. *There should be more soldiers*, Brenwar thought. A dozen. A few more maybe and that was it. Other cities this small had three times as many.

Squawk!

Silence was shattered.

Squawk!

The sound was loud. Abrupt. It wasn't a bird that made the sound, either. It was something larger, at ground level.

Shoulda stayed on the mountain, Brenwar thought.

Gorlee and Pilpin were back alongside him.

"What do we do?" Pilpin said.

Brenwar nodded his chin and headed back toward the bottom of the mountain. Pilpin followed, but Gorlee was gone. *Drat it! Now, one listens but not the other.*

Squawk!

Pilpin tugged at Brenwar's elbow.

"Do I hear what I think I hear?" Pilpin said, pulling the small shield off his shoulders.

"Aye," Brenwar said, readying his War Hammer. "It be dragon hounds, and more than one of them, I suspect."

"So, it's a trap then?"

"And a problem. A big one."

CHAPTER

3

IN AN INSTANT, NATH'S CLAWED fingers locked around the throats of the wide-eyed orcs. He lifted them up, choking and feet dangling off the ground.

"Quiet now," he said, squeezing a little harder.

Orcs. He hated them. They were like men, but with hard muscles covered in thick skin and coarse hair. Some of them had a lot of lard in their bellies too. And they stank. Nath should have caught the scent sooner.

They kicked at him.

He rattled their necks.

"None of that now," he warned in a whisper. He wasn't certain they understood him so he rattled them again, jogging their eyeballs in their sockets. "Aw, drat."

Nath was crafty, but completing tasks without inflicting blunt force trauma wasn't a skill set he had mastered. His objective was simple: Move into the town. Scout. Go back and report. The conditions couldn't have been any better. There was fog. Rain. Everything he needed to conceal himself. And he'd blown it.

This isn't my fault!

He glared at the orcs. This pair wasn't where they were supposed to be. They should have been posted somewhere. Standing guard. Maybe sleeping. A clay jug fell from one's hand and spilled onto the grass. Nath could smell ale.

"Well, if you thought that ale would give you a hangover," he said, wait till you feel this." He slammed their heads together.

Clok!

One orc went out cold. The other's eyes bounced inside his head.

Stupid orcs. Even rocks are softer than their heads. He slammed them together again.

Clok!

Both orcs were out and he lowered them to the ground.

"Great," he whispered to himself.

At some point, the orcs would wake up and they'd remember what had happened. Killing them wasn't an option. Hiding them wasn't a good one either. A senior patrol would come looking for them, wondering why they weren't at their post. That could be any minute now.

Great move, Dragon. Great move.

Nath felt eyes on his back. Only the cabin was behind him. He eased himself backward and heard the door start to close. He lashed out, stuffing his hand inside the door jamb. The door slammed on his fingers. *Whack! Whack! Whack!*

He pushed the door open, stepped inside, and eased the door shut behind him. A little boy stood looking up at him, gaping. A young woman had her arms around him, sobbing.

"Please don't—"

Nath wrapped his hand around her mouth.

"Sssssh," he said. "You don't want to wake the orcs." He winked at her and smiled. "Do you?"

Her posture eased. The little boy reached up and felt the scales on his arms.

"Feels like a snake, Mommy."

"No," Nath corrected, rubbing the boy's tawny head, "It feels like a dragon."

The boy jerked his hand away.

"Like the ones in the barns?"

"Barns?" Nath said. His heart jumped a little. He looked at the young woman. "What barns? What dragons?"

She drew her son back into her arms and stepped backward.

Nath felt her fear. Terror. His eyes searched the room. A small lantern glowed dimly on a corner table. There were cupboards, a sofa, and a few wooden chairs. Blankets were spread over a decent-sized bed. He turned his gaze to the woman.

"Where's your husband?"

She didn't say anything, but the boy did.

"They killed him."

The young woman covered her son's mouth and shushed him. Nath took a moment to get a better look at both of them. The young woman had a pretty face and long brown hair that hid a dark mark around her eye. Her lips were cracked, either from the heat or from being smacked. The boy she held had lash marks on his bony arms. The clothes they wore, once colorful, were now dirty and tattered.

Nath kneeled down.

"Who killed them, the Overseers or the dragons?"

"You should go," the woman said. "Just leave us alone."

Nath shook his head. So many towns. So many cities had fallen to the lash of their oppressors. Armies, battalions, legions invaded. They ravaged, pillaged, and took over. The wells of life ran full of despair in small places such as this. Nath's blood ran hot.

"I'll go," Nath agreed, "as soon as you tell me what I want to know. Who did this? Who's in charge? What dragons and where are they?"

The little boy looked up at his mother and said, "Tell him, Mommy. Tell him."

She shook her head. Closed her eyes. "Just go. Please!" She whispered.

"I can rid you of this menace," Nath said.

"You are just one man."

"Oh," he said, shaking his head. He extended his clawed hands. "I'm no man, and I'm not alone either."

"The Overseer, a large sluggard of a man, killed my husband. He threw a spear into his back after my husband had words with him." Tears streamed down her cheek. "He murdered him right before my eyes. Right before my son. No child should see that. None." She sobbed. "I'll never forget that look in my husband's eyes when he fell."

The boy turned around and hugged his mother. "It's alright, Mommy. Don't cry anymore."

Looking at Nath, she said, "I don't want to see anyone die anymore. Nor my son either."

"Where is this sluggard? This Overseer?"

"They stay in the main assembly near the middle of town," the boy said. "If you listen, you'll hear their coarse songs and laughter." He slipped from his mother and headed for the window. "They say the strangest and ugliest words. And I've heard ravens carry a better tune." He looked at Nath. "Some people just shouldn't be singing. Or speaking."

"And these dragons? Tell me about them. Are they big like a horse or small like a dog?"

The Overseers didn't concern Nath so much as the dragons. It was no wonder there weren't so many soldiers keeping the city under wraps if they had dragons keeping a terrifying eye on things. Of course, that was assuming that the dragons were indeed dragons and not something else. If they were indeed dragons, then who controlled them? It couldn't just be a handful of common soldiers.

"They stay in the barns outside of town facing the mountains. They have six legs and tiny wings. Dark purple and black-tailed." The boy shivered. "They scare me."

"Are you certain?" Nath said.

The boy nodded.

Nath reached behind his back. No Akron. No Fang. Ben had Akron. Nath and Fang hadn't been getting along, so he had sheathed his sword and set it aside. It troubled him that Fang didn't feel comfortable in his clawed hand anymore.

"How many?" he asked.

Squawk!

The boy's eyes popped open. He dashed into his mother's arms.

There was a dragon out there alright. Not all dragons were quiet. They had to communicate, and many used bird sounds. Others made sounds that would freeze the blood in your veins.

Squawk!

The sharp sound cut through the streets. Vibrated the cabin. The dragon out there was terrible. Plain terrible. A six-legged bluu dragon. A real predator. No wonder the people were terrified. *Drat!*

There was very little that Nath didn't know about dragons. Born of dragons in Dragon Home, or The Mountain of Doom as the commoners called it, he'd learned all there was to know. Their sounds. Their scales. Habits. Weapons. Magic. His father the Dragon King had educated him on all that during Nath's first hundred years.

Nath gazed at the boy, nuzzled in his mother's arms. His father was gone. Their provider. Protector. It made him thankful he still had his own father, even though he couldn't see him. That made him wish he'd spent more time with him when he had the chance. Made him wonder if he'd ever see his father again and made him miss Dragon Home more than ever.

Squawk!

The young woman gasped.

"That sound. That horrible sound."

Nath didn't remember hearing the sound the night before.

"How often does it come out?"

"Every few days or so," she said. "It picks through the streets."

"It eats people," the boy said. "It ate my friend."

"Dragons don't eat people," Nath said.

"Uh-huh."

"No, they don't, at least, not any that I've ever known. But they do like orcs. I'm certain of that. Your friend wasn't an orc, was he?"

The boy shook his head.

Did giants and some of the other fowl races and creatures eat people on Nalzamblor? Yes. But dragons, much like people, did not. They might kill them by the bushel. Or roast them. But they didn't eat people. At least, that was how it had always been.

Perhaps things had changed.

Nath walked over to the boy and woman, saying, "I'll take care of this." He patted the boy's head. "No dragons will be eating any people."

"Promise?" the boy said.

"Indeed," Nath said. "Now stay with your mother." Headed for the back door, he turned back one last time and nodded.

As Nath headed out the door, he heard the boy speak one more time.

"I hope you don't get eaten."

Squawk!

CHAPTER

4

SQUAWK!

"Brenwar," Pilpin said, "What is that thing, a giant bird?"

Hunkered down at the edge of the mountain, Brenwar said, "Hush."

"But it bothers my ears. Rattles the hairs in my beard." Pilpin scrunched up his face. "I want to make it stop."

Brenwar had as much patience as a stone, but it began to wear. Something strange was in the small town, and Nath was in there. Gorlee had disappeared as well. *Can't take anything that's not a dwarf anywhere!*

"I think what yer hearing isn't any bird. That's a dragon calling."

"Sounds like a bird."

"Aye, a featherless bird with a hide like iron."

"Oh," Pilpin said, glancing upwards. "It sounds like it's coming from everywhere. Do you think it's calling more dragons?"

Brenwar grumbled. *Trap!* He had a feeling their luck would be running out soon. The Clerics of Barnabus wanted Nath Dragon. They had made that clear. He'd slipped past them for twenty-five years. Now, rumors of a black-scaled, red-haired man's exploits had begun to spread. Now, the walls were closing in. And Brenwar was sure what the next step was. Soon enough, they'd have to join the wars that waged all around. Would Nath Dragon be ready? That worried him.

He pulled Pilpin over by the neck of his armor and looked him in the eye. "Are you ready?"

"Does my beard have hairs?" Pilpin said, getting excited. "Does a dragon have scales? An orc, a malodourous hide and breath? A giant, hair in his nose? Do roosters crow? Do—*mrph*?"

With his had clamped over Pilpin's mouth, Brenwar said, "Alright." He grabbed a small horn of bone that dangled like a necklace over Pilpin's chest. "Be ready to use this. Come on."

"We're going in then?"

"Were going in for a closer look. Stay close to my side, Pilpin. I've a feeling there's a lot more in there than we're hearing."

Gorlee changed. He was no longer an ancient dwarf adorned in heavy robes, but something the opposite and less distinguished. His hands were ruddy. His hair coarse and black.

Uck! One of these days I fear I might not change back. How horrible would it be? An orc is me.

On the edge of the town stood an orcen sentry with a helmet of Barnabus on his head and a spear resting at his side. Gorlee approached with a toothy smile.

The orc lowered his spear. Spoke in orcen.

"Who are you?"

Gorlee shuffled in his armor. Imitating the bodies of others was one thing. Natural. Instinctive. Imitating their garb and armor was another. That took more effort. *Armor's the worst.*

"Why," Gorlee said back in orcen, coming closer, "Can't you see I'm you?"

He could see the yellow of the orc's eyes now. Confusion filled them. It should have been fear, but orcs were hard-headed and stupid. It was hard to scare an orc. Even when one was looking at an exact replica of itself.

"You're," it started, leaning its big chin forward, "me?"

"No, no," Gorlee said, "I'm your cousin. It's good to see you. How's the family been?"

"Uh," the orc said, blinking.

Squawk!

"My, what was that?" Gorlee said in common.

"Dragon," the orc said. It jumped back and lowered its spear. "Say, you didn't speak orcen. What's the password?"

Great! Soldiers on post always had a password. Anyone that didn't know it was challenged and killed. It was common. Even for orcs. Assuming they could remember the word.

"Chicken Feet," Gorlee said.

"No," the orc said, shaking his head, "that ain't it."

"I'm certain it is."

"No."

"Think about it," Gorlee said, in orcen. "It's late. You're standing at your post talking to an exact replica of yourself and you've forgotten your own password. That's not right, is it?"

The orc looked left and right. It bared its teeth and growled.

"What's the password?"

"Chicken feet. I'm certain of it. Now before you act, are you willing to kill yourself?"

"Huh?"

"I am you, after all," Gorlee said. "And you are asleep and dreaming."

The orc shook his head. "I never sleep on post."

"Haha. Never. Now, I know better. I sleep when you sleep. But," Gorlee came closer and spread out his arms, "if you want to wake up, just pierce yourself. Well myself. Yourself. It's all the same. But you need to wake up now."

"I am awake."

"Well, then you need to go to bed now. The sheep are calling."

"What sheep?"

Gorlee locked eyes with the orc. Summoned his magic. Made a suggestion in orcen.

"Sleep."

The orc collapsed to the ground with little clamor.

Gorlee removed its helmet, grabbed its leg, dragged it farther from town, and donned the helmet.

Uck! Picked up the spear and resumed the orc's post. Only one thing bothered him. He still didn't have the password.

Squawk!

The sound was closer.

What kind of dragon is that? Sounds terrifying and fascinating. Can't wait to see it!

CHAPTER

5

NATH DONNED HIS HOOD AND headed straight for the middle of town. His clawed toes sunk deep into the muddy streets and the rain became heavy. *Be smart about this.* Someone controlled the dragon. Or dragons? And that person, most likely, was the Overseer. The sluggard the boy mentioned.

Squawk!

The sound came from the other side of town. Nath kept going and made a bead for the steps of a large wooden building. Outside the double doors were posted two soldiers that lowered their spears on his approach. They were men. Sizable.

"What are you doing out of your room, Villager?" one said in a rough voice. "You want killed, do you?"

Nath ripped the spear out of the man's hands and drove the butt of the spear into the chin of the other soldier, who sagged to the ground just as Nath wrapped his fingers around the bewildered first soldier's throat. The man's face turned purple.

"Is the Overseer in there?"

The soldier nodded.

"Does he control the dragon?"

The soldier nodded again.

"Blink for every person inside the assembly room."

The soldier's bulging eyes blinked five times.

"Including the Overseer?"

The soldier nodded.

Nath hauled the man over to the porch post. "Ever kiss a post before?"

Wide eyed, the soldier shook his head.

Nath shoved his head forward.

Bonk!

He dropped the man to the ground.

He opened the double doors, stepped inside, and closed them right behind him.

Two candelabras hung above the room. A large fireplace on the opposite side was filled with burning wood. A long table stretched out in front of the mantel from one side of the room to the other. The place smelled of wine, sweat and old food.

A man sat at the table, back to the fire, chewing on a rack of meat. He was big-boned and heavy, with greasy black hair combed over the side of his head. A large bright crystal hung from a heavy gold chain on his neck outside his heavy leather armor. Two dog-faced gnolls in plate mail armor stood on either side.

"Can I help you?" the heavy man said in an arrogant voice.

Two lizard men shifted in the corners closer to Nath.

"I'm not of the impression that you are the kind of person that helps anyone," Nath said. He kept his hooded head down. He raised his clawed finger. "But if you truly want to help, you can stop eating and start leaving."

The Overseer's head popped up from his food. "Huh-huh," he laughed. "Do my ears deceive me? Are you another upstart villager? A foolish troubadour passing by, perhaps?" He dropped his rack of meat on the platter with a bang, stood, and drew his heavy shoulders back. "I am Overseer Dormus. I am not amused. Remove your hood, or I shall have my soldiers remove it for you. Head included."

Nath heard the lizard men's swords sliding out of their scabbards. The gnolls hopped over the table and stood between him and the Overseer, leaving a man-sized gap between them.

"I am unarmed," Nath said, holding his hands out wide. "Certainly I'm no threat to you, Overseer Doorknobs?"

"It's Dormus!" he rapped his fist on the table. "And you just came into my assembly room and told me to stop dining." He grabbed his goblet and took a slug of wine. "And to start leaving?" Overseer Dormus leaned closer. His beady eyes squinting. "My, what long fingernails you have. You speak too well to be a lizard man, but your build as that of one. Interesting."

The Overseer didn't seem one bit nervous. His stern face overcompensated for his sagging jaw. At one time, the man might have been a seasoned soldier, but now he didn't look the part. Still, Nath sensed something dangerous about the man. He was sly. Unpredictable. Nath's eyes slid over the gnolls. Each carried a flail with three spiked balls and a chain.

"Feel free to take your men and leave now," Nath said, walking into the center of the room, "and no harm will come to you what-so-ever."

Overseer Dormus yawned, resumed his seat at the table, and poured another glass of wine. One of his hands slipped under the table. The other hoisted up the goblet.

"They say brave men are fools that survived." A pair of gold teeth showed when he grinned. "I say brave men are fools that die."

Clatch-Zip!

A crossbow bolt zoomed from underneath the table.

Nath snatched it out of the air.

"Impossible!" Overseer Dormus yelled. He jumped up and banged his knee on the table. "Kill him! Kill him now!"

CHAPTER

6

PILPIN PASSED THROUGH THE FOG and strode right up to a pair of orcen soldiers who had their spears lowered.

"I don't suppose either of you know where the nearest shower is?" he said, fanning his nose. "Because you smell worse than ogre dung."

"What!" one orc said.

"Skewer that hairy halfling," the second orc said.

"Halfling!" Pilpin swung his mace into the orc's knee, socked the other in the groin, and took off running.

"Kill that rodent!"

A spear zinged by Pilpin's ear.

"Oh my!" He darted between the storehouses with the orcen soldiers on his heels. He pumped his short legs as fast as he could, but the orcs were gaining.

"Oomph!"

An orc tackled him to the ground.

He busted it in the nose.

"Ow!"

The orc jerked Pilpin up over his head, slammed him into the ground like a sack of grain, and drew a dagger from its belt.

The other orc pinned Pilpin down with a spear.

"What are you doing here?" the orc said, chuckling. "I've never seen so small a dwarf before. Huh-huh." He kicked Pilpin in the gut. "Didn't think dwarves could make even smaller runts."

"Didn't think orcs could speak so many words," Pilpin shot back.

The orc kicked him again.

"Ooph!"

"Go ahead," the Orc said. "Kill him. There's probably more around here anyway."

"Ahem."

The orcs turned.

Brenwar stood behind them with War Hammer over his shoulder.

"Ye be right about one thing," Brenwar said, raising War Hammer over his head, "There's more of us alright." He slung it from his hand.

Whop!

The first orc flopped on the ground.

The second orc lowered its spear and charged the grizzled dwarf.

Crack!

The spear tip shattered on the chest of Brenwar's armor.

Brenwar swiped the orc's legs with his knotty arms and knocked him to his knees, saying, "You're just as ugly short as you are tall."

Pilpin hopped to his feet and swung his mace into the back of the standing orc's head.

Clok!

It fell face first to the ground.

"That was fun," Pilpin said. "Why don't we do that more often?"

Squawk!

The dragon sound was close.

"'Cause if we make too much noise," Brenwar said, peering back between the buildings, "a bunch of evil things start coming."

On the road ahead, something slithered through the mud and fog.

Brenwar stayed Pilpin back with his hand. A pair of bright eyes was looking right at him.

Squawk!

Gorlee Stood on the road near the outskirts of town, watching the muddy waters run between his boots. The town was dark and foggy, but lanterns glowed outside the buildings along the streets. The warm glow of fire could be seen in many windows, but the atmosphere was still gloomy. The dragon sounds were startling. It made him more curious than fearful. Being a chameleon, he didn't fear much of anything. Still, his fingertips were tingling.

Squawk!

He felt the sound inside his chest. A few lights in the buildings went dim. The dragon was coming. Two lights hovered down the road like glowing moths. Closer they came, swaying in the fog, back and forth. Dark silhouettes appeared next. Then large figures that carried the lanterns. Lizard men.

Judging by their gait, they were making their rounds. Heading right toward him. He edged closer to the road and waved. *Hopefully, they'll move right on by me.*

A long serpentine head stretched out between the two lizard men. Gorlee caught his breath. The dragon's body was big enough to ride. It had six short, powerful legs. It looked more like a great lizard with a long neck and small horns on its head. Its scales were purple and maroon. Its long tongue whipped over razor-sharp teeth. It had small wings folded down over its back. Its eyes shone bright and evil.

Gorlee took a half step back. Dragons fascinated him and he'd studied them for years, but he was still getting accustomed to the more aggressive sort. The evil dragons didn't value the lives of the other races. They'd rather snap men in two or incinerate them just for staring. A sweep of their tail could break a man's back in an instant. Yet somehow, the men, the Clerics of Barnabus, were controlling them.

Gorlee remained still, awaiting their approach and watching the dragon's long black tail sweep back and forth. He rubbed his hands together. He was exposed at the moment. His fleshy form would not hold against the dragon, but becoming something thicker such as stone or metal could be detrimental. Dragons were very sensitive to magic. Things out of the ordinary did not escape their notice.

The dragon's eyes grazed over him. It snorted and stopped.

Gorlee kept his eyes down. Waved at the lizard men again and stepped back.

Squawk!

The sound shook his bones.

A lizard man approached and pulled off his helmet.

Gorlee blinked wide eyes.

I'm still an orc. I'm still an orc.

The dragon turned and faced him. Eyed him up and down. A rumble started in its throat, and it stepped back.

I can fool men, but can I fool dragons?

It snorted a blast of hot steam in his face.

Gorlee choked and spat. Spit the foul taste in his mouth on the ground. He cringed. This dragon was a hunter. A predator. He could tell by its legs and the small wings on its back. Like a great cat it prowled, and it probably ran like an antelope.

I bet it hates orcs. I'm going to die. Everything hates orcs but orcs.

Its jaws opened wide and snapped shut again.

Gorlee flinched.

Its tongue rolled from its mouth right toward Gorlee's eyes.

Drat! I might look like an orc, but I don't smell and taste like one. I'm done for!

CHAPTER
7

Nath snapped the crossbow bolt in half and tossed it to the ground.

Speed. I love speed!

The gnolls rushed in with spiked balls of steel whirling in the air. They both swung at the same time. Nath ducked beneath the lethal blows, popped up, and punched the first gnoll in the belly, lifting him off the ground. The second gnoll struck him across the back with a fierce blow.

"That didn't even tickle," Nath growled. He snatched the flail out of the gnoll's face and slung it to the floor, then lifted the gnoll and slung him across the room and into the wall. His keen ears picked up the heavy steps of the lizard men coming right at him.

Nath whirled.

A sword blade arced down toward his head. He caught it in the palm of his dragon-scaled hand. The other lizard man chopped into his ribs. Nath laughed. It took more than ordinary steel to hurt him. His scales were as hard as black diamonds. The power of a dragon was awesome. One lizard man soared through the window. The other busted through the front door.

"So much for being subtle."

He turned to the Overseer. Sweat dripped off the man's face. His greasy fingers fumbled with the amulet around his neck. He licked his lips and said, "Who are you?"

Nath removed his hood.

"Nath Dragon?" Dormus said, swallowing hard and eyelids fluttering like a girl's.

Nath grabbed the edge of the large wooden table and flipped it aside.

Dormus sunk back toward the fireplace. "They said you might come, but I didn't believe it. So many small towns and villages for you to save, and you pick this one. I must admit you surprised me." He pulled out a long dagger that had a glow around its blade. "But word of your exploits is well traveled. The Clerics of Barnabus are well prepared. Heh. Heh." He ran his forearm over the sweat in his eyes. "But you cannot stop armies that control the dragons."

"I'm not here to stop any armies," Nath said, coming forward. "I'm just here to stop you."

Dormus squeezed the amulet around his neck. "I'll be a bit more challenging than gnolls and lizard men." The crystal glowed bright red. "Come, dragons! Come!"

Squawk!

Brenwar remained still. His heart thumped loudly in his chest. The dragon made its way through fog and rain right toward them. He readied War Hammer. The dragon's head slid back and forth between its great shoulders and stopped between the buildings.

Squawk!

The sound rattled the shed.

"Come on then, Dragon. Let me bop the ugly nose on your head."

The dragon took a deep breath.

Brenwar shoved Pilpin and scurried away. He took a moment. Gathered his thoughts. The sound of heavy footfalls was moving away. He peeked around the corner of the shed. The dragon had made its way into the street and was moving onward.

Squawk!

Another dark-scaled dragon with six legs appeared. The pair seemed to converse with one another and then they moved on, deeper into the town.

Squawk!

Squawk!

Squawk!

"There be two of them," Pilpin said.

"Nay," Brenwar said. "I hear three."

"Why would this little town have so many dragons?" Pilpin asked.

Brenwar's muscles knotted in the small of his back. "Because it's a trap."

"What kind of trap?"

"A Nath Dragon trap." Brenwar grabbed Pilpin's horn and stuck it between the little dwarf's lips. "Blow and hope it isn't too late."

The dragon's hot breath felt like a furnace near Gorlee's neck. He couldn't help but notice the numerous razor-sharp teeth. *One bite. One bite and it's "Goodbye, Gorlee."* The tongue eased in like a snake, just inches from his face. *Just turn to stone, Gorlee.* But he couldn't do that fast enough. The dragon would detect it. Before he could change to stone, its claws would rip him apart like a rake rips into a bale of hay. *I'm an orc. I'm an orc. I'm an orc.*

The dragon's head reared back.

Gorlee hunkered down. *This is it!* He summoned his magic and his skin began to gradually turn to stone.

The dragon's six legs stomped in the mud. It turned, lowered its head, and squawked.

Others squawked back.

There's more of them! Oh no!

The dragon stomped onward into the town.

Whew!

Its tail cracked back as it went, striking Gorlee full in the chest and flinging him through the air. Pain filled him from head to toe where he landed in the wet grass, cracked stone that was unable to move.

A six-legged bluu dragon crashed through the front doors of the assembly room and made an awful sound.

"SQUAWK!"

The glass panes shattered.

Nath's spine shivered and his knees buckled. He teetered back against the wall and braced himself. Normal weapons might not hurt him, but dragon fangs and claws were made of different matter.

The dragon came inside, eyes narrowed, claws scraping all over the floor.

Blast!

Nath could handle most things, but having his sword and bow, Fang and Akron, would have been extremely helpful right now.

"Not feeling so invincible now, are we?" Dormus yelled over from the fireplace, dangling the crystal amulet. "My, won't this be interesting, seeing you eaten by one of your own."

Drool dripped on the floor from the dragon's fangs and sizzled on the planks.

Perhaps dragons have *begun eating people like the little boy said. Things change.*

"We'll see," Nath said. He straightened himself on the wall. Beckoned the dragon on. "Come on, Fella. Show your cousin what you've got."

The dragon charged, jaws wide, claws ripping up the wooden planks like a chicken's beak rips through straw.

Nath leapt into the rafters and watched the dragon crash through the wall.

Dormus howled, but inside came another dragon.

Great Guzan!

There were two of them.

Another came inside the busted front doors right after the other.

Three of them! The boy was right. *Tell me there are no more!*

Nath and his friends had fought plenty since they'd taken down the hull dragon, a titan, outside of Troghlin, but that was mostly people. These dragons were ferocious predators. Real killers. Powerful. Mature. Magical. Their black tails banged into the walls and off the floor with a thunderous sound.

Squawk!

Squawk!

The dragons reared up on their back four legs beneath him. Jaws snapped open and shut like giant bear traps.

Nath clung to the rafters. *Need a plan! Need a plan!*

The first dragon popped his head back inside the wall and climbed back in. The room was filled with dragons now. Dark eyed and dark tailed. Possessed. Controlled.

"Hahaha," Dormus howled, holding up the amulet. "Such power in the palm of my hand. Rip him to pieces, dragons. Iddy biddy pieces!"

A dragon jumped up and snapped at the rafters, landed, and burst through the floor.

Nath scurried from rafter to rafter. The dragons crashed through the room. Out of the corner of his eye he spied Dormus heading for the front door. *I need to get that amulet.*

The dragons jumped up one after the other. Their great jaws clamped on the wood beam rafters and ripped them down, where they broke the planked floor. The entire assembly room shook and the building started to sway. Nath found himself cornered in the rafters above the fireplace.

One of the dragons took a deep breath inward.

Guzan! I've got to get out of here!

A stream of fire shot right at him.

CHAPTER

8

PILPIN BLEW THE HORN, BUT no trumpet blast came forth. The little dwarf shook it. "Awfully quiet for a horn, don't you think?"

"Blow it again. Harder this time!" Brenwar said, taking off at a run straight into town.

Pilpin took a deep breath and gave it all he had.

KA-KA-ROOOOOOOOOOOM!

It sounded like something a giant moose would say.

"Good!" Brenwar said. "That ought to do it."

"Do what exactly?" Pilpin said, running along his side. "You've never let me use the horn before. You just make me wear it like a necklace, which wouldn't be so bad if it were made of gold perhaps. Not a lot of bling to it."

They splashed through the muddy streets, following the dragon tracks and rounding the corner.

"By my beard!" Brenwar exclaimed. "There's more of them!"

Dragons, one by one, burst into a large building.

"Nath must be in there!"

"Why do you say that?" Pilpin said.

A streak of flames shot through the room.

"Because where there's fire, there's Nath Dragon." He readied War Hammer. "You stay back, Pilpin. Wait."

"I'll certainly not. I'll fight when I want to. I'll die when I want, too."

It wasn't easy, telling a dwarf to stay away from a fight. It was like telling a bear he couldn't have honey, and it didn't matter how big or small a dwarf you were. But orders were orders and Brenwar gave the orders.

"You'll be in the fight soon enough. Wait."

A jangle of armor caught his ears. Soldiers of Barnabus filed into the streets from out of nowhere. Brenwar hadn't thought there were a dozen in the whole town, but a full score showed up, fully armed for battle, orcs, gnolls and lizard men. One race just as ugly as the other. Their dark eyes locked on the two dwarves. Their faces turned to snarls.

"So," Pilpin said, toying with a mace in one hand and a hand axe in the other, "do you still want me to wait?"

"I think you've waited long enough," Brenwar said, lowering his powerful shoulders. "Charge!"

Gorlee pushed his face out of the grass and rolled onto his back. Everything in his body tingled. Stung with pain. It was the first time he had felt the full wrath of a dragon's tail.

"I hope that never happens again," he said, sitting up and rubbing his head.

Squawk!

Squawk!

His head snapped around. No dragons were there. Just pain and rain. He heard a sound in the field behind him. A lone barn stood isolated from the others. Its massive doors swung open and soldiers came out.

Not more of those guys.

The soldiers of Barnabus. A mishmash of the rotten races working together in the battle for evil. Gorlee was sick of seeing them. Determined. Obnoxious. Dangerous. Every last one of them. They cut through the grasses, armor and weapons rattling, and went into the streets.

Gorlee groaned and forced himself up on his feet. He checked his hands. One was stone and one was still orcen.

"I'm going to have to do better than this if I'm to go after them."

He summoned his power and staggered into the streets behind them.

Nath jumped away from the shower of fire onto the floor.

The roof and rafters burst into flames.

"Kill him!" Dormus screamed. "Stupid lizards! Kill him!"

Nath hopped over a swishing tail.

A second tail lashed out.

Whop!

He left his feet and hit the wall.

Crack!

He fell to his knees, clutching his chest. He had felt every bit of that. He shook his head and stood up with clenched teeth.

"That's enough of that now."

A dragon jumped on top of him, pinning him to the floor by the chest.

"Get off me!" Nath pushed back its great neck with both hands.

Saliva dripped from its fangs and sizzled on his chest.

"Argh!" he said, "You're making me mad now!"

Memories flashed in his head. Childhood. He'd wrestled with dragons then, and they had walloped him good, time and time again. Sometimes in fun. Sometimes not. He could tell way back when that some dragons liked him but many dragons didn't. They didn't respect him for some reason. Maybe because he looked more like a man than a dragon. Maybe something else. But he had learned one thing: every time they beat him down, he had better get back up again.

He threw a roundhouse punch into the dragon's nose.

Pop!

The dragon reared up with a roar.

Nath rolled away and sprang to his feet. He ducked and dodged claws and teeth. Pieces of the roof fell down in big chunks of burning wood. The room filled with smoke and heat. Nath jumped on the back of one and wrapped his arms around its neck. He squeezed with all his might. His muscles bulged and popped.

Squawk!

The dragon thrashed. Wood splintered. Flames and smoke were everywhere. The dragon slung its head back and forth, but Nath held on. He squeezed harder. The dragon slammed him into the fireplace, ripping out the rock. Still Nath held on.

The dragon staggered on its feet and sagged to the ground beneath the ruined floor.

"That's it! Go to sleep!" Nath said. He didn't want to kill it. And he didn't have to. He could put it to sleep if he could hold on long enough. His arms started to quiver. His dragon heart gave him a lot of power, but he couldn't hold on forever.

He peered through the smoke and fire. He couldn't see anything. All he heard was the dragons squawking. They were still looking for him.

Nath closed his eyes and heaved one last time. He could feel the dragon's heartbeat and breathing begin to slow. It slumped to the ground and moved no more.

"Good boy," Nath said, blinking and fanning the smoke. It was thicker than water, but it didn't bother him to breathe it. "One down and two to go." He slipped off the dragon's neck and waited, ready to spring on the next dragon that passed.

A resounding crack came from above. He looked up just as the entire flaming building came crashing down on him.

CHAPTER

9

BRENWAR SENT TWO LIZARD MEN flying with a single blow.

"Who else wants to kiss my hammer?" he yelled. He pointed to an orc that had long hair in its eyes. "You!" He swung again.

The soldiers jumped back.

The soldiers were a well-trained unit. Cautious, but confident. They formed a ring around the dwarves, two deep, maybe three.

"Surrender, dwarves," the lead orc said. He was a tall one. Big muscles like the gnolls had. Covered in hair and heavy leather armor. His dark eyes beamed from behind his helmet. "Surrender, and we won't take the scourge to you. We'll just kill you."

Pilpin huffed behind his back. The little dwarf bled and limped. A nasty gash was on his head. The handful of soldiers they'd charged had become a horde.

"You won't be killing anyone, Snaggle Teeth," Brenwar warned. "It's you that best surrender, not we."

Spears with long curved tips lowered at their chests.

"I'm going down swinging, Brenwar," Pilpin said through his little brown beard. "And I'm killing that orc." He spat on the ground. "He clipped my beard."

Whoosh!

Crackle!

The assembly building collapsed. Fire and cinder exploded everywhere. Smoke, dust and debris filled the air.

"Hah! Hah! Hah!" the orc laughed. "We'll just toss them in there." He gloated to his men. "Dwarves burn like coal. We used to use them to warm our stoves back in Thraag." He snorted. "No good for eating, but good for cooking. Just be sure and shave their beards first. Smell bad burning. Awful bad."

"No one shaves my beard! And I'm not a lump of coal for baking loaves!" Pilpin charged. He hopped between two jabbing spears and brought his axe and mace around full circle.

Whack! Chop!

A gnoll barked out and fell to the ground. The soldiers piled on Pilpin, crushing him into the ground with their superior weight.

Brenwar raised his hammer over his head.

The knife-like spears licked out and cut his wrists. More spears pressed at his throat and neck.

"Don't even think about it, Dwarf," the orc said. "Drop it, and we'll let the little one live."

Gnolls had Pilpin's arms locked behind his back and his feet kicking above the ground. A knife was on his throat.

"Bring it down, Brenwar!" Pilpin said. "They'll kill us anyway! Gorla Mon Chok! Gorla Mon Chok!" The words were dwarven. *Death before surrender.*

Pilpin was young for a dwarf. Only a couple hundred years old. He didn't understand the burden that Brenwar carried. That Brenwar had to survive, and that sometimes in order to survive, you had to surrender.

Brenwar lowered his hammer and set it on the ground.

"Brenwar?" Pilpin said, blinking.

The soldiers chuckled.

"Seems the dwarves are no longer stubborn as stumps in the ground, as they used to be," the orc said with his nostrils flaring. "Like I said, they're nothing but bearded halflings anymore."

"Why you—" Brenwar started.

The butt of a spear clocked him in the back of the head.

"Settle yourself, Dwarf. Else we cut the little one's throat."

"Why don't you anyway?" Pilpin said.

"Because the dragons like their meals live and kicking. It does their bellies well."

Three six-legged bluu dragons crawled out of the flames of the ruined assembly building. A man in dark armor stood outside with a bright amulet on his neck, waving the dragons toward him. There was no sign of Nath. Brenwar felt his belly churn.

"Hark!" the orc soldier yelled over to the man with the amulet. "We've dwarves! Shall we toss them in the fire or feed them to the dragons?"

The man walked over, cutting through the ranks, and looked down on Brenwar. He wore the mark of an Overseer. His slung his greasy hair over his shoulder. He had a sharp nose, sagging chin and dark features.

"My," he said, "is this Brenwar Bolderguild?"

"Yes!" Pilpin said, struggling. "And you better think twice if you think you can stop him."

"Well, if I can stop Nath Dragon, I'm pretty sure I can stop his friends." He looked over at the orc commander. "Just kill them."

The orc pulled out a knife and said, "Can I keep his beard?"

"You can keep his toes for all I care," Overseer Dormus said, walking away. "Just get it over with. I need Nath Dragon's bones recovered once this fire is out."

Gorlee stood alongside a storehouse nearby. He'd seen most of everything but not all. The soldiers had Brenwar and Pilpin surrounded but the roar of the fire drowned out their words.

What to do? Think, Gorlee. Think!

Gorlee was a chameleon. A gifted and powerful race. He could change himself to look like any of the races. He could even turn his skin into stone or metal. But he couldn't always think of the right thing to do at the right time. He watched the dragons drag their tails out of the flames and begin to prowl around the building, with their great tails sweeping the muddy streets. He clutched his chest.

Is Nath in there? Is that what they're looking for? Is he buried in the timber and flames?

An idea struck him. He changed form. Black scales and sharp claws formed over his hands.

Nothing brave about being a fool and nothing foolish about being brave.

He ran out into the streets, waving his scaly arms high. His red hair was blowing in the wind.

"Here! Over here, dragons! Hah! Hah! Hah!" Gorlee laughed. "Catch me if you can!"

The man with the bright crystal on his neck whirled. Hatred filled his eyes. He held the amulet up high.

"Kill him! Kill Nath Dragon!"

The soldiers turned their focus from the dwarves and started to run.

"Not you!" the Overseer said. "Stay put! Let the dragons handle this."

Gorlee sprinted for the fields, taking quick glances over his shoulders. Dragons were fast. Six-legged dragons were even faster.

Stupid idea! This isn't going to do it!

The dragons were gaining.

Ah, if I could only turn into a rover horse. Why can I only do races and not the animals? Why can't I make stuff up? Be strong as stone and still able to talk and fly? I wish I could spread wings like an eagle and fly away. Guzan!

He glanced over his shoulder. The dragons would be on him at any moment.

Never thought I'd see the day when I might not see the next.

The farmlands stretched out all around. The plowed fields were muddy, slowing him down. Gorlee's breath started to labor. *Go for the cornfields.*

I never run!

He stumbled and fell into a mud hole.

Splash!

He scrambled up, feet deep in the mud, and found himself eye to eye with three dragons.

Sultans of Sulfur!

CHAPTER

10

A LL THE SOLDIERS TURNED TOWARD the voice of Nath Dragon, who waved his arms in the air yelling like a fool and dashed away like a deer. Brenwar didn't hesitate. He batted the spears away and snatched War Hammer off the ground. He swung. *Bang!*

An orc lay on the ground with a large dent in its helmet.

Brenwar swept the hammer left and right, knocking the soldiers aside, cutting a path right through them. Nath was out of sight, and the dragons raced after him.

Glitch!

A spear jabbed into the back of his shoulder.

Brenwar whirled.

A gnoll's flail caught him full in the chest. Down Brenwar went.

One by one, the soldiers of Barnabus piled on top of him, clawing, biting, and stabbing. His dwarven armor was the only thing keeping him together.

He jammed his fist in a lizard man's snout one last time before they pinned his arms and wrists down.

The orc stood over him and kicked him in the ribs. With its knife, it shaved the hair off his coarse arms. "Any final words, Dwarf?"

"It's raining," Brenwar said.

"Huh?" the orc grunted, holding out his palm, watching the rain splatter on it. "That's it. Sounds like you rattled his skull, men! Ha!"

They let out a round of throaty chuckles.

"I'm not finished," Brenwar growled.

"Oh, please do finish before you die."

"It's raining … Dwarves!"

Thoom! Thoom! Thoom! Thoom! Thoom! Thoom! Thoom! Thoom!

Dwarves fell out of the sky like giant bearded pumpkins and landed on the soldiers. Bone crunched. Guts squished. They started swinging and singing. The Soldiers of Barnabus were overwhelmed. And then the dwarves cried out at the same time.

"GRAADA-STOOK-SAAY!"

It was hot. Smothering. Nath was pinned down underneath the heavy burning beams. Fire engulfed everything around him. His eyes were filled with smoke. The fire was blistering hot. Painful. Agonizing. But dragons don't burn. Not by normal fire. But that didn't mean he couldn't suffocate and die.

He shoved up on the beams with all his strength. "Urk!"

The beams started to rise.

He gathered his knees under himself and put his back into it.

Push, Dragon! Push!

The air was thin. His head became dizzy. The hot lights started to dim. He started sagging toward the floor.

Crash!

The burning wood beneath him caved in and down he went into the crawl space beneath what was left of the assembly room floor. The movement of cool air greeted him. A glimpse of darkness gave him hope. He pushed away the burning beams and fought his way through the debris. Flames rolled under the flooring like a bright orange roof. Crawling on hands and knees, he headed out. Fiery holes emerged above him. The entire floor warped and crackled. He found the edge of the crawl space and kicked it open. Fire rushed out over him, feeding off the night air.

Nath felt his energy fleeing him and despair moving in. The flames had him. His fingers hung off the edge of the wood, and he moved no more.

Of all the ways to go.

Something seized his arm and dragged him through the hole and away from the flames. He figured one of those dragons was ready to take him apart one limb at a time. He could see the inferno now, blazing high. He gulped in a lungful of sweet night air. The rain felt delightful on his face. Strength returned to his limbs.

"Huh?" he said, looking back at the man that held his arm. "Ben!"

Ben heaved him up to his feet and slapped him on his back.

"You must weigh a ton!" Ben said. He reached behind his back and grabbed something.

Snap. Clatch. Snap.

Akron's string twirled up along the bow. Ben slipped an arrow from the quiver and nocked it.

Twang!

The arrow buried itself in the chest of a gnoll attacker.

"Are you finished resting yet?" Ben said, loading the string again.

Twang!

The arrow zipped into another.

There was fire, fighting and screaming all over. Dwarves slugged it out with the gnolls, orcs and lizard men. Overseer Dormus shouted orders to his men. Nath sprang to his feet.

"That's the one we want," he said to Ben. He took off at a run.

Dormus caught him out of the corner of his eye and gaped. Then his face turned to rage.

"Impossible!" the Overseer shouted. "Stop him! Stop him!" He wrapped his hand around the amulet and started chanting.

Nath lowered his shoulder and drove Dormus to the ground. He snapped the amulet off of Dormus's neck.

"You can't control it!" Dormus said. "It is I that controls the dragons. Dragons, come back to me!"

A dragon dangled Gorlee upside down with its tail and swung him gently like a chime. The other pair sniffed and snorted at him.

"Easy, dragons," Gorlee pleaded. "I'm not worth killing. It's those orcs—gah!"

One dragon snorted a blast of hot steam in his face.

Squawk!

Squawk!

Their eyes were intent on him. Intelligent. Murderous. One cocked its great neck. Ran its long tongue over him like wet fingers.

"Ewww," Gorlee shivered. *They're going to kill me. But I don't have to make it easy on them.*

One dragon inhaled a great breath. Another stepped back.

"No! No! Don't roast me!" He summoned his magic. Started to change his skin and bones to hard stone.

Whoosh!

Fiery dragon breath engulfed him from head to toe. The heat was so intense it felt like he was baking alive.

When the dragon finished, Gorlee crossed his arms over his chest. His stony skin smoldered and it hurt but he lived.

The dragons growled. The one that held him slammed him in the mud. Up and down. Up and down.

Smush!

Smush!

Smush!

Gorlee's breath left him. They were dragons and he was a mouse. Up in the air he went. He saw the sky, then the mud hole they made with him.

Squawk!

The dragon's long-necked head popped up and looked back toward the town.

Oh thank goodness!

Something had their attention. Two of the dragons headed back for town. The one that held him snapped at him, then flipped him high in the air.

I'm free! I'm free!

When Gorlee stopped at the zenith, he managed to turn and look down as he fell. The dragon was still there. Its great black tail behind its back was poised like a giant cobra.

"No, not again!"

As Gorlee approached the ground, the dragon's tail lashed out.

Whap!

Gorlee screamed and sailed, far and long, head over heels. "Aiiiyeeeeeee!"

CHAPTER

11

THE TIDE HAD TURNED. THE dwarves had routed the Soldiers of Barnubus. Nath had the Overseer by the throat and the amulet in his hand.

"Send the dragons away," Nath ordered.

"Never!" Dormus said. "I'll see our deaths first!"

Nath took the amulet and smashed it on a stone. The stone cracked.

Dormus laughed.

Squawk!

Squawk!

Squawk!

The dragons weren't far and he knew they moved fast. It would be open season on him and the dwarves.

"Brenwar," Nath yelled, "get over here!"

Brenwar pushed his way through the skirmish. Nath tossed the amulet on the ground.

"Smash it! Hurry!"

War Hammer went up and came down.

Krang!

The hammer hummed like a great chime, but the stone remained.

The dragons arrived. No sooner had they, than the dwarves initiated a full-scale assault. The first three of them were flung aside like toys. Others were stomped into the ground.

A white bolt shot from the sky.

Ka-Room!

A dragon roared. A smoking hole was in its side.

Bayzog hung in the air above. He yelled down. "I can't hold them off! Do something!"

The Elderwood Staff sparked to life. White-hot light blasted from it and smacked into another dragon.

One by one, the dragons' wings hummed to life and slowly they sailed up and surrounded Bayzog.

"Dragon," Ben said holding arrows, "I need your spit on these."

Nath spat on the tips. They glowed to life.

Ben nocked and fired.

Whiz—Boom!

The arrow exploded into one dragon's neck. It bucked in midair and crashed through the roof of a building below it.

Above, Bayzog tried to float away, but the dragons cut him off.

Nath couldn't get up there. He couldn't do anything. His friend would be dead any moment.

He slammed Dormus into the ground.

"Call them off!"

Dormus licked his bleeding lips and smiled. "No." The Overseer might not be that formidable, but he made it clear that he was stubborn as an orc and loyal as a hound to the cause of Barnubus.

Ben nocked another arrow.

"No," Nath said, "Bayzog's too close." Out of the corner of his eye, he caught Fang's dragon hilt glimmering on Ben's hip. He yanked his sword out.

It burned hot as a furnace on his fingers.

"No, Fang! I won't let go this time!"

Sweat burst on his forehead. He hefted the sword over his head with both hands. Even though it weighed a ton, resisting him, he brought the blade down on the amulet.

Dormus screamed.

The stone shattered with a gale-like blast of air, knocking everyone off their feet.

Nath still held the burning hot sword in his hands. "You need to trust me again, Fang!" He slid it in back in the sheath. Peeled off his smoking hands.

Bayzog floated down beside him.

"You did it," the elven wizard said. He pointed skyward. "See?"

The dragons landed, scurried through the muddy streets and disappeared into the farmland.

Nath saw a couple of smaller dragons fly through the night. "Did you see that?" Nath said.

Bayzog nodded.

Nath squeezed Bayzog's shoulder. The elf had a nasty gash on his arm.

"Is that a flesh wound I see on you?"

"Better a flesh wound than a death wound," Bayzog replied.

"Well it took you long enough to get here, Elf," Brenwar said. "We blew the Horn of Summons an age ago. What took you so long?"

"Dwarves are heavy. And the giant bats didn't like them. But they got them here, didn't they?"

"Humph."

"Of course, if I could summon dragons," Bayzog said, reaching down and picking up a shard of the amulet, "that would be fascinating. I need time to investigate this." He narrowed his violet eyes. "Interesting. It's warm. Almost living."

Everyone leaned in for a closer look.

"Say," Nath said, "where's Gorlee?"

Glitch!

Pain erupted in Nath's side.

Dormus had jammed a glowing dagger between Nath's ribs. "Death to Nath Dragon!" the Overseer yelled. "Death!"

CHAPTER

12

NARNUM. THE FREE CITY THAT wasn't so free anymore.

"Any news?" a woman said, looking over the balcony of the tallest tower in the city.

The tower stood hundreds of feet tall. The proud centerpiece of civilization that housed some of the finest citizens of Narnum and Nalzambor. The Clerics of Barnabus controlled it now. They came. They conquered. They hurled those who resisted from the tower, one right after the other. She could still hear their screams. Their terror. Lamentations.

A man approached from behind and stood at her side. She was a tall woman, but he was still much taller than she. A great heavy mace hung by his side. He had tattoos all over his forehead and some on his face. His voice was deep and powerful.

"Nay, my queen," he said. "No confirmation that he lives."

She turned toward him with narrowed eyes. Her black satin hair spilled over her shoulder. In her robes and décor she was everything a queen should be. An evil queen. She was Selene.

"You still can't help the flattery on your tongue, can you?" she said, placing her hand on his broad chest. "And after all that I have put you through."

He bowed his ugly head. "I worship you. That's why I die for you."

Selene chuckled and tipped up his chin. "Kryzak, you've done almost everything a queen could ever ask. You've conquered cities. Crushed our enemies. But you have not found me Nath Dragon."

Kryzak stiffened. His face snarled a little. "I am not the only one to fail. Just let me have one more chance," he pleaded. "One more chance to kill Nath Dragon."

Her black-scaled tail slid over to his cheek and stroked it.

Kryzak's hard face showed faint little scales. His great hands were like a lizard man's. She had killed him decades ago when he failed, and she had brought him back part draykis.

"These scales have served you well, Kryzak, but I will not waste my creation in vain." Her tail fell away from his cheek and rested on the balcony's edge. "We've conquered most cities, but now a glimmer of hope remains. Gorn Grattack is not pleased. Dragon Home still stands. Nath Dragon still lives." Her clawed fingers dug into the rail. "We cannot have this."

A dragon swooped by. It was coppery in color, with a black tail and faintly glowing eyes. Bigger than a man, it perched itself on one of the towers nearby. It wasn't alone either. Dozens of dragons sat perched and flying through the city like great birds of prey.

One dove into the streets, snatched a man up from the ground, and dropped him a hundred feet.

Selene chuckled. It was her way of keep a firm grip on things.

"I found him before, Selene. Let me find him again. With the aid of the dragons—"

"No," she said. "Come with me."

She went back inside her room and made her way to a map of Nalzambor on the wall. Bright spots sparkled in a variety of places.

"These villages and towns are where it is rumored that he was seen. He's smart. They move all over this world like ghosts. But now, I've placed more dragons inside these nuisance cities." She frowned. "He'll hit one of them soon enough, and when he does, we'll be ready. He can't hide forever."

"Then can I take him?"

A small feathered dragon flew inside and landed on a large perch that hung from the ceiling above the map. It stretched its neck out.

"Ah, my pet returns," Selene said, stroking its feathers. "And it has a little something in its mouth."

It purred.

She removed something from its mouth. A small glass bottle with a note in it. The tiny scroll became larger the more she unrolled it. It had an image of a man on it and a map below it.

"Humph," she said, handing it to Kryzak. "Is this who I think it is?"

He took the scroll and stared at it. "Aye, it's Nath Dragon, and he's just outside the settlement. This is great news. I will not delay."

"No, Kryzak," she said, snatching back the scroll. "I need you here. I'll send my own dragons out to play."

CHAPTER

13

"STAY PUT," BAYZOG SAID, HOLDING Nath down by the shoulder.

They were inside one of the homes of the settlement. Nath lay on a small bed with his head propped up by some pillows. For the past two days, Bayzog and some others had been tending to Nath. The wound Overseer Dormus had given him was deep. Nath's situation had turned grave.

"I want to see Dormus," Nath said, brushing the long hair from his face. He coughed. "I have questions I want answered."

"Brenwar is handling that," Bayzog reminded him. "You need to keep your blood down. The poison still works its magic yet."

Nath snarled and grunted.

The healthy gleam he always had in his face had faded, but it had been much worse a day ago. The mortal wound had put Nath into a coma of sorts. They had applied salves and administered potions but nothing took at first. Anyone else struck by the blade would have certainly died from it by then.

"Have you made anything of that blade yet?" Nath said. He reached over, coughing, and grabbed a jug of water. "How did that sluggard come to acquire it? It's almost as if that blade was designed for me."

Bayzog plucked the blade out of a nearby table. "It's a Dragon Skinner. You know them well. Usually, the Clerics lend them out to poachers, with strings attached, of course."

Nath sneered and held out his hand. Dragon Skinners were made by the Clerics of Barnabus from enchanted and carved dragon claws. It was said that a well-forged one could peel an eyelid from a gnat and the edge was difficult to notch or chip.

"Let me see it."

Bayzog hesitated. His friend had been in bad shape, the worst he'd ever seen him. Yet it didn't seem possible that such a small blade could kill him. It was several inches long with a stout blade and handle with two notches on the end. He handed it to Nath, who eyed it with suspicion.

"Strange. I remember it had a glow to it. Like a firefly." He flipped it around in his hand and thumbed the edge.

"Nath!"

"What? It can't still be poisoned, can it?" He coughed again. Harder this time. His face flashed in pain. He stuck it back in the table. "I hate those blades. And those Clerics."

"Me too," Bayzog agreed. He lifted his robes over his toes, sat down in a chair by the bed, and thought about the dragons they'd seen flying away the night of the battle. At the time, he had assumed they were flying off because they no longer were under the power of the crystal amulet. But given the evidence now, he wasn't so sure. "I think we have some problems that need discussing."

"Go on," Nath said.

Bayzog leaned forward with his black brows furrowed.

"They're on to us. Why else would they let someone like Dormus have an enchanted Dragon Skinner? The evil curse of a Cleric of Barnabus is what poisoned it. The evil courses through the blood and right into the heart. It can kill," his eyes flicked up at Nath's, "or corrupt."

"I'm fine, Bayzog," Nath assured him.

Bayzog wanted to believe it. Nath's behavior had been nothing short of brave and exemplary of late. Still, it seemed Nath had taken the bait. Placed everyone in danger. He'd been sent to scout, but something had gotten to him. He should have waited. Bayzog let it go. *He's done well. I'll trust him for now.* He reached inside his robes, grabbed something, and tossed it on the bed. It was a shard from the amulet. The light was dim that once glowed.

Nath picked it up, inspected it, and said, "What do you make of this?"

"It's crystal from beneath the cities that float above the rivers."

"What? Floating cities?"

"They're near the river cities far in the west. I've never seen them, but I've come across the histories plenty. These crystals store magic and hold it a long time. I believe the Clerics of Barnabus have cast spells in them that control and charm the dragons." He leaned back. "At least, the dragons who are not willing." He ran his fingers over the wound on his head. "The dragons, to my good fortune, weren't entirely evil."

"But they had black tails," Nath said. "Are you saying the black-tailed dragons aren't all evil? They didn't have black tails before."

It was a good question. Bayzog wasn't entirely certain about it either. Dragons, good or evil, had personalities of their own. Just because they were aligned with evil didn't mean they would do everything they were told.

"I think they had to follow the commands of Dormus, but when the spell was broken, they decided to conduct other business they might have been given."

"That being?" Nath said, toying with the shard.

"I suppose they were looking for you."

Nath's expression didn't change. They both knew it was only a matter of time before the Clerics of Barnabus figured out who was behind the raids, but at least he and his friends had managed to fortify some of the forces of good in the land.

Nath sat up with a groan, holding his side. "We'd best be leaving then, Bayzog."

They'd spent enough time in the settlement. However, they always waited for help before leaving, and no soldiers or Legionnaires had yet arrived.

Nath made his way over toward the door and donned his cloak. "You coming?"

"Where are we going? To liberate another city? The risk, I fear, is too great. And you aren't fully well yet." Bayzog waited. He wanted to see what Nath decided. He was the one who had led them this far, and they'd accomplished much for it. But what would his next step be?

Nath folded is arms across his chest. "Do you really think they have dragons in every town, village, and city?"

"Their numbers are great and the black-tailed dragon sightings are increasing. Sasha says they pass through the skies like flocks of birds." It was Bayzog's turn to sigh. He missed Sasha. His sons. It had been far too long since he'd seen them. "The good dragons are sights unseen."

"The good dragons burrow. Wait." Nath shook his head. Disappointment marred his face. "Good for them." He leaned against the door. "If we've been rousted, then maybe it's time to try another tactic." He tossed the shard to Bayzog. "I think it's time we learned more about these stones. Get to the heart of who's creating the amulets. Dragons should not be so easy to control."

Bayzog agreed. "They just need to be a little willing, Nath. The rest is surprisingly easy."

"Are you saying it's easy to control people?"

Bayzog went after the Elderwood Staff that leaned in the corner of the room. Its polished wood felt soft in his hand. He tapped it on the floor.

"The heart is easily misled. It wants what it wants and can fall prey to that. To a mouse, it's all the cheese it can eat. To a dragon, all the precious stones it can have. A dwarf, precious metals. These things don't fill you, but these things can fool you. Evil promises all of that …"

"… but it's love and goodwill that last forever," Nath said, finishing Bayzog's sentence. "Yes, I know. It's not the first time I've heard that." His gold eyes brightened. "I say we head east to this floating city. Maybe we can put a stop to some of this. It can't be easy to mine those crystals. It must take special skill to do that."

Bayzog nodded. "It will be heavily guarded and very risky."

"So is everything else," Nath said, opening the door. "Perhaps our prisoner can add some insight to this."

An ancient dwarf stood in the doorway, ready to knock. He had a worried look about him.

"Gorlee?" Nath said. "What's wrong?"

"Overseer Dormus … he's escaped."

CHAPTER

14

"BRENWAR, WHAT HAPPENED?" NATH SAID.

The town didn't have a jail or a dungeon, but a barn had been set up with stockades and chains that dangled from pegs mounted into the posts and rafters. One of the stockades was open. Brenwar had a deep crease between his eyes, and his bearded face frowned. Two dwarven warriors lay on the floor. There was blood in the hay and they weren't moving. Several dwarves were gathered around. Some of the townsfolk were inside as well. Brenwar didn't reply.

Gorlee and Bayzog had sad looks in their eyes.

"Were they sleeping?" Bayzog said.

"No dwarf ever sleeps on his post," Brenwar growled. "Something tricked them. Magic." He kneeled down beside them. His thick shoulders sagged and he closed his eyes. "I'll avenge this. We'll catch that Overseer and kill him."

An orc prisoner snickered. One of the commanders. He was one of a few Soldiers of Barnabus that still lived. His hands were bound behind a post. The others rattled their chains, laughing from the floor.

Nath made his way over to him. His blood was boiling. "Who did this?"

The orc licked his lips and looked up at him through a busted eye. "Someone that did what should have been done. Killed the little bearded halflings like sleeping children." The orc smiled. "I thanked them, I did."

Nath drew back his fist.

Gorlee caught his arm. The changeling was strong as a dwarf, even in his ancient form. "We'll find them," Gorlee said. "We don't need his help and they haven't been so long gone anyway. Ease yourself, Nath."

Nath pulled his arm away. He got in the orc's face. Eye to eye. "Who did this? The Overseer, or someone else?"

"Ha!" The orc spat on the ground. "Even if I saw everything, I wouldn't tell you." The orc stretched his muscles against the bonds that had him chained to the post. His hairy chest swelled. He sneered with his chin jutted. "And you couldn't make me, Demon."

Nath had heard that word before, but it had been a long time. Sometimes, he forgot he'd been asleep for twenty-five years. They had called him a demon in Quinley and Quinktuklen. He hadn't liked it then, either. He grabbed the orc by the metal collar on its neck and lifted it to its toes.

"Are you sure you don't want to tell me anything?"

The orc chuckled, snorted, and spat at him.

Hock-too!

Nath shifted his head aside. Avoiding it.

He hated orcs and it wasn't the first or last time they'd tried to spit on him.

"Let me take him," Pilpin said. "I'll beat the answers from him! Beat him like a castle rug, I will."

The dwarves stirred. Their faces were angry. Anytime a dwarf died, they took it personally. It was even worse when the crime was in cold blood. This wasn't a battle. It was murder. It was a wonder the imprisoned soldiers weren't already in pieces.

"Heh, heh," the orc said. "Go ahead. Turn the little one loose on me. I'll squash his fuzzy head."

Nath stepped in the way and the dwarves held Pilpin back.

"Unbind him," Nath said.

The orc's eyes got wide. "What is this?"

"A game."

"What sort of game?" the orc said with his throaty voice.

"Let's call it a game of strikes."

The orc cocked his head.

A dwarf grumbled and unbound the orc's hands.

It rubbed its wrists and spat again, yellow eyes wary. "Keep talking, Demon."

Demon. No, Nath still didn't like that word. The fact that the orc said it was worse. It was something the Soldiers of Barnabus had been told to use against him, he assumed. Paint a picture of the hero as a demon. Put doubts in the minds of women, children and men.

"I'll give you the first strike." Nath stuck out his chin and tapped it with his finger. "If you knock me out, you win. You and your men can have your freedom. If you don't knock me out, I get to hit you back." He stepped over to the post the orc had been tethered to a moment earlier and took aim with his fist.

The orc grunted.

Nath balled his fist, cocked his arm back and punched the heavy post.

Wham!

The post broke and doubled over.

Crack!

The roof sagged. The entire barn shook. Hay fell from the rafters.

The orc's eyes were as wide as ever. He cringed a little.

"Now remember, Orc," Nath said, dusting his hands, "you get the first shot. Make it a good one. If it doesn't work, then it's my turn. Just hope my strike won't kill you."

The orc took a giant swallow, balled up his fists and raised them up. Sweat dripped from his heavy brows. His eyes drifted over to his wide-eyed men.

"You aren't scared to hit me, are you?"

The orc lowered his shoulder and shifted his feet. His eyes were hard and ready. His fists looked like they could hammer nails, with callouses and scars all over them. He'd probably cracked a few skulls with them. He cocked back his elbow and started to swing.

Nath grinned.

The orc dropped his fist and blurted out, "It was the satyrs! It was the satyrs!" He fell to his knees. "Please don't hit me in the face. Please!"

CHAPTER

14

ON HORSEBACK, NATH AND COMPANY rode from the settlement and beyond the farmlands. It was quiet. The skies were darkened by grey clouds, and a cold drizzle fell all around them. Nath led, his keen eyes picking up on the satyrs' hoof prints. There were two of them and Dormus must have been riding on horseback with them. The gait between the tracks was long. They'd galloped and fled, through the farmlands and into the mountains.

Nath pulled his horse to a halt and hopped off. It jolted his side and it burned a little.

"What are you stopping for?" Brenwar said, pulling a small horse beside him. "We need to keep moving."

"I don't want to lose the tracks," Nath said, putting his hand in an impression in the ground. He glanced at the sky. "Heavy rains are coming. We'll catch them, Brenwar."

"We should have caught them already." He led his horse away, barked an order to the dwarves, and made a bead for the mountain range.

Ben, Bayzog and Gorlee sat on their horses, staring at him. Gorlee's dwarven expression was sad. Ben's stern face with its solid demeanor was still something Nath was getting used to. It was hard to believe Ben the rugged warrior was the farm boy who had followed him ... well, more than twenty-five years ago. Bayzog had his arms tucked inside his robes. Always polished and refined, his skin and robes were more like a scuffed up piece of pottery. His shoulders were heavier and his violet eyes carried power and confidence.

Nath stood up and stretched out his arms. Eyed the dwarves that were riding away. Brenwar was a fine tracker. He didn't need Nath to track down the satyrs. The dwarves were more than capable of doing that on their own.

"I know what you're thinking, Bayzog."

Bayzog's sharp brows popped up. "Well if you can read minds, then how can any enemy stand against us?"

Ben and Gorlee chuckled.

"No," Nath smiled a bit, "that's not what I mean. You think we should depart from this pursuit, don't you."

"Absolutely."

"What?" Ben said. "And let those murderers run free? They killed our friends in cold blood! There is not a more heinous crime than that. The dwarves were sleeping!"

Nath's neck muscles tensed. He agreed a hundred percent. Justice needed to be served. But it wasn't always up to him to dispense it.

"Dwarvenkind can take care of dwarvenkind," Nath said.

"What!" Ben said, his face filling with fury. "Am I hearing you right? You're going to abandon your friends? Brenwar and his men need our help. They might be riding into greater danger."

"Yes," Bayzog agreed, "they probably are riding into greater danger. We all are."

"Ben," Nath said, "if you want to go with the dwarves, you can."

"No," Ben shot back, "We are staying together!"

"Ben, we all have the same enemies here."

"Do we?" Ben said. His voice was deep and angry. He pointed to the mountains. "My enemies are that way."

"Our enemies are everywhere," Gorlee said, his bright eyes shining. "And they close in. This pursuit is dangerous. There is no reason for satyrs to come to the aid of a single Overseer. Or to murder the likes of dwarves in cold blood."

Ben's demeanor softened a little. "They incite us?"

"Aye," Nath said, dejected. It was a hard thing to admit. So many had sacrificed so much over the years. They'd given life and limb. There was nothing Nath wanted to do more than put an end to all of it. "As much as I hate to say it, Ben, our battle needs to be fought elsewhere. This is bigger than tracking down and punishing a couple of satyrs and a simple Overseer. The game board is much bigger than that. Our moves must be well planned and executed."

Ben's horse nickered.

"But the dwarves?"

"The dwarves will do what the dwarves want to do. Have you ever met a dwarf doing something he didn't want to do?"

Ben shrugged his shoulders. "How can you tell? They're so moody."

Nath laughed. "They like being moody. You should know that by now."

"So," Ben said, "what are you planning?"

Nath looked at Bayzog. "We're going east to the river lands. We need to investigate the crystals that our enemies use to control the dragons."

"Wouldn't that kind of resource be well fortified?"

"We're certain of it," Bayzog said.

"You don't need to come, Ben. You can pursue the satyrs all you want. You've been with the dwarves a long time."

Ben shifted in his saddle. "I don't know, Dragon."

A thunder of hooves started their way. It was Brenwar. His beard waved like black smoke in the wind. His horse came to a halt.

"I know what you're thinking!" Brenwar yelled at Nath. "I know every bit."

"It seems we have two mind-readers now," Bayzog said.

"Watch yourself, Elf!" Brenwar turned back to Nath. "Are you planning on sharing your plan?"

"Well—"

"Well, nothing! I could see your back wasn't in it when we started moving. I thought your gray matter was going to fall out, from thinking so hard," Brenwar bellowed out like a minotaur gone mad.

Everyone covered their ears.

Brenwar finished red-faced with a heavy sigh.

Alarm filled the eyes of all around him.

Brenwar faced Nath. "You aren't going anywhere without me." He grunted. "And where you go, I'll follow. We'll all follow."

"I can't ask that of you and the dwarves. You have a blood hunt to fulfill."

"Since when do you think you have the right to ask a dwarf to do anything? We do what we want to. When and how we want to." He held up and flexed his arm. It was thick and knotty like an oak. "Ask. Pah!"

"I don't think it's best that we all go where we're going."

"So you want my dwarves to chase whilst we evade."

"It's not a bad idea," Bayzog said. "And night will fall soon."

"I'd like to go with the dwarves," Gorlee said. "I'd be curious to see what the enemy has in store for us. And I can throw them off course." His form changed from dwarf to Nath Dragon.

"Well, one thing's for certain. I can never see enough of me." Nath laughed. Pain shot between his ribs. He fought against his grimace. "Ben, do you want to come with us or go with the dwarves?"

Ben sat tall in the saddle. Shoulders back, chin up. Nothing short of a formidable warrior. It made Nath feel good that Ben was on his side and had always been.

"Seeing how dwarves aren't much for conversation, I guess I'll go with you, Dragon."

CHAPTER

15

"THEY SLOW. WAIT. HESITATE," FINLIN the satyr said. He stomped his hoof rapidly on the ground. "We should stretch the distance. They may track in the night as well."

His sister Faylan stood with her fists on her hips nearby. Her hoof dug in the ground.

"The rain comes down, Little Brother. It washes our tracks. Gives them little to follow." She combed her fingers between the horns on her head. "We need to keep the trail fresh. Fresh enough for them to follow."

"Do you really think Nath Dragon will fall for that?" Overseer Dormus said, sitting perched on his saddle. "I say we stretch the distance like he says. I don't want to be around when those dwarves catch up with us." He scoffed. "After what we did." He eyed the satyrs. "Rather, after what you two did. Killing them. There'll be no such mercy shown to us."

"Ha!" Faylan said. She paced around Dormus and his mount. "You fear them? The dwarves? Have you not yet met the High Priestess of Barnabus, Selene? Failing her is a far worse thing." She pulled out a dagger. "She'll turn your thews into harp strings."

"Those are stories," Dormus said. "Told by the likes of you to frighten children. I know all about you two. Faylan and Finlin. The lowly spies. Dreaded henchmen." He swung his horse around, bumping Faylan.

"You dare!"

"I am an Overseer."

Faylan's eyes narrowed. Finlin knew that look. It was murder. Over the decades, his sister had become one of Selene's most loyal hounds. Cold blooded. Calculating. She'd been underestimated before. She lived. Her enemies didn't. Finlin trotted between them.

"Yes," Dormus said. "Protect your kin, little satyr. I figure you keep her oversized mouth out of plenty of trouble." He eyed Faylan. "Let me tell you something, you little horned goat. That man ... or dragon, whatever he is, should be dead. I delivered a lethal blow. Yet, he still breathes. And he's coming for me. He's coming for us. Let us put more distance and safety between us and him."

"I thought you said the blade you used was poisoned," Faylan said.

"Indeed it was. With a curse. A drop of evil that will one day take form, but I know not when. I don't want to be anywhere near him in the meantime. We keep moving. Through the dark if we have to."

"Your plan is my plan, Sister," Finlin said.

She shoved his chest. "My plan is the only plan. We wait. You will wait as well, Coward," she said to Dormus, reaching into a leather pouch that hung on her hip and pulling a tiny figure out. She had a pixie pinched by its wings. It was a small one. Maybe six inches tall. A she with skin like a pale pink rose. A tiny golden collar was on her neck. "Little one. Spy out the dwarves. Come back to us when they move again."

The little thing nodded her head of white wispy hair.

"Let me see that!" Dormus demanded, leaning forward. He pushed his greasy hair back over his head. "I've always wanted my own pixie."

Faylan held the pixie up before his eyes and shook the tiny thing. Fairy dust sprinkled in the air.

Dormus leaned back, blinking his eyes, and sneezed. "Achoo!" His eyes became dreamy, his limbs loose. He fell out of his saddle.

"What did you do that for?" Finlin said, aggravated. His sister always had to pull one over on someone. "He'll not wake up for a day."

She released the pixie.

Zing.

It was gone.

Sighing, Finlin walked over and pulled Dormus's foot out of the stirrup and then rolled him onto his back. His face was covered in mud and his nose was bent.

Faylan laughed. "Good. A shame his jaw is not busted as well."

"We can't move quickly with him in this condition. They'll gain on us for certain."

She tossed her knife to Finlin.

"Who says we still need him?"

CHAPTER

16

BEFORE THE BREAK OF DAY the next morning, Nath, Bayzog, Ben and Brenwar were on the move. They rode east until the sun was hot on their backs and then stopped for water at a stream. Everyone was quiet. Bayzog sat in his saddle with his staff crossed over his lap. Ben refilled canteens with water. Brenwar stood by his mount, not moving at all, staring at the ground. The dwarf hadn't made the slightest complaint or suggestion to Nath about anything.

Nath wasn't used to that. But he also wasn't used to feeling the heaviness in Brenwar's heart. Murder, such as things were, had always been a rare occurrence in Nalzambor. Things had changed indeed.

Nath made his way over to Ben and refilled his own canteen.

"This would be a nice place for fishing," Nath said.

"Indeed," Ben said, slinging his canteens over his shoulders. He looked into the sky. "We don't have many days like this it seems. Clear skies and warm weather when it's usually cold or wet. It almost makes me uncomfortable."

"Has the weather really changed that much while I slept?"

"It's certainly gotten darker, or at least I think it has. I'm just so used to it." Ben led his horse to the water. "I'll be honest, Dragon. Things do seem brighter since you're back. Dwarves haven't started to smile or anything, but some of the other folks have."

Nath waded into the waters. It always felt like he became a part of Nalzambor whenever he did so. As if life was rushing through him. He felt like he was part of something. Something good. He dunked his head under. Watched the fish swim by and scatter. There didn't even seem to be as many fish as before. He popped up, slung his red hair over his shoulder, and wrung it out.

He watched the water slide off his scales that seemed to sparkle like coal in the light. It fascinated him. Even though it had been over a year, he still hadn't had much time to get acquainted with his new body yet.

He sloshed out of the water toward Bayzog. The wizard's eyes were full of inquiry.

"My side's fine," Nath said.

"So you *are* a mind reader."

"No, I'm a good study. You know that." He looked over at Brenwar. The dwarf hadn't budged an inch. Nath said to Bayzog, "Any suggestions?"

Bayzog's narrow shoulders offered a little shrug.

The group had been fighting hard for months. Planning. Executing. Day and night. It was exhausting. Now that they had a few spare moments, it seemed no one knew what to do with themselves. He wasn't so certain either.

"Will somebody say something?" Nath said, exasperated. "Anything at all?"

Brenwar pulled himself back into his saddle with a grunt.

Ben did the same.

"You lead," Bayzog said, turning his horse east, "We follow."

The statement was matter-of-fact. Chilling to some degree. Nath moved over to his horse and stuffed his clawed foot in the stirrup.

"Who *are* you people?" he said, pulling himself up.

Ben's brown eyes brightened a little.

"Well," Nath said, "whoever you are, it's good you recognize a good leader when you see one." He snapped the reins. "Yah!"

CHAPTER

17

ORLEE AND PILPIN KNEELED OVER the corpse of Overseer Dormus. Two knife wounds were in his chest. His eyes were closed.

"He was sleeping," Pilpin said. He stretched himself up to almost a full four feet in height. "They slaughtered him the same as our brethren."

The other dwarves grumbled. Some were sitting and sharpening their axes. Others waited on horseback.

"Should we bury him?" Gorlee said, checking the surrounding trees and branches.

"Let the critters have him," one dwarf said. Many others nodded and grunted confirmation.

It surprised Gorlee. Though dwarves had no love for their enemies, a proper burial was given when time and circumstances permitted.

"I'll bury him," said another dwarf, walking over with a shovel. He had a square-ish battle helmet on with a horn in the middle of it. One eye was missing and half his fingers were gone. He shoveled his little shovel into the soft dirt. "No sense in stinking up the woods."

Grumbling, some of the other dwarves got up and pitched in. Shovels and picks were digging and swinging. Minutes later, a hole big enough for three men was finished. One by one, they pulled each other out.

Gorlee gaped. He'd seen the dwarves dig plenty of graves over the years, but every time they did, it amazed him. It was as if their tools were magic.

In a single heave, two dwarves tossed Dormus's body into the deep grave. The dwarves started filling the hole with dirt, and minutes later it was done.

"Now what?" Pilpin said, getting into the saddle of his horse. It wasn't just any horse either. It was the biggest one of them all. The dwarven saddle had three sets of double stirrups that helped them get on and off. "The wounds were the same as our brethren's. The satyrs must be behind all this."

"Indeed," Gorlee said. He scanned all the dwarven faces. Not a one would be turning from any of this. The satyrs had poked them in the eye. The dwarves would make them pay for this.

But the dwarves were all looking at him. Waiting. Gorlee was scratching his hairy chin when it hit him. They weren't looking to Gorlee. They were looking to Nath Dragon.

"We keep tracking them, of course," Gorlee said.

The biggest dwarf led the way. His armor was covered down to his chest in brown hair and beard. His dark green eyes were penetrating and inquisitive. He went by Devliik because his dwarven name was too long.

Gorlee followed along quietly in the middle. His thoughts were heavy and his instincts wary. This was the first time he'd taken on a mission without Brenwar, Ben or Bayzog, and though he'd been around a long time, the chameleons weren't the most responsible people. Their awesome shape-shifting power pretty much allowed them to do whatever they wanted while easily avoiding harm to themselves. He shivered. The recent encounter with the six-legged bluu dragons had shaken him up. His ribs were still plenty sore from it.

They wound through the mountains at a brisk pace, with Devliik stopping to dig at the ground from time to time. All the dwarves were silent and hard-faced, their determined debating character dulled by the tragedy that had happened to their brethren at the settlement. Gorlee felt for them. He wasn't used to losing family. None of his kind had ever died and he'd never spent enough time with the mortal races to get attached to any before. The chameleons were very reclusive. Small in number. For the most part, they only mixed with the other races to humor themselves.

Gorlee stretched out his fingers in front of him. The black scales and claws were each a unique color that he'd only been able to master by being close to Nath. He wondered what that felt like, being a dragon, the most powerful creature in all the world. Much like Bayzog, it was his fascination with dragonkind that drew him out into the world. That and the danger that had grown after Nath Dragon disappeared. He clenched his fist. He could feel power in it.

I wonder how much power Nath feels. It must be great, but miserable that he can't unleash it.

He'd seen the struggle in Nath's face. The fire that built and had to be extinguished. Having to pull back against mortal enemies that did not draw such a line seemed an impossible feat. Yet Nath did it and he handled it well at that.

If I had that kind of power ... oh mercy. He shook his head. *I don't think I could do that. There would be rows of corpses in my tracks.* He looked at his hands again. *How does he do it!*

"How does who do what?" Pilpin said.

"What do you mean?" Gorlee said. "Did you hear me thinking?"

"No, but I looked over and your lips were moving."

"Interesting."

"I see people doing that a lot. Talking to themselves."

"I wasn't talking to myself," Gorlee corrected, "I was thinking to myself."

"Aye, but your lips were moving."

Gorlee eyed Pilpin. "That's a special gift you have, reading lips."

Pilpin eyed him back. "Not as special as yours." Pilpin adjusted himself in the saddle. "So how does who do what?"

"I just don't understand how Nath contains all that power he has. With that kind of power, I'd decimate the Clerics every time I crossed them. Wouldn't you?"

"I do anyway," Pilpin said, patting the weapons hooked over his saddle. And then nodding, he said, "Nath wasting his power seems stupid to me, too."

They kept riding. Gorlee's forehead was creased between his brows. Taking Nath's form seemed different than taking other forms, somehow. It made him want to be more responsible. Careful. Normally, he was carefree and easy, but inside him things had changed.

I'm not sure if I can get used to this or not.

He felt like he had to help the dwarves find their tormentors. He wanted to help them. Prevent any more harm from coming to them. And being curious, he wanted to see face to face what such an evil person would be like. One who killed both enemy and ally with no remorse whatsoever. He pulled his shoulders back and kept his head high. *I can do this.*

Later, Devliik the dwarf came to a stop and the rest of the party gathered round. The brown-faced dwarf directed his comments to Gorlee.

"They split up. One heads toward the top of the mountains and the other heads below."

"Are we gaining any ground on them?"

"A little," he spit tobacco juice from his mouth, "perhaps that's why they split."

Gorlee noticed that all the dwarves were looking at him again. He felt awkward. *This is tiring!*

"Uh," Gorlee said.

"Uh," Devliik said back, glaring a little.

His Nath Dragon form was confusing them perhaps. He confused himself, but he felt compelled to make a decision. *Make it a good one.*

"Follow one or the other, Devliik," Gorlee said. "We'll stay together."

"Uh-huh," Devliik said. He spat again. He combed his fingers through his beard, turned and climbed back into his saddle. He said something in dwarven and lurched forward.

Down the hill they went.

Pilpin was looking back at him. "You coming?"

Gorlee nodded and nudged his mount onward.

Am I in charge of this thing now? Wouldn't the higher ground be better? I should've paid more attention to Brenwar.

The pink pixie hovered at Faylan the satyr's ear.

"I see," she said, opening her pouch.

The pixie dropped inside and ducked out of sight.

Faylan closed the flap and tied it down.

She stood in a narrow ravine at the bottom of the mountains. Water ran down the middle of it and wound through great rocks covered in moss and then ran out of sight. She splashed through the creek around the next bend. Mossy rocks, green trees and lush foliage stretched up both sides of the massive crevasse. The creek water flowed over her hooves and straight ahead as far as the eye could see.

She scanned both sides. Nothing out of the ordinary appeared. Wild life chirted and hooted all around. Bugs buzzed in the air. They traveled a little farther until a rustle in the foliage lifted her ears. She turned. A rock started to move and take a humanoid form. Boulder-shaped hands revealed sharp claws. A head the size of a small boulder revealed a row of sharp teeth. It was a draykis. Covered in grey scales and heavy muscles.

"Do they come this way or the other?" it said,

"They come this way," she said. "But both paths lead to death."

"The High Priestess doesn't want Nath Dragon dead," the draykis said. "But the dwarves are of no consequence."

"I know this," Faylan said with a sneer. "Just secure our spot."

The draykis stretched out a paw big enough to envelop her head.

She stood her ground and patted the amulet on her neck.

"Don't even think of such an offense. I'll have you declawed."

Slowly, it pulled its arm back. "Don't be so sure of yourself," it warned, slipping back into its spot. "Death comes to all from many corners."

She started to back down the stream. "Just see to it that you and the rest of your kind are ready."

She heard a laugh of sorts from the foliage.

There were two draykis in the woods for every dwarf. But the Nath Dragon factor she wasn't so sure of.

She made her way up the bank and tucked herself away in the bushes.

Certainly, there are enough of us.

She smiled.

And if not, I've another trick up my sleeve.

CHAPTER

18

EAST. CLOUDS. THROUGH STIFF WIND and stinging rain they galloped. Ben was right: the good pauses in the weather didn't last very long. Still, the travel hadn't been difficult. Nath's biggest concern was encountering adversaries. The enemy seemed to have eyes and ears everywhere and when they passed people, they said little to them or nothing at all. Nath kept them in single file most of the time. Quiet. Halfway into the next day, he slowed to a trot.

"Shouldn't we traverse the mountains?" Bayzog suggested more than asked.

"You can't gallop in the mountains," Nath said.

"You can't hide in plain view either," Bayzog responded.

"Well that's what we have you for. Certainly you can hide us?"

"Well, I suppose—"

"It's a joke, Bayzog," Nath said. "Stop riding so close to Brenwar."

Bayzog showed him an unhappy look. "I don't think we need to make haste to get there."

"Well, I'm excited to go somewhere different. And I don't like looking back."

Bayzog rode closer along his side. "What do you mean?"

"This is difficult. We are leaving so many opportunities behind. The people. Who will protect the people?" Nath said.

"Thanks to you and our efforts as well, more people are starting to take better care of themselves." Bayzog poked him in the shoulder with his staff. "You can't protect them all. But you can give them courage. And this isn't all about them, Nath. What about the dragons. How shall we liberate them?"

Nath nodded. All his life, he'd dedicated himself to protecting the dragons. Lately, he'd been more focused on saving people. But there were more people than dragons. And the dragons were really well hidden. He hadn't even seen a good one since he'd woken up from his last hibernation. He hoped they were at Dragon Home. A pit formed in his stomach.

Nath forced a smile.

"Are you truly worried about galloping in the open, Bayzog, or is this about something else? After all, I thought I was leading."

"I just fear the skies have eyes."

"The forest has even more."

Bayzog nodded. He seemed content. Perhaps he just wanted to make conversation.

Nath continued. "If we're in no rush, maybe we should go to Quintuklen. I'd like to see Sasha."

Bayzog's hand went to an amulet that was hidden under his robes. Nath had seen him use it to communicate with Sasha several times before. He knew that Bayzog could hear her voice, but didn't know if he could see her too. Nath wished he could see her. There was nothing better than her company. It would warm a day like this.

"Don't tempt me, Nath. And don't tempt yourself. You are leading, after all."

"Well, we'll see this through first. And we'll reward ourselves with a trip to see Sasha."

The tight-lipped wizard showed all his teeth with his smile.

"Easy," Nath said, blocking his eyes with his hand, "You'll blind me. I hope our enemies didn't see that smile."

"I hope they did. The sooner we deal with them, the sooner I can see Sasha." Bayzog dug his heels into his mount. The horse reared up. "Onward."

They galloped through the plains, staying just outside the edges of the forests and the mountains. Nalzambor was a vast world and it wasn't uncommon for Nath to travel sight unseen for days. Their enemies, though great in number, couldn't control everything. What they could control were the places where most of the people were gathered. The largest cities had fallen victim to that already. At least that was what Nath had been told. No one wanted him to get too close to those cities. Those places tended to get him into trouble, and he could admit to that now.

Narnum and Quintuklen were lost. The dwarves in Morgdon held their own and the Elves in Elome battled with the orcs from Thraag daily to maintain their foothold. The people of the world went about their daily lives the best they could. Some fought for good. Others were recruited by evil. Families were split and divided. Seeing the change in people left Nath's heart heavy. So much had changed in such a little time. He was astounded by it all.

They galloped until the first light of the moon, slowed, and then trotted in the shadows of the mountains.

"Jordak's Crossing nears," Bayzog said to Nath. He sounded concerned.

"Since when did you become such a world traveler?"

"It's been twenty-five years, remember?"

Nath felt a little small for a moment. The Bayzog he'd known had spent all of his time inside the walls of his home. The elven wizard had been anything but inside ever since. He'd even become adept at hunting and fishing.

"Have you gotten accustomed to swimming yet?"

"Humph," Bayzog said. "I've gotten accustomed to many things that would surprise you."

"You've surprised me plenty already." Nath turned to Ben, who had drifted back along their side. "Have you been to Jordak's Crossing as well?"

Ben shook his head. "No, should I have been?"

"No."

"Nath," Bayzog said, "the Crossing is not what it once was. Our enemies control that spot. Just as well as most of the major bridges and intersections."

"Your point being?"

"There are other ways across."

"And I was counting on the fact that you didn't know that," Nath said with a smile. "I'm certain we can handle any obstacles in our path. Besides, any other avenue would be two more days out of the way."

"The war is long," Bayzog said. "We need patience."

"My patience thins," Nath said. "But I'm willing to entertain your worries, Wizard. Let's ride and get a better look at your concerns."

Hours later, in the dark, they stood on the edge of a deep chasm overlooking a river of what looked like lava. Nath could see its shadowy glow in his friends' faces. Hard lines. The river Jordak was the only river of its kind. Its bright bubbling waters disintegrated skin from bone, and withered away bone thereafter. There was no swimming in the Jordak. There were no boats that crossed it either. The heat rising up from it felt like a fireplace, even from here.

Nath wiped the sweat from his brow and stepped away.

Ben held his nose. "Ew, that sulfurous smell is so strong. Do any fish swim in that thing?"

"Some things live within," Nath said, "but you wouldn't want to catch them."

"I didn't have that in mind at all," Ben said, "Guzan, that's hot! And deep. How do we cross it?"

Nath pointed.

North of them was the outline of a great stone bridge that stretched out like a fallen limb over the fiery gap. Massive rock columns supported it from waters below.

"That's a bridge," Ben said, gaping. "It must be huge."

"It's dwarven," Brenwar said. "Some of our finest work in Nalzambor."

Nath caught Brenwar's eye for a moment, but the dwarf moved on. It left an uneasy feeling in him. They made their way within a couple hundred yards of the bridge and stopped. Nath could see soldiers shifting in the darkness of their posts. Odd shapes outlined the tower tops of the bridge that were stark in the night.

Ben closed his spy glass.

"There must be thirty soldiers." He looked at Nath. "Maybe fifty."

"We can take them," Brenwar said.

Nath rubbed his chin. He had to admit that he hadn't expected so many. The bridge was long and wide, and during the day it was full of people crossing back and forth. Perhaps they could blend in, but no doubt the soldiers were thorough and checking everybody.

"Can you get us across?" he said to Bayzog.

Bayzog huffed. "I can take one, but not another for over a week." He frowned. "I could summon some bats, perhaps?"

"No bats!" Brenwar said. "I'll not trust some winged rodent to carry me over fiery waters. Are you planning on flying the horses over too?"

"Good point, Dwarf," Bayzog said.

"I suggest," Nath said, making his way toward Brenwar. He tapped the chest on Brenwar's horse. "We wait until morning and see what we can use that is inside here."

"A potion?" Ben said. His eyes brightened in the darkness. "I wouldn't mind trying something like that."

Brenwar slapped Nath's hand away.

"It's not a toy chest."

"Certainly not, but it does make for an interesting experience," Nath said. "What do you think, Bayzog?"

"It bears us many options, but I hate to use the magic on such a simple matter. I would just as soon take a longer way around. Exercise caution." He looked at Nath. "But I support your decision."

"I'm with the elf," Brenwar said.

"You support me."

"No, we don't use the potions. Last time I took one, it left my stomach turning like a grindstone. *Blecht.* Take the longer way. Enjoy the journey."

Nath turned his attention back to the bridge, squinting his eyes. There were plenty of soldiers, and through the hot haze that rose from the river, he couldn't see what was on the other side. There would be at least as many men. Maybe more perhaps. He nudged his horse toward the bridge.

He could make out the long tips of halberds and spears. Fangs and gritty teeth. There was nothing he'd rather do that charge the bridge and toss those fiends over the edge into the flaming waters. But he'd lost enough friends already and he wasn't about to lose the ones that were with him now. Still, urgency stirred inside his head. He ignored it.

"Caution it is then," he said, starting to turn. "We go south—"

He caught movement out of the corner of his eye and froze. Slowly, he turned his head back toward the bridge. One of the tower tops of the bridge moved. A pair of windows spread.

A dragon dropped from its perch and glided right toward them with fire in its eyes.

Nath's words froze on his lips.

Great Guzan! That thing is big!

Chapter
19

FAR AWAY FROM NATH, HORSE hooves splashed through the water of an ordinary creek, making the only notable sound in the ravine. Gorlee's teeth tingled. He wasn't used to being a major player in these adventures. He pretty much kept a low profile, only showing up to help out when needed. He scanned the trees for birds and other creatures. Things seemed so quiet, like the moment before a storm. He swallowed and fanned a flying insect from his face.

They were on foot now, reins in hand. The dwarves, four in back, four in front, all in pairs, had him well protected. It made him feel like a prince or something. Each had a small shield in one hand, an axe, hammer or mace in the other. All their helmets had been donned the moment they entered the ravine.

He ran his fingers through his hair. *Perhaps I could use one of those.*

Ahead, the creek bent and couldn't be seen anymore. He could hear the waters cascading over the rocks, but nothing more. Usually Nath would lead. His eyes and ears seemed to pick up everything. Brenwar was no slouch either.

Gorlee sniffed the air.

It smelled like water, mud, horse, leather and dwarf. He frowned. He might look like Nath, but he was anything but that right now. Even blindfolded, Nath could find a particular flower among hundreds. Little things like that. Nath did many, and Gorlee hadn't thought much about them before. Not until now. Without Nath or Brenwar or Bayzog, Gorlee had to admit he felt a bit naked.

A sword and scabbard bumped against the saddle of his horse. He didn't often fool with weapons. They weren't needed. He usually relied on his powers. Something crept between his shoulders. He looked around. The dwarves were looking too. He slid the sword free. The blade sounded really loud scraping out of the scabbard.

Pilpin looked back at him and winked.

Devliik and another followed the creek around a huge rock that formed a bend and disappeared. Ten feet ahead, Pilpin and another dwarf were waiting on him.

"I'm coming," he muttered under his breath.

From the other side of the rock, a dwarf cried out. A loud splash followed.

Everyone burst into motion and pushed onward. Pilpin's pair disappeared; two more dwarves passed Gorlee with weapons hoisted high. He dragged his horse through the creek toward the sound of the skirmish. Blood rushed through his ears.

"Get off me!" a dwarf cried out.

Gorlee bustled around the massive boulder, sword ready. The dwarves had gathered at the edge of the creek, where a pool of water had formed. Devliik and his horse were submerged to their necks in the middle. Devliik slung off a rope that had encircled him.

"I don't know your rope," he bellowed. He urged his mount forward, but it continued to sink. "What manner of creek is this! It's deep as a river!" His head whipped around, checking the waters. "I see stones where there are none."

Another dwarf tossed a rope around the horse's neck and they began to tug.

"One, two—Heave! One, two—Ho! One, two—Heave!"

The horse nudged forward. Its hooves found solid footing and surfaced from the pool of water. Water ran out of Devliik's armor and over the horse. The husky dwarf eyed the pool along with the rest of them.

Pilpin tossed a stone into the middle. It sunk in the clear water and settled only a foot below. All the dwarves were still with weapons ready. Gorlee breathed heavily and felt amazed. There were plenty of treacherous things in Nalzambor. Ways nature preserved itself. Or fed itself, perhaps.

Devliik said something in dwarven and moved onward.

"What did he say?" Gorlee said to Pilpin.

"Avoid the pools."

"That's it?"

"Is there anything else that needs saying?"

The dwarves formed columns on the left and right of the creek. Gorlee took the middle of the right column. He scanned the sides of the ravine. The faces were steep and ran upward hundreds of feet. He couldn't help but feel that eyes were watching them from somewhere up there. At any moment, they would be trapped. Hemmed in on one side or the other. But he also had the feeling that Devliik wasn't worried about a satyr. Not that dwarves would be worried about anything.

The soft rattle of dwarven armor came to a stop. Gorlee stopped as well. Something cried out ahead, like a wounded cat. Slowly, the dwarves proceeded forward. Ahead, the creek water rushed over the rocks, forming another pool of water. A woman hung on to a vine in the middle. She struggled and splashed. Something deep in the waters was pulling her down.

Her green eyes found the dwarves and she mewled again.

Gorlee forced himself up to the pool's edge. The dwarves had funny looks on their faces. The woman in the pool wasn't just any kind of woman. She had golden fur and was spotted like a leopard. Her long whiskers rested on the waters.

"My, look at her," Pilpin said. He looked up at Gorlee. "Have you ever seen such a woman?"

Nalzambor was huge and there were plenty of rare creatures that the eyes of commoners had never seen before. In the case of this feline-like woman, he didn't know.

"No, not like that." He squinted his eyes. "I'd say we need a closer look."

"She's pretty," Pilpin said. His hard eyes were wide. He started to wade into the waters. Others stomped their boots into the water as well.

She's pretty?

The muscles in Gorlee's back started to knot. Something wasn't right. He'd never heard a dwarf call anything pretty before. He scanned the woodland. The trees, bushes, and giant ferns all seemed undisturbed. Everything was pleasant. Normal. The insects and critters chirped. Everything seemed to be in harmony. Even the wind that whistled through the ravine sounded like a flute.

The dwarves edged closer. Devliik tossed the cat-like woman a rope. Pilpin waded in. Gorlee pulled him back by the shoulder.

"What are you doing?"

"Don't you think she's pretty? She's the prettiest I've ever seen."

Gorlee looked at the woman in the water and scratched his head. "You're certain? She doesn't seem like your type."

"Will you let go of me?" Pilpin said, jerking away and marching into the water. "I want to help her first. It's been quite some time since I saw such a fair dwarven maiden."

"Dwarven?"

Gorlee's stomach began to knot and his forehead beaded in sweat. The ground felt loose beneath him. The horses nickered and stomped backwards. Shook their necks. The music of the wind became louder. The woman he saw in the water's eyes drew him closer.

This isn't right. Isn't right at all.

His fingers loosened around his sword, and the blade slipped free. The musical breeze licked at his earlobes, urging him toward the waters. He took a step closer, but kept one hand on the reins.

"Pilpin," he said, raising his voice, "I don't see a dwarf."

Pilpin didn't turn. He kept going.

The windy music tugged at his ears. Gorlee's legs slackened. He felt it: magic. Rushing through him. Subtle. Seductive. Dangerous. He cried out to the dwarves but they heard him not. Their eyes were glossed over. The woman's face in the waters darkened and shifted. Gorlee covered his ears. The woman sneered at him. The waters stirred and shifted.

"Get out!" he yelled.

Something terrible was about to happen. Spots in the forest began to stir.

Gorlee's mind raced. He was Nath Dragon. What would he do? He summoned his magic powers. He couldn't do most of what Nath could do, but he could do a fine impression of most of it. He sucked in his chest and let out a mighty dragon-like roar until he could roar no more.

Every dwarven head turned toward him.

"That's no dwarven maiden!" He yelled. "It's a trap! Get out of there, you fools!"

The dwarves shook their heads and turned back to the woman in the pool. She was gone.

"Where'd she go?" One dwarf said, wading through the waters.

Something jerked him under.

"What goes!" Devliik cried.

The woods and waters came to life.

Draykis, scaly and grey, were all over them.

CHAPTER

20

THE DRAGON SWOOPED DOWN ONTO the grass. Nath's neck tightened. He didn't fear anything, but he respected danger.

"Stay back," he said, dismounting and putting himself between the dragon and the others.

The dragon was a grey scaler. The biggest he'd ever seen. Twenty feet long. Thirty feet with the tail. He had a crown of four black horns on his head. Hundreds of sharp teeth filled his great mouth. His scales were grey and hard as steel. He was black-winged and black-tailed.

Arms wide, Nath approached him.

"What are you doing?" Brenwar said in a forced whisper. "Get back here."

It was too late for that. Nath kept going.

The dragon's serpent eyes widened bigger than Nath's head. Grey scalers made excellent enforcers. Guardians. Hunters. This one probably didn't want to do anything more than check them out. Maybe kill them if bored. Nostrils the size of his fists snorted and flared. A throat bigger than Nath's whole body growled.

The muscles along Nath's spine knotted up.

"A moment please," Nath said, holding out his hand and speaking Dragonese. He slipped off his cloak, revealing his fully-scaled body. The dragon's great neck reared up over the top of his head. Jaws gaping. "You know who I am, don't you."

The grey scaler didn't speak, but Nath could feel words forming in his mind.

Yes. The Dragon Prince. Death to the Dragon Prince.

The moment the dragon swooped down, Nath had known he would probably be recognized. He was unique, which left him as flat-footed as a shoed horse. Their objective was to cross Jordak's Pass unnoticed. Now, any commotion with the dragon would bring the entire regiment from the bridge on them. Any chance of slipping toward the river cities and investigating the mystic shards would be gone. The armies of Barnabus would comb all the hillsides in pursuit of them. Nath would have to try something else.

"I am your prince," Nath said.

You are a cursed prince. A failure. As is your father.

The dragon blood in Nath's veins ignited. His claws lashed out across the dragon's nose.

"You dare!" The dragon hissed and recoiled back. And then in Nath's mind, he heard, *I serve Gorn Grattack. You and all of Dragon Home will as well. Nalzambor is ours.*

The dragon boasted, which wasn't anything uncommon among dragons. After all, they were the most powerful creatures in Nalzambor. But this dragon was on another level. A different place. Nath could feel him oozing with confidence. Feel his heartbeat thundering behind his mighty breast. This dragon wanted glory. The glory of bringing down Nath Dragon.

"Not without me," Nath said, stepping forward. He poked the dragon's chest and felt the hot breath behind the scales like a fireplace mantle. "*Gorshamishultru...*" It was a long word he started quickly that went on and on. *You would be wiser to surrender,* Nath said to him. *Your body is no match for that of a full dragon.*

The dragon stirred. His tails stopped sweeping the grass when Nath finished.

"So then you submit?"

He huffed a hot blast of air in Nath's face.

It had been over a hundred years since Nath had heard what he said to the grey scaler. It was an ultimatum. A contest. Dragons were proud creatures. Many times too proud. And their pride could rub one another raw. It would take more than a conversation or a contest of prowess to settle a dispute that might last centuries. His only option was to take a match. A death match.

"You are no full dragon," the grey scaler said, sliding his neck from side to side.

"You hesitate," Nath said, "so you submit?"

He didn't say anything for a few minutes. Nath could hear his heart racing though.

And then the grey scaler said, "Death for you it is," and laid his neck on the grass, pulling back his wings.

Nath climbed on.

"What," Brenwar started, aghast, "is going on?"

"I've offered a Dragon's Ultimatum," Nath said.

"You what!" Brenwar said. "Get off that dragon, Nath."

The grey scaler took several steps, lifted off, and glided over the grasses toward the hilltops.

Nath took one last glance back at his friends. One expression was as dumbfounded as the next. He took a deep breath and wondered if he'd ever see them again.

CHAPTER

21

*LANG!*

Crash!

Splash!

Dwarves and draykis battled. Gorlee himself battled. The surprise attack was as fierce as it was sudden. Gorlee was at a loss what to do. Right before his eyes he watched a draykis pin Pilpin underneath the waters. Its scaly back faced him.

Do something, Gorlee!

He charged with his sword and pierced the back of its hide.

It reared up and whirled on Gorlee with wary eyes. It wasn't Gorlee it saw, but Nath Dragon, sword in hand.

Pilpin popped up out of the waters and struck it between the legs with his mace.

Whop!

The draykis wobbled on its legs and fell to its knees.

Gorlee struck again, chopping it.

Pilpin hauled back and clobbered it in the head.

It splashed face-first into the creek, unmoving.

The victory was hollow.

Dwarves cried out. Their short arms delivered biting blows with dwarven steel, but they were overwhelmed. The draykis were bigger, faster, and greater in number. The dwarves normally fought in tight ranks and circles that carved their enemies up, but they were scattered. One on one, no dwarf was a match for a draykis, which fought like three lizard men in one.

Hivluum, the dwarf with a square helm and horn in the middle, had two draykis pulling his arms. Another dwarf was picked up and slammed into the ravine rocks. Devliik went down as three draykis pounced on him at once. There was blood. There was death. The dwarves were being slaughtered. Soon they'd all be dead.

Sultans of Sulfur! What do I do!

Gorlee held up his arms and cried out, "I surrender!" He dropped his sword. He summoned his magic and yelled louder. "I surrender!"

The woods shook.

Everyone stilled. A dwarven helmet slipped off one's head and into the water.

"What are you doing?" Pilpin whispered.

"What must be done," Gorlee said.

A voice spoke out from the forest.

"Bind his hands."

"Let the dwarves walk away first," Gorlee demanded.

"You are in no position to negotiate now," the voice said.

The voice was that of a woman, husky. Gorlee assumed it was the satyr. His eyes scanned the ravine, but nothing noticeable was moving.

"You've revealed your location," he said. "And I can get to you faster than any of you can get to me. I'll give you a few more seconds and then the fight will be back on."

"And all of the dwarves will die," the voice said.

"And all my vengeance will be on your head," Gorlee growled.

Nothing was said for a moment. Only the air stirred and the insects hummed.

"Dwarves, depart from us then," she said, "and make it quick."

The dwarves remained still, but were staring at Gorlee.

"Do as she says," he said.

They grumbled.

"But, Guh—" Pilpin started to say his name.

Gorlee cut him off. "Do as I say, Pilpin."

Pilpin shook his beard and stuffed his weapons in his belt. "As you say, Nath!"

One by one, the dwarves trudged out of the pool and up the banks of the creek. Their faces were battered and pride bruised. Blood was in their beards and armor and one spit out a tooth. Two carried one that was dead with a hard look in their eyes. Vengeance had been denied them once again.

Devliik was the last to pass.

"Ye should know better. It's our right to die when and how we want to."

The brown-bearded dwarf mounted up and led his men back up the creek, around the boulder in the bend, and out of sight. Gorlee listened until he could hear the horse hooves splashing in the water no more. When he turned around, the draykis had him surrounded.

"I don't see any rope," Gorlee said, shaking his mane of hair. *Got to be convincing.* "Or was I supposed to bring that myself?"

A figure of a part goat and part woman appeared on one of the rocks above nearby. Two small horns of a goat protruded from her head. She had a nasty look about her. A set of wooden pipes hung from her shoulder and a dagger hung from her belt. Gorlee couldn't help but think that she was the one who had murdered the dwarves in their sleep. One of them at least.

"I must admit," Gorlee said, "you're more pleasant to look upon than expected, for a goat woman that is."

A draykis walloped him in the belly, lifting him on his toes.

"Oof!"

Ugh, that hurt! Try not to show it so much. He fought to stay on his feet and blocked the stars from his eyes. He patted his belly and said, "You don't hit very hard. Are you a girl draykis?"

The draykis's lips pulled back over its large sharp teeth and it drew back again.

"Enough," Faylan said. "The High Priestess wants him alive, every last piece of him." She tossed a rope down that splashed in the creek. "Bind him with that. Its mystic tethers will hold him."

The draykis stared up at her while the rope sank into the water.

"I don't think they know how to tie a knot," Gorlee said. "Have you seen their fingers?"

The big clawed and scaly hands were more like paws than fingers.

"I'd be more than happy to do it myself." He shrugged. "I'm *really* good with knots."

Faylan's face bunched up in fury. She jumped off the rock and into the creek right by him. The tops of her horns came up to his chest. She bent down and snatched the rope from the water.

"Not a move," she said.

Gorlee lifted his brows and offered his hands. He noticed the satyr looked much better far away than up close. Hard lines and ruddy skin covered her face. Her eyes were dark and beady and she smelled a little funny. *No wonder she's mean.*

She coiled the rope around his wrists, made a full loop around his neck, and then wove around each leg. She knotted it around his foot, staring at his scaly toes for a few seconds. She looked up and eyed him again.

"I know," Gorlee said, "they need clipping. You wouldn't happen to have a file on you would y—*ulp*!"

The rope constricted around his neck, legs, and wrists like living iron. He was choking.

Guzan! What is this!

He tried to cry out, but the bonds got tighter. He sagged to his knees.

Now, Faylan was looking down on him.

"Keep your tongue still," she said in his ear. "You don't want the rope to kill you. I don't like your talking, and it doesn't like it either. Do you understand me?"

Gorlee, purple faced, managed a nod.

"Good," she said, lifting up his chin. "Get up now. Slowly. It doesn't like much moving either."

Gorlee froze and the draykis hissed and snickered. The rope that bit into his skin slackened, but remained taut.

"Put him on his horse," she ordered the draykis. "It's time to go. I want to put as much distance between us and the dwarves as we can."

A draykis spoke up. "Let us finish them."

"Later," she said. "First, we need to secure Nath Dragon."

The draykis heaved him up into his saddle and took the reins. Gorlee started to speak, but thought the better of it. He could still feel his tongue in his throat. A sudden darkness took over inside him. The dwarves were on their own and now he was as well. *Maybe getting a closer look at my enemies wasn't such a good idea after all.*

Another draykis dropped a sack over his head. Now Faylan was laughing.

"We can't hurt him, but that doesn't mean we can't make him miserable on our long journey."

CHAPTER

22

"WHAT WAS THAT ALL ABOUT?" Ben said, scratching his head. "What's a Dragon's Ultimatum?"

Bayzog and Brenwar were silent, watching the night sky. Glum.

Ben turned his sights toward the sky and clouds in the air. Nath and the grey scaler were a black dot that disappeared into the distant hills. He felt empty and turned back to his friends. Their faces were empty.

"They're going to fight, aren't they." Ben said.

Brenwar huffed and jumped off his horse.

Bayzog frowned. "It's a battle that doesn't end well for one or the other."

Ben's hand fell on Fang's hilt. "But he doesn't have a weapon. He needs Fang. That dragon will kill him!"

"Keep yer voice down," Brenwar said. "You're not some child anymore and neither is Nath. He made his decision. He'll live or die by it. As will the rest of us."

"You always have the most spirited words, Dwarf," Ben said, walking over to Brenwar clutching his fist.

"Watch yourself, Man."

"The both of you watch yourselves. Nath is gone, and there's no point in arguing about it now, especially with one another." Bayzog left his horse and searched for wood. "Let's make camp. Wait it out."

"Pah," Brenwar said, picking up a stick and snapping it. "Never listens."

"I apologize, Brenwar," Ben said, walking over. "I'm certain Dragon meant well."

"He always means well. That's the problem," Brenwar said. "But it doesn't always end well. That fight will be to the death. There's no more Nath Dragon if he's dead."

"But why would he do that?" Ben said, shaking his head. "That's a big dragon. As big as I've ever seen. And … Nath has no weapon. No weapon at all."

Even though he was a hardened soldier, Ben hadn't been able to help but marvel at Nath's prowess since he'd awakened. Fast. Powerful. Strong. He did things that even extraordinary men couldn't do, but fighting a dragon five times as big with no weapon? That wasn't a death match. It was a funeral.

"We should be there to help him," Ben mumbled. His fingers toyed with Fang's hilt. "You should be there to help him. Why don't you like him, Fang?"

Brenwar's brows perched with a grunt. "Fang's got sense. There's still too much darkness in Nath, I fear. Though, he does seem to be getting better."

Bayzog dropped some wood in front of them.

"What are you doing, Elf? We aren't building a fire," Brenwar said, "not with our enemies all around us."

"It's become a habit, I suppose."

Thunder and lightning cracked in the sky. All eyes went toward the distant hills.

"Why don't you make a tent?" Brenwar said. "It's going to rain. Heavy."

"I didn't think the rain bothered you," Bayzog said.

"It doesn't. I'm just giving you something to do."

"Do you think the battle will last long?" Ben said. "What if Dragon loses? How will we know?"

"We'll know," Brenwar said, "because if that grey scaler finishes Nath, he'll be coming for us next."

Ben punched his fist into his hand. He'd been fighting hard alongside Nath for months and losing him didn't seem possible. He was a grown man. A veteran. Tried. Tested. Tough. He'd let those things keep a wall between him and Nath. Not getting as close as he once was long ago. Now he wished he'd taken the time to say a few more kind words to him. To let Nath know that even though he'd lost his wife and children, now he had hope. A distant flicker caught his eye.

"We're going to have visitors."

Brenwar and Bayzog turned their attention to the great bridge. Soldiers with torches were coming their way. A squad of a dozen, by the looks of them.

"Let's ride," Brenwar said, going to his horse.

Bayzog met him at the saddle and said, "I've a better idea." He patted the small chest hitched on Brenwar's saddle.

"Oh no," Brenwar said, pushing Bayzog back. "I'm not taking any potion."

"Time is fleeting, Dwarf. It's probably this, or a dive into the burning waters below."

Brenwar peered over the chasm, grunted, and shook his head.

"Alright then. Get it down."

Bayzog untied the chest and handed it to Brenwar, who popped it open.

Ben leaned over Bayzog's shoulder. He'd only gotten a couple of peeks inside the chest over the years and was always fascinated by it. He shielded his eyes from the illumination within the chest that was filled with many colors.

Quickly, Bayzog rummaged through the potion vials. His slender fingers pulled out a vial filled with a sparkling blue liquid. He closed the chest and Brenwar set it down.

"Drink a third," the elven wizard said, handing it to Ben. "Just a sip."

Ben did. Its taste was wonderful sliding down his throat and into his belly. Everything tingled. He blinked his eyes. "What does it do?" It seemed funny that he'd taken a drink of it without giving any thought to what it was.

Bayzog sipped his portion.

"A moment," he said to Ben, turning to Brenwar, "Now you, Dwarf."

Brenwar grabbed the vial with his stubby hands, eyeing it.

"Hurry," Bayzog urged.

"Dwarves don't hurry," Brenwar said with a frown. He sucked the vial down and pitched the bottle into the chasm. "And it better not turn me into an orc. If it does—"

"Would an elf ever turn himself into an orc?" Bayzog admonished.

"They're almost here," Ben said. He looked at the torches and then his hands. Nothing was happening. "Am I supposed to turn into something?"

"You're already something," Bayzog said, "you'll just be turning into something else." A wart sprung up on the elf's nose.

Ben stiffened. His feet and ears had a burning sensation. His knuckles became hairy. Skin ruddy. Across from him, Bayzog's body contorted. The slender elf shrunk and widened. His garments changed from robes to roughly-hewn clothes. The Elderwood Staff became a walking stick of sorts.

"What have you done, Elf?" Brenwar exclaimed. His fingers clutched at his beard that was shrinking into his face. Sharp ears with little knots in them popped out on his head, and his wide features became more slender and hairless. A yellow gleam was in his eyes and teeth as well. He looked between Ben and Bayzog. "A goblin? I'm a stinking goblin. Horn blasted potions!"

"Well, we all have something in common," Ben added, fighting the queasiness and funny taste in his mouth, "we're all pretty ugly."

"Ugly yerself," Brenwar said. He shook his fist at Bayzog the goblin. "Tricky elf."

"It's no trick, Brenwar. Now settle yourself. They come," Bayzog said, running his fingers through his ratty hair. "They come." He tossed the Cloth of Concealment over the chest.

"Who does the talking?" Ben asked. He noticed his voice sounded strange, and his words were too.

"I'll do that," Bayzog said, stepping forward to greet the oncoming soldiers. There were twelve of them. Heavily armed. All lizard men, but led by an orc with neck muscles up to his ears. He towered over Bayzog the goblin.

Ben found the moment surreal. *This is madness.* His fingers rubbed the hilt of a knife behind the back of his belt. *How long do potions last, anyway?* His stomach gurgled.

"What are you doing out here?" the orc growled, eyeing them all with suspicion.

"Camping," Bayzog said, sounding every bit like a nasty goblin. "We cross the bridge tomorrow. Make camp tonight." He wrung his hands. "Problem, Orc?"

The orc made its way over to the horses. Checked the saddles.

"Where'd you come by these horses, goblins? Fine steeds they are."

"Stole them," Bayzog said. "We cross the bridge and sell them to the Clerics of Barnabus in the morning."

"Is that so?" The orc eyed Ben. "And who'd you steal these horses from? They don't look like easy pickings for goblins such as you to come by." IT towered over Ben with its hands on its hips. "Well, goblin?"

Ben swallowed.

"Er … we stole them from an awful dwarf and two humans." He pulled out his knife. "And now they be dead." He licked the blade. "The blood of dwarves tastes awful."

The orc laid a heavy hand on Ben's shoulder and snickered. "Aye, but not as awful as the ale they drink. Har. Har. I hate dwarves."

Brenwar stiffened.

The orc turned its attention back to the horses. "Hmmm … we could use these horses. And I don't like seeing those Clerics of Barnabus getting the first offer at everything." It grabbed the reins. "Come with me."

"But," Ben stammered, "where are we going?"

"Across the bridge to barter for your horses."

Ben's eyes went to Bayzog. *Think of something, Wizard!*

"We already have a buyer," Bayzog said, "that expects us."

"We'll see about that, now come on."

"But," Ben started.

The orc poked him in the head. "I could just kill you all," the orc grinned, jangling a necklace of bone fingers around his neck. "You know that, don't you?"

Ben nodded.

Away they went toward the bridge, leaving the chest and the hope of Nath Dragon's return alone in the darkness.

Ben rubbed his forehead.

How much longer will this potion last? Once it wears off, we're done for!

CHAPTER

23

THE DWARVES' SHOULDERS WERE HEAVY. Pilpin rode behind Devliik with the others and the dead behind them. It was the grimmest Pilpin had ever felt. Not only had another brother dwarf fallen to the hands of their enemies, they'd lost Gorlee as well.

"Why do we go this way?" Pilpin questioned Devliik.

The thickly-thewed dwarf didn't turn, but went on steadily back the way they had come.

Pilpin looked back at the nearest dwarf, who shrugged in return. He ground his teeth. All the dwarves were banged up in one way or another. A bloody sling held up a wrist that dangled. Ears and teeth were missing. Eyes were swollen black under heavy brows, and a couple of dwarves were coughing with a nasty rattle in their chests. It made Pilpin realize something.

Gorlee had made a sacrifice.

Otherwise, they'd all be dead.

We should go after him. Perhaps I can convince Devliik.

They made it all the way back to the place where the tracks of the satyrs split. Devliik climbed off his horse, adjusted his dented helmet, and limped through the woods. Pilpin did the same. When he caught up with Devliik, the brown-bearded dwarf kneeled in the pines.

"These tracks are still good," Devliik said.

"Good for what?" Pilpin replied.

Devliik stood up and slapped Pilpin in the shoulder.

"We may have missed our opportunity to kill one satyr, but we won't miss another." Devliik limped back over to his horse and climbed on. "Pilpin, you're coming with me. Two of you take our brother back for a proper burial."

The grimness in Pilpin's chest eased. One satyr would certainly lead to another. One trap had been sprung by the pipe-playing fiends, but would there still be another? *There's only one way to find out.* Pilpin snapped his reins and rode with a slight smile on his face.

"We'll make them bury twenty of theirs for every one of ours!"

All the dwarves huffed in the rain.

"Morgdon!"

CHAPTER
24

NATH FELT STRANGE. IN A twisted way, the ride on the gray scaler's back reminded him of the days when he rode on the back of his father. The moment of reflection stirred him. Sometimes they'd spent days flying over Nalzambor without even landing. It was then Nath had seen some of the most incredible things he ever saw. Now it all seemed long forgotten.

I can't let you down, Father. I won't let you down anymore.

He could feel the might underneath the scales of the dragon's back. The heart thumping like a blacksmith hammer underneath. The power of the grey scaler's beating wings that lifted them higher and faster with a single flap. Nath took a deep breath and tried to block out the pain that still bit in his side. The dagger's cursed wound had not fully healed. It still felt like rusty nail in his ribs.

The dragon made a slow spiral into a clearing on top of the hills and landed.

Nath slid off of his neck and backed away.

"It's not too late to succumb," he said, stretching out his arms. "You can fly away and never be seen again."

The dragon's eyes were dark with fury. He huffed a burst of flame and a cloud of smoke.

Today the son of the King Dragon dies. And soon the King will as well.

His black tail lashed out.

Thwack!

Nath jumped back. The tail clipped his chest, spinning him around and hurling him into the trees. Nath got up just in time to see the tail striking again. Sweeping across the grove like a striking snake. Nath hopped over the top and dashed away into the woods.

Be smart, Nath!

Without a weapon, he knew it would take more than brute force to slay the dragon. All of his cunning as well. Nath could hear the grey scaler's voice in his head.

You flee like a rabbit? The Prince of Dragons … a coward.

The words stung a little, but his ribs hurt more. Nath gathered himself behind a great tree. Waited. There was one rule in a Dragon's Ultimatum. One must be vanquished. How long that took was entirely a different matter. Battles were known to take hours, days or even weeks. Still, Nath had friends that needed him and other pressing matters to deal with.

I see I have erred, the grey scaler said in Nath's mind. *The woodland will delay your death and my flight to glory.* The dragon pushed his way through the woods, snapping and uprooting small trees with his weight, sniffing and snorting. *I can smell you. You can't hide forever.*

Nath could feel the grey scaler's presence. Fiery breath came from behind the other side of the tree. Out of the corner of Nath's eye, he saw the dragon's long tongue lick out.

I bet you'll taste good. It's a shame I will not eat you. A nibble when you're dead perhaps, the dragon said in Nath's mind, licking his tongue out again, on the other side of the tree this time.

Nath snatched the tongue with his claws and jerked it with all his might.

The dragon's neck snapped back, freeing the tongue and howling a painful roar.

Nath moved behind the distracted dragon, took a deep breath, and burst out with his own flames into the scaly haunches of the dragon.

The grey scaler bucked and roared, louder this time, splintering and felling more trees.

Yes! Nath thought, *I've wounded him. Hurt him. Angered him for certain.* Nath raced back into the center of the grove with his dragon heart pumping, feeling like his entire body was on fire. *I can do this!* He spread his arms wide. "What are you waiting for, Dragon? I'm here, and unlike you, I'm not scorched! Perhaps it is I that will be sampling you when this is all over."

The dragon stormed out of the forest, eyes angry but wary. Without warning, a stream of fire shot out.

Nath twisted away. Flames still caught his back. He cried out. His ears caught the dragon's paws digging up the earth and bounding toward him. He scrambled away and dashed headlong for the forest. A blast of fire caught him square in the back, driving him to the ground.

Nath screamed.

Fire was one thing. Dragon fire was quite another. Dragon scales or not, the fire hurt. Nath twisted himself onto his back just as the dragon's paw came down.

Whap!

Pinned by the waist to the ground, Nath felt the dragon's head butting his back.

It's over for you, Human!

"No," Nath managed to say, "it's over for you. I have you just where I want you."

The dragon's head leaned back. *I don't believe so.*

Buy time. Buy time. Buy time, Nath thought.

A huge clawed paw began to crush him with raw power.

Nath took a short breath and breathed fire on the claw.

The dragon jerked Nath up and slammed him on the ground. *You shall pay for that!*

The dragon's neck reared back—maw full of teeth open—and struck like a serpent.

Fighting the pain, Nath leapt away. *Got to finish this!* he thought.

Everything hurt, from his head to his toes. The grey scaler was pummeling him like a cat pummels a rodent. Nath dug his claws into the dragon's hide and climbed onto his back.

What are you doing, Flea?

Nath jumped onto the grey scaler's head and locked his hands on the horns.

The head shook like an angry bull's.

Nath held on with all his strength. He was like a tick now. *I'm not coming off.*

The dragon's tail lashed out and beat his back, jarring him blow by blow.

"I'm not letting go, Dragon!" Nath yelled.

The dragon's wings expanded and flapped like gusty winds. Up in the air they went.

We'll see about that!

Higher and higher they went, swooping, twisting, turning, and barrel rolling through the air.

Your arms will tire long before my wings will.

Nath's arms already ached. It was one thing to fight something weaker than you, but quite another to fight an opponent much stronger. *What am I doing? I can't hold on much longer.* He didn't have a weapon. He had nothing but the horns of the dragon in his grip. Each was three feet long and could gore a stone golem to death. *That's it!*

Summoning all his strength and power, Nath pushed one horn and pulled another. Muscles bulged in his arms and neck. His dragon heart pounded like thunder.

What are you doing? the grey scaler cried. *Stop it!*

Nath heaved and hoed.

Snap!

A dragon horn broke off in his grip. Nath raised it over his head, and like a spear, he jammed it between the dragon's neck and wing.

The dragon's entire body shuddered, then stiffened. The wings went limp. The two of them spiraled toward the ground. At the last possible second, Nath leapt off.

Crash!

The dragon lay in a heap on the ground, chest still rising and falling, wings crushed underneath.

Nath forced himself up to his feet and staggered over toward the dragon's great belly.

Huge eyes rolled over on him. *You truly are the son of the King Dragon, but I don't wish you well.* There was the rasping sound of fires stoking.

Nath plunged the horn into the dragon's heart, and his fire died.

It was almost morning when Nath found his way to the camp where he'd left his friends. Everything hurt, but he lived. He eyed the dried blood on the dragon's horn. *I can't use this. It's sacrilege.* He tossed the horn into the burning Jordak River.

With a sigh, he hobbled back to where he last stood with his friends. *Even the horses are gone.* He kneeled down and surveyed the land. The tracks of many people were on the ground. He got up, started walking, and tripped over something unseen.

"What in the name of Dragon Home is this?"

He reached out and felt a hard object. It was Brenwar's chest, covered in the Cloth of Concealment.

He rubbed his aching head. Eyed the bridge.

"How in Narnum am I going to get across that bridge and find them?"

CHAPTER
25

GORLEE'S BACKSIDE WAS SORE. THEY'D ridden mile after mile, league after league. The sack over his head was suffocating. For the first time, he smelled and tasted his own sweat, which dripped from his head. He wasn't even sure if he'd ever sweated before. He'd never felt so miserable.

Is this what heroes do?

He had plenty of time to think. Plan. Scheme. But he was exhausted. Blinded by the sack, the only comfort he had was the pounding rain that came and went. He could feel the sun between the clouds sometimes on his face and back. Sometimes that only made the stuffy air worse. Everything was bad, but at least he lived.

Suffer. I guess heroes suffer. Not sure I want to be a hero anymore.

Wrists tied, fingers aching, he kept a tight grip on the saddle. The satyr woman, Faylan, didn't speak much. Sometimes he wondered if she'd left him altogether, only to hear her bark an order or scold a draykis.

And to think, if I don't hear her, I miss her. I actually miss her. That's a sick thing.

Faylan was all he had. The link between him and the world. The draykis were something different. Part dragon. Part man. Part living and dead. They made his skin crawl. They smelled like death. Colorful conversation was out.

Who'd have thought I'd miss all that dwarven grunting and frowning?

It wasn't all bad, however. Gorlee had hope. But he couldn't imagine what it would be like to a person that didn't. The armies of Barnabus treated plenty of people the way they were treating him. Moved people from place to place in caged wagons. It was horrible, all the things he'd seen since the takeover started. The desolate. The desperate. The depraved. There was no hope for them except people like him, the dwarves, the elves, Legionnaires, Bayzog and Nath Dragon. Those numbers seemed to be dwindling, though. And in his case, he could shape-change and make a run for it the moment the opportunity presented itself. At least, he could if he got out of his mystic bonds, if only for a moment.

Have to stick it out. Do something meaningful. Help the cause.

He wanted to change. Be more comfortable in the saddle. He'd gotten used to riding, but not so long and never blinded, suffocating, or with his wrists bound. For the first time in his life, his back ached and his muscles were sore. It made him wonder what race made for the most comfortable riders. He rode often as a dwarf and their bodies were durable and hardy, but the lithe frames of elves always seemed at ease in the saddle. It was hopeless though. Any change, and those cords would still constrict him. It left him feeling helpless and afraid.

How much longer can I suffer? Your first significant plan might have been your worst plan, Gorlee.

The daylight slowly dimmed through the sack, and eventually his horse came to a stop. He could still sense the presence of the draykis holding the reins and there were other sounds farther ahead.

"This is far enough," he heard the voice of Faylan say. "Get him down."

A powerful arm shoved him out of the saddle. He landed hard on the ground and cracked his head on a rock, drawing bright spots and a burst of pain.

Faylan chuckled. "Maybe you draykis aren't so bad after all. Now get him up and follow me."

"Get up," a draykis said.

Gorlee made it to his knees and started to rise to his feet.

A heavy foot slammed into his back, sending him to the ground again. He wanted to scream.

"Enough of that," Faylan intervened. "We need to get moving. I'm certain you'll get a chance to play with him later. Or at least get to watch something else play with him. It'll depend on what the Priestess wants done with him."

"What about the horse?" a draykis said.

"I'll let you and your kind decide. I'm not sure if horse meat tastes good to you or not."

"No!" Gorlee blurted out. Instantly, the cords constricted on his throat. *Urk!* He couldn't breathe. He fell back to his knees.

"Ha! Ha! Ha!" Faylan laughed. "It's always good to see Nath Dragon on his knees. Get used to that position of submission."

Gorlee could see her in his mind. Her stout frame with her hands on her hips. It infuriated him.

"Now get up," she said. "I can't have you crawling on your hands and knees already. There'll be plenty of time for that later."

CHAPTER

26

JORDAK'S CROSSING. THE FRAMEWORK OF the stone and iron bridge was nothing short of enormous. Spectacular. Ancient. Foreboding. Bayzog sweated. The heat from the fiery river below made all his clothes stick to his body. It was humid. Hot. Nasty. His enemies that led them from one side to the other had never smelled worse either. He fought the urge to cover his nose.

You're a goblin, remember?

And that was what bothered him. The potion. Normally, the enchanted liquid would last a day, maybe longer, but in this case it was split three ways. Morning approached. If anything, they maybe had an hour. Probably less. And it had already taken half an hour to get across the bridge.

What do I do when we change?

He held the Elderwood Staff close to his chest. It didn't look like much now, but it gave him comfort. He ran through an inventory of spells in his mind. *I know what I can do. But what will they do?*

Brenwar and Ben stood nearby. They weren't the worst pair of goblins he'd ever seen, but they weren't the best either. Their yellow eyes were watching all around and their ruddy fingers fidgeted with their weapons. The orcen soldier had left them under the guard of the lizard men minutes earlier, and had taken their horses into the darkness of another campsite.

Bayzog wandered closer to Brenwar. The lizard men eyed him, but remained still with their spears crossed over their chests and tongues flickering out of their mouths occasionally. He spoke in Goblin to Brenwar.

"This magic will not last much longer."

Brenwar's goblin brows lifted and he said, "Good, then we can start killing them."

"Hush, goblins," a lizard man hissed.

"Hush yourself," Brenwar spat back in Goblin.

The lizard man lowered its spear on Brenwar's chest.

Brenwar slapped it away. "I'll make new boots from those scales of yours and a necklace with your teeth, Snake Belly."

"Quiet," Bayzog said to Brenwar in Goblin. He stepped in front of the spear and pushed Brenwar back. "Sorry," he said in the common tongue.

The lizard man's tongue flickered and it stepped back. Suddenly, the lizard men snapped to attention. The orc leader approached, swords rattling on its wide hips. It stopped and tossed a small sack that Brenwar snatched out of the air.

"That's your payment," the orc said, "Now you go."

Bayzog could sense a smile behind the orc's throaty voice.

"What's this?" Brenwar said in Common. "Coppers and a few silvers? That's insulting."

"Perhaps you feel our forces are being unfair … little goblin?"

"We had a price arranged already," Bayzog said. He had to sell it. Goblins were just as greedy as anyone else in Nalzambor and they weren't bad negotiators either. He snatched the sack away from Brenwar and tossed it to the orc soldier. "We'll have the steeds back or you'll bring us back twenty times that."

The orc's big chin bobbed back and forth and it showed some rotting teeth. It pulled out two smaller sacks and tossed them over.

"No more negotiating. Be on with you."

Bayzog checked the bags. It wasn't enough to cover the cost of a donkey, but that didn't matter at the moment. Moving on did. He tossed one sack to Brenwar and one to Ben. Something caught his eye. Brenwar's beard was growing.

"We go!" Bayzog said with anger. "But I'll let my buyers from Barnabus know about this!" He pointed to Ben and Brenwar and started to head up the road. "Come, goblin brothers!"

"I'll certainly not be going without more gold for those horses," Brenwar argued back. "Now give me back my horses or give me more money."

Bayzog wanted to take his staff and whack Brenwar in the head, but he should have known. Dwarves were as fierce as negotiators as they were as fighters. Dwarves parting with their possessions was a serious matter. Sleeping with a snoring bugbear would have been easier.

"*Come,* brothers!" Bayzog demanded.

Ben came, but Brenwar ignored him. He was almost on the orc's toes when the dwarf's beard started growing faster.

"Say!" the orc said with its eyes popping open. "What's going on with that face of yours?"

"What do you mean?" Brenwar said. He followed the orc's eyes and looked down. Filled his fist with a handful of hair. "Oh...."

"Yer not no Goblin," the orc roared. Its meaty neck turned toward Bayzog. "What are you?"

Bayzog felt his limbs stretch taller and taller. All the lizard men hissed. He locked eyes with the orc and said, "Yes, I am an elf, Orc." He raised his staff over his head, closed his eyes, and yelled. "*Gustoovanleeght*!"

A sunburst brightened the sky.

Shock and dismay shouted from the lips of the orc and lizard men.

Brenwar swung his hammer in devastating fashion.

Crack! Bang! Whop!

The orc soldier went down. Several blinded lizard men screeched.

"I can't see," Ben cried out.

Bayzog took his hand. "Come." He led them down the roads into the woods. Brenwar's heavy footsteps were right behind them.

"You better have more than pretty lights up your sleeve, Elf," Brenwar shouted from behind. "I could always stay back and fight them."

"Come on, Dwarf! There's no time. We have to move! We have to hide."

Bayzog could hear the soldiers scrambling. Orders shouted. In moments, the forces of Jordak's Crossing would be on top of them.

Hiding and escaping are not my best skills. And without the horses, they'll be on us in moments.

He pulled Ben along. The rangy, blinded man stayed with him stride for stride.

A war horn sounded and a great bell rang.

"Guzan!" Ben said. "We're in for it, aren't we."

CHAPTER

27

FIFTY YARDS FROM THE BRIDGE, Nath took cover and waited. His keen dragon sight could pick out most details, day or night. Only one detail mattered. Jordak's Crossing was armed. Heavily armed. Soldiers of Barnabus were posted all along the bridge in pairs.

There must be thirty of them.

He sighed and rubbed his aching ribs, shoving two of them back together. *Pop! Pop!*

He eyed the bridge. Its towers were like black obelisks against the stark night sky, with more than twenty yards between them. The bridge itself was over a hundred yards long and twenty wide. A marvel over the fiery Jordak River.

He shook his head and took a breath. He was tired. Hurt. All of his bones felt like jelly under his skin. He needed rest for the first time since he'd awoken from his twenty-five year hibernation.

Did fighting that grey scaler take so much out of me?

He felt something burning inside him where the blade had entered his side at the settlement. The irritation was worse. He opened up Brenwar's chest and peered inside. Several vials popped into view, in tiny racks. He rummaged through them one at a time. There were things he could use, but didn't want to waste any. It wasn't as if he could go back to Dragon Home and get more, and something told him not to ask Bayzog to make any.

Can't always rely on potions, and the Cloth of Concealment is too small for me.

He fingered a bright yellow vial.

These I don't mind so much.

As much as he hated to do it, he grabbed the healing vial and drank. Tingles erupted inside him. His ragged breathing eased. He closed the chest, stood up, and tucked it under his arm.

Got to get over there.

The biting in his side had eased. He rolled his shoulders and pulled them back.

Huh, I just vanquished a full-grown dragon. With no Fang and no Akron.

He nodded. Another rush went through him. There were many dragons, and they came in many shapes and sizes, but though grey scalers were not the biggest, they were contenders for toughest and deadliest. Nath's chest swelled. Pride overtook him. His head was rushing. He ran his fingers though his mane of hair and walked out into the middle of the road, headed straight for the bridge.

"If a dragon can't stop me, then those soldiers certainly can't."

Ready for anything, he approached with a smile. He made it about ten yards and stopped.

What am I doing?

It hit him. Wisdom. It conquered his pride. The objective was to get over the bridge without drawing any attention to himself or the others.

What are you doing, Nath? If the soldiers have them and they hear me coming, they'll be put in further harm's way.

He slid back off the road and hunkered down. He could imagine Ben, Bayzog and Brenwar tied or caged up somewhere. He squinted his eyes, but the heat from the river obscured his vision almost halfway across.

Time, Nath, Time.

Suddenly, a Battle Horn sounded. An iron bell rang. His thoughts raced.

Brenwar!

The soldiers turned their backs to him and peered toward the other end of the bridge. Nath rushed through the high grasses along the road. The soldiers were moving. Organizing. Shouting orders back and forth among them. Seconds later, two-thirds of the soldiers trotted across the bridge and out of sight.

Now that's excellent timing.

Still hiding in the grasses near the bridge entrance, he waited a moment longer. Four soldiers were left standing guard, talking softly to one another. The twos and threes posted along the bridge were now ones.

All lizard men. Good and not good.

Lizard men were stout soldiers, but they weren't the better trackers. They weren't very good on horseback either. Horses and lizard men didn't get along well. It was a good sign.

They're chasing someone.

Orcs and gnolls were other cases. The gnolls were like hounds and the orcs had a keen sense of hunting things. Brenwar, Ben and Bayzog were formidable, but being hounded by thirty, maybe more? If that was the case, that would be deadly.

Quietly, he moved out of the brush and walked onto the bridge.

The lizard men continued speaking to one another, facing the other side of the bridge.

"Ahem," Nath said, keeping his distance.

Startled, the lizard men turned with spears lowered.

"I say, can you tell me, does this bridge lead to Narnum?"

"Getss," one said, poking a spear his way. "Leaves chest."

"And part with all my personal belongings?" Nath said, turning the chest away. "Why, I need to return my new trousers and boots back to Narnum. They don't fit these scaly legs and feet of mine."

All four of the lizard men peered at him. Their reptilian eyes narrowed even further.

"You have scaless," one said. "How iss that?"

Stupid lizard men. Orcs with scales.

"I was going to ask you that," Nath said, "but why are yours so drab and ugly? And those faces on top of them. I hope that's a mask. It's hideous."

A lizard man took a jab at him.

Nath slid away.

"Easy now," he said. "So is this the bridge to Narnum or not?"

One lizard man whispered to another. It nodded and grabbed the horn hanging on its neck.

"What's that?" Nath said, "I didn't catch it?"

"Leaves the trunk."

Nath grabbed the iron handle on the side of the trunk and swung it back and forth gingerly.

"I'm afraid I cannot part with it."

All the lizard men crept closer.

"We kills you thens."

Nath's trunk laden arm kept swinging. He smiled.

"Alright thensssss," he mocked. "You can have it." He wound the trunk around in a huge windmill circle and let the chest fly. It struck the nearest lizard man in the ribs and toppled him over.

Spears sailed through the air.

One soared by Nath's ear. The second bounced off his chest. The third he snatched from the air. He snapped it in half like a twig.

"You are the worst bridge greeters I've ever met." He dropped the broken spears and they clattered on the bridge. "Who is your superior? I wish to speak with him."

The lizard man with the horn raised it to his lips.

Nath leapt the distance between them. Snatched the horn and crushed it in his fist. "Now, now," Nath said. "It's rude to blow your horn when no one else has one to play as well."

The lizard man gaped and blinked.

"Did you just wink at me?" Nath said, grabbing the lizard man by its armor's collar. "That's strange." Behind him, swords scraped out of their scabbards. The one he held slipped out a dagger.

Simultaneously, all the lizard men struck.

Gick. Gick. Gick.

Nath didn't feel a thing. He shoved them all away.

"Really?" he said. "You just saw a spear bounce off me and you thought you could still harm me? What are you, lizard men?"

One charged, sword raised to strike.

Nath ducked inside in the blink of an eye and punched.

Whop!

The lizard man and his sword bounced on the bridge walk.

"Next," Nath said, dusting off his claws. He yawned. "I'm waiting."

Wary, both lizard men approached with their swords ready.

"I don't think that is going to work." Nath shook his head. "You should have figured that out by now."

"Diess!" one said.

Both charged. Both lunged.

Nath leapt high in the air.

Below him, the lizard men's heads snapped up just as he landed on top of them. Nath knocked them out with single blows.

Whack! Whack!

All four lizard men were out cold, but more stormed over the bridge right toward him.

One. Two. Three. Four. Five. Six. Seven. Ah, that's a good number. Nath felt better than ever. Stronger. Faster. His dragon blood rushed through his body like a geyser. *I've never felt so wonderful before.* He picked up the dwarven chest and faced the oncoming horde. *Good for me.* His eyes narrowed. *Too bad for them.*

Nath took the chest by the handle and smashed it right into the lizard men. They hissed. They flew through the air. Their limbs were busted and broken. Nath swung the chest like Brenwar swung his hammer. He busted their snapping jaws. Broke the fingers on their scratching claws. He sent one flying into the bridge wall.

Seconds later, they all were down and Nath wasn't even breathing hard. No more were coming either. It was just him and the haze on the bridge.

"Huh."

He set the chest down and opened it. Everything inside was in perfect placement. "Dwarven. The ultimate craftsmanship." He closed the lid, tucked it under his arm and strolled across the bridge.

He didn't know what was different about him, but something was. Something had happened when he defeated the grey scaler. He'd grown. Not in size, but in something else.

What is it?

He crossed the bridge at a slow pace. One clawed foot in front of the other. Thinking. Contemplating.

I could have fought an entire army of those lizard men. They used to be able to hurt me before.

Halfway across the bridge, through the haze he could see the other side.

Troops were gathered at the end. He could smell them just as well as see them: orcs, gnolls, and lizard men. The rush of the fiery Jordak River no longer covered their voices. The hunt was on for a man, dwarf, and elf. A piece of gold for each head.

We'll see about that.

Nath kept walking. One quarter from the end, the soldiers saw him coming. Grunts and fervor started.

Nath set down the chest and watched them come in a frenzy.

I now know what the difference is.

He spread out his arms and opened his clawed fingers.

I'm a dragon. They are not.

CHAPTER

28

GORLEE'S LEGS WERE TIRED. HE'D never marched so long and hard before. Walking without sight was ten times harder than with, but he tried to make it look easy. Still, he stumbled. Fell. Only to be jerked up by the brutish claws of the draykis. He hated those things.

"Wait here," he heard Faylan say.

They stopped. Gorlee picked up more sounds. People. Things. Moving not so far away. His stomach growled. *If I could only make my ears bigger and my stomach smaller*. He didn't even dare ask for food, because of the biting rope that bound him tighter if he even thought about speaking.

Not one for eating much, he now hungered and thirsted more than ever before. He felt ashamed that he had mocked the dwarves, saying that eating was overrated. But a single dwarf ate like many. Gorlee, by comparison, was a much lighter eater. But now for the first time ever, he felt the bite of hunger.

An aroma caught his nose. He sniffed. There was something fragrant beyond the sweaty burlap sack. His stomach rumbled again.

Is that meat? It's never smelled so divine before.

He shuffled forward.

A rough hand shoved him down to his knees.

"Be still," a draykis rumbled. It sniffed the air. "Smells like burning halfling over there."

Ew ... but it smells so good. He shook his head. *Oh, I hope if they do feed me, they don't feed me people.* His stomach constricted. *Maybe a nibble.*

He tried to empty his mind and block things out. Focus on all around him. Changelings were highly intuitive people. It was a natural-born part of their magic. It took more than just magic to imitate people. It took strength in many other attributes as well. Gorlee, for that matter, was as good at many things as any man, orc, gnoll, or dwarf could be. Highly durable. Intelligent. Apt. He could mimic many skills and trades just by watching, but for the first time in his life, his abilities were put to the test.

I suffer from this blindness.

He learned however. He used more of his other senses. The sounds of the draykis walking left a clear vision in his mind. The birds in the trees were more numerous than he once believed. Chirps and hoots were from many sorts. His nose tingled before new rain started. He was even pretty certain of the direction they headed. North.

At least I changed before this started.

Changing from one form to another took power, but once the change took form, maintaining it required minimal effort. Still, he couldn't maintain it forever. At least he didn't think he could. He wasn't sure what the longest amount of time was that he'd spent in another form.

Just keep this ruse up long enough and you'll be free. Must stick it out until I find out more about who the High Priestess is.

On his knees, he remained still. The draykis were like giant tree stumps around him. They hardly moved at all, but occasionally one would shift or rattle its metal.

They make for fine statues.

Minutes later, he heard Faylan's hooved approach. It brought him relief for some strange reason.

"All is arranged," she said.

He could feel her right in front of him. She patted his head.

"I almost hate to see you go."

Go?

He heard her slip a knife from her belt and make her way behind him. He felt her hand clutching the top of the sack that covered his head. He heard and felt her saw the cords that bound it, and he gasped when she pulled it free from his face.

The dim light of the day almost blinded him. He blinked and squinted. They were overlooking a small valley with hills rising all around. It was foggy as much as it was rainy. Campfires glowed dimly farther away and tent posts peeked out above the fog. At least a hundred soldiers of Barnabus awaited him below. Maybe a lot more.

Slit.

Faylan cut off a lock of his hair.

Ow!

He jumped to his feet. The ropes constricted, but he held his ground. He eyed the lock of auburn hair in her hand.

"Just a souvenir," she said, tucking it in her pouch.

Gorlee eyed her fiercely. He had to sell his anger. Contempt.

Why did she have to do that?

This was a problem. The lock of hair she put in her pouch probably wouldn't be the same lock she pulled out. Faylan was no fool. She'd be able to figure it out or she'd find someone that would.

She strutted by and down toward the valley.

"Come along."

Gorlee followed her and the draykis followed him. The soldiers of Barnabus formed two ranks on either side of them. Their faces were harsh. Their comments coarse, but none came within a horse length. Gorlee kept his chin up and strode with his chest out. Inside he was rattled.

As they made their way deeper into the camp, a strange structure could be seen rising in the fog. A metal cage with thick iron bars sat on a high slab of stone. Faylan stopped in front of it, climbed up the stone steps, and swung open a creaking iron door.

"Inside," she said, smiling a fiendish little smile.

"Aren't we going to have dinner first?"

"No."

Gorlee walked up the steps and walked in. Circled inside the cage. It was big enough for twenty men. The heavy iron bars were big enough to hold a dragon or even a cyclops. There wasn't even enough room for a halfling to squeeze through them.

He gestured with the mystic ropes that bound him.

Faylan laughed.

"The High Priestess will handle that." She closed the cage door, set the bolt, and locked it with a key. "I hope you like your new home," she smiled, "or should I say your chariot."

Chariot? What does she mean by that? There's no wagon or wheels?

Faylan hopped off the rock and marched over to a draykis that awaited her. It held a hollowed out dragon horn in its clawed hands. The horn curved not once, but twice. Faylan put the small end to her lips and blew.

Ba-ah—rooooooon! Bah—ah—ah—rooooooon!

She handed the dragon horn back, folded her arms over her chest, and locked her eyes on Gorlee. Everyone else was looking toward the sky.

A black shadow fell over the army. Something whooshed through the air. Gasps and murmurings spread through the camp. Many soldiers hunkered down. Gorlee's spine froze.

Don't look. Don't look.

Slowly, he lifted his chin upward. A dragon circled in the sky above. The scales on its belly were dark and bronze. Its wings and claws were darker than night. Gorlee felt his heart beating in his ears.

That's a big dragon.

All of his life, he'd hardly seen any, and now they were everywhere.

He wrapped his clawed hands around the bars and eyed it.

It was eyeing him back.

I think this cage is a good thing.

It dropped out of the sky and landed on top of the cage. It rattled and shook everything as its giant claws grabbed hold of the cage. Gorlee held on and watched Faylan wave goodbye.

The bronze dragon's wings beat in the air, parting the fog and stirring the tents. Up, up, up the dragon went, taking Gorlee and his cage along and leaving the tiny creatures below. Gorlee felt sick to his stomach. He belched and felt queasy.

I never thought I would fly!

Below the clouds and above the mountains they flew, hour after hour. Gorlee marveled at the world below. At the world the dragons saw.

No wonder they rule the world.

He hung onto the bars, facing the direction they were headed. A sense of dread filled him. He wasn't worried about being dropped, burned or eaten. Something else terrified him.

I'm going to face the High Priestess. She'll kill me the moment she finds out I'm not Nath Dragon. You can pull this off, Gorlee. You have to.

"Take your time," Gorlee shouted at the dragon. "My time in the air will be much more splendid than my time back down there."

CHAPTER

29

THE ROAD TO THE RIVER cities was long and wide from the Jordak Bridge, winding through towns and villages for miles on end. But the next town wasn't for miles, and staying on the road was too dangerous. After an hour of hard running, Brenwar came to a stop. Huffed for breath.

"I'm not running anymore."

Bayzog and Ben came to a stop as well. Ben rubbed his eyes.

"We need to hide then," Bayzog said.

"Well, we can't very well hide on this road, can we?" Brenwar shot back. He took in his surroundings. The other side of the Jordak was rolling hills and green meadows. It would be easier to track them through the grass than on a heavily traveled road. He shook his head. "Let's just wait on them." He dropped the head of War Hammer on the ground and rested his hands on the handle. "Put an end to them."

"Our goal is to remain sight unseen," Bayzog reminded him. "Otherwise, they'll be crawling all over the landscape looking for us."

"They can't find us if they're dead," Brenwar retorted.

Ben shuffled over to Brenwar and unhitched Akron from his shoulders.

Snap. Clatch. Snap.

The bow string twirled into place.

"I'm with Brenwar. We can handle that lot from the bridge."

Bayzog's face lit up. "And the dragon? What if it comes back?"

Brenwar turned to face him. "Which dragon are you talking about, Elf?"

Bayzog sighed. "I'm sorry."

"Dragon will be alright," Ben said. He patted Fang's hilt. "He'll not leave his sword with me for that long."

"We need to wait on him anyway," Brenwar said. "I don't want to go on without him."

"So your plan is to wait for him to come waltzing down the middle of the road. While the armies of Barnabus run us through and over." Bayzog shook his head. "I don't think I've ever heard of a worse dwarven plan before. Why don't you build us a castle out of the grass while we wait?"

Brenwar stiffened and pointed his stubby finger.

"Are you using sarcasm with me, Elf? A wizard at that. Making some sort of jest. To a dwarf?"

Bayzog walked right up on him. "I suppose I am."

Brenwar grunted a laugh.

Ben chuckled.

Bayzog showed a grin.

"Good then," Brenwar said. "I'm glad it only took you two centuries to find a sense of humor."

"And what about the dwarves then?"

"We don't have humor, we have mirth."

"In short supply, I'd say," Ben commented.

The three of them fell silent, gazing at the long road behind them. Brenwar fully expected Nath to come walking down it at any moment. In truth however, he had doubt inside his belly. How in the world would Nath Dragon survive a battle with a fully grown grey scaler without a weapon? It angered him. He should be there for Nath. He'd promised Nath's father he would be.

"We need to go back for the chest," Brenwar said.

"We'd have to walk leagues to the next crossing," Bayzog reminded him. "It would take days. Listen, assuming Nath survives, he'll be coming this way anyway. He'll catch up, eventually. I say we keep going."

The soldiers will catch up with us too, eventually," Brenwar said. "I say we set up an ambush. After all, they don't want us. They might want us dead, but they don't want us."

Ben spun around, eyeing the landscape.

"There's no good ground here. It's all open." He peered down the road. "And I think someone is coming."

Brenwar pushed up on his tiptoes. It was dark, but torches could be seen coming their way in the distance. The distant rumble of trotting boots and horse hooves hit his ears.

"The night still gives us good cover, and the sun will rise on our backs." He looked back at Bayzog. "It will gives us a fine element for surprise if we time this right."

The part-elf wizard nodded.

"They move slowly. Cautiously."

"They are not so eager to find us. Perhaps they fear us."

"I'm sure they fear men," Ben said, smiling.

They trotted up the road until the sun peeked over the horizon, and then they came to a stop. Behind them, Brenwar could see the sun shining off the dull metal helmets of the soldiers that pursued them. His heart beat harder. His grip on War Hammer tightened.

Ben and Bayzog took positions on either side of the road and kneeled down in the high grasses. Brenwar stood in the middle of the road, resting War Hammer two-handed on his shoulder. He was angry inside. Nath was gone. Maybe for good. Someone was going to pay and it might as well be a bunch of orcs.

"Brenwar," Bayzog hissed at him, "are you really just going to stand in the middle of the road and greet them like a sailor's maiden?"

"You do your thing, Elf. I'll do mine."

He could hear the troops coming up the road, but they were still out of sight. Brenwar was on the higher ground. The sun now warmed his back. A banner appeared, rising above the road. The flag of Barnabus. A gold dragon against a red and black background. Next rose a horse and rider. Followed by two more.

Brenwar spat on the ground. He suspected it was the orc they had bartered with before. It was in full armor now. Its shoulders were heavy, covered with muscle under metal. The gnolls were just as big and there were maybe another score of soldiers behind them. One by one, they appeared over the crest of the hill with hands up and heads down. The sunlight was bright on their metal. And on their ugly faces.

Brenwar's black brows furrowed.

"They're going to regret coming this way."

Brenwar glanced at Ben and nodded.

The warrior stretched the bow string along his cheek and released to fire.

Twang!

Like a streak of sunlight, the arrow buried itself in a gnoll rider's chest, toppling it over so it hit the ground.

The orc leader ripped his sword from the scabbard and bellowed.

"Trap! Ride through it!"

It was a good move. Brenwar had hoped they'd scatter, but instead they lowered their heads and ran right at them.

Twang!

Another arrow zipped through the air, catching the second gnoll rider in the leg. Onward the soldiers of Jordak's Crossing came.

Thirty yards away, the orc leader locked eyes with Brenwar. It made a nasty grin and thundered his way.

Brenwar braced himself and set down his hammer.

The orc let out a triumphant howl.

"Brenwar," Ben yelled, "what are you doing?"

The rugged dwarf clenched his teeth and lowered his shoulder.

The horse closed in.

Twenty yards. Ten. Five.

Crash!

Brenwar tackled the horse's leg. The beast and rider plowed over Brenwar and crashed into the ground. Brenwar shook his bearded head and scrambled for War Hammer. He snatched it off the ground.

"Try to run me over, will you? No one tramples a dwarf!"

Across from him, the orc rolled back to his feet and hopped up with his blade ready.

"Fool of a bearded one!" It spat blood on the ground, raised its weapon and charged.

Brenwar yelled back and rushed forward.

The warriors collided. Dwarven metal against orcen steel.

Chang! Chang! Snap!

The orc's blade broke in the middle. Brenwar swung his hammer full circle.

Pow!

The orc left his feet and was dead before he hit the ground. An angry chorus of cries rose up behind him. Brenwar whirled. Soldiers closed in from all directions. Ben and Bayzog were not heard or seen.

"Come at me, then!"

Ben kept shooting. If Brenwar wanted to tackle a horse, so be it then.

Akron was a marvel in Ben's hand. Easy to use and deadly accurate.

Twang! Zip!

Twang! Zip!

A soldier of Barnabus went down, clutching the arrow in its chest. Another soldier died with one in his next.

Ben drew another and fired once more.

Twang! Zip!

It punched a hole in the metal belly of a gnoll soldier and dropped him to the ground.

Ben pumped his fist a little. He hated gnolls. They were worse than rabid dogs to him. They were rabid dogs that could talk.

A howl rose up among the soldiers. One pointed less than twenty yards away.

"Seems the surprise is over," Ben said, dropping Akron to the ground and drawing his own sword. Fang still hung on his other hip. He'd used the mystic blade before, long ago, and had not used it since. He hadn't even tried. It was Nath's. "Maybe next time."

He set his feet in the grass.

A lizard man charged with a spear.

Ben spun.

Chop!

Hacked its leg.

Another lizard man followed. It stabbed. Ben jumped. *Whack!* It lost its tail.

Something clipped Ben's leg, spinning him around. He jerked back. A club clipped his head. He saw stars and blood, ducked and swung back.

Slash!

A gnoll fell, holding its wounded belly.

Ben struck again and again. His sword banged off metal. Cut flesh. Hit bone. But the soldiers hit back.

Slash! Stab!

Ben parried and punched.

The soldiers crowded him. A gnoll dove onto his legs. A lizard man tackled his arms. Down into the high blood-slicked grasses he went.

Madness.

Bayzog cast his hands over his head and let the first onslaught of magic fly. Bees of bright light erupted from his fingertips. With an angry buzz, they assaulted the faces of the oncoming attackers.

The soldiers of Barnabus swatted, cried out, fell and writhed on the ground. They kicked up dust, screamed and moaned.

Bayzog backed away. He had stopped a few of them, but more were coming. He needed time to summon his energy. A gnoll burst out of the chaos, snarling and making a straight line for him, spinning a spiked flail over its head.

Bayzog didn't have a spell ready to counter.

I should run.

He stayed and lowered the Elderwood Staff before him.

The gnoll slowed to a stop ten paces away, its evil eyes wary.

"Wizard," it barked while rattling a necklace of bones on its neck. "Elf. I have no elven trinkets, either." It barked again and darted straight for Bayzog.

Bayzog jumped aside. Ducked.

Whoosh!

The spiked ball of steel passed over his head. Bayzog tried to recall a spell. Anything.

The hulking gnoll swung the flail like a toy, knotting up its muscular arms. It struck.

Bayzog jumped.

Whoosh!

The spike ripped through his robes.

The gnoll barked and laughed. It spun its mace again.

Bayzog backed up with his staff guarding the front of him.

"With a single word I can destroy you," Bayzog warned.

The whirling of the flail stopped. The gnoll paused in thought. It rested its big shoulders.

Bayzog took a breath. Wiped the sweat from his eyes.

Suddenly, the gnoll wound its arm, flung the flail and struck him in the belly.

Bayzog groaned and went down on both knees. Pain exploded in his stomach. He looked up. The gnoll stood over him, holding a dagger. It kicked him in the jaw.

"I can destroy you as well, and I will."

Bang!

Down went an orc.

Bang!

Down went a lizard man.

Bang!

Down went a gnoll.

Brenwar showed no mercy. He busted up heavy armor. Broke bones like twigs. He and War Hammer were a war machine. Striking with the fury of a storm. Wreaking havoc on enemies.

"Had enough dwarf yet?"

Bang!

A gnoll's dented helmet flew from its head and bounced down the road. Wide eyed, the gnoll started to run, teetered and fell to the ground.

Chest heaving and bleeding from several wounds, Brenwar scoured the area for his friends. He didn't see them. He saw something else. A shadow from the skies above on the grounds below. He looked up.

"Bloody beards."

CHAPTER

30

GORLEE SHIVERED. HIS DRAGON SKIN was thick but the chill winds still bit. He covered his ears and puffed misty breath. The picturesque scene below him got old after the first few hours. Snow-capped mountains and lush valleys covered in shadows or golden sunlight, all of it became a blur. Now he lay down on his back, glancing up at the dragon's belly.

I guess they're living armor, those scales.

Thousands of hard scales covered every inch of the dragon from gut to neck. Clean rows of bronze, shifting and rippling in rhythm to the dragon's mighty wings. The dragon flew effortlessly through the air, holding Gorlee in the heavy cage like a fish in an eagle's talons. Gorlee, always fascinated with dragons, fought the urge to reach up and touch its great claws. Thick and heavy like wrought iron, with tips as sharp as razors. Gorlee envisioned the dragon ripping rocks asunder.

Please don't try to talk to me.

It was a concern. Dragons could talk to dragons. Sense things about one another that others could not. Dragonese was their language, and Gorlee didn't know it. He recalled a few words Nath had said, at best. He sat up and pulled his knees into the chest.

Wherever I'm going, what to do when I get there?

He sunk his head between his knees and tried to ignore the moaning in his stomach.

Cold and hungry is no way to live.

The dragon jerked the cage. Gorlee bounced across the floor and into the bars. He caught the dragon gazing at him. A smile lifted over its oversized teeth. It shook the cage again. Gorlee's head dashed across the bars. He rubbed the lump on his head.

Really? As if I'm not going to suffer when I get wherever I'm going.

The dragon turned away and spread its wings wide. A rush of wind caught Gorlee. They were descending, and fast. He pressed his face to the bars and held on. A series of tiny structures appeared below. The make-up of a town. Downward they drifted in a large winding circle. Gorlee could see the square made up of farms and roads below. What he thought were small streams turned into rivers. Huts became villages, towns, and cities.

Is that what I think it is?

He saw the tops of large buildings now. They looked like toys beneath him. *No wonder dragons look down on us. They're used to being so far above us.*

Gorlee's heart raced. The once small buildings became massive. The containment of the cage and the freedom of the air gave him a false sense of security, but he now realized that peace was about to come to an end. The evil world was ready to greet him once again and he had no idea what to expect.

Suddenly, the dragon dipped, rattled the cage, and snorted.

Gorlee clutched at the bars. "Don't drop me now, you terror!"

He heard a rumble in its great throat.

Maybe that's what a dragon laughing sounds like.

He turned his attention downward. In seconds, the city was much closer than it had first appeared.

Narnum?

Gorlee didn't spend much time in the great cities. He preferred the isolation of the less-traveled paths and places, but Narnum, the Free City, was certainly unforgettable. Tall and magnificent towers jutted from the ground and reached for the clouds. The roads were wide and many. People moved like tiny ants below, working on more great structures, heavy stone and metal towers like he'd never seen before.

What is going on down there?

Slowly, the dragon spun in a tighter circle. Gorlee picked up the outlines of more dragons roosted on rooftops like birds. Some looked right at him and some did not bother, instead casting their eyes downward, warding the people below like hawks warded their prey. Gorlee felt his chest crush. Freedom was gone from the Free City.

The dragon beat its mighty wings and set Gorlee's cage down on a raised dais in the middle of the roof of the tallest building. It's great claws unclamped and without a final glance, off it went, up into the sky, disappearing into the grey clouds.

Gorlee spun around in his cage. The rooftop was huge. Big enough to hold hundreds of people, maybe over a thousand. There were benches, railings, and gardens, but no people, leaving him alone with a view of the world in all directions.

He checked the rope on his wrists that coiled around his legs and neck. It was still snug. Uncomfortable. *Gives me a reason not to talk anyway. But how will I ask for food?*

Thunder rumbled overhead. The stiff winds whistled through his cage bars and the building parapets. Gorlee focused on an entryway that was well concealed in the distance. He didn't notice any others.

One way up and one way down.

His eyes drifted to the outer wall.

Well, maybe two ways down.

He made his way over to the cage door and played with the lock. He picked at it with his claws. It had an intricate key slot on the heavy lock.

I fear this is beyond me. The lock clattered against the bars and he backed off.

He found it strange that Faylan had the key and she wasn't here. *There must be another that someone else has. The High Priestess, perhaps.* He tried to picture what that woman would be like. Would she be a large demonic hag or something else entirely?

Minutes passed. Dark clouds drifted overhead. The heavy rain came with bitter wind.

Great.

An agonizing hour passed with Gorlee's thoughts racing every minute.

Perhaps they're on to me.

Maybe they wait for me to change.

Or try to escape.

They're trying to starve me into extraordinary feebleness.

Thunder boomed. Lightning flashed. His innards groaned and jumbled.

Must it be so miserable?

He huddled and rested his back against a corner. Closed his eyes and shivered. Hours went by one after the other. The pouring rain brought coldness, not comfort.

CHAPTER

31

BEN PUNCHED AND KICKED. THE weight of the soldiers overwhelmed him. A mailed fist struck him in the face. A strong arm tore his sword free from his hand. Ben head-butted one with his rock-hard chin, drawing forth a groan.

Whop!

Pow!

He saw bright lights. His limbs went numb. Ben was strong, but his strength was no match for the other soldiers. Lizard men and gnolls were brutes by comparison. Ben curled up into a ball. They wailed on him with hard kicks and heavy fists. His armor was the only thing keeping his bones from being splintered. Finally, the beating stopped.

"Get me a flail," a gnoll said, glaring at him. It had a mouthful of big yellow teeth like a dog.

Ben struggled up to his feet, huffing for breath, swaying, and bleeding. There were four of them and only part of what was left of him. He could feel his face swelling.

"What's the matter, Dog Face? Don't you know how to finish a beating?"

Another gnoll kicked him down to the ground. It barked and howled in his face. Gnolls liked to torment their foes.

He spat blood and got back to his knees. Spread his arms wide. "Say, get an orc over here to do your job. At least they hit harder."

The gnoll strolled over, swishing its flail from side to side. It pointed its long hairy finger. "Break jaw. Break body. Break spirit," it said with a fiendish grin. "They kill."

Ben lowered his hands. Fang still hung on his belt.

"Well," Ben began, clutching his side, "you might want to let an orc in on it if you want to succeed in all three things. So far, you've not succeeded in a single one."

The gnoll snarled. Its flail whizzed to life. It jumped at Ben's swing.

In a flash, Ben slid Dragon Claw out of Fang's hilt, and ducked.

Swish!

He jabbed Dragon Claw in the gnoll's belly, drawing a fearsome howl.

The other gnolls and two lizard men froze, watching their comrade fall. A split second later, Ben ripped Fang out and charged his stupefied attackers.

Fang's blade cut the air with an angry howl. Its sharp blade cut the lizard men down in two strokes. A shadow closed in on Ben's back with heavy feet. He launched Dragon Claw out of his hand and into the last gnoll's chest. Down it went. Dead.

Ben wiped the blood and sweat from his forehead with the back of his forearm. Fang, once cold in his hand, was getting hot. He shoved it back in the sheath, staggered across the grass and collected Dragon Claw. Its steel almost burned to the touch.

"Mercy, Fang," he said, stuffing it back into its hidden spot in the hilt. He blew on his hand. "But thanks." He scanned the grass for his own sword and picked it up, turned and locked eyes on Brenwar. The dwarf was looking up. Ben lifted his head. Circling dragons were looking down.

"Great Guzan."

The last two decades had toughened Bayzog up, but he still tried to avoid getting his robes dirty at all costs. That effort had failed him today. A gnoll snarled over him. Chomped its teeth. Raised its dagger with murder filling its eyes.

Bayzog summoned his strength and swung the Elderwood Staff at its feet.

It hopped over the staff in a single bound and landed by his head. Dropping to its knees, it pinned Bayzog to the ground by his neck and squeezed. Drool dripped from its mouth and the small bones rattled on its necklace.

"You'll make a fine prize, Wizard."

Bayzog clocked it in the head with his staff again, making a hollow bonk sound. The blow wouldn't have hurt a squirrel.

The gnoll sneered and laughed. The dagger rose over its head—Bayzog's life flashed in his eyes. Sasha. His boys. In a flash, the blade came down.

Chuk.

The gnoll missed his ear by inches.

"Not yet. No, no. Not yet," it said, choking Bayzog until his face turned purple. "Don't move." A clawed fist punched him in the gut.

"Oof!"

The Elderwood Staff fell from his grip. The gnoll snatched it from the ground and let out a triumphant howl.

"More pleasure busting your bones with your little staff until I break it on your head."

Bayzog held a shaking finger out. "Wait," he croaked, sitting up and clutching his stomach.

"Death cannot wait," it said, swinging the Elderwood Staff to its full zenith.

Bayzog forced out a word of power.

"Gaarmahngee."

The Elderwood Staff flashed.

The gnoll's wolfish eyes widened. *Pish!* Its entire being incinerated. The staff fell through its dusty fragments and onto the ground. The wind took the rest of the gnoll specs away like ash.

Bayzog crawled to his staff, used it like a cane and pushed himself up to his feet.

"Would have been nice if Brenwar had seen that."

Whump! Whump!

Bayzog jerked around, wincing.

Ben and Brenwar stood back to back with a pair of grey scalers surrounding them.

A shadow glided overhead.

He didn't want to look up, but he did.

I can't believe there are three of them.

CHAPTER

32

NATH GRABBED AN ORC BY the backs of its arms and slung it into two others. A lizard man popped up on his right, swinging a heavy iron blade. Nath caught the blade with his fingers and yanked it free of the lizard man's grip. Its snake eyes widened, watching Nath slowly bend the blade in half like a piece of cheese.

"If I can do that to steel, imagine what I can to do you," Nath said, frowning.

The lizard man looked left, then right. No one else was around. It backed away toward Jordak's Bridge, turned, and ran.

"And the smartest shall survive," Nath said, scanning the area.

He'd been fighting for minutes and it showed. The soldiers of Barnabus were heaps on the ground. Some groaned. Others crawled. Many were still like stones. He didn't care. He'd had enough of them tormenting his friends.

Nath jogged over to the barracks and camp of the soldiers of Barnabus and made a quick inspection. He checked all the small buildings and tents. No sign of his friends. He nodded.

Good.

He took a deep breath.

And goodbye.

He exhaled fire from his lungs. Instantly, the camp of Barnabus caught fire. Flames roared all around. The entire camp would be cinders within the hour.

Nath pumped his fist and sprinted down the road.

My friends better be fine.

Foot and horse prints were plentiful and fresh in the mud. As best as Nath could tell, the soldiers didn't have too much of a head start. He lengthened his stride and ran near the pace of a galloping horse, ignoring the nasty itch in his side.

That should be better by now.

He buried it in the back of his mind. He had friends to help. As he ran, he scanned the soft green edges of grass along the road.

Maybe they doubled back.

He and Brenwar had done that often in their days roaming Nalzambor alone together. It was effective in losing pursuers if you were smart and quick about it.

One clawed foot after another, he splashed over the mud and slowed. He noticed the impression of Brenwar's boot along the edge. A thrill went through him.

He's alive. That means they're probably all alive.

The soldiers were numerous, however. Two dozen and heavily armed, clearly pursuing. Nath wondered if his friends might split up and divide the forces. There was no sign of that and it made him wary.

What is Brenwar doing?

He picked up the pace. Ahead, the sun began to peek over the meadows. Wild flowers in bright colors popped out among the grasses. The wind whistled in his ears as he ran. Something troubled him inside. A nagging feeling in his neck. A tightening between his shoulders. He glanced toward the sky.

Far away, a small flock of black birds circled like vultures. They dipped and dove in the sky. Nath ran harder. It was difficult to see what kind of birds they were in the bright sunlight. A half mile farther up the road, he could see the long necks and great wing spans.

Those aren't birds. Those are dragons!

He went into a sprint.

One dove out of sight, followed by another, leaving one alone to keep watch from above.

They're attacking!

CHAPTER

33

"WHAT DO YOU SAY?" PILPIN said to Devliik.

They'd tracked the second satyr high into the mountains, only to start another weaving downward trek again. Now they stood on a crag in the rocks overlooking a deep valley. Devliik was propped up on one knee with a long brass spy glass to his eye. He handed it over to Pilpin with a grunt.

"Got a host of them down there," he said, rubbing his wooly brown beard. "That'll be a mighty amount of graves to dig unless we can bury them all at once."

"Bury them?" Pilpin said, peering through the spy glass. "What if Gorlee's still in there?"

"We've been watching for hours. He ain't."

"We can't know that for sure," Pilpin said. "He could be in any one of those tents."

"I don't think so," Devliik said. "Why, are you wanting to go snoop around?"

"Well," Pilpin started, but stopped.

Devliik was in charge. A fine and experienced commander in the field. Pilpin followed him without question, but he wished he knew where the big dwarf stood in terms of finding Gorlee.

"I want those murdering satyrs," Devliik said, making a spit. "I want to find our friend too, but I don't see any sight of him down there. I don't see any of them scaly lizard soldiers either. They've moved off to somewhere and must have Gorlee with them."

"Shall we go around and peek?"

"Maybe that's what they want us to do," Devliik said. "Perhaps we should flush them all out."

"The entire host? There must be over a hundred. Quite a risk when all we want is the satyrs."

Devliik spat.

"This is war and those are orcs and such. We don't make friends with them. We kill them, else they kill others, like our friends."

CHAPTER
34

*B*ANG!

Gorlee jumped.

Bang!

Up on his feet he went, head whirling.

The ropes constricted and down he went again.

He groaned and slowly made his way back to his feet.

The rain had stopped and sunrays split the clouds in the sky.

Bang!

He turned and faced the sound of the aggressor. A tall figure with huge shoulders shrouded in a dark purple robe stood in front of the cage. A heavy war mace swung back and forth like a pendulum in his gauntleted hand.

Gorlee didn't say a word. He just stared back.

Heavy eyes went up and down him, eyeing his scales. Most of the man's face was shadowed, but Gorlee could see the tattoos. A hard expression. A glimmer of metal armor under the big man's neck. The man stared at him as if he should know him or was waiting for him to speak.

This is your test, Gorlee. This is your fate.

His stomach groaned. His legs felt weak and his neck was heavy. He checked his hands. Still clawed. Still scaled. *Good.* It wasn't uncommon for a changeling to wake up as someone else. Dreams, especially bad ones, could do that to them. But it had never happened to Gorlee. Not yet at least.

Moments passed as he tried to think of things Nath would say.

I accept your surrender.

It seems the flies like you.

I know an orc that is taken with you.

Nath had an unusual way of finding humor in the gravest things. He also had a sharp tongue and wit about him too.

I guess when you're a dragon, it's easier to get away with those things.

The cleric wasn't alone. Behind him stood several more acolytes with their hoods pulled down. Colorful tattoos decorated their heads in bright and exotic colors. They had chains and shackles in their hands. Moorite, by the looks of the metal.

Great.

Two other figures stood looming in the back with black wings folded over their backs. Draykis. A higher order of the lizard mankind. The part man, part dragon undead creatures were something Gorlee had come to dread. Their cold eyes disturbed him. They had no value for life, as true life was no longer in them. He thought of the dwarves.

I hope they are free and clear of those evil goons.

The lead cleric raised his war mace up and brought it down on the lock.

Whack!

It fell to the dais on the roof in two pieces.

"Step back," the man said in a heavy voice.

Gorlee backed up a few paces, while the other robed servants opened the door. In moments, they hand Gorlee's arms and legs chained and shackled. His wrists were bound behind his back. Tight. Uncomfortable.

"Come out," the large man said.

Gorlee stepped out with a flutter in his stomach. He felt less free and secure.

An incantation was muttered by the hooded man.

The mystic ropes that bound him slipped off his body and coiled up on the ground.

An acolyte picked up the rope, held it out bowing, and said to his leader, "For you, Kryzak."

Kryzak grabbed the rope and smote the man across the face with his mailed fist, knocking him to his knees.

"Lord Kryzak," the war cleric said. "Imbecile." He turned his attention to Gorlee. "You may speak now."

Gorlee said nothing. His thoughts raced in his head. *Kryzak.* He should know that name. He'd heard it before in stories. But there were so many. *Kryzak. Who is that?* He eyed the man with defiance. His stomach made a loud rumble.

"Too hungry to speak, Dragon? Has your sharp tongue weakened over the years?" Kryzak pushed his shoulder. "And you seem so much more, uh, formidable with all those scales. I'm certain they'll fetch a fine price on the market, along with that lovely head of hair of yours."

"Still envious, are we?" Gorlee said without thinking. "Perhaps you can buy it, assuming you could afford to on whatever the paltry wage is for being an ugly goon of Barnabus these days."

Kryzak cracked him in the back with his mace. Not too hard, but a warning.

Gorlee held his tongue but felt every bit of it.

Blast! They only look like scales. I wish they were real.

"Glad you found your lizard's tongue, Nath Dragon," Kryzak said, making his way around and facing him. The man's eyes were as haunting as his deep voice. "I wouldn't enjoy this so much without it. Come."

Across the roof they went and down the steps. The draykis held him by a metal leash on his waist. Kryzak led the way down the long steps that zigzagged down the huge tower hewn from large alabaster stones, talking most of the way.

"I've been waiting for this day," he said, "but I'm surprised you haven't resisted further. You were always so temperamental." He cleared his throat. "And how are your little friends, Dragon? Do the ones that survived me still live, or have our forces killed them? We've killed so many since you went into hiding. Twenty-five years of dying." He stopped and waited for the acolytes to open a pair of great bronze doors. "But don't feel so bad. It was always going to lead to this. And it's better than drowning."

What? Drowning? Kryzak! He recalled the story that was told to him by Bayzog and Brenwar one night. *The man who murdered the elven rover and tried to kill the others in the crater. They always wondered what happened to him.* Gorlee took a hard look at the man. *He's purely diabolical.*

A large room greeted him with high arches in vaulted ceilings. Dark curtains were pulled open around huge bay windows, and beautiful tapestries hung on the walls. On the far side, a grand opening led out onto a large terrace. In the middle, a giant oval table stood alone with high-backed mahogany chairs around it. A map hung on a separate wall and a large padded chair with lions carved in the arms sat like a throne on a dais nearby. It faced a window and a woman was seated there facing the terrace. She did not turn when they entered.

Gorlee swallowed hard. The room felt cold. Unnatural. The pungent smell of death lingered. He gazed around, just moving his eyes, high and low. Blood stained the marble floor. Dark spots blotted the carpets. His breathing thinned. His hunger froze. Power, evil power, crawled in his skin and bones.

A large bird swooped inside the room. Its feathers were dark and colorful. It landed on top of the woman's throne-like chair, facing Gorlee.

What is that thing? A bird, or a dragon? Oh no. A drulture!

Those, he knew about. Feathered dragons. Small dragons that preyed on the dead and the living like vultures. They were known to terrify gnome and halfling villages from time to time. They ate pixies like frogs eat flies.

Gorlee held its gaze with blood frozen in his veins. Drultures, unlike most dragons, actually did eat people. Of course, he was never clear if they were more dragon than bird or more bird than dragon. They were the best of the worst in both. Nasty.

It glared back at him. A restless hunger filled its bright eyes.

He had seen drultures on a battlefield full of the fallen once. Their jaws opened up like a python's and swallowed up parts of men whole. It had left him empty inside.

"Is he well secured?" the woman said. Her voice was deep, dark, and powerful.

"The moorite is intact as it pleases your will," Kryzak said, bowing with the others to a knee, "my Queen."

"Good. Now," she said, still sitting, still without turning, "you may all leave us."

Kryzak stood up and stiffened. His mouth opened to speak but didn't.

"Are you still here?"

The war cleric bowed and slowly backed away through the doors with the others, glaring at Gorlee. Gorlee offered a smile. It didn't last. It felt like a tomb was sealed when the doors closed behind him.

Nothing was said for moments until finally the High Priestess spoke. Her voice turned his blood to ice water.

"My, aren't you clever…"

Oh no, she knows!

CHAPTER
35

"BRENWAR," BEN SAID, GLANCING BETWEEN dragons, "what do we do?"

If ever there was a time that he should use Fang, it was now. He hadn't stood toe to toe with dragons before.

"Watch my back," Brenwar said. "And that dwarven steel should cut them."

The dragons snorted blasts of hot air at them and circled. 'Great lizards with wings' Brenwar called them sometimes. They crept like cats with scales. Their claws dug up the muddy ground like sharp metal rakes. A deep rumble came from their bellies, ready to unleash the thunder that waited inside.

Ben's knuckles were white on his sword grip. The dragons that ruled night and day had come out to play.

"We can take 'em, Brenwar said. "Just stay close. I don't think these grey scalers are big enough to be breathers. Just go for the neck and nose. And watch out for their—"

Swat!

A black dragon tail lashed out, lifting Brenwar from his feet, sending him head over heels on the ground.

Ben chopped downward and scored a deep cut in the tail.

The beast let out an angry growl and whirled on him with hot saliva dripping from its mouth.

He swung back and forth, keeping both dragons at bay.

They clawed and swatted at him. Their heads slid back and forth with cat-quick eyes.

Ben struck at one's nose.

Its long neck recoiled from harm with ease.

A tail swept at his feet. He jumped high over the tip of the tail.

Whack!

The other caught him full in the chest. It felt like it loosened his body from his bones and down hard he went. His sword flew from his fingertips. A second later, the dragon, twice the size of him, had him pinned down. Its claws dug into his shoulders. Ben screamed.

Zzzzt! Zzzzt! Zzzzt! Zzzzt!

The dragon jerked away from him. Golden shards of light were buried in its face.

Ben scrambled for his sword, dove and rolled back onto his feet. The angry dragon came right back at him.

Ben swung a two-handed blow with all his strength, splitting its nose.

The beast went into a mad frenzy. Its eyes flashed with anger, and on it came.

He braced himself for the charge, but the dragon didn't charge him, it leaped.

Gads! I can't catch that thing!

Brenwar rolled like a metal ball, onto his feet with War Hammer ready. It wasn't the first dragon he'd fought, and it wouldn't be the last. Not if he moved fast. He rushed the back side of the nearest dragon. In a split second it turned.

"Too late, Lizard!"

Brenwar brought War Hammer down with all his might and all his power, striking it in its backside. It sounded like a crack of thunder.

Ka-Pow!

The grey scaler's entire body shuddered. Its wings jolted, stretched and shuddered.

Brenwar struck again.

Pow!

And again.

Pow!

His battle-lusted mind heard the cry of an elf. He turned.

"Brenwar!" Bayzog yelled, pointing above.

A dragon dove from the sky and snatched him up.

"Let me down, you filthy lizard!"

Woozy, Bayzog's mind raced on what to do. Ben and Brenwar were both in grave danger. He himself was almost too weak to move. Brenwar was being lifted away toward a certain doom. He envisioned the dwarf being dropped into the fiery Jordak River.

No!

The Elderwood Staff glowed hot in his hands. He pointed it at the flying dragon. He swore he could hear Brenwar screaming in the air, "Don't you dare, Elf!"

The half-elf wizard unleashed the staff's power in a long hot burst of mystic flame.

Sah-Razzzz!

It streaked across the sky and struck the dragon in the shoulders. Brenwar tumbled toward the earth.

"Soft landings, Dwarf," he muttered, eyes searching. He found Ben just as the grey scaler leapt on top of the rangy warrior. Fangs and claws tore into him. "No, Ben, no!"

The dwarven armor lasted a few seconds before the dragon ripped it all off. Ben didn't think. He fought. His strong country thews were no match for the might of the dragon. All he could do was hang on to its horns. Push back against its great neck. A moment passed and his battle-hardened muscles began to shudder and give.

I won't die without giving it everything I've got.

Burning saliva dropped on his chest and the dragon let out a triumphant rumble and opened its jaws wide.

Ben put forth a great heave with his last ounce of strength.

The dragon lurched backward with an alarming howl.

Ben gasped. He was free. Exhausted, but free.

The dragon clawed at the ground. It roared in anger. Something had it by the tail.

Ben's heart pounded.

That something was Nath Dragon.

CHAPTER

36

GORLEE'S NAILS DUG INTO THE palms of his hands.

She knows. She knows. She knows.

He wanted to make a dash for the patio. To jump.

Surely I can turn into something that can fly. A draykis, perhaps.

She rose from her chair and stood on the dais. Her body was tall and magnificent. Her robes were dark, ornate and finely crafted. Her black hair was pushed up under a crown of silver leaflets.

"Cleverness is a survivor's skill," she said coolly, walking down the steps. Her dark beautiful gaze met his. "Are you a survivor?"

He had never felt panic until now. The woman had presence. Her words were powerful and hypnotic. He wanted to fall on his knees and beg for mercy. Confess everything. His knees started to bend.

I can't do this.

She came closer.

"Well?" she said.

Gorlee's tongue clove to the roof of his mouth. Every joint in his body had frozen, but his eyes remained on hers. *She's going to kill me. So beautiful. So frightening.* He stirred but did not speak.

She stopped a foot short of him, eye to eye. Her dark eyes searched his from underneath lavender eyelids. Her thin lips were pursed in curiosity. Her fragrance drifted into his nose. A sweet musk. Invigorating. She licked the top row of her white teeth. Ran the fingers of one hand through his hair.

He tingled.

She knows. She knows. She knows.

"Twenty-five years I've been looking for you," she said.

She doesn't know! Yes!

She circled him and a long black tail gently swept side to side behind her.

Whoa! Black scales! What did Bayzog say about the return of the black scales?

She ran her fingers over his scaled arms and said with a purr, "I see the rumors are true. You have indeed become more dragon." She put her lips to his ear. "Now we just have to finish the rest of you, Nath Dragon." She strolled toward the table with an unusual sway in her tail-laden hips. "Come. Sit. Talk." She glanced over her shoulder at him. "And I'll fill you like you've never been filled before."

His stomach gurgled.

She threw back her hair, laughed, and took a seat at the backless head chair.

"Come. Come."

Gorlee's limbs loosened and he took his first step forward, keeping his eyes on hers the entire time. *I can't believe I'm about to be seated at the table with the most powerful person in Nalzambor. Be Nath Dragon. Be Nath Dragon. Be Nath Dragon.* He sat down opposite her.

She clapped her hands.

A pair of young women in knee-length deep purple robes appeared from behind the curtains. Covered silver platters and a carafe of wine were carried to the grand table and set down. The young women stood silent and pretty with their hands down at their sides.

"Even dragons can get hungry," Selene said. "And they get very difficult when they hunger, don't they now, Nath…"

Oh no, is she saying Nath's entire name?

She was. On and on it went. Fascinated with dragons, Gorlee had requested that Nath repeat it to him once. Nath had obliged. That day had been more regrettable than enlightening, and he was a patient one. Now, he was starving. Frightened. His thoughts raced.

No person has ever recited a dragon name before, therefore, she's a dragon! And I know what they say. It takes a dragon to know a dragon. How long can I fool her? I'm in for.

The smell of food seeping out from under the silver lids was torture. An hour went by. He wanted to stop the woman, but interrupting a dragon was rude. Very rude among their kind. The second hour passed. One of the serving girls swayed. Her knees buckled and she collapsed on the ground.

Selene's lips continued to utter one intricately long syllable after the other.

Gorlee's head bobbed. His chin dipped down. He caught himself nodding off time and again.

Almost over. Almost over. I think it's almost over. Does she talk slower than Nath?

The second girl collapsed.

The sun dipped down on the west-facing patio and finally Selene stopped. Her engaging eyes waited on his lips.

"So," Gorlee said, reaching for the silver platter, "I guess I'm not the only one." He lifted the lid off it. "I hope you don't mind if I serve myself, seeing how your non-dragon servants," he peeked over the table, "have pillowed on the floor." He shook his head. "Maybe your draykis would make for better servants. They're horrible fighters."

"They caught you," she reminded him.

He lifted the lid off the plate. Sliced hunks of meat and cheeses were on there.

Ah, yes! He grabbed the platter with both hands. He picked the entire thing up, set it before himself, and ate, chewing up one large chunk at a time, barely keeping his ravenous hunger under control.

Selene's eye's widened. "Your manners are surprising, even for a hungry dragon."

He barely heard the words she said.

Food, I'll never undervalue you again.

"Sorry, but I'm so hungry I could eat a dragon."

She huffed a laugh. "Fine, fill yourself. You'll need it."

He tossed a meatless turkey bone on the platter and went for the wine. Not because he thirsted, but to let her know he didn't fear her. He filled a goblet for him and one for her.

"Thanks for the food," he said, smiling and sitting back down. "Aren't you drinking?"

She pushed the goblet away.

"I'm not thirsty."

He shrugged, tipped the goblet to his lips, and finished it in one gulp. He set the goblet down, leaned back, tapped his chest and burped. He picked his teeth with his claws.

Don't seem so formidable. Keep her off guard. Guessing. Nath says women are captivated by that.

"Now, what were you saying about the draykis capturing me? Hah. Is that what they told you? I surrendered."

"And why would you do that?"

He leaned forward on the table and said, "So I could meet the one who is behind all this."

Her face brightened. "I knew you would come!" she said, picking up her goblet. She made a slight toast. "You think you can save the world, don't you?"

"Who better than me?"

She took a long drink. "Well, Nath, you will be disappointed."

"And why is that?" he said.

"Because I'm not trying to destroy the world."

"Then what are you trying to do?"

"I'm just trying to run it." She set her goblet down. "And I want you to help me, but first there is one last test that you must pass."

"Wait a moment," he said. "I'm not going to help you do anything. There's no reason to test me."

"Oh," she said, cocking her head. "But you did so well on the first two. The roof. Starvation. Your name that I speak. But I'm still not sold you are the true Nath Dragon."

She does know! Gads!

"And I'm not sure you are the true High Priestess, but I'm not going to test you on it. You seem plenty wicked to me, judging by all the ugly faces. Why test me?"

She slammed her fist on the table.

Gorlee's strength had returned with the food, and he wanted to laugh. *Evil is so impatient.*

"Because you are my prisoner!" She got up and walked away. "Kryzak! Come!

The brass doors opened, and in the war cleric came. He did a quick up and down kneel.

"Yes, my Queen."

"Secure him in The Deep."

The Deep?

"As you wish." He motioned the draykis over with his arm.

The dragon-like men jogged over and picked him up by the arms.

"And I thought you were going to fill me with interesting conversation," Gorlee said, being hauled away.

"I did fill you, Fool. And it's only a matter of time before it takes effect."

Gorlee got a bad feeling.

Great. She's toying with me. That food must have been undercooked.

CHAPTER
37

"AH," FAYLAN SAID, SITTING INSIDE her tent and chewing the meat off a ham bone, "my little brother returns." She chucked the bone at him.

He swatted it away.

"Can you ever offer a kind greeting?" he said.

"I greeted you," she said. She got up and strolled over. Butted horns with his head and pinched his cheeks. "Is that better, Little Brother?"

No.

"Yes, for you it is anyway." He sniffed the air. Scanned the tent. He hungered. "Is there anything left of your feast?"

"Check with the soldiers. I'm sure they saved you some, Little Brother."

Finlin stomped his foot. His sister had become more and more unbearable over the years. Pushy. Greedy. She had always been rotten but not to this degree. She'd even pushed him to murder. He wanted take to his hoof to her butt.

He checked his anger. There were better ways to deal with his sister.

"So, the camp stirs in victory," he said, "and word of your great capture spreads."

She turned to him, excited, hands clasped together.

"Really, what have you heard?"

"Brilliant trap," he said. "That's what the orcs say. I heard that as I traveled in, not knowing what to make of it at first until I—"

She grabbed him by the armor.

"What else?"

"inquired," he finished his last word. "Inspiring, I heard another say. A gnoll said, 'Faylan did what a hundred generals and dragons had not, captured the greatest dragon of them all.'"

Her eyes were wide and feverish.

"And?"

"Something about a great hall in your honor," he added. He was making things up now, but she'd buy all of it. She always did.

"A Great Hall?" she let him go and looked up, grabbing her chin. "I like that." She turned to the tent entrance and yelled. "Guards. More rations and wine!" She made her way over to a small table and set of chairs. A moment later, a half-orc man entered with a wooden tray of food and wine, set it down, and left.

"Eat," she said.

Finlin reached over.

She grabbed his forearm, squeezed it, and said, "*and* talk."

"Hmmm, there was so much chatter and excitement to sort through," he said, spreading honey on a roll. He stalled as long as he could. The armies couldn't stand her. Not one bit, and it ate at her. It was fun to tease her with the opposite. "Something about underestimating you and that soon the war would be over. Ah!" He wiggled his finger and stuffed bread in his mouth. "Many want to be your henchmen when you get your own town or castle."

She hitched her elbow over the back of her hair and smiled.

"Really?"

Finlin nodded but not too much.

"Hailed by all the rotten races," she said, "there's not much better praise than that."

Except maybe being hailed by all the good races.

Her face lit up and she snapped her fingers.

"Wait till you see this!"

Quickly, Finlin buttered another roll and stuffed it inside his mouth.

"Whff is if?"

She pulled something from her pouch, tossed it on the table and pointed at it.

"That's a lock of Nath Dragon's hair."

Finlin swallowed.

"It is?"

"Yep."

Finlin leaned forward and eyed it.

"I thought his hair was auburn as a rooster."

"It is. Are you blind, you fool?" She looked at the lock of hair and gasped. "What!"

The hair was white and withered.

Faylan picked it up for inspection.

Finlin could feel the heat rise in her. Her cheeks reddened. Her eyes filled with worry. He couldn't keep from saying his next thoughts.

"That wasn't Nath Dragon, was it?"

She swatted the tray across the tent and screamed.

"Not a word of this to anybody!"

Certainly, dear Sister, certainly.

CHAPTER

38

IT WAS A SIGHT.

Nath dragged the dragon backwards. It screeched like an angry kitten.

Bayzog kept his distance, staff ready, breathing heavily. His emotions conflicted with relief and terror.

He lives!

Ben caught his glance. The rangy warrior poked his sword at the dragon's head.

"Stay back, Ben," Nath bellowed out. "I'll handle this!"

The dragon shook and shuddered. Snorted and roared. Nath held its tail fast in his bulging black-scaled arms. His eyes flickered with golden fire. Savagely, the dragon beat its wings. Its serpentine body lifted from the ground.

"No you don't," Nath said with anger. He released the dragon's tail, made a great leap onto its neck, and punched it in the head.

Whop! Whop! Whop! Whop!

The dragon flopped onto the ground.

Bayzog gasped. The powerful beast was over twice the size of Nath, and down it went. It coiled up like a serpent and crawled back and away from its aggressor.

Nath charged straight at it.

Like a snake it struck. Jaws wide, then snapping shut.

Nath slapped it.

Whack!

Bayzog felt the blow where he stood.

The grey scaler recoiled and whined. Its neck rolled from side to side and it shuffled off the road's edge.

Nath walked right at it.

"You know what happened to your great brother now, don't you?"

Its tongue flickered in and out of its mouth with a hiss, making Bayzog want to slap the evil thing.

Nath beckoned with his claws and said, "Come, let's finish this, Wicked Serpent."

Its serpent eyes were full of hate, but there was something else behind its fires. Respect. It backed farther from Nath and beat its wings. Up it went.

Nath turned back to face his friends.

"I'm glad to see everyone is alright."

The dragon dropped from the sky.

"Dragon!" Ben yelled, "Look out!"

Nath leapt out of the way a split second before it crashed to the ground. He was on his feet in an instant. His hair a red streak behind him. The dragon struck. Nath leapt over its head and locked his arms around its neck. The grey scaler writhed like a scaly worm. Its wings flapped with anger. It bucked like a maddened bull.

Nath held on, squeezing its great neck until its tongue juttered from its mouth.

Crack!

Its body sagged, and it died.

Nath tossed his head back and huffed for breath. His body trembled.

Ben approached and said, "You killed it."

Bayzog didn't know if Ben was shocked that the feat was accomplished or horrified that Nath had actually killed a dragon. He himself was already bewildered that Nath had survived a battle with the full-sized grey scaler.

Nath sagged toward the ground, but Ben caught him up.

"You alright?" Ben said, handing Nath his canteen.

Nath drank. "I'm fine." He straightened himself upright, clutched his side, and said with worry, "Where's Brenwar?"

Bayzog pointed where he had seen him land.

"I like to assume he's mostly alright. He took quite a fall."

Nath nodded and took a long look at all the dead dragons on the muddy road, and at the soldiers too. "It's sad it's come to this." He slapped Ben's shoulder. "Looks like you all fought well."

"It's us or them now, Nath," Bayzog said. "Not much of a choice now. So, I'm assuming we should get moving, that more are coming."

"No," Nath said, walking back down the road and picking up Brenwar's chest. "I took care of that." He heaved it onto his shoulder. "And we have our horses back. So, to the Crystal Cities it is, then?"

Bayzog caught movement in the corner of his eye. Brenwar marched through the grasses with War Hammer on his shoulder. His mouth twitched when he saw Nath, and his brows buckled.

"What happened?" the dwarf said.

"I'll tell you later," said Nath, walking on ahead.

"Where'd all the blood on you come from?" said Brenwar. "It's not that dragon's."

Nath didn't break his stride.

"The bad guys."

Strife in the Sky

-BOOK 7-

CRAIG HALLORAN

CHAPTER
1

ESCAPE.

The Tower of Narnum was more than it appeared to be. After they led him out of Selene's chambers, the draykis soldiers led Gorlee down the great tower's stairs. At the bottom of the tower he caught a glimpse of the Free City. The markets. The banners. The unhappy faces on the normally robust people. It seemed only the orcs smiled out there.

"Keep going," Kryzak said, shoving him forward.

It took almost an hour to walk down the steps, and Kryzak nudged him the entire way. He wasn't sure if the draykis was just mean or if he held some sort of grudge against Nath Dragon. For whatever reason, it seemed personal.

"I've kept pace every step," Gorlee said, shaking his shackled arms and legs. "Your pushes aren't making me any faster." He sniffed the air. "How about I buy you a meal, Kryzak? We'll take some time and settle things. Perhaps you can fill me in on this place, The Deep, that you've been talking about."

"We'll have plenty of time to talk when we get down there," Kryzak said. "Plenty of time. But enjoy the sounds, smells, and fresh air, Dragon." He made a gruff snicker. "Things aren't so pleasant in The Deep, and the food's far from refined."

Gorlee continued shuffling forward with the chains dragging on the floor.

"Oh, so there will be food then. That's good news. Are the draykis cooking?"

A guard shoved a spear between his legs, making him tumble onto the tiles.

"Always talking," Kryzak said, kicking him in the gut. "You talk too much." He kicked Gorlee again. "Shut it."

Gorlee rose to his feet with a groan. Things hurt, but he couldn't let on. He was Nath Dragon now, with scales. Sort of. High Priestess Selene had said there would be another test for him to pass. She'd said she wasn't convinced he was indeed Nath Dragon, and she'd hinted that the food he'd eaten might have some kind of effect.

"Will you quit with all the violence," he said, eyeing Kryzak. "Such actions are beneath a Warrior Priest like yourself."

"Everything is beneath me. Including scaly worms like yourself." He shoved Gorlee. "The Deep awaits, Nath Dragon."

Led by his escort, they traversed the lower plaza of the great tower. People were doing business there. All sorts. Food. Wine. Tapestry. Robes. Tools. Many of them eyed Gorlee and the group of soldiers, muttering and whispering but keeping to themselves. Gorlee could hear their haunting whispers though.

"To The Deep he goes."

"Into The Deep he disappears."

"Never the same again."

"His mind will be twisted in fears."

"I hear their screams in the ground at night."

"Mercy, Overlords! Mercy!"

Kryzak's penetrating stare sent them away.

Gorlee's belly fluttered.

I need to run for it. I don't want to know what this Deep is!

He glanced around. Women, men, children. He could mimic any of them. Mimic a child whose limbs were too small for the chains and slip away, blend in, and vanish. He had the strength for it. He slowed.

But he could feel Kryzak's eyes still glued to him.

They don't expect me to run. I gave myself up willingly. What to do? What to do?

One of the guards shoved him forward.

Gorlee shoved him back.

"I'm going!"

Kryzak grabbed him by his head of hair and jerked his chin back.

"Don't get antsy around all of these people." Kryzak pushed him onward. "But it happens when prisoners get their first look at The Deep." He pushed Gorlee's head in another direction.

A cone-shaped structure made of metal bars that crisscrossed in odd designs jutted from the ground. Several armored guards stood inside and outside of it. It was tall. Tall enough to reach the high point of the Plaza's great vaulted ceiling, which was high enough for a giant to walk under. Gorlee felt a chilling breeze coming from the structure.

"Take a look around," Kryzak said. "You won't have this kind of atmosphere for quite a while." He made a nod. A pair of guards unlocked the metal door and swung it open.

A strange howl filled Gorlee's ears, coming from within the cage. He stepped closer and raised up on his toes. A black hole with a rock rim gaped in the center. The fine hairs on his neck stood up.

I don't like this. Not one bit.

"And I thought that was you howling." Gorlee laughed. "But the hole is just as big."

Kryzak sneered and shoved him down.

Gorlee fell to his hands and knees.

This is it, Gorlee. Make a run for it, or you'll have to play this out. His mind raced. He was certain Selene had every intention of seeing him again. But had she done something to him? *What is this test?* He felt pixies fluttering in his stomach. *Is it in that hole, or is it in me? What if she discovers who I really am? Will she kill me? Let me rot in The Deep? I'm not ready to die yet.*

"Not so eager to go in there, are you?"

"Quite the contrary. Dragons love caves. Certainly you know that, don't you, Kryzak?"

Kryzak chuckled.

"I think you're scared."

"I'm not scared of anything. You know that." *Sultans of Sulfur. There's no turning back now.* There was a tight-knit group of draykis and guards around him. Even if he changed and confused them, it would be hard to make a break through them. They were armed and ready. He wasn't.

I should have tried this move back there. I had a window. I blew it.

"And if you'd quit pushing me down, I'd be in The Deep by now." He got up. "You know, Kryzak, I'm beginning to think you'll miss my company. Is that it?" He walked inside the cone and stood along the rim of The Deep. It was pitch black, and the breeze was cold on his toes and neck. He shook his mane of hair and combed his fingers through it. "A nice touch."

Smiling, Kryzak stepped over the rim and stood on the darkness.

"Impressive," Gorlee said, raising a brow. "I guess it's not as deep as I thought."

Kryzak nodded.

The draykis grabbed Gorlee by the arms and legs and hurled him into The Deep.

Gorlee landed at Kryzak's feet and slowly sank into the darkness.

What madness is this!

CHAPTER

2

THE TRAVEL WAS QUIET. PEACEFUL. The sun peeked through now and again, only to be snuffed out by grey clouds. Bayzog kept his chin up and eyes alert, but his lids were heavy. His body ached and his mouth was sore.

I don't want to ever engage in melee again.

The half-elf combed his hair behind his ears. His thoughts wandered to Sasha and his sons. He needed to know how they were doing. He wanted them to know that he was well. Alive, despite the efforts of some dragons and a troublesome gnoll. He cracked a smile. *I wonder if she'd ever believe I almost beat a gnoll in hand-to-hand combat.* He rubbed the polished wood of the Elderwood Staff. *Sort of.*

Ahead, Nath led, following the tree line an arrow-shot away from the distant road. Bayzog had faith that Nath's eyes could keep a lookout on things. Ben rode alongside Nath, chatting with him from time to time. It gave him some comfort. Sometimes Nath liked to be left alone, but at the moment he didn't seem temperamental. But there was plenty about Nath that was unpredictable.

I wish Sasha were here. She has a way with him that we don't.

Brenwar, who usually rode on Nath's other side, drifted back on his horse. The chest was secured on the back of his mount. Bayzog was relieved to see it. His feelings weren't the same for Brenwar, however. After all, he had knocked the dwarf from the sky a day earlier.

Brenwar grunted and eyed him with bushy brows.

"I only did what I felt I had to do," Bayzog said, avoiding his eyes. "And I figured you to be every bit as hardy as you look." He could hear Brenwar squeezing the leather of his reins. "And you don't seem hurt, aside from your limp … Wasn't that better than being carried away and dropped elsewhere?"

"Dwarven bones don't break as easily as elven," Brenwar said, taking his gaze away. "And…" He huffed. "And I'd have probably done the same. But only because you're as light as a feather and would have drifted down in like fashion."

"Is that a jest?"

"Aye, but never a truer remark."

Bayzog sat up in his saddle and cracked a smile.

Brenwar added, "But don't do it again." He grunted. "You seem rattled. Would you like to peek into the chest? We've a ways to go yet, and it'll ease your bones."

The dwarf's comment filled a void inside him. Bayzog always felt like an outsider. Odd. He wasn't the warring type. Not a master of steel. Not a soldier in armor. It was difficult for him to relate to the others because he trusted in magic and they trusted in what they understood: metal.

Today however, it was different. He and Brenwar had been searching for Nath for years and even though there was a worthy degree of trust between them, this was the first time he felt Brenwar was not just an ally, but a friend.

"I've a feeling we'd better preserve our resources, but it's a fine thing we have them." He pulled back his shoulder. "And I'm sure the longer I stick with you, the more likely I'll mend."

"Now you're thinking like a dwarf. Ye might just make it yet."

Bayzog allowed a laugh but kept his eyes ahead on Nath.

"He killed that grey scaler without a weapon, Brenwar," Bayzog said. "And he slapped another around like an orc."

"I wish it had been an orc."

"Well, I think he slapped plenty of them around too. To death, it seems."

"Let's hope not," Brenwar grunted. "But like you, it troubles me. That look in his eyes. The power in his voice. It reminds me of someone."

"And who might that be?"

"His father."

"Really?" Bayzog said, excited. "That's a good thing, right?"

Ben eyed Nath's scales.

Dark and beautiful, they had a way of winking in the sunlight. There was a quality about Nath and his presence that was unexplainable. Admirable. Captivating. Ever since the first time Ben met Nath, he'd been amazed with him. That was twenty-five years ago. And now, himself a hardened warrior and a battle-scarred veteran of over a hundred battles, he felt like a young man again.

"Dragon, how far can you see?"

Nath showed a pleasant smile over his strong chin and pointed into the sky.

"You see that cloud, the white one with a ring around it?"

"Yes."

"Keep an eye on it," Nath said, "something is about to pass through it."

Ben squinted and shielded his eyes. Waited. Several seconds later, a flock of birds passed through the cloud. "Huh," Ben said, then smiled at Nath. "But maybe that was a guess."

"A guess huh," Nath said, extending his hand. "Then hand me Akron."

"Why?"

Nath eyed him.

"Alright," Ben said, unhitching the bow from the lock on the back of his armor and handing it to Nath.

Snap. Clatch. Snap.

The bowstring twirled up and stiffened into place.

"And an arrow," Nath said, opening his palm.

Ben reached into the quiver and felt the feathers of a shaft.

"Moorite," Nath added.

"But there's not that many—"

Nath snapped his fingers, popping Ben's ears.

"Fine," Ben said, handing it over, "moorite it is."

Nath brought his horse to a halt, and Ben did the same. Slowly, Nath loaded the arrow and scanned the horizon. His red hair drifted gently in the breeze.

"I don't know what you're shooting at, but please don't waste that arrow."

Nath nocked the arrow and drew the string back along his cheek.

His pull is so smooth, and he pulls with such ease!

Nath closed one eye, aimed high, and released the shaft into the sky.

Twang!

Ben watched it sail one hundred yards, two hundred yards, and out of sight. He gawped.

"Uh, no disrespect, Dragon. But you just wasted an arrow."

"Well, it's my arrow," Nath said. *Clatch. Snap. Clatch.* He handed Ben Akron. "Come along." He directed his horse in the flight path of the arrow.

Two hundred yards later, Ben said, "Are you going to find the arrow? A black sliver among the high grasses? It would be an impressive feat."

Nath didn't reply.

"We *are* going to try to find it, aren't we? Aren't we, Dragon? Brenwar will be mad."

"He's always mad."

"I suppose," Ben said. "Does he have a difference between mad and happy?"

Nath was smiling.

"I guess if he's happy, he'll let you know."

Ben looked over his shoulder. Brenwar and Bayzog were far behind.

"Have you ever seen him smile or laugh?"

"He's always told me that he does it on the inside. 'The inside matters more than the out,' he says. I think he'd been drinking when he first said that." Nath pulled his horse to a stop. An elk with a great rack of horns lay dead on the grass with an arrow in its heart.

"Impossible!" Ben exclaimed, getting off his horse.

"I told you I had good eyes." Nath slapped Ben's shoulder. "Be of good cheer. You will all eat well tonight."

"What about you?" Ben said.

Nath turned to him and said, "I need Fang."

Ben unstrapped it from his shoulder and handed it over.

Nath buckled the sword's scabbard around his waist and climbed back on his horse.

"I'll be back," Nath said.

"Where are you going?" Ben said.

Nath dug his heels in and rode away.

"Where's he going?" Brenwar said, frowning. "Why didn't you stop him?"

"I'd like to see you stop him," Ben replied. "Don't worry, he'll be back. I think."

CHAPTER
3

SASHA SIGHED.

"What is it, Mother?" asked her eldest son, Rerry.

Rerry was a fine young part elf, little more than twenty years old. He had sandy hair and violet eyes like his father and was spry and well-built, taking from his human side. He sat on a stool at Bayzog's great table, rubbing oil on the blade of his longsword. He wore a light vest and fine trousers and always looked relaxed.

"I think it's these walls," she said, rubbing a trinket on her necklace. It was enchanted. Something Bayzog had given her in case of trouble. It sparkled like a star when it hit the light right. "I miss my walks in the gardens."

Rerry hopped off his stool.

"Let's go then."

"It's late," Sasha said, brushing her auburn locks from her eyes, "and it's dangerous." She rubbed her son's shoulder. "You know that."

He backed off and whipped his blade around.

"I can handle it. I'm already a top swordsman in my class."

"Yes, I know. You tell me every day."

"Well, I am," he shrugged, slashing more patterns in the air. "And many don't like me, being so young and all. But I practice. That's what being the best is all about."

"Just put it away," she said, pulling her sleeves down her arms. She shivered. There was fighting everywhere, and Bayzog was out in the thick of it. *I think Rerry inherited the bravery that Bayzog kept buried.* She yawned and fought it.

"Why do you do that?" Rerry asked.

Sasha looked puzzled. "What?"

"That," he said, setting his sword aside and pointing out her mouth. He mimicked her yawn.

"What, yawn?" she said, feeling startled.

"Is that what you call it, a yawn? Do you do that when you're tired?"

His words hit her like a bag of sand. She walked over to the great mirror that hung over one of the fireplaces and studied her face. Her eyes had the slightest hint of crow's feet, and there were faint wrinkles on her forehead. *Oh my.* She'd never thought about it before! *Elves don't yawn.* She fixed a glass of Wizard Water and sat down on the sofa. *I'm getting older while they all stay so young.*

Rerry hopped up on the sofa arm and said, "Let's go to the gardens. You need some fresh air." He twitched his lips. "A horse ride in the country, maybe. It's been years since we rode."

It was true. They used to ride all the time, but now things were dangerous. The soldiers of Barnabus were everywhere, and Sasha and her boys had to be careful. Given their elven heritage, they had to conceal it. In the case of Rerry, his features were more man than elf, but his energy was extraordinary.

"Maybe tomorrow."

"Ah, Mother, you always say that. You can't stay cooped up so much, and you can't worry so much about Father."

She took a drink of Wizard Water. The revitalizing nectar warmed her skin. She looked at her son.

"I don't worry about your father so much. He can handle himself. It's you and your brother I worry about." *And myself. I'll be old and gray before they've even grown up.* She took another sip.

"Mother, we can't live in fear of what is to come. If we live in fear, then our enemies win."

"Is that what your father said?" she asked.

He sat down and put his arm around her shoulder. "No, that's what you said about ten years ago." He took her by the hand and pulled her up. "Now let's go."

She kissed his cheek and said, "You're a fine boy, Rerry."

"I know."

She laughed.

"What about your brother? Should we ask him along?"

"No, I want this to be fun."

CHAPTER

4

THE DEEP. TRANSPARENT DARKNESS COVERED Gorlee's entire body from head to toe. His mind raced. His flailing was futile. He couldn't move. *What is this blackness?* Above him, Kryzak showed a triumphant sneer. That man hated Nath Dragon. Gorlee wondered why. *I should have escaped! I should have escaped!*

Coldness covered him like damp snow. He couldn't feel his breath, but it wasn't lost either. The only thing he could feel was his heart racing inside his chest. *Thump! Thump-Thump!* The murky blackness began to move. Kryzak's form swirled out of sight.

As if he were in a drain, Gorlee swirled downward faster and faster. Black waves rushed by his ears.

Madness! Pure madness!

His belly churned. His toes and fingers tingled at the tips as he spun in the vortex.

Noooooooooo!

It went on. Spinning and spinning. Minutes. Maybe hours.

Please stop! Please stop!

The spinning slowed. The darkness lifted. His body came to a stop.

Sultans of Sulfur! Thank you!

On hands and knees, he felt the cold ground beneath him. Holding his stomach, he struggled to rise, but the room was still spinning. He collapsed on the floor, spinning and spinning. Gradually, it came to a stop.

Finally.

He pushed himself up into sitting position and rubbed his neck.

Where am I? What test is this?

He tilted his head upward. A tiny round light shone impossibly high above him. The entrance.

"Gads!"

His voice echoed off the rocks that formed the inner ring of The Deep.

A blackness hovered above. It moved like a cloud. Bright spots in it stared down on him like eyes.

A chill crept down Gorlee's spine.

Not again!

The blackness drifted down until it stood above him in a man's shadowy form. A smoky arm lifted from its ethereal body and pointed down a great hall.

Gorlee's eyes were glued to it.

A phantom!

There were legends about the phantoms of Nalzambor. A race in their own right. Mystical. Powerful. Keepers and guardians of many things.

Gorlee swallowed and shook his head, summoned his courage.

"Are you the warden of The Deep?"

It didn't speak so much as it breathed a cold and eerie *Yes*.

The illness in his stomach returned.

This is horrible.

He glanced upward again. The Deep appeared to be as far below ground as the Great Tower of Narnum was above.

Dwarves must have done this. But I have no Brenwar!

The phantom raised its ghostly arm again.

Go ... or ... die ...

Gorlee turned and faced the hallway. There were green torches—magic, he surmised— running as far as he could see.

"You know, Selene will be very upset if you lose me," he said, chains rattling on his ankles as he stepped forward. "And I can only assume you are the only way in and out of here ... so don't oof—"

A blood-curdling cry echoed down the hall. Gorlee stopped, looked, and listened. He noticed one thing. The phantom was gone. He had never felt so alone in his life.

CHAPTER

5

NATH ABANDONED HIS HORSE AND trudged into the forest with the scabbard of Fang in his hand. He eyed the finely-crafted hilt of the blade. Ornate dragon-heads with gemstone eyes stared back at him. He leaned it against a tree and stepped away.

Fang hadn't been kind to him of late. He rubbed his palms. He could still feel Fang's burning hilt in his grips. This 'sword with a mind of its own' had been made for him, but something was wrong. The great blade didn't like him anymore. Not since his last long hibernation. And change.

He rubbed his chin. Kneeled down and eyed it.

"Fang," he said. He grumbled and stood back up. "What am I doing?"

Fang had always been unpredictable. It unloaded its great powers when it wanted to and not when Nath wanted it to. He'd never had control of it.

They say I'm unpredictable too. Hmmm. Perhaps that's it.

Nath walked over to the sword, took a breath, and pulled it out of the sheath. The metal was cool on his palm.

"That's better," he said. He cut the weapon through the air in circles. "Much bett—*ouch*!"

He jammed the blade into the ground and blew on his hands.

"Blast you, Fang! I'm your master, you are not mine!"

He kicked some pine needles off the ground.

"Aw, I don't need you anyway! I can do this without you!"

He ripped a hunk of wood from a tree.

"Stupid sword!"

Nath was angry. He was hurt more. It seemed that Fang didn't trust him anymore. Even worse, Fang was a blade that his father made for him. It was special. Fang's resistance reminded him of his failures. It didn't like the bad inside him.

"I'm not evil," he said through clenched teeth. He took a seat and leaned back against a tree. "This is no way for a man to behave." He rubbed his side. That nasty little splinter in his ribs started to bother him. He combed back his mane. "Great."

Earlier in the day, Nath had felt all powerful. Stronger. Faster. Invincible. His confidence had risen to new heights when he beat the grey scaler. But there were more dangerous things in Nalzambor than grey scalers. What if there had been two of them? Could he have handled them both?

I am strong but am I not wise.

He needed every advantage to protect himself and more importantly his friends. He needed all of his friends. Fang in particular.

"What good is a sword that you cannot hold?" He eyed the sword. "Father made you for me, didn't he?" Nath got up and pulled his shoulders back. "Didn't he?"

His father's strong voice echoed in his head. *You make things to serve yourself as well as others.*

Nath stretched out his fingers and held them close to the hilt.

"I'm not letting go this time, Fang," he said, bringing his fingers closer. "Not even if my hands catch fire."

He wrapped up the hilt and squeezed. His fingers felt like they were cauterizing in fire. He screamed.

"Eeeeeee—Yaaaaaaaaah!

Wood burned. A small campfire glowed and crackled. All the faces around it were glum. Bayzog huddled in his tattered robes. Brenwar sulked and grunted.

Nath Dragon was gone again.

"He said he'd be back," Ben said, turning a spit of elk meat over the fire. "And at least he left us dinner." He smiled at Brenwar. "Lordy, that was something."

Brenwar huffed and chewed on a hunk of meat.

The dwarven warrior looked like he'd fought a thousand battles in a day. His black beard was raggedy, and his chest plate was dented and beaten. The remnants of his clothes were in tatters, and his boots had holes in them.

"What are you staring at, Man?" Brenwar said, ripping off a hunk of flesh with his teeth from the bone. "You don't like what you're seeing. Don't like my boots? They're two years old, you know, and just worn through."

"Don't *Man* me, Dwarf," Ben said. "I don't want to hear all of your fussing. You should be grateful Dragon is alive. I know I am."

"Ah yes, you're just so giddy. A child playing with fire."

"What are you talking about?" Ben said. He wanted to shake Brenwar.

"I see that look in your eyes, Human," Brenwar said, slipping his hand onto War Hammer's handle. "You think you can tangle with me? Do you?"

"I'm just making conversation," Ben said, getting to his feet. "But if you want to—"

"I think that is quite enough," Bayzog interjected. He'd been sitting quietly, eyeing the flames. "We have to focus on our enemies, not making enemies of one another."

Ben resumed his seat on the grass, eyeing Brenwar.

"Don't you stick your lip out at me," Brenwar growled.

"Brenwar, you'd bicker with a tree," Ben said, fixing a piece of meat.

"And I'd win."

"Only a dwarf would claim to win an argument with a tree," Bayzog said.

Brenwar glared at him.

Bayzog raised his palms.

"And I see nothing wrong with that."

Bayzog rubbed the amulet under his robes. It was times like this he missed Sasha and his sons the most. He hadn't seen them in a long time, and that wasn't so bad for the elf in him, but the human inside him missed his wife. Every time he got to see her, she had changed so much. *Focus, Wizard. Focus.*

"Brenwar," Bayzog said, "why don't you finish telling me about Nath's father?"

"No."

"Well, tell us about Dragon Home."

"You mean The Mountain of Doom?" Ben said. "Brenwar, you've been in it? And you've seen the King Dragon?"

"Of course I have."

"All these years and nobody tells me anything," Ben said, frowning.

"Stop complaining," Brenwar huffed. "And you didn't ask, did you?"

"Well, it would have been nice to have known," Ben said.

"Dwarves don't gossip."

"It's not gossip! It's just conversation among friends. I'd like to have some understanding of who and what I'm fighting for."

Brenwar stiffened.

"If you don't know what you're fighting for, then you shouldn't be fighting."

"Well," Ben said, "I've been fighting so long, I guess I've lost track of all of that. Please remind me."

"Wizard," Brenwar said, tossing an elk bone away, "you fill him in. My mouth is too sore for this chatter."

"But it's not too sore for eating," Ben said.

Brenwar got up, clenched his fists, and disappeared into the woods.

"You'd think," Ben said, "given his years, he'd be less temperamental."

Bayzog opened his mouth to speak, but Ben cut him off.

"I know, he's a dwarf."

Bayzog liked Ben, but he envied the man too. Ben had faith in Nath. Much more than he did. Bayzog had doubt. Concern. And those were not good things.

"Ben, evil destroys love, joy and peace. Wouldn't you agree, based off what you've seen?"

"I know," Ben said, shaking his head. "I know. It's not patient or kind or good, so to speak."

"And it lacks self-control. It lies. It twists. It digs at each and every one of us." Bayzog sighed. "But we have to resist those temptations it offers. Ben, I miss my family. I love them more than anything, and there is nothing I'd rather do than go home and huddle with them and let the world end how the world ends. But I can't."

Ben bobbed his head.

"Well, you could," Ben said, "But I understand. I had a family too, only to see those minions take them. If I'd been there, then maybe I could have saved them. It eats at me every day. I miss them."

"So why do you fight?" Bayzog said. "Why do you go on?"

"Because I don't want other families to go through what I went through. I want to help end this. I want peace on Nalzambor again."

"Then you do know why you fight this war. Your reasoning is sound and wise. You are a good friend, Ben."

"Do you think we'll win?" Ben asked.

"All I know is that we have to."

CHAPTER

6

THE WALLS WERE STONE. THE corridor long. The green torches didn't flicker, and the howls were like banshees in the night. One foot at a time, Gorlee stepped forward. He'd never been so deep in the ground before in all of his decades. Not even with a dwarf. He'd never felt so small, either. Above, in the light, he felt confident and invincible. Now he felt like a child frightened by the howls of the night.

His stomach groaned. The fullness he had experienced earlier at Selene's table had dissipated and been replaced by something else. Fear.

Be brave. She won't keep you down here forever. Will she?

Gorlee's chains rattled when he stopped. He hadn't thought about that. Maybe she knew he wasn't Nath Dragon. Maybe she knew what he was and had abandoned him down here forever. *No. Can't be. Please, it can't be.*

He jumped.

A pale white rodent scurried over his toes and disappeared into the wall.

A cry echoed down the tunnel, sending a chill down his spine.

Get it together, Gorlee. You've never met anything you couldn't handle. He took a breath and continued forward. The tunnel was murky and damp. Water dripped down the slime-coated walls, forming many small puddles. He covered his nose. *What is that?*

An angry cry rang out. The sound of a scuffle ensued. Gorlee kept going. Ahead, a light glowed beyond the torches. Shadows flickered in its essence. *What kind of place is this? Are there prisoners? Do they all run free?*

He thought about Selene. So far as he knew, she was the most powerful woman in the world. Beautiful. Dark and exotic, she was. Beyond human, and different. He could picture her in his mind and see her as if she were right there, smirking and toying with him. *She knows I'm not what I appear to be. But she said this was a test.* His stomach gurgled. He felt uncomfortable. *That's odd.* It gurgled again. *What was in that food she gave me?* He looked at his black-scaled hands. They shifted and changed a little. *Control it, Gorlee. Control it.* His hands seemed to solidify once more, but he had a feeling something was at work inside him. Probing what he was all about.

A bend in the tunnel started. The murmuring of many voices assailed his ears. Onward he went with his hand on his stomach, fighting down the fear inside him. *Is it possible that I missed another phantom?* The smells got stronger, the voices louder, and steps led ... *upward*?

Up he went, chains dragging over the stones. All the mumblings went silent. Gorlee looked at his shackles. *How can I defend myself in these things? I could make myself smaller. Change to something lither and slip out of these things.* He shook his head. *It's a test, remember. It's a test.* On heavy legs, he followed the light up the long rows of stone steps. He took fifty of them and came to a stop on a broad marble platform. Ancient runes and symbols covered the floor, but most were covered by the wet murk.

"COME," a cavernous voice said.

Gorlee remained frozen in place.

"COME," the voice said, "and I don't like to repeat myself."

"Come," other voices chanted. "Come," all sorts of voices said.

Gorlee's legs seemed to move of a will that was not his own. Toward the lights. Toward the voices he went. A great chamber opened up. Hundreds of eyes blinked and sought his from the shadows of ledges and side caves. A great figure stood in the middle with its arms crossed over its chest.

I've never seen anything like that before.

Its long large fingers beckoned Gorlee forward.

"COME," it said, calmly, "let me have a better look at you."

Gorlee made his way into the chamber and took a glance back over his shoulder. He could hear all the voices say:

"Nothing leaves The Deep."

CHAPTER

7

Nath ripped Fang out of the ground. His fingers felt like fire, but he held on. His head beaded in heavy drops of sweat.

"I will not let go!" he said, fighting the agony.

Fang's blade shimmered and winked with life. Orange and blue colors swirled in the metal of the blade. It hummed. Moaned. Angry. Urging Nath to release it.

"I will not!" Nath said. He staggered in the grove. "You'll have to burn my fingers off first!"

Water. Nath wanted water to douse the blade in to cool his fingers. But no stream nor any creek trickled nearby.

Don't think about water. Think about control.

Fang! You are mine! A gift from my father. You serve me. I do not serve you!

The blade flared with mystic fire and let out an angry moan.

Nath could feel the scalding heat up to his elbows. His great arms juttered. His teeth clenched.

Fang! Listen to me! Stop this! Stop this madness now!

The blade shook in his hands from a force of its own.

"I will not let go, Fang! Not until you succumb to me!"

The dragon heads on the hilt started to move. Streams of smoke poured from their nostrils. They let out tiny roars.

Nath's hands started to smoke. The white scales on his palms burned.

"Fang! Enough of this!"

Nath's body trembled. His great muscles convulsed. He fell to his knees, with his scales sizzling. His own mind screamed. His fingers begged to recoil.

I cannot! I will not!

Nath fell on his back screaming. Birds scattered from the trees. Branches shook. He held on, fighting the pain until his mind began to black out.

"Fang," he whispered. "You are my friend. I need you. But you must trust me."

The bladed metal swirled with scintillating colors and heated up in one great burst. Nath felt every ounce of its power rush through him like lava, and it swept him across the ground. He held on and on and on. Everything hurt from head to toe, but he held on.

"Fang," he managed to say, "trust me again."

The blade winked out. The metal cooled in his hands. Nath let out a long sweaty sigh and said, "Thank you, my friend. Thank you."

He rolled to his knees and pushed himself up with the blade. He peeled one hand away.

"Uh."

His hand was swollen and it trembled like a leaf, but there was no burn on it. He checked his other hand and it was the same.

"Whew," he said, dashing the sweat from his eyes. "I'm glad you got that sorted out. And I'm gladder to have you by my side. I never would have made it this far without you."

He hefted Fang over his shoulder, picked up the scabbard, and searched for his horse. Minutes later, he was riding back toward his friends. When he got there, doubtful faces greeted him, but he was all smiles.

He stretched Fang out over his head and let the steel blade shine in the sun.

"Saddle up. It's time to vanquish evil."

Bayzog rode easy, studying a piece of mystic shard in his hand. The bright fragment's powers were gone, but some mystery remained. How did the forces of Barnabus harness its power? The crystals were almost impossible to mine and shape, but somehow they managed to do it. It was a grave concern.

"Worried, I see," Nath said, riding up alongside him.

"Is it that obvious?"

"Well," Nath said, "you always look concerned about something."

"It's that bad, is it?"

"For an elf, maybe, but for a man, maybe not so bad. So, tell me, what are you thinking?"

Bayzog wanted to ask the same thing, but Nath had made his plans quite clear. He was heading straight for the River Cities to find out what was going on with these crystals. Not a subtle strategy but a bold one instead.

"I'm thinking only one person is capable of making these things," Bayzog said. "Maybe a few, and the more we close in, the more heavily guarded they will be." He glanced back at the forest and fields behind him. "Not to mention, we are most likely being pursued from all angles, thanks to your efforts at the bridge."

Nath sat tall in the saddle with a calm look in his eyes and said, "The path is broad to where we go, and we won't be so easy to find."

"And when we get there?"

"We'll come up with something."

Nath pulled his horse to a stop and craned his neck toward the sky.

Bayzog scanned the sky, but heard nothing.

"Get into the woodland," Nath said. He made a sharp whistle ahead.

Brenwar and Ben turned in their saddles.

Nath pointed toward the woods and mouthed the words, "Quickly."

They all led their horses deep into the edge of the forest, where Nath stopped and waited.

Bayzog peered up through the pines. A distant sound caught his eyes and came closer.

Whump. Whump. Whump. Whump. Whump.

Wings beat against the wind in the sky, dragon shrieks called out in the air, shadowy forms glided over the branches, and his heart beat in his throat. It sounded like more than a dozen of them. He turned back at Nath.

Nath held his arm out and finger up.

Splintering shrieks were like bells in his ears. The horses shifted, snorted and stammered on their hooves. Bayzog rubbed his horse's neck and whispered in its ear. The fine beast calmed.

After the dragon shadows passed, the shrieks faded. Bayzog heard Ben sigh.

"Noisy things, aren't they?" Nath said with a smile.

"That was awfully close, wasn't it?" Brenwar remarked.

"True," Nath said, "but I'll always hear them coming."

"Is that so?" Brenwar said.

"Yes, yes it—"

A shadow circled above and dropped just outside the tree line with a *whump*. A dragon crept toward them with its long neck swaying back and forth. With its piercing eyes locked on Bayzog's, it charged forward.

CHAPTER

8

GORLEE STOOD FLAT-FOOTED, LOOKING UP. The monstrous figure looked down on him from twelve feet above. Its head was bald, and its broad face rested on a thick neck like an ugly troll's. Its chest was broad and hairy, and its grey skin was clammy like a fish. Its arms were long and thick like an ape's, and its knuckles almost clawed the floor.

What are you?

"What am I?" it said. "I know you wonder."

Gorlee shrugged and tried to ignore the stench of its breath.

"Confident this one is, ah ah ah," it said. It pointed a fingernail tipped like a spear at him. "Perhaps you think me a troll, but trolls don't speak like me and you, do they?"

"I wouldn't know," Gorlee said. "The only trolls I've ever known are dead."

"Ooh," the creature said with a smile of broken teeth, "I like that. Hmmm … maybe you think me a giant?"

Gorlee gave the monster a closer study. He knew the races. He'd spent his entire life mimicking them, and he thought he'd seen all of them. But this thing was different. The eyes of trolls were dull and stupid. This thing's eyes showed cunning. He'd seen plenty of giants too, but none with arms so very long before either. Its legs were short, and there were strange ridges in its skin, but its mouth looked a mile wide. *Maybe it's cursed. Maybe it's a demon from the depths.*

"I don't care what you are," Gorlee said.

Its pinkish eyes widened and blinked.

Gasps and hisses could be heard among the other voices. Slowly, they came forward from the shadows into the cavern's light. Most of them were long-haired and unkempt, but normal in size. What was left of their clothes was in shambles. Men mostly. Orcs, gnolls, and goblins were among them.

It poked him in the chest.

"I am a triant. My name is Bletver. My mother was a troll and my father a giant."

"I think that is one of the worst things that has ever been bred, er, I mean said." Gorlee yawned and covered his mouth. "I guess that explains the present company of scary faces you keep. He yawned again. "And what a fine establishment you have set up. How much to rent one of these caves?"

"Oh ho ho," the monster said, "I'm going to enjoy you." It crept closer and eyed his chains. "My, you must be special." It flicked Gorlee's shackles. "I've not seen moorite in an age. Take a look at this, boys."

The faces crowded in.

"Indeed you are special. Very special as the phantom did say." It huffed and leered at Gorlee. "Who are you, and how did you get those scales?" It brushed its arms with the back of its fingers.

Gorlee felt ill, and his stomach was still turning. The multitudes were pressing in and tugging at his chains. It took everything he had, to not take a swing at them. To not change and escape the chains. But the desperation in their eyes left a feeling of pity in him. These people were condemned. Some of them might have been soldiers that fought against the forces of Barnabus. Others might have been failed enforcers of the same. The monstrous humanoid was their warden, and he probably already had his henchmen scattered among the crowd, feeling him out. And the phantom, that was the gatekeeper of the deep.

"I'm just one of you now, it seems," Gorlee said. "When do we eat?"

The monster clapped his hands.

"You are a delight to my dungeon." It laughed. "A man of wits and games. Well now, let's see what we can do to make our guest more comfortable. Let's get you out of those chains."

"That would be kind."

"Bring an axe and block!" it shouted.

The crowd parted, making a pathway for a large humanoid that approached. Its head and shoulders were covered in shaggy black fur, and it stood taller than the others. Broad and muscular, it came with a large block of wood tucked under one arm and a great axe slung over its shoulder.

A bugbear. They have all the worst down here. How quaint.

It dropped the heavy block of wood down on the ground with a snort and clutched its axe in both hands.

"I don't think that blade is of much use against moorite," Gorlee said. He laid the chains across the block. "But you are welcome to take a whack."

The monster's chuckle was low and wicked.

"Oh, we know our plans can't break those chains. But removing your hands from your wrists? That's another thing."

Gorlee jerked his hands away.

"What!"

"Grab him!"

A surge of bodies seized him, pinned him down, and held his arms in place. "Aw, don't worry, *Nath Dragon*, with any luck, your dragon skin will hold."

No it won't!

"And," the monster continued, "you will have passed your test. Of course if you fail, you'll be doomed like the rest of us." He signaled to the bug bear.

The axe flashed up over its head.

CHAPTER

9

FINLIN THE SATYR KEPT HIS joy to himself.

I love it when she makes mistakes.

He tossed a small rough sack over his shoulder and belted his scabbard around his waist. He carried two daggers only and kept his pipes tied close to his neck. The rest of the camp bustled with activity, and the march to seize another city began. One hundred motivated soldiers of Barnabus in heavy gear and arms moved through the hills like an invincible python. The draykis could be seen positioning themselves in the fore and middle of the ranks. Their eyes were alert and their commands not subtle.

"Perhaps you should tell them," Finlin suggested to his sister.

She clenched her fist in his face.

"I said not a word of this."

The pair remained behind. Quiet. Faylan toyed with her hair and chewed on her lip. She didn't like to make mistakes. In the case of their capturing Nath Dragon, neither one of them could be certain who that really was.

"Well, perhaps it was him. Maybe his hair is just different. I don't see how you could have suspected anything different." He tried to sound reassuring. "Whoever it was, it fooled everyone. Even the draykis. I'm proud of you, Sister."

"Oh shut it, you little horned toad." She punched him in the arm. "I don't need your reassurance. I just need you to keep your mouth closed and do as you're told. I'll deal with the High Priestess if the time comes. And you will not admit to knowing anything otherwise." She patted the dagger on her chin. "I'd hate to think my brother would turn on his sister."

"No, never," he said.

"Good," she said, trotting away, "Idiot."

Watching her go, Finlin entertained two schools of thought. If the High Priestess discovered what they had hidden, they'd both be punished. He was certain it would be a fatal thing. Another thought occurred to him as well. *If we are caught, no doubt my sister will turn on me.* He noted the draykis heads towering among the ranks. The hulking dragon-like humanoids should have known, if they'd captured someone other than Nath Dragon. *Wouldn't they have said something?* Maybe they had kept quiet about it, wanting Faylan to fail. No one really liked her that much, particularly the draykis. After all, she controlled them. A stubby goat-legged woman ordering such renowned monsters around couldn't sit too well.

Finlin caught up with the ranks and walked alongside. The faces of the races were far from pleasant. Hard, grim, mean and not a smile among them. Metal rattled on their shoulders and hips. A sizable force to take over a small town or city.

When we take over, I wonder what happens after that? What kind of reward is in it for the likes of us?

He thought of his home at The Crater. He longed to be back there.

If only I could slip away without notice. The smell of this army is becoming alarming.

He trotted toward the front and caught up with his sister.

"Shall I scout ahead?" he asked.

She frowned at him and said, "Be back by dusk and not a crack of light later."

"They move," a dwarf said, reporting back to Pilpin. It was Horn Bucket. He had a rusty beard and half an arm left on one side. "Southeast and winding toward the villages. A strong force, and those oversized lizards are with them." He adjusted his wooden helmet with the elk horns sticking from it. "Shall I head back out?"

"Come with me," Pilpin said.

They'd been keeping a close eye on the satyrs and the small army, probing for opportunities and weaknesses. So far, nothing had presented itself, but it was only a matter of time. The dwarves had a saying, "If it's not dwarven, then it has a weakness." A motley army of the wicked races couldn't be cohesive. Especially under the lead of a woman satyr. But they were strong. Merciless. They'd pummeled town after town with iron gauntlets.

Back at their camp, Devliik accepted the news and gathered all his men.

"Smaller bands of dwarves have taken greater numbers," he said, thumbing the blade of his axe. "But it's those draykis I'm concerned about. At the moment, we are outmatched by them. Their skin is thick as steel." He huffed. "It's the satyrs we want to extract, but once we do, we'll have the entire army after us."

"Better they come after us than after the next village," Pilpin said. "A good thing."

"Aye," Horn Bucket added.

"I agree," Devliik said, "and, we ride, but they don't."

"Perhaps they won't miss the satyrs if we take them," Pilpin suggested. "And the one seems to control those draykis. Perhaps if we finish her, we can finish them. Or scatter them maybe."

"How far to the next settlement?" Devliik asked.

"At their rate," Horn Bucket said, "I'd say four days. Six if they move toward a greater city, and they're more than capable of taking one. They're slow, but they're in no hurry either."

"Death is never in a rush," Devliik said.

"And what of that dragon?" Pilpin said. They'd witnessed Gorlee being snatched away by a great dragon. It was part of the reason they needed to follow the satyrs: in order to find out what had become of him. "What if it comes back?"

"We just better get this done before it does come back," Devliik said, "or there might be a toasty grave for all of us."

CHAPTER
10

T HE DRAGON TORE THROUGH THE brush and barreled toward Bayzog. It was a young grey scaler, but bigger than two men put together. Its claws tore through the dirt and brush, and its mouth opened to roar.

Nath went for Fang.

Twang! Zip!

An arrow streaked into its neck, cutting off its roar.

It reared up.

Twang! Zip!

Another arrow stuck in its belly.

The dragon thrashed on the ground, its tail swiping around. Nath leapt over the tail and brought his sword down. The dragon moved no more.

Sadness overcame Nath. His heart was grieved. He kneeled down and closed the dragon's eyes.

"There is no other way," Brenwar said, stepping up behind his shoulder. "It's us or them."

"I'm not supposed to kill my kind," Nath replied, holding back tears. "I'm not supposed to kill at all. What have I done?"

"We're at war," Brenwar said.

Nath looked back at Brenwar and said, "Do dwarves kill dwarves? Do elves kill elves?"

"It happens. We all squabble and skirmish," Brenwar reminded him, "and it's a shameful thing when it happens. And this isn't the first time. Dragons have fought and killed dragons before. I was there when the last war happened."

Nath sighed. He knew the stories. The history. The tragedy. There had always been good and bad dragons. He'd spent a lifetime trying to rescue both. In the case of the grey scalers, there was little good in them, but that didn't mean they weren't worth saving.

He got up and said, "Ben, you'll need those moorite arrows." He tilted his head and listened. If more grey scalers were coming, he didn't hear them. "We'd better get moving." He took a lasting look at the dead dragon. *How many more have to die before this is over?* He got on his horse. "Let's go."

For the better part of the day, they rode through the forest with solemn expressions. Nath could feel the weight of the war that was upon them. His goal was to do anything in his power to prevent that. If he could, he would redeem himself.

The splinter in his ribs bit into him. He grimaced.

"You alright, Nath?" Bayzog said.

He nodded.

"It's that wound from Egdon. It hasn't healed, has it," Bayzog said with a concerned look.

"Just a splinter. It won't slow me down."

"I'm not concerned that it will slow you."

"Then what is your concern?" Nath said.

"The Dragon Skinner blades don't splinter," Bayzog said, "and that cursed blade left a mark inside you. I told you, that poison can lead to the heart."

Nath could still feel the blade that Overlord Dormus struck him with. He'd almost died from it.

"I just don't think the wound is fully healed."

"You are a dragon, Nath," Bayzog said, "and I've never seen you slow to heal."

"It was a fatal strike," Nath said.

"So it was," Bayzog said with a smile. "And I'm glad you are still with us. Just make sure you stay focused, Nath. We've been through much, but the most dangerous part is what lies ahead."

"I hope the Floating City will provide some answers. Give us an edge. We need it."

"Agreed, but I have no idea what to expect."

Thunder rumbled overhead, and the sound of rain pelting the leaves in the forest followed.

"Good," Nath said. "This will make it harder for them to find us."

Ahead, Ben covered himself with his cloak and Bayzog did the same. Brenwar sat like a rock in his saddle with rain dripping off his beard.

He's bearded iron.

Brenwar had stayed by his side during his best and worst days. Stalwart. Loyal. Nath had been with him so long, he'd taken his friend for granted. Had Brenwar ever taken him for granted? He couldn't remember the dwarf ever doing so. There were times he wished he could be more like Brenwar. *"Dwarves do what must be done."* Nath never understood why he couldn't live by that motto. It might have put an end to all the orcs, if he had.

Ah Father, it's so hard to tell when I'm right and when I'm wrong sometimes. I guess that's why Brenwar is here. To remind me. He rubbed Fang's pommel. *And you too. Make sure I get it right.*

CHAPTER
11

THE BUGBEAR SLUNG THE AXE over his head.

Gorlee's thoughts raced.

They're really going to cut off my hands! No! I can't let that happen!

The axe crested.

Instinct took over. His body shrank and shifted.

The axe came down in a flash.

He jerked his wrists out of the shackles.

Chok!

The axe stuck into the block of wood.

A collective gasp followed.

Gorlee twisted from his aggressors and slipped his feet from his shackles. Gasps and exclamations followed.

"What is this treachery!" the triant yelled. "Where is he?"

Gorlee, smaller than a child, dove between the legs of one man and darted through another's.

"There he is!"

"He shrunk!"

"Get him!"

"Kill him!"

Dirty fingers clutched at him. Jabbed and poked at him. The frenzied throng piled on top of him, shouting and encouraging one another.

"I've got him!"

"No! I've got him!"

Gorlee kept changing. Squirming. Growing.

Figure this one out, you smelly warthogs!

"I lost him!" Gorlee said. "I lost him! There he is!" He grabbed someone by the leg and pulled them down. "That's not him!"

Others murmured and groaned.

"Where did he go!"

"He's gone!"

One by one, the pile of the doomed people stood up and looked around. Their dirty faces were blank and confused. Gorlee stood among them, a lizardman now.

The triant eyed each and every one of them. His face was confused and angry. He snatched Gorlee's shackles and banged them on the floor.

"Search this place! Every cave! Every tunnel!"

All the prisoners scurried. Gorlee played along.

It worked! At least for now it did.

He followed the others and assisted in the search. Tunnels led up and down the catacombs. New faces turned up. Old dead ones too. There were tombs and bones. Many dark and unknown places. For hours they searched, but with every passing hour, Gorlee's belly felt worse.

What did that woman feed me?

He found an abandoned cave that they'd searched earlier, crawled inside, and lay down. *I just need to rest.* His belly moaned, and his eyes became very heavy. *Rest for a little while.* He shifted his skin into a rocky form, yawned, and fell fast asleep.

"Wake up!"

Gorlee blinked his eyes.

"Wake up!"

He sat up straight.

He was back in the large chamber, surrounded. The triant stood nearby with his arms crossed over his chest in triumph. Gorlee's shackles were draped over his thick neck.

"Did you enjoy your nap?"

Gorlee rubbed his blurry eyes. He felt like he'd slept for over a week. And he didn't feel right.

"I could have used a little more time," he said, gathering his feet under him. "What did you wake me for, anyway? Is it dinner time?" He eyed the crowd. The bugbear with the axe wasn't around. *That's a good thing.*

"You've been either hiding or sleeping for days. We just found you, now that you turned."

Gorlee checked his arms. The dragon scales were gone. His skin showed: a hairless soft pink with tiny little scales like a lizard. *Great Guzan! I'm me!*

"What are you?" the triant demanded.

Did he say days? I've been asleep that long? And I turned?

"I'm a triant," Gorlee said. "I'm just not all brawny and big."

The triant stormed forward and flicked him in the head.

Gorlee's head rocked back.

"I've had quite enough of your humor," Bletver the triant said. "Now tell me what you are."

Gorlee eyed the moorite chains around Bletver's saggy neck.

"I said I'm a triant!" Gorlee yelled. He felt better. Whatever he'd eaten had passed. His belly no longer moaned, and he felt good, despite being a little hungry.

The crowd made angry howls. He could feel them wanting to tear him apart.

"Don't believe me? I'll show you!" Gorlee summoned his power. He started to grow and transform. Seconds later, he stood eye to eye with Bletver the triant. He was an exact duplicate of the monster. "Now do you realize how ugly you are?"

Bletver gawped and stepped back.

"How did you—"

Gorlee drew back and punched Bletver in the face.

Pop!

Bletver's head rocked back, and he fell to the cavern floor. He got up and snarled.

"You dare!"

"I do!"

Bletver lowered his shoulder and charged.

Gorlee caught the full force of the triant, and the two rolled around wrestling, punching, and kicking.

The crowd of prisoners urged the two triants on.

Bletver punched him in the belly and slugged him in the jaw.

Gorlee drove an elbow into Bletver's ribs, stood, and flipped the triant over his shoulder.

It had been a long time since Gorlee was in a fight, but he knew plenty of moves. He side-stepped a punch and then countered.

Crack!

Bletver's body shook. The triant's strength was great, his endurance endless. Fires stoked behind Bletver's beady eyes.

"You think you can take me?" Bletver retorted. He closed in. His great arms flailed like hammers.

Whop! Pow! Crack! Boom!

Gorlee felt every bit of it and staggered around the floor.

"You are no fighter!" Bletver said, throwing a haymaker.

Gorlee blocked it with his arms and winced.

"You are a hopeless imitator."

Wham! Wham! Wham!

Gorlee dropped to a knee. The prisoners went wild. His chest heaved, and drops of sweat splattered on the ground. His chin dipped down in his chest. *This fighting is exhausting.* He huffed. *I'm tired.*

"Don't you know that the only way to stop a triant is to kill it?" Bletver said, gloating over Gorlee. "I'm putting a stop to you, Imitator." He raised both fists over his head and brought them down with all his might.

Gorlee's hands shot up and caught Bletver's wrists.

"Still have some fight in you, I see," the triant said, leering down at him. He drove his foot into Gorlee's gut.

"Oooof!"

A second later, Bletver was on Gorlee's back, wrapping the moorite chains around his neck.

Gorlee was choking. He tugged at the chains.

No! No! I'm not going to die like this!

Bletver heaved on the chains.

The prisoners went into a frenzy.

Gorlee's eyes bulged out of their sockets. He strained against his bonds.

Enough of this!

He summoned all of his power.

"Eh!" Bletver cried out. "What's this?"

Gorlee's body popped, cracked, and grew even bigger. His head almost hit the top of the cavern, and he slung Bletver off his back like a child. Twenty feet high he stood, and he was mad. Mad at the stink. Mad at the filth. But mostly he was mad at Bletver.

Bletver raised his arms up and said, "Surely we can talk about this? Can't we?"

Gorlee raised his foot and stomped it down on Bletver.

"NO!"

He picked him up and threw him into walls. Grabbed him again and stuffed him in a cave that was one size too small. Then Gorlee turned to the stunned crowd and said, "Anyone else want to tangle?"

They scattered like water off cats, leaving Gorlee alone in the great chamber. He nodded.

That felt good. The snap of his fingers sounded like a clap of thunder. *I have an idea.*

He left the chamber, headed back down the stairs, and followed the great tunnel below the well. He could see a faint light a thousand feet up. He peered around.

No phantom at the moment.

He hopped up into the tunnel with his enormous body and started to shimmy toward the top. Halfway up, darkness fell from above, and he found himself face to face with the phantom. He kept going anyway.

CHAPTER

12

RERRY FROWNED AT HIS BROTHER, and his brother frowned back.

"Please," Sasha said, taking each by the arm, "can't the pair of you get along? For your mother? You'll ruin the mood of such a pretty day."

They walked through Quintuklen. The streets were busy, the faces and voices filled with tension and worry. Sasha tried to ignore the dire comments, but it wasn't easy. It was part of the reason she stayed inside so much.

"It's not me, Mother. It's Toad Face over there," Rerry said. "He makes sunny days seem like rainy ones."

"Oh, don't be ridiculous," Sasha said. "He's just quiet is all, and there is nothing wrong with that." She squeezed Rerry's brother's arm. "Nothing at all, Samaz."

The part-elven boy beside her had his head downcast. He was meaty and round-faced like a butcher's boy. He wore heavy olive-green robes that dragged on the ground, and his thick fingers were locked together. His eyes were deep and spacy, but he still looked a little elven. Sweat dripped on his brow.

"It's hot," Samaz said.

"You need fresh air," Sasha said. She reached up and stroked the thin brown hair on his head and gave it a tussle. "You work too much."

Samaz didn't reply, staying intent on putting one foot in front of the other. Samaz was a quiet and peaceful boy, while Rerry was a spry as a pixlyn.

"Mother," Rerry said, "just let him go home and study his scrolls. He'll be exhausted before we make the wall to Quintuklen.

"No I won't," Samaz said, coming to a stop. "I just don't want to go."

"Why is that?" Rerry said with a flare of drama. "Are you afraid a dragon might get you?"

"Enough of that, Rerry," Sasha said. Rerry, the younger, always wanted to pick a fight with his older brother, but Samaz never took the bait. Over the years, Rerry had always resented him for it, not so much because he was mad, but because he never had a brother to play with. "Your brother is your brother, and you are what you are. He can't change what he is."

"He could show some courtesy. I do the same for him."

"Yes," Samaz said.

"Yes what, you talking toad stool," Rerry said.

"Rerry!" Sasha exclaimed. "Stop with the insults."

"It's just a little one."

Sasha pinched his arm.

"Ouch!" Rerry said, wincing. "Mother?"

"I warned you," she said, eyeing him.

"See what you made Mother do, Samaz?"

"Rerry, don't be incorrigible," she said, trying to pinch him again.

Rerry slipped away and said, "Alright. I'm sorry, Mother."

"Good," she said, turning her attention back to Samaz. "Yes to what, Samaz?"

"Yes," Samaz said, looking up into her eyes. "I am afraid that a dragon might get you."

Goosebumps raised on her arms.

"No dragon is going to get you, Mother. Not when I'm around," Rerry said, scanning the skies. "Samaz, you should know better than to say that."

"Why do you say that, Samaz?" Sasha said, barely able to contain her breath. "Did you have a dream? A vision?"

"No," Samaz said, staring up into the sky. "Just a really bad feeling."

CHAPTER

13

NATH CUT THROUGH THE FOREST like a black stag. He'd spent the last several days scouting ahead for his friends. He could feel every creature. Small critters. Bears. The birds nested on high. He could sense their fear. They were as troubled as he was.

He padded through a clearing, pushed through a thicket, and nearly slipped down the side of a cliff. The valley below him was deep, green treetops mile after mile with rippling rivers flowing right through them like blue-green snakes, weaving around the bends. He traced the river to where it disappeared. Something else caught his eye.

"I'll be," he said, putting his clawed hands on his hips. "Didn't think I'd ever notice natural beauty again. It's something." He took a moment to take it all in. The bright sun and wispy clouds made for quite a setting over the lush valley. It was so big and peaceful, it was hard to believe that war had taken over the land at all.

Ben burst through the brush and barreled toward the ledge.

"Whoa!" he said, arms flailing like windmills.

Nath snatched him by the arm and gently pulled him back.

"Careful," he said.

Ben huffed and dashed the sweat from his eyes.

"You sure are something to keep up with," Ben said, with his hands on his knees. "You move like a ghost. But I kept up with you. Whew!"

"I let you keep up with me," Nath said, "but you did well, considering."

"Considering what?" Ben said, rolling his big shoulders and stretching his back.

"Do I really need to answer that?" Nath said.

"Well, I still did better than most men ever could … have … " Ben's eyes fixed on the enormous object that hung in the sky. "Is that … ?"

"A city? Yes. Yes Ben, that's a city."

"But, it floats?"

"Why do you think they call it the Floating City?"

"I just figured it was some sort of expression. I didn't really think it'd be floating." He squinted his eyes and shuffled back a little. "But it does. How's that possible?"

"Magic. Lots of magic."

The city floated in the air like a cloud atop a rocky moon. Below the rock, bright blue shards of crystal glowed with brilliant life. Nath could count hundreds of rocks suspended in the air, some small and some huge, but only one hosted a city.

"And we are to go there?" Ben asked, shaking his head in disbelief. "And how do we get up there?"

Even miles away, Nath's keen sight could make out catwalks and bridges that went from rock to rock once you got to the city, but there was no answer how to get up. He shrugged.

"We'll let Bayzog think of something."

"Do people live there?" Ben said, rubbing the whiskers on his rugged chin.

"They did once, but that was long ago. Long before my time."

"What happened?"

"It's cursed," Nath said, "Abandoned."

"Haunted?"

"I don't know about that, but it's foul, they say."

"There looks to be some life. Look at those birds flying from the spires," Ben said.

"Those aren't birds," Nath said, gazing their way, "those are dragons."

"Dragons? So many? Are you sure?"

Nath eyed him.

"I don't think we should venture where so many dragons are about. They'll find us for certain."

"I'm not worried about those dragons," Nath said. "Those are small ones. They roost. They sleep. There are ways around the dragons. It won't be a problem."

"If you say so."

A dragon roar echoed down the valley.

Ben looked at Nath. "That didn't sound so small." He peered over the edge, into the valley.

Nath did the same.

A red-orange dragon glided over the river. With a beat of its great wings, it soared upward into the sky.

Ben gulped and hunkered down. His eyes enlarged when another dragon burst through the clouds and crashed into the other. The titans roared and clashed, filling the valley with thunder. The great monsters spit fire and clawed at one another.

"Are they fighting?"

"No, they're sparring. Dragons do that, too. Hone their battle skills. Test one another."

Shards of fire scattered in the sky and drizzled toward the ground.

"What kind are they?" Ben asked.

"Bull dragons."

"They seem awfully big. Are they a problem?"

Nath looked down at him and nodded.

"They're a problem times ten."

CHAPTER

14

BAYZOG GOT OFF HIS HORSE and let it drink from the river. All the others in the company did the same. Hours earlier, Nath and Ben had come back to share what they had discovered. When he found out the Floating City hosted dragons, his stomach had sunk into his toes.

"Do you really think it's that bad?" Nath said ironically, wading into the waters. He scooped up a drink. "What's a few dozen dragons? ... Including a couple of bulls."

Bayzog slumped on the Elderwood Staff.

I feel old. I should not, but I do. He rubbed the pendant under his robes.

"You miss her, don't you?" Nath said. "I would too. Well, I do. After all, I've not seen her in twenty-some years."

Brenwar stormed over.

"So, do we have a plan? Or do we wait to become dragon toast?" He eyed the sky. "I don't think it's the best idea to be in the wide open."

"I don't hear anything," Nath said. "Take a moment and relax, Brenwar."

"Do you see a barrel of ale around here?"

Nath shook his head.

Ben walked over with his thumbs hitched in his belt and said, "Do we have a plan?"

Bayzog liked to plan. He lived for it, but at the moment he was at a loss.

Giving it a shot, he said, "We're here to find out who mines the crystal shards. And I'm not so sure angling for the Floating City is the best route." He pulled the shard out of a pocket in his robes. "But I think a visit to the citizens of the River Cities might garner some answers."

"An excellent idea," Brenwar said with a snort. "We just waltz in there and ask them. A dragon, an elf, and a dwarf. Ha!"

"We have our advantages," Bayzog said, eyeing Brenwar's chest.

"No, no, no," Brenwar said, "I'll not be drinking any more potions again. No."

Bayzog missed Gorlee. The chameleon was priceless at times like this.

"We can send Ben," Nath suggested. "He'd fit in, and I bet he could discover a few things."

Ben shrugged.

"I can do it."

"No sense splitting up now," Brenwar said. "We lose one and we all might be lost. I'm not for it." He turned his nose up at the sky. "Let's just climb up there and see what we find."

"I thought you'd show a little more patience, Brenwar," Nath said. "We won't end this war in a day."

"Maybe not, but I want to. And you should too. Time is our enemy. The deeper evil burrows, the more difficult to extract it."

"Another day won't hurt anything," Nath said.

"Lives are over in a second, Dragon," Brenwar said.

Bayzog had never seen Brenwar so impatient before. It bothered him.

"I know," Nath said, "but we've made it this far being patient. That saves lives just as well."

Brenwar harrumphed.

"Ben," Bayzog said with a nod, "I think it's time you got a closer look at the River Cities."

"Agreed."

A mile upriver, farmlands and rolling terrain stretched as far as the eye could see on their side of the river. They released the horses there and waited long enough to watch them gallop out of sight. Brenwar hefted the dwarven chest on his shoulder and Nath led the way. Bayzog had gotten used to Nath's senses. It was as if he could see and hear everything. He tripped on his robes catching up to him.

"Nath, something disturbs me," Bayzog said.

"Oh, and what is that?"

"Are the senses of other dragons as keen as yours?"

"Good question," Nath said, stepping over a fallen tree. "And I'd like to think not, but I can't say for sure. Their eyes are better than those of eagles, but I don't think them so motivated to find us."

"Why not?"

"Dragons don't worry about things as much as the races do. They are aloof. Not stupid, not by any means. But other than a love for people's treasure, they have little care for people. Don't bother them, they don't bother you, unless you're a gold or ruby statue." He sliced some branches down with his claws. "It's the soldiers we need to worry about."

"And those bull dragons," Bayzog said, "are they of no concern?"

"Well, they're guarding the Floating City for a reason. I assume your hunch about the crystals is right."

"And after what happened at Jordak's Pass, they'll figure we're coming this way." He checked the sky. The Floating City's tower-tops hung behind the mountains, but he could see other chunks of rock that floated in the air. "And they probably have eyes everywhere?"

Ben gazed upward at his side and said, "If the crystals float like that, then why don't people use them to fly like birds?"

"It's not a property they have," Bayzog said, sipping from his flask. "Though they are the rarest and most precious stone in Nalzambor. It's called Jaxite. And what you see in the sky is where it comes from."

"It looks alive," Ben said.

Bayzog nodded. "Jaxite means 'living rock' in the old tongue. The histories say that whoever controls the jaxite controls the world. So the Wizards of Renown built a city on top of it and guarded it closely. But not all agreed on how the rock should be used. The races from all Nalzambor came to claim it. They warred for years, and the peaceful River Cities ran red with blood. The Wizards of Renown were wise. War prompted them to place a curse on the jaxite."

"What kind of curse?" Ben asked, fingering the hilt on his sword.

Bayzog cracked a smile.

"A powerful one that is as plain as you see. Unifying their powers, they cast a great and mighty spell that lifted the jaxite from the earth to the sky. That is what you see now. And they added another spell as well. One that made the jaxite even harder to mine than moorite. It took a few years, but the races finally gave up after that. The jaxite had become useless."

"But it seems useful now," Nath said, climbing up a rock and lending a hand one by one to the others.

"Hence the reason for this quest," Bayzog said, taking Nath's hand. "And every bit of information we can acquire from the River Cities will be of great use before we venture above."

He found himself overlooking the river that flowed through the majestic River Cities. Buildings of stone and wood lined the sandy edges of the riverbank clear off into the distance. The wharfs were busy with people who looked as small as insects they were so far away, loading and unloading cargo, mostly from small craft and barges. But a few big suppliers dipped great oars in the water.

"Seems like a nice place to live," Ben said, starting down the other side of the rock. "I'm ready to go."

"Wait, Ben," Bayzog said.

Ben clamored back up the rock with a groan.

"Time's wasting."

Bayzog gestured to the dwarven chest on Brenwar's shoulder.

"May I?

Brenwar set it down with a grunt and opened it up. The vials of potions popped up in rows. In the bottom of the chest was an assortment of other things. Clothing, pendants, rings, scrolls and many other baubles and trinkets.

"How can so many things be inside a chest that is so small?" Ben asked.

"Magic," Nath said, patting his shoulder.

Inside, Bayzog found a small jar of dark green ointment. He pulled the lid off and dipped his fingers inside it. "Come, Ben," he said, holding his fingers out.

"What are you doing with that?" Ben said, frowning.

Bayzog rubbed it on Ben's cheeks and muttered some mystic words.

Ben's face shone brightly, then dulled.

"Is that it?" the warrior said.

Bayzog capped the jar and set in back in the chest.

"That's it."

"What does it do?"

"It's Adderack's Aversion Balm. It will keep the soldiers from pressing you."

"Does it make me ugly?"

"You're already ugly," Brenwar said.

Nath laughed.

"You're fine, Ben," Nath said, staring at him. "Just different. The balm works well."

Bayzog nodded. Ben's visage had gone from something strong to something forgettable.

"You should go," the part-elven wizard said.

"Agreed," Nath and Brenwar said.

"But," Ben said, but Nath was already shoving him along.

"Find the Water Dog Inn," Bayzog said, "and don't ask too many questions."

"Be back by dawn," Nath said, waving him onward, "Now hurry on."

Ben looked back over his shoulder a couple times, then disappeared into the woods.

"That was strange," Nath said, "but really effective. And he's going to need it."

"Why do you say that?" Bayzog said.

"Because those little people in the cities you can't see," Nath said, pointing down the river, "most of them aren't citizens. Those are Barnabus soldiers."

"Are there many orcs?" Bayzog said.

"Some. Why?"

"Oh, well, let's just hope he doesn't cross too many of them. They aren't often disturbed by uncomely anything." He shrugged and glanced down the path Ben took.

"Should I go after him?" Nath said.

"I'm sure it will be alright. Ben is a cautious man."

CHAPTER

15

THE PHANTOM DROPPED DOWN ON Gorlee, covering him instantly in darkness. His big triant body shuddered from the cold, and fear sunk into his bones. The phantom's voice was an eerie howl in his head.

Keep going, Gorlee. Keep going!

He squeezed his eyes shut and steadied himself. Pushed hard on the rocks that supported his enormous frame. Brenwar's voice spoke in the back of his mind.

Courage frightens evil.

He dug into the rock and surged upward.

The phantom tore at him like a mighty black wind.

I have courage!

Up Gorlee went.

I hate evil.

The phantom pulled at his arms and legs. It felt like icicles were forming on them. He shook. He dug in.

I have courage. I hate evil.

No longer shackled by the moorite chains, Gorlee climbed a dozen feet at a time. Straining against the dark force, he continued his ascent up the great pipe that led out of The Deep.

I have courage. I hate evil.

The phantom let out more angry shrieks the higher he climbed. He could feel its hatred. It stabbed at his heart with frigid hands.

He screamed but no sound same. He slid downward, toes and fingers clawing at the walls. He pushed his mighty arms into the sides of the hole.

No! I have courage. I hate evil.

His ascent began again. Up, up, up the deep well he went.

I have courage! I hate evil!

I have courage! I hate evil!

I have courage! I hate evil!

Blinded, he kept going. One hundred feet. Two hundred feet. Minute after agonizing minute.

I have courage. I hate evil. Five hundred feet. Arms trembling and legs shaking, he summoned all of his strength.

The phantom passed through him. Shocked him. Burned him. Poked icy holes in him. Gorlee did not stop.

I have courage! I hate evil!

I have courage! I hate evil!

I have courage! I hate evil!

I have courage! I hate evil!

Every minute was agony. Forever. Tormenting.

I have courage! I hate evil!

I have courage! I hate evil!

His hand felt a rim.

Can it be?

He swung his elbow over the ledge. The phantom howled and yanked him back down to his fingertips. He hung there with all the phantom's power and hate pulling him back down in. Gorlee's grip slipped. He hung onto the lip with one hand.

The phantom howled in triumph.

No! I will not fall! I will not fall!

His fingers started slipping.

I have courage! I hate evil!

I have courage! I hate evil!

He channeled his reserve power. His bones popped and crackled. His hulking form grew once more. He tore his arms away from the phantom's grip, grabbed the rim, and heaved himself upward.

The phantom covered him like a black slime. It felt like being in a tar pit. He pulled one arm free from the blackness then another. His head burst into the light. The phantom screamed. One leg at a time, Gorlee climbed out. He sucked in the fresh air.

The air was like a long lost friend. The bewildered faces of the guards were not. Two lowered their spears and charged. Gorlee snatched them up in his hands, bopped their heads together, and tossed them into The Deep.

He turned and found himself inside the cage. His head peered over the fifteen-foot-tall gate. He looked at all the startled faces and growled, scattering the gathering crowd. The soldiers readied weapons and spears. One shouted up at him.

"You get back in that well! That's an order!"

Gorlee grabbed the metal bars and ripped them out of the floor one by one. He stepped through the threshold, throttled all the Soldiers of Barnabus he could get his hands on, and fled into the night.

I'm free!

CHAPTER

16

HIGH PRIESTESS SELENE BROKE THE grand table in half with her black tail.

Crack!

"How did this happen?" she demanded. "Escape from The Deep is impossible!" She walked up to Kryzak and wrapped her tail around his neck. "Isn't it?"

The big draykis was rather calm when he said, "It was until now."

She squeezed a little harder, turning his face purple, and released him.

Kryzak gasped and rubbed his throat.

Selene's tail swished back and forth. Her lip curled. She didn't completely understand what had just occurred. Days ago, she'd sent Nath Dragon into The Deep. She had doubts it was really him. Something was not quite right, but time in The Deep would reveal any man's secrets. And The Deep held its own secret. She resumed her seat on the throne and sat down. The drulture flew over and nestled on her lap. She shooed it away. With a growl, out the window it went.

"Tell me what happened once more," she said to Kryzak. The war cleric wasn't alone, either. Ten guards were there that witnessed the event. Four draykis stood ready in the room.

Kryzak cleared his throat.

"A triant emerged."

Selene huffed.

"Tore out the bars of the cage like candlesticks off a table and throttled a dozen guards."

"And it wasn't the triant Bletver?" she said, toying with her silky hair.

"The phantom states that Bletver remains below," Kryzak said, taking a breath, "but he's incapacitated. And there are no signs of Nath Dragon. We just have these." He held out the trousers that Gorlee had been wearing and draped them over the back of the chair.

"And what is the phantom's excuse?"

"It offered none."

"And the triant," she said, "it just disappeared? All fifteen feet tall of it, assuming your little soldiers aren't exaggerating."

"A hundred soldiers comb the streets," Kryzak said, "and I swear we'll catch this—"

"You'll catch nothing!" she said, rising to her feet. "You suppose you can find anything The Deep cannot contain!" Her voice echoed in the chamber. She rubbed her head. She sighed. "But you can try, Kryzak. And I'll even offer your soldiers some incentive." She eyed the soldiers kneeling face first on the floor. "For every hour you do not find him, two soldiers will die. And I believe an hour has passed already."

"As you wish," Kryzak said in his deep voice. He nodded at the draykis and pointed at two soldiers on the floor.

The draykis pulled their swords.

"No blood on these floors," Kryzak said, nodding at the terrace.

The draykis picked the two men up by their arms and legs and dragged them to the terrace.

"Mercy, High Priestess! Mercy!" the soldiers begged.

She resumed her seat on the throne and watched them squirm in the clutches of the draykis. One by one, the draykis heaved each soldier's body over the balcony. She could hear their screams until they hit the bottom.

"That should motivate them," she said to Kryzak. "I suggest you get moving. Another hour will be upon you by the time you reach the bottom."

"I was just thinking the same thing." He pointed to two more.

The draykis snatched them up, hauled them to the terrace, and heaved them over the balcony wall. Selene offered a faint smile.

"I'm fond of people screaming. It soothes me on bright and sunny days."

Kryzak bowed and led the rest of the draykis and soldiers outside, leaving her alone in the grand chamber.

"Something is amiss," she said to herself. She made her way to the terrace and looked below. A crowd had gathered around the soldiers' corpses. Her sharp eyes could see their faces, and her sharp ears could hear their cries. She shoved a planter off the railing and watched it crush someone. "That's better."

She leaned back against the terrace rail and wondered. The man she met could not have been Nath Dragon, or could he have been? Did Nath Dragon have powers she didn't know about? Who should she ask? Gorn Grattack? Her dragon master might not like that, not that he liked anything, other than destruction.

Who was he? Who was it?

Not knowing felt like needles in her spine. She had her suspicions, and that's why she had sent him to The Deep, but the creature had escaped. That was unforeseen. It rattled her. Control had slipped from her grasp.

She made a high-pitched whistle with her lips and waited on the terrace, watching the dark clouds drift over the city and into the country. Her drulture flew over and landed on the rail. She gave it a command. It flew away and contacted the roosted dragons in the city. They'd help keep a look-out for anything that was not ordinary. She crossed her arms over her chest and said, "I'm not sure that will do." She let out another whistle, different than the last, and made her way over to the map.

"So, Nath Dragon, if you are not here, then where might you be?" She circled a spot with her black fingernail. "Perhaps that was you after all, making a statement at Jordak's Pass. I've a missing grey scaler to show for it, and a host of soldiers wiped out." She traced her finger over the map and stopped on the River Cities. "When you show your claws, we'll be ready."

Something roared behind her and she turned.

The feline fury prowled inside from the terrace. Its lion face had very long whiskers, and smoke rolled from its nose. The horse-sized creature brushed along her side. She stroked the mane above the neck and rubbed the scales on its back.

"How are your wings working out?" she said, toying with the leathery things. "You continue to mature into a fine, fine beast. And your new wings are just what we needed." She pointed to a spot on the map. "Do you remember our old friend Nath Dragon?"

It snorted a blast of smoke.

"We need to find our guest, who was his imposter." She grabbed the trousers that Kryzak had left on the chair and held them under the feline fury's nose. "I need you to hunt our guest down, immediately. Can you do this?"

Its cat eyes narrowed, and the scales on its back rose. On silent paws, it headed for the terrace and bounded over the rail.

"You might have escaped The Deep, but you won't escape me." She eyed another spot on the map. The City of Quintuklen. "Perhaps it's time to play another card of mine."

CHAPTER

17

B EN HEADED INTO THE RIVER town with his eyes up and shoulders down. His dagger felt heavy on his hip, and his hand drifted to the hilt from time to time.

Should be easy, shouldn't it?

He rubbed his face, which still tingled.

It has to be working, right?

He peeled through some branches and found himself on a road that ran along the river, about three miles from where he left the others behind. He kept his eyes forward. Ahead, people were coming and going from what looked to be a hard day of work. The faces he passed were weathered, and their eyes were weary. They shuffled by with little urgency, and their glances went right over him and beyond.

It is working.

He lengthened his stride, passing a pair of old men pushing a cart of produce. They grumbled at his glance.

Yes, it is working.

Small storage buildings and cottages lined the road the closer he got the city. Hard voices were moving commerce on the loading docks. Hoists and pulleys and sweaty bodies on loaded barges. Armored figures watched over it. The glint of armor and weapons caught his eye. He slowed his pace.

Soldiers were everywhere. Orcs and men. The blazoned dragon-head banner waved high in the air. A lonely feeling sunk into Ben's belly, and he shuffled from the road into the shadows.

At first glance, the River Cities were picturesque, appealing. Up close though, the whitewashed buildings weren't so bright, but gray. Mold covered the roofs. Overgrowth blocked the windows. If not for the river breeze, the foulness in the air would not be bearable.

A stone archway hung over the road leading into the city. Several guards stood watch with spears, checking the people coming and going. They patted men down and shoved others to the road. They chuckled with wickedness, watching the people go.

From the back of the line, Ben eased his way forward while another group's cart was kept behind and inspected. A half-orcen man with a warty face cut him off. He was tall and lean for the breed.

"Where do you think you're going?"

"I have no gear to inspect," Ben said, "and I'm just passing through."

The soldier poked him in the chest.

"Not with that hardware, you're not," it said, peering closer at him. "Take it off."

What is going on? Why is this orc bothering me? Avert! Avert!

Ben's hand slipped to a dagger hidden under his cloak.

He said, "I'm just passing through. Looking for work. I can work the docks or sell my services with a sword."

A pair of other soldiers flanked him.

This is bad in so many ways.

"What seems to be the problem, Harvath?"

"This one carries a dagger," Harvath said, poking Ben in the chest again.

"Oh," the soldier said. He was a beefy man, but stout and seasoned, "he has a dagger, does he? And let me guess, you think he's going to take it to us. The hundreds of us?" He laughed and so did the other.

"Methinks you just don't like this fella cause he's a might more," he stared at Ben for a moment, and blinked his eyes, "unappealing than you are."

"I'm a hard worker," Ben interjected.

"Uh," the soldier said, shaking his head, "I'm sure you are. Just head on through."

"But," Harvath objected.

"No buts, Harvath. Let this poor fellow go. I've more important things to do."

"I can help you," Ben said with a grin. "I'm a really hard worker. I really am."

The sergeant's eyes got really big.

"Don't make me turn you around. If you can find someone who'll hire you, then good fortune to you. But you won't be working for me. Now go!"

Ben nodded and headed into the city. He could still hear Harvath arguing with the sergeant with each and every step.

"Something about that man," Harvath said, "I tell you."

"Find someone else to bother, Harvath."

Ben kept his smile to himself, walking along the wharf until he found the sign that read: The Water Dog Inn. He pushed the door open, and inside he went. Dozens of hardened stares greeted him and at the same time looked away. Their rugged conversations continued. Ben sauntered up to a stool at the end of the bar. A man the size of two people glanced over at him and moved one stool farther away.

This must be how Brenwar feels.

A bartender came over wiping his hands on a rag and said, "What will it be?" His eyes were smoky, like darkened glass.

"Coffee," Ben said.

"Better make it ale," the old man said under his breath. "I may be blind, but I can still see, Stranger."

Ben swallowed.

"Ale it is."

The blind bartender shuffled away and returned with a large tankard.

"I can't drink all of this?"

"You will, and that will be twenty bits of gold."

"What?"

"Twenty gold," the old man warned, "else I expose your sorcery."

Ben stiffened.

"But I don't have twenty gold."

"That's too bad then," the old man said. "Heh, heh. Too bad indeed. Riik!"

A shadow rose behind him and busted a club over his back. Everything went black.

CHAPTER

18

DAWN BROKE OVER THE RIVER, and Ben had not returned.

"He should have been back by now," Brenwar said, pacing back and forth.

"Just give him some more time," Nath said. "An hour, and if he doesn't return we'll do something.

"Certainly he made it to the Water Dog Inn," Bayzog said. "If we go in, we can start from there."

Nath's thoughts drifted to Gorlee. The Chameleon should have been with them. They'd come to rely on him heavily. He wondered how he and the dwarves were doing.

"So who goes in?" Brenwar said, combing his beard. "We can't send one more in and risk losing another. Those soldiers are bound to recognize us, aversion balm or not."

"There's always a potion," Bayzog said, "And I have spells."

"Keep your trickery to yourself," Brenwar said. "But since you're volunteering ... " Brenwar gave Bayzog a shove. "Get going."

"Are you mad, Dwarf?"

"Am I mad? Is my beard black? Are your ears pointed?" He stomped his foot. "You bet I'm mad!"

"Keep your voice down," Nath said. "Someone's coming."

Each one of them concealed himself in the forest. Nath could hear two approaching pairs of footsteps. One heavy. Another light. Two figures emerged from the grove. An old man hung on the arm of a brute the size of two stout men.

"You can come out," the old man said. He wore common clothing, and his eyes were smoky. "I might be blind, but I still see everything."

"They fear us, Father," the brute said. His head was shaven, and his bare arms bulged like tree trunks out of his leather jerkin. A long heavy club hung from his free arm. "As they should. I'll break them the same as I broke their comrade."

Nath stepped out from behind the tree. Brenwar did the same.

The brute grunted and sneered at Nath.

"This one has hair like a woman's."

"Mind your manners, Horse Neck," the old man said. "We are not here to make enemies, but allies."

Horse Neck spat on the ground.

"As you wish, Otter Bone." He leered at Brenwar. "I've never tussled a dwarf before. You look like an oversized beaver."

"You dare, you undersized troll?" Brenwar said, coming forward. "I'll break you piece by piece."

Nath cut off his advance.

"Otter Bone, is it?" Nath said.

"It is." The blind mind came forward and reached out toward Nath. "Be still. I can sense what you are, Dragon, but I want to feel for myself."

"And how can that be?" Brenwar said.

"He's a sage," Bayzog said, moving out of the clearing and into view. "A formidable one at that."

Otter Bone gaped and his face brightened.

"Well played," the blind old man said. "I did not sense you, Wizard. Hmmm. Part-elven. Unusual."

Nath glanced at Bayzog and the wizard nodded. It let him know Otter Bone was someone to contend with.

"Tell us about Ben?" Nath said.

"He is well, quite well. Just has a large knot on his head, but those lumps are good for readings. That lump told me many things, it did." Otter Bone moved closer to Nath, reaching out. "May I, please?"

Nath spat a small fireball on the ground.

Horse Neck jerked the old man back and stamped it out.

"Tell me about my friend and what you want with him. What you want with us."

Horse Neck stuck his wooden club in Nath's face.

"Don't do that again," he warned. "Or I'll—"

Nath spat fire on it. It burst into flame and turned to ash, leaving Horse Neck's hand an empty mitt.

"Next time," Nath warned, "it is you that will feel heat and not some part of a tree."

The brute's arms flexed with muscle and his chest heaved with angry breaths.

"Enough, Horse Neck!" Otter Bone said. "I can't take him anywhere without him wanting to fight something. Please understand, the siege we are under can be quite stressful and my temperamental nephew gets pent-up from all our unpleasant captors."

"We don't care about that!" Brenwar said. "Where is our friend?"

"Why, in the River Cities, of course."

"Whose prisoner is he?" Nath said.

"Ah, now that is the question," Otter Bone said, "and you have many? I have foreseen this. That's how I knew you were coming."

Nath looked to Bayzog. He hadn't dealt with sages before. Bayzog shrugged his eyebrows.

"You've come to visit the Floating City," the old man said, "to see who cuts the stones that cannot be cut. To see who controls the dragons. Am I right?"

No one spoke.

"I am not your enemy. I'm not friend or ally to Barnabus either, but I'll not leave my home on account of them. You," he pointed to Nath. His voice became haunting, "are the one to stop all of that. You are the Black Dragon. I've seen you. I've seen Nalzambor destroyed and saved. I'll help if you will."

"What kind of ally holds an ally hostage?" Brenwar said.

"A desperate one. A selfish one. I crave jaxite crystals for myself. Bring me three, and I'll free your friend."

"What will you do with them?" Bayzog asked.

"That is no concern of yours," Otter Bone said, raising his voice, "but I will have what I will have, and you will get it for me."

"Or what? You'll kill our friend Ben?" Nath said. "You don't seem the type. Nor your oafish nephew."

"I might not have the blood on my hands that you do," Otter Bone said, "but my—"

"I tire of this," Nath said. He grabbed Horse Neck by the wrist and twisted it behind his back. He shoved the towering man to the dirt and put a knee in his back. "Let me tell you what is going to happen. You will stay with us, and this troll will bring back our friend."

Brenwar sat on the big man's back and pinned War Hammer under his neck. "Don't make a sound or move," he said in Horse Neck's ear.

Nath towered over Otter Bone and folded his arms over his chest.

Otter Bone cleared his throat.

"Well, I saw this coming. I'm a sage, after all. And I have given you my terms. I will not relinquish them." He took a quick breath and started to whistle.

Nath closed his fingers over the man's mouth.

More men were out there. He could hear their breathing in the woods. *How did I miss that?* He could now sense that Otter Bone had a strange power. *He dulled my senses!* But now that had changed. He heard swords slide from sheathes and bowstrings being drawn back. Otter Bone was well prepared. Nath uncovered his mouth.

"You are fast, Nath Dragon. But are your friends?" Otter Bone said.

"Hurt them and who will fetch your crystals?"

"I only need you to get the crystals. The others will just slow you down. Now let's talk about this, shall we?" Otter Bone lifted his brows. "No one has to get hurt."

Nath could sense sincerity, but desperation too. He wondered if there were more out there that he hadn't noticed. *It doesn't matter. I am a dragon, and they are just men.*

"No," Nath said.

"Disappointing, then. Very disappointing."

Bow strings stretched and fingers released.

Twang! Twang! Twang!

CHAPTER
19

ORLEE STOOD AMONG THE GAPING crowd. Soldiers of Barnabus were falling from the sky. He pushed his way closer and eyed the broken bodies on the street. A man shoved him out of the way.

"Excuse you," Gorlee said in an old man's fragile voice.

A rugged character looked down into his eyes.

"Go back to your quarters and knit some trousers, why don't you?"

Gorlee pulled a shawl over his narrow shoulders and moved on, taking a moment to lean on a lamppost. His body quavered a little. Typical of older men he'd seen before. *They'll be looking for someone bigger. Someone stronger.*

"Out of the way!" a soldier said, leading squads of them out of the great tower. He dispatched them throughout the entire city in groups of four. Their eyes were wild and fearful. He could hear them whispering among themselves. Two of them were to die for every hour he was not found. It chilled him. They started shaking everyone down and questioning them about the triant and where it went. Fingers pointed in all directions.

All of this over me. How twisted Selene is.

He fought the urge to look up. He swore he could feel Selene's eyes on him from above.

A terrible sound filled the air, causing him to shudder. Screams came forth from the crowd, and people scrambled through the streets. Dragons dropped from the rooftops and onto the road. They roared at everything that moved. People fell to their hands and knees, cowering in front of the terrifying beasts.

Dragons and soldiers are looking for me now! Guzan!

Gorlee shuffled in with a mob and went with the flow. He had no idea where to go.

Need a safe place to hide. Away from the commotion.

The farther the crowd went, the more it thinned. He sighed and took a seat on the porch of a storefront. All the doors were closed and the streets were becoming empty. Gorlee wrung his withered hands together and dipped his head. He was exhausted. Drained.

Need rest. Need much rest.

Escaping from The Deep had taken it all out of him. And then the long trek here. He could barely move.

Dragon roars echoed down the street, causing him to jump.

Sultans of Sulfur! There are dragons and soldiers everywhere. Working together! This is madness!

He swore he could feel the great presence of Selene above.

She certainly must be the most powerful person in the world.

A person who controlled both men and dragons. And her tail. Blacker than coal and full of scales. The scales looked just like Nath Dragon's. He and Bayzog had talked much about the return of the black dragons. Now, he had no doubt he knew of two of them. They were the most formidable people he'd ever met in the world.

"YOU!" a hard voice said. "Get over here!"

A pair of soldiers approached. Both had swords out and nervous looks in their eyes.

Gorlee struggled to rise and sat back down.

"I said get over here," the soldier said.

"I can barely move my withered legs," Gorlee said, holding out a trembling hand, "can you help me up? That mob ran over me."

The soldiers marched over. One grabbed him by the wrist and jerked him up.

"Oh!" Gorlee exclaimed. "My bones are brittle. You'll break me in two."

The soldier grabbed him by the collar and pulled him up to his toes.

"I don't care if I break all your bones. What I want to know is if you've seen anything strange."

The soldier held his sword to Gorlee's throat. Desperation was in the man's eyes. Gorlee's head beaded with sweat.

The soldier said, "Someone like you would notice when strange things happen. Did you or did you not see something odd coming out of the Great Tower of Narnum?" He pressed the sword into Gorlee's wrinkled neck. "I'm a good judge of character. I'll know if you're truthful or if you're lying."

"I've no desire to lie," Gorlee said, pushing himself into a sitting position. "I've always wanted the best for this city. I saw a monster—Great, huge and scary—running through the streets. It fled toward the stables." He pointed. "The roadway out perhaps. Even with my old eyes I could see him, but when the ground shook under his great feet, I trembled and hid my eyes."

The soldiers looked at one another and one said, "How could something that big disappear so fast?" He looked up. "And with all these dragons around too. Lousy overlooking lizards! No, we have to find him."

Gorlee withheld his smile. He had pulled off quite a feat.

A dragon roared from above. The soldiers' heads snapped up. The dragon had a soldier in its claws, and it circled the great tower. Gorlee could hear the soldier scream when the dragon dropped him and he was falling. The soldiers glanced at him and each other with terror in their eyes.

The soldier here stuffed his sword in his scabbard and grabbed Gorlee by the hair. "If you see anything, you'd better tell us!" He let go gruffly, and they both took off running toward the stables.

Gorlee shook his head.

I almost feel sorry for them. Should I?

Once he was sure they were gone, he got on his feet with a groan. At the moment, he really did feel old. Every bit of his energy was sapped. *At least I made it this far.* He shuffled down the street, heading away from the sounds of commotion and dragons. *I just need a nap. There must be somewhere safe a man can curl up around here.*

All around, soldiers pounded on doors and kicked them in. Dragon claws, blue, grey and yellow, clicked on the cobblestones as the dragons slunk through the streets. From the tops of buildings they watched, making piercing cries like hawks. There wasn't sanctuary anywhere in the city.

He slogged through the town, peering into storefronts, down alleys. His entire body was shaking. His stomach groaned and he rubbed his belly. *How long did Bletver the triant say I slept? A week? No wonder I'm so weak and starving.* If he could, he would have changed into a soldier and blended in, but he didn't have the strength. That would be the easy way, assuming a dragon didn't snatch him, fly him up, and drop him for dead. *I've flown with a dragon once, and that should last a lifetime for me.*

He sighed, shuffled along, and continued on his quest to find rest. Narnum the Free City was huge. Wide open. There must have been a thousand places to hide, but without any friends or allies, he couldn't find one. He kept walking until he found himself face to face with the edge of the city. The countryside, its farms and green hills, looked like freedom, but it was anything but that. Towers, bulwarks, and great weapons of war surrounded it now. He could see dragons crawling through high grasses and soldiers marching through the fields. He shook his head.

Is there anywhere peaceful left in this world? He leaned against a building. *If I were a triant, where would I hide? That's where they'll be looking.* Narnum had bridges, huge barns and storehouses. The rivers were said to be as deep as they were wide.

While running through town with the crowd, he'd seen soldiers rowing up and down the rivers, poking sticks into the water, and a dragon slithering through the grass to slip into the river.

He pulled the shawl tighter around his shoulders. *If you can't hide in the river, where can you hide?*

He scanned left and right. No one was about. It was just him leaning back against a building that overlooked the river. *Maybe the best place to hide is right in front of their faces.* He pulled his knees up to his chest and tucked his head between them. His belly growled. *Just rest, Gorlee, rest. You can find something to eat later.* A gentle breeze stirred, bending the reeds along the river. The sweet sound of the wind put him right to sleep.

Gorlee hadn't moved for hours when his head popped up and hit the building.

"Ow," he muttered. It was dark now. He could hear the voices of soldiers and see lanterns and torches in the fields, and others cast shadows in the streets. He was rubbing his eyes and yawning when he heard a rumble nearby. The blood in his veins turned to ice, and his heart pounded in his chest. A large black creature moved toward him. A lion-like face emerged from the shadows and came face to face with him.

Gorlee swallowed hard.

The feline fury touched him nose to nose. Its scaled paws pinned his toes to the ground, and smoke rolled from its nose. Hot saliva dripped from its mouth and sizzled on his leg.

Gorlee screamed.

CHAPTER
20

"WHAT IS IT, BROTHER?" FAYLAN said to Finlin.

Finlin stood inside her tent just inside the flap, hands clasped and one thumb rolling over another. They'd been marching hard for days and were finding things difficult to navigate from time to time.

He cleared his throat.

"And don't tell me more scouts have been lost."

He remained silent.

She slung her plate of food into a tent wall.

"What! How many this time?"

"Two," he mumbled with his head down.

"That makes for seven of my soldiers in three days!" She grabbed a dagger out of her belt and jammed it in the table. "How did it happen this time?"

"Logs."

"Logs!"

"Rocks," Finlin added.

"Rocks! Logs and rocks!"

He nodded.

She made her way over to him and pinched his cheeks with her fingers.

His eyes started to water.

"Tell me about these logs and rocks," she huffed. "What, no deep pits this time?"

"Well," Finlin said, "they fell in the pit first and then the rocks and logs came."

"And did you see where the logs and rocks came from?"

"The trees," he said.

She clenched her teeth and pinched his cheeks harder.

"You're hurting me," he said.

"I don't care!" she said with a curse. Then she released him.

He backed away. *I'm going to knock her out one day.*

"I told you to let me scout alone. You see that I am unscathed. Those soldiers you sent are as clumsy as they look. And they made too much of a racket in the woods." He raised a finger up. "But I have good news."

"Really," she said. "I can't imagine what that might be."

"On my own I have discovered the nature of our threat, and I know just how to find them."

She raised a brow.

"And?"

"Dwarves."

"Hah!" She said. She poured a goblet of wine and picked at some food still on the table. "It must be those ones we encountered before. The ones that traveled with Nath Dragon or whatever it was. Hmmm, it seems they want to slow our army's movements and take us out one by one."

"And they can't hurt us when we stay together," Finlin added. "Just let me scout. I can find and spring their snares." He smiled. "Even better, I think we can catch them in the act. Snare them and take them."

"What do you propose?"

"The dwarves can't detect me as quick as I can find them," Finlin said. "They live in rocks, and we're bred in the woodland. No, I'll find them, lead them on a chase, and where we wind up..." He punched his fist into his hand. "...the draykis will be waiting to pounce."

Faylan twitched her lips and scratched the side of her cheek.

"I suppose it will work. How many do you need?"

"I need them all," he smiled, "and I will let not a single dwarf get away."

"So be it then," she said with a wave, "but you'd better not fail me again."

Pilpin ran a stone over the blade of his axe. Most of the other dwarves were doing the same. For the past few days, they'd been harassing the scouts of the soldiers of Barnabus with pits, snares, and other traps, but they had yet failed to get their prey.

"We'll get them," he said, thumping the edge of his blade. "We'll get them both."

"Aye," one said, followed by another.

Pilpin nodded. So far, their efforts had been successful, but the satyrs had evaded all the tricks and traps. The little goat-man was faster than a jackrabbit in the forest, and he noticed anything out of the ordinary. He could sniff them out in the breeze. *Must get that satyr and that satyr woman. Justice will be served the dwarven way, or it won't be served at all.* Every dwarf, one and all, would die if necessary, to bring to justice the enemies of their friends.

Horn Bucket rode up to them from deep in the woods. He sat tall in the saddle, looking like a bear with a wooden helmet on his head.

"We have him," Horn Bucket said. "Devliik wants us to make our move. All of us. It's now."

The dwarves scrambled out of the dirt and climbed into their saddles with determined looks in their eyes. Pilpin followed Horn Bucket's lead into a pass at the bottom of the hill. Horn Bucket signaled for them to spread out. Once they did, they came to a stop where two more dwarves on horses waited. One was Devliik.

"He's up there," Horn Bucket said, pointing with his missing hand. Ahead was more forest and rocky terrain. He eyed the others and then Pilpin. "No path through the way we came except through us." He winked at Pilpin. "This time, I think he's wandered too far away."

Devliik raised his arm and dropped it down.

The dwarves spurred their mounts forward at a trot. Two remained back with small crossbows ready. Pilpin could feel his blood charging through his veins. Peering ahead, he saw two small horns peaking around a large oak tree.

"Don't let him flank us again," Devliik said.

The satyr had evaded them before. Two at a time and sometimes three, they had gone after him on horseback, and they had come so close. But this time, all of them were ready. They maintained their trot. The satyr didn't move. Pilpin could see his brown eyes shifting from side to side.

Run for it, you little horned fiend! Run for it!

They closed in. Thirty yards. Twenty yards.

The satyr bolted up the back. The dwarves dug their heels into their mounts and charged after him.

"East ten!" one dwarf yelled.

"West five!" said another.

"Southwest fifteen!" Pilpin shouted out with his eyes on the satyr.

The dwarves might not be as quick, but they were tactical. Everyone shouted a direction and a measure, cutting off the satyr's path wherever it turned.

Back and forth the dwarves shouted.

The satyr dashed through all sides of the pass, only to be cut off time and again. Desperation filled its eyes. It snarled and barked at them. They closed in and started to surround it. It turned and sped straight down the pass, away from them and its army.

"After him!" Devliik said. "This is just what we wanted!"

Horses thundered through the pass fifty yards, then a hundred. Devliik led them to a stop where the pass almost dead ended in a cliff of huge rocks.

"Well, well," Devliik said, looking above.

The satyr hung suspended above them upside down with its leg in a snare.

"Your days of running are over, Murderer," Devliik said, getting off his horse. All the dwarves did the same.

Pilpin pulled the rope that held him, and the satyr landed hard on the ground. It sprung on its feet and started to run.

Whop!

Devliik punched it in the jaw, and it fell to the ground. In seconds, the dwarves had its arms and legs bound with rope.

"What do you have to say for yourself, Murderer?"

Finlin flashed them all a grin and said, "You didn't trap me, you bearded fools. I trapped you."

The horses nickered and bolted back down the pass.

Pilpin and all the dwarves readied their weapons, scanning the area.

Hidden in the rocks, the draykis emerged with claws and teeth that looked like razors.

Finlin laughed and said, "There won't be any dwarven justice, but there will be more dwarven deaths."

CHAPTER

21

TWANG! TWANG! TWANG!

Nath snatched one arrow out of the air. Another splintered off his chest.

"Gads!" Bayzog cried out.

The third arrow buried itself in Bayzog's leg. The part-elf crumpled on the ground. Nath rushed over.

"Are you alright?"

"I'll be fine. Go!" Bayzog said.

Nath pointed his finger at Otter Bone.

"You'll regret this!" He dashed into the woods.

Twang!

He swatted an arrow away and made a bead toward the tree in which sat the man who fired it. He jumped up high, grabbed the man's leg, and jerked him off the branch. The archer scrambled to his feet and reached for another arrow.

Nath snatched the bow and snapped it in half. *Whop!* He knocked the man out.

Twang! Twang!

Arrows skipped of his back. He whirled and pounced thirty feet through the air into the trees.

"How'd you—" the archer said, "—*ack!*"

Nath slung him to the ground.

The last archer tried to climb away.

"Where are you going?" Nath said, grabbing the man by the belt and hurling him downward.

The man crashed on top of the other.

Several men with swords ran beneath his feet, straight for the camp.

Nath leapt out of the tree and ran straight at them. He slung one right after another to the ground and held his laugh when they got up from the ground. He narrowed his eyes.

"You should have stayed home tonight."

They gang rushed him.

Whop!

A man fell gasping for air.

Wap!

The next spun like a top to the ground.

Crack!

A jaw went loose.

Wap! Wap!

A man's eyes rolled up in his head.

Boom!

The last man's feet left the ground, and he crashed out of sight in the forest.

Nath headed back for camp.

Bayzog and Brenwar were fine, but Otter Bone was shaking.

"My patience thins," Nath said, picking him up by the collar and lifting him from his feet. "Have your nephew go and fetch my friend."

Otter Bone coughed and sputtered.

"You are fast, Dragon. Very fast indeed."

Nath shook him.

"Tell your nephew to get moving now." He glanced at Bayzog. The half-elf seemed hurt. "How's the leg?"

Bayzog's face turned clammy and a sheet of white. He fell onto his back.

Nath let go of Otter Bone and rushed over.

"Bayzog!"

The wizard's eyes were weak, and his breath was thin. He started to say something.

"P-Poison."

Nath whirled toward Otter Bone, who had a thin smile on his cracked lips.

"You are fast, but wise as a serpent you are not," the sage said, pointing at the arrow in Bayzog's leg. "You missed one."

"Brenwar!" Nath said. "Get the chest!"

The dwarf got off of Horse Neck and punched him in the back of the head. The man sagged into the ground. Brenwar headed for the chest.

"It will do you no good, Nath Dragon." Otter Bone said. "Only I have the cure for the bane that ails him. And I'll never tell without those crystals."

Nath's fires burned deep inside. His chest heaved. His nostrils flared. He fought the urge to turn the man to cinder.

"I'll find a way with or without you, Sage."

Brenwar set the chest down and opened it up.

"That won't help," Otter Bone warned. "He's been hit with poison, not magic. But a potion will probably heal his leg. Not that he's going anywhere."

Nath put a healing vial to Bayzog's lips.

Bayzog sipped. A moment later, he coughed and sputtered. His violet eyes rolled up into his head, and his body went limp.

Nath crushed the vial in his hand.

"Cure him now, Old Man."

"Old Man, am I? I'm certain I'm not older than you. You are old, but you are not wise, Nath Dragon. So many decades you have wasted." He shook his head. "You should have seen this coming."

"I'll get the cure from him," Brenwar said, stepping forward.

"Brenwar Bolderguild. If you only used your wits as much as you used that hammer, you might not have ever been in this predicament. You or the young black dragon."

"Why you—"

Nath stopped him with is hand.

"I'll get the crystals."

Otter Bone eyed him.

"And?"

"And I'll give them to you," Nath said.

"Now you are learning," Otter Bone said.

Bayzog groaned. The part-elf looked miserable, sinking Nath's heart. As much as he didn't want to cooperate with Otter Bone, he had no choice but to comply. He had to save his friend. And another thing bothered him too about Otter Bone. The things the sage said seemed to voice concern. But deceit was often clouded in mystery.

"Is there something specific about these crystals you want to share with me?" Nath said, "Or am I supposed to find this needle in the haystack without any idea what the needle looks like?"

"Ah, now I know you are committed," Otter Bone said, scratching the scraggly whiskers on his chin and combing his frosty hair back from his smoky eyes. "I've seen visions of these things. Three the size of eggs should suit me. Above, there are many common things and many terrors as well."

"Like dragons?" Brenwar stated, folding his arms over his chest. "How do we roam streets that are filled with dragons?"

"Well, what was your plan to begin with? Obviously you were going to go up there," Otter Bone said, "and try to find a way to stop the dragons."

"Bayzog was going to help out with that," Brenwar bristled, "and that's why we sent Ben into the city, to get some insight on what we are dealing with!"

"I'm a sage. I know these things already. Please don't repeat them—"

"Why you—"

Nath held the deep-chested dwarf back.

"Get on with it, Sage!" Nath said.

Otter Bone cackled.

"Alright, alright then. My, your patience does not match your longevity." He sighed. "I know you want to free the dragons from the control of Barnabus. The stones of jaxite are many that they use, but," he held his finger up, "there are not that many. The jaxite is difficult to cut, but doers up there get it done."

"Who are the doers?" Nath said.

"That I do not know, but the dragons are not the only thing that guards them. There is something else. Something stark I've seen. Dark and deadly. Malevolent. The curse on the Floating City makes it hard to see, but I get drifting visions from time to time. Stands my hairs up on end, it does." He shook his head. "I'm not sure what lurks up there can be stopped or killed."

"Dragons and dark forces," Brenwar huffed. "How much worse can it be?" He swung War Hammer around. "Either way, I'm ready."

Otter Bone laughed.

"You cannot go, Bolderguild. There is no time for turtles to fetch my fare."

"I certainly will."

"You'll never make the climb in time."

Bayzog moaned.

"Brenwar, someone needs to keep an eye on him and Bayzog. You're all I have."

The older dwarf grunted and made a quick nod.

"And you better get moving," the old sage said to Nath. "The longer he stays sick, the more damage is done. I cannot reverse the effects beyond a period of time."

Nath glanced at Bayzog. The mage looked miserable.

"How much time?" he said.

"I cannot say for certain. Just make haste. Find the ones that carve the crystals and bring me three of what they have."

"I don't even know how to get up there," Nath said. "Can you tell me?"

"You have good eyes, Nath Dragon. You'll see."

Nath rummaged through the chest and grabbed a few things. He reached for Akron.

"That will only slow you down," Otter Bone said. "Use your mind. It's much faster."

Nath vanished into the forest.

CHAPTER

22

THERE WAS DARKNESS. THERE WAS gloom. The dank smell of a dungeon lingered in Gorlee's nostrils.
Oh no, not The Deep again.

He was sprawled out on a slab of stone. His ankles and wrists were constricted by an unseen force. A fog-like mist rolled over him like a ghostly hand, and chill bumps raised on his pinkish limbs. Fear assailed him.

What if Bletver has me?

His fuzzy mind began to clear. Exhausted, he'd fallen asleep against the wall on the edge of the City of Narnum only to awaken and face a dark terror in the night. Longer and heavier than a great cat, a fanged cat-like creature had slavered over him. Smoke of a languid scent had spilled from its nose, and his sight had turned into flowers and then black. Now he awoke, bound on a cold hard slab.

"This is tiresome," he said, straining against his bonds. His limbs felt weak and his bones like jelly. He sighed. "Awfully tiresome."

He could hear the sound of a torch nearby, and it gave off a faint yellow light in the dreary chamber. Somewhere, something metal scraped over stone.

"Who's there?"

His voice echoed off stones. Stillness was his answer.

He closed his eyes. His mind raced.

Don't panic. Don't panic. Don't panic.

Just when Gorlee thought he'd gotten control of things, the world had slipped out from under his feet. Even in all the years he spent protecting Nath Dragon with Brenwar, Ben and Bayzog, he'd never encountered fear like this before. The past two days had stifled him. And now it seemed his captors knew what he was.

And they had him.

Metal scraped over stone again.

His eyes snapped open.

Dark-robed figures formed a hem around him. The tattoos on their bald heads glowed with eerie colors that seemed to move and swirl.

"Where did you come from?"

They chanted and swayed.

Nausea assailed Gorlee.

"Stop it! Stop it! What are you doing?"

A metal footstep resounded over the stone, and a shadow fell over his head.

Gorlee's head twisted around.

"Kryzak!"

The man's steady glare was heavy on him. His eyes were wild with fire. He joined the chants in the acolyte circle and stretched his long fingers over Gorlee's head.

"What are you doing?"

Kryzak's hands burst with glowing purple flame. His chant became louder and louder. He waved his flaming fingers over Gorlee's eyes, shouted out, and dropped them on his face.

Gorlee tried to jerk away, but the mystic hands seized him. His scream was muffled.

NO!

His fingers and toes curled. Something invaded his mind and his body. Like dark waters bursting through a dam into a previously calm lake, it roiled him inside. Kryzak's burning hands engulfed his head, and mystic violet immersed his body. The acolytes' chants turned into howls, and his body shook on the great stone.

What is happening to me?

Gorlee's mind recoiled. Something dark had entered. Had peeled the bars away that guarded his mind. Now that it was inside, he felt powerless to stop it from rummaging around.

What are you doing to me?

Memories flooded through his head. Friends. Cities. Countryside and mountain peaks.

He screamed.

Everything he'd ever known seemed lost.

The fires went out, and he lay there, cold and shaking. The chants ended. The acolytes dispersed, leaving only him and Krysak. The large man held a glowing crystal over his head and said, "You are one of us now."

Gorlee's lips were glued shut, but his mind asked many questions.

One of what? Who am I? Where is this?

Why does it smell so bad?

CHAPTER

23

THERE WON'T BE ANY DWARVEN *justice, but there will be more dwarven deaths.*

Trapped and flatfooted, Pilpin glared at the laughing satyr and readied himself for the draykis advance. The hulking creatures were almost three times the size of the dwarves, and their sharp claws clutched in and out like razors.

Devliik raised his battle axe up high over his head and shouted a battle cry.

"For Morgdon!"

The dwarves formed a battle wedge behind Devliik and shouted in return.

"For Morgdon!"

"Charge!" Devliik roared in Dwarven.

The dwarven force careened into the nearest draykis with ram-like force, toppled him over, and kept on going. Pilpin stepped on its ugly face and slipped through its grasping claws. It was the fastest he'd ever run before. He cast a glance over his shoulder. The draykis stood flatfooted, and their huge fanged jaws were gawping.

"Get after them!" Finlin screamed, sawing at the rope that held him. "Get them! Kill them all, you grey-skinned fiends!"

The dwarves scurried up a rocky hilltop, darted under hanging branches, and ran straight into the mouth of a large cave.

Pilpin could hear the satyr Finlin's rage-filled scream.

"They're getting away!"

Into the darkness the dwarves plunged, with the draykis fast on their tails. One by one, they each burrowed into a smaller cave barely big enough for a dwarf to fit through. Pilpin squeezed inside the gap and his brethren pulled him in.

"Ulp!"

A draykis grabbed his ankle and pulled him back out. He dangled in its mighty arm like a stubby, bearded child.

"Ha! Ha! Ha! Ha!" Finlin laughed, entering the cave. "Another prisoner." He beat his chest like a drum. "I suggest the rest of you come out if you don't want to see another dwarf die."

Pilpin eyed the approaching satyr.

"My," Finlin said, "you are a small one, aren't you. And you almost have more beard than body." He shook his horns. "That's gross. Now, call out your brethren so we can get this over with."

"It's over with already," Pilpin said with a gleam in his eyes.

"It's good to know that you've come to terms with your circumstances," Finlin said. He cupped his hands over his mouth. "Come out, come out, you little husky men. Or else I'll feed this bearded morsel to my draykis."

"They won't come," Pilpin said, folding his little arms over his chest.

Finlin stood eye to eye with him and said, "Is it because you'd rather die than see them surrender?"

Pilpin shook his head.

"No, not at all."

"Then why is it then?"

Pilpin scanned the cave. All the draykis had converged around him and Finlin.

"Well," Pilpin said in a hushed voice, eyes darting from one draykis to the other, "it's because the dark skies are falling."

"What?" Finlin said, craning his neck.

"Dark skies are falling," Pilpin said with a wink.

"I don't catch your meaning," Finlin said while his ears wiggled all around and bent.

Tink. Tink. Tink ... Tink. Tink. Tink.

Pilpin made an odd dwarven giggle and reached into his pocket. He held a large nut shell in his hand.

"Is that your last meal?" Finlin said, eyeing the cave.

Tink. Tink. Tink ... Tink. Tink. Tink.

"No, it's for the draykis." He stuffed it in the nearest draykis's mouth, closed his eyes, and covered his ears. "Enjoy!"

The draykis chomped down.

Boom!

The entire cave shook.

Pilpin fell free and scrambled for the narrow gap they pulled him from before. He took one last glimpse into the cave. One draykis was missing a head, and its body was smoking. Finlin and the others staggered onto their feet, eyes searching the darkness above.

Tink. Tink. Tink ... Tink. Tink. Tink.

Tink. Tink. Tink ... Tink. Tink. Tink.

Tink. Tink. Tink ... Tink. Tink. Tink.

Finlin the satyr's eyes widened.

"Get out! Get out!"

He dashed for the cave mouth just as the dark sky crashed down.

"We found something," a sergeant of Barnabus said. He was tall and wiry with tangled brown hair. He saluted and stood at attention.

"Finally," Faylan the satyr said. She waved him off and shoved by him and out of her tent. She turned and looked back at the tent flap. "Well! Show me what you found."

The man scurried out with a nod and made his way through the camp, gathering a host of men.

Faylan eyed each and every one. The muscles between her shoulders were tight, and the corner of her lip twitched. She hadn't seen her brother or the draykis in the past two days. She rubbed the amulet around her neck and summoned its power, but nothing came.

"Brother, I will kill you if you failed me again."

She had followed the soldiers on hooved feet miles through the forest and ravines when they came to a stop. She could see scouts standing up on the rocky hillside farther ahead. She noticed a rope hanging from a tree nearby. Her gaze fell to the ground.

One scout pointed at footprints and said, "Dwarves, draykis, and your brother. They lead that—"

"I can see that!" She marched forward with her heart beating inside her throat. Something was wrong. Amiss. She picked up her pace and trotted up the rocky climb underneath the overhanging pine branches. A few soldiers in dusty and stained armor who stood on a crag turned to face her with widening eyes. They scooted back and dipped their heads, turning toward the rock face of the mountain.

Her head beaded with sweat. Her breath was hard to find. Before her, what was once a large cave mouth that opened wide was filled with huge stones and rubble. Her hooves clacked over the rocky crag and came to a stop in front of the cave mouth. A glint of steel in the sun caught her eye. A smear of red did too. She shuddered a breath and her eyes swelled with tears. Holding the knife was the cold dead hand of her brother. The rest of his body was buried in the rubble. She fell to her knees.

"NOOOOOOOOOOOOOOOO!"

She sobbed, cried, and screamed for minutes, maybe an hour, until she could cry no more. Shaking like a leaf, she managed to stand up and eye the rock-filled tomb. She could only assume the draykis were in there too.

High Priestess Selene will have my head for this!

The sergeant cleared his throat and spoke with his head cast to the ground.

"I'm sorry for your loss," he said, "but at least the dwarves are gone too."

She stabbed him in the chest with her brother's dagger.

He fell dead to the ground. All the soldiers shuffled backward. She glared at them and shook her head. "Leave him for the vultures. Let's get back to camp."

Tink. Tink. Tink ... Tink. Tink. Tink...

Tink. Tink. Tink ... Tink. Tink. Tink...

The sound of metal striking stone echoed all around.

"Are you finished crying yet, you goat-horned, mule-hooved, hairy-backed fiend?"

Faylan's head snapped upward and hatred blazed in her eyes.

A small dwarf that sounded like ten spoke.

"Your brother's dead, and soon you will be as well, but until then, it's never too late to surrender."

"I'll kill you!"

"Eh," the dwarf said, cupping his hears, "Were you talking to your brother again? Don't you know the dead can't hear you?"

High atop the rocky hill, she could see a small group of dwarves. Their hands were filled with picks and shovels.

"Only a fool would follow a dwarf into a cave." His voice echoed. "Or a satyr."

"You'll pay for this!" she shouted, shaking her first. "My army will hunt you down and slaughter the lot of you!"

"We'll see about that," the little dwarf said. He raised a pick over his head and started swinging. "Brethren, let us deliver her a nice rocky grave." The dwarves rattled their picks and began to chant and yell.

Tink. Tink. Tink … Tink. Tink. Tink…

Tink. Tink. Tink … Tink. Tink. Tink…

Huge chunks of rock broke off and started to fall.

"Rockslide! Run!" one soldier yelled.

Faylan sprinted down the hill. Behind her, the rockslide covered the entire face of the hill. Only the soldiers at the bottom survived. Above, she could see the small dwarf waving his hand.

"Don't worry, we'll get you next time, Little Horned One."

CHAPTER

24

NATH CUT THROUGH THE FOREST quicker than a jungle panther. Heavy thoughts and urgency rattled around in his mind. He leapt over a wide creek and weaved through the trees and brush. He was miles west of the last River City now, and the Floating City hung like a great moon in the daylight above. Almost directly beneath the edge of the gargantuan rock that hung in the air, he came to a stop.

Need to save Bayzog.

The jaxite glowed with a strange blue light, making odd life-like shadows on his surroundings. Nath stared up in wonder. He could see the outlines of towers and buildings built from marble and limestone. They twisted into the stark blue sky. Cable bridges swayed in the wind, bridges from one floating rock to the other. They led into the city, but from way up high. A dark shadow streaked across the sky like a great bat. He hunkered down.

Need to be a little more mindful.

Despite his concern for his friends, his dragon blood still raced with exhilaration. He could never say it out loud, but Otter Bone was right about one thing. His friends did slow him down and hold him back. There was nothing like the freedom of being a dragon. He reached behind his back and caressed Fang's steely hilt. *Not you, my friend.* Nath rubbed his scruffy jaw and surveyed the expanse above.

How do I get up there?

Otter Bone had been vague, but also clear. There was a way, and he'd find it, or else. Nath couldn't figure the man. Good or bad. And he never had problems reading people.

A long sleepy roar scattered the birds from the trees.

Bull dragon.

Another slightly different roar followed.

Great, they're both prowling.

Nath could hear trees falling over, where the two bull dragons pushed through the forest. Without hesitation, he waded into the river that ran beneath the Floating City. Bull dragons didn't care much for water, but there were plenty of dragons that did.

Neck deep, he made his way toward rocky cliffs that hung over the river. Green and brown vines twisted downward like lush waterfalls over the river. Nath slipped behind them and waited, ears perked and eyes alert. His golden eyes widened when they came.

Two golden brown-red dragons pushed out of the woods. Their great iron-scaled bellies dragged over the ground. They both sniffed and snorted smoke and fire. One made an ear-shattering roar to the other. The other's great chest heaved. Fire shot from its mouth like molten lava into the water, smoking up the river.

Nath dipped his head a little deeper into the water. The bull dragons were each bigger than the grey scaler he'd defeated, and their girth was even greater. They weren't the fastest fliers, but they were certainly one of the toughest dragons to kill. Their scales were more than just iron and razors. They were harder than the hardest metals, and their bones were like steel. Nath had tangled with one of the baby ones when he was a boy … once.

Great, they smell me, but I don't think they know who I am.

The bull dragons locked horns with a great clack and shoved their great necks back and forth.

Clack!

Clack!

Clack!

They drew their heads back and struck one another again and again, like claps of thunder.

It was a warning. The bull dragons wanted whoever lurked in their territory to know who was boss. Minutes later, they broke it off and spat streams of flame high into the air.

Always snorting and blowing like the bullheads they are.

All of a sudden, their tails lashed into the leafy forest and smote a large tree into splinters. It tumbled down with a crash. One dragon chomped down on the trunk and slung it into the river.

Splash!

Nath allowed himself a smile.

At least they're not as smart as they are strong and skull-headed. That's when he noticed something else. Their tails, long and mighty like great snakes, were not black. *How did I miss that? Interesting.*

As the tree floated by past the corner of his eye, the dragons barked two roars and leapt into the sky. Their wings spread out and beat, and slowly their hulking forms rose into the sky and disappeared from sight.

I'll never understand how those fatties can fly.

Nath twisted his head upward and peered into the air. Many boulders floated up there, with layers of jaxite below them. There were dozens of them, maybe hundreds, spread out through the sky between here and the city. He smiled, bobbed his head, wrapped his arms up in the vines, and climbed toward the top of the overhanging cliff. *For Bayzog.*

CHAPTER
25

"ARE YOU HAPPY WITH YOURSELF?" Brenwar said, glaring at Otter Bone.

The wiry old man shrugged.

"It's what is best," the sage said, glancing into the sky, "for the long run. You should know that, being a dwarf."

Brenwar sneered under his beard and tipped a canteen to Bayzog's thin lips. Half a day had passed since Nath left, and every minute seemed like an hour. The mage slumped against the tree with red rings around his weak eyes. Brenwar dipped water into his mouth. Bayzog spit it out and groaned.

"That's touching," Otter Bone said, "seeing a dwarf tend to an elf. Do you do that often?"

Brenwar shot him a look.

"What kind of man uses poison? You're evil ilk."

"I'm desperate. We're all desperate." Otter Bone untied a small cloth pouch from his belt and tossed it up and down in the air. "And I'm not evil. Well, mostly not, just twisted. Horse Neck!"

The large brute of a man lumbered out of the woods with a cautious eye on Brenwar. He rubbed a large knot on the back of his head. Otter Bone stared oddly at the knot for a minute and then whispered something in his ear. The man's lazy eyes enlarged.

"But, why?" he said.

"Just do it," Otter Bone replied, waving him off with his hand. "And take the others."

"What was that all about?" Brenwar said. "Where's he going?"

"We need to move," said Otter Bone, helping himself up to his feet. His joints crackled as he stretched and yawned. "I swear I feel as old as you are some days. Do your bones get cold when it rains?"

"Dwarves don't ache."

"Of course they don't. And I suppose they don't feel pain, either."

Brenwar shrugged his heavy shoulder and said, "We aren't going anywhere with him like this. And where are your people going?" He bristled. "I'm tiring of your games."

Otter Bone tossed the pouch onto Bayzog's chest.

"Just give him a couple pinches of that, and your wizard friend will be fine."

Brenwar flung the pouch back.

"You take it first."

"It will cure the poison that ails him," Otter Bone said, tossing it back. "Well, it's not really poison. He was just hit with an arrowhead carved from Gortt Root. It's just a paralyzing tummy-ache that will pass on its own in a few days. But if you want your friend to suffer longer..."

Brenwar hurled it back.

"I'm not a druid. I don't know what Gortt Root is."

"If it was a tankard of ale, you would have."

"If it was a tankard of ale," Brenwar growled, rising to his feet, "I'd dash yer head in with it."

"Point taken, Dwarf," the sage said, removing a pinch of mossy-yellow powder. He stuffed the pinch under his lip and smiled. "Happy?"

Brenwar snatched the pouch out of his hand and took a whiff of it. His eyes watered.

"Strong, isn't it?" Otter Bone said.

"What is it?" Brenwar asked. He felt good but light headed.

"Alleck Moss. Very rare, like Golden Ore. It's a natural remedy for most world-born poisons. Your friend Bayzog was struck by the Gortt Root. Its fibers are dark and twisty. Rooted poison that kills off the fish in pond waters. Just another dirty little secret in this world of ours."

"You know a lot of odd things," Brenwar said.

"I'm a sage. We are odd people."

Brenwar kneeled down and grabbed a pinch out of the pouch.

"A little more," Otter Bone suggested. "Just stuff it inside his cheek."

"This better work." Brenwar stuffed the Alleck Moss inside Bayzog's mouth.

The part-elf's chin wriggled a bit.

"Give him a few moments," Otter Bone said, "and while he recovers, I'll reveal a few things to you." Otter Bone felt his way around until he found a log and took a seat. "You'll have to forgive me. Usually,

Horse Neck assists me with these minor things." He craned his neck in Brenwar's direction but not directly at him. "Come sit."

"I'll stand," Brenwar said, making his way closer. It was odd. Otter Bone was not only blind, but all alone, but he seemed far from helpless. "Go ahead. Spit it out."

Otter Bone cleared his throat and tapped his chest.

"As I said. I knew of you coming. I've seen the darkness that comes and closes in." He pointed upward. "Floating above are grave perils that not all of you were prepared for. Brenwar Bolderguild, I could not allow you and your friends to continue on with Nath Dragon. It would have been your peril. And you are still needed. Alive, not dead."

"Ha!" Brenwar barked. "A likely story. More likely, you are a servant of Barnabus, and now you've divided our forces. Kidnapped one. Poisoned another. This is not the work of good people."

"I serve Nalzambor, and Nalzambor is good, but I have a very different way of going about it. Either way, what must be done must be done." He slapped his hands on his knees. "You should be thanking me. If you'd gone with Nath Dragon, you'd be dead already."

Brenwar scoffed. His beard itched. The ring of truth in Otter Bone's voice was clearly heard. He hefted War Hammer over his shoulder. His heart pumped in his chest. Not having Nath within a glance ate at him. What kind of danger was Nath facing?

"Your friend," Otter Bone continued, "is very powerful and resourceful. But there is a lot more darkness up there than there is light. He will be tested. Let's just hope he survives."

"If you know so much," Brenwar said, "then you know that I am charged to never leave his side. If something happens to him … " He gently popped Otter Bone in the head with his fist. "Then something bad happens to you."

"If something happens to him," Otter Bone replied, "then it won't matter what you do."

CHAPTER

26

SASHA SAT ON HER SOFA in front of a fireplace, picking at her lip. At her sides her boys sat, Rerry on the right and Samaz on the left. Her thoughts were on her husband, Bayzog. She could feel something wrong.

"Mother," Rerry said, pushing her hand away from her face. "You should stop that. You're making Samaz nervous."

Samaz leaned forward with a glum look, and then nestled back into the sofa.

Sasha's hand drifted back to her pendant.

"You're thinking about Father, aren't you?" Rerry said. "And you aren't sleeping well, are you?" He glared at Samaz. "It's his fault. Every time he says weird things, you're unsettled for days." He pointed to Samaz. "I should take you out and give you a good throttling."

Samaz huffed a laugh and said, "Don't forget what happened the last time you attempted that."

Rerry popped up out of his seat.

"That was years ago!" He whisked a small dagger from his belt. It flashed and twirled in the air. "I've gotten bigger and stronger, while you've gotten fatter and slower."

"Enough of this, please," Sasha said, rising from her seat.

"Mother," Rerry said, taking her by the hand, "I'm sorry. Let me fetch you some Wizard Water. It will refresh you."

She pulled away, crossed the room, and stood in front of a mirror that hung over the fire. She noticed something. *What is that?* She rubbed the winkles in the corners of her eyes. *I have crow's feet!* Her head dipped into her chest. She was almost fifty now, and she felt like a hundred. She made her way over to Bayzog's grand table, a great circle made of elven wood inlaid with precious things such as topaz, sapphires, onyx, emeralds, silver, and gold.

"What are you doing, Mother?" Rerry said. "Are you going to give us a lesson?"

"No," she said, grabbing one of Bayzog's ancient books.

"No?" Rerry looked back at his brother. Samaz had a concerned look on his round face.

"Why don't you go play with your sword or something?" she suggested.

"But," Rerry said, "you never want me to play with my swords."

Sasha didn't hear what he said. She was thumbing through the pages.

There must be a way to get rid of these wrinkles.

CHAPTER

27

"HE'S EXQUISITE, ISN'T HE?" HIGH Priestess Selene said from her backless throne chair.

Kryzak shrugged his wide shoulders. In his heavy hand he held a large yellow stone that swirled with mystic energy.

In between her and Kryzak stood Gorlee. The changeling wore dark grey robes that covered everything but his head, hands, and wrist. His pinkish skin and white hair intrigued Selene. In all of her centuries, she'd never encountered a changeling before, so far as she knew. She knew of them, but like most, she knew little about them. The changelings were even more introverted than the dragons. She tapped her fingertips together and showed a wolfish smile.

"I can't imagine why this creature would aid Nath Dragon," she said, "but I'll understand soon enough." Her eyes ran up and down Gorlee. "Like finding a diamond in the sewer." She rose from her chair, made her way down the steps, and studied Gorlee. He stood tall but listless as an empty vessel. His face was well-featured, his frame lithe but well-knit. His pale green eyes sparkled with intelligence and curiosity, but the fires that had ignited them with derision toward her were gone. "Do you understand me?"

Gorlee nodded.

She rubbed his arms with her hand and caressed his body with her tail.

"Do you have a name?"

He shook his head.

"Do you have a tongue?"

He shook his head again.

"Speak," she demanded. "Do you have a tongue?"

"Yes," he said in a soft voice as polished as stone.

"What are you?"

"A changeling," he answered.

"But you don't know your name?"

"I cannot recall it."

She glared at Kryzak and said, "I hope you did not overdo it."

He held out the bright yellow stone.

"The Chamal Stone has a mind of its own."

Selene turned her back on Kryzak and faced Gorlee.

"Change into an orc."

"A what?" Gorlee said.

Selene's eyes flared and her fists clenched.

"He doesn't even remember what an orc is?"

She spun Gorlee toward Kryzak.

"Change into him!"

Gorlee's pale eyes narrowed to slits, and his body changed and contorted. In seconds, he was a mirror image of Kryzak, but in different robes.

"Excellent!" She clapped her hands. "You're going to need to escort him through the city and let him familiarize himself with people and the races. Take him through the towers and into the galleries. He's sharp. It won't take him long to figure things out."

Kryzak stood glaring at Gorlee, and Gorlee glared back at him. Every little move Kryzak made, the changeling mirrored.

"Please tell him to change back."

"Please tell him to change back," Gorlee's voice, the same as Kryzak's, echoed.

Selene laughed.

"Seems you can be replaced after all, Kryzak. How nice it would be to have a man who can change the scenery." She rubbed Gorlee's tattooed head and played with his ear.

Kryzak's eyes became hot with jealousy.

"Does that bother you?" she said, rubbing Gorlee's bulging arms and back.

"My queen," Kryzak said, "you know this is torture for me. I've died for you, and this thing has done nothing."

"Nothing yet, Kryzak, nothing as of yet." She stretched out her arm and opened her palm. "I'm certain that will change. Now depart from me and see that he is well trained."

Kryzak laid the Chamal Stone between her fingers, took a knee, and bowed. With a grunt, he led Gorlee out of Selene's chamber.

Selene drifted up the stair and resumed her place on the backless throne. The Chamal Stone was warm and living in her hands.

Let's see what kind of memories were stored in that wonderful mind.

She closed her eyes and started to chant in Dragonese. Smoke rolled from her nostrils and over her lips. Her eyes snapped open, glowing with bright purple fires. The Chamal Stone flared and lifted from her hands, glowing like a yellow star.

Selene clutched the arms of her throne and inhaled the mystic energies of the stone. Gorlee's memories became hers. She saw his parents, his home, his decades wandering alone. The way he toyed with people thrilled her. His great powers chilled her. Gorlee. That was his name. Good natured. Curious. He wanted to stop her. Stop evil. Give aid to the good in the next dragon war.

I won't let that happen.

Minutes went by. Almost an hour. She savored every bit of him. She saw his friends as if they were standing right there: Brenwar Bolderguild and a bunch of other dwarves, Bayzog the Wizard, Ben the Warrior, and the great Nath Dragon. All the names and locations of their friends and loved ones became hers.

STRIFE IN THE SKY

My weapons can never have enough edges.

No doubt she would need to isolate them all from each other, similar to how she had the elves under wraps with the orcs so that it wasn't likely they'd leave their lands. The part-elf wizard Bayzog made an impression in her mind. He was more than formidable with the power of the Elderwood Staff.

We can't have too many heroes running amok and ruining my plans. Perhaps I shall take a closer look at who his wife Sasha is. It seems Bayzog and Nath Dragon both talk about her much. Love makes an excellent weapon when you know how to use it against them.

She watched the pounding he'd given Bletver and the escape he'd made from the phantom.

It would have been nice to have him as an ally all these years. But at least I have him now.

She closed her eyes and broke the connection to the stone. The mystic memories that drifted sparkled and fell onto the dais and disappeared.

Selene clasped her fingers together and rested her elbows on the arms of her throne.

"And now I know precisely where Nath Dragon is. Poor Gorlee the Chameleon. He couldn't have given me a greater gift." She chuckled. "Once again proving that heroics which don't work are only foolish efforts."

She squawked in Dragonese.

Moments later, her pet drulture flew in and landed on the arm of her chair. Its scaly feathers were bright and colorful.

She showed it the Chamal Stone and said, "Take this to the phantom and have him take it to Bletver. He's to keep it safe until I call for it."

The drulture let out a throaty little roar, snatched the Chamal Stone in its mouth, and flew outside through the terrace.

Selene sat straight up and showed a confident smile.

"I think this war just might be over before it's even begun."

CHAPTER

28

CONCEALED IN THE BRUSH, NATH kneeled on one knee, scanning the skies above. The Floating City hung ominously in the air. A monolith beyond expectations. Its tall buildings and high spires hosted dragons, colorful and with dark tails.

There must be at least twenty of them up there.

He reached behind his back and grasped Fang's hilt. The metal was cool to the touch. It put Nath's mind at ease. Having Fang on his side again gave him an edge, and that would have to be enough.

In one of the stone archways in the city, a dragon with deep blue scales stretched its wings and yawned. Little bigger than a man, the blue streak dragon dropped out of the archway, glided between the towers, and disappeared behind the cover of the buildings, only to appear again streaking high into the clouds above.

If I just had wings, getting into that city would be a lot easier.

He eased his way through the brush and forest to another vantage point facing the eastern part of the city.

One. Two. Three. Four. Five. Great Dragons!

Dragons were scattered the same on this side as everywhere else. Some of their eyes gleamed like diamonds, and others were closed. Nath dug his nails into his palm. He had to get moving and help Bayzog. Otter Bone had even said there was a greater menace within than the dragons. Not to mention that even if he managed to make it into the Floating City and out, he'd still have to navigate through the bull dragons. They had his scent. They'd be looking for him.

He scanned the great rock the city floated upon. There were catwalks high above that led from the city onto other rocks floating on jaxite above. But they were a hundred feet above him, maybe more.

I can't jump that high. If Bayzog were here, he'd take me up.

He eyed the stones that hung in the air. There were many small ones the size of boulders that hung suspended in the air.

Like the rocks that help you cross a rushing river.

That's interesting.

There were hundreds of stones scattered over the expanse. Nath could see a path leading upward toward the city. But it was no simple feat. The distance from one rock to another looked to be over twenty feet.

Alright then. That's one option. But how can I climb them without being seen? Is this the way Otter Bone meant for me to take? It hardly seems safe. Only one way to find out.

He scanned the tops of the city buildings, eyeing the dragons roosted and gliding through the city. *But what do I do about them?*

He combed his fingers through his mane of red hair, buckled his brows, and snapped his fingers. He slipped the potion vials he'd taken from Brenwar's chest out of his clothes. Each was colorful, but not bright. He put the royal blue and lavender mixtures back and kept the emerald green. He shook its contents in front of his eyes. It began to bubble, fizz. A tiny tornado formed inside with bright sparkles. *I can't believe I almost forgot about this. Now I just need something to use it on.*

Nath crept back into the forest. The potion would work on many things. Living things. But he needed to find the right subject. He stopped at a burrow in the grasses and put his ear to the ground. *Nothing in there.* He trekked around with his head on a swivel. Shoved leafy branches from his face. *Has to be something I can use here.* He lifted his chin up. Something buzzed overhead. A hornet nest. He smiled. *Perfect.*

He scaled the tree and crawled out on the limb that held the nest in place. The nest was bigger than Nath's head, and the black-and-gold-winged hornets buzzed with more fury the closer he crawled toward them. Nath huffed a plume of smoke at them. The buzzing subdued. It didn't stop a few dozen hornets from landing on him, though. Each was big, about half the length of his finger, and he knew their stings were almost lethal to most people.

Nath chuckled. He remembered a time when he'd dropped a hive onto a camp of orcs. He could still see them scrambling and flailing their arms and kicking their legs. A camp of thirty-some orcs, reduced to nothing in seconds. He had freed a pair of green lilly dragons that day. It had been over fifty years ago, maybe longer.

"I didn't have my scales then," he said to himself as several of the hornets tried to sting him. "I had to be more careful. One of your brothers still managed to put a knot on my chin."

He blew another ring of smoke, scooted over the branch, stretched out his arms, and plucked off the nest. The hornets started to cover his arms, chest and face. He hopped out of the tree, landed on cat's feet, and made his way back toward the river canyon's edge.

"This better work," he said, eyeing the mystic vial though the coat of hornets he wore. He flipped the cork off the vial, stuffed the vial into the nest, and poured.

One ... two ...

The nest sprang to life.

Three!

He slung the nest high in the air. Over a hundred feet up it went, reaching its zenith, where the entire nest seemed to hover for a moment.

Come on, now, work!

The hive exploded in a burst of buzzing golden light. Dozens of hornets, maybe hundreds, grew ten times in size and streaked through the sky. Their golden wings buzzed with roaring fury. They zigzagged like sparkling gold fishing lures in the air, scattering everywhere.

A dragon roar caught Nath's ear. Followed by another and another. He dashed beneath a leafy overhang in the rocks.

Dragons streaked through the sky, jaws wide and snapping. Their eyes were wild, and their wings beat in chase.

The golden-winged hornets looked like huge flying gold nuggets to the dragons.

The skies filled with chaotic roars that echoed off the rocks. The hornets buzzed in fury. They flew through the skies, into the forest, and beyond. Hundreds of hornets and dozens of dragons.

Nath stepped out of his hiding place and dusted off his hands.

"That should keep them tied up for a few hours. Just like fish, dragons love shiny things."

He sauntered over to the ledge and faced the nearest hanging rock. It was a twenty-foot leap away and about ten feet up. He stepped back a few paces.

I'd better get a run at this.

He dashed over the ground and flung himself upward.

Too far! Too far!

He glided over the floating rock, stretched out his arms, and splashed into the river. Emerging, he yelled, "Great Dragons!"

He swam to the riverbank and climbed the vines. Standing on the ledge again, he flung water off his arms and said, "Let's try that again."

He leapt up in a perfect arc and landed flat on his feet on the floating rock. It teetered. He steadied himself with his arms, and with his keen eyes he traced a path to the city, on the floating stones.

It took another long hop impossible to man, followed by another and another. Every rock was different than the last. Some were big enough for many, and some barely big enough for him. One slip, and he'd have to start all over again. Halfway across, he looked down at the river rushing far beneath him. The wind whipped his hair, and every rock he landed on wobbled and teetered.

There must be another way they came up here.

He crouched, craning his neck toward the sky. If a dragon saw him, he'd be an easy mark.

Keep moving. Halfway there.

He leapt onto stone after stone after stone. Some went up. Some down. Some left. Some right. His path spiraled, but he was getting closer. He stood on a smaller stone, barely wider than his shoulders, balancing himself. The next stone was a big one twenty feet wide and ten feet high, but it was more than thirty feet away. He gathered his legs under him. Tried to steady himself in the wind.

I can do this.

His legs exploded upward. Up he was going with his arms stretched out when a gust of wind hit him. He landed on his chest on the rock, with his legs dangling off. His fingers clawed at the rock. The rock titled toward him. When he started to slide off, Nath caught a glimpse of the water rushing beneath him.

I'm not doing this again. For Bayzog!

He raised his arm up and slammed it down like pounding a nail. By digging one set of claws into the rock after another, he heaved himself up, legs and all.

"Whew!" he said, drawing his arm across his forehead. He stood up, looked down at the river, and waved. "That should be the worst of it."

A growl rumbled behind him.

He whipped his head around.

"Sultans of Sulfur!"

All he saw was dragon teeth and scales.

CHAPTER
29

"WHAT IS THIS PLACE?" BRENWAR said.

Otter Bone had led them for hours through the forest, using Brenwar and Bayzog as eyes. Bayzog couldn't help but be impressed. Considering the fact that the sage was blind, he gave excellent directions.

"A hideout," Otter Bone said in his firm but smoky voice. "Of sorts. We'll wait here until the others arrive."

Bayzog rubbed his belly. He'd been nauseous the entire walk, but he was getting better. He took a seat on small wine barrel and leaned back against the cave wall. They were a few dozen feet deep in a cave that opened like a mouth into a forest. He closed his aching eyes and took deep breaths through his nose.

"The queasiness will pass," Otter Bone said, shuffling over and staring right past him with glassy eyes. "Most likely by tomorrow." He stretched out his work-laden hands with heavy knots for knuckles.

Bayzog grabbed one of those hands and led him down into a sitting position.

"Your hands are awfully rough for a sage," Bayzog said.

"Yours aren't exactly soft for a wizard, or an elf," Otter Bone said back. "I used to be a fisherman until the gift came to me. Over fifty years from birth I'd fished, when blindness struck me and a new sight was revealed to me. This cave," he said, craning his neck around, "I lived here alone for over a decade. Everyone thought madness was upon me." He sighed. "So did I. Those were dark times."

Brenwar picked up a wine casket, shook it, and tossed it down. One by one, he went through a dozen of them.

"Your hideout doesn't have any rations."

"They will come," Otter Bone said. "They will come." He nudged Bayzog. "I thought dwarves were more patient."

"They are," Bayzog said. "They're just testy around strangers."

"Are you jesting, Wizard?"

"It's not a normal thing for me, but it's been known to happen."

"Heh," Otter Bone chuckled. "You might have made for good River Folk in more peaceful times." He laid a hand on Bayzog's shoulder. "I apologize for making you sick, Bayzog."

Bayzog could sense the man's sincerity, but he was still uneasy. Otter Bone knew things, and by and large, sages weren't trustworthy. They considered themselves servants of the world more than champions for good over evil. They were known to align themselves with whichever side suited them at the moment.

"No need to apologize. I'm sure you did what you felt you had to do."

"I did."

"Well, no, you didn't. There is often more than one way to achieve a common goal, if indeed the goal is common."

"You wouldn't have made it," Otter Bone hissed, shaking his head. "I have seen it."

"Are your visions always right?"

Otter Bone shrugged.

"I've never known one to be wrong so far."

Brenwar kicked a wine casket farther down the cave, sat down, and sulked in gloom.

Bayzog left it at that. He'd already discussed Otter Bone's visions with the sage and Brenwar. It didn't sit well with him. It didn't seem possible that Nath would be safer without them. *Certainly, a formidable party of many is better than a party of one?* He'd give it some time for now. Otter Bone had his ways, and he had his own. *Nath at least needs to know that I am all right.*

Hours had passed when Brenwar stirred. Figures entered the darkness of the cave. The outline of Horse Neck's burly form took shape. A moment later, Ben appeared. He shoved his way past Horse Neck and came right at Otter Bone.

"Don't trust this lying old man!" Ben said, holding his bound wrists in front of Brenwar. "He's a deceiver!"

Brenwar slit the cords on Ben's wrists and said, "We've established that much."

Ben poked Otter Bone in the chest.

"He's treacherous—*ulp*!"

Horse Neck wrapped his big arms around Ben's wide shoulders and squeezed.

"Don't ever touch my father—*Ow*!"

Ben drove his boot into Horse Neck's shin. The goon's arms slackened. In a flash, Ben grabbed him by the arm, twisted his hips under him, and flipped him over his shoulder, where the brute landed hard on the ground. Ben's fist pounded on Horse Neck's ribs.

Jab! Jab! Jab!

Slobbering cries of anger came from the man's mouth.

"You'll pay! You'll pay!"

Ben locked him up in an arm bar and applied pressure.

"OOOOW!"

"What was that?" Ben said, twisting harder. "Are you calling for your cows?"

"OOOOOW!"

"Stop this!" Bayzog said, rising to his feet. "His cries will carry to the town."

Ben snarled and released the man. Brenwar gave him an approving nod. Horse Neck moaned and pushed himself up from the stone floor of the cave. His heavy eyes glared at Ben.

"Let it go, Nephew," Otter Bone said, "Let it go."

Horse Neck rose up, spat dirt from his mouth, and lumbered out of the cave.

"He's protective," Otter Bone said, staring blankly at Ben, "and he's not such a bad man, most of the time."

"Do you care to tell me what is going on?" Ben said to Bayzog, wiping the dirt from his elbows. "Where's Dragon?"

While a pair of Otter Bone's henchmen brought in some rations, Bayzog filled Ben in on the details. Ben's brow stayed furrowed the entire time, and his glare remained hot on Otter Bone.

"We should be done with this sage," Ben said, scooping Akron up from its spot alongside Brenwar's chest. "You can't trust a thing he says. They stuck me in a hole, Bayzog. A dirt hole with a wooden crate and ratty carpet over it.

"It was for your protection," Otter Bone said. "You were a danger to yourself and others. Whose idea was it to send this man into the River Cities with aversion balm on him?"

"It worked!"

"Hah," Otter Bone said. "It did no such thing. The overseers of Barnabus have eyes and ears on everything. They would have sniffed you out soon enough. I saved you from a certain doom. All of you."

"You keep saying that," Brenwar said with his mouth stuffed with jerky, "But I don't believe a word of it." He took a slug of wine from a bottle the henchmen had brought. "But this wine is not so horrible." He shared the bottle with Ben, who shared it with Bayzog, who took a sip.

"Not so bad," the wizard said. "Not elven, but not so bad at all."

"Good that you think so," Otter Bone said. "It should ease your minds and settle your bones. We've a long wait ahead."

"Nath Dragon moves fast," Ben said, rummaging through the rations and grabbing a clay jug of water. "He'll be back tomorrow. You'll see."

"I wish I did see," Otter Bone said, his voice low and eerie. "I don't see anything, but I'm certain of this. His journey into the Floating City, it won't be over in a day. It will take many days, if not weeks."

Ben dropped the clay jug onto the ground, where it shattered with a crash.

"What!"

CHAPTER

30

NATH JERKED AWAY.

"Argh!"

A claw snapped down on his arm with the power of an iron trap. A dragon had a hold of him.

Nath drew his free arm back and socked it in the ribs. The dragon shook him like a rag, slamming his head into the stone. Bright spots of light burst in his eyes, and blood trickled down his scalp, over his nose. He eyed the creature.

A spiny-backed crawler. Cripes!

Half the size of Nath, its burgeoning abdomen dragged over the stone as it tried to sling him back and forth. With a neck thick as a tree trunk, its snout was long and wide. It had four short legs with six claws each, and its sandstone-colored wings were clawed as well. More like a lizard, no horns adorned its wide flat head. Rows of small spikes covered its back, which looked glassy in the sunlight.

"Let go!" Nath said, punching it again.

It shook him like a dog tearing away a bone.

Eyes watering, Nath held back his cry and drew back his fist once more.

The spiny back's eyes followed the move. Jaws locked, its thin lips curled up over its sharp teeth. It rumbled a growl.

"Great Dragons!"

Spiny-backed crawlers—a smallish breed—tended to hide along riverbanks and dry stretches of land. They liked to dig and tunnel. Patient, they'd wait for their prey from beneath the grit and strike quicker than a flying arrow. Once their jaws locked, there was no unlocking them unless their prey killed them.

Nath tried to dash the sweat out of his eyes by blinking. He shook his head, looked deep into the dragon's eyes, and spoke in Dragonese to it.

"Release me."

The dragon bit down harder.

Nath's tongue clove to the roof of his mouth. The dragon was moments away from taking his arm off at the elbow. Spiny-backs' teeth were some of the hardest and sharpest of them all. They could bite through steel with them.

Think, Nath Dragon, Think!

The dragon shook its thick neck again.

Nath heard Fang rattle on his back. With his good arm, he reached back and slipped Dragon Claw out of the hilt. He waved the glimmering blade in front of the dragon's watching eyes.

"Don't make me use this," he said in Dragonese. If he had to kill a dragon to save Bayzog, then so be it. Blood racing, he drew Dragon Claw back. "I'll do what I must do."

Its jaws bit deeper.

Nath groaned, brought the dagger down, and stopped inches from its back. He eyed its wings. One dangled on its side, broken. The other, hemmed into its side, was fine. It fluttered a bit and stopped. Nath jabbed Dragon Claw into the rock.

"Your eyes, tail and wings," he said, swallowing, "they aren't darkened." He reached over and stroked its broken wing.

The dragon jerked a little.

Nath sucked through his teeth and said in more Dragonese, "Easy ... friend." He inspected the wing more. It had been gnawed up, and the joint between the wing and back was broken. It would take a long time to heal. Flying dragons without their wings were not only vulnerable but insecure as well. Ignoring the pain exploding in his head, he stroked the dragon over the eyes. "Who did this to you?"

The scaly brows on the dragon lifted up toward the city in the sky.

"I see," Nath said, looking up and around, not forgetting the hornets and dragons were still in chase. "Great." He took a seat on his rump, with the dragon attached to his forearm. It seemed that along with its injury, the spiny-back had received new orders. Another dragon must have flown down and ordered it to guard the pass over the rock with its life. Nath stroked its eyes again. A blast of smoke came from its nostrils. "Despite your effort to detach my arm from my elbow, I do consider this good fortune. Your bite is far less revealing than your lack of roar. If you'd roared, dragons certainly would have swarmed me."

The spiny-backed dragon's eyes remained intent on his, fierce and unblinking.

Alright, Nath Dragon, there's no time for this. All those dragons will return soon enough. What options do you have? He eyed Dragon Claw. *If I must, I must.* He peered over the rock. He could always plunge into the river waters below and hope to shake the dragon off. Perhaps then it would let go.

"That's your stupidest idea ever, Nath Dragon!"

Great. Now I'm talking to myself.

At the moment, he was at the mercy of the dragon. He wasn't going anywhere. He closed his eyes and sighed. Suddenly, he heard his father's voice speaking inside his head.

Sometimes compassion can be a friend to your enemies.

His head snapped up.

"Father?"

He searched the skies. The clouds. Only the wind howling through the rocks answered. He looked at the dragon and said, "Did you hear that?"

The dragon didn't move. Nath had chills on his neck, and it felt like the scales on his arms stood up. As much as he had dreaded his father's throne-shaking voice in the past, he longed for it now.

Perhaps I'm just recalling something I've long forgotten.

He patted the dragon. Rubbed the scales around its neck in the tender spots they enjoyed. Even dragons had places they couldn't scratch that itched. He heard a growl and stopped.

"Was that your belly?"

The heavy belly rumbled and groaned.

"My, you've been up here awhile. Years perhaps, judging by that moan." Nath's brows buckled. A fire ignited inside and drowned out the piercing pain in his arm. "Whoever did this is a cruel master." He thought of the poachers. The hunt. The chase. For more than a hundred years, he had protected the dragons. Freed them from bondage. Freed them from chains. He felt ashamed. He'd lost sight of that somehow in the greater scheme of things.

"You know where you belong?"

It didn't answer.

"Dragon Home," he said, but in Dragonese. A lengthy and exotic name that had more bends than a river and syllables only heard in dreams.

A wink of golden light zipped high overhead. The sleek silhouette of a dragon streaked right behind it. Nath's fingertips tingled. The chase of the golden hornets was almost over.

"Please let me go," he urged.

The dragon's eyes were stone cold.

"Ah, moving a mountain would be easier. Great Dragons!"

He looked at the next floating stone he needed to leap upon along his path to the Floating City. It didn't look so bad. Perhaps this was the breaking point. The place no other had ever gotten past.

"Fine then," Nath said to the dragon. With his good arm, he scooped up the spiny-backed dragon and pulled him to his chest. The dragon remained still as a steel trap. It was awkward. Like carrying a big scaly dog.

"Gads, I'm strong! You must weigh over two hundred pounds."

He eyed the next rock, floating fifteen feet away and five feet up. Nath gathered his legs underneath him and leapt. A second later, he landed and slid on the stone. The rock teetered. Nath flailed his good arm for balance and righted himself.

"Whew! I have this now … I think."

He made the next leap. Three. Five. Ten more. Bounded from stone to stone like a black-scaled frog. The Floating City greeted him. Stark and Vast. A mountain in the air. Nath felt small. *It's much bigger up close.*

Across one more chasm, a set of stairs was carved into the great rock, leading up into the city. *So this is a pathway, after all.* He judged the distance between him and the narrow steps on the other side. It was farther than it had looked from below, every bit of thirty feet. With a dragon latched onto his arm.

"This wouldn't be hard if you just let go," he said to the dragon. Its eyes were closed. "Enjoying the ride, are we?"

A chorus of roars echoed above in the towers of the city. The dragons were coming back from the chase. His mind raced, arguing with itself.

You have to do this, Dragon. You have to. But how? It's too far. This blasted dragon is too heavy. Bayzog's going to die if you don't get moving. What choice do I have? I've done my best.

He slipped Dragon Claw out of his belt where he'd tucked it in earlier.

The dragon's eye popped open.

CHAPTER

31

FAYLAN THE SATYR STOOD INSIDE her tent, arms crossed over her chest with her bottom lip trembling. Her hooved feet had worn a track in the dirt floor where she'd paced for hours. Her brother, Finlin, was dead. The draykis, all of them, had been wiped out. And she'd have to answer to the High Priestess for it.

"But not just yet," she whispered, resuming her pacing.

Everything had been going so well! She'd captured Nath Dragon, so she'd thought, and sent him straight to Selene. However, things had gone downward from there. The lock of hair from the man's head had withered away, leaving doubt whether or not it was Nath Dragon at all. If it wasn't, then certainly the report from Selene would not be good, but no bad news was forthcoming as of yet. However, she could feel trouble in her hooves.

"I hate dwarves," she snarled. "And I'll kill them all."

It wouldn't be easy. Now, with the draykis gone, the army she commanded had become loose in discipline. Many had deserted. Her authority had already been challenged before, but now she very thinly held command.

She did hold command of her army, though. Although she was a woman, she was still stronger and quicker than most men. A half-orc had died horribly under her hooves, making him an example to others.

A tall man in partial-plate armor stepped inside her tent. His hair was braided, and he had a dark and swarthy look about him. He brought his heels together and nodded.

"I've rounded up a few deserters," he said.

"Hang them," she said. She grabbed her girdle off the planning table and buckled it on. "Before the sun sets."

He nodded and his eyes slid back and forth to hers.

"What is it?" she said, aggravated.

"The troops are uneasy and keep asking about our orders. They fear the craftiness of the dwarves, now that the draykis are gone."

"The High Priestess wants the dwarves eliminated," she said, toying with the gem amulet around her neck. "Tell them the death of the dwarves is their orders."

He nodded, said, "Yes, Commander Faylan," and disappeared through the tent flap.

Faylan rubbed the hair between her thorns. She'd lied about the High Priestess giving that order, but they didn't know that. She fingered the amulet. So long as she had the object that helped control the draykis, she had some control. The soldiers didn't know what it did, and for now that would be enough.

"Fear the dwarves?" she said. "There's only a handful of them, and we're a hundred strong. We'll get them soon enough—*ack*!"

She jumped aside.

The body of the tall man in partial-plate armor burst through the tent flap and collapsed on the floor. He was dead.

She pulled out her knife and backed away from the entrance.

A scaly arm shoved the flap aside, and the hulking form of a draykis stepped inside. Its beady eyes glowed like emeralds in their sockets. Great leathery wings were on its back, unlike on other draykis. It glared at her and said, "The High Priestess demands a report."

Looking up at the towering figure, Faylan swallowed hard. Her fingers wrapped around the amulet. "Watch your tone with me, Draykis."

Its lips curled back over its fangs, and it stepped forward. Reached for her.

She summoned the amulet's power.

It wrapped its huge clawed paw around her neck.

"Your amulet does not work on me," it said, lifting her toes from the ground, "only on those under its enchantment. Where are they, Goat Feet?"

Faylan didn't want to say. She'd rather die than admit the truth to the draykis. The High Priestess would kill her anyway. She croaked out unintelligible words.

"What's that?" it said. "And bear in mind, your answer will bear your life or death, and the High Priestess demands the truth." It released her.

She gasped for air and finally craned her neck upward.

I've no choice but to be truthful. I hate that!

"Dead," she said, dejected. "Dwarves killed them … and my brother."

"Dwarves?" Its knuckles cracked. "*Dwarves* killed all the draykis?"

"Buried them in a mountain," she said. "It was my foolish brother's fault."

It swatted her across the face, knocking her into the table and sprawling her on the tent floor. Her entire horned head rang. She shook it.

"You are responsible for this," it said. "Not your dead brother. Unfortunate for them."

It came forward, flexing its layers of scaled muscles. Faylan had never feared death, or anything, for that matter, until now. At this moment, death felt inevitable. She raised her arms and prepared to beg for mercy, but how does one receive mercy from the dead?

"Get up," it said. "We've work to do."

"What?" She said, rising to her hooved feet, heart jumping.

"Selene is pleased with your prisoner," the draykis said. "Come." It disappeared through the tent flap.

It was him. It was Nath Dragon! I did it! She pumped her fist, held her chin high, and strode outside. *Yes!* She stopped in her tracks. A great shadow covered her. Her body trembled. *Oh my!*

A great bronze dragon leered down at her. Its great wings were black, and its dark tail swept the ground behind it. It was the one that had flown off with the cage that carried Nath Dragon in it. At least she thought it was. The winged draykis stood facing her, with its back to the dragon.

It could eat him in a single bite. Me as well.

Only the High Priestess had ever made her feel smaller.

"This dragon," the draykis said, glancing back at the great creature, "the High Priestess has sent to assist you with things. Myself as well. And unlike the draykis, I don't think the dwarves will be able to bury this dragon."

"What kind of dragon is it?"

"The kind that crushes people."

"Dwarven people?" she asked.

"Like eggs."

The bronze dragon reared up its serpentine neck and let out an ear-splitting roar.

Ears covered, Faylan smiled.

CHAPTER
32

DRAGON CLAW IN HAND, NATH said to the dragon in his arms, "This would be easier if you could fly. Are you sure you won't let go?"

The spiny-backed crawler's eyes were wide and still.

Nath shook his head. Not so long ago, he had defeated a fully grown grey scaler and felt invincible. Now, he was humbled by a small dragon. It made him angry. Fueled his blood. He eyed the steps and snarled.

"I can do this."

He shuffled back to the farthest edge of the floating rock.

"If you aren't going to let go, then don't start moving now."

Summoning his anger, pulling the dragon closer, and holding the ready dagger in his hand, Nath dashed over the rock, one step, two steps, and leapt with all his strength. He sailed through the air on target. *I'm going to make it!* A gust of wind knocked him off course. *No!* He collided with the rock to the right of the stairs.

But Dragon Claw bit into the stone, and with one dragon arm, Nath hung on, dangling over the river.

"Great Guzan!"

The steps were several feet away.

"Would you let go of my arm!"

The spiny-backed crawler didn't respond. Nath knew dragons were smart, but he was convinced this was the stupidest one he'd ever met.

"An orc has better sense," he barked at it.

Its teeth bit deeper.

"Gads that hurts! At least I know you're listening."

He looked down at the river. The only thing to do was start all over and hope he could somehow get this dragon off his arm.

"I hope you like water. You're about to get a snout-full of it." He shook his mane. "If only I had wings."

He slackened his grip.

The dragon grrrr'd.

"What?"

The dragon's long tail stretched out, wrapped around the top post of the stone banister, and pulled them toward it. Nath could feel it taking some weight off him.

"You'd better not let go now, Crazy Dragon."

Nath jerked the blade from the rock and used his arm attached to the spiny-back to swing over to the stairs. He jabbed the blade into the rock, steadied himself, and crawled up from there.

"Thank Guzan!"

He gritted his teeth. The pain in his arm was killing him, but at least his arm was still there.

"I don't guess you're going to let go now either."

He swore it shook its head.

"Fine."

Nath gathered the dragon in his good arm again and started up the stairs, but the dragon's tail was still tethered to the post.

Nath wanted to scream but didn't.

"You really do want me to kill you, don't you?" He sat down on the steps and slid Dragon Claw through his belt. "This is ridiculous."

It seemed the dragon was intent on doing its job and alerting its masters to his presence and that no method of coercion or compassion was going to change its mind. Nath logged through his memories. Dragons had weaknesses. He didn't know them all, but he knew many. He poked at it. Tried to tickle it. Pried at its jaw with his claws with no avail. Stout as stone, the dragon didn't move. It just breathed softly through its nostrils. In and out. In and out.

"Hm," Nath said, grimacing. The dragon was wearing on him. The shard in his ribs throbbed, too. "Let me try this." He covered the dragon's small nose holes up with his fingers.

The dragon's glittering eyes widened. Dragons could hold their breath a long time, but not forever.

They were nose breathers, too. Exhaling through the mouth would bring forth a breath weapon of fire. Nath was mindful of that.

"This might take hours," Nath sighed, eyeing the sky.

Dragons glided above, returning to their roosts in the towers, out of sight. Nath remained crouched in the stairwell. *Stay focused. For Bayzog, remember.*

The spiny-backed crawler flinched. Its jaws popped open.

Nath jerked his arm away.

Yes!

The dragon filled its lungs with air, and a stream of hot flames shot out, blasting into the rock.

Nath leapt away from the scorching heat and bounded up the stairs. The dragon scrambled after him, claws scraping over the stones. He whirled to confront it.

It lunged.

Nath leapt over its head, snatched its tail, and dragged it down the steps.

"I've had enough of you!"

With a quick powerful jerk, he slung the dragon by its tail over his head and into the open sky. One wing spread wide and flapped feverishly, but it didn't slow. It spiraled downward and plunged into the water with a small splash.

Nath hated to do it. He'd hoped to make an ally of the dragon, but that plan had failed.

They can be stubborn things.

He checked his throbbing arm.

Deep teeth marks gashed his flesh. Blood seeped onto his scales. He could barely move his trembling fingers.

"At least I still have my arm."

He lumbered up the steps and made his way into the city. It was desolate. Dark and dreary. The deteriorating buildings blocked the light of the setting sun and cast enormous shadows throughout the city. The winds howled through the streets like banshees. What was once magnificent was now cold and unwelcoming. A foreboding feeling overcame him. Nath stepped into an archway, concealing himself from the skies.

I'm here. Now what?

He pulled Fang out. The metal was cool and welcoming. He slipped Dragon Claw from his belt and held both weapons out before him. He could barely move the arm that held the gleaming dagger.

"I've a feeling I'm going to need both of you."

He slid Dragon Claw back inside Fang's hilt and removed a vial from his jerkin. The yellow liquid sparkled with energy. He had pulled off the cork and put the vial to his lips when he stopped himself, replaced the cork, and tucked the potion back inside his jerkin.

Closing his hand in and out a few times on his bad arm, got up and started moving.

"I've handled worse."

This enormous floating rock was more of a graveyard than a city. Skeletons of fallen warriors were scattered throughout, decorated in death, weapons, and armor. Doors creaked and groaned. Shutters banged into the buildings. The wind howled like ghouls, stirring the fine hairs on Nath's neck. He stayed under the porches, awnings and overhangs, walking on cat's feet with every step. He knew that the dragons above, wherever they were, had eyes and ears just as sharp as his.

Nath stood inside the great stone archway of a cathedral. The great wooden door with brass fixtures was closed. He tugged on it, but it didn't budge. He'd been in and out of dozens of buildings already. Most all of them were open. Doors busted down. Windows shattered. Walls burned to the ground. It looked like war had run roughshod through it.

He combed the hair out of his eyes with his wounded arm. The pain wasn't as bad, but his frustration was getting worse. Whoever mined the jaxite had to get here somehow, but he'd yet to find a single stairway down. Certainly there had to be a tunnel of some kind near, or something.

A dragon's roar rang out above. It was followed by another and another. They were talking to one another. Bickering. Bragging. One had consumed more golden hornets than the other. Dragons liked to do that. Boast to one another. Nath was glad to hear it. *They aren't on to me yet. A good thing.*

He pressed his ear to the door. *Maybe only the dead are inside.* He heard nothing. He'd never been in a city so quiet before. The normal sounds were gone: rat claws scratching over wood or stone, a cat mewing, birds roosting in rafters and spires. Nothing ordinary was there at all. He pulled his ear away.

This is maddening. There has to be some living thing here, mining.

He looked down the streets. They ran over a mile from one side to the other. The buildings numbered in the hundreds, the streets in dozens. Nath never had a problem finding a needle in a haystack, but now he couldn't find anything.

I wish Brenwar were here. He could find a hole into the ground blindfolded. He shook his head. He'd been mean to Brenwar. Difficult. Disrespectful. He never thought about it much, but recently he'd come to realize why. Brenwar was a constant reminder of his failure to please his father. The dwarf knew everything. His triumphs. His failures. And Brenwar himself was sort of a father-figure to Nath as well. He'd not only failed his father, but his friend too. He opened up his hand and rubbed the white scales in his palm with his fingers. They hadn't gotten any bigger or smaller. No change at all.

Am I doing anything right?

Sheathing his weapons and then clenching his fists in frustration, he stormed down the steps and into the street, where he kneeled down and put his ear to the ground. Minutes passed, but the only thing he heard was his breathing.

Gads!

He wanted to scream. Even with all of his powers, he felt helpless. There was nothing to see. Nothing to fight. No one to talk to. Building by building, door by door, he searched one street at a time. Stopping. Looking. Listening. Sometimes he jogged. Sometimes he sprinted, dashing from one cover to another from the eyes above. He didn't sense that the dragons had any idea he was here, but he did feel something. An unsettling presence that tightened his shoulders.

Someone has to be here doing something. Keep searching, Dragon. Keep searching. Hmmm. Maybe I need a better look at things.

Earlier, he'd noticed bell towers that stood dozens of feet tall. Most cities had them in Nalzambor. They were a message system that could be heard from one side of the city to the other. The rhythmic ringing of the bells could bring cheer or spell doom. Nath headed for the nearest one he had seen, an enclosed stone tower about ten feet wide, with a single door that led inside. It was open.

At least I won't be running into any pigeon hawks in there.

Inside he went and headed up the wooden steps that hugged the wall of the stone bell tower. Everything was pitch black above, but he could make out the outlines of the wall. The steps creaked a little under his weight. He stopped. Lifted his foot and tried another step. It was more solid. He continued his ascent, some steps groaning, others not.

Just keep moving. The dragons shouldn't be able to hear you over all these high winds. Or through these stone walls.

Platform after platform, he headed toward the top. The only things he sensed were his wounded arm and the shard in his ribs.

Truly a sad thing when only pain will keep your company.

He made it to the top, where a trap door greeted him. He took a moment to listen, then pushed the door open. The whistling winds greeted him with a cold blast of air. Nath eased himself through the portal onto the tower-top, where a great brass bell hung. An armored skeleton lay in pieces on one side of the wooden floor. The skeleton's helmeted skull was on the other side, and the spine was still attached. Nath's jaw dropped.

Grizzly.

Unlike the rest of the fallen, this soldier showed no other wounds. It seemed his head and spine had been torn up from his body.

What would have done such a thing?

Keeping his head low, he spied the towers above. Tall buildings surrounded him, but no dragons were in sight.

Good.

From his knees, he peeked over the wall into the streets below. All the main streets ran parallel to each other. The alleys crisscrossed between them. It was ordinary. The structures were well-crafted, some magnificent, but he didn't notice anything unique. And just like everywhere else in this floating city, nothing was moving but him and the wind.

There has to be something. Guzan! Something.

He wanted to hit something. Instead, something icy hit him. He jerked around, teeth chattering. The ghostly form of a soldier stood there with a dagger.

Nath swung right through it.

Its body parted and re-emerged. Nath felt nothing but cold water in his veins. His movement became slow and sluggish.

"*What are you?*" the ghost said. "*How did I miss your presence?*"

"I think you were asleep at your post," Nath said, grimacing. "You must be a lousy guard. That's why you died the first time."

The ghost stood wavering in the wind. A black look was on its face.

"*I must tell the others,*" it said, reaching for the rope that sounded the bell. "*They need to be awakened.*" It wrapped its ghostly fingers around the rope and started to pull.

Nath ripped out Dragon Claw and slit its arm.

"My metal bites." Nath got closer. "Now tell me, what others? And how do you get to the jaxite mines?"

This wasn't the first time Nath had dealt with the undead. They could be hurt if you had the right weapon. They would talk, too, if you got them to listen.

Its hollow eyes fell on the dagger's glimmering blade. It eyed it and Nath Dragon.

"*I failed my post once. I'll not fail it again.*" It drifted like a cloud up to where the bell hung.

Great, Nath thought, *nothing like a ghost with a sense of duty.* "Get down here and talk, Apparition!"

He could see the ghost sawing at something.

"What are you doing?"

"*What I must.*"

Snap!

The ropes that held the great brass bell gave. It plunged straight through the trap floor with a crash. The entire floor went with it. So did Nath Dragon.

"No!"

Nath clutched wildly in the air. Down he went, right after the bell and through the stairs. Wood shattered and crashed under his weight. He grabbed at everything he could to slow his fall. Darkness and splinters swallowed him whole.

"Oof!"

He hit hard, landing beside the bell. The stairs collapsed onto him. The skeleton landed right on top of him. Groaning and gasping for air, Nath shoved it aside. Sluggish, he pushed himself off the floor.

I hate ghosts.

DONG! DONG! DONG!

He could hear other bells sounding in the city.

I really hate ghosts.

Dragon Claw still in hand, he staggered toward the door. His entire body ached, and it also felt like molasses. A sword-wielding skeleton with glowing green eyes met him in the doorway.

"Sorry, we're closed," Nath murmured.

It struck.

CHAPTER

33

NATH SLUNG HIS BODY TO the side. The skeleton's rusted blade still hit home, skipping off his scales. He spun around and back-fisted it in the jaw, knocking its head from its shoulder. The skeleton sagged to the ground in a bony heap.

Nath shook his head and lumbered through the doorway. The streets were alive now, with undead soldiers closing in.

Nothing living moves, but at least something moves. He drew Fang, pulled his shoulders back, and started counting the undead. He reached a hundred and gave up.

Bong! Bong! Bong!

It seemed Otter Bone was right. There indeed was a great evil here. But someone or something had to be at the helm of it. Nath had to find it, and to do so he'd have to wade through an undead army.

Don't get cornered.

A skeleton carrying a spear closed in and lunged the tip at him. Nath batted the weapon away and drove Fang through its ribs. The glowing lights in its eyes went out, and it slumped lifeless to the ground.

Three more were flanking him. Behind them, Nath could see more closing in from every street and alley. Spread out as they were, Nath had room to run past them. Find safety and cover. Skeletons moved as fast as men, but they didn't run well. That gave him an advantage, aside from the frozen blood in his veins. He felt like he was moving in quicksand.

A skeleton jabbed its sword at him. Another blade arced over his head.

Nath swung Fang with all his might. The blade whistled through the air and struck two down in one blow. The third poked its sword at his chest and skipped off his scales. Nath jammed Dragon Claw in its skull. The bone exploded.

Pow!

Nath blanched. He said to the blade, "I didn't know you had it in you, Claw." His words came out slow and slurred, and his vision was a bit hazy.

Five more skeletons closed in.

Nath took off in a half run, half jog. *Great Dragons!*

The ghost had done a number on him. Its touch would have killed most people or at least knocked them out. Ultimately, the undead, especially an army of them, were impossible to overcome. Their touches could kill or paralyze. A single nick could be fatal in some cases. It was no wonder none had ever fooled with the Floating City. It was well-prepared for any trespassers.

Rushing through the wide streets, Nath weaved his way through the armies of the dead. A skeleton soldier erupted from an alley and barred his path.

Fang arced up and hewed it down. Nath's feet stomped its bones and jogged on.

Something's not right.

Nath glanced up over his shoulder. He caught a glimpse of two dark-green dragons leering from the building above. Nath's thoughts raced.

Why aren't they attacking? Whoever or whatever controls the skeletons probably doesn't control the dragons. Barnabus might be behind some of it but not all of it. What is going on?

Armed skeletons sealed off the street ahead. Nath turned down the next one. A rank of skeletons greeted him with rusty steel. They came at him with deliberation and force, boney arms flailing and chopping.

Nath dodged. Swung. Sheared through arms and torsos. The bones clocked off the cobblestone road. He carved himself a path, only to see it filled with the undead again.

Fang severed arms and legs. Shattered weapons and armor.

Dragon Claw wrought havoc with every blow.

Hemmed in, Nath fought with subdued fury. Frustration. His quickness and speed had been negated by the touch of the ghost. And overwhelming forces.

A sword clipped his forehead. Sharp steel jabbed and poked all over him. Bony fingers clutched and pulled at his hair. Blood ran into his eyes.

I'm getting sick of this!

He swung harder and harder. His arms felt like lead. His legs like anvils.

One skeleton fell after another. His mystic steel ripped through rotting armor, shattering hollowed bones.

Unrelenting, the skeletons fought without fear of consequence. Silent. Cold. Determined. Their weapons didn't cut through Nath's scales, but they stung like mighty bees time and time again.

Nath's fury and aggravation continued to build. His dragon blood exploded through his veins, shattering the ice within. His limbs loosened. He felt imaginary shackles on his arms and legs breaking free.

"Now you're going to pay!"

He hacked into the skeletons. Fang ripped through their legs. Dragon Claw popped holes in their skulls. The skeletons fell in heaps, but more kept closing in. A mob of metal and bones.

"This is getting ridiculous!"

Nath jammed Dragon Claw back into Fang's hilt and wrapped both dragon hands around it.

"I've had enough!"

The great blade flared with blue and purple light. Nath swept it from side to side with fury. He mowed them down, two, three, four at a time. The lights went out inside their heads. Their bones snapped and cracked under his clawed feet. His anger and temper flared. The street was filled with the skeleton horde. Dozens had him surrounded. Hundreds more were coming.

I could take the high ground but then go where?

He chopped. Ripped. Hacked and pummeled. Blood streamed down his face. He was being suffocated by the dead. Boney arms locked up his legs and wrapped around his waist. Skeletons climbed over each other to get at him.

They jumped on his back and shoulders, driving him to the ground. He was trampled under a mass of decayed bodies. He held Fang tight but could swing no more.

"Nooooo!"

CHAPTER
34

THE SKELETONS CLAWED AT HIS face. His eyes. The stench of their rotting bones and decayed skin was suffocating. Nath felt he was in a living prison of bones, and even with all his great strength, he could not get out.

"Get off me!" he spit out.

Their green eyes glimmered. Their jaws bit at his ears. Bony fingers pulled out his hair. Nath couldn't imagine a worse way to die. Surrounded by a living tomb of the undead. Their horrible faces reeked of death and evil. He struggled. Stretched. Strained. Rose to his knees only to topple over again.

Skeletons were hard to stop. Not for him, but there were too many. He was trapped.

I've got to be smarter than mindless skeletons.

In his writhing fury, a puff of smoke billowed from his nose. His golden eyes widened.

Stupid!

He sucked in a great gulp of air.

Burn, undead, Burn!

Whoosh!

A geyser of hot flames erupted from his mouth. Supernatural screams filled the streets. Skeletons burned and twitched. Body parts fell off. Tendons were incinerated. A burning skull's jaw fell from its face.

Nath shoved his way up, opened his arms wide, and took another deep breath.

From all directions, the skeletons closed in.

Whoosh!

Flames blasted into them. Slowly, Nath spun in a circle with dragon fire blazing from his mouth. An inferno of burning skeletons surrounded him, screeching in bizarre misery. The fire spread from one skeleton to another. He kept blowing until everything burned and he could breathe no more fire for a while.

Hundreds of skeletons fell in small pyres of fire, rattling once and rattling no more.

It was a beautiful thing, watching evil burn. The stench was almost pleasing.

Nath snorted, pulled his shoulders back, nodded, and waded through the flames down the street, brushing aside a burning skeleton that wandered into his path. His ears picked up the sound of rotting shoes and bony toes scraping over the cobbled streets. He picked up his pace and trotted toward the edge of the city.

With the back of his arm, he wiped the blood from his eyes. His limbs were throbbing. Fighting endlessly was one thing, but exhausting your fire was another. It drained him. That's why younger dragons were easier to capture. They didn't have as much fire as the older ones, and Nath, for all accounts, was still a young dragon. And he'd overdone it.

But I cooked them good.

Ears peeled, he shuffled through the streets, avoiding any sounds of skeleton soldiers. He tilted his head upward, keeping in mind the ghosts in the towers that he assumed would be on the lookout for him.

Still, it was odd. That ghost had seemed surprised it hadn't noticed him earlier. He wondered why that was.

Perhaps it's because I'm a dragon. They wouldn't be looking for dragons, but instead, people. Ignorant ghosts.

He realigned his thoughts. In the throng of battle earlier, a thought had struck him. Perhaps the entrance to the mines didn't lie on the surface of the city, but below it. From ground level, by the river, he'd observed many stairs on the edge of the rock, similar to the one he came up when he battled the spiny-backed crawler. It never occurred to him that one might mine something from below, rather than above, but this city was different, to say the least.

Why not? Nothing else makes any sense.

Finding the edge, he jogged over the rocky terrain. Unlike the rest of the city, which was well laid-out, the edge was the beginning of a cliff. Here, it was clear that this enormous rock had been ripped up out of the ground. As far as he understood it, the Floating City moved, but a bit slowly. It stayed its course along the wind currents of the river. There was a crater where the city had originally lain in the earth. He hadn't seen it, but he'd heard about it.

With whipping winds in his face, he pushed forward along the edge, scanning for any signs of a stairway. He'd walked hundreds of yards through the rubble, finding nothing out of the ordinary. He halted. He could feel eyes on his back. Everywhere. Above, he noticed dragons on the roofs of buildings, glaring down at him like hungry vultures.

"Come on," Nath said, wagging Fang's steel at them, "get a closer look."

These dragons weren't big. Some were bigger than him, others smaller, but he counted almost a dozen of them, watching his every move. Their long serpentine necks stooped down, and their faces wore hawkish looks. Their dark wings and tails told him they'd been turned by Barnabus.

Waving his sword once more, Nath turned his back to them and continued on.

I wish we could have one final fight right here, right now. I'm sick of these monsters.

He came across another stone-cut staircase leading down the side of the Floating City's cliffs. The staircase was wide enough for three men, and the slope was easy, curving along the cliffs. Gradually, it narrowed, and the stairs became steeper. Nath could see the river again, a blue-green line between the trees. The wind tore at his hair and slammed into him. He dug his claws into the cliff to steady himself.

"This almost makes me miss those skeletons."

He felt small again. An ant on a hillside trying to save the world from destruction. He eased his way down to the last step, which ended at the edge of the rock. The next step was the river.

Why would they even have steps here? They have to lead somewhere.

He started back up the stairs. The scraping of bone on stone caught his ear. He dashed up and peered around the bend. Skeletons advanced, filling the stairs as far as he could see.

Great!

Down the steps he went. A stair of rocks floated nearby, similar to the one that got him here to begin with. The first step floated no more than twenty feet away and several feet downward. It wasn't very big though. Not quite as wide as the span of his arms.

I can make it.

The first skeleton appeared. Its body rattled with every step on shaky legs. Its eyes were bright green fire.

I have to make it!

Winds whistling through his ears and battering his clothes, he squatted into position, eyeing the distance. If he missed the mark, he'd start all over again.

This might be my worst idea ever.

The skeletons closed in, crowding one another. The gusty wind ripped two off their feet, hurtling them over the edge of the cliff.

Good. Two down, one thousand to go.

Steps away, the first skeleton was almost there.

He jumped. Having accounted for the wind this time, he sailed and landed right on target. He hugged the stone.

"Yes!"

He sat on the stone, a big dragon man on a tiny island.

The first skeleton took the leap. It sailed several feet and plummeted downward. One right after the other, they plunged to their second deaths into the depths of the river.

Nath laughed. *It's true, what the old dwarves say. 'Every glum day has a cheery outline.'*

He'd watched over a dozen go when the madness stopped. The skeletons, one and all, stopped moving. The nearest few began to commune with one another. Seconds later, they set their weapons aside. Some actually sheathed them in their scabbards. They locked hands and arms, forming a chain, and started lowering themselves over the edge. Seconds later, they were swinging like a rope. Coming his way.

Nath popped up into standing position.

It's always back to another thing dwarves say, 'Evil is unrelenting'!

CHAPTER
35

WITH THE PALM OF HIS hand on his forehead, Nath shook his head. There were more floating rocks nearby, but where would he go? No matter where he went, the skeletons would follow. And they clearly wouldn't stop until he vacated the city. And the dragons, they were probably just the guardians of the jaxite. If he didn't take it, they'd leave him alone, but he had to take it.

I'm not stopping now.

Dangling from the steps, the chain of skeletons kept swinging back and forth, the end getting closer and closer to the rock he stood on. Two skeletons swung at the bottom of the chain with their arms stretched out like branches. They swooped backward under the stairs and forward underneath his rock.

The undead chain stopped when their bony hands locked onto the sides of the rock. A bridge was formed. Skeletons started across. Nath whipped out Fang and chopped the fingers away. The bridge twisted and tossed. The skeletons plummeted through the air, then it started all over again. Skeleton climbed down skeleton, and the chain resumed its full form.

Stubborn as dwarves as well!

Searching for another rock, something caught his eye. The staircase continued to run beneath the city, inverted, and accompanied by a solid iron railing.

I'll be. I knew there'd have to be something.

He could almost jump and reach it, but the skeletons were in the way. Swinging like a rattling trapeze in the air. He wished he had Akron and some of those special arrows. They'd make a fine hand right now.

Hmmm…

Back and forth they swung.

Nath snapped his fingers.

This might work.

The next time the skeletons swung forth with outstretched arms, Nath snatched them by the wrist, hoisted them up, jumped off the rock and swung himself underneath the staircase and rail. The skeletons bit at him, but the chain held. Underneath the rock they swung, and he grabbed hold of the iron rail with one hand and jerked his other arm free from the skeletons. Away they swung. Without hesitation, Nath worked himself down the railing, hand over hand, following the steps. Glancing back, the skeletons had swung to a stop.

Let them figure this *out.*

Toes dangling over the river, he shimmied down the rail. The staircase led into a cavern, and then the warm blue-green glow of the jaxite was everywhere. The stairs kept going, winding and winding with no up or down.

What madness is this?

Nath reached over to the rail on the other side and hung suspended from both of them. His weight came from torso to toe, bearing down on his head. He brought his toes to the stairs with ease. He let go of one rail, then the other. He stood on the stairs, upside down but not falling anywhere.

I hope those skeletons never figure this out.

Inverted, he continued along the stairs. Jaxite was everywhere. A world of it, and nothing else. Beautiful, magnificent, living. With mystic radiance. Its colors were of many gemstones in one. It reminded him of Dragon Home.

The stairs came to a stop on a large landing tiled in dark-blue marble. A stone archway twelve feet high gaped open like a dragon's maw.

Chink. Chink. Chink. Chink.

Something lived, moved, breathed, and worked in there.

Nath got Fang ready and strode straight through the archway. Little hairy bearded men were hard at work. Glowing chisels and hammers were in their skilled hands, but they weren't dwarves.

Gads! Gnomes!

Shorter and leaner than dwarves, the gnomes hammered and chiseled away. Ten of them was all Nath could count, wearing long working smocks and leather aprons. Their beards were neatly trimmed to a point in most cases. A few didn't have beards at all. The best way to tell a dwarf from a gnome, if one didn't know better, was that gnomes smiled. Dwarves didn't.

It's a good thing Brenwar isn't here.

Nath remained still. The gnomes continued working on chunks of jaxite. Pieces large and small were scattered all over the cavern floor, with much of the mystic light of the jaxite gone. A shirtless gnome with a bald head and a leather apron held a polished piece of jaxite in front of his grey eyes and smiled. Polishing it with a cloth, he said something to the others in Gnomish. They crowded around the man and stared with wonder. Their comments were excited and incredulous. They passed the glowing stone around.

That'll do. I just need a couple more. And some questions answered as well.

Nath made a quick glance around the room and saw nothing suspicious.

I've killed dozens of skeletons. A few gnomes shouldn't be a problem.

Fang secured, he strolled over and looked down at the circle of gnomes. He noticed a strange blue hue to their skin.

Odd.

With Nath towering over them, the gnomes continued talking, heads down, lips moving with excitement as if a newborn baby had arrived. They went on and on in Gnomish gibberish. Not a single one made a glance up at him.

"Ahem," Nath said, crossing his arms over his chest.

Not a single chin turned up his way.

These gnomes were just as engrossed in their work as dwarven builders got. Once they started, they didn't stop, often to the point of death. Nath recollected a time when dwarves were building a bridge and were under attack. Volley after volley of arrows came, but the dwarves weren't any more distracted by them than they would be by a mosquito. They worked wounded, dying, and even falling to their deaths. Nath could still see one hammering away with several arrows in him until the blood loss let him fall to his death.

Nath cleared his throat again. Same result. He reached over them and snatched the vibrant stone from one of their hands. Blinking, they all murmured back and forth at one another and started to shove and push each other. Nath understood bits of it.

"Where did it go?"

"Who took it?"

"I didn't get to see it."

Nath growled in his throat and spoke in his best Gnomish in an unfriendly tone.

"Excuse me!" he said, dangling the stone over their faces.

One by one, their heads turned up toward him. All of their looks were puzzled.

"Who made him?" one said, scratching the hairs on his head.

The circle of gnomes encircled him.

"He's so lifelike, and my," said another gnome with bright white teeth, "these scales are marvelous craftsmanship."

They started poking and prodding. That was another thing about gnomes. Their inquisitive and obnoxious nature. They treated every living creature like a specimen for their amusement.

"And his eyes are perfectly aligned in his head."

"And rivers of gold flow in them."

"Let me fetch my chisel. I'll have a closer look at them."

His lips curling up in a snarl, Nath hoisted that last one by the collar and shook him like a rug.

"I'm no creation. I'm Nath Dragon. No more musings. You've been warned."

"That's not possible," the gnome said, stretching out its arms and feeling Nath's face. "No man can invade this cavern. My, you really are real." It shook its head and looked down at the tall bald one with knotty arms. "What do you think, Snarggell?"

"Yes," Nath said, looking at the gnome he presumed to be the leader. He dropped the other gnome to his feet. "What do you think, Snarggell?"

Pecking at his teeth, the lead gnome didn't say a thing. Then, it broke out speaking in Common, but so fast a normal man might not have understood.

"Ithinkyemayhavegotteninhere,butyouwon'tgetout.Howdidyoumakeit?Butdieyouwill.Still,I mustknowwhoyouareandwhyyouarehere.Weneverhaveanyvisitorshere.Nicetohavesomecompany,e venthoughtheybealreadydeadones.Thefirstintwentysomeyears.We'lltalk,dine,andchiselyourgrave. Thelurkercomessoontosuckthemarrowfromyourbones."

Snarggell spoke fast, but not too fast for Nath. Still, the gnome's last words crawled through his veins like mud.

"Excuse me, but what's going to suck the marrow from my bones?"

CHAPTER

36

NATH SWATTED SNARGGELL'S FRISKY HANDS away. The persistent gnome continued to poke and prod.

"What is this thing, this monster you mentioned?"

"It's no matter. No matter at all. The end of your presence is inevitable." He grabbed Nath's elbow. "This skin is fascinating. I hope there's enough left so we can keep it."

Nath shoved him back.

"That's enough."

"No matter. I'll inspect when you're dead."

"I'm not going to die," Nath said, pointed to his chest.

The gnomes giggled.

"Stop that. I assure you I've faced tougher monsters than this *lurker* you've mentioned."

The gnomes gaffed. They all spoke Common now, fast, but plenty understandable to Nath.

"Nothing can defeat the lurker," one said, shaking his head.

"Nothing," said another.

"Not ever," said the third.

Nath wasn't used to anyone telling him that he was going to lose or die to anything. If he could handle a full-scaled dragon, he could handle just about anything else. Nath's arms tensed at his sides. His scales rippled.

The gnomes ooh-ed and ah-ed.

"You might as well sit. Have something to eat," Snarggell said, tugging at his arm. "Enjoy our company before the lurker comes."

Nath pulled away.

"I'm not here to chat. I've somewhere to be, and I'll see this finished."

"See what finished?" Snarggell asked.

"I've two demands. First, I need two more of these," he said, holding the glowing stone up.

The gnomes reached into their aprons and each handed him a stone. The small haul made for plenty.

"I said two more," Nath said, sticking the three for Otter Bone inside his jerkin. He tossed the others back. "Don't be so zealous to drop your booty."

They giggled at him and one another.

The tall bald one said, "What is your second request?"

"You will cease making any more stones, and you'll destroy what you already have. And you'll have to come with me."

They froze. Their little gnarled hands twisted at their beards. Suddenly, they burst out laughing. Red-faced guffaws followed one right after the other. Two fell to their backs on the floor kicking. They laughed so loudly, it was resounding off the jaxite walls. This was one of the things dwarves hated about gnomes. They were always cheery and laughing.

Embarrassed and taken aback, Nath felt uneasiness seep into him. He had what he wanted. All he had to do was leave and jump for the river, but their laugher convinced him that wasn't going to happen.

They all got up, grabbed their tools, and got back to work, talking and laughing back and forth with one another, leaving only him and Snarggell all alone.

"Your quest is foolish. Futile, my friend," Snarggell said, stroking his hairy arms. "Nothing comes to the Floating City and lives for long. Just us gnomes."

"You live."

"Aye, we live, but we are cursed," he said, frowning. "The lurker will kill us if we try to leave."

"Or the dragons?"

"The dragons? Hah," Snarggell laughed, "they fear the lurker just as much as any do. They come and collect the stones for Barnabus. Come." Snarggell led him through the mines, stopping at a small well made of jaxite rocks. It was barley big enough for a cat to squeeze through. Dark colors swirled in the hole.

"We put the stones in here. On the other side, dragons pick up them up. They won't come inside the cavern. Too dangerous. The lurker can be temperamental."

Dragons didn't fear anything except other dragons. What could be so bad that a dragon would fear it?

"Why you?"

"Why me, what?" Snarggell said.

"Why doesn't someone else prepare the stones?"

"Hah! Only we *can*. We are crystal gnomes. Masters of precious stones. We work the blue rock and make it willing. It is our craft. But it still takes the hardest metals and magic to chip it. Most people don't understand. This jaxite is harder, but especially hard when you don't understand it. We do. We talk to it, and it talks to us." He rubbed the skin on the back of his hand with his finger. "We aren't blue for just any reason. We're special."

"What you're doing is serving Barnabus. The stones are used for evil, to control the dragons. You'll have to stop."

"We cannot. It's what we do. We're here. We cannot leave."

"And if you die?"

"They just bring more gnomes. Everyone is expendable."

"Can more gnomes do it?" Nath said.

"Any crystal gnome can, with the right tools," the gnome said, leading him back through the jaxite catacombs to where they had stood before. "We've always done this for the wizards, for generations. They were wise doing what they did. Cursing this city and freeing it from control. It worked for a long, long time, but Barnabus figured it out. The undead protect the city above, and the lurker is the guardian in the mines below. Barnabus made a deal with it."

"What kind of deal?"

"They feed it."

"Feed it what?"

"Whatever it wants, but mostly the river folk," the gnome said, picking up his hammer and chisel, "but it gets a craving for other things from time to time. Elves, dwarves, gnolls, you name it. Horses, cattle, pixies. The dragons fetch them. The one reason why they roost like hawks in a nest. Sometimes it even feasts on the dragons themselves. That's why they hate it." He eyed Nath's scales. "I can only imagine the lurker will be looking forward to a taste of you. I've heard every marrow has a different flavor." He rubbed his belly. "Still makes me a little sick to my stomach when I hear those horrible sucking sounds. Worse than an orc licking its fingers, thanks to the accompanying screams." His bald head shivered. "Ugh, still hear the screams."

Nath folded his arms over his chest, glowered at him, and said, "You wouldn't be stretching the truth, would you?"

Gnomes, unlike dwarves, weren't quite so honest. Not only were they crafters, they were well-known tricksters as well.

Snarggell eyed him back and said in a dire tone, "I assure you, this is no tall tale."

Nath looked back over his shoulder. The inverted staircase was gone.

"Where did ... "

Snarggell held his palm up and pressed a finger to his lips. His eyes widened like saucers, and the chiseling of the other gnomes stopped.

"It was nice talking to you, Nath Dragon," the gnome said, extending his hand. "I'll do what I can to preserve your skin. There's no salvation for your bones, however. The lurker knows you're here."

CHAPTER
37

NATH'S SENSES IGNITED. THE CRYSTAL gnomes set down their tools. Huddled together murmuring, they turned into an odd-looking statue of jaxite stone. He caught Snarggell peering at him. The gnome winked just before he solidified. All that was left of the gnomes was a hunk of lifeless stone, odd in fashion, but similar to the rest of the cavern.

"Thanks for the help," Nath said. He eyed the place where the inverted steps once were. The entire cavern landscape had changed. The series of caves had become catacombs of blue-green stones.

He sighed, drew Fang, and wandered into the oppressive silence.

Dragons were patient. Mature ones were, anyway. They had all the time in the world, but of late, Nath wasn't so patient. Being trapped in the catacombs reminded him of the tomb he'd lain in for twenty-five years. Again now, it seemed to take forever to get from one place to another.

What if I go into a deep sleep again? With this lurker near?

Worry. It was the enemy of the brave. It wasn't something Nath was accustomed to either, yet it was there. Same as the shard of a dagger that bit between his ribs, courtesy of Overlord Doremus.

I must help Bayzog.

Nath wandered into the depths of the catacombs. The jaxite illuminated his way. It was a strange place, dayless and nightless, and it reminded him a little of Dragon Home. The stark silence was misery, however. Unsettling like a rash that ran through his bones. Only his steps penetrated the silence. The tunnel twisted left and sloped down, taking him right back to where he'd started what seemed like an hour ago.

Not much of a monster if it's afraid to face me.

Nath tried to envision it. *It must be big if it eats horses and dragons.* A shadow or a shade, perhaps. Would it have many arms, legs or heads? Could it cast fire from its breath? Was it a giant of a man or some hideous beast? He'd never heard of the lurker before. Perhaps Bayzog would have read about it in his histories and been able to tell Nath something about it.

Nath walked on for hours, but the landscape didn't change. Jaxite. Jaxite. And more Jaxite. A glimmering rock that was clear like glass. He stared into a piece that was smooth as a mirror. His reflection faced him. He could see blood dried on his face, and his lips were split and swollen.

Gads, my hair's a mess. He combed his free hand through it and winced. His chewed up arm was still tender, agonized and stiff. *The long days just get longer.* As he turned from the polished stone, his image turned into something dark and ugly, then faded away.

Nath felt a chill in his scales. A foreboding presence neared. The faint smell of decay filled his nostrils.

Follow that malodorous smell. Where there's stink, there's evil.

Trusting his instincts, he tracked the scent. Winding, turning, rising and dipping, the lurker's course resembled a crooked river. The farther Nath followed, the worse the smell became.

If there are orcs at the end of this, I might be glad to see them.

He rounded a deep bend into a vast cavern that opened up like a huge auditorium. Bones were piled up high all over. A horrifying sight. Flesh rotted on busted bones. Skulls of horned dragons and other beasts lined the walls. The heads of all the races were scattered all about, just as Snarggell had said. The elves, dwarves and humans made him think of his friends. Most of the others he didn't care so much about.

He journeyed through the massive cavern, surveying all the atrocities. Decades of death as far as his keen eyes could see. A graveless tomb for the unburied. The lurker, whatever it might be, was detestable.

He stopped. A disturbing sound tickled Nath's ears. Sucking. Long, slow slurping draws. His irritation for the gnomes rose. It seemed they'd been truthful about everything. He started onward. The sounds became clearer. More distinct. More terrible.

Snap. Crack. Pop.

Ahead, bones were being snapped like branches. Slurping came in deep draws. A satisfied moaning followed. He heard bones tossed onto bones.

"Mmmmmm…" something completely alien to him said. "It seems I've an eager guest to dine with. Come…" It made a sucking sound. "Come … I yearn for a new flavor." It sniffed at the air. "A sweet fragrance unlike all before. Come…"

Nath's legs moved with a will not his own. He felt dreamy and light. He didn't feel his toes touching the ground. The voice. The disconcerting voice was irresistible. His arms hung at his sides. Fang dangled in his clawed fingers.

"Come," the lurker said, growing in strength. It sounded like many in one voice. It inhaled, making a great sniffing sound. "No fear in this one. So, so delicious. Strong. Powerful. We must have it. Come," it commanded.

Nath's eyes rolled up. His eyelids fluttered. Fang flared to life in his hand.

We?

The recesses of his lulled mined begged the question.

We? Is there one lurker, or are there many?

Nath waded through the bone pyres, dragging Fang behind him.

"Come," it said, so strong, soft and soothing. "And release your shiny toothpick. We won't require that. Come… "

"What are you?" Nath said, forcing out the question. Curiosity assailed him.

"I am all that I consume," it said. "Now, come … gaze upon me."

Nath's languid eyes lowered. His gaze tilted upward. A monstrosity lounged on a throne of jaxite many times the size of him. Its wide face was terrible and ever changing. He saw men, dragons, and orcs in its burning eyes. A rack of great horns rested on its head. Its arms were many, of all the races. Its many legs were hooved, scaled and taloned. Tentacles writhed like hair around its neck with little mouths hissing like snakes. Coarse hair and scales covered it all over. Its jaws were wide and filled with great sharp teeth. The lurker was the abomination of all abominations.

Nath's knees locked when it opened its enormous mouth and said, "Come, make this easy. Hop in."

A startled cry escaped his lips. Fang slipped from his fingertips.

CHAPTER
38

NATH HAD NO SENSATION IN his arms or legs. His heart thundered in his chest. He felt like a child who'd been told the most terrible of stories. Horrors that struck in the night, leaving children terrified of the dark. Yet there was no darkness. Only desolation. He stepped toward the lurker's gaping mouth.

Come. Come. Come.

The suggestive words repeated in his head, driving him forward.

The long snake-like tentacles spread about its head like a glorious raiment. The lurker pushed up off its throne and came forward. It had no neck, no chest, just a body with a head, arms, and legs. Its face shifted between dragons and ogres. Dwarves and orcs. Curiosity and suggestion compelled Nath forward.

Come. Come. Come.

The recesses of his mind became fuzzy. Unclear. There was something welcoming about the gaping maw and writhing tentacles coming toward him. He took a long step forward.

Come. Come. Come.

"Be part of my oneness," it said. "Join the others and feast on bones forever." Its arms stretched outward. The rows of fangs glistened in its mouth.

Nath's thoughts were lost. His will was not his own. It bothered him. He took another step and stopped.

This is not right. This is not right at all.

"Come," the lurker urged him. "Come now. There is no turning back. It is inevitable, Friend."

A black-bearded dwarf appeared in his mind. Words followed.

"If it eats people, kill it."

Nath stumbled backward. He tore his gaze away. Covered his ears with his paws.

"So be it then," the lurker said, scurrying like an insect from side to side. "I never tire of executing dragons." It pounced.

It covered Nath with its bulk. Tendrils tied him up. Punching fists assaulted him. The lurker slammed him on the ground and slung him across the floor.

"Hmmmm," it said, "seems your bones don't break so easily. The tougher the bone, the more delicious the marrow." A great tongue rolled out and licked its lips. "A feast of the delicious."

Nath scrambled to his feet, sucked in his breath, and shot a ball of fire from his mouth. It struck its cheek and sizzled out. *I've nothing left.*

Its laughter was awful.

"Oh how I like that fire in dragon bellies." Its face turned into that of a dragon, and it sucked in and blew out. Roaring flames gushed out, enveloping Nath.

He cried out.

The lurker stormed into the flames, jerked him out, and dangled him in front of its eyes.

"I don't like my dinner roasted!" It opened its mouth wide, stuffed Nath in, and chomped down. Nath squirted out.

Its teeth clattered and its angry yell was deafening.

"Quick you are! But nothing is quicker than me!"

Nath dashed through the cavern and bolted for the nearest tunnel.

I don't care how many legs it has, it's not faster than me!

The lurker charged after him and slammed into the tunnel. Its ear-splitting yell caught up with him. "None escape me!"

Nath kept running. Aching all over, he bore one thing in mind. *Sultans of Sulfur! What about Fang?* He churned through the tunnels until the echoes of the lurker's screams died out. He stopped and rested against the cave wall. Took a breath and gathered his thoughts. He found relief in his thought that the hex it had put his mind under was broken, but the rest of him hurt. The jaxite was harder than metal, and he'd been slammed several times into it. He sucked a painful draw of air through his teeth and staggered onward.

How can I beat that thing without Fang?

Every creature had a weakness. If it had been a dragon, he could have coped, but the lurker was many things in one. It fed and grew in stature, and was of so many creatures. Each weakness was masked by the other strengths.

I have no choice. I'll have to think of something.

He tried to think of what Brenwar or Bayzog would do. It wasn't so long ago they defeated a larger creature. The hull dragon. But they'd had magic and worked as a team on that one. Now it was only him. One dragon against a bizarre thing that became everything it had beaten. It was like fighting all those creatures at once.

Certainly it can be wounded.

Nath retraced his steps. *Find the gnomes. Maybe they have a clue.* But he was lost. He took another turn and gasped. He was right back inside the lurker's lair. The tunnel he'd just come through disappeared. There across the room, the lurker sat with a disturbing smile on its face.

"Welcome back," it said, holding up Fang in two of its many hands. "Looking for this?" It waggled the sword and passed it through its hands. "It's a hot thing. I don't like that." Fang went from one tentacle to another. "I can handle this pretty little thing. It will make a nice trophy to go with your skin and bones." Its tongue licked out over its teeth. Its arms and tentacles fanned out. "Come now. Why don't you take it?"

Nath shrugged.

"Why don't you just give it to me and save me some trouble? Once I take it, you're dead, you know."

"Ha!" it said. "There is nothing that can kill me."

"Nothing that you know of."

"I just get bigger and stronger. Once I finish dining on you, I'll be stronger than ever."

"Once I kill you, I'll be stronger too," Nath said, coming forward. He noticed Fang being passed from hand to hand more quickly. The lurker's face showed frustration. Fang's blade glowed with dark angry light. "I'd drop that sword if I were you."

It jammed the sword into the ground behind it and snarled.

"There it will stay forever!" It skittered forward, blocking Nath's path to Fang. It towered over him, arms and tendrils ready. "And today your fate is forever sealed." It charged.

Nath dashed right.

It cut him off.

He went left.

It cut him off again, laughing.

Nath zigzagged through the cavern. The lurker crashed through the piles of bones, following him like a shadow. It was the biggest and fastest thing he'd ever seen. But it made a miscalculation. Nath caught a glimpse of the pathway to the sword.

You might be fast, but I'm not moving my fastest.

Nath juked to one side.

It lunged.

Nath twisted away from its clutch and sprinted for the sword.

Its yell was awful. It bore down after him. Thundered over the stone.

Nath bounded away, making a straight line for the blade. He glanced back.

It's gaining!

Its legs churned beneath its girth, propelling it forward at an impossible speed. Its tendrils lashed out.

Nath dove for the blade. His fingers wrapped around the hilt and gripped it tight. The tendrils snagged his feet and pulled him. He now hung parallel to the floor between the lurker on his feet and his own hands on Fang, who remained stuck in the floor. The lurker towed back, stretching Nath's spine, laughing.

"Almost," it said, snapping its hideous jaws. "But it's time to be eaten."

Nath held on with all his might and tried to yank the blade free. He had no leverage. His muscles groaned and popped. More tendrils wrapped around his legs and body.

"Say goodbye to your burning sword, Dragon."

The powerful monster jerked him all at ounce.

Nath's fingers ripped free. The lurker stuffed him inside its mouth and its jaw clamped down forever.

CHAPTER

39

T HERE WAS DARKNESS. THERE WAS pain. Nath felt hands and fingers clutching at him. Pulling him deeper into the inner core of the creature. His mind ignited with the stark realization that he wasn't going into the belly of some beast, but rather of something horribly supernatural. He screamed in his mind. His surroundings suffocated him with the thoughts of the fallen. Their existence was angry. Miserable.

Nath squeezed his eyes shut. Tried to block it out. The terror tore at his mind.

There must be a way! There must be a way!

Fear squeezed him. His breath was lost. He hung suspended in a blanket of darkness, struggling fiercely against unseen bonds.

"Don't fight it," the lurker said from within. "You'll soon be one of us now."

NEVER!

Nath felt something beating. Pulsating. A heart of some sort.

Pulling those who held him along for the ride until one by one they fell away, he swam through the dark muck right toward it. A green light glowed in the murk. He spiraled toward it. Scratched at it. It was hard as stone. Tougher than steel. Powerful magic encircled it.

"The essence of all," the lurker said all around him, "Thousands of hearts beating as one, controlled by my thoughts. Embrace it."

A vision of him being part of this monstrosity formed. His glorious mane on its hideous head. Nath pulled something out from concealment within his clothes. Dragon Claw's light cut through the darkness.

"Where did that come from!" the Lurker roared.

More bodies that were there but not there swarmed him, grabbed onto him, restrained him.

Nath sent his thoughts to them. He could sense their torment and pain.

Be free.

The essences of the beings that held him struggled with one another. Their good essence got the upper hand and released him.

"Nooooo!" the lurker said.

Nath struck. Dragon Claw buried itself into the heart of the monster. It shook like an earthquake.

"I gave you everlasting life!" It roared. "You betrayed me."

They didn't want everlasting life. They wanted peace.

Nath twisted the blade.

The heart exploded. Thousands of voices cried out. Some in anger. Others in joy.

The lurker spoke no more. Its inner core collapsed around him.

Nath struggled to breathe. To rise. To anything. But he could move no more. His thoughts were rattled.

Where am I?

He passed out.

Nath felt something on his face. It was cold. Icy. His mind was foggy.

Please tell me the dragon sleep didn't hit again. Last time, I lost twenty-five years. Now would it be fifty?

He shot into an upright position and opened his eyes.

Snarggell was there along with the other gnomes. He had a bucket of water in his hand.

"You're dirty," he said in Gnomish. "Alive, impossibly. But dirty."

"Where's the lurker?"

"Where you left it. Dead. We had to fish you out of it. Now we're all dirty. Don't like it. We're not dwarves or orcs. You got muck all over us."

"Shouldn't you be glad it's dead and I'm alive?"

The gnome sighed.

"Now more trouble comes."

EPILOGUE

SASHA RESTED IN ONE OF the gardens, enjoying the view and fresh air. She needed to get out now and then. Time to think and ease her thoughts. Rerry and Samaz were driving her crazy with worry, and she'd made it a habit to slip out from time to time, drawing their angst. But she always came here. There were people. Life. Not all the sorts she liked, but it was close enough to normal to hold her.

"Pardon me," a woman said. She was tall, pleasant-faced, and adorned in black robes that covered her from toes to the top of her head, leaving only her face open. "May I sit?"

"Certainly," Sasha said, scooting over on the bench. "It's too lovely a day not to share."

The woman sat down and eyed the white clouds in the bright azure sky.

"Aye, it is. It's so nice when all those horrible grey clouds are gone. I don't like them."

Sasha said, "I love the warmth that it brings. It just seems like it's been so long." She looked at the woman. "But aren't you hot in all that black? That's heavy cloth you have on."

"No," the woman replied, with a light giggle. "It absorbs the sun and warms me to the bones. I chill easily." She eyed Sasha. "Is something bothering you? For such a pretty woman, I can see so much trouble on your brow."

Sasha leaned away and looked at her funny. *Is it that obvious?*

"Please, no offense, Dear. I'm just a good judge of character." The woman's voice was warm and soothing. "I spend a lot of time with a lot of people."

Sasha found comfort in the woman's voice. She'd been so isolated, she'd almost forgotten what it was like to converse with another woman. It excited her.

"No, it's alright. I just haven't been out much."

"Well, I can understand why," the woman said, eyeing a spire that hosted a dark green dragon. "And as much as I hate to say it, I've almost gotten used to it. That's dreadful to say, isn't it?"

"No. You sound like someone who's found peace amidst the chaos. I think that's commendable."

"Well thank you," the woman said, smiling "And what about you?"

For reasons unknown, Sasha started talking. A dam inside burst open. Her troubles with age and being human with part-elven boys spilled out of her mouth.

"I'll die before they even grow up. And look," she pointed, "look at these crow's feet decorating my eyes."

"Is that all that bothers you?" the woman said. Looking around, she spread her arms wide. "This is Nalzambor. It has answers to everything. You're a sorceress, are you not? You should know that."

"I cannot reverse time," Sasha said with a sigh.

"Well, maybe not," said the woman, "but you can lengthen it."

Sasha was intrigued.

"How do you know this?"

"I'm a woman," she said, "But I'm well over one hundred." She whispered in Sasha's ear. "But how far over the century I will not tell." She rubbed Sasha's shoulder. "But I like you, and I'm willing to tell."

Sasha started to pull away. Something wasn't right about the woman.

"Easy now," the woman said, rising to her feet. "I'll be here the rest of the day and all day tomorrow, but after that I must go." She started to walk away. "And I felt as you did once, but today I've never felt better." She walked into the gardens and disappeared.

Sasha stood there gaping. There was truth in the woman's words.

I'm tired of feeling old.

She followed after the woman.

Otter Bone gasped, and his eyes popped open.

"What is it?" Bayzog said. It had been days since the old man had even spoken.

Brenwar and Ben came forward.

"Yes, what is it?"

Otter Bone smiled.

"Your friend lives. But he needs our assistance." He got up. "Come."

Horse Neck guided him toward the mouth of the cave, but something blocked the exit. It was a dragon, but not Nath Dragon. Copper-scaled. Vicious, with a long sharp tail that matched its teeth. The dragon struck, its speed blinding and the blows precise. The dragon's jaws clamped down. Its tail lashed out. The river folk fell in heaps.

Brenwar rushed forward and smote the dragon in the skull with his hammer. It recoiled and dashed outside the hole. Brenwar chased after it and shortly came back.

"How are they?" the dwarf said.

Bayzog shook his head.

Otter Bone and Horse Neck were dead.

Fight and the Fury

-BOOK 8-

CRAIG HALLORAN

CHAPTER

1

"WHAT DO YOU MEAN, *MORE trouble comes*?" Nath said to Snarggell, flinging off the lurker slime that coated him. "How could there be more trouble than that thing?" He eyed the monstrous corpse behind him. It smelled as foul as it looked.

Snarggell blinked his eyes repeatedly and said, "Have you forgotten the undead army that awaits? And the dragons? There are many, are there not? Once they sense the lurker is dead, they'll come."

Weary, Nath grabbed Fang and pushed himself to his feet. He stuffed Dragon Claw back inside the hilt.

"I suppose we had better get out of here then."

"And go where?" Snarggell said. "I'm fine chipping away at jaxite until I'm dead. So are the rest of us."

The gnomes huddled around him, murmuring in agreement. Clenching small tools and chisels between their fingers, they moved on and started picking at the stones.

Nath sighed.

"I didn't come here to help you continue your work for Barnabus. I came here to put an end to that," he said, slinging more muck off his hand. "And the end has come. Put down your tools and stop picking."

"That is not possible," Snarggell said. "We are crystal gnomes. This is what we do."

"So you serve an evil cause, then?" Nath said, eyeing him.

"We've no proof of that, only your word, and we hardly know you, Scaly One."

"No proof," Nath argued. "Were you not brought here against your will? Are you not unable to leave? Snarggell, don't be absurd."

Snarggell stormed away, picked up his hammer and chisel, and joined the others.

Tink. Tink. Tink ... Tink. Tink. Tink.

Nath felt every little tap inside his skull, and a headache coming on. Sometimes, slaves are uncomfortable with the thought of freedom. Prisoners aren't kept well, but they know what to expect. Freedom can be scarier, because you have to fight for it. His father had told him that. Nath rubbed his finger under his lip and paced the cave. It wasn't long before he found himself standing underneath the inverted staircase that had appeared once again. He rubbed his forehead.

What was that thing, the lurker? What kind of power was that?

He ran his claws through his slimy hair and slung muck to the floor.

"Yech."

He could smell himself. Taste a nasty grime in his mouth. He took a path under the inverted stair and stopped at the edge where the cavern's mouth opened. The winds were refreshing. The river far below looked refreshing.

I could go for a bath about now. A long one.

A dragon streaked through the sky beneath him, followed by another, two emeralds no bigger than Nath. Necks low and wings spread wide, they glided in circles, screeching back and forth at one another. Nath scratched his back.

If only I had wings!

He headed back for the gnomes, deep in thought. It was time to put their work to a halt, one way or another.

Snarggell peeked up at him, turned away, and kept on chipping.

"This ends now, Snarggell. We're leaving."

The gnome's huff bristled his beard. His hands continued in a flurry of motion.

Nath marched over, snatched the tools out of his hands, and slung them aside.

"What are you doing?" Snarggell blurted out, face reddening. "We aren't going anywhere! Nothing awaits us but death out there."

"Nothing awaits you but death *in here*!" Nath said, snorting small flames from his nose.

All the gnomes stopped what they were doing, eyes wide as saucers. They looked at Snarggell. He looked back at them, folded his knotted arms over his chest, and said, "We're staying right he–*ulp!*"

Nath snatched the gnome off his feet and tucked him under his arm like a satchel.

Snarggell kicked and screamed.

"Let me go! Let me go!"

Nath grabbed another one and started carrying them toward the inverted staircase. Their struggles were fierce but in vain. Nath's powerful arms held them tight.

"Stop him! Stop him!" Snarggell screamed at the others.

The remaining gnomes attacked like a swarm of bearded bees. They climbed on Nath's legs and on his back. Muttered curses. Tried to pull his arms away.

Nath dragged them one slow step at a time. Toward the inverted stairs and beyond.

"You've no right to do this!" Snarggell yelled. "You'll get us all killed. Kill yourself!"

Snarggell did all the talking. The others fought in a furious frenzy, like wild children oblivious to anything going on around them except bringing the giant down.

Nath lumbered on. He made it ten steps from where the jaxite cavern dropped off into the river. The dragons that circled below were gone. *No time like the present.*

"You remember how to swim, don't you?" he said.

Snarggell's head whipped around in desperation.

"What! Of course."

"But you haven't bathed in almost forever, have you?"

"Huh? But you can't be doing what I think you're doing."

Nath made a fierce grin.

"Oh, but I am."

"Get off him, brethren!" Snarggell yelled. "Get off him. Run!"

It didn't register with the gnomes. Like a pack of loyal dogs, they only wanted to rescue their leader, giving no thought to the consequences, one way or the other. They clung to him like burs from the brush.

Nath slogged his way over the next few steps and leapt into the air.

"Dragon Home!"

The plunge went fast. Wind whistled in his ears, and Snarggell's screams could barely be heard. Nath just hoped no one would get hurt. Headfirst he fell, watching the river rush up to meet them. Suddenly, two emerald dragons swooped underneath them, jaws open wide.

CHAPTER

2

RUNNING HIS SLENDER FINGERS OVER the cool wood of the Elderwood Staff, Bayzog sat and caught his breath. He, Brenwar, and Ben had been on the move, cutting through the woods, ever since the copper dragon's lethal attack left Otter Bone and Horse Neck dead. And they weren't the only ones, either. Many others were dead. He could still see them in his mind, broken and twisted like a tornado had run through them. He held his staff tighter.

"Can ye keep up, elf?" Brenwar said, combing his stubby fingers through his beard. "Or do I need to carry you?"

"A moment, Brenwar," he said, taking a deep breath. "A moment."

"Life and death happen in moments."

True.

The part-elf wizard had seen it several times with his own eyes, but that last assault had shaken him. The dragon—copper, black-winged and black-tailed—had struck like an assassin. He still saw the murderous look in its snake eyes. It was a predator. A killer. It had snapped the two men like chicken bones. He tightened his grip on the Elderwood Staff and let the power of the ancient wood fill him.

"Here," Ben said, handing him a canteen, "take a drink. A long one."

He drank, said, "Thank you," and handed it back.

"We're still heading after Dragon, aren't we?" Ben asked, taking a sip himself. "He needs us. Otter Bone said so himself."

"Aye," Brenwar said, "that's what we should have been doing all along. Let's move, elf." He slung War Hammer over his shoulder. "We've got a copper on our tails, and I get to protect you all the time."

"I can take care of myself just fine," Ben said. Holding out Akron, he nocked an arrow. "I think it's *you* who need *our* help. If a dragon attacks from the air, how will you hit it with that ugly hammer? Your ability to jump is a bit lacking."

"Watch yourself, human," Brenwar said, buckling his brows. "I've pulled you from the pit more than one time. Now let's get moving."

Brenwar led, marching through the forest like a bearded bear. Ben remained close behind. The sun dipped behind the Floating City, and the forest became dark and quiet, the hum of bugs silent. Even the hoots of the owls were missing.

Bayzog had finally become accustomed to sensing differences in nature. This should have been elven instinct, but it had taken decades. And that wasn't all he had developed. There was a greater sense of awareness. Meditation and the Elderwood Staff helped with that. The suffocating grip of evil was always in his midst.

Brenwar halted. Hunkered down.

Bayzog and Ben flanked the dwarf. Ahead in a clearing, a wide creek's trickling waters ran toward the river. A dragon's long neck was lowered into the waters.

"That's the one," Brenwar said. "The one I should have crowned. Slippery lizard."

Ben's bowstring stretched.

Brenwar pushed it away, saying, "What are you doing? They be upwind of us. Watch and wait, foolish boy."

Ben's rugged taciturn face scowled at him, but Brenwar kept his eyes fixed ahead. More movement slithered through the shadows: dragons, two more, weaving through the trees with their necks low and tongues licking out. Bayzog could see the muscles rippling under their scales. Fear filled him, more than ever before. The dragons had gone from fascinating to horrifying.

The dragon with his head in the stream jerked his neck out and choked down a fish. The other two waded into the waters and dipped their scaly heads in.

"We should strike now," Ben said in a low voice. "While their guard is down."

"So ready to risk death, are you?" Brenwar said. "We wait. They'll move along."

"In a day. Maybe two. They wait for us. Those dragons are no fools."

Ben was right. The dragons were biding their time. With such long lives, they could afford to. But

Bayzog wasn't sure if the dragons were hunting them or not. Why had they killed Otter Bone and Horse Neck? Was that who they hunted, or were they hunting all who opposed Barnabus now? He felt time pressing inside his chest. He and his friends needed to move. Find Nath. Bayzog couldn't believe what he said next.

"We might have to take them out."

Brenwar twisted his neck around.

"What?"

"It's us or them now."

"Are you feeling alright, elf?"

"Never better," he said. "And we can't avoid these conflicts forever. I say we take them out, as quickly as we can."

"Are you sure it can't wait a little longer?" Brenwar said. "They may pass."

"They'll have our scent soon enough. You know that. And since when do you prefer stealth over an attack?"

"Argh, since never." Brenwar nodded. "What is the plan?"

"Just remember," Bayzog said to Ben, "they have a breath weapon. Keep your distance." He looked down at the stream full of dragons. "Wait for my signal. I'm going in."

CHAPTER

3

BAYZOG'S SON RERRY STROLLED BAREFOOT through their home in the city of Quintuklen. His stomach rumbled, and the smell of his mother's cooking didn't linger in the air. His brother, Samaz, sat at Bayzog's great round table with his nose in a scroll. One of many that were scattered about.

"Where's Mother?" Rerry said. He slid on his shoes near the fireplace, buckled on his sword, folded his arms across his chest, and waited for Samaz to answer. His brother slept even less than he did, so if their mother, Sasha, had left, then he'd know. He tapped his foot on the floor. "Samaz, you toad, where is Mother!"

Samaz's head eased up. There was a sad look in his bigger, brooding, older brother's eyes.

"What is it?" Rerry said. His blood raced. "What is wrong?"

Samaz wiped his robed sleeve across his brow and said, "She has not come home yet. She's been gone since yesterday." He swallowed. "That feeling ... that feeling I've had, it's gotten worse."

In two quick steps, Rerry grabbed him by the collar and started to shake him.

"Why didn't you wake me? Why didn't you wake me, you oaf!"

With a single move, fast as a fly, Samaz brushed Rerry's arms away and forced him backward.

"Because I've been trying to find her." He tapped his meaty fingers on the table. "Using these scrolls. This feeling, Rerry," he clutched his robes. "It won't go away."

"Then we need to find her," Rerry said, taking a mail coat out of an open closet and buckling it on. "We need to go now."

"Where do we start?" Samaz said.

"The gardens. Certainly someone saw her in the gardens."

CHAPTER

4

MAN-SIZED DRAGONS. EMERALD. BLACK TAILED. Dark winged. They greeted Nath's descent with open maws filled with sharp teeth. Plummeting through the air, Nath didn't think. He reacted. He let go of the gnomes, crashed into one of the dragons, wrapped his arms around its neck, and squeezed.

Its wings flapped vigorously, but not for long. Nath pinned them down with his legs. The emerald dragon's claws tore at him. They fell fast and hit hard.

Splash!

Deep into the water they sank. Fighting. The dragon's tail coiled around his neck. It felt like an iron bar, choking him. Nath continued squeezing its serpentine neck. It snapped at him. Clawed at him as they sank deeper into the water. Nath sent his thoughts out to it.

I'm not giving in!

He didn't know if they registered or not, but the tail did not loosen. His arms didn't either. He was a dragon. His scales were steel. His muscles stronger than iron. He wrestled the dragon's neck into the nook of his arm and put everything he had into it.

It's me or you!

The dragon fought.

Nath fought back.

You cannot win! I'm Nath Dragon!

There was no give in the dragon. It was proud. Devoted. Its tail flexed and tried to pull Nath's head from his shoulders.

It made him mad. He summoned his strength and wrenched its neck.

Pop!

The great green lizard went limp. Nath released it and watched it sink to the bottom, its beautiful form coming to rest on the great river's floor. Lungs burning, he swam for the surface and emerged, gasping for air. Treading water and spinning around, he spied the gnomes, who were paddling their way toward the bank with a poor effort. They screamed back and forth at one another.

Great dragons!

The other emerald dragon slithered through the waters like a great snake, quick after the gnomes.

Nath yelled and waved his arm over his head, "Over here! Over here!"

The dragon's neck snaked around, and evil intelligent eyes glared back into Nath's. It went back and forth between him and the gnomes for only a moment before gliding after the gnomes.

No!

Nath swam, arms churning like paddles as fast as he could. He cut the distance in half while the gnomes scrambled up on the sandy riverbank, coughing and wheezing. One helped another and cried for the last to hurry along.

The dragon closed in on the last gnome in the water, and like a snake, it struck. Its jaws clamped down on the gnome's leg and pulled it underneath the waters in a violent surge. All the gnomes screamed in horror.

Nath filled his lungs full of air and plunged into the waters. In seconds, he made out the shape of the dragon. The deeper he swam, the more he saw.

Swim faster!

He pulled Dragon Claw out of Fang's hilt and closed in. He could see the gnome's stubby fingers clawing for the surface, its little leg pinched between the dragon's jaws. Nath reached out and locked one paw around the dragon's arm, and with the other he struck. Dragon Claw's glowing tip went deep. Straight into the head of the dragon beast. The fire in its eyes extinguished, and its jaw went slack.

Hurry!

He scooped the unmoving gnome up in his arms and swam for the surface. Seconds later, he carried the gnome's limp form onto the riverbank, where the gnomes waited with tender looks on their faces, one and all.

They pushed Nath away and huddled around their friend. The throng of small river-soaked bodies started to chant and sway. Moments later, Snarggell stepped away with his head down.

"Flupplinn is gone."

"I'm sorry," Nath said. "I tried."

"You hurried us from our home and into death," Snarggell said, balling up his fists. "You've failed yourself. You've failed us all. Most of all Flupplinn."

"Sorry," Nath said, raising his eyes to the sky. He could see more dragons perched in the Floating City's towers above. The shadow of the great city sent a chill through him. "We must go."

"Go! We must have a burial, Rescue Murderer."

"There's no time for a burial," Nath said. "I'll carry Flupplinn. We can bury him later." He moved toward the fallen body that lay still on the ground. The gnome's small form was like that of a child, and Nath felt sadness run through him. He started to stoop down, but the gnomes stopped him.

"We'll carry our own dead," one said, "Rescue Murderer."

"Be on with you now," said another.

"Go, go away."

"Rescue Murderer."

"Safer with dragons, we were."

"The lurker was safer too."

The comments stung. Bit. But Nath didn't have time for any of it. He didn't have time to explain himself, and it wasn't surprising that the gnomes didn't see the truth of it. They'd gotten settled in their jaxite home.

He turned and faced Snarggell.

"I know this is hard, but it's going to be much harder if you don't come with me."

"Are you going to snatch me up like a child again?"

Nath's golden eyes flared. Smoke rolled from his nose.

"Alright," Snarggell said, eyeing the city in the sky. His ancient eyes narrowed a little. "We'll go with you then."

"Good."

Nath led them along the riverbank for about a half mile, keeping his eyes on the city behind him. The dragons remained still as gargoyles in their perches. Not a wing in the sky. His mind raced, wondering why they didn't come. What were they waiting for? He glanced back at the gnomes. Four of them carried one dead friend. All of their faces were dour. It left a guilty feeling in him. But he hadn't invaded the city to make friends. He had done it to put an end to the jaxite mining that allowed the Clerics of Barnabus to control the dragons. And to save Bayzog from Otter Bone's spell.

My friend had better be in good order.

He pushed his way up the riverbank, through the clinging briars, and into the forest. The frozen stares of the dragons were now gone from his mind. He focused on catching up with Bayzog, Brenwar, and Ben.

A hundred yards deep in the forest, he pushed through the foliage and into a grove of pines. He came to a stop. The ground rumbled beneath his feet.

"What is it?" Snarggell said, squinting his eyes in the growing darkness. "Why did we stop?"

"Sh," Nath said, staying the gnomes with his hand. He kneeled and put his palm on the ground. His nostrils flared. A moment later, birds exploded from the tree and the forest shook.

Ear-shattering roars filled the valley like thunder. Nath shrank back. The gnomes fell to their knees, quivering.

"What in Nuh-Nalzambor was that?" Snarggell said.

"Dragons," Nath said, unsheathing Fang. "Bull dragons."

CHAPTER
5

"A MAD ELF," BRENWAR SAID TO Ben, lifting his brows. "I thought I'd never see such a thing. The war's gotten to him. He goes to feed himself to the dragons."

"Maybe he's being brave," Ben said. His strong features shone well in the dimming light. Rugged. Battle worn. He readied his bow.

"An elf, brave?" Brenwar said. "A wizard, at that? You know this is not a time for jesting."

Ben shrugged and positioned himself for an open shot. Brenwar kept his eyes on Bayzog.

The elf glided through the forest on cat's paws, a shade of himself.

He grunted. He'd seen elves move with plenty of stealth before, but not Bayzog. The part-elf was clumsy by such standards, except today. Today, Bayzog was as graceful as a ghost.

"Magic," he muttered under his beard. "I heard you use it, you tricky one."

Still, his heart pounded beneath his breastplate like a hammer. He wasn't used to watching another take the heavy risk.

"It's not dwarven-like."

Bayzog weaved through the trees, blending in with everything he passed, becoming more difficult to see with every step. Straining his eyes, Brenwar lost Bayzog in the forest. At the same time, the copper dragons froze there wading in the waters. One barked an awful sound to the others. The others barked back. Their serpent eyes shone like yellow moons, narrowing while their necks swayed from side to side.

Brenwar's knuckles turned white on War Hammer's handle.

"What are ye doing, elf?"

He glanced over and caught Ben glancing at him. The well-knit warrior pointed at the stream, his lips mouthing the words, "He's there. He's there. Right in front of them."

Brenwar inched forward, squinting.

There!

Bayzog stood like a sapling on the edge of the stream, easing his staff into the waters.

A copper dragon stood in the waters no more than twenty yards away, eyeing the spot where he stood. It barked. A sharp dreadful sound.

Bahhhct! Bahhhct!

It waded deeper into the waters.

"'Wait for my signal' he says," Brenwar grumbled. "He can't signal if he's dead."

With fire charging through his veins, Bayzog eased the Elderwood Staff into the waters. He could feel the power of the dragons, who were strong like iron, powerful like a gale, but little bigger than a large man. But he'd already seen one rip Horse Neck apart like a cat does a mouse.

Don't think about that. Block it out.

He'd already used magic to conceal himself. An old elven spell he'd learned when he was young. But now, so close, there was only so much you could hide from the powerful sense of a dragon. The most excellent hunters in the world.

Feeling the dragon's eyes burning a hole right through him, he summoned his power and fed the Elderwood Staff that rested in the waters. The silvery stream burbled a bright spark of blue under the surface. The spark spread. The waters began to crystalize, crackle, and turn to ice. In seconds, the mystic power raced from one side of the stream to the other, forming a huge slab of ice.

The dragons barked back and forth, thrashing in their frozen bounds. The giant ice slab held their legs and bodies fast. They roared at the frozen waters. One of the three's neck was frozen under. The nearest dragon showed Bayzog a vicious stare and opened its jaws wide. A stream of acid shot forth.

Bayzog dove, but failed to beat the acid, which burned into his legs.

Ben heard the waters crackle and watched in amazement. The waters turned to a sheet of ice, damming up the stream in seconds. The cold expressions of the dragons he'd never seen on their serpent faces before. Surprise that quickly turned to anger. A black stream of liquid sizzled from the copper dragon's mouth, and he heard Bayzog cry out.

Twang!

The first arrow went into the copper dragon's neck.

Twang!

The second clattered off its horns. He reloaded and aimed. Brenwar charged between the dragon and his sight with War Hammer waving like a banner.

"Shades! Get out of the way!"

Brenwar barreled through the forest toward the riverbank. His knees sprang into action the moment the dragon opened up its maw. Instantly, he knew he'd be too late to warn Bayzog to get out of the way. Instead, he watched the part-elf fall in a heap of agony.

"I'll give you a fight, lizard!"

Brenwar's boots hit the ice, and Ben's arrow whizzed into the dragon's neck. The dragon's head recoiled back. Another arrow ricocheted off its horns. Brenwar slid across the ice and swung.

Pow!

He caught the beast full in the chest, rocking it back. He drew his arms back to strike again.

Whap!

The dragon's tail knocked him across the ice. He scrambled to his feet, slipped, and fell down again. He popped up just in time to see the dragon's lungs fill with air.

"Uh-oh." It was one of those moments he wished he carried a shield. Flat footed, he curled up into a ball. "This is going to sting."

Twang!

Boom!

Brenwar's head popped up. The dragon was in smoking pieces. He twisted his head around and saw Ben charging his way with the bow held high. He was yelling something, but Brenwar's ears were ringing.

"What's that?"

Ben pointed and waved frantically.

Brenwar turned. The frozen dragons on the other side of the ice were breaking free.

Brenwar huffed through his beard and said, "No you don't."

He slung War Hammer across the ice with all his might.

Kachoom!

It blasted into the dragon's chest so hard that it shook all of its scales. Its eyelids fluttered. Streams of acid exploded from its mouth. It struggled, squawking like a drowning animal. Droplets of acid showered the air, sizzling on the ice and everywhere.

"Get away from there, Brenwar!" Ben yelled.

"Stay back!" Brenwar yelled at the same time. He'd had enough of this. He was putting an end to the dragon. He stormed right into its path, ignoring the burning acid that sizzled off his skin. He snatched up his hammer and struck the wild beast again and again until it moved no more. He combed his fingers through the smoking holes that burned in his beard.

"Drat!"

The ice cracked between his feet, and the third dragon ripped its head out of the frozen waters. Its eyes locked on Brenwar's. War Hammer locked on its eyes and sailed straight into its nose.

Krang!

The muscles in its steel-hard neck went limp and sunk onto the ice. Brenwar strode over, picked up his hammer, and finished it in one quick blow. He wheeled around. No more dragons. All three were dead. He saw Ben assisting Bayzog. The elf's chiseled face was filled with pain. Brenwar headed over and kneeled down. The acid had eaten through Bayzog's robes and into his flesh. Nasty bubbling wounds.

"Yer legs never did you much good anyway," he said. "I'll get the chest and see if we can stop that."

"Thanks," Bayzog said, grimacing. His face was beaded in sweat. "Feels like its eating right through me."

"Brenwar," Ben said, eyes wide, "your head is smoking." He started patting it out.

"Stop that!"

"But?"

"It will go out soon enough."

"Doesn't it hurt?" Ben said. "I would think it hurts."

"It doesn't hurt as much as the sound of your yapping." He eyed Ben. "Say, make yourself useful and fetch the chest."

"That was a good plan, elf," Brenwar said.

"Thanks," Bayzog said. He'd never been in so much pain before. "Maybe you can make me a suit of armor one day," he continued, trying not to look at his wounds.

"Maybe," Brenwar said, peeling the remains of Bayzog's robes away from his acid-burns.

Bayzog sucked in sharply.

"But, it won't do you any good if you don't fill us in on the plan," Brenwar said. "No good at all. Why didn't you just tell us something instead of running off like ye did?"

"Well, I didn't really have a plan. I just felt I needed to do something. I followed my instincts." He surveyed the dead dragons. Ben had blown one up, and Brenwar had walloped the other two. Despite his burns, he felt good for playing a part in that. Too often, he felt like he did nothing at all. It was as if they were protecting him and he was never protecting them. "Seems it worked."

"Aye," Brenwar said, unfurrowing his brow. He laid his hand on Bayzog's shoulder. "Sometimes you have to trust your instincts. Yours are getting better. Much better. Just not better than mine. I shouldn't have let you go. I shouldn't have let Nath go either."

"You did right."

"We'll see." Brenwar dusted off his hands. He'd peeled all the robes away from Bayzog's legs. The flesh was nasty underneath. "Well, at least we have plenty of ice to put on it," he said, doing just that.

Bayzog choked a laugh and wiped away his tears.

"Where's Ben? We've got to get moving, help Dragon."

"You don't think there could be another dragon out there, do you?" Bayzog said.

"No, not after all that squawking they made. Aid would have come by now. The forest covers the racket farther out. I think we're safe." He stood up and peered through the forest. "Where is he?"

Bayzog scooted around. The movement made the pain worse, and the pain made him queasy. He squinted. Ben emerged from the overhanging brush. He had his fingers locked behind his head. Bayzog reached for the Elderwood Staff. Someone beat him to it.

CHAPTER

6

THINGS WERE COMING TOGETHER. It was no wonder the other dragons hadn't come after Nath and the crystal gnomes. They were going to let the bull dragons do the dirty work for them. Nath wanted to kick himself. He'd forgotten all about them.

"What do we do?" Snarggell whispered. His eyes blinked continuously, and his fingers fidgeted. "What do we do, Rescue Murderer?"

"Stop calling me that," Nath said, irritated. "Just be still."

The gnomes, typically chatterboxes, were silent. They huddled together in the brush in some sort of protective circle. Snarggell merged with them, whispering quickly in Gnomish.

Nath paid them no mind. Instead, his thoughts raced through his memories of the dragons. He knew each kind's weakness, most of them anyway, but the bull dragons didn't have much of one. They were brutes: flying, fire-breathing juggernauts. Only the titan dragons, the hulls, were a greater match.

It could be worse I suppose. It could be raining.

The bull dragons had Nath's scent already. He didn't have much doubt that the other dragons had told them he and the gnomes were near.

"I'm glad I have you," he said to Fang. "And that you are cooperating. I need you."

The great blade winked blue. The hilt warmed in his hand.

"Let's not have that again."

The hilt stayed warm, not scalding hot.

Nath focused. *I have to help Bayzog.* He'd defeated the grey scaler without a weapon. Could he defeat *two* bull dragons, even *with* weapons?

Perhaps I can reason with them. He smiled. Bull dragons were anything but reasonable.

Another pair of ear-shattering roars erupted, louder this time than the last. He could hear trees toppling. Branches breaking.

"They come closer!" one of the gnomes squealed.

Nath grunted. The bull dragons had the scent. They would be upon the party soon. He'd have to hold the dragons off until the gnomes made their way to safety. But where would that be? Up along the riverbank? He could at least catch up with them from there. If he survived.

"Snarggell, lead the gnomes up river, along the bank," he said, turning, "I'll hold the dragons off as long as I can."

The gnome didn't reply. None of them. Their bodies formed a tight knot of people.

"Snarggell?" He reached over and grabbed one of the gnomes. Its body and clothes had turned to stone. He found Snarggell's eyes twinkling at him. "What are you doing?"

Snarggell's stony lips retorted, "Surviving. Goodbye, Rescue Murderer." His features solidified again.

"Blast my scaled hide!" he said, staring at the statues of bodies. The crystal gnomes' plan was a good one, assuming the dragons couldn't sniff them out and crush them. But at least they were safe for now.

I wish I could do that.

A fleeting thought of running drifted through his thoughts. He was fast. But that would only endanger others. He moved away from the gnomes to another clearing in the pines. The great trees swayed in the darkness. Timbers cracked and groaned under the power of the scaled bulk that pushed through them. The claws on Nath's fingertips tingled. He wasn't scared of any man, dragon, nor monster. Nor of death. But one thing did scare him: failure. Especially when the entire world depended on him.

Two pines crashed left and right, and the first bull dragon emerged. Huge. Bigger than a pair of elephants. The great horns twisted on its head like spears. Its face was large. Fierce and terrible. Red-orange scales shimmered like steel armor. Its mouthful of teeth a bunch of giant white icicles.

Nath felt its hot charred breath on his face. Heard its thoughts inside his head, in Dragonese.

"Well, what have we here?"

The second bull dragon pushed through. Just as big and just as ugly and terrible. The pair hemmed him in.

"Why, it's the precious son of the dragon 'king'."

Bellies scraping the ground, they both came closer.

"Doesn't look like a dragon to me," the first one said.

Eyeing Fang, the other bull dragon replied, *"Look, he brought us a toothpick. Now we can see if he tastes like one."*

CHAPTER

7

BAYZOG'S LIPS DREW FORTH POWERFUL mystic Elvish words. The butt of the Elderwood Staff jammed in his throat and cut him off.

"Uh, uh, uh," said the tall figure that held his staff, wagging his finger at Bayzog. "Not another syllable if I were you."

Bayzog's eyes flitted around. Tall stout figures held Ben and Brenwar at sword point. Their heads were all hooded, and they wore cloaks. Dark green and grey. One of them had Brenwar's chest tucked under his arm, and another carried the bow, Akron. Bayzog couldn't imagine how men so big had gotten the drop on them.

The one above him said, "Did you kill those dragons?"

Bayzog nodded, noting the strange accent.

"We killed those dragons, and we'll kill you too," Brenwar said. "I suggest you move on, if you know what's good for you."

"Says the fat bearded one," the stranger said in a cool sanguine voice. "Are you a dwarf? You sound gnomish, but you're too fat for a gnome."

Brenwar shook his fist, snarled, and pounced. He grabbed the first hooded stranger's legs and drove him into the ground. His fist came up and down.

Another cloaked stranger tackled him.

Bayzog heard his captor chuckling.

"Dwarves. Love a good insult. Love a good fight," the stranger said. He eased the Elderwood Staff off Bayzog's neck. "Enough!"

The two cloaked figures brawling with Brenwar skittered away, leaving the dwarf swinging at empty air.

The two figures, swords ready, kept Brenwar hemmed in.

"Enough," the lead stranger repeated. "Secure your weapons. I've no interest in wounding old friends." He removed his hood. Bright eyes and pointed ears revealed a stony elven face.

"Shum?" Bayzog said, shocked.

Brenwar's eyes shone big as moons.

"Yes," Shum said, kneeling alongside Bayzog. "Now, let's take a look at those legs."

"But, you're dead."

"*Was* dead. Sort of," Shum said. "Sansla Libor saved me."

The name pricked Bayzog's ears. It had been so long, more than twenty-five years, since he'd even thought about the cursed elf king, Sansla Libor. Cursed into the form of a great winged ape.

"Is he still under the curse?" Bayzog asked.

Shum nodded while inspecting Bayzog's legs.

"He's only gotten worse. It seems the nature of this world hastens things." The stone-faced Elven Ranger reached into a pouch and withdrew some multicolored grains, which he sprinkled all over Bayzog's acid burns.

"Ah!" Bayzog exclaimed, eyes watering. "What is that?"

"Give it a moment," Shum said, holding his long finger up.

The pain in Bayzog's legs eased. He sighed as relief filled him.

"You should be able to stand now." Shum extended his arms and pulled him up.

Bayzog fought his grimace.

"Try to walk," Shum said, folding his hands over his belly.

Leaning on his staff and showing a grim smile, Bayzog limped along the edge of the stream and said, "At least I'm moving."

"The dragon's acid is often life ending. You're fortunate we came."

"We aren't helpless," Bayzog said, eyeing the dwarven chest that Ben now rummaged through. "Not that I'm ungrateful."

"Maybe we soon will be," Ben said, holding up a yellow vial that was less than half full. "Dragon took the other one."

"Well!" Brenwar said, marching forward with his meaty hands on his hips. "Look who shows up after the battle is over. A fat-bellied elf! Ha!" He spat in the ground. "What's the matter? Do you need us to track down your ape-king again?"

"Mind your tongue, dwarf," Shum said, glowering at him with steely eyes.

"Mind your business," Brenwar fired back. "And get on with you, Fat Belly."

"Brenwar!" Bayzog said. "Our friend now lives. Can you at least welcome him back from the grave?"

"No," Brenwar grumbled. "He had no business dying in the first place. He just needed to hold his breath a little longer."

"Brenwar, really?" Bayzog said. He couldn't believe his ears. "You're colder than a mountain snowcap."

The husky dwarf made his way over to Shum and poked him in the chest.

"Don't you die on me again, elf," Brenwar said. "I'll bury your corpse myself the next time."

Shum looked down on him with flashing eyes.

Brenwar picked Shum up in a bear hug and bounced him up and down a few times.

"Alright, alright," Shum said, pushing Brenwar's heavy shoulders. "It's good to see you too, dwarf. Now set me down, will you?"

Brenwar obliged, dashing the sweat from his eyes.

"Are you crying?" Ben asked.

"Dwarves don't cry." He mopped his brow again. "Now, what are ye doing here?"

"Yes," Bayzog said, "I don't believe in coincidence."

"We were sent," Shum said, gesturing to the others. "All of us. You remember my brother Hoven?"

Nearby, Hoven stood adorned in his riding cloak, elven steels on his hips.

"And the other Roaming Rangers came to heed the call as well."

There were another half-dozen Roaming Rangers. These were Wilder Elves, a more rugged and durable kind of elf. Heavy bodies exposed to harsh elements of all sorts. Their entire presence was eerie, but welcomed.

"So, again I ask," Bayzog said, "who sent you? The elves? Sansla Libor?"

"We cannot say yet," Shum said, shaking his head. "All I can say at this time is we are here, well meaning, and seeking Nath Dragon."

"What do ye mean, *well meaning*?" Brenwar retorted. "I don't like the sound of that."

"I don't think Nath Dragon will like the sound of it either, but know this," Shum said, "your friend is in grave danger. The worst of all our fears."

"Such as?" Brenwar growled.

"The clutches of the high priestess of Barnabus, Selene, are close. We're here to make sure she does not capture him," Shum said. "And we must go." He made a sharp whistle, as did the other Roaming Rangers. Seconds later, their Elven Steeds emerged from the brush. "Find a ride. We must hurry."

"I'm not riding on your beast with you, or any other," Brenwar said.

Shum nodded to one of the other Roaming Rangers. One hopped off, took his reins to Brenwar and doubled up with another.

"Satisfied?" Shum said.

Brenwar couldn't get his foot up high enough to reach the stirrup.

Shum whistled again, and the horse lowered to its knees.

Brenwar climbed on, saying, "You didn't have to do that."

Bayzog helped himself up behind Shum, and Ben climbed on with Hoven. As soon as they settled, they shot off over the icy stream, deeper into the forest. The wind whistled through Bayzog's ears. Onward the horses galloped, cutting and leaping through the brush. He could hear the urgency in the Wilder Elf's voice when he spoke.

Shum's words shook him.

CHAPTER
8

DRAGON KING. NATH'S FATHER. THE bull dragon's mockery ignited his blood.
  "And I'm the prince," Nath said, resting Fang on his shoulder. "And I'm more dragon than the both of you."
  "Is that so?" the first one said in his mind, lowering his head, coming eye to eye with Nath. *"I've never seen a dragon use a sword before."* It opened one of its paws to showcase its claws. Nath could almost fit inside its palm. *"Dragons fight with claws. Do you have claws, little Dragon Prince?"*
  "I see his claws," the second bull dragon said. *"My, they look as vicious as pine needles. Perhaps he plans to tickle us."* It rested its head on the ground. *"Is that your plan, little dragon?"*
  There was venom in their thoughts. Hatred. Ancient, but not buried. The bull dragons weren't like the others, whose wings and scales had been turned black. No, these dragons were the bad ones. Survivors of the last dragon war. Soldiers for evil.
  "You sound bitter," Nath said. "Perhaps you can still taste my father's victory, shoved down your throats centuries ago."
  Bright orange eyes flashed. Great bellies swelled.
  "Your father is far from innocent," the first one said, lashing out with his tail to snap a tree in half. *"He's every bit the murderer the rest of us are."*
  Murderer?
  "That's absurd," Nath said, "And I'd expect nothing short of lies coming from the tongue of an oversized lizard." He stepped forward, pointing. "Did my father bust those horns of yours? Why is one eye half shut? And you," he pointed to the second. "You've got scales missing from your belly and your hide. And half your claws are missing. Did you bite them off from the shear fear of his presence?"
  The dragon pair glanced at one another, but no expression changed on their scaled faces. Nath could feel some confusion, however. Such terrifying creatures weren't accustomed to anything challenging them. Lava started to drip from their mouths.
  "Today you will die, Nath Dragon," the first said, drawing back a sneer.
  "Yes, die," said the second. "Prepare yourself."
  "No, prepare your—"
  Claws swiped the ground.
  Nath leapt high, but caught the full force of a whipping tail. He tumbled through the air and smashed into a tree with bone-jarring force. Thunder came his way, shaking the ground. The first bull dragon pounced at him. He sprang underneath it, rolled onto his back, and swung. Fang clipped its armor-plated belly scales, drawing an angry growl.
  He scrambled away, sword ready. The second dragon cut into his path. A whoosh of flames erupted from its mouth, lighting up the night. The scorching heat was suffocating. Nath charged with Fang held high, bursting through the flames, yelling, "Dragon! Dragon!"
  He chopped claws from its hand.
  The great beast recoiled back. Making an ear-splitting roar, it crashed through the trees in the forest

and destroyed everything in its path. Nath's scales were smoking, his face and hair singed, but he lived. He was the Dragon Prince.

A shadow fell over his shoulder. He twisted around.

Stomp!

The first dragon pinned his body to the ground underneath its clawed foot. Nath lost his breath. It started grinding him into the ground.

"It seems the cat has caught the mouse," it said.

His sword arm was free, but his feeble strikes were useless.

"Scratch me all you can," it said, licking its lips, "you'll be dead in seconds." Golden lava dripped through the cracks in its teeth. "And I thought the Dragon King's son would be a challenge. It seems he didn't have you prepared."

Nath struggled and strained. His efforts were in vain. He didn't have the size or the leverage. His grip began to slip from his sword.

The bull dragon pushed him deeper into the dirt.

"Die, Dragon Prince! Die!"

Lava dripped onto Fang's blade and sizzled on the metal.

Help me, Fang! Help me!

With tremendous effort, he took one last swing, nicking Fang's tip between the dragon's steel-hard scales.

The great blade hummed with life. The steel flared like a star. The sound grew louder and louder.

The first dragon lurched.

"What!"

Nath pointed Fang right at it.

"Stop that!" it growled. Stop that!"

The sound grew and lashed out.

WRAAAANG! WRAAAANG! WRAAAANG!

The vibration caught the first dragon's outspread wings and sent it sailing into the forest.

Nath crawled out of the dirt. Fang poured it on.

WRAAAANG! WRAAAANG! WRAAAANG!

Leaves and pine needles scattered. Rocks flew through the air. Trees bent, cracked, and shivered. All the while, the mystical sound pounded into the second dragon. Its roars could not be heard. Even its thrashing was muted.

WRAAAAAAANG! WRAAAAAANG!

The blade winked out. The sound was over.

The first dragon rolled through the toppled timbers, blinking and dazed.

"Thank you, Fang!" Nath caught his breath. "Now finish it!" He had just started his charge when his senses exploded. He jerked around.

Whap!

The second dragon's tail separated Nath's paw from his sword. He went careening into the forest with stars exploding inside his head. Swordless, he rose to his feet and gaped at his empty dragon paws. Fang was nowhere to be seen. He rubbed his aching chest, swearing he could hear his bones rattle. Nearby, the dragons rummaged the forest, searching for the spot where the dragon's tail had flung him.

What do I do now?

He felt something in his tunic. A vial from the dwarven chest remained sealed and unbroken.

Thank the dwarves and their iron glass.

He drank the entirety of the sparkling blue contents and tossed the vial aside.

I hope this works.

Both dragons appeared with angry looks on their monstrous faces.

Fast!

"Where is your toothpick, little dragon?" the second one said, waving at him its paw whose claws were missing. "I want to skewer and roast you on it."

A tail lashed out in a downward arc.

Nath jumped aside and scurried deeper into the woods.

The dragons bounded after him, crushing everything in their path. They were big, but also fast. Their monstrous strides caught up with Nath in seconds and hemmed him in. Their tails struck like cedars, smiting everything around him.

The ground shook.

Nath jumped. Dove. Dodged.

Whop! Whop! Whop! Whop!

Their tails beat the ground like striking snakes and cut him off wherever he jumped or dived. It was two cats toying with a mouse, and he had nothing to defend himself. He cleared one tail and got hammered by another. Its strike was planned. Well timed. It flattened him on the ground. A massive paw pushed his body into the dirt.

"Time is up, Dragon Prince," the first one said, scooping him up in its claws. "Now we feast on your bones." Its tongue licked over its lips, and lava dripped from its jaws. "But I have to share with my brother, so we'll need to split you apart."

Nath squirmed and strained, but the dragon's great strength kept him restrained.

Sultans of Sulfur!

"No, Brother," the second dragon said, sitting back on its haunches. "You eat him. I enjoy the sound of crunched bones. Feast, Brother. Feast. We don't want this slippery one to get away."

"So be it then," the first dragon said. He held Nath up and gazed in his eyes and shook him vigorously. "I don't like my meals staring at me." It slammed Nath onto the ground and hammered on him with its fist a few times. "And I don't like my meat too chewy either. Needs softening up a bit." It smiled. "Now, let the feast begin."

Nath's head rolled along his shoulders. His red hair was matted to his head, and blood dripped from his nose. His face was swollen. His lips split. He hurt. He ached. But he wasn't done yet.

"I don't think you got me soft enough. I don't think you broke a single bone," he sputtered through his lips. "You ugly oversized lizard."

"Is that so?" it said, eyes narrowing. "We'll see about that." It opened its mouth wide and stuffed Nath inside.

Chomp!

CHAPTER

9

"I KNOW THERE HAVE BEEN MANY battles," Shum had said, "but the one coming might be the most important of all."

The Elven Steeds cut through the woodland with the ease of a straight path. Ben found himself hanging on for his life. He'd never ridden on a horse so fast, let alone with two people on it in the darkness. It assured him of one thing … the Roaming Rangers were good company, and he was glad to be among them.

I need one of these horses.

An hour into the ride, they slowed and came to a halt. He squinted in the dimness. Bayzog and Shum strolled along at his and Hoven's side. Bayzog had a weary look in his violet eyes.

"Are you well, Bayzog?" Ben asked.

"Well enough, just weak." Bayzog grimaced. "This riding jars my legs, but I'll make it. Much better than walking so far."

Brenwar reared his horse around and said, "Why are we stopping fer? Time's wasting."

Shum held up his hand and tilted his head, saying, "I heard something."

"Over all the riding?" Ben asked.

"A moment of quiet please," Shum said.

The Elven Roaming Rangers sat poised in their saddles like dark statues. Unmoving and stony. If he didn't know they were there, he'd probably walk right by them. He noticed Bayzog perk up and bend his ear toward the sky.

Am I missing something?

He cupped his ear and closed his eyes. It bothered him, the better senses the other races had. They could see better in the dark and hear trickles and scuffles where none could be heard. He continually had to find ways to improvise.

A minute went by, maybe two, and when he was about to pull his hand from his ear, he heard something. East, farther downriver, a howl, maybe a roar erupted in the woods. His heart started pounding. It sounded big. Huge perhaps. Goosebumps rose on his arms.

"That's where Nath is," Brenwar growled.

"How do you know?" Ben said

"Only Nath could make something *that* mad." Brenwar wheeled his horse around. "And we better get over there before that monster kills him. Ee-Yah!"

CHAPTER

10

STILL DAZED, NATH FELT SOMETHING stir inside him. Outside of him, something else stirred. The dragon had him wedged inside its mouth. Its great teeth ground at his scales. The pressure was building, and his body popped and cracked. He screamed.

The dragon shook him.

Nath punched its nose with all the power he had. He could feel the dragon's throaty laughter.

I can't go like this. I can't!

His stomach buckled and knotted. Something inside him grew and stirred. He let out an awful bellow. His limbs popped and stretched.

The dragon's bone-splintering pressure eased.

Nath felt magic course through him. The potion had ignited and was rushing through his blood. He expanded. Head, torso, and limbs groaned and enlarged. He caught the second dragon's bewildered look and watched it back off.

"What trick is this!" the first dragon thought, releasing Nath from its jaws.

Nath convulsed and thrashed.

The dragons backed away.

Finally, the stretching stopped. He gathered his feet under him and stood erect.

"Sweet salamanders!"

He was a tower. A great wall. He grabbed a tree and ripped it from the ground.

"COME, DRAGONS," Nath beckoned, looking down in their eyes. "THE BATTLE ISN'T FINISHED YET." His voice thundered. "AND WHEN IT'S OVER, PERHAPS *I'LL* EAT *YOU*." He swung the tree like a club into the haunches of the first dragon. It scurried and hissed.

Nath laughed. He was bigger than them. Taller by a head. He was a man fighting two giant lizards.

A geyser of flame erupted from the second dragon's mouth, burning into the scales on Nath's legs. He couldn't contain his scream. Angered, he spit his own larger geyser of flame right into its face. It thrashed in the flames.

The first dragon's great tail swept Nath's feet out from under him. The pair of giants wrestled back and forth. Trees fell. Rocks crumbled behind their bulk. It wrapped its tail around Nath's neck. Nath locked his claws around its throat and squeezed with all his power.

"You cannot kill me," it thought in his mind. "You don't have the willpower. Just like your father, who spared us once before, you are a fool, Nath Dragon."

Nath released its neck and started punching. Harder and harder. He loosened its jaw. Dotted its eyes. He walloped it in the soft spot behind its wings. Its tail around his neck slackened. Nath tore the tail away, scooped up the dragon, and slammed it to the ground. His next blows were a thunderous flurry that shook everything in the forest. He beat the dragon to death. It lay still with its tongue hanging from its mouth.

Nath drew his arms across his busted mouth with his chest heaving. His giant limbs quivered, and his closed-paw fists had dragon blood on them.

"What have you done!" the second dragon said. "Impossible!"

"I did to it what I'm going to do to you," Nath said, turning to face it.

It beat its great wings, lifting its body from the ground, and a whoosh of flame came out. Nath balled up under the searing fire at first, and then slowly he rose. All around him, the forest burned. Turned to char and cinder. He gazed up at the dragon, shrugged off the blistering heat, and jumped high in the air, grabbing the dragon by its paws and jerking it to the ground.

Whoom!

He pinned it to the ground by the neck and unleashed the full fury of his dragon fire. Its claws raked at his scales. Its thoughts cried mercy. But nothing could save it from Nath's wrath-filled heat. It died with its own eyes scorched inside its sockets.

Nath slumped over. He lay on the ground shaking. The night sky wavered. Smoke and firelight made an eerie look in the sky. He hurt. He bled. The dragon's claws had torn through his scales into his flesh. There were even black blisters in many spots. He clutched his queasy stomach.

I'd be dead if not for that vial.

Getting on his monstrous hands and knees, he searched for Fang, lifting up burning trees and tossing them toward the river. But there was no sign of Fang.

Sultans of Sulfur! Could I have lost him?

Perhaps being bigger was the problem. Maybe he just needed to wait until he got smaller.

He can't be far.

He stared into the sky at the Floating City that hung above. He could see the dragons, still perched on their roosts. Not a single one had moved. He beckoned for them.

Come. Come and play.

Thumping his chest, he coughed a little. At his feet, the first bull dragon lay still. Wings broken. Nath wondered what it had meant when it spoke about his father. Why had his father spared them the first time? How do you spare something that wants to kill you?

He'd spent the majority of his life saving dragons, and now several had died by his hands. He wasn't supposed to kill. He'd been told it was different when a war was going on, but he couldn't make sense of the difference.

Isn't the war between good and evil always being fought?

He felt sadness. Despair. He stroked the bull dragon's horns. Despite the dragon's ferocious and terrible nature, it was still a beautiful thing. A spectacular mix of power and beauty. A shame it had been corrupted. A shame for them all.

Nath let loose and bellowed. After that, he pushed through the burning woods and located the crystal gnomes, who still formed a lump of stone. He picked them up with a grunt and walked back into the woods. He set them down and renewed his search for Fang. Perhaps the gnomes could help, if they ever thawed out, so to speak.

He tossed more burning trees toward the river, stomped and patted some fires out. Others he made into a huge bonfire until all the flames were under control. But there was no sign of Fang. Even with his excellent dragon vision, things were still harder to find in the dark than in the light.

He yawned, stretched his arms high into the sky, and sat down. Horses galloping through the forest caught his ear. They were coming his way. Seconds later, the riders emerged. Three of them had astonished looks. It was Brenwar, Bayzog, and Ben. The others were stone-faced Wilder Elves, and to his surprise one of them was Shum.

"What have you done to yourself this time?" Brenwar bellowed.

Nath kneeled down in front of them with his eyes fixed on Bayzog. His heart swelled.

"You're alright then?" he said.

Looking a little squeamish, Bayzog climbed from his horse and said, "Never better."

Nath slapped his hands together in a clap of thunder.

"Will you contain yerself!" Brenwar yelled. "You'll wake our dead enemies with all that racket."

"Oh, they're awake alright," Nath said, lowering his voice. He pointed back at the Floating City. "Green eyed and bony tailed." He smiled. He was so happy to see all his friends alive and well. He pointed at Ben.

The strongly built man held Akron in his hands and offered an approving nod.

Nath continued. "Seems we have some things to sort out. I suppose we should start with you, Shum. How is Sansla Li—"

Nath's vision spun, and a moment later everything went black.

CHAPTER

11

"I CAN BARELY STAND THIS PLACE anymore," Rerry said to his brother Samaz. "Look at all of these melon heads. It's revolting."

"Keep your voice down," Samaz said. The big-shouldered part-elf sat on a bench beside him, head low, eyes up. They'd been sitting for over two hours, looking for any sign of their mother, Sasha. "You know their ears are as big as their heads."

Rerry rose up in his seat a little, violet eyes bright.

"Was that a jest?"

"More fact than jest," Samaz replied, adjusting the sleeves on his robes, "any fool can see that."

"Watch what you say, Brother."

"Watch how loud you say it ... Brother."

Rerry eased back on the stone bench and started drumming his fingers on the hilts of his swords. He had the steel frame of a man but the grace of an elf. They sat in Quintuklen's Gardens of Worship, in the favorite spot of their mother. Over the years, it had become the lone spot among hundreds that was their favorite spot to share. There had been a time, years ago, when Rerry ran away, only to be found by his mother, sleeping on this very bench.

"This will be our safe spot," she had said to him. "If there is any trouble, this is where you come. But when we get home, you'll have to do all of Samaz's chores and some others."

It was one of the few times Rerry didn't bother to disagree. He hadn't wanted to run away, but pride hadn't let him go home either. He was just glad his mother found him. Plus, he'd been hungry.

"So you sense anything?" he said to Samaz, back in the now.

Samaz shook his head, his pale eyes flashing a little. The deep-chested part-elf rolled his eyes and sighed.

"I told you it doesn't work like that."

"Don't be so dramatic," Rerry said. "Find a way to make it work. You're just sitting here doing nothing."

"And you're just sitting here doing nothing as well, aside from the bickering."

A very tall man walked by, glowering at him. He wore a dark robe, was bald-headed with tattoos all around, and had a crow-like quality about him.

Rerry hoisted up his boot on the bench and tugged on the laces. "Good day," he said to the crow-faced man. "How's the weather up there?"

The man lifted a brow, shook his head, and vanished into the gardens.

Rerry scowled.

"Bald-headed tattooed freaks," he muttered under his breath. "Need to stick a sword in all of them."

"Watch what you say," his brother warned under his breath.

"Who's listening? The plants? The trees?" He grabbed a sunburst daisy and spoke into it. "Hello, flower, I want to skewer all the Clerics of Barnabus. Now run along and tell them about it." He released the flower. "Sheesh."

"Your silly mouth isn't doing Mother any favors."

"Pah," Rerry said, turning away. He didn't care. Every year, more people joined the ranks of Barnabus. They shaved their heads and got tattoos. They filled the gardens with chanting, praying, and pestering. They filled the streets with horrible singing. Rerry had friends once, but now most of them had fallen into the clutches of the disturbing acolytes of Barnabus. They made his stomach crawl.

"How much longer should we stay?" Samaz said, dashing sweat from his brow. "She could be anywhere by now. Perhaps one of us should wait at home in case she returns."

"So you can read more scrolls?"

"I might find something useful. You never know."

"You tried that," Rerry said, frowning, "and it didn't bear any fruit whatsoever. We wait here until the next crowing."

Samaz pulled his legs up into a cross-legged sitting position and closed his eyes.

"Oh great," Rerry said, shaking his head, "sleeping upright will help."

He waited. Watched. People of all sorts were milling about, babbling about Barnabus and the war. They said the same things they always did.

Barnabus will overcome evil.

Barnabus will crush the dragon hordes.

Barnabus will win the war. Save us all. Hail Barnabus.

It was lunacy. The last dragon Rerry saw had been chasing people through the city with a bald rider on its back shouting commands while it wrought havoc. He knew which dragons were good and which were bad. His father Bayzog had told him how to tell the difference between good and evil.

"Just watch and listen to the things they do," Bayzog had said. "Evil cannot hide its nature for long. It always outs itself. Just be careful that you don't get too close to the web it spins. If you get caught, you might not ever get out."

He rested his head in his hands.

Aw Father, I wish I were fighting at your side. I wish Mother would hurry back, too.

"Excuse me," a pretty voice said.

Rerry's head popped up. A mature woman of stunning beauty stood before him. Her lustrous black hair was peppered with white. Her peach gown clung to the generous curves of her body, and her features were elven. Rerry swallowed hard, and his heart started racing.

"Yes?" he said, coming to his feet. He smiled. "Can I help you?"

"I don't believe so," she said, taking his hand, "but I believe I can help you."

"How…" Rerry started, blinking. Her beauty filled his eyes. Her touch was so soothing, and a strange melody tickled his ears. "How can you help me?"

He didn't notice, but Samaz stood by his side, just as entranced as he was.

"I'm going to take you to your mother, Sasha." She brushed her fingers over his ears. "Would you like that?"

All Rerry wanted to do was nod, and that was all he did.

She led them both by the hand, deeper into the gardens, underneath the overhanging tulip vines into a tunnel encircled in flowers and thorns. Rerry took a quick glance back. The city he'd known as home had vanished. He didn't care one bit.

CHAPTER

12

"WELL, IT'S NOT MORGDON, BUT it will do," Brenwar said. With a small torch he carried in his hand, he lit a lantern hanging from a wooden support post, eyeing the surrounding structure's craftsmanship. "Certainly not dwarven."

He, Ben, Bayzog, and the Roaming Rangers had traveled without stopping for two days now, south of the Floating City. The Roaming Rangers had led the way to an ancient and long-forgotten location, a small fortress carved in the mountains. They all agreed it was the safest place to keep Nath Dragon while they waited for him to shrink from his enormous form. The Elven Steeds had towed him here, deep into the fortress.

"He'll be safe here with us," Shum said, tilting up a chair that lay on the chamber floor. "You are all welcome to stay as long as you like."

"Stay as long as we like? Har!" Brenwar said. "He's not staying here for long. If anything, he's going to Morgdon."

"But we agreed," Shum started, setting his swords on the dust-ridden table, "that he would stay with us."

"For a spell," Bayzog said, moving between the two. "Not for an unknown duration."

"We have our charge," Shum said, touching his fingertip to a candle sitting on the table. He muttered and the wick lit up. He nodded to Hoven, who took the flaming candle and worked his way around the chamber, lighting the lanterns. The light alleviated the dimness, but the mood did not lighten.

"I have a charge as well," Brenwar said. "And I won't be going anywhere without Nath. Not now. Not ever."

"I said you could stay," Shum said, "as long as you like, but he stays with us."

Brenwar bristled. His fists bunched up at his sides. "We'll see about that!"

"Hold on," Bayzog said. "Who gave you this charge, Shum? You never told us that."

Shum dragged a couple of wooden chairs their way, took a seat, and said, "Please sit. I've a feeling we'll be here awhile."

That's when Ben entered the chamber, dragging the now-shrunken Nath on a stretcher behind him. He lowered the braces of the stretcher to the ground, mopped the sweat from his brow, and started rubbing his shoulders.

"Whew! Even normal size, he weighs thrice as much as he looks." Ben shook his head, and a sad look crossed his face. "I don't like this, Bayzog. It was twenty-five years the last time. I'll be ancient if I live another twenty-five more." He loosened Fang from his shoulders, kneeled down, and lay the blade down by Nath's side. "We have to wake him up this time. We need him."

Brenwar grunted. He could agree that they needed Nath now more than ever. He'd never seen such large forces of evil before. Without Nath, he didn't think Nalzambor would hold up much longer.

"As you were saying, Shum," Bayzog said, breaking the silence, "who gave you this charge? I'm guessing Sansla Libor."

Shum shook his head. Hoven returned the candle to the table and took a seat beside his brother, resting his hands on his belly.

"The King," Shum said.

"Sansla, then," Bayzog said.

"No," said Shum, "*the* King."

"You mean the Elven King, then?" Brenwar said. "Pah! I don't follow the orders of elves. You'll have to do better than that. The king of Morgdon, perhaps. Or are you following the orc king now? Pah! Pot Belly."

"You know the king I am speaking of, Brenwar, personally, but you have not spoken with him in a long time." Shum's eyes drifted and rested on the dwarven chest. His chair groaned when he leaned forward. "He told me this: 'Tell Brenwar Bolderguild I have not forgotten that he has borrowed something of mine.'"

Brenwar's fingers froze in their search of his beard, and his fuzzy mouth formed an "O".

"The *Dragon* King," Bayzog said, rubbing his hands on the thighs of his robes. "You saw him?"

"I've spoken with him, or rather, he spoke to me," Shum said, glancing at Brenwar, "rather clearly."

Recovering, Brenwar folded his arms across his chest and said, "Preposterous. What else did he say, then?"

"He said we were to find Nath and aid him and his efforts in any way we could." He gestured to all the Roaming Rangers in the room. "That's why we are here."

"Humph, anyone can say that. Besides, I'm the one charged with aiding him, not you. Ask Nath," Brenwar said. He walked over and kicked Nath in the ribs with his boot. "He'll tell you."

"Is it so hard to believe?" Shum said.

"We have your word, but have no proof."

"What about the chest?"

"I'm sure Nath blabbed to you about that. As much as he talks, I'm sure he told everybody." Brenwar kicked him again. "Wake up, Dragon!"

"Stop doing that," Ben said. "You could hit him with your *hammer* and it wouldn't do any good. You know that."

"Agreed," Bayzog said. "Now sit, Brenwar. Let's finish this conversation."

"Oh! Well certainly," Brenwar said, hustling over to his chair and resuming his seat. "Why don't all of you deceitful elves continue to humor me?"

"Deceitful?" Bayzog started.

"Yes, deceitful!" Brenwar hopped back to the ground and punched his fist inside his hand. The Elven Roaming Rangers didn't bother him. It was the fact that the Dragon King had spoken with them that bothered him. It made him doubt himself. Feel like a failure. The Dragon King must not be pleased with his efforts. And Brenwar was ever confident. The dwarf had never doubted his efforts until now.

"Brenwar Bolderguild," Shum said, "I assume you'll be by our side for the duration. We all have to protect him."

"And what about this war? There won't be anything left to fight for by the time he wakes up again," Brenwar said, now pacing. "And I don't want to spend the next several decades with elves, Roaming Rangers or not."

"Hoven," Shum said, turning to his brother, "would you mind? I think now is the time."

"Aye, Brother."

As Hoven departed, Brenwar took to Nath's side. His friend had dried blood on his face, and his scales were blistered and ruptured. He appeared dead, other than the gentle fall and rise of his chest.

"Let's clean him up," he said to Ben. "I don't like seeing him like this."

Brenwar had been looking after Nath for over one hundred twenty-five years, and he'd never seen him in such bad shape. It hurt him. He felt like a failure.

"Brenwar," Ben said, wiping the blood from Nath's face. "If I'm not around the next time he wakes up, will you tell him … just tell him that it was good knowing him. I was honored."

The words sank into Brenwar's heart, softening it like a pillow. He squeezed his eyes shut and shook his head. "I'm going to make sure you're here to tell him yourself." He patted Nath's chest. "He's going to wake up. Soon. He has to."

The chamber fell silent, the firelight flickering in the draft, casting shadows on the solemn faces of the men. No one was ready for another twenty-five-year dragon sleep. None had yet recovered from the exhausting efforts of the last one.

Hoven returned with a small wooden chest in his hands. He handed it to Shum, whose chin rested on his fist and elbow.

"Ah, excellent," the Wilder Elf said. "Brenwar, come. This is for you."

Without looking up, Brenwar said, "I'm not interested."

"But you should be," Shum replied. "It's for you, from the King."

Brenwar perked up and said, "Is that so?"

Shum nodded.

"What is it?" Brenwar asked, making his way toward the table.

"I don't know. All he said to me was, 'Give this gift to Brenwar with my thanks. And tell him job well done, but it's not over. Do not fret. Aid comes. But this will help in the meantime.'"

Brenwar set the box on the table and opened it, with Ben and Bayzog watching over his shoulders. His brows popped up. A pair of metal bracers woven in intricate patterns with lustrous metal gleamed within the velvety box. Rugged, but beautiful.

"Whoa," Ben said, "I've never seen anything like that before."

Brenwar rubbed his fingers over the smooth configurations of the polished metal. The craftsmanship was beyond excellent. He'd seen them in the Dragon King's chambers and commented on them once, only to never see them again. He'd wondered what happened to them.

He turned to Shum and said, "Everything is true that you said."

"Indeed, Brenwar. Indeed."

One by one, he snapped the bracers on his thick wrists. Power and security coursed through his skin and sank into his bones. The corner of his bearded mouth turned up into a smile. When he punched his fist into his hand, it sounded like thunder in the room.

"I like that," he said, forming a battle grin. "Where's the nearest outpost of Barnabus?"

A larger fire had been lit in the chamber's fireplace, and a deer was roasting. The Roaming Rangers had been in and out the better part of the day, while Ben, Bayzog, and Brenwar made themselves as comfortable as possible. Bayzog had isolated himself in the farthest corner of the chamber, meditating on the jaxite stones he'd found on Nath. Brenwar, Shum, and Hoven discussed other locations to take Nath Dragon.

Ben sat at the end of the table, sharpening a knife with a stone, staring at Dragon.

Wake up! Will you wake up!

Over the past few months, his hopes had gone up. They were winning. Defeating the forces of Barnabus. It had seemed everything was going right, but now it had turned wrong so fast. And he knew in his heart that things truly did rest on Nath. With Dragon, victory was sure to come. He believed.

He set the stone and knife on the table and dragged his chair closer to Nath. The dragon man's face was bruised and swollen. His lips were cracked and split in three places, and two of his claws were broken. It hadn't seemed possible that anything could hurt Nath before, but it was clear now that Nath suffered as much as the rest of them.

"We can't wait forever on you," Ben said. "The war must be fought, with or without you." He took Nath's stiff paw and wrapped it around Fang's hilt. "Whenever you wake up, you're going to need this. Be ready."

Leaning back in the chair, Ben noticed something. The rise and fall of Nath's chest was gone. His features were stiff and rigid. Ben shook his head, and with sadness he announced to the others what was going on.

Brenwar was the first one there, and he said, "It's happening again. He's hibernating."

CHAPTER

13

NATH DREAMED. HE STOOD IN a cavern of darkness before a gigantic throne of stone. Two great urns glowed with wavering green fires on both sides of it. The walls howled and moaned. He tugged at his unseen bonds. His frozen limbs would not be freed.

Where am I?

His head twisted in all directions.

What is this place?

There were bodies strewn along the floor. All the races were represented. They were corpses, rotting flesh and bones. Their bodies were twisted and mangled. Their weapons shattered and broken. Everywhere.

Nath screamed, but no sound came out.

Something started laughing at him. Above him, high above in the darkness of the cavern, dragons hunched in the arches like scaled gargoyles. They laughed as only dragons can laugh. As only dragons can understand. They made it clear they were laughing at him. At his friends. At all of their futile efforts.

"Nalzambor is ours," they said in a ghostly form of Dragonese. "The Dragon Prince will soon be ours as well."

"Never!" Nath's yell was stifled by silence again. He fought at his bonds with all the might in his dragon arms. He was strong, yet powerless. "Who are you?"

A great colorful mist erupted behind the throne of stone. Something lurked inside the swirls. Its glaring eyes were bright suns. Its sharp teeth shone like stars. It emerged from the mist and took a seat on its throne. It was a dragon. One of the biggest he'd ever seen. Its horns were pointed and many, its head more skull than scales. Lightning danced all over its body and skipped between its claws. Its voice was greater than thunder.

"I am Gorn Grattack! King of this world!"

Its claws dug into the arms of its chair.

"I'm coming," it said. "I'm coming for you soon, little meddler." Gorn lifted his foot and stomped it into the ground, crushing every fallen victim into powder. "I cannot be stopped." It pointed at Nath. "And your friends will all die…" It stooped down its great head and opened its mouth wide. The fiery pit inside transformed into a vision.

Bayzog's body and staff were broken on the rocks.

War Hammer lay in a pile of ashes shaped like Brenwar's form.

Ben swung from a tree with a noose around his neck.

There were others, countless others, busted and mangled. Sasha. Pilpin. The Roaming Rangers. And hundreds of good dragons in bright shining colors.

Gorn Grattack ran roughshod through every town and village. His breath and his stare turned everything to rubble and cinders.

Gorn's mouth closed, and the huge dragon resumed his seat on the throne.

"I cannot be stopped. But you can save your friends and many others if you join me."

Nath's shock turned to rage. He redoubled his efforts against the forces that held him. Smoke and flames frothed from his mouth. He screamed at full power.

"Noooooooooooooooooooo!"

Nath snapped up, bathed in sweat. His broad scaly chest was heaving. Blinking, he rubbed his blurry eyes. He was in a poorly lit chamber that looked in deteriorating condition. Fang glowed in his paw.

Great Guzan! How long have I been gone this time?

He tore off the sheet that covered him and rose to his feet, headed toward the warm glow of an orange fire in the corner, bumping the edge of the table. A wooden tankard clonked the tiled floor. A mass of nearby figures stirred. Silently, they rose to their feet and came straight for him. He cut them off with his sword.

"Put that thing away before you cut my beard off!"

"Brenwar?" he said.

"Aye," the gruff dwarf said. He stood with Shum and Hoven beside him. "And what are you doing up already?"

"Already?" Nath said. "How long as it been? Years? Decades?" He swallowed hard. "Centuries?"

"Perhaps you should sit down," Brenwar said.

Nath sat in a chair that groaned. It felt like it would give at any moment.

Brenwar laid his hands on his shoulders. Looked him in the eyes and said, "It's only been a matter of hours. Maybe a day or so."

"Are you jesting?"

Brenwar offered the rarest smile. His stern expression was almost joyful.

"Would I jest with a dragon?"

"No," Nath said, "but I've seen you joust with them."

Brenwar let out a gusty laugh and hugged him.

"Come on! Let's go tell the others. Ben and Bayzog will be as excited as a dwarf in an ale house." Brenwar dragged Nath to his feet. "Let's get some air. Hah! Let's get some ale!" He marched forward taking the lead, arms swinging.

"Are you well, Nath?" Shum said, sliding in at his side with an easy gait. "You look flustered."

"I'm stiff and sore," he said, moving his healed jaw in wonder, "but I've been worse."

"You're sweating … like a fever," Shum added.

Nath recalled his dream. The dragon enemy Gorn Grattack. It was so real. So vivid. Images of his dead friends flashed inside his mind. Something else was eating at his mind as well. Something he'd forgotten. Something important.

"Bad dream," he said to Shum. "And I don't often dream. Not like that anyway."

"Perhaps I can help," Hoven said. "I have understanding of such things."

"Perhaps," Nath said. Something gnawed at his stomach. "How far are we from the bull dragons I battled?" His mind was hazy about the entire thing. It had been so brutal. Why had he fought the bull dragons, anyway? It seemed like forever ago. He started to retrace his steps.

"We are not far," Shum said. "Why? We found the sword you'd left behind."

Then it hit Nath like the swipe of a dragon's tail.

"The gnomes!"

"What gnomes?" Shum said.

"The crystal gnomes I rescued from the Floating City!"

CHAPTER

14

"THEY'RE GONE," NATH SAID, GLANCING back at the others. "We have to find them." He reached down and touched the stone-hard face of Flupplinn. *Why didn't they take him?*

Shaking his head, he sauntered back to the rest of the party. After leaving the ruins of the fortress, they'd ridden a full day nonstop. Nath had run, keeping pace with the Elven Steeds that hadn't broken from full speed. All rode but him.

"Surely we'll find them," Shum said, "even if they have a day or two's lead. We can find anything on two feet."

"That's not what bothers me, Shum," Nath said, looking toward the Floating City in the sky. Its dark towers shimmered in the morning sunlight, but not one single scaled monster could be found. "I fear they've been taken back there."

"Then we'll just have to get them back," Ben said to him. "If you did it once, you can do it again."

Nath rested his paw on the armored shoulder of his friend and said, "It's not so easy, I'm afraid."

"Why?" Ben asked, glancing upward. "What is up there?"

"Unimaginable terrors and perils," Nath said, "and that was only a portion of what I found. I can't risk the rest of you as well."

"But there are more of us," Ben suggested.

"True, but strength in numbers cannot overcome the overwhelming hordes of evil."

"Tell us about it then," Bayzog intervened, holding the jaxite stones in the palm of his hand. "I need to understand more about what is up there. Tell me everything."

When Nath released Ben's shoulder, the veteran warrior said with alarm, "Shades! Nath, look at your hands!"

So concerned he'd been that he hadn't even noticed the white scales that speckled all over. His palms were white, and there were white speckles and jagged lines around his claws. His heart started to swell.

"You're doing right, Nath," Ben said, gazing in wonderment. "I knew you were."

There were changes to his hind claws, as well. He grabbed Ben's shoulders and let out a joyous laugh. He gaped at the white scales and even counted each and every one. There were only two hundred and fifty-three white scales among tens of thousands of black scales, but it was a start. A good one.

All who gathered there congratulated him: Brenwar, Bayzog, Shum, Hoven, and the other Wilder Elves. They slapped his back and shook his paw. One of the Roaming Rangers even hugged him. There was a great deal of excitement inside the throng of well-tempered men.

"Nath," Bayzog said, "tell us. What happened up there? Maybe that explains this."

His mind raced through everything from the moment he had left on his quest to save Bayzog: the bull dragons, the spiny back sand crawlers, the skeletons and ghost soldiers, and ...

"The Lurker," he said.

"The what?" Ben said, leaning closer. "What is a lurker?"

Nath's mind drifted, however. He still couldn't shake the memory of that foul creature devouring him. The foul smell of its rancid breath still lingered in his nostrils. *That had to be it.* So many minds had been freed from the horrible being. Hundreds. Men, women, children of all the races, even dragons the lurker had devoured.

Snap. Snap. Snap.

"Huh?" Nath said, blinking.

Ben was snapping his fingers in his face.

"Are you still with us?" the warrior said.

"Yes," Nath said.

"Well," Ben said, hitching his leg up on a log. "Get on with it, unless you've lost your chattering tongue. And don't leave out any details."

"Alright, Ben, alright."

Nath went through everything. The floating rocks. Spying from the towers. Fighting and then running from the skeletons only to have them almost catch him on the floating rocks. The inverted stairs. The fall from the cavern into the river before finishing his battle with the bull dragons.

"You really plunged hundreds of feet with the gnomes attached to your britches?" Brenwar said, sniggering. "Tell me that again. I'd love to have seen their faces. Stupid gnomes. Always trying to be like dwarves without wits about them. Har!"

"That's quite a story Nath," Bayzog said, holding the egg-shaped stones. "Now I just have to figure out what Otter Bone needed with these."

"Well, I'm sure you'll figure it out," Nath said. "It is a shame what happened to him though. And it's disappointing he was so deceitful. I'm glad you are well now, my friend."

"I just wish you hadn't needed to risk your scales on my behalf. I don't think anyone else could have survived what you did," Bayzog said. "At least Otter Bone was honest about that."

"I would have made it," Brenwar said.

"*Sure* you would have," Ben said, laughing.

"Let's go then," Brenwar said, jumping up and heading back toward the Floating City.

Nath walked over, grabbed Brenwar, and said, "You'd never make it up the floating rocks. Give me a moment, everyone."

Nath made his way through the forest to the spot where the bull dragons had fallen. The piney forest was a disaster. Huge divots were clawed up in the ground. Any trees not fallen or broken were burnt. If he didn't know better, he would think an army of giants had stormed through there.

"They should be buried," he said, running his fingers over the great horns of one fallen foe dragon. Guilt seeped into him. A tear formed in his eye. "They're still my brothers."

He could see poachers arriving after he had gone. Perhaps they lurked in the forest already. Dragon scales, horns, claws, teeth, and meat were individually worth a fortune. The lot would bring a small kingdom. He didn't want to let the evil Clerics of Barnabus get their hands on it, but there were other things he had to do.

He sighed.

For decades, he had protected the dragons. They'd been nearly impossible to find. Now, they cropped up everywhere. And they wanted to kill him.

Where in Nalzambor are the good ones?

Again, he spied the city looming above the river, between the clouds. He could see the skeletons still searching the streets for him. Countless heads of the undead clawing for his throat.

Perhaps there is another way. A flying potion, perhaps.

His instincts fired. He wheeled around and found himself facing Shum and Hoven.

"One of our brethren found tracks," Shum said. "Gnome tracks."

"Up the riverbank?" Nath said.

"Yes."

"Good," Nath said, "they listened to me. How far?"

"Two miles upriver, toward the River Cities. I've dispatched more Roaming Rangers to follow after. He said the trail was only hours old, but that they moved in a hurry." Shum said.

"In a hurry how?" said Nath.

"As in, something else was already tracking them. Big. Heavy. "

"What?"

"Tracks he'd never seen before."

Nath's blood raced. If anything happened to the gnomes, it would be his fault.

"Let's go then!"

CHAPTER

15

"NATH," BAYZOG SAID, "TELL ME more about the dream. What did you see?"

"A moment," Nath said.

Bayzog caught him by the elbow.

"We might not get another moment," he said. "Let the Roaming Rangers handle this. They're more than capable."

Nath pulled away with a fierce look at Bayzog. A dangerous element lurked behind his golden eyes. Power ready to lash out at any moment.

"You have to be able to rely on others," Bayzog said, easing the Elderwood Staff in front of his chest. He drew strength from it. Readied words of power on his lips.

Nath avoided his eyes. "They might miss something."

"They won't," Bayzog said. "You know better than that."

It had been half a day since they departed. The gnomes' trail drifted from the river and went deeper into the forest. According to Nath, whatever chased the gnomes wasn't trying to kill them. It wanted to trap them somewhere.

"We're close," Nath said, flaring his nostrils. "I picked up the scent minutes ago." He'd been running hard, with Bayzog following on horseback. Brenwar, Ben, and one more Ranger were behind them, somewhere. When Nath slowed, he clutched his side, wincing. He clutched at it again.

"That shard in you," Bayzog said, "it's gone deeper."

"I'm fine."

Bayzog could see the weight of the world in Nath's eyes. And something else. Worry.

"No secrets, Nath. Tell me about the dream you mentioned."

Nath shook his head and kept on walking.

Bayzog could tell his friend had let something slip out that he didn't want to explain. But the excitement of the conversation led right to it.

"Nath," Bayzog said, catching up with him. "I must insist."

Nath jerked around.

"Alright!" He took a breath. "Alright then." Nath sat on the pine-needled forest floor and leaned against a tree. "Gorn Grattack."

Bayzog recoiled and lost his breath. Recovering, he kneeled by Nath's side and said, "What about him?"

"He appeared in my dream. He spoke. He said he was coming to get me," Nath said, rubbing his forehead. "Why would I have a dream about that, Bayzog? Why?" He glanced at his claws. His eyes traced the white patches of scales on them. "If I'm doing right, then why do I feel so wrong?"

Bayzog felt a chill inside his chest. His hand rested on the amulet he shared with his family. His son Samaz often had dark dreams. He never told Bayzog, but he did tell his mother, Sasha, who in turn confided in him. He worried how they were doing.

"You've been through much, Nath," Bayzog said, trying to sound reassuring. "And we cannot understand the changes you've been through or the weight on your great shoulders. But Nath, we believe in you. We wouldn't have made it this far if we hadn't."

Nath gazed up at him with a long look in his eyes and said, "I'm going to have to leave."

"No, we've talked about that."

"But Bayzog, Gorn Grattack said he was coming for me. He called me a meddler. He said he would kill all my friends." Nath's hand fell on Fang's hilt. "I can't protect you from him. His might, Bayzog. I could feel it. Nothing ever shook my marrow before, aside from my father." He shook his head. "How can that be? How can Gorn Grattack still live?"

Bayzog wanted to pinch Nath's lips shut. Gorn Grattack had been the greatest dragon in the last dragon war. The champion of evil. The enslaver of the world. So far as the wizard knew, none had uttered the evil dragon's name or even written it in five hundred years. Since the last Great Dragon War was won. Saying the name, the old ones said, was the same as saying a curse. Few even knew about him in today's world, except for the older elves, dwarves, and dragons. But careful measures were taken to make the name be forgotten.

Bayzog patted Nath's knee and said, "Remember Nath, evil lies. I'd venture that he wants to separate you from those who look out for you. You'll be easier to conquer alone. That's what they want. That's what they always want."

"I don't want to see my friends die because of me," Nath said.

"That's not your choice. It's ours."

Nath sulked for a bit, then stretched out his arm and let Bayzog help him to his feet. Placing his dragon paws on Bayzog's shoulders, he said, "You're a true friend, but I have to put an end to this."

"No, *we* have to put an end to this, Nath. And don't forget, your father says more help is coming." Bayzog rubbed Nath's corded forearms. The scales were smoother than wet river stones. "But it would be nice if we all had tough skin such as this. Perhaps I can create a spell for that one day."

"Ho!" From high in his saddle, Brenwar yelled.

Ben and one of the Roaming Rangers fell in behind them. There was an Elven Steed for each of them now, aside from Nath.

"What's going on here?" Brenwar said.

"Speaking of thick skin," Nath mumbled.

Bayzog allowed a grin.

"Harrumph! What's so amusing?" Brenwar's nose twitched. "I smell secrecy. Out with it."

"Bad dreams," Nath said. "Bad dreams. Let's walk and talk."

Clearing the air did little to ease Brenwar's disposition, or Ben's either. They wouldn't let Nath out of their sight for anything, especially now, after what he'd told them. However, unlike before, it didn't bother him so much. The freedom Nath longed for was replaced with something greater: the companionship of his friends.

"Gnomes," Brenwar huffed. "Of all the silly things, I'm tracking gnomes. Why don't we chase after some bearded kobolds next? Hmmm?"

The dwarven fighter had been grumbling about it for almost an hour. He referred to the gnomes as "short men without stature" and "goblins' stupid cousins." There was a litany of things dwarves didn't like, and they loved to talk about them all.

Shum returned. His horse was lathered up, and there was a spark behind his stony eyes.

"You found them," Nath said.

"Indeed. Less than a league."

Nath hated to ask the next question, but he did. "And what is their condition?"

"Alive, we believe. They've managed to traverse the cliffs farther east, and we think they are hidden in the caves." Shum shook his head. "The caves are many."

"And what of the creature that pursues them?" Nath said. "Any sign of it?"

"Its tracks stop at the edge of the cliff and vanish."

"So, the Roaming Rangers have initiated a search in the cliffs."

Shum shook his head.

"Why not?" Nath said.

"Above the cliffs ... there be dragons."

CHAPTER

16

THE CLIFFS WERE SHEER, BUT manageable. The stone surface was cut away in parts, forming level paths carved out long ago by another civilization. It reminded Nath of the rock-carved goblin fort in the Shale Hills where he had battled the necromancer Corzan. That seemed a lifetime ago.

The footing wouldn't be difficult, even for a gnome. Vines hung over the rocky edges, and trees were abundant for climbing. Any cautious person could make the climb. A desperate person just as well. And there were plenty of caves dotting the cliff face, any of which was big enough to provide shelter.

But dragons circled above.

A dozen grey scalers.

Bigger than men.

The hunters of Barnabus.

"Brenwar," Nath said, "can you make anything of the cliffs? Could the gnomes find another way to escape?"

"Solid," he said. "Those caves aren't carved, just porous spots in the rock face. Those ledges were roads once. Nothing more." He squinted. "That's why they remain. Only one way up and down, and we're looking at it. If gnomes had any sense, they'd head back down."

The gnomes had gone up for a reason, though. Something chased them. A predator. Swift and cunning. Nath had seen strange paw prints in the dirt. It was the faintest marking. Almost ghostly. Neither he nor the Wilder Elves could make out the full print, but Nath felt he should know it.

"Something else lurks down here," he said to them all. "Be alert. I'm getting an odd feeling."

Above, a grey scaler dove through the sky and neared one of the caves. A hovering bird of prey, it screeched at the hole.

Nath's ears caught the twang of a bowstring loosed, and he watched an arrow whiz through the air and tear through the dragon's wing.

It squawked, wings batting in fury and lifting it higher into the sky's safety among the others.

"Rangers are posted along those rocks," Shum said, pointing the way. "We've been fending them off since we got here. They can provide cover while we search the caves, but at some point or another we will have to battle those dragons. And there's more of them than us."

"Well, Barnabus wants the gnomes back—" Nath said,

"And I say we let them have the gnomes," Brenwar interjected.

Nath glared at Brenwar and continued, "and *we* won't let that happen. Shum, have your Rangers keep their bows ready. I think Ben can help keep them off our backs."

Ben nodded at him.

"Shum, Hoven, and I will go up."

"And what will I do?" Brenwar said. "Stand down here and throw rocks at them?"

Shum glanced at Brenwar's new bracers and said, "I think that's an excellent idea."

Brenwar looked at his wrists.

"Ho! I think I like how yer thinking, elf!" He clapped his hands together. "Come Ben, help me fetch some stones."

"Look!" Ben said, pointing toward the sky, loading his bow.

Two grey scalers dove toward the rocks where Shum's archers were posted. Arrows ricocheted off the dragons' hides and horns. A third dragon slipped behind them. Arrows zinged through the air. Some found a soft spot, others skipped off their hides before all three dragons soared back high in the air. It all happened in seconds.

"They test our forces," Shum said. "Rousting us from our roost. But we can hold them. The Roaming Rangers are outstanding marksmen, and our elven arrows seek their soft spots and slow their efforts."

"Yer arrows need to kill them," Brenwar said.

"Easier said than done," Shum said. "I've seen dragons fly with a dozen arrows in them. I've even seen heavy crossbow bolts skip off their bellies. That's why we go for the wings. It makes them mad, but it slows them."

"Alright then," Nath said, "then let's get moving." He then said to Bayzog, "And I expect you to come up with something to deal with those dragons before we find those gnomes."

"I will," Bayzog reassured him.

Nath nodded, headed for the cliffs. He halted at the sound of a blood-curdling cry.

"That was one of mine," Shum decried. He rushed toward the sound, swift as a gazelle.

Nath kept close a half step behind.

In seconds, they arrived at the spot in the rocks were the scream came from.

"NO!" Shum cried out, rushing to his friend's aid. It was too late.

The Ranger was mauled to pieces.

CHAPTER

17

THE ROAMING RANGERS, STEELY IN resolve, had long looks on their stony faces. Shum and Hoven knelt beside their fallen brother, laid on hands, and began chanting in ancient Elvish. As they did, other Roaming Rangers filed in, smooth in gait, bright elven steel on their broad hips. A dark fire burned in their eyes. They joined the chanting.

Bayzog closed his eyes and did some chanting of his own, and a magical shield covered the mourning Wilder Elves. He beckoned everyone closer.

Brenwar and Ben moved in closer only because Nath did, they were so entranced by the ritual.

Nath felt a pit inside his gut. He recalled the last time a Roaming Ranger fell. Shum. Somehow, Sansla Libor had brought him back from the dead. He checked the sky. There was no sign of the winged ape, but the dragons crowed evil sounds. Mocking. Taunting. But it was not them who had done this. It was something else.

Over a minute had passed when Shum stood up again and said, "He is gone." Some of the Roaming Rangers lifted the bloody body of their brother and vanished into the woods. "They will return, shortly," Shum said, watching them go. "And then we shall hunt this menace down and end it."

The Roaming Rangers Shum and Hoven, dressed in heavy cloaks and woodland garb, stood broad and rangy. Long flaxen hair braided and beaded. Well framed, broad, and as rugged as the wilderness they called home.

Nath had no doubt that whatever took their brother would pay, if he let them chase after it, but he thought that might not be the best plan.

"We have a plan to save the gnomes from Barnabus," Nath reminded them, eyeing the cliffs while another dragon dove, landed, and began prowling the ledges. "And we need to act quickly, regardless of the circumstance. What do you suggest, Shum?"

Roaming Rangers were hard to read, both Shum and his brother Hoven. But what Nath could not see, he could feel. Anger. Anxiousness. The Roaming Rangers wanted to let loose on something. Nath couldn't blame them.

Shum's long fingers drummed the hilts of his swords. Eyeing the sky, he said, "You and I will still go up. Hoven will stay here and keep an eye on the rest." His narrow eyes scanned the woods. "Whatever skulks in these woods, we'll be ready for next time."

"Are you sure?" Nath said.

"We are Roaming Rangers, young dragon," Shum said, whisking out his swords. "We pledge our lives to the greater good of Nalzambor. Chaldun's death honors his life." Without another word, he sprinted for the cliffs.

Bayzog's mouth hung open. He wanted to speak with Nath. Instead, he found himself gaping at Nath and Shum's sprint for the cliffs. The pair of warriors didn't slow, climbing the brush-heavy cliff-face like a pair of monkeys. He'd never seen men so large move so fast and fluidly.

"What are ye thinking, elf?" Brenwar said, holding a large rock on his shoulder.

"I'm thinking we need to stay close," he said. "I believe our enemies are determined to divide our forces."

"That's what I would do," Brenwar said, dropping his stone, "and I don't assume I'll be able to do any rock fetching without an escort." He punched his fist into his hand. "But I don't need one. And those Roaming Rangers need more armor on."

"I thought they had armor?"

"Light armor," Brenwar said, tapping his breastplate, "and not dwarven."

Bayzog surveyed the spot where the Roaming Ranger Chaldun had fallen. A pair of his brother Wilder Elves had returned and begun covering all the blood with dirt. It left him with a sick feeling. He could still see the elf's body, torn and broken. Just like Otter Bone and Horse Neck. Life taken like a branch snapped. He found Ben's eyes.

"Let's get our backs to the rocks and keep our eyes on the sky," the warrior said, unhitching Akron from his back. *Snap. Clatch. Snap.* "And everywhere else we aren't looking."

Hoven walked over and said, "Follow my men and secure your positions."

"What are you going to do?" Bayzog asked.

"I'll be near." The big elf hopped on his horse and eased into the trees.

Moments later, the other Roaming Rangers led them and the horses into the outcroppings near the bottom of the cliff. One laid his hand on Bayzog's shoulder. His face was long and heavy, more so than the others. Younger too. "Stay close to the steeds. If trouble comes close, they'll tell you." He rubbed one under the neck and scanned the surroundings. "They were too far when the creature struck. An error on our part." He dropped a heavy sack near Brenwar's feet, smiling. "Perhaps you can use these, dwarf." He drifted away, set his back to the bottom of the cliff, and loaded his long bow. All the Roaming Rangers Bayzog could see were poised and waiting.

Brenwar dumped the sack over and picked it up. Dozens of fist-sized round stones tumbled out.

"Was he being wise with me?"

Ben chuckled. "It's better than nothing, and probably more accurate than the rocks in your head." He nocked his first arrow. "I'm ready to get on with it."

Brenwar threw the stones back into the sack and hefted it over his shoulder, saying, "Soon enough, we'll see who hits the most dragons with what."

With a tight grip on the Elderwood Staff, Bayzog tried to look past all the recent horrors he had seen. He was formidable now, and it was not time to get rattled, but he couldn't shrug off the dread his body felt.

A spell, perhaps.

Out of the corner of his eye, he caught another dragon diving out of the sky. A volley of arrows loosed.

Twang! Twang! Twang! Twang! Twang! Twang!

Pummeled and feathered, the dragon spiraled downward in a tight circle, crashed into the cliff, and tumbled to the surface.

The other dragons let out a feverish howl, folded their wings, and streaked toward the earth.

Bayzog summoned his powers.

Brenwar cocked back his stone-filled hands and roared.

"Incoming!"

CHAPTER

18

RUNNING FULL SPEED, NATH TRAVERSED the ledges and cut into the grey scaler's path.

The black-winged dragon's dark tail whipped fiercely into the rocks. Its eyes glowed with fire.

It reared back, hissing. Eyes narrowing, jaws slavering, it clawed its way toward Nath.

He beckoned it onward with his claws.

"Come on then," Nath said in Dragonese. "I have something for you."

Serpentine neck down, horns lowered, it charged.

Nath snatched it by the horns and shoved its face into the ledge. Jaws snapping, the dragon thrashed and bucked. The awesome strength of its power tried to sling Nath off the cliff. He held on. Dug his clawed toes into the dirt and started shoving it backward. The man-sized beast roared. Its neck jerked. Its tail flashed over its back and smote Nath on the head. Once. Twice. Fresh blood ran in his eyes.

"Enough of this!"

Nath slammed its head into the rock face. Once. Twice. He cranked its horns around and twisted the creature to its back. Its front legs and arms clawed at him like a wild cat's. Pinning it down, he kept twisting.

"Yield!" Nath said. "Yield or die!"

The muscles inside its scaly neck strained and resisted.

Muscles pumping, Nath twisted harder. Its claws scraped all over his body. Blood dripped in his eyes. *It's me or him.* He heaved.

Crack!

The grey scaler went limp. The glow in its eyes extinguished.

Lathered in sweat, he raised his fist into the air and yelled up to the other dragons, "Which one of you traitors is next!"

He shoved the dragon off the ledge.

"No mercy for him! No mercy for any of you!"

Nath had had enough. These dragons were vicious killers. Controlled or not. And he wasn't about to risk any more of his friends dying if he could help it. He spat blood. Eyed the dragons. Some circled. Some dove into a volley of arrows and stones. Torn, he rushed for the nearest cave, calling for the gnomes.

Shum dashed along the narrow ledges, ducking in and out of the small caves. He hollered, whistled, and crept inside, but so far all of the shallow caves were empty. Fleet of foot, he sped to the next cave. A grey scaler dropped out of the sky, hovering in the air by the blustering power of its wings, cutting him off. Swords first, Shum darted in. Elven steel struck in a fury, driving the beast backward out of range.

Shum slid by and into the next cave.

In a second, the dragon had hemmed him inside. A stream of liquid fire spewed from its mouth.

Shum twisted away, lunged forward, and hacked into its nose.

The dragon retreated, filled its lungs again, and spewed dark smoke into the hole.

Blinded, Shum started coughing and hacking. He chopped his swords at any sound of movement. He fought to hold his breath but couldn't. His coughing increased, and his eyes began to burn. His elven hearing picked up the sound of claws getting near. He focused on what he'd already seen and readied his elven blades.

His coughing stopped.

All fell quiet.

He hacked again.

The dragon pounced right on top of him.

From horseback, Hoven removed a short spear packed behind his saddle. He flipped it hand over hand once, lengthening it. A second time it lengthened once more, extending over six feet in length. It was a special weapon of the Roaming Rangers, elven made magic called a Dragon Needle.

Trotting through the forest with the ongoing battle ringing in his ears, Hoven scanned the ground. There were no tracks of the monster he believed killed one of his brothers, nor any strange impressions in the ground, just a gentle wind with the smell of death in it.

His steed snorted and nickered to a halt before moving forward again.

Hoven, heavy and well-built like his brother Shum, towered in the saddle. He was everything a Wilder Elf represented: stalwart, alert, formidable. An extension of the wild land he thrived in. Covered in skins, leather, and light elven armor, there wasn't anything the wilderness soldier was unprepared for—until today.

Something had slaughtered one of his brethren. Something he could not track. It was as allusive as Sansla Libor. His mind ran through the catalog of everything he had tracked and hunted over the centuries. Giants and orcs. Witches and warlocks. Pixlyns and nymphs. Dragons and dalumphs. But nothing as curious as this.

He tugged on the reins. Something had pushed through the underbrush, and there were fresh drops of blood on the ground. He lowered his spear, poked it into the thicket, and pushed it aside. There were bloodstains on the leaves. There had been blood on Chaldun's blades as well. It was Hoven's hope that the creature bled, but how had it come this far without letting blood until now? Perhaps it was Chaldun's blood he saw instead.

He poked the brush and scanned the higher branches. Horse hooves stamped beneath him. The supple muscles in his back tightened. He could feel a heavy gaze on his neck. He eased his head around.

Large burning cat's eyes locked on his, sending a chill through Hoven's bones.

He jerked the reins and wheeled his spear around. The dragon cat creature was gone, but he'd heard a description of the strange beast before.

"Feline Fury ... come, kitty, kitty, kitty..."

Dragons diving, Brenwar launched his first stone. The creature spiraled away, but the stone exploded into the cliffs beyond it. He grunted with approval. The mystic might from his bracers surged through his arms. He scooped up more rocks and started chucking them one right after the other. One caught a flying dragon square behind the wings. It squawked and spun into the cliff.

"Yes!"

Above, the dragons dove and spit fire.

The Roaming Rangers and Ben volleyed arrow after arrow.

Bayzog's fingers unleashed shards of fire that blasted into the dragons.

They dove, spit. Fire charred the rocks. Burnt through armor and flesh. The fighting force held its ground. Unloosed everything they had, filling the skies with the roaring sounds of angry dragons. They were repelled again and again.

"Eat that!" Brenwar yelled, hurling a rock into a grey scaler's spitting mouth. It tumbled from the sky and crashed into the ground.

Two Roaming Rangers rushed in with fine elven steel and cut it down. It was one of several dragons that died, but they kept coming. The skies became thick with them.

"Keep fighting!" Brenwar yelled, chucking another rock. "We have to hold them off long enough for Nath to find those blasted gnomes." He noticed a dragon snaking along the cliff ledges. He hefted up a large stone over his head and heaved with all his might. It exploded into the dragon's side, knocking it off the ledge. "Woohoo!"

The others let out a cheer, hoisting their bows high in the air. The grey scalers retreated and hung high in the sky.

"Well done, Brenwar," Ben said, slapping him on the shoulder. "I don't think a catapult could have launched that rock with such power."

"Of course not," Brenwar said, "unless it was a dwarven catapult."

"Of course," Ben said, mopping the sweat from his brow. His armor was charred black in spots. Eyeing the sky, he added. "But there are still many more of them."

"Bah," Brenwar said, "they cannot handle my great feats. And the next rock I toss will be bigger than the last. Ha!"

A great shadow blotted out the sun, covering them all. It glided past them.

"What in Narnum is that?" Brenwar said, lifting his bearded face to the sky. He glimpsed a pair of claws as great as he'd ever seen.

"Dragon ..." Ben said with dismay. "Big dragon!"

CHAPTER

19

NATH SCRAMBLED FROM ONE CAVE to the next, calling out in the fragments of Gnomish he knew. More than a hundred caves dotted the steep cliff face. Hollowed holes. Dens. Cavities. Some deep, most shallow. Unless you could fly, it would take at least a day to search them all.

"Snarggell! Snarggell!"

His keen eyes scanned for traces of their passing. His nostrils flared. But their scent was gone. Ears peeled, he listened for anything out of the ordinary, but his search had garnered nothing. Coming out of another cavern, he cursed, "Sultans of Sulfur!" He glared down at the treetops over a hundred feet below. The battle raged on. He struck the rock face with his fist.

"Ooch..."

Nath's golden dragon eyes popped wide. He poked at the rock with his clawed finger, tracing an abnormal outline. *How'd I miss that?* A gnomish body had melded with the rocks. Two stony eyes gazed at him.

"Snarggell?"

"Go away," it said. "Go!"

"It *is* you," Nath said, staring into the hardened eyelids. "Listen, Snarggell. You have to come with me. Those dragons won't stop until they have you."

"No," the rock retorted.

"You can't stay like this forever," Nath pleaded.

"We can outlast our enemies like this," the gnome said. "Now go!"

Nath stuck his clawed finger on the crystal gnome's nose, applied a little pressure, and said, "I will claw you out of there if I have to."

Snarggell's eyes crossed, but his rocky lips fell silent.

Nath wasn't about to abandon the gnomes to their stubborn and over-preserving nature now. Barnabus wanted the gnomes back, and Nath vowed to himself that would not happen.

"Snarggell," he said, "you must come along. Your kind, my kind, and every kind is in danger. Can you not see that now?"

Snarggell squeezed his eyes shut.

Nath leaned back against the rock wall. He hadn't spent much time with gnomes in the past. He wasn't sure what made them tick.

"The people below are giving their lives for you. I just wanted to make sure you knew that." He sighed. "And by the end of the day I might be dead too."

"Good."

"What!" Nath turned and glared at the gnome. "What do you mean, 'good'?"

"Rescue Murderer," the gnome's rocky lips mumbled. "Rescue Murderer."

Nath popped Snarggell in the belly.

"Oof!"

"Well, I'll tell you this much," Nath said, voice rising, "there's about to be another gnome murdered." He got face to face with Snarggell, buckled his brows, and said in his most threatening voice, "You had better come with me now, gnome. I'm not fooling around." He drew his fist back, squeezed it so tight that his knuckles cracked, and added. "Don't make me repeat myself."

"Alright," Snarggell said, but it was barely audible.

"What!"

"Alright. Just give me a moment."

The crystal gnome eased out of his spot. In moments, his rocky skin resumed its fleshy form. "Happy?"

"No," Nath said. "Where are the others?"

In gnomish, Snarggell called out names, one by one. They were closer than Nath thought. A few seconds later, they'd all gathered near the ledge. Many remained tucked inside the caves and dens, with nervous faces.

"Well," Snarggell said, "when are you going to finish off the rest of those ... those ..."

"Dragons," Nath said.

All the gnomes froze with their little necks twisted up.

Nath thought a great cloud had blocked the sun, but the enormous beating of two wings proved otherwise. Eyes to the sky, he exclaimed in awe, "Great Dragon!"

Thrashing in the dark smoke, Shum somehow seized the dragon claws tearing at his throat.

The dragon's jaws snapped. Its hind claws ripped through his garb. Its relentless strength pushed Shum's reserve to the limits.

Choking, gasping, fighting, he gathered his feet under the grey scaler's belly and launched it into the cave wall.

The monster let out a shrill shriek and came clawing after him again.

Eyes squeezed shut, Shum's fingers searched through the dirt for his blade. Finding the hilt crafted for his hand, he lashed out. Steel penetrated scale.

The beast recoiled with a fearsome howl.

Shum forced his way along the wall toward the mouth of the cave, finding the fresh air outside. With blood all over his tattered Roaming Ranger garb, he backed down the berm and opened his burning eyes, still coughing.

Smoke rolled out of the cave, and the grey scaler slithered out, hissed at him, leapt off the ledge, and took to the sky.

Shum was glad of it, pressing his back to the rock wall and watching it go upward to join the ranks of the other dragons. Shum gasped. Something else loomed over the top of the cliff. An immense dragon. Dark-winged, bull-horned, and bull-necked, its iron hide was many shimmering colors. Plated bronze scales covered it from neck to belly. Its oversized claws were the biggest Shum had ever saw. It opened its great mouth wide and let out an ear-splitting roar that shook the valley.

Nothing moved until the humongous dragon's neck stretched out. Its piercing eyes scoured the green channels below. A huge dragon eye fixed on Shum. Intelligent. Cunning. Burning with evil.

Shum's heart raced.

The dragon's eye drifted away, and Shum's gaze drifted back, eyes probing the monstrous beast for weakness.

There seems to be none. But if it can breathe, it can bleed.

The feline fury, a monster with the face of a great cat and the body and wings of a dragon, had disappeared. Hoven spun his horse around, full circle, with his great spear lowered. He sniffed the air. Perked his ears. But the monster, bigger than his horse, had simply vanished.

Nothing moves that fast, except magic.

With a gnawing feeling in his gut, he galloped back to the rest of the party.

CHAPTER
20

Along the ledge, Nath and the gnomes behind him hung back with bated breath. Even Nath couldn't withhold his surprise at the shear enormity of the beast that surveyed them all. Though it didn't have the girth of the wingless titan dragons, it was still almost as big. A terror of the skies. And Nath knew the dragon beast the moment he saw it. Its name was Inferno. A Sky Raider. An armored flying fortress. Nath had heard of him but had never seen him before.

Snarggell punched him in the back.

"What have you done?" the gnome cried. "What have you done? How will we protect ourselves against that?"

"I'll protect you," Nath said.

"Against that?" the gnome leader shook his head. "No, Rescue Murderer. An army of you could not stand against that."

Nath tossed his hair back.

"Watch it."

Inferno. Of all the great beasts. He makes most dragons look like featherless chickens. Nath didn't think the likes of Inferno would join the ranks of anyone. The sky raiders were highly individual. Harriers of the sky. Nath had dallied with some in his past, but they had been smaller. Iron-scaled braggarts that boasted about their leader. And talked down about Nath's father. They mocked his father. "What kind of king rules beneath the ground?" they said. "A cowardly king, perhaps?" The memories stirred Nath.

"We're leaving," Snarggell said.

"There's nowhere to go now," Nath said. "You had best stay with me." He cocked his head. A figure in dark robes traipsed along Inferno's neck. *A woman!* She didn't stop walking until she stood between the horns of Inferno's monstrous head. A waterfall of smoke poured from its mouth. Nath absorbed every detail of her being. Long raven-black hair pinned up in a crown of silver leaves. A stunning face with soft crimson lips. *Who is she?*

She parted her lips and spoke in a voice of thunder that echoed over the valley.

"I AM THE HIGH PRIESTESS OF BARNABUS." She spread her arms wide. "I AM SELENE!"

Nath's cheeks flushed red. Fire erupted inside his veins. The leader of his greatest enemy stood right there. *If I only had Akron!*

A black-scaled tail snaked out from beneath her robes and slithered side to side.

The rising heat inside him cooled. His blistering thoughts turned to ice.

"No," he muttered, glancing at his own scales. "It can't be."

In her enhanced voice, Selene continued.

"LEAVE MY GNOMES. MOVE ON!" Her lips turned up in a sneer. "OR THIS VALLEY WILL BE FILLED WITH YOUR BURNING FLESH!" Her tail rapped Inferno's skull. A volcanic blast of fire burst from his snout. "AND ALL THE RIVER CITIES WILL BURN AS WELL!"

"Never!" Brenwar bellowed, hurling a stone into the sky. Zinging through the air, it bounced off the sky raider's nose.

The gigantic dragon's thin lips curled back, revealing its enormous teeth.

All of the Roaming Rangers held their bowstrings tight along their cheeks. Elbows cocked back. Eyes alert and ready.

"Hold," Bayzog said to them all. "We need to make sure the gnomes are secured."

"They're with Nath," Ben said, pointing with his eyes. "And that's safe enough." He glanced over toward the great dragon and the woman standing on its head. "Guzan, that beast is big."

"We've taken bigger," Brenwar growled, "and not so long ago, if you care to remember." He cocked back another stone.

Staying the dwarf's arm, Bayzog said, "Don't. The slightest provocation might have a dire consequence."

Brenwar let the stone drop and picked up War Hammer and twirled it around.

"The beast will feel this."

Bayzog rose his voice.

"Perhaps, but not without severe repercussions! I say hold!"

Brenwar scowled and said, "Then you need to think of something, Wizard. And think of something quick." He glanced into the sky. The hard-boiled dwarf's eyes enlarged like moons. "I mean quick!"

The part-elf wizard twisted his head around. Dragon's wings beat from high in the sky. There were at least another half dozen sky raiders. They weren't bigger than the great one on the cliff, but all were the size of bull dragons. Flames and smoke puffed from their mouths.

"I'm going to need another hammer," Brenwar said.

Ben loaded an exploding arrow that Nath had licked and said, "Maybe you should check that chest of yours."

Brenwar shrugged. "Perhaps."

"This has suddenly become more severe than I ever imagined," Bayzog said.

It wasn't a moment. It was *the* moment. Bayzog's first inclination was to get the gnomes to safety. But they were too far away for him to do that. His next option was to protect the others from forces the likes he had never faced before. He would need all of his might and the Elderwood Staff as well.

He held his staff tight to his robes and harnessed its power. In moments, he became aware of everything at once. Nath and the gnomes. The dragons and High Priestess Selene. A rushing threat from the forest.

The Elven Steeds nickered, stamped their hooves.

"Be alert!" he said, pointing with his staff, "More danger nears!"

A large cat-like dragon appeared, perched on a nearby rock.

A circle of defenders formed around Bayzog. It was the beast from the caves inside the crater, but bigger. And with wings.

"I remember you," Brenwar said.

Twang! Twang! Twang!

Arrows ripped through its body harmlessly, disappearing into the forest.

"A ghost," Ben said.

It bared its teeth and pounced over everyone's head, landing right on top of Bayzog. Claws dug into his shoulder, pinning him to the ground. Its jaws clamped down on the Elderwood staff.

Blinded by pain, Bayzog didn't hear Brenwar and Ben's screams, but in the moment of life or death, he belted out a cry of his own.

"*Evvarynnosst!*"

Arcane energies erupted through his body into his staff.

The feline fury leapt ten feet off the ground. It landed in a maelstrom of striking swords and hammers. Smoking, the feline fury went wild. It screeched and howled. Claws and tail lashed out.

Roaming Rangers fell and flew through the air.

Brenwar swung War Hammer into its head.

Whiff!

The hammer passed right through it.

"By my beard!"

The dragon-cat sprang away, spread its wings, and few toward the clouds. Arrows whizzed right through it.

"Bayzog!" Ben said, rushing toward him, "Are you alright?"

There was blood all over the wizard's robes, and his shoulders burned like fire. He couldn't lift his arms. The Elderwood Staff trembled in his hands.

He blocked out the pain and said, "It knew."

"It knew what?" Ben asked, propping up his head.

"It wanted the staff," he replied. "It wanted to kill me. I could feel it. See the murder in its eyes." He stared at Selene. She stood looking down with her arms crossed over her chest. "She sent it to kill me. She set this trap for us all."

The sky raiders dropped from the sky. Their scaled hides crushed the trees, snapped branches under their bulks. Each and every dragon had a hungry look in its leering eyes. The small party was hemmed in between the dragons and the cliff wall.

Just then, Hoven returned with a great spear in his hands. "They play games with us," he said, scanning their enemies. "And they can do that with superior forces. Well played."

Bayzog wondered if Otter Bone set them up. Was he killed by the dragons because he was a threat, or because he had something to hide? He feared they had given the armies of Barnabus exactly what they wanted. *By the Elves of Elohim!* Nath Dragon.

CHAPTER
21

SMALL. FOR THE FIRST TIME in his life, Nath felt that way. It was the first time he felt pinned in by a situation that overwhelmed him. Below, his friends were pinned to the cliffs by sky raiders. Fierce winged behemoths whose myriad of scales glinted in the sun. Their spiked tails swished back and forth like cedars.

Feeling despair, Nath glanced up at the woman fixed on Inferno's head, clenched his fists, and looked back.

"Get in that cave," he ordered the gnomes.

"But—"

"Now!"

Shum pulled himself up on the ledge using the vines that hung over the rim. His steely eyes never left the terror that lurked above. "Danger comes in many shapes and sizes, but even a needle can be the gravest threat," he said.

"I'm going up," Nath said, grabbing a vine. "You stay with them."

"Nath," Shum said, "I don't think that is wise. We don't even know what may be concealed beyond the rim of the cliff."

"Well," Nath said, hoisting himself up. "It couldn't be any worse that it is."

Shum grabbed his ankle, and with a fierce tug, he pulled him back down.

"We came to help," the Wilder Elf said. "Not to turn you loose. Help is coming, Nath. We just need to hold out."

Nath eyed him.

"What kind of help?"

"That, I do not know."

"TIME IS SHORT," Selene said from her perch. "BRING FORTH THE GNOMES."

"Do you see any other way out of this?" Nath said. "We can't run. We can't hide. Any sudden moves will destroy us, Shum." His jaw muscles clenched. "That's Inferno up there. A killer. There won't be any mercy from him or his murderous brothers. Sultans of Sulfur! Are the good dragons ever coming?"

Shum's expression remained frozen when he said, "The dragons have capricious timelines. Of course, you know that."

Nath needed to hit something. Lash out. If another dragon war was about to start, then where in the ten lakes were the good dragons? Had Barnabus overtaken them all? Killed them? Could the jaxite stones win them back? He needed answers.

But first, he needed to secure the safety of his friends.

"I can at least go up there, meet our enemy face to face, and buy time." He grabbed the vines. "You have to figure something out."

Snarggell popped his head out of the cave and said, "Just turn us over. It's our lives, and we can do what we will. And no one else has to die."

"Countless have died already thanks to the jaxite stones, you fickle gnome." He pointed at him.

"Don't try to go anywhere, because I'll be coming back for you." He grabbed some vines and surged up, leaving the others behind.

Ben watched Nath climb up the cliffs with Fang strapped to his back. He glanced back at the dragons that sat poised to strike less the fifty feet from him. His heart pounded in his chest. The heat from the dragon's breath stung his eyes. He wiped them and resumed his focus on Nath.

"What is he doing?" he said.

"Is he going to fight that dragon without me?" Brenwar added.

Bayzog shook his head, saying, "I hope he's not doing what I think he's doing."

"What's that?" said Ben, dressing Bayzog's wounds.

"Buying time."

"That's not such a bad idea, is it?"

"He'll have to bargain," Bayzog said, wincing.

The last of Nath's red hair and black scales disappeared over the rim.

"Bayzog, didn't you teach me that you can't bargain with evil?"

Brenwar tossed his hammer down.

The elf just nodded his head yes.

Clearing the ledge, Nath unslung Fang and rested him on his broad shoulder.

Only a fool approaches man-sized dragon fangs without a Fang of his own. Or an orc.

Nath took a breath and made a bead through the tall grasses where Selene and Inferno waited, overlooking the valley. His dragon heart pumped hard and fast, heightening his senses. He had never feared anything but failure and harm to others, until now. He was facing her. A woman with scales the same as his.

Bayzog's words echoed in his thoughts: *The black dragons shall return again, and the final war shall be waged.*

Above, the grey scalers circled.

A stiff breeze from the distant woodland cooled his hot neck. Nath stopped short of Inferno's tail, which coiled like a snake in the grass. The great dragon's head remained at a steady perch, but its eye glared back at him.

That's when Selene turned and Nath caught his breath.

She was glorious. She was a dragoness.

She parted her crimson lips and said, "Where are my gnomes? Are they hidden in the sheath of your pretty sword?"

Nath's tongue clove to the roof of his mouth. Her speech was ancient, hypnotic, mysterious.

"Well," she added, walking down Inferno's neck and standing between his wings. "Where are they? Or did you come to surrender?"

Her words jolted his mind from its slumber and revived his sharp tongue.

"No, Selene," he nodded and looked side to side. "And you are correct. There are no gnomes with me." He lifted his chin and smiled. "But it's good to know that we have something in common."

"Oh," she said, perching a brow, "and what might that be, our scales?"

"Ha! No," he chuckled, "not at all. But I would like to talk about that sometime." He chuckled again.

"So you find your hopeless situation amusing?"

"I just find it funny that you assumed that I came up here to offer my surrender, but," he paused, holding his chuckling stomach, "in all truth, I came up here to accept your surrender."

The polished features on her gentle face formed a dark scowl. Inferno's neck raised up, and his throat rumbled.

"You are every bit the fool they say you are!"

"Fool?" Nath said. "Who says I'm a fool?"

"The dragons," Selene said through clenched teeth. "You are the fallen Dragon Prince. The heir of folly." She walked farther down Inferno's back along his curled tail and stopped, staring at his arms, legs, and claws. "Oh, and look. You have white scales. I bet you don't even know what those mean. Do you, Nath Dragon, son of Balzurth..."

Nath's father's name rolled from her tongue, smooth and easy, but less than a minute into it she stopped. Her point was made. She knew much more about dragons than he did. And perhaps more about himself as well. Nath was torn. He wanted to kill her, but he also wanted to learn more about himself.

"Well," she continued, "do you know what your white scales mean? Do you understand why your father banished you? Why they call you the demon in the towns? The cursed serpent in the cities?" She let loose a haughty laugh. "I can see you still know nothing."

Nath eased back a half step. His fingers fumbled on the hilt of his blade. This felt like a scolding from his father, and his emotions were split between anger and shame. His thoughts drifted. Became unfocused.

Then he blurted out, "I'm sorry, does this mean you are surrendering or not? I'm uncertain."

Her eyes flashed like torch-lit fires, and a dark energy formed about her entirety, like a second skin. A dragon-like shroud.

"You think you can toy with me, Nath Dragon?" She traipsed to a spot between Inferno's wings and grabbed the saddle rope around his neck. "I'll dull that sharp tongue of yours. And if I can't have the gnomes, nobody will." She barked a command to Inferno in Dragonese.

The great dragon expanded its wings, leapt from the ledge, and glided down over the rim. His armored belly skimmed the treetops, and up, up, up he went, over the forest, turning and racing right back at the cliff.

Nath ran to the rim.

What is she doing!

Inferno's wings beat the air. His chest glowed with fire. The dragon pulled up short of the cliff and hovered in the air.

Nath locked eyes with Selene.

He saw her lips say, "I warned you."

A tunnel of dragon fire erupted from Inferno's huge mouth and struck the rock-face full force. The roaring flames scorched every vine and tree. They filled every cave with flame. Ash, smoke, and fire covered the steep mountainside.

Inferno kept going.

Flames gushed into every hole. Every crevice. All life was incinerated.

Nath cried out, "Nooo! Stop it!" He could not see the gnomes, nor Shum. Just scorching hot fire and black-grey smoke.

He fell to his knees.

"I've killed them. I've killed them."

CHAPTER

22

"Have you anything else to say?" Selene said from atop Inferno's back. They had returned to the spot they had left.

Nath kneeled in the thick grass. An empty vessel, trembling. Smoke filled his eyes, and his face was coated in soot and sweat. Through the hazy heat, he could make out his friends at the bottom, still surrounded by the sky raiders. A single command from Selene, and they'd all be burning corpses.

What have I done? What have I said that unleashed such evil?

Shum, Snarggell, and all the gnomes were wiped out.

Shaking, he rose up with Fang gripped in two hands.

"Why did you kill them, if you needed them?"

Inspecting her nails, Selene said, "I had to make sure they could not be used against me. And besides, I have enough stones already. And there are plenty of crystal gnomes, we just have to dig more out of their holes."

"That doesn't make any sense," Nath said, torn and advancing.

Inferno lowered his horned head between the two of them. A blast of hot air came from his nose. Selene walked up to his crown of horns and sat down between them.

"Do you want to end this war before it blossoms further?"

"I'm not the one that started this fight," Nath replied.

"True, but you are the cause of it."

"That's a lie," he said.

"Is it now?" Her eyes grazed over his scales. "But you and I are black dragons, Nath. We're destined to fight for dominion over the world. But together we can stop that. Together, we can end it all today."

Usually, Nath had little trouble telling truth from a lie, but he was having trouble today. Selene was seasoned. Intelligent. Clever. He wanted to believe her. And he was drawn to her power. *Evil twists the truth into a well-spun lie. It will catch you before you see it.*

"What do you propose?" Nath said, looking down over the rim before fixing his eyes back on hers.

"A truce," she said, "with conditions."

"Such as?"

The feline fury drifted out of the sky and landed alongside Inferno. Its eyes were bright. Nath remembered tangling with it before, in the caves where he battled Kryzak. It had grown and sprouted wings, making for a unique beast, both feline and serpentine.

"You come with me," she said, "for five years. The war ends, and none of your companions below will die. And I assure you, Nath Dragon: else, all of them *will* die."

"Five years? As your prisoner? I'd rather die first."

"Oh, don't think of it like that. You will have limited freedom, assuming you don't interfere." She stood, walked down Inferno's nose, and put one arm around the fury. Its purring rumbled in its throat. "And thousands, tens of thousands, won't have to die, assuming you stay true to your word." Her eyes bore into his. "There is much I can teach you, Nath. There is much you need to know." She breathed a ball of fire into her hand and tossed it over the rim. "Take some time and let me show you. Unlock your great powers."

"And who taught you, Gorn Grattack?"

Surprised, she said, "Ah, so he's visited you."

"He said he'd destroy me."

"And he will, and all of your friends, unless you come with me."

This wasn't how Nath had envisioned the final battle. He had pictured himself leading one great dragon army into battle against another. Now it was just himself versus all of them. He felt the sword warming his hands. *Any ideas, Fang?*

Another presence entered his mind.

Nath.

The voice of Bayzog was in his thoughts.

You cannot surrender. They are deceivers. Defilers.

I cannot let all of you die either, Nath replied with thought.

We fight for you, Nath. For Nalzambor. Dying is part of that. Our sacrifice. Our call. Don't let all we've fought so much for be lost.

Nath thought back, *There will be another time and place to fight again. I promise.*

Nath, don't do this. Don't do this. They can destroy us, but don't let them destroy you. This is all a trap, using us against you. Help will come, Nath. You must be patient.

Maybe so, but I won't watch my friends die today, Nath thought.

Then all our efforts are in vain.

I'm making a truce so no harm will come to any of you.

Don't.

Forgive me, but I must, Nath thought before breaking his connection with Bayzog.

"Selene."

"Yes."

"Send away the dragons as a sign of good faith."

"So be it," she said, then uttered a word.

The grey scalers disappeared into the sky. The sky raiders lifted from the earth and flew beyond the forest. The feline fury glided over the hills until it was gone, leaving Nath, Selene, and Inferno all alone on the plain at the top of the cliff.

I might not have an answer to this today, but I will have one soon enough.

"Are you satisfied?" Selene said, climbing onto Inferno's back.

Nath nodded and said, "Five years of peace."

"Assuming there's no provocation," she said. "Do you agree to this truce, Nath Dragon?"

"I do," he said.

"Then come," she said, "but there is one more thing. Your sword. You won't be needing it anymore."

Nath swallowed, eyed the mystic blade, and stuck it in the ground. He rubbed the dragon pommels before he walked away, saying, "Goodbye, old friend."

Brenwar watched with exasperation. His friend, his charge, Nath Dragon, climbed onto the back of the great dragon with High Priestess Selene. Inferno's wings spread, flapped, and lifted him into the air.

"No you don't! No you don't!" Brenwar roared. He snatched a stone from the pile and hurled it with all his might. Nath's flame-red hair ducked it. The dragon lifted up, up, up, and out of sight. Brenwar's heavy shoulders sagged. "How can he do this? How can he do this?"

"He did it so we could live," Bayzog said, sighing.

"It's bad, isn't it, Bayzog?" Ben said. *Clatch. Snap. Clatch.* He locked Akron away. "But at least those dragons are gone. I'd be lying if I said I didn't see my life getting short." He rubbed his grizzled chin and eyed the sky. "I would have died for him though."

"Now what?" Brenwar said. "Do we go after him? We must, shouldn't we?"

"It's up to him now," Bayzog said, leaning on his staff and grimacing.

"Are you there? Are you there?" Hoven yelled inside the scorched cave.

Cough. Cough. Cough.

Hack. Hack.

"Yes," a voice cried from behind a strange wall of stone. Hoven could also hear sobbing on the other side. "We're here." It was Shum's voice. He was certain.

Hoven could barely make out the muffled voices, but one spoke fast, sobbing with distress.

"They've died. They've died. All of them."

It was a gnome.

"We have to dig them out of there," Hoven said to the other Roaming Rangers. He ran his fingers along the strange glob of stone that sealed off the small cave. The rock was charred and singed, and it had an odd aroma to it. *How did he get behind this?* Running his hands over the strange formation, it hit him. *On my!* The rocks were small bodies knotted together. *The gnomes!* In the dim light, his eyes adjusted and could make out their small bearded faces, frozen in pain and anguish.

A Roaming Ranger arrived with a pick and started to swing. Hoven barred his path and said, "We must wait."

Eight small graves covered in wildflowers rested in the falling light. Snarggell spoke for more than an hour, with tears streaming from his eyes. Ben barely understood a word of it, but he did understand one thing the bald gnome said.

I live because they died. I wish it was the other way around. And all these years I didn't think they much liked me. I will remember. I will do right by them.

It was evening. Bayzog, Ben, Brenwar, Snarggell, Shum, Hoven, and the rest of the Roaming Rangers had led the horses up the roads to the meadow at the top of the cliff. Nath's sword, Fang, had been recovered, but the warm glow of a campfire did little to lift the gloom.

"You have no Nath Dragon to assist now, Shum," Bayzog said. "Now what will you do?"

Shum stood with his back to the fire, staring beyond the dark.

"It is all unfortunate and unforeseen. I cannot answer that," the Wilder Elf said. "But the battle is still going on. And there are plenty more that need saving. We'll focus on that." He turned and faced Bayzog from the other side of the fire. "And what will you do?"

He looked at Brenwar and Ben. "It's been a long time since I've been home. I'll probably start there."

CHAPTER

23

"SHE'S PERSISTENT. I'LL SAY THAT," Pilpin said to Devliik. The dwarves of Morgdon had kept their distance from Faylan the satyr and the Barnabus soldiers for the past several days. Pilpin wanted the falling of Faylan's brother and the draykis to soak in. To let the little horned murderer feel their pain. "But I'm not sure there will be justice for this one, aside from that which comes from death."

"Agreed," Devliik said, sharpening his axe with a stone. "But the time has come to end this." He dropped the stone, stood up, and sauntered into the trees.

The rest of the dwarves were spread out in the camp, sharpening weapons, feeding themselves, and stitching up each other's wounds. Devliik had marched them nonstop for two days, winding through mountains and valleys, looking for something that he did not name.

Pilpin stretched his limbs and clawed at his beard. He wondered how the others were doing. Brenwar. Nath. And most of all, Gorlee. *Wherever he went is where we should be headed. But that could be anywhere.*

The dwarf called Wood Helm signaled to him.

"I suppose it's time to go," he said, gathering his gear. "On we march. On we march. On we march. Ho! Ho! Ho!"

In less than a minute, they were off.

Hours into the trek, the party of dwarves stopped on the bank of a stream that raced between the hills. A dragon's roar sounded from above. Every thick neck bent up toward the sky.

"Fill yer flasks," Devliik said, peering through the trees. "And get moving."

A dark shadow darted through the clouds. Pilpin swore it had a bronze glimmer to it.

"It's not looking for us," Wood Helm said, "but if it does come looking, I've got something for it." He shook his axe. "I'll scale it like a flying fish, I will."

Pilpin slapped him on the back and said, "You and I both will. And they say dragon skin makes for excellent armor."

"Only one way to find out," Wood Helm joked.

They filled their flasks, splashed through the stream, and up another hillside they went. Devliik's path was difficult, but not impossible for an army to follow. And the dwarves were taking turns scouting the rear and making sure they were still being followed. As of yesterday, there were signs that Faylan's army had slowed or backed. If anything, they came after the dwarves more determined than ever.

Huffing it up the slopes, Pilpin wondered if there wasn't a better way to take Faylan out. They'd managed to trick her brother, Finlin, and the draykis and defeat them, so he thought there might be a better way to get at her. But Devliik seemed to be determined to try and set another trap, similar to the last. Pilpin was certain that she'd be too sharp for that.

We should just stage one grand ambush and end her.

He had shared those thoughts with Devliik, but the brown-bearded warrior shook his chin at him. "When the terrain favors us, we'll get them," he'd said. "Just keep those legs churning. We'll march 'em until their legs fall off."

Pilpin obeyed. They all did. Stalwart. Unceasing. They'd bring Faylan to justice, but it would take more patience this time.

"Report!" Faylan said to one of her scouts. She stood on the edge of a stream. She and her army had been pushing through the brush for days, a tiresome task through rough terrain, and a handful of her soldiers had fallen.

A half-orc man in a buckskin vest and boots with a belt decorated in knives saluted.

"We gain," he said, wiping the greasy hair from his eyes. "In a week, we'll catch them." He patted a knife on his belt. "Shorten their beards, we will."

Faylan cocked an eyebrow.

"Did I ask for your commentary, orc?"

"No," the half orc said with a bow of his head, "apologies, Commander."

"Continue your charge and be away with you." She shooed him with her hand. "And never try to amuse me with your jests."

The half orc saluted and darted into the woods. Her soldiers, less than a hundred now, lined the stream, filling flasks and skins. Even in their heavy armor, they had moved well, but not well enough. Alone, she would have caught up with the dwarves within a day. This course simply took too long. She wanted vengeance, and she wanted it now.

"Azklan," she said, rubbing a jaxite amulet the winged draykis had given her. "Come. Come to me." The stone's inner fires came to life, tingling the fingers on her hand. "Azklan, the time has come."

A dragon-shaped shadow dropped out of the clouds that filled the valley and splashed into the stream, crushing two soldiers. The armored warriors scrambled up the banks, but no farther. The bronze dragon paid them no notice. Eyes focused on the amulet Faylan wore, it dragged its massive body through the waters until its head, crowned in horns, stopped just a few feet from her face.

Faylan's heart raced. Her grubby fingers clutched the amulet. She swallowed, stepped forward, and placed her hand on Azklan's snout. The scales were cool. Its breath hot. Everything about it was magnificent.

"I want to see the dwarves die," she said. "I want to see it with my own eyes."

Azklan lowered his neck. She sensed his thoughts saying, "Climb on then."

She stepped on his shoulder, climbed up, straddled his neck, and grabbed the harness configured around him. She yelled out to her soldiers and pointed up the mountains, "Meet us at the top."

The bronze beast dashed down the stream, spread his wings, jumped up, and took off. Into the clouds she went, screaming with joy, soaring in circles. Her face lit up with an exhilaration the likes of which she'd never experienced before. She felt awesome. She felt invincible.

"I see them," Azklan told her.

Her windblown face made a fierce grin.

"It's time to kill them and avenge my brother."

Folding back his wings, Azklan, a bronze bolt, a nightmare in the skies, crashed through the trees and landed in the midst of the dwarves. Fire, smoke, and death erupted from his visage.

Never surprise a dwarf if you don't want your skull cracked.

The saying was ancient. A warning to dwarven enemies. If you surprise them, then you had better kill them, else they unleash their wrath on you.

But that saying was made for orcs, lizardmen, gnolls, and bugbears. Not full-grown dragons.

Trees splintered, and the mountain shook when Faylan and the dragon dropped from the sky. Pilpin didn't see it coming. None of them did. Head down on the trails, Wood Helm died first, smashed by the dragon's scaled belly.

Flames roared from the dragon's mouth, setting two dwarves on fire. The flaming dwarves charged with their axes before they fell. A spiked tail lashed out and skewered the fourth dwarf through his armor. Another strike sent the fifth dwarf through tree branches and out of sight.

Pilpin could see the satyr on the dragon's neck. Screaming. Gloating. Pointing.

Dwarves drove their weapons into the beast. The dragon swept them aside with its tail.

Blood spilled.

Wood burned.

No one screamed except the satyr. In elation.

"Kill them! Kill them all!"

The bronze dragon loosed death upon them. No dwarf fled. They stood their ground and battled. Dwarven steel versus dragon scales. The hearty fighters were no match.

Pilpin slung his axe with all his force. It glanced off the dragon's eyelid.

The dragon's head snaked around, tongue licking out.

"Save that one!" Faylan yelled. "I want to kill the little one that taunted me myself!"

In one swipe, the dragon scooped Pilpin up and caged him with his claws. It fought on. Dwarves struck. Dwarves fell. Fire raged from the dragon's mouth with raw heat.

Pilpin's eyes stung and burned. Flames roared all around him. But nothing else. The battle cries of the dwarves were no more.

No!

Pilpin thrashed in his prison, to no avail.

The dragon held him in front of the satyr Faylan. She stood on the dragon's neck with her arms spread out, triumphant. A dagger glistened in her palm. She advanced with murder in her eyes.

"This is for you, little one!"

Behind her, a figure appeared. His beard smoked, and his armor was burning.

Pilpin's eyes widened. *Devliik!*

Faylan halted her advance and turned.

Devliik smote her right between the horns.

Chok!

The dagger fell from her grasp as she tumbled off the dragon's neck.

Devliik!

The brown-bearded dwarf came at the dragon in a rush and struck between its claws. It let out a belly-full of fire and loosened its grip on Pilpin. Devliik snatched him by the neck and said, "Live to tell our tale! We have avenged!" He shoved Pilpin away, latched onto the dragon's horns, and started chopping at its head.

Shaking with fury, the dragon spread its wings and leapt into the sky with Devliik still attached. It thrashed in the air until it vanished in the smoke and flames.

"I will, Devliik. I will," Pilpin said, stumbling among the dead. He came across Faylan. Her face was as cruel in death as it had been in life. He took the amulet from her neck and dragged her corpse into the flames of the forest.

"It's better than what you deserve."

Over the next half day, he collected his brethren's trinkets and built a pyre beneath their bodies. He said words, ancient and meaningful.

And then alone, Pilpin headed down the other side of the hill.

CHAPTER

24

Narnum. The Free City. There was a time when Nath hadn't thought he'd see it again. Its great towers. Its wondrous sights. Now, he stood on the balcony of its tallest tower, overlooking everything, particularly the people of all the races that roamed the streets.

It was different now. All the races thrived, to include the likes of orcs, lizardmen and goblins. There were soldiers too. Thousands of them scattered on the streets and even more in camps set along the rivers. And there were dragons. Dozens perched on rooftops and others gliding through the sky.

Narnum had changed. It was no longer the Free City, rather the City of Fear. He could feel it. See it on the citizens' faces.

I have to do something about this.

He turned away and faced the chamber within.

Selene sat on her throne, her piercing eyes fixed on him. Even as beautiful as she was, it was unsettling. He'd been forced to trust a woman permeated in evil. On the arm of her chair squawked a drulture, a creature with colorful scale-like feathers.

Nath wanted to choke the strange bird. He had never liked them. They were carnivorous spies and tattletales.

Your time will come.

At the foot of Selene's dais lay the feline fury. A quiet rumble roused inside its belly. Its feline eyes watched Nath's every movement.

Nath's paw fell to his naked hip, where Fang once hung. *I hope he is taken care of.*

"Are you alright, Nath?" Selene said. Her voice echoed. The chamber felt lifeless. Empty.

He folded his arms behind his back. It had been over a week since he arrived, and he'd done absolutely nothing.

"Is this the plan?" Nath said. "I stare out from this balcony for the next five years and then you let me go?"

"Those were our terms, more or less."

Your terms. Like a fool, I countered with nothing other than my friends' lives, and I still have no idea if they live.

"You said there would be peace," he said. "How can I know there is peace from this tower? For all I know, the entire world burns, aside from this city."

A chilling smile stretched over Selene's lips before she said, "Barnabus's forces are at rest. I assure you."

"I'd rather see that for myself," he said, easing his way inside her chamber. Everything was exquisite—the tables, the chairs, the food on the table—but lifeless.

"That would be a vast undertaking."

"I have plenty of time on my hands," he said, picking a grape from the table.

The drulture squawked.

"That's an annoying pet you have." He crushed the grape and flicked it away. "Can I kill it?"

"Absolutely not," Selene said. "Not my dear baby." She stroked its back and pecked its beak with a kiss. "It's one of the family. A brother."

"A rodent. A rat with wings."

The drulture's wings fluttered. *Squawk!*

Nath paced around the table, whistling a dwarfish tune. It was an inspiring melody they whistled when marching into war. He kept at it over an hour.

Selene sunk into her throne.

"Will you stop that?"

He kept whistling, another fifteen minutes more this time.

Selene's nails dug into the arms of her chair.

"Stop it!"

Nath's golden eyes brightened. He paused, touching his chest, saying, "I'm sorry. Did you say something? I couldn't hear over all that whistling." He cocked his head. "Ah, it seems to be gone now." He walked behind the feline fury and stepped on its tail.

It jumped up, whirled, and roared.

"Heel!" Selene commanded in another tongue.

The cat-like dragon's ears bent back. Its lips curled over its fangs.

Nath glared right back in its eyes.

"You are a child!" Selene said.

"You are treating me as such, sticking me in here with all of your animals." He folded his arms over his deep chest. "How long do you think I can be kept like this?"

"There are worse places you can be put," she said. "And I'd be more than happy to shackle those limbs of yours."

"No one will be shackling me, now or ever, Selene. Try it, and I'll destroy this tower and your brood in it." His chest heaved. "Do we have an understanding?"

She rose from her throne.

"You think you can test me?"

"I say the same to you."

Her eyes flashed, and down the steps she came. Standing toe to toe with him, she looked him in the eye and said, "You have much to learn, young dragon. Much to learn about the error of your ways."

"Go on," Nath said, "I'm listening."

She put her hand on his chest and said, "You're all brawn and mouth. You need refining. Composure."

"Most women like my composure."

Selene smiled.

"Do they now?"

"Ask any of th—"

Her hand exploded with power.

He flew across the room and smashed into the wall. Nath jumped up, woozy, holding his burning chest. And fell down again.

Sultans of Sulfur! I've never felt anything like that.

Shaking the debris from his hair, he noticed Selene standing over him. Her eyes and hands crackled with bright energy.

"That is power, little dragon. That is composure. Focus. Everything you lack."

Grimacing, Nath rose to one knee and said, "You are a wizard."

"No, *I* am a *dragon*." Her tail swished over the tiles and lifted up his chin. "A creature of magic. You are as well." She chuckled. "Your father didn't teach you anything at all, did he?"

"He taught me plenty."

"Hah. He gave you a sword. And a dwarf holding a leash around your neck. He told you to stay out of trouble." Her tail stroked his hair. "Precious time wasted. What I just did to you, you should be able to do to me by now. Gorn Grattack taught me. Why didn't your father teach you?" She turned and resumed her seat on the throne, blowing the mystic fires from her hand. Her glowing eyes returned to normal. "My, that felt good."

Quietly, Nath resumed his place on the balcony, thoughts confused and racing.

CHAPTER

25

A WEEK BECAME TWO. TWO BECAME four.

Nath and Selene sat and ate at the table. No drulture. No feline fury. No draykis nor guards. Just the two of them. Alone.

The High Priestess of Barnabus carved the roast on her plate and stabbed it on her fork.

"It smells delicious, doesn't it?" she said, taking a bite, then washing it down with her wine. "You should try it. Eat. Keep your strength up."

Nath stared at the plate of food, the steaming aroma drifting into his nostrils. His stomach rumbled.

"My," Selene said, "was that you? You have to eat, Nath. You don't look well. And that's not your style, is it?" She dabbed the corners of her mouth with a napkin. "I never would have imagined you could be silent so long. A cathedral mouse makes more noise with cats around." She sighed. "Oh Nath, would you speak. Have I wounded your pride? Hurt your feelings? Does it bother you to know that I am your superior?"

Nath's claws stretched out.

"Or rather, that you are my inferior?" she added.

He could feel her eyes on him and retracted his claws. Over the past month, he had not said a word. Not since she loosed her powers on him. It shook him, to be up against powers he did not understand. Words he could not comprehend. He had to believe it was all lies, but it sounded so convincing.

And sometimes the best strategy was to say nothing, do nothing, don't engage at all. Let your enemies reveal themselves. In vain, he struggled with his curiosity.

He pushed himself back from the table, headed for the balcony and into the rain. It had been raining on and off all week. Flash storms. Gusty winds. The weather kept him inside more, when he'd rather be out. He clutched at his side. The shard still dug in from time to time.

"What is that?" Selene said, walking up beside him. "I see you digging at it."

He didn't respond. He kept his eyes fixed on the flashes in the distance.

"Is it a wound? I can fix that. I am a priestess." She reached over and touched the vest he'd been given. "Look at me."

He balled up his fist and pulled away.

"That wound can fester. Come, let me take a look at it."

It riled him. It had been her overlord who wounded him with a poisoned dagger. And he'd be lying if he said it didn't bother him. It had gotten worse over the past two weeks. Digging deeper. Becoming more painful. Making him angry.

"Nath, five years is a long time," she said. "It doesn't have to be like this. We have a truce, remember? There is no reason I cannot offer care to one of my, well, prisoners. I want you taken care of. Allow me to show you things are not as bad as they seem."

He moved to the farthest corner of the balcony and turned his back to her.

"So be it, Nath Dragon. Be as miserable as you want. So be it."

He heard her footsteps walking away and let out an inward sigh.

How can this be? How can I live in peace with my enemy?

Nath wanted to know how his friends were. Wanted to know where the help his father had promised was. Why hadn't his father taught him how to do the things that Selene could do? Was any of that even true? He scraped at the stone railing with his claw, digging through the stone as easily as dirt.

How much longer can I put up with this? I want answers. I want the truth!

He huddled down behind the balcony wall, pulled his legs up to his chest, tucked his head in between his knees, and fell asleep. And dreamed.

Dragons filled the sunny skies. Their scales were scintillating colors. His father's voice echoed in his thoughts. *Stay on the higher road, Son. The low roads are full of danger.* He awoke, gasping. The pain in his ribs throbbed.

"Uh!" he groaned, wiping the hair from his eyes and stretching out his scaly arms. The rain had stopped, and the sky was bright and clear. He shielded his eyes.

"How are you, Nath?" a woman said. The voice was familiar but not Selene's.

He grumbled and rubbed his eyes. Pressing his back into the wall, he pushed himself up. A woman stood in front of him, wearing a wizard's gown the color of purple lilies. She smelled nice, even more familiar. He stared. She stared back.

"Nath," she said, "are you not going to speak to me?"

He blinked.

"Sasha?"

She glided over, smiled, and clasped his hands.

"Have I gotten so old after all these years that you do not know me?"

"No, absolutely not," he said, unable to hide his surprise. "You haven't changed at all." His heart pounded. "I-I can't believe it. How?"

She didn't say a word. Instead, she wrapped her arms around him, gave him a strong hug, and held on.

Nath looked down at her red-brown hair, closed his eyes, and hugged her back.

"I missed you," she finally said, releasing him. She rubbed her hands up and down his arms. "And your scales."

Nath withdrew a little.

"No Nath," she said, grabbing his paws, "they are so handsome. They go perfectly with the rest of you." She hugged him again. Her body was soft. Warm.

"I missed you too, but Sasha, what in the world are you doing here?"

"It's a long story, Nath." She kept ahold of his hand and pulled him along. "Come, let's eat, and I'll tell you all about it."

He followed, almost in a trance, and took a seat beside her. A feast was on the table. She put a napkin on his lap. His belly groaned.

"You need to eat," she said, pouring wine into a goblet from a carafe. "You eat; I'll talk. Fair enough?"

"Certainly," he said, scanning the chamber. "Where is Selene?"

"Gone," she said, "for the time being. I convinced her you would be more comfortable if it was just me." She made a face and winked. "It wasn't easy, but she agreed." She began stacking his plate with bread, racks of meat, and cheeses. "Eat."

Reluctantly, Nath started in.

Sasha eased back into her seat and said, "That's better."

With his mouth full, Nath said, "How is Bayzog?"

"I'm getting there," she said. "You just eat."

Nath's face darkened.

"He's well, Nath. Very well," she reassured him. She toyed with a jasmine amulet on her neck. "And I have this. It keeps him close to my heart at all times."

"You shouldn't be here. You should be with him and your sons."

"Nath, they are all in Quintuklen, and I'll return there soon enough." She took a sip of wine. "But for the time being, per Selene's request, I am here to serve as your liaison."

"Liaison?"

"Selene knew she couldn't keep you on a leash without you knowing what was going on," Sasha said, brushing her hair from her eyes, "so she contacted us. Not directly, but through some emissaries. Bayzog and I discussed it and felt it would be best if I came. I'm not the threat that Bayzog is."

Nath shifted in his seat.

"They're still our enemies, Nath. This is only a truce, not peace. But since your arrival here, the upheavals are down. Over the past few weeks, I've traveled from the Settlements to Morgdon and back. The armies of Barnabus have quieted their forces, but they have not retreated." She cleared her throat and took a drink. "Sorry. But the people in the towns and cities are encouraged. The overlords have turned most of the control back over to the people. They just keep watch."

"Brenwar is fine and back in Morgdon, for now. The orcs still wage war on the borders with the elves. Dragon sightings and attacks are far fewer." She patted his knee. "All of these things, I have seen with my own eyes."

"It would be more believable if I saw it with my own eyes," Nath said. "Can that be arranged?"

"Nath," Sasha said, exasperated, "I would not tell you tall tales. I never have. I never will."

"You can always be forced to say what you don't want to say. Coercion is a common game in this world."

"Do I seem coerced to you?"

He paused, frowned, and said, "No."

Sasha continued with her observations. Each word, every sentence, was well-stated and described the ideal truce—short of their dark enemy's actual surrender. It was more than he had hoped for.

But it didn't sit well with him. Something didn't smell right. He just couldn't detect what that was.

He cut her off and asked, "So when did you arrive here?"

"Me? Uh, yesterday. Why?"

"Just asking."

"Nath, is something bothering you?"

"I thought you would have come to see me sooner." He leaned forward. Pain shot through his side. He doubled over.

Sasha jumped out of her chair, "Nath!"

"I'm fine."

"You are not fine," she said. "Let me see your side."

"No," he groaned.

"Yes," she insisted. "Get up. Take off that vest."

He did so.

Sasha's eyes grew two times.

"It's swollen. Festering." She laid her fingers on it and pressed.

"Ouch," he said, "please don't do that."

"Well, I must do something," she said. "That must be fixed. What happened?"

"Nothing," he said. "I'm surprised Bayzog didn't tell you about it."

She blanched and said, "He doesn't tell me everything."

"Funny," Nath said, slipping his vest back on. "I thought he did."

"Would you tell me about all the terrors in this world if you didn't have to?"

Nath shrugged. "I suppose not, but you're his wife. I'd think you would know."

"Well," she said, "he protects me. Especially after all that has happened since you were gone." She patted his hand. "Nath, you need to get that wound looked at. It's only getting worse."

He leaned back with a groan and said, "I'll think about it."

"You do that," she said. "Now, if all goes well, I'll convince Selene to give you your own quarters."

CHAPTER
26

ANOTHER WEEK WENT BY. SASHA had been in and out, but had no luck getting Nath his own quarters. He was alone now. Standing on the balcony hundreds of feet above the streets of Narnum, he counted dragons. Dozens had become less than ten. The armed forces of Barnabus had moved on, leaving an oversized garrison of soldiers. Sasha had explained that it was all in good faith. He couldn't allow himself to believe it.

The massive door to the main chamber popped open.

Nath peered over his shoulder.

Selene and Sasha came in side by side, wearing white and golden robes. Two men, bald, tattooed, and crimson robed, accompanied them from behind. Their eyes were content, and they carried a smoking incense urn by the chains.

"Are you ready, Nath Dragon?" Selene said, pushing up the sleeves of her robe. She had black scales on every exposed part but her head. She waited for his reply and said, "It won't take long."

Sasha glided over and locked her arms around his.

"You need to do this, Nath. I can't stand to see you in pain any longer. Come."

With hesitation, and a little stooped over, Nath sauntered to the table, grimacing. The shard inside him used to feel like little more than a pinprick. Now it felt like a hot nail digging deeper and deeper.

"Lie down on the table," Selene said, touching his shoulders.

Nath stayed her with his hand and said, "Easy now."

The last few days, he had been more open to conversations. Selene and Sasha talked, and Nath listened. He spoke more, asked questions, but didn't delve too deeply.

Against his will, Selene fascinated him. She was radiant. Dark. Exotic. Her voice could be soothing like a warm bath or piercing like a knife. He wanted to figure her out—without appearing to be interested.

He got up onto the grand table and lay flat on his back.

"I'll need to restrain you," Selene said. "The extraction will be painful."

Nath propped himself up on his elbows and said, "I don't think so."

"Nath," Sasha said, coming to his aid, "nothing will happen to you. I promise. Let's get this thing out of you. I can cast a spell and relax you, if you like?"

"I don't need to be shackled," he growled. "I'm no mere mortal. I can take the pain." He lay down on his back, clenched his fists, and closed his eyes. "Do it, before I change my mind."

He could feel their tension. Hear the rustle of their robes. Smell their soft breath. If there was a whisk of a knife, he'd know it. Or another presence in the room.

But his chest rose up and glided down, easy. The scent of Sasha's perfume eased him. He had to trust someone, and Sasha had always been an excellent confidante. He felt her warm hand on his head and heard her whisper "I'm here, Nath."

His breathing eased even more.

The acolytes began to chant. A bright light flared.

Selene placed her hands over his ribs.

"Be steady," she said, and began her own chanting.

Her hands turned hot. He felt a fiery spade in his side. His jaws clenched. Every muscle tightened. An anguished moan came from his mouth.

"Be strong, Nath. Be strong," Sasha said.

The incantation became louder. The pain excruciating.

"Argh!"

"Hold on, Nath! Hold on!" Sasha said.

Deeper and deeper Selene's powers dug, through muscle, bone, and flesh.

Nath shuddered. His forehead beaded in sweat.

Be still, he told himself. *Be still.*

A hot poker plunged inside him and ripped something out. A burst of fire exploded in his head.

"Aaaaaaaah!"

He lurched into a sitting position, golden eyes wide with horror.

Selene stood away from the table, hand aglow, holding a bloody fragment of steel in her hand. The splinter he believed was inside him was no splinter at all. It had branched out with jagged talons as big as his fingers. Blood dripped from it onto the floor.

"That thing was in me?"

Selene nodded.

Nath glanced at the oozing hole in his side.

"It will heal up," Selene said.

Nath's head became light and woozy. He collapsed headfirst on the table.

"You are well now," Sasha said, seated at the grand table. It was just the two of them.

It had been over a week since Selene extracted the shard from Nath's body.

"I am," Nath said, smiling. "And I'm almost ashamed to admit that I am better off for it. The poisoned barb took a toll on me, it seems. But now, my head is clear. My stiff scales have loosened." He glanced around. "But don't tell you-know-who about it."

Sasha giggled.

"You know I won't. I'm as much a prisoner here as you are."

"But you can leave," Nath said. He adjusted the robes he wore. Well-knitted sleeveless garb with intricate designs.

"It looks great on you," Sasha said. "Fitting for a prince. A Dragon Prince, that is."

"It's not bad," he said.

"Well, you will want to look your best among the people. They've been talking about you, you know," she said.

"About what?"

"They see you standing on the balcony. They know who you are: Nath Dragon, the legend. Your presence here has brought peace to the city. To the world."

He liked the sound of that. But it couldn't possibly be true.

"I haven't done anything," he said, heading for the balcony.

"Exactly," Sasha said, eyes trailing after him. "The truce. The agreement. You kept your word. Selene kept hers. Officers and soldiers return home. You are The Peace Maker. They credit you with that."

"It makes no sense," he said. Beneath him, the Narnum he had known had become revitalized. Windows were open. Doors unlocked. Colored banners and flowers were in ample display. The sweet aroma of seasoned meats and delicious sweets filled his nose. Heads were lifted and fingers pointed at him. Many of them waved. He made the slightest gesture. An excited clamor rose.

"What are they doing?" he said to Sasha, who had slipped over to stand by his side.

She peeked over the balcony holding her ear and said with a smile, "Cheering."

He could hear them. He watched more gather. It was a far cry from the days when they had called him a demon. Now they chanted his name like a hero.

Nath! Nath! Nath! Nath! Nath!

He rose his arms up high in the air.

The cries of the citizens exploded. His dragon heart swelled.

Sasha wrapped her arm around his and leaned her head on his shoulder.

He liked it. All of it.

Later that week, there was a soft knock at the door of Nath's new quarters.

"Come in," he said, setting down his comb and closing the doors to the mirror.

"Nath," Sasha said, slipping inside and closing the door behind her. Her pretty smile was upside down. "It's time for me to go now."

"What?" he said, clasping her hands, heart racing. "How come? Why now?"

She dangled her amulet in front of his eyes and said, "I need to return to Bayzog. You didn't forget about him, did you?"

"Uh, no. Of course not." His blood went cold. He felt ashamed. He'd become so fond of Sasha that he'd lost himself. He released her hands. "He misses you. Certainly. I just hate to see you go. How long will it be?"

"A month. Maybe two," she said, taking him by the hand and leading him over to a sofa and sitting them both down. "I think Selene is getting a little jealous of me and you. I don't think she understands what friendship is. I feel sorry for her."

"Don't," Nath said, shaking his head. "She is still our enemy, and the truce won't last forever. I don't think she can hold her forces back another year. She's temperamental."

Sasha giggled.

"And you aren't?"

"No. Thanks to you, I'm not." He grabbed and tickled her.

She erupted in laughter.

"Stop it! Stop it!" she squealed.

"Oh, alright." He pulled her up from the bed. "I can't have your thrashings messing my hair up."

"I'm glad you're back to your old self again," she said. She stood up, leaned over, and kissed him on the cheek. "I'll miss you." She made a bead for the door.

"Sasha!" he cried. "You're leaving *now*, just like that?"

She popped open the door, looked back into his eyes, and said, "I must, Nath. It's hard enough to leave as it is."

"But," he said, trying to object, but the door clanked shut, and he was all alone. He plopped back down with a hundred emotions coursing through him. "Sultans of Sulfur."

CHAPTER
27

ROBES HIDING HER FEET, High Priestess Selene glided through her throne room. Having it to herself again, aside from the drulture and feline fury, was soothing. The coddling of Nath Dragon had become a bore, and she needed some entertainment.

On the grand table a box lay, wooden and trimmed in colorful paints. The hinges squeaked as she opened it. The shard she had extracted from Nath lay inside on a lavender bed of cloth. The steel, now corroded and stained with blood, throbbed inside the box. She grinned and closed the lid.

Knock. Knock. Knock.

The knock on the grand doors echoed in the chamber.

"I need more curtains," she said to herself, then louder, "Enter."

A large figure donned in dark crimson robes entered with two draykis on either side of him. They all kneeled, and he bowed.

"You summoned me, my queen."

"Yes," she said, "yes I did, Kryzak. Your old friend Nath Dragon is getting quite comfortable." She snickered. "Arise and walk with me." She eyed the draykis. "Depart from us and send in the changeling."

With a bow, the pair retreated.

Outside on the balcony, the feline fury basked in the sun. Its eyes locked on Kryzak, and its lips curled back over its teeth. Selene walked over, sat on its back, and toyed with its mane of hair.

"Are you ready, my dear, dear, servant?" she said to Kryzak.

Kryzak slipped his battle scepter out from underneath his robes.

"I'd wait a hundred lifetimes for this," he said, pulling back his hulking shoulders. "A thousand just to see a glimpse of your face."

"You're so sweet, Kryzak," she said, rubbing the purring tiger-dragon, "but my lifetime is many of yours. Fortunately for you, I've become bored with this charade. I'm ready to put Nath Dragon to the test. And I want to test my favorite servant as well."

"Anything for you, Selene," he said. "What would you have me do?"

"Your test shall be a reward for you. I want you to kill Nath Dragon."

Kryzak dropped his hood from his oversized head. The tattoos all around it glowed with fire. He smacked his battle mace into his palm. His throaty voice could not contain his excitement. "It will be an honor. It will be my pleasure."

"I knew you would feel that way. And if you win, an entire kingdom will be yours."

He dropped to a knee and bowed.

"You *are* my kingdom, my queen."

His eyes glanced up. Sasha entered the room. Her eyes were weak and drained.

"Ah," Selene said, "if it isn't my little sorceress." Her belly chuckled. "Tell me, Sasha, are you ready to depart for your trip? Is our guest Nath Dragon well?"

"Everything is as you please, my queen. He suspects not a single thing."

"Are you certain?" Selene said.

"I am, but I am weary as well." Sasha pressed her palm onto her head. "This deception is draining."

"Come now," Selene said, getting up and putting her arm around Sasha's shoulder. "You may rest. The hard part is over, and you've done exceptionally well."

"I'm not so sure I could have pulled it off without this," Sasha said, holding the amulet hanging from her neck. "But what is done, is done. For now."

"So it is," Selene said. "So it is. Now, go, back to your room and take your rest. The next time I need you will be soon enough."

Sasha nodded, and with her chin dipped down she said, "May I go now?"

"Certainly." Selene glanced at Kryzak. "I always find this so fascinating."

Sasha's face shimmered and contorted from a splendid woman to the bald, pale pink form of Gorlee the Changeling. His lids fluttered over his bulging eyes. He swayed and steadied himself against the wall.

"Ah," he said, rubbing his head, "that's better. Being a woman is hard." His eyes blinked rapidly in the direction of Selene. "I'm not sure how you manage it."

"I'm no ordinary woman," she assured him. "I'm a dragon."

CHAPTER

28

BAYZOG'S APARTMENT WAS COLD. EMPTY. He sat on a stool, elbows propped up on his round table, his head resting in his hands. He cracked his weary eyes open and thumbed through the pages of his tome. The pages of the grand book bound in dark hide leather flipped on their own, each folding slowly over the other, suspended through the air. Bayzog uttered a sigh, grabbed the book, and flung it through the air. It smacked off the wall and fell on the stone floor.

"What was that?" Ben said, popping his head up from the sofa.

Stooped over, Bayzog walked to the tome, picked it up, and returned it to the table.

"Sorry," he said, resuming his seat and rubbing his blurring violet eyes.

Ben made his way over, put his hand on the part-elf's sagging shoulder, and said, "We'll find them."

"I've failed them," Bayzog said, shaking his head. "I should have been here with them. I just don't understand what happened. And now they could be anywhere."

He and Ben had returned to Quintuklen weeks ago, but there was trouble long before that. After Nath departed with Selene on the back of Inferno, Bayzog had tried to contact Sasha, but hadn't been able to. With haste, he had returned home, accompanied by Ben. The two of them had been met with a foul greeting. Acolytes of Barnabus greeted them at the gates. They had Rerry's swords and a ring he'd given to Samaz. Their warning was firm.

"Remain in the city, go nowhere else" they had said, "and when the time comes, we'll contact you with our demands. Cross us, do anything suspicious, and you will never see them alive again."

That was over a month ago, and Bayzog had been frosty ever since. The waiting game was torment, and there hadn't been any word from Barnabus's camp. There was nothing worse than fighting an opponent that you could not see while he held your loved ones.

Ben slid the tome over to himself and thumbed through the pages.

"So there isn't any way to track them down? I know you've been pouring through this day and night, but can't you summon pixlyns or something?"

"Too risky," the part-elf wizard said. "There are too many dragons that would gobble them up."

"I wish they'd gobble some of those soldiers up," Ben said. "They keep coming. I thought this was a time of truce. It looks more like a siege to me."

Bayzog brushed his long black hair out of his eyes and said, "Indeed."

Every day, he and Ben walked the streets and overheard the conversations of people. The armies continued to stretch their grip through the land, invading city after city, without fire and force, but filling them with armed soldiers. Armies of thousands camped outside the cities. High-ranking officers and overlords worked with the leaders of Quintuklen from within. Everything seemed backward. Something strange was going on. It twisted Bayzog's stomach.

As for Sasha and his sons, he had no idea if they were even in the city of Quintuklen. Were they well cared for? Tortured or starved? He and Ben had walked the streets hour after hour, trying to find signs of anything without asking any questions. They had to be careful. The eyes of Barnabus were everywhere. No one could be trusted.

"Do you want to go for a walk?" Ben said. He stood by the mantle, near where Akron and Fang hung from the wall. "I could use some air, and I need to stretch my legs." He buckled a belt with a sword to his waist. "Can never be too careful when you pop your head out these days."

Ben had been good to him. A stalwart, rugged, and seasoned soldier, deep-chested and lean-hipped, the durable fighter was always ready for any takers. The streets were safer when he was around.

"Let me gather some things," Bayzog said, heading back toward the bedrooms. Inside by his bed sat Brenwar's chest. He popped it open, grabbed a few items, set them on the bed, and closed the lid. On his way out, he stopped and ran his fingers over the Elderwood Staff. The gemstone eyes inside the woven wood at the top of the staff twinkled at him. He wanted to set its power loose on his enemies, but they had his family, and at the moment he didn't even know where they were. *Patience. I must have more patience. Let time reveal their plotting.*

Shackles dragged over the dank corridor's floor. Samaz, Rerry, and Sasha, one behind the other, followed two guards up front and were harried by two behind. Lizardmen, coated in metal armor and carrying spears, prodded the three of them along.

For weeks they'd been moved from one location to another. Marched. Dragged. Transported in barred wagons. They slept in dungeons, barns, stables, and forts filled with their vile enemies. Their captors didn't say a word to them. The woman who had bewitched them was nowhere to be found. Samaz didn't understand any of it.

The lizardmen opened a pair of double doors. The air was stale and rank within. A cool breeze wavered the flames on the torches they carried. The guards shoved them along into the darkness.

"What is this place, serpent?" Rerry said, pushing back against the lizardman.

A second lizardman came and locked up his other arm. They picked Rerry up off the floor. "Unhand me, snake face!"

The lizardman walloped him in the gut.

"No!" Sasha cried out, rushing toward him.

A lizardman jerked her by the chain collar, right off her feet.

"Mother!" Rerry cried out. Samaz rushed to her aid.

She choked and coughed.

"I'm alright," she said, rubbing her neck. "Just, just do as they say."

They tossed Rerry into the room first, followed by his mother, and then Samaz. The door closed, and they bolted it shut from the other side. The only light came from torches outside the barred window.

Samaz covered his nose. So did Rerry, who squinted in the dim light. Someone else was in the dim chamber with them.

"Gad!" Rerry said, shielding his mother.

The dead eyes of a goblin's rotting corpse stared right at them.

"I'm sorry, my sons," Sasha said, "so sorry."

Wham!

The giant toppled over.

Thud!

Brenwar eyed a large dent in the giant's bronze helm and grunted.

"That's the last of them," he said, hopping down from the giant's chest. "But with any fortune, we'll run into another nest of them tomorrow."

Shum spun his great spear around. It retracted with every twirl. He wiped the blood that wetted its tip off on the grass.

"I'm surprised they are so many," Shum said. He put his fingers to his lips and made a sharp whistle. "But times are changing."

"Times are going to be changed back then," Brenwar said, hefting War Hammer over his burly shoulder. "Even if I have to crack the skulls of all of them."

Two massive men, over fifteen feet tall each, lay dead on the ground. Each carried a club of iron as heavy as a man. Their armor was steel, forged by men and orcs.

Brenwar could tell by the craftsmanship. He shook his head. "I miss the days when I hunted the giant raiders. Now they hunt us."

Shum's steed trotted from the woodland to his side. Other figures on horseback followed, Hoven and the other Roaming Rangers.

"How many?" Brenwar asked.

"One."

"One? I swear I heard at least three."

"You did," Hoven said, holding a rag against a bloody gash on his head. "And the other two lie at your feet."

Brenwar harrumphed. He hadn't parted with the Roaming Rangers since they battled together near the River Cities. Every day had been a battle of sorts ever since. Worst of all, he'd gotten used to their company. Now, having escorted Bayzog and Ben back to Quintuklen, they had been chased south of Morgdon, his home. He wiped the sweat from his head.

"Any of you pot bellies have a horn of ale to spare?"

The stone-faced Wilder Elves didn't bat an eye.

"Didn't think so." Brenwar turned and faced south, looking toward the Mountain of Doom, or Dragon Home. Shum had said the Dragon King, Balzur, would send help. He hadn't seen any yet. It tore at him. Nath's departure was even worse. Shum reminded him often that help was coming, and Brenwar believed it, but would it get here before they all met their end?

It started to rain.

"Good," he said.

A chestnut steed with double stirrups nuzzled his side. Brenwar climbed on.

"Lead the way," Brenwar said.

"Where?" said Shum.

"I don't know," he said. "I need to think, but I'm sure we'll run into something that wants to kill us soon enough. Oversized lizards and oversized men. Pah. What's next? Oversized orcs?" He grunted. "Just ride toward Morgdon. I'm tired of looking at you elves."

Without a word, Shum led the way. Within minutes, sheets of rain were soaking the forest, but Brenwar didn't notice a single drop. His thoughts were far away. The armies of Barnabus were everywhere, growing like ivy that crept up castle walls. Dragons cruised the skies. Perched in the high rocks. Dove through the towns and cities, sometimes snatching people off the ground. The war might be on hold, but the torment was not.

Uncertainty filled Brenwar's mind. Doubt churned in his stomach. Not for himself, but for Nath Dragon. His friend had bargained with the dark forces of Barnabus and saved them all from the sky raiders and Inferno. Brenwar would have rather fought and died than seen Nath go the way he did. Evil had a way of changing a man.

I don't think he's ready for it.

In the meantime, the armies of Barnabus didn't strike, but every brooding race and monster popped out of the thickets. Hill giants. Cave trolls. Bug Bears. Rogue Poachers.

Certain there was a bounty on their heads, they avoided the towns and cities. Occasionally, he and the Roaming Rangers would get within earshot of troops that were moving or farmers in the fields. They knew enough.

They rode day and night until the clean edges of Morgdon's walls were in sight.

"Are you going in?" Shum said to him.

Brenwar ran his stubby fingers through the greying hairs on his beard. His life in Morgdon was another lifetime ago. He grunted a small laugh. He hadn't been back since Nath turned himself into a bat and flew away.

He shrugged his armored shoulders.

"Might as well. It's time they knew everything that I know."

CHAPTER 29

"ALL HAIL THE DRAGON PRINCE!"

"Nath the Great!"

"Peace Bringer!"

The shouts and praise came from all over. The people of Narnum cheered and smiled from ear to ear. They laid wreaths woven with flowers in the streets. The crowds pressed against the soldiers—armed with swords and spears—that shielded Nath and Selene. The pair rode on a chariot being pulled by a wingless purple dragon with a short stumpy tail.

"Harmony, Nath," Selene said in his ear. "We can have that. Always. Especially when the people love you."

But I haven't done anything.

Something stank. But Nath decided to play along with it. It was the only way he'd find out what was truly going on. Eyeing the purple dragon that pulled the chariot, he said, "This isn't right."

"You know he doesn't mind," she said. "The groog dragons are work horses. And the brethren don't mind. You can feel them, can't you?"

There were half a dozen dragons perched on the buildings along the road. Blue and green, and dark winged. Nath had barely managed to get along with any of them before, but now they seemed to respect him. They buzzed to him at the balcony and nodded at him from time to time.

"Sure," he said, "but I can still feel the antipathy."

"That's normal, even for me," she said.

Nath lifted his hand and waved at the crowds. The cheers and cries were deafening. Men, women, and children on their parents' shoulders waved flags with dragons emblazed on them. It was the third time they'd done this since Sasha departed, and that was two weeks gone. The crowds became bigger and bigger every time. Even the lizardmen and orcs were cheering. Bizarre was an understatement.

There can't be this kind of harmony. It's insanity.

"You certainly have a way with the crowd, Nath." Her eyes glossed over him. "I can see why. That hair, those eyes."

"And don't forget the scales," he said, flexing his arms.

"I'm glad to see you loosening up," she said. "There's no reason to make passing the time miserable. We're all tied up in this, Nath. Let's make the most of it."

"We'll see," he said. *We'll see.*

Nath was doing his best to keep his distance, but he and Selene had become closer. She had told him things about herself and how Gorn Grattack raised her. That she didn't know who her mother was, but that Gorn had fathered her. She felt that Gorn feared her, or any black dragon. And she also felt there might be a third black dragon somewhere.

Nath wasn't sold on any of it. He kept in mind that evil lies, but every day it seemed more difficult to understand it. Good things were happening in the City of Narnum. How could good come from bad?

"Where are we going?" Nath said.

"I thought you could use some entertainment," she said.

"This is entertainment," he said, dusting confetti from his hair. "At least to me it is."

The chariot wheels clattered over the cobbled roads toward the edge of the city. Nath eyed faces in the crowd. Joyous. Jubilant, despite the pushing and shoving going on. But not every face in the crowd was full of mirth and cheer. There were many dissenting eyes within, not so much on Nath, but rather on Selene and her troops. Not everyone was happy in Narnum. Something else was going on.

The company of soldiers came to a halt. A large oval structure, five stories tall, made of limestone and circled in marble pillars, loomed before them.

"The Arena," Nath said. He'd been by it a dozen times in his adventures in the city, but never once had he been inside. It made him think of dragons that were pitted against each other for gambling and sport, thanks to the poachers. His efforts to free dragons seemed like ages ago. "This is what you call entertainment?"

"It's alright, Nath. No dragons fight in there. Only warriors and soldiers, and they are all *volunteers.*"

"Sure they are," he said, stepping off the chariot. "I'm curious to see what you consider amusement." He held out his hand.

She took it and stepped down, holding it for a moment before she let go.

"Thank you."

Thousands were gathered inside, cheering and ranting.

Nath and Selene sat side by side on thrones carved from stone. The arena waited below. It was a hundred-foot-long oval of grass, blood, and sweat, mixed with soil. Dozens of bodies were lined around the outer wall. Fighters. Warriors. Scrappers. Men, lizardmen, orcs, dwarves, goblins, gnolls. Hard faced. Scarred. Embattled. Many of which strutted back and forth, pumping their fists at the crowd.

"What sort of contest is this?" Nath said, eyeing the pile of crude-looking clubs in the center of the arena.

"Have you never watched the legendary Battle Royale of Narnum?"

He shook his head no.

She clutched her chest and said, "You? Nalzambor's greatest hero? I'm shocked."

His muscles pulsed under his scales. He'd fought plenty of battles but didn't recall watching many.

Eyeing the warriors and leaning forward, he said, "Tell me about this."

"Once a year," she said, "a champion arises from a group of warriors who all want to prove they are the greatest fighter. They come from all over."

"It seems brutal. And only once a year in this oversized yard?"

"Now Nath," she said, "the arena isn't always used for fighting. The people of Narnum are more sophisticated than that. They have jousts and concerts most of the time. But this time of the year is special."

Nath recalled hearing some of the women he'd known blabbering about it before, but he never paid it any mind. Soldiers were tossing helmets, gauntlets, and shields over the wall into the arena. Some of the brawlers were picking them up. Others were ignoring the soldiers. That's when the name-calling started going back and forth.

"What are the rules?"

"At my word, or yours perhaps, they'll rush into the middle and beat one another until only the last fighter is standing."

There were big men in there. Bigger than Nath in some cases. Others were smaller. Lean and muscular. The bug bears and gnolls had muscles up to their necks.

"People will die," he said.

"Only if they don't submit. And there is no shame in submitting," she said, taking a goblet of wine a serving girl offered her. "They can even fight again next year if they want." She chuckled. "Assuming they've recovered."

"People will die," he said again. "I see no way around that."

"It's their choice. Warriors wage war. It gives their life meaning."

With that, Nath agreed. He'd been around enough fighters to understand their way of life. But a mad dash for a pile of clubs? By the look of things, skulls would be crushed. Except for the dwarves'.

Still, Nath's blood was charged.

"So, what does the winner receive?" he said.

"I'll let that be a surprise." She nodded to one of her acolytes. He motioned to another, and a moment later, brass horns trumpeted. The crowd sat down and fell silent.

Selene rose from her chair and said to Nath, "Stand up and say it for them."

Slowly he came to his feet and said, "Say what for them?"

"Say, 'Let the battle royale begin'," she said, "and use your dragon voice. Say it with some flare."

Caught up in the moment, Nath raised his arms over his head and shouted with his power,

"LET THE BATTLE ROYALE COMMENCE!"

CHAPTER
30

I T WAS A MAD DASH to the middle. The smaller, quicker warriors arrived first, snatched up clubs of metal and wood, pooled their forces, and started swinging. Three men, wiry and lean, clubbed down a lizardman and an orc in seconds.

Nath clenched his fists.

"Yes!"

He hadn't considered that the smaller warriors would form teams and take it to the bigger threats.

"You *like* this," Selene said, keeping her eyes fixed on the games.

"I am a warrior."

Clubs went up and down, banging off shields and metal helmets.

An orc broke a wooden club on a red-bearded dwarf's head. The dwarf ripped the club away and dashed the brute across the knee. It teetered into a heap, and the dwarf whacked it into submission.

The fast, hard-fought spectacle ignited screeching cheers from the crowd.

Man fought gnoll.

Orc fought lizardman.

Women fought men.

Speed verses skill versus strength.

Four fell in the first seconds. Soldiers scrambled in, wearing yellow smocks draped over full armor. They dragged the wounded out by their arms and legs, but one man managed to walk on his own power, holding his broken arm by the elbow.

"Once you surrender, you cannot return," Selene said, "but so long as you are in the arena, you are fair game. The games are merciful."

Three warriors, two men and one woman who carried shields and swung clubs, hemmed in another warrior, a brute who swung two clubs like a wild man. He busted one man's shield, knocking him to the ground, and caught a striking blow in his ribs by the woman.

Whack! Whack! Whack!

The club came down with wroth force on all three of them, splintering chips off her shield. She collapsed on her knees. The third warrior slammed his club into the back of the towering fighter's knees, dropping him.

Sticks clattered on sticks with feverish madness.

The woman rolled out of harm's way from a thunderous blow. She scrambled back to her feet and twisted behind the third fighter and slipped behind the brute.

Well played, Nath thought.

The monster fighter didn't see it coming. She clobbered him in the back of the skull. His clubs slipped from his fingertips. The pair of small men dashed him from knees to shoulder.

Whap! Whap! Whap! Whap! Whap!

The frenzied crowd howled.

"Yield!" the brute cried from bloody lips. "Yield!"

The three warriors paused, conversed, and pounced back into the fracas.

Nath felt his blood churning in his veins. The fighters were rugged, hardy, and well-trained, all of them. They were fierce. Some showed compassion. Others did not.

A gnoll crushed a man's helmet with a two-handed blow.

An orc had a long-haired woman in a choke hold.

They bit, they scratched, they smashed.

Wang!

A large man adorned in dark purple robes and wearing a helmet of iron clocked a gnoll in the head. Its body collapsed and shuddered. He slung the blood from his gauntlets and eased into the fray once more. The heavy-shouldered warrior caught a club in his armored hand, ripped it away from a lizardman, and struck.

Crack!

The lizardman crumpled and threw his arms up.

Crack!

The warrior broke his wrists and moved on.

"He's quite the fighter," Selene commented. "Size, skill, and speed."

Nath's eyes darted from battle to battle. Over a score of fighters had fallen and withdrawn, leaving less than a dozen. His fingers twitched.

"You want to jump in there, don't you?" Selene said, sipping her wine.

"It wouldn't be fair," he said.

"So sure of yourself, are you?" she replied.

He glanced at her, then back in the arena.

"They might surprise you," she added, "if things were a little more even. After all, you'll still be here next year. Maybe we can make the stakes higher."

He huffed a silent laugh. He'd battled and killed full-grown dragons. It was absurd to think one of those warriors could best him.

"Why? Next year do you plan to have dragons fighting dragons?"

"That would be interesting," she said.

"That's what poachers sell them for," he said, glaring at her. "Being a dragon, you should be ashamed of what you say."

She shrugged it off and said, "I say if they want to do it, as warriors, then let them. No one is making them do it. If you wanted to fight, wouldn't you want me to let you?"

He didn't reply. Instead, he kept his eyes intent on the battle in the arena. Iron Helm held the dwarf down by the neck and hammered into his ribs. It stirred Nath's blood. Dwarves never yielded, whether you were beating them to death or not. The battered dwarf struggled to rise, only to be beaten down again by the superior foe until it moved no more.

The three warriors walloped a pair of orcs that had been fighting as a team. A swift clattering of sticks disarmed the dismayed orcs, and another succession of blows drove them to their hands and knees. Knotted and bruised, covered in dirt and sweat, hairy chests heaving, the pair feigned surrender and tossed dirt into the eyes of the three aggressors and pounced.

The crowd went wild, pumping their fists up at the sun.

One of the team of three warriors went down under the weight of the two orcs. His head slammed into the ground. The orcs stomped and kicked him. The warrior curled up under his shield, screaming for help. The woman charged, ramming her shield into the back of one orc and barreling him over. A swift strike of her club caught him in the chin, knocking him out cold. She whirled back toward the remaining orc.

She's a fine fighter. All three are.

The warrior on the ground wrapped his arms around the second orc's legs. The second warrior wailed on the orc with his club until it pleaded for mercy.

Thunder boomed, startling the crowd. The skies darkened. Drizzling rain came.

"They'll be fighting in the mud soon enough," Selene said, holding out her hand to feel the rain. "I like this weather. It's so … soothing."

It could have been raining buckets, and Nath would not have noticed. His eyes were glued on the conflict. Amidst the moans and groans, only four fighters were left standing: the large robed man in the iron helm, and the three crafty warriors, one of which, a man, was limping. Shields raised and clubs ready, they surrounded the larger fighter and barked commands to each other.

Interesting, Nath thought, *if they defeat this goon, they'll have to battle one another*. Nath rested his chin on his knuckles. *Humph.*

The rain came a little harder, plittering off the three warriors' metal helmets. In perfect synchronization, they advanced. They struck.

Cat quick, Iron Helm caught a club of the flanking men in each mailed hand. The woman, in the middle, smote him in the chest with a thud. In a heave, Iron Helm twisted the clubs from the men and slung them to the ground. He drove his boot into the woman's gut, knocking her off her feet.

The crowd exploded. The big warrior was fast.

Too fast, Nath thought.

The warriors scrambled over the muddy dirt, snatched more clubs off the ground, and charged.

Wood clocked off wood. Iron Helm parried, deflected, and countered. Clubs licked out, popping him in the arms, knees and legs. The woman rapped on his helmet with a metal rod, clanging it like a bell. The mighty fighter waded through it all. His blows became fierce. Harder. The three warriors' chests were heaving now. They looked back and forth at one another. It was fatal.

Iron Helm attacked the limping man, drumming him all over with his mighty clubs. Snakes couldn't have struck faster.

Crack! Crack! Crack! Crack! Crack!

The man crumpled.

A blistering series of blows rained down on Iron Helm's backside. He spun, grabbed the nearest man's arms, jerked him off the ground, pushed him over his head, and slammed him head first into the ground.

"Ooooooooooh," the ignited crowd said.

Iron Helm was a giant compared to the woman. Her shoulders sagged, and her arms were shaking. Slowly, she raised her sticks up.

"She should yield," Selene said, leaning back, "don't you think?"

It would be wise, Nath thought. Be he didn't see it happening. She'd fought harder than anybody.

"Someone once told me, 'The best surprises come in small packages,'" he said.

Iron Helm dropped his clubs and beckoned the woman with his metal fingers.

She let out a battle cry and charged. Her clubs slammed into his ribs. His fingers locked around her throat and hoisted her off the ground. With his free hand, he ripped her helmet off.

The crowd gasped.

She was dark-haired and pretty, but one eye was missing. She kicked at Iron Helm's chest. His grip was a vice, and her skin began to purple. Life drained from her face.

Selene leaned toward Nath and said, "You were saying?"

Nath's jaw muscles tensed.

"He should release her!" he said to Selene, astounded.

"She hasn't pleaded. She hasn't withdrawn."

"She can't speak. He holds her by the neck."

Selene leaned back in her chair and said, "There are no rules against that."

Nath rose to his feet, watching the woman slap at Iron Helm's arms.

"She's tapping his arms. That's a submission!"

"She'll be well remembered," Selene said, looking at her nails. "A funeral. Flowers, perhaps."

"This isn't a death match! End this!"

"Mercy!" someone screamed.

"Release her!" shouted another.

"If you won't stop it, I will!"

Selene shrugged.

Nath turned to leap into the arena. The woman stopped flailing. Heart sinking into his toes, he fell down into his seat.

Crack!

CHAPTER

31

"YOU ARE A MONSTER," NATH said to Selene. "A monster."

"Oh come now. She died with honor. And with a bad eye, she didn't have much to live for." Selene huffed. "Nath, I didn't kill her. That warrior did. Perhaps you should speak to him about it."

The emptiness inside him stirred. His claws dug into the arms of his chair.

"But first," Selene said, "we must honor the champion." She rose from her seat and quieted the crowd with her arms. Heavy drops of rain pelted her face.

Nath's eyes were fixed on the warrior woman's broken form, lying still in the mud.

She didn't deserve that. His scaly biceps flexed. *But he does.*

"Champion!" Selene said. "You have won the Battle Royale. Your skills are without equal. And now, anything in the city is within your grasp. Fame. Fortune. Notoriety. An army of your own men to lead, perhaps."

Boots sinking into the mud, the warrior came forward and stood before the thrones. The eyes behind the helmet leered at Nath and focused back on Selene.

"High Priestess," the champion said. His voice was gruff and throaty. "I do not desire any of those things."

"Then what is it you wish?" she said.

"I want to fight Nath Dragon … to the death!"

The silent crowd ruptured in howls and cheers.

Nath glanced at Selene. Her eyes were wide, and her jaw hung open. In a moment, she recovered and focused on him.

"That isn't part of the custom," she said without batting an eye, "but the champion is entitled to such a bold request." Her eyes flitted toward the champion. His big arms roused the crowd. "I'm sure they wouldn't think any less of you if you declined. And I'm certainly not going to make you do it. That's up to you."

Nath's eyes narrowed. It wasn't what Selene said that bothered him. It was what she didn't say. Omission was one of the best ways to hide the truth and bury a lie. Wrap meaningless words around it.

She's hiding something. I can feel it. His eyes drifted to the fallen warriors in the mud. Why would he avenge people he didn't know? They knew what they were in for. And that man in the arena, he would love to teach him a lesson, but it was beneath him. At least it should be.

"I think I've seen enough," he said, getting up and turning away. "I wish to return to the tower."

"Understood," Selene said, "understood." She addressed the citizens. "Citizens, the Battle Royale is over. And you, Champion, will have to make another request. Nath Dragon is our guest, and we dishonor him by challenging him to a death match."

The crowd became restless and started to boo and shout.

"Teach him a lesson, Nath Dragon!"

"Avenge that brave woman!"

"Feed that brute his helmet!"

"Stuff those gauntlets in his mouth!"

The comments stirred his blood, making him turn and look down on the challenger.

"Yes, teach me a lesson, Nath Dragon," Iron Helm said, "or be a coward and walk away."

Nath set his jaw and headed for the wall.

Selene grabbed him by the crook of his arm and said, "It's not worth it. You're right. You are better than this. Let's go. The crowd will forget about it soon enough, and who knows, maybe you can dazzle them someday with other awesome feats."

"He called me a coward," Nath said.

"A word, a meaningless word. Come," she said, "Come."

As Nath began to turn away, the champion removed his helmet and said, "Come back and play, Dragon, or are you afraid I might kill you!"

Nath's face flushed red. He recognized the face. The voice.

But it was Selene who spoke first.

"Kryzak!" she yelled. "You traitor! You dog! How dare you infiltrate this honorable event! I should have your head for this."

"I only wish to please you, High Priestess!" the war cleric said. "To win my honor back. Return to your side. I've learned the error of my ways. "

Nath glared at the man with the tattooed forehead, taking it all in. The war cleric had changed. And he was bigger. Uglier, with scales on his head. Ah, part draykis. Barnabus had to have done this. Why would he not side with Selene?

"You are a failure, Kryzak," she continued. "Trying to overthrow me was a fatal mistake. I rule this army, not you. I am done with you."

"But I am the champion now!" He thumped his chest. "Let me fight him. Let me earn the right to rule by your side."

"You have no right, aside from one. A champion's request. And if you have any wisdom left, you should plead for your life." She motioned to her soldiers. They surrounded Kryzak. "I suggest you move on."

Kryzak laughed. "My request stands." He shot a look at Nath. "Come down here, big mouth. You know you want to. Please the crowd. Please yourself."

The crowd began the chant.

Nath! Nath! Nath! Nath!

His claws dug into his paws. He hated Kryzak after what he'd done, drowning Shum and almost killing Brenwar, Sasha and Bayzog.

He has it coming!

He leapt into the arena, and the crowd went into a frenzy.

"Nath!" Selene yelled. "You don't have to do this!"

He glanced back at her and said, "Yes, I do." He turned, oblivious to the veiled smile on her lips, and faced Kryzak. The war cleric stood tall, his girth thick and unnatural. A crooked smile crossed over his lips. He said, "Anything goes?"

Nath replied, "Anything you have won't be enough."

The fighters squared off in the middle of the arena, and the soldiers disbursed along the wall. Selene rose her arms and hushed the crowd.

"The Champion of Narnum versus the great Nath Dragon."

The people cheered. The rain poured down.

"Anything goes. This match is to the death."

"Aren't you going to put your helmet on?" Nath said to Kryzak. "You're going to need it."

Kryzak sneered and strapped it on.

Selene dropped her arms, and the brass trumpets blared.

Nath sprang and knocked Kryzak's helmet from his head.

The big man staggered back, wiping the blood from his jaw and shaking his head.

"You looked better with it," Nath said, "I'll say that much."

"Try that again," Kryzak said.

"Am I supposed to wait for you to put the helmet back on?"

"That's not what I meant." Kryzak shook his head. "You and that tongue of yours. It's time I ripped it out." He muttered an incantation, lowered his head, and charged.

Nath braced himself. A smacking collision of bone, muscle, and scales followed, jolting Nath's entire body.

Sultans of Sulfur! What is he made of?

Kryzak punched hard. Swift. A donkey didn't kick that hard.

"Oof!"

The war cleric socked his belly, doubling him down. A nasty uppercut followed.

Clack!

Nath's feet left the ground. He splashed back-first into the mud, his jaw loosened and his face hurt. The roaring crowd surged in his head. He pushed his fist in the mud and gathered his feet beneath him, teetering a little. His skin tingled.

Treachery! Magic!

But it was an anything-goes match.

Across from him, Kryzak raised his fists up, working the crowd and beating his chest.

"I am the champion! I will kill Nath Dragon!"

Nath's eyes slid over to Selene. She leaned back in her chair: smug, satisfied.

Treachery alright.

Kryzak dug his iron helmet out of the mud and tossed it over.

"Perhaps you need this helmet more than I do! Ha, ha, ha!"

Nath crossed the distance between them in a second.

Wham! Wham! Wham! Wham!

The war cleric absorbed every hit and dished out his own.

Pow! Pow! Pow! Pow! POW!

Nath's head snapped back over his shoulders. He stumbled through the mud, reeling, and splashed down on his knees. His head rang over the frenzied crowd. Nath shook it. Kryzak was a rock. His punches great hammers.

Think, Dragon!

With a groan, he rose up in the pouring rain.

Kryzak held the iron helmet. He crushed it in his hands.

"That will be you, Nath!" He slung off his gauntlets and tore off his robes. His hulking frame was dragon-scaled and ridged. An abomination of man and dragon. Similar to the draykis: part living, part dead, and radiating a dark aura. "I'm more dragon than you. I'm more everything than you." He slammed his clawed hands together. "Come, let me show you I am invincible."

"Everything has a weakness," Nath said, sloshing through the muddy arena, "and certainly something as ugly as you does."

Nath approached, mind racing. *I should be able to handle this. I'm a dragon, and no ordinary one at that. He can't be stronger than me. He can't be.* He closed in.

Kryzak punched.

He shifted aside and jabbed Kryzak under the chin.

Kryzak countered.

Nath blocked and rammed an elbow in Kryzak's temple. A flurry of punches followed, driving the cleric backward and off balance. Nath's foot swept his legs.

Splash!

Kryzak laughed and got up.

"Fool! You cannot hurt me! Haven't you figured that out yet?" He dashed the muddy water from his eyes. "Everything you do makes me stronger. I'm stronger than a giant now. Stronger than a dragon. Ha, ha! Of course, you can walk away, like a coward, but will your pride let you? Do you fear a true life-or-death battle?"

"I fear nothing!"

"You do fear! You are a failure! And you are about to fail in front of all Narnum and let the entire world down!"

The crowd began to boo. Their chants became ugly.

"Ha!" Kryzak continued. He lorded over the fallen woman. "Did you think you would avenge her? Did you think you would teach me a lesson, be the noble Nath Dragon? Ha! You jumped right in without thinking, and now it will be your doom." He flung a club at Nath and stuck his ugly chin out. "Come on. Take your best shot. I'll give you a free one. Or would you rather run, *coward*."

The sneer on Kryzak's scaled and tattooed face enflamed Nath's rage. He charged into the cleric with ram-like force. He put everything he had behind his punches.

The titans battled all over the arena, using fists, feet, knees, clubs, shields, and helmets. One heavy-handed blow after the other, the pair rocked each other back and forth.

Nath punched until his paws ached, probing for a weakness. He struck knees, temples, eyes, ribs, ankles. Everything he could think of.

Whop!

Kryzak drove him down with two fists in his back.

Nath bounced up and slugged into his ribs.

They twisted in the mud. Pummeled one another. Slammed into the dirty waters. Clubs busted off heads and shoulders. Shields splintered.

"You fight hard, but you cannot win!"

Wham!

Nath's knees wobbled.

Wham!

He landed in the mud again.

The war cleric leapt high and descended toward Nath, jamming his clawed toes into Nath's gut.

The pair of giants wrestled in the muck, raising the cry of the crowd to its highest crescendo. They grappled and fought.

Nath spat mud.

Kryzak head-butted him in the nose.

Bright stars erupted inside Nath's eyes. Blood ran down his nose. Dazed, he felt his arms fall limp for a moment.

Kryzak spun behind him, locking both arms behind his neck in a full headlock. "It's over for you, Nath Dragon!" The cleric cranked up the pressure. Two dozen men in one.

Nath strained. His arm and neck muscles bulged and cracked.

"No!" he yelled.

"Yes!" Kryzak said, forcing Nath's chin into his chest.

Nath surged back. His feet dug into the mud, and he pushed back against the force.

Kryzak slipped in the mud, but his mighty arms held.

"No," the war cleric said, "I'll never let go until you're dead!"

Iron thewed muscles bulged underneath Nath's black scales. Wriggling and shaking, he raked his claws over the cleric's skin.

Kryzak would not give.

This can't be happening!

"Once this is over," Kryzak said in his ear, squeezing harder and harder, "I'll find all your friends and kill them."

Red-faced, soaked in mud, rain, and sweat, and nose bleeding, Nath choked out, "Never!"

He drove both elbows into Kryzak's rib cage.

The cleric didn't budge.

Nath's paws stretched out toward the crowd. He started choking.

"It's over, coward!" said Kryzak's voice. Eerie. Throaty. Annoying.

Nath's gold eyes flared. His dragon heart raced. Smoke rolled from his nose. He summoned every ounce of strength within and turned it loose in a super-human heave.

"GRAAAAAAAAAAHHH!"

Fire exploded from Nath's mouth, turning the rain to steam.

Kryzak's grip loosened.

Nath tore free.

"Impossible!" Kryzak said.

Nath didn't hear a thing. He cut loose his rage. He hit hard and fast.

Whop! Whop! Whop! Whop!

Kryzak's body sagged. Pain filled his eyes.

"How?"

Nath snatched the bigger man off the ground and hurled him into the wall, driving the crowd wild. The surge of energy consumed him. He was bigger, stronger, and faster than ever.

Kryzak gathered his feet and lumbered forward, arms raised.

"You cannot beat—"

Pow!

Kryzak's aura faded.

Nath wailed away with fury in his eyes. Kryzak battled back a few more seconds until his entire body gave out. Nath locked the war cleric's tattooed head in the nook of his arm and dragged him out of the mud.

"To the death," he said, amping up the pressure.

Kryzak's grey eyes bulged.

Krack!

He dropped Kryzak in the mud, took a deep breath, and with a whoosh of torrential fire burned all of his enemy's skin, scale and muscles to the bone.

"…and then some."

The crowed hailed him all day and long into the night.

Nath! Nath! Nath! Nath! Nath! Nath! Nath! Nath! Nath…

CHAPTER
32

NATH LAY IN BED. THE sheets and pillows were soft. Every bit of his body was sore. It had been almost a week since he battled Kryzak in the arena. A long week. With a groan, he sat up on the bed's edge and stretched his long, sinewy scaled limbs.

"Ah!" he said, wincing.

Whatever spell Kryzak had cast, it was a powerful one. Fighting dragons had been less trouble. The war cleric had almost beaten him to death. Nath could still feel the blows thundering into him. He stood up, rubbing his neck, cracking it from side to side, and then checked his hair in the body-length mirror.

"He never should have gotten mud in my hair," he said, smiling a bit. His lips were cracked, and his cheeks were bruised and swollen. He eyed himself toe to head. "I'm still the finest looking dragon in this town." He took a seat at the edge of the bed and rested his chin on his fist.

What is she doing to me?

Now, after the fight, the bewitching woman had few words to say to him. "I'm disappointed," was all she had said. It threw him. He spent days wondering what she meant by that, but still angry, he didn't want to speak. Selene had guile. And he had trouble being able to tell whether she set up the entire incident with Kryzak or not.

It's best to assume she did, he thought. *Evil lies, always.*

In the meantime, he rested. Despite the lumps, he felt better than ever. The splinter was gone, and he had a nasty knock-down drag-out fight behind him. It had roused him. He squeezed his paws into fists. Something had broken loose inside him. He felt like he could take ten dragons. He lay back on the bed with his paws behind his head and wondered how his friends were doing.

Knock, knock, knock.

He lurched up, his thoughts racing to Sasha, and rushed over to the door. He stopped short, cleared his throat, and said, "Come in."

Knock. Knock. Knock.

He grabbed the handle, pulled the door open, and said, "I said, come in … oh."

It was Selene.

"You're supposed to open the door for a lady."

He shut it in her face and walked away.

She opened the door, walked in, and closed it behind her.

"Funny," she said, "for a child. Are you still a child, Nath?"

"No," he said, but when he was around her, he felt like one. "What do you want?"

Exotic and mysterious, she eased her way into his room and took a place on a long sofa. Her robes were white, inlaid with a gold pattern sewn with satin. She made herself comfortable and said, "Sit."

"I've been sitting all day, for several days," he answered, pacing. "And I prefer standing when you're around."

"Is that so?" She rubbed her hands on her knees. "Why don't we take a walk then?"

"The last time we took a walk, I almost died."

She laughed and shook her head.

"Such a shame."

"What is?"

"Your confidence, Nath. It's weak."

He pulled his shoulders back.

"It doesn't seem weak to me, or to anyone else."

"Well, you are the one who is scared to take a walk with me, not me with you. Hah," she said, rising. "Perhaps it's for the better. You probably couldn't protect me from muggers."

"I'm sure you'll do just fine on your own."

She walked up and stood toe to toe with him, staring deep into his eyes.

"I will teach you things. I will teach you how to deal with powers like Kryzak had."

"You probably taught him," he said. His mind told him to pull away, but his body was drawn to her.

She brushed against his chest. "You are a creature of magic, Nath. You must learn to use it." Her tail stroked his hair over his ear. "I don't know why your father never showed you, but I will show you what I can."

She smelled so good and sounded so convincing.

Why not? The more she shows me, the more I learn about her.

CHAPTER
33

OUTSIDE, BEYOND THE RIVERS, THE City of Narnum was gone from sight. It was Nath and Selene, riding side by side on horseback over the plains, into the sunlight. Behind them, a score of followers trailed on foot. Draykis. Some armed and wearing heavy armor. The others clawed and scaled. Acolytes shuffled through the grass, too, barely making any sound.

Nath kept his eyes ahead. The rolling hills, flowers, and greenery were a welcome sight. It almost felt normal.

It had been morning when they started, and it would be dusk before long. Nath had many questions for Selene. Where are we going? Why? But he didn't ask. He enjoyed the silence. A reprieve from his suffocating situation. Still, he was curious. Where *were* they going, and why the long ride? Perhaps she was taking him to another location. A prison perhaps. A dungeon in the ground. He surveyed everything they passed. He knew the lands better than most people did, and nothing was out of the ordinary. Trees, shrubs, forest, mile after mile of high grasses and prairies.

Selene stopped her horse and got off. She motioned a draykis over and handed him the reins.

"You do the same," she said to Nath.

"Why?"

"Humor me, please," she said.

He shrugged his shoulders and slipped off, glaring at the draykis that took the reins. The dragon-men were eerie. Wicked. Every one of them made him think of Kryzak.

"All of you go, return to Narnum," she said, shooing them with her arm. "Nath and I need to be alone."

What? Why?

"As you wish," the lead draykis said with a bow.

Slowly, the procession wandered away and disappeared into the grassy fields. Nath's arms tingled. Selene, appearing to enjoy the wind in her face, looked stunning. Beautiful. Nath's breath became uneasy.

"An amazing world, isn't it, Nath?" she said, toying with her hair. She walked through the meadow and looked back over her shoulder at him. "Come. We have plenty of time. After all, we are dragons."

Chest out and shoulders set, Nath took his place by her side, uncertain what to say. He'd been around plenty of women in his lifetime, but never one such as Selene. She was dynamic. Enchanting. Precarious. It roused his curiosity. Drew him in. He'd never felt this way around any woman before.

"There is freedom everywhere, Nath," she said. "The birds don't worry where they nest. The rest of the world should not either. There is plenty of room for everyone, but some take too much."

"Such as Barnabus," he said.

"We don't take, Nath Dragon. We protect."

"No, you invade. Interfere. That's not how life should be."

"Is that so?" she said. "You are a dragon, Nath. If everyone is so free, why are the dragons hiding?" She perched a brow. "Hm?"

"Because your kind is selling them? Poaching them? Killing them?" He felt angry. "I've seen what Barnabus has done to the dragons. I've seen them caged. Mutilated. Horrible things. And Barnabus is behind all of it. At least, that is most of what I've seen."

She stopped, turned, and met his gaze. She draped her arms around his neck, and he could feel her gentle breath on his face. His heart raced.

"We are dragons, Nath, and I want to see the dragons as free as me and you. It hurts me when dragons are put through such vile things." Her thumbs brushed over his cheeks. "Together, we can put an end to all of that."

Nath swallowed. His mouth became dry. She drew closer. Her lips almost touched his.

"I need you, Nath," she said, softly. "You need me. The world needs us." She ran her fingers through his hair and searched his eyes. "I'm lonely, Nath. Have you ever felt lonely?"

Always.

"What are you thinking Nath?" she said with a dark twinkle in her eye.

Something popped within him. A warning of some sort. His distracted wits began to gather. He took a breath and pushed her back. "I think that you're the most gorgeous liar I've ever met. And I'm not interested in this ..." He gazed around "... seductive trap you've set."

"Nath," she moaned, "what kind of dragon do you think I am?"

"The worst kind," he said, backing away, "and you brought me all the way out here to seduce me? To play more games?"

"I'm merely going about this the easy way," she said, checking her painted claws. She sighed. "But as usual, you want to go about things the hard way. But, perhaps that is for the better." She started loosening the buttons on her robes.

"What are you doing?"

Her tail lashed out and smote his cheek.

Smack!

Nath's blood ignited.

"Are you mad?"

"You could say that, Nath. But I think that's an understatement." Her face contorted, and her body began to grow. Larger scales popped up all over her arms, neck and face. "Do you remember me telling you how disappointed I was after you battled Kryzak? Do you!"

Gawping and backing away, he nodded. His eyes were glued to her. Her robes ripped, revealing a dragon's belly. Wings sprouted on her back, and her neck stretched long and serpentine. Her voice deepened and resonated with power.

"Do you think that buffoon, Kryzak, would have lasted ten seconds with the likes of me? I'd have killed him in an instant. Yet you," her tail slashed over the grass, "almost died! You are an embarrassment to our kind!"

She spread her wings and blasted green fire into the air. Selene's body had changed into that of a full dragon. Twenty feet long with black scintillating scales. Claws, fangs, wings. She had it all. Spectacular. Riveting.

Nath clenched his fists and backed away.

Selene's face snaked down toward his. He could count the long lashes on her eyes.

"How did you do that?" he demanded.

"You are such a fool, Nath! You hold back. Are you a man wanting to be a dragon or a dragon wanting to be a man? I think the later, and that is truly sad." She head butted him with her curled horns.

Whack!

He stumbled to the ground, seeing stars and reeling.

"Pathetic, Nath Dragon," she said, shifting side to side, "and that is why you must die." Her tail came up, and down it went.

Wham! Wham! Wham! Wham! Wham!

Confused and stunned, pain lancing through his body, he tried to figure out what was going on. He rose.

Her claws ripped across his chest, drawing blood.

He cried out.

"Scream all you want, but no one will come to your aid!"

Nath shuffled side to side. His gold eyes were fixed upward, to where she towered over him several feet, sitting back on her haunches as her tail slithered like a great snake in the grass. He became angry. Jealous. How could she turn into a dragon and not he?

She spit gobs of green fire at him.

He jumped out of the way.

"Come on! Fight me, human!"

There was nowhere to run. No blade for his hand. No friends to come to his aid. He clenched his teeth and rushed in, swinging for her nose.

Her neck slid away. She laughed.

"Pathetic." She batted her eyes and stuck her chin out. "Care to try again?"

He swung.

She dodged. He'd never seen a big thing move so swiftly.

She swatted her paw at him.

He ducked under.

She slapped him head over heels with the other paw.

He crawled through the grass and started rising to his feet.

She pounced right on top of his back, crushing him into the ground.

"Are you a man? Or are you a dragon?" she said, shoving him down harder. "Are you a man? Or are you a dragon?"

He couldn't speak with his face pushed into the ground. He strained to push up. No avail. He grunted.

"WHAT DO YOU SAY?" she roared, lifting a paw off of him. "YOU ALWAYS HAVE SOMETHING TO SAY. WHAT HAVE YOU GOT TO SAY FOR YOURSELF NOW?"

He rolled onto his back, sucked in his breath, and shot flames from his mouth.

Selene leapt into the air, wings beating, and soared into the sky, making a great wide circle.

Gasping for breath, Nath watched with envy. It seemed every dragon could fly but him.

She flew higher and higher, turned, and dove downward straight for him.

He set his feet and gulped a lungful of air.

So be it!

She closed in.

A geyser of flame shot from his mouth.

Selene the dragon plucked him from the ground. Her talons dug deep into his shoulders. High into the air she soared, and flung him across the sky.

Spinning head over heels, he crashed into the earth.

It went on like this: once, twice, three more times. Nath struggled to his feet every time, shrugging off the searing pain that wracked his body.

"WHY WON'T YOU DIE?" Selene roared. "TELL ME, NATH! WHY WON'T YOU DIE?"

Blood seeped over his scaly chest and dripped onto the grass as he staggered through the meadow. His paws were numb. His mouth was dry. Painful bright spots leapt in his head. He teetered face-first into the ground, bewildered.

CHAPTER

34

SELENE THE DRAGON LOOMED OVER him. Her shadow covered him in a cloak of death.

"Pitiful dragon," she said, spitting green fire, "Just pitiful."

Swollen, bloody, and with a mind full of mud, Nath fought his way back to his feet and faced off with her, swaying.

"You are no dragon," she said. "You are a disgrace. You are a little worm. Nath Worm."

Her words stung. If he had Fang, he'd ram him through her chest. Instead, she played with him as a cat toys with a mouse. He'd be angrier if he had more energy.

"Are you tired, Nath Worm?" she said, sliding her head from side to side. "Tired, and you haven't even put up a fight yet?" She flicked him in the chest with her claws, knocking him back down. "Crawl into the ground and sleep with your brethren, O' Worm Prince."

He put his fist to the ground and rose again. His mind began thinking.

I should be dead, yet I live.

"I'm a dragon," he said.

Selene stuck her face in his and said, "No, *I* am a dragon. *You* are a scaly worm."

Nath struck her in the nose.

Whack!

She reeled back.

"YOU DARE!" Her chest expanded and glowed.

Something ignited in Nath. A deeper furnace now burned within. His mind triggered a mystery, and his thoughts shouted.

I'm a Dragon. I'm a Dragon. I'm a Dragon!

Swat!

Selene slapped him across the grass and dropped her foot down on his chest. She glared down at him and said, "I'm going to rip you apart."

Nath shot her a fierce grin and said, "No, you are not!" *I'm a Dragon!* He slammed his fists into the ground. Shot fire from his mouth.

Selene recoiled back, dodging the flames. Nath bounced up to his feet. *I'm a Dragon, the same as she!*

Selene shot another blast of green fire at him.

Nath blasted his own, bright red.

Fires collided, gushing flames from both mouths. A great plume of blue fire erupted between them.

I'm the Dragon!

Nath kept breathing. With every passing second, he felt bigger and stronger. His limbs stretched. His head rose taller. The flames kept gushing out.

Selene smiled on the other side of the flames. She extinguished her fires and jumped away.

Nath cut his own flames out and stared down at the charred circle of grass. It seemed so far down. Everything seemed smaller. Even Selene. She prowled over the grass with her neck hanging low. Her dragon eyes were wary. She hissed. Her tongue flicked out of her mouth.

Something swooshed over the ground behind him. He jerked his neck around. A great tail and wings lurked behind him.

"Gah!" he said, leaping and landing hard on the ground.

Whump!

He circled in the grass, chasing after the tail. His neck stretched behind the wings. *Oh my!* He stopped. Focused. Beat his wings. His own wings! *Oh my!* A great thrill shot through him. He eyed Selene.

"Worms can't fly, but dragons can," she said, "Fly, Dragon. Fly."

He stretched his wings out. Grand and beautiful they were. Their thin dragon skin glowed in the setting sun. He flapped them, *whump, whump, whump,* and took off running.

Nath's talons lifted from the ground.

He soared over the fields and up toward the mountains.

Zoom!

No words could describe it. There was peace. There was power. The wind lifting him higher and higher. He could see everything for miles and miles. Towns, farms, animals, people. He caught it all. He cut through the clouds. Looped. Barrel rolled. Blasted through flocks of birds. He spied a lake of crystal-clear water and glided for it, half landing, half crashing into the ground. He shook it off, strolling his great form into the waters and staring at his reflection.

The water settled, and his image became clear.

Great horns crowned his head. His eyes were living gold. The scales over his face revealed only a shade of the man he once saw in the mirror. Black scales traced in white coated his entire mammoth body.

Nath knew this much: he was all dragon.

Whump!

He turned.

Selene landed in the grass by the lake, and he said, "You meant for this?"

"I did," she said. "You had buried deep inside you what should have come out long ago."

"That's why you had Kryzak try to kill me? Wanting this outcome?"

"That was one step."

"And this was step two, you trying to kill me as well?"

"No," she said, "I was merely trying to beat you into turning dragon. You, however, seemed determined to die. Good thing you're tougher than you look. I had started to worry."

Nath waded back out of the waters, drew closer to Selene, and slashed his tail across her face.

She gasped.

"Why did you—"

His gold eyes narrowed.

"Don't you ever call me a worm again."

EPILOGUE

SAMAZ'S EYES POPPED OPEN. IN the dungeon cell across from him, his mother and brother slept. He sighed and swallowed, mopping the sweat from his brow. The dream that woke him had been fierce. Terrible. Horror unleashed in the land.

He ran his fingers over the cold metal bars of the cell, thinking, *Perhaps it's safer within than beyond.*

Bayzog and Ben watched a flock of dragons streak across the sky, zipping over the rooftops of Quintuklen. Their visits had been more frequent.

"That's not a good sign, is it?" Ben said, squinting his eyes. "Even I can feel it."

"So can I," Bayzog said, "so can I."

The pair took a seat on a bench in the city's grand garden. They'd spent much time there of late. An investigation of sorts. Bayzog was tired of waiting on word about his wife and sons. He had to take action. He had to outsmart their enemies.

He slid his hand inside his robes and rubbed the jaxite stones. During his studies, an idea had blossomed. He was learning how to harness their power.

I will find you, Sasha. I will find you soon.

Brenwar sat inside the walls of Morgdon on a chair carved from stone, staring into the night sky. War Hammer rested on his lap. Home among thousands of his brethren, he'd never felt more out of place. He needed to be with Nath Dragon. Nath Dragon needed to be with him.

THE CHRONICLES OF DRAGON

War in the Winds

-BOOK 9-

CRAIG HALLORAN

CHAPTER

1

I**T WAS EVENING**. A **STIFF** breeze billowed the curtains of Selene's chamber inside the highest tower of Narnum, the Free City. Alone, Nath sat on her throne, long returned to his human form. He blew a ball of fire the size of an apple into his dragon-scaled palm. After tossing the red-orange ball high in the air from one hand to the other for a few moments, he blew another ball of fire, followed by another and another—and began to juggle the four of them with ease.

Eyes wide and with exhilaration fueling his veins, he said, "I'm amazing. Simply amazing."

The great doors popped open. Selene came in, alone. She wore a grand sleeveless white gown with symbols of Barnabus woven into it. Her arms were scaled the same as his, and she no longer wore the crown of silver leaves. Instead, her raven hair cascaded unadorned down past her shoulders. She approached with a sensuous walk and a beguiling smile on her face.

"My prince has great mastery of his flames, I see," she said, stopping at the bottom of the dais. "It pleases me to see it."

Nath let the fireballs drop and extinguish on the floor.

"I have you to thank for that," he said, rising from her throne. "Please, have your seat."

"No, you sit. I'm comfortable with you in my chair. After all, we *are* both dragons."

"Then maybe we should get another chair," he said, smiling and brushing his red hair over his shoulders.

"I like the way you think," she said, rising up the stairs to him and giving him a brief embrace. She kissed his cheek. "I like it very much."

"Great dragons think alike," he said, smiling at her.

"Indeed," she said, sitting down.

The drulture flew in from the balcony, followed by the feline fury. The winged dragon-cat prowled up the steps and nuzzled Nath. He stroked it behind the eyes and horns. Its purring was like that of a coming storm.

Nath went down the steps, took a seat at the great table, and dug into the abundance of food.

"I could eat a herd," he said, biting off a hunk of turkey leg.

He almost always felt hungry. Selene said she'd teach him to control it. She'd been patient with him so far, saying the most difficult test wasn't becoming a dragon, but resuming and maintaining the form of a man.

In dragon form, he had flown for hours. It had taken Selene just as many hours to coach him down out of the skies, and another week to teach him how to turn back into a man again. At first, Nath hadn't understood the need to retake human form. But Selene said it was important to earn the trust of people, and even more, he needed to master his powers.

"When do we fly again, Selene?" he said.

"Soon," she said, tapping her fingertips together. "I just have a few more matters to attend to, and then the open skies it is."

"You said that last week."

"Oh, Nath, don't think like a person. A week is but a second for a dragon."

This was another agonizing step in his training: patience. He'd been in the company of people most of his life. He was accustomed to moving at their pace. Selene was persistent in slowing him down and often suggested that he sleep. It made sense. There were plenty of dragons he'd known that slept years at a time, in some cases decades. Even he'd done that once already, for twenty-five years, but if he slept too long, it was possible he'd awaken with the Truce gone. For all he knew, at that point the world would come to an end.

His thoughts drifted to his friends. He missed them. *I hope they are alright.*

"Selene," he said, "I'm ready to fly again now."

"Oh," she said, touching her hand to her chest. She gestured to the balcony. "Then by all means, transform and go."

Nath dropped the turkey leg on the table, where it landed on the gold plate with a *clank*. His red brows crinkled. He'd only been in dragon form once. He hadn't been able to resume it since. His eyes narrowed on Selene. Had she tricked him into becoming a man again so that she could control him? Did she fear his power in full form? Was he a threat to her?

"You're too old to pout, Nath," she said, checking her nails. "You know you can turn into a dragon, but you're going to have to do it under your own power. Your own motivation. Not mine. It's your body. You must control it."

"And you said you would teach me how to control it, but you've been very quiet about that. If I didn't know better, I'd say you were avoiding it."

"And why would I do that?"

"That's what I'm wondering." He shrugged. "And there could be many reasons."

"Such as?"

"Fear," he said.

"Of what?"

"Not being able to control me."

"I'm not controlling you now," she said. "You decided to take the Truce to spare your friends, and you are doing well to honor that. Other than that, you have complete freedom, do you not?" She came down the steps and stood behind him, resting her hands on his shoulders. "A city full of people chant your name," she whispered, "Nath Dragon, Dragon Prince … the Peacekeeper. The Truce Bringer."

In spite of himself, Nath smiled.

Rubbing his shoulders deeply, she said, "Long before the Truce ends, there will be no more talk of war at all. The councils of men, elves, dwarves, orcs, and gnolls bring greetings and salutations to one another."

He could feel the power of her grip through his scales. He leaned back into her and closed his eyes. Her voice was so soothing.

"Think about it, Nath, the last great dragon war. What if it never happens?"

"I never thought about that," he mumbled.

"But I have," she said. "No one would die in a war that never happened. Together, we can bring peace to the land."

"I don't think Gorn Grattack wants that." He twisted his neck toward her. "Are you turning traitor?"

"I cannot say," she said, still rubbing. "But being with you, Nath, I've … well, I've begun to think about things differently."

"Differently how?"

"I've always served Gorn. Been loyal. Faithful. I've been one of his own. But through you, I've glimpsed a side of things I've never seen before." She swallowed. "You have friends you care about. I've never had any of those. In all truth, after centuries of life, I think you are the closest thing I've ever had to a friend."

"Friend, huh," he said. "Well, if you want to be my friend, you're going to have to take me out to fly."

She shoved his head and laughed.

"I open my heart to you, and this is how you respond."

Shrugging, he said, "I don't think you have a heart, just a beating lump of coal."

Her chuckle was wicked and delicious as she strode toward the balcony, mainly in the form of a sensuous woman. She was something. An awesome kind of something.

Standing with her back to the terrace wall, she said to him, "Watch and learn, Dragon Prince."

Her lips moved, and the words were soft and quiet. It was an ancient form of Dragonese. Selene spoke many such things, and Nath was beginning to pick up on them. Her body shuddered, and her flesh groaned. Two black shapes heaved up behind her back and spread out.

Nath's eyes shone like golden moons.

Dragon wings. With a beautiful wide span. Everything else about Selene's form was the same. She pushed herself up onto the wide ledge of the balcony and showed an enticing smile.

"You can join me," she said, stretching out her hand. "Come and join me right now."

Nath hesitated. He was angry. Jealous. Confused.

"You can do this, Nath," she said. "Just focus. Envision it. Think dragon!"

He closed his eyes.

If she can do it, I can!

He felt a glimmer of dragon magic within. Calm. Dormant. Dragons had powers that no others had. Great mystic powers. Breath. Spells. Many little things. Nath's mind probed deep within, and he tried to take command of his powers. *Obey me!*

Nothing stirred, without or within. His eyes opened. Selene was there beckoning for him.

"Come," she said. "I will take you elsewhere and teach you."

"I should be able to do this myself."

"True," she said, batting her wings to hover in the air. "But it even took me a long time to learn it. Remember, Nath, be patient. Dragons should always be patient."

He sauntered over to her, long in the face.

"Come," she said, landing on the balcony. "We all fly here: me, the fury, the drulture, and soon you as well. Now, climb up here and stand by me."

He did. Peering down into the darkness below, he could see the lanterns glowing, making a grid through the streets. Selene clasped him behind his waist and spoke into his ear.

"Have you forgotten the exhilaration of flying so soon? It is within you. Don't you want to do it again, like us, like even the draykis?" She squeezed him. "Surely they are no better than you." Her wings stirred the air, and his feet lifted from the ledge. "There is nothing that I can do that you cannot do, Dragon Prince."

Nath needed to believe that, but he was having his doubts.

"What about the words you speak?" he said. "I need to know them."

"No, you just need to find those words within. But," she said, soaring far from the edge, "if you think it will help, then repeat after me."

He nodded.

She spoke in Dragonese once again.

"I, Nath Dragon, do solemnly swear," she started.

"I, Nath Dragon, do solemnly swear…"

"That I will grow my wings…"

"That I will grow my wings…"

"Before I hit…"

"Before I hit…"

"The ground down there…"

"The ground down—*what*?"

Selene released him with a cackle.

Claws clutching, Nath plunged a thousand feet toward his death.

"Noooooooo!"

CHAPTER

2

F ROSTY.

That's how Ben saw the condition of Bayzog, the part-elf wizard. The Clerics of Barnabus hadn't sent any word regarding Bayzog's family in months. Every passing day further iced the part-elf's demeanor.

Ben sat on a stool with his sinewy forearms resting on the rounded edge of Bayzog's grand table. The wizard had been hard at work for days, with his nose inside his great book and his violet eyes glued to the pages.

How does he do this and not sleep?

Ben yawned.

Bayzog flipped another page.

Ben turned his focus to another set of objects on the table, the jaxite stones. There were three of them, large and egg-shaped, each with a warm blue radiance. They flared and pulsated from time to time, depending on Bayzog's utterances. Ben couldn't make heads or tails of anything Bayzog said. He had tried once, but it had given him a headache.

He plucked purple grapes from a fine bowl on the table and chewed slowly. Bayzog didn't mind him being there, so long as he didn't create any type of *disturbance*—what his parents would have called a *ruckus* in Quinley, but that was a lifetime ago. His thoughts drifted.

He didn't have any family now. He'd checked years ago. His mother and father had passed. Many of his other kin had died in the war or moved on. His wife and children were dead at the hands of Barnabus. He clenched his fists, thinking about the last time he stared into his wife's soft brown eyes. Sometimes he didn't sleep well at night, with nightmares of the day he had shoveled his children's graves. *I should have been there to protect them.*

He wasn't alone in his loss. Families all over had lost. In a strange way, he found comfort in that. Motivation. He had to do everything he could to help put an end to all of this. Every time he vanquished one of their enemies, perhaps more senseless deaths were prevented. Bayzog had helped him see that. So had Brenwar. They were the only family he had left.

Bayzog's neat black brows were buckled as another page flipped over. The book, or tome rather, was a monstrosity, maybe thousands of pages long. The wizard seemed intent on reading all of it. Searching, digging deeper and deeper, trying to find help. Ben felt for his friend, who was tormented over the safety of his captured wife and children. It was a cruel game the forces of Barnabus played with Bayzog. Ben felt his pain.

I don't know how he does it. I'd have unraveled long ago.

They'd talked little about it. Bayzog seemed to have taken the servants of Barnabus at their word—that his family wouldn't be placed in any duress or danger. That all he had to do was remain quiet and still, within the city. All the wizard said was that longsuffering was something elves were accustomed to, even though it did drive the man inside him a little crazy. He would endure, and he had faith that Sasha and his sons, Rerry and Samaz, would endure as well.

On its own accord, the book closed, lowered, and rested itself on the table. Bayzog rubbed his eyes. Ben wanted to speak but held his tongue. He reached for the Wizard Water in a nearby pitcher.

"I'm fine," Bayzog said. "I drank my fill hours before you arose." He pulled his narrow shoulders back. The whites of his eyes were cracked. "But I've discovered some information that could be helpful."

Ben leaned forward and said, "Tell me about it? And I hope it involves getting out of this place."

Bayzog stretched out his long fingers and wrapped them around the jaxite stones.

"I have a handle on their unique power," he said. His eyes smoldered the color of the stones. "And we can use that to our advantage." When he released the stones, the glow went out. He turned to Ben and locked eyes with him. "Our enemy watches us everywhere, so we will incorporate aid from sources they will not suspect. We will use that aid to seek out my family and my enemies."

"And what kind of aid might that be?" Ben said.

"Dragons," Bayzog said. "I'm going to summon dragons."

Tired, hungry, and thirsty, Sasha and her boys endured. Shackled, on foot, and tethered to horses, the three of them followed behind a train of soldiers. It was the third move in a month. Sasha didn't understand the reason for it. Why not leave them locked up in one spot? Was that too easy? Was this mild torture? No one had spoken a word to them.

Arms and hands encased in metal cuffs tied to her waist, shoulders sagging and sore, she glanced behind her. The gait of her boys was easy, but their heads were downcast. She was proud of them. Neither complained. Both stayed close, quiet, and determined to protect her, and they'd done well. A pit was in her stomach, however. She was the mother. She should protect them. Instead, she'd let them down and gotten them all captured.

I just wanted to be younger. Her teeth dug into her lip. *What a fool I was!*

Lizardmen and acolytes led the way up the rocky steppes with no sign of resting. They'd been to ruins, abandoned camps, and temples, stopping very little for rest. Above, the skies were dreary and the clouds thick and lazy. A misty rain fell on her face.

Oh how I miss you, Bayzog.

Navigating between two rocks, she slipped. Pain jabbed into her knee.

"Guzan!" she cried out.

Rerry and Samaz rushed to her side.

"Mother," Rerry said, "are you alright?"

"I'm fine," she said, trying to force herself up to her feet. "Just help me up."

"No," Samaz said, pinning her down by the shoulder.

"But," she said, glancing at the nasty gash in her knee. She grimaced, and her eyes watered.

"Look away, Mother," Rerry said, "while we clean it."

"Alright—*ulp!*"

The horse she was tethered to jerked her onto her back, dragging her away.

Rerry sprang to his feet, yelling, "Stop the horses! Stop the—*woof!*"

A lizardman drove his spear butt into Rerry's belly.

Rerry dropped to his knees.

An acolyte, small and ghostly with bright colors on his head, brought the horse to a halt. The rest of the small caravan came to a stop. Plum robes dragging the ground, he eased his way over to Sasha and inspected her knee. He offered her a smile full of gaping teeth and said, "You can walk or be dragged."

She wanted to spit on the oily man's face, but instead, she pushed off the ground onto her feet and looked down at him.

"Well done," he said. "See to it you don't lose step again. There will be no stopping next time."

Struggling with the metal cuffs, she eyed him as he went away.

If I could reach my magic, I'd set fire to your tattooed head.

Rerry and Samaz held each other's gaze for a moment as the group resumed its movement. Rerry, the younger, light-haired and fair, scooped up a stone. Avoiding the guard's eyes, he tossed the stone back to Samaz, who snatched it out of the air and slid it under his robes.

"Mother," he said, catching up to her, "are you alright? You are limping."

Two lizardmen cut him off and shoved him backward.

"Enough!" he said, surging forward. "I'm just checking my mother, serpents! You're the ones slowing us down, not me!"

The lizardmen, both of which had thick muscles bulging under their scales, hemmed him in dangerously, spears lowered between neck and belly.

Rerry raised his hands and backed away, glancing at his ailing mother. "Alright. Alright." He fell back in step with the horse that led them. The lizardmen stayed close, to either side of him. He checked out the steel on their hips.

One day, I'll turn you all into boots.

He took a quick glance over his shoulder at Samaz. The thickset part-elf dropped the stone on the ground and returned a quick nod.

Good, Rerry thought, *good.*

For weeks on end, at every opportunity, he or Samaz had been leaving markings on stone or in wood by any means they could. It was an elven distress sign that Bayzog had taught them when they were little. The problem was, Rerry didn't think there were any elves for at least a hundred miles except them. He trudged along.

No harm in trying. No harm at all ... unless we get caught.

CHAPTER

3

BRENWAR'S HAMMER CAME UP AND banged down. Orange sparks danced off the red-hot steel. Sweat dripped from his forearms and sizzled on the blade's hot metal. Sleeveless and with his leather apron soaked in sweat, he'd been hammering on and off for hours, working day and night in the forge. His mind was restless. He took out his aggravations by beating on steel, day in and day out.

After cooling the blade, he laid it in the corner with other fine weapons he had made and took a seat on a three-legged wooden stool. Head down and sighing, he mopped the sweat from his brows. He felt empty inside. Restless. The great halls and mighty walls of his home, Morgdon, did little to dull his edge.

"Ahem."

Brenwar lifted his chin and found himself looking into the bright eyes of Pilpin.

"What is it?" he said.

"I just thought I would stop by and see how you were doing," Pilpin said. He walked over to the racks of weapons Brenwar had made: hammers, knives, swords, and axes. All well fit for dwarves. Pilpin picked up a pair of matching hand axes and twirled them around. "These are excellent."

"Then make excellent use of them elsewhere, will you?"

Pilpin stuffed them in his belt and adjusted the neck of his chainmail armor. "Don't mind if I do." He sauntered a little ways through the forge. It was a large room with three bright furnaces glowing orange. It was Brenwar's personal forge, and he'd been using all three. "Say, are you sure you can't use some help down here?"

"No," Brenwar mumbled. "But I'm sure someone could use your help elsewhere." Brenwar rose from his stool and glared down at Pilpin. He towered over the small dwarf by over a foot.

"Nope."

It was clear Pilpin wasn't going anywhere, and why should Brenwar want him to? They were the last of the dwarves sworn to protect Nath Dragon. They had done so together for more than twenty-five years.

Brenwar had been distraught ever since Pilpin arrived, alone and with the news that a dragon had killed Devliik and all the others. But it did him some good to know that justice had been served to the murdering satyrs, Faylan and Finlin. Of course, there was still the issue of Gorlee having gone missing. The changeling was a mystery, but the best candidate to take care of himself. Shum and Hoven, the elven Roamers, would keep an eye out for him in their travels. Snarggell the Crystal gnome had gone on his own. That was one thing Brenwar was glad for. And then of course Nath… All of this gave Brenwar plenty to think about, and he didn't like company that interrupted his thoughts.

He shrugged his heavy shoulders and said to Pilpin, "Alright, grab a hammer. Let's forge."

Pilpin's small bearded face brightened.

"Really?"

With his oily forearms, layered in muscle, Brenwar picked up a smallish anvil and tossed it to Pilpin.

"Put that over there." He pointed. "And straighten those blades yonder."

"Aye," Pilpin said, lumbering toward the spot and resting the anvil on a stout wooden block. "Brenwar, have you heard any news of late? Or rather, have you had any other visitors?"

Brenwar poured molten steel into an oversized war-axe mold. It was shaped with twin blades and had a long spike at the end. Nasty thing. "No," he said, "other than my wife." He nodded toward another corner. "Help yerself."

A small table was layered in food, making Pilpin's mouth water. Sweet cakes, breads, cooked meat, cheeses—and a small barrel of ale on either side.

"Seems you do have all you need down here," Pilpin said, driving his hammer down on his first blade. "But, I was wondering if she reported any recent news to you."

"Such as?"

"Well…"

Bang! Pilpin drove the hammer down.

"…there have been dragon sightings. Strange ones."

Bang!

"There are all kinds of dragons," Brenwar said, "many of which have never been seen or will never be seen."

Bang!

"Yes…" Pilpin said.

Bang!

"…But these dragons are special, they say. They soar blacker than night in the sky."

Bang!

Brenwar's brow furrowed.

Bang! Bang! Bang!

"How do you mean, blacker than night?"

Bang!

"Black. Black-scaled. Such as the legends say." Pilpin swallowed. "The likes of Nath Dragon."

Brenwar froze. A chill went through his veins. *It can't be. It cannot be.* Unsure of what to do with himself over the passing weeks, he had holed himself up in Morgdon, waiting for word. A sign from Bayzog. From the Roamers. Something. Dwarves were patient, Brenwar as patient as any, but now his patience ebbed.

"Who says they saw these dragons?" he said. "Men? Orcs? There are terrible rumors all over the city."

"They say terrible things are happening everywhere," Pilpin said, switching out one blade for another, "and all the sources say the rumors are true, despite the 'Truce.' The dragons and armies of our enemies thicken." He slapped another blade on the anvil.

Bang!

"Our forces thin." *Bang!* "So it seems."

"When did you hear of this?" Brenwar said, pushing the vat away.

"On and off over the past week."

Bang!

Brenwar eyed War Hammer. His weapon rested on a nearby steel table, along with the box that held the bracers given to him by Balzurth. His breastplate and other gear adorned a dwarven mannequin.

"Let me finish this axe," he said, "and you temper those blades."

"Then what?" asked Pilpin.

Bang!

"Then we go."

"Go where?"

"Wherever my hammer takes us."

Pilpin nodded and smiled.

Bang!

CHAPTER

4

THE ROAMERS. ANCIENT. ELVEN. STALWART. Vulpine. Trapped.

Shum dived for cover.

A dragon swooped over his head, tail lashing out and striking the rocks, before soaring up into the air again. Bigger than two men, the dragon and one of its brethren had cornered them in a narrow chasm. The dragons, cherry scaled with barbed black wings and tails, hissed and spit blasts of fire at them. Flame tongues, they were called.

Shum dashed across another chasm behind another rock. Hoven was there. His arm dangled at his side, and his sleeve was seared to his skin.

"Can you fight?" Shum said.

"Certainly," Hoven said, wincing. "I just wish I had my spear with me."

Whoosh!

The second flame tongue dragon whipped overhead, blasting a streak of fire into the stone and then darting back up in the air. Its serpentine neck twisted around. Its eyes were glowing red flares. Tail and wings black. Cursed. The dragons struck quickly, again and again.

Shum peered over the rocks and up the walls of the chasm. He and Hoven had opted to split from the other Roamers in an attempt to divide the dragons. Instead, both dragons had followed the two Wilder Elf brothers. The flame tongues were crafty. Patient. Capable of setting the entire chasm on fire.

"Suggestions?" Hoven said. His elven sword, keen and fanciful, was white-knuckled in his grip.

"If we can take one, we might scare the other off."

Above the rim of the chasm, the dragons circled and spat flames. The small bushels of brush quickly caught fire, and the chasm was full of smoke. Shum squinted his eyes. The big elf handed his brother a spear and said, "I'll lure one in."

Hoven spun the spear around, lengthening it one-two-three times. He eyed the sky and nodded. Shum crawled up on the rock, blades ready at his sides. Dragon hides were tough, but his elven steel was a match for the smaller flame tongue. He stretched his blades in the air, shouted a challenge in Elvish, and muttered an incantation.

The dragons dove, two red darts streaking toward him, closing in. Flames shot from their mouths. A wash of fire covered Shum from head to toe. The first dragon's mouth rushed at him, wide open.

Shum struck, cutting the dragon's nose with one blade and clipping its wing with the other.

The dragon barreled into him, backing him into the rocky chasm. The beast skittered over him. Claws tore into his face, gashed his thigh.

"Agh!"

Shum rolled to one knee.

The dragon squared off on him, rearing back on its hind legs, towering over him. Its neck coiled back, its lungs filled, and dragon fire whooshed out.

Shum hunkered down. The heat was excruciating, suffocating, but nothing burned. His spell held, for now. He rushed in. The first blade skipped off the dragon's dark cherry underbelly. The second lanced into the dragon's shoulder.

The dragon snarled, hind claws flashing.

Shum ducked, rolled, struck, dodged, and struck. Claws clipped him. Teeth snapped at him. The speed of the bigger foe was amazing. Swift. Fluid. Punishing. Shum parried its claws.

The dragon turned its hip and swung its tail around.

He jumped. The spiked tail caught his booted heel and flipped him onto his back.

The dragon pounced. It pinned his arms to the ground. Its claws dug into his flesh.

"Have at it, dragon!" he said.

The dragon's head coiled back.

Sshlunk!

Hoven's spear lanced through its neck.

The dragon bounded backward, wriggling its neck. Its claws dug at the spear. Fire exploded from its mouth, engulfing its head in flame.

Hoven locked his good arm under Shum's shoulder and dragged him away.

The dragon exploded.

An earsplitting roar filled the sky, and the second dragon dove at both of them with flames surging from its mouth.

Sshlunk!

A great spear penetrated the dragon's belly. It veered left and crashed into the side of the chasm.

Another Roamer appeared on the rocks. He bounded through the chasm with the supple ease of a wild animal. Two blades sprung from his hips. The Roamer pounced on the back of the flame tongue and put the beast's thrashings to an end.

Glitch!

A puff of smoke came from the great lizard's lips, and its bright eyes winked out. The younger Roamer cleaned his blades and sheathed them. A warm smile was on his face that went well with the rugged ranger garb he wore.

Hoven nodded and said, "Well done."

"Well done indeed, Liam," Shum said, steadying himself.

Without a word, Liam nodded. Then his eyes drifted toward the sky.

Another flame tongue circled.

Blood dripping to the ground, Shum gathered his swords.

"Roamer up," he said.

A moment later, the dragon dove.

Liam went for the spear in the dead dragon's belly, but the beast had wedged it into the ground.

"On guard, Liam, or take cover."

Eyes flame-ridden with hatred, the third dragon closed in.

A great flying bulk slammed into it, driving it into the chasm wall. The two monstrous creatures rolled down the cliff side and into the gorge.

The Roamers rushed over.

The cherry-scaled dragon had locked up with a great winged ape. Massive fists pummeled the dragon, heavy blow after heavy blow. The dragon reeled. Recoiled.

The winged ape tore into it with savage power. Dragon claws tore at the hairy beast. Fire scorched its hide. The ape locked its arms around the dragon's neck and slammed the dragon's hornless head into the wall, full force.

Fire spewed from the dragon's mouth.

The muscular arms of the great ape bulged.

The dragon roared one last time before its neck snapped.

Shum, Hoven, and Liam kneeled as the great Sansla Libor walked over. He towered over them a full eight feet in height. The savageness was gone from his eyes, but not the power.

"Arise and be healed," Sansla said in a distinctly elven voice. "We have much more work to do."

CHAPTER

5

"THEY'RE SO SMALL," BEN SAID to Bayzog, eyes fixed on the dragons. "Almost tiny, like field mice." Bayzog rubbed his eyes and held his head. Weary, he rested his arms on the table and eyed the dragons with intent. They were wondrous. Three of them, scales bright in color. A citrine yellow, a scarlet red, and a cobalt blue. Sharp and scintillating as the sun. Each prowled over his table, and they growled back and forth at one another.

Ben stretched his index finger toward the citrine one. "Can I touch one?"

"I wouldn't advise that."

The tiny citrine dragon widened its jaws, and a bolt of lightning flashed out.

Zap!

Ben lurched up. Eyes wide and hair standing on end, he collapsed on the floor. Shaking, he crawled up to his elbows.

"Are you alright?" Bayzog said, holding back a chuckle.

The rangy warrior shook his head, peering at the table.

The dragons peered back at him. A puff of smoke came from the red one's mouth, and a puff of blue acid from the cobalt's.

Ben eased up and away from the table. "They pack a punch."

"I'm sure it's not personal," Bayzog said. "Dragons in general aren't too trusting of people. You should know that by now."

Ben shrugged and took a stool farther down the table. He smacked his lips. "I taste metal."

"That's better than death," Bayzog said. "You should be more careful."

"Aye," Ben said, rubbing his head. "So, are they really *dragons*?"

"Yes, and I didn't even know that such a breed existed until I came across them in my studies."

"Why did you summon such small ones?" Ben said. "I thought you'd need something bigger?"

"I need something our enemies won't notice."

"Are they easier to control?"

Bayzog shrugged and said, "I don't know. I've never controlled a dragon before." He rested his fingers on the jaxite stones and concentrated. *Come*, he thought. *Come*.

One by one, the dragons paraded over and sat back on their haunches. Their tails swished behind their backs, heads cocking.

"I think they like you," Ben said. "What are they called?"

"The Elvish word is long, and I'm not sure how to pronounce it in Common."

"Eh, well, how about I call them dragonettes?"

"I don't see why not."

"So, what do these tiny dragons eat?" Ben asked. "Flowers and such?"

"People."

"People!"

Bayzog smirked.

"It's good to see you in better spirits," Ben said to him. "But honestly, how can they help our cause?"

"They are small, fast, and virtually undetectable," Bayzog said. "And remember, dragons are outstanding trackers." He set some articles of clothing on the table, items from Sasha, Rerry, and Samaz's wardrobes. "Seek," he whispered to the dragons. "Seek."

The dragonettes snorted and sniffed the items. One by one, they raised their heads to him in a sort of salute.

"I have to admit," Bayzog said, "this is going better than I expected."

Ben nodded.

It had taken Bayzog hours to cast the summons, and upon completing it, he had fallen over in exhaustion. That was three days before this morning, when the dragonettes appeared. How they'd gotten into his home, he didn't know. All that mattered was they were here and they seemed to be doing his bidding. He took a breath and sent his thoughts to them.

I'm seeking my wife and my sons. I miss them. I need them. Can you help me?

The dragonettes growled back and forth at one another and traipsed around. They butted heads with their tiny horns.

Bayzog felt the jaxite stones warming under his palm. He had control of the tiny dragons! At least, he thought he did. Still, better to ask than to order in such delicate circumstances. He wanted to earn their trust and respect. It was better that way. He couldn't control them forever, or at least, he didn't want to. With or without the jaxite stones.

Their wings buzzed to life the same as a hummingbird flies. They lifted off the table and darted through the air, zipping back and forth in the wink of an eye. Briefly, they circled Ben's head, causing him to duck. They zipped in front of Bayzog, roared, then headed upward through a crack in the wall and disappeared from sight.

"Did they flee, or are they doing what you told them?" Ben said, peering up at the rafters.

"We'll see," Bayzog said, stuffing his hands into his sleeves. "We'll see."

"Huh, I think I miss them already." Ben hitched his elbows on the table. "To think, you can actually hold a dragon in your palm. That's amazing! And the way they fly! Fast. Fast as lightning."

They sat in silence for a long moment. Ben's eyes were fixed on the rafters. Bayzog gazed at his book. He'd just summoned three dragons. *What other wonders can I do?* He stretched out his fingers. The book slid off the table into the air and opened up before his eyes.

"Are you already reading again?" Ben said. "Don't you get tired from all that reading?"

"I won't stop until my family is found," he said. "You should know that by now."

"I do know that, but let us get a breath of fresh air, at least." Ben made his way to the closet and stuffed his boots on. "Our enemies might be missing us anyway. Best we give them something to see."

With a wave of Bayzog's finger, the tome closed and lowered back onto the table.

"Perhaps you're right," Bayzog said, sauntering over to the closet to slip his shoes on. "You're a good friend, Ben."

"As are you, Bayzog." Ben buckled on his sword belt. "I just wish there was more that I could do."

"You've done more than enough already. Come, let's stretch our legs a little, shall we?"

They made their way out of the mystic apartment and back to the gardens. A misty rain fell, wetting the flower petals. Bayzog took a seat on the bench, with Ben standing near his side. It was here he always waited, in plain sight, hoping the servants of Barnabus would check in with him. It was his way of letting them know he was desperate and under their command. At least that's what he wanted them to think.

Ben's fingers tapped on the pommel of his sword. His eyes were busy, drifting from person to person. It seemed they all avoided his stare, avoided walking by him, even.

Are they all in on this?

They sat for almost two hours, talking little. Ben, as usual, commented on the flowers and chatted a little about the time when he had worked on his parents' farm. Bayzog could feel the tension in the man. Ben had become a man of action. A soldier. Fighter. The waiting game must be torment to him.

"Perhaps you should spend a little time among the other folk," Bayzog suggested. "Unwind. So long as you are within the city, I don't think our unseen captors will mind. Go. Be normal."

"I'm not so sure I want to spend time among these people," Ben said, sucking his teeth and eyeing a vulture of a man walking by them with a stone-cold stare. "And I always have this feeling they want us separated. We're all split up enough already. Only the Sultans of Sulfur know where Nath is, and Brenwar's probably arguing with a tree somewhere. No, I'm staying."

"As you wish," Bayzog said, "and I hope no offense."

"None taken."

A figure approached. She was beautiful. Crimson robes. Tall, dark, and eerie. Her voice was soft and commanding.

"Bayzog." She nodded. "I bring word of your wife and sons ... "

CHAPTER

6

BRENWAR TUGGED AT HIS REINS. Into the stiff winds they rode. Their dwarven horses nickered and stomped their hairy hooves. Behind him, Pilpin led his horse to a stop and opened his mouth. Cutting his utterance off with his hand, Brenwar squinted his eyes and sniffed the air.

In a low voice he said, "You smell that?"

Pilpin cocked his head. His eyes widened.

"Orcs."

They'd been riding north, toward Narnum, for two days, keeping their eyes on the skies. Brenwar knew there was little chance he'd see a black dragon. He was certain the story was half-cocked to begin with, but dwarves claimed they had seen them. And if you couldn't trust the word of a dwarf, who could you trust?

He dug his heels into his horse's ribs and plunged deeper into the forest. He and Pilpin traveled the remotest of areas. The forces of Barnabus were along all of the major roads and scattered throughout the cities. Armies of thousands camped miles from Morgdon's borders, keeping an eye on things. They were everywhere, making their presence known in irritating but unforceful ways.

The Truce.

The word irritated Brenwar. *You cannot have a truce with evil.*

After traveling another twenty yards, he stopped and dismounted. Pilpin did the same. Like two stout barrels walking, the pair lumbered through the woods, pushing through the briars and brush. Rough orcen voices caught Brenwar's ear. He crept behind the next tree and peered toward the source of the sound.

Two orcs wandered the woodland. Scouts, by the look of them. In chain hauberks and bearing crossbows. Swords hanging from their hips. It wasn't a good sign. Where there were scouts, there were armies.

"We can take them," Pilpin whispered, pulling his axes from his belt. "Let me do it."

Brenwar shook his grey-streaked beard.

"No, I can take them," he said. "You stay here."

"But—"

"Stay," he said, low and forcefully. He took a step and stopped. There might be others. Perhaps he needed to draw them out. He rubbed the bracers on his wrists. His blood began to race. He hated orcs. He needed to take his frustration out on something. "Be ready."

He crept behind a tree. It was a small tree, but a tree nonetheless. He placed his hands on it and began to push with the might of the bracers.

"Hurk!"

The roots popped from the ground, and the tree began to tilt toward the orcs. Fueled by mystic strength, Brenwar's stout legs kept pressing. His face flushed. Sweat dripped from his nose. Roots ripped from the earth and the tree toppled over, crashing right behind the orcs. Brenwar moved into new cover.

The bewildered orcs sprang to either side of the branches with their crossbows ready. Brenwar could see the yellow in their eyes. The confusion. Where two had gathered, four more quickly came.

Six!

The orcs were big, greenish, and layered in scars and muscles. Their hair sprang out in greasy black tangles. They fanned out and began a search.

Brenwar caught Pilpin's stare and nodded. The little dwarf waddled out of his hiding spot and banged together his axes.

"Greetings, uglies!"

Clatch-Zip!

Clatch-Zip!

Crossbow bolts rocketed through the air and splintered on Pilpin's axe blades and chest plate. Brenwar burst from his spot and clocked the nearest orc in the chest with War Hammer. It sailed from its feet and into the next tree.

Clatch-Zip!

Clatch-Zip!

Two bolts whizzed by Brenwar's bearded face.

Clatch-Zip!

The third buried itself inside his leathered thigh.

"Ya shouldn't have done that!" Brenwar yelled. He ripped the bolt out of his thigh and advanced. The orcs tossed their crossbows and went for their swords. Brenwar closed the gap, swinging.

Pow!

One orc left his boots.

Pow!

The second crumpled on the ground.

Brenwar scooped up a handful of dirt and rubbed it into his wound.

"That'll do."

What Pilpin lacked in size, he made up for with heart and speed. He rushed in between the pair of orcs that shot at them and chopped into their legs. The pair crashed into the ground and fumbled for the blades on their hips.

Hack! Hack!

Pilpin's blades slashed fingers and hands. The orcs howled.

"No, no, no," Pilpin said, wagging his index finger in their faces. "None of that now."

One orc bit at him. The other punched with its fist.

Pilpin rapped the flats of his blades upside their heads, knocking them out cold.

The last standing orc stood between him and Brenwar. It eyed them both, raised its sword high with an alarming battle cry, and sprinted for the woods.

"Drat it all!" Brenwar roared. The barrel-chested dwarf wearing the mystic bracers swung War Hammer in the orc's direction and let loose. His favorite weapon busted though the smaller trees and slammed into the back of the orc. It moved no more. "Bind them up," Brenwar said, storming off to collect his hammer.

Pilpin unraveled some dwarven twine from his pack and bound the orcs together. Brenwar returned with an angry look on his face.

"What are you orcs doing here?"

Their bellies rumbled in hefty chuckles. Brenwar picked up one of their swords and rested it on his shoulder.

Pilpin had no idea what Brenwar was up to, but he had a feeling it might be painful.

"This is your leg and what I'm about to do to it," Brenwar said to the orcs. He grasped the sword by both ends and started to bend it. The metal groaned and bent.

The orcs' eyes widened.

"We're scouts!" one blurted out. "We're scouting!"

"I know yer scouts. Now, what are you scouting for?"

"Enemies of Barnabus. We hunt them down. Kill them."

"Well," Brenwar said, "yer doing a lousy job." He clamped his hands down on both orcs' shoulders and squeezed. "Tell me, what else does Barnabus have planned?"

The orcs' faces flushed red. They squirmed in their seats.

"Burn. Destroy. Disrupt," one said.

"Take the outer cities one by one," said the other.

"Why the outer cities?"

The orcs clammed up.

Pilpin banged them on the knees.

"Speak up!"

Brenwar pressed his fingers harder through the armor.

One orc's lips burst open and said, "'So he cannot see,' they say!"

"Who cannot see?" Brenwar shouted.

"The Dragon Prince!" said one.

"A fool he is," said the other.

"Where is he?"

"With the High Priestess."

"In Narnum."

Brenwar clocked their heads together. His fingers combed through his beard. This was information he'd heard already, but he hadn't believed it until now.

"Are we going to Narnum then?" Pilpin said.

"I don't think we can do much good in Narnum. It's the edge of the world I'm worried about."

CHAPTER
7

Sansla Libor. The Roamer King. An elf cursed.

Shum was grateful for him.

On foot, Sansla led. His heavy feet landed softly on the grass, and the rest of the Roamers followed. Silent. A little in awe. The last time they'd encountered Sansla, he'd been more savage. Now, despite his appearance, he was more elflike.

They stopped at the edge of a stream, where many refilled their canteens. Sansla scooped water into his big paws and drank. The winged ape was a magnificent figure. Layered muscles bulged under his fur. He radiated power.

"Gather," Sansla said.

The Roamers—over a score in number—hemmed in their king and took a knee.

"As you know, the Dragon King, Balzurth, has enlisted our aid in these dire times. Many of us were here for the previous dragon war. This one is to be the last." Sansla's wings fluttered and collapsed behind his back. "As before, we are to play a part in this, and our mission will be perilous. Barnabus and his evil continue to spread. The dark dragons thrive everywhere.

"In Elome, the elves battle the orcs, goblins, and gnolls all over the borders. The dragons aid the orcs. The Pool of the Dragons, the River Cities, the Settlement, and Borgash are all besieged. Deceived. The men of this world have put their faith in the Truce."

Liam raised his fist and started to speak.

Sansla Libor shook his head, his ever-serene ape face contorted and strained. "We cannot aid them. We must focus on the heart of the matter."

Liam gave his king a questioning look.

The strain on the ape's face began to ease. "Our ancient enemy, Gorn Grattack the Transgressor, is behind all of this, and his vanquished spirit has taken form. We must search him out. He no longer walks in darkness but among us, roaming the dirt."

The hairs on Shum's neck rose.

The utterance of Gorn Grattack's name was an incantation in itself. Most all of the races had banned the words, but now the evil words were out and let loose on Nalzambor.

"He is a dragon of many forms," Sansla continued, "and we must look for the signs and be wary. He can consume any of us. Summon undead armies. Command dragons that bring wroth heat. He lies in wait, but his patience will run out. He must be found. We'll search the world in pairs. I'll go alone, however." He cleared his throat. "My condition comes and goes, and I have other missions."

"How will we know it's him?" Liam asked.

"A chill, and you will know it." Sansla's wings fanned out. "I must go now, brothers. Call me when you find something."

The wings beat, and the great ape lifted into the air. Moments later, he vanished into the night sky.

Shum nodded to his men. He was their leader. He stretched his limbs upward and began with the assignments.

"Pair up. Find aid in all creatures. Befriend our allies. Warn them of the dangers," he said, clasping hands with each and every one. "May your steeds run like the wind."

Within minutes, all of the Roamers had departed, except Hoven.

"What do you make of all this?" Shum said to his brother.

Hoven shrugged and said, "Well, at least the trees are not yet our enemies."

"Most of them at least." He called for his horse. The great steed trotted over to him. He mounted, eyeing the sky again. "Where do you think Sansla goes now?"

"He's the king. Wherever he wants, I suppose."

The Roamer King seemed strange to Shum. Sansla had been able to resurrect him, but he'd been unable to cure himself. Perhaps, Sansla had been unwilling. Maybe the Ocular of Orray only healed those who wanted to be healed. Perhaps Sansla had refused its aid. After all, Shum had mentioned it before.

Perhaps unwillingness is Nath Dragon's issue.

As they rode, Shum had Nath heavy on his thoughts. The Dragon Prince was the key to everything, and now he stood in the company of evil, willingly. In the meantime, it seemed every city in Nalzambor was hostage to the Truce. If Nath broke it, many would die. But in Shum's heart, breaking this false truce would be the right thing to do.

People have fought and won their freedom before. And what is life without freedom? I hope Nath Dragon realizes that soon.

CHAPTER

8

BAYZOG SAT IN FRONT OF his fireplace with the Elderwood Staff in his lap, violet eyes glaring into the fire. He was infuriated. The woman, tall and shady, had offered little news. All she had said was that Sasha, Rerry, and Samaz were doing well. She had told him to be patient and they'd be returned soon. That had been three days ago. He'd been fuming ever since.

"Pah!" he said. Pah indeed.

"Can we not depart, search them out," Ben said, "and return unnoticed? Certainly you have something inside your spellbook."

Bayzog didn't respond. There were such spells, but at the moment, he didn't even know where to begin his search. And it was risky. He needed to put his faith in the dragonettes, for now.

He let his own powers merge with those of the Elderwood Staff. Mystic energy coursed through his veins. There was nothing he'd rather do than turn that garden for acolytes into a pile of ash right now.

"How much longer can you trust them?" Ben said, scratching the trim beard on his face. "I hope you're not thinking five years. My bones get sore as these days wear on. I'm not an elf."

"We'll see," Bayzog muttered. "The rendezvous is within the year. If we don't arrive, well, our friends will know something is awry."

"I want to be there," Ben said. "I want to see who shows up. For all we know, the dragons have hunted Brenwar and all the Roamers down."

"We'll have to get word to them or of them by some other means. However, for now, all I guess we can do is wait." Bayzog looked to Ben. "Go into town. Enjoy yourself."

Ben slumped down on the sofa and propped his feet on the table.

"When you start enjoying yourself, I'll start enjoying myself."

Sasha stirred. Cold and dirty, clothes in tatters, she lay on the cold dirt floor in the dimness of indirect moonlight. She and her sons had been sitting inside this large cave for days. Lizardmen and acolytes kept watch on them, and something else. A draykis. One of the most horrible creatures she'd ever seen. An abomination of man and dragon. It called the shots now.

She struggled into a sitting position with her metal-clad hands fastened to her waist. Her ankles were also bound. Both her sons lay still, resting. The cave mouth opened to the starry night sky with its full moon, and against it, all she could see were the silhouettes of the lizardmen who guarded the entrance with spears. Her stomach groaned. Little food. Little water. Little comfort. That was life now. Each new day miserable.

She scooted toward her sons. Rerry moaned as she bumped him. She could see the swelling on his face in the dimness. He and Samaz had attempted another escape days earlier. They had taken down two lizardmen and three clerics when the draykis appeared. It had struck hard. Fast. Ferocious. The boys' skills could not prevail against it.

All was lost again.

But the excitement! That brief feeling of freedom had charged her blood.

Anger now pumped inside her chest. The draykis would pay for her sons' suffering!

Her eyes rested on Samaz. His heavy chest rose and fell. He coughed and sputtered a little. He'd taken as many lumps as Rerry. The brothers, though at odds, fought like wild tigers for each other and their mother.

She shuddered a sigh.

She curled up between them, lay down, and closed her eyes, absorbing the warmth between them. *I might not have a rock to my name, but I have them, and that's everything I need.* Her heavy lids began to close.

Scratch. Scratch. Scratch.

Her eyes snapped open. Something gnawed on something somewhere.

Rats!

She jerked and shimmied. A yellow glimmer caught her eye. A tiny creature gnawed at the bonds on her feet. No bigger than a mouse, it had tiny wings and bright yellow eyes.

Her heart leapt inside her chest.

A dragon!

Its little claws sawed through her bonds. It let out a dragony squeak.

Sasha gazed down at her metal-clad and tethered hands.

Its wings buzzed to life, and it floated over to Samaz's feet. A second tiny dragon, cherry colored, joined it. In seconds, the cords were cut and Samaz's feet were free.

The gnawing continued at her wrists. The cords snapped at her waist, and she freed her arms.

The two continued to the cords on Rerry's ankles. The boys woke, blurry eyes filled with wonder. The two tiny dragons sat in front of them and started marching toward the front of the cave.

"What do we do?" Rerry whispered.

The dragons stopped and turned. The red one let out a tiny roar then turned and marched onward again, straight for the guards at the cave entrance.

Meanwhile, a third tiny dragon, cobalt in color, landed on one of Sasha's metal gloves. It spat a glowing blue substance onto the metal, which dissolved.

Before the tiny blue dragon even landed on her other hand, Sasha pressed her newly bared hand into the dirt. As she at last tapped into the world's arcane energies, exhilaration rushed through her. After a while, she stood up and whispered, "Let's go."

Silently, they crept toward the silhouetted lizardmen at the cave entrance.

The tiny dragons buzzed in front of the lizardmen, who tried to shoo them away.

Rerry sprang behind one, Samaz the other. Rerry slipped the lizardman's sword from its scabbard and chopped it down. Samaz pounced on the other's neck and choked it to the ground. It was quiet. It was quick. It wasn't without notice.

A bolt of power blasted into the cave rock, singeing Rerry's hair. Sasha's eyes locked on the lead acolyte. His head glowed, and his eyes blazed with fire. Lizardmen rushed up the slopes. Acolytes muttered and moaned. Sasha understood their ways. They channeled energy into the small, ghostly leader in plum robes.

We'll see about that!

Raising her hands above her head, she flipped her fingertips out. Bright shards of blue light sprayed from her hands and cut through the mass of men. The leader howled in rage and flung an arc of power up the hill. It slammed into the three of them, lifting them from their feet and back into the cave.

Dazed, Rerry shook off the blow and popped back on his feet. Steel swords from the guards filled both his hands, and he twirled them with grace and ease. Two more lizardmen arrived at the mouth of the cave.

"Ah, what a pleasant surprise," he said. "Dying lizardmen."

The lizardmen lunged with barbed spears.

Rerry hopped high over them and struck, sinking his blades in one chest each.

"So nice to meet you."

Samaz rolled past a lizardman's lunging sword. Catching it by the wrist, he wrenched the blade free, cranked up the pressure, and broke its wrist. The lizardman's large mouth of sharp teeth snapped at him. Samaz drove his boot heel into its jaw and laid it out on the ground.

The second lizardman sliced at his head. Samaz crouched beneath the decapitating blade and launched both fists into the soft spot in the lizardman's belly. The swords dropped from its hands, and its jaw fell wide open. Samaz roundhouse kicked it in the jaw and watched it collapse on its nose.

Acolytes and lizardmen fell. The dragonettes swarmed. Bright sparks of lightning and lancing acid burned through robes and skin. Smoke from the red one caused sluggishness and confusion. Though tiny, their attacks were nevertheless a whirlwind of terror unleashed on evil.

Sasha rushed down the slope with power-filled hands. The greasy acolyte greeted her with his own power. Mystic forces collided. Weak and starved, Sasha fell to her knees. The haunting man cackled.

Sasha swayed on the ground and watched the man come closer.

"I do have to keep you alive," he said, "but only barely. Let's have some fun, shall we?" He raised his arms in the air—

Sasha sprang to her feet and locked her fingers around his neck.

"Yes, let's have some fun, shall we?"

She channeled her sorceress energies. The veteran acolyte twisted and fought. His hands locked on her wrists, burning them. Sasha held on.

"No you don't!"

A torrent of energy coursed through her.

The acolyte gaffed. His eyes shone like moons. His body stiffened, cracked, and turned ashen.

Sasha shoved him away. His body fell and broke into pieces.

Gasping, she searched for her sons. The first thing she saw was the draykis. Armored to the neck in heavy metal, horns twisting on its head, it engaged her sons once again. Rerry's blades glanced away. Samaz's punches and kicks were futile. The dragonettes were discharging everything they had. Nothing slowed it.

It struck hard.

Rerry fell.

Fast.

Samaz collapsed.

It flicked the dragonettes away and faced off on Sasha.

"Don't you hurt my sons again!" Sasha said.

It cocked its head and strolled right at her with a demonic look in its eyes.

She summoned everything she had left, lifted her arms over her head, and unleashed it at him.

The draykis stopped.

Nothing happened.

The draykis laughed and came right at her again. She sagged to her knees.

Rerry came. Samaz came.

The draykis pounded them down with supernatural strength.

Crying out, Sasha rushed over and covered her boys.

"It's too late for them," the draykis said. "It's too late for all of you."

The tiny citrine dragonette blasted lightning in its face.

"Argh!"

The draykis swatted it away.

"Fleas! Be gone! I have death to deliver to these other feisty ones."

Its sword scraped from its scabbard. The metal glinted in the moonlight.

"For Barnabus," it said, raising the sword up high.

A shadow dropped from the sky.

Whump!

A cherry-scaled dragon landed behind the draykis. The draykis was to it as a dog is to a horse. The draykis spun and struck. Its steel glanced off the dragon's armored belly. Fast as a snake, the dragon's maw clamped over the draykis entirely. Metal and bone crunched. The draykis squirmed then squirmed no more. The crimson dragon slung the mangled corpse into the dirt. Fire surged from its mouth. It disintegrated every evil being in the camp.

Sasha gaped when the dragon turned to her. Its belly was a lighter shade of red, and it had small twisting horns and long black eyelashes. "Th-Thank you," Sasha managed to say.

The dragon dug its claw into the earth and made a circle with two slashes through it. Sasha knew that symbol. Bayzog had shown it to her before. A thrill rushed through her. It was the sign of Balzurth, the Dragon King.

CHAPTER

9

ORLEE THE CHANGELING STOOD GUARD inside the cage of The Deep. He was one of half a dozen, guarding just outside the rim of the well that led down there, past the phantom, into the realm of the damned. He wore a uniform of Barnabus and was in the form of a man, the same as all the other guards. Now, he stood near the lip of the stone pit, staring into the blackness.

"I wouldn't get too close," one man said. His face was rugged and sad. "The phantom's been known to snatch guards once or twice."

Gorlee didn't respond. His eyes were fixed on the blackness.

The guard grabbed him by the shoulder, saying, "Young fella, you'd be wise to listen to me."

"Huh?"

"I said, get back from that pit," the guard said, "and that's an order."

"Oh," Gorlee said as the older guard hooked his arm and pulled him away. "Sorry."

"You'll be sorry alright if you wind up down there. Nothing but a city of torment down there." The guard wiped his forearm on his brow. "Say, what's your name, anyway?"

Gorlee didn't have an answer to that. He didn't know. All he knew was what Selene told him. "Uh, Jason," he said.

"Well, Jason, stop being so stupid." Some of the other guards laughed, but the moment was cut short by a frightening wail that came from within The Deep. "Great Guzan, I hate this place," the guard said. "The entire world's run by monsters now."

Some of the guards gave the older one a disapproving look. Others looked away.

"Yeah, I said it," the guard said. "You'll say plenty more of what's on your mind, too, if you ever get to be my age." He glanced at the pit. "And I don't think my words will wind me up in there. But I might get fed to a dragon nest, maybe." He cracked his neck and slapped Gorlee on the shoulder. "You're young, Jason. You should be marching the borders. This is just a dead end here."

"I think I would like that," he said. "I think."

"Well, you really need to work on the *thinking* thing. I wish *I'd* done more thinking when I was younger." He sauntered away and said to another, "What are you looking at?"

Thinking. That was the problem. Gorlee had become a dullard. Without purpose. Drifting. The High Priestess Selene controlled all of that. Whenever she called, he went. Whatever she ordered, he did. But none of what she asked came easy. Something inside of him resisted. Something within himself had led him here, to this pit. There was still a remnant of whoever he really was hidden inside him, and he wanted to find it.

Taking a position between the pit and the cage, he teetered on his feet. He'd been imitating many people. Their manners. Habits. Voices. All in pursuit of something. His memories. Selene and Kryzak had taken them. He knew. He could remember parts of that day. They'd taken almost everything , but not gotten all of it, and tucked it away. He'd played along for months, but every day he felt more parts of him fading away. He had to find his memories. Fix what they'd done to him.

The Deep. It was the perfect place to hide what they had taken. And he could sense that his memories were down there. He edged closer to the pit again.

"What did I say?" the older guard said, marching over. "You don't want a kiss from the phantom, son. Now stay back. All the way to the bars!"

"Sorry," he said. "Just curious."

"Just stupid is more like it."

Gorlee felt stupid. There were only bits and pieces. It stirred him. He saw Nath Dragon's face. *There is something wrong with what I am doing. I can't live like this any longer.* He edged toward the pit.

"Fine," said the guard. "It's not as if you aren't expendable."

CHAPTER

10

F*OCUS. FOCUS. FOCUS!*

Nath had no wings. Nothing changed. Thoughts rushed through his head.

Will this fall even kill me?

Through the evening darkness he plunged, headlong toward the street.

I'll know soon enough.

He covered his head with his arms. Something jerked him up by the ankles, snatching him a few feet from impact with the cobbled street. People screamed. Then up, up, up he and Selene went. Nath crossed his arms over his chest and scowled. Selene dropped him back on the balcony.

"You are an evil lady," he said.

"Am I?"

"You might have killed me," he said, gathering his legs under him and standing up again.

"Maybe, but I don't want you dead. I want you alive. I want you to embrace the dragon within, and I must say, you seem reluctant to do that."

"I'm not reluctant. I've always wanted to fly." The feline fury cruised to his side. Nath dug his fingers into its mane. The fur was thick and soft. The cat that had tried to kill him before had become his only comfort. "I've always wanted to be a dragon."

Selene's wings collapsed behind her back and disappeared.

"I was taught these things when I was a little girl. I imagine things were easier then. More of a second nature. Your problem is still the same. You think more like a man than a dragon. You need to stop that, Nath."

She was right. He'd spent most of his life fitting in with people, not dragons. He simply got along with people better. The dragons had shunned him for some reason. Up until now, anyway.

"I just don't understand why your father withheld so much from you, Nath," she said, coming closer. She kneeled in front of the feline fury and petted it. "He had plenty of time to show you. Why would he hold you back? Gorn Grattack pressed me from the moment he first saw me. I mastered the magic within when I was young."

"Good for you," he said. It ate at him that his father had never taught him these things. He didn't understand why. He turned away. "I'll see you later."

"You are departing from me so soon? Oh Nath, don't leave."

He kept going.

"Nath, wait!"

He stopped and bent his ear over his shoulder.

"Next week, Nath. We'll take leave. We'll see the cities. The wide open spaces will do your scales good. I think there's a good chance things will come alive for you out there." She approached and patted his shoulders. "Just a little longer. Rest till then."

He rolled his eyes.

"Don't be so hasty. You don't want to miss Sasha, do you?"

He turned to face her.

"You expect her back. When, exactly?"

"Any day now. Perhaps that will help you relax, seeing an old friend."

"We'll see," he said, leaving. "We'll see."

When the heavy double doors slammed behind Nath, Selene caught her breath. Deceiving him wasn't easy. He doubted her despite all she did. She scratched the fury's head and said, "Keep close to him. He needs a friend."

The feline fury slunk outside onto the terrace and leapt into the night.

Selene moseyed around the table, tracing her fingers along the tops of the chairs.

"Thank goodness for crafty spells."

The food was tainted in magic. It left Nath hungry and unable to change into his dragon form. It also inhibited his magic powers. So far, he didn't suspect a thing.

She couldn't have him flying from one side of the world to the other and seeing what was going on. The outskirts of the world were under siege. The Truce was a lie. She couldn't risk him finding out, at least not until she had a firm hold on Nath as well as Nalzambor. Then it would be too late.

He trusts me enough. I just need to finally win him over.

She didn't want Nath to cross paths with Gorn Grattack, either. The Dark King would kill him. She needed him.

Oh Nath, we can rule this world together. I just have to get you to see things my way. Then we both can have whatever we want.

A knock came on her chamber door.

"Enter," she said, resuming her throne.

A lone draykis came in, winged and wearing partial plate armor. His face was a twisted lizardish scowl. One of her captains. He held a scroll in his hand and kneeled after he approached.

"Awfully late for bad news," she said. "What is it?"

"High Priestess," he said in a deep and guttural voice, "we have found several of these signs, and we thought that you should be informed."

"What sort of sign are you speaking of?"

He unrolled the parchment and held it out before her.

Her eyes became saucers. It was a painted circle with two slashes through it.

"Where have you found this?" she demanded. "How many places?"

"We've found dozens. My draykis, the soldiers, and the clerics are quick to take them down."

"Who is putting them up?"

"That we do not know."

"Find the culprits and kill them," she said. She leaned forward and pointed at him, saying, "I had better not see any of these signs in the city." She slammed her fist on the arm of her chair. "Notify every member from here to Borgash to the Pool of Dragons and beyond that I don't want to see this symbol anywhere. And you had better bring me the culprits by sundown tomorrow. This is unacceptable!"

"As you wish," he said, bowing.

An alarming cry arose from the streets below. Selene headed for the balcony and gazed down. The fire burned in a most peculiar way. A great circle with two slashes glowed brilliantly in the street, dazzling the onlooking crowd.

"Great Guzan!"

She grabbed the draykis commander and shoved him off the balcony.

"Get down there and put that out!"

She rubbed her head.

"Sultans of Sulfur! I hope Nath didn't see that." She slammed her fists on the rail. "I need the changeling!"

CHAPTER
11

BAYZOG'S EYES WERE GLUED TO the tome when a tiny creature crawled over the pages.

"What have we here?" he exclaimed.

It was the tiny citrine dragonette. Its tongue flickered out of its mouth as it sat on the edge of the pages. Bayzog's heart leapt inside his chest. The tiny dragon dropped something out of its mouth. A gold ring clanked off the table and rattled to a stop.

"It can't be…" Bayzog said, reaching down and picking up the golden ring between his fingers.

"Can't be what?" Ben said, stepping alongside his shoulder. "Oh my. One of the dragonettes is back. Already? It's been but a few days."

"It's Sasha's ring," Bayzog said. "Her ring of betrothal."

Ben swallowed and said, "Do you think … well … you know … "

"I don't know," Bayzog said, eyeing the tiny dragon. It eyed him back, cocking its head. "Can you take me to her? Is she alive?" He dreaded his next words. "Is she dead?"

The dragon continued to tilt its head back and forth. Its tongue flickered from its mouth. Bayzog reached for the jaxite stones on the table and wrapped his fingers around their warmth. He could feel his control over the dragon, but he couldn't understand its thoughts.

"Can you speak to it?"

"I can't."

"Is there a special way to communicate with it?" Ben asked. He started tapping on the table. "Maybe it understands code." He rapped his knuckle on the table. *Tap.* "One for yes." He rapped twice. *Tap. Tap.* "Two for no. That should suffice. What do you say, little fella?"

The dragon hissed at him. Lightning crackled inside its mouth.

Ben edged away and said, "Alright, I'll let you handle this one."

Bayzog nodded at him and said, "It's a good idea, Ben. Let me try something along those lines." He searched his mind for the proper incantation. He tried to thumb through the pages of his book, but the dragon's tail was blocking it. "Do you mind?" The dragon remained still. Its tail dropped over the pages, back and forth. Of course, it was entirely possible the tiny dragon understood everything he said but was unwilling to reply. Nath had told him that much about dragons. Many were familiar with the common tongue, but it wasn't always easy to prove it.

"Ben, will you go into my quarters and fetch the small box that rests by the mirror?"

"Sure," Ben said, wandering away and quickly back again. "Is this it?" he said, setting down an ebony box trimmed in silver. "It's the only box I saw."

"Thanks, Ben," Bayzog said, scooting the box in front of him. It was Sasha's jewelry box. He opened it up and stared inside. It was half-filled with rings, bracelets, and necklaces. Elven made. Each a treasure of precious metals and sparkling stones.

"That's a nice little dragon hoard you have," Ben said with bright eyes. "What do you plan to do with it?"

Bayzog turned the jewelry box around to face the dragon.

It let out an excited hiss and dove right in, wallowing in the treasure.

"He's a greedy little thing, isn't he?"

"They all are to some degree," Bayzog said, "and some more so than others." He glanced at Ben. "They say there are trenches filled like this in Dragon Home."

"It's hard to imagine, and I can imagine plenty," Ben said. "Nath told me about some of it once, but I wasn't sure I believed it. What would you need that much treasure for, anyway?"

Bayzog smiled.

"Good question." He clapped his hands. "But the real question is, 'Where are Sasha and my sons now?'" He started thumbing through the pages. There had to be some way to get the dragon to communicate with him. The only thing he had done before was to give them his commands, or rather, to ask for their help. At least one of them had responded. Now he had to unravel the mystery that surrounded the fruit of his work.

"Look," Ben said. "He's wearing a ring around his neck." He bobbed his head. "That would make for a fine portrait. Especially if you put me in it."

"If you say so," Bayzog said, immersing himself in his work. He blocked out every sound and utterance. His mind became the narrow edge of a razor. Time lost all meaning until Ben started tapping him on the shoulder.

"What!" Bayzog said, irritated, still focusing on the huge open book.

"I think you need to see this," Ben said.

Bayzog huffed, rolled his violet eyes, and turned, saying, "What is so important that I—"

A dragon sat perched on each of Ben's shoulders. One cherry in color and the other citrine. They cocked their heads back and forth at him.

"I told you that you needed to see this," Ben said, careful not to move any other muscles. "They've been here over thirty minutes."

"Thirty!"

"I didn't want to bother you, and I don't think they're going anywhere, but their claws are digging holes in my shoulders," Ben said, wincing. "Do you think you can lure them off?"

The dragons' wings buzzed, but they didn't lift off. Bayzog noticed the cherry dragon had a tiny parchment inside his mouth. It was rolled up like a scroll. He leaned forward and said, "That's interesting."

"Oh," Ben said, "I noticed that too, but he won't let loose of it. What do you think could be written on such a tiny letter?"

"Hmph," Bayzog said, rubbing his finger under his nose. "It's either a tiny letter, or it was shrunken by someone."

"Shrunken?"

Bayzog's eyes lit up. It wasn't the first time he'd seen a tiny scroll.

"Are you alright?" Ben said.

"Just … reminiscing."

"About what?"

"A little something from years long past. A good thing." He held his slender hand under the dragon's snout. "Give it."

The dragon held the scroll fast in his mouth.

Bayzog harnessed the power of the jaxite stone.

"Give me the scroll, please."

The dragon's mouth popped open, and the scroll dropped into Bayzog's palm.

"Thank you," he said, inspecting the tiny object. "Now, can I remember how this goes?"

"How what goes?"

Bayzog paid Ben no mind and began reciting quick intricate words. The scroll expanded in size. Sasha used to send Bayzog tiny messages when he courted her long ago. It was her way of showing off what she'd learned about sorcery. It did his heart good to see her using it again. The tiny red dragon growled at it. It flew from Ben's shoulder onto Bayzog. Its ruby eyes were intent on the parchment. He unrolled it. The parchment had a circle with two slash marks cut through it and words in the middle that read:

We are all safe. You know where to meet up. Sasha.

His eyes misted over.

"What does it say?" Ben asked.

The tiny cherry-scaled dragon spit a ball of flame at the parchment. The scroll caught fire and disintegrated in a whoof of flame.

"That little scaled varmint!" Ben cried out.

"It's alright," Bayzog said, staying the man with his hand. "We have everything we need now."

"So, what did it say?"

"It said it was time to go."

"Go where?" Ben said, shooing the dragon. "And how do I get this dragon off my shoulder?"

Bayzog pointed at the crack in the wall, and all the dragonettes took off. He said to Ben, "Get your gear. We have one quick stop before we depart from here."

The Grand Gardens of Quintuklen. Ben followed Bayzog back toward their bench. With determination and a dangerous look in his eye, the part-elf wizard almost glided through the streets. Ben had seen it a few times before. He'd seen those violet eyes put a shimmer in a man's bones.

Ben hitch-stepped to keep up, and his gear jangled. He had his heavy pack strapped over his shoulders. Two swords hung from his hips, one his own and the other Fang. Akron was snapped behind his gear along with a quiver filled with arrows. He had Brenwar's chest tucked under his arm.

I think Bayzog could carry a little more than his staff. By the sultans, this is heavy!

Bayzog carried the Elderwood Staff and nothing else. As soon as he passed beneath the iron archway of the Grand Gardens, leery eyes slipped his way. Ben could feel a presence now. Something he'd never felt before. He thought about the dragonettes. *Wouldn't mind having them with me now.*

Traipsing through splendid walkways lined with bountiful plants and flowers, he followed Bayzog back to their usual bench. Again, the odd men and women in strange garb of many colors shunned them. That was fine with Ben. He didn't want anything to do with their weird and haunting faces. There was just something so strange and uncouth about the manners of all of them.

"Stay close," Bayzog said, scanning the garden. "No farther than arm's length. And keep your sword inside its sheath, no matter what."

Ben pulled his head back, looked down on Bayzog, and said, "What do you have in mind, Wizard?"

"When she comes, I'll do all the talking and all the doing. Just stay close to me."

The muscles in Ben's jaw clenched. He plucked a piece of spiced rawhide from his pouch and started chewing. He didn't have any idea what Bayzog was doing, but the part-elf could be odd like that. He'd gotten used to it. But if it were up to him, he'd have left Quintuklen already and headed after his wife and family. *He must be setting them up for something.*

An hour passed, then two. Ben's back and knees began to groan. He couldn't stand for days on end the same as he used to. He was almost fifty now.

Bayzog remained a statue. Hard-eyed and focused.

Certainly by now, their enemies knew they were ready to go somewhere. Ben stretched his back and twisted his waist. Kept switching the chest from arm to arm. *This is worse than my Legionnaire days.*

"Bayzog," he said, "I don't know what you're planning, but let's just go."

"Perhaps you're right," Bayzog said. His eyes drifted up the left path. "Ah, company is coming. Just a moment longer, Ben. And remember, stay close."

The same woman as before came down the path, but she was not alone this time. Two large men, both bigger than Ben, flanked her backside. Tall and heavy shouldered, they were the biggest acolytes of Barnabus he'd ever seen. Each had a sword belted to his robe. Ben's hand drifted to the pommel of his own sword. Bayzog eyed him. He pulled it away.

"It's your show, then," Ben whispered to him.

"Are you going on a journey?" the woman said. Her dark ghostly features were intent on the Elderwood Staff. "You know that you are not to leave the city."

"I thought it was time you took me to my wife," Bayzog said. "I need some good faith this time."

"I'm sorry," she said, "but that is not how this works. I've been very clear about that."

Ben wondered if the Clerics of Barnabus had any idea that Sasha and her sons had escaped. It seemed they did not.

"Do you have a family?" Bayzog said to her.

"Barnabus is my family," she said.

"Have you a husband? Or children, perhaps?"

"Let me say, Bayzog," she began, cocking her head, "I believe I can relate to your circumstances. But these circumstances will change for the worse if you become persistent about leaving." Her eyes kept drifting back and forth between Bayzog's eyes and his staff. She backed between her men. "And this public garden is no place to start anything. That would be foolish."

Ben felt the muscles between his shoulders begin to knot. The air thickened with tension.

"I agree," Bayzog said, easing his stance. "That would be foolish."

Ben's breathing eased.

"But," Bayzog continued, "it wouldn't be nearly as foolish as taking the wife and sons of a very powerful wizard." His eyes sparked with bright fire. His staff flared with brilliant life.

Swords ripped out of men's belts. The woman recoiled back, and mystic red claws sprang from her hands. Her voice became a shriek.

"Don't be a fool, Bayzog!"

Bayzog and his staff erupted with fervent white power. The air shimmered. Ben shielded his eyes. A disintegrating force exploded forward in a thunderous flash. Ben gasped for air inside his lungs, coughing and gagging. A strong hand seized him.

"Are you alright?" Bayzog said.

Ben looked into the part-elf's eyes and then behind him. The woman and two guards were skulls and bones, piled on ash. Similarly ashen was most of the garden behind him. Ben gaped.

"You did that," he said.

Nearby, terrified onlookers stared. Others fled on unsteady feet.

"I did!" Bayzog yelled, raising his staff. "And I'll do more if any more of you murderous deceivers comes any closer!"

More ran, but some stayed, evil eyes flicking to the skies now and then.

"Great Guzan, Bayzog! I didn't know you had it in you."

"Hang on to my robes," Bayzog said.

"Why?"

The dark-haired wizard pointed his staff toward the sky. A flock of black-winged dragons were whooshing through the air right at them. Ben counted at least a dozen of them. He clasped Bayzog's arm.

"Now what!"

Streaks of fire erupted from the dragons' mouths.

"Hold on!"

The Elderwood Staff blasted lightning into the sky, tearing a hole through two dragons. Flames exploded all around them. A split second later, Bayzog brought the end of the staff to the ground—and everything Ben saw disappeared.

CHAPTER

12

NATH SAT CROSS-LEGGED ON HIS bed, eyes closed. He hadn't meditated since he was a boy. It was something his father had taught him. A tool to maintain focus. Nath had never considered himself a deep thinker, but now it seemed time to be one. His brow furrowed. He envisioned himself with wings. He envisioned himself as a dragon.

He slammed his fists into the bed.

"Drat it all!"

He slung a pillow across the room.

"I can make fireballs out of flames, but I can't turn into a dragon again. This makes no sense!"

He stormed out to his balcony, tripping over the feline fury's tail.

"Will you go away?"

The big dragon-cat, lying down, yawned and reclosed its eyes.

Nath shook his head and leaned over the balcony's edge. It was nearing midday, and people milled about the streets, staying uniform to their daily business. He could even hear some of them singing songs and praises in his name. He folded his arms over his chest. *That's right, heap praises on the dragon who is not a dragon at all. Preposterous!*

The citizens of Narnum had been in unusually high spirits since the day he defeated Kryzak in the arena. Nath, after all, *had* been named the champion. And the people loved their champions. Still, everything seemed too ordinary. The smiles were too big. The laughter too loud. And there were odd disturbances. Fires and small riots that were quickly snuffed out.

Nothing is ever as good as it seems. He sighed. *Four more years of this. I'm not sure I can take it.*

He glanced back at the feline fury. The dragon-cat filled up half the balcony. Nath rubbed his chin and said, "You're pretty big. Maybe you can take me for a ride, perhaps."

The fury rose upon its paws and arched its back. Smoke snorted from its nose. It brushed by Nath, leapt straight off the balcony, and soared away.

"Great Dragons!" Nath said, yelling after it. "I'm not that bad of company!"

The fury vanished among the buildings.

Nath went back inside his room and closed his balcony doors, muttering, "I don't need your company anyway."

"Well that's a shame. I came all this way to see you."

Nath's head snapped up.

"Sasha!"

He rushed over and hugged her.

"Easy now," she said, patting his back. "I'm breakable."

"Oh, sorry," he said, letting go. "I didn't hurt you, did I?"

"No," Sasha said, laughing. "I was just teasing you." She hugged him again. She wore a traveling cloak. Leather boots covered her ankles. Her auburn hair was soft and fragrant. "I've missed you."

"I've missed you," he said. "It's been so boring here."

"Boring?" she said, eyeing him. "I've heard nothing but talk of your exploits in the arena since I got within five leagues of here."

"Really?"

She clasped his hand, looked at him with soft eyes, and said, "It does my heart well to know that Kryzak is vanquished, and that it was done by your hand makes the tale even sweeter."

"He had it coming."

"He did," she said, toying with the pendant on her neck. "How about we sit? Talk?"

"Maybe we should go for a walk," he said. "I could use it."

She grabbed his arm and dragged him over to a sofa and sat down.

"I've walked more in the past few weeks than I've walked all my life." She patted the spot next to her. "You don't mind, do you?"

He smiled and said, "No, certainly not. I assume you're tired."

"That's an understatement, but I made it a priority to come and see you as soon as I returned. I was worried."

"About me? Nath Dragon?" He nudged her. "You know I'll be fine."

"I can see frustration in your brows, Nath," she said. "I can feel the tension. I know you. You know that. What is going on?"

"Sasha," he said, "I actually became a dragon! A full-sized flying dragon!"

"You did?"

"Yes, and I could fly and everything!"

"So, what's the problem?"

"I turned back into this, and now I can't turn back into the dragon," he said, frowning, "and I don't understand why not. I *am* a dragon. I should be able to turn whenever I want, the same as Selene." He brushed his own auburn hair out of his eyes. "It's frustrating. More than frustrating."

"Maybe you're trying too hard," she said. "I think you need to relax. You always put too much pressure on yourself. It makes me think of Bayzog."

"Hmmm," Nath said, rubbing his chin. "And how is he?"

"He's holed up in Quintuklen, spending time with his sons and doing well enough. But he is a little crankier these days." She pulled her legs up underneath her. "He sends his regards. That's about it, seeing how he's a man of little words."

"And how are other things in this world?" he said. "I'm only getting bits and pieces. Selene says we are soon to travel abroad, but I'm not so sure I believe her."

"You'll be pleased, Nath. The Truce has brought about many great things. Honestly, Nalzambor hasn't felt so wonderful in a long time." She yawned and stretched her arms. "And I've tried the most wonderful foods from all around. I even had a conversation with a pixlyn named Gorgy. A black-haired little sprite with plenty more attitude than size."

"I'm happy for you," he said, "but have you seen any dragons? Not the ones that are black winged and tailed either. My kind."

"They are hard enough to find as it is," she said. "And I can only say I've heard a few tales. Nothing noteworthy."

It didn't sit well with Nath. Not one bit. Something was going on out there, and he needed to see it.

"How well do you know Selene?" he asked Sasha.

"Well enough to not get too close." She shrugged her eyes. "Why?"

Rubbing the back of his neck, Nath said, "I just don't know how much I can trust her. She has shown me so many things, and I feel we have so much in common, but ... I can't explain what it is about her."

"You like her."

"Guzan no, Sasha!"

"She's beautiful."

"She's evil."

She shrugged and said, "We all have evil in us, Nath. We all have good in us, too. You know that. Besides, she is of your kind. It's normal that you would be comforted by her. Nath, I can see it in you. You are now more dragon than man. Before long, you might not relate so well to this world of men at all."

"No," he muttered. He couldn't imagine not being friends with her, Brenwar, Ben, and Bayzog. Not to mention so many others. He liked people. Dragons often talked too much and were boring. Well, at least his father, Balzurth, was that way. *Perhaps I am too attached to being a man instead of a dragon.*

"It will be alright, Nath," she said, patting his knee.

"I think this conversation has helped me," he said. "I'm so glad you came. It really means a lot to me. You always know the right things to say."

She got up.

"What are you doing?"

"I need to rest, Nath," she said, yawning again.

"You can rest here. I have the most comfortable bed, but I don't ever use it."

"It looks like a good bed for brooding," she said. "I bet Brenwar would like it."

"Not if it's softer than a rock, he wouldn't."

"Ha! There's never been a truer statement."

Gently, he grabbed her wrist. "Don't go just yet, Sasha. There are so many things on my chest. The people chant my name, yet there's strange commotion in the streets. You say things are better, but I find things disturbing. Even my lost neck hairs are prickling. And I can't put my clawed finger on any of it."

"It's change," she said. "Good change, at that. And I wouldn't worry about those happenings in the streets. The races who are new to town have gotten settled and begun feuding with the locals. It will pass. Selene will see to that."

"I'll take your word for it, Sasha."

"Good," she said, heading for the door. "And I bet Selene will take you out of here soon so you can stretch those scaled legs of yours. Don't worry, Nath. You'll figure things out soon enough."

"I hope so," he said. "Say, Sasha, do that sorceress trick for me? It's been a long time, and you know how much I love it."

Her brows lifted.

"Uh ... Nath, I'm so weary. How about next time? And I have to admit," she said, touching the pendant hanging over her chest, "I haven't been practicing magic as much as I should. Bayzog would swat me for it." She glided over and gave him a quick hug. "I must go before my eyes fall from my head."

"I understand," he said, frowning. "Just don't be gone so long this time."

"I won't," she said, opening the door and walking out down the hall. She glanced over her shoulder at him. "I won't." Two Barnabus soldiers in chain armor escorted her down the hall and out of sight.

Nath closed the door and took a seat on the bed, filling his nostrils with a deep draw of air. Something smelled funny. The perfume Sasha normally wore was gone. Her eyes shimmered a little when she spoke. And she had said she would perform the trick later. The problem was, there had never *been* a trick. But everything seemed right about her otherwise.

Nath's fingers drummed on his knees.

She's trying to deceive me. Or Selene's forcing her to deceive me. Don't let on too much. Patience, Dragon. Patience. You'll put it all together soon enough.

He got up to pace the room, his mind restless and angry. He flung the balcony doors open wide and scanned the streets below. Soldiers stormed back and forth through the streets, looking for something. Or someone. He wanted to know who it was. He climbed on the balcony wall and hung his legs over the edge. The stiff breeze billowed his hair. Looking down, he considered something.

Perhaps I can unlock my powers if I don't rely on anyone else being around. He scooted closer to the rim. He could feel his dragon heart thumping in his chest.

Are you a man, or are you a dragon?

CHAPTER

13

A MAN IN HEAVY ARMOR WEARING a commander of Barnabus's insignia kneeled and bowed at the bottom of the dais. Selene sat on her throne, eyes elsewhere, and said, "Speak."

"High Priestess, we have captured several of the culprits," the man said in a deep but nervous voice. Sweat dripped from his brow. "I'm bringing the news directly to you as ordered."

"Hmmm," she said, "is that all the news that you bring?"

"They are shackled," he said, "three in all. Ready for torment."

"And are they the leaders of this movement?"

"I fear not," he said, "but I'm certain they'll lead us to them."

"Certain, Commander?"

His downcast head lifted the slightest and drifted back downward.

"I'm fully confident in our methods," he said. "They've never failed before."

"Everything fails," she said. "Especially people."

The commander, a stout veteran judging by his appearance, trembled.

"Commanders," she continued, "take me to them. I want to see these culprits for myself."

"Er," he said, standing up as she came down the dais, "it would be an honor."

"Yes, yes it would."

She made her way out of the chambers, followed by an entourage of acolytes, the commander, and a draykis. Taking the steps down the Great Tower took almost an hour, but Selene was in no hurry. She had plenty on her mind. Word had come earlier in the day. Bayzog had obliterated one of her finest servants in Quintuklen. The real Sasha and their sons had escaped. She rubbed her temples.

It's starting. And it hasn't even been a year yet.

She and her escorts bottomed out at the street level pavilion and were now passing by the gawking onlookers. It wasn't often she came down from the tower. Many people kneeled and bowed, most averting their eyes from her gaze. Across the market, another series of steps under heavy guard led down below the tower. They stopped at a double gate of iron bars guarded by two lizardmen. Both saluted.

"Open," the commander said.

The doors creaked open, and inside the dungeon they went. The air was rank with rot, mold, and sweat. A staleness hung in the air. The commander led Selene and her entourage toward the back, where they passed many cells crammed with moaning people. Many hollow eyes were pressed to the bars. Stomachs groaned. The miserable cried.

Selene's breathing eased.

Ah, the sound of suffering. It does my heart well.

She stopped inside a cove carved out of stone, lit by two torches on the wall. Three prisoners huddled on the ground, shivering in heavy metal shackles. A table with many crude devices was pressed against the cove's wall, and a burly man with a dropped shoulder and a crooked jaw stood alongside it.

"Well," Selene said to the commander, "let's see these torments you boasted about."

"Yes, High Priestess," he said, nodding to the tormentor.

The man grabbed a lash and shuffled toward the huddled crowd. He grabbed one man by the hair and pulled him aside.

"Tell us," the tormentor said, glaring into the man's weary eyes, "who were you putting those signs up for?"

"A man," the prisoner said, trembling, "a man paid us. I swear it! We just did it for the money."

The tormentor lashed the man.

Wupash!

Wupash!

The prisoner squealed, and the other two wailed.

"You're lying," the tormentor said.

"No, I swear it!"

"What did he look like, this man who paid you?"

"He was just a man, as ordinary as I am, with deep green eyes."

The tormentor glanced back at the commander.

The commander nodded.

Wupash!

Wupash!

"You lie!"

"I don't lie!" the prisoner said. Tears streamed down his face. "We just needed the money."

"Don't you raise your voice to me!"

Wupash!

Selene folded her arms over her chest and said, "Oh please. Do you expect me to stand here all day while you beat him until he cries himself to death?" She pointed at the prisoner. "Do you know who I am?"

"Y-Yes," the disheveled man said, "you are the High Priestess."

"And you wouldn't be stupid enough to lie to me, would you?"

He swallowed and shook his sweat-soaked hair.

She approached within arm's length of the prisoners and turned her stare toward the tormentor.

He backed away and fixed his line of sight elsewhere.

She stared deep into the first prisoner's eyes, but he twisted his head away.

"Why won't you look at me?"

"I don't want to catch fire."

"Ha!" she said. "Is that what they're saying now?" She looked back at the others. "Well, are they?"

No one uttered a word.

"I see." She bobbed her head. "So then, you put the signs up because you were hungry and you needed money. Hmmm. How much did this green-eyed man pay you, then?"

"A silver and a few coppers."

"I have a feeling you are lying."

The prisoner shook his head.

"You aren't supposed to lie, you know. Bad things happen when you lie."

"I know."

"Remove his shirt," she ordered.

With a few stiff tugs, the tormentor ripped it off. A few voices in the room gasped.

The prisoner had a circle with two slashes tattooed to his chest.

Selene recoiled.

"You!"

The prisoner looked her dead in the eye. Fearless.

"The king is coming, High Priestess. You can't stop it. King Balzurth is com—"

A wash of fire erupted from her mouth. The man howled inside the fiery blaze. His flesh disintegrated from his bones, which collapsed into a pile of ash.

Everyone's eyes were wide, their mouths breathless.

The other prisoners shuffled and twisted in their bonds.

Scowling, Selene backed away.

Metal cuffs and links snapped. The figures bound in them transformed into the sleek forms of metallic green dragons.

"You dare!" Selene roared.

Lightning blasted from the dragon mouths. A bolt slammed Selene off her feet. Another ripped through the draykis, dropping it stone-cold dead.

Selene gathered balls of flame in her hands and hurled them at full force. An explosion shook the room. Soldiers and acolytes charged the magnificent dragons with swords and spell work.

The green dragons—little bigger than men—shot lightning, swung tails, and clawed through robes and armor. The prisoners clamored. The scent of blood and burnt metal filled the air. Quick and sleek, the dragons felled every servant of Barnabus one by one. Seconds later, they hemmed Selene back inside the cove.

"I will feast on your flesh for this, you sacrificial fools!"

Lightning blasted from their mouths.

Selene absorbed it. Her body enlarged and filled with power. She unleashed it.

Lightning and fire pierced the dragons' scales and clean through their hearts. Their bodies juttered and teetered over, lifeless as stone.

Hands smoking, Selene dropped to her knees. Huffing for breath, she said, "Great Grattack, that was close!"

CHAPTER

14

ONE OF THE GREATEST OF dragons in the realm soared above the clouds with his great wings beating. His scales were a colored blend of iron, copper, brass, and traces of silver. He was the leader of the sky raider breed, who were some of the largest dragons. Flying fortresses in the sky. All the dragons knew him by name. Inferno.

He hadn't landed in days. Instead, he watched Nalzambor from above, spying on enemies. He and his breed thwarted efforts wherever good people rallied. Farmland and villages burned. Lives were snuffed out in the moon and sun light. When he dropped through the clouds, the wind made a terrifying whistle between his horns. His armored belly rumbled.

Below, a herd of cattle began to stampede. Inferno bellowed a monstrous sound that bent the grass and shook the leaves from the trees. Stunned, some of the cattle staggered, shaking the horns on their heads. Others doubled over on their knees and rolled over.

Ten times their size, Inferno landed among them. His eyes were burning coals. He snatched a bull from the ground and tossed it into his mouth whole.

Crunch! Crunch! Crunch! Gulp!

Inferno grabbed another and ate, and another. One more he swallowed whole. When he had finished, he'd eaten over twenty head of cattle. His neck swayed from side to side, and his eyes narrowed.

Burrrrrrp!

The noise was so loud, even more leaves fell off the trees. Inferno ate three more and moaned. His claw patted his belly. He blew a fog of smoke from his snout.

Puff!

Picking his teeth with the long claw on his left forefinger, he strolled through the grasses, head lowered. He took a deep draw through his nostrils and smelled something living that was not cattle. Men. Fear. Sweat. He could smell it all.

When Inferno neared a grove, a rider on horseback burst free.

Inferno spat flame, setting both man and horse on fire. A clamor of cries rose within the trees, and Inferno pressed within. Trees snapped and fell, uprooted. A volley of arrows zinged off his nose.

A small regiment of Legionnaires lurked within the woodland.

Inferno's chest expanded and glowed with a bright orange light right before he unleashed a flood of fire.

Man and horse screamed.

Inferno stomped everything that moved and burned. Metal armor and strong bones collapsed under his great might. In seconds, the grove was a blaze of fallen wood ruins.

In his great dragon voice, he chuckled. Scanning left to right, he snorted, spread his wings, and lifted himself up and out of the blaze.

Whump. Whump. Whump.

He lifted toward the clouds, a bit slower this time. His belly hung a little low, and there was more effort in his wings. He sounded another triumphant roar down at the valley. Cattle still stampeded, trampling anything in their path. Fear. Inferno thrived on it. He recalled the last dragon war. All he had terrified. All he had killed. Man and dragon alike.

Soon won't be soon enough.

He loved war. He loved battle. The mere thought of it made him salivate. Lava dripped from his jaws.

He tilted his head toward the heavens and beat his wings a little harder. His great frame and bulging belly lifted upward and began to pass through the first layer of mist.

A blue streak zinged out of the clouds, right past his nose.

What!

Inferno dropped his neck and turned in the air toward it. It was a dragon. A blue streak, no less. One of the good ones.

I'll have you for a snack!

Behind him, more blue streaks darted out of the clouds and latched onto his wings.

You dare!

Lightning burst from their mouths, singing his scales.

Inferno roared, spun, and writhed in the air. Wings pinned by a dozen smaller dragons, he plummeted toward the ground. A second before he hit the rocks, the blue dragons fled him.

WHAM!

The entire valley shook.

Hot with rage, Inferno reared up.

I'll kill every one of you little fleas!

The blue streaks, fast and sleek, peppered Inferno with jolts of lightning that lanced through scales and skin.

His tail lashed out, knocking two from the sky. His great claw swatted another from the sky. He gushed out fire and terrible roars.

The blue streaks darted in and out of his fury, striking his eyes and blasting his nose. The wounds were more annoying than fatal.

You rodents cannot kill me!

He slapped another blue dragon from the sky with his tail and stomped it under his great claws, grinding it into the ground.

Only half of the small dragon force remained, and many of them were wounded. They broke off the attack and jetted skyward, vanishing in the clouds.

You will not escape me!

He spread out his great wings. The veils of skin that made up his wings were shredded.

Noooo!

He lifted his great neck skyward. The blue streak dragons reappeared, circling wide above him.

You dare mock me! You think you can end the great Inferno! My wings will heal in no time!

Suddenly, his eyes shone like fiery moons.

Another dragon dropped through the clouds and right through the ring of blue dragons. Big and vast, the steel dragon, half the size of Inferno, led a train of good dragons—more than he could count—of all colors and sizes. They swooped down, hovered in the air, and surrounded Inferno.

You'll pay for this!

It was the steel dragon's thoughts that responded.

Perhaps, but you won't be around to see it. Annihilate him! it ordered.

Dragon breath—flames, balls, lances, shards, and bolts of power—blasted from hundreds of dragon mouths, pounding Inferno into the ground. The wroth heat bubbled his scales. His horns caught fire. His wings disintegrated. Drawing up all his power, he let out the greatest blast he had in him. Fire erupted from his mighty jaws, coating three dragons with liquid fire in the sky.

I'll take you all! I'll take you all with me! I'll—ulp!

A blue streak dragon flew inside his mouth with a green orb of energy carried in its claws. A moment later it zipped out—empty handed—narrowly missing Inferno's snapping teeth.

The dragons in the sky pounded him with their fierce breath once again. Geysers of power came from green, yellow, red, and blue dragons of many varieties and colors.

Sluggish, Inferno raised his weary head. Pain throbbed in every scale. He leered at the steel dragon and filled his breath once more. All the dragons had landed and surrounded him.

I wouldn't do that if I were you.

Inferno scoffed.

Why? Because there is an orb in me?

It will kill you instantly. Surrender and go home to the king. Ask for mercy.

Never.

Then you will die.

Then I'll take all of you with me.

The steel dragon's eyes went wide.

Move!

Inferno let out a gust of flame. And exploded.

Most of the good dragons survived, recovered, and stared down into the smoking crater. Only scales, horn, and pieces of bone remained of the vanquished Inferno and almost half their comrades.

A threatening roar came from high in the sky.

On the ready, dragons! the steel dragon said, twisting his great neck in the air.

Inferno's brood, the sky raiders, blackened the sky in the dozens.

"Vengeance comes!"

CHAPTER

15

NATH SNAPPED UP INTO A sitting position.

"Agh!"

Shards of pain lanced through his body.

"Oh," he moaned, slowly collapsing back down on the bed. He tried to rub his sore head, but could barely move his sore arms. He narrowed his aching eyes and turned his chin from the candlelight that blurred the distance. "Where am I? What happened?"

"You jumped off your balcony, you fool," a harsh woman's voice said.

It was Selene, but Nath couldn't see her.

As his memories rushed back to him, every bit of his awakened body began to throb. He'd jumped and plummeted a thousand feet. He hadn't meant to. His intent had been to regain his dragon form and fly. Halfway down, he panicked. Mouth screaming and arms flailing, his life flashed in clips of his two hundred twenty-five years. In a split second, he met the sweet kiss of the bone-crushing street. Lucky for him, he didn't feel a thing, until now. And he wasn't dead. At least, he didn't think he was.

"So, I live?"

"Call it a miracle. They often favor the foolish." Her face appeared before him. A hard scowl. A look that wanted to kill him herself. But there was worry behind her dark eyes. "Patience, Nath. It's no wonder you can't take dragon form. You have no patience."

He propped himself up on his elbows.

"Ugh! How long have I been out?"

"That does not matter," she said. "What matters is that you breathe again."

"Breathe again?" His heart jumped. "Did I die?"

"Sorry," she said, brushing his hair out of his eyes. "It was a figure of speech, but I can only assume at some point you stopped breathing. Falls from tall towers typically knock the wind from a fellow."

"Heh," he said, unable to contain his smile.

"What is that for?"

"Well, it's good to know."

"What's good to know?" she said, lifting her brow.

"That I'm so hard to kill."

"It's not that, it's because your skull is ten times thicker than others."

"And that's a good thing."

"Being thick-headed is not a good thing!" She huffed. "Will you ever outgrow your boyish charm?"

Wincing, he swung his legs over the bed and said to her, "Are you saying I'm immature?"

"That's exactly what I'm saying."

He rolled his neck and cracked it from side to side. Her words had the sting of truth in them. But he thought he'd been more responsible than ever. After all, he'd agreed to the Truce and spared all his friends. Hundreds and thousands of lives had been spared. But now he sat in the tower, feeling much like a child again.

I never should have transformed back into a man. I wouldn't have all these problems then.

"Come with me," Selene said. "If you are able to walk, that is."

With a groan, Nath stood up and wobbled. Selene caught his arm and helped straighten him up. Shaking her head, she said, "I can't believe you jumped. Perhaps I should shackle you somewhere. After all, you *are* my prisoner."

"Don't you dare," he said, limping after her.

"Why not? You are a prisoner, and I am responsible for your care."

"Hah," he laughed, glancing around. He wasn't familiar with his surroundings. "You shoved me off the terrace in the first place. You had me fight Kryzak to the death. And then you tried to kill me."

She stopped and pushed him back.

"Yet you live. Why don't you quit brooding and take a moment to think about that?"

Taken aback, he said, "Wow, I can't die."

"Now you jest." She rolled her eyes. "Of course you can die. I could have killed you if I wanted. And I'm not the only one, either." She ran her claw over his chest. It sent a chill through him. "Every dragon has a weakness." She patted his chest and walked away. "You know that."

She walked on outside the chamber he'd never been in before. The Great Tower had hundreds of rooms, and he'd only been in a few of them. Anything could be going on in any one of them. He followed her down the hall. She was escorted by a pair of draykis guards that leered at him. He sneered back.

I wonder how they'd fare if I tossed them out a window. I'll find out soon enough if they cross me.

Selene knocked on the next door in the hall. Nath heard the soft scuffle of feet on the other side and watched the door open. Sasha's head popped out.

"I thought you should know that Nath is now awake," Selene said, motioning his way.

"Nath!" Sasha said, running to him and giving him an embrace. "It's so good to see you!" She patted his shoulders. "Alive!" Her face became confused. "Why-Why did you do that?"

"Long story," he said, "but it's good to see you, even though I just saw you moments before I ... well ... fell." He glanced at Selene then back at her. "How long has it been?"

"I've been tending you for more than a week."

"A week!" He glared at Selene. "I was of the impression it wasn't quite so long."

"Oh Nath, I'm so glad you've awakened. I would have been tormented in my travels had you not."

"What travels?"

"I'm going back home," she said, squeezing his hands.

"I'm glad to hear it," he said, "but I was hoping you'd be able to travel with me across the lands. Say, maybe I can come with you."

"We are going south," Selene injected, "and she is headed north. And with haste, I might add."

"What's the hurry?" Nath said.

"This is Bayzog's request. It's between her and him, and something to do with their children."

"What has happened, Sasha?"

"Oh nothing, Nath. It's a family celebration. Rerry and Samaz have upcoming years-of-life celebrations, and they urge me home. My return will be a surprise to them, but I'd been tending to you."

"Sasha, you didn't have to do that. Please, get home to your family. I'm alright."

"But I worry," she said, brushing his cheek.

"I did something foolish, and I promise it won't happen again," he said, giving her a little hug. "*I should be worrying about* you. It should never be the other way around. Now go. And don't let me be a burden to you any longer."

She squeezed him tight.

"Thank you, Nath. Thank you!" A tear dropped from her eye. "I'm relieved."

"Tell Bayzog good-bye for me. He'll know what I mean."

"I will," she said, scurrying by Selene. The pair met eyes. It left Nath with a strange feeling. Then Sasha, tugging at her pendant, scampered back through her door.

"Oh my," Selene said, "you sound so grown up all of a sudden. Humph. Come with me, Nath. Come with. It's time to travel."

Gorlee–disguised as Sasha—stood with his ear to the door. Selene, Nath, and the draykis shuffled by, and then he heard them no more. He wiped the tear from his eye. Selene had told him he needed to work on being more convincing in his role. But Nath's golden stare had begun to penetrate his disguise. The ruse became harder to maintain the longer they were in company with each other. He had shared this with Selene, and she had decided it was time Sasha moved on.

Moving away from the door, he sat down at a desk and rested his head on his arms. Tired and confused as he was, scrambled thoughts bounced back and forth in his head.

What do I do? What do I do?

Selene controlled him. What she wanted, he did. And posing as Sasha was only one of those things. She'd made him do other things. Despicable acts. He'd hurt people. Cheated and deceived them. And deep down inside, it ate at him. *Why?*

The Deep. That was where the answer lay, and he knew it. He wanted to wait until Selene left, but what if she took him along? *I can't wait any longer. I can't live like this anymore.* He sat several long hours and started to cry. *What am I? Am I a lie?* Gathering himself, he removed the yellow stone pendant, left his room, and headed for The Deep.

I will find the answers, or they will find me.

CHAPTER
16

"It's a strange place to meet," Ben said, sitting down and emptying the water from his boots. He and Bayzog had been traveling by foot for days and just finished wading through a waist-deep stream of icy water. His teeth chattered. "And you're sure this is where they'll be?"

"That's what her note said," Bayzog replied, ringing out his robes. "Barring any changes in the circumstances." He coughed. Eyed the ridgeline. A range of rocky steppes surrounded them.

"Be nice if we had horses, but you had to rush us out of there. My guts are still churning." Ben rubbed his head. "How can there be power to do *that*? It's not right."

"It's magic, and it does plenty of things we don't understand. How do so many dragons fly with such small wings on their backs?"

"Huh, I've even seen dragons fly without any wings." Ben stood up and dusted off his trousers. "Point taken. Just give me fair warning before you … uh … what's the word?"

"Teleport."

"Yes. A warning would be nice." Ben picked up Brenwar's chest and slung it over his back with a grunt. "Best we get going."

"Is that chest a burden?" He eyed the cast iron bandings strapped over the darkened wood.

"Oh, *now* you ask?" Ben shrugged. "No. It's not as heavy as it looks." He narrowed his eyes at Bayzog and laughed. "Must be magic. Not very burdensome at all." He groaned. "Light as a feather. Yep. Light as a feather."

"You jest?"

"Let's keep moving," Ben said, huffing his way up the slope. "I'm starting to understand why Brenwar parted with it now. The bearded buzzard got tired of lugging it around. Good for him. Bad for my back."

"I can assist."

Ben waved him off and started his trek up the slope. He looked back at Bayzog and said, "This *is* the right way, isn't it?"

Bayzog nodded. Pointing, he said, "Just head straight toward the split in the peaks, and soon we will arrive."

Ben set his chin and nodded. The rangy man, stalwart as they come, had taken care of most everything on the trek. He hunted, fished, and trapped. Bayzog might have starved without him, despite the last twenty-so years of survival. Although part-elf, the old wizard's city ways had never quite acclimated to the woods. But he could recognize plants that were edible and maybe catch a fish from time to time.

He slipped. Ben caught his arm.

"You really need to be more thoughtful in your gear," the warrior said, looking at Bayzog's shoes. "You'd almost be better off in bare feet than those things."

His friend's shoes were little more than leather slippers. But that was all part of being a mage. The lighter you traveled, the better. Bayzog had explained, but Ben hadn't fully understood. It had something to do with how the energies were harnessed from the world.

Two more hours they trudged up the slope into the setting sun, winding left to right along the rocky edges.

"You realize we're exposed, don't you?" Ben said. "Marching right up into the high ground with the sun in our eyes—"

"It will be alright."

"How do you know that?"

"I know." Bayzog gave his friend a reassuring look.

Ben shrugged and mopped the sweat from his brow.

The sun eased its way between the split, and the slopes became heavy in shadow. Bayzog could see the rock faces ahead, less than a mile away. Natural stone columns were in the rock, and many of them looked like giant faces.

"That's odd," Ben said, glancing back at Bayzog. "So you and Sasha have been here before?"

"We used to ride horses a lot and take trips for days at a time. We came across this place by accident." He smiled. "She fell in love with it."

"With the rocks?"

"More or less. But it's what's on the other side that impresses."

"Impresses you? I've seen Elome, and I've never seen anything more impressive than that."

"This is not like that. It's different, and she's fond of it. That's all that matters." His eyes watered. Doubt seeped into his heart. *What if she's not there?*

"She'll be there," Ben said, drifting back and squeezing his shoulder.

Eyeing the rock faces, Bayzog explained, "We took our vows there."

"Well, perhaps you can renew them, now. Come on. I'm excited to see this place. The place that stirs the heart of the Grand Bayzog."

They entered the split in the great stones after traversing a jagged pass over half a mile long. Ben set the chest down and stared into the valley. The sun was a big orange eye overlooking a huge lake surrounded by great trees and abundant forest life. Some of the trees were colored with golden leaves. Others were violet, white, or red.

"I like it," Ben said. "So, are we heading down"—he looked left and right—"or around?" The rocky steppes and pinnacles formed a crescent moon around the lake. A narrow path led along the rocks either way. "I find it hard to believe no one lives here." He lifted a brow. "Giants, maybe?"

A shadow dropped behind them from out of nowhere.

Whump!

Bayzog twisted around.

Snap. Clatch. Snap.

Ben hustled to his side, with Akron ready.

A cherry-scaled dragon filled the chasm. Magnificent. Beautiful. It had small twisting horns and rose-colored belly scales. Long black lashes over its eyes. He could feel the heat of its breath.

Bayzog stood behind his staff and held Ben an arm's length behind him. His heart pounded between his temples. "Hold," he said.

Ben kept his arrow nocked. "If you want to teleport me out of here, I'm alright with it."

"Be still," Bayzog said. "I'm not so sure she aims to harm us."

The cherry dragon shook its scales and wings.

"She?" Ben said.

"Aye—"

"Father! Father!"

Bayzog's head snapped up. His eyes fixed on Rerry climbing down the rock.

"Son!" Bayzog said.

Rerry, light-haired and lithe, scrambled to the bottom. He embraced his father. The young part-elf's wiry arms squeezed him tight.

"You've grown well, Son!" Bayzog said, unable to contain his elation.

"Father, I've missed you so much!" Rerry hugged him again.

"Ahem," Ben said to them both, eyeing the dragon.

Rerry looked at Ben, nodded, then looked over at the dragon. "We call her Shayleen. She's been with us many days. Was it you who sent the tiny dragons?"

"Yes."

"I knew it was. Come, come," Rerry said. "Mother waits."

"What about ... er ... Shayleen?" Ben said, lowering his bow.

Rerry shrugged.

"She'll be fine, I'm certain. She's a dragon, you know."

"Rerry," Bayzog said, "this is my dear friend, Ben."

Rerry looked Ben over, and his eyes widened.

"Oh! Is that Akron? Is that Fang?"

"No, it's Ben," Ben said, pulling the bow away. *Clatch. Snap. Clatch.* His hand fell on Fang's hilt.

"Rerry, where are your manners?"

"Ah, they're somewhere around here," Rerry said, scratching his head. He extended his hand. "Hello, Ben."

Ben squeezed it, and Rerry winced. Ben picked up the dwarven chest and handed it to Rerry.

"Oof!"

"I'd be obliged," Ben said, stretching his back and eyeing the dragon.

"I wouldn't stare too long if I were you," Rerry said, grinning.

"Why?"

"Because she might kill you."

"Rerry!" Bayzog said.

"Come along, Father and Father's friend, Ben," Rerry said, teetering with a happy gait. "I can't wait to see Mother's face when she sees you!"

Rerry led the way around the rim of the valley until they stopped at the mouth of a small cave overlooking the lake. Bayzog saw Sasha standing just outside it, auburn hair blowing in the gentle breeze. Bayzog strengthened his knees. Shayleen soared by and darted up, disappearing into the clouds high over the lake.

"Mother! Mother!" Rerry yelled.

Sasha's chin turned. Her eyes locked on Bayzog, and his heart jumped in his throat. The pair collided halfway to the cave. Sasha buried her head in his shoulder, sobbing.

"Bayzog..."

He stroked her hair, trembling a little. "I've missed you," he said. "But my heart has never ached so much as it does now. I'm not parting with you again."

"Good," she said, still hugging him. "Good." She tilted her chin up, and they kissed.

"Not in front of the children," Rerry started.

Ben backhanded his shoulder.

"Oh, come on," Rerry said to Ben, rubbing his shoulder. "Might as well let sour face know his father has arrived."

"Let's go in," Sasha said. "Our spot will make you feel right at home."

Holding her hand, Bayzog ducked inside the cave after Ben and Rerry. Mystic flames reflected on the walls, which were coated in bright oily colors. There were beds made from giant leaves and tall grasses and nothing more. The cave went back as far as he could see, and the ambiance was soothing. He glanced back outside the cave mouth, beheld the spectacular view he and Sasha fell for so many decades ago, and sighed.

"You need rest," she said, rubbing his hand between hers.

He brushed her hair over her ears. Her face was scuffed up and swollen. It angered him. His wife and sons had been through quite an ordeal. He could feel it.

"Never again," he said. "To the end."

"Mother! Father!" Rerry's voice echoed in the cave.

They rushed deeper within. Samaz lay propped up in Rerry's arms, with the whites of his eyes showing. Bayzog knelt alongside his son and squeezed his knee.

"What's wrong?" Ben asked.

"He does this when he dreams," Rerry said, "and his dreams seem to be getting longer and worse."

Samaz stiffened and popped upright.

His eyes rolled so that only the whites were exposed, and he started mumbling, "Gorn Grattack comes … Gorn Grattack comes … Gorn Grattack comes…"

CHAPTER
17

BRENWAR SHOVED A BOULDER FOUR times his size.

"Hurk!"

The boulder shifted in the dirt.

"Brenwar! You're pushing it! You're pushing it!" Pilpin said. He scurried over to the mountain rim and peered over. Barnabus soldiers waited below, breaking camp. Pilpin rushed back. "Hurry! They're moving on."

Brenwar's dark eyes were popped wide open, and sweat beaded his face. He straightened with everything he had. The mystic bracers aided a great deal, but they still needed fuel from his iron will. He clenched his teeth. "Grrrrrrrrrrrrr … "

The dust and dirt below the great stone shifted more, and the rock began to grind over the dirt.

"You're doing it!" Pilpin exclaimed.

"Keep it down!" Brenwar grunted.

"Oh," Pilpin said, hopping up and down and covering his bearded lips. "Is there anything I can do?"

"Push!"

"Certainly, Brenwar, certainly!" Pilpin lowered his shoulder, dug his boots in, and gave the rock a shove.

The boulder started to eclipse the edge.

"We've almost got it, Brenwar!"

Red-faced, Brenwar eyed the little dwarf that was half the size of him. Shaking his head, he took a deep breath and put more back into it.

"Hurk!"

"Come on, Brenwar!" Pilpin blurted out. "Push it!"

The rock moved another half foot. It was inches from the rim. He dug in and shoved it another half step. The rock teetered back toward Brenwar and Pilpin.

"Oh no!" Pilpin said, stepping away.

"No you don't!" Brenwar added.

The rock slipped inches farther, teetered more over, and …

Whoosh!

It slid off the rim.

Bam! Bang! Crack!

It bounced down the hillside, crushing rocks and breaking off jagged limbs. The soldiers of Barnabus—men, orcs, lizardmen, and gnolls—cried out at the rolling hunk of terror. Weighed down by armor and lacking quick-thinking brains, they caught the doom full force.

Over a dozen Barnabus minions were pulverized as the great stone rolled on toward the river.

Huffing for breath, Brenwar picked up a stone larger than his head and hurled it down on a lone survivor. Pilpin chucked a few rocks of his own.

"We did it," the little dwarf said. Slapping Brenwar's shoulder, he stuck his chest out. "I couldn't have done it without you."

"Aye," Brenwar added. "Now let's go. There's certain to be survivors. Let's see what we can squeeze out of them." He rubbed his wrists. "Such marvelous toys."

As the pair traversed the slope, Brenwar still had much on his mind. Black Dragons. Nath. Sightings of Gorn Grattack. Skirmishes far away from the cities in a secret war that was going on. There was only one thing he liked so far in his quest: there was plenty of fighting to be done. He just hoped his friends fared as well as he did.

CHAPTER

18

"THIS IS STRANGE," SHUM SAID to Hoven. His stone-faced countenance was sad. He held a pixlyn no bigger than a doll in his hands. The pixlyn, a small winged figurine of a man, breathed no more. Its once vibrant body was now stiff and lifeless. "And tragic," he added.

Nodding, Hoven slid a hunting knife from his belt and began carving in a tree. The pair had trekked into the foothills south of the Shale Hills, stopping only to rest the horses. The Roamers, horse and elf, required little sleep, but Hoven yawned.

"Brother, are you well?" Shum said, tucking the pixlyn under his arm.

Hoven dug his blade deeper into the knot in the tree.

"This land is cursed. See how this tree bleeds?" Black sap seeped from the knot and down the bark of the tree. There were brown moldy spots all over it. Hoven put a dab of sticky sap on his finger. His face turned sour, and he spat. "The soil is tainted."

"And the waters." Shum removed a small shovel from his horse and tossed it to Hoven. "We need to bury him."

"Here? In this unhealthy ground?"

The fertility of the forest had ebbed. The colorful leaves dried up and fell out of season. The bark of the trees was peeling, and fallen branches were scattered on the ground. Chipmunks, moles, and such lay dead in their tracks. Predators such as foxes didn't eat them. Not even vultures did. Shum's skin crawled. Unseen forces lurked all about.

"We'll find another spot where the ground is more fertile."

The Roamers winded through the woodland, passing through bountiful spots and others dreary and grey. The wildwood divided. Some groves thrived, while others moaned for light, dark undergrowth and weeds overwhelming them. Shum didn't remember such places from the last dragon war, but he did remember the devastation. Forest and city burning with fire. Desolated. What he saw now was different.

"Here," Hoven said, dipping his shovel into the soft earth. It was a nice clearing, under the sun and a couple dozen yards from the glass surface of a pond. "This spot is better than most I've seen. It should give it a chance."

Hoven put his back into it, long sinewy arms scooping out heaps of dirt, braided hair dangling down over his ample shoulders.

Shum brushed his thumb over the pixlyn's face. The little person was a creature of earthen magic. Sometimes, the soil could revive them. He'd witnessed it before, but that was with other pixlyns handling the burial. There were no other pixlyns now. Just a still, quiet forest, where nothing breathed but them.

A horse nickered and headed for the pond.

Shum craned his neck and swallowed. The cool waters of the pond looked refreshing. Hoven stopped his digging, and, eyeing him, he lowered the small body into the small but deep grave. Kneeling, he followed with a few Elvish words.

The wind stirred.

Shum nodded, and Hoven began refilling the grave. Nearby, a horse whinnied.

"I'll fill the canteens," Shum said, making his way toward the pond. The horses' necks were bent toward the water, but they did not drink. Their hooves became restless on the soft ground. Shum's hands fell to his swords. He let out a sharp whistle.

A dragon's head surfaced and struck. Its great jaws clamped down on Shum's horse's neck. A second dragon head burst from the water and latched onto the other horse. The Roamer steeds whined and bucked.

"No!" Shum cried, rushing for the water's edge. He struck into the dragon's neck. An oily beast coated in slime and muck. The blade bit, but not deeply, and the dragon jaws crunched farther downward. "Hoven!" He struck again and again.

The dragon's neck rose, lifting the horse higher, and the full body of the dragon began to emerge from the waters. It towered over elf and horse. Two serpentine necks were attached to a large four-legged body coated in mud and scales. Its wings and tail were coal black.

Shum slid his spear out of his pack and twirled it three times over. It lengthened from two feet to eight. He waded into the waters and plunged the spear into the beast's belly. It sank in. The dragon heads roared. Both horses fell to the ground in a heap.

The dragon struck at him.

Spear in one hand, sword in the other, Shum parried the assault with fury. Hoven emerged and chopped vigorously at the other dragon head. Both elven blades chipped away through the scales and into the bones. The wingless, hornless dragon beast slunk deeper into the waters. Its striking heads collided with razor sharp steel.

"Don't let him get away!" Shum yelled.

He rammed the spear up through the bottom of its jaw, piercing the gray matter in its head. The second head let out an ear-splitting howl. Hoven cut it deeply through the throat and neck. The dragon slunk back into the pond, and the waters began to bubble over its dying bulk.

Shum and Hoven rushed out of the waters to the sides of their gravely wounded mounts.

"No! No! No!" Shum cried. He laid his bare hands on his beast and recited mystic prayers in Elvish, but it was too late.

CHAPTER

19

"Man, are you slight in the head?" the older guard of The Deep said. "Get back away from there, Jason!" It was the same man who had warned Gorlee about his musings days ago. Older. Gruff in nature.

Gorlee continued to stare at the glassy black surface that covered The Deep. The oily image shimmered and warbled. He teetered closer to the edge. What he needed was down there. He could feel it. He also knew somehow that he had been down there before. If he could only get back down there, he knew he would find his memories. His booted toes stuck out over the edge.

"Get back here, you fool!" the senior guard said. "We already have one to feed him. We don't need two."

Gorlee turned.

A tall, rangy man with a thick black beard stood shackled between two guards. His clothes were ornate but disheveled, and he had a weary look about him.

"Tell you what, rook," the lead guard said, spitting juice from his mouth. "I'll let you lead this man to the edge. You can even watch the phantom snatch him up."

"Ph-phantom?" the prisoner said, cringing. The guards shoved him forward. "No! No! I'm supposed to be put in a dungeon, not The Deep! My sentence is only—*oof*!"

The guard walloped him in the back of the head with a small club. The prisoner collapsed in a heap, and the two men dragged him over to the rim.

"Go ahead," the senior guard said to Gorlee. "Roll him in there."

Gorlee hooked the man beneath the arms.

The wind stirred, and a whoop of cries came up and out of The Deep.

The center of the black water stirred and started spinning in a swift circle. A dark oily form rose in the middle, dripping with sludge and goo. The guards scurried to the other side of the bars and slammed the gate shut. Gorlee heard one guard's armored knees knocking.

"Get away from there!" the veteran guard said. "Get away!"

The phantom, a towery faceless ghoul, stretched its elongated arms out and made a shrieking howl. The ghostly hands engulfed the unconscious man's entirety and pressed him deep down into the sludge.

Gorlee stood chin up, facing it.

The phantom tilted its head and shrieked again.

Gorlee hunkered down, covering his head and waiting. At last, Gorlee felt the phantom's hands engulfing *him*, too. Ice raced through his veins, and down he went, spinning and spinning and spinning.

Coughing, Gorlee struggled to his knees. The prisoner lay beside him, wide eyed and shaking. Above, the well of The Deep showed a dim light hundreds of feet up. All signs of the phantom were gone. He reached over and touched the man. The prisoner jerked and sputtered.

"Eh," Gorlee said, wiping slime from the man's face. "I'll check on you later." He rose to his feet, swaying, and staggered forward until he regained his balance. A long corridor of cut stone and ancient symbols let out into several illuminated tunnels. He could hear shrill cackles, rustling chains, and the scuffle of bare and booted feet.

Hmmm…

He rubbed his chin, summoned his power, and shape-shifted. His mannish frame shrunk a foot. His arms corded up with muscle. Long yellow nails grew from the tips of his fingers. He tore off his uniform shirt, ripped up his pants into tatters, then said in a raspy voice, "I'm a goblin."

Though he didn't remember much about The Deep, he knew there were plenty of creatures from all the races down here. He'd heard the guards and their stories. He hobbled along the corridor and followed the stairs up into another level of caves that led to an overlook over a grand chamber hundreds of feet wide and deep.

He took a few quick breaths.

Even in this cavernous expanse, the stale air was rank with sweat. Suffocating. Covering his nose, he spied down below. Scores of prisoners milled about: men, orcs, half-orcs, gnolls, goblins, lizardmen, and even a few halflings. More lay still on the ground. Others, blemished and shaking with fevers, huddled in corners. Some sat with their legs dangling over the ledges up here, near the small tomb-like caves that encircled the arena.

Hunched over and dragging a foot, Gorlee made his way along the rim and climbed down one of the ladders that led to the bottom floor. Not a single eye drifted his way. He wrung his goblin hands.

Excellent.

Now he just had to find the part of him that was missing. The part that called to him from its burial down here. He milled about, staring at faces and listening to conversations.

The prisoners were all marred in some way or another. An orc was missing both eyes and one leg. A bugbear had no teeth. A halfling was covered head to toe in warts and chattering rapidly to himself. Many were hapless, but some were formidable. Another goblin with ruddy skin and both fingers missing from one hand bumped into him and muttered a curse. Its beady eyes bore into him.

Gorlee turned away. He'd spent months blending in. Imitating anyone and everything. Serving Selene's dark purposes. The last thing he needed to do now was to draw unwanted attention to himself. Disguised or not, until he found whatever it was he was looking for, he needed to lay low. At least until he figured it out.

A firm hand grabbed and squeezed his shoulder. He turned and found himself face to face with the goblin.

"I don't remember you," it said in Goblin. "What is your name?"

Some of the other prisoners gathered around, hemming the pair of them in. Gorlee balled up his fists and slugged the fingerless goblin in the jaw. A raucous chorus of cries went up, and a circle of bodies closed in.

The goblin, dismayed, picked up a stone and lunged at Gorlee. It drove the stone into his gut and socked him in the head. Gorlee punched and kicked. It clawed and bit. Blood dripped over his eyes. He wrapped the goblin in a headlock.

"What you do!" the goblin cried. "What you do!"

There was fear in its voice.

The crowd chanted, arms pumping, at the two of them.

"To the death! To the death! To the death!"

Gorlee squeezed the goblin's neck, making its eyes bulge. It tugged and pulled at his arm, but Gorlee held him fast. He had no love of goblins.

But he was no killer, either. Not yet at least. He released the goblin.

It felt to its knees, coughing and wheezing.

A bugbear shoved him forward. Other prisoners began shoving him as well.

"To the death!" they demanded. "That is how we live."

It seemed there was a code in The Deep. That in order to keep the peace, such squabbles among the prisoners were made fatal.

Gorlee set his jaw and filled his hand with a stone.

The rank bodies resumed their clamor.

"Kill him! Kill him! Kill him!"

It was a dark and depraved moment.

The goblin dove onto his legs and drove him to the ground. Gorlee struck a blow to its back, drawing a howl. Back and forth they tussled, one rolling over the other. The goblin locked its claws on his neck. Gorlee swatted it in the ribs with the stone, bringing forth a grunt. The pair locked up arms and legs. It butted its mangy head under his chin. He held on.

Buy time. Buy time.

Gorlee glanced through the faces in the crowd. He could turn into any one of them and get away, if they closed in just a bit more.

Need another escape.

Suddenly, the crowd dispersed at the sound of a thunderous voice.

"WHAT HAVE WE HERE, A BATTLE?"

The triant, Bletver, lorded over them, leering downward with hairy knuckles dragging the ground. Part giant. Part troll. Gorlee knew something of what it was, based off the stories he'd overheard. But deep inside his mind, a spark flashed.

"He started it," the goblin squealed. "Mercy, Lord Bletver. Mercy!"

"I DO NOT RECOGNIZE THIS GOBLIN." Bletver snorted the air. "BUT ALL STINK TO ME." He bent his great mass downward.

A bright yellow stone dangled from a chain on his neck, catching Gorlee's eyes.

That's it! I can feel it!

His grip on the goblin loosened, and it twisted from his grasp. It went down on knees and elbows.

Bletver's arms lashed out, snatching them both from the ground in his oversized hands. Gorlee's eyes bugged out, and his bones groaned.

"PERHAPS I KILL YOU BOTH!" The triant's eyes fixed on Gorlee. "YOU ARE UNFAMILIAR. AND A STRANGE SCENT CONSUMES YOU." His throat rumbled. "ODD, YET FAMILIAR."

Gorlee stared at the yellow stone hanging on Bletver's sagging neck. Inside, the stone throbbed and swirled. He stretched his fingers toward it.

"Eh … you like that?" Bletver said. "Well, that is mine!" It heaved Gorlee up and slammed him to the ground. Its hand began to grind him into the stone floor.

Gorlee absorbed the stone's features and became harder than the rock itself.

"WHAT IS THIS?"

Gorlee regained his feet and now stood a stone goblin. And kept on growing.

Bletver's dark eyes widened.

"NO! NO, IT CANNOT BE!"

Gorlee stood eye to eye with the triant now and watched it back away.

"YOU!" Bletver chanted. "IT CAN'T BE!"

"Give me that stone," Gorlee said, holding out his hand.

Bletver engulfed it with his great hands.

"NEVER!"

Gorlee pounced. He picked up Bletver and slammed him to the ground.

Some of the other prisoners gathered what they could and attacked Gorlee. He grew another size larger than Bletver and let his stone fists loose.

WHAM!

WHAM!

WHAM!

WHAM!

Bletver reeled. The Chamal Stone slipped out of his fingers.

"NO," Bletver whined, "NO, not again..."

Gorlee smashed the yellow stone on the rock floor, into a thousand pieces.

Its essence filled him. His memories flooded his mind.

Tears streamed from his eyes. He dropped to his knees with his face lit up with elation. A broad smile formed on his rock-goblin face.

"Time to go," he said, swatting away his assailants. He turned back to Bletver. The triant sagged against the chamber wall, chin buried in its chest. It didn't even glance his way.

"Go," Bletver grumbled, "and return never again."

Gorlee sauntered out of the chamber and squeezed back down the corridor that led him to the pit. The other prisoner was gone. He rubbed his chin and looked up into the well of The Deep. He recalled the icy grip and daunting powers of the phantom.

I did it once. I can do it again!

He reached up, dug his rock hands into the rock walls, and started shimmying up the well. The howl of the phantom shrieked in his ears. Its black ghostly form coated him like black ice and tried to force him down.

"We meet again," Gorlee said.

He scrambled up the tunnel with the phantom shrieking inside his mind. The blood in his veins became icy water, but he did not slow. He could feel the phantom's anger and hatred tearing at him from the inside.

Gorlee's goal was the beacon of light at the top of the well. He had to get up there and help his friend, Nath Dragon. His own deceptions and guilt fueled his inner fire of determination to make things right.

"You couldn't stop me last time," Gorlee grunted, "and you won't stop me now!" He laughed. "Ha! Twice I will have escaped your precious Deep!"

The phantom was a force. A guardian with a mission. It had little intelligence of its own, just a mission: don't let anything escape this tunnel. That was all it had ever known.

The higher Gorlee climbed, the more the monster's energy faded. Near the top, it drifted away, its mission a failure.

"I'll be," Gorlee said with a grin. The phantom was gone. His fingers reached the rim, and he changed form again, back into the guard named Jason. Climbing out of The Deep, he found himself standing naked in front of the other guards. They all gaped at him. He covered himself and said, "Sorry, Commander, but I seem to have lost my trousers."

Gawping and scratching his head, the veteran guard said, "I can't believe that's *all* you lost. Now fetch yourself a new uniform and stay away from the rim." He tossed Gorlee a cloak. "Sultans of Sulfur, young men do the most foolish things!"

CHAPTER

20

RIDING ON HORSEBACK SOUTH OF Narnum near where the three rivers met, Nath and Selene shook off the drizzling rain. A host of soldiers rode and walked before and after them, weapons and armor creaking and jangling. They'd ridden for days, visiting small towns and cities, and the people heaped his praises. By all of his observations, things were becoming prosperous and back to normal. The people smiled and cheered. The children showed no long faces. But the armies of Barnabus were always near, like slow-moving rainclouds in the background.

He shifted in his saddle, eyeing the sky. The feline fury circled in the air. It wasn't alone, either. Dozens of grey scalers swooped through the sky in tight formations, accompanied by red horned dragons as well.

"How do you control them?" Nath said. "I see no jaxite stones in your possession."

"Those stones are for the overlords," she said. "These dragons you see here, they serve the same cause as me. Their service is voluntary."

Nath thought about Snarggell and all they'd sacrificed to put an end to the jaxite stones. He'd killed the lurker and removed the crystal gnomes from the cursed Floating City, but it seemed the damage had been done already.

"Do they speak to you?" he asked her.

"How do you mean?"

He shrugged.

"I see," she said. "No and yes. I've earned their respect, and that's why they stay. It's not easy to control dragons."

"That's why you need the stones."

"Even without the stones, the dragons would have made their choices sooner or later," she said. "All dragons ultimately serve themselves."

Nath had rescued countless dragons over the years, so he knew they did have selfishness in common. They could be good, greedy, selfish, nasty, and surprising. Only one that he recalled in all his years had ever thanked him. The dragons, even to him, were still a mystery. His father said dragons were good, but many were fallen. That's why you needed to watch out for them. They could be deceived as easily as men.

"They are our brothers and sisters, Nath," Selene continued, "and they want the same peace that we want. Give it some time, and you will see that."

"And what of Gorn Grattack?" He eyed her. "Does he want peace, or does he want power?"

"It takes power to maintain peace. At least, that is his way. Don't get power confused with force, Nath. Don't get distracted. We are making progress, I believe."

The feline fury landed between them. Its mane of hair rose on the back of its neck, and its eyes were intent on Nath.

"Seems this dragon is talking to you," Selene said. "What does he say?"

The fury didn't communicate as most dragons do. Not through thoughts or speech. Instead, it nudged his leg, and Nath could feel the heaviness within its being.

"He's seen something ahead. It's treacherous and worrisome." He tugged the reins of his horse. "Lead the way!"

The feline fury sprang into the air, wings beating. Nath kicked his horse into a gallop and trampled by the soldiers, keeping the fury in sight. The magnificent dragon diminished into a speck and joined a circle of grey scalers that drifted in the sky. Behind him, Selene rode. Galloping through the high grass, he slowed. Smoke rose over the tree line. Thick and yellow. A strange pungent stink lingered in the air.

"I know that smell," Nath said. He whipped the reins. "Ee-Yah!"

Another two miles of hard riding, and his horse and thoughts came to an abrupt halt. The forest valley was a battlefield. Soldiers. Dragons. And none of them moved.

"No," Selene said, horrified. "No, it can't be." She trotted her horse alongside the smoking corpse of a huge dragon and hopped off the saddle. "Inferno!" She lay down between his scorched skull and broken horns, sobbing. "I-I can't believe it."

Nath felt numb. Inferno wasn't the only fallen dragon in the valley, just the biggest. There were dozens scattered all over. Some torn to pieces and others smoking corpses. Blue streaks, grey scalers, green lilies, sky raiders, white lotus flares, and even an orange wizen. Trees were crushed and uprooted. Craters were blasted in the dirt. He covered his nose and coughed, eyes watering. He'd never seen or imagined such a spectacle of war before. A war between dragons! Their blood drenched the earth. He clenched his jaw and fists. A swell of anger pounded inside his chest.

A host of soldiers rode in behind them. Nath stopped the leader and said, "No one better pluck one bone, horn, scale, or anything from any of them." Nath poked a hole through the man's chest plate with his claw and rent a rift in it. "Do you understand?"

The commander in full plate armor nodded.

"As you wish. Any defilers will meet with their deaths." He bowed and dispersed his men. "I'll put my best men on watch at once." He glanced at the sky. "And ready our troops for any other circumstances."

Nath dismounted and made his way through the carnage. It wasn't natural, dragons killing one another. Oh, he had seen dragons scuffle before, but this was different. This, indeed, was war.

He kneeled alongside an orange blaze dragon, much like the one he'd rescued in the orcen outpost so long ago. He pushed the lids down over its frozen stare. He stroked its metallic orange neck.

How can this be?

Other races fought all the time. They battled, warred, and skirmished, but this battlefield left a great hole inside him. He stood up and wiped his eyes.

I can't let this continue to happen. I can't.

"You should eat something, Nath," Selene said, motioning to a plate of food that was piled in front of him. "It will comfort you in times like this."

"I've no appetite," he said, leaning back on a small chair made for travel. He sneered at his meal.

The pair of black dragons sat inside an extravagant tent big enough for twenty people. Carpets lay on the ground. Deep colorful tapestries were hung. It had all the comforts of the city, aside from a bed. There were large plush cots instead.

Selene made her way out of her seat and poured steaming hot liquid from a kettle.

"Some tea, perhaps," she said. "It helps my mind rest."

He frowned.

"Nath," she said, easing her hips on the table, "there is a Truce, at least there is on our end."

"You mean your end."

She shrugged. "As I see it, it was not my dragons that struck first. Inferno was ambushed."

"There must have been a reason," Nath said.

"There is a war, and not all wars are fought with battle. There are more subversive tactics than that." She pushed the tea toward him. "Drink. Talk. Listen."

He took a sip from the cup. "Happy?"

"Now is not a time to be happy," she said. "Now is a time for mourning the lost. And a time for planning." She stroked his hair. "Nath, we've made a Truce with the races, but a truce with the dragons is another thing entirely. And I don't think they would have acted on their own without orders."

He cocked an eyebrow at her and said, "What are you trying to say?"

"I think you know what I'm suggesting."

He stiffened in his chair and pushed her hand away.

"You think my father is responsible for this? Do you?"

"You are thinking the same thing, Nath," she said, grabbing his chin and staring straight into his eyes. "My dragons were attacked without provocation. You saw that."

"What I saw was a battle." He pushed himself out of the chair.

"A senseless slaughter!" She banged her fist on the table. "You saw Inferno. He's one of the most ancient dragons in the world, and he was picked off in a battle without honor."

Nath's stomach churned. She was right. The dragons had hit Inferno hard and fast. The great beast had been blindsided.

"I have no doubt you have used similar tactics." Nath tore off a leg of turkey and bit into it. Selene lifted a brow. He waggled the leg at her. "And it was under your orders that this war began in the first place."

"Hah!" She tossed her head back. "You are a fool! This war started long before me or you. If anyone initiated it, it was your father."

"You dare!"

"I do dare!" She seized his arm. "Nath, I know you love your father, but what has he ever done? He sits in the Mountain of Doom and dispenses orders to his minions."

"What minions?"

"Oh Nath," she sighed. "Are you so naïve? Do you think in all the land you were the only one rescuing dragons and keeping an eye on things? Your father has as many spies as I. Likely more. And not just dragons. There are elves, humans, and what about your dear friend Brenwar? What do you think Balzurth *does* inside that mountain home when you're not around?"

"Sleep?"

She held her gut and broke out in laughter. "Ah-aha-ha-ha-ha!"

Nath tossed the turkey leg onto the table. "Pah!" He scowled. "You don't know everything."

"And you do," she said, chuckling. She caught her breath. "Oh, I needed that laugh. I don't think I've laughed so hard in years. You amuse me, Nath."

His jaw muscles clenched. Again, Selene was pointing out things he'd never considered before. Why wouldn't his father have other spies? How else did he keep such a close watch on things? There were times, so many times, when he spoke with his father and his father seemed to know everything. It only made sense that he had help with it.

"Why would my father want war?"

Selene cleared her throat and took a sip of tea.

"Balzurth has one way of controlling things, and Gorn Grattack has another. It's a fight between the two of *them*, if you ask me," she said, "and I think it should be the two of *them* fighting it out and not us, their ... oh, how shall I put it?" She tapped her clawed finger on her chin. "You don't like minions—you made that clear, so how about henchmen? Yes, we are their henchmen. Or foot soldiers? Do you like that?"

"No," he said.

"Nath," she said, resting her elbow on the back of his chair, "Gorn Grattack raised me to serve his purpose, and Balzurth raised you to serve his own. It's as simple as that. Are we special? Yes, I suppose. We can both do things other dragons cannot do, but we are just pawns, in the larger scheme of things."

"I don't believe that," he said. "I'm supposed to take my father's throne one day."

"And if you aren't worthy," she said, "then it will have to be another."

The blunt statement stung, and his eyes drifted to his hands. Black scales with a little mix of white.

"No one is perfect, Nath, and that includes our sires. They just want us to think they are."

He rubbed his temples and said, "So what is the point in all this?"

She shrugged and said, "I suppose to them it's entertainment, but I think we can change that. I think *you* can change it."

"I'm tired of all this fighting!" he said, balling up his fists.

"Then put an end to all of it, Nath. You and I can bring peace among the dragons. I believe it."

Everything had become more difficult and more confusing. One day, he could turn into a dragon. The next day, he couldn't. He was banished by his father yet accepted by his enemy. He had black scales, white scales, and could make balls of fire with his mouth. He had fallen a thousand feet and survived. But now, at this very moment, he felt...

Nath glared at Selene. She had a way of making him feel as helpless as an infant. And a way of combining the truth with lies. Still, he found himself agreeing with what she said.

"Are you suggesting we rebel against our sires?"

Selene got up and rested her hands around his neck and shoulders.

"Now you are starting to think the way a true dragon prince should think."

CHAPTER

21

WHISTLEDOWN. IT HAD BEEN EITHER a large village or a small town; one could no longer tell. Buildings were shattered or burned to the ground. The streets were empty of life, the farmland and vineyards overgrown with weeds.

Sasha kept her hand clasped to Bayzog's. The husband and wife had not parted company for more than a moment since they reunited over a month ago. They walked hand in hand, arms swinging a little. Behind them, Ben and their boys followed.

"A strange place," Rerry said. He eyed his brother Samaz. "I'm sure you like it."

"I do," Samaz said softly.

"Of course," Rerry said, dusting his light hair out of his eyes. "Must be the lack of people."

"Behave yourself," Sasha said. She nudged Bayzog's shoulder. "They never stop unless it's something else they fight."

Bayzog bumped her back and nodded.

"They are as feisty as their mother," he said, looking into her eyes, "and that's a quality I always admired about you."

"That's not a good thing," she said, lowering her eyes. "Sometimes dangerous."

"Sasha, let it go," Bayzog said. Sasha had been apologizing profusely for days, and Bayzog had forgiven her profusely even though he didn't think there was anything to forgive. "You are too hard on yourself. Everyone makes mistakes."

"You don't."

"I have," he said.

"Name one, then," she said. "I'd like to hear."

"Me too," Rerry said, catching up.

"Count me in," said Ben, strolling along Sasha's side, smiling.

Bayzog swallowed the lump in his throat. He'd made mistakes—he was certain of it—but they eluded him. Finally, he said, "I never should have left my wife's side, nor my children's."

"Mmmm..." Sasha started. "I can accept that."

Bayzog's eyes enlarged.

"I'm joking, Bayzog. A jest. You did nothing wrong with that." She hugged the robed sleeve of his arm. "You had a greater duty."

"Greater than family?"

"You know what you did was right," she said. "I know it, too. We all do. And we can't win this battle with you thinking like that."

Bayzog appreciated her words. They rang true in his heart, but it ached anyway. His boys were men now, and he hadn't been there to see it happen.

"We are ready to go where you go now, Father," Rerry said, laying a hand on his shoulder. "Even my overly knit brother can handle himself."

Bayzog glanced over his shoulder. Samaz sauntered behind them, dark hair covering all but the small elven tip of one ear. His sleepy eyes seemed to watch both everything at once and nothing at all. The Samaz he saw now was a far cry from the one in the cave, ranting about Gorn Grattack, sweating and chest heaving. Now, Samaz moved with perfect peace.

"Son," Bayzog said, releasing Sasha's hand and drifting alongside Samaz, "what are you feeling?"

"Nothing at the moment," he said, "but there was a tremor earlier. Gave me the bumps."

"I'll give you a bump," Rerry injected.

Bayzog's violet eyes narrowed on his younger son.

"Sorry," Rerry said.

"Anything else?" Bayzog said to Samaz.

"No, I just hope I feel something before it's too late."

A brisk gust of wind slammed into them, howling.

Whistledown, north of Quintuklen, rested on the plains inside of leagues of canyons. They walked toward a mostly dry riverbed where much water had flowed not so long ago. Now there was but a tiny stream.

"How can an entire river be gone?" Samaz said. "I remember coming here as a boy."

"The giants and dragons drank it up," Rerry said. He picked up a smooth river stone and chucked it to the other side. "Or monstrous beavers made a dam. So, now that we're here, what do we do, Father, start a new village?"

"We wait," Bayzog said, looking toward the darkening skies. "Now, let's make some shelter."

"Let me see that," Brenwar said, holding out his hand.

"A moment, if you please," Pilpin replied. He held up to his eye a spyglass cast in iron. He peered into the valley below the canyon's rim. "My eyes are better than yours anyway."

"They certainly are not."

"They certainly are too," the feisty little dwarf replied.

Brenwar snatched it away.

"No need to be so rude," Pilpin said.

"I gave you an order. You ignored it." With a grunt, Brenwar surveyed the demolished town of Whistledown, and his heart sagged. It had been one of the nicest places in Nalzambor, even though it wasn't dwarven. The people were warm and so was their food. They made fine ale too, for common folk. Now, it was a heap with little sign of life. "Truce, my behind."

"What's that?" Pilpin said.

"Seems you don't hear so well, Pilpin."

"You grumble so."

Brenwar slapped the spyglass so that it collapsed, and then he spit through his beard, saying, "Grumbling is what dwarves do."

"But you do it worse than most."

He shook his head. Pilpin was a good companion, but his chronic comments became cumbersome.

"Why don't you go check on the horses or something?" Brenwar said.

"They are fine."

"Then go crack rocks on your head."

"*Well* then!" Pilpin sauntered off.

Brenwar could still envision Whistledown with its cheery voices and smiling faces. Fishermen came from all over to wade in the wide but shallow river. Nath loved to go fishing there when he was younger. They'd walked the sandy riverbanks for weeks at a time on occasion. Now those days were gone. The knuckles on Brenwar's fist turned white. It had all happened so fast.

Backing away from the canyon's rim, he took a seat on a pile of rocks and unwrapped the blood-soaked bandage on his leg. He and Pilpin had fought their way through every forest, hillside, and meadow between here and Morgdon. The hidden landscape crawled with evil. He scooped up some dirt and rubbed it in the wound.

"Ah … that'll do."

He took the bandage, found a clean spot, and polished his breastplate. The leather bindings creaked, and he could feel a loose spot where one of the buckles was busted. A dragon's claw had ripped through it, but Brenwar's war hammer had dotted it in the head. He'd never seen so many dragons before, not even in Dragon Home. It left him uncomfortable. Closing his eyes, he leaned back against the rocky ledge. The canyon winds stirred his beard. Combing his fingers through it, he fell asleep.

"Ugh!" Brenwar jerked up. It was pitch black, and rainfall was soaking him. Harshly, he whispered, "Pilpin!"

No reply.

He scanned the darkness and cocked an ear.

Where is that little bearded monster?

Wiping the rain from his eyes, he had rolled up onto his knees when his instincts fired. He clutched for War Hammer—and found nothing.

"Woe is me."

Two shadows closed in on either side of him, hemming him in. Spears pointed at his neck.

Brenwar tried to grab one of the spears by the shaft, but the steel head eased away, and the other cracked against the back of his skull.

"Fast for a dwarf," a hollow voice said, "but slow for anything else."

"I'll show you slow," Brenwar said. His knees bent, and he readied to spring.

"Even naps don't do you well." The cloaked figure tossed something at his feet. *Thunk.* "Here's a pillow."

War Hammer lay at his feet. Brenwar snatched it up, saying, "You're a piece of work, pot belly." He huffed. "I thought I was rid of you."

Shum pulled his hood back and offered a stony smile.

"And I you, but it seems a season passed."

Hoven, the other ranger, offered Brenwar a hand.

He took it. It was good to see them, so long as they didn't know it was.

"Where's that bearded runt?" Brenwar said.

"He sleeps."

Brenwar stretched out his thick arms and yawned.

"What is *with* this place?"

"How long had it been since you last slept?"

Brenwar shrugged and nodded.

"So, have you gathered anything on the others?"

It had been a year. The time to meet had come. It was good to know the rangers were fine, but he wondered about Bayzog and Ben. And Nath…

"We caught wind of your horses," Shum said, resting his hands on his stomach, "as we traveled in."

"You walked?"

"We lost our steeds to a black-winged dragon some time ago," Shum said.

Brenwar's heart fell. Losing a mount, especially a Roamer steed, was contemptible. And he knew the steeds were more than the best. They were friends that would die for you.

"Sorry for the loss," he said. "Now let me go dig Pilpin out of whatever hole he burrowed himself into."

"And we head down then," Shum said.

"Aye," said Brenwar. "Aye."

The dwarves claimed that the rain had washed out any signs of passersby, but the Wilder Elves' keen eyes still picked up a trail worn in the dirt back and forth to the river. In the dark, he could feel it through his soft leather boots. Someone still prowled the area. A man, or men.

"Care to wait?" he said back to Brenwar.

"Suit yerself," the dwarf said with his arms folded over War Hammer on his chest. "But don't stir a fight without me, elf."

Through the rain, Shum and Hoven slid through the dark down the path. There were plenty of dangerous creatures that lurked in the ruins these days, waiting for food to spring upon. He and his brother had the wounds to show for it.

Almost a hundred yards from the river, he came to stop. A pair of cellar doors were closed over the ground behind a ramshackle house. Shum's nose twitched, and in the darkness he could see the warmth within. He nodded to Hoven.

His brother slid over to the doors and grabbed one of the handles.

The doors burst upward, knocking Hoven backward. Three shrouded figures emerged.

Shum's hands felt for his hilts, but it was too late. A sword shimmered beneath his chin.

The second figure stood within the cellar and had an arrow nocked and pointed at Hoven's chest. "Don't budge."

"Well done," Hoven said.

The figure stretched the bowstring back farther and leaned closer.

"What did I say?"

"Ben," Shum said, "you're among friends." He turned his eyes down on the figure with the sword on his neck. "You're quick. I'm impressed. I don't believe we are acquainted."

The young part-elf's violet eyes didn't blink.

"It's alright, Rerry," Ben said. He eased the string and quivered his arrow. *Clatch. Snap. Clatch.* "It's the Roamers we told you about."

All parties were in the cellar now, out of the rain: the two dwarves, the three part-elves, the two Roamers, Ben, and Sasha.

Bayzog was more than pleased to see his old friends.

"It's been months we've waited," he said. He told them the entire story about what happened when he returned. How Sasha and his sons were kidnapped. How the dragonettes and the jaxite stones aided in their rescue, and about the conflict in the garden with the mysterious female Cleric of Barnabus.

"I like that last part," Brenwar said. "'Tis good to know I've rubbed off on you some, heh, heh."

Bayzog wasn't the only one with adventures to tell.

"The woodlands are thick with enemies, and the armies of Barnabus are choking the life out of all the outer cities," Brenwar told everyone.

"And Gorn Grattack roams," Shum added, relaying his quest that the winged-ape Sansla Libor had given them, to find their greatest enemy. "And I believe my brother and I have caught wind of him."

"You have?" Bayzog said. The fine hairs on his arms stood up. "And?"

"He's near," Shum continued. "We've felt the chill of him. Seen the unnatural devastation." The Roamer elf went on in detail, telling how branches curled and grasses blackened. Forest varmints dropped dead in scores. Streams ran mixed with dark water. "East of Quintuklen, burrowed in the thickness of the forest."

There was talk that had been spreading of black dragons seen in the sky, too. It sent chills through Bayzog.

"Yet," he said, "Balzurth's dragons are on the move. His word is good."

"Aye," Brenwar said, "dragons fight and skirmish, but this war must be fought by all the races, not just them. The elves wait too long. The dwarves burrow. Men bicker among themselves. The other brood races gather and strengthen. Lay siege on the outlying lands. The dragons' coming should have been a grand enough sign that the war is upon us, but they've all dug their heels in on this false truce."

"They must know cities still burn," Ben said.

"They ignore it and blame it on the dragons," Shum said.

Sasha stepped in and said, "We will have to convince them."

"No," Shum said, "that is not for us to do. Others already try. We need to strike at the heart of the evil and expose it." The torches flickered in the oversized cellar, and all went quiet. "We need to assault Gorn Grattack."

Brenwar huffed. "Madness." He thumbed the edge of War Hammer. "But I like it."

CHAPTER
22

BACK IN NARNUM AFTER TWO months' absence, Selene sat on her throne, clutching her head. The incompetence of her guards was like a nasty spike into her skull.

The changeling, Gorlee, was gone, slipped right through her grasp. Worse yet, he'd managed to break into The Deep and not only regain his memories but wreak havoc while she and Nath were gone.

She reeled from the effects of it. Her control over things was slipping.

"You!" she said to one of the two guards who flanked her great doors, decorated in fine armor and carrying halberds. "Come! Stand before the dais."

The lump in the man's neck rolled. With a glance at the other guard, he marched over and kneeled at the dais.

She locked her fingers together and rested her chin on them.

"Show me how you use that weapon."

Water beaded on his brow as he nodded. A moment later, the grand weapon jabbed and cut and flashed all over. He bowed again in less than a minute, lathered in sweat.

"Excellent," she said. Then she pointed to the other guard. "Now go and kill him."

"High Priestess?" he remarked.

Her eyes blazed, and flames erupted from her mouth, incinerating the man. The dragon fire left only the metal from his armor and weapons. Glaring at the other guard, who trembled at the door, she said, "Looks like you win. Now leave me!"

The guard vanished, and the doors locked in place behind him.

Selene walked down the steps, swatting her tail through the ashes and warped metal. She still seethed.

Gorlee had made a mess of things. Disguised as her, he'd had her top priests, acolytes, commanders, and aides taken to The Deep with orders to be fed to Bletver.

Faced with the task of explaining all this to Nath Dragon, she'd drugged him. A sleep potion, powerful as could be made, filled his belly. He would not wake up until she countered the spell. At least she hoped. All dragons had some resistance to magic, but she had been very careful. So in his room he slept, while she got Narnum back under control.

She called for her drulture. In moments, it swooped over the balcony and landed on her shoulder. She petted its head.

"Good dragon. Good dragon."

The rebels in the streets were being found and cleared. The graffiti of Balzurth—two slashes and a circle—was all gone. The feline fury she had sent again to find Gorlee, but the changeling had vanished. It worried her. What if the fury could no longer sniff the changeling out? It could be anyone and anywhere.

Worst of all, Gorlee could warn Nath Dragon.

She needed to keep Nath close and make sure Nath wouldn't believe what anyone else told him. That might not be so difficult. Lucky for her, he was busy brooding over the war among the dragons and doubting his father. Her seed had taken root. She'd created enough doubt to gain more of his trust. Nath was primed to make a bold move. She just had to be careful how she led him. His bold move needed to be in her favor.

She went out onto the terrace. It was a cool night, heavy in dark cloud cover. Below, the streets were empty of the citizens, now that a strict curfew was enforced at nightfall. The absence of the carousing sounds of citizens that time of night was strange, leaving her alone with the gentle howls of the wind that whipped through the towers.

"*Selene ...* "

Her head snapped around, followed by a chill that raced down her spine.

An apparition emerged from the shadows. It had long wispy white hair, horns in its skull, and a green hue around its body. A dragon wraith, somewhat like a man, a lich, torn between the living and dead worlds. Its features were gaunt, and its scales stretched in the semblance of wrinkled leather. It stood as a man, wore robes, and had eyes that flickered with power. It pointed a crooked clawed finger at her. Its voice was a ghostly hiss.

"*Gorn Grattack summons you...*"

Lifting her chin, she said, "I cannot leave at this moment."

"*Now,*" the ghostly lips hissed. It pulled a sword from the belt strapped around its tattered robes. Its blade was pitch black. "*Now, or death.*"

Selene's lips curled back.

"Don't threaten me, you little wraith." She summoned her power. A ball of flame formed in her hand. "I'll banish you with a thought, you undead courier."

"*Now,*" it warned, drifting closer. The sword winked lightning. "*Now, or all will be lost.*"

Resisting Gorn Grattack's wishes was a fatal thing to do, but she didn't like how she received the invitation.

"Lead," she said, crushing out her ball of flame.

The wraith lifted from the terrace and glided quickly up into the night sky.

Selene summoned the dragon within. Great wings sprouted from her back. She was in one of many dragon forms she could assume, a secret she held from Nath. She leapt into the air, wings flapping, catching up to the wraith in an instant.

While the pair flew hour after hour, all she could think about was what Gorn Grattack wanted with her now, in person. There were dozens of other ways they could communicate that weren't in person.

He always wants something different than what I think he wants. Be strong, Selene. Be strong.

The wraith dropped out of the sky and spiraled toward the ground somewhere east of Quinktuklen in the mountain ranges. Scores of dragons of all sorts were scattered along the peaks. It petrified the blood in her veins. Gorn Grattack had his forces rallied. She had none of hers.

As soon as they landed, she had to change back into human form so that the wraith could lead her into a temple entrance she'd never seen before. It was grand but had fallen into ruin, and it led deep into the mountain. The darkness chilled her robed shoulders.

Her fingertips tingled more than the last time she'd encountered Gorn Grattack. He had still been in spirit form that last time, and she wondered what form he'd taken now. Ahead, a giant-sized throne sat empty between two massive urns that sprouted blue flame.

The wraith turned to her and said, "Wait." Then it promptly left.

It seemed she waited an eternity, but it was probably a few minutes.

"How are you, Selene?"

She twisted around.

A striking man stood before her, dark haired and dark featured, with a serpentine look about him. He stood much taller than she did, broad and lean, wearing the attire of a commoner, but a fanciful sort. His eyes had a radiant glow.

All of her blood rushed through her. She dropped to one knee.

"My Lord," she said, bowing.

"Rise and embrace me, Daughter," he said. His voice was as strong and steady as the rivers. "I've missed you."

She did. His arms locked around her waist and held her tight. His natural strength was crushing. He let her go and brushed her cheek.

"You look marvelous, as always," he said, "and those wings are a nice touch." He waved his hand, and dozens of torches came to life. He led her to a table cut from purple marble and sat down in one of the chairs. "Sit. Eat if you like." There were many tureens of different stews, and carafes of various wines. He dropped some grapes in his mouth. "I've been wandering among the races of late, trying to get a better feel for things. I can't fail this time, as I did the last time."

"And why did you fail the last time?" she said, avoiding the food.

"I didn't have strong enough adversaries, but this time, well, this time things are better planned." He crushed a grape between his fingers. "And we'll be more deliberate about things." He locked his fingers on the table and leaned in her direction. "So, tell me, how are things going with Nath Dragon?"

His piercing eyes bore into her. Seeing him in monstrous dragon form was one thing, but his current form seemed more dangerous somehow. Crafty. Insidious. Omnipotent. She had no idea what to expect.

She pulled her shoulders back and said, "I'm gaining his trust."

"And what will you do once you have it?" Gorn asked. "Join forces with him and turn against me?"

He can't know that!

"Certainly not, my Lord," she said. Her heart was jumping. *Think. Think. Think.* "But the thought has occurred to me."

Gorn didn't speak. Instead, he just tilted his head. After a long moment, he said, "I've raised you well, Selene. Ambition. That's the key to conquest. I would be sorely disappointed had you answered differently."

"As well you should be."

Gorn slammed his fist on the table, creating a crack through it.

"Don't tell me how I should be!" he said firmly. "Ever." He stared her down.

Selene gulped, but she did not avert her eyes, staring right back at him.

After a pause that would have been awkwardly long to anyone but a dragon, Selene gave her father the briefest of nods, and Gorn Grattack went on.

"As for Nath Dragon, the uppity son of Balzurth, how do you think we should handle him, hmm?"

"The Truce keeps him at bay," she said. "I have his dragon powers harnessed, but he is getting stronger and learning to understand his powers. In but a little more time, he will cross over."

"So certain, are you?" Gorn said.

"Indeed. He cannot stomach dragons warring among ourselves. He'll fight to prevent it." She shrugged. "He's too naïve to understand."

"And how long is this truce to hold him?"

"Four more years, but my work will be done long before then."

"Oh," Gorn said, "your work will be done much sooner than that, Daughter. Balzurth's servants move on us now, and I like how you are using that against him. Turning his son's feelings inside out. You are wise, Selene." He smiled. "But, we can't hold back while Balzurth picks us apart one unit at a time. He attacks where our forces are weak, from the inside out. We need to step up our timetable."

"Whatever you wish, my Lord."

"I'm sure you've grown fond of Balzurth's son, but he's only of use to us if he's fighting on our side. You must assure that, or kill him."

The words were an invisible blow across her cheek.

"I'll have him serving faithfully in no time."

"There is only one way to make that happen, Selene. Nath Dragon needs dragon blood on his hands. Virtuous dragon blood. He must kill one of his father's own faithful followers. Only then will he cross over to the victorious path which is ours."

"It will be done," she said.

"Easier said than done, but I have faith in you, Daughter."

He rose from his chair calmly enough, but then he grew to another size, towering over her. Scales rose on his arms, horns sprouted from his head, and claws popped from his fingers. Towering over her, he spoke in a voice of thunder.

"EXECUTE THIS IMMEDIATELY. IF THIS PLAN FAILS, THEN BRING NATH DRAGON TO ME PERSONALLY—FOR HIS DESTRUCTION. GO NOW." He pointed outside the mouth of the temple. "YOU HAVE NO TIME TO WASTE."

CHAPTER
23

INSIDE A NARNUM TAVERN, GORLEE lay low. Hunkered down over a table illuminated by a lone candle, he'd taken the form of a half-orcen man and could even see one of the warts on his own nose. Ruddy-skinned and hairy, he finished off his tankard of spiked sap and drew his sleeve across his chin. He banged his mug on the table.

"Waitress!"

The tavern was crowded. Sweat-soaked bodies milled back and forth late in the day, cursing the curfew that High Priestess Selene had set in place.

He chuckled to himself. He'd fouled her plans up something awful!

A waitress, ragged in appearance with a mop of long blond hair, dropped another tankard on the table. He offered her a smile filled with rotten teeth.

"How are you this day, pretty woman?"

A ghastly look filled her face. She did a double take and scurried off to murmur to the bartender.

Gorlee huffed and leaned back in his groaning chair. He'd made himself the least appealing person in a room where most of the races were represented, the more notorious ones being gnolls, goblins, orcs, and such. There were men, too, and just as many, all swarthy and misaligned. None of them wanted anything to do with him, and that was just what he wanted.

People are so ... fascinating!

He took a drink and made a bitter face. The spiked sap was strong. It didn't have any effect on him, but even though he was a changeling and capable of many amazing things, he realized he had to get the details right. The manners. The smells. Selene had taught him that, and it had helped. Especially when he was certain the feline fury was prowling the city for him. He had avoided the dragon-cat for weeks.

He peered through the window where he sat. He could see up the street all the way to the Great Tower. It was tall, broad, and magnificent. He was certain Nath was back in there, so he needed to stay close. Soon enough he'd catch him and warn him.

Not easy, even for someone such as me.

He wished he could take the form of a draykis with wings and just fly up to Nath's room. It didn't work that way, though. He could duplicate forms but not abilities. He recalled Nath almost sniffing him out when he asked Gorlee to display the sorceress powers of Sasha. All of that left a guilty pit in him, and he was determined to make it right.

He took another sip, gazing at the tower and the rooftops along the street. Dragons had returned. Great lizards with black wings and tails watched the street like hawks. It was clear to him: Selene wanted him back. Soldiers scoured the streets for him—and for any citizens who made the mark of Balzurth. Selene had it under control now, which worried him because there was no sign of Nath Dragon.

I need to go in. I can't wait much longer.

The rebellion Selene had quashed was little more than a handful of men and women leaving the two slashes through a circle mark. It had stirred quite the reaction from Selene's Great Tower. Punishment had been swift and deadly. Several people still hung from the neck in grisly town square scenes. As quick as the rebellion began, it ended.

Yet, Gorlee saw things that others did not. Rebels yet roamed the streets of Narnum, and he was trying to decide who he could trust, if any, among them.

A small group of men and women huddled at a table adjacent to his. He'd been keeping tabs on them for days. They were a rugged bunch, judging by their garb, but their voices were as polished as river stones. His ears were tickled by bits and pieces of their conversations. Balzurth was spoken of more than one time, and Gorlee had noticed something else that was odd. Another man came and quickly displayed an 'O' with his right hand and two fingers up with his left before he sat down.

Clever.

Over coarse voices in many languages, he siphoned out their conversation. It was another skill he'd been working on for years.

"We are found out," a woman said, "and the time to leave is now. Our brethren hang, and we will soon be next."

"Aye," a man said, stroking his grizzly beard. "Only a matter of time until these dragons sniff us out, and we've had enough close calls already."

"We hold until the last," a third man said. He was taller than the rest. A hood covered his head, and he sat with his back to the wall. A sword, long and heavy, was strapped to his waist. He had a soldier's look about him. "We have our orders, and we'll die for the cause. For Balzurth."

Gorlee's heart skipped a beat. Something special moved behind the scenes. Men were working with dragons. It was fascinating. He shouldn't be shocked. After all, the evil dragons were working with Barnabus. Still, it seemed odd. He shifted in his chair, moving his back and ear toward them.

"Balzurth will deliver. All will hold true," another woman said. A hood was draped over her head as well. Her garb was faded and dirty, but she hand beautifully manicured hands, with indentations where she usually wore jeweled rings. "We must await new orders."

"I hope we aren't just going to leave more marks," the bearded one said. "We need greater action. I want to do something bold."

"Not while the Truce holds," the tall man said. "It aids our cause."

"Pah," said the bearded one. "I say we take Nath Dragon and run him home."

"He's a thousand feet up in the tower," the first woman said. "It's not possible. Selene won't let him out."

"We'll push him out. Hah!" said the bearded one. "He survived that fall. He'll survive again, and we'll scurry him away."

"Not with a dozen dragons watching him." The leader sighed. "He must take care of himself. We take care of ourselves."

The group became quiet, and the air seemed to thicken. Gorlee scooted his chair back toward the corner and rested his hairy forearms on the table. Feeling eyes on his ugly half-orc form, he glanced up and found the hooded woman's gaze locked on his. Her features were striking. She whispered to the taller man at her side. He glanced Gorlee's way with hard brown eyes, nodded to the bearded one, and dropped some coins on the table. The group headed for the door.

Go in peace, Gorlee thought, avoiding their eyes.

As the group closed in toward the door, another figure stepped through the entrance: the brawny form of a winged draykis, with two more on his flanks. The small party froze. The rest of the patrons gasped. Chairs scraped the floor.

The winged draykis, decorated in plate-mail armor with the insignia of Barnabus, blocked the exit while the other pair drifted through the room, bumping bodies and tables.

Gorlee's breath became heavy. The draykis were outstanding hunters. Bounty hunters, in this case. They'd strung up more than a score of rebels in the past few weeks. Clearly, they weren't finished.

"Any traitors here?" the draykis commander said in a deep, garbled voice. "A sack of coin for reward." The dragon-faced man scoured the crowd. His fanged face was lean and terrifying. His eyes bright coals. "The High Priestess is known for her generosity."

Everyone averted their eyes. The citizens were certain that many who had already been hung were innocent of the crime, but the soldiers of Barnabus didn't care. The slightest doubt about your allegiance, and they'd drag you out for hanging.

A draykis stopped at Gorlee's table and stared down at him. Its tongue flickered from its mouth, and it said, "You're even uglier than me. I think a noose is best suited for your neck."

Gorlee drew his arms back, tucked his chin in his chest, and turned his head away.

Keep silent. Keep that sharp tongue silent.

Well, you are *part orc.*

"Hanging doesn't scare me. I'd rather be devoured by a dragon, given the choice."

The draykis leaned down in his face and said, "That can be arranged, foul one." He shoved Gorlee in the shoulder and moved on.

Sad, I'm getting the hang of this orc thing.

Several onlookers in the crowd stood tall and guiltless. Others cringed. The draykis rough-handed them all. Checked markings on their arms and faces. Stood them up and shoved them back down again. The tension intensified with each passing moment. The air became rank with fear and dripping sweat.

The draykis commander spoke up again.

"I've a quota to make before the curfew, or the High Priestess will have my head." He stepped close to the small group that Gorlee had listened in on, who were trying to leave. "Take those hoods down."

The first man and woman dropped the heavy cloth back off their heads. The pair's chestnut hair fell on their shoulders. Their features were sharp and inquisitive, but scuffed with dirt and soot.

Towering over the man, the draykis commander shoved his chest.

"I don't like the smell of you, or this woman either." It eyed all of them. "Not a one of you. You remind me of those others we hung."

"We're lifelong citizens," the man said.

The draykis lashed out.

Whap!

The man spun and collapsed on the ground. It was an awesome display of the draykis's supernatural power.

The party of humans helped the man to his feet. His mouth was bleeding. His hand fell to his sword.

The draykis folded his arms across his chest and said, "By all means, unsheathe that blade of yours, human." It eyed its scaly arms. "Many have tried, but no steel can cut my skin." It grunted an unnatural laugh. "Shackle them and take them to the gallows. Send word there will be hangings after first light."

The other two draykis approached. One went outside, and the other stayed in. A moment later, the other draykis entered with shackles and chains.

"If you must have blood, arrest me then," the man said, holding out his wrists. "My family doesn't deserve this, but I'll give my life for theirs."

"Bravery, humph," the draykis commander said, spitting on the floor. "I think I'll let you watch as I hang them first."

Gorlee's fists turned to stone. *Evil bloodthirsty monster!*

"Now," the commander continued, holding out his clawed hand, "hand over your sword."

The man's shoulders slumped. His head dipped when he said, "As you command…" A blade of bright light whisked from his sheath and lanced into the chest of the nearest draykis. "Abominations!"

CHAPTER
24

SELENE TRACED THE LINES OF the white scales on Nath's arm. They were smooth to the touch yet tougher than iron. It was a fascinating feature of dragons. He stirred the slightest, and it gave her a shiver. He'd awaken soon. She had discontinued the sleep charm she'd put on him.

And the lies will resume once more. Her cherry lips formed the slightest smile. *I like lying. And this one hates it. Why is that?* She brushed his red hair away from his face and admired his strong handsome features. She rested her other hand on the gentle rise and fall of his deep chest.

So much power and such little understanding.

A gust of wind blasted into Nath's bedroom, extinguishing one of the torches. She made her way to the balcony and secured the door. Outside on his terrace, the feline fury's paws were propped up on the balcony and its head was cast downward. Her face drew tight. *Gorlee.* Once the war was won, she'd see to it every changeling died. They were too dangerous. Too much of a threat, alive.

She relit the extinguished torch with her fingertip, resumed her place by Nath's side, and lay down on his chest. His heartbeat galloped.

"Oh, Nath." She sighed. "I really hate doing this to you." She rose and began tracing the white lines on his scales again. "I'm going to have to make up an explanation for this. A really good one, as I promised."

She clasped her fingers with his. Her scales were coal black with not a single trace of white. Why was he different? Was it the good in him? Or something else? Gorn Grattack had never explained. The thought of her dark father gave her a shiver. He'd brought her up, but she knew little about herself. She was a dragon, born a girl human. How, she did not know. From her earliest memories, Gorn had been the one to show her everything. How to hunt. To fly. To kill. He told her she was filled with wondrous powers and that with her by his side, he'd take over the world.

Nath moaned, and her body became rigid.

She'd have to lead him into darkness. Convince him to kill a good dragon. Maybe she could make Nath think it was an accident. That might get the job done. Surely he would defend himself. She had no choice. If Nath didn't fall in step with her, Gorn Grattack would kill him. Nath could not survive Gorn and all his forces.

Nath's fingers tightened around hers.

"Ah," she said, freeing her hand. She gave him a kiss on the cheek. "See you soon." Then she departed from his room.

Nath woke with a funny taste in his mouth. Next, his sight was fuzzy. Holding his head, he grunted and slung the sheets from the bed. His first step wobbled. With the second one, he found his strength, headed for the balcony, and slung the door open. The piercing eyes of the fury greeted him.

"Great Guzan! Are you going to just gawk, or finally eat me?"

When the beast did nothing, he pushed past it and glanced down into the streets. It was quiet. No one was moving. Dragons perched like gargoyles on the rooftops. The guards barely even shifted at their posts.

"How long?" he said. "How long this time?" He leaned against the balcony and rubbed his eyes, trying to figure out the last thing he had done. He had been in Selene's throne room, talking and ... His stomach rumbled. And *eating!* They had been discussing the war among the dragons and how he could put an end to it once and for all. Nath's blood turned fire red. He balled up his fists and snarled so loudly the whole town heard him.

"SELENE!"

He charged off the balcony, through his chamber, into the corridor, and up the stairs to the doors of her throne room. A pair of draykis barred his path. One started to speak.

"The High Priestess—"

Nath slung one draykis right into the other and flung the doors wide open.

Inside, Selene sat on her throne. Her face lit up with surprise.

"Nath!" she exclaimed. "You have awakened! Thank the dragons!" She rushed down the dais and right up to him. "I feel ... joy, I think." She embraced him.

Her embrace felt ... too good. Fighting to keep his wits about him, he grabbed her shoulders and pushed her backward, asking, "What's happened? How long was I out, Selene?"

"Nath," she said, taking his arm. "Come and sit. It hasn't been so long. Just a few months."

Relieved that the Truce hadn't passed by while he slept, and stirred anew by the feel of her hand on his arm, Nath fought to stay alert, to remember why he was angry.

He pulled his arm from her hand and said, "Are you certain?"

"As certain as the scales on my tail," she said, swiping it along his side, "and I am relieved. I feared you'd sleep through the Truce." She pulled a chair out for him. "And that would have been a disaster, after all the work you've done."

With a furrowed brow, Nath took a seat. Waking from this sleep didn't feel the same as waking from the other long ones. He felt groggy, not bright-eyed and energetic as before. He held back a yawn.

"It's alright, Nath," she said. "You've been through much. Even dragons get tired. I know I am."

"You never seem tired to me," he said.

"I'm a woman, so to speak. We hide it well. Now eat."

He grabbed some cherries in his clawed fingers and ate them one by one. He noticed Selene eyeing his scales.

"What is it?"

"You have even more white scales now," she said. "I envy them."

He glanced at his hands and said, "I don't notice any difference."

"I do, and I think it's a good thing."

"Why is that?"

"I think it's the Truce you have sworn, Nath. It's making an impact. Not just on you, but on all the people. You are growing."

"I don't see how sleeping is doing a good thing."

"Sometimes, the best action is no action. Sometimes, the best words are none at all. Silence is often an excellent answer." She poured him a glass of wine. "Enjoy the peace we live in, Nath. Your patience is changing you. Your wisdom makes you stronger."

"And that's why I have white scales?"

"Nath, many dragons have scales of different colors. You see how they change as they grow. You are growing, and with growing comes change. That's all."

"You're growing," he said. "How come all your scales are black?"

"I like black. It suits me. Besides, there is no change in me. I am what I am."

"You are what you *want* to be, Selene. Anyone can change, even a dragon." He took a sip of wine. "You just have to want it."

Selene's eyes became distant, and she turned her gaze away. He'd never seen that look before. She was strong. Confident. Striking. But not at this moment. He eyed his scaled arms and fingers. "Huh?"

"What?" she asked, turning back toward him.

"Maybe that's what's happening to me. I'm finally learning."

"You're young, but you're not a fool."

He dug into his food. Maybe he had been too hard on himself. That was his problem. He needed to trust his instincts and be patient.

I need to end this war among the dragons. If I can change, they all can change. They just need a good leader.

"So, what has happened while I've been out?" he said.

"Well," Selene said, resting her hand on his arm, "the citizens miss seeing their champion, and they've been restless. You have such an effect on them."

"I'm not worried about them, so much. I'm worried about the warring dragons. What has happened with them?"

"Nath, you need to not worry about so much. You just woke up. Ease your way into things."

"I'm not going to sit here and do nothing, Selene."

"We can do some things. Perhaps a walk through the city—"

He rapped his fist on the table.

Bam!

"Don't be childish!"

Nath got up from the table and said, "Then don't play games!" He made a bead for the door.

"Alright, Nath," she said. "Alright!"

He stopped but didn't turn.

"The skirmishes are becoming more frequent, more large-scale in some places." She sighed a long breath. "But you can't go chasing the winds. You aren't ready yet."

He turned and said, "I want you to take me to the nearest battlefield. Will you do it?"

"I'm not going to resist you, Nath. I've held you back enough already, and I support your cause. Our cause. I'll gather a legion, and we'll leave at first light."

"Good," he said, turning and walking back through the doors.

Selene smiled as he walked out.

Perfect.

CHAPTER

25

THE ENTIRE TAVERN ERUPTED IN brilliant flashes of light that sent the draykis commander careening into the door frame.

Great Guzan!

Gorlee gravitated toward the fireplace at the back of the room and wrapped his hands around an iron fire poker.

The small party of humans, heroes by his reckoning, had exploded into action. One draykis stood in astonishment with the leader's sword in his chest. The bearded man, hard-faced and well-built, swung a flanged mace into the other draykis's face. The tall and lovely woman's slender arms were entwined in snakes of mystic power, while the last woman, smaller in stature, held arcane symbols over her head and shouted words of power. Everyone else in the room scrambled. They crashed through doors and windows and scurried through the streets.

The draykis struck back. The commander ripped a sword from his side and charged.

"You won't hang! You'll die here and now."

"Try it!" the lead human said.

The draykis's steel clashed into the man's magic weapon, and bright sparks flew. The two swung and parried back and forth, rambling through tables and knocking over chairs.

The bearded man pressed his swift attack. He bashed the draykis over its hard skull—once, twice, three times—knocking it to its knees. The taller woman blasted brilliant yellow fire into its chest. The draykis squealed as its scales erupted into smoke and ash.

Two draykis were down, and their commander battled for its undead life.

Who are *these people?*

The group converged on the lone draykis commander, hemming it in.

"Your life comes to an end, abomination!" the leading man said. "Balzurth's forces are at hand." He lunged.

The draykis, quicker than a snake, side stepped and cut the warrior in the chest. His heavy fist rocked the man in the jaw, dropping him to his knees. His glinting sword clattered off the planks, and its brilliant light went out. In a flash, the draykis slid behind the man and pressed a dagger to his throat.

"Overconfident fools," it said. "Step back."

The small party eyed one another and backed off.

The draykis let out a high-pitched whistle. Barnabus soldiers flooded into the room, carrying heavy swords and wearing heavy armor. With them, a wingless dragon scaled in deep purple prowled in. Its back was waist-high with tall, scaly ridges. Horns swooped back along its neck, and a pair of tongues flickered from its razor-sharp mouth.

Guzan!

Gorlee channeled his power. His skin turned as hard as the iron poker he held.

The leader jammed his elbow into the draykis's belly and yelled, "Get out of here, everyone! Escape!" He went for his sword, but the bigger, quicker draykis jumped on his back, pinning the man to the ground. His fingers stretched for the hilt of his sword, juttered, and went still.

One woman gasped, while the taller woman blasted a swarm of golden hornets into the fray. The soldiers of Barnabus swatted and clutched at their arms and faces.

The bearded warrior hammered into them with his mace. He dropped three frantic soldiers to their knees and turned just in time to face the deep maw of the purple dragon.

Chomp!

Its jaws clamped on his legs, and the bearded warrior yelled and struck out his mace with ferocity.

"If I'm going down, you're going down with me, you wicked scaled beast!"

Two handed, he wailed on the dragon's head, one heavy blow after another. The dragon held him fast while two soldiers slipped behind the man and drove swords into his back.

"Urk!"

His mace fell from his fingers. The smaller woman let out an ear-splitting scream. Windows and glassware shattered. Gorlee's knees buckled. Soldiers fell to their knees. The draykis headed right for her, unhindered.

Gorlee's mind reeled, and something within took over. He snatched up the fallen warrior's sword, and its blade became hot with fire. He charged the draykis, lunged, and chopped through its wings.

"Who dares?" the draykis said, whipping around, sword ready.

Gorlee, never a practiced swordsman, hacked at him.

The draykis, skilled as they come, parried and countered. A deadly arc of steel bit into Gorlee's shoulder and skipped off it.

"What manner of race are you?" the draykis said. "Your skin's thick as metal."

Gorlee swung again. Sword met sword.

Clang!

"You have to be tough when you're this ugly," he said. "You should know that by now!"

Clang! Clang! Clang!

Striking harder and faster, he banged the draykis's sword down.

The draykis twisted inside and jammed a dagger at his belly. It snapped off at the hilt.

"Impossible!"

Gorlee slid the shimmering sword through the draykis's ribs.

Its eyes popped open and simmered to dust inside its head. It collapsed to the floor, unmoving.

Guzan, what a sword! Maybe I should learn to use these things!

He turned and squared up on the dragon. The hulking beast stood on top of the smaller woman. Her body was broken. Its tail lashed out, striking the last woman. Her body crashed into the fireplace hearth.

"No!" Gorlee said. He raised the blade and charged.

The dragon lowered its horns and rushed straight for him.

Gorlee smote it with the blade. Unhindered, the dragon trampled over him, pinning him to the floor. Its hot breath snorted in his face, and its jaws clamped down on his shoulder. The pressure blinded him with pain, but his iron skin held.

"What's the matter, dragon, not chewy enough for you?"

The dragon released its bite and filled its lungs with air.

Sultans, what does this creature breathe?

Gorlee grabbed the creature by the neck and tried to push it away. Green fire erupted from its mouth in streams that dripped all over him.

"Ow!" Gorlee cried out. "That burns!"

Chairs and tables caught fire. The tavern filled with smoke.

Gorlee wriggled beneath the beast, but its paws kept him pinned down. Clothes and iron skin burning, Gorlee cried out, "Enough of this!"

Power inside him ignited, and his half-orcen body of iron expanded. In seconds, he towered the height of ten feet and locked his arms around the dragon's neck and squeezed.

"No more toying with you, lizard!"

The dragon thrashed and flailed. Its claws scraped at his chest, but Gorlee held the dragon fast. Its tail slithered around his neck and squeezed.

"No you don't!" Gorlee grunted. He cranked up the pressure.

Flames spread across the tavern. Soldiers scrambled for the doors, coughing.

The dragon's neck was filled with muscle harder than stone. Even with his great strength, Gorlee's efforts seemed futile. The beast was a knot of muscle. His giant fingers fumbled for the sword. Eyes bulging from his head, gasping for air, Gorlee clutched the hilt with his oversized fingers. He raised the blade and drove it through the dragon's back into its heart.

The knot of scales went slack.

"Whew!"

Coughing, he peered through the mess. He couldn't make out anyone through the smoke and the roar of the flames. Making his way toward the rear of the building, he stumbled over the man who had fallen to the draykis. He scooped him up and busted through the back wall that led into the alley. It was just him and a woman, the tall hooded one, coughing.

"Are you alright?" he said to her.

She leered at him. He changed his form, shrinking down into a human to look more pleasant, and set the dead man's body down.

"Sorry about your friend," he said. He lay the sword across the man's body. "I'd take him somewhere, if I had a place to go."

She limped over and knelt beside the fallen man's body.

"Thanks for the help," she said, "but we'll be alright. It's you who should go." She unhitched the man's sword belt, slid the blade into the scabbard, and offered it to Gorlee. "Take this."

"I don't have need of it," he said. "I'm not so good with them."

She shoved it in his chest and said, "Keep it safe then. I can't take it with me." She reached in a pouch, sprinkled dust over the man, and began chanting. She sprinkled dust on herself next.

"Again, thank you. May Balzurth be with you."

She and the man shimmered, faded to dust in the wind, and vanished.

How interesting. Seems I'm not alone in this fight after all.

Gorlee strapped on the sword belt and assumed the form of a battered Barnabus soldier moments before dozens swarmed into the alley.

"Did you see anything?" the commander said.

Gorlee coughed and pointed at the flaming hole in the wall and said, "Something ran over me and went that way. Big as a troll. *Cough-cough.* Fast, too." Scratching his head, he added, "No idea what it was, but it was ugly."

"Get yourself to the infirmary, eh..." The sergeant paused. "I don't know you. What's your name?"

"Jason."

"So be it. Now get those wounds looked at."

Gorlee trudged along the wall, averting his eyes from the soldiers. Sadness swelled in his gut. He'd watched good people die for a great cause and realized something.

I have to keep close to Nath Dragon more now than ever. As Bayzog says, without him, everything is lost.

CHAPTER

26

Nath, Selene, and a battalion of soldiers departed Narnum and headed south again. A parade of cheers followed them all the way out of the city. Nath said little that next couple of days. Selene remained silent as well. They'd spoken enough already. Talked about many things. The War. The Truce. His scales. He eyed his hands wrapped around the reins of his horse.

I'm doing good. I know I am.

Several times, Selene had traced the outline of his white scales. There was a flicker of jealousy behind her eyes when she commented on them. It made him wonder if her scales could turn white as well.

Maybe I can help her.

He snapped the reins and trotted toward the front of the army. The battalion consisted of nearly a thousand heavily armored soldiers with swords and shields, pole axes, bows, and spears. They marched in steady ranks whose armored footsteps had the rhythmic sound of a dangerous army. Others accompanied them, too—robed men and women in the dozens, all with tattooed foreheads. They chanted, murmured, and carried burning canisters of incense.

There had been a time when Nath's skin recoiled at the sight of them. Now, it didn't seem so bad. Wasn't peace what everyone wanted?

He glanced toward the sky. Dragons with dark wings and tails flew in tight formations. His fist tightened on the reins.

I should be up there.

He'd given up even trying to change into a dragon for now. Selene said it would just have to happen one day. More than likely when he least expected it.

The army remained on foot, with the commanders on horseback, cruising up and down the ranks and barking commands. They were a fit army, as fit as he'd ever seen. Banners and edged weapons gleamed in the sun's dim light. Selene said the sight of Nath with an army at his back would make quite an impression on the commoners. It would encourage them and raise their hopes. So far, his presence had been well received by those they passed as word of his great deeds spread, but there was also fear of the dragons that battled in the skies and tore into their flocks. It was happening more often all the time.

He rode alongside one of the commanders in the front of the ranks. The man was tall in the saddle and protected by full plate armor. His helmet was dark and menacing, and a well-crafted sword hung from his saddle. He was one of the biggest men Nath had ever seen.

"Have you seen Selene?" he asked.

"She rides with the scouts," the man said in a deep voice. "Departed at first light with them."

Nath stiffened. He'd figured Selene was giving him space. She said he needed it. But this didn't sit well with him. He'd been staying toward the front, figuring she remained in the rear with her acolytes and priests. But not seeing her after a half day had him circling the ranks, finding no sign of her.

"First light, you say?"

"Yes, Dragon Prince."

Nath glanced at the hard eyes inside the man's helmet.

"A simple yes or no will do," he said.

"Yes, Dragon Prince."

Nath spurred his mount ahead with a grunt. Selene had the entirety of her army calling him Dragon Prince, and it was beginning to have a nice ring to it. That and Peace Bringer, Truce Forger, and The

Champion. He grinned, thinking about that, and then squinted his eyes. The roughshod road ran for miles up and down rocky plains and tall grasses.

Why would she leave without me? He eyed the sky. *I bet she's flying.*

He stretched the distance between himself and the army. A squad of horsemen galloped after him, one being the commander, who pulled up short of him.

"What are you doing, Dragon Prince?"

"I should ask you the same."

"We are not to leave you from our sight," the commander said, shifting in his saddle. "It's the order of the High Priestess."

"Alright," Nath said. "Fine then. Just make sure you can keep up." He whipped the reins. "Ee-Yah!"

In seconds, the wind whistled through his ears and his hair billowed like a flag over his back in a streak of red.

It's not my army. It's Selene's. She can watch after it herself!

He continued at a full gallop until his keen eyes picked up deep impressions going off the road in the tall grasses. He slowed down. Not waiting for the soldiers to catch up, he trotted down the newly formed trail.

"Dragon Prince," the commander said. "We should not travel so far from the army."

"Then go back," Nath said.

The big commander let out a whistle, and several of the other men headed back toward the ranks. The commander kept pace behind Nath.

"The High Priestess won't approve of this," the commander said. "I advise you to return."

Nath slowed his mount and turned. He pointed toward the sky. Dragons circled in the air.

"Selene has much better eyes on me than you, Commander. Perhaps it is *you* who should return to the ranks. I'd hate to be the one who leaves her army exposed."

"Er ... well…"

"Of course, you're all being replaced by the draykis anyway. Just think, if you die in battle, that just might be your fate. A fate worse than death."

"Dragon Prince," the commander said, "I'm following orders. I mean no offense."

Nath turned his mount and headed down the trail. He didn't care what the commander thought, or Selene. He was tired of being babysat. It stirred him. Made him think of Brenwar.

I wonder how ol' Grizzly Beard is doing?

The trail led on another league and dipped down a hill into a narrow crevice. Mossy rock faces were steep on either side, and the trail was darkened by overhanging branches. The trail of the scouts and Selene's men faded.

"This is interesting," Nath said.

"What's that?" the commander said, leaning forward on his horse.

"If you took that ugly helmet off, you could see better."

The commander's head creaked as it twisted toward the sky.

"Are you afraid of dragon droppings?" Nath said.

"Er ... no, Dragon Prince. Just unneeded exposure."

Nath slid out of the saddle and led his horse by the reins. The commander did the same, hopping off and raising a clamor with his armor.

"Big and loud," Nath said, shaking his head. "Armor slows a skilled man down. It makes the instincts lazy."

"You have scales."

Nath's head turned halfway back, and he said, "And what of it?"

"That's armor."

"I sense something odd about you," Nath said, forging ahead. "I'm not sure I like it."

He cut through the pass with the commander's heavy armor licking at his ears. Brenwar's gear never made a sound. This man behind him sounded like an entire army. Even his breath made noise.

Big. Heavy. Slow. Maybe I'll throw him at something.

They had pushed through the crevice for another hour when Nath came to a stop, peering forward into a clearing. A rank smell drifted into his nose. The horses nickered. Something burned and reeked.

"What is it?" the commander said, trying to cover his nose with his mailed fist. "It's foul."

Nath pressed on, eyeing the rock walls that rose on either side. Anything could be hiding in the cliffs. The crevice opened up into a canyon. There was heavy brush and cave mouths everywhere. He happened upon the dead bodies of three soldiers. Scouts of Barnabus. Armor was torn. Bodies were broken. One was burned to cinders and still smoldered.

"Death is a rank smell," the commander said. "Those wounds. Looks as if dragons did this." He grabbed his sword belt and buckled it on. "We must find the High Priestess."

Nath placed his hand in the large impression of a dragon's paw. He could see signs of their passing everywhere.

Ambush! Another Ambush! There is no honor in that!

His nose twitched in the air, searching for the lingering scent of Selene.

Surely she can handle herself.

He traipsed through the canyon. Signs of battle were all over. Above, trees jutted toward the top of the canyon, but the skies were mostly hidden, and a strange yellow mist hung in the air, obscuring his vision. The scent of death lingered everywhere. He forged ahead, following a scuffled trail that smashed down the grasses.

"Where are you going?" the commander said.

"Stay with the horses," Nath replied.

"I'm coming with you."

"No, you won't be able to keep up." He turned and faced the commander. "I've a feeling Selene's in danger, so you can wait or you can go for help."

"I insist I go," the big man said, coming forward.

Nath shoved him backward, and the man toppled over.

"Stay put," Nath said, turning away. "If she's within these caves, I'll bring her back. If not, we'll resume the search elsewhere." He started off.

"Dragon Prince, please … "

Nath kept moving on until the voice and figure of the commander vanished into the strange fog.

CHAPTER
27

NATH FOLLOWED THE IMPRESSIONS IN the ground. Something was being dragged. Selene, perhaps. He couldn't tell, but there were dragon prints. He dug his claws into the rock and started his climb. It didn't seem possible that anything could surprise Selene. *The dragons or whatever took her must have been clever. Sprung a perfect trap.* Dragons were capable of that. They didn't often work together, but with the war, things had changed.

He ran his hands over the loose rocks and noted claw marks scraped into the stone. The markings led him to a large cave mouth. Brush and trees were crushed down and pushed aside. Heart pounding, he made his way into the pitch black cave and traveled dozens of feet within. Coming to a stop, he closed his eyes and let his dragon instincts take over.

He could smell them, sometimes. Dragons. They were hard to track on the rock and in the air, but they did give off the faintest odor. Only the keenest noses could detect it. Dragons blended in well with their environments in all aspects. They were flowers among flowers. Part of the landscape. Part of the terrain. They melded into cave walls. Burrowed under the grasses. Nestled in the trees. Even insects didn't note them.

He took a breath.

Alright, Selene, where are you?

Of all the people in Nalzambor, Selene would have been the last person he ever thought he would miss, but things change. She was the closest thing to him that he'd ever known. He needed her. He recollected something Brenwar had said.

'Women are always trouble. Be mindful.'

The cave coiled through the rock at a gradual slope, twisted, and began to deepen. Eyes squinted, Nath traversed the tunnel that became slick with dirt and grime. There were many passages, some narrow, others wide and tall where giant bats rustled on the ceiling. Nath's keen dragon eyes glowed with a faint golden light, and he could make out the outlines of the walls that were slick with water and glittering minerals. His hand fell to his sword Fang, but it was not there.

Guzan! I wish Fang were here!

The magnificent blade always gave him comfort, even when they didn't get along. He set his jaw, waded through shallow waters, and scaled slippery walls. One thing about caves, they often became much bigger inside than out. He clambered up into another chamber and weaved his way through stalagmites that reminded him of giant chess pieces.

A gust of hot air stung his face.

Sultans of Sulfur!

A glimmer of light shone far below, a streak of lava flowing through a crevice. An eerie whining nipped his ears.

Selene!

Nath leapt down the next level and followed the river of lava deeper into the cave. The bubbling magma glowed on his face, lighting up the room and casting shadows through the cave. The whining continued on, a strange howl of the wind, or maybe a woman, or the call of a crafty dragon. Something moaned. Familiar. Distraught. He picked up the pace, jogging along the flaming stream, hopping over the rocks, and dashing from side to side. The lava spat and hissed at his trespass, but Nath did not slow until he came to an abrupt stop where the stream turned into a fall and splashed into a molten lake a hundred feet below.

Sweat beaded Nath's head. The flaming cauldron of fire burbled and gurgled, beckoning for him. Scanning the steaming haze, he caught a glimpse of a figurine pinned down on an island of rock in the middle of the molten pond. The body sagged down in a crumpled heap, weighted down by great chains. Nath caught the glitter of the prisoner's eyes.

Selene!

She stirred in her bonds, and he could see blood on her face. His heart jumped. He climbed down the rock face of the lava fall and jumped the last thirty feet onto the banks of the pond. A path of rocks led to the island where Selene lay still. Scathing bubbles of lava popped up between the rocks and splashed back down. Nath dipped his toe in the lava. He took a sharp draw of air through his teeth.

Great Guzan!

His toe throbbed, but his scales didn't burn. He scanned all around the lake and everywhere around the rock island.

There must be a guardian somewhere.

His mind raced. What manner of creature had dragged her into this cave and dropped her on the island? Red rock dragons might have been the culprits, but they couldn't fly.

Need to move!

A geyser of lava erupted between him and the next rock on the path. He hopped thirty feet across the lava, landing just as it exploded again.

Sultans!

He timed it. Lava blasted. He hopped, rock to rock to rock. The lava blasted his tail end on the final heave to the island.

"Yipe!"

Crashing to the ground, he scrambled up and straight for Selene. He scooped her up in his arms and pushed her matted hair from her battered face.

"Selene," he said, shaking her gently, "Selene."

Her eyes fluttered open.

"Nath?"

"What happened?" he said, helping her into a sitting position.

"I sensed something," she said, holding her head. "Took the scouts and wanted to see what it was for myself. We were ambushed inside the canyons." She shuddered. "Hit hard and fast. Dragons. Bright ones. Tore into the men. I had started to take dragon form when a boulder the size of a city blasted into my head. At least that's what I thought it was." She looked up into his eyes. "They were waiting for me, Nath. They were ready." She held up her arm.

"What is that?"

"Huh," she said, rubbing the bright metal bracelet adorned in jewels cuffed to her arm. "It's something I should have used on you. It crossed my mind, but I trusted you. They call it Nalzor's Band of Negation. It blocks my magic powers."

He grabbed her wrist and started to pull it off.

Selene shrieked and jerked her arm away.

"Don't you think I tried that already?" She clutched her wrist. Agony was on her face. She said to him, "Don't do that again!"

"Well, let's get you out of here at least then," he said, reaching down and trying to lift her up. She resisted. "Get up, Selene."

"We aren't going anywhere!"

"What do you mean?"

"Nath, don't you think I would have walked out of here if I could have?"

"I saw none of your captors, Selene. Let's go."

"You'll see them soon enough," she said, brushing her jet-black hair aside. "You're trapped here the same as I am."

"Trapped by what?"

She huffed the hair out of her face. "Nath, I'm pretty sure whatever they put on this island stays on this island."

"Again, I don't see anything, Selene." He reached for her. She jerked away. "I'll carry you out of here over my shoulder if I have to."

She shot him a look.

"You wouldn't dare!"

"Don't test me," he said, crossing his arms over his chest.

"Tell you what, Nath. Go ahead and step toward the flaming pond's edge."

He shrugged and made his way toward the lake of lava.

Plop! Plop! Plop! Plop!

The stones he had crossed on sunk into the magma.

"Guzan!"

"Told you," she said, "and I don't think Guzan will be of much help, either. Pretty sure he's dead, to begin with."

Nath leered at her over his shoulder.

"What?" she said, shrugging. "He's just a legend. All legends are dead." She laughed and said, "Except you."

"Funny, Selene." He sat down and crossed his legs, staring out over the blazing lava lake. "Very Funny."

CHAPTER

28

NATH PITCHED A LOOSE ROCK into the lake.

"Great."

His frustration was mounting. None of this would have been so bad if he could transform and fly.

"Any suggestions?" he said, twisting toward Selene.

"Maybe the draykis will show at some time. Maybe some dragons, but by then I figure it will be too late."

"You think your captors are coming to kill you?"

"They went to great length to capture me," she said. "I'd say they have a contingency for everything."

Nath dashed the sweat from his eyes. Any lesser person would have died from the suffocating heat of the molten lava, but dragons could survive in the harshest environments. Above, he could see bats hanging among the stalactites of the cave. He recalled the time he had drunk one of Brenwar's potions and turned into a bat. He'd been blinded by it. It had almost killed him.

He scooted back alongside Selene and asked, "Who do you think is behind all of this?"

She rolled her eyes his way and said, "Are you really asking me that? Certainly you know who I think."

"My father?" He shook his mane. "No, I don't believe it."

"Your father is as ruthless as he is good, Nath. Why wouldn't he take me out? I'm the leader of his enemy. I'd take me out too, if I were him."

"I don't think my father does things this way."

"Hah! Of course he does. Or he has someone else do it *for* him." She shrugged and pulled her knees to her chest. "I can live with my fate, Nath."

It was the only time he'd seen her vulnerable. He felt for her. He put his hand on her shoulder and said, "I don't think it's him." He didn't say anything for a moment then added, "Perhaps you can teach me something about my powers that can help us."

"There's not much I can think of, and besides"—her eyes pointed toward the ledges—"I think it's too late for that. They come."

Nath stepped in front of her. Fiery eyes burned within the distant crevices. Humanoid globs of lava emerged from the fiery lake.

"What are those things?" he said.

"Fire goblins and lava trolls," she said. "My guardians, but not my captors. As I said, this was well thought out. The dragons will come at any moment. You had better grab some steel. I don't think your fire breath will be much help."

"I don't have a sword," he said.

"Look around," she said. "Many have perished here long before I came around. This island is full of strange treasures. Small amount of use most of them are now."

"MAAAAAH—ROOOOOOOO!"

The lava troll came forward out of the red-hot sludge. Lava slid off its ghastly grey form as it stood towering over the lake. Its head was a monstrosity, its mouth foul with busted teeth. Its lumpy skin was as smooth as a fish belly.

Nath rummaged through the decayed bones and rusting weapons.

Great Dragons! I wish I had Fang!

"Nath, look out!"

The troll splashed a wave of lava right at him. Nath dove away and rolled.

"Argh!"

Drops of lava sizzled on his scales. Wading through the bones of the dead, he found a spear and jerked it out of a skull.

"This'll do."

The troll splashed another wave of lava and lumbered onto the shore.

Nath danced away, squared up on the towering monster, and threw the spear.

"URK!"

The troll thrashed and flailed with the spear jutting from its chest. It teetered backward, and its head splashed into the lake of lava.

"Nice shot," Selene said.

Nath walked over to the troll's body and retrieved the spear. He tossed it to Selene, who plucked it from the air.

"Defend yourself, Selene. There's plenty of weapons around here."

"What can I say, Nath. You spoil me. I like seeing you in action..." She tossed the spear back to him. "Champion."

An ear-splitting shriek caught his ears.

"Now what?"

A dragon the size of three men streaked through a hole in the ceiling of the cave. Its belly scales were a pale shade of red, and its body scales were cinnamon. Its claws were long, thick, and sharp as razors. It circled its prey from above.

"That's the one, Nath," Selene said, eyes wide. "That's the one that's going to kill me."

"Her?" Nath said. "I think I can handle her."

"Well, I can't. Not without my power. It's me or her, Nath. Me or her."

Nath lingered by Selene and said, "I think you'll be just fi—*uh!*"

A lightning bolt knocked him from his feet, and a blue streak buzzed right over him. Its talons tore a gash in his cheek. Nath sprang to his feet, only to catch another bolt in the chest. His teeth clattered off his chin, and he fell face first on the ground.

"Ugh, that hurts!"

From her knees, Selene watched Nath battle against the blue razor dragons.

It's working.

Grasped inside the palms of her hands, an egg-shaped blue stone glowed. Jaxite. And her mind was attached to it.

She wanted to laugh. All of her planning had worked to perfection. Nath believed it all. Everything from the dragons capturing her to Nalzur's Band of Negation was a complete sham. She had all of her powers and then some, including control of the good dragons that she was setting Nath up to kill.

Just a little longer, Selene. A little longer. She gave another command to the blue streak dragons. *Keep him at bay as long as you can, and await my signal.*

The blue razors reared up on their hind legs, spitting jolts of lightning at Nath. He lunged with the spear at one only to get blasted in the back by another. The blue streaks were the fastest living dragons. They could keep Nath corralled for a time.

Selene glanced up at the dragon circling over her head. It was a rose blossom. She was one of the most pure and innocent breeds of the dragons, and Selene had captured her quite some time ago for just such an occasion.

The shedding of her innocent blood will make him mine. He'll serve Gorn by my side forever.

The stage was set. The weapons among the dead laid out for him. There were swords and spears, all forged from dragon claws and enchanted into dragon skinners. It was now or never to turn Nath Dragon.

She harnessed the power of the jaxite stone and turned loose her next command. To the rose blossom she said, "Attack! Attack me, the High Priestess Selene, without mercy."

The rose blossom swooped in front of her, and a hot blast of purple energy blasted from her mouth. The force pounded Selene into the rock.

"Save me, Nath! Save me!"

CHAPTER

29

NATH'S SPEAR CLIPPED THE BLUE streak's wing, drawing forth a shriek. Another jolt of lightning struck his back.

Szzzz!

A tail lashed out and cracked him in the back of the skull, toppling him over.

Smoking, he rose to his feet again. The blue streaks were lightning quick but not overly powerful. Speed and cunning were his skills.

"Get off me," Nath yelled in Dragonese. "Have you gone mad?"

He bounced to his feet. Jabbed at one with his spear, twisted around, and warded off another. Another blast of bright lightning lit up his scales.

"Argh!" He shuddered. "Enough of this!" He drew back his spear.

An explosion of purple rocked the island. He stumbled, and the blue streaks scattered into the air.

"Save me, Nath! Save me!"

Gathering his senses, Nath dashed across the small island toward the voice of Selene.

"Guzan!"

The rose blossom dragon had Selene pinned to the ground under her weight.

Nath blew a fireball into his hand and slung it into the beast. The ball of flame exploded into its side. The female dragon roared but maintained her ground. She picked Selene up in her claws and slammed her hard into the rock.

Nath rushed in and poked the dragon's shoulder with his spear. It bit in.

"Be gone, blossom!" he shouted in Dragonese.

Her purple eyes glared down on him, and her tail lashed out.

Swat!

The blow sent Nath skipping over the island, and he rolled partially into the lake of lava.

"Agh!" he screamed, flinching out of the molten rock. He got up snorting fire.

"I tire of this!" he yelled. "Get off of her now!"

The dragon's paws slammed Selene into the ground again and again.

The High Priestess moaned.

"Kill her, Nath! Kill her, before she kills me!" Selene howled out in pain. "She's killing me!"

Nath closed in and unleashed a gust of fire from his mouth. The flames splashed off the dragon's scales. She turned her neck and unleashed a cone of purple energy of her own. Nath sprang to the side.

"Great Dragons!"

He needed to distract the dragon and get Selene free, but the dragon seemed determined to kill her.

"Nath please! End this!"

Still pinned, Selene struggled underneath the weight of the dragon. Her claws pushed Selene into the ground, and her serpentine neck bent so that her snout snapped in her face.

"Kill it, Nath! Use your spear and kill it!"

He charged again, saying, "You give me no choice!" He jabbed the spear into its hide again and again. The spear tip went deep.

The dragon's assault on Selene didn't falter. The dragon's eyes blazed with purple fire. Her mouth primed to tear Selene apart.

"Strike her heart, Nath! The heart! Strike the heart!" Selene screamed.

Blood pumping, he gathered the spear up to his side and readied to charge. The heat of battle blurred his mind. The rose blossom was a fair breed of dragon. Peaceable. Loving. Female. It was a twist in reality, watching her try to tear Selene to shreds. It had to be one or the other. Nath set his shoulders, aimed for the heart, and charged.

Selene's eyes lit up, but he didn't catch it. He caught something else. The dragon's long lashes. The beautiful softness deep inside the dragon's eyes. He pulled up.

What am I doing?

He dropped the spear.

"Nath! What are you doing! Kill it!" Selene yelled.

I cannot kill this lady dragon. His clawed fingers clutched at the air. *But I can wrestle her down, I bet.*

He leapt onto the dragon's head and locked his arms around the horns. With a heave, he twisted the dragon's neck around and rode the great beast to the ground. The dragon's wings flapped and fluttered. Her tail lashed into Nath's back, but he held on.

"Selene!" he yelled. "Get out of there."

The dragon, bigger than a great horse, twisted and bucked.

"Easy, girl. I don't know what my father put you up to, but it's time to settle down."

Scaled muscles bulging, Nath twisted the dragon's neck by the horns. The dragon flopped to her back and thrashed and roared on the ground.

"Selene!" Nath yelled again. "Are you free? Selene!"

Glitch!

The dragon's body lurched with violence, slackened, and went still.

"What?" Nath looked into the eyes of the beautiful dragon and watched her rosy fire go dim. "No!" He saw Selene standing over the dragon's chest, the spear jutting out of it.

"You saved me, Nath," she said, swooning. "For now, that is." She teetered and fell onto the ground and lay still.

"Selene! Selene!"

He rushed over, picked her up in his arms, and brushed the hair from her face. She was bruised and bleeding. A tremor shook inside the cavern, and the path of rocks popped up from the lava lake once more.

Dare I try it?

He noticed the eyes of the fire goblins were gone from within the caves, and no more trolls or dragons were to be found. He edged toward the burning shore. Geysers blasted, but the rocks remained. He glanced back at the rose blossom dragon. Sadness filled him. *This is madness.* In his arms, Selene's battered face was unconscious. He hopped from rock to rock until he reached the shore.

He didn't notice the jaxite stone she tossed into the lava.

An hour later, they emerged from the grave once more.

"We made it," he said. The cool air was refreshing, and he let out a long breath, shaking. With Selene slung over his shoulder, he could feel her breathing and her heart beating. She'd be alright for now. "Let's get you back to the army."

Traversing the ledge, he made his way down to the bottom of the canyon and headed back for the horses. The commander, tall and heavy, was still there.

"High Priestess!" he said, rushing toward them. "What have you done, Dragon Prince?"

"I've saved her," Nath said, "as I said I would."

"It's suspicious."

Nath's golden eyes narrowed, and smoke rolled from his nose.

"Er," the commander continued, "let me ready a horse for her."

Suspicious, Nath thought. *Isn't every bit of it?*

EPILOGUE

CURSE ME!

Selene stood with her acolytes, rubbing the wrist where the Band of Negation had been. Her dark brows were furrowed. Her face was swollen. She'd taken the beating of a lifetime in order to fool Nath Dragon, but he had turned the tables on her. He had failed to take the life of the innocent.

There is no way he'll be turned.

She took a seat inside the tent and said, "Secure that treasure and leave me."

The men and women scurried away. Nalzur's Band of Negation did work, but she had full control of it. She always had full control of everything. Except Nath Dragon.

Blast his white scales!

They seemed even whiter now, what he had anyway, but she'd only had a glimpse, recently. He'd come to visit, but she'd pretend to be sleeping, and the clerics would hurry him away. She ran her fingers along a jagged gash on her forehead and smiled.

I actually took a beating for that man. That dragon! What have I become?

The plan had failed. Had it succeeded, she was certain Nath would have remained by her side forever. That there was no way Balzurth would have been able to stop them. Nalzambor would have been theirs. The Mountain of Doom would have been their palace.

Her fantasies had evaporated, however. Her body ached as she sighed. Soon, Gorn Grattack would be calling, and Nath Dragon would have to die.

-BOOK 10-

CRAIG HALLORAN

CHAPTER

1

NATH SLUNG HIS FISHING LINE into the stream. Wading in ankle deep, he could see fish swimming in the rippling waters but not taking the bait.

"Perhaps we should return," the commander said, standing behind him on the bank with his arms folded over his chest. "The skies darken. Rain comes."

Nath didn't reply. He had other things on his mind, particularly the rose blossom dragon that Selene had killed. And Selene as well.

"The High Priestess will not care for this, Dragon Prince," the commander added.

The man was very ominous underneath his dark helm. Peculiar, too. He'd stayed with Nath like a fly on glue.

Nath felt a nibble on his line and jerked his wrist. A fish snapped up out of the water. "Got him!"

He swung the fish over the bank, hitting the commander in his chest plate.

"It's a big one," Nath said. "Ever fish before, Commander?"

"Certainly," the commander said, batting the fish aside. "Don't be foolish."

"Foolish," Nath said, cocking his head. "Did you call me—"

"Apologies, I meant no disrespect." He bowed. "A slip, Dragon Prince."

"Aw, don't call me that," Nath said. He grabbed the fish, poked inside its mouth, and pulled the hook out. "I'm hungry." He puffed a blast of fire, charring the fish. "Mmmm!" With his clawed finger, he gutted it, picked the meat off clean, and ate. "Want some?"

"No."

"Funny, I never notice you eating anything. You're a big man. I figure you eat plenty, too. Yet I never even hear your stomach growling."

"Runs in the family."

"Family, huh?" Nath said, chewing a mouthful. "Why don't you tell me about them? Do you have a wife? Did you marry with or without that ugly metal bowl on your head?"

"I don't have a wife."

"Tell me about your father and mother, then. Do they wear bowls on their heads?"

The commander shifted in his armor. His head twisted in other directions. He turned away and started walking up the bank.

Good.

There was something odd about the commander that Nath couldn't figure out, but he had other things on his mind. Selene. She'd been evasive. Normally, she stayed close by his side, but now she was distant. She had been ever since they had come out of the cave where she'd killed the rose blossom, the beautiful dragon that had attacked him along with the blue streaks.

Why did they attack me? Why?

He inspected his arms. Bands and streaks of white scales adorned them now. Even the patches of white in his palms had grown fuller. He glanced upward. A flock of dragons flew high in the sky in a V formation.

I should be up there.

He'd tried every day to turn into the dragon he'd once been, but he couldn't harness the magic. He didn't understand why. He snapped his fishing rod and tossed it into the water. "Bah." He glowered at the stream that rushed swiftly by. "Commander, any idea where we're headed? We seem to be doing circles."

The armored man came back his way and said from underneath the helm, "We go where the High Priestess says."

"Do you always do what you're told?"

"I follow orders."

"Have you ever not followed orders, say, when you were a boy?"

"Let's get back to camp," the commander said. "Perhaps you'll find the answers you seek there." The commander started to pass by.

Nath grabbed him in the nook of his arm.

"Let go," the commander said.

"Say, what is your name, Commander?" Nath said, nostrils flaring.

"You know that. I'm Commander Haan." He tried to pull away, but Nath held him fast.

"No, what is your first name?" Nath said, eyeing him. "And take off that helmet. How can you always wear such an ugly thing? Is your face so horrible that it must be hidden?"

Commander Haan stiffened and tried to twist from Nath's grip. He couldn't break it. He shoved Nath backward.

Nath shoved him back off his feet, onto the ground. "You're a big man, but don't be a fool, Haan." Nath stood over him. "Now, show me your face and tell me your name."

"No."

Nath's nostrils flared. His dander rose. Frustration set in. "Fine. I'll remove it myself, then."

CHAPTER

2

SELENE SOARED ABOVE THE CLOUDS with one thought in her mind.

Nath Dragon must die.

It didn't sit well. She'd have lost sleep over it if she slept at all, but that was always very little. Gorn Grattack had been clear. If Nath didn't turn to their side, then she was to bring him to Gorn, who would put Nath to death. Flapping her massive black wings, she streaked through the clouds.

A year ago, she'd have been thrilled to see Nath go. She would have killed him herself. She'd relished manipulating him.

But now, she'd gotten used to him. He was the only one like her, in so many ways: a black dragon who could also be human, the child of a powerful and distant father... She'd watched many die before, but such an outcome for Nath didn't seem possible. He had become large in her life.

She circled the skies, hour after hour. She'd marched her armies through the hills and beyond the valley on the longest path she could take toward Gorn Grattack.

She broke through the clouds again, dipping below their midst. Parts of the green lush lands were still intact, while other portions were dead and broken. The battle blood of men and dragons seeped into the ground all over, and the world trembled. The edges burned. Elves and orcs were in full battle. Dwarves marched out from Morgdon. The Legionnaires combed the lands. The races were restless, yet the Truce remained intact.

But it will not hold with Nath Dragon dead.

She glided to the earth and took her place on a spire in the mountains. Her keen dragon sight could pick up anything for miles. The forces of good were being spread out just the way Gorn Grattack had planned.

No more Nath Dragon. No more Truce. A new world will be ushered in.

Her black heart skipped a beat, and with a sigh, she puffed a plume of fire into the sky.

Gorn Grattack's will must be done. I will obey. Nath Dragon must die.

CHAPTER

3

"WHAT KIND OF MAN DOESN'T get hungry?" Nath said, reaching for Haan's helmet. "And doesn't sweat—or even stink, for that matter." He locked his fingers on Commander Haan's collar and started jerking at the dark helm. "Oof!"

Haan launched his metal gauntlet into Nath's belly, shoved him away, and rose up from his knee, reaching for his sword. "Stop this, Dragon Prince, I urge you."

Nath coughed and patted the iron-hard muscles under his scales. "You hit awfully hard for a mortal, too." He glared into Haan's hard eyes. "Harder than a big man even your size could. Explain that, and tell me what your name is." He pounced on the commander, smote him to the ground, and yanked off the helmet.

Haan cocked his arm back and struck Nath in the ribs.

Nath grimaced. "You can't hurt me when I'm ready for it. Now, who are you?"

Haan struggled.

Nath strained to hold him fast.

"Haan. Jason Haan is my name. Are you happy now?"

"No," Nath said. He groaned. "Still you don't sweat. How can that be?"

Haan's stern face grimaced under a head of short, black hair. His dark eyes shifted away from Nath's.

"Look at me," Nath demanded.

"No, I'll not." Haan flailed at him.

Nath grasped Haan's wrists and pinned them over the man's head. He squeezed the gauntlets until the metal bent and dug into flesh.

"How am I supposed to get those off now?" Haan said, rolling his eyes. "Sultans! Will you just let go of me—Nath. You're messing everything up."

Haan's voice had changed. No longer harsh and deep, it was lighter. And familiar.

Nath loosened his grip and leaned back.

Whop!

Haan's metal fist cracked him in the face. The big man effortlessly regained his feet and towered over Nath, to his dismay.

"Gorlee!"

Forming a sheepish grin, the big warrior nodded. "It's me." He reached down and pulled Nath up to his feet. "Sorry."

Nath rubbed his jaw. "Think nothing of it. If anything, I'm glad to see that kind of fight in you. But how long, Gorlee, how long?"

CRAIG HALLORAN

Gorlee scanned the surroundings.

"It's all right," Nath said, "no one is near."

Gorlee let out a breath, and his shoulders eased. "Good."

"Gorlee, how long have you been near? Have you been spying on me?

"Protecting you would be a better word."

Nath's eyes narrowed. Something didn't set with what Gorlee said. The way he said it wasn't right. "Sasha!" Nath stepped toward Gorlee. "That was you!" His hand lashed out, and his fingers locked around Gorlee's neck. "Why? Why?!"

"Keep your voice down," Gorlee managed to croak out. "Please." He clutched at Nath's arms. His face turned purple. "I can explain."

"How can you explain posing as my friend, looking me in the eye, and lying to me?"

"Please, Nath. I came to save you. Selene caught me, captured my essence, and made me her vessel." He choked. "I swear it."

Nath shoved him down.

For all Nath knew, Gorlee was still under her power. No matter what he did, she was there. How could he trust Gorlee now? How could he trust anyone? And what about Sasha? Bayzog? Where were they now?

Coughing, Gorlee started to speak. "Nath, you have to believe me. I'll tell you everything I know. And I know much. It's Selene."

"I don't want to hear it," Nath said. "I know she lies."

"It's more than that. She was ordered to turn you, and she failed. Do you know what that means?"

"Turn me?" Nath said. His anger subsided as confusion set in. "Turn me into what?"

Gorlee made his way to one knee, shaking his head.

"Into what, Gorlee? A draykis? Hah. I'm already a dragon. And I'm fully alive, not dead."

Gorlee swallowed as his eyes looked up.

"Kill me? And turn me into one of those monsters?"

"I believe it means something like that. It's very confusing."

"Why didn't you tell me this sooner?"

"I couldn't risk being discovered. I escaped. They still search for me, but I think I have them fooled, for now." He glanced around. "That's why you mustn't reveal my cover. We must play along."

"No. I must confront Selene about her plans for me," Nath said with a sneer.

"She's a liar, Nath. She'll twist your clear thoughts into the mud of worms."

"*You* are a liar."

"Not of my own volition."

"Hah, a changeling is nothing but a deceiver."

"Nath, you know me better than that."

"Do I?"

There was silence between them for a moment. Only the cool breeze that pushed down the tall grasses whistled by their ears. Nath had no one to trust now but himself. He grunted within. *I wish Brenwar was here.* He never had to doubt Brenwar. But even so, Gorlee's words had a ring of truth to them.

"Nath, there's more. The acolytes, they prepare for something. I fear Gorn Grattack is near."

Nath remembered his dream. The evil Dragon Overlord was coming for him, and he could feel a great presence of evil in his scales.

"So this is why Selene hesitates," he said, almost with a smile.

"Pardon?" Gorlee said, picking up his helmet.

Things fell into place. Selene's capture had been a ploy. Setting his jaw, he ground his teeth, clenching his fists.

"We need to keep this charade going, Nath," Gorlee said. "The way I see it, we need to get to the heart of the matter. That is Gorn. I was waiting for that moment. The moment to strike."

"And what exactly were you going to do? As I understand it, Gorn is every bit as powerful as my father."

"I was going to be your backup against him or Selene ..." He put on his helmet. "Let's play along while we can." He extended his hand. "I am your true friend, and I can explain much more later."

"I'd be interested to hear it." Nath stretched out his hand, but he still felt uncertain. A shadow grazed over the grasses. He jerked his head up. "Look out!"

The feline fury dropped out of the sky, right on top of the both of them.

CHAPTER

4

NATH FELT THE FULL WEIGHT of the feline fury on him. Its claws dug into his back. Peeled at his scales. He screamed. Out of the corner of his eye, he saw Gorlee pinned down underneath its other paw, wide eyed.

"Get off me," Nath said in Dragonese.

The beast stuffed his head into the dirt.

Nath pushed himself up, straining underneath its power and weight, inching his way up off the ground. "I said get off me!" Nath snarled.

The dragon cat clocked him in the back of the head with its horns.

Stars burst in bright spots before his eyes.

"Sultans of Sulfur!" Nath twisted underneath the cat dragon.

It pinned him down on his back, crushing his chest. Its jaw opened and struck.

"Gah!"

It bit down on his arm and flung him away.

He skipped over the ground and into the stream. Slinging his mane of auburn hair over his shoulder, he dashed the water from his eyes.

The feline fury was all over Gorlee. It ripped his armor off and dug its paws into his flesh.

"Great Guzan!" Nath blew a fireball into his hand and flung it at the monster.

The ball of flame exploded into its hide, and it let out a crying, cat-like howl, but it kept pounding away.

Gorlee was up on his feet. In a flash, he drew a gleaming blade from his scabbard. He flashed it at the fury.

It crawled backward, head low, yellow eyes shifting back and forth. They had it flanked.

Nath blew a fireball into each hand.

The feline fury's ears flattened on its head. It made an eerier howl. It crouched back, ready to pounce.

"You all right, Gorlee?" Nath said.

"I've a few hunks out of me, but nothing I can't heal. This beast, Nath, it's been hunting me for weeks." He stepped closer, slicing the blade through the air. "It will notify Selene, Nath. It seems I'm exposed. We both are, for that matter."

Nath figured Gorlee was right. If Selene found Gorlee, she'd kill him. If they killed the feline fury, she'd know that one of them was involved. Perhaps now was the time to make a break for it? No, with all the dragons and her army, it wouldn't take her long to hunt him down.

"Gorlee, I think it's time you left."

"What?"

"I'll handle the fury."

"No, Nath. We're in this together." Sword high, Gorlee advanced.

"No! Stop!"

Gorlee froze.

The feline fury drew back, ready to spring at any moment.

Nath flicked the balls of flame into the rippling water. They sizzled and disappeared. He kneeled down, eyeing the dragon cat. Summoning a power he felt deep inside, he said in Dragonese, ""Come. Come, great dragon cat. I'm a friend. You should know that," Nath added, lying flat on the ground.

"Nath, what are you doing? He'll gore you."

Growling at Gorlee, the feline fury eased out of its stance and slunk closer to Nath.

Nath spread his arms wide and welcoming. "Come, great dragon cat. Come." He felt power. A connection with the dragon. Something he'd not felt before. Unlike Selene's other dragons, the feline fury had a cunning mind of its own, no longer under the influence of a spell or jaxite stones. He stretched his fingers out as the beast inched closer. "Come, friend."

"Nath, get away. You're mad," Gorlee said in a loud whisper.

Nath felt the tips of the dragon cat's whiskers and its lava-hot breath on his face. Its citrine-colored cat eyes bore into his. A purr rumbled in its great scaled belly, and it lay down beside him and licked his hand.

"I'll be," Gorlee said.

Nath smiled at Gorlee. "Father once told me, 'You'll never make new friends unless you try.'"

As the dark clouds rolled over the skyline, Nath headed back toward camp, heavy in thought.

Is Selene really going to kill me?

Gorlee had made his case, filling in details Nath hadn't known. The ruse of Gorlee posing as Sasha in order to gain his trust had infuriated him, but he believed Gorlee now. The changeling had no reason to lie. But how would he deal with Selene?

The feline fury nuzzled past him and took to the air.

"Are you certain that beast is on our side now?" Gorlee said, marching at his side. "It nearly ripped me apart a few times."

"Me too," Nath said. "But he's an ally now. He's made his choice. He just needed a reason, and now he has one." He frowned. "Poor creature. All these years, Selene kept him through fear, rearing him for wrong, but a little kindness, a tad of submission turned him."

"Do you think that will work with the rest of the dragons that want to tear out our throats?"

"Probably not."

They walked on, pushing along the path, less than a mile from the main camp now. Inside, Nath simmered. He'd been manipulated. He'd trusted in the Truce, and now he knew it was all a lie. A ploy to keep him on the sidelines. Selene had used him to fool everybody, and it had worked quite well.

"Nath," Gorlee said. "I'm sorry."

"For what?"

"Deceiving you as Haan."

"It wasn't your fault, Gorlee."

"I was foolish," the changeling said.

"You were brave. Don't start doubting yourself now, Gorlee. You risked your life for me. For the land. That's ... well, that's something." He slapped his hand on Gorlee's shoulder. "That's the mark of a true friend."

"Thanks Nath," he said. "So, do you really think we can fool her?"

"I don't see why not. After all, you fooled me. Plus, now we have another ally in the fury. I think it will be a good one. We'll see." Still, something stirred in Nath's belly. He needed to be at full power, and he hadn't been for quite some time. Not since he'd flown that first time.

Selene has done something to me. Hah! I'm a fool not to have realized that.

Heavy raindrops began to pelt them from above. Soon the path became muddy. Gorlee kept chattering about things. He talked about Bletver the triant. Even Nath hadn't heard of such a creature. Gorlee also told him about the heroes in the tavern, the ones who fought in the name of Balzurth. It made Nath's chest swell. Men, the most unpredictable of all, fighting in the name of his father did his heart good.

"Things are going to have to come undone soon, Nath. The farce called a truce must end. I think that's on you."

It seemed sacrifices were being made all over. Nath felt like everyone gave something but him. He frowned as Gorlee continued speaking. He couldn't stop thinking about Brenwar, Ben, Bayzog, and Sasha. Did they still even live?

As they reached the edge of the camp, a group of acolytes, tattooed and bald, greeted them. "You must come with us, Dragon Prince."

"Why?" Nath said. "Has something happened?"

"Peace Bringer," said another acolyte, "High Priestess Selene has an urgent summons. She awaits you in her tent."

"I see. All right, then." He glanced at Gorlee, but the helmet on his friend's head hid any expression. "Let's go then." He nodded as he left. "Commander."

CHAPTER

5

"I SEE YOU ARE WELL," NATH said to Selene.

She wore all-black robes traced in gold. Her crown of silver leaves was on her head. She took a seat at a long table inside the tent. There was no one else there but them.

"Please have a seat, Nath. Eat with me."

"I'm not hungry." He took a place at the table and pushed a plate of steaming food away.

"Interesting," she said, placing her cloth napkin on her lap. She took a sip of wine. "Not drinking either, I imagine."

"I'm fine." His stomach rumbled.

Her eyebrows lifted. "Are you sure about that?"

"Probably some fish I must have eaten too fast."

"Fish?" She tapped her fingernail on the glass goblet. "All right, then."

"Selene, what is this all about? You summoned me, after all, not I you. As a matter of fact, I've hardly seen you in days." He draped his elbow over the back of his chair. "Why is that?"

With a look of sadness, she scooted her plate away, rested her elbows on the table, and locked her fingers together. "Nath, I've been avoiding something."

"Is that why you march this army in circles?"

"So you've noticed."

"I know the land as well as anyone." He looked at his clawed fingers. "So why is that? Hmmm? I think you are avoiding Gorn Grattack."

She raised her head. "Why would you think that?"

"We've had many conversations, Selene. And you've made it pretty clear that you don't care so much for him. I seem to recall you mentioning that the two of us could defeat him."

"Oh," she said with a small smile, "did I say that?"

"You know you did," he said. "And I believed you."

"Believed?"

Careful what you say, Nath. She still has to believe she has you duped.

"Yes. Selene, I think you felt we could take Gorn down together, but now ... well, now you doubt me. After all, I can't even turn into a dragon, and I showed mercy to that rose blossom that wanted to kill me." He shrugged. "Maybe you fear I don't have the killer instinct needed to carry out a fight with the likes of Gorn—"

She held up her palm. "Let's not say his name too many times. His name evokes attention."

"I see. So, am I right?"

"You are wise as a serpent."

"Of course, we still have my father's forces to contend with. They are liable to make another attempt on your life, and we can't let that happen. Not if we're going after, well, you know who."

Selene stared at him with silence. Finally, she said, "I admit I am surprised."

Not as surprised as I am. I can't believe she's swallowing this.

They marched onward, mile after mile, league after league. Nath and Gorlee rode on horseback side by side, Gorlee's lips silent under the ominous metal helm that he wore. Behind them was the rest of the army, troops numbering in the thousands now, their bootsteps splashing through sloppy mud holes. The heavy rain rang off their metal armor. It made for a dreary sound, creating an unforgiving itch down Nath's spine.

Am I a fool, rushing headlong into the mouth of Gorn Grattack?

And there was Selene.

Why would I believe anything she said? She lied every time before. Does she really want to face Gorn Grattack now?

Faith urged him forward. He didn't know why, but he had to move on. Confront his fears. Face Gorn Grattack and save the world or doom it. He'd been looking inward for quite some time. Perhaps that was his biggest problem: fear of failure.

Am I to let the world down the same as I did my father?

It ate at him, the thought of not seeing his father again—nor Dragon Home. Nor any of his friends, for that matter.

Guzan! I wish Brenwar were here. He'd be fired up for this final battle.

He glanced at Gorlee.

At least I'll have one friend to witness my death. I hope it's a grand funeral.

CHAPTER

6

"HIT 'EM!" BRENWAR YELLED. HE hefted up a rock as big as himself. "Now!" With a heave, he hurled the huge missile through the air.

Beside him, Ben nocked an exploding arrow, took aim, and fired.

Twang!

Coming right for them was a hull dragon, bright green and orange scaled, more than thirty feet in height, stomping through the valley.

Brenwar's boulder rocked it in the jaw.

Ben's arrow skewered its neck.

Boom!

The massive monster staggered backward and let out an ear-splitting roar.

Ben fired again.

Boom!

Brenwar ripped another hunk out of the ground and said, "Quit showing off!" He chucked it. The rock smashed off the monster's nose. "Perfect hit!"

With an important look on his face, Pilpin picked up a smaller rock and threw it at the hull.

Around Ben's arrow, the hull sucked in a mouthful of air.

"Uh oh," Ben said, "here it comes!"

"Bayzog!" His head whipped around. "Where are you, elf?"

A bluish-green light glowed to life inside the dragon's great maw.

Brenwar and Ben glanced at one another.

Pilpin made as if to advance on the hull.

"Take cover!" Brenwar yelled, snatching Pilpin by the collar.

"Where?" Ben said, looking around.

The hull dragon's scales charged with light. Mystic fire dripped from its jaws.

Bayzog dropped from the sky with the Elderwood Staff in hand. "Get down!" he commanded.

Whooooooosh!

A firestorm of energy erupted from the dragon's mouth.

With a wave of Bayzog's hand, a great wall of yellow mystic energy formed, shielding them all. The torrential flames sizzled angrily against the wall. Sparks and specks of bright energy burst in the air. Bayzog's stern face beaded in sweat.

Brenwar could feel the intense heat through his armor. "Get out of there, elf, before it roasts you alive!"

The geysers of flames came on. The shield started to pop and crack.

"Run!" Bayzog said. "Run!"

"I'm not running!" Brenwar picked up his war hammer. "Forward. Onward," he said, still holding Pilpin back by the collar. He wound the hammer up, spinning it like a pinwheel.

The shield crackled and wobbled. Bayzog drifted to the ground. Flames spilled through the shattered holes, setting fire to his lily-white robes.

"Mrurumrah Hooooooooooo!" Brenwar bellowed. Then, with all of his bracer-enhanced might, he let the ancient hammer fly. It burst through the shield and straight through the flames. A great clap of thunder popped the air and shook the ground.

Kra-boooooooom!

Bayzog's shield dissipated, and the dragon's fiery breath was gone, leaving only a smoky mist that covered almost everything.

Somewhere in the mist, the hull dragon made an awful moan, and a tremendous *thud* shook the ground.

Brenwar scurried forward and lifted Bayzog back up to his feet.

"I better not have lost my hammer."

Bayzog dusted off his robes. "I didn't think dwarves ever lost anything."

"Hrmph," Brenwar and Pilpin both said.

The four of them stood on the cliff's edge in silence. A stiff breeze cleared the air, revealing the monstrous form of the hull dragon collapsed on the earth. Trees and branches were crushed beneath it.

"Do you think you killed it?" Ben said, leaning over the edge.

"Why don't you go down there and tickle it?" Brenwar said. "Or pinch its scales, maybe."

The great monster didn't stir, not in the slightest. It was tons of scales and muscle, with great armored fins on its back, wingless and formidable. Brenwar looked at the bracers on his wrists, the ones that Balzurth had gifted to him. They pulsed with an eerie yellow light. It gave him a rush. Filled him with power. With the war hammer and the bracers, he felt like he could take out an entire mountain. With the hull dragon down, he practically had.

Filling his lungs full of air, he pounded his chest and let out a tremendous bellow.

"Hooooooooooooooooooooooo!"

"What are you doing?" Ben said, covering his ears. "Are you trying to wake it?"

Brenwar's great voice continued to fill the valley as he broke out in song.

"*Home of the Dwarves! Morgdon! Home of the dwarves! Morgdon! We have the finest steel and ale! Our weapons will never fail! Morgdon!*"

"Look," Bayzog said, pointing down at the great dragon.

Brenwar stopped and looked.

The hull dragon was moving.

"By my beard!" His brows buckled as his eyes scanned for his war hammer. "Fetch my weapon, mage!" he yelled at Bayzog.

The dragon snorted a blast of smoke and let out an angry groan.

"He looks mad, Brenwar," Ben said, loading up Akron. "I don't think he likes your singing."

"Aw, shut it, human," Brenwar said, scraping a hunk of stone out of the earth. The sound of hooved feet caught his ears, and he stopped.

Shum and Hoven galloped by, holding up spears at least eight feet long. Dragon Needles.

"Don't you dare kill my dragon!" Brenwar shouted, but they were gone.

Each Roamer leapt off his horse and climbed up the dragon. Without hesitation, they rammed their Dragon Needles into the dragon's armored chest. The tips pierced the thick hide and plunged straight into the heart.

The dragon's bright eyes glared with intensity. It lurched a few times, but then the eyes went dim.

Brenwar was furious. In a rush, he stormed down the hillside and greeted the Roamers alongside the dragon, shaking his fist at them.

"That was my dragon!"

Shum twirled his Dragon Needle around—once, twice, three times—shrinking it. Looking over his shoulder, he said, "You can still have it. Just so long as you remember it was us who killed it."

"Why you pointy eared, fat—"

Shum lowered the tip of his spear in Brenwar's face. "Watch what you say, dwarf."

Brenwar slapped it away. "Don't ever stick that stick in my face again, pot belly!" He stormed away and scoured the valley until he got his hands back on his war hammer. He hugged it to his chest and stepped alongside the head of the hull dragon. Its magnificent horn was cracked off at the top of its head, which had a dent in it. "You did that, not them," he said to the war hammer. "Dragon Needles? Pah."

CHAPTER

7

"NO SMILES? NO JOY?" SASHA said. "You men should be happy. You saved another town."

Brenwar and Pilpin each snorted a grunt. Shum and Hoven remained expressionless, and Bayzog's face was creased in concentration.

"I'm happy," Ben said, tossing some firewood into the smoking pit. "Who wouldn't be, after surviving a battle with a monstrous dragon? Woo, I'm relieved!" He stirred the fire with a stick and rubbed his beard. "Don't pay any mind to those sour faces over there. Especially the bearded ones."

"I'd be happy, too, Mother," Rerry said, stepping out of the woodland and dropping a stack of sticks on the ground, "if I'd gotten a few licks in on that hull dragon." He drew his sword. Lightning-quick strokes cut the air. *Swish. Swish. Swish. Swish.* He slammed the blade back inside his scabbard. "But again I missed it, thanks to Samaz. I can't always be his keeper, you know."

Bayzog spoke up. "You did well, Son. It was your duty."

"Does it always have to be my duty? After all, he's older. He should be watching over me and not me over him. I sicken of it, Father. I want to fight, not sit watching Glum Face all the time."

Bayzog lifted his eyes to the sky, shaking his head. The stars and moon twinkled behind the drifting clouds, but that wasn't all. Winged silhouettes drifted through the sky, sending a chill through him. He noticed Shum and Hoven glancing upward as well. "Sasha, how about you conceal these flames?"

Warming her hands, she was just about to sit down beside him when she paused and kissed him on the head. "I'd love to."

She scratched up a handful of dirt from the ground, rubbed it in her hands, and began muttering a quick incantation. Tossing the dirt into the air, where it sparkled bright with energy, she said, "Azzah!"

A dimness formed over them, stretching from tree limb to tree limb.

"Well done," Bayzog said. He took her by the hand and kissed her. "I couldn't do better myself."

"I know," she giggled as she took her place beside him. She clasped her warm hands around his. "Some things take a woman's touch."

"Like your cooking," Ben piped in. "Please don't let Brenwar and Pilpin make supper again. It tasted like baked bark."

Pilpin tossed a metal pot in the fire and chomped his teeth. "You cook, then. We don't need as much food as you anyway, do we Brenwar?"

Brenwar groaned in agreement.

Rerry plucked the pot out of the fire and tossed it back and forth until the metal cooled, saying, "I'll make it. Something with some elven zeal will lift these dour spirits." He patted his belly. "And I'm too hungry to wait for all this bickering to end." He walked away with a sigh.

Bayzog could feel something he didn't like: pressure. There was fatigue in everyone's movements. Heavy concern in their faces. None more so than Brenwar's. Losing his charge, Nath Dragon, had unsettled the ever-stout dwarf. He'd been edgy ever since Nath took things into his own hands. It left everyone uncertain.

"How much farther, Shum?" Bayzog said.

The ranger was sharpening his elven blade with a rune-faced whetstone while Hoven hummed a gentle tune. "A few more days. You'll see. The land starts to decay. Darken. Leaves fall from the trees out of season. I assume there'll be more encounters on our way. Let's hope we can avoid most of them."

"That hull dragon was unavoidable, that much is certain," Ben said. "It was its own city. Do you think there will be more hulls? I'm running low on exploding arrows."

"Then take better aim with them," Brenwar growled. "Unless Bayzog can conjure up more."

Bayzog shook his head.

"Oh," Ben continued, "maybe I need some practice. Why don't you put an apple on your head and let me shoot it?"

"You'd like that, wouldn't you?"

"Other than it being a shame to waste a good piece of fruit, why yes, I think I would." Ben chuckled.

Brenwar folded his arms over his chest and said, "Pah. All you do is waste arrows and your breath."

Pilpin barked a laugh.

Bayzog tuned them out. They'd gone on like this for hours, but it wasn't the worst thing. It kept an edge about them, and they needed that. It had taken Sasha some time, but she'd gotten used to it. He squeezed her hand. She looked over and smiled at him. Regardless of the darkness, doubt, and despair that surrounded them, she seemed happy.

"I'd better go check on Samaz," he said. "It's been awhile. Would you like to come along?"

She stroked his long black hair, rubbed his back, and said, "No. I'll help Rerry prepare our supper. He's a horrible cook, but he tries. You go. Take all the time you need with our quieter son."

"Save me some stew." He patted her knee and departed.

Samaz sat cross legged out on the end of a rocky crag. The stiff breeze bristled his short black hair and played with his robes, which were snug around his body. He didn't turn as Bayzog approached. Instead, his chin was tilted up and his eyes were glassy and dreamy.

Of all the things I've dealt with, this always seems the most strange.

Samaz had always been like this. He'd sit up in his bed, late at night, eyes open, staring at nothing yet everything.

I'd love to see what's in that mind of his.

Quietly, Bayzog eased down into sitting position. It was best not to disturb Samaz from his slumbers. He'd broken Rerry's wrist for it once. It was no wonder the brothers bickered so much and Rerry resented him.

Bayzog crossed his legs the same as Samaz, closed his eyes, and relaxed. They used to do this all the time, have long whiles of peace and quiet. It soothed him, and he was certain it brought comfort to Samaz as well. His thick-set son, though aloof and distant, no doubt knew he was there. Samaz had amazing intuition. Rerry could never sneak up on him, nor beat Samaz at hide and seek, either.

The crickets chirped, and the distant pixies played. Bayzog could feel his elven roots stretching out and acclimating to the sound of the woods: the rustling of branches, hooves that scurried through the night. He'd gotten more in tune with his elven roots over the past twenty-five years, and it had been good. He started to breathe easy. His taut shoulders relaxed. He became one with his son. One with nature.

Moments went by.

"Father," Samaz said, softly.

Bayzog opened his eyes, turned, and faced his son. Samaz's features were covered in sweat, and his dark eyes were wide. Placing his hand on his son's chest, he felt the young part-elf's heart pounding.

Thump-thump ... thump-thump ... thump-thump ...

Unable to hide his worry, he asked, "What is it, Son?"

A silvery tear dripped down Samaz's cheek. His body trembled. "I–I saw a dragon die." He pointed toward the sky.

Bayzog followed his finger.

A large black object dotted the sky, blotting out a small part of the rising moon. It sent a shiver through Bayzog. He stood up, and his slender jawline dropped. It was too big to be a dragon, yet it moved too slowly to be anything else, and something propelled it forward, dragging it over the mountain treetops.

"What is that, Samaz?" He shook his son by the shoulders. "Have you any idea?"

Teary eyed, Samaz spoke again, his voice more haunting this time. "I saw a dragon die." He looked at Bayzog. "I saw Nath Dragon die."

CHAPTER

8

THE GREEN AND COLORFUL FIELDS were in a state of decay. Leaves fell from branches. Branches fell from trees. At night, the pixies no longer sang.

Nath stood in the morning mist and sighed. His clawed fingertips tingled. He felt tired. He never felt tired.

"Time to move," said Gorlee, posing as Jason Haan. He was buckling his armor over his big frame. His sullen face with its hard eyes showed no sign of worry. "Seems we're getting closer to something."

"Yes," Nath said, donning a leather tunic Selene had given him. It was plain, with no insignia of Barnabus, which was odd, seeing how everyone else was marked. It did have a special crest on it, a crown resting on wings. "I'm curious as to what that something is."

He was speaking of Gorn Grattack.

Gorlee came closer, careful no one else was within earshot, and said, "It's not too late to move on."

"Nervous?"

"I feel something I cannot describe."

"Does it make you feel any better that I feel the same way?"

Gorlee managed the grimmest of smiles on his warrior's face. "It does."

"Good then. Now listen, Gorlee. I'd just as soon you left to go find our friends Brenwar and Bayzog. You of all people have the best chance of coming out of this, and the fury no longer hunts you. I'd just as soon you slipped out, first chance you got. Someone else will have to fight this war if I fail."

"I wish you wouldn't say such things," Gorlee said, buckling on his helmet.

"Things need to be clear."

Without another word, Nath mounted his horse, and Gorlee followed suit. The army finished breaking down the camp, loaded up, and was on the move again. Through the misty rain they went, mile after mile, league after league.

Nath felt incomplete. He forged on through his doubts. Could he trust Selene at all? Could he trust himself? He'd made plenty of bad decisions. The Truce he had agreed to might have been the worst of them all.

But I couldn't let my friends die, even though they were willing to. What kind of friend would I be if I had let them die?

He must not have done the right thing, though, because the farther they went, the smaller he felt inside.

Near evening, when they were cresting a hill made up of fallen trees and dried-up and broken branches, Selene appeared. She rode on the back of a dark grey horse. Her robes were deep violet woven in red, and her black dragon tail hung over both sides of the saddle. Draykis were on either side of her.

"We are near, Nath," she said, coming along his side and leading him away. "Come." She glanced at Gorlee and then spoke to the draykis commanders. "Stay here with the rest of the army. We shall return. Wait."

Without a glance back, Nath followed Selene through the barren mountain range. It was a territory he was unfamiliar with. They would be hard pressed to push an army along this pathway, which cut through a thick comb of briars, thickets, and dying trees. And even though the forces of Barnabus were anything but his kind of people, he felt abandoned without them. A little more so without Gorlee in tow.

No one watching my back now.

Ahead, Selene rode tall in the saddle as always. She had a gentle sway in her body as she rode, plodding along, patient, eyes forward. The tip of her tail lay flat over the saddle. Sometimes he noticed that it would whip back and forth, caress her hair, or coil along her waist. Not now.

She's nervous? Perhaps she is *on my side.*

After miles of riding through the dank day, she stopped her horse and looked back at him. "Are you ready?"

"There's never been a moment that I wasn't," he said, smiling weakly.

"Huh," she said, dismounting. "We'll leave the horses here. Are you all right with that, or are you more comfortable around pets?"

Nath slid off his horse and hitched the reins over a branch. "Walking is fine by me, company or not." He stretched out his long arms, rolled his shoulders, and cracked his neck. He puffed a ring of smoke. "I'm ready to greet him."

Selene came closer and locked her arm around his. There was a warm-soft texture to her scales. Standing almost as tall as he, she looked up into his eyes. "Don't do anything rash."

"Me?"

"Just keep your tongue in place and let me do the talking. Follow my lead."

"Silence and inaction aren't my better qualities."

"No, no they aren't. But it's your life, Nath. Your actions will determine how much longer you keep it."

He squeezed her hands and held them to his chest. He wasn't sure why. He just did it.

She didn't resist.

That's when he said to her, "Isn't your life worth something, too?"

"I can live with my choices, Nath. I've lived for them. I'll die for them. Not even you can change that."

The morbid statement created a void inside him.

Her fingers slipped out of his, and she walked away, tail dragging over the path.

An ominous dragon-woman puzzle, that's what she is. If I live, I might just write a poem about this.

CHAPTER

9

ORLEE FIDGETED INSIDE HIS ARMOR. He was of no use to Nath now. Selene had him. His effort to stay close had been blocked. They'd been gone for hours, and darkness had come.

"Get back with the rest of the troops," one of the draykis commanders hissed. He had great black wings on his back, and he was very tall and ominous inside his patchwork of metal armor. "We'll watch the pass."

"I don't recall the High Priestess removing my authority. I'm to watch after the Dragon Prince, so far as I can."

"There is nothing to watch now," the draykis said, looking down the path Nath and Selene had taken. "But soon, I'm certain, there will be a funeral."

"Until I see a body, I'm just fine right where I am."

The draykis grabbed Gorlee's horse by the harness and jerked its neck. The horse nickered.

"Ride your beast away," it said. "This army is under the watch of the draykis now, not men."

Gorlee looked into its face of scales and beady eyes and said through his teeth, "Let … go."

"Move along, human," the draykis said, releasing the harness and walking away. "Huh-huh, move along. There are four of us and just one of you, and any one of us can tear you in two."

Gorlee didn't doubt he meant it. Very few mortals could handle draykis. But he wasn't mortal. He clenched the reins of his horse and nudged it away.

"Enjoy your sleep, human, while we who need no sleep watch over things. Huh-huh," it said, following with a hiss.

Gorlee moved deeper into the ranks, where the army made camp. There was little reason to begin a scuffle with the draykis. After all, they were Selene's most trusted. Them, and a handful of acolytes. He'd been clever enough to fool her. He had fooled them all, taking on the identity of Jason Haan. Selene and the draykis didn't pay much attention to the men in the ranks. She'd grouped the different races of followers among themselves. In the ranks were goblins, orcs, gnolls, and men as hard as you'd ever meet. Fat, big, ugly, or rangy, they fought for greed. Gold. A twisted form of glory. Now he sat among them, listening to their coarse talk. Their usual tone, one of ruthless mirth, was now replaced by a dull sort of melancholy. It seemed that the draykis weren't the only ones pushing them around. So were the other races, not to forget the lizard men.

"They're showing their colors," one man said. His scarred face was shadowed in the fire. "Pushing us around."

"The orcs have been hoarding our rations."

"The goblins slide away with our steel," said another man, whose beard hung to his knees. "I caught one with a quiver of my arrows and throttled him." He looked up at Gorlee. "Commander Haan, may I ask what in Narnum is going on?"

Gorlee didn't have the answer to that. The truth was he'd been more concerned about Nath. But he was aware that some of the captains, the human ones, had been kept out of some of the meetings. It happened from time to time, but of late it had been more frequent. "Don't fret. I'll speak with the acolyte chiefs at first light."

The bearded man spit a wad of tobacco on the ground and looked into the sky, shaking his head. "Something is not right about this," he muttered.

All the others continued to mumble and grumble and complain among themselves.

Gorlee didn't entirely understand it all, but he'd been around the races long enough to know that humans weren't born with as much wickedness as the other kinds. They just had an unpredictable flair about things.

He started away toward the edge of the human camp and took a walk. The entire time, he was listening to the other races. After all, he understood all their languages. Languages were second nature to him. He didn't hear much, however. The boisterous orcs were quiet. The gnolls gnawed on bones. The goblins stitched up their crude armor and painted themselves with bright, ghastly images. And the lizard men, who talked little at the best of times, now hardly breathed a hiss.

Gorlee kept walking, keeping his distance, but he could feel their eyes on him. The night air with its dripping rain contributed to an already very heavy tension.

Something is wrong, he thought. *Very, very wrong.*

He wondered if he'd been discovered. Perhaps Selene had known his identity all along. Maybe the feline fury had tipped her off after all. The dragon cat was as cunning and quick as any dragon. He tried to shake the feeling. Rubbed his hands together. He felt chilled.

Perhaps it's time to change. Surely I can make off through the woods as something undetectable. Nath Dragon needs my help.

A commotion caught his ear. A small group of goblins barreled their way into the human camp, carrying torches and making a fuss. In an instant, a crowd of angry men gathered around the goblins, shouting.

Gorlee pressed his way into the throng. "What's going on?" he yelled. "Get out of my way, men!"

The surge of bodies didn't part. Instead, the knot of men tightened, and their voices became angrier. Standing taller than all of them, Gorlee could see the goblins standing in the middle of the fray, screaming and waving their torches back and forth. They yelled in Goblin. Gorlee's blood froze as he recognized the words they said.

"Kill them, dragons! Kill them all!"

Suddenly, a large ring of dark shadows dropped from the sky, surrounding the human camp. The dragons, bigger than horses, spread their wings, corralling the dumbfounded men. Gorlee heard a sharp draw of air fill all the dragons' lungs. The dragons' eyes glowed with light, and he screamed, "Get down! Get down!"

Bright red-orange flashes roared from their mouths, setting fire to everything. To everyone. Including himself.

"No! Stop! What are you doing?"

The sound of agony. The intense heat. The horrid scramble of bodies overwhelmed him.

CHAPTER
10

THE PATH BOTTOMED OUT. SELENE stopped. The valley ahead was a barren half moon, surrounded by more mountains. Nath's stomach became a little queasy as the stench of decay riled the air.

"What is this place?" he said to Selene.

Ahead, towering stones that only giants could have lain jutted out of the ground. They stood upright in a pattern, though some of them had fallen long ago. Many were coated in vines, and some of the blocks were covered in moss and weeds. Nath figured if he could fly and look down on them, the stones would spell out something.

"More temple ruins," Selene said, taking a few slow steps forward. "I think you are familiar with them."

Nath was, but these were bigger. Some of the stones stood as high as forty feet. He noticed that on some pairs of them, other great stones rested on top, forming massive gateways. It would take a hundred horses, maybe more, to move any one of them. He followed Selene, noting the ancient rune markings on the stones. He was familiar with the ancient use of portals. The scales on his neck tingled.

"This isn't your typical ruin," he said, looking up at the top of one. A live dragon with a slithering tongue sat perched up there. A grey scaler. Its glowing green eyes narrowed on him.

Nath's eyes narrowed back. "He *is* here, isn't he?"

"You can feel him," Selene said. "Can't you?"

Dark power. Deep. Penetrating. Suffocating. Evil. It would have taken a man's breath away, dropped the stoutest warrior to his knees. A mist drifted over his ankles, hugging his scales and giving him a chill. Above, he noted more dragons perched on the stones: grey scalers, sky raiders, iron tusks, copper hides. The moonlight twinkled off their scales and claws.

"I hate to admit it, but I almost can't feel at all."

But the feeling wasn't unfamiliar to him, either. There had been days when he'd had to face his father, Balzurth, knowing he had done wrong. The power that radiated from Balzurth was unimaginable sometimes. At times, it seemed his father's mere thoughts could shake the room.

Nath swallowed. Summoned up his courage. Now he was facing a power just as great but unfamiliar. A power that wasn't warm and fiery, but instead an icy breath of death.

He then heard his father's voice inside his head. *"You can have faith in me or in your friends, but don't forget to have faith in yourself, Nath."*

"Are you scared, Nath?" Selene said, glancing back at him. "I think I see fear in your eyes. It worries me."

"And I note a tremble in your voice," he said, pulling back his shoulders and stepping to her side. "But I'd be lying if I said didn't feel fearful."

"Fear is good. It can give us an edge."

"Us?"

She didn't say anything, but it felt like a slip. A good one, the kind that gave his spirits a lift. Maybe Selene wasn't going to double-cross him? He took a deep, silent breath through his nose and into his chest, stoking the dim fires within. Onward he went with Selene, through the network of colossal stones where dragons loomed like large gargoyles on top. Selene's hand even gently brushed against his a couple of times.

"Remember," she said, slowing her pace as they approached another rectangular archway, "don't do anything unless I do something first."

"I won't," he nodded. Gawking up at the archway, forty feet tall and twenty feet wide, he noticed a great chair of stone in the distance. On either side, great urns burned with the glow of a purplish-red fire. He'd seen such thrones before, and the sight sent another sliver of ice through his scales.

A dragon, bronze and long necked, squawked above them. Other dragons squawked in return. It seemed their arrival had been announced.

"Let's go, then," Nath said. And through the archway they went.

CHAPTER

11

"**W**HAT IN GUZAN'S BEARD IS that?" Brenwar said, staring up into the sky.

Bayzog had returned with Samaz, but he'd kept Samaz's dream to himself. After all, dreams were open to interpretation.

"It looks like a rock," Ben said, craning his neck and shielding his eyes.

The sun was rising again, and Bayzog hadn't bothered to say anything until now. Everyone needed all the rest they could get, especially Sasha. Her pale eyes were bleary, and she stood by everyone else, gaping and yawning.

"How can this be, Bayzog?" she said. "It glows. Is it a dragon? A monster?"

Shum and Hoven crept along either side of her, staring as intently as everyone. Neither of the pair was ever rattled, so calm and poised in their expressionless demeanors. Now there was a puzzled, almost amazed look in their eyes. They glanced at each other and then at Bayzog.

Shum said, "Can you see it now, Bayzog?"

"It should seem familiar," Hoven added.

"Well, if you can see what it is, then why don't you spit it out?" Brenwar said, holding Pilpin by his ankles and up on his shoulders. "Does it kill the elves to be forthcoming about anything?"

"Why would that kill us?" Shum said.

Bayzog glided in between as Pilpin hopped off Brenwar's shoulders and bared his axes.

"A moment, everyone," Bayzog said, irritated, "if you please. We can wait, or I can shed some light upon this for all to see."

"Do it then, wizard," Brenwar said with a growl. "And make it quick. I'm about to pull the answers I want from a pair of elven skulls." He glared at Shum and Hoven. "That's no jest."

Bayzog spread his arms out wide, revealing his slender hands from the wide necks of his sleeves. His fingers drummed the morning air, and he started an incantation. Before his eyes, the air shimmered with new life. The distant view of the land and sky twisted and warbled. He summoned more power within and muttered the final word of the spell in Elven.

"*Ishpahlan!*"

Ben gasped the loudest of the group. Some of the others stepped back.

"By my beard, what have you done?" Pilpin said in wonderment.

"It's a wall of enhanced imagery," Bayzog said, "making everything appear much closer than it is."

"You can do that?"

"Fantastic, Father!" Rerry said, stepping closer to the wall. "Why haven't you shown me this before?" Everything was closer, ten times at least. The trees, the rocks, the birds that flew in the sky. Rerry stretched his hand out.

"Don't touch it!" Bayzog warned. "And don't stare so long, either. It'll make you dizzy."

Brenwar stood close by, clawing his beard and grumbling to himself. "Where'd that rock go?"

Bayzog narrowed his eyes. It took time to adjust to looking through the magic wall, but just when he saw it, Brenwar cried out.

"It's the Floating City!"

"That city?" Ben said, stepping closer. "Great Guzan! I see it now!"

The Floating City was there, floating straight toward them through the sky. Where it had seemed miles away, now it seemed as if it was right on top of them.

"Dragons are pulling that thing, Father," Rerry said. "Hundreds of them!"

There they were, shackled by enormous chains to collars around their necks: dragons. All sorts. Black winged. Black tailed. All their eyes had a soft, green, radiant glow. Their leather wings labored over their backs as they pulled the city forward.

Bayzog felt Sasha's hand on his arm.

"Dearest," she said, "you have goose bumps. Never in my life have I ever seen you so stricken before."

"What do we do, Father?" Rerry said, drawing his sword. "What do we do?"

"I'll tell you what I'm going to do," Brenwar said. "I'm going to follow that city!"

CHAPTER

12

WHEN THE SQUAWKING OF VULTURES roused him, Gorlee's eyes fluttered open. He coughed, spat, and wiped the grit from the melted eyelets of his helmet. He rolled onto his back, wondering what was happening. A foul stench lingered in the air. He coughed again, louder this time, scattering the vultures that had landed.

How long have I been out?

He remembered the dragons. The intense heat. The screams. He had channeled his powers, changed, and blacked out, moments from his own flesh being charred to the bone. He pulled off the helmet he wore and studied the warped metal. The leather straps of his armor cracked and fell away. He peeled the remnants of metal from his stony skin and surveyed the area.

Oh my!

The human camp was smoke and ash now. Piles of bones and armor. Crawling on hands and knees, he looked around. Every man was dead. No survivors. The human ranks of Barnabus were gone.

So were the dragons, to his relief.

"What happened?" he gasped. "Why did they do this?" He staggered to his feet and stumbled through the ash. "Why did they leave so suddenly? I couldn't have been out that long, could I?"

Judging by the sun, it was nearing the end of the next day, or so he thought. But he wasn't sure. He broke off more of the stony cocoon that had formed over his skin, saving him from a certain end. Feeling weak and drained, he glanced at his pinkish skin.

"I'll need something thicker than that." He held his stomach and took a knee. "That dragon fire really sapped me." With the ghost of a new instinct born of playing Jason Haan for months, his hand fell to his waist and searched for his sword. He broke the brittle scabbard from the belt. The sword was gone. "Great. But when did I ever really need such a thing?"

Forcing himself up to his feet, he made his way through the camp. It seemed the army had taken a turn away from the path Selene and Nath had followed. He checked the sky.

No dragons. Good.

Heavy in thought and trying to figure out what was going on, he headed down the path Nath had taken.

I don't know what's happened, but I hope I'm not too late to aid Nath Dragon.

CHAPTER

13

Passing under the huge stone, Nath's senses caught fire. The landscape, the great throne, the colors of everything changed. He swore the sun rose and set. The moon emerged, dimmed, and made way for the sun to come out again. Holding his head, he squeezed his eyes shut and fought for his balance.

"What trick is this?" he said, reaching out for Selene. "Where are you?"

"I'm here," she said, clasping her arm in his. "Easy, Nath. The feeling will pass."

He pulled away and straightened himself. The moving ground seemed to settle beneath him. He glanced back at the monstrous portal. This side of it was still there, but changed somehow.

"Tell me," he said, "what is that?"

"A barrier in time. It can move you forward or move you back. In this case," she said, tilting her head toward the sky. "It moved us forward."

As Nath looked up, every fiber of his being became taut. "Impossible!"

The Floating City hovered above. The jaxite stones, bright and brilliant blue, pulsated with eerie power.

"Isn't it magnificent?" Selene said, checking her nails. "It was one of my better ideas, actually. Using a few small stones only controlled a few dragons, but with the entire city of stone, well, I believe Gorn Grattack can control them all."

Nath gaped. This wasn't something he would have ever imagined. Control of the entire city's worth of powerful jaxite just might bend the will of all dragons who came near. Nalzambor wouldn't stand a chance.

"I thought we were in this together, Selene."

"Don't misunderstand me," she whispered, looking around. "I came up with this beforehand. I didn't expect it to bear fruit already, but seeing it now, well." She sighed. "It's exhilarating."

"You cannot control all of that power."

"No, Nath, you're right, I cannot."

Golden eyes as big as moons, Nath watched the dragons who rested on their perches atop the buildings in the city. They had great metal chains around their necks.

"Did they pull it here?" he said to Selene. His blood became hot, and smoke rolled from his nostrils. "Was that your idea, too?"

"No, Nath Dragon," said a powerful, self-assured, bone-rattling voice. "It was mine."

Nath twisted his hips around and found himself facing the monstrous form of a dragon man.

"Allow me to introduce you to my master, Nath." Selene opened her palm out for display. "This … is Gorn Grattack."

Nath felt his heart skip and then pound like thunder. This dragon man's evil aura disrupted every scale and every fiber of his makeup. Gorn stood eight feet in height, with great horns combed back from his head. His penetrating eyes burned with ice-cold fire. His countenance had hard, terrifying features. His scales shifted between white, grey, and black. His hands were great paws with steel-rending claws. Chin high and shoulders broad, there was an omnipotent air about him.

"Time to talk, Nath Dragon," Gorn said, turning his back on him. A great tail swept over the ground behind him as he headed toward the throne. "Come."

Nath had fought creatures far bigger than Gorn—giants, ettins, dragons, and the lurker—but he had never felt as small as he did now. Unlocking his frozen knees, he moved forward as if with a will not his own. The commanding power of Gorn's voice was overwhelming, much like that of his father, Balzurth.

Selene's firm but gentle touch pushed him along.

His eyes met hers.

They spoke to him through his muddled thoughts. *Don't do anything until I do.*

She had said that, but it might be too late to do anything by then. He'd have to trust her for now. He took a breath. Forced himself forward. He could handle being in the presence of his father, the most powerful dragon of all.

Certainly I can handle Gorn.

Blood rushed through him. His aversion to evil ignited over and over. His thoughts raced. What would become of Nalzambor under Gorn's rule? It would be devastated.

I must stop this monster! he thought, but the conviction was not there. *But how?*

Gorn stopped at the stone throne—which was still far too big for him—and turned.

"Can you feel it, Nath Dragon?" Gorn said. His tongue licked out, tasting the air.

"Feel what?"

"Defeat," Gorn said, hissing somewhat. "Inevitable defeat."

Nath pulled his shoulders back a little, lifted his chin, and said, "I'm surprised, Gorn. I thought you'd be more confident than that. I'm more than happy to accept your surrender." He looked at Selene, dusted his hands off, and added, "That was easy."

Gorn laughed a booming laugh. "Ha!" Flames shot from his nose. "I must admit, I've not done that in centuries. I give you credit, foolish gnat."

"It's Nath!"

Gorn's clawed hands clutched in and out. His black tongue licked over his snout. He then said, "I bet your father doesn't appreciate your clever tongue, but I find merit in it. The same as I do in a jackal when it laughs. Ha-ha-ha. Nath Dragon, Balzurth's lone spawn, born with a foul tongue. It's no surprise he is so disappointed in you."

"Everything can be disappointing. It just depends on your perspective of things. For example," Nath said, moving closer. "I'm disappointed in you. I expected you to be bigger. Scarier. But you're hardly a monster at all. I've seen worse." He glanced at Selene. "I've faced more terrible. Are you sure this is the Dark Dragon Lord?"

"Mind yourself, fool!" Selene said, drawing her hand back. "Silence your tongue!"

Nath couldn't. He tended to run his mouth when he was scared. It was a reflex of sorts. Something about his mouthing off soothed him within. Dropping his hands to his hips, he faced Gorn. "What do you want of me, Gorn? Do we fight? Talk? Bicker like old women at one another? Does my death give you victory in this war?"

"I don't need your death to win," Gorn said. "I won the moment you stepped through that portal. Ha-ha-ha."

Nath felt his scales stand up on end. What had happened? What had he done? "I don't see how."

"Oh," Gorn said, rubbing his chin, "you don't see it? Well then, let me show you." Gorn stretched his arms out toward the great stone portal and huffed in Dragonese. A brilliant mirage of dark colors twisted and turned within.

Slowly, images formed.

Nath turned and gaped.

Dragons covered the world in flame.

CHAPTER

14

THERE IT WAS. DRAGONS. DEVASTATION. Towns burned. People dead. Prisoners shackled. Nath had to catch his breath. Never had he imagined such horrors.

"How can this be?" he said in little more than a whisper.

The dwarves marched from Morgdon. The elves from Elome. The orcs of Thraag and their horded army descended from the north. The image in the great portal gave Nath glimpses of the entire world. He'd watch long enough, enthralled, only to see the image change into another. His blood raced.

"What of the Truce?" he yelled a Selene. "You knew of all this!"

"As I said," Gorn began, "the Truce, or rather, the Lie, has ended. It ended before it even started."

Nath turned back to the portal. Dragons soared the skies, scraping the building tops with roaring flames gushing from their mouths. Towns he'd seen before were now cinders, the people dead, enslaved, or lost.

"What is the meaning of all this?" he said, turning and not holding back his anger. He clenched his fists, chest heaving. "Tell me why you do such wretched things!"

"I do this because dragons were meant to rule this world. Not men. Not elves. Not dwarves. Dragons!" Gorn said, stepping closer. He poked Nath in the shoulder, knocking him a step backward. "All will submit to me. Those who don't will perish. Especially your friends, Nath Dragon." He pointed at the grand mural. "Take a look. See."

He saw Brenwar wielding his war hammer and barking orders. Ben unleashed exploding arrows from Akron. Bayzog stood behind them, face in distress, arms shaking, shielding them and the others behind them. Dragons had them pinned down in the mountains, raining down blasts of fire upon them. They wouldn't last. They needed his help. Now. The image faded from one form to another. In Quintuklen, the city of humans, tall towers burned. The Legionnaires fought dragons and giants on the hillsides. Wave after wave of gnolls and goblins assaulted them.

Stretching his hand toward the portal, Nath said, "Wait!" He needed to see what happened to Brenwar, Ben, and Bayzog.

"I've waited long enough," Gorn said with a sneer. "The end is what it is."

Nath's knees weakened. It wasn't supposed to be this way, was it? How had everything happened so fast? The portal must indeed have moved him through time. He needed to move it back. The image changed from one scene to another. He saw a blast of dragon fire shatter Bayzog's shield and drive Brenwar to his knees.

"Nooooo!" Nath yelled. He gathered his legs and sprang through the portal. The image faded, and he fell face first on the ground. Spitting the dirt out of his mouth, he glared back at Gorn and Selene.

Gorn was laughing. "Fool!" the dragon warlord said, crossing his arms over his chest. "A fool indeed. Perhaps this fool would like to make a bargain."

Nath came to his feet. "I don't bargain with evil."

"Is that so?" Gorn lifted a scaly brow. "Even if it could save your friends? Save most of the world, perhaps?"

"No."

"I think you should at least look and see what I have to offer, Nath." Gorn turned and started to walk away, and Selene followed. "Come."

Eyeing the dragons perched on the stones above, Nath followed after them with a heavy heart. His friends were in danger. Possibly dying. And all he was doing was nothing.

This can't be happening. It can't be!

Above, he heard a rattle of chains. He stopped to look. The dragons tethered to the Floating City took flight. With great effort in their wings and angry growls coming from their throats, they began pulling at the chains tethered to the city. Slowly, inch by inch, foot by foot, the city began to spin clockwise.

Sultans of Sulfur! What are they doing?

He followed Gorn and Selene behind the great stone throne. Ahead, Gorn had stopped. His broad, muscular, scale-ridged back blocked the view of something that captured his attention. Selene stood at the monster's side, tail sliding side to side in unison with Gorn's. She seemed insignificant beside him. It reminded him of how Nath felt ofttimes when he stood beside his father.

Could he be her father? That would explain a lot.

If that were the case, his cause might be lost already. Nath proceeded, coming to a stop beside Selene, where a large altar of stone sat on the brown and dusty ground. A dragon was chained down on the bloodstained slab. A gold one.

"You dare!" Nath said. He jumped up on top of the dais and tugged at the moorite chains, straining.

The dragon's eyes fluttered open. She had long lashes and beautiful pink- and gold-flecked eyes. She moaned, soft and miserable.

"Release her!"

"No," Gorn said, slowly shaking the great horns on his head. "I cannot do that. But you can, Nath Dragon. You can release her from this life that offers only a horrible end." Gorn reached over and grabbed a great spear that was stuck in the ground. It was eight feet in length and had a large, barbed head and a razor-sharp tip. "Her life for your friends' lives."

Still tugging at the unbreakable links, Nath groaned, "Aaarererer!" and his brow beaded with sweat. "I don't do your evil deeds!" he said through clenched teeth. "Not now! Not ever!"

Gorn eyed the spear tip. "Please. Settle yourself. You're in no condition to break those chains." He thumbed the edge. "Sharp. Now Nath, do you know the best way to kill a dragon? After all, we have scales, harder than steel. Armor all over. We are fast, but we can still be defeated. What is it that kills us so well?"

Nath didn't answer. Instead, he eased his efforts and rubbed the dragon's head. She snorted a little. Selene had already tried to fool him into killing one dragon, a rose blossom, before. Why would they tempt him now and try to make him kill a magnificent golden-tailed lady, the sweetest and gentlest of all the dragon breeds, if not the rarest as well?

"The heart," Gorn continued. "One swift, hard strike will do it. But not with just anything. It takes magic steel, or an enchanted dragon part, such as a horn. That is what this fine tip is crafted from, the horn of a steel dragon. I think you knew this one once."

Nath sneered. All he could think of was the one he had met guarding the tombs in the Shale Hills. That dragon was a powerful one. More powerful than inferno, maybe.

"Take it," Gorn said. "Better her life be lost to a friend than to my kind." Somehow, the dragon warlord smiled. "Consider it mercy, far better treatment than what I have in store for your friends."

A lump formed in Nath's throat. He glanced at Selene.

There was a glimmer of sympathy in her dark eyes.

"I'm not feeling very patient, Nath Dragon." He held the spear out toward Nath. "Her life for your friends' lives. You must decide now."

CHAPTER

15

"Hold on! Hold on!" Sasha yelled. She'd locked her hands around Bayzog's waist and now began feeding him power. "I'm with you!"

They'd followed the Floating City for three days, trying to keep up as it moved swiftly beneath the clouds. The dragons that hauled it along had paid them so little mind that for a long time, Bayzog had no reason to believe they even saw them. Then they had struck.

Huddled inside a small ravine in the hills, Bayzog secured them with his shield. It had begun to crack under the blistering heat. Dragons dove from the air, blasting fire one right after the other.

"We have to find a way out of here," Brenwar yelled. "Pilpin, find us a hole!" The grizzled dwarf wound up his war hammer. Beside him, Ben reloaded his bow. "Let them have it!" He released the hammer. Ben shot his bow.

The war hammer shattered the teeth of a diving grey scaler.

Crack!

An exploding arrow busted the wing of another.

Boom!

Both dragons spun out of control and slammed into the rocky slopes of the mountain.

"For Morgdon, lizards!"

Another series of flames danced and sizzled on Bayzog's shield. Gripping the Elderwood Staff with all his might, he summoned more power. The cracks in the shield strengthened. Above, in the nooks in the rock, Shum and Hoven went to work with their Dragon Needles, jabbing at anything that came close enough to attack, keeping some of the smaller crawling dragons at bay.

"Father," Rerry said, brandishing his sword, "let me fight!"

"No, Son! Stay back."

"But—"

"I said *no*."

"Brenwar," Ben said, firing another shot, "what about your hammer?"

"Guzan!" Brenwar yelled. He dashed away and disappeared over the edge of the ravine.

"Get back here!" Ben yelled. "You'll get slaughtered out there!" He looked back at Bayzog. "I have to go after him."

"Don't," Bayzog said, starting his argument, but Ben was already dashing out of the ravine. Rerry followed, lithe as a gazelle. "Rerry, come back!"

"Rerry!" Sasha screamed after her son. "No!" She released Bayzog, stumbled over the loose stones in the ravine, and fell. Pain erupted in her face.

"Sasha!" Bayzog said, reaching out for her.

A roar of flame coated the shield. The bright-orange, blistering flames blinded his eyes. A bolt of lightning lanced through the shield, and again it began to crack.

Ssszram!

Another bright blast came, shattering the shield into shards and knocking Bayzog from his feet. Numb and shaking, he rolled off his back and tried to gather his feet. Strong hands hoisted him up. He looked back and saw Samaz.

"Look!" Samaz said with wide fear-filled eyes. "Mother!"

Twenty feet away, Sasha was hemmed in by a pair of dragons, a blue streak and a grey scaler, each standing one head taller than Sasha. Tongues licked from their mouths, and angry hisses came forth.

Brow buckled, Bayzog unleashed power from the Elderwood Staff.

Kra-Cow!

A blinding bolt of intense golden power erupted from the staff, incinerating the grey scaler. The blue streak darted away.

Bayzog and Samaz rushed over to Sasha and helped her stand. Her robes were torn, and one knee was bleeding.

"Are you all right?"

"Yes," she said, dusting off her robes. "I should have been able to handle that. What a fool I am. I had a spell on my lips and could not—"

A great shadow filled the ravine, and all parties looked up. A huge sky raider descended, its great jaws wide open. In an instant, Bayzog finally realized his shield was gone. The scales on the beast's chest became bright like flame, and it blasted the ravine with an ear-splintering roar. Covering his ears, Bayzog fell to his knees. Sasha was shaking, and the heat alone from the great dragon's breath was suffocating. A snort of flame shot from its nose, and the blackness of its massive maw began to glow.

"Do something, Father!" Samaz said.

Bayzog's thoughts went blank.

"Did you find it?" Ben said to Brenwar, bow ready, eyeing the sky.

"No," Brenwar yelled, ripping a small tree out of the earth.

A dragon burst from the foliage, little bigger than him. Its mouth filled with flames that began to gush out.

Brenwar stuffed the small tree into its mouth. "Chew on that, fire breather!"

A copper dragon head emerged from the woodland and dashed into the clearing. Its tail swiped the ground and lifted Brenwar from his feet.

Brenwar's head cracked a rock. "I've had enough of you lizards!" He snatched up the rock his head had broken and hurled it at the dragon.

The monster slithered aside and pounced on Brenwar. Claws tore at his eyes and limbs. Its tail curled around his throat.

"Now yer making me mad," Brenwar spat at the beast. He cocked back his arm and punched it with all the power of his bracer.

Whop! Whop! Whop!

The dragon hissed. Acid flames dripped from its mouth, but the stubborn monster held on, dripping acid onto Brenwar's armor so that it sizzled and burned holes in his now-smoking beard.

"Now you've done it!"

Whop whop whop!

Whop whop whop!

The dragon's ribs cracked, making tree-like splintering sounds.

Cri-crick crick!

Its body softened and wavered. Its tail went slack around his neck.

Brenwar grabbed its tail and slung the two-hundred-pound dragon like a man slinging a cat.

It crashed into a tree and moved no more.

Nearby, Ben loosed another arrow into a dragon's neck, dropping it from the sky. The warrior locked eyes with him and nocked another arrow.

"Brenwar, look out!"

Out of nowhere, a grey scaler pounced on his back, driving him face first to the ground.

"Blasted lizards!" Fighting to regain his footing and ignoring the clawing at his back, Brenwar twisted over. He shoved the limp form of the dragon off him. "What happened?" he said. "I didn't even hit it." And then he noticed Rerry.

The young part-elf warrior brushed his light hair from his eyes, staring at the blood on his sword. "I—I killed it," Rerry said, staring down at the dragon. "With my sword."

Brenwar got up on his feet. "You did well, part of a part-elf. Now stop gawking and help me find my hammer." His eyes scoured the landscape. "Ah, there it is." Making his way toward the brush, he stopped and picked up his war hammer.

Above, a great dragon blotted out the light of the sun and landed over the ravine. Another one circled over the first.

"Sultans of Sulfur," Ben said. "Not another one."

"We have to get back," Rerry said, "Mother and Father are up there!"

CHAPTER

16

A STORM BREWED INSIDE NATH DRAGON. The mere idea of shedding innocent blood infuriated him. After all, he was the one destined to protect the dragons from such horrific things. Now Gorn and Selene had tried in a more subtle way to get him to kill an innocent dragon, a female. It was madness. Why would he ever do such a thing?

He looked the dragon in the eye and petted her snout. She wasn't young, but perhaps the same age as him. Bright scaled and beautiful. A beautiful vision most people only dreamed of seeing.

"I'll save you," he softly said under his breath. "Somehow." He closed his eyes and thought of his friends. They were dying out there, all because of him. Gorn offered to save them if he killed this one dragon. And then what? His thoughts raced.

Think it through, Dragon. Think it through.

"Time is up, Nath Dragon," Gorn said. "And I'm certain your dear friends' lives hang by a thread. Seconds remain, maybe."

Lies!

Evil always lies.

Perhaps, Nath thought, *everything I've seen is a lie. Why should I do anything Gorn says? Or Selene, for that matter?* His mind turned it over in those moments. What of his friends, who he feared he'd never see again? They'd made it clear to him before that they were ready to die for him. He had never understood what that meant until right now.

He turned and faced Gorn Grattack. Stepping forward, he grabbed Gorn's spear by the tip and held it to his chest.

Gorn leered down at him, brow lifted.

"You win, Gorn. But I offer you something better. My life for hers and the lives of my friends. I need your word on that."

"What?" Selene said, coming forward, hands balled up into fists. "Don't be a fool, Nath!"

"Back away, Selene!" Gorn said, sneering at her. "You disappoint me!" Gorn pulled the spear away from Nath and rested it on his shoulder. Glowering at Nath with blazing eyes, he said, "You disappoint me as well."

"My father, Balzurth, didn't raise me to kill dragons. He raised me to save them." He swallowed. He could feel something swelling inside his chest. A wonderful epiphany of sorts. "I understand that now."

"What sort of fool would die for those who don't even care about him? All your life, have the dragons not rejected you?"

"I'm over it," Nath said, stepping forward and taking a knee with a newfound inner strength. "If I have to die for them, then so be it."

"Nath, don't!" Selene said.

"Silence!" Gorn said, in more of a roar than a word. His rumbling voice shook the ground. "Nath Dragon, do you know what a pawn is?"

"Of course I do," Nath said, looking up at Gorn's terrifying face. "And I suppose you're going to tell me I've been a pawn all along. A tool of my father's. Even so, I stand by my word and his words. If it's his will for me to be his pawn, then so be it. I believe in him."

Gorn sneered and tossed back his head and let out a frightening roar.

Nath wasn't sure if Gorn felt angry or triumphant.

Above, the Floating City continued to spin around and around, getting faster and faster.

"Your father has his pawn," Gorn said. "And I have mine. The jaxite combined with my power will bring even more dragons under my control. Once I have them, I'll take over your father's precious Dragon Home and make it once again my Mountain of Doom."

"Not without a fight."

"He won't put up much of a fight after you're gone, let me assure you." Gorn bounced the spear off his shoulder. "Huh," he said, snorting smoke, "part of me wants to thank you, but I don't thank anyone." He started to lower the spear. "And I've waited long enough for this."

Nath lifted his chin and closed his eyes. He heard his heartbeat in his ears and felt Gorn poised to strike. He didn't flinch when the spear sliced through the air.

Glitch!

He heard the tip pierce through scales, separating bone and marrow. He didn't feel a thing.

A soft, painful moan caught Nath's ears.

His eyes snapped open, and he screamed.

"Selene!"

CHAPTER
17

AFTER THE SLAUGHTER, GORLEE HAD scraped up fragments of armor, strapped them on, and taken on the form of a lizard man. He'd pushed though the heavy brush of the hillside, avoiding the path Selene and Nath had taken. Wingless dragons patrolled the path along the harsh woodland, escorted by draykis. He'd already had enough close calls the past few days. He'd gotten close, only to be pushed back again. His thick lizard hide saved him aggravation when hiding in the thorns and thistles.

Why do I have the feeling I'll not get within a mile of Nath Dragon?

He kept hoping a human patrol or squad of the army would come down the path, but it didn't happen. It was just draykis and dragons, not to mention the fiery eyes that peered down at him. The valley he sought to invade was a well-fortified hole.

Through the trees, he eyed two armored draykis leading a pair of six-legged blue dragons the size of ponies. The dragons snorted at the path, sniffing the leaves on the trees and growling.

Gorlee hunkered down deep into the brush. His heart started pounding. He'd been evading the dragons for days, but he couldn't keep it up much longer. They knew he was near. They'd figure him out.

Be still. Don't take any chances.

"Come on," a draykis said, tugging on the chain that held the dragon by a heavy collar on its neck. "All you're doing is sniffing branches." He jerked the chain.

The dragon blasted fire at his feet.

The draykis hopped over the flame toward the dragon and swatted its horned head.

Whop!

"Don't do that again!"

The dragon's throat rumbled, but its neck bent down. Slowly, it turned and headed back down the path. The other draykis and dragon followed.

Gorlee gave it a few minutes and let out a breath.

Whew!

Once again, he pushed through the thickets and came to a stop on a crag that overlooked a crescent moon–shaped valley. It was distant, but among the treetops he could make out great stones standing tall in the valley. At least a dozen dragons were perched on those rocks, and more were coming. They glided in and landed while others departed and disappeared. But that wasn't what enamored Gorlee at the moment.

I never would have believed it if I wasn't seeing it for myself.

The Floating City hovered above, with the jaxite stones twinkling and throbbing with life. Nath Dragon had caught him up on a few things, and the Floating City this had to be. He also recalled the undead army that waited inside, and he started to count all the dragons perched on the building tops. There must have been at least a hundred that he could see, and others that weren't tethered by chains were still flying in and out. A chill went through him.

What kind of army can stand against such a fortress?

Ignoring the trepidation within, he renewed his descent to the bottom of the mountain and the crescent-moon valley below.

I don't know if Nath Dragon needs me, or if I need him.

Gorlee had made it another hundred yards or so when a loud commotion cut through the trees. It sounded like a fire and a skirmish of sorts. He swore his keen ears heard a woman cry out. He shook his head.

It's a trap. It must be.

Nath had told him how some dragons played games when they baited their prey. He needed to be careful when he heard strange calls that cried out through the darkness. He glanced down the hill. He was getting closer to his goal, and he felt drawn to those great stones, but the sounds he heard were too tempting. Trusting his instincts, he rushed off toward the sound of danger.

Heroes do stupid things like this all the time.

He hopped a fallen tree, sped down into a clearing, and surged toward the other side.

Ssslap! Ssslap!

Dragon tails hanging like vines from the branches knocked him onto his backside. Two forest-green-scaled dragons plopped to the ground, heads low and hissing. In an instant, they had scrambled over the ground, and fierce jaws seized him by the leg and arm.

Gorlee screamed. The pain was blinding.

Change form! Change form!

The jaws of the black-tailed emerald dragons locked, and like angry bulldogs they tried to tug him apart.

"Nooooo!"

CHAPTER

18

BLANK. BAYZOG, WHO PRIDED HIMSELF on being prepared for anything great or small, was dumbstruck.

"Father!" Samaz said again.

Eyes filled with destruction, the sky-raider dragon's chest glowed with new light. Flames shot out of its nose.

Screaming, "Give me that!" Sasha snatched the Elderwood Staff from his grip and held it out before them.

The ancient piece of polished wood glowed with an intense, brilliant white light.

The dragon roared and recoiled.

"Be gone, monster!" Sasha yelled as the staff's light became brighter and brighter.

Samaz rushed alongside his mother and yelled as well. "Go!"

The dragon turned its neck and shielded its eyes with its wing, letting out an awful-sounding roar that shook the mountain.

Bayzog shook his head, blinking. *What am I doing?*

Suddenly, the radiant light winked out, and he heard Sasha say, "Oh no!" She didn't have control over the staff, but she'd had just enough to distract the dragon.

Baring its claws, it turned on them again with a nasty angry growl.

They were still cornered.

Gathering his wits, he bounded over and grabbed the staff.

"I'm sorry, Bayzog," Sasha said, "I tried."

"You did well! Now get behind me and hold on to me and the staff. Both of you!"

As the dragon started to let loose its breath, Bayzog felt power surge through him like never before. The wills of Sasha and Samaz forged a desperate bond with his and let loose a cannon of power.

Sssrazz-Booom!

A blast of blue-white energy punched a whole clean through the dragon and sent it spinning in the air. It flopped in midair and tumbled crashing through the trees, toppling timbers and pines in its death throes. Its ear-splitting howl was knee bending.

Bayzog took a deep breath and let both his own power and that of the staff fill him. He'd been holding back for years, decades even, but he couldn't hold back now. This was it.

"Stay close," he said to his family, "And thank you. Your bravery saved us."

"We are here to help," Sasha said, catching her breath, "I'm more than a lovely face, you know."

"Father," Samaz yelled, pointing toward the sky. "Another dragon comes!"

"Kill that dragon!" Brenwar yelled, winding up his hammer. "I've had my fill of them!"

Just as he finished saying it, a bolt of power ripped through the back of the sky raider that landed, sending it hurtling through the trees.

The second dragon sailed downward in its place, its claws and fangs bared.

Twang!

An exploding arrow rocketed through the air and hit the dragon underneath its wings, which sent it spinning out of control.

"Good shot," Rerry said, "but we need to finish it."

Ben and Rerry darted ahead and sprinted for the ravine. Legs churning, Brenwar huffed along behind them, dragging Pilpin along with him. He glanced above and noted that the skies were clear. Only the Floating City remained behind them, and it had dragons whizzing out of it and draped all over it. He clambered up the hill as fast as his stout legs would take him, following the busted trees in the forest.

"Where'd you go?"

Crack!

Out of nowhere, a tail whipped out and sent both Brenwar and Pilpin spinning head over heels. He pushed his face out of the dirt and shook his beard. Head low, a grey scaler crept in with its tongue slithering out of its mouth.

Brenwar swung and missed.

Whoosh!

Pilpin was going in when a bolt of lightning shot from the dragon's mouth and hit Brenwar square in his chest plate.

Zap!

Every hair stood up on end, and he staggered back into the trees with a painful tingling from head to toe. He shook his head like an angry bull and said, "Now you've made me mad!"

The dragon darted in at full speed, knocking Pilpin clean away with its tail.

"Aaaaahhhhhhhhhh!" Pilpin cried as he sailed over the trees.

Timing it, Brenwar brought War Hammer around with all his power. A thunder clap followed.

Ka-Pow!

A dragon horn shattered, and the beast sagged to the ground.

Still tingling, Brenwar forged ahead.

The sky raider, ten tons of scales and towering twenty feet high, fought everything coming. Shum and Hoven darted in and out with their Dragon Needles. Ben volleyed arrow after arrow, and Rerry taunted the beast.

Mad and confused, the dragon struck. Its claws tore up the ground as it pounced after Rerry.

"Eep!" Rerry said, springing away from the snapping jaws of the dragon at the last second.

Shum knifed inside and jammed a Dragon Needle in its eye.

The dragon reared up with a roar, and a blast of yellow flames shot out of its mouth. In a flash, its great tail swept over the ground.

Ben and Rerry moved, but not fast enough. The tail swept them aside and flung them across the ground. Both man and part elf lay still and broken.

"No!" Brenwar yelled, charging straight for the dragon's belly. Speeding underneath its swinging tail, he smashed it in the belly. Ancient metal powered by magic bracers met ancient scale.

Krang-Boom!

Scales shattered. Bones splintered. The dragon staggered backward on its haunches and fell.

Hoven, like a shadow, moved in and struck.

Glitch!

He pierced the dragon's chest, straight into its heart.

The beast huffed one last breath of fire, and its glowing eyes went out as it died.

"Ben! Rerry!" Brenwar rushed over to them. They were breathing. "Wake up!"

"Perhaps a gentler approach," Shum said, strolling over.

Brenwar shoved him away and kneeled down to pinch Ben.

Ben's eyes snapped open. "Ow!" The warrior started to his feet. "Ow!"

"I didn't even touch you that time," Brenwar said.

Ben winced. "I think my arm is broken."

"Well, you should have been paying better attention," Brenwar said. "Ducked, jumped, or something."

"Not everyone is made out of stone like you dwarves."

"Oh!" Rerry said, as Shum and Hoven jostled him up, "and I think my leg is broken."

Brenwar shook his head. "Great, just great. Now I'm going to have to carry the both of you."

"You aren't carrying me," said Ben, "My legs are just fine."

A branch cracked from somewhere nearby. Everyone's stance became battle ready. Shum and Hoven crept forward and spread out wide just as a figure emerged.

It was Pilpin. "Save any dragon for me?" he said, lifting his brow.

"Did you find us a cave yet?" Brenwar said.

"No, did you?"

"Pah!"

A moment later, Bayzog, Sasha, and Samaz emerged from the brush.

"Rerry!" Sasha said, rushing over to his side.

"I'll be fine, Mother. I'm just glad you and Father are well." He looked at his brother, who had the faintest smile on his grim face. "Even Samaz."

Change form! Change form!

Gorlee could feel the emerald dragons biting down into his flesh, sinking their teeth in deeper and deeper. He screamed. "Ee-yah!"

One tugged on his arm and the other pulled on his leg, stretching his body taut as a bowstring.

Come on, change, Gorlee!

It was hard to concentrate and fight the blinding pain at the same time. All his life, he'd been clever enough to avoid such unpleasant circumstances. But today, this very minute, it had all caught up with him.

They're going to eat me! Guzan, no!

He squeezed his eyes shut, blocked out the pain, and thought of the hardest thing that he knew. He saw the great stones in the valley, and his skin began turning to living stone. His pain faded, and his strength renewed. With his free arm, he punched one of the dragons in the head. Its jaws loosened, and it recoiled with a hiss. He grabbed the other one by the horns and twisted its neck until it released his arm. Its claws raked at his stony skin. Gorlee flung it away.

"Be gone, lizards!"

With leery eyes and tongues flickering from their mouths, the dragons flanked him. Their black tails slithered from side to side.

Gorlee kicked at them. "Go away if you know what's good for you!"

Together, the dragons opened their mouths and spat out blasts of bright-green fire. The flames engulfed Gorlee from head to toe.

"Argh!"

His stony skin was tough, but nothing was completely resistant to dragon fire. The suffocating heat dropped him to his knees, and he curled up into a ball. His stone-hard skin sizzled.

Hang on, Gorlee! They can't breathe out forever! Hang on!

The roar of fire filled his ears. Every second felt like ten. The heat was excruciating. Unbearable. He felt faint and dizzy. He tried to concentrate on something else, anything else, but he couldn't focus.

I'm not going to make it.

Whoosh!

The flames stopped. The air felt ice cold on his smoking skin. He opened his eyes and started to rise.

"Stay still, lizard man," a voice said. It was familiar, dwarven.

Two tall elven men with pot bellies stood over the emerald dragons with spears driven into them. The dragons were dead, and the dwarf who spoke was …

"Brenwar?"

"What kind of lizard man are you?" Brenwar said.

Another dwarf, much smaller than Brenwar, rushed in and chopped his axe into Gorlee's leg. The blade skipped off.

"This lizard man is a living statue," Pilpin said. He swung his axe into the back of Gorlee's legs this time, sweeping him off his feet. "A fallen statue."

Suddenly, Gorlee was hemmed in with spear tips and axe blades.

One of the elven men spoke, pointing a spear tip at his neck, saying, "This will penetrate anything."

Brenwar jostled his axe over him, saying, "And this will do much worse than what this elf thinks he can do."

Gorlee swallowed hard. His friends weren't toying with him. And judging by the hard looks in their battle-scarred faces, he'd better be careful how he chose his next words. Slowly, he held up his palms, closed his eyes, turned his cheek and said, "I'm Gorlee. Please don't kill me, friends?"

CHAPTER

19

"Y OU SAY HE'S DOWN THERE?" Bayzog said. He stood on an overlook, hidden by the trees. All the others were there except Ben, Sasha, and Rerry. She was treating the wounded. "The Half Moon Valley of Stones. Interesting."

"What's so interesting about it?" Brenwar said, looking through a spyglass. "Just roughhewn stones."

"They're portals."

"To where?"

Bayzog ignored him. He was more interested in what Gorlee, who stood beside him in the form of a large roughhewn stone himself, had to say. He stared at the changeling.

"What? Better than a goblin—or a dwarf," Gorlee said to Brenwar.

"Hah!"

"Perhaps you'd prefer an orc," Gorlee said. "I expected you'd be glad to see me."

"Glad … har, never!"

"It's not your appearance," Bayzog said, "it's your story. Nath Dragon and Selene. Why would he do such a thing?"

Gorlee had already told them about his abduction and Selene's betrayal, but he still didn't understand Nath's motivation.

"I guess Nath needed to see what he was up against."

"You should have stopped him," Brenwar said.

"And blown my cover? I couldn't do that. They'd have killed us all, not that they didn't try once already." Gorlee towered over Brenwar with his hands on his hips. "Hundreds of men died just after he left."

"Back up, changeling, or whatever you are." Brenwar poked at him with the war hammer. "I'm not going to mourn men who served on the side of evil. Now, get out of my way. I'm going down there and dragging him out myself."

"There's scores of dragons down there," Bayzog said, stepping in his way. "Not to mention the hundreds that watch from above in the city. Set your frustration and anger aside. Let's think about this. At least we know Nath is close, and I'm grateful for that."

"Hrmph!"

"We need a plan," Shum said, stepping in. "But I fear we might be too late."

"Why do you say that?" Brenwar said.

Shum pointed toward the Floating City. The jaxite glowed with new life, and the dragons tethered to the chains were flying again, with their great wings beating. Slowly, the city began to turn in the sky. Little by little, it picked up speed.

Eyes tilted upward, Bayzog said, "I have a bad feeling about this."

"What do you mean?" Brenwar said. "Spit it out, elf."

"If I were to guess … that city and all that stone, it's a beacon."

"A beacon for what?"

"A beacon that will not only attract but control more dragons."

"And how many of those do you think it will control?" Gorlee said.

"With that much jaxite? I'd say all of them."

Brenwar stormed away, found his chest, and picked it up by the outside handles. He headed back to the rest of the party and dropped it at their feet. They all stared.

"What are you looking at me like that for?"

"What do you propose we do with that," Shum said, eyeing it, "put our boots in it?"

Hoven laughed.

"Brenwar," Bayzog said, kneeling down and opening the chest up wide. "I understand what you're thinking, but even this and all the powers stored within, I don't think it will help us enough."

"Nath went in there with nothing at all, as I understand it. At least we have this. Now is the time to help him." Brenwar looked into the darkening sky. Lightning streaked across it, and more dragons flew into the city. "Now is the time. I feel it in these bones of mine."

Bayzog fingered the items in the chest. There were rows of potions in small, bright vials, ornate tokens and objects, strangely woven cloths, wands, orbs, tools, and stones of many colors. He plucked a yellow vial from the shelf and tossed it to Hoven.

"Take that to Sasha and tell her to use it on Ben and Rerry, if you please."

Hoven started to slide away, but Ben's strong voice stopped him.

"I'll take it from here," he said, coming closer and looking into the chest. His arm was in a sling, and his bearded face was scratched up something fierce. "I think what you have in there can certainly help us, but this is what Dragon needs."

Ben held out Fang, who was still sheathed in his scabbard. The dragonhead hilt's tiny gemstone eyes were glowing, and puffs of smoke flared from their nostrils. "Fang's trying to talk to me. I think he misses Dragon."

Eyes resting on Fang's hilt, the wizard's face brightened a little. He was certain Nath was alive. The possible futures shown in Samaz's dreams didn't always come to pass. It was clear to Bayzog, inside his gut, that Nath still lived. He'd been hesitant before to let his friends rush in, fearing the venture might be futile, that Nath was gone. For now, this was not the case. There was still time to help their lost friend.

"That settles it, then," Brenwar said, standing tall and picking up his war hammer, "we're going down there now."

And then the ground shook. Stones cracked. A gut-wrenching dragon bellow rose up out of the valley and swayed the trees and timbers.

"BAH-ROOOOOOOO!"

"What in Guzan's beard was that?" Brenwar said.

Another thunderous dragon cry rose up. Dragon flames blasted into the sky down from the valley.

"*What* was it?" Bayzog said, unable to hide his bewilderment. "'*Who* was it' is more like it…" All of his fears came to life. "I don't know why, but I'm certain that was—"

Brenwar stepped out on the overlook and finished his sentence.

"Nath Dragon."

CHAPTER

20

"SELENE!" NATH CRIED.

Gorn ripped the spear out of her chest. "Fool of a traitor!"

Nath caught her as she teetered backward, gasping, and fell into his arms.

"Why, Selene, why?"

Her dark eyes were spacey as she touched his cheek. "Because you are the only one who can stop him, Nath." She coughed and spat a little blood. "Only you can." Her tail snaked around his shoulder and stroked his mane of hair. "And because"—*cough-cough*—"I…"

Her tail slipped off his shoulders. Her eyes turned glassy. Selene was gone.

Tears swelled in Nath's eyes as his thoughts raced and he tried to make sense of it all. "Noooooooooo!" he yelled at the top of his lungs. "Nooooooooooo!"

His bloodshot eyes locked on Gorn, who stood nearby leaning on the bloody spear.

There was a smile on the dragon warlord's face. "She was a pawn, nothing more. Her weakness was her end." He flashed a face filled with razor-sharp teeth. "I see you share the same weakness as hers." He shrugged. "Oh well, it seems now I have to finish this." He flicked up the spear. In a snap, he flung it at Nath Dragon.

Nath shifted his shoulders and snatched the spear out of the air. "No! Now it's your time to die, Gorn! I'm going to make you pay. For this, and for everything else you've done!" He lowered the spear point. In a blur of motion, he charged.

The spear plunged through Gorn's chest with ram-like force, pinning his back against the rock.

Gorn groaned, and then suddenly he started to laugh. Loud and thunderous. "Ha! Ha! Ha! Ha!"

Slap!

Gorn's backhand sent Nath flying through the air.

After crashing into the throne, Nath scurried to his feet. His chest was heaving.

Gorn pulled the spear out of his body and flung it aside. "No stick can kill me, boy. Nothing can kill a heartless dragon."

Nath glanced at Selene's broken body. She was dead. It was impossible to believe. Eyeing Gorn, all he could do was scream at the top of his lungs, "BAH-ROOOOOOOO!"

His dragon heart charged. His dragon blood pumped like never before. His scales popped and rippled. Gorn, the stones, and Selene started shrinking. Power filled him. Awesome power that he had never felt before. At least not since that time he flew with Selene.

Gorn cocked his horned head and stared at him with suspicion. Then he glanced down at Selene with anger in his eyes. "Traitor of a daughter! You did this! You let the poison wear off!" He dipped his chin. "So be it, then."

Nath's enraged thoughts clicked into place. The food she fed him. It stifled his powers and his ability to change into a dragon. Selene had always fussed about him not eating enough, and now he understood why. But these last few days, she hadn't made him eat.

Gorn clenched his fists at his sides. His horns charged up with power. He grew and transformed, from a huge draykis-like being to a full-sized dragon and then some. He had gigantic arms, powerful legs, and a beastly and ancient smile. He let out a roar the sound of a hundred dragons in one.

"BAH-RHOOOOOOOO-THAAAAAAAAAAAAA!"

It shook the valley.

Nath Dragon, still growing, let out a thunderous roar of his own. "BAH-RHOOOOOOOO-THAA!" Nath charged.

The dragon titans, each thirty feet tall, collided.

BOOM!

Gorn's tail caught Nath behind the neck and jerked him down to the ground. A bright blast of deep-purple power shot from his mouth, pounding into Nath. It sent him skidding across the ground and back into the throne. Bright, painful spots formed in his eyes.

"Stay down, foolish Nath!" Gorn said, lording it over him. "You might have a dragon's body now, but you have no experience in how to use it. Let me teach you."

Nath shook his head and started up on his feet. He glared at Gorn. "Teach me? Hah! I'll teach you!" His chest charged up in brilliant yellow light. He unleashed the fury within. Dragon fire blasted from his mouth, slamming Gorn in the chest.

The dragon warlord teetered backward, covering his face, and fell.

Nath pounced. Landing on Gorn, he started punching with all his might. He landed one earth-shaking punch after the other.

Gorn flailed wildly and tried to scurry away, but Nath held him down and kept hammering.

Whop! Whop! Smack! Smack! Smack!

Gorn groaned. His bright-yellow eyes became wild with fear. "Yield! I yield, Nath Dragon!"

Nath paused. His dragon chest was heaving. He started to speak, changed his mind, and started to hit.

Wham! Wham! Wham!

"Please stop!" Gorn cried out. "Please stop!"

Nath held back.

"Your powers, Nath, I underestimated them. You have more mastery than I imagined." Gorn's yellow eyes turned bright as the sun. "But not more mastery than me!"

Beams of power blasted from Gorn's eyes.

Nath jerked away a split second too late.

The blast ripped through his shoulder and sent him backward.

Holding his burning shoulder, Nath forced himself up to one knee.

"Dragons," Gorn ordered to the sky, "Kill the prince. Kill Nath Dragon!"

The dragons who were patiently waiting perched on the stones spread their wings and attacked.

One of the stone portals flared with a strange swirl of mystic life nearby.

Gorn dashed through it and disappeared.

Nath raced after him, stopping short as a hull dragon, dark purple, launched itself out of the portal.

The two collided with a thunderous crash and became an angry knot of scales battling for their lives on the ground.

CHAPTER

21

IN HIS DRAGON FORM, NATH smashed his clawed fist into the hull dragon, rocking its head backward.

It regained its balance and unleashed the churning forces of its powerful breath.

Nath ducked under the searing heat and tackled it. It was bigger and slower, and Nath's superior speed and claws tore into it.

It howled in pain and fury.

Nath howled back. Angry now, he clutched its neck, pinned it down, and unleashed the fires within. The flames engulfed the hull dragon's face.

It writhed and twisted, but Nath held it fast, letting his flames do the work until the monster moved no more. Nothing but a searing, smoking skull remained when Nath stood up and pounded its face in triumph.

The celebration was cut short.

Sa-Boom! Sa-Boom! Sa-Boom!

Fireballs, lightning, acid bombs, and mystic needles assaulted him from above, where dragons filled the air, circling and diving: sky raiders, grey scalers, bull dragons, blue streaks... One right after the other, they dove and nipped, unleashing breath weapons from their mouths.

The furious assault overwhelmed Nath and dropped him to his knees. He covered up with his arms.

There must be a hundred up there!

A bull dragon flew straight into him, knocking him over. Grey scalers latched onto his legs with their teeth. Fireball after lightning bolt and lightning bolt after fireball rocked every scale on his body.

Nath punched. Clawed.

The dark dragons bit and spat.

"Get off me!"

He grabbed hold of a bull dragon and busted its wings. He ripped a grey scaler off his leg and smashed it into the stony ground.

The valley had become a furious knot of muscle and scale gone mad.

A sky raider almost as big as him landed on him and spat hot lava in his face.

Nath rammed it with his horns and blasted it with fire of his own.

It screamed and then withered away.

Shaking his back, he slung a small horde off him.

This is madness! Guzan's beard! They're everywhere!

Bigger, stronger, faster than all of them, Nath tried to take them out one at a time. Tooth and claw penetrated his scales. Dragon blood dripped everywhere. For every two he downed, four more appeared from the frenzied dragon horde.

"Enough of this!"

He gathered his feet under him, spread his wings, and took to the air. He made it up one hundred feet, then two.

Zazz-zap! Zazz-zap! Zazz-zap! Zazz-zap!

The blue razor's lightning ripped through him. Smoke and explosions filled the air. One by one, two by two, and four by four, dragons latched on, pinning his wings, tearing at his body and his legs.

"No!"

Nath twisted out of control and plummeted toward the rushing ground below. He hit one of the arches in the great stone square and plowed right through it. Through the smoke and haze, pushing the rubble and crushed dragons aside, he rose to his feet once more, great shoulders slouched. Aching. Exhausted.

A bright red bull dragon swooped right at him and unleashed its fiery breath.

Nath unleashed his.

The forces collided and exploded.

Boom!

The bull dragon made a rough landing and shook its head. Nath's breath scorched it into the earth, leaving only bones among the ashes.

Nath staggered back and braced himself against the towering stones, feeling empty inside from head to toe. His fire was gone, and he had little breath at all remaining. He glanced up at the sound of the roaring dragons that now descended by the dozens like a swarm of angry hornets.

He lifted his fists and lowered his chin, prepared for his final stand.

CHAPTER
22

"WE HAVE TO GET DOWN there and help him!" Brenwar said, eyeing the sky.

Dragons were pouring down into the valley like rain, and their breath weapons were lighting up the air.

Brenwar's chest tightened. It seemed like the entire world was assaulting his friend, Nath Dragon. "Do something, wizard!" he commanded. "Teleport us or something!"

"Patience," Sasha urged. "He's trying."

Bayzog's eyes were locked on a scroll. His lips moved quickly and spoke at a hastened pace, the words ancient and in Elven.

"Now is not the time for talk! It's the time for action."

"I'm with you, Brenwar," Ben said, rolling his shoulder and checking his arm. He tossed the potion vial to Rerry. "It'll mend you and make you feel great. Finish it." He unhitched Akron from his back. *Clatch. Snap. Clatch.* He tested the string. "Let's go, Brenwar!"

"Don't be foolish," Shum said, stepping in front of them. "Patience. There's nothing but dragons and death down there."

"Get out of our way," Brenwar growled. "Dragons. Death. Aye. And our friend is in it. Move!" He had started to shove past when Hoven stepped in as well.

"Patience!" the Roamer urged. "See what Bayzog unfolds."

"Not when I'm this close," Brenwar said, pushing his way through.

Ben fell into step behind him. "Dead or alive, I'll see you where the battle is."

Suddenly, Bayzog's violet eyes filled with light and radiated with power. His Elven words cut short. The wind picked up like a storm. A black vortex-like tunnel opened up a dozen yards behind him.

"This will take us there," Bayzog said. "Exactly where we'll come out, I'm not certain." He picked up the Elderwood Staff and grabbed Sasha's hand. "Stay here, love."

"I can't," she said, shaking her head. "I'm in this with you to the end."

"We all are," Rerry and Samaz said together.

Bayzog took a deep breath and nodded. "Brenwar!" he yelled out, "lead the way, then!"

Black beard streaming over his shoulder, Brenwar was the first one through the hole. No one was close behind him.

"I've never seen him move so fast before," Ben said, rushing after him. "But we'd better catch up—"

A large bronze dragon dropped out of the sky and blocked the path into the vortex.

"Move," Bayzog yelled, raising his staff and summoning its power.

Hot fire blasted from the dragon's mouth, bouncing off Bayzog's shield and scattering everyone.

The nearby trees erupted into flames.

Shum and Hoven burst into action. One Dragon Needle caught the bronze dragon in the neck.

Its tail whipped out and sent Hoven flying.

Ben fired two arrows.

Twang-Thunk! Twang-Thunk!

The moorite arrows sank into its chest, just missing its heart.

The dragon filled up another lungful of air.

Sprinting out of nowhere, Shum rushed in and lanced his Dragon Needle through its heart.

Its glowing eyes flashed, and its great hulking form toppled over into the vortex—which was no longer there.

"Oh no!" Ben said. "It's gone!"

All eyes gazed from the overlook down to where the battle in the crescent-moon valley raged.

"What do we do?" Sasha said to Bayzog.

He shook his head with disbelief. "I have no idea."

CHAPTER
23

NATH SWATTED HIS TAIL. HE punched. Kicked. Grabbed two grey scalers by their necks and slammed their horns together. They wilted in his grip, and he tossed them aside and prepared for the next onslaught.

Fire and lightning raced down from above, pelting him. It seared his smoking scales. Two sky raiders dropped out of the sky and flanked him. Tails coiled around his legs, they tried to pull him down. Another bull dragon landed, charged, and rammed him.

Nath toppled over, shaking the ground.

Thoom!

Small dragons swarmed him like a hive of angry bees. They pinned themselves to his arms and legs. They bit and clawed. Razor-sharp talons tore at his scales. Acid, fire, and jolts of lightning spewed from their mouths.

Nath swatted at them and peeled them off, but his strength was fading.

Keep fighting! Keep fighting!

He gave it everything he had, but their numbers and strength were overwhelming. Claws dug into his ribs. Teeth bit into his legs. It was excruciating. He let out a painful gasp as a dragon stuck a pointy tail into his neck.

Somewhere, he swore he heard Gorn Grattack laughing.

His vision began to fade.

Keep fight …

His body gave.

Krang!

A bull dragon wailed an awful awakening sound.

Krang! Krang!

A clamor of hisses erupted from the dragons.

Krang! Krang!

Nath opened his battered eyes and spied a small bearded hurricane unleashing his full fury.

"Brenwar?"

"Get off yer scaly behind, Nath Dragon!" Brenwar roared. He brought his war hammer full circle and crushed a snapping dragon's face. *Krang!* "I can't do this alone!" *Krang! Krang! Krang!* He pounded three grey scalers into submission and whirled to face the wrath of the busted-horned sky raider. "Haven't had enough, I see!" Brenwar hefted the war hammer over his head and slung it into the dragon's chest full force.

The missile of moorite howled through the air.

Ka-Chow!

The dragon roared and tumbled.

Nath was on his feet, heart pumping and legs churning, fighting through the frenzy to help his friend. "Look out, Brenwar!"

"What?" Brenwar said, turning around as he retrieved his hammer.

Another sky raider stood behind the battle with jaws the size of a tunnel stretched open.

"Don't you dare!" Brenwar said, shaking his fist at it.

The great dragon's mouth came down, and Brenwar disappeared inside.

Gulp!

"Brenwar! Nooooo!" Nath fell to his knees.

The dragons pounced.

Angry and disheveled, his thoughts a blur, he fought on until his last ounce of great strength was gone and the dragons once again pinned his trembling, broken body down.

I gave it all. I swear I did.

He felt his body being dragged over the ground as he stared weakly into the sky. He saw dragons, black winged and tailed, circling everywhere. Their eyes were green and glowing as they swooped in and out of the clouds around the Floating City.

I should have killed Gorn when I had the chance. I failed.

A flash of gold streaked through the sky. A blurred streak of silver followed. A clamor of roaring dragons filled the air like roaring thunder.

What is happening?

A tight-knit wedge of golden flare dragons sliced through the dark-winged ranks. Two gold dragons peeled off the rear of the wedge and tore a sky raider's wings asunder.

Can it be? Can it be?

A score of silver shade dragons breathed lightning bolts that blasted blue razors out of the air. The swift strike caught the evil dragons off guard, and the wave cut through them like ribbons. Seconds after the chaos, the evil dragons rallied. Gathering their superior forces, they chased the gold and silver dragons through the sky.

The golden flares and silver shades disappeared into the clouds.

Nath felt his excited heart begin to sink.

And I thought they were going to rescue me. I should have known better. I rescued them and they never even thanked me. Why would they save me now?

Out of the clouds another dragon appeared, bigger than a sky raider, pewter with purple scales and dark-red wings. His rack of horns looked like a helmet on his battle-scarred head. Magnificent was an understatement for the grand beast.

Nath sat up gaping.

The dragons that held him released him and leapt into the sky.

Is that? It cannot be!

It was. An immense flying dragon almost bigger than the land-dwelling hulls. A strange flap of scales on his chin made him look bearded. Underneath his scales were knots of rippling muscles like the bull dragon's. He blasted out a roar that drove the dark dragons away, and his grand rack of horns flared like firelight.

Rising to his feet, Nath felt his heart speed up again. *It is him.* "Great Guzan! You live!"

Guzan was the greatest dragon fighter of all. Most believed him to be a man or a dwarf, but he was all dragon, armed with tons of fury and devastation.

The dark dragons were feeling his wrath now. A rush of flame engulfed an entire flock of grey scalers and dropped them from the air.

"Yes!"

Guzan wasn't alone, either. The golden flares zipped out of the clouds, not a dozen but a hundred this time. The silver shades erupted from the mist in the same manner. There was an accompaniment of rose blossoms, green lilies, yellow streaks, blazed ruffies, steel dragons, and many others of all shapes and sizes.

Guzan led the charge, and the sky erupted in scintillating colors of flame.

Nath blinked and shook his head.

They came!

Only one dragon could have command so many.

With an exhausted sigh, Nath dropped to a knee. "Thank you, Father. Thank you, Balzurth."

He spread out his wings and started to flap. "Ow!"

His wing bones were busted, and the skin between them was torn.

"I need to help. I need to fight."

He tilted his head up and watched the carnage in the air. Dragons were dropping from the sky and crashing into the earth. Good dragons, bad dragons, they plummeted, spiraled, and spun out of control. Never in Nath's worst dreams could he have imagined such a horrible scene. The good dragons were taking it to them, in the air and on the ground. Trees shattered into splinters and hilltops burned.

It was war.

It went on for minutes that seemed like an hour.

Suddenly, the dark dragons retreated. They darted for the Floating City and disappeared within the buildings. The Floating City quickly began drifting away under a power of its own. The good dragons did not give chase.

"Finish them!" Nath yelled. "Finish them!"

He locked eyes with Guzan. The ancient dragon's scales were torn, and his wings beat with effort.

Guzan nodded, turned, and led the surviving dragons away.

Nath could hear Guzan's voice inside his head.

This battle is won, but the war is not over. Prepare yourself, Nath Dragon.

Nath surveyed the smoking carnage. Just like men after a battle, dragons lay dead everywhere. Broken. Busted. Bleeding. Scores of them had died. Perhaps hundreds. His head ached and his body shuddered. When he gazed into the sky once more, the good dragons were gone and the Floating City was disappearing over the next mountaintop. He could feel that Gorn was inside the Floating City. Plotting. Hiding.

"This isn't over."

He pushed away the carnage until he located Selene's broken form lying near the throne. She seemed so small and fragile. He shrank down to his man-sized body. Only mildly surprised to find his clothes magically on him again, he kneeled down and brushed Selene's hair aside. His chin touched his chest, and tears filled his golden eyes.

CHAPTER
24

SHUM AND HOVEN LED THE party down the mountain, through the spreading smoke and flames, toward the towering rocks. Everyone was quiet, and Sasha held Bayzog's hand tightly. He had no idea what to expect when he arrived down there, but he sensed the danger was gone for now. But what about Nath and Brenwar?

Witnessing a full-scale dragon battle for the first time had left his senses jangled. He felt so small and insignificant. At the same time, he couldn't make out whether the good dragons had won or lost. The battle had ended abruptly, with both parties moving on.

The Roamers stopped and signaled for everyone to stay back. Hoven pulled back some branches. Shum stepped though. A copper dragon with black wings lay on the ground wounded. Its wings and legs were broken. Using his spear, the Dragon Needle, Shum put it out of its misery, and the party moved on.

Branches crackled and pine cones popped, the flames were so hot.

"This entire mountain will be ablaze soon enough, Bayzog," Ben said. "It's spreading."

"Have you ever seen an entire mountain burn?" Bayzog said.

"Well, no," *cough-cough*, "I haven't."

"Have faith, then," Bayzog said, "and we should be safe in the green grasses of the valley. Make haste now."

When they were nearing the bottom and making their way onto the main path, a strange humming pricked Bayzog's ears. Shum and Hoven turned and looked back at him and nodded. All around where the flames licked at the trees, strange insect-like creatures snuffed them out.

"Do you see that?" Rerry said with wide eyes. "They're putting the flames out."

"It's fairies and pixlyns doing that," Samaz added.

"You don't know," Rerry said, limping along and bracing himself with the Elderwood Staff. His hand snatched out and caught some sort of fly. He opened his palm.

A tiny winged woman sat inside with her arms crossed over her chest, frowning.

"Er ... sorry," Rerry said with a smile.

She stuck her tongue out and buzzed away.

"Told you," Samaz said. "Pixlyns."

Rerry didn't argue.

They made it through the flames into the valley and traversed between the massive stones, searching for any signs of Brenwar and Nath.

Passing through the largest portal, Bayzog noted the massive stone throne, big enough for a titan. Nath Dragon stood beneath it, cradling a black-scaled woman in his arms. His head was down, and tears were streaming down his face. His powerful chest and shoulders shivered, and a brisk wind blew his tangled red mane over his face.

"I've never seen such a look about him before," Sasha whispered to him. Sasha slipped her hand out of Bayzog's and quickly made her way toward Nath. "Nath," she said. "Are you all right?"

Nath didn't respond.

Sasha glanced back at Bayzog and shrugged.

Gorlee found his way to Bayzog's side and whispered in his ear, "That's the High Priestess, Selene."

"She's dead," Nath said, abruptly. "And it's my fault. She saved me. I should have saved her."

"Easy, Nath," Sasha said. She reached over and rubbed his shoulder. "You're alive, and I cannot hide the joy I feel from that." She smiled. "It will be fine. Don't be so hard on yourself. I'm sure you did all you could."

Nath's face, marred with strain, frowned. His chin trembled when he said, "Brenwar's gone."

Bayzog felt his heart sink. Pilpin gasped. Even the Roamers' chins dipped down.

"It's my fault," Nath said. "All my fault. I battled Gorn. I had him. I lost." His head shook sadly from side to side. "I learned a hard lesson today: never let up on evil."

A moment of silence followed.

Bayzog contemplated things. The strained expression on Nath's face told him a horrible story. His friend was wrought with guilt and failure. But the fight wasn't over yet. He needed to lift Nath up. They could regroup. Fight again soon enough.

Pilpin waddled up to Nath. "Can you tell us what happened to Brenwar?"

Nath set Selene down and wiped his eyes. He swallowed a lump in his throat and said, "I was near my end when he arrived and saved me. He took out several dragons, and then a sky raider swallowed him. When the gold dragons arrived, that sky raider took to the sky." He surveyed the carnage. "Now the sky raider is either dead or inside that city with my friend in his belly." He kneeled down and rested his hand on Pilpin's shoulder. "I'm so sorry."

"Humph," Pilpin said. "I'm not worried about his death. He'd die for you, for me, for dwarven kind at least a hundred times. It's his funeral I'm concerned about. We can't have one without a body. I have to find that dragon. His body." He rubbed his bearded chin. "Sky raider, you say. I seem to remember quite a few of them falling." Pilpin sauntered off.

Hoven followed.

Nath sat down and buried his face in his hands, weeping.

"And I have to bury *her*."

CHAPTER

25

"WE'LL FIND THE RIGHT SPOT for her," Sasha said, wiping tears from his eyes. "A beautiful one."

"Perhaps he needs some time to mourn," Bayzog said, extending his hand to Sasha.

Nath's thoughts were racing.

"No," Nath said. "I'll feel better looking for Brenwar." He started up and eased back down. "Oof, I'm stiff." He glanced at the torn scales on his arms and legs. "But I'm alive. Just paying for it." Grimacing, he took Bayzog's hand and pulled himself up. "Would some of you mind watching over her while I look?"

"Not at all," Bayzog said. "I'll stay here with my family while the rest of you go and look for Brenwar."

Ben came forward. "I believe this is yours." He held out Fang. "And it's good to see you, Dragon."

"You too, Ben," Nath said, extending his hand. They shook and then he took Fang. The polished dragon pommel was warm in his hand. Invigorating. He caressed Fang briefly and strapped his scabbard around his waist. "I missed the both of you." He noticed two men with strong elven features he hadn't met before. "And this must be Samaz and Rerry?"

"Indeed," Bayzog said. "And that man is..."

"Gorlee," Nath said. "Yes, I know. Glad to see you survived, my friend."

"I'm glad you made it through. I had my doubts when you departed for the valley."

Nath nodded to Shum and Hoven, and they made slight bows in return.

"Well, let's go find Brenwar. As much as it hurts, it will only be worse if we don't give him a proper burial." He glanced at Bayzog. "The next step in this war will have to wait, for now."

"Agreed."

Nath and his friends started off after Pilpin. He'd made it beyond the great stone portal he'd passed through before when his scales began to prickle.

"Nath!" Sasha yelled after him. "Nath!"

He whirled around. Shum and Hoven had their elven blades ready and had formed a wall in front of Selene. Bayzog and his family had backed off.

"What are you doing?" Nath said, jogging back toward the throne.

Shum and Hoven's expressionless faces didn't speak. Behind them, a monstrous winged ape appeared with Selene in his hulking arms.

"Put her down!" Nath yelled. He started to run, but he was so weak. His legs were like lead, and he was tired. So very tired. "Shum! Hoven! What are you doing?"

Sansla Libor's eyes locked on his. A snarl bared his white fangs. He spread his wings and leapt into the sky.

"No!" Nath said, stretching out his hand, trying to change. "Bayzog! Use your staff! Stop him!"

Bayzog raised the Elderwood Staff over his head but then slowly let it down.

Sansla disappeared into the coming night.

Gathering what strength he had left, Nath rushed over and confronted Shum and Hoven.

"Traitors! What did you do that for?"

"He is our king," Shum said, sheathing his sword. "He knows what is best."

Gold eyes blazing, Nath grabbed Shum by the collar and picked the Roamer up off of his feet. "He's a monster!"

"He is our king!"

Nath slung Shum away. "No!" He fell to his knees and started pounding the ground with his fists. "No! No! No! No! No!" Chest heaving, he said. "Where is he taking her?"

"Where it is best."

"That is not an answer."

"I don't know, but it will be for the best."

"Is he going to bring her back?" Nath said, hopeful now that he remembered, "like he did you?"

"I'm afraid not. His magic only works on Roamers, and at that only every century or so. I was fortunate." Shum rested his locked fingers on his belly. "I'm certain the High Priestess is gone. But evil still lives within her. It must be destroyed."

Head down, kneeling, fists resting on the ground, Nath shuddered a breath. Selene had tormented him. Lied to him. Abused him. Was it even possible for her to be redeemed? Had she really given her life to see Gorn destroyed?

He pushed himself off the ground, swayed, and then straightened himself. All eyes were on him. He could feel the essence of his friends. They were resolute. Determined. Ready. Capable. Patient. Faithful. He lifted his chin and nodded.

"No looking back now," he said. "Let's find Brenwar. I can already hear him complaining about missing his funeral."

CHAPTER
26

THE MOUNTAINSIDE HAD BECOME A cemetery for dragons. Nath had never seen so many dead before. His stomach turned. It would be a poacher's field day.

"They all need to be buried," he said, picking up a blazed ruffie little bigger than a dog. Its orange scales still had a bright sheen to them.

"Won't the dragons return and take care of that?"

Nath shrugged and laid the dragon corpse back down. It made little sense to see dragon fighting dragon. No more sense than seeing men fighting men. Sure, dragons didn't always get along with one another, but they weren't prone to killing each other, either. *No wonder the last dragon war was so horrible.* And by the looks of things, this one would be worse. He had to end it.

"Come! Come!" Pilpin said somewhere deep in the forest.

Nath limped through the trees toward the sound of the dwarf's voice and found a sky raider in a patch of broken trees. His body still smoked, and his scales were in cinders. Both his horns were broken.

"Guzan must have taken this one," Nath said, cocking his head and looking at its eyes.

"Does it look like the one that ate Brenwar?"

Nath shrugged his shoulders. "I don't know."

"I've never seen such a huge dragon before," Rerry said. He put his hands on the dragon's head, which was bigger than a horse. "They seem smaller in the sky and so much bigger up close." He swallowed and looked at Nath. "I'm sorry about your friend." Using the pommel of his sword, he tapped on one of the dragon's teeth, which were almost as tall as him. "One swallow, huh?"

"Rerry!" Sasha admonished. She took her son by the arm and led him away.

"Is it dead?" Ben said, cocking his head. "I swear I think it's still moving."

"Sometimes a dragon's body, being so big, doesn't go right away. It fights, but it will pass."

"I can hear inside it," Pilpin said. He had his ear pressed against the dragon's great belly. "It sounds hungry, the way it's groaning. Let's cut it open. I say Brenwar is inside there, giving it a sour stomach."

Again, all eyes fell on Nath, and he wasn't certain what to say. With some effort, he shrugged again. "Do what you have to do."

Shum and Hoven walked over and unleashed their elven blades. Nath turned away. He abhorred the thought of any dragon being carved into, but he hated the idea of his friend being in there more.

"What's that?" Rerry said.

Nath turned. With a sparkle in his eye, the young part elf was staring at the dragon's great neck. The scales were rippling.

"A spasm," Nath said. "I'm certain."

The spasm started at the lower end of the dragon's neck near the belly and moved upward.

"Strangest death spasm I ever saw," Shum said, tilting his head.

A knot of rippling scales made its way toward the head.

"It's still alive," Rerry said.

"I bet its fire's coming back up," Nath added, following the moving bulge. "Everyone should stand clear. His body might buck, and the entire forest might go ablaze." The moving stopped in the next instant, and with bated breath everyone was silent.

Nath stepped in front of the mouth.

"Be careful, Nath," Sasha said, gripping Bayzog's arm.

"I hear something," Nath said, looking at Shum. "Can you hear it?"

Shum rested his ear on the dragon's upper neck. "It sounds like horrendous singing."

"Singing?" Ben said. "What song is it singing?"

"I'm not sure," Nath said, leaning closer, "wait …. It can't be."

Inside the dragon echoed a song that gave his white scales chills.

Home of the dwarves—Morgdon. Home of the dwarves—Morgdon!

We have the finest steel and ale—Morgdon! In battle we never fail—Morgdon!

Nath's jaw dropped.

Kapow!

The dragon's teeth shattered, leaving a gaping hole between them. Coated in dragon saliva, Brenwar stepped through the gap and slugged the dead dragon in the nose with his hammer.

"Nothing swallows a dwarf and lives!"

"Brenwar!" Nath cried.

Brenwar wiped the slime from his eyes and shook his bearded face like a dog. "Aye!"

"Brenwar!" Pilpin exclaimed.

"Brenwar!" injected Ben, rushing toward him.

Nath scooped his slime-coated friend up in his arms and hugged.

Brenwar eyed him. "Put me down, Nath Dragon."

Nath squeezed him harder. "I know, I know. 'Never hug a dwarf.'"

More than a mile away from the battle site, the party came to a stop and set up a small camp. The smell of death and battle didn't reach this far. The smoke from the burning trees had faded. The pixlyns and fairies had done their job and disappeared back into the woodland.

Ben, Samaz, and Rerry returned with cut branches in their arms. They dropped them by the circle of stones Brenwar had set. The dwarven warrior patted the pouches outside his armor and growled.

"Sultans of Sulfur! That foul beast swallowed my striking stones." He got up. "I'll fetch them."

"Brenwar, please," Nath said. "Sit. I think I can handle it."

Brenwar lifted a brow. "Is that so?"

Nath rubbed his index finger and thumb together, igniting a ball of orange flame. "Toss those sticks in there," he said.

Brenwar did.

Nath flicked the ball of flame, igniting the wood. In seconds, it began to crackle and pop.

"That feels good," Sasha said, nearing the fire and rubbing her shoulder. "I haven't felt warmth for days." She glanced at Bayzog. "Excluding your company of course."

Bayzog showed a quick smile and turned to Nath. "You should save your powers. You need rest."

"I'm tired, no doubt," Nath said, stretching out his arms and yawning.

Bayzog's violet eyes widened.

"What?" Nath said. "It's been a long day."

"We need to discuss things," Bayzog said. "Many things."

"Let's break some bread first," Nath said. "I'm sure everyone is hungry."

Bayzog bowed a little. "As you wish."

Nath combed his fingers through his mane and let out a sigh. Everyone needed rest. Clearly everyone had been through some dire things. Still, Nath felt better than he had earlier. Watching his bristling friend Brenwar grumble orders at everyone did his heart good. Losing Selene was one thing, but losing Brenwar might have been unbearable. He couldn't be happier that his friend was alive.

Edging away from camp, he let the others go about their business. Bayzog and Sasha produced food and water. Ben, Rerry, Samaz, and Pilpin stuffed their faces. Shum and Hoven were nowhere to be found, but Nath could sense them nearby, watching in the woods for other dangers. And Brenwar, he leaned against a rotting stump and stuffed tobacco into a small pipe.

You can judge a dragon by the friends he keeps.

Bayzog had told him that. Nath painted a mental image of the scene and locked it away in his mind. Quietly they ate, speaking little, and before long they bedded down for rest. Sasha was the first asleep, covered in a dark-green blanket with her pretty face turned toward the fire. Rerry and Samaz lay on either side, and Bayzog sat behind them, staring into the fire.

Ben was lying down and talking to Pilpin. Seconds later, he fell asleep mid-syllable. Pilpin snorted, "How rude," and waddled away. He stopped and started talking to Gorlee, who hadn't said much of anything to anyone at all.

The forest became alive with nature song. Soothing. Strong. They were safe for now. Above, the moonlight cut through the dark leaves, darkening the shades around the camp. Through the foliage, Nath saw dragons streak through the night in winks of gold and silver. Balzurth's forces were with them after all.

Still stiff limbed, Nath slipped into the forest. He passed through a clearing and stopped at another rocky overlook. His keen eyes searched the lowlands, looking for any bad signs at all.

Booted feet crunched up behind him. "Not thinking about running off again, are you?"

"Certainly not," he said, turning around and facing Brenwar.

"I think you said that last time."

"No, not with such certain effect."

"Adverse effect is more like it," Brenwar said, puffing on his pipe. "The Truce. Pah!"

"Well, it's over now. You should be relieved."

"I am," Brenwar said. "But I'm more relieved to have you back in my line of sight. And I aim to keep it that way until the end. Do you understand me, Nath Dragon?"

"I do … now." Nath yawned.

"Stop doing that," Brenwar said as he blew three rings of smoke.

"Why?"

"I don't like it. It makes me jittery."

"*You?* Jittery?"

Brenwar grunted. "Just don't go running off again, Nath Dragon. We have a war to win, and we need you to win it. I think you need us, too." Brenwar turned to walk away. "I'm certain of it."

"I'm not going anywhere," Nath said. "I promise."

Brenwar stopped and turned. "That's a first. You've never promised me before. I think you've finally learned the importance of keeping your word."

Nath smiled, covered his yawn with his elbow, closed his tired eyes, and fell down. He didn't hear what Brenwar said next.

"Sultans of Sulfur! Not again. Bayzog! He sleeps again!"

CHAPTER

27

DREAMS. NIGHTMARES. LIGHT. DARKNESS. NATH'S slumber was nothing short of restless. He saw Nalzambor burning and revived. Armies decimated: men, elves, dwarves, orcs, gnolls, lizard men, goblins, all races. Cities and towns were torched and burned. Giants marched over the wasteland. The dark dragons soared toward Dragon Home. The last of the good dragons were gathered there. So he dreamed.

Nath's eyes popped open. Hay tickled his nose. He struggled against his unseen bindings.

What is this?

The last thing he remembered was talking to Brenwar.

What's going on? How long did I sleep this time?

He squirmed, but the chains around him did not give.

Moorite!

Scenario after scenario rushed through his thoughts. Was he captured? Imprisoned? Where were his friends? How much time had passed? Another twenty-five years? A hundred maybe?

Guzan, no!

He fought harder against his bonds until he gathered his wits about him.

Why am I covered in hay?

He concentrated. Eased his breath. Listened. He heard the wheels of a cart rolling beneath him.

Am I in a cart?

He sniffed the dampness in the air. Heard heavy footsteps. The distant chirping of birds.

At least I'm outside, not inside. That's a good thing, I think.

He listened longer to the wheels rumbling over a rough road that made them bounce and jangle other things.

Who in Nalzambor is pulling this thing? And why am I in a hay cart?

The golden fibers tickled. He twitched his lips. Crinkled his nose.

Don't sneeze. Don't sneeze.

Nath didn't have any idea if he was among friends or enemies. He pictured draykis in his mind. Perhaps lizard men.

"Achoo!"

The cart came to an abrupt stop.

Great Guzan!

Footsteps approached.

Nath's body went taut. He flexed his muscles against the tight chains. He had to burst free. He felt hands feeling their way around in the hay. Clump after clump was being pulled off him. A rough hand dusted off his face. Nath held his eyes shut. Held his breath.

Let them think they were hearing things.

He could feel light on his face. Sunlight. The figure that loomed over him blocked out a portion of the light. A stiff finger poked his cheek. Poked his nose. A staff of some sort, or maybe a sword hilt, poked at his ribs. Nath didn't flinch. The person continued the poking and prodding.

Enough already!

He heard a sigh that sounded like a man's. A moment later, the figure covered him up again.

That was close. I think.

Nath wanted to wait things out before he revealed himself. He needed to know more about his captor.

But why did he sigh?

The cart lurched forward. The rumbling of the road began anew. Nath's nose began to tickle again, too.

Uh oh, I can't hold it, again!

"Achoo!"

The cart stopped and hasty feet rushed over. Handfuls of hay were scraped from his body. Fingers poked at his face.

Oh, enough of this game!

Nath popped his eyes open and said, "Boo!"

"Dragon!" a friendly voice exclaimed.

"Ben?" Nath said, squinting. Ben's face was hidden behind a beard mixed of brown and grey. The thick muscles of his shoulders were leaner, the armor on his body looser than it had been before. Still, Ben's happy countenance was in there. Nath dreaded his next answer. "How long has it been?"

"Seventy—"

"Seventy years!"

"No, no," Ben said, waving his comment off. "So sorry. Seven years, Dragon. Seven. Sorry, but it's been so long since I've spoken. My tongue was confused by the question."

Nath felt the slightest bit of relief, but still … "Seven years?" He swallowed. "Ben, get me out of here! And why am I chained up like a prisoner?"

"Bayzog's idea," Ben said, raking off the hay.

"That figures. And where is Bayzog?"

"I don't know."

"What do you mean, you don't know? When was the last time you saw him?"

"Uh, almost seven years ago."

"Ben, just get me out of these chains, will you!"

"Hold on now, I have to find the key. Or remember the word."

Ben shuffled around the cart, looking for something, and Nath lost sight of him. He could see the cloud-darkened sky, but that was about all.

"Ben, will you at least sit me up so I can take a look around?" Nath huffed. "Seven years? Where is everybody?"

Ben climbed into the cart and propped him up. He hugged Nath. "I can't believe you're back! It feels like it's been a hundred years."

"Ben, what's going on?" Nath scanned the area. The landscape didn't seem familiar. A faint road followed alongside the hills and mountains. Few leaves were left on the branches, yet the weather was warm. The tall grasses, normally the color of golden wheat, were grey. "And where are we?"

"North of Quintuklen," he said, wrestling with the lock on Nath's bonds. "Or what's left of it."

"Left of it? What do you mean by that?"

"They destroyed it."

"You mean, Go—"

"Don't say his name!" Ben whispered harshly. "Never utter it!"

"Fine, but what happened to Quintuklen?"

"Not more than a week after you fell asleep, the Floating City drifted to Quintuklen and burned it to the ground." Ben looked him in the eyes. "Maybe one in ten remain in the ruins. All the rest are dead."

"Get me out of these bonds!"

"It seems I'm missing the key."

Nath snorted out a blast of fire. "What was Bayzog thinking?"

"He couldn't have you squirming around. Said something about you moving too much could upset the cart's magic."

"Magic?"

"Sure, it conceals you and me from prying eyes. I keep moving you, from town to town, farmland to farmland. I get stopped a lot. The lizard men and draykis poke and prod a lot."

"A habit you picked up."

"Huh?"

"Never mind," Nath said. "So you've been pulling me all over Nalzambor?"

"Bayzog says they won't search for you in the open, and it's worked up until this point."

"And you've been doing it all alone?"

"Yep."

Nath was moved. Ben was only a man, and seven years was a long long time in a man's life. Hauling a cart along. Day in and day out. For his protection.

"I'd hug you if I could, Ben. Thanks."

"You're welcome," Ben said. "Ah, here's the key."

"Say, Ben, why didn't the army of Barnabus kill you? I thought they were after humans."

"They don't see me as a man." He shrugged and held out a small talisman. "It's from the chest. It took some getting used to, but it works. It makes me look like a half orc, I think. Hmmm."

"What now?" Nath said.

"Seems I'm having trouble with this lock. It's rusted, jammed, or something."

Nath gasped.

"What?" Ben said, drawing his sword and checking the skies. "What do you see?"

"My scales. They—They've changed color!"

Indeed they had. No longer black, they were pearly white, woven with gold and flecked with red.

Ben smiled. "Yes, and that was years ago. I thought you'd wake up when they changed, but you didn't."

Nath's dragon heart warmed inside his chest. It told him that somehow, he'd made his wrongs right.

"Oh no," Ben said, pointing. "Get back in the cart, Dragon."

"Why, what's wrong?"

A band of soldiers armored in dark grey metal galloped toward them.

"Riders of Barnabus," Ben said. "And by the looks of them, draykis! Quick, get back under the hay. I can handle this."

"Perhaps you could have, but I think they've already seen me."

CHAPTER

28

"B EN," NATH SAID, MANAGING HIS way onto his knees. "We don't need that key." Nath set his jaw and flexed his muscles. The moorite chains started to groan, pop, and stretch.

Eyes widening, Ben gasped, "You're bending the moorite."

Chink. Chink. Snap!

The loose chain fell into the hay around Nath's feet.

"Cover yourself up, Dragon," Ben said. "They're looking for you."

In the distance, Nath could see the riders coming hard. Indeed, the five of them were draykis, and the sight of them churned his blood now more than ever before. He inspected the garb he was covered in. A hood covered most of his head, but the cloak that covered his scales hung open. Grabbing a length of moorite chain and tying it around his waist, he stepped out of the small cart and stood by Ben.

"That's a lot of draykis," Ben said, slowly shaking his head. "I've never encountered more than one before, Dragon. We can't let them know who you are. If one gets away, the entire army of Barnabus will be on us."

Narrowing his eyes, Nath said, "Good." He then reached into the cart and filled his hands with the other length of chain.

"Brenwar's not going to be happy that you busted his chain," Ben said.

"When's the last time you saw him?"

"Five years ago," Ben said, "And it's been pretty peaceful since."

Nath stepped in front of Ben. "When this is over, you have a lot of explaining to do. Now wait here."

Nath started up the road. The closer the draykis came, the harder his heart pounded. He could feel the evil. His aversion was enhanced like never before. In the past, their presence had been bothersome, but now that his scales had turned white, they were downright intolerable. Nath draped the chain over his neck and tucked his scaled hands into his cloak.

The draykis pulled their horses to a stop a mere twenty feet away. Their faces were covered in a patchwork of scales, and tiny horns cropped up on their heads. They were big and endowed with thick layers of muscle. Tongues licked from the mouths of half-dead, half-dragon men. One by one, they dismounted and gathered around Nath in a circle. All of them were tall, but not as tall as him. They wielded heavy, crude swords, clubs, and axes.

Nath jangled his chains. "I've some moorite to sell. Are any of you lizard faces interested?'

"You jest, mortal?"

"I'm only breaking the tension in the air. I'm not sure what to call your kind, but I've heard many things: smelly serpents, clawed ogres, ugly fiends, dragon rumpkins... Hah! The children use that one. Yes, it's all in jest, of course."

"We are draykis. We are death," the leader said. It had a jagged scar on its bare chest. Its spiked metal shoulders were heaving. "Hand over those chains."

"You'll have to pay first, and I don't think we've discussed a price."

One of the draykis shoved Nath from behind.

"Last warning, mortal."

"I don't seem to recall the first warning, so how can that be the last?"

Another hard shove from behind knocked Nath to the ground. He lifted his chin, gold eyes blazing. "You shouldn't have done that." He took the chain from his neck and tossed it at the draykis's feet. He undid the chain around his waist and tossed it aside as well.

The draykis laughed. "Not so mouthy now, are you?"

"Look at his hands," another draykis said. "They have claws and scales."

"What?"

Nath rose to his feet, lowered his hood, and dropped his cloak. The wind bristled his mane of red hair.

"Nath Dragon!" the leading draykis said, gaping. It recovered quickly and said to the others, "Kill him!"

Perspective can change in an instant.

One moment, Ben was slinking behind the cart and gathering Akron, ready to defend his friend, the outnumbered dragon. In the next, he was gaping in wonder.

Nath transformed. In seconds, he went from a seven-foot man to a thirty-foot dragon. Great horns and wings sprouted as he turned into the fiercest, most majestic creature Ben had ever seen. Nath's tail whipped out.

Wupash!

It sent two draykis flying, head over scales.

The horses scattered.

The draykis fought back, striking their swords and axes into Nath's scaled armor.

Nath crushed one down into the ground with his paw. Another he crunched in his jaws and slung away. The last one standing turned to run. Nath consumed it with a mouthful of bright-blue flames. One by one, Nath scorched every draykis to the bone. It happened in seconds.

Nath the dragon turned toward Ben and looked down at him. As smoke rolled from his mouth, he said in a great dragon voice, "That felt good."

Trembling the slightest, all Ben could say was, "That was awesome."

"Ah," Nath said, dusting off his hands, "Stomping out evil, one draykis at a time. A good start for my return." He fastened his eyes skyward. "Perhaps it's time we took to some shelter. I sense more danger is near."

"As you say, Dragon," Ben said, unable to contain his smile. He grabbed the handles of the small cart and started to pull. "There's some sanctuary a few miles beyond the next bend. We can hide in there."

Nath nodded as he checked his garments. Once again, his shirt and trousers were still intact. He eyed Ben. "Something Bayzog did?"

"I believe."

Nath donned his cloak, pulled on the hood, retrieved the chains, and resumed his trek alongside Ben. He felt great. Strong. Mighty.

"That was something else, Dragon."

"Indeed. I can't help but be impressed, myself. I feel so … free." He glanced at the sky. "You know Ben, I could fly us wherever we need to go."

"I'll pass. I flew on a dragon once already, and my stomach still feels queasy. Perhaps if I was younger." He frowned. "Walking and riding do me just fine."

"When did you ride a dragon?"

"Oh, not long after you slept. She was a very pretty one, too. Gorgeous eyes, pearl-horned with turquoise scales. Something I'll never forget."

"Are you serious? A dragon let you ride her?"

"Rescued us, is more like it. We were trapped. Penned in near Jordak's Pass. We were taking you to a new place to hide. Then wham! Dragons closed in." Ben shook his head. "We escaped, barely. After that, Bayzog came up with another plan."

Nath let Ben continue talking. He studied Ben. His friend's brown hair had become greyish and wispy. There was a hitch in his step and a slight wheeze in his breath. Wrinkles lined his eyes, and more scars marked his face. It seemed like Ben had gone from a vibrant young man to an old iron war horse in an instant. But there was still light in Ben's kind brown eyes and an avid curiosity.

"I see you looking at me, Dragon, but don't fret. I've lived more than I've lost. And I live for what I've lost. My wife. My children. I miss them, but I understand that no matter what, this battle must be fought. And I'm honored I have a part in it, be it a small one or not."

"Ben," Nath said, "you have been everything a friend should be and more. I'm grateful."

"So am I, Dragon. The things I've seen. The adventures we've shared. It's been wonderful. But Dragon?"

"Yes."

Ben looked him right in the eyes. "Promise me we'll finish this before I die."

Always keep your promises, His father always said. *Never make a promise you cannot keep.*

Nath shook his head no. "I wish I could promise you that, but all I can promise is that I'll try my best."

Ben nodded yes. "Well, that's good enough for me."

"Now, Ben, tell me everything I need to know."

CHAPTER
29

BEN WARMED HIS HANDS OVER a small fire just inside the mouth of a cave.

"Every time the sun drops, my bones get cold. And the rain makes my knuckles ache and my scars throb." He glanced at Nath. "Do you have any aches and pains?"

Inside, Nath hurt. Selene had been gone seven years, but it felt like she had died yesterday.

"I'm fine." Nath tossed a stick into the fire. "So get on with it. Where is everyone?"

"Barnabus has the world under its thumb. Men have been wiped out. Women and children enslaved."

"All men?"

"Of course not. But after Quintuklen was stifled, it scattered them all. The Legionnaires that numbered thousands strong are maybe a few hundred now."

It riled him. But men, always so conflicted with one another, were so easily scattered, unlike the other races that clung tightly together.

"Morgdon and Elome work together, though," Ben said, shaking his head in disbelief. "Never imagined they'd team up as they did, but it was either that or annihilation. For seven years they've defended their lands from the wicked humanoid forces. Orcs, gnolls, and goblins swarm over and over. I've seen it for myself.

"Is that where Brenwar and Bayzog are?"

Shrugging, Ben stirred a stick in the fire. "I suppose. But I never know what they're thinking."

"What of the dragons?"

"They still war all over. Some with the races. Others without. It depends. I've seen quite a few while you've been asleep. But the battles are one thing and the search for you is another." Ben combed his fingers through his beard. "Barnabus's forces still search for you. I don't think the dragon warlord is fully committed in his triumph until he knows you're through. Things are at a standstill of sorts. Like the Truce, but worse." His eyes reflected the firelight. "They're sharpening their claws. Holding their foul, furnace-hot breath. Waiting for you to surface."

"I'm here now," Nath said, looking at his hand. His golden-yellow claws were as sharp as ever. His scales twinkled in the firelight. He was hungry. Hungry for another crack at Gorn Grattack. "So what was the plan once I awakened?"

"Ah," Ben said, nodding. "I almost had forgotten." He yawned. "Or have I forgotten? I haven't thought about that for quite some time." He shook his head. "I'm not so old, am I? Only fifty seasons."

"Ben," Nath said, aggravated, "how did you go about taking turns watching me? Was there a signal? Something? Anything?"

"Normally someone would just show up. Rerry and Samaz did. But now, I'm not so sure. Maybe something happened to them? I can't be certain."

"Ben, do you feel all right?"

"I'm just tired, Dragon. It's been a long day." Ben lay down on his blanket and fell fast asleep.

"Ben?"

Nath was surprised that his friend was out cold. And even more surprised that Ben seemed so old. Something was out of place that he couldn't put his finger on. The world was off. Out of place.

Am I still dreaming?

Ben stirred and rustled in his armor. The beaten breastplate from his brief stint with the Legionnaires had held up quite well. It was good work for something that wasn't dwarven.

Nath grabbed a blanket out of Ben's pack and covered his friend. He then headed out of the cave to stretch his legs. The air was brisk, and a cool drizzle was coming down. The sensation felt soothing for a change.

Learn to appreciate the little things.

He glanced up the hill. The firelight in the cave was dim. Nath fought the urge to wake Ben back up and ask more questions. He needed to know where everyone was. Where to start? Where to go? It seemed Ben didn't know anything. Perhaps that was by design. It was the best way to keep everyone safe. The less everyone knew, the better. It was the best way to protect Nath and everyone else.

But I can't just stand around. Not after seven years.

Nath wanted to take flight. Get a good look around. He glanced back again.

He never left me. I can't ever leave him. Just let him rest. I'm sure he'll have answers tomorrow. I slept seven years, so what's one more night?

Nath sat on the hillside and reflected on things. He could turn into a dragon now and still just as easily maintain a man's form. He tossed a small ball of orange and blue fire from palm to palm, wondering what other powers he might have. He needed to understand them, but he had no one to teach him. Selene could have, and had to some degree, but she had also deceived him. And where had Sansla Libor taken her? He closed his eyes and took a long draw of breath through his nostrils.

Focus, Nath. Trust your instincts.

He heard Ben's heartbeat, slow, steady, and strong. Animals prowled the night. Pixlyns sang the song of crickets. The gentle wind tickled the leaves. The night could bring terror, but it could also bring peace. He eased his clawed hands into the ground. He felt the trepidation deep in the bowels of the world. Its life was in jeopardy. It was on a course that ended in death.

Where do I resume this battle? Where do I start?

He meditated until the dawn's light caught his face.

He felt an unnatural tremor nearby. A rustle of armor. He cocked his head.

Two men approached on cat's feet. He felt their hearts pounding in their chests.

Thump-thump. Thump-thump. Thump-thump.

Nath remained still.

Let the bandits strike. Their blades can't cut my scales.

The soft shuffles came closer and closer. Nath could feel hard eyes on his back.

"If you're going to kill me," Nath said, raising his arms above his head, "Make it swift."

CHAPTER

30

GORN GRATTACK'S EYES POPPED OPEN. Smoke rolled from his nose. He lifted his ten-foot-tall frame from his throne and stepped down off the dais. Standing as a man, he stroked the horns on his head and spoke to one of the many draykis that guarded the throne room inside the Floating City.

"I sense our enemy has awakened." He lifted his chin toward the glass dome above. "I can feel him." He clenched his clawed fists. "And I hate it."

"Shall I send more out in the search for him?" the winged draykis commander said.

"No, I will see to it that he comes to us. Come."

Gorn's tail slithered behind his back as he headed out of the throne room into the city. Legions of skeleton soldiers waited outside the cathedral that Gorn departed. Their black eyes flared with life and hunger. Gorn's towering frame waded through them and down the street. Above, dragons crowed and snorted. Hundreds could be seen perched on spires and rooftops. Their eyes glowed green with energy. They were under Gorn's control, thanks to the power of the jaxite stones, and for seven years his army had been growing.

He strode down the streets toward the Floating City's edge. A grey-stone building stood in his path, dark and grim. Skeleton soldiers pulled open the tall iron doors as he approached. Unaccompanied, Gorn went in. He stood in the inner courtyard of a small covered prison. There were barred chambers three stories tall, open, most of them abandoned and empty.

Gorn's rough voice echoed in the cold chamber. "I have great news."

Several torches that illuminated the cages that lay in the room flickered at the sound of his voice.

Gorn headed for the largest one in the center. A lone figure leaned against the bars, huddled in tattered robes, shivering. There were other cages, but they were empty. Lying on the stone floor nearby were dragons, grey scalers. Heads down, their tongues slithered from their mouths.

"I said, I have news." Gorn banged on the cage. "Nath Dragon is awake. How does that make you feel? Hopeful?"

From underneath the hood, a pair of violet eyes fastened on Gorn's.

"I'm hopeful? Aren't you, Bayzog?"

The part-elf wizard rose to his feet and coughed. Shackled, he teetered toward the bars, clasped his grubby hands on them, and faced off with Gorn. "The end nears, and I couldn't be gladder."

"I'm thrilled you share my thoughts," Gorn said. "And now it's time to draw out our needle in the haystack."

"I've told you everything. I don't know where he is."

"Don't toy with me, Bayzog! You might not know where he is, but you do know how to find him!"

"We've danced this dance before, to no avail. And it's not my life I'm worried about. Even if I could help, I would never yield."

"No, I'm certain you won't." Gorn snapped his fingers. The iron doors opened, and the draykis marched three hooded figures inside. "But perhaps they will."

Bayzog stiffened.

Gorn stepped back and grabbed the hood on the nearest one. "We recently came across some persons you might be interested in."

Bayzog's eyes shone like moons as he pressed his face against the bars.

Gorn pulled off the hood, and there stood Sasha.

"No!"

"Yes," Gorn replied. He plucked off the other two hoods, revealing Rerry and Samaz. "Tell me how to find Nath Dragon, or I'll make your family pay."

CHAPTER
31

"I OUGHT TO KILL YOU," BRENWAR's strong voice said, "fer falling asleep again."

Nath twisted around and jumped to his feet. "Brenwar!"

With War Hammer slung across his back, the dwarf stood as tall and stout as ever. His beard was still mostly a prominent black, but more grey had taken over.

Pilpin stood beside him. "Enjoy your nap?"

"It's good to see you, too," Nath said. He stepped forward and clasped Pilpin's hand. "The both of you."

"It's good to see you on your feet, Nath," Pilpin said, combing his beard. "Especially during the exciting times we live in. I'm glad you're back."

Both of the dwarves were worse for wear. Their breastplates were dented, scars raced along their corded arms, and their other garments were tattered and rumpled.

"You knew where to find me, didn't you?" Nath said to Brenwar.

Brenwar pulled a spyglass from his pocket and rattled it in the air. "I wasn't letting you out of my sight no matter what Bayzog said. Not again. I've always been around, and if not me, Pilpin kept an eye out."

"Does Ben know this?"

Brenwar shook his head. "He's a bit daffy after he took a hard shot on the head. A giant clipped him good a while back." Brenwar spied the cave. "Asleep is he? Hmmm."

"He did seem a bit off. Is he all right?"

"He's fine. Just fuzzy on the details of things. Nothing to worry about. He's as good a fighter as ever."

"Are you sure about that?"

"He's fine."

"Perhaps that's why he couldn't tell me anything. I asked and asked, but he was a bit clueless."

Brenwar sank the axe end of his war hammer into a fallen log. "We're here to fill you in. What do you know?"

"It's only been a day ..." Nath proceeded to tell all that Ben had shared. "And I'm eager to get on with things. Where's Bayzog? He still lives, does he not?"

Brenwar looked away at Pilpin, who was staring at him.

"He's dead?" Nath asked.

"No, just missing. It's been a few years."

Nath's heart sank. "What happened?"

"Don't know. We've had a rendezvous set up years in advance and he hasn't been at the last few."

"We think Gor—"

"Don't say it," Brenwar said to Pilpin.

"You really think that?"

"He's not with the elves, and not even Shum and Hoven can find him."

"At least the Roamers are still with us," Nath said. "What about my father? Is he still aiding in all this?"

"Your father's forces thin, Nath, but they still fight. Many have been tempted and taken by that city that floats on the jaxite."

Nath rubbed his forehead and sighed. "Don't you think we should rally one massive army to defeat them?"

"I believe that's where you come in."

"Me?"

"The dragons won't listen to *us*."

"They never listened to me before."

Brenwar eyed his scales. "I've a feeling they will now."

"Perhaps."

"Pilpin, go and rustle Ben up, we need to get moving."

The small dwarven warrior hopped to his feet and scurried away.

"I saw what you did to those draykis," Brenwar said.

"And?"

"You should've had enough sense to bury them. Not long after we came along, others started to pick at them." He scratched his beard. "I don't think it will take long for the forces of Barnabus to figure out you are near."

"You said we needed to get moving. If so, where are we going?"

"You woke up at the right time, it seems."

"Why is that?"

"It's near time for the next rendezvous."

"And where might that be?"

Brenwar rubbed his face and muttered under his beard, "Near the City of Waste and Ruin."

"I've never heard of that."

"Quintuklen."

Nath swallowed. "Ben says the Floating City is there. Why would you pick such a risky place to meet?'

"Because it was still a city when we made the plan. Can't help the fact it's not there now. It's still the plan. Now let's get moving. I've got a strange feeling in my bones."

So do I, Nath thought. *So do I.*

CHAPTER

32

LATE AFTER NIGHTFALL FIVE DAYS later, traversing harsh elements and avoiding prowling enemies, Nath and company arrived a league southwest of Quintuklen. They had moved day and night, taking little time to sleep, which only Ben seemed to need. His friend slept in the cart half the time while Brenwar and Nath took their turns pulling it.

"I can see it," Nath said, peering skyward.

"See what?" asked Pilpin.

"The Floating City."

It hung like a small moon east of Quintuklen, mostly hidden by a strange mist. He could see the jaxite that ebbed with glowing light beneath it. Dragons darted swiftly through its cloud.

Nath's strange feeling only got stronger. "I can feel him."

"Him who?" Brenwar said, glancing at the sky.

"Him."

"Aye, I suppose you do."

Nath looked at Brenwar.

Brenwar added, "Being a dragon and all." He set the cart handles down and used his glass to spy the small farm they approached. He readied his axe. "We'll go take a look."

Nath started to object, but Brenwar and Pilpin were too quick to scurry away.

"Great."

He leaned against the cart. Ben lay in the hay, snoring softly. Nath closed his eyes and stretched out his senses. He didn't sense evil or danger. That ability had come in handy as they traveled, alerting them to take cover whenever dark forces approached. It took everything Nath had to hold his powers back. He was eager to unleash them, test them out. It was torture.

What else can I do? I need every edge I can get.

Almost an hour later, he noticed Ben beginning to stir.

"Dragon," Ben said, sitting up in the hay and rubbing his blurry eyes. "Have we arrived?"

"They're checking it out."

Ben slid out of the cart and buckled on his sword. He stretched his arms and yawned. "I wish I didn't get tired, like you."

"Oh, I get tired. I just sleep for years when I do," Nath said, laughing. "Come on, let's catch up with the others. There's no danger out there waiting."

Together they wheeled the cart toward the farm until they found Pilpin standing outside the barn, waiting.

"I suppose they're inside?"

Pilpin nodded. "Waiting on you. Ben, they want you to stand guard with me."

"I'd rather—"

"I'm sure it's for the best," Nath said, patting Ben's shoulder.

He proceeded inside the barn door, and Pilpin pulled it shut behind him. The ramshackle barn was typical, with stables and a loft. Brenwar sat at a large table lit by a lantern in the middle. Three other figures sat there as well, with hoods pulled over their heads. That strange feeling returned and knotted his stomach. He stopped at the edge of the table.

"Is there a need for secrecy?"

Two of the three cloaked figures that sat across from Brenwar dropped their hoods. It was Shum and Hoven. He almost didn't recognize them. Their faces had been burned by fire and scarred by battle.

"Apologies," Shum said, "we aimed to spare you displeasure."

"Never say such a thing, my friend. I see only beauty, inside and out. But I hurt from all your suffering on my account."

"It is our honor to serve," Hoven said, adding a smile. "And these marks fill me with honor."

Nath nodded and fixed his eyes on the person at the end of the table. "Are you scarred as well, my friend Bayzog?"

"Nay," Bayzog said, dropping his hood. Tears were in his eyes. He wiped his sleeve on his cheek. "It is my shame that I hide, for I have failed."

"What happened? Where is Sasha? Where are your sons?"

Bayzog rolled a crystal orb down the table. It hopped over the lantern and hovered above.

"It was here when I arrived, two days ago."

It grew and brightened in swirls and colors until a clear image formed. Bayzog's face emerged. He was inside an iron cage. His voice was pleading, "He has us. He has us all."

The image panned backward, revealing the disheveled Sasha, Rerry, and Samaz in small separate cages. Sasha's fingers were stretched through the bars toward her sons and theirs toward hers, but they could not touch.

Nath's heart ignited. "We have to save them!"

The image altered, and Gorn Grattack's terrifying countenance appeared. "I want Nath Dragon's sword, Fang, or all of them die! You have one week." The image vanished.

"Gorlee!" Nath said, pushing his hair back. "That was him, not you!"

Bayzog nodded. "Gorlee went there on his own in hopes of discovering more about the enemy by the time you awoke. That was years ago. This is the first I've seen him." Bayzog sighed. "My family was separated from me, but only recently did I lose track of them. When I saw this, my horrors were confirmed."

"We'll save them, Bayzog." Nath said. "We're here, and we'll go and save them today."

Bayzog shook his head no. "We are not ready to rush into this. Too much is at risk."

"They'll die."

"Perhaps, but they know the risks. We all do. So much is at stake. They'll understand."

"You'll see them alive again," Nath said. "I swear it."

"Nath, heroes and dragons have tried to get in, and none of them have survived. Not one. The Floating City is impenetrable."

Nath rapped his knuckles on the table and stood. "I've been inside it."

Brenwar scowled at Nath.

Bayzog said, "Our kinds are working on something so we can go with you. It's unknown if it's ready yet, but we can check."

"And why did he ask for my sword and not me?"

"I'd say your confrontation is inevitable, but I don't follow why he would need Fang. It's an odd request," Bayzog said.

A thought struck Nath. "Perhaps it is the only blade that can kill him. I battled him once before, lanced him through the heart. He only laughed."

"He might not have a heart as we understand it," Bayzog said.

"Makes sense," Brenwar added, shrugging his shoulders. "Or maybe he needs it to kill you."

Nath leaned over the table. "Regardless, we have to give it to him."

"Nath, that's too dangerous," Bayzog said.

"Your family is at risk, and time is short. I've made my decision. Where is it?"

The creaking barn doors opened and Pilpin burst through. "I tried to stop them, but eh," he glanced back over his shoulder as two ominous figures entered the barn. The hulking winged figure of Sansla Libor emerged, and beside him stood Selene.

CHAPTER

33

WIELDING HIS WAR HAMMER, BRENWAR rushed between Nath and Selene. Shum and Hoven stood ready on either side of him.

"The dead rise against us!" Brenwar said. "Stay back, Nath!"

Selene let out a soft chuckle, opened her palms, and took a knee. "I assure you I am not dead, Brenwar Bolderguild. And I'm not here to fight against you, either." She rose back up, eyeing Nath. "I come to join you."

Selene had changed. The hard lines on her face had softened. The black scales that had dressed her body were now lavender mixed with white. Her presence was soothing, almost radiant. And beautiful.

Nath's heart pumped hard inside his chest. He sensed that hers rang as true as there had ever been.

Behind Selene, Sansla Libor let out a grunt.

Shum and Hoven sheathed their swords and backed away.

Nath folded his arms over his chest. "You have much to explain."

"It would be my pleasure." She grabbed the necklace around her neck and pulled it out from underneath her white robes, revealing a brilliant white amulet that illuminated the room.

Everyone shielded their eyes but Selene and Nath.

"The Ocular of Orray!" he said in amazement.

"I died," she said, "but Sansla, Laedorn, and the elves redeemed me."

Nath stepped closer. His eyes slid from hers to the amulet. "Why would they?"

"To help you, I believe." She forced a smile. "The Ocular sustains me so long as it is in my possession. It's temporary."

Nath looked solemnly into her eyes. "You'll die without it?"

"It's uncertain, but most likely." Selene tucked the Ocular back inside her robes. "That's why I need to teach you all that I can in the little time we have left together."

Nath reached out and held her face between his hands. She was warm and more real than she had ever been before. He felt the light within her. "Bayzog, did you know about this?" he said over his shoulder.

"I knew they had her. I did not know she was revived. It's a wondrous thing that the elves would use the Ocular on Selene. A good sign, I believe."

"A great sign." He studied Selene's eyes. "I'm glad you have returned, and I hope it's not temporary."

She squeezed his hand. "So do I."

"Are there any other surprises?"

"Dragon!" Ben said, bursting inside. "Dragon! Come quick!"

Nath rushed outside the barn.

Dragons in flocks like birds were landing in the fields. Their bright eyes and colorful scales twinkled in the moonlight.

"Your army comes," Selene said in his ear. "Are you ready to lead them?"

"Can you feel that?" Selene said to Nath. "What is she thinking?"

It was still nighttime. Nath stood facing a golden flare dragon. She had long lashes over her pretty eyes, and he could feel her heart beating under his fingertips.

"She thinks I'm handsome," he said, showing a broad grin.

Selene rolled her eyes. "Uh-huh, and what else?"

"She's ready to fight. Eager."

"Tell her to do something. Bend her will."

Nath didn't like the sound of that. "I'd rather ask."

Selene folded her arms across her chest. "A general doesn't ask his soldiers to fight in the war. He's a commander. He gives orders."

"True, and they follow a commander they respect even better."

"You're proven, Nath. They wouldn't be here if you weren't."

"Fine." He cleared his throat and spoke in Dragonese. "Golden flare, trip Selene."

The dragon's tail whipped out, making the sound of a cracking whip.

Wupash!

Selene was upended and crashed onto the ground.

Nath nodded in satisfaction. "I think I have it. What other lessons will you teach me now?"

Selene walked him through the steps of changing form. As a man, he grew a tail and wings. He added horns even.

"Fascinating."

She taught him to blow different kinds of smoke, acid, fire, and even ice. He froze trees and shattered them with ease.

"Summon enough power, and your roar alone can split rock and splinter trees," she said. "But your power is limited. You control great magic and can do many things; just don't overdo it." Her face darkened. "Our enemy is ancient, Nath. He'll tempt you to burn up your powers until you weaken, and then, like a monstrous asp, he'll strike you in the neck, burrow inside your body, and poison the heart within." Her expression became distant. "That's what he did to me."

Nath nodded.

"You surprised him once before," she said. "He won't be caught off guard a second time."

"Could I have killed him then? When I had him?"

"His body maybe, but not his spirit. It takes a special weapon to sever the spirit from the body. That's what Barnabus did."

Nath remembered the legends of the man Barnabus that Bayzog had shown him long ago. Barnabus had wielded a great sword that lanced and banished Gorn after the last Dragon War. Barnabus's heroics had been twisted ever since and turned against the good.

"Do you know what happened to Barnabus and that sword?" Nath asked of Selene.

She chuckled. "Do you not yet know who Barnabus is?"

"No, should I?"

"Yes, you should. Barnabus is your father."

Nath's limbs went numb. "What?" Inside, it all felt true, and then he realized there had been a time when his father was a man, too.

Selene puckered her brows.

So did Nath. "But the sword, Fang, he made for me. Fang can't be the same sword that he used before. Is he?"

"I don't think the last sword did the trick, and I believe your father forged another. I've heard it told that the other blade snapped the last time he used it. It vanquished the dragon warlord, but not entirely."

"So that's why he wants Fang?"

"That blade in the right hands can destroy both body and spirit," she said. "He fears it."

"All this time, I had the key in my claws," he said, eyeing Selene. "And you knew it."

"I suspected."

"Why didn't you try to take Fang, way back when?"

Selene gazed up at the Floating City. "He wanted me to turn your will. With you on his side, the blade's power would have been useless. He took a calculated risk, I failed at my task, and now he just needs the blade." She turned her gaze back to him. "Sorry, Nath."

"I guess I'll have to forgive you," he said, holding her gaze, "but I have one other question. Where is Fang?"

CHAPTER
34

"I'M NOT SO CERTAIN THIS is the best course of action," Bayzog advised. The part-elven wizard held his chin and rubbed his finger under his eye. "The entire world is at stake."

"Where is the sword, Bayzog? I haven't seen Fang since I woke up!" Nath pushed his back off the support post in the barn and unfolded his arms. "This is my choice, not yours. And if I want to save your family at my risk, I will."

Bayzog's violet eyes flashed. "Do not insist that I don't want to save my family, Nath Dragon. I'm considering other options."

"I know you want to save them more than anybody. But we don't have the time. They don't have the time!"

Brenwar stepped between the pair. "All right now. We're on the same side. But Nath, I'm with Bayzog on this. We can try another way."

Nath stiffened. "I say we give them the sword. Period. Now where in Nalzambor is it?"

Bayzog looked him in the eye and said, "I don't know."

Nath looked down at Brenwar.

"I don't know either."

"Who does know, then?" Nath turned and looked at Ben, who sat on the cart sharpening his sword. "Ben, certainly you know."

Ben scratched his head. "I haven't seen it since … I don't know, when?"

Nath spun around, looking at everyone. "Well, who was the last one to have it?" He caught Brenwar and Bayzog's eyes meeting and looking away. He raised his voice. "I'll storm the Floating City alone if I must! I'll not fight beside those I cannot trust. And you, Brenwar, always on me about my tales, and now you're telling one yourself. By the Sultans! Sasha, Rerry, and Samaz's lives are on the line!"

"I don't know where it his!" a bristling Brenwar said.

"Nath," Bayzog intervened, "we took precautions so that the sword would never be found unless absolutely needed. I don't know where it is. No one here does."

Nath started to pace. "*What* precautions?"

"When we learned the Dragon Warlord desired it, we had it hidden." Bayzog fetched his staff from the table and started to walk away. "For exactly this reason."

"So, if I weren't threatening to ransom it to him, would you get it for me?"

"We would, but we can't with your current intent."

Nath's claws dug into his palms. Bayzog was hiding something, but he wasn't lying.

Think like a dragon, Nath. Outwit this wizard.

"I'm sorry, friends," Nath said as Bayzog headed toward the barn doors, "I believe you. You clearly would never lie in such dire times. Whatever you have done, I know you have done it for my protection as well as others. I'm grateful. But …" Bayzog stopped. "Perhaps I have not been asking the right question. I think I'll ask another. You say you don't know where the sword is, but I now ask, do you know how to find it?"

Bayzog gently nodded and turned. "I do." He glanced at Brenwar. "We need the chest."

Brenwar looked over at Pilpin. Pilpin dug his fingers into one of his pouches and produced a tiny replica of Brenwar's chest. He spoke in Dwarven. "Iidluumkraaduum." He rapped his knuckles on the chest. Its banding crackled and popped, and the chest expanded until it stopped at normal size.

"It's in there?"

"No," Bayzog said, stepping to the chest and kneeling. He opened the lid and fingered the rows of small vials. He plucked out one filled with liquid the color of plums. "Ben, come and drink this."

"Me?" Ben said, setting down his sword and walking over. "Why me?"

"Because I'm tired of you being daffy," Brenwar said. "Now drink it!"

Ben snatched the vial, popped the cork, and drank it down. He blinked, thumped his chest, burped, and swooned.

Nath reached over and steadied his friend. "What did you give him?"

"I think I need to lie down," Ben said, holding his head. He sagged back in Nath's arms and burped again. He steadied himself. "Maybe not."

"Care to explain, Bayzog?" Nath said.

"We had Ben hide Fang. When he finished, we gave him a potion that makes him forget things. It kept us all innocent in case our enemies captured us. The sword is as safe as it ever was."

"And what if it's in a place so far off we can't get it?" Nath said. "Great Guzan, Bayzog! You overthink these things. Time is pressing. We only have one day."

"Ben," Bayzog said, "where is the sword?"

Ben ambled over to the cart and picked up his sword. "Here it is."

"No, you daffy idiot!" Brenwar said. "Bayzog, I told you this was a bad idea. He's permanently forgotten."

Bayzog rose up. With a serious tone in his voice, he said, "Ben …. Where is Fang?"

Ben gazed up into the rafters with a glassy look in his eyes.

Brenwar and Pilpin slapped their foreheads. "Oy!"

Nath glared at Bayzog. "Well done, old friend. Well done."

Ben started to laugh.

"What's so funny?" Brenwar said.

Ben slapped his knee and said with a smile on his face, "I know where Fang is." He got down on his hands and knees and crawled underneath the cart.

"He's gone loony," commented Pilpin.

There was a rustle of metal on wood and wood on metal. Something snapped. Ben crawled out from under the wagon and popped up on the other side. He raised his arms high. In one hand he held Fang, and in the other was Akron.

"All this time I thought I lost them, and all this time they've been right under my nose."

"That's the dumbest hiding place ever," Brenwar remarked, tugging at his beard.

Bayzog added with a smile, "Yet brilliant at the same time."

CHAPTER

35

THE FELINE FURY HAD MADE his way to the small farm and gone, only to return hours later. The dragon cat lay on the grass at the feet of Nath, who sat on a stone bench in the garden. It purred, and fragrant petals of smoke wafted from its nose.

"It seems you are making new friends in the dragon world all the time," Selene said, taking her place by his side. "It's comforting to see."

"It certainly is, seeing how you used the fury against me."

Selene bent forward and stroked the great cat's mane. "I raised him. Did you know that?"

Nath shook his head.

"He was my prized hunter. Tracker. One of the most gorgeous dragons I'd ever seen. And even in captivity, these dragons are hard to tame. But I bent him to my will." She glanced up at Nath. "But in the end, it was your will that won him over. Did you know that?"

"No."

"I learned of the fury's deception, Nath. I felt it. It preferred you over me, and for the first time in my life, I doubted myself. I doubted Gorn as well." She locked her fingers inside the fury's mane. "I lost my pet—not out of fear, but out of adoration. I saw for the first time that good things don't take a shine to evil. Your light turned the fury's light on as well. Balzurth is proud."

Nath looked at her. "Have you ever—"

"Met him? No. Never. But I think I have a fine idea what to expect of him."

Down the road, Bayzog and Brenwar approached. The part-elven mage leaned on the Elderwood Staff, and his eyes were still weary. Brenwar frowned over his folded arms.

"They approach," Bayzog said. "Nath, you don't have to go through with this. Not on my account and not theirs. They are willing to die for what is right: saving Nalzambor."

Nath's golden fingertips toyed with Fang's dragon-headed pommel. The mystic metal, no longer hotter than fire, was cool in his hands. The tiny gemstone eyes of the dragons twinkled in the daylight. Fang was one of the most precious things his father had given him, which technically, he should not have. He'd let Brenwar borrow it, and Brenwar had lent it to him. He stood up, handed the sword to Brenwar, looked at Bayzog, and said, "I have faith."

Brenwar grunted.

Bayzog gave a nod.

Nath came forward.

Brenwar stayed him with his hand. "You wait. We'll deliver this. We meet now in the valley. From up there," he pointed to a crag on a hillside, "you can watch."

Nath started to object but held his tongue. After all, this was his idea. "As you wish, Brenwar." He turned and looked at Selene. "Coming?"

Nath, Selene, and the feline fury made their way to the crag. He couldn't fight off the uneasiness that twisted his belly. Giving up Fang, the only weapon that might kill Gorn Grattack, was a gut-wrenching task, but he had to believe it was the right thing.

"That was a brave thing you did," Selene said. She patted him on the back. "I don't think anyone else in this world would have done that."

Nath's chest tightened. He could see his friends entering the valley, where a score of draykis awaited them, accompanied by half a dozen horse-sized dragons. Behind Brenwar, Pilpin, a hooded Bayzog, and Ben, were Shum, Hoven, and the hulking Sansla Libor. A more than formidable party, but they were vastly outnumbered by a superior force.

"I should be down there," he whispered. "I feel a trap in the works." He started forward.

Selene grabbed his arm. "They'll be fine. Wait it out."

Nath swallowed and eyed her. Selene's dark eyes had a twinkle of excitement in them. Sansla's appearance with Selene had been suspicious. She'd been able to deceive him before. She could certainly do it again. His blood ignited, and he jerked away.

"Nath? What are you doing?"

He peered down in the valley, keen eyes alert to everything. His friends were now surrounded by the draykis and dragons. Brenwar did the talking.

"Don't you move a muscle!"

"All right," she said.

"Not a word, Selene."

The feline fury's purr became a hearty rumble.

Nath's senses tingled.

What is going on? Something is going on!

He squatted down on the rock, ready to spring. So much deceit. So much betrayal. He'd somehow talked himself into giving Gorn Grattack everything he wanted. The draykis commander gave a nod. The other draykis led four hooded figures over. They had the builds of Sasha, Samaz, Rerry, and Bayzog.

Shum came forward and removed the hoods.

All their faces were clear: Sasha, Rerry, Samaz, and a part elf that looked like Bayzog.

Brenwar handed over the sword to a winged draykis commander, who eyed the blade.

"Everything is fine." Selene sat down on the rock and added, "You're the one who said you had faith. Now practice it."

Nath clenched his jaw as the dragons crowded the circle. Suddenly, the draykis commander, Fang in hand, took to the sky. Covering the area in a puff of smoke, the dark dragons took flight and escorted the draykis commander back to the Floating City. When the smoke cleared, all the draykis were gone, leaving Nath's friends coughing but reunited with Bayzog's family.

Brenwar was grumbling at Ben and Ben back at him.

Nath sprang like a cat and dashed down. In seconds, he was down inside the valley. "What is it? What is wrong?"

Ben had one arm and Brenwar had the other of a lone man who stood between them. A hood was crushed in Brenwar's free hand. The man had tattoos on his bald head and face. His teeth were grey and crooked.

"Ah," the acolyte said, licking his teeth, "you must be Nath Dragon. I've a message for you from the great Gorn Grattack himself. These friends are delivered as agreed. But your other friend, Gorlee the Deceiver? Well, if you want him, then you'll have to get him yourself. All by yourself, that is. Heh heh heh!"

CHAPTER
36

"YOU THINK IT'S FUNNY, DO you?" Brenwar leveled the acolyte with a fist to the gut.

Whop!

The man doubled over and fell to his knees.

"What happened, Brenwar?"

"Magic," Bayzog intervened, "a well-crafted illusion. It seems we've been deceived."

Nath looked at Sasha.

She was meek and disheveled, as were her sons. "It's me, Nath," she said, hugging Bayzog. "All me and my sons. Thank you, Nath. You didn't have to do that, but I'm glad you did."

Nath stepped over and stretched his long arms around them both. "So am I."

The happy reunion was short. They all headed up the hillside, back into the barn. Inside, Nath had no doubt he'd done the right thing, giving up Fang as ransom for his friends. But there was another surprise when they returned. Selene was gone.

Brenwar and Pilpin dragged the acolyte into the barn and shackled him up in the moorite chains.

"Hah, I'm honored," the greasy cleric said. "All this trouble over little me. I always knew I was a large threat. Gorn will be pleased."

"Shaddup!" Brenwar said. He started to stuff a handkerchief in the man's mouth.

"Oh, I wouldn't do that. I have something to say. Something you must hear today, before it's too late."

Pilpin shoved the man's head back into the post.

Conk!

"Spit it out, then."

Blinking and rolling his eyes, the cleric finally looked up at Nath. "Your changeling friend will die at the last light. That's not long from now, Nath Dragon. Go soon, and go by yourself. Gorn will free your friend, and then the two of you can be alone."

Nath kneeled down. "Is that all of your message?"

The acolyte's eyes brightened. "It certainly is."

Fuming, Nath flicked the man's chin with his index finger, rocking his head back and knocking him out cold. He rose, headed outside the barn, and spied the Floating City. The setting sun was reflecting off the windows.

Bayzog glided to Nath's side. "It seems your hand is being forced. Doing what he wants you to will be a bad move." Bayzog laid his hand on Nath's shoulder. "You've been patient thus far; don't be hasty now. We'll think of something."

"I've done enough thinking. The time has come to act." Nath surveyed his surroundings. His dearest friends were there. Dozens of dragons huddled nearby, perhaps more inside the hillsides. "Everyone gather."

His friends crowded around him, and many dragons slunk inward.

"I want to thank you all for being here for me. No dragon could ask for a better group of friends, but I have to do what must be done. I have to face our mortal enemy one on one, and I am ready." He glanced down at Brenwar. "Do not interfere." He took Brenwar's hand inside his. "There is no one I'd rather have by my side in this battle, Brenwar, but you know it cannot be."

Brenwar grumbled, but nodded his head.

"I'm going into that city to end this war, but I need you around to finish it in case I can't." He made his way around the circle and hugged each and every one of them. He stopped at Sasha and wiped away the tears that rolled down her cheeks.

She hugged him tight, sobbing and saying, "Don't go. Don't go yet. Gorlee will understand."

Nath shook his head no. "Gorn will just pick off one friend after another. I have to put an end to this madness now." He released her and stepped away. Channeling his power, he made dragon wings sprout from his back. He beat them and lifted off the ground. "Remember, no one does anything until you know Gorlee is safe, or I am gone."

The higher he rose, the smaller his friends became.

Then he heard Ben's strong voice shout into the sky, "Take it to him, Dragon, like I know you can!"

Brenwar watched his flying friend turn into a speck and disappear into the Floating City. His stubby fingers clawed at his beard. "How in Nalzambor does he stand a chance against those odds? There's a thousand jaxite-controlled dragons in there, not to mention Gorn Grattack. Pah!" He punched his fist into his hand. "It's madness."

"I don't know how he beats those odds, but have some faith in him, why don't you?" added Ben. "I believe, and you should believe as well."

"I'd believe better if I could get in there with my war hammer."

The dragons stirred, squawked, and beat their wings.

Sansla Libor took to the sky. The Roamers unsheathed their blades.

"Someone comes," Rerry said, eyeing the crest of the road that led down to the farm. "Look."

Brenwar's eyes went wide, and his fingertips turned numb. A waving dark banner of black and gold appeared on the horizon.

CHAPTER
37

SOARING THROUGH THE SKY, NATH Dragon stretched out his arms. There was nothing more liberating than the sound of the wind rushing by his ears. Heading to his doom or not, the feeling was exhilarating.

His wings beat, slow and powerful. He circled the remains of Quintuklen below. Every tower, every spire was rubble. The walls—which circled the city in a labyrinth—were half torn down. They were of little use against flying dragons.

Men scurried from broken building to broken building. Survivors. Even though Quintuklen was in ruin, most people would not abandon their homes until they died. The sight of the desperate scavengers stirred Nath's heart and angered him. What gave Gorn the right to take homes away from anyone?

He swooped through the air and sped toward the ominous bulk of the Floating City, which hung like a dreadnought in the sky. Nath carefully weighed his thoughts. He could accept Gorlee's sacrifice. After all, he would do the same. He could muster an army of men, dwarves, and dragons and attack the forces of Barnabus like a juggernaut, but how many more would die? Thousands? Tens of thousands? He made his decision.

Better one of me than all of thee.

Bearing down on the city, a lone figure dropped to his side. It was the feline fury.

"Away now," he said in Dragonese, pointing at the cat. "It's my fight alone."

The cat dragon's eyes narrowed as it growled in response and veered away.

Nath watched it go, realizing the fury didn't even have a name.

If I survive this, I'll take care of that. It's something Selene should have done.

Ahead, the dragons stretched their necks from their perches and crowed. The Floating City was still spinning, pulled by the dragons shackled by the neck. Nath clenched his fists. It fired his furnaces within. Smoke rolled from his nose, and his golden eyes smoldered. He cut through the building tops, whizzed over the streets. Dragons hissed and coiled. Armies of the undead gathered in the streets, pressing around the large cathedral-type building he remembered from his visit here.

Nath landed on the stairs.

Armored skeletons and dragons of all sorts crowded near with their eyes glowing. Armor rustled and dragons hissed and slithered.

It rankled Nath, their hatred. Evil. He turned his back on them and placed his hands on the massive doors. His heart thundered inside his chest.

This is it, Dragon. This is it.

A thought lingered in his mind.

Selene. Will she be at Gorn Grattack's side? Was this the plan all along?

Weaponless aside from his dragon claws and magic, he shoved the massive doors open.

Gorn Grattack waited inside. His monstrous voice echoed as he spoke. "Come. Come and die."

Nath stepped within, and the door shut behind him.

Thoom!

Massive cauldrons of fire illuminated the room. Windows stained in dark colors let little sunlight show through. There were cages, empty ones, scattered throughout the room. The smell of death and decay lingered. Fang was nowhere in sight. Neither was Gorlee. Selene, to his relief, was nowhere either.

Nath's scales tingled. Cried out.

Danger!

In front of him once again waited his greatest enemy. Seated on a throne of stone was the foul foe of Nalzambor. Gorn towered ten feet tall. He was covered in brawn and greyish scales. Razor-sharp horns crowned his head, and his eyes had an evil glow.

"Nothing to say, Nath Dragon?"

"Where is my friend Gorlee?"

"Ah, I see," Gorn said, holding his chin. "You still are concerned about these mortals. Tsk. Tsk. Tsk. Such a weakness."

"Where is he?" Nath demanded.

"You do realize it's only a matter of time until all of your *friends* are dead, don't you?" Gorn folded his arms over his chest. "I control most of the dragons in this world. Only a small remnant of free dragons remains. A paltry force stands against me at best. I control the jaxite, and this city is shielded from the attacks of mortals. Why, I even have your precious sword. Once I finish you, I'll melt it down. Then I'll wipe out all of my enemies—the elves, dwarves, and those pesky Roamers—and it will be onward to my Mountain of Doom."

"You might defeat me, but you won't defeat my father. You couldn't the last time."

"Hah! Your father withers while I grow stronger." Gorn clenched his fists and leaned forward. "He fades from this world. He sent you to fight this battle. A battle he knows he cannot win. You cannot win either. You'll never leave here alive. And all of your friends combined cannot save you. You are doomed, Nath Dragon."

"It's you who are doomed."

"Really, how so? I'm in control of everything."

"If that were the case, then I wouldn't be here to fight you now."

"Ah, so you are ready to battle, then? You look ill prepared in your current form." Gorn showed an oversized smile of dragon teeth. "You might want to try bigger, like me." He stood up, and his form increased. From the other side of the room, he sneered down at Nath. "You don't stand a chance."

"Release my friend!"

Gorn reached behind the throne, grabbed something, and brought it forward. It was Fang. "This friend?" Gorn pulled it from the sheath, revealing the bright glow of the blade. The scales on that hand sizzled and smoked. "Isn't that quaint?" he snorted. "It doesn't seem to like me. I can handle that."

Nath's eyes narrowed as he drifted closer.

Gorn studied the blade as he squeezed it with his monster-sized, clawed hand.

Fang's blade hummed and throbbed with light, turning from a bright golden sheen to blue as night before fading to a dark blackish purple. The hilt stopped smoking.

Gorn Grattack laughed. "That was easy." He shrugged. "There is nothing I cannot control in this world. It all lives and dies under my command." He raised the sword high. "I'll make this interesting." He jammed the blade down into the throne. "If you want it, come and take it."

"I didn't come for Fang. I came for Gorlee."

Gorn sighed. "So be it then. Draykis!"

Two winged draykis emerged from the dark beneath the balconies, dragging a figure. The pinkish form of Gorlee sagged between them, head dangling. They dropped him on the floor in front of Gorn and departed.

"Yes, Nath, your friend, the changeling," Gorn said as he started to snicker, "is dead."

Nath's face turned blood red.

"Nooooooooooooooooooooooo!"

CHAPTER

38

"IT CAN'T BE." BRENWAR SLUNG his war hammer over his back.

"It is," Bayzog said.

The waving black and gold banner showed a hammer and anvil. Another banner appeared, showing a sun shining over a land of blues and old gold. A stout dwarf in plate armor from the neck down carried the black and gold banner of the dwarves. An elven warrior wearing a green tunic over a suit of chain mail carried the other banner. Behind them, twelve dwarves and twelve elves came.

"Haarviik!" Brenwar shouted out.

A dwarf bigger than Brenwar marched forward and clasped his hand. He wore heavy armor, and his lustrous beard was more white than brown. Haarviik was one of the highest commanders of Morgdon. Higher than Brenwar, even.

"Great to see you, old warrior," Haarviik said. "No other dwarf I'd rather fight beside at the end."

"Are the armies with you?" Brenwar said, peering over Haarviik's shoulder.

"Nay, certainly you would have heard them marching if they were."

"Aye, there's no sound greater than dwarven boots. But your voice will have to do." He slapped Haarviik's shoulder. "So, what can you share with me?"

A tall elf made his way over. His silvery light armor gleamed in the sunlight. His helm of hammered leaves twinkled. He offered his hand to Brenwar, who shook it, then to Bayzog.

"Your arrival is both pleasing and surprising, Laedorn," Bayzog said.

"Greetings," Laedorn said, making a slight bow. "We've marched day and night." His gaze drifted toward the Floating City. "And I believe our timing is just right." His light-green eyes scanned the farm. "Where is Nath Dragon?"

"You just missed him. He's taken to the Floating City. I could not delay him," Bayzog said.

"That is unfortunate," Laedorn said. "But we must not tarry."

"The time to strike is now," Haarviik grumbled. "Now, they won't be looking."

"What are you getting at?" Brenwar said, scowling. "You said you don't have an army. Only two score warriors are with you. Did the elves bring magic ropes and ladders to climb into that spinning city? No disrespect, but I say, 'Hah!'"

"It's ready, isn't it?" Bayzog said to Laedorn.

"What's ready?" Brenwar said.

"The weapon," Haarviik said to Brenwar. He clasped Brenwar's shoulder. "The one we've been working on."

Brenwar's eyes went wide. "I thought you only had two of the three pieces."

"We did, but now we have the third."

"Bayzog, what is your understanding of all this?" Brenwar said.

"I know little more than you, but I know this is a dangerous plan, only to be used as a last resort. I don't think we are there yet. What has changed, Laedorn?"

Laedorn motioned toward the troops. The elves and dwarves marched forward with their packs. Each carried several metal pieces marked with intricate patterns. Quickly, they got to work assembling a contraption that pointed at the Floating City. Busy dwarven hands tightened large bolts with metal wrenches. Heavy hammers pounded pins in. The elves slid small slivers of metal into place.

"What are they building, Bayzog?" Sasha said with fascination.

"They call it the Apparatus of Ruune."

"What does it do?"

"It destroys things."

"What things?"

Sasha, Rerry, Samaz, and Ben came closer.

"Everything."

"You can't use that when Dragon is in there," Ben objected.

"And they won't," Brenwar added.

"Brenwar," Haarviik said, "our counsels have agreed. It's been almost five hundred years since we've agreed on anything. We will carry out this service."

"You must delay!"

"Oh, we must not, Brenwar Bolderguild," Laedorn said. "And know that my affection for your friends is the same as for my own kin. But we must strike before the opportunity is lost. We've lost many lives hiding the Apparatus and getting it here." Laedorn's chin dipped. "Two of my brothers are gone, among a hundred others. It is agreed we must strike, or thousands more will die. We must smite that city from the sky."

Bayzog approached Laedorn, looking him in the eye. "Why such urgency? You don't even know for certain the amount of power that you wield yet. What if it fails?"

"Urgency is the utmost, Bayzog. Surely you know that. Powerful artifacts are at work here, and it's only a matter of time before Gorn Grattack senses that. His forces will be upon us at any moment. That's why we travel small and discreetly. We cannot appear to pose a threat. And now, with Nath Dragon up there, Gorn is distracted. This might be our only chance to take him."

"And risk killing our friends? Nay!" Brenwar said. "Give him more time!"

Laedorn sighed. "We can't put our fate in the hands of the dragons, just as the dragons cannot put their fate in ours. We must act."

Brenwar's eyes slid over to the Floating City. Bright lights flashed. Something was stirring. He shook his head. "Give him more time."

"Once the Apparatus is finished, we will unleash all of its fury."

"You can't let them do this, Brenwar," Ben said. "You can't!"

Brenwar grumbled. The Apparatus of Ruune was almost finished. It was a massive cannon standing eight feet off the ground on a tripod of thick iron legs. The elves and dwarves had put large sections of moorite tubes together, wide enough to fit someone's head inside. It was braced down on the tripod, sitting in a bracket that could swivel left to right and up and down. An oversized spyglass was perched on the top. Two seats were lined up behind it. Below it was an iron stomach, a furnace waiting to be fed. There were gears and handles laid out in an intricate array. An oversized stepladder led up into the seats. The marvelous contraption towered over them all.

"You really think this can knock that city out of the sky?" Brenwar said.

"I don't know," Haarviik said, offering a dwarven grin, "but I can't wait to try."

CHAPTER
39

RED WITH ANGER, NATH ROARED. Hot as fire, he summoned his power and charged. Crossing the span between him and Gorn Grattack, he transformed into a full-size dragon.

Gorn lowered his head and shoulders and grew.

The two behemoth dragons collided with a roof-shaking *boom*!

Nath pinned Gorn to the floor and unloaded a blast of green dragon fire.

Gorn's tail slithered around Nath's neck and jerked him away. With a heave, he sent Nath skipping over the tiles.

"You'll pay!" Nath said in an all-powerful dragon voice. "You'll pay for all this!"

Each almost thirty feet tall, the two titans circled, their heads almost grazing the rafters of the massive cathedral.

Ready to spring, Gorn flashed a wicked smile. "You're a fighter, Nath Dragon, but you lack my killer instincts."

Nath said as he charged, "We'll see about that!"

Gorn's eyes bore into Nath's chest, and a blast of purple fire shot from them.

Nath ducked. Fast was good. Big and fast was not the same. The blast caught him in the shoulder and spun him to the tiled cathedral floor. Nath roared and pushed his dragon body upright.

Gorn rammed him with his horns and drove him into the tiles once more. "You are still a boy!"

Whop! Pow! Smash! Smash! Smash!

Gorn's blows were a furious storm. They smote Nath's face, his jaw, his belly. His dragon claws ripped into Nath's scales. Each blow was lightning. Each impact was power.

Wham! Wham! Pop! Crack!

Nath felt Gorn's clawed hands wrapped around his neck. Claws dug in. He was being choked to death.

No. No. No. Nooooooooo!

With a powerful blast from his eyes, Nath let loose the furnace within.

The white-hot blast snapped back Gorn's head, and Gorn's fingers loosened around Nath's neck.

Nath gathered his legs between them and thrust with all his power into Gorn's belly. The Dragon Warlord was catapulted through the air, blasting through the roof and onto the streets.

Nath sprang to his feet, gathered his breath, and crashed through the great doors of the cathedral. Gorn lay in the street holding his head. At least a dozen skeleton warriors were crushed beneath him.

He rushed Gorn again.

A sky raider dropped between them. A blast of fire came from its mouth, catching Nath in the chest.

He stormed right through it and locked his arms around the sky raider's neck. "Are you fighting this battle yourself or not, Gorn?"

Gorn staggered up and waved the crowding dragons aside. "It's just me and you!"

Nath popped the sky raider in the jaw and slung it away. "No," he responded. "It's just me!" He pounced on Gorn and started hammering away, one heavy blow after the other.

Pow! Pow! Pow! Pow! Pow!

The two of them slammed through the streets and tore through the city. The buildings shook. Glass shattered. Ancient statues toppled over. The entire city trembled. The pair of titans thrashed back and forth. Nath pressed with punches. Gorn flailed back with his tail. Nath drove Gorn through building after building. He pummeled his enemy down.

Whop!

Gorn's dragon head crashed with Nath's fist and into the street. Nath's chest was heaving.

Gorn started laughing. "Ha ha ha! You tire already, and I haven't even begun fighting."

"Neither have I," Nath gasped.

Whop!

He punched Gorn.

Gorn got bigger.

Pow!

Gorn got bigger.

Wham! Wham! Wham!

Gorn got bigger and bigger and bigger. The monstrous dragon lord shoved Nath aside like a doll and rose to his full height.

Shoulders sagging, Nath looked up and swallowed.

Gorn stood more than fifty feet tall. He was almost twice the size of Nath. Bigger than most buildings. "You are such a fool, Nath Dragon! My power is ten times yours. Now taste what true power is!" He open his mouth, and a blast of dark-purple fire came out.

The scale-blistering heat made Nath let out an awful blood-curdling roar. "Bah-Ha-Rooooooooooooo!" He fell to his hands and knees. He couldn't breathe. Coated in excruciating flames, he was suffocating. The roar of flames was deafening, the unbearable heat terrifying. Stunned, he couldn't think. He couldn't counter.

Hang on, Nath Dragon! A voice inside his head said. *Hang on!*

Who said that? Was it him? Was it his father?

The flames stopped. Smoke rolled off his cooling scales. But the pain was still there. Mind-numbing pain. It was bad, but not as bad as Gorn's laughter.

"How is that for a baptism by fire, Nath Dragon? Torture, isn't it?" Gorn reached down and lifted up Nath's chin. "That is what is in store for the rest of the world, and it seems there is nothing you can do about it. Ha! You are not ready yet. You could have been if you were patient and let your friends die, but you chose their lives for your death. How fitting for a fool."

Gorn released him and let out a triumphant sigh. He slithered his great neck from side to side and bared his razor-sharp claws and teeth. "Now it's time to pluck your beating heart out, one scale at a time." He stepped around Nath and grabbed his tail. "But let's soften you up a bit more first."

Eyes swollen shut, Nath felt himself being dragged through the streets. He heard the dragons taunting him and praising Gorn. All of his strength had evaporated. Where had it gone?

I'm beaten. But I can't be beaten. I can't be!

Gorn slung him like a club into the buildings, one right after the other, and then dragged him back inside what was left of the cathedral.

CHAPTER

40

"IT'S READY," LAEDORN SAID, SLIDING a small pack off his back and setting it on the ground. Haarviik did the same. The packs were made of a pale green elven wool that had a soft glow to it. "Within lie the Thunder Stones. Once we load them in the Apparatus of Ruune, we must unleash their power without delay."

"I thought you said there were three of them," Bayzog said, rubbing his neck. "Who carries the third?"

"I do," said a strong female voice. Selene waded through the elves and dwarves and stood among them. A stone wrapped up in dark crimson cloth filled her hands. "I'd been saving it for other plans, but now it is yours to master."

Bayzog waded in closer as they unwrapped the stones. His skin tingled. His heart flinched. Such power would make him or anybody invincible. He took a deep breath and found Selene staring at him.

The corner of her lip was turned up in a smile. "Tempting, isn't it, Bayzog?"

He wasn't sure what to make of her, or any of them for that matter. This historic alliance was strange indeed. It seemed the elves, led by Laedorn, had chosen to save her with the Ocular of Orray. But had they done it so she could help Nath Dragon, or had they done it because they needed her help with the Thunder Stones? It was an unlikely unification.

"Yes, it is tempting." His neck hairs prickled. His violet eyes narrowed. "Imagine what you could do with the stones under your power. You would be just as powerful as Gorn Grattack himself." He readied the Elderwood Staff in front of him. "Perhaps that was what you were saving your stone for."

"What are you getting at, Bayzog?" said Brenwar, stepping along his side. "Do you smell treachery among us? Do you doubt her scaly hide?"

Laedorn and Haarviik stopped unwrapping the stones and fixed their eyes on Selene.

Her eyes were aglow. The clawed fingers at her sides flexed and stretched out. Eyes fixed on the stones, she swayed forward.

Bayzog and Brenwar's knuckles whitened on their hilts. There was the scrape of weapons sliding from sheaths. The sounds quieted. The sky turned dim.

"What are you thinking, Selene?" Bayzog said.

Her dark eyes blinked. She shook the locks on her head. "I, I'm thinking it's time to take down Gorn Grattack, but not at the cost of Nath Dragon." She took two steps backward from the stones. "But I will not interfere."

The tension eased, but the doubt in Bayzog's mind remained.

"Laedorn, Haarviik, can you wait another hour? That would be enough time for our friend Gorlee to be released and returned. Perhaps he'll bring news that can be useful."

"Such as?" Haarviik said.

"Such as where in the world do you aim that thing?" Brenwar responded. "Pah. This plan is as bad as an ogre's stench."

"Bayzog!" Sasha exclaimed. "It's Samaz. Look!"

Bayzog whipped around and fastened his eyes on his son, who stood alone and away from the crowd. He's eyes shone a solid white, and he stood with his arms wide and on his tiptoes. He spoke quick words in Elven, repeating the same phrase over and over.

"What is he yammering on about?" Brenwar said to Bayzog. "My Elven is horrible."

"He comes," Bayzog said, glancing over toward Laedorn. "Fire the weapon. He comes. Fire the weapon."

"We can no longer hesitate," Laedorn said. He filled his hands unwrapping his stone. It was pearl in color with ancient gold runes engraved on it. Inside, it beat with mystic life.

Haarviik unwrapped his stone. It was a marble rock with red runes engraved on it. A red glow pulsated inside.

"Take the third," Selene said to Bayzog. "They'll need your wizard's touch for this."

Bayzog hesitated, then ambled over. He picked the stone up off the ground. The power he felt enlightened him from fingertip to toenail. Elation. Exhilaration. Temptation. His violet eyes flashed. A struggle within ensued. The vibrant man inside him collided with his pious elven self. A storm raged.

Laedorn and Haarviik, radiating power, lugged their stones toward the apparatus and fed them into its iron belly. Up the ladder they went, from there to take the bench seat behind the cannon. Haarviik grabbed the handles and turned the many bare gears. The Apparatus of Ruune's barrel shifted over, rose, and aimed at the Floating City. The old dwarf eyed the line of sight and nodded. The elf and dwarf each slipped on a pair of leather goggles.

"It's time, Bayzog," Laedorn said. "Unwrap yours and load it."

Bayzog felt his heart thumping in his ears. Could the weapon destroy everything inside the city? Nath would die, Gorlee would die, and hundreds of dragons who had been turned to the evil side would die. He glanced over at Sasha. Tears stood in her eyes, but her warm, pretty face had no answers. He turned away and removed the cloth from the stone. It was onyx marked with silver runes. He stepped over to the contraption and opened the door to its stomach. Inside, the pair of Thunder Stones throbbed in unison, beckoning for the third. Trembling, Bayzog set it inside the waiting furnace.

The belly glowed with life.

Whuuuuuum!

The ground shook, the trees bent, and Bayzog fell down. A stiff breeze swirled around them all, stirring the hairs on Haarviik and Laedorn's heads. The Apparatus of Ruune hummed a tumultuous tune. A swirl of bright, mystic colors spilled from the barrel.

"Father! Father!" Rerry shouted over the howling winds. He was pointing down the road that led into the valley. "Someone comes!"

The other elves and dwarves pushed Bayzog out of the way. They latched their hands on the apparatus and began chanting.

Whuuuuum!

The sound became louder and louder.

Squinting, Bayzog watched Brenwar and Pilpin rush at the stranger coming up the road. He was waving his hands over his head, staggering as he ran forward. Brenwar and Pilpin cut him off, threw him down, and dragged him forward.

"Who is it?" Bayzog said.

The figure locked eyes with him, blinked, and started to turn. His skin was pinkish. His eyes were wide.

"Gorlee!" Bayzog exclaimed.

Huffing for breath, Gorlee said, "I escaped, but they know you're here and they're coming!" He glanced at the pulsating apparatus. "What is that thing? Where is Nath Dragon?"

"He's in the city!" Bayzog shouted over the wind. "Looking for you!"

"No! No! It's a trap! It's all a big trap! We have to get him out of there!" He tried to pull away, but Brenwar held him fast. "Let go! Let go!"

Bayzog and Brenwar started shouting at Laedorn and Haarviik and waving their arms.

"Stop! Stop!"

Haarviik, beard billowing, shouted, "Cover your ears!" And then with all his dwarven might, he shouted, "Fire!"

Kah—Kah—Kah—Rooooooooooom!

A bright ball of energy blasted out of the barrel and soared through the sky. Bayzog watched in awe. The blue-green torpedo of energy was on a direct path into the very heart of the city. Bayzog sank to his knees. Sasha huddled at his side, watching with dread-filled anticipation. He barely heard the words she said.

"Balzurth be with you, Nath."

CHAPTER
41

APUMMELING. A BEATDOWN. NATH FELT like a child fighting a man. Gorn was bigger. Gorn was stronger. It took everything Nath had to keep himself together.

He can't be this powerful. He can't be!

Gorn wailed on him. He felt every blow in his bones. He struck back only to be swatted aside and assaulted again.

"I can't kill you this way, but I enjoy delivering the pain!"

Nath, sprawled out on the ground, struggled to rise.

Gorn kicked him in the gut. Blasted him with more fire.

"That's for your father! And after I finish you, I'll finish him!"

Gorn drove his fist into him and kicked him once more.

Listless and wrought with pain, Nath lay on his back in the supine position as Gorn walked away. He'd hardly put up a fight. He was ashamed of it. It angered him. Selene had told him to hold back his powers, and as far as he could tell, he'd exhausted them all. Gorn's powers seemed unlimited. They seemed to be growing. What was feeding the monster that made him so strong? He heard a voice inside his head.

Fear and doubt are our enemies. Evil feeds on them.

Bayzog had said that.

Sometimes you have to set your faults aside and be a hero.

Brenwar had lectured that.

Nothing can stop Nath Dragon.

Nath rose to his feet with a groan and pulled his shoulders back.

"I said that."

"What's this?" Gorn said, stomping over the throne where Fang was embedded. "Still some fight in you, I see. Hah hah hah!" Gorn plucked the tiny sword from the chair. "Let me show you true power, my full power."

Fang sparkled and hissed in his palms and began to enlarge.

Nath's golden eyes widened. "Impossible!"

"You think small, Nath Dragon. And with your precious sword, I'm going to sliver off your scales and skewer your heart."

Nath crouched back. He felt more odds stacking against him.

How is he doing this? What can't he do? Think, Nath. Think.

"You'd think you'd have your own sword," Nath said. "Sad thing you have to use mine. It seems you lack many skills my father has."

Gorn sprang across the room and swung Fang at his belly.

Slice!

Nath skipped away.

Guzan! That was close.

Gorn jabbed Fang at him again and again.

Nath twisted, ducked, and dodged. The cathedral was collapsing all around him.

"Stay still, you fool!"

Nath did no such thing. Gorn thrust. He moved. Gorn jabbed. He sidestepped. He narrowed his eyes. *Nothing is faster than Nath Dragon.* His dragon heart surged inside his chest, his confidence renewed. Gorn cut and chopped. He anticipated and moved.

Evil is overconfident.

Brenwar had once said that.

The wicked are powerful but often sluggish.

Bayzog's memory reminded.

Nath felt his senses coming together now. Wary, Gorn waded through the city. He'd close in on Nath, only to see him slip away time and again.

"I tire of this!" Gorn growled. He looked up into the spires. "Dark dragons, pin him down!"

The dragons spread their wings and dropped from the sky.

Nath acted. He summoned his power and unleashed a cone of icy dragon breath.

Distracted, Gorn slipped on his next step and thudded into the street.

Nath unleashed his full fury, freezing Gorn's legs and covering his chest and arms.

The dragons flew at him and latched onto his arms and legs.

He slung them off and pounced on Gorn Grattack.

Fang was frozen to Gorn's hands.

Nath tried to pry him out.

"Ha!" Gorn said from his frozen cocoon. "You think to fool me, do you? Admirable try, but my grip is solid iron." Flexing his scales, Gorn busted the ice off. He slugged the gaping Nath in the jaw with the hilt of his own sword. "Fool!"

Smaller dragons clawing all over him, Nath crashed to the ground. "No!"

Gorn was on his feet towering over him with Fang resting on his shoulder.

Nath strained against his living coat of dragon armor. They had him pinned. Gorn had him right where he wanted him.

Nath's father's words entered his head.

Evil is deceitful. Don't close your mind for a second.

"Let go of me, brothers and sisters! You don't know what you're doing!"

"Save your breath, Nath. They don't listen to you, they listen to me." Gorn readied Fang over his head. "They listen to me from now on, forever!" He started into his swing.

BOOOOOOOOOM!

The entire Floating City shook. Nath felt it tilt beneath him. Above, some sort of meteor skipped off a mystic shield he hadn't noticed before. Gorn stumbled backward, and a sneer formed on his lips. He opened his mouth to speak again.

BOOOOOOOOM!

The Floating City trembled again.

"Dragons!" he roared. "Find that weapon and destroy it!"

Dragons by the hundreds took to the sky, darting through the shield and away.

Gorn leered down at Nath. "I suspected such a thing, but I control the jaxite's power. Nothing but dragons can get in or out of this city." He waggled Fang in the air. "The more dragons come, the more I control. And in moments, those distant heroes, no matter their force, will be torn into pieces." He readied the sword for the final blow once more. "Don't worry, Nath Dragon. You'll never get to see it."

CHAPTER

42

As HE WATCHED THE MAGIC torpedo fly, Brenwar's chest tightened. Thoughts of not seeing Nath again raced through his mind. As the great missile sailed up, he ground his teeth and braced his mind for impact.

Behind him, everyone watched with rapt fascination.

Brenwar's keen eye caught a quavering bubble that he hadn't noticed before. It surrounded the city.

"Great Guzan! What is that? A shield? Bayzog, do you see that?"

The mage squinted.

Careening through the sky, the bright blast sailed toward the city, barreling down on the mass of buildings. There was a bright flash followed by a thunderous boom. An invisible dome appeared, saving the city. The ball of power skipped off the greenish dome and skittered into the sky before fading.

"Buckle my boot! It ricocheted!" Brenwar yelled. He felt relief. He turned back toward Haarviik. "*Now* what are you going to do?"

Haarviik stood up in his seat and pulled up his leather goggles. His weathered face was painted with fury. "It cannot be!"

Suddenly, coming out of the Floating City, dragons by the hundreds filled the sky. Black tailed and winged with glowing eyes, they soared straight for the Apparatus of Ruune.

"Fire again!" Haarviik bellowed, plopping down in his seat. "Fire!"

Laedorn and Haarviik pulled back on their triggers and let chaos fly.

Kah—Kah—Kah—Rooooooooooom!

Kah—Kah—Kah—Rooooooooooom!

Kah—Kah—Kah—Rooooooooooom!

Torpedoes ripped through the dark dragons, incinerating them before blasting into the dome protecting the city. But the blast only took a few of the hundreds that remained. The dragons swarmed toward them, roaring in fury.

"Pilpin, fetch the chest!" Brenwar yelled.

"Aye!" Pilpin said, scurrying into the barn.

The Apparatus of Ruune continued to rock, blast after blast after blast.

Kah—Kah—Kah—Rooooooooooom!

Kah—Kah—Kah—Rooooooooooom!

Kah—Kah—Kah—Rooooooooooom!

The torpedoes destroyed dragons in their path but continued to ricochet off the dome.

Bayzog appeared at his side. "They'll be on us at any moment. What do you plan to do?"

Brenwar cocked his eyebrow. "Fight! One last glorious fight!"

A series of roars erupted behind them. The good dragons who had been huddled in the hills took to the sky and surged toward the oncoming enemy. Brenwar could see that the good dragons were outnumbered at least four to one.

"When they get here, they'll rip that apparatus apart," Bayzog said, "and then it will be over. We have to protect it!"

"I thought you didn't like it?" Brenwar said.

"Quite the contrary. It's fascinating. I just don't like Nath being on the other end of it."

Pilpin scurried back with the dwarven chest in his arms. He set it down and peeled the ancient lid open. Bayzog kneeled down and started plucking out vial after vial. He tossed them to his family, the Roamers, Ben, and Pilpin.

"Just drink," Brenwar said, pulling the cork off one and draining it down. "No time for questions." He thumped his chest and burped. Eyeing a hesitant Pilpin, he said, "If I can drink, you can drink."

Pilpin gave a quick bearded nod and swallowed the greenish potion down.

"Everyone, form a circle around the apparatus and stay close," Bayzog said. He stepped underneath the weapon's muzzle and readied the Elderwood Staff. "Have faith this isn't the end."

Kah—Kah—Kah—Rooooooooooom!

Kah—Kah—Kah—Rooooooooooom!

Dragons tore at one another. The sky was filled with firework-like destruction: lightning, fire, black acid, streams of lava, smoky eruptions. Dragons big and small battled for it all. Wings were torn and shredded. Dragons fell like great scaled birds from the air. Once so beautiful and majestic, now they were razor-clawed, fire-breathing terrors. The roars of battle were angry, painful, deafening. It was mayhem. Carnage.

"Stay close to me," Bayzog said to his wife Sasha, "no matter what."

"I will." Rising up on her tiptoes, she kissed his cheek. "But I have to admit, I feel great. What potion did you give me?"

He looked into her eyes. They were aglow with radiant fire. Her hands tingled with mystic life in his. "One that will increase your powers."

"How much?"

"Did you drink the entire thing?"

"Yes."

He showed a little smile. "Five-fold at least. But remember, its effects are only temporary. "

Sasha faced the oncoming wave of dragons in the sky and clenched her charged-up fist. "Then temporary will just have to do. It's time to let those rotten lizards have it!"

Bayzog summoned the power of the Elderwood Staff. The gemstone carved into the ancient wood flared with brilliant tangerine light. It fed him. Empowered him. His eyes smoldered with mystic light.

"Everyone!" Bayzog yelled. "Don't strike until you see the green of their eyes!"

The clamor of battle in the sky subsided. The swarm of steel-hard, dark-scaled beasts would be on them at any moment. Bayzog heard Brenwar cry out.

"What are you waiting for, Haarviik? Get to firing that thing!"

Bayzog turned and looked. Something was wrong. Laedorn and Haarviik were frozen.

Selene! he thought. *Where is Selene?*

CHAPTER

43

NATH'S MIND WAS A RACE of thoughts. Gorn loomed over him with his beloved sword Fang, whose keen blade reflected dark powers. All over Nath, dragons pinned him down. They'd latched onto his legs, his arms. Tails encircled his neck, ankles, and wrists. Other dragons, strange ones of a dark-green hue, bit into his body with a leech-like quality. They drained his power.

He groaned. He strained.

For decades he'd fought to save them, only to see them destroying him. His friends would die as well. Gorn was right. He didn't want to see it. So many things he considered that he didn't even notice the blade descending.

Booooooooooooooom!

Booooooooooooooom!

More blasts shook the city. Gorn lost his balance. The sword missed its mark, cleaving into a copper dragon, who exploded.

Nath swallowed the lump in his throat.

That was close!

Gorn held his free clawed hand up in the air and said with venom, "Perhaps I should rip your heart out of your chest myself!"

Nath started to reply, but, choking, he couldn't speak. But another voice did.

"I wouldn't do that."

Gorn's head twisted to the side. A dragon, lavender and white scaled, stood nearby. It was Selene.

"You!" Gorn said. "Impossible!"

"Oh, Gorn, you should know better than that. After all, you came back from the brink of death. Why can't I?"

He huffed a blast of fire at her feet, but she remained still. "What game are you playing, Selene?"

Her magnificent lavender wings spread out and fluttered, then folded behind her back. She was as captivating as a dragon as she ever had been as a woman. Her eyes were dark-purple gems, pretty. She batted her lashes.

"I've brought you a gift," she said.

"A gift," Gorn growled. "What sort of gift?"

Nath couldn't believe his eyes. His ears. Selene had betrayed him … again!

She opened up her dragon hands, and bright brilliant light spilled out.

Gorn's eyes widened like moons. "You have the Ocular!" he said, excited.

"It was worth dying for, my lord. And it's all yours."

"You have exceeded my grandest expectations, Selene. My most diabolical plan has come to fruition. You fooled the elves, the dwarves, and Nath Dragon most of all." He belted out a monstrous laugh. "Ha ha ha! You have restored your lost honor."

Her eyes slid over to Nath's before she said, "Sometimes, you just have to have a little faith."

Gorn stretched his fingers out and started to wrap them around the Ocular of Orray. He paused and withdrew.

"A moment, Selene." He turned his attention to Nath. "I have some business to finish first. I'll deal with the Ocular and its uncanny powers next." Once more he towered over Nath. "Do you have anything you would like to say before you perish, Nath Dragon?"

Nath fastened his eyes on Selene. "I have nothing to say. Just kill me."

CHAPTER

44

DRAGON FIRE RAINED DOWN TOWARD the apparatus.

Bayzog unleashed the power of the Elderwood Staff. A powerful arc of energy scattered the ranks of dragons. Beside him, Sasha deflected fire and lightning with shield after shield.

"There's too many!" she yelled.

Dragons landed and rushed.

Two towering figures, more than twenty feet tall, stepped into their path. It was Shum and Hoven. Their Dragon Needles had become gigantic lances. They skewered one dragon after the other. There was smoke and fire, and the dust of battle began to roll. Bayzog heard Brenwar shouting out in the clamor.

"Take that!"

Wham!

"And that!"

Crack!

"And that, you foul lizards!"

Crunch!

"War hammer! War hammer! Hooooooooo!"

A grey scaler, little bigger than him, slid between Shum and Hoven's ranks and charged at Sasha's blind side. Bayzog swung his staff around and connected with its head.

Ka-Koom!

The dragon sagged into the ground, dead, leaving Sasha gasping.

"Are you all right?" he said.

Sasha nodded. "Yes, now keep fighting!"

Wupash!

A dragon tail licked out of the smoke and swept Bayzog from his feet. His head hit hard on the ground.

"Oof!"

A dragon pounced on him, copper scaled and copper eyed. It pinned Bayzog under his staff and snapped at him with its jaws. Its breath was as foul as the acid that dripped from its mouth onto Bayzog's chest.

He moaned. He heard Sasha scream for help. His power ignited. The Elderwood Staff flared, and the copper dragon exploded into ashes.

Chest burning, Bayzog scrambled to his feet. Sasha strained to fend off two grey scalers with her mystic shield. Superior in size and power, the dragons pressed in for a lethal attack. One of the dragons' long tails coiled back to strike. Bayzog wouldn't make it in time.

"Sasha! Watch out!"

A blur whizzed by Bayzog and sliced into the nearest dragon. It was Rerry. His body and blades moved at impossible speeds. He was a whirling dervish of flashing steel. The grey scaler growled and hissed as Rerry ripped through his scales.

Slice! Slice! Slice! Slice! Slice!

"Get away from my mother, dragon!" Rerry cried out.

On the other side, a bulk fell out of the sky, landed on the other dragon's neck, and wrestled it to the ground. It was Samaz. He punched at the dragon with fists made of iron. With tremendous punches, he pummeled the beast into submission.

Whop! Whop! Whop!

Bayzog caught Sasha up in his arms. Her forehead was beaded in sweat. All around them was the clamorous chaos of battle.

"Can you still fight?" he said to her.

"I still have plenty left in me, I've just never fought two dragons before." She squinted. "And these dragons better not hurt my boys." Her hands charged up with blue light. She summoned a fireball and hurled it at a dragon engaged with Rerry. The blast knocked off its scales.

"Mother!" Rerry said. "I'm a big elf! I can take care of myself!" In a flash of speed, he assaulted another.

Whump!

A sky raider landed on top of the barn, crushing it to splinters. Another one landed behind it, followed by another. There was enough fire in them to lay waste to the farm in one breath.

"Everyone to me!" Bayzog yelled. "Everyone now!"

The giants Shum and Hoven kept fighting the dragons that hung all over them. They both bled from at least a dozen wounds. Valiant. Unfailing.

Bayzog heard the first sky raider taking in a breath. Any second, it would wipe them out. Then, out of the sky, a blur of fur and muscle appeared.

Sansla Libor, fists ready, flew into the dragon and smote him in the face with ram-like force.

Another figure ran through the streets toward the sky raiders, getting bigger with every stride. It was Gorlee, transforming into a giant made of stone. He tackled the sky raider and drove it to the ground. The other sky raiders pounced Gorlee the Stone Giant. They attacked with fire and claws.

"No!" Bayzog yelled. "Come back! Come back to me!"

Shum, Hoven, Sansla, and Gorlee kept fighting. So did Samaz and Rerry, close by.

"Samaz! Rerry! To me!"

The sons broke off their attack and hurried back to their parents. Bayzog jammed the butt of his staff to the ground.

Wuh-Wuuuuuuuuuum!

A mystic yellow dome formed around them and the apparatus, protecting them, with a few dragons inside.

Sasha unleashed her power on the dragons.

Sssraz! Sssssraz! Sssssraz!

Rerry and Samaz cut and pounded down the others.

Slice! Whop! Slice! Whop! Slice!

Rerry stuck his tongue out at Samaz. "I whipped many more than you."

"Wizard!" Brenwar said, emerging from behind the apparatus with Pilpin. The pair were bloody and battered. "What do we do?"

Dragons, eyes glowing green, pressed the mystic dome from all over. Bayzog could feel their full weight on him. Sweat dripped down his face.

"I don't know," he said. "I don't know."

His violet eyes darted around their surroundings. The Apparatus of Ruune sat quiet. Laedorn and Haarviik's bodies sat behind it frozen stiff. How could a weapon so powerful fail?

The protective dome began to crack. The dragons were too many. He could only hold them off for seconds longer.

Sasha wrapped her arms around his waist and lent him all the strength she had left.

"You did your best, husband. You did your best. Being your wife has been an honor."

Shards of magic cracked away from the shield. His sons joined in the hug as well.

"Keep fighting, Father!" Rerry yelled. "Keep fighting!"

Bayzog found new strength, and a desperate thought emerged.

"Brenwar!"

"What!"

"Aim the Apparatus of Ruune at the jaxite!"

"Then what?"

"Fire it!"

Pilpin scrambled up the ladder and shoved Laedorn and Haarviik out of their seats.

"Sorry, Commanders."

Brenwar huffed up behind him.

More shards of energy fell. Dragon horns pounded through the mystic dome. Dragons squirmed through.

"Hurry, Brenwar! Hurry!"

Pilpin and Brenwar worked the gears with the handles, and Brenwar yelled, "I can't even see what I'm aiming at!"

"Just do your best for the love of Morgdon and fire!"

CHAPTER
45

"IT'S OVER," GORN SAID. "NALZAMBOR will be mine forever!"

Nath, straining with all his might, gave one final heave against the dragons. The effort was futile. He glared at Selene. "You picked the wrong side."

"Oh, did I?" she replied with a smirk on her face.

Fang flashed in the sun.

Selene spoke a word of power, and the Ocular of Orray burst with brilliant blinding light.

"Argh!" Gorn said, staggering back and covering his eyes in his elbow. "What are you doing, Selene?"

Tendrils of energy stretched out from the Ocular and ripped into the dragons that held Nath down. The dark dragons screamed and scurried. Others darted into the sky, and several suddenly died.

"Ultimate betrayer!" Gorn bellowed. "You shall pay for this!" Gorn blasted Selene with the fire of ten thousand furnaces. It buried her in the buildings, leaving her out of sight beneath a smoking pile of rubble. "Fool!"

Nath sprang to his feet and charged.

Gorn turned on him and swung. The blade sheared through Nath's wing and into his side.

Nath screamed. "Argh!" He blocked out the pain. He kept fighting. He grabbed Gorn's wrists and blasted him in the chest with his own dragon fire. He and Gorn butted horned heads.

Klock! Klock! Klock!

"You are no match for me!" Bigger and stronger, Gorn scooped the exhausted Nath up in one arm and slammed him down hard.

Fang's blade flashed in the sun and came down.

Nath rolled to the side, avoiding a fatal blow that still sank into the meat of him. "Ugh!" He twisted his body around and swept Gorn from his feet with his tail and sprang up, clutching the side of his dragon body. It was bleeding. Bleeding badly. It burned, too. Nothing felt worse than being wounded by a friend. It angered him.

Gorn made his way back to his feet with ease and laughed. "Ha ha ha! Give up, Nath Dragon. I've too much power. I have your sword. The jaxite. Thousands of dragons under my command." He lifted his chin and snorted smoke. "I have more than your father ever had. I am disappointed. It seems you are less of a fighter than he."

"Maybe so," Nath said, "but I'll fight you to the end. This fight isn't over yet." He summoned all of his courage and all of his strength and charged. "Dragon! Dragon!"

Fang licked out faster than a snake's tongue.

Nath stopped short of its tip, spun to one side, and countered with a punch to Gorn's chin.

The Dragon Warlord staggered back and howled.

Nath unleashed radiant beams of fire from his eyes, striking Gorn in the throat.

Again the dragon lord fell back. "I see you learned one of my tricks," Gorn said, "but it will take more than that to save you."

Nath pressed his attack. He brought fire. Rays. Punches. Claws. He gasped in pain with every offensive blow but kept on swinging. He used his speed. All of his energy. He was a hornet stinging a larger enemy.

Gorn chopped one heavy swing after the other. He missed time after time. "Stand still!" Gorn roared. "You annoying fly!"

Nath filled Gorn's face with his dragon fire, but then his inner fires went dim.

Guzan!

He'd used all of his breath up. His body became weak and wobbly.

"Tired," Gorn said, leering down at him, "little dragon?"

Nath punched Gorn in the face with arms that felt like lead.

Gorn unleashed a final blast from his eyes.

Ssssraaaaat!

Nath's body skidded down the street, stopping when he crashed into an ancient fountain. Everything hurt. Everything felt broken. He forced open his swollen eyes. Fifty feet of Gorn towered over him.

What happened?

He'd exhausted his powers and shrunk back down to the size of a man.

"I should squash you like a bug," Gorn said. "But that won't do."

Gasping for his breath, Nath watched Gorn and Fang shrink in size, but he still stood a full ten feet in height.

Gorn reached down, grabbed Nath by the neck, and hoisted him up high. He squeezed Nath's neck in his grip.

Nath kicked his feet, and his face turned beet red, almost purple.

"Oddly silent now isn't it?" Gorn said with a hiss. "The lonely sound of death. Ah, but is that the distant screaming of your friends that I hear? I believe it is. They are dying. But don't fret, Nath Dragon, I'll give all of you a fiery funeral." He rested Fang's tip against Nath's chest. "How nice. I can even feel the last beats of your heart in your chest."

Nath tried to speak, but all he could do was squirm and think about his friends.

Keep fighting until the end.

He felt Fang's tip begin to sink into his scales, but in the distance he heard something else.

Kah—Kah—Kah—Rooooooooooom!

"Ah, it seems your friends got off one final shot before they died," Gorn mocked. "A pity it will do neither them nor you any good." He glanced up at the protective dome. "Let's watch the final ricochet together, shall we?"

Nath's golden eyes made their final glance. The magic torpedo soared overhead and kept on going, a shooting star in the night. His heart sank. They'd missed.

Kah—Kah—Kah—Rooooooooooom!

A second torpedo skipped off the shield, making a blast of fiery sparks.

He heard another shot and closed his eyes.

"Oh well," Gorn said, "at least they still fight. That's more than I can say for you."

BOOOOOOOOOOOOM!

The entire Floating City shook so hard that it half tilted over.

"What?" Gorn cried out.

BOOOOOOOOOOOM!

The city shook again, and he dropped Nath on the ground. Out of control, the city started rocking back and forth and spinning in an wobbling fashion.

"Impossible!" Gorn said, shaking his head. "No matter! The end of you is the end of this world."

"You know what your problem is, Gorn?" Nath said, rubbing his neck.

"What might that be, foolish little dragon?"

"You talk too much!" Nath lunged for Fang and jerked Dragon Claw from the hilt. In a flash, he buried the blade in Gorn's chest to the hilt. "And you're too darn slow!"

"No!" Gorn cried out with widening eyes. "Impossible! Noooooooooooo!"

Gorn's body crackled and fizzled, illuminated with light. An eerier cry went out.

Kah-Poooooooof!

Nath stared down at Gorn's corpse, now turned to bone and ashes that the wind quickly took away. He took Fang from Gorn's disintegrating grip. "I don't ever want to do that again."

Boooooooooooooom!

Boooooooooooooom!

Boooooooooooooom!

Everything was collapsing all around him.

"Selene!"

He rushed over to the pyre where she had last been and dug his claws into the dirt. He found her out cold in the smoking rubble. He took her up in is arms, spread his wings, and took to the sky. His battered wings kept on pumping, barely keeping him aloft. He heard Selene gasp and cough. "Hang in there," he said.

Teetering out of control, the Floating City careened toward the ground. An earth-shaking, horrendous crash smote the mountain tops. The city was destroyed, leaving only giant plumes of smoke and rubble.

Nath said to Selene, "Looks like we did it. We're going to make it."

Her eyes found his. "Of course we are. I had faith, did you?"

CHAPTER
46

THE APPARATUS OF RUNE STOPPED firing. Bayzog's shield collapsed. Dark dragons climbed all over them, the Apparatus, everything. Brenwar swung his hammer into a copper dragon's nose.

Krang!

"Get off me, lizards!"

There was a blinding flash! A thousand bolts of lightning in one.

Boooooooooooooom!

Boooooooooooooom!

Boooooooooooooom!

The dragon surge ended. The dark lizards shook their necks and flapped their wings. The glowing green lights in their eyes went dim.

"Direct hits! Directs hits!" Pilpin said, sliding down the ladder to the smoking barrel of the apparatus. "Look!" he said, waving his arms. "Look!"

The Floating City split into two massive hunks. It teetered and warbled in the sky, sputtering and smoking. Slowly, it drifted toward the earth, dragging the chained dragons down with it.

BAMmmmmm!

It crashed into the mountains with thunderous impact. Smoke billowed up in huge plumes of dust and rubble.

"I'll be," Brenwar exclaimed, mopping the sweat from his brow. "You were right, wizard!" He scanned the area around the apparatus. There were dragons everywhere, some dead, others alive. "Where are you, wizard?"

"Perhaps I can help," Shum said. The giant-sized Roamer elf began picking dragons up from the pile and tossing them aside. Bayzog and his family lay underneath the pile, unmoving.

"Bayzog!" Brenwar jumped off the apparatus and rushed to his friend's side. He scooped him up in his arms. "Wake up, elf! Wake up!"

Bayzog's violet eyes fluttered open. "I was right, wasn't I?"

"About what?"

"Shooting the jaxite."

"It was my shot that did it, elf. Not your advice. Your words had little effect."

Grimacing, Bayzog eyed him, starting to rise. "If you say so, dwarf. Ouch.

"Are you all right?"

"Just a few broken ribs, and possibly my leg. Hardly a wound of note."

"Hah!" Brenwar said, slapping him on the back. "Glad to see I'm finally rubbing off on you. A wizard turned soldier! Too bad the war might be over." He helped Bayzog to his feet, and together they gazed into the sky, where all the bright colors of the rainbow lingered.

Everyone seemed to be all right, especially Rerry.

"What kind of potion did you give me, Father?" Rerry said. "I was so fast!" He jabbed his sword. "Quick!" *Swish!* "My strikes were lightning-filled power! I want to drink that again. Please, please, tell me what it's called."

"In Elven," Bayzog said, "It's called *Cafleiyn*. And no, you can't have any more."

"Aw!"

Gazing toward the distant mountains, Brenwar frowned.

"Do you think he made it?" Bayzog said.

Kabooooom!

Kabooooom!

The Floating City exploded, shaking the ground beneath them.

"What in Nalzambor is that?" Brenwar said.

"The jaxite. Its energy is activated. The Apparatus of Ruune made it unstable."

"We need to get Nath out of there," Brenwar said.

"We need to get us out of here!"

BOOOOOOOOOOOOOOOOOOOOOOOOM!

A dome of fiery light covered the mountains. Everyone standing fell from their feet. Dust and debris rained down on them, coating everything.

Coughing, Brenwar stood up and wiped the grit from his eyes, gaping. The mountains were gone. He swallowed hard, and through a cracked voice he said, "I guess that's it then."

Everyone stood in silence.

Tears streamed down Sasha's cheeks.

Pilpin sniffled.

The dragons, of all sorts and colors, made sad honks and drifted away until all of them were gone. Almost an hour passed before Brenwar said, "I suppose we need to go and look for him. Come on, Pilpin."

"Look for who?" someone said.

"Nath," Brenwar grumbled. "Who said that?"

"I did," a voice from above responded.

Every chin tilted upward. Nath hovered in the sky with Selene in his arms.

"You get down here, you … dragon!"

EPILOGUE:

WEEKS LATER, NATH STOOD INSIDE the throne room at Dragon Home. The piles of gold and treasure were as high as ever. Gemstones twinkled and winked in the grand torchlight. Balzurth sat on the throne, resting his great jaw on his clawed fist.

"Why, you're not even 250 years old," his father said. "You don't really think your days of adventure are over yet, do you?"

"Well, we defeated Gorn Grattack. Stopped the war. What else is there?"

"You don't really think men, elves, orcs, and dwarves are going to start getting along, do you?"

"Well," Nath said, scratching his mane, "I don't suppose, but..." He glanced at Selene.

"Son," Balzurth said, reaching his great clawed hand down and patting him on the head. "You've done so well. But evil never rests. Not only must you be vigilant for all, but also yourself. Don't think for one moment that all the dragons are going to behave."

"I'll keep them in line."

"Ha!" Balzurth's short laugh shook the throne room, loosening the piles of gold like shale. "Just like I kept you in line, eh, Son?" He turned his great frame and head toward the enormous mural in the rear of the throne room. "Every living thing has a mind of its own. Remember that. It's their choice to do right or wrong. Same as it was yours. Same as it will be with your children."

"Children?" Nath said, jaw dropping.

Selene locked her fingers with his.

"You will have children," Balzurth said. "Nothing prepares you for that. They are full of so many wonderful surprises. They can be trouble as well, just as you were to me, I was to my father, and my father to my grandfather. Be firm, just. But always love them, no matter what. "

Balzurth turned his great scaly neck back toward him. His golden eyes were watery. "It's brought me nothing but joy, watching you grow up and become fully dragon, Nath. It aches my heart to have to go, but my time on this world is at its end. I'll see you soon. Never forget how much I love you, Son."

Nath's heart burst in his chest. Tears streamed down his cheeks. He didn't want his father to go. So much time had been missed, wasted. Now he was going, just like that.

"Don't go, Father! Not yet!"

"Oh," Balzurth said, his eyes brightened.

"Stay for a little longer at least?"

"I wish I could, Nath, but there is an appointed time for all, including me."

Nath fell to his knees and laid his hands on his father's tail. A flood of emotion overcame him. He trembled.

"Son, have no regrets. It's quite natural for the child to leave his parents and live life on his own. We'll be together soon enough on the other side of the mural. Have faith, Son."

Nath sniffed. Even with all the power he'd mastered, he felt like a child once again.

"Father, can you tell me something?" He looked up in Balzurth's eyes. "Was I really hatched from an egg?"

A smile cracked on Balzurth's face. "You need to ask your mother that."

"My mother?" Nath stood. "I really have a mother?"

"Yes, and when I leave, you'll have the power to find her." Balzurth headed closer to the mural.

Nath watched in silence. Stunned, his tongue clove to the roof of his mouth.

With one last wave goodbye, Balzurth slipped into the mural.

"I love you, Father!" Nath blurted out, but Balzurth was already gone.

Nath's chin dipped down to his chest.

Selene rubbed his shoulder.

He patted her hand. "Well," his said, lifting his chin and tossing back his mane. "I guess we should search out my mother."

Selene hugged him and spoke in his ear. "I'll see you later, Dragon King." She kissed his cheek, turned, and headed out of the throne room. The great doors sealed shut behind her.

Nath stood gaping for a while before he climbed up on the throne. There he sat, a dragon-scaled man, fist under his chin on a seat meant for someone ten times bigger than him. He contemplated all he had done. All that had happened. He snapped his fingers, and a ball of flame appeared. With a huff, he blew it out. "I'm bored."

Bong! Bong! Bong!

The pounding on the great doors stirred the piles of coins in the room.

Nath sat up and said, "Open."

The great doors swung inward. The stout, black-bearded figure standing in the threshold seemed so tiny in comparison.

A broad smile formed on Nath's lips. "Brenwar! What are you doing back here?"

In a new set of black plate armor, Brenwar marched into the room and took a knee.

"Rise," Nath said, "and don't ever do that again." He hadn't gotten used to the formalities of being king yet. "Unless you have to. So, what brings you back to visit?"

Brenwar rose to his feet and gazed up at Nath sitting on the throne. "If you get off your hind end and come down here, I'll tell you."

"Oh," Nath said, hopping down out of the massive chair. "Better?"

Brenwar nodded and grumbled, "A little bird called me out. It says to me, 'We need to find Nath the Dragon King's mother.' Unless you'd rather sit on that throne up there."

"You know where she is?"

"I know enough. Are you coming or not, your majesty?"

"Will it be dangerous?"

"Of course."

"Then what are we waiting for?"

THE ADVENTURES OF NATH DRAGON CONTINUE IN SERIES, 2, TAIL OF THE DRAGON.

ABOUT THE AUTHOR

Craig Halloran resides with his family outside of his hometown, Charleston, West Virginia. When he isn't entertaining mankind, he is seeking adventure, working out, or watching sports. To learn more about him, go to: www.thedarkslayer.com

WORKS BY THE AUTHOR

The Darkslayer Series 1
Wrath of the royals (Book 1)
Blades in the Night (Book 2)
Underling Revenge (Book 3)
Danger and the Druid (Book 4)
Outrage in the Outlands (Book 5)
Chaos at the Castle (Book 6)

The Darkslayer Series 2
Bish and Bone (Book 1)
Black Blood (Book 2)
Red Death (Book 3)

The Chronicles of Dragon Series
The Hero, The Sword and The Dragons (Book 1)
Dragon Bones and Tombstones (Book 2)
Terror at the Temple (Book 3)
Clutch of the Cleric (Book 4)
Hunt for the Hero (Book 5)
Siege at the Settlements (Book 6)
Strife in the Sky (Book 7)
Fight and the Fury (Book 8)
War in the Winds (Book 9)
Finale (Book 10)

Zombie Impact Series
Zombie Day Care: Book 1
Zombie Rehab: Book 2
Zombie Warfare: Book 3

The Supernatural Bounty Hunter Files
(Coming 2015)
Smoke Rising
I Smell Smoke
Where's there's Smoke
Smoke and Mirrors
Smoke on the Water

Connect with him at:
Facebook – The Darkslayer Report by Craig
Twitter – Craig Halloran